Books by Daniel Peters

Border Crossings

The Luck of Huemac: A Novel
About the Aztecs

THE LUCK OF HUEMAC

THE LUCK OF HUEMAC

A Novel About the Aztecs

DANIEL PETERS

Random House   New York

Library of Congress Cataloging in Publication Data
Peters, Daniel.
The luck of Huemac.
1. Mexico—History—To 1591—Fiction. 2. Aztecs—
Fiction. I. Title.
PS3566.E7548L8   813'.54   81–40221
ISBN 0–394–51313–4   AACR2

Manufactured in the United States of America
2 4 6 8 9 7 5 3
First Edition

To my mother and father

Acknowledgments

The author wishes to express his deep gratitude:

To my sources: Fr. Bernadino de Sahagun (Arthur J. O. Anderson and Charles E. Dibble, trans.), Fr. Diego Duran (Fernando Horcasitas and Doris Heyden, trans.), Bernal Diaz, J. Richard Andrews, Burr Cartwright Brundage, Alfonso Caso, Nigel Davies, Frances Gillmor, Miguel Leon-Portilla, Ignacio Marquina, Jacques Soustelle, and George Vaillant; also to the University of New Hampshire Library and the University of Utah Press;

To my friends and readers: Matthew and Susan Epstein, and Gary and Judy Lindberg;

To my *agente extraordinaire,* Susan Lescher;

To Gnossos, for his unflagging support and inspiration, and to B. D. Gregory, for his generosity, expertise, and companionship in Mexico;

To Annette, who heard all this first and made me do it right, a task only true love could sustain for 1500 pages;

Finally, to the gods who presided over this work, as they do over all things upon the earth.

Contents

The People

Acapipioltzin (A-ka-pee-pee-ol-tsin); Texcocan; the son of Nezahualcoyotl and Regent of the heir.

THE ACOLHUAS (A-kol-was): Inhabitants of the lands east of the Lake, with major cities in Texcoco, Huexotla, Coatlinchan.

Acolmiztli (A-kol-mis-tli), Lion's Paw (1441–99); Tenocha; the older brother of Huemac; a Jaguar Warrior, warchief, and judge.

Ahuitzotl (A-wheet-sotl), Water Monster; Tenocha; the grandson of Moteczuma I and the middle brother of Tizoc and Axayacatl; warchief and eighth Speaker of the Tenocha (1486–1501).

Atototl (A-to-totl), Water Bird; a daughter of the ruling house of Ixtapalapa and the first wife of Acolmiztli.

Axayacatl (Ash-a-ya-kotl), Water Face; Tenocha; the grandson of Moteczuma I and the younger brother of Tizoc and Ahuitzotl; father of Moteczuma II; warchief and sixth Speaker of the Tenocha (1469–81).

Axolohua (Ash-o-lo-wa), He Who Has the Axolotl (as a nahualli); Tenocha; a priest attached to the Tlillan calmecac; Huemac's third teacher.

Azcatl (Ahs-kotl), Ant; Texcocan; adviser to Nezahualcoyotl and superior of the young Quinatzin.

Azcatzin (Ahs-kot-sin), Ant Prince (1474–1510); Tenocha; the younger son of Cocatli and the nephew of Huemac; a Jaguar Warrior and a ball player; captain of the royal ball team under Moteczuma II.

Cacalotl (Ka-ka-lotl), Raven; Texcocan; an apprentice ball player under Icpitl and later Texcocan champion; captain of Tizoc's team in the game of augury against Huemac.

Cacama (Ka-ka-ma), (1494–1520); Texcocan; the son of Nezahualpilli and brother of Ixtlilxochitl and Coanacoch; nephew of Moteczuma II and puppet ruler of Texcoco under him.

Ce Malinalli (Say Mal-i-nal-li), One Grass; Texcocan; a woman of the streets.

Chalchiuhnenetl (Chal-chwee-ne-netl), Jade or Precious Vulva; Tenocha;
(1) the granddaughter of Moteczuma I and the sister of Tizoc, Ahuitzotl, and Axayacatl; the wife of Moquiuix of Tlatelulco.
(2) the daughter of Axayacatl and the sister of Tlacahuepan and Moteczuma II; the second wife of Nezahualpilli of Texcoco.

Chalchiuhtona (Chal-chwee-to-na), Shining Jade; Tepanec; the wife of Xolotlpilli and the mother of Cuauhcoatl and Xiuhcue.

Chimalman (Chee-mal-man), Shield Hand (1468–?); Chichimec; sorceress and great-great-granddaughter of Oztooa; the mate of Huemac and mother of Tepeyollotl.

Chimalpopoca (Chee-mal-po-po-ka), Smoking Shield; Tepanec; the Speaker of Tlacopan in the time of Axayacatl, Tizoc, and Ahuitzotl.

Chiquatli (Chee-kot-li), Screech Owl (1464–?); Tenocha; Puma Warrior and ball player; apprentice and teammate of Huemac; later Master Trainer of Texcoco and member of Texcocan rebel forces.

Chopilotl (Cho-pi-lotl), Fine Crystal; Tenocha; the youngest daughter of Quinatzin and Teuxoch.

Cipactonal (Si-pac-to-nal), Alligator; Tenocha; the second youngest son of Quinatzin and Ome Xochitl; died in famine years (1450–55).

Citlalcoatl (Sit-lol-ko-atl), Snake of Stars; Texcocan; the father of Quinatzin.

Coanacoch (Ko-a-na-coach); Texcocan; the son of Nezahualpilli and brother of Cacama and Ixtlilxochitl; ruler of Huexotla; ruler of Texcoco (1520–25).

Coatleztli (Ko-atl-est-li), Snake Blood; Tenocha; a priest attached to the Tlillan calmecac; Huemac's second teacher.

Cocatli (Ko-kot-li), Mountain Flower (1450–1519); Tenocha; the youngest daughter of Quinatzin and Ome Xochitl and sister of Acolmiztli and Huemac; wife of Tlacateotzin and mother of Illancueitl, Omeocelotl, and Azcatzin; a priestess of Quetzalcoatl.

Colotl (Ko-lotl), Scorpion; Tenocha; Jaguar Warrior and enemy of Huemac; died in Michoacan.

Cuauhcoatl (Kwa-ko-atl), Eagle Snake (1501–?); Tenocha; the son of Xolotlpilli and Chalchiuhtona, brother of Xiuhcue and grandson of Huemac; a member of the Arrow Warriors.

Cuauhpopoca (Kwa-po-po-ka), Smoking Eagle; Totonac; ruler of Nauhtla and subject of Moteczuma II; burned by Spanish.

Cuauhtemoc (Kwa-te-mock), Descending Eagle; Tenocha-Tlatelulca; the son of Ahuitzotl and grandson of Moquiuix; warchief and Speaker of Tlatelulco (1520); the Speaker of Tenochtitlan-Tlatelulco (1520–25); captured and later hanged by the Spanish.

Cuauhtlatoa (Kwa-tla-to-a), Talking Eagle; Tlatelulca; the Speaker of Tlatelulco in the time of Moteczuma I.

Cuetzpaltzin (Kweets-palt-sin), Lizard Prince (1443–1511); Tlatelulca; head of the Guild of Vanguard Merchants and friend of Quinatzin and Huemac; father of Pinotl.

Cueyatzin (Kwee-yat-sin); Tenocha; adviser to Axayacatl and ambassador to Moquiuix during time of civil war (1473); killed in Tlatelulco with Quinatzin.

Cuitlahuac (Kweet-la-wock); Tenocha; the son of Axayacatl and half brother of Moteczuma II; warchief and tenth Speaker of the Tenocha (1520); died of smallpox following escape of Spaniards.

Ehecatzin (E-he-kot-sin), Wind Prince; Tenocha; a member of the Arrow Warriors and comrade of Cuauhcoatl.

Ehecatzitzimitl (E-he-kot-si-tsi-meetl), Wind Demon; Tlatelulca; spy for Tlacaelel during time of civil war (1473).

Eptli (Ep-tli), Pearl; Chontal-Mexican; a woman from Xicalanco and the wife of Pinotl.

Eztetl (Es-tetl), Bloodstone; Tenocha; Supreme Commander of the Eagle Warriors and Huemac's superior.

Huactli (Wock-tli), Night Heron; Matlatzinca; warrior captured by Hue-mac; sacrificed to Tonatiuh (1477).

Huemac (Way-mock), named for last Toltec ruler of Tula (1454–1520); Teno-cha; youngest son of Quinatzin and Ome Xochitl and brother of Acolmiztli and Cocatli; father of Quetzal Papalotl, Xolotlpilli, and Tepeyollotl; Eagle Warrior, ball player, sorcerer.

THE HUEXOTZINCANS (Weh-shot-sin-kans): Inhabitants of the lands beyond the eastern mountains, with major cities in Tlaxcala, Huexotzinco, Cholula, Atlixco.

Icpitl (Ik-peetl), Firefly; Texcocan; ball player and Master Trainer of Texco-can team; Huemac's teacher.

Illancueitl (Il-lan-swaytl), Splendid Feather (1469–?); Tenocha; the daughter of Cocatli and the sister of Omeocelotl and Azcatzin; Huemac's niece and the wife of Michpilli; emigrated to Teloloapan (1488).

Iquehuac (E-kwa-wock); Tenocha; the only legitimate son of Moteczuma I.

Itzcoatl (Its-ko-atl), Obsidian Serpent; Tenocha; uncle of Tlacaelel and Moteczuma I; warchief and fourth Speaker of the Tenocha (1428–40).

Itzquauhtzin (Its-kwat-sin), Obsidian Eagle Prince; Tenocha-Tlatelulca; Eagle Speaker (appointed ruler) of Tlatelulco under Moteczuma II; killed by Spanish prior to their escape (1520).

Ixtlilxochitl (Isht-lil-show-cheetl), Vanilla-Flower Face; Texcocan;
(1) the sixth ruler of Texcoco and the father of Nezahualcoyotl; killed by Tepanecs (1418).
(2) son of Nezahualpilli and brother of Cacama and Coanacoch; leader of Texcocan rebel forces.

Iztacxochitl (Is-tak-show-cheetl), White Flower; Tenocha; the eldest daughter of Quinatzin and Ome Xochitl; died during time of famine (1450–55).

Lady of Tula (Too-la); a daughter of the ruling house of Tula; the third wife of Nezahualpilli and a composer of flower songs; the sponsor of Quetzal Papalotl.

Lord Malintzin (Mal-int-sin); Spanish; the Conqueror Hernán Cortés.

Malintzin (Mal-int-sin), Grass Princess; a woman from Teticpac; interpreter for the Spanish and the mistress of Hernán Cortés.

Matlatzihuatzin (Mat-lat-si-wat-sin); Tepanec; the sister of Chimalpopoca of Tlacopan and the first wife of Nezahualcoyotl; mother of Nezahualpilli.

Maxtla (Mash-tla), Loincloth; Tepanec; the son of Tezozomoc and the former ruler of Coyoacan; overlord of the Tepanecs and oppressor of the Mexicans and Acolhuas (1428).

Michpilli (Mich-peel-li), Baby Fish (1462–?); Tenocha-Tlatelulca; Eagle Warrior, apprentice, and assistant to Huemac; married Illancueitl and emigrated to Teloloapan (1488).

Moquiuix (Mo-kee-wheesh), Intoxicated One; Tlatelulca; warchief and Speaker of Tlatelulco during time of civil war (1473).

Moteczuma (I) Ilhuicamina (Mo-te-soo-ma Ill-wee-ka-meena), Angry Lord Who Shoots at the Skies; Tenocha; nephew of Itzcoatl and half brother of

Tlacaelel; grandfather of Tizoc, Ahuitzotl, and Axayacatl; warchief and fifth Speaker of the Tenocha (1440–69).

Moteczuma (II) Xocoyotzin (Mo-te-soo-ma Show-ko-yot-sin), Angry Lord the Younger (1467–1520); Tenocha; son of Axayacatl and brother of Tlacahuepan and Chalchiuhnenetl (2); half brother of Cuitlahuac; nephew of Tizoc and Ahuitzotl; warchief and ninth Speaker of the Tenocha (1502–20).

Nahuicoatl (Na-wee-ko-atl), Four Serpent; Texcocan; a warrior and comrade of Quinatzin.

Nahui Olin (Na-whee O-lin), Four Movement (1499–?); Tenocha; dwarf; jester to Moteczuma II; friend of Huemac and Cuauhcoatl.

Nezahualcoyotl (Ness-a-wall-ko-yotl), Fasting Coyote (1402–72); Texcocan; warchief, sorcerer, and composer of flower songs; the seventh ruler of Texcoco and Lord of Acolhuacan; father of Acapipioltzin and Nezahualpilli; father of Ome Xochitl and grandfather of Huemac.

Nezahualpilli (Ness-a-wall-peel-li), Fasting Prince (1465–1515); Texcocan; the son of Nezahualcoyotl and Matlatzihuatzin; warchief, sorcerer, and composer of flower songs; the eighth ruler of Texcoco and Lord of Acolhuacan; father of Coanacoch, Ixtlilxochitl (2), and Cacama.

Nopaltzin (No-palt-sin), Cactus Prince (1456–73); Tlatelulca; the son of Tezcatl and brother of Taypachtli; Huemac's friend; killed in War of Defilement.

Ocomatli (O-ko-mat-li), Monkey; Tenocha; warchief and adviser to Axayacatl; spy and agent of Tlacaelel.

Omeocelotl (O-may-os-se-lotl), Two Jaguar (1471–1520); Tenocha; the elder son of Cocatli and the brother of Illancueitl and Azcatzin; Huemac's nephew; a traveling merchant and later head of the Guild of Vanguard Merchants.

Ome Xochitl (O-may Show-cheetl), Two Flower (1424–1510); Texcocan; the daughter of Nezahualcoyotl and second wife of Quinatzin; a composer of flower songs and the mother of seven children, including Acolmiztli, Cocatli, and Huemac.

Opochtli (O-poach-tli), Left-Handed One; Tenocha; a Puma Warrior and ball player; Huemac's comrade and teammate.

Oxomoco (O-show-mo-ko); Tenocha; the second youngest daughter of Quinatzin and Ome Xochitl; died during the time of famine (1450–55).

Oztooa (Oss-too-wa), Gray Fox; Chichimec; sorcerer and chief of the hillpeople; great-great-grandfather of Chimalman; also known as the Old One.

Patecatl (Pa-te-kotl), He from the Land of Medicines; Tenocha; High Priest of the Temple of Quetzalcoatl; confidant of Huemac and superior of Cocatli and Quetzal Papalotl.

Pinotl (Pee-notl), Stranger (1479–?); Tlatelulca; the son of Cuetzpaltzin; a member of the Guild of Vanguard Merchants; the friend of Huemac and Quetzal Papalotl and the comrade of Omeocelotl.

Poyahuitl (Po-ya-wheetl); Tlatelulca; High Priest of Huitzilopochtli and member of the Tlatelulca war party during the time of the civil war (1473).

Quetzal Papalotl (Ket-sal Pa-pa-lotl), Precious Butterfly (1479–1519); Teno-cha; the daughter of Huemac and Taypachtli and the sister of Xolotlpilli; a priestess of Quetzalcoatl in both Tenochtitlan and Cholula.

Quinatzin (Kee-not-sin), named for a former ruler of Texcoco (1410–73); Texcocan; a warrior and spy for Nezahualcoyotl; Chief of Protocol for Tlacaelel; married to Teuxoch and Ome Xochitl; father of ten children, including Chopilotl, Acolmiztli, Cocatli, and Huemac.

Taypachtli (Tay-patch-tli), Seashell (1458–1496); Tlatelulca; the daughter of Tezcatl and sister of Nopaltzin; the wife of Huemac and mother of Xolotl-pilli and Quetzal Papalotl; a singer and composer of flower songs.

Teconal (Te-ko-nal); Tlatelulca; warchief and brother-in-law of Moquiuix; member of Tlatelulca war party during time of civil war (1473).

THE TENOCHA MEXICANS: Inhabitants of the island of Tenochtitlan, in the western part of the Lake.

THE TEPANECS: Inhabitants of the lands west of the Lake, with major cities in Azcapotzalco, Tlacopan, Coyoacan, Tenayuca.

Tepcyollotl (Te-pay-yol-lotl), Heart of the Mountains (1488–?); Tenocha-Chichimec; the son of Huemac and Chimalman; warrior, hunter, and apprentice sorcerer-chief.

Teuxoch (Too-shosh), (1415–84); Tenocha; the daughter of Tlacaelel and the first wife of Quinatzin; the mother of three daughters, including Chopilotl; the adoptive mother of Huemac.

Tezcatl (Tess-kotl), Mirror Stone (1411–73); Tlatelulca; the father of Tay-pachtli and Nopaltzin; warrior, artisan, and friend of Quinatzin.

Tezozomoc (Te-so-so-mock); Tepanec; ruler of Azcapotzalco and overlord of Tepanecs; father of Maxtla; died prior to Tepanec War (1428).

Tizoc (Tee-sock), the Pierced One; Tenocha; the grandson of Moteczuma I and brother of Ahuitzotl, Axayacatl, and Chalchiuhnenetl (1); Defender of the Temple and member of the Council of Four Lords; the seventh Speaker of the Tenocha (1481–86).

Tlacaelel (Tla-kay-lell), He of the Demon's Heart (1398–1489); Tenocha; the nephew of Itzcoatl and half brother of Moteczuma I; father of Teuxoch and Tlilpotonqui; warchief, High Priest of the Snake Woman (Cihuacoatl), and vice-ruler during reigns of Moteczuma I, Axayacatl, Tizoc, and Ahuitzotl.

Tlacahuepan (Tla-ka-way-pan), Pillar of Men; Tenocha; the eldest son of Axayacatl and brother of Moteczuma II and Chalchiuhnenetl (2); killed in flower war in Atlixco (1496).

Tlacateotzin (Tla-ka-te-ot-sin), Godlike Man (1448–78); Tenocha; the husband of Cocatli and father of Illancueitl, Omeocelotl, and Azcatzin; warrior, commander, and warchief from the ward of Moyotlan; killed in Michoacan (1478).

Tlaltecatzin (Tlal-te-kot-sin), He Shakes the Earth; Texcocan; Master of Arms of the Young Men's House and military instructor of Huemac.

THE TLATELULCA MEXICANS: Inhabitants of the island of Tlatelulco, in the western part of the Lake.

THE TLAXCALANS (Tlash-kal-ans): Inhabitants of the city of Tlaxcala, east of the Lake.

Tlilatl (Tlil-atl), Black Water; Tenocha; the second son of Quinatzin and Ome Xochitl; died during time of famine (1450–55).

Tlilpotonqui (Tlil-po-ton-kee); Tenocha; the son of Tlacaelel and his successor as High Priest of the Snake Woman (Cihuacoatl); adviser to the Speaker and Regent during the ruler's absence.

Tonatiuh (Tow-na-tee-wa), He Who Goes Forth Shining (the Sun); Spanish; Mexican name for the conqueror Pedro de Alvarado.

Tzotzoma (T'so-t'so-ma); Tepanec; sorcerer and ruler of Coyoacan; killed by Ahuitzotl in dispute over water rights (1498).

Xicotencatl (Shi-ko-ten-kotl); Tlaxcalan; ruler of Tlaxcala during time of Moteczuma I (1440–69); enemy-within-the-house to the Mexicans.

Xiuhcozcatl (Shee-wa-kos-kotl), Turquoise Necklace (1398–?); Chichimec; warrior, sorcerer, and agent of Nezahualcoyotl; Huemac's instructor in sorcery and the sacred plants; later the chief of the hill-people; also known as the Old One.

Xiuhcue (Shee-wa-kwa), Turquoise Skirt (1506–?); Tenocha; the daughter of Xolotlpilli and Chalchiuhtona and the sister of Cuauhcoatl; Huemac's granddaughter.

Xolotl (Show-lotl), Monster, Prodigy, Double; Chichimec warchief and first overlord of the Acolhua (1200?); first in the line leading to Nezahualcoyotl.

Xolotlpilli (Show-lotl-peel-li), Monster Prince (1481–1520); Tenocha; the son of Huemac and Taypachtli and the father of Cuauhcoatl and Xiuhcue; apprentice warrior to Chiquatli and member of the order of Cuachic (Shorn Heads); the brother of Quetzal Papalotl; commander and member of the Council of Lords; also known as Xolotl Mexicatl, the Monster of Mexico.

The Places

(present-day locations are approximate)

Acapulco (A-ka-pul-ko); Yopi; on the Pacific coast southwest of Mexico; in the present-day state of Guerrero.

Achiutla (A-chee-ut-la); Mixtec; northwest of the city of Oaxaca; in the present-day state of Oaxaca.

Acolhuacan (A-kol-wa-kon); the province of the Acolhuas, on the eastern side of Lake Texcoco; capital at Texcoco.

Acolman (a-kol-man); Acolhua; town north of Texcoco; in the present-day state of Mexico.

Ahuilizapan (A-wheel-li-sa-pan), There by the Waters of Delight; Totonac; southeast of Mexico, near the Gulf coast; near the city of Orizaba in present-day state of Veracruz.

Alahuitzlan (A-la-wheets-lan); Tlalhuica; southwest of Mexico, in the present-day state of Morelos.

Anahuac (A-na-wock); the mountain valley containing Lake Texcoco and its surrounding cities.

Atlixco (At-lish-ko); Tlateputzca; city beyond the mountains to the southeast of Mexico; in the present-day state of Puebla.

Ayotlan (A-yot-lan); Quiche Maya (?); city on the Pacific coast south of Xoconochco; in the northwest corner of present-day Guatemala.

Azcapotzalco (As-ka-pot-sal-ko), Ant Hill; Tepanec; Tepanec capital just west of Lake Texcoco; in the present-day state of Mexico.

Aztlan (Ast-lan), Place of Herons; legendary ancestral home of the tribes of Anahuac, to the north and west of the Valley.

Cempoalla (Sem-po-al-la); Totonac; city on the Gulf coast east of Mexico; in the present-day state of Veracruz.

Chalchicuecan (Chal-chee-kwa-kan); Totonac; site of the first Spanish encampment on the Gulf coast; the present-day city of Veracruz.

Chalco (Chal-ko); Chalca; lakeside city southeast of Mexico; near the present-day city of Chalco, D.F.

Chapultepec (Cha-pul-te-peck), Grasshopper Hill; mainland promontory southwest of Mexico; site of Maximilian's Palace in present-day Mexico City.

Chiapan (Chee-a-pan); Mazahua; city north of Mexico, in the present-day state of Mexico.

Chiconauhtla (Chee-ko-na-wat-la); Acolhua; lakeside city northeast of Mexico; in the present-day state of Mexico.

Cholula (Cho-lu-la); Choluteca; Holy City beyond the mountains southeast of Mexico; in the present-day state of Puebla.

xx

Coaixtlahuacan (Ko-a-isht-la-wa-kon), Plain of Serpents; Mixtec; city north of the city of Oaxaca; in the present-day state of Oaxaca.
Coatlinchan (Ko-at-lin-chan), House of the Serpent; Acolhua; city on the eastern side of the Lake; in the present-day state of Mexico.
Cosamaloapan (Ko-sa-ma-lo-a-pan); Mixtec; city on the Papaloapan River, near the Gulf coast; near the city of the same name in present-day state of Veracruz.
Coyoacan (Ko-yo-wa-kon); Tepanec; lakeside city to the south of Mexico; now part of Mexico City.
Cuauhnahuac (Kwa-wa-na-wock); Tlalhuica; city beyond the mountains to the south of Mexico; the present-day city of Cuernavaca.
Cuetlaxtlan (Kwet-lasht-lan), Leather Land; Totonac; trading center southeast of Mexico, near the Gulf coast; in the present-day state of Veracruz.
Cuitlahuac (Kweet-la-wock); Chinampaneca; island city in the southern portion of the Lake; now part of Mexico City.
Culhuacan (Kul-wa-kon); Culhua; lakeside city south of Mexico; now part of Mexico City.

Huexotla (Whe-shot-la); Acolhua; city south of Texcoco, on the eastern side of the Lake; ruins south of the present-day city of Texcoco.
Huexotzinco (Whe-shot-sin-ko); Huexotzinca; city beyond the mountains southeast of Mexico; possibly the site of the present-day Huejotzingo, in the state of Puebla.

Ixtapalapa (Ish-ta-pa-la-pa); Chinampaneca (?); lakeside city at the end of the causeway south from Tenochtitlan; near present-day Ixtapalapa, D.F.

Mexico (Me-shee-ko), In the Navel of the Moon; Mexica; the islands of Tenochtitlan and Tlatelulco, in the western part of Lake Texcoco; now Mexico City.
Meztitlan (Mes-teet-lan); Huaxtec; city northeast of Mexico, in the present-day state of Veracruz.
Michoacan (Meek-wa-kon), The Place of Those with Fish; Tarascan; independent province beyond the mountains west of Mexico; the present-day state of Michoacan.
Mictlan (Meek-tlan), Land of the Dead, Region of the Fleshless, Place of Our Common Sleep; mythical underworld; site of present-day Christian hell.
Mizquic (Mis-keek); Chinampaneca (?); lakeside city at the southern extremity of Lake Texcoco; near present-day Xochimilco.
Moyotlan (Mo-yot-lan), Place of Mosquitoes; Tenocha; the southwest quarter of the city of Tenochtitlan.

Nauhtla (Nowt-la); Totonac; city on the Gulf coast, northeast of Mexico; possibly near the present-day city of Nautla, in the state of Veracruz.
Nonohualco (No-no-wal-ko); Mexica; a small island to the west of Tlatelulco, crossed by the western causeway.

Oaxaca (Wa-sha-ka); Mixtec-Zapotec; highland city south of Mexico; the site of the present-day city of the same name.

Otumpan (O-tum-pan); Acolhua-Otomi; city northeast of Texcoco; in the present-day state of Mexico.

Oztoma (Os-to-ma); Tlalhuica; city southwest of Cuernavaca, in the present-day state of Morelos.

Pochtlan (Poach-tlan); Tlatelulca; calpulli (ward) of the merchants in Tlatelulco; speculatively placed in the southwestern quarter of the city.

Tehuantepec (Te-wan-te-peck); Zapotec; isthmian city on the Pacific coast; near the present-day city of the same name, in the state of Oaxaca.

Teloloapan (Te-lo-lo-a-pan); Tlalhuica; city southwest of Cuernavaca, in the present-day state of Guerrero.

Tenayuca (Te-na-yu-ka); Tepanec; lakeside city northwest of Mexico; now part of Mexico City.

Tenochtitlan (Te-noach-teet-lan), Place by the Hard Prickly-Pear Cactus; Tenocha-Mexican; island city in the western part of Lake Texcoco; now downtown Mexico City.

Teotihuacan (Te-o-tee-wa-kon), Place of the Gods; Acolhua; ancient ceremonial site north of Texcoco; ruins near the present-day town of San Juan Teotihuacan.

Tepechpan (Te-pesh-pan); Acolhua; city north of Texcoco; near the present-day town of Tepexpan, state of Mexico.

Tepeyac (Te-pe-yack); Mexica; small mountain at the end of the causeway north from Tlatelulco; a ceremonial site.

Texcoco (Tesh-ko-ko); Acolhua; lakeside city to the east of Mexico, capital of Acolhuacan; the present-day town of the same name.

Texcotzinco (Tesh-kot-sin-ko); Acolhua; hill east of Texcoco and site of Nezahualcoyotl's gardens; ruins in a national park outside the present-day town of Texcoco.

Tizaapan (Tee-sa-a-pan); Culhua-Mexica; first home of the Tenocha, near Culhuacan.

Tlacopan (Tla-ko-pan); Tepanec; mainland city to the west of Mexico, capital of Tepanecs during time of the Three-City Alliance; now part of Mexico City.

Tlalocan (Tla-lo-kon); mythic paradise of the Rain God, home of those who died by lightning or drowning; not to be confused with Cancun.

Tlatelulco (Tla-te-lul-ko), Mound of Earth; Tlatelulca-Mexica; island city in the western part of Lake Texcoco; ruins at Plaza de Tres Culturas in Mexico City.

Tlaxcala (Tlash-kal-la), Eagle Crags; Tlaxcalan; four confederated cities beyond the mountains to the southeast of Mexico; near the present-day city of the same name, in the state of Tlaxcala.

Tlaximaloyan (Tla-shee-mal-o-yan); Tarascan; city in the province of Michoacan, west of Mexico; near the present-day city of Ciudad Hidalgo, in the state of Michoacan.

Tochtepec (Toach-te-peck); Mixtec; trading center on the Papaloapan River, near the Gulf coast; possibly the present-day city of Tuxtepec, in the state of Veracruz.

Toluca   (To-lu-ka); Matlatzinca; city and valley to the southwest of Mexico; near the present-day city of the same name on the outskirts of Mexico City.

Tula   (Too-la), Place of the Rushes, Toltec; ancient capital of the Toltec empire, northeast of Mexico; ruins near the present-day town of the same name, in the state of Hidalgo.

Tullantzinco   (Tul-lant-sin-ko); Acolhua-Otomi; city northeast of Texcoco; possibly present-day city of Tulancingo, in the state of Hidalgo.

Tzintzuntzan   (Seen-soon-sahn); Tarascan; capital city of the province of Michoacan; present-day village of the same name on the shore of Lake Patzcuaro, in the state of Michoacan.

Xicalanco   (Shee-ka-lan-ko); Chontal-Mexican; trading port on the Gulf coast south of Coatzacoalcos; near the present-day city of Ciudad del Carmen, on the Laguna de Terminos, in the state of Campeche.

Xilotepec   (Shee-lo-te-peck); Mazahua; city to the northwest of Mexico; possibly the present-day city of Jilotepec, in the state of Mexico.

Xiquipilco   (Shee-kee-peel-ko); Mazahua; city to the west of Mexico; possibly the present-day city of Jiquipilco, in the state of Mexico.

Xiuhcoac   (Shee-wa-ko-wock); Huaxtec; city to the northeast of Mexico; near the present-day city of Tuxpan, in the state of Veracruz.

Xochimilco   (Show-chee-meel-ko), Flower Fields; Xochimilca; island city at the southern extremity of Lake Texcoco; the city of the same name, south of Mexico City.

Xoconochco   (Show-ko-noach-ko); Maya (?); trading center on the Pacific coast, south of Tehuantepec; possibly near the present-day town of Escuintla, in the state of Chiapas.

Yanhuitlan   (Yan-wheet-lan); Mixtec; a city north of Oaxaca; near the present-day city of the same name, in the state of Oaxaca.

Zacatula   (Sa-ka-too-la); Yopi; a city near the Pacific coast, southwest of Mexico; in the present-day state of Guerrero.

Zinacantlan   (See-na-cant-lan), Place of Bats; Tzotzil Maya; highland trading center in the isthmus between Xicalanco and Tehuantepec; near the present-day town of Zinacantan, in the state of Chiapas.

The Gods

Acuecueyotl (A-kwe-kwe-yotl), Goddess of the Waves; an aspect of Chalchihuitlicue.

Camaxtle (Ka-mash-tle), Lord of the Chase; Hunting and War God of the Tlaxcala and Huexotzinca.

Ce Acatl (Say A-kotl), One Reed; ancient celestial version of Quetzalcoatl; one of the war gods of Teotihuacan.

Centzon Huitznahuac (Kent-son Wheets-na-wock), The Unnumbered Ones of the South; the stars of the southern sky; the uncles and aunts of Huitzilopochtli.

Chalchihuitlicue (Chal-chee-wheet-li-kwa), She of the Jade Skirt; Water Goddess and consort of Tlaloc.

Chicomecoatl (Chee-ko-me-ko-atl), Seven Serpent; Goddess of Maize and Sustenance.

Cihuacoatl (See-wa-ko-atl), Snake Woman; Earth Goddess, ruling over childbirth and death by sacrifice.

Coatlique (Ko-at-leek), Skirt of Serpents; Earth Goddess and mother of Huitzilopochtli.

Coltic (Kol-teek), The Twisted One; War God of the Tepanecs.

Coyolxauhqui (Koy-ol-shwa-kee), Painted with Bells; Moon Goddess and sister of Huitzilopochtli.

Ehecatl (E-he-kotl), Wind; God of Wind; major aspect of Quetzalcoatl.

Huehueteotl (Way-way-te-otl), The Old God; ancient God of Fire.

Huitzilopochtli (Wheet-si-lo-poach-tli), The Hummingbird from the Left; War and Sun God; chief god of the Mexica.

Ilamatecuhtli (Ee-la-ma-te-koot-li), The Old Princess; ancient Goddess of Maize; patron of the month of Tititl.

Ipalnemohuani (Ee-pal-ne-mo-wanni), The Giver of Life; esoteric aspect of the Creator God, Ometeotl.

Macuilxochitl (Ma-kweel-show-cheetl), Five Flower; God of Flower and Song; an aspect of Xochipilli.

Mictlancihuatl (Mict-lan-si-watl), Lady of Mictlan; Goddess of Death and consort of Mictlantecuhtli.

Mixcoatl (Mish-ko-atl), Cloud Serpent; ancient Hunting God; also known as Camaxtle (Tlaxcala) and Taras (Michoacan).

Moquequeloa (Mo-kay-kay-lo-a), The Mocker; an aspect of Tezcatlipoca.

Moyocoyani (Moy-o-koy-a-ni), He Who Creates Himself; esoteric aspect of the Creator God, Ometeotl.

Nahui Olin (Na-whee O-lin), Four Movement; birth sign and name of the Fifth Sun, Tonatiuh; especially sacred to the Eagle and Jaguar Warriors.

Nanahuatzin (Na-na-wat-sin), The Pimply One; god who sacrificed himself to create the Fifth Sun at Teotihuacan; identified with Tonatiuh.

Necoc Yaotl (Ne-kok Ya-otl), The Enemy of Both Sides; an aspect of Tezcatlipoca; creator of strife.

Ometeotl (O-may-te-otl), Lord of the Duality; Creator God, male and female in one; also known as Tloque Nahuaque, Yohualli Ehecatl, Moyocoyani, Ipalnemohuani.

Quetzalcoatl (Ket-sal-ko-atl), Plumed Serpent; God of Knowledge and Learning; patron of the priesthood and the calmecac; Wind God in his aspect of Ehecatl; patron of the traveling merchants in his aspects of Yacatecuhtli and Naxcitl; chief god of the city of Cholula.

Quetzalcoatl-Topiltzin (Ket-sal-ko-atl To-pilt-sin), Our Lord Quetzalcoatl; mythical god-king of the Toltecs of Tula.

Quilaztli (Kee-last-li); Goddess of Childbirth, an aspect of Cihuacoatl.

Tecuciztecatl (Te-kwa-kis-te-kotl), Lord of the Shells; god who sacrificed himself to create the moon at Teotihuacan; identified with the moon.

Telpochtli (Tel-poach-tli), The Youth; an aspect of Tezcatlipoca; patron of the Young Men's House.

Tepeyollotl (Te-pay-ol-lotl), Heart of the Mountains; Jaguar God and God of the Mountains.

Tezcatlipoca (Tes-kotl-i-po-ka), Lord of the Smoking Mirror; War God and God of the Night Sky; also known as the Sower of Discord, the Decider of Fates, the Dark One; aspects as Yaotl, Telpochtli, Necoc Yaotl, Moquequeloa; chief god of the city of Texcoco.

Tlaloc (Tla-lock), He Who Makes Things Sprout; Rain God.

Tlaltecuhtli (Tlal-te-koot-li), Lord of Earth; personification of the earth as a devouring monster.

Tloque Nahuaque (Tlo-kay Na-wa-kay), Lord of the Far and the Near; esoteric aspect of the Creator God, Ometeotl.

Toci (To-si), Our Grandmother; Earth Goddess and Great Mother.

Tonatiuh (To-na-tee-wa), He Who Goes Forth Shining; The Sun; also known as Nahui Olin; patron of the warrior orders; identified with Huitzilopochtli by the Mexicans.

Xilonen (Shee-lo-nen), Young Maize Mother; Goddess of the Young Maize; patron of the eighth month.

Xipe Totec (Shi-pee To-teck), The Flayed God; God of Seedtime and Planting; War God; important to the warrior orders; chief god of the Yopi.

Xiuhtecuhtli (Shee-wa-te-koot-li), Turquoise Lord; Fire God and God of the Year and Time; patron of the eighteenth month; also known as Huehueteotl.

Xochiquetzal   (Show-chee-ket-sal), Flower Feather; Goddess of Flowers and Craftsmen; patron of the ball game.

Xolotl   (Show-lotl), Monster, Prodigy, Double; god of the underworld and twin (nahualli) of Quetzalcoatl; patron of the ball game.

Yacatecuhtli   (Ya-ka-te-koot-li), Lord Who Guides, Lord of the Vanguard; patron of the traveling merchants and an aspect of Quetzalcoatl.

Yaotl   (Ya-otl), The Enemy; War God and an aspect of Tezcatlipoca.

Yoalticitl   (Yo-al-tee-seetl); Goddess of Childbirth, an aspect of Cihuacoatl.

Yohualli Ehecatl   (Yo-wal-li E-he-kotl), Night and Wind; esoteric aspect of the Creator God, Ometeotl.

THE LUCK OF HUEMAC

Prologue: The Gods

ABOVE the twelve heavens, it is said, is Omeyocan, the Place of Duality. Here is the abode of Ometeotl, the Creator of All Things, the god both male and female, known to the people as Ometecuhtli and Omecihuatl, the Lord and the Lady of the Duality. And out of himself, Ometeotl created four sons, one to rule over each of the directions upon the earth. His sons are these:

The Red Tezcatlipoca, god of the East, also known by the names Xipe Totec and Camaxtle.

The Black Tezcatlipoca, god of the North, Lord of the Smoking Mirror, also known by the name Yaotl.

Quetzalcoatl, god of the West, the Plumed Serpent, whose color is white, also known by the name Ehecatl.

The Blue Tezcatlipoca, god of the South, also known by the name Huitzilopochtli.

Many other gods were also created, but these four remained the most powerful, and they vied with one another to be the Sun who gave warmth and color to the earth. Four times, the Sun was created and then destroyed in the struggle between the sons of Ometeotl. The first Sun was destroyed by jaguars; the second by great winds; the third by a rain of fire; and the fourth by storms and rains that flooded the earth. Each time, everything upon the earth was utterly destroyed, and there was blackness.

After the destruction of the Fourth Sun, when the earth was dark and still, the gods gathered at Teotihuacan. There, in the Place of the Gods, they took counsel among themselves as to what should be done. And they cried to one another:

"Speak, O Gods! Who will do this? Who will take on the burden, the glory of being the Sun?"

And one who was great among them, a splendid god whose name was Tecuciztecatl, Lord of the Shells, stepped forward and spoke proudly: "I shall be the one, O Gods. I will give myself to the fire."

"And who else?" the gods asked, but no one answered. They were all afraid, and drew back from being chosen. But at the edge of the circle was one who had listened without speaking, a small god whose body was covered with sores and pustules. His name was Nanahuatzin, and the gods now turned to him and said:

"You, Nanahuatzin, you should be the one to try."

And Nanahuatzin was gladdened, and he accepted their decision with gratitude: "Let it be as you say, O Gods; let me be the one who sacrifices himself."

For four days, Tecuciztecatl and Nanahuatzin fasted and did penance, seated upon the great pyramids of earth the gods had built for them, there at

Teotihuacan. And all of Tecuciztecatl's materials and offerings were precious and costly: the fir branches with which he swept his hill were made of quetzal feathers; the spines of penance were made of jade, and the straw balls into which they were stuck were made of gold; the reddened, bloodied spines were made of red coral, and his incense was the finest white copal.

As for Nanahuatzin, his fir branches were merely bundles of green reeds, and his spines were those of the maguey plant. He reddened the spines with his own blood, and stuck them into balls made of aromatic grasses. For incense, he used only the scabs from his sores, which he tore off with his own fingers.

At the end of the four days, Tecuciztecatl and Nanahuatzin burned their sacred implements and came down among the gods to be arrayed for the ceremony. Tecuciztecatl was given a round, forked headdress of heron feathers and a sleeveless shirt of white cotton. Nanahuatzin's headdress was of mere paper and was tied onto his hair; he was also given a mantle and loincloth made of paper.

When midnight had come, the gods formed themselves into two lines, one on either side of the teotexcalli, the sacred hearth, where a great fire had been kept burning for four days. Tecuciztecatl and Nanahuatzin stood between the lines of gods, facing the hearth, and the gods spoke:

"Tecuciztecatl! Now is the time! Cast yourself upon the flames!"

Tecuciztecatl stepped forward, but when he was at the edge, the flames flared up and the enormous heat of the fire made him afraid, and he could not bring himself to jump. In his fear, he whirled about, stopped, and went back to where he had been. Then he hardened himself and went forward to try it again. He exerted himself and struggled against his fear, forcing himself nearer and nearer to the flames. But he could not bear the awful heat, and again he leapt back instead of forward. Two more times he tried and failed, and then the gods would allow him to try no more.

Then the gods called to Nanahuatzin, the pimply one, the little one with the sores on his skin, and they said to him: "You, Nanahuatzin, have courage! You try!"

And Nanahuatzin stepped forward with determination, hardening himself against the terrible heat of the fire. The flames roared up before him, but he braced himself, and closed his eyes, and with a great leap threw himself all at once into the heart of the fire. His body sizzled and crackled noisily as it burned, and hearing this, the splendid Tecuciztecatl was stricken and rushed forward to throw himself into the fire.

At this time, as well, an eagle flew up and cast himself into the fire after the gods. Thus are the eagle's feathers always blackened as if scorched. And then a jaguar came and followed the eagle into the fire, but since the flames were no longer so great, he was only singed and blackened in places. Thus is the jaguar's skin always spotted, as if splashed with black. And therefore, the bravest of warriors are always called Eagles and Jaguars, because the eagle and the jaguar followed the gods into the fire that made the Sun.

When the bodies of Nanahuatzin and Tecuciztecatl had been consumed by the fire, the gods seated themselves around the sacred hearth to await the rising of the new sun. For a long time they waited, wondering where, from what direction, Nanahuatzin would appear. Each had his own opinion, and they agreed on nothing, arguing among themselves. Some said that the Sun would come from the north, and when the red glow of dawn had begun to spread over the earth, these stood and looked to the north. Others had predicted the west or the south, and so faced in those directions. It is said that Quetzalcoatl and Xipe Totec were two of those who had pointed toward the east, and it was from that direction that the Sun finally came into the sky.

The Sun was red, and appeared to wobble as he came into the sky, swaying from side to side. His light was very intense and penetrated to every corner of the earth, stealing the sight from the eyes of the gods. And then Tecuciztecatl rose behind him from the same direction, and he was exactly the same in size and brilliance. And the gods cried out:

"How can this be, O Gods? Can both of them follow the same path, can they both shine upon us like this?"

So the gods deliberated among themselves and issued a judgment. And one of their number came running, swinging a rabbit over his head by its ears. And he threw the rabbit at Tecuciztecatl, wounding him in the face and destroying his brilliance, so that he is darkened to this day.

But when this was done, the gods saw that both hung motionless in the sky, and could not follow their paths. And they cried out in alarm:

"How will we live, O Gods? The Sun does not move! Are we meant to live down here among the common people? Let all of us die, and with our deaths revive the Sun."

And the task of slaying the gods was given to Ehecatl, the Wind, who slew them one by one. Only Xolotl, the twin of Quetzalcoatl, wished not to die, and had to be pursued before he could be slain. And it is said that when this had been done, when all the gods had died, the Sun still could not move. So Ehecatl rose up and blew with all the force and violence at his command, and at once the Sun began to go on his way. When he had completed his path across the heavens and had come to the place where he set, only then did the moon begin to move and follow him. Thus, the Sun comes forth first and does his work during the day, and the Moon rises behind him, and labors all of the night.

Here ends this legend, which was told in times past, and was in the keeping of the old ones. And the name that they gave to this sun, the Fifth Sun, was Nahui Olin, Four Movement, after the day and sign of its birth. And it is said that under this Sun there will one day be famine and earthquakes, and our end will come . . .

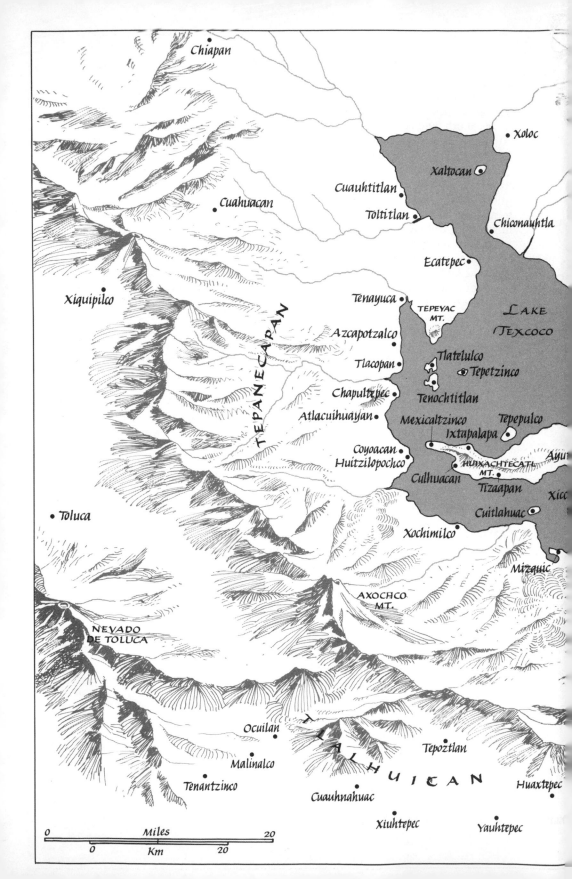

Chiapan

Xoloc

Xaltocan

Cuauhtitlan

Cuahuacan

Toltitlan

Chiconauhtla

Ecatepec

Xiquipilco

Tenayuca

TEPEYAC
MT.

LAKE
TEXCOCO

Azcapotzalco

Tlatelulco
Tepetzinco

Tlacopan

Chapultepec

Tenochtitlan

TEPANECAPAN

Atlacuihuayan

Mexicaltzinco

Tepepulco

Ixtapalapa

Coyoacan
Huitzilopochco

Ayu

Culhuacan

HUIXACHTECATL
MT.

Tizaapan

Xicc

Toluca

Cuitlahuac

Xochimilco

Mizquic

AXOCHCO
MT.

NEVADO
DE TOLUCA

Ocuilan

Tepoztlan

TLALHUICAN

Malinalco

Tenantzinco

Huaxtepec

Cuauhnahuac

Xiuhtepec

Yauhtepec

0   Miles   20

0   Km   20

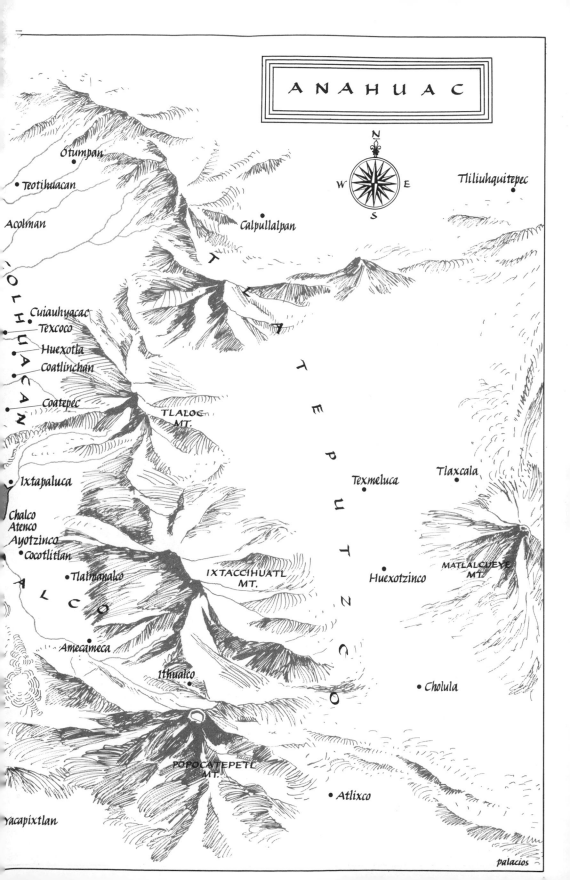

A N A H U A C

N
W · E
S

Otumpan
· Teotihuacan
Acolman
Calpullalpan
Tliliuhquitepec

Cuiauhyacac
Texcoco
Huexotla
Coatlinchan
Coatepec
TLALOC MT.
Ixtapaluca
Chalco
Atenco
Ayotzinco
· Cocotlitlan
· Tlalmanalco
Amecameca
Ithualco
Yacapixtlan

IXTACCIHUATL MT.

POPOCATEPETL MT.

· Atlixco

Texmeluca
Tlaxcala
Huexotzinco
MATLALCUEYE MT.
· Cholula

COLHUACAN

TLALTEPUTZINCO

ALCO

palacios

Behold the Land of Anahuac;
There between the mountains,
There by the shores
Of the Lake of the Moon.

Here live the descendants
Of the Toltecs;
The descendants of the Chichimecs:
Those both wise and fierce,
The people from Aztlan, the Place of Herons.

Here the years are counted,
And bound in sheaves;
Here offerings are made to the gods;
Here the Eagle and Jaguar Warriors
Feed the Sun with their blood.

Behold the Land of Anahuac;
There where the shining water
Reflects the heavens.
Smoke rises from the temple fires;
Dark clouds gather
On the mountain called Tlaloc;
The warriors go forth singing
To the fields of blood and burning.

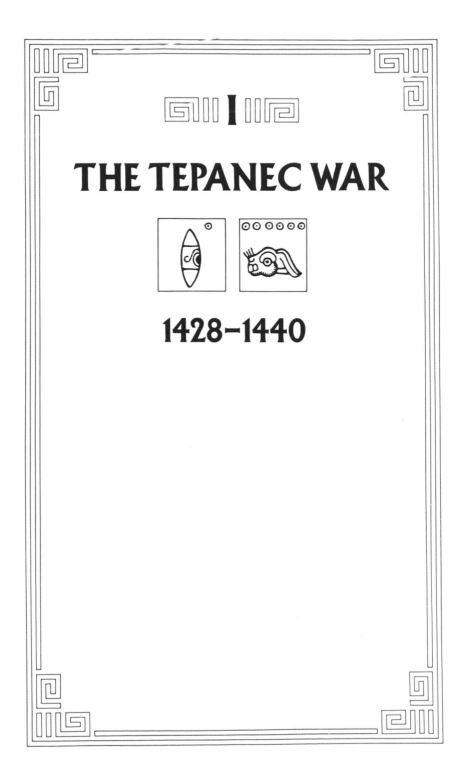

I

THE TEPANEC WAR

1428–1440

1

THE MEXICANS will come to me soon. This was the one thought in the mind of Nezahualcoyotl, Lord of the Acolhuas, as he stood on a high ridge in the mountains of Tlaloc, looking west over the Valley of Anahuac. Mist rose from the surface of the great lake that filled the valley floor, and the cities dotted along its shores shone white in the early morning light. But Nezahualcoyotl had no eyes for the beauty before him. Squinting, he could just make out, in the far western part of the Lake, the islands of Tenochtitlan and Tlatelulco, the homes of the Mexicans. Beyond, on the shore, were the lands of the Tepanecs, Nezahualcoyotl's enemies, the people who had driven him from his own home ten years ago.

Yes, the Mexicans will come to me now, he thought coldly, and they will remind me of our ties of blood, and of the protection they gave me when I was young and new to my exile. We will call each other brother, and we will pretend that we have never been enemies ourselves. We will pretend that they were not the willing servants of Tezozomoc, the tyrant of the Tepanecs, the man who murdered my father and stole my lands; we will pretend that they did not join in the slaughter of my people and the burning of our cities.

All this will be forgotten, out of politeness. We will not even speak of Tezozomoc, but of his son Maxtla, who hates the Mexicans as dearly as his father once loved them. They will tell me how Maxtla assassinated their leaders, and how he has closed off the Tepanec marketplaces to them and cut off the supply of fresh water to their islands. And I will listen to their complaints with sympathy and the proper display of outrage; I will not make it difficult for them to admit their oppression, for I know their pride. Yet they will be made to speak of these things at length, so that the true extent of their desperation will be hidden from no one. Then, when they finally ask me to join with them against the Tepanecs, they will not remember that they had to beg, but only that they had no other choice. I will let them keep their pride, so that their gratitude will not turn to bitterness, and give them cause to turn against me in the future.

Satisfied with his calculations, Nezahualcoyotl opened his eyes to what lay before him. Directly below was Acolhuacan, the land of his birth, and as he gazed at the deep forests and the rich maize lands that led down to the shore of the Lake, he felt the powerful presence of his ancestors. There, among the trees of the forest, he could feel the spirit of Xolotl, the first of his lineage, the great Chichimec warchief who had brought his band of wild nomad hunters out of the northern wastelands and settled them in this green valley. Xolotl, the Prodigy, Lord of the Chichimecs, who had gathered the marauding tribesmen into armies and had led them in conquest over the previous inhabitants of the Valley.

And there, Nezahualcoyotl thought, looking farther west, to where the city of Texcoco rose from the water's edge. There strode the ghost of his great-grandfather, Quinatzin, the fourth after Xolotl, who had coaxed the Chichimecs out of their caves in the hills and made them live in cities and learn the civilized ways of the Toltecs. Quinatzin, who had founded Texcoco and had filled it with craftsmen and teachers, initiating his people into a tradition of learning and culture.

But you, Ixtlilxochitl, my father, Nezahualcoyotl wondered sadly, where does your spirit reside? Do you haunt the Place of the Wolf, the canyon deep in the mountains where I saw you die? You fought bravely against the Tepanec assassins, as I saw from the tree where I hid. But even had you saved yourself, it was too late to save your kingdom. You had no weapons against the treachery of Tezozomoc, who brought his army to Texcoco under a false banner of peace. And you had not thought to arm yourself against the treason of your own lords, who betrayed you and threw open the gates of your city to the invaders. Your innocence and trust were your undoing, my father, Nezahualcoyotl thought grimly, but they will not be mine. I will bring these Mexicans to my side, but I will not turn my back to them. Or to anyone else, be they friend or enemy.

It was the year One Flint-Knife, and Nezahualcoyotl, Lord of the Acolhuas, was twenty-six years old. He was the seventh of his line, one, it was said, who had been destined for greatness from birth. He had suffered much hardship and survived many attempts on his life during the last ten years, and now that destiny loomed large for him, written in the stars that hung over the Valley of Anahuac, and echoed by the sounds of war that drifted across the Lake. It would not be long now.

As Nezahualcoyotl turned to go, his guards stood up from their hiding places and came to escort him back to his camp. There, his loyal Acolhua warriors waited, along with their allies from Tlaxcala and Huexotzinco, the cities that lay to the east, beyond these mountains. It was to this camp that the Mexicans would have to come, offering themselves as allies. Then the war against the Tepanecs would begin again.

THE YOUNG Texcocan warrior, Quinatzin, was among those in Nezahualcoyotl's camp when the Mexicans were brought in, surrounded by the sentries who had intercepted them in the darkness and had taken their weapons. He joined the others who crowded in around the captive ambassadors, whose leader bore a banner of white plumes attached to his broad shoulders. Word quickly spread through the crowd that the one with the banner was the Tenocha warchief, Moteczuma Ilhuicamina, the Angry Lord Who Shoots at the Skies, and Quinatzin strained against those around him for a better look. He had heard stories about this stern warrior, who was related to Nezahualcoyotl by blood, and who had more than once helped him escape from the assassins of Maxtla.

Moteczuma strode through the crowd of onlookers as if he did not see them, as if they were not armed and he empty-handed, as if he could not hear the hostility in some of the voices. His heavy face remained unchanged until Nezahualcoyotl stepped from his tent to greet him, and then the Mexican warchief scowled with such force that many hands in the crowd tightened on their weapons, their owners not understanding how Moteczuma showed his pleasure. But though the speech he made to Nezahualcoyotl was blunt and unrefined, the tones of friendship were unmistakable, and the warriors surrounding Moteczuma relaxed when their ruler came forward to grip the Mexican's arm and call him brother. Nezahualcoyotl ordered that the Mexicans be given back their weapons, and then he led Moteczuma and the other Mexican leaders into his tent.

The Mexican warriors left outside the tent clutched their bows and warclubs tightly and stood together, not speaking to the Texcocan guards who had been stationed alongside them. They know that there are many in this camp who hate them, Quinatzin thought, examining the Mexicans suspiciously. He had reason to hate them himself, knowing the role they had played in the sacking of Texcoco. But all of Quinatzin's hatred was reserved for the Tepanecs, for the bushy-headed warriors who had hunted him like an animal in the darkness, so many years ago. These Mexicans, with their high topknots, could never inspire a similar hatred in him, no matter what they might have done. Let them join with us if they must, Quinatzin decided, glancing at the tent of his leader; I will be the friend of anyone who hastens the day of my revenge upon the Tepanecs.

As gifts, the Mexican ambassadors had brought fish and waterfowl from their cities in the Lake, and Quinatzin's mouth began to water as he saw these things being prepared for the spit. But it was time that he went to his guard post, so he put his thoughts of revenge and his hunger out of his mind and collected his weapons: his bow and quiver of arrows, a flint knife, and his macana, the flat wooden warclub set with razor-sharp edges of obsidian. Though Quinatzin was only eighteen years old, his weapons showed the effects of much hard use, for he had been fighting in these mountains since he was fourteen. He had come here as a child of only eight years, fleeing in terror from those who had burned his home and made him an orphan. Nezahualcoyotl had then been sixteen, and had seen the Tepanecs burn the body of his father before he had escaped over the mountains and taken refuge in the city of Huexotzinco. There, he had gathered his people and found them shelter, and made them live again.

There, too, in a city of strangers, Quinatzin had grown and been educated at the hands of the same old men who had taught Nezahualcoyotl, and sometimes at the hands of the Fasting Coyote himself, who was wise beyond his years, and known to be adept at various kinds of sorcery. Quinatzin had been taught how to read the stars and interpret the symbols in the painted books, how to observe the rites of the gods, and how to speak properly and conduct himself in public. He had also been initiated into the mysteries of the cult of the Black Tezcatlipoca, Lord of the Smoking Mirror, the high god of Texcoco. Only then, when the old men were satisfied with the strength and straightness of his character, had he been ready to learn the ways of a warrior, and to take his place at the side of Nezahualcoyotl.

Once he was beyond the range of the campfires, the darkness closed in around him, for the sky was blackened with clouds and the moon had not yet risen. Picking his way between the rocks and cactus, the young warrior climbed to the ridge, making small noises to alert the sentry of his coming. When he was almost to the place, he coughed once, like a coyote, and an answering sound came from the darkness. Then the guard, a Tlaxcalan, appeared from behind the rocks and stepped close to Quinatzin, so that he could see his face.

"So . . . it is you, Texcocan. What happens below? Who were those I heard coming to the camp?"

"The ambassadors of the Mexicans have come to sit with our leaders. Among them is the great Tenocha warchief, Moteczuma Ilhuicamina. It is said that they have come to join hands with us against the Tepanecs."

The Tlaxcalan grunted in the darkness. "These Tenocha," he said scornfully. "They squat on their island of mud, saying that they will rule the world, yet they cower at the feet of Maxtla. I say, let them save themselves."

"There are many who say this," Quinatzin replied tactfully. "But it is well known that the Mexicans are wild and angry fighters, and that Maxtla hates them more than anyone. If he chooses to tire the arms of his men killing Mexicans, how can we be harmed?"

"How indeed?" The Tlaxcalan laughed. "You are crafty, Texcocan, like your leader. Still, *someone* should kill the Mexicans. Everyone knows of their vicious treatment of the people of Culhuacan, when they were Tezozomoc's overseers there. They are a filthy people, and perverse in their beliefs . . . someone should put an end to them!"

"Perhaps," Quinatzin said agreeably. "But these filthy people have brought us gifts of fish and waterfowl, and the other good things from the waters of the Lake. Even here, I can smell the ducks cooking over the fires . . . "

"I go now," the Tlaxcalan said, and disappeared. Quinatzin smiled to himself in the darkness. These Mexicans and Tlaxcalans are much alike, he thought: Their hearts are in their arms and their stomachs. They would each rule the world in order to feed themselves and their gods.

Taking a sheltered place among the rocks, Quinatzin faced west, looking down the mountainside to the darkness below. In that direction lay the city of Texcoco, the place of his birth, the home that had been stolen from him by the Tepanecs. For many years after his flight, he had not even been able to think about Texcoco, due to the terror the memories of fleeing brought up in him. He had made himself forget and adapted himself to exile, learning to smile at strangers and to make his home among them.

But lately he had begun to dream of returning to Texcoco, tantalizing dreams that left him restless and yearning when he awakened. Always, the city was as he remembered it when he first entered its gates, but then began to change as he walked through the streets. The buildings and temples lost their familiarity, there were paintings and stone-carvings he didn't recognize, and the people began to rush past him without speaking. He always woke before he found the house of his parents.

But it has been ten years since I left, Quinatzin consoled himself, and I no longer look through the eyes of a child, even in my dreams. He wondered now if Nezahualcoyotl shared his yearning, and would strike first at the Tepanec garrisons that held Texcoco. Or would he choose to return with the Mexicans to the other side of the Lake, to the islands that lay so close to the territory of the Tepanecs? From Tenochtitlan and Tlatelulco, the warriors could drive straight at the Tepanec cities of Tlacopan and Azcapotzalco, confronting Maxtla before he had time to summon his allies.

Yes, Quinatzin decided suddenly, that must be what is in Nezahualcoyotl's mind. I know his heart, I know the patience he has learned in exile. He will fight the battle on the enemy's land, and save his own fields from burning. He will leave the garrisons in Texcoco and destroy those who posted them there. When he returns to this side of the Lake, there will be no one to menace him from behind. This is a patience the Mexicans and Tlaxcalans will never learn, Quinatzin thought proudly.

With his face still pointed toward the west, Quinatzin crouched in the darkness, his macana ready in his hand and his senses alert to the smallest sound or movement. But in his thoughts, he was already traveling across the water to Tenochtitlan, to the island city where men like the stern Moteczuma lived and prepared for war. Where he, too, would prepare for war, for the war that would end his exile and bring him home at last. He looked west, toward Tenochtitlan, and was ready for the fighting to begin.

BEFORE the Acolhuas and their allies left for Tenochtitlan, Quinatzin was summoned to the tent of Nezahualcoyotl. The king was wearing an embroidered loincloth, a deerskin mantle trimmed with black thread, and an eagle-feather headdress bearing a shining circle of black mirror-stone, the insignia of Tezcatlipoca, Lord of the Smoking Mirror. Quinatzin looked upon the long, angular face that he knew so well, with the bright, gentle eyes beneath the furrowed brow, and the long nose and pointed jaw that seemed to reach out to those whom he addressed. And he again felt the power of the king's personality, a force of presence that made the eight years' difference in their ages seem like eighty. Quinatzin wondered how he could ever have imagined that he knew this man's heart. He bowed low to Nezahualcoyotl, and called him Lord.

"It has been some time since we have spoken, Quinatzin," Nezahualcoyotl said, his voice smooth and comforting. "You have grown into a man worthy of the name you bear, a name that is honored in my heart. But still, I remember you best as the child who fled with us to Huexotzinco. I remember the child who smiled for us when we were homeless and our hearts were broken."

"Children cannot cry forever," Quinatzin said modestly. "They quickly forget their pain."

"Yes, but even among the children, your cheerfulness was exceptional, and enabled you to make friends easily. Your face has always proven pleasing to strangers, and they speak openly in your presence. I have seen this myself, and my guards tell me that even among the Tlaxcalans, you are known and liked."

"It was from you, Lord," Quinatzin reminded him, "that I learned the secrets of reading men's hearts and gaining their confidence. The Tlaxcalans are men like any others."

Nezahualcoyotl laughed, a high, whinnying sound. "There are some who say that they are beasts who only fight like men. No, Quinatzin, I have taught you some things, but others have come to you naturally. And I have need of your talents."

Quinatzin bowed to show his compliance, and Nezahualcoyotl gestured that he should seat himself on the reed mat opposite his own.

"As you know, I have formed an alliance with the Mexicans," the king said gravely. "Today, the ambassadors of Maxtla came to me here, offering me my lands and the title of my father if I would join with them and turn against the Mexicans. I sent one of the ambassadors back with my answer and had the others spitted on stakes, so that there should be no uncertainty about my loyalty."

Quinatzin straightened slightly, shocked by this violation of custom concerning messengers, and by a ruthlessness he had never seen in Nezahualcoyotl before.

"You know that my father—and your own—were betrayed by those they trusted," Nezahualcoyotl continued, his voice like flint, "as well as by those they should never have trusted. I shall never be so careless about my friends, even those who are related to me by blood. And so, although my mother is a Mexican, and I have spent time in their cities, I desire to know more about them. You must use this face of yours, Quinatzin, you must be my eyes and ears in Tenochtitlan."

Quinatzin bowed again, swelling with pride at this show of trust. He waited expectantly for Nezahualcoyotl to go on.

"You must learn all you can about the disposition of the people toward this war, and their morale. Find out what kind of allies they will make. As you do this, bear in mind that the Tenocha and the Tlatelulca are separate peoples, though both call themselves Mexican, and both claim Huitzilopochtli as the high god of their cities. Listen carefully for the signs, and the causes, of the differences that exist between them."

Nezahualcoyotl paused, to allow Quinatzin to absorb what he had been told, then continued:

"You are familiar with the orders of the Eagles and the Jaguars, the warriors who have taken vows to Tonatiuh, the Sun. They have their lodges in every city in the Valley, and they are dedicated, above all else, to the sacred task of providing captives for sacrifice to their god. They are not well established in our ranks because of our exile, but it is said that they are particularly numerous and influential among the Tenocha. You must determine, if you can, the true extent of their power in Tenochtitlan.

"Finally," Nezahualcoyotl concluded, "you must learn all you can about the one called Tlacaelel, He of the Demon's Heart, the brother of Moteczuma. I know little of him myself, except that he is very powerful. Make no mistakes in how you inquire of him."

Quinatzin bowed to indicate that he had heard and understood, and rose to leave. Then he hesitated, frowning involuntarily.

"What is it?" the king demanded sharply, but then smiled. "Ah, yes, you are a warrior, and eager for glory, and revenge upon the Tepanecs. Do not be anxious, Quinatzin, you will have your turn in the fighting. You will be there when we put the torch to the temple in Azcapotzalco, I promise you this. But first you will make the acquaintance of these Mexicans."

"Yes, Lord," Quinatzin said gratefully, and bowed, and went to gather his weapons.

2

THE islands of Tenochtitlan and Tlatelulco lay in the shallow, salty part of the Lake, less than a mile from the western shore. The canoe in which Quinatzin was sitting was heading for Tenochtitlan, which lay slightly to the south of its neighbor, and seemed the larger of the two islands. Through the clouds of water birds hovering overhead, though, Quinatzin could see that Tlatelulco was much the grander city, the tops of its temples thrusting high into the air above houses that shone cleanly under a coat of white paint. Tenochtitlan, on the other hand, presented an unimpressive vista of flat-roofed, dun-colored buildings crowded one after another, with few taller buildings rising out of their midst.

Quinatzin's canoe was one of three that had come from Acolhuacan, each carrying a dozen Texcocan warriors, and as they glided through a channel between the dense cane thickets and reed beds, they were the object of much curious staring by the Mexican fishermen and fowlers. The Texcocans were all fully armed and were wearing their thickly padded cotton armor, and Quinatzin raised his head proudly between thrusts with his paddle, knowing that he presented a brave and warlike figure.

Closer in to the island, the water opened out again, cleared of the reeds and rushes, and they began to pass isolated hillocks of earth, over which huts of reeds and mud perched precariously on high stilts, with canoes tied up underneath. Here, there were an incredible number of people working in the water: men with long spears stood motionless in the shallows, stalking frogs; women with reed baskets on their backs gathered newts and fish eggs among the rushes; gangs of young boys dredged mud from the lake bottom and piled it onto rafts woven from reeds, building the floating chinampa plots that were everywhere along the shore, anchored by young cypress trees. All these people worked steadily, in silence, seemingly oblivious to the war canoes passing behind them.

Quinatzin observed it all with eager eyes, struck by the similarity of this scene to the descriptions he had heard of Aztlan, the Place of Herons, the mythical homeland to the north from which the seven major tribes in the Valley had come. There, too, the people had lived by fishing and capturing the waterfowl, and since the Mexica had been the last tribe to journey south, it seemed appropriate to Quinatzin that they should gain their livelihood in the old way. It is plain that they have no maize lands here, he thought, so it is only natural that they have made the Lake their garden, and work it like farmers.

But then the canoes left the open water and entered a canal lined with mud-brick houses raised over the water on pilings, and the stench of the city seemed to descend upon them in a cloud. It was a smell like no other Quinatzin had known, an odor of fish, mud, rotting vegetation, and human excrement. After the high, clear air of the mountains, it came to his nostrils like a blow, and he coughed harshly, fighting back the urge to gag.

"These Tenocha do not *smell* of greatness, anyway," the man behind Quinatzin said, and the warriors in the canoe gave vent to their discomfort in a chorus of scornful laughter.

The banks of the canal widened and grew higher as the canoes went forward, passing rows of houses set back behind narrow streets, which were filled with people. Only the warriors among the crowd stopped to look at the canoes, the others hurrying along with baskets in their arms or tumplines stretched around their foreheads to the loads on their backs, all moving at a pace too rapid and purposeful to permit curious dawdling. It is best that we be ignored, Quinatzin reminded himself, to assuage his disappointment at this lack of a reception. Nezahualcoyotl had not wanted to give the appearance of having come here to save the Tenocha, an appearance that would have been as enlightening to the Tepanec spies as it was offensive to the Tenocha themselves. So the Texcocans had come in small groups, and it was rumored that many would be hidden away until the fighting actually began. But not I, Quinatzin thought, and his spirits were lifted by the importance of the secret task with which he had been entrusted.

Azcatl, a white-haired old man who was one of Nezahualcoyotl's chief lieutenants, met them as they disembarked at the canoe dock in the center of the city. After assigning some young boys to see to the canoes, Azcatl ordered the warriors into their ranks and marched them quickly to the telpochcalli, the Young Men's House, where they were to be quartered. Quinatzin had just finished rolling up his armor and arranging his weapons next to his sleeping mat when he was summoned to the main hall by Azcatl.

"You are being given the insignia of a messenger of the second rank," the old man informed him, "which you will wear at all times when you are on duty. The Tenocha are very particular about such things, so see that you do not forget, or try to enter places forbidden to your rank. You will be made to spend much of your time waiting, and will no doubt be abused by those above you, but you must not allow this to distract you. Even from abuse, there is much that can be learned."

"I understand you, Grandfather," Quinatzin said courteously.

"You will report only to me, but not until you feel you have learned all that you need to. Until then, you are a messenger like any other, and I will treat you as such. Do you have any questions?"

"No."

"Good. Then tell me what you have learned so far."

Quinatzin thought quickly, realizing that he should have been prepared for this kind of examination.

"I have noticed that Tlatelulco has better temples and houses," he said slowly, "and that the Mexicans, like our ancestors in Aztlan, harvest their food from the Lake, as if its waters were their fields. They are very intent on their work."

"Anything else?" Azcatl asked, giving no clue as to whether or not he was satisfied. Quinatzin cast about in his mind, but he could think of only one thing.

"Their city stinks very badly," he said impulsively, and the old man laughed.

"We would not have much use for you, if you had not noticed *that*. I would not mention it to the Tenocha, however," he added dryly, and nodded to Quinatzin, indicating that he was satisfied. "Go and rest now, my son. Tomorrow, your work begins . . . "

IN THE middle of the night, Quinatzin bolted upright out of a dream, awakened by a rumbling, clashing sound that made him reach for his macana in alarm. The war has started, he thought wildly. But then, as his heart quieted, he could make out the individual sounds of drums, gongs, and shell trumpets amid the din, and he realized that what he was hearing were the midnight ceremonies of the Tenocha priests. He had forgotten that the telpochcalli was so close to the precinct of the temples, and he looked around in embarrassment, to see if anyone else had been awakened. On the next mat was a comrade from the mountains, a man a few years older who was called Nahuicoatl, Four Serpent. He had propped himself up on an elbow and was smiling at Quinatzin, his teeth a thin, white line in the near-darkness.

"You have been living in the wild for too long," Nahuicoatl whispered in an amused tone. "You have forgotten the sounds of a city. Even in this stinking place, the priests observe the ceremonies of the gods."

"Indeed," Quinatzin said gruffly, and lay back down.

"No doubt they are calling on Huitzilopochtli to fulfill his promise and make them the rulers of the world. Then perhaps they would not need *us* to fight for them."

Quinatzin grunted softly, indicating his displeasure with this kind of jesting, and Nahuicoatl laughed and rolled over on his side away from him. Quinatzin stared into the darkness, wondering about the high god of the Mexicans, Huitzilopochtli, the Hummingbird from the Left. He had asked one of the priests in the camp about this god, but the priest had not been able to tell him much, for little was known about Huitzilopochtli among the other tribes in the Valley. He had led the Mexicans to this place from Aztlan, and he was their war god, a god who fed on the hearts and blood of men. There were some among the Tenocha, the priest had said, who claimed that he was the Blue Tezcatlipoca, the last of the original four sons of Ometecuhtli and Omecihuatl, the Creators of All Things. But there was nothing in the sacred books, the priest had added, that proved this to be true.

So their god, like their city, is young and unestablished, Quinatzin thought, listening to the rapid beating of the teponaztli, the two-toned wooden drum. Is it you, Huitzilopochtli, he wondered, who has stirred up this conflict? Or is it your brother from the north, the Black Tezcatlipoca, the god of my people, the Lord of the Smoking Mirror? He is the second-born and much the stronger, recognized everywhere in the Valley as the God of the Night Sky, he who sees the fates of all men in the black depths of his smoking mirror. And though we weep and make offerings to him, he laughs at our hopes and creates strife and discord upon the earth, promising only death. Yet you, Huitzilopochtli, you promise your people the whole world! Is such a thing to be believed of one so little known?

Quinatzin stirred restlessly, disturbed by this incongruity, yet able to find little comfort in Nahuicoatl's scorn. They are our allies, he thought, and they fight as much for us as we for them; it is improper, and foolish, to treat their god with disrespect. The sounds suddenly began to die down, and Quinatzin relaxed his muscles and closed his eyes. A shimmering, turquoise-blue hummingbird blossomed in the middle of a circle of blackness, hovering effortlessly on vibrating silver wings. May you be as mighty as you claim, Quinatzin prayed wearily, as he sank into sleep. May you be strong and true, Huitzilopochtli, for our fate has been joined with yours . . .

QUINATZIN spent the whole of his first day carrying messages from one chamber to another within the Tecpan, the sprawling complex of buildings where the official business of the war was being conducted. The rooms and hallways were filled with warriors, priests, and other messengers like himself, and it was from these that Quinatzin began to form his impressions of the Tenocha. They seemed, at first, very much like the man he had seen in the mountains: grave and taciturn, showing little curiosity in their surroundings and no interest whatsoever in making the acquaintance of a stranger. They did not seem to know that it was natural for men to pass the time of waiting in conversation, and all of Quinatzin's attempts at friendliness were met with rude remarks or a stony silence.

Yet behind the rudeness, he sensed a great impatience, an overriding urgency that distracted them from the demands of politeness. They are in a hurry even when they are standing still, Quinatzin decided; they have no time for proper greetings or idle talk. That must be why their speech is so blunt and crude, and why they react suspiciously to the greetings used in Texcoco and Huexotzinco. They cannot even find the time to smile. But what is this impatience that consumes them? Quinatzin wondered; can they truly be so eager for war?

He returned to the telpochcalli at dusk with his questions unanswered, feeling baffled and frustrated in his mission. He could learn nothing about these people while their faces remained closed to him, yet he had no notions as to how to make them open up. Nahuicoatl, though, who had spent the day standing guard in various parts of the city, had already resolved the matter of the Mexicans for himself.

"They are savages," he stated flatly. "They have nothing, and they know nothing. Never have I seen so many blank, unpainted walls in a city, and so many faces that are equally blank."

"I have seen nothing outside of the Tecpan," Quinatzin confessed gloomily.

"You have missed nothing," Nahuicoatl spat. "Their palaces and temples are all half-finished. The temple of Huitzilopochtli, their great god, is little more than chalk lines and stakes in the earth. And their gardens are all dead."

"But that is because they have no water," Quinatzin pointed out, having noticed the same thing in the courtyards of the Tecpan. "Maxtla has cut the aqueduct to the springs at Chapultepec, and there are only a few springs on the island. The lake water here is salty, and undrinkable."

"And stinking," Nahuicoatl added, then smiled slyly. "They also have no maize or beans, since the Tepanecs have refused to trade with them. Some of us took our extra rations to the marketplace today, and it was as if we had brought bags of precious stones! It was thievery, the things that were offered to us for a mere handful of beans . . . "

Quinatzin frowned. "We were warned against cheating the people."

"Is it cheating to take what is offered?" the older man demanded, looking at Quinatzin with annoyance. "Besides, the Tenocha warriors who were policing the marketplace stopped the bidding just when it was getting good. They made the people so ashamed of their eagerness that afterward they would not trade with us at all."

"Not at all?" Quinatzin asked curiously.

"They would not even barter. They shunned us completely."

"Had the warriors forbidden them to trade with you?"

"They did not have to," Nahuicoatl said with disgust. "These people have enormous pride, once they are made to remember it."

"Ah!" Quinatzin exclaimed softly, suddenly seeing the stony faces of the Tenocha in a different light. Their pride *must* be enormous, he thought, remembering the people he had seen laboring in the water. To have lived here this long, without land or fresh water or even the stone with which to build their temples—in this *stench*—and to still dream of ruling the world! Quinatzin shook his head in amazement. Mere friendliness would not be enough to capture the attention of a people so hard-pressed, and so stubborn in their ambitions. I, too, must remember this pride of theirs, he told himself, but I must never use it to shame them. I must approach them with the caution and respect appropriate to such proud savages.

ON HIS third day of duty, Quinatzin was finally given an assignment that allowed him out into the city. His destination was the temple of Huitzilopochtli in Tlatelulco, and he could tell from the contents of the message that it was not urgent, and that he could travel at his leisure. Though he maintained a properly somber expression upon his face, there was an unmistakable eagerness in his gait as he left the Tecpan and crossed the open space that separated it from the palace of Itzcoatl, the Speaker of Tenochtitlan. Ahead was the south gate of the Coatepantli, the Serpent Wall that surrounded the great plaza that was the precinct of the temples. Quinatzin had no authorization to enter this area, but his curiosity had been so aroused by Nahuicoatl's description that he had to try to see it for himself.

The large, stone head of an eagle, painted red, stared down at him as he approached the entranceway, which was split by four rows of plastered columns. Presenting himself to the Tenocha guards, Quinatzin described his mission briefly and asked for directions, pretending that he was in a hurry and did not know that it was possible to walk around the enclosure. Nor did he use the elegant Texcocan form of address that was natural to him, because he had learned in the last day and a half that the Tenocha found elegant speech intimidating, and therefore offensive from one of his low rank. Instead, he tried to speak as they did, directly and plainly, affecting a pose of studied indifference to the response, as if a refusal or rebuff could not touch him.

He had been having some success with the Tenocha guards and messengers in the Tecpan, speaking with a practiced abruptness that made them attend to his words before they could react to his presence. These guards proved no different, one of them turning automatically to point north, across the plaza. Quinatzin followed the man's arm and stepped past him into the enclosure, nodding seriously at his words.

"That is the way I will go, then," Quinatzin said matter-of-factly, as if the judgment had been made for him. "I am grateful for your advice."

The guard nodded magnanimously and waved him toward the gate at the far side of the plaza, some three hundred yards away. I am learning, Quinatzin congratulated himself, as he walked out of the shadow of the Serpent Wall and into the bright sunlight flooding the enclosure. The rich, resinous aromas of pine smoke and copal incense filled his nostrils, and he slowed his pace instinctively, affected by the great hush that hung over the activity in the plaza. The faint sound of chanting voices drifted through the air like the echo of some timeless and constant music, punctuated by the sharp, chipping sounds of stone chisels and the low rumbling of stone blocks being dragged on wooden rollers.

There are as many workmen as priests, Quinatzin thought, and they have much work to do. All the temples within his immediate view were in some stage of construction, some still surrounded by wooden scaffolds and earth ramps, others receiving their first coats of plaster and paint. To his left were two small temples, both nearly completed, one bearing the Flower Feather insignia of Xochiquetzal, Goddess of Flowers, and the other the seven serpents of Chicomecoatl, the Goddess of Maize. A line of young boys with shorn heads climbed the steps of this second temple, their backs bent double under loads of wood for the temple fire, and Quinatzin nodded respectfully at their holy labors, though he knew that only the god of war could put maize back into the marketplace of Tenochtitlan.

To his right, as he moved ahead, a much larger edifice was in its first stages of construction, its shrine already in place on a small platform in front of the pyramid being raised for it. From the shining black stones surrounding the portals of the shrine, Quinatzin could see that this was the temple of his own god, the Black Tezcatlipoca, and he was pleased with the size of the projected pyramid. He glanced up at the sun, then across the vast expanse of the plaza, noticing the way the shadows fell in precise, orderly patterns. They have much work to do, he thought, but they have planned well. Perhaps they do indeed have a vision of their future greatness, and it is this that makes them impatient with the present.

Directly ahead of him now, in the very center of the plaza, was a raised platform surmounted by a large, cylindrical building with a conical roof of thatched straw. Quinatzin recognized this immediately as the temple of Quetzalcoatl, the Plumed Serpent of the Toltecs. Quetzalcoatl's temples were always round, for he was also known as Ehecatl, the God of Wind, and it was not fitting to obstruct his swirling presence with sharp corners that cut the air. As Quinatzin came abreast of the main entrance, he had to pause for a procession of black-robed priests and barefoot apprentices, who were coming down the platform steps waving braziers of incense and carrying long staffs covered with white paper streamers. Quinatzin bowed his head and offered a silent prayer to the Plumed Serpent, the Giver of Knowledge, the god who had promised to return one day to reclaim the kingdom he had abandoned in the time of the Toltecs of Tula. O Lord, Quetzalcoatl-Topiltzin, Most Perfect Priest, he prayed; give me the wisdom for this task, guide me to the knowledge I seek, open the hearts of your people here, so that I may learn their secrets.

After the priests had passed, Quinatzin lifted his head and examined the temple. One side of the roof was still under construction, and several of the attached buildings were also unfinished, their walls as empty of plaster and paint as Nahuicoatl had claimed. But the stone serpent's heads flanking the steps were excellently carved, and the low entranceway into the shrine had been cunningly painted to resemble the gaping jaws of a great snake. What they have been able to do, Quinatzin thought, they have done with skill; Nahuicoatl was wrong to mistake their poverty for an indifference to craftsmanship.

Knowing that he should not linger idly, Quinatzin began moving again, his eyes sweeping over the temples beyond that of Quetzalcoatl, identifying those of Tonatiuh, the Sun, and Cihuacoatl, the Snake Woman, among others he could not recognize. To his right, alone at the far eastern end of the enclosure, was the first stage of what was obviously intended to be a massive pyramid. The temple of Huitzilopochtli, Quinatzin guessed, noticing the stakes and markers that Nahuicoatl had mentioned. A flight of perhaps twenty steps led up to the top of the platform, and set well back upon it were two wooden shrines with raised, ornate roofs. The one to the north was painted blue and decorated with scalloped shells, the color and symbol of Tlaloc, the ancient God of Rain. The southern shrine was red and painted with golden butterflies, and standing before its veiled entrance was the familiar, ridged shape of the techcatl, the sacrificial stone. Next to the platform was the tzompantli, the skull rack, where the heads of those who had been sacrificed to the god were displayed.

For a poor, oppressed people, they have been generous to their god, Quinatzin reflected grimly, counting several hundred heads impaled on the horizontal poles of the tzompantli. He glanced again at the red shrine. So, Huitzilopochtli, he mused, you are a god of fire, and you share your platform with the water god who has been worshiped for so long in this valley. It seemed a wise accommodation, a fitting acceptance of the gods who had ruled here before Huitzilopochtli had even led his people out of the caves at Aztlan. Such a pairing cannot have come about by accident, Quinatzin decided; this is not the work of ignorant savages.

But then he was close to the north gate, and his thoughts were interrupted by the challenge of a Tenocha guard. Quinatzin displayed the yellow plumes attached to his shoulder and spoke in his Mexican voice.

"I carry a message to Tlatelulco," he said abruptly. Then, struck by a sudden intuition, he gestured admiringly at the temples behind him. "Have they temples in their city as impressive as these?"

The guard scowled, but satisfaction showed in his narrowed eyes as he looked past Quinatzin at the plaza.

"Some that are bigger," he admitted grudgingly, "but none as finely crafted. We are Culhuas; our craftsmanship comes from our ancestors, the Toltecs. The Tlatelulcans are like their brothers, the Tepanecs; they admire anything gaudy and large."

"Have they as many heads in their skull rack?"

"No!" the guard snorted, and laughed scornfully. "You can be sure of *that.* They wear out their arms in paddling their canoes, instead of in fighting."

"That is shameful," Quinatzin agreed earnestly, and the guard waved his hand in disgust.

"Ah, they are the whores of the Tepanecs! We would be better off to fight this war without them."

"Surely, though," Quinatzin suggested, allowing himself a smile, "there is room for my people alongside the Tenocha. We also have reason to hate the Tepanecs."

"Then you may join us!" the guard said expansively. "There will be killing enough for everyone. Go now, Messenger, but watch over yourself in that city of quackers."

Quinatzin nodded confidently, as if he indeed knew what quackers were and how to defend himself against them, then went through the gate and turned left, following the Serpent Wall toward the causeway that led to Tlatelulco. In his heart, he was thanking Quetzalcoatl for the inspiration that had led him to speak to the guard as he had, and to learn the power that flattery gave him with these people. But many of the things the guard had said were puzzling to him, and he wished that Nezahualcoyotl or Azcatl had told him more about the history of the two tribes of Mexicans. What did it mean that the Tenocha considered themselves Culhuas, and spoke of the Tlatelulca as brothers of the Tepanecs? Quinatzin had yet to meet anyone clearly identifiable as a Tlatelulcan, and he had assumed that this was due to his own inability to distinguish them from the Tenocha. Can it be, he wondered now, that I have not seen any, because none were present? Can it be that the two tribes are separated by a hostility much greater than the stretch of water between their islands?

The street to Tlatelulco began at the western end of the Coatepantli, and was the widest thoroughfare that Quinatzin had so far come across in the city. As he joined the crowd moving north, the sweet smells of the holy precinct were left behind, and the powerful odor of dirty water came to him from the canals. He quickly discerned, as he crossed over bridge after bridge, that the area of the palaces and temples was the only high, solid ground on the island, and that the common people lived in a constant state of struggle with the waters of the Lake, which flowed beside, beneath, and sometimes completely around their houses. Wooden pilings banked with earth provided only a minimal protection against flooding in some sections, and the side streets were often little more than narrow dikes of earth and mud. Quinatzin stopped noticing the crude construction of the houses and their lack of paint, marveling at the mere fact that they were kept standing with so little real foundation.

The long bridge to Tlatelulco loomed ahead, and about one third of the way along its length, a barricade had been erected across it. This was being guarded by a heavily armed contingent of Eagle Warriors, recognizable by their identical beaked headdresses of eagle feathers. They were a fierce-looking group, and they stared boldly into the faces of all who tried to pass, questioning them as to their credentials and business.

"I carry a message to the temple of Huitzilopochtli," Quinatzin explained to the warrior who stopped him and peered into his face.

"You are one of the Fasting Coyote's men?" the Eagle Warrior asked, then nodded before Quinatzin could answer. "You may pass, then. They will provide you with a guide to take you to your destination," he added, pointing to a similar barricade that had been set up a short distance farther down the bridge.

Assuming that the guard was referring to the Tlatelulca, Quinatzin looked in the direction of the second barricade, and what he saw there made his blood freeze. Suddenly, he was a child again, running for his life through the leaping shadows of burning buildings, with the shrieks of the dying ringing in his ears and the wild, uncomprehending terror of an eight year old squeezing his heart.

"What is it?" the Eagle Warrior demanded, gripping Quinatzin's arm to steady him. Instinctively, Quinatzin knocked the hand away and whirled to face the man, assuming a fighting stance. Then he blinked and realized where he was: the Eagle Warrior was holding his deadly macana waist-high and ready to strike, and his comrades had closed in around Quinatzin on all sides.

"You should not raise your hand to an Eagle, my friend," the Warrior said in a cool, menacing voice. "Even if you *are* unarmed and only jesting. What is this madness that has come over you?"

Quinatzin slowly straightened up and let his hands fall to his sides, and the warriors around him relaxed and broke their circle. Feeling exceedingly foolish, Quinatzin pointed toward Tlatelulco.

"Those are Tepanecs," he said harshly, forcing himself to look again at the warriors behind the second barricade. All had shaven foreheads and large tufts of hair sticking up on the backs of their heads, presenting the bushy silhouette that Quinatzin remembered all too well from that terrible night ten years earlier. A great coldness came over his limbs as he stared at them, and he flexed his empty hands uselessly.

"Those are Tlatelulca," the Eagle Warrior corrected him, smiling grimly. "But you were not *far* wrong. They have been the slaves of the Tepanecs for so long that they have even come to look like them. It is only the oppression of Maxtla that reminds them that they are Mexicans like us."

"I must go now," Quinatzin said, realizing what a spectacle he had made of himself. I will be of *no* use to Nezahualcoyotl, he thought disgustedly, if I continue to call attention to myself in this way.

"Perhaps you would like a weapon," the Eagle Warrior suggested slyly. "*They* would not like it, but I doubt that they would dare to take it from you."

"It would not be proper," Quinatzin demurred. "I am only a messenger."

Taking his leave of the Eagle Warrior, Quinatzin passed through the barricade and walked down the bridge. His emotions began to rise again as he neared the crowd of tufted heads, but he repressed them angrily, stiffening his back and fixing his face into a stern expression. When he stated his business to the Tlatelulca guards, he used the cold, haughty tones he had learned from the warrior lords of Huexotzinco, looking past them with eyes that were veiled and condescending.

"Tezcatl will take you there," one of the guards said, and suddenly Quinatzin was confronted by a man too large to look past. Quinatzin was not small himself, but this man was half a head taller, and his chest and shoulders were massively muscled. He was about Quinatzin's age and had a handsome face, though his huge head was completely bald and shone like a beacon in the sunlight. He smiled at Quinatzin, showing broad rows of large, white teeth.

"I am Tezcatl," he said, in a voice as large as himself. "I would be honored to escort you to the temple."

"Let us go, then," Quinatzin said curtly, so determined not to be intimidated by Tezcatl's size that he missed the man's smile, which vanished abruptly at his rude reply. Tezcatl turned and led the way down the bridge, and Quinatzin followed at his own pace, still too conscious of the bushy heads to observe anything around him, or to feel the anger emanating from the Tlatelulcan. The next thing he knew, they had turned off the bridge and entered a narrow passageway between two houses, and Tezcatl had turned to face him.

"I would not challenge you before the others," the Tlatelulcan said with barely restrained fury, "but now you will answer my greeting with the respect due to a warrior of your own rank. You are not Tenocha, so there is no excuse for this lack of manners."

Quinatzin stared at him in surprise and then anger, gauging his size and weight and the possible success of a sudden blow to the throat. But he realized just as quickly that he was no match for this man unarmed, and that entering into a brawl while on duty could earn him only disgrace. Besides, the man is right, he thought with sudden remorse; I forgot myself, there on the bridge; he smiled at me and I treated him rudely.

"I am Texcocan, and my name is Quinatzin," he said evenly. "I greet you, Tezcatl, and I ask that you forgive my rudeness."

Tezcatl bowed ceremoniously, his great bald head glistening under a fine sheen of perspiration, and Quinatzin returned the bow without hesitation.

"That is more like the way allies should conduct themselves," Tezcatl said gruffly, looking into Quinatzin's face. "No doubt the Tenocha have been telling you lies about us, and have caused you to act this way."

"I do not believe all that I am told," Quinatzin said stiffly, disconcerted by the man's candor. No one had spoken to him so openly since he had come to these islands, and he was not sure that he should allow himself to trust it. But there was something in the man's face that made him want to, and something in himself that made him want to explain the cause of his rudeness.

"It was the sight of your comrades that made me forget myself," he blurted impulsively. "They looked to me like Tepanecs, and I cannot be polite in the presence of those I consider my enemies."

"I would look like that myself," Tezcatl said evenly, without apology, his eyes on Quinatzin's face, "had I not inherited my father's baldness. But we are Mexicans, my friend, do not mistake us for the enemy. When the fighting begins, there will be no question of our feelings for the Tepanecs."

This last was uttered with fierce conviction, and, despite the lingering discomfort of his forced apology, Quinatzin found himself liking this man, whose outspoken dignity was so different from the taciturn pride of the Tenocha. And there was such sincerity in his face and words! Can I really be so lucky, Quinatzin wondered, for surely, this is an exceptional man. Who has sent him to me?

"I was wrong to let appearances deceive me," he said finally, seeing that Tezcatl was waiting for his reply. "I would be honored if you would lead me to your temple."

Tezcatl smiled with open satisfaction, bowed again, and led the way back to the street. Relaxed for the first time, Quinatzin was able to open his eyes to the city around him, noticing the relative abundance, after Tenochtitlan, of stone and white paint, and the greater solidity of the foundations of the houses. The canals were also wider here than in the city to the south, and there seemed to be many more canoes. Quackers, Quinatzin thought suddenly, seeing several fowlers expertly poling their canoes through the traffic in the canal. Remembering the scorn of the precinct guard, and feeling the attentiveness of the man beside him, Quinatzin decided to give Tezcatl's frankness a further test.

"Your city is older than that of the Tenocha," he observed aloud. "Did you not come to these islands together?"

"You have not heard the tale of our journey from Aztlan?" Tezcatl inquired skeptically. "I am surprised that the Tenocha have not told you their version of it, to impress you with their importance."

"I have been in Tenochtitlan only a short time."

"That is usually long enough for them to begin their bragging," Tezcatl said dryly. "But let me tell you, then, what *we* know to be true: The first of our people to come into Anahuac, over a hundred years ago, settled near the springs at Chapultepec, the Grasshopper Hill, which you can see to the southwest of Tenochtitlan. But they were a small tribe, and the land there belonged to others. Eventually, they were attacked by their neighbors and forced to flee for their lives. Some—*my* ancestors—came here, to this hill of earth in the Lake, this island they called Tlatelulco.

"The others," Tezcatl continued, warming to his story, "fled south and sought protection from the ruler of Culhuacan, which was then a powerful city, the last remnant of Toltec greatness. They lived there for thirty years, fighting for the Culhua lords and marrying their daughters. But then they did a terrible thing to the daughter of the Culhua king, and they were forced to flee again. It is these who came to live on Tenochtitlan, and who now call themselves the Culhua Mexica."

"What was this terrible thing that they did?" Quinatzin asked, unable to restrain his curiosity.

"*That* you must ask the Tenocha," Tezcatl said with a superior smile, "when they tell you *their* story."

I will, Quinatzin vowed, if I ever find a Tenocha as talkative as you, my friend. They had left the street and entered a large market area, laid out in neat rows of merchants' stalls with wide aisles in between. As they wound their way through the crowds of customers, Quinatzin noticed that there was no shortage of goods here, including seashells, rare stones, parrot feathers, and other precious items that must have come from a great distance. The Tlatelulca merchants also had maize and beans to trade. Not great quantities, surely, but neither were the maize sellers attracting large and eager crowds. Nahuicoatl could not have cheated anyone here.

"How is it that your people have maize and beans?" Quinatzin asked, careful not to make his statement sound like an accusation. "The Tenocha have none."

"They hoard theirs for the war, then," Tezcatl said flatly, "for we have shared our stores with them since the Tepanecs closed their markets to us. But they do not have our skill with the canoe, and their traders are not as resourceful as ours. They have learned enough from us to keep themselves alive, but they have always preferred warfare to fishing and trading."

"And you, my friend?" Quinatzin inquired boldly. "Do you not also welcome the chance to win glory in battle?"

"As much as any warrior," Tezcatl vowed, holding Quinatzin's eyes to make sure he was believed. "But fishing and trading are also honorable pursuits, and someone must feed the warriors. It is the Eagles and Jaguars who give the Tenocha this attitude, for there are a great many of them in Tenochtitlan, and they live only to fight."

Quinatzin's ears pricked up at the mention of the warrior orders. "Are there not Eagles and Jaguars in Tlatelulco?"

"There are some, but our highest order is that of the Otomi Warriors," Tezcatl said proudly. "They are those who shave their heads to look like mine, and wear splendid mantles and lip-plugs. My father was an Otomi Warrior, and I shall be one myself with one more captive. But my father was also an artisan, and he taught his craft to me. When this war is over, Quinatzin, you must come to my house in the calpulli of Atezcapan, and I will show you the fine mirrors and mosaics I make from the black and silver mirror-stones. But enough of this idle talk, ahead of us is the temple . . . "

Tezcatl's commanding presence earned them a swift passage through the guards at the gate of the temple precinct, and then they were standing before the temple of Huitzilopochtli, which towered over all the buildings surrounding it. Steep stairs rose in three successive flights to the platform high above, where the two wooden shrines sat side by side. But the shrine next to Huitzilopochtli's red house was painted black, and was decorated with the black mirror-stone of Tezcatlipoca. Tezcatl nodded in response to the startled expression on Quinatzin's face.

"We do not claim, like the Tenocha, to be the heirs of the Toltecs," he said simply, "so we have not placed the Toltec rain god next to the god of our people. We pray to the Lord of the Smoking Mirror, the Decider of Fates, as you do."

And has Huitzilopochtli made you the same promise that he made to the Tenocha? Quinatzin wondered. But Tezcatl was leading him into the hushed courtyard beside the temple, and it was not the place to be asking such questions. I have learned much today, Quinatzin told himself, but I have also been very lucky. Had this man not had the boldness to remind me of my manners, I would have abused him, and would have learned nothing. I must be patient, and treasure his frankness like the gift that it is.

Waiting in the courtyard for the priest to appear, Quinatzin stared upward at the twin shrines of Huitzilopochtli and the Black Tezcatlipoca, the brother gods who seemed to be looking over his fate in these island cities. Which of you has shown me this favor, he wondered, and sent me this man who corrects my manners and makes me learn? Which of you would have me know these Mexicans despite myself?

Twin columns of smoke rose from the shrines, darkening the sky above the temple. All was silent within the courtyard, where Quinatzin waited patiently to deliver his message. Tezcatl stood next to him with his head bowed respectfully, assuming that Quinatzin was praying to the god of his people. But it was of his king, not his god, that Quinatzin was thinking, preparing, in his mind, the message he would one day deliver to Azcatl.

3

AND after the Mexica had lived at Tizaapan for thirty years, Huitzilopochtli again became restless, for he always preferred strife and unrest to peace. So he called to his priests:

"Mexica! It is time for you to go to the place I have promised you as a home. But you cannot go there peacefully; you must go there in a warlike way, with many dying. Be brave, my people, and show me the strength of your arms! Go now to the king of the Culhuas, and ask him for his daughter as the bride of your king. Tell him that she will also be married to your god and will rule as a goddess in your city. This woman will be the Woman of Discord, and it is she who will provide the reason for your leaving here."

And so the leader of the Mexica went to the Culhua king, Achitometl, and asked for his daughter, telling the king that she would be worshiped as the bride of the god of their city. Achitometl loved his daughter greatly, but he could not refuse the honor the Mexica offered to pay her, so he agreed. There was great rejoicing in both cities, and the bride was brought back to Tizaapan and seated upon the icpalli, the reed seat of the ruler. Then Huitzilopochtli again spoke to his priests:

"Now that you have this woman, you must dress her as my bride and sacrifice her in my name. Then you will flay the skin from her body and give it to one of the youths to wear in her place. You will dress this boy in all the regalia of the goddess and place him upon the icpalli, and after this you will invite Achitometl to come to your city and see how you have honored his daughter. Then you will prepare yourselves for war."

The Mexica were filled with fear at this command, but they dared not disobey their god, so they did as he had instructed. Achitometl was at last invited to visit his daughter in her place of honor, and the king of the Culhuas called together all the dignitaries of his city and brought them with great ceremony to Tizaapan. After many gifts had been exchanged, the king was invited to enter the chamber where his daughter resided as the goddess of the Mexica, who called her Toci, Our Mother.

Achitometl did so proudly, and once inside the darkened chamber, he sacrificed quail and scattered their blood in the four directions, and he threw incense onto the coals of the divine fire. When the incense flared up, there was light in the room by which to see, and Achitometl reverently raised his eyes to the figure upon the icpalli. But there, instead of his beloved child, he saw the awful sight of the youth dressed in his daughter's skin, wearing the jewels and feathers of the goddess. Screaming in horror, the king rushed from the chamber, calling to his people to arm themselves. Then the Culhuas came against the Mexica in force, and drove them in flight from Tizaapan, killing many . . .

Thus the people came at last to the place the god had prophesied, the place in the swamp where the waters ran white, and the willows and junipers were also white, and so were the fishes, frogs, and snakes in the water. And then they found the rock upon which grew the great nopalli, and at the top of the high cactus was the eagle, spreading his wings in the bright light of the sun. In his talons was the serpent upon which he fed, and when he saw the people, he bowed his head to them. Then the Mexica knew that the prophecy of Huitzilopochtli had been fulfilled, and they had come to their home, to the place where they would one day rule over all the lands between the Divine and Unlimited Waters. To Tenochtitlan, the Place by the Hard Prickly-Pear Cactus . . .

QUINATZIN had heard the story enough times by now that he knew it by heart, yet he had not stopped thinking about it, or pondering its meaning. He understood now why the other tribes in the Valley considered the Tenocha to be perverse, and feared having them for neighbors. It was indeed a terrible thing that they had done to the daughter of the Culhua king, yet they regarded it with a reverence and awe that did not let them see the hideousness of their actions. It was the command of their god, and they could not question its holiness, especially since it had led to the fulfillment of Huitzilopochtli's prophecy.

It was a barbaric legend, Quinatzin felt, yet it gave the Tenocha their sense of being indomitable, for all of them believed it to be true. Quinatzin had tested this himself, on all kinds of people, from warriors to fishermen, for he had become adept at flattering the Tenocha and loosening their tongues, and now had contacts in many parts of the city. Every one of them knew the story of the Woman of Discord and the founding of Tenochtitlan, and it had never taken more than a little coaxing to get them to repeat it to him. Quinatzin was fascinated by the trance they all seemed to fall into during the telling, forgetting his presence entirely, as if they were calling up the story from the deepest sources of memory.

He now knew most of the stories of the Tenocha, and had fixed in his mind much of what he would tell Azcatl. But he was still not satisfied with what he knew of the man called Tlacaelel. Certainly, the exploits of this brother of Moteczuma were the subject of much bragging, and the fiery words with which he had shamed the Mexica and urged them toward war were repeated over and over, as if he, and not Itzcoatl, were the Speaker of the city. Yet Quinatzin knew only the barest facts about the man himself, and he mistrusted the stories, because they were told in the same, trancelike way that seemed to more properly belong to the legends of the gods and the ancients. This man was alive and breathing, yet the only thing visible in these tales was the common perception of his bravery and prestige.

With the day of the war approaching, security had tightened around the city, and Quinatzin's movements were confined more and more to the Tecpan, where the activity was intense. On those occasions when he could get out to visit his sources, he pressed them for information with increased boldness, knowing that his days as a messenger were numbered. He used every opportunity to bring up Tlacaelel's name in conversation, always expressing his admiration as the excuse for his interest. But all he heard were the same stories and speeches, repeated with a veneration that quickly turned to nervous suspicion if he demanded to know more about the man's life and personality. Even the faces of his most talkative informants turned blank at the mention of Tlacaelel, no matter how subtly he approached the subject.

Shortly after he had begun to make these inquiries, Quinatzin became aware that he was being watched, and followed whenever he went out into the city. It was easy enough to shake the watchers, when he wished to, but he soon saw that such evasive action was useless. Contacts who had spoken freely to him earlier now turned their faces away at his approach, even some to whom he had never spoken of Tlacaelel. He is indeed a powerful man, Quinatzin realized, and he is moving ahead of me. He decided that he'd learned all that he could, and that it was enough. So he went about his business plainly, and did not try to elude his pursuers, and ceased making inquiries that might arouse suspicion. At the close of one day, he slipped away from the Tenocha warrior who had been shadowing him and found his way to the room of Azcatl.

With the care and patience of a good messenger, Quinatzin told him first of what he had learned of the histories of the two tribes, and of the separate lineages they had established, and of the differences in the gods they worshiped. He described the advantages enjoyed by the Tlatelulca, due to their trading abilities and skill with the canoe, and the scorn and jealousy felt by the Tenocha on this account. He talked of the predominance of the warrior orders in Tenochtitlan, and of how the cost of their maintenance was being borne by the macehuales, the common people.

"The streets in the calpullis, the districts, go unswept and the canals and dikes unrepaired," Quinatzin said, "because the young boys from the telpochcallis are all at work building defenses along the western shore, or making arrows for the warriors. But I myself have seen the women scraping the eggs of the waterflies from the reeds for food, and very young children, only years in age, up to their necks in the water, pulling up reeds to build their precious chinampas. And they do this while gnawing on roots and drinking the troubled water of the Lake, starving themselves so that the gods and the warriors may be fed."

"There is praise in your voice, Quinatzin," Azcatl said shrewdly. "Have you come to admire these people?"

Quinatzin shrugged, as if such a possibility were beneath him, for he had heard the veiled scorn in the old man's voice.

"They are not Texcocans," he said bluntly. "Their temples are half-built and their palaces have no gardens. Besides this, they are crude in their manners and speech, and they have a great weakness for flattery. But they will make good allies, because although they are poor and oppressed, they have not lost their pride, or their belief in their destiny."

"Yes, everyone knows of their ambition," Azcatl agreed impatiently. "Will they betray us?"

"Even the Tlatelulca, who have ties of blood with the Tepanecs, know that Maxtla desires their destruction. They are fighting for their lives. And everyone knows what our Lord Nezahualcoyotl had done to Maxtla's ambassadors. He could not have given the Tenocha a better proof of his friendship, because those who are in power here admire strength and fearlessness above all else."

"And how firm is their power?"

"The Eagle and Jaguar Warriors command great respect in this city, and it is said that Itzcoatl himself, and all those who surround him, are from the ranks of these orders. They are gambling everything on the success of this war, and it is rumored that Itzcoatl and Tlacaelel have promised the Eagles and Jaguars much in return for withholding themselves from battle until the day of the war. The priests of the Sun are said to be very angry that a flower war has not been arranged to provide captives, and they remind the warriors of their vows to Tonatiuh. But the rulers hold them fast, and the common people see no other choice but to support them; they speak of the Eagles and Jaguars as their shade, their shelter."

"And of this man, Tlacaelel? What do you hear of him?"

"Everyone speaks of his exploits and repeats his words. They boast of how he went alone to Maxtla and presented him with weapons and anointed him with the chalk paint of the dead, as a declaration of war, and of how he fought his way past the Tepanec guards to return to Tenochtitlan. They tell of how he shamed those who suggested surrendering their images of Huitzilopochtli to the Tepanecs, and how he stirred the people to war. These stories have been repeated to me many times."

Quinatzin paused before going on.

"Of the man himself, though, little is said. His father was Huitzilihuitl, son of Acamapichtli, the first of the Tenocha rulers, and his mother was from Chalco. They say that he and his brother Moteczuma, whose mother was a woman from Cuauhnahuac, were born in different places on the same day, at the same moment. As a warchief, he holds the rank of Atempanecatl, Guardian of the Shores, but he is also called Cihuacoatl, because he is the priest of the Snake Woman, she who lives in the House of Darkness. Beyond this, and the stories, the name of Tlacaelel freezes people's tongues. They are afraid of this man. It was after I asked about Tlacaelel that the men began to follow me through the streets."

Azcatl raised his eyebrows, but Quinatzin dismissed his concern with a shake of his head.

"They are not skillful at such things, these Tenocha," he said condescendingly. "They do not have the humility necessary for stealth. I can evade them at will."

"Do not be young and foolish, Quinatzin," the old man scolded. "Tlacaelel is a dangerous man, and this is his city. You are no longer a messenger. Go tonight to your comrades in the telpochcalli and stay with them, and do not mingle with the Mexicans. The fighting will begin soon, and you must prepare yourself."

"I have heard you," Quinatzin said stiffly, and Azcatl smiled.

"Do not be offended, my son," he said gently. "You have done well, and you will be rewarded. But you must not rush to meet your fate. We need you in this fight."

"Can Tlacaelel be so dangerous a friend?" Quinatzin asked, only partially mollified by the old man's soft words. Azcatl nodded emphatically.

"Yes. And you must tell no one of the duties you have performed, or that you are in any way interested in this man. Go now, Quinatzin," the old man said gravely. "But watch behind you . . . "

THE WAR was now very near. Already, a combined force of Acolhuas, Tlaxcalans, and Huexotzincans, under the command of Nezahualcoyotl, had clashed with the Tepanec garrison at Tenayuca, the city that commanded the end of the causeway that went north from Tlatelulco. The Mexican warriors and the rest of the Acolhuas were massed along the causeway that led west toward Azcapotzalco, and the Tenocha and Tlatelulca war canoes, commanded by Moteczuma and Cuauhtlatoa, the Tlatelulca warchief, were ready for an attack on the Tepanec city of Tlacopan, on the western shore. Maxtla's allies among the Xochimilca were said to be wavering in their loyalty, and no troops had arrived from Coyoacan, where the inhabitants of Maxtla's former home were fighting among themselves. Soon, it was said, a fire would be lit on the mountain called Quauhtepec, on the northern shore of the Lake, and the war would begin.

For several days, Quinatzin had not stirred from the telpochcalli, where he and the other warriors of his company awaited the call to battle. He had gathered his provisions, filled all of his quivers with arrows, and honed the edges of his macana to a deadly sharpness. His fasting and penance to the gods had been completed the day before, and he had had his consultation with one of the soothsayers who daily visited the warriors' quarters. This had only added to Quinatzin's restlessness, because the soothsayer, while promising him glory, had warned that it might come at the cost of his life.

Quinatzin did not feel that he deserved to spend what might be his last days in the confinement of the Young Men's House, listening to his fellow Texcocans repeat the same tired stories. Because of Azcatl's order, he was forced to limit himself in conversation, and could not talk about all the things he had seen and learned in the past weeks. So he had to sit silently and listen to Nahuicoatl and the other warriors speak scornfully of the Mexicans, out of ignorance, calling them savages, and mud-eaters, and people who stank of fish. He heard them complain, in their elegant Texcocan accents, of the poorness of the food and the shortage of water, when he knew they were getting the best the city had to offer. He remembered the fisherman whose hut he had visited near the shore, a man who plied his nets from sunrise to dusk, yet was allowed to take home only a little to his hungry children. "Our warriors and their allies must eat," he had said to Quinatzin, and had turned over all of his fish to Itzcoatl's provisions collectors, hiding nothing for himself.

There is more to these people than you know, Quinatzin wanted to say, but could not. He began to resent Azcatl's orders, remembering how he had been scolded, and how the old man had ridiculed his admiration for the Tenocha. And he does not know these people as I do, Quinatzin thought; that is why he fears them. Was I so young and foolish that I did not notice that I was being followed, and immediately cease making suspicious inquiries? And are we not the guests of these people, and their allies? Though he is my superior, Quinatzin decided pridefully, he was wrong to have spoken to me like that, and to have confined me so closely.

The urge to once again wander through the muddy streets of Tenochtitlan began to grow in him, and he decided that he at least deserved the right to look upon the stars before he went into battle. Late one night, he was given his chance. Azcatl was suddenly called away from the telpochcalli, and he took with him the two sentries who had been guarding the door to the street. Quinatzin found himself alone in the room where he was stationed, with no official duties until the morning watch. For several moments, he could not believe his good fortune, but then he got up and moved toward the door. Making sure that he was not observed, he slipped from the telpochcalli and into the dark streets, taking only a flint knife for protection, because the Tenocha sentries were nervous and might react harshly to an unauthorized, armed warrior at loose in their city at night. Almost immediately, Quinatzin was aware of a pursuer behind him, but his desire to be out overwhelmed his misgivings, and he fled into the shadows with the sound of soft footsteps following after him.

At ease in the darkness, Quinatzin quickly outdistanced his pursuer and then doubled back on him, hiding beneath a house raised on stilts at the water's edge until the Tenocha warrior had gone past. Circling wide along the shore, Quinatzin drank deeply of the damp, salty air, reveling in his freedom. Frogs boomed in the shallows, and the water birds squawked and splashed off into the reeds at his approach. The sounds and smells of the city seemed familiar to him now, and he felt no trepidation as he left the shore and moved through the streets, pausing frequently to avoid sentries, processions of priests, and the movement of troops. It was some time before he realized that he was again being followed.

Disturbed by his own carelessness, Quinatzin doubled back and hid himself in the darkness, remaining motionless as the time passed and the mosquitoes hummed over his exposed flesh. The priests blew their conch trumpets, signaling the middle of the night, but he still had not seen his pursuer. When he crept out of his hiding place and again began moving toward his goal, his senses quickly told him that he was not alone. Sweat began to form on his body as he dodged between houses and ran through the shadows beneath the temple walls. Then he caught his first glimpse of the man behind him, and shortly afterward, he was able to lead the man into the view of two Tenocha sentries, who accosted him with loud cries as Quinatzin slipped away into the darkness.

Breathing hard, Quinatzin at last came to his goal, which was the mecatlan, the mud-brick building where the Tenocha stored the drums and flutes used in the festivals of the gods. It was a one-story building standing upon a raised mound of earth, not far from the palace of the Speaker. Quinatzin climbed to the roof and crouched at the edge, listening. The throaty *huac-huac* of a night heron came to him from the water, but otherwise all was silent. In the middle of the roof was a garden that had been abandoned for lack of water, and Quinatzin walked through the weeds and broken stalks to the center of the plot, where he stopped and gazed up at the night sky.

It was a clear night with little moon, and Quinatzin stared upward in awe, having never seen such a spectacular commotion in the sky. Stars wheeled across the heavens as if they had been thrown, and the stars to the west seemed to shrink and flee before all the others. Quinatzin felt his heart swell with confidence and pride, for he saw in the stars a great victory for the Acolhuas and their allies, who would blaze their way westward to Azcapotzalco, driving the Tepanecs and their war god, Coltic the Twisted One, before them.

And Quinatzin saw the wisdom of Nezahualcoyotl confirmed in the stars that shone over Tenochtitlan. The stars of the Tenocha pierced the night sky like fiery darts, making those to the west and south seem to tremble in their movements. Even the silver-clawed Jaguar of Tezcatlipoca, hanging high over Texcoco, was no match in brightness. Nezahualcoyotl must have seen this long ago, Quinatzin thought; he has known all along that there is no denying these people.

But Quinatzin was suddenly aware that he was no longer alone on the rooftop, and he turned to find a man standing almost at his elbow. How he had approached so closely without being sensed, Quinatzin never knew. He was shorter than Quinatzin and perhaps ten years older, a slender man yet physically very powerful. The muscles stood out on his bare arms like taut bowstrings, and his face in the near-darkness was that of an eagle, cruel and hungry, a hunter of men. His hair had been cut in the manner of the highest of Tenochan warriors, with just a lock left over the left ear, but his face was blackened like a priest's. He was wearing a long white mantle, and his ears and forearms had been recently bled with the thorn of penance. Quinatzin knew, though he had never seen him before, that this was the Man with the Demon's Heart: Tlacaelel.

"What do the stars tell you, Texcocan?" the man asked, his voice a harsh rasp that buzzed in Quinatzin's ears. Quinatzin quelled the instinctive movement of his hand toward the flint knife at his side, telling himself that he could never save himself in that way. Only with my tongue, he thought.

"There will be a great victory, my Lord," he said confidently, as if he had been sent here to gather just this information. "We will drive the Tepanecs before us like so many rabbits." Quinatzin felt the hungry eyes upon him and added: "And the Tenocha will be the greatest of all in this fight."

"Yes," the man agreed, turning his eyes upon the sky. "Yes, there will be much glory for the warriors of Tenochtitlan, and many captive hearts for Huitzilopochtli. But come closer, young lord," the voice rasped, "my throat is tired from much talk, and I would know what is in your face and your heart. I found you here only by accident; I must know how you eluded my men."

The hungry face was now very close, and the talons of an eagle gripped Quinatzin's arm. Desperately, he sought to calm the beating of his heart and drive off the fear that clouded his mind. He knew that he dared not show any fear to this man.

"I do not know the men of whom you speak, Lord," he said, using the deliberately courteous tones of the Texcocan nobility, who were experts at feigning innocence. "I came here alone, to view the stars, and I brought no one with me. And why should I desire to elude the Tenocha, who are my brothers in this war?"

"Even brothers have their suspicions of one another," Tlacaelel said harshly. "Maxtla had *his* brother killed. Do you know who I am, Texcocan? Yes, I can see that you do, so do not anger me with your false innocence. How is it that you move so easily through the darkness?"

"My god is the God of Night; he guides my footsteps."

"And your tongue?" Tlacaelel demanded. "What god has driven you to these questions that you ask of my people? Speak, Texcocan. You have asked of me, and now I am here to answer your questions. What is it that you desire to know?"

"You must forgive the natural curiosity of a young man," Quinatzin said, with a sincerity that came from desperation. "I merely wished to know more about the man whose name is upon everyone's lips, the man who is said to be the fiercest of the Tenocha. I did not believe that any man could be more formidable than Moteczuma, whom I saw in the mountains. But I know now that what they say of you is true, for I can feel it in your presence, beyond all questioning."

There was a long silence, and Quinatzin realized that he had not fooled this man, and that he himself was here alone, far from the strong arms of his comrades. His body would be found among the reeds, food for the vultures, and it would be said that he had been killed by Tepanec spies. And always, after this, Azcatl would speak of him as the example of what happened to those who were young and foolish enough to disobey orders.

But then Tlacaelel laughed: a hoarse, heavy sound, without mirth. Quinatzin repressed a shiver.

"You do not fool me with your flattery, Texcocan. But I understand now how you were able to loosen the tongues of my people, and elude my guards. You are young, but already you are as slippery as your king. What is your name, young lord?"

"Quinatzin, Lord."

"Then know, Quinatzin, that this night you have looked upon your death, and it has not claimed you. I came here to kill you, but I am not a wasteful man. I know the value of a brave captive."

Quinatzin realized that his arm had been released from the cruel grip, and he forced himself to ignore the urge to rub away the pain that lingered behind.

"If you are not killed in the fighting," Tlacaelel continued, his voice proud and commanding, "you will come to me afterward, and I will give you one of my daughters as a wife. We are going to rule the world, Texcocan, and my city will need men like you, men whose tongues are as subtle as their hearts are strong. Our young warriors are bold in their actions and words, but they do not know how to mask their faces with cleverness and respect. We will need your slipperiness before we are through. When you come back to Tenochtitlan after this war, Quinatzin, you will stay here and teach it to them."

"I am honored, Lord, and if the Decider of Fates, Tezcatlipoca, does not steal my life from me, I will come to you when the war is over. But the city of Texcoco is the home of my birth, and it lies in ruins, weeping, waiting for the return of her men."

"You will not refuse my wishes, when the time comes. Believe that with all your heart, Texcocan. Huitzilopochtli will watch over you, and Tenochtitlan will be your home and the home of your children. You will live here and teach your sorcery to your father-in-law, Tlacaelel."

It was as Quinatzin had suspected, yet the very name struck fear in his heart, and made him believe what he had been told. Bowing low, he put his fingers into the dust of the garden and touched them to his tongue. Tlacaelel laughed hoarsely.

"Go back to the stars, Texcocan," he commanded. "Believe what you read there, and forget your lost home. Your fortune lies *here,* Quinatzin . . . "

WITH the strength of the Mexicans and their allies growing daily, and still no allies of his own having come from Xochimilco and Coyoacan, Maxtla decided to strike the first blow. Shrieking their war cries and blowing on bone whistles, the plumed and painted Tepanec warriors, in their cotton armor of many colors, launched themselves against the white-clad warriors who guarded the island cities. The Mexicans and Acolhuas under Itzcoatl and Tlacaelel met the Tepanecs at the place where the causeway entered the western quarter of Tenochtitlan, showering the enemy with darts and arrows from behind the earthworks they had constructed of reeds and mud.

To the north, Nezahualcoyotl again led his forces against the Tepanecs at Tenayuca, to prevent them from sending reinforcements to Maxtla. Moteczuma and Cuauhtlatoa brought their war canoes across the water and attacked the lakeside city of Tlacopan, which surrendered to the Mexicans without a fight. The Tepanecs of Tlacopan had long been friendly with the Mexica, and Maxtla had angered them by cutting off trade between the cities out of his own personal spite, without consulting them. Now they paid him back by opening their city to the Mexicans and giving them aid against the Tepanecs of Azcapotzalco.

Day after day, the fighting surged back and forth along the causeway, spilling over into the reeds of the Lake, and sometimes reaching into the streets of Tenochtitlan. The warriors threw themselves against one another in a confusion of bodies and weapons, the Tepanecs following their multicolored standards and the Mexicans recognizing their allies by their white armor and the red thongs they wore around their heads. The water of the canal called Petlacalco, where the fighting was the worst, was stained red with the blood of the fallen, and clouds of carrion birds hovered over the corpses that lay uncollected in the shallows. Many times, the outnumbered Mexicans seemed on the verge of being overrun, but then Tlacaelel would rally his warriors, or Moteczuma would attack with his canoes, and the threat would be beaten back.

Finally, the white-clad warriors won command of the causeway and fought their way to the shore. Badly hurt, the Tepanecs retreated to Azcapotzalco, the Ant Hill, where they fortified their capital and prepared to defend themselves. But it was not a long siege, with no supplies coming from Tlacopan and the full force of Mexicans and Acolhuas holding the fields surrounding the city. Nezahualcoyotl's warriors pressed down from the north, and after one hundred and fifteen days, the siege was broken and the defenses breached. Soon the fighting reached the streets, and circled in around the temple of Huehue-teotl, the Old One, the high god of Azcapotzalco.

Quinatzin, his face painted with the black and yellow stripes of Yaotl, the Enemy, and his macana well-bloodied, was among those who first reached the summit of the temple. He and his companions, a mixture of Acolhuas and Tlaxcalans, slew the last of the Tepanec guards and priests and burst into the shrine, which was empty, the image of the god having already been taken down and carried off. The Tlaxcalans in the party immediately fell to looting, breaking open the reed coffers that had been left behind and using their macanas to pry the precious stones from the walls. But Quinatzin and the other Acolhuas set about destroying the relics of the Tepanec god, the god who had ruled over the land of Acolhuacan when they and their god had been hiding in the mountains of Tlaloc. Crying "Texcoco!" and shouting the names of their fathers and brothers, they toppled the altar and tore down the carved wooden façade that stood behind it. Then they ripped down the wall hangings of cloth and feathers and threw them onto the pile, and shredded the vestments of the priests on the edges of their warclubs. Lastly, they overturned the brazier next to the altar and watched the pile catch and leap into flames.

As the fire reached the wooden roof, the Acolhuas retreated from the shrine with the Tlaxcalans not far behind, still gathering loot. Some of them joined together and with a mighty heave toppled the techcatl, the sacrificial stone, and sent it crashing down the temple steps. Quinatzin stood on the edge of the platform and watched the shrine burn, brandishing his macana and ululating into his palm, savoring his revenge. In the flames, he thought he could see the face of Nezahualcoyotl, and the face seemed to smile, reminding him of the king's promise that he would be here for this. And then behind the face of the Fasting Coyote appeared another, a face filled with the joy of killing and destruction, a face that stared out at him with hungry eyes. Defiantly, Quinatzin shook his warclub at the face of Tlacaelel.

"This war is not over yet, Demon Heart," he cried aloud, and turned to run down the steep temple steps, seeking new victims, and careless of his own death.

SPREADING south and east, the war continued for another five years after the fall of Azcapotzalco. Maxtla had escaped and fled south to Coyoacan, which was the next city to feel the combined weight of the Mexicans and Acolhuas, who were supported in this venture by their new allies from Tlacopan. Then Nezahualcoyotl took his warriors and returned to his lands on the eastern side of the Lake, conquering first the northern cities of Teotihuacan, Otumpan, and Acolman, before sweeping down to drive the last of the Tepanecs from Huexotla, Coatlinchan, and the city of his birth, Texcoco.

Quinatzin was not with Nezahualcoyotl when Texcoco was recaptured, because he had been sent with the company that went to Huexotla. From there, he marched south to help the Mexicans subdue the Xochimilca, who had failed to help Maxtla yet had responded threateningly to the Mexican movement southward. Quinatzin performed bravely on the Flower Fields of Xochimilco, adding several captives to his credit, but his luck deserted him in the streets of the lakeside city of Mizquic. There he was surrounded in battle and slashed at from all sides, until he fell with his legs badly mangled and blood pouring out of him in many places. His comrades saved him from capture, but he lay near death for several weeks, and it was thought by the healers that he would never walk again.

In the time of his delirium, before the fever broke, Quinatzin again dreamed of returning to Texcoco. And in these dreams, the city was as he remembered it from his youth, with its beautiful gardens and great temples. He was happy in these dreams, and the people he met were friendly. Once more, he ate in the house of his father. When he finally awoke, he thought about what he had dreamed, and he realized that the city he had dreamed about before the war was not Texcoco, but Tenochtitlan. Can it be that Huitzilopochtli was reaching out for me even then? he wondered. He thought often of Tlacaelel, hoping he had been forgotten, as the days passed and he lay on his mats, too weak to move.

The house where he was quartered was among those occupied by the Tenocha garrison that had been left in Mizquic, and when he had gotten stronger, Quinatzin had himself carried out into the courtyard, where he could converse with the warriors and learn the latest news from the other cities. Most of the talk, naturally, was of Tenochtitlan, which now possessed lands of its own, and had sovereignty over other cities. The Tenocha warriors boasted endlessly of the wealth that was pouring into their city, and they discussed to the smallest detail how the captive lands had been distributed among the leaders, temples, and calpullis, with the largest shares going to the supporters of the war party, and the warrior orders. New titles and insignia had been given to those who had distinguished themselves in the fighting, and a council of four lords had been elected to sit next to the Speaker and advise him. These included Moteczuma and three of his close relatives, and it was from their ranks that the next Speaker would be elected.

There was also a fifth adviser to the Speaker: the Cihuacoatl, he who spoke with the voice of the Snake Woman, informing the ruler of the goddess's thirst for fresh blood and the hearts of men. A chill came over Quinatzin's body whenever the warriors spoke of Tlacaelel, calling him always by his priestly title, though his powers were really those of a secondary ruler. It was he who had advised Itzcoatl to burn the painted books of the tribe, so that the memory of their servitude should not live on to shame the conquerors. It was he who had devised the new titles of the warriors and the powers of the Council of Lords, creating a leadership dedicated totally to the divine mission of Huitzilopochtli. He had made war the highest calling of the Tenocha, and whenever the warriors spoke of him, their voices were hard and cruel, and their words were filled with the images of conquest and death.

He will not want me, Quinatzin thought hopefully; he will never permit a cripple to teach his warriors. But as his strength grew and he gradually regained the use of one leg, Quinatzin knew that the time of decision was drawing near. He summoned the soothsayers and sign readers to his room, one after another, hoping for some sign that the fate Tlacaelel had predicted for him was not to be. But always, the straws fell in a northwesterly direction, and the signs indicated water, and blueness, and the influence of eagles and serpents. The Jaguar of Tezcatlipoca had no power in the alignment of his stars, which hung like a net over Tenochtitlan.

During this time, fresh troops arrived to relieve the Tenocha garrison, and one of the new warriors came to Quinatzin with a message.

"I come from the Cihuacoatl," the man said. "He has sent me to tell you that he awaits your return to his city. He has also ordered that I repeat to you the story of the birth of Huitzilopochtli, which has only now been found, painted in the sacred books."

"You may tell me," Quinatzin said, stretching to relieve a sudden pain in his bad leg. The Tenocha warrior drew himself up and began to recite from memory:

"Hear then, that Huitzilopochtli, the Hummingbird Wizard, the Blue One from the Left, is the son of the one called Coatlique, She of the Serpent Skirt, the Goddess of the Earth. It is said that Coatlique was sweeping the temple on the mountain of Coatepec when a ball of feathers descended from the heavens. She picked it up and placed it inside her clothing, but when she looked for it again later, she could not find it. Soon afterward, Coatlique became pregnant, and her sister, Coyolxauhqui the Moon, and her brothers the Centzon Huitznahuac, the unnumbered stars of the South, gathered to kill her for the disgrace she had brought upon them.

"But as the killers approached, Huitzilopochtli called out to his mother from inside her womb, telling her not to be afraid, for he would protect her. And at the last moment, just as the killers were about to strike, Huitzilopochtli sprang fully armed from his mother's womb and slew Coyolxauhqui. Then he did battle with the Centzon Huitznahuac and drove them from the sky.

"Thus," the man concluded proudly, "it is said that Huitzilopochtli is our Sun, and it is he who rises every day to vanquish the stars of night and bring light to his mother the earth. And so that he should have the strength for this fight, his people, the Tenocha, labor to feed him with the hearts and precious blood of men. It is by this sacrifice that we maintain our Sun, the Fifth Sun, the one that was born by the sacrifice of the gods at Teotihuacan!"

Quinatzin remained politely silent, for the man had raised his voice and appeared openly moved by his own recitation. So *this* is the god the Mexica serve, Quinatzin thought, and the one that I am to serve, as well. He glanced up at the warrior, who had recovered himself and was awaiting Quinatzin's reply.

"You must tell your master that I am grateful to know these things, and that I respect his desire to see me in his city. But you must remind him that I am a Texcocan, and that I must await the orders of my lord and ruler, Nezahualcoyotl."

"That is proper," the warrior concurred, and rose to leave. "I will tell him."

When he was alone in his room, Quinatzin rolled to one knee and pulled himself up hand over hand, using a series of niches he had chipped into the plastered wall. His bad leg buckled under him, and he had to brace himself against the wall with both hands to keep from falling. I do not even have the power to stand on my own, he thought desperately, sweating from the effort of simply rising. How can I meet the eyes of that man, when I cannot even stand to face him? I will truly be his captive, without even the means to flee.

Groaning from the strain on his good leg, he lowered himself to the mat on the floor, and lay back with his eyes closed. It is your fate, he told himself wearily, and fell into a deep sleep.

IT WAS early in the year Six-House when Nezahualcoyotl came to Mizquic on his way to Tenochtitlan. He sent two of his warchiefs ahead of him to Quinatzin's room, each bearing an armload of the honors that had been conferred upon Quinatzin for his bravery in the war. These were in the form of finely embroidered mantles, bands of gold for his arms and legs, necklaces and earplugs of amber and crystal, bunches of eagle and hummingbird feathers to be worn as insignia, and a round, spoked shield covered with the scarlet feathers of the macaw. There were tears in the eyes of the warchiefs as they made their speeches, for the extent of Quinatzin's injuries was clearly visible, and they knew that he would never add to these honors on the field of battle. Quinatzin accepted their praise with dry eyes. The king has been generous, he thought, examining the precious feathers on the shield after the warchiefs had gone. I would make an impressive sight in all this, if I were able to walk.

Then Nezahualcoyotl himself entered the room, carrying a long wooden staff in his hand. The king was wearing jade earplugs and a mantle embroidered with gold, and his long face under the royal headdress seemed weary and much older. Quinatzin was sitting with his back against the wall, his bad leg stretched out in front of him, and he managed an awkward bow as Nezahualcoyotl squatted across from him and laid the staff on the floor.

"It has been two years since I have seen you, my friend," the king said, "and many more since we last spoke. I have not commended you for your valor in the war, or thanked you for the services you performed in Tenochtitlan. You deserve rewards greater than these."

"Revenge upon the Tepanecs was reward enough," Quinatzin said modestly. "As for the other, I would have forgotten Tenochtitlan long ago. But there is one who reminds me . . . "

Nezahualcoyotl nodded solemnly. "And me, as well. He would have you by my order, if not by your own choice."

"And do you so order it, Lord?"

"It is not prudent to refuse Tlacaelel what he wants," Nezahualcoyotl said, then paused before going on. "But the choice will be yours, Quinatzin, for it was in my service that you drew the attention of this man."

"No, my Lord, it was not. I disobeyed Azcatl's orders that night. It was Tenochtitlan itself, that city of fishermen and fowlers, that lured me into its nets."

"Is the leader not responsible for the temptations put before his men?" Nezahualcoyotl asked rhetorically. "You were young and impetuous, and I sent you there knowing this. Texcoco is now ready to receive me, and after the ceremonies in Tenochtitlan I will return there, to stay until I die. I will take you with me, if that is your wish. You must accompany me to Tenochtitlan, and there you will decide."

Quinatzin bowed awkwardly to show his gratitude. "I am honored that you would risk offending Tlacaelel for my sake. But I have had much time to consider this matter, and I have consulted all the soothsayers in Mizquic. There is no escaping it; I am fated to this. It is useless to struggle against the hand of Huitzilopochtli, or the one who serves him."

"It is wise, and proper, that you accept your fate," Nezahualcoyotl commended him. "You have lived among strangers for most of your life, Quinatzin. Sometimes, when you have lost your home, it is better to find another. Tlacaelel values you highly, and you will be honored in Tenochtitlan."

"Honored?" Quinatzin reflected with sudden bitterness. "A man without legs in that city of warriors?"

"That is why I have brought you those," Nezahualcoyotl said, pointing to the jewelry and insignia. "And this," he added, pushing the staff toward Quinatzin. "Your weakness will be your strength, when the Tenocha see how calmly you bear your injury."

Quinatzin was silent, staring at the staff, seeing himself leaning upon it, looking into the hungry eyes of Tlacaelel. He did not know, still, if he could bear that calmly. He looked up into the sympathetic eyes of the king, the man who had been his teacher and protector since he was a child.

"It would be of great value to me, as well, to have a friend such as you in Tenochtitlan," Nezahualcoyotl said slowly. "Perhaps your skill as a messenger has not left you."

Quinatzin started at the idea. "It would be very dangerous," he said hesitantly.

"Did not Azcatl warn you once of a similar danger, long ago?" Nezahualcoyotl said insinuatingly, a small smile playing around his lips. "Could I have foreseen that you would ignore his warning, when I called him to me that night? Clearly, the old one must have underestimated the courage, and the independence, of such a young messenger."

Quinatzin glanced sharply at his king, suddenly understanding why he had been scolded as he had, and why the door of the telpochcalli had been left unguarded that night. The snares of his fate had been set before he had even left the mountains. Seeing the challenging expression on Nezahualcoyotl's face, Quinatzin felt himself entangled in the webs of ever-larger nets, against which he could no longer struggle. He braced himself with an arm against the wall and reached out for the staff.

"Teach me how to stand," he asked.

5

S EVEN years passed, years of great growth in Tenochtitlan and of relative
peace in the Valley of Anahuac. The Triple Alliance of Texcoco, Tenochtitlan, and Tlacopan had been held together by the skillful hand of Nezahualcoyotl, who had negotiated a fair division of the tribute collected from the
conquered cities and had seen to the mapping of the boundaries of the lands
that belonged to each of the Alliance members. Now the three cities conferred
regularly and participated in the election of each other's leaders, and each had
built temples in their cities dedicated to the gods of their allies. Together, they
had conquered the lakeside city of Cuitlahuac and had marched south to
subdue the Tlalhuican city of Cuauhnahuac, opening a route into the Hotlands
beyond the mountains. And they had not fought with one another, perhaps
the greatest of Nezahualcoyotl's accomplishments, since the Tenocha had not
forgotten their mission to conquer the world, and demanded the continual
acknowledgment of their military superiority. The Fasting Coyote gave them
this acknowledgment freely, anticipating their whims and responding to the
demands of their pride with such tact and precision that his compliance could
never be mistaken for cowardice.

In the year Thirteen-Flint-Knife, the Tenocha Speaker Itzcoatl died. From
the Council of Lords that had advised him, his nephew Moteczuma Ilhuicamina was chosen to replace him upon the icpalli, the reed seat of the
ruler. A flower war was arranged with the warriors of Chalco to obtain the
necessary captives for sacrifice, and the soothsayers were consulted to find a
propitious day for the ceremonies. Demands for extra tribute were sent out
to the subject cities, and as the materials for the feasting began to pour into
Tenochtitlan, invitations to the coronation were sent to all the tribes,
friendly and unfriendly, whom the Tenocha considered important enough to
attend.

When the day arrived, Nezahualcoyotl came across the water in a fleet of
war canoes decorated with flowers, and a long line of dignitaries came out of
the city to meet him at the Tetamatzalco, the canoe dock on the eastern
shore of the island. At the head of the procession were the black-robed
priests of Huitzilopochtli, waving braziers of incense, their long hair matted
with the blood of sacrifice. Behind them came Tlacaelel, wearing the white
robe of the Cihuacoatl, and with him were all four members of the new
Council of Lords, as well as the Speaker of Tlacopan, Totoquihuaztli.
Ranged in order behind these were the subject kings and lesser lords, including many of the high priests and elders of Tenochtitlan. The only important
person not present was Moteczuma himself, who was still completing his
fasting and penance to the gods.

Quinatzin was also there to greet the king, though he had come not out of
friendship, but in his capacity as Tlacaelel's chief of protocol. It was he who
had arranged the order of the greeters, and he who would have to answer for
any indiscretion or irregularity in the proceedings. Though he no longer leaned
upon his staff, Quinatzin walked with a permanent limp, and the face he wore

in public had hardened considerably over the years, taking on the aspects of arrogance and disdain favored by the Tecuhtli, the warrior lords of Tenochtitlan.

Nezahualcoyotl stepped ashore in his fine jewels and feathers, with the stiff crown of blue cotton upon his head, and as he greeted Tlacaelel and the other lords, the languid, elegant tones of his voice carried to Quinatzin's ears. The Texcocan accent seemed overly refined and disagreeably soft, and Quinatzin frowned involuntarily. He no longer spoke in that accent himself, except to impress foreigners to the court, or when Tlacaelel found it amusing to remind him that he was a foreigner here himself. He had become accustomed to the abruptness of the Tenocha, who had little patience for flowery language.

Tlacaelel and Nezahualcoyotl came down the long line of greeters, followed by Nezahualcoyotl's retinue of lords, warriors, and gift-bearers, the latter carrying armloads of jewels, feathers, flowers, and cotton mantles. Nezahualcoyotl stopped frequently to exchange greetings with those in the line, affecting even the stern Tenocha warchiefs with his compliments and his fine figures of speech. Especially eager for his recognition were the elders known as tlamatinime, wise men, for Nezahualcoyotl's wisdom and love for learning were held in the highest esteem throughout the Valley, and his court was always filled with teachers, and sorcerers, and men of knowledge.

Tlacaelel looked on with undisguised contempt as Nezahualcoyotl paused to speak to several of these old men, telling them of the poems, the flower songs, that were being composed in his city. His long face was suffused with happiness as he spoke of these things, and Quinatzin marveled, with some disdain of his own, that the king could lose himself so easily in the presence of Tlacaelel. It did not seem wise of the Fasting Coyote to be so unafraid of the Mexican's scorn.

Then they were standing before him, and Quinatzin bowed low with those around him, straightening up on his bad leg with some difficulty. Nezahualcoyotl came forward and gripped his arm in a friendly fashion.

"The gods of this city have protected you, my friend," the king said, his face again filled with happiness.

"And you, my Lord. The Dark One, Tezcatlipoca, looks on your city with kindness."

They stared deep into one another's eyes as they exchanged these courtesies, and Quinatzin knew that Nezahualcoyotl could sense his hardness, his inability to permit his joy to show upon his face. The king's brow furrowed momentarily, then smoothed again so quickly that only Quinatzin had perceived the alteration.

"This is a great day for your city," Nezahualcoyotl said formally. "We will talk after the ceremonies are concluded, and I will tell you about Texcoco, and your people there."

"Yes," Tlacaelel interrupted loudly, "and he will tell you of his people here, the Tenocha, the People of the Sun!"

"With pleasure, Lord," Quinatzin said, ignoring Tlacaelel's rudeness and bowing to both of them. Then Nezahualcoyotl moved on, and the retinue passed, and the procession began to move toward the plaza in the center of the city.

DURING the ceremonies for Moteczuma and the feasting that followed, Quinatzin had charge of the guests who had come from the lands not yet subject to
the Alliance. These had been given private audiences with the new Speaker,
and were later kept apart from the other guests in the plaza by means of
latticed partitions that had been covered with flowers to keep out curious eyes.
Screened off from one another in a series of small bowers were delegations of
Huaxtecs, Huexotzincans, Tlaxcalans, and Matlatzincans from Toluca, as well
as a small, hostile group from Chalco, which was perpetually on the verge of
war with the Tenocha. Quinatzin's main responsibilities were to see that all
were sufficiently impressed with the wealth and generosity of their hosts, and
that no incident of provocation marred the celebration. For this reason, he had
hand-picked all the guards and servants who waited on these particular guests,
choosing only those with the humility to bear the inevitable insults in silence.
He had also made certain that all weapons were carefully stored, and that the
Eagle and Jaguar Warriors, who would look for a fight even in the midst of
a celebration, were not allowed into the guests' banquet rooms.

As Quinatzin expected, all went smoothly until the captives were led out
into the plaza and formed into a long line at the base of the steps that led up
to the Tlacatecco, the main temple of Huitzilopochtli. There were nearly a
hundred captives, mostly Chalcans taken in the recent flower war, and they
stood between their guards with their heads bowed, weeping loudly and singing their death songs. At this point, Quinatzin ordered all the servants to
withdraw from the guests' bowers, and he went along from one to the next,
arousing the guards to full alertness. The last booth belonged to the Chalcans,
and had the clearest view of the temple. This had been arranged according to
the wishes of Tlacaelel, and it was here that Quinatzin took personal command, surrounding himself with his most trusted guards.

Since the great pyramid planned for Huitzilopochtli was still being built, his
shrine and that of Tlaloc stood at the front of what was only the second level,
low enough so that those in the plaza could clearly see the techcatl that stood
before the red shrine. The Chalcans fell silent as the first captive, one of their
own people, was led up the steps and thrown onto his back upon the sacrificial
stone, with a priest holding each of his limbs. Then Moteczuma, wearing the
shining turquoise headdress of the Speaker, stepped forward with the heavy
obsidian blade held high over his head. With one swift stroke, he ripped open
the taut chest of the captive and reached in to tear out the man's heart, which
he held up to the sun. A muted murmur of approval swept through the crowd
in the plaza as the captive was swiftly decapitated and his body sent tumbling
over the side of the temple, falling as did the sun in its western descent.

Nezahualcoyotl sacrificed the next victim, and he was followed in order by
Tlacaelel and Totoquihuaztli. Then the kings stood back and let the priests
wield the knife, and the bodies began to roll down the side of the temple in
swift succession. When it became clear to the Chalcans that all the captives
were going to be sacrificed, they rose angrily from their mats, spilling gourds
of cocoa and scattering food in their surprise and disbelief.

"Is this how the Tenocha honor their god?" the Chalcans cried. "Can
Huitzilopochtli really be so hungry?"

"This is outrageous, and they have done it only to mock us!"

"There is no holiness in this butchery. We will tell our ruler of this insult," they vowed, "and we will kill all the Tenocha held captive in our city!"

They turned as one to leave, and Quinatzin was ready for them. Without discussion, he provided them with an escort who could be trusted to guide them safely out of the city, and with bearers already loaded with the gifts they had been given by Moteczuma, gifts they might otherwise have left behind. That would have been an insult to Moteczuma, and while Quinatzin had played his role in delivering Tlacaelel's insult, he did not wish to do the same for the Chalcans. Such was the nature of his position in this city, and he returned to his duties with his face set into the hard lines of a man who must bear much without complaining.

LATE THAT night, while the dancing still continued in the plaza, Nezahualcoyotl's lieutenant, Azcatl, came to Quinatzin.

"My master asks for you, Lord," the old man said humbly, paying deference to Quinatzin's rank among the Tenocha.

"Grandfather," Quinatzin greeted him. "It is good to see your face again, and to know that you are alive after all these years."

"The years seem few to one who has as many as I, my son. Then you have forgiven me for helping to bring you here?"

"A young man runs after his fate," Quinatzin said with a shrug. "You warned me of that, but my ears did not hear you. Where is the king?"

"In his apartment. She will take you to him."

Azcatl turned and a young girl stepped out of the shadows behind him, her eyes lowered before Quinatzin's gaze. She was perhaps sixteen years old, with beautiful dark skin, and black hair that had been braided with small yellow flowers. She glanced up at him with the proper shyness, showing him the youthful curiosity in her dark, oval eyes. Azcatl abruptly made his farewell and departed without explaining the girl, who turned to indicate that Quinatzin should follow her. He did so, but slowly, limping painfully from the strain that the day had put upon his legs.

"Slowly, my child," he said to the girl, bringing her back to his side. "What is your name?"

"I am called Ome Xochitl, Lord, Two Flower."

"And how do you serve the king, Ome Xochitl, apart from guiding me?" Quinatzin asked with a smile, thinking that she was one of Nezahualcoyotl's women, and envying the king his good fortune in possessing one so beautiful.

"I do not serve the king," the girl said meekly. "I am his daughter."

Quinatzin looked at her in surprise. "And who is your mother?"

"My mother is dead, Lord. She was a slave woman from Cuitlahuac, the City of Sorcerers."

"Where were you born, then?" Quinatzin asked, wondering how the existence of this princess had escaped his notice, and irritated at displaying his ignorance before one so young. He also had the impression, which he found impossible to believe, that she was enjoying his discomfort.

"In Huexotzinco, Lord, where my father was in exile. Where you were also a child," she added with sudden boldness.

Quinatzin sought her eyes, but she kept her face averted as she led him into the palace where Nezahualcoyotl was quartered. In the light from the flickering torches on the walls, Quinatzin could see a certain resemblance to the Fasting Coyote in the fine lines of her jaw and lips, but the beautiful darkness of her skin and eyes must have come from Cuitlahuac.

"Oh?" he said coolly. "So your father has told you of me?"

"Only that in Huexotzinco you were known for your smile," the girl said mischievously, and then would say no more, for they had entered the chamber that belonged to Nezahualcoyotl.

"Bring us fruit, and cocoa," the king said to his daughter, then bade Quinatzin to sit on a mat against the wall, where he could lean back and stretch out his leg. Nezahualcoyotl sat down across from him and studied his face for a long time without speaking, and Quinatzin returned his gaze at intervals, as was proper in the presence of the ruler. He noticed the narrowed eyes and furrowed brow, obvious signs of the Fasting Coyote's displeasure, but they did not move him as they might once have. I have met the eyes of Tlacaelel for seven years, Quinatzin thought scornfully; does he expect a mere show of displeasure to affect me now?

"So, Quinatzin," Nezahualcoyotl said finally, as if he had reached some decision. "You are to be congratulated. Both the ceremonies and the festivities have been conducted flawlessly."

"The Chalcans did not think so," Quinatzin said with a grim smile. "But then, they were not meant to."

"It is good to be precise in one's provocations," Nezahualcoyotl said, veiling his eyes and lifting his eyebrows inquiringly. "Is it not?"

"Twenty captives would have sufficed, had they all been Chalcans," Quinatzin said with deliberate coldness, sensing that the king was toying with him.

"You told this to Tlacaelel?"

"As my superior in the court, he listens to my advice." Quinatzin shrugged. "As the Cihuacoatl, he hears only the famished cries of the Snake Woman, calling for blood. Had there been a thousand captives, he would have given them all to the god."

They fell silent as Ome Xochitl came in carrying cups and a pottery jug of hot cocoa. She was followed by a Tenocha serving girl bearing a basket of cherries, watermelon, and cactus tunas. Quinatzin recognized the girl as one of Tlacaelel's spies and gave her a significant glance as she entered, making sure that Nezahualcoyotl saw him and caught his meaning. But then he found himself distracted by the presence of Ome Xochitl, who had poured for her father and was now kneeling before Quinatzin with the painted jug in her hands. The sweet aroma of her skin rose lightly to Quinatzin's nostrils as she bent to pour the frothy cocoa into his cup, and he felt the blood quicken in his veins. The women went out, and Quinatzin looked up at Nezahualcoyotl in confusion, trying to remember what he needed to say.

"The girl will not overhear us," Nezahualcoyotl supplied for him. "Ome Xochitl is with her, and she has learned from me how to occupy the thoughts of others. We can speak plainly."

Quinatzin nodded and waited patiently for the king to begin, wondering when he would indeed begin to speak plainly of his displeasure.

"You showed no joy in seeing me today, Quinatzin," Nezahualcoyotl said abruptly, his face stern and reproving. "Why was that? And why were you embarrassed that I spoke as I did to the tlamatinime?"

"I apologize for my rudeness," Quinatzin said automatically. "I saw only that you needlessly exposed yourself to the scorn of Tlacaelel."

"And is there some way to *avoid* his scorn?" the king demanded. "Is the earth a large enough place in which to hide from it? Surely, it is useless even to try. Why, then, Quinatzin, do you attempt to hide yourself behind this face of stone?"

"It is the face I have learned, living in this city, and serving a master such as Tlacaelel," Quinatzin said coldly. "He knows that I serve you as a messenger, and he permits this because he knows me, and knows what it is that I can tell you. Yet he also spies upon me, and kills those I trust too openly, and sets traps that would mean my death. Perhaps, Lord, you can explain to me how these things can be borne with a smile?"

"As a child in Huexotzinco, you knew this without asking," Nezahualcoyotl said with sudden gentleness. "You were filled with life then, your heart did not know the hardships you suffered. Where has your heart wandered, Quinatzin? Has it deserted you on this island?"

"I do not know, Lord. I have not had the time to think of such things."

"No time!" Nezahualcoyotl exclaimed sadly. "We are not forever on the earth, my friend. In time, even the hardest of stones is broken, and crushed into the earth. The flower songs tell us these truths, and help us to bear them. It is wrong to scorn them as Tlacaelel does!"

"He hears only those that praise Huitzilopochtli and sing of the glory of his people. The truths you speak of are left to the old men who can no longer fight. Surely, I am crippled and cannot fight, but would you have me number myself among those whom he despises?"

"Long ago," Nezahualcoyotl reminded him sternly, "I told you that your weakness would be your strength. But you have forgotten this; you have become infatuated with your own cleverness, as if that alone could protect you from everything. You think that because you have hidden your heart from yourself, you have also hidden it from Tlacaelel. But never do you show him more, Quinatzin, than when you pretend to be as hard and scornful as he!"

Quinatzin lowered his eyes and did not reply. He felt the truth of the king's words, as well as his anger, and he was chastened by the thought of Tlacaelel reading his hardness as easily as Nezahualcoyotl had, and laughing as he used it against him. I was brought here to change these people, Quinatzin thought sadly, and I have taken pride in doing so. But I did not see how they were changing *me*.

"Do not accuse yourself," Nezahualcoyotl said abruptly, breaking into Quinatzin's thoughts. "You have served me well here, and it has been hard for you. I have seen the woman Teuxoch, your wife," he added pointedly. "Tlacaelel brought her to me, along with your daughters, so that I might see the cause of your contentment here."

"She is a good wife," Quinatzin insisted loyally, in a low voice.

"No doubt. But she is her father's daughter; you might as well whisper your secrets to Tlacaelel himself. And I have heard that she will bear you no more children. Is this true?"

"So the midwives say."

"Your daughters are like precious green stones, they smile as you once did. They will give you great joy in your old age. But you must also have some sons to lean upon, and that is why I have brought Ome Xochitl to you."

Quinatzin felt the heat rise to his face, and he drank from the cup of tepid cocoa to cool himself. It did not seem possible to him that a wish of his could be answered so readily, that such beauty could find its way into a life that had grown unaccustomed to its presence. It did not seem possible, and therefore it did not seem right. Quinatzin frowned and put down his cup.

"You seek to reward me, Lord, and I am honored. But the girl is so young. Teuxoch would make her life a thing of misery, for my wife is *much* like her father. Would you have your daughter share such a bitter fate?"

"You pity yourself, Quinatzin!" Nezahualcoyotl exploded in disgust. "Your bitterness has rendered you foolish, so that you reject your good fortune! Listen, then, you who are so bitter: when I came to you in Mizquic, I, too, had read your fortune. And there was death in it—*certain* death if you went to Texcoco. You had consulted the soothsayers of Mizquic, but you did not think to ask me," he said wonderingly. "I would have told you that death hovered over Tenochtitlan, as well, but that there were ways for you to avoid its grasp. But even had I chosen to tell you, I would have relied upon you to find those ways for yourself. And you *have* found them, Quinatzin, you have kept yourself alive. What I am offering you now is another of the ways."

"The girl?" Quinatzin said stupidly, wearing so stunned an expression that Nezahualcoyotl laughed.

"Is she not *my* daughter? She is young, but you do not have to fear for her. She will be more to you than the mother of your children, Quinatzin. She will be your friend, and the keeper of your heart."

Quinatzin bowed low, and when he looked up, his face wore the beginnings of a smile, tentative and amazed.

"You have softened me, Lord. I will consult the soothsayers for the proper day on which to hold the ceremonies."

"Good. I will make the announcement myself, so that Tlacaelel will have no way to oppose it. And for your wedding, I will establish a contest: I will offer a prize of gold and precious stones to the composer of the most beautiful flower song honoring the occasion."

"I am a poor messenger to deserve so much," Quinatzin said gratefully.

"I have not been blind to your suffering," the king said brusquely, and gestured Quinatzin to his feet. "Find my daughter and bring her to me. I must tell Ome Xochitl of the life that awaits her, here in Tenochtitlan . . ."

6

THE marriage of Quinatzin and Ome Xochitl took place in the Cillan, the Royal House of Texcoco, on the propitious day of Three-Alligator. Since she was to be Quinatzin's second wife, parts of the ceremony had to be omitted, and he could not knot the corner of his mantle to hers, as he had done with Teuxoch. This could only be done once, with the woman whose children would be the first to inherit.

At sunset, the old women bathed Ome Xochitl and washed her hair. Then they pasted red feathers to her arms and legs, and, because she was so young, they painted her face with a yellow powder, like the pollen of a new flower. When she was seated before the hearth in her father's house, the old men who spoke for Quinatzin came before her and addressed her. They told her that she was no longer a child, and that she must carry herself with honor and respect now that she was abandoning the house of her parents. They admonished her to have respect for the elders who had gone before her, and they urged her to enliven her heart, for never again would she give it to her mother, or her father.

Ome Xochitl replied with weeping and expressions of sadness, thanking her parents for having inclined their hearts to her, and for having shown her favor. Then the old women, the kinswomen of Quinatzin, came to Ome Xochitl, and one of them, a strong one, wrapped her in a black mantle and bore her upon her back to the house Nezahualcoyotl had given to Quinatzin as his own. They were accompanied on this journey by the members of Ome Xochitl's family, who carried torches and made a great clamor as they went, arousing passers-by to the beauty and fitness of the bride.

The wedding couple greeted one another with welcoming words, each waving a brazier of incense over the other. Then they were brought together before the hearth, and the bride was placed to the left of the bridegroom. Ome Xochitl's stepmother then presented Quinatzin with a mantle and a loincloth, and Quinatzin's kinswoman likewise gave a mantle and a skirt to Ome Xochitl. This woman then washed out the bride's mouth and fed her four mouthfuls of the tlaxcalli, the maize cake, which had been soaked in a special sauce. When she had eaten, Ome Xochitl took the polished bowl from the old woman and fed four mouthfuls to Quinatzin. In this way, the ceremony was completed, and the old women took the couple to the marriage chamber and closed them in.

They were not to leave this room for the next four days, except to burn incense before the altars of the household gods at noon and midnight. And during this time, they were not to touch, but only to talk and become familiar with one another. At first, Ome Xochitl and Quinatzin were nervous and awkward, inquiring too frequently as to the comfort of the other, and often lapsing into silence. Then Quinatzin, as the elder and the man, rose from his mat and began to talk as he paced the room, taking slow, deliberate steps so that his limp would not be so noticeable.

He told her first of his lineage, and who his father and mother had been, and how he had been given the name of the famous grandson of Xolotl. He explained how his father had been slain by the traitorous Texcocan lords, and how he had been separated from his mother and sisters, and had been hunted through the night by the bushy-headed Tepanec warriors. He told her of his education in Huexotzinco, and of the years spent fighting in the mountains with her father, before they had come to Tenochtitlan for the final battle with Maxtla.

Hearing the change in his voice at the mention of Tenochtitlan, Ome Xochitl raised her eyes to look upon her husband, this man nearly twice her age, a man who had fought in foreign cities and had taken lives and captives, a man who had had other women before her. She saw the vivid scars on the backs of his legs as he walked away from her, and the tension in his face as he turned back in her direction. His voice had grown suddenly hoarse, and she poured water into a cup and held it out to him, so that he would stop his pacing and come to sit with her.

"Your throat is tired, my husband," she said, as he lowered himself onto the pile of mats against the wall and took the cup from her gratefully. "You must rest a while, and then tell me more about this island, this city that will be our home."

Quinatzin stared at her intently over the rim of the cup, as if drinking with his eyes as well as his lips.

"There is none so beautiful as you in Tenochtitlan, my flower," he said softly, staring until Ome Xochitl was forced to lower her eyes. "But you must tell me of yourself, and of your own childhood in Huexotzinco."

"I was sheltered there," she said simply, "and taught the things that girls must know, the cooking and weaving, and how to care for myself. I was taken back to Texcoco when I was nine years of age, and I was placed in the care of the priestesses of Tezcatlipoca for a period of three years."

"How is it that you were not promised in marriage during this time?"

"My mother had died in childbirth, and to honor her memory, my father chose to keep me by his side. He made me his maidservant, so that he could teach me, and so that I could listen for him in the court."

"So you are another of his messengers!" Quinatzin exclaimed, and laughed heartily, leaning his head back against the wall. Then, forgetting the weariness of his throat, he again began to speak about Tenochtitlan, describing how he had come there as Nezahualcoyotl's messenger, and how he had made himself a student of the Mexica, which had led to his fateful meeting with Tlacaelel. He told her of his dreams of Texcoco, and of the face he had seen in the flames in Azcapotzalco, and of the other signs that had revealed his fate to him. Ome Xochitl encouraged him with her eyes, using her attention to calm the air between them, as her father had taught her. Quinatzin's voice rose and fell, sometimes bursting forth with an abruptness and candor that shocked her, and other times relaxing into the courtly Texcocan tones with which she was familiar. His eyes were turned inward as he spoke, and some of what he remembered seemed to surprise him, as if he had never tried to remember it before.

"There is a man called Tezcatl," he said slowly, "a Tlatelulcan I met before the war. His frankness was valuable to me, but more than that, I came to trust him completely. I know that he is still alive, and living in Tlatelulco. But I have never attempted to renew our friendship."

He shook his head, amazed at himself, and Ome Xochitl waited before she spoke.

"Has Tlacaelel made it so dangerous for your friends?"

"Friends? I have no friends. There are those I trust to serve me, and supply me with information, but I dare not make them my friends. Too many have died, or simply disappeared, while doing my bidding."

"Do you not protect them, if you can?"

"As much as I am able," Quinatzin said with conviction.

"Then it is not your friendship that killed them," Ome Xochitl said flatly. "And surely, Tlacaelel could have no interest in those who were simply your friends, and not in your service?"

"I do not think he would understand that such a thing is possible. I had forgotten myself . . ."

Ome Xochitl sat quietly, knowing that she had said enough, and that he was best left to reach his own conclusions. She refilled his water cup, watching his face as he sat thinking. He is handsome, she thought, and he has been lonely for too long—he has not yet made a home for himself. When she again felt his attention upon her, she decided that it was time to ask him the question her father had given to her before the ceremony.

"I must ask you one other thing, my husband," she said softly, with her eyes lowered. "This is the first time that you have returned to the city of your birth since you left it so many years ago. How do you find the city of Texcoco now?"

Quinatzin glanced at her sharply, then lapsed into thought and was silent for a long time.

"The gardens and temples are even more beautiful than I remember," he said at last. "Yet . . . they do not seem as large as they once did. I know that is because I no longer see with the eyes of a child," he added hastily, "but the buildings are older here than in Tenochtitlan, and their carvings are sometimes worn, and the paint faded. I have also noticed that the air here is dry and cold, and hurts my nose. And I cannot hear the water birds, or the waves lapping against the reeds . . ."

Quinatzin stopped abruptly, and Ome Xochitl looked up into his eyes. He smiled knowingly.

"You *are* your father's daughter, Ome Xochitl. You have me speaking like a Tenocha."

"Is that not your home, and mine? Our children will have the blood of Texcoco in their veins, my husband, but they will be Tenocha in their hearts. We will not be able to teach them if *we* remain foreigners in our own hearts. It is our fate to become Tenocha."

Quinatzin stared at her with open pride, no longer startled that one so young should also be so wise. He knew now that Nezahualcoyotl had spoken truly, that this one would have nothing to fear from the jealousy of Teuxoch.

"Come lie beside me, and rest a while," he said happily. "We have much time until the fifth day, and I would not know all of your secrets too soon . . ."

WHEN THE fifth day arrived, Quinatzin and Ome Xochitl left the marriage chamber and went to the temazcalli, the sweathouse, where they crouched in the steamy darkness and flogged their bodies with maize husks to cleanse their skin. After they had washed themselves thoroughly and put on clean garments, they were blessed by a priest and led back to their room. Here, the old women had prepared a bed for them by piling soft, clean mats on top of one another, placing feathers and small pieces of jade between the layers as charms that would help bring the couple many beautiful children. Again, the bride and groom were closed in together, and they could hear the old women talking and laughing in the next room, where they were drinking octli and preparing the food for the feasting that would begin the next day.

Ome Xochitl had tinted her cheeks with yellow powder, and her black hair was braided with the same yellow flowers she had worn on the day of their first meeting. She smelled slightly of copal from the priest, but it seemed to Quinatzin that a thousand other tantalizing scents rose from her body and filled his head. Her dark eyes glowed in the dim light of the room as he put his arms around her and drew her close, feeling the fullness of her breasts against his chest.

With deliberate slowness, Ome Xochitl untied the knot at her shoulder and let her mantle drop to the floor. Then she removed her skirt and lay naked on the bed, watching as Quinatzin took off his mantle and unwound the loincloth from between his legs. He came to her eagerly, running his hands over the trembling softness of her limbs and feeling the heat rise in their bodies as she opened herself to him. He stared into her eyes as he stroked her thighs and caressed the dark, silky nipples of her breasts, seeing that she had no fear of him, but only a desire that matched his own.

Manipulating her body gently, he brought her beneath him, pressing his belly against the roundness of her buttocks. Her breath caught in her throat but she did not cry out as he entered her, slowly and tentatively, and finally with a force that filled her completely and stained the mat beneath them with the evidence of her virginity. Sweat ran off their bodies as Quinatzin plunged and Ome Xochitl rose to meet him, again and again, until their vision blurred and they did not hear the sounds they made. Quinatzin's arms suddenly came around her ribs, and his breath was hot upon her neck as he came shuddering to a finish, and was still.

"My flower," he gasped as he lay upon the mats, smiling happily at the face so close to his own.

"Now you have taken me, my husband," Ome Xochitl said softly, with joy in her voice. "Now I am yours . . ."

THE FEASTING that followed the fifth day continued for three more days, during which gifts were exchanged, many speeches were made, and there was much singing and dancing by the guests. Octli was consumed in great quantities, and the old men and women, to whom it was permitted on such occasions, became drunk and foolish, making lewd jokes about the stained mat that hung over the hearth. Quinatzin smiled continually and never left the side of his bride, who wore a headdress of white plumes as the symbol of her new status.

On the third day, the composers of flower songs rose, one by one, and recited their compositions before Nezahualcoyotl, who sat upon a raised reed seat, directly behind the wedding couple. Most of the composers were Texcocans, and Quinatzin sat with his eyes lowered, listening to the elegant modulations of their voices as they sang of the beauty and hardship of life upon the earth, and of the power and mystery of the gods, whose very names echoed their strength and the darkness of their purpose. Quinatzin was aware, suddenly, of the immensity of space that surrounded him on all sides, extending in all directions, and he felt something move and separate, deep inside him, as if the fibers of his being were plucked and stretched. I have been deaf all these years, he thought in amazement, yet my heart still knows how to hear.

But then there was a movement next to him, and Ome Xochitl rose and stepped forward to stand before her father. Quinatzin straightened up as the room fell silent and Nezahualcoyotl gave the order for her to begin. Looking first at Quinatzin, then at her father, Ome Xochitl began to speak in a manner that surprised her listeners, for her tone was sober and the rhythms of her speech were very abrupt, nearly masking her Texcocan accent. This was her flower song:

> "We are all the captives
> Of the Giver of Life.
> We dream here, on the earth,
> Thinking we are free.
>
> The captives are brought in
> To Tenochtitlan.
> Some come crying aloud;
> Some come with tears in their eyes.
> They are taken to the House of Eagles;
> They are given to the Snake Woman.
> They know there is no escape.
>
> These, too, are the captives
> Of the Giver of Life.
> They dreamed here, on the earth,
> Thinking they were free."

Shouts of approval rang out in the room when Ome Xochitl finished, and there was a general clamor among the guests, who appealed to Nezahualcoyotl to grant her the prize. Quinatzin sat with his head high, feeling that his heart would burst with pride. When Ome Xochitl returned to his side, he took her hand and pressed it to his breast, so that she might feel the movement inside him.

Nezahualcoyotl decided, since there had been many fine flower songs, that he would award several prizes. Calling the singers to him, he gave them quills filled with gold dust, armbands and necklaces of beaten silver, and richly embroidered cotton mantles. And to his daughter, he gave the finest gifts of all: a necklace of blue flowers, all of turquoise, and an amulet in the shape of a rabbit, carved in jade by the craftsmen of Xochimilco.

"Now, may I take *my* prize?" Quinatzin asked, as he stood with his wife before the king. Nezahualcoyotl gazed down upon his daughter with a sad smile on his face.

"Be kind, Quinatzin," he said. "Protect this precious stone, this beautiful flower that once was mine. Be her shelter, and her shade, and exert yourself so that hardship does not overtake her. And you, Ome Xochitl, be correct in your duties to your household, and see that your words and your actions bring honor, and not disgrace, to your husband and children. Go with your husband, my daughter, for already I leave you."

Weeping at her father's words, Ome Xochitl bowed with the others as Nezahualcoyotl left the room. Then she gathered the jewels that were her prize and looked to her husband.

"Come," Quinatzin said, his voice firm and confident. "Let us go to Tenochtitlan."

"To our home," Ome Xochitl said with equal firmness, and followed after him, drying her eyes as she went.

NECETOCHHUILOC:
When People Died in One-Rabbit

1450–1455

1

IN the early spring of the year Ten-Rabbit, the midwives again came to the house of Quinatzin, there within the Royal Compound, carrying with them the blankets, the herbs, and the obsidian knives of their calling. Since they were the servants of the Snake Woman, Cihuacoatl, who ruled over childbirth as Yoalticitl, Grandmother of the Sweatbath, the midwives were compelled to pay their respects first to Teuxoch, Quinatzin's first wife. Though a disagreeable woman, Teuxoch was the daughter of the high priest of the Snake Woman, and was thought to have powers useful to the deliverers of children. Indeed, though Tcuxoch herself had only borne three daughters, the young wife, Ome Xochitl, had given birth to three boys and two girls in the ten years she had lived in this house, and had only once borne a child that had not survived.

In any case, it was always wise to placate the daughter of Tlacaelel, so the midwives went first to the rooms on the western side of the courtyard, where Teuxoch lived with her two unmarried daughters. Teuxoch greeted them and gave them her blessing with great ceremony, and then led them across the courtyard to the room where Ome Xochitl lay, breathing deeply against the pains that had just begun. The midwives greeted her familiarly and made jokes to distract her as they massaged her swollen abdomen and felt for the position of the baby. Teuxoch gathered Ome Xochitl's children and sent them into the courtyard, with her own daughters to attend to them. Then she dispatched servants for wood and fresh water, and set others to work making food for the midwives.

When Ome Xochitl's pains had become more persistent, the midwives bathed her and washed her hair with soap, and they arranged her on her mats, with clean cloths beneath her. Then they carefully swept the room and put everything in order for the ordeal that was to come, while Teuxoch bustled about importantly, giving them useless instructions and generally getting in their way. The midwives did not like this sharp-eyed woman with the narrow face, this woman whose keening voice was stilled only to replenish the yetl leaves she chewed constantly, a habit that stained her teeth brown and gave her breath a sour odor. They did not like her, but they could not show her any disrespect or ask her to leave, since she was there at Ome Xochitl's request. So they worked around her silently, admiring the honor Ome Xochitl paid the older wife by seeming, even in her pain, to welcome Teuxoch's presence.

When the labor had begun, the midwives built a fire at the back of the round sweathouse in the corner of the courtyard, which they called on this occasion the xochicalli, the Flower House, the sweathouse of our Grandmother. Taking care that it was the right temperature, they carried Ome Xochitl inside and massaged her abdomen gently, praying to the Goddess of Childbirth, who was called by the names Cihuacoatl, Yoalticitl, and Quilaztli. Then they gave Ome Xochitl a potion made of the herb called ciuapatli, in order to hasten the delivery, and when she had drunk it, she was carried back to her room.

The sounds of the young mother's struggles carried clearly to the courtyard, where Teuxoch's daughters comforted the smallest of the children and told them not to be afraid. Their mother was a brave warrior, they explained to the children, and she had battled like this to bring each of them into the world. It was the small death exacted by the Snake Woman as the price of a child, they said, and the women who died in this battle were taken up as warriors to live with the Sun. The two oldest boys understood this already, and they did not tremble when they heard their mother cry out.

But finally the sounds from the room ceased, only to be followed by the joyous shouts and loud war cries of the midwives, signaling that Ome Xochitl had fought a successful battle, and had captured a baby.

"It is a girl child," Teuxoch said to Ome Xochitl, who lay on her back with her eyes closed, her breath coming in short gasps. "It is healthy, and has your skin."

Mumbling prayers under her breath, the midwife who had delivered the child cut the umbilical cord with her obsidian knife. Then she held the child up for all in the room to see and spoke to her: "Now you have arrived upon the earth, my young one, my precious feather. Your beloved father, Tloque Nahuaque, the Lord of the Near and the Far, has sent you here, to this place of suffering. Here your kinsmen suffer exhaustion, and thirst, and hardship, and this, too, will be your lot. But do not be sad, my young one, weep not! Rest now, repose yourself, for truly you will endure much torment and fatigue upon the earth. Thus has the Lord arranged it, thus he determines what is, and so it must be."

Then the midwife was given clean water, and she breathed upon it, and sprinkled it on the baby's head and chest, and made the baby taste it with her mouth. As she continued washing the child, the midwife prayed in a low voice to Chalchihuitlicue, She of the Jeweled Robe, the consort of Tlaloc. And she asked the Water Goddess to cleanse this child, to wash away the filth and vice that the child had worn into the world, and to make her clean and pure. When the baby had been completely bathed, the midwife wrapped her in soft cloths and gave her to Ome Xochitl, who held the child close and spoke to her lovingly.

With great ceremony, the midwives took the umbilical cord and the afterbirth in which the baby had been enveloped and buried them in the corner of the room, next to the hearth, signifying that the place of this girl child was in the house, and that she was not to wander. Her place was here beside the hearth, the midwives proclaimed, where she would prepare food and drink, and do her weaving. Thus was the sixth child of Ome Xochitl and Quinatzin brought into the world, in the year Ten-Rabbit.

FOUR DAYS later, a second bathing ceremony took place, during which the midwife bestowed upon the young girl the implements of womanhood and gave her her name. This occurred in the courtyard, and though he was very busy with his duties, Quinatzin attended out of respect for his daughter, and for the guests who had been invited to join in the celebration. These included several of Quinatzin's colleagues and aides, one of the Texcocan ambassadors and his family, who were the kin of Ome Xochitl, and the parents of a number of eligible young men with whom Teuxoch was hoping to match her daughters. A great quantity of food and drink had been prepared for the feasting that would come later, and the smells of spiced cocoa and roast fowl hung over the courtyard like a rich perfume, adding to the pleasure of the ceremony.

The day of the naming had been chosen carefully by the soothsayers, who had studied the day signs of the child's birth in their painted books and had found them favorable. She had been born under the rule of the sign xochitl, flower, which was also her mother's sign, and gave promise that she would have the skills of an artisan. So this child, this third daughter who had her mother's dark skin and oval eyes, was being given the name Cocatli, after the beautiful mountain flower that puts forth its single, delicate blossom.

"So that she will remember the mountains where her mother and father were born," Ome Xochitl had explained to Quinatzin the night before, when they had been alone for the first time since before the labor had begun. He had wanted to comfort his wife and share in her joy, so he had pronounced it a good name and had indulged in the wishful conversation of parents who consider the future of their child. He had not spoken of the things that troubled him, though he had been carrying them with him for many days.

Now, as he sat in the shade of the huehuetl tree with his wives and children around him, listening to the words of the midwife as she washed the baby, his worries came back to him as if a cloud had passed before the sun. It did not seem possible to him that disaster could visit this house, which was so happy, or this city, which had become so strong and prosperous. The Tenocha now had maize lands of their own, and tribute coming from as far away as the Hotlands. The marketplace in Tlatelulco had become one of the largest in the Valley, attracting goods from everywhere, and the Tenocha warriors fought their wars in distant lands, with no one to menace the people on the island.

And we have built new temples to Quetzalcoatl and Cihuacoatl, Quinatzin thought, and completed the first level of the great temple of Huitzilopochtli. How could our priests, who are so rigorous in their fasting and penance, and so generous in their offerings, how could they have offended the gods? All the festivals were properly celebrated, all the necessary sacrifices performed. Even the smallest gods were not slighted, for these, too, had their priests and temples in Tenochtitlan.

Yet the anxiety would not leave him, for he knew that the Lord of the Duality, he who lived above the ninth heaven and was called Ometecuhtli and Omecihuatl, did as he pleased with the people upon the earth, and that his sons and daughters, both the great and the small gods, did likewise. Men could not speak to the gods as they did to other men, nor could they know what suffering might be inflicted upon them, or why. They could only show their devotion and lament their sins, and hope that the gods would grant them favor.

The people of the Valley were now close to the end of the cycle of the years, when the sacred calendar of day signs, the tonalpohualli, and the calendar of the seasons would be in conjunction. In five years' time, the fifty-two-year cycle would be completed, and the years would be bound with the celebration of the New Fire Ceremony on the Hill of the Stars. This was a dangerous time, for it was said that at the Binding of the Years, the Sun might be extinguished as had the four suns before it, and the stars would be turned to ravenous beasts who would descend from the sky to devour the people.

According to the sacred books, the years had been bound five times before this, and each time the Sun had been rekindled and the earth saved. Yet all knew that this Fifth Sun, Nahui Olin, whose sign was movement, was destined to end with earthquakes and famine, and it was this knowledge that preyed on Quinatzin's spirit. Because recently, and quite suddenly, it seemed, predictions of just these disasters had begun to be heard in many places in the Valley. This had created turmoil in some cities, with prophets rising out of the ranks of the fortunetellers to accuse and challenge the priests, and people breaking the images of their household gods in despair. The same predictions had been made in Tenochtitlan, but Tlacaelel had suppressed all discussion of them, and his agents had moved in other cities to eliminate the prophets of doom.

Still, the rumors persisted, and even while Quinatzin had done his duty in suppressing them, he had sent to Nezahualcoyotl for confirmation. Yes, the word had come back, there would be great famine, and possibly earthquakes as well, and many people would die, though no one knew if it would mean the end of everything. Nezahualcoyotl had already begun storing extra food for his people, and had suggested to Quinatzin that the Tenocha do the same. Quinatzin had been turning this suggestion over in his mind for days, wondering how he could evade the ban on discussion and broach the subject to Tlacaelel, who had made it clear that his confidence in Huitzilopochtli did not allow for such fears.

"You frown, my husband," Teuxoch said reprovingly, leaning close so that he could smell the yetl on her breath. Quinatzin saw that the midwife was placing Cocatli in her cradle, and that the ceremony would soon be over. Ome Xochitl, on his other side, did not look at him, but he knew she had heard, and was listening.

"My mind was elsewhere," he said, smoothing his face automatically, though he did not doubt that Teuxoch had also heard the rumors, and had guessed where his thoughts had been. He never tried to hide them from her anymore, or from her father, though he had mastered many ways of not explaining them.

"Perhaps it was on your eldest daughters," Teuxoch suggested, "and the fact that they are not yet married."

"They are of age," Quinatzin agreed, and smiled, as he always did when he had overestimated her craftiness. "Perhaps some of the guests here could be made aware of that."

Then Quinatzin broke off the conversation, for the ceremony was over, and the midwife had to be greeted and thanked, and a speech made to the guests. Quinatzin did all this while leaning upon his staff, for his legs had stiffened with age, and he could not stand unaided for long without fatigue. But when he had finished his speech, he laid the staff down and lifted the cradle with both hands, and carried it back to his wife under the tree.

"Here is our mountain flower," he said, seating himself next to Ome Xochitl, with the baby between them. Teuxoch, he saw, had already gone off to introduce her daughters to the guests. Ome Xochitl rocked the cradle with one hand and stared solemnly at Quinatzin.

"Has the world changed, my husband, while I have been gone from it?" she asked curiously, without reproach.

"It has gotten older, but it has not changed. A campaign against the Huaxtecs has been decided upon by the war council. The warriors will leave for the east after the festival of Toxcatl."

"May the god protect them and grant them success. And what of those of us who stay behind and raise children?"

"There have been omens of famine, and earthquakes," Quinatzin said bluntly, and felt less fear at finally having said the words aloud. "Your father has confirmed this. Tlacaelel continues to deny it."

Ome Xochitl stared thoughtfully at her child and did not speak for several moments, during which Quinatzin shooed the other children away and gave orders for the servants to begin bringing out the food. Ome Xochitl's face was calm, and Quinatzin studied it with pleasure. Time and childbirth had thickened her body and made it more womanly, but her face was as fine and beautiful as on the night he had first laid eyes upon her.

"The little ones must not be allowed to starve," Ome Xochitl said suddenly. "And it cannot be left to Moteczuma or Tlacaelel, for they will never admit that there are enemies the warriors cannot fight."

"No," Quinatzin agreed. "We have stored extra rations for the armies, should it be a long campaign, and I have added to these stores as much as I could. But Tlacaelel expects his warriors to be feasting in the houses of the Huaxtecs within the month, so storing too much would be a sign of too little faith."

"Do not the warriors also need extra weapons for such a long campaign?" Ome Xochitl suggested slowly, showing him the idea forming in her mind. "And are not my father's people among the finest makers of arrows and darts?"

"Yes," Quinatzin said excitedly, "and we could as easily turn to him as to the Chalcans, who are our enemies, though they make fine arrows. Perhaps your father, in his wisdom, would desire his payment in the form of maize and beans."

"It is possible. And it might take a long time for so many arrows to be made, and the food would have to be collected and stored here until they were delivered."

"We might forget we wanted them, if the war goes well," Quinatzin concluded, and smiled at his wife. "I will make the arrangements."

"I, too, will store extra food," Ome Xochitl said. "I will tell Teuxoch that you have ordered it in anticipation of the marriage of your daughters."

A fresh wind blew up in the courtyard and a few drops of rain began to fall, bringing the guests crowding in under the shelter of the tree. Many commented that the rains came early this year, and that it was a good sign. Quinatzin looked at his wife, and at the child between them, but he did not speak. Nor did he smile, though his eyes were tender.

2

THE rains that had come early that year did not stop, but continued intermittently through the months that were normally dry. The many rites of Tlaloc, the God of Water, which were always held at this time, were often interrupted by sudden downpours, and the required ceremonial journeys to the mountains behind Texcoco were made treacherous by the flooding of the passes. The priests were amazed, and none could account for it, though extra offerings were made to Tlaloc and Chalchihuitlicue to repay them for their unexpected generosity.

Then it was summer, and still the rain did not stop. Day after day, Tlaloc sent his clouds across the Lake, and the rain beat down on the earth with such force that it drowned the sound of Tlaloc's thunder. The level of the water in the Lake rose to a dangerous height, and the chinampa gardens anchored to the shore of the island were torn from their moorings and washed away. The reed huts of the fishermen and common people were the next to go, and homeless people began to crowd into the center of the city.

Soon the canals overflowed into the streets, and water began seeping into the courtyards and houses of the nobles. Food became scarce, for no one in the Valley had been able to plant, and the volume of water pouring into the salty southern part of the Lake was overflowing into Tenochtitlan's part, and the increasing saltiness of the water was killing the fish and other water creatures. Even the maize that had been stored for the army began to spoil in its granaries, and people started to leave the flooded city for the shore, fearing for their very lives.

Moteczuma sent for aid to Nezahualcoyotl, who came across the Lake accompanied by his best engineers, and by those who had studied and charted the currents of the Lake. Nezahualcoyotl suggested that a dike be built on the eastern side of the island, running north and south, so that the salty flood from the south would be diverted to the eastern portion of the Lake. The dike was to be built of logs, stone, and earth, and it was to be nine miles long and more than eleven arm-spreads wide.

All of Tenochtitlan's allies and subjects were called on to aid in this great project, and long lines of workers went out from the city each day to struggle against the waters of the Lake. A large part of the army had been recalled from the land of the Huaxteca, and the Eagle and Jaguar Warriors took their places on the dike next to the macehuales. The stern Moteczuma himself commanded the laborers, and often he and Nezahualcoyotl were seen stripped to their maxlatls, loincloths, carrying stone with the others.

A warm rain was falling steadily on the day that Quinatzin came to the place on the dike where the kings had raised a canopy over themselves. He had come on official business, but with him in the canoe was his eldest son, Acolmiztli, the Lion's Paw, who had been named for his grandfather Nezahualcoyotl.

Digging into the mud with his staff, Quinatzin climbed the bank and made his way to the canopy, where the two kings stood alone, since even the guards had been put to work. Gesturing for Acolmiztli to remain behind, just under the canopy, Quinatzin went up and bowed low before the kings.

"Rise, Quinatzin," Moteczuma said gruffly. "What does my brother say?"

"Tlacaelel sends to tell you," Quinatzin said formally, without attempting to meet their eyes, "that our labors here must not cause us to ignore the gods. He suggests that a flower war be arranged with Chalco or the Tlaxcalans, so that the gods may again have proof of our devotion."

Moteczuma scowled and wiped the moisture from his neck, looking past Quinatzin to the work going on in the rain. Quinatzin gave Nezahualcoyotl a respectful glance, allowing his concern to show only in his eyes. The king stared back at him bleakly, his angular features so sharpened by fasting that deep shadows gathered in the hollows of his cheeks. Quinatzin lowered his eyes and saw the mass of fresh scars on Nezahualcoyotl's forearms and shins, where he had pricked himself with the thorn of penance. He wears the proof of his devotion upon his face and skin, Quinatzin thought bitterly, yet Tlacaelel refuses to see.

"And what of Nezahualcoyotl's suggestion?" Moteczuma said abruptly. "Is the tribute to be lightened?"

"Tlacaelel does not deny that the people of Xochimilco and Coyoacan may be hungry. But he asks: Are not the people of Tenochtitlan hungry? And are we not their masters? He suggests instead, Lord, that they be allowed to renew their pride by being invited to participate in the flower war."

Quinatzin's voice was toneless, and his mouth felt soured by the cruel advice he had just been required to pass along. Nezahualcoyotl turned expectantly to Moteczuma, who looked at him once and then glanced away.

"My brother is wiser than I in matters concerning the gods," Moteczuma said finally. "And he knows the feelings of the priests and the Council of Lords. I do not rule here alone. Tell Tlacaelel to make the arrangements," he said to Quinatzin, and then stalked off into the rain, shouting to the workers to apply themselves as he was about to.

Nezahualcoyotl passed a hand over his long face and arched his back wearily. He glanced at Quinatzin's staff.

"You will need your staff, my friend, in the times ahead," he said gently. "We will all need something to lean upon. But do not concern yourself with Tlacaelel's displays of willfulness. No one fights for long on an empty stomach, not even a Tenocha. Soon enough, we will all be fighting starvation."

Nezahualcoyotl's eyes glazed over as he spoke, but then he blinked and stared straight at Quinatzin.

"But it will not be the end of everyone. It has exhausted me, but I have ascertained this much. Those who are strong and brave will survive. You must see that my grandchildren are among them."

Quinatzin nodded solemnly. "Ome Xochitl will be glad of this news; it will give her strength. She asks that she be allowed to bring our new daughter to you for your blessing."

"It would gladden my heart. But who is this young warrior you have brought with you today? Can this be the grandson who was named for me only days ago?"

Quinatzin motioned his son forward, and smiled proudly as the boy bowed gracefully before the king.

"It was ten years ago, my Lord," Quinatzin said. "I have brought him to you because in two days' time he enters the calmecac."

"So, Acolmiztli, my young lion, soon you will go to live with the priests, in the House of Quetzalcoatl, the House of Penance. There you will hear the words of the old men, and you will learn how to live properly in the sight of the gods. You must be humble, my grandson, and diligent, so that you never have to be summoned a second time."

"Oh no, Grandfather," the boy said seriously. "I will run when I am called. I am very good at running."

"That is good." Nezahualcoyotl laughed, and patted the boy fondly on the shoulder. Then he stared out at the workers and seemed to lose himself in thought. The rain drummed hypnotically upon the canopy, and Acolmiztli, with his grandfather's hand still lying on his shoulder, looked questioningly at Quinatzin. Finally, Nezahualcoyotl came to himself and released the boy with a parting pat.

"Only the bravest, Quinatzin," he repeated softly. "Only those who can live with the emptiness they will feel inside . . ."

THE RAINS continued to fall well into the time of the Festival of Xocol Huetzi, the Fall of the Fruits, when the hot sun of ripening should have been shining over Anahuac. This was the feast of the God of Fire, Xiuhtecuhtli, also known as Huehueteotl, the Old One. As a special measure of supplication to the god in this desperate time, Tlacaelel ordered the priests to resurrect the ancient hearth sacrifice, which was said to have been practiced by the gods themselves at Teotihuacan. The captives taken in the flower war with the Tlaxcalans were dressed in the garments and feathers of the gods and led to the temple of Xiuhtecuhtli, where a great brazier of coals had been kept burning for a day and a night. One by one, the captives were thrown onto the fire, where they writhed in the burning hand of the god, their flesh crackling noisily. Then the priests pulled them out of the fire with hooks and sacrificed them, still living, upon the techcatl. The priests also pricked themselves with maguey thorns and bled upon pieces of paper, which they gave to the fire along with quantities of rubber and copal incense. Despite the rain, the black smoke was seen to rise in a great pillar to the heavens, carrying the prayers of the people with it.

When the rain stopped, the people of Tenochtitlan waded out into the streets and fell on their knees to give thanks for their rescue. Gradually, the flood began to recede, and those who had left for the shore returned to begin repairing their homes. The farmers went out to plant the few crops that might be harvested before winter, and Moteczuma sent out the traveling merchants of Tlatelulco, the pochteca, with loads of his own goods, ordering them to trade for maize and seeds for next year's planting.

"The dike is nearing completion," Tlacaelel said. "Let the warriors take up their arms and again go against the Huaxtecs, so that the gods may be fed with the blood of warfare."

During these dry autumn months, when the city seemed to be returning to its former health, matches were made for both of the remaining daughters of Quinatzin and Teuxoch. The weddings were held in consecutive months, and though Quinatzin prevailed upon Teuxoch to limit the feasting, she would not hear of it.

"Would you have our daughters be disgraced?" she demanded angrily.

"I only think of the future," Quinatzin replied.

"You *worry* over the future," Teuxoch said scornfully. "Our daughters are Tenocha, Huitzilopochtli will feed them, and their children. My father would not be pleased that you show so little faith in the god."

So Quinatzin had to watch helplessly as course after course was brought out to the guests, and as bags of beans and strings of chilies were given to them as gifts when the feasting was over.

"Can she be right?" he asked Ome Xochitl later, staring at the empty bags and baskets with distracted eyes.

"Let us hope that she is," Ome Xochitl said, then quietly rose and began to take down the bags she had hidden in the rafters, and the baskets stored behind her loom, and the food she had wrapped in cloth and concealed in the reed chests that held ceremonial garments. Even the children's rattles had been filled with kernels of toasted maize. Quinatzin looked at his wife in mute astonishment.

"Still," she said matter-of-factly, "one cannot eat hope."

LATE THAT winter, snow fell on Tenochtitlan for the first time in memory. For six days, the air was filled with whiteness, and the people huddled around their fires to escape the cold that bit at their skin. When the weather finally broke, the whole city was blanketed in white, and the Lake had frozen over in places, trapping the waterfowl in the ice. Though the snow melted quickly, many of the Tenocha began to walk with their eyes on the ground, fearful of looking upward at the sky.

The first days of the year Eleven-Reed brought news of victories over the Huaxtecs, and there was a general sense of relief as some of the spoils of the war began to flow back to the city. But the supply of seed remained low, and the farmers went out to plant with uneasy hearts, taking special care in their offerings and pleadings to Tlaloc, and to Chicomecoatl, the Goddess of Maize and Sustenance. They watched the rains come and the green shoots begin to push their way through the soil, and they worked feverishly to protect the tender plants from the weeds and insects.

But then they awoke to find that a frost had come during the night, and that their crops lay flat in the fields. Again they tilled the soil, but now the rains refused to come, and as the farmers watched the sun bake the earth into brick, they despaired of risking what little maize they had left on another planting. They saw the merchants returning empty-handed, or with only a small amount of food among their other goods, and they began to hoard their seeds for themselves, to eat. As the summer wore on and still there was no rain, the shallows surrounding the island became wetlands, then mudflats, and, finally, desolate stretches of cracked, dry earth. The water birds vanished, and though the fishermen ranged further and further out onto the Lake, they returned with less and less.

By the winter, the macehuales were dying of starvation in their huts, and the effects of the famine were being felt by even the greatest of the lords. The house of Quinatzin was quiet, for although he was given food from the royal stores, it had to be rationed so strictly that none of the children had the strength for play. Acolmiztli was in the calmecac yet had to be supplied by the family, so Ome Xochitl had continued nursing Cocatli past the normal time of weaning, so that there would be more for the other four children. She kept the youngest boy and girl, Cipactonal and Oxomoco, close at hand, to prevent them from filling their mouths with earth or the painted plaster from the courtyard walls, and she had to scold her second son, Tlilatl, and her oldest daughter, Iztacxochitl, so that they would not follow the example of Teuxoch, who had taken to chewing the bark from the huehuetl tree in place of yetl leaves. She gathered them around her and told them stories, and sang to them to keep their minds off their hunger.

Occasionally, Quinatzin would return from the palace of the Speaker with some delicacy that had been brought back from the land of the Huaxtecs, and the family would sit down and share it out equally, savoring its goodness slowly, with the restraint that Ome Xochitl and Quinatzin had made a way of life for themselves and their children. The words of their grandfather Nezahualcoyotl were repeated so often on these occasions that Cipactonal and Oxomoco, who were still learning to speak, did not know that the word for hungry was not "brave."

But the new speech of these young ones did not gladden the hearts of their parents for long. Early in the year Twelve Flint-Knife, the coughing sickness swept through the houses of Tenochtitlan, and Cipactonal and Oxomoco died within a day of each other, coughing out their lives in their mother's arms. It was another year without rain, and even the desert plants, the maguey and the prickly-pear cactus, bore no fruit. The springs on the island dried up, and only a trickle ran through the aqueduct from Chapultepec. The sun burned down upon the lines of people who left Tenochtitlan with their possessions on their backs, heading east or south, wherever they had heard there was no drought. Many of these died of thirst along the trail, with their tumplines still tied around their foreheads.

Others sold themselves or their children to the Totonac slavers, who gave them maize and promised that they could buy their children back later, if they could pay for the food the children ate as slaves. Helpless to alleviate the suffering of the people, Moteczuma and Tlacaelel could do nothing to prevent this migration, though they set and enforced a price of two hundred ears of maize for a child and four hundred for a full-grown man, so that the city might gain something from the loss of its people.

In that same year, the moon rose suddenly into the day sky and bit into the sun, partially blackening the earth, and causing the priests to sacrifice dwarves, albinos, and hunchbacks in their terror at the sun's deformity. Quinatzin's eldest daughter, Iztacxochitl, was out on the mud flats digging roots with her brother when the eclipse occurred, and it so frightened her that she fell to the earth and her heart stopped beating. When Tlilatl could not rouse her, he pried the roots from her dead hands and walked slowly home to tell his mother.

The next year, Thirteen-House, brought hailstorms and an earthquake that opened a crevice in the dry bed of the Lake and rocked the temples of Tenochtitlan. Tlilatl caught the coughing sickness and died quietly in his sleep, without the strength to make a sound. Now Acolmiztli, who had been sent home from the calmecac, and the infant Cocatli were the only grandchildren left to Nezahualcoyotl, but even he could send them no food. They moved like old people, their skin hanging in wrinkles on their shrunken bodies, and Ome Xochitl climbed the tree in the courtyard herself to feed them on the tender bark of the upper branches.

In the year One-Rabbit, the vultures roosted on the rooftops in Tenochtitlan, and the coyotes and mountain lions came out of the hills to feed on the bodies that lay uncollected in the streets. It was the last year before the New Fire Ceremony, and all those still living thought that surely the end must come. Over half the population had already died or left, and the priests went through the motions of the festivals in solitude, watched over only by the gods and the vultures.

To her horror, Ome Xochitl discovered at this time that she was again pregnant. But though she was troubled by pains from the beginning, she refused to abort the child, or to leave Tenochtitlan for Texcoco. Nezahualcoyotl had built aqueducts to bring water from the hills behind his city, so there was some food in Texcoco, and he urged his daughter to come and let him feed her, because he dared not send food out of his city. Even Teuxoch encouraged her to go, but Ome Xochitl was steadfast.

"A captive must not flee his fate," she reminded Quinatzin, as the child grew within her and she no longer had the strength to rise on her own. "I am Tenocha. If I am to die, I will die on this island, among my people."

SEVERAL MONTHS before, at the suggestion of Tlacaelel, Moteczuma had begun dispensing food from the royal stores to the poorest people in the city. Because of his ability to deal with delicate situations, Quinatzin was put in charge of the operation, and he was given a contingent of Eagle Warriors to help maintain security. For it was known from the outset that there was not enough food for all who needed or wanted it, and the potential for rioting and theft were great.

To avoid this, Quinatzin had his own people overseeing every phase of the operation, from the opening of the granaries to the baking of the maize cakes, and the time and place of distribution were secrets known only to Quinatzin himself. Each night his staff was assembled according to a fixed schedule, with none knowing until the last moment whether they would indeed be working. Then, sometime after the middle of the night, orders would be issued to the keepers of the granaries and the bakers, and trusted messengers would be sent out simultaneously to the officials of the calpulli selected as the beneficiary of the next day's feeding. These officials were given only a few hours to gather the poorest people from their district and lead them to the appointed place, and the messengers stayed with them constantly, to make sure that no favoritism was shown to the well-off, or to those who were the relatives of the officials. A penalty of death had been set for anyone who took more than his share or tried to enrich himself at the expense of the truly needy.

At dawn, twenty canoes would be loaded with the maize cakes, made as large as a man's head, and the jugs of gruel that had been prepared in the kitchens of the palace. With the Eagle Warriors trotting alongside in the street, the canoes would be poled through the canals to the distribution point, where the people continued lining up until all the food was gone. By keeping himself aware of the rumors circulating in the city, and by adopting a seemingly random schedule, Quinatzin was able to complete several deliveries without incident, emptying the canoes and retiring from the scene before the crowd of the disappointed grew too large or unruly.

But the diminishing number of unvisited calpullis and the sharp noses of the hungry eventually began to undermine his ability to take the people by surprise, and Quinatzin came more and more to rely on the intimidating presence of the Eagle Warriors. There would be enormous crowds at each of the remaining possible places before the canoes even arrived, and it would be all the Eagle Warriors could do to force the people into orderly lines and prevent them from trampling the children and shoving each other into the canal. The food would be parceled out quickly, and then the fights would break out, and the Eagle Warriors would have to use the flat edges of their macanas to beat back those who attempted to jump into the canoes after scraps.

Finally, Moteczuma announced that his granaries were nearly empty, and that all the food that remained would be given out the next day, at the main canal that ran beside the Great Plaza. Quinatzin had protested the wisdom of such a move, but Tlacaelel had insisted that it was a necessary gesture, so that no one could later question the magnanimity of the Speaker, or the reality of his emptied stores. A second detachment of Eagle Warriors was assigned to the operation, and the cooks worked through the night to empty the granaries.

The sun rose the next day over a scene such as Quinatzin had dreaded from the very beginning. Thousands of people milled in the narrow street next to the canal, all pushing, shoving, and shouting accusations at one another. The noise was so tremendous that the Eagle Warriors could only make themselves heard with the blunt ends of their warclubs, and the sun had risen well into the sky before space was cleared at the edge of the canal and Quinatzin allowed the canoes to be brought over. The people pressed forward and were met by the strong arms of the Eagle Warriors, who gradually established a corridor through their ranks and began allowing the people through. Five empty canoes were drawn up abreast in the canal to form a bridge, and those given food were allowed to cross over by stepping from canoe to canoe, rather than being made to fight their way back through the crowd. Soon a crowd began forming on the other side of the canal, and Quinatzin had to assign part of his second detachment of Eagle Warriors to help the fortunate ones escape with their rations, and to prevent an assault from the rear.

Since the stream of loaded canoes in the canal appeared endless, there was relative calm in the street until well into the afternoon. But no matter how quickly Quinatzin's men emptied the canoes, the crowd never seemed to grow any smaller. Quinatzin strode nervously behind the lines of Eagles, gripping his staff tightly and ignoring the shouted appeals of those in the crowd who knew his name. The air around him was hot and seemed heavy upon his skin, as it sometimes had in the thick of battle. He glanced to the west, where the canal made a turn and disappeared under a bridge. Until this moment, the line of canoes had been solid all the way to the bridge and out of sight. But now there was open water visible between the bridge and the last canoe in the line, and when no further canoes appeared to fill the gap, voices were raised in the crowd:

"The food is running out!"

"Let me through! Give me mine!"

As the line of Eagles began to give ground before the renewed pressure of the crowd, the men unloading the canoes realized their danger, and each tried to speed up his task, without regard for those in front or behind. Men got in each other's way, food was dropped in haste, and the effort lost all coordination. Anxious to get away, the canoe drivers banged their vessels into one another, dislodging the canoe bridge, so that those who had received food had no way to escape, and began pushing back the way they had come. The Eagles attempted to close the corridor but were thrown back, and suddenly a man in the middle of the crowd leapt upon those who were in front of him, slashing wildly at their heads and shoulders with his warclub. Screams of pain and terror rose above the shouts of the hungry as the man cut a bloody path through the crowd, blindly attacking anyone who stood in his way. With a desperate cry, he struck at the first Eagle he reached, catching the warrior off-balance and wounding him in the shoulder.

The other Eagles reacted instantaneously, leaving their places to rush to the aid of their fallen comrade. The man who had struck him was quickly surrounded and methodically hacked to pieces. Then the Eagles turned all their pent-up fury upon the crowd, slashing right and left with their deadly macanas, felling the armed and the unarmed alike. But the people rushed past them heedlessly, their eyes on the remaining canoes. In their panic, the men unloading the canoes began throwing the food into the surging crowd, which fought over it like wild animals. The ground became slippery with blood and spilt gruel, and anyone unfortunate enough to fall was quickly trampled underfoot.

Striking out with his staff, Quinatzin struggled desperately to hold his ground, shouting to the Eagles to regroup. But his words were lost in the din and his staff was torn from his hands, and the people closed in around him, pushing and kicking. He saw his men being thrown back into the canal and the last canoes being capsized by the people who jumped into them from above. Food was being dumped into the water, and soon the canal was filled with struggling bodies. Held upright by the crowd, Quinatzin freed a hand and reached for the bone whistle he wore on a thong around his neck. Hoping that the Eagles would remember their orders, he blew as hard as he could on the hollow piece of bone, producing a high, keening shriek that pierced the ears of everyone around him and brought them to a momentary halt.

Then a second whistle sounded, and another and another, until the air was filled with the ear-splitting sound of a chorus of war whistles. Suddenly there was silence, and the crowd stood still, and began looking around them as if they had just awakened from a dream. Quinatzin found his staff and raised it over his head, and the Eagle Warriors began moving toward him, with the people parting to make way for them.

"People of Tenochtitlan!" Quinatzin shouted hoarsely. "There is no more food. Take what you have and go. It is better to die of starvation than to kill one another in the streets. Go now, before the Speaker is further disgraced on your account."

The crowd dispersed in silence, the people walking slowly with their heads bowed in exhaustion and shame. The street was littered with the bodies of the dead and wounded, and more floated face down in the canal. Quinatzin ordered some of the Eagles to tend to the wounded and help them to their homes.

"Burn the bodies of those who lie dead in the street," he said to the other Eagles. "And bury the ones who have drowned in the canal. Remember that they are Tenocha, and see that it is done properly."

Then he turned to see the line of children standing against the plaza wall, hungrily eying the bits of food that lay in the street, but too afraid of the Eagle Warriors to make a move for it.

"Take what you can find, my children," Quinatzin said. "But do not fight with one another as your parents did. Do not make us bury you, too."

THOUGH IT was only a short distance to his house in the royal compound, Quinatzin walked there slowly, leaning on his staff and taking small steps to ease the pain in his legs. His mantle was torn, his body covered with cuts and bruises, and he had not eaten since the previous evening. Nor had he slept, but these things were not the source of the distress he felt in his heart. It was the emptiness at the very center of his being, the absence of any real hope, that made it so difficult to go on. Were these the people who were going to rule the world? Were these the chosen people of Huitzilopochtli, these wretches who fed their children on witch grass and old deer hides and killed one another for a handful of food?

This, Quinatzin knew, was the real emptiness of which Nezahualcoyotl had spoken. How could men go on when the gods no longer heard their pleas? How could they be brave when the Sun burned them without mercy, and the earth itself had turned hard? What could sustain them? It was no wonder the people went mad; they were not made to live alone upon the earth.

Distracted by a sound overhead, Quinatzin glanced upward at the vulture flapping through the air above him. It flew low, borne down by its unusual weight, its head the color of a raw wound against the blackness of its feathers. Ahead, others were circling, and beginning to settle in the topmost branches of a tree. *My* tree, Quinatzin realized with a flash of fear. Forgetting the pain in his legs, he broke into a lurching run that carried him, gasping for air and nearly blind from the exertion, to the doorway of his house. The courtyard swam before his eyes. He saw figures: one, two . . . and another lying on the ground.

"Who?" he managed, before the words caught in his throat and choked him. He stood with his head bowed, unable to bring himself to look. Then he heard his son's voice, and forced himself to raise his eyes.

For several moments, he could not believe what he saw before him. At the foot of the huehuetl tree, Teuxoch was kneeling with a knife in her hand, and Acolmiztli was standing next to her, speaking softly and staring downward at the thing on the ground. Neither of them had heard Quinatzin or noticed his presence, and they did not look up as he approached. The thing on the ground, Quinatzin saw, was a coyote, and there was an arrow sticking out of its side. Teuxoch was skinning it with her knife, while Acolmiztli watched with eyes that shone with hunger, and coaxed her to work faster. Teuxoch glanced up at Quinatzin briefly, then returned her attention to the coyote.

"Go to the young wife," she said curtly. "She needs you."

Quinatzin nodded and walked across the courtyard to the rooms belonging to Ome Xochitl. She lay near the door on a pile of mats, her swollen belly thrust into the air. The four-year-old Cocatli huddled next to her, her tiny arm bandaged with cloth.

"Have we all been spared, then?" Quinatzin wondered aloud, kneeling on a mat next to his wife. Ome Xochitl turned her head toward him and took his hand. Her voice was a whisper.

"Acolmiztli left the little one in the courtyard to come help me rise. When we came out, the coyote had her cornered against the tree. We shouted at it, and threw things, but it was bold and unafraid, and it tore the stick from Acolmiztli's hands when he tried to attack it. Our son was very brave, but he did not have the strength to keep fighting. The beast had its teeth on the little one when Teuxoch put an arrow through its heart."

Ome Xochitl turned her head back to her daughter, and roused her gently with her hand.

"Show your father your wound, my little warrior," Ome Xochitl said. "Even when the coyote had her, she did not cry out."

"Come, my precious flower," Quinatzin said, and the little girl ran into his arms. He held her against his cheek and stroked her head and shoulders, feeling the sharp outlines of her bones through her skin. She began to cry, and Quinatzin patted her back soothingly, feeling the tears come to his own eyes.

"I must rest," Ome Xochitl said weakly. "Take the child, and let her see what has become of the one who tried to eat her. We must not let fear overtake her now that the danger is past."

Lifting Cocatli in his arms, Quinatzin went back into the courtyard. The hide of the coyote now lay in a bloody heap, a few feet away from where Teuxoch was cutting chunks of meat off the carcass. The vultures in the tree overhead rustled their wings expectantly and squawked at one another. Acolmiztli was holding the bowl into which Teuxoch was putting the meat, but when he saw his father looking at him, his face lost its hungry expression and he lowered his eyes in shame.

"Do not be ashamed, my son," Quinatzin said firmly. "You were brave to attack the coyote without weapons."

"They are Tenocha," Teuxoch said proudly, and when Quinatzin looked at her, he saw that there were tears in her eyes.

"Yes, but there are no other Tenocha like yourself, my wife," he said gratefully, and the tears began to flow down Teuxoch's narrow face.

"I have always kept your weapons for you, my husband," she said softly, her wet eyes glittering. "Though you have not used it in many years, the bow still knew how to kill."

Quinatzin put Cocatli down next to Teuxoch and lifted the bow and quiver from the ground. He turned to Acolmiztli.

"We were lucky to have this woman to protect us, my son. You must honor her in how you use this," he said gravely, handing the bow and quiver to the boy, who swelled with pride at the gift. "When you have eaten, you can begin practicing on these scavengers who watch us from above," he added, gesturing toward the vultures in the tree. "Even the death-eaters must be food for us now."

Then Quinatzin retrieved his staff and walked slowly toward the doorway of the courtyard.

"Where do you go, my husband?" Teuxoch asked anxiously. "We will soon eat."

"I will join you," Quinatzin promised, and bowed to Teuxoch in parting. "But first I must go to the temple of Huitzilopochtli, and thank him for the courage he has put in the hearts of my loved ones . . ."

3

THERE were periods during this time of famine and death when Quinatzin would not see or speak to Tlacaelel for several days. Messages and orders might come, but the Cihuacoatl himself would be sequestered within the Tlillan, the House of Darkness, home of the Snake Woman. This was a long, low building in the northwest corner of the plaza, and it had only one entrance: a low, round, cavelike opening that was always covered with a cloth. It was said that inside, the hideous image of the Snake Woman, the Earth Mother, stood in complete darkness, surrounded by representations of the mountains of Anahuac, and by the other gods whose images had been captured by the Tenocha.

Here, Tlacaelel remained alone for long periods of time, praying in the darkness to the Snake Woman and drawing his own blood in penance. He had fasted so strenuously in his pursuit of visions that his face had become as thin and sharp as a knife blade, and his body looked as if it had been made of sticks. Quinatzin did not know when he slept, if he did at all, and there were times, now, when he did not seem to be in control of his own thoughts. He would order massive sacrifices, when there were no prisoners. Or he would suddenly command his servants to bring him a meal such as had not been seen in Tenochtitlan in three years, detailing how his cocoa should be prepared and what spices should be added to the fish and fowl. When the terrified servants returned later with a handful of toasted maize, expecting to be put to death for their failure, Tlacaelel would have forgotten, or would be gone.

Other times, he would be seized by the conviction that he was the target of traitors and assassins, and he would carry a macana everywhere and surround himself with a troop of heavily armed Eagle Warriors. Twice, in such moods, he had ordered Quinatzin's death, accusing him of treasons that existed only in his own, tortured mind. Moteczuma had intervened in both instances, and he had become so concerned that he had made it an unspoken rule in the palace that his brother was not to be obeyed too hastily when the madness was clearly upon him.

But Tlacaelel was also visited by moments of tremendous lucidity, when all his powers seemed magnified by a composure so deep and otherworldly that the force of his presence was irresistible. Quinatzin feared these moods almost as much as the madness, for he felt himself to be totally in the other man's power, without the ability to dissemble or win his way with words. In these states, Tlacaelel had no need for trickery or intimidation. He had only to explain what was in his mind, and the clarity of his vision swept all arguments out of the way, as if there could be no other way to see things.

It was in such a state that Quinatzin found him when he went to make his report on the riot at the canal, several days after it had occurred. He had been summoned to await the Cihuacoatl outside the Tlillan, and as he crossed the plaza in front of the temple of Huitzilopochtli, Quinatzin knew that he might not return this way alive. The incident had been disgraceful, and he had been in charge. His protestations before or after the fact would not save him, if Tlacaelel had decided that the honor of the Speaker and his city had been injured. So as Quinatzin waited at the base of the steps that led up to the House of Darkness, he reconciled himself to his fate and prepared no words in his own defense. He kept his eyes on the ground, for the mere sight of the Black House made his flesh crawl with forboding.

Finally, Tlacaelel was led down the steps by his priests, his eyes blinking furiously in the bright sunlight. Yet when he was able to focus in on Quinatzin, his face broke immediately into a smile.

"So, here is the great warchief Quinatzin," he said sarcastically, "the hero of the War of Maize. Only why did you bring the killing to a halt? The Eagles were grateful for the chance to exercise their arms."

"It did not seem right for the Tenocha to kill their brothers," Quinatzin said. "I acted out of concern for the Speaker's reputation."

"Of course. And you were correct; it was enough." Tlacaelel laughed hoarsely. "Ah, but even in their hunger and weakness, the people showed themselves to be warlike. Our Mother, the Snake Woman, was pleased. She has sent me a vision."

Quinatzin waited politely, knowing that his response was not required. Tlacaelel smiled again, his eyes turned inward, and when he again looked at Quinatzin, his face was very calm.

"The New Fire Ceremony will soon be upon us, and time will begin again.

We must decide how we will proceed. Summon the lords of the Alliance to Tenochtitlan, in the Speaker's name. Also summon our vassels from Coyoacan, Xochimilco, Cuitlahuac, and the cities of the Tlalhuica. Send invitations to the people beyond the mountains, the Tlaxcalans and Huexotzincans, and tell them we have need of their counsel. Do this immediately, and then prepare the palace for their arrival. You may have the use of whatever is in my storehouses and those of the Eagles and Jaguars."

Tlacaelel looked at Quinatzin's face and laughed knowingly.

"You wonder how I will obtain their permission," he said, his eyes bright with pleasure. "But I have already *seen* the way. This is a powerful vision, Texcocan. Be sure that your father-in-law is adequately alarmed. We would have use of all of his famous eloquence."

Quinatzin bowed and turned to go, but Tlacaelel caught his arm and made him face the empty plaza. He gestured broadly at the still-uncompleted temple of Huitzilopochtli, which lay surrounded by abandoned piles of stone and timber.

"Tell the Fasting Coyote that before the years are bound for the seventh time, the priests of Huitzilopochtli will look down upon the earth from a great height, and all that they see will belong to him. Tell the king this, and let him prepare himself."

AFTER ALL the religious ceremonies and the required courtesies—the speeches of greeting and the exchange of gifts—had been completed, the invited chiefs began to assemble in the council chamber. The stone floor of the great room had been swept until it shone, and the carved wooden rafters overhead were decorated with pine boughs, since there were no flowers to be had. The red mats had been laid out in a circle in the middle of the room, and Quinatzin's aides guided the various delegations to the places that had been reserved for them. Tlacaelel had drawn the arrangements precisely for Quinatzin, as if recalling them from memory:

Moteczuma, on his reed seat, sat at the westernmost point of the circle, and to his immediate left was Tlacaelel himself, and then Nezahualcoyotl and the other Acolhua leaders. Further left were the newly subject kings of the Tlalhuican cities, people who knew of Nezahualcoyotl by reputation only, and could not be expected to side with him.

To Moteczuma's right was the third leader of the Alliance, Totoquihuaztli of Tlacopan, and beside him was Cuauhtlatoa, the Speaker of Tlatelulco. The two tribes of the Mexicans had been on uneasy terms since the end of the Tepanec War, and it was Moteczuma himself who had insisted that the Tlatelulca be given a place of honor, despite Tlacaelel's vehement objections. Tlacaelel had complained bitterly of this to Quinatzin, as if it spoiled his entire arrangement to have "quackers" so close to the Speaker. But the extremity of the situation had made him bow to Moteczuma's wishes and allow the reconciliation of the Mexicans to take place, though he had refused to have any part in it himself.

Further to the right, beyond Cuauhtlatoa, were the subject rulers from the cities around the Lake: the Xochimilcans, Cuitlahuacans, Culhuas, and the Tepanecs from Coyoacan and Azcapotzalco. These tribes were naturally friendly to Nezahualcoyotl, and thus had been placed as far away from the Fasting Coyote as possible.

Finally, facing Moteczuma across the central space were the rulers of the Tlateputzcan cities, the cities beyond the eastern mountains: Tlaxcala, Huexotzinco, Atlixco, and the Holy City of Cholula. These powerful tribes had ambitions of their own, and little fear of the Alliance, whom they had aided against the Tepanecs. Their delegation was led by the young ruler of the Tlaxcalans, Xicotencatl, a loud, arrogant warrior who made no secret of his scorn for the Tenocha.

"He has isolated me from my friends," Nezahualcoyotl had remarked earlier, when Quinatzin had revealed the arrangements to him. "But it does not matter; my voice will carry. But what can he mean by this prophecy of his?"

"I fear that he intends to goad you into open opposition, my Lord," Quinatzin had offered, "so that he can engage our cities in warfare. This is no small vision he has had. The power of it has not left him, but only increased."

"That may be so, but he is in no position to provoke me now. And why invite the Tlaxcalans and Huexotzinca? He knows that they would side with me in any conflict. No, my friend," Nezahualcoyotl had assured him wearily. "It is never wise to read Tlacaelel's motives too plainly. You know this yourself: he causes alarm with his right hand while preparing true disaster with his left."

"Forgive me, Lord," Quinatzin had said, expressing his own weariness. "But this power of his frustrates my senses. His heart is truly that of a demon, and I cannot fathom it. I do not know what he may propose next."

"Whatever," Nezahualcoyotl had concluded grimly, "it will no doubt be worthy of his name . . ."

Now, from his place behind Tlacaelel, Quinatzin watched the Cihuacoatl greet Nezahualcoyotl with an elaborate show of friendship, smiling without a trace of his usual sarcasm. Tlacaelel was wearing the white robe of his priestly office, but on his head was the turquoise crown of the Speaker, an honor that had been granted to him by Moteczuma and the Council of Lords in recognition of his true importance to the city. The force that possessed him was so strong that his face and body showed none of the debilitating signs of his fasts, and he spoke and gestured with an animation Quinatzin had seldom seen him display, except when the subjects under discussion were war and killing.

Moteczuma rose first, and spoke in his usual blunt manner: "My Lords, you know why it is that we have assembled here. The famine has visited great suffering on all our peoples. Surely, the gods must be greatly angered with us, to punish us in this way!" The Speaker paused and lowered his voice. "Very soon, we will once again bind the years, if the gods so will it. We must act now to appease them, if we are to continue upon the earth. I ask you to listen to what my brother, the Cihuacoatl, proposes."

Tlacaelel rose from his mat and stood silently, allowing his gaze to travel slowly around the circle of lords.

"I tell you frankly, friends and enemies alike," he began, in a tone of candor that sounded genuine even to Quinatzin, who saw heads straighten up around the circle. "I tell you that if there is again no rain, all my people will perish, and you can come to Tenochtitlan at this time next year to count our bones. Even if our Sun is not destroyed, the Tenocha cannot survive this punishment much longer!"

Tlacaelel paused, and Quinatzin could see, on the faces visible to him, the signs of astonishment at this unusual confession of weakness. The lips of Xicotencatl, the Tlaxcalan, curled upward in derision, and his comrades did little to conceal their contempt.

"Your priests have told you of the gods' anger," Tlacaelel continued, "and of the hunger that has come to them, as it has come to us. Oppressed as we are, we cannot allow this to continue! Therefore, I say to you: Let us pledge ourselves with our blood. Let us take a vow to the gods, *now,* before the years are bound. Let us promise them that if we are allowed to survive, if we are given the food and water we need to sustain *our* lives, we will then feed *them* as never before! We will give them twice, three times, a hundred times the number of hearts we have offered to them in the past!"

Tlacaelel sat down, and a low murmur swept through the room. Only the Tlaxcalans openly approved of the suggestion, though there were obviously other sympathetic listeners around the circle. The subject kings did their best to hide their consternation, for some of them were already forced to supply captives as part of their tribute, and they could only see their burden growing heavier. The other members of the Alliance, whose backs were to Quinatzin, seemed to neither agree nor disagree. When there was again silence, all the faces around the circle turned toward Nezahualcoyotl.

The Fasting Coyote rose with a grace that belied his fifty-two years, though the lines had deepened in his face and there were streaks of gray in his topknot. He drew himself up to his full height and began to speak in a thoughtful tone:

"Lords, I have listened to the words of our brothers the Tenocha, and I have been impressed by their concern, and by their foresight. Truly, something must be done to appease the gods; there can be no question of this. But what is it that we should do? Is it not necessary, first, to determine *how* we have offended them, so that we may know how best to regain their favor? Warfare and sacrifice are our sacred duties, and we have always performed them with enthusiasm and correctness. Particularly have the Tenocha been zealous in this regard. Can we say then, with *certainty,* that this is the area of our dereliction? Perhaps our error lies elsewhere; perhaps we have made our offerings incorrectly. It is difficult to know these things for certain. Let others speak to this, so that I may be enlightened."

As Nezahualcoyotl seated himself, Quinatzin was reminded of a piece of advice the king had once given him: "Never oppose a man when it is enough to cast doubt upon his words." Clearly, the Fasting Coyote was a master of this, as he had just demonstrated. But Quinatzin had no confidence that it would be enough on this day. Tlacaelel sat calmly, showing no desire to regain the floor and press his point. He *knows* something, Quinatzin thought, or else he would want to destroy Nezahualcoyotl's argument himself. Who is his ally? Can it be Totoquihuaztli?

But the Speaker of Tlacopan, who had always had close ties with Nezahualcoyotl, continued in a questioning vein, suggesting that it was Tlaloc, the Rain God, who had been offended, rather than the gods who ate the hearts of men. He was not a good speaker, though, and he was afraid of even the appearance of disagreement with Tlacaelel, so he did not make a strong impression. There was a mood of indecision in the room when Totoquihuaztli sat down, but this was shattered instantly when Cuauhtlatoa, the Speaker of the Tlatelulca, leapt to his feet and began speaking in an impassioned voice:

"*Surely,* Tlaloc is angry with us," he agreed scornfully. "But Lords! Is it not the Sun who burns the earth until it cracks, and heats the sky so that the clouds perish? And is it not the Mexicans, the People of the Sun, who have been punished most severely? The signs are clear, my Lords. Can we accuse the priests of incorrectness, when they have told us time and again that the gods, too, are famished? Tlacaelel is right! I say, let us shed our blood now, at this moment, so that there may be no question of our sincerity!"

There was an uproar in the chamber as Cuauhtlatoa sat down, and several people jumped to their feet at once, clamoring for the right to speak. So *that* was the price of reconciliation, Quinatzin thought sourly, angry at how thoroughly Tlacaelel had fooled him. I should have known that it was not Moteczuma's doing, Quinatzin accused himself; never before, after all, had the Speaker acted without his brother's consent.

The Tlaxcalan, Xicotencatl, had been given the floor, and he proceeded to pour forth his contempt for doubters, proclaiming loudly that only weaklings and cowards could fail to see the need for more blood. After he had finished, the other rulers rose one by one, anxious to assert their courage by joining the cry for more and greater sacrifices. Finally, Moteczuma ended the discussion by declaring that the decision had been made, and the chiefs solemnly pledged themselves by pricking their earlobes with pieces of bone and smearing their blood onto long strips of white paper, which were then gathered by the attendant priests and taken off to be burned in the hearths of the war gods.

Moteczuma again inclined his head toward his brother, but Tlacaelel declined the opportunity to speak and turned to Nezahualcoyotl.

"I would have the benefit of your enlightenment," he said unctuously, "now that the others have spoken."

"Surely," Nezahualcoyotl said as he rose, "the gods will be moved, as I have been, by the courageous words spoken here today. Now we must establish the way in which our vow will be fulfilled. Few are the enemies who remain close to our lands, and when we war far from our cities, as we have against the Huaxtecs and the Mixteca, many of the captives die of their wounds during the long march back. Besides, many of them are savages, who do not even speak the tongue our gods understand. Can we feed the gods on the hearts of such men? And what of slaves, and those of our own blood? Surely, these would not be fit offerings. We have made our vow as warriors," Nezahualcoyotl concluded in a powerful voice. "Let it be only warriors, then, who go to the stone in our name!"

"I agree," Moteczuma said emphatically, as Nezahualcoyotl resumed his seat. "The gods will not be satisfied by the hearts of filthy savages. But it is also true, as the Fasting Coyote has said, that we have few enemies close at hand. Must we war upon one another, and bring ruin to our lands and our people? Speak, my brother, if you have the answer."

Tlacaelel rose eagerly, as if he had been waiting for this very moment. Quinatzin felt the trap closing, and his stomach tightened with dread when Tlacaelel began speaking in that tone of deadly assurance that had come to him with his vision.

"Lords, I have given this problem much thought, and I have prayed to the Snake Woman for guidance. And she has given me the answer, she has shown me a vision. And what I saw in this vision was a marketplace—a place where we can go to purchase the food our gods crave!

"No, I do not mean a slave market," Tlacaelel went on quickly, to silence the stir his words had created. "This market will be stocked only with warriors. Listen to me, and I shall explain: When you go to the marketplace in your city, and you see a beautiful pair of jade earplugs, or a fine shield of feathers, do you not wish to possess them? And do you not pay the price that is asked by the artisans? Of course you do, for such is the way things have always been done.

"But let us make a change, Lords," he suggested, "for the sake of our vow. Let it be ordered in your cities that from now on the lip-plugs and earplugs, the golden armbands and beautiful feathers, the shields, weapons, and insignia of the warrior—let it be ordered that all these things may no longer be bought, but may *only* be dispensed by the ruler of your city. Tell your young men that there is only one marketplace for these things, and that that marketplace is upon the field of battle. Tell them that they must purchase these things with their bravery and their blood, and that no man who does not fight—even though he be the son of the Speaker himself—will be allowed to wear the feathers and jewels of the warrior. Cowards and weaklings will have no rank, and they will be made to dress in the coarse garments of the macehuales and to work with their hands. They will not be allowed to speak to the proven warriors, and they will have no yetl or octli or cocoa, and they will eat whatever is left after the warriors have finished. All will know who they are, and they will be pointed out and despised!"

Shouts of approval greeted this plan, and Tlacaelel waited patiently until there was quiet once again.

"Let it also be ordered, if you think it is wise," he continued, "that those born of slaves or the common people be given their legitimacy, and that they, too, be allowed to rise to rank and wealth by the strength of their arms and the courage of their hearts. In this way, should the sons of the lords lose their eagerness for fighting, we will never lack for warriors."

"It is wise!" Xicotencatl shouted rudely, but no one saw fit to correct his manners. When Tlacaelel resumed speaking, Quinatzin imagined, from his tone, that the Cihuacoatl's face wore one of its rare smiles.

"But the problem still remains," Tlacaelel cautioned. "Where is this market-place to be established? Can it be in the lands of savages? The Fasting Coyote has convinced us otherwise, and the truth of his words cannot be doubted. Let me suggest, then, that when there is no war, or when we war on people unfit for our gods, let us then contend with one another in the Xochiyaoyotl, the War of Flowers. Let there be those among us who will consent to be our enemies in times of peace, so that we may trade with them in the marketplace of death!"

Tlacaelel looked straight at the Tlaxcalans as he said this, and both Xicoten-catl and the ruler of the Huexotzinca leapt immediately to their feet.

"Our warriors crave the sweet death of which you speak," Xicotencatl declared boldly. "Let *us* be your enemies when you need them. We will designate fields on our borders for this purpose, and we will meet you there to barter with our lives!"

"It is settled," Moteczuma announced, after a sufficient number had expressed their agreement. "Let us retire now, and cleanse ourselves before the feasting begins."

Quinatzin rose with the others, but saw that Nezahualcoyotl remained seated, lost in thought. He has defeated us, my Lord, Quinatzin thought, gazing sadly at the dejected king. He has shown his vision to Anahuac, and the rulers have accepted it. Now the whole Valley will serve Huitzilopochtli, without even the need for conquest. His power was too great for us.

A servant came to Quinatzin and told him that Tlacaelel had gone to the next room, and was asking for him. Putting his sympathy for Nezahualcoyotl firmly out of his mind, Quinatzin went through the doorway into a small chamber, an anteroom where the scribes had been recording, in painted pictures, the substance of the lords' speeches. The room was now empty and the torches had been extinguished, and Quinatzin was surprised to find Tlacaelel lying on a pile of mats in the corner.

"Come closer, Texcocan," he whispered hoarsely, and Quinatzin squatted next to him. His eyes were sunk deep into his face and all his limbs trembled visibly, revealing the extent of his fatigue. Quinatzin was struck by the impossible thought that the man was dying, and was shocked into speechlessness.

"Have you no words of praise, then?" Tlacaelel said mockingly, trying to focus on Quinatzin with eyes that kept closing of their own accord. He waved a hand wearily. "It does not matter. The will of the Goddess has prevailed. You must thank Nezahualcoyotl for me; his eloquence was useful."

"Yes, Lord," Quinatzin said numbly, and Tlacaelel mustered the strength to look at him fully.

"We are saved," he whispered feverishly. "We will rule the world . . . there is nothing that can stop us now."

"Yes, Lord," Quinatzin repeated, as the eyes closed and Tlacaelel slipped into unconsciousness. Quinatzin leaned close, and heard the soft but steady murmur of his breath. He will not die now, Quinatzin thought, and even if I were to kill him, he would live on in his vision. He has given his heart to Anahuac, and it will beat on forever.

Quinatzin slowly straightened up, then bent again to cover Tlacaelel with the blanket that lay nearby. He did it without thinking, feeling, somehow, that if he could not kill this man, he would have to serve him. Then he turned and went out to join the rulers in their celebration.

THE last five days of the year were those called nemontemi, the Useless Days, the vain and idle days that hung between the old year and the new. These were the unluckiest days in the sacred calendar, days with no signs, and thus no purpose. No business was conducted during this time, and the people stayed in their homes and did nothing, not even sweeping the floor.

It was thought that should one stumble or fall during this period, or pick up bad habits, such accidents and habits would plague the person for the rest of his life. If someone were to fall ill, it was believed that he or she would never recover.

The sky turned gray over Tenochtitlan as the nemontemi began, bringing the year One-Rabbit to an end. But no rain fell, and the starving people felt a deep apprehension as they waited for the time when their lives might begin again. At sunset on the fifth day, the New Fire Ceremony would be held, and then they would know if the Sun would be rekindled to burn for another fifty-two years, or if the sky would turn black and the monsters would descend to destroy them. In accordance with custom, the priests had extinguished the fires that had burned continuously in the temple hearths since the last ceremony, and the people put out their hearth fires and broke their household utensils and the images of the household gods. The sky was empty of smoke, and in all of Tenochtitlan, no one, not even the priests, stirred from his home.

On the second day of the nemontemi, Ome Xochitl felt the child begin to move within her. Despite the discomfort, she told no one, praying to the Snake Woman that the child not be allowed to come at this unlucky time, when it could have no hope of happiness and good fortune. But the pains only increased, overwhelming her in her weakened condition, so that she would fall unconscious and only awaken some time later, bathed in sweat. She became delirious, imagining that she had died giving birth, and was being carried through the streets of Tenochtitlan on Quinatzin's back. There was an honor guard accompanying them that included her father Nezahualcoyotl, and these were fighting with the young warriors that chased after the burial procession, hoping to steal a lock of hair or a finger from her hand, for the body of a woman who had died in childbirth contained much power.

Indeed, Ome Xochitl felt this power within her, and wished that it was she who could do the carrying, for Quinatzin's back and legs were bent with her weight. Then she began to glow with heat and felt herself rising into the air, into a golden light, and she knew she was in the place called Tonatiuhilhuicac, the dwelling place of the Sun. Coming toward her was a great crowd of warriors, Eagles and Jaguars in all their brilliant plumage, and those in front were dancing and waving their weapons and singing war songs, while those behind bore the bright burning globe of the Sun upon their shields.

Ome Xochitl found herself surrounded by women, among them her mother, who greeted her with tears of joy. Then the warriors dispersed, some transformed into hummingbirds, and the women lifted the Sun upon a litter of quetzal feathers and carried him across the western sky, waving fans of the emerald-green quetzal feathers and shouting their war cries to gladden the heart of the Sun. Down, down, they bore him, finally down to Mictlan, the Land of the Dead, where all became blackness . . .

Then she dimly heard voices, and felt a cool wetness against the skin of her face, and once more there was the terrible pain that seemed to push out from the center of her. She forced open her eyes, but only gradually could she see. Teuxoch was squatting next to her, bathing her forehead with a wet cloth, and Quinatzin towered somewhere above her, his voice seeming to come from the staff she could see planted between his legs.

"We must send for the midwives," he was saying, the uncertainty in his voice betraying his anxiety.

"They will not come during these days," Teuxoch said curtly, then smiled when she saw that Ome Xochitl was conscious. "So, my daughter, you have returned to us. The time is near, is it not?"

Ome Xochitl managed a weak nod and tried to smile as Quinatzin squatted next to Teuxoch and took her hand. Then she grimaced and had to close her eyes against the pain.

"We must try to get them," Quinatzin insisted to Teuxoch, who snorted scornfully.

"And if you *could* get them to come," she demanded, "how would you pay them? No one accepts promises anymore."

"With these," Ome Xochitl gasped, and directed her husband's hand to a cloth-wrapped bundle that lay on the mats beside her. Quinatzin held the bundle in his palm and unfolded the cloths, revealing the necklace of turquoise flowers and the jade amulet that Ome Xochitl had won as the prize for her flower song. Teuxoch fingered the necklace briefly and held the amulet up to the light to examine it. Then she dropped them unceremoniously back into Quinatzin's hand.

"The craftsmanship is excellent," she said brusquely. "But they have no value in these times. The midwives would want food. Have you any of that to give them?"

"You know we have none," Quinatzin said despairingly. Teuxoch reached over and once more plucked the amulet from his hand.

"And this. Is it not a rabbit? Would anyone who has lived through this year want such a reminder? Already, the people think of starving as 'rabbiting.' Put this away, and let it be your gift to the new child. *I* will be the midwife."

Quinatzin glanced uncertainly at Ome Xochitl, who gave him her consent by closing and opening her eyes. Folding the jewels back into the cloths, he rose slowly to his feet. The thought of losing his young wife suddenly filled his heart with pain, and he had to blink to keep back the tears.

"My wife . . ." he began, but Teuxoch cut him off impatiently.

"Bring me clean water," she commanded without looking at him, and began to arrange Ome Xochitl upon her mats.

THE LABOR continued for most of the day, with Teuxoch continually having to rouse Ome Xochitl and urge her to push back against the struggling child. At last, Teuxoch gave a great cry of victory, and Quinatzin rushed into the room and threw himself on the mats next to Ome Xochitl. Her eyes were closed, but the breath whistled noisily through her nose and open mouth, and her breast rose and fell with rapid regularity.

"My flower," he said softly, and moistened her lips and forehead with the wet cloth. Ome Xochitl sighed and looked at him briefly out of exhausted eyes, before falling back into sleep.

"It is a boy child, this unlucky one," Teuxoch said, holding the squirming infant out to Quinatzin with a strange, stoical expression on her face. Quinatzin left Ome Xochitl's side and came to take the tiny creature, which was about as large as his hand, and seemed to weigh nothing. He was as emaciated as his mother—as they all were—but his limbs were straight and moving. Then Quinatzin turned sideways into the light from the doorway and looked closely at the child's face, and nearly recoiled in horror.

Even for a newborn, it was an exceedingly ugly face: bloated and wrinkled, with a prominent forehead and a flat nose, and a chin that disappeared into a roll of misplaced flesh. His skin was a mottled copper color, and his head was crowned with a curly mass of thick black hair and a pair of ears that stuck out from the sides of his face like a tiny pair of scalloped hands. Quinatzin stared at the creature in his hands and did not see his own son, or even a child. In his shock, he saw something inhuman, a grotesque joke of the gods, as deformed in its flesh as it was in its fortune.

"Will it live?" Quinatzin asked dully, turning back to Teuxoch. Snatching the child from his hands, she glared at Quinatzin with sudden fury.

"You forget yourself!" she snapped angrily, her narrow face contorted with displeasure. "Must this poor child add the lack of his father's love to his store of misfortunes? He is Tenocha! He must not come into the world without respect."

Turning away from Quinatzin, she raised the child to the four directions, and spoke to him in the words of the midwife:

"You have been born here, my young one, my precious son," she said sternly. "Here, where your cradle is, and your blankets, here in the house of your father and mother. But your real place is out there, on the plains, upon the field of battle, where the Eagle Warriors and Jaguar Warriors give their lives to war. Warfare is your inheritance, my young one, it is your rightful task upon this earth. Here you will give nourishment to your father, to Tonatiuh, the Sun. Perhaps you will be a great warrior, and take many captives. Or perhaps you will merit the flowery death, the sweet death by the obsidian blade. Thus is your fate, that someday you will go to your real home, there with the Sun, in his dwelling place in the heavens."

Teuxoch set the child down on a clean blanket and held up the umbilical cord she had cut with her flint knife.

"This, which I have taken from your side, this is the gift, the property of the Great One, Tonatiuh. When there is again war, this gift will be entrusted to the great warriors, to the Eagles and the Jaguars, and they will take it with them to the battlefield. There, they will bury it in the middle of the plain, planting your name in that place, and pledging your life to the Sun. You must labor, my precious child, and pray that the Lord of the Near and the Far will watch over you, and provide for your life."

Then she began to bathe the baby, who immediately started squalling with a force that seemed impossible for one so tiny. Teuxoch held him in the basin of clear water and washed him all over, murmuring the prayers to Chalchihuit-licue under her breath. Quinatzin stood to the side with his head bowed, still filled with shame at the way he had acted. It was the madness of my hunger and fatigue that spoke, he told himself sadly, finding little consolation for the enormity of his son's bad luck. To be born on one of the idle days, in this awful time of famine, when the world itself might soon perish! How could such a one survive? How could there be any honor or joy in his life? It would have been kinder to let him die now, before he could begin suffering all the pain and misfortune that would be his lot.

Teuxoch finished bathing the child, dried him, and bundled him in blankets. Then she handed the squalling bundle to Quinatzin, refusing to meet his penitent gaze.

"You were right to correct me," Quinatzin said softly, but Teuxoch brushed his apology aside.

"Tomorrow, at sunrise, I will bathe him for the second time," she said decisively. "There is no point in sending for the soothsayers. Even they are not clever enough to find a propitious sign for this child. But I will not allow him to be called Nemon or Mentlacatl or any of the other names that would indicate the worthlessness of his fortune. I will go now to the temple of the Cihuacoatl, and I will pray to the Snake Woman, and hope that a suitable name will be whispered in my ear."

Teuxoch left the room, and Quinatzin stood holding the child, who had quieted in his arms. Ome Xochitl called to him softly, and he knelt beside her, and put the bundle next to her breast. She, too, saw the child's face, and looked up at Quinatzin with tears in her eyes.

"We must labor, my husband," she said. "We must protect him from the bad fortune he has brought with him into the world."

"I will do all I can," Quinatzin promised sadly. "If such a thing is indeed possible . . ."

THE SUN was just rising over the courtyard the next morning when Teuxoch bathed the child for the second time. After cleansing him of his sins, she dressed him in a miniature mantle and loincloth, and she presented him with a tiny shield, a bow of the same size, and four little arrows, one for each of the directions. Again, he was dedicated to Tonatiuh, to the sacred warfare that sustained the Sun. Then Teuxoch gave him the name Huemac, the name that had come to her in a dream the night before. This was the name of the last great king of the Toltecs, the ninth ruler of Tula, a tormented man who was said to have sacrificed his own children during the Rabbit years of famine in Tula, and who had been driven to take his own life after the fall of that ancient city. It was the proper name, Teuxoch had insisted, prophesying that the life of this Huemac, like that of his namesake, would be filled with the greatness of misfortune.

"You must teach him to guard against the petty accidents that might disrupt his fate," she said when the ceremony had been completed, and she reluctantly returned the child to his mother. Ome Xochitl gave the baby to Quinatzin and turned to bow low before Teuxoch.

"We are grateful to you for all you have done," she said humbly. "You must have this as a gift."

Ome Xochitl brought out the necklace of turquoise flowers and placed it around the older woman's neck, and again bowed low. Teuxoch beamed proudly and turned to show off her gift to Acolmiztli and Cocatli, who did not shy away from her approach, but complimented her with childish politeness. Shifting the bundle from one arm to the other, Quinatzin noticed that the child's eyes were open for the first time. They were large and round, dark brown, with golden rings around the pupils and heavy lids that gathered in folds within the deep sockets formed by the powerful brow. They stared back at Quinatzin without fear, unblinking in the new light.

"Ah, he has brave eyes, this Huemac," Quinatzin exclaimed with sudden pride, holding the baby up for the others to see. "Look upon your people, my son. Show your brave eyes to those who call you their kin."

The baby's head wobbled and he blinked at the sudden movement. But then he opened his eyes to their widest, and seemed to stare directly at Teuxoch, making a sharp, sucking noise with his mouth. She reached out for him, and Quinatzin, after a brief, reluctant glance at Ome Xochitl, handed the child over.

"Yes, my child," Teuxoch crooned, holding Huemac against her breast. "I am also here for you, my little Tenocha . . ."

"Can it be unlucky to have two mothers?" Ome Xochitl suggested softly, seeing the troubled expression on Quinatzin's face as Teuxoch cuddled the child possessively. Quinatzin turned hesitantly toward his young wife, and noticed that Teuxoch was now watching him carefully. Her face wore an expression of such vulnerability that Quinatzin's heart was softened, and he rested a hand upon her shoulder to reassure her.

"No, it cannot," he agreed, and put his other hand on Ome Xochitl's shoulder, drawing her and the other children in around Teuxoch. "Let us guard him well, my family. Let us deliver our Huemac from his unfortunate beginning . . ."

AT SUNSET on the last day of the nemontemi, the final day of the year One-Rabbit, the Fire Priests went out from Tenochtitlan in a long procession, each dressed in the regalia of one of the high gods. They moved with great solemnity, and the people watching from the rooftops of Tenochtitlan said of them that "they walk as gods." They went south along the causeway to Ixtapalapa, arriving in darkness at the temple on the hill called Huixachtlan, the Hill of the Star. Here the priests waited, their eyes fixed upon the eastern sky, praying for the appearance of the stars that would confirm the renewal of time, and assure the salvation of the people. The Fire Priest of Copulco, he who would draw the New Fire, tested his painted fireboard, whirring the firesticks between his hands.

The night was cloudy, and for a long time it was difficult to see anything in the sky above. But then the wind blew a hole in the clouds, and gazing upward, the priests saw the stars for which they had prayed. Crying out in gratitude, they set feverishly to work. At the precise moment when the stars came into the center of the sky, a captive—a Tlaxcalan of high rank taken in the last flower war—was led to the sacrificial stone. After the man's chest had been opened and his heart torn out, the priests placed the sacred fireboard into the cavity where the heart had been, and everyone present prayed to Xiuhtecuhtli, the God of Fire and Time, as the firesticks spun in the hands of the Fire Priest of Copulco.

Suddenly, there was smoke, then a flame. As tinder was fed to the growing fire, the blazing firesticks were thrown skyward in joy. From this first flame a great bonfire was built, large enough to be seen in all the corners of Anahuac. Then runners lit torches from the fire and raced down the hill, carrying the New Fire through the night like flying stars. They brought it to the hearths in the temples and palaces, and to the bonfires in the temple plazas, where the tired and hungry people of Tenochtitlan gathered to rejoice, and to carry away coals with which to rekindle the fires in their homes. The years had been taken, and the people were once again safe.

That spring, the rains came to Anahuac for the first time in three years, and the land was once again clothed in green. Maize and beans were found growing wild along the trails, pushing up through the bones of those who had died trying to leave the city. The young plants were cherished as a gift from the dead, and they were cultivated wherever they were discovered. Sweet water once again poured into the Lake from the mountain streams, and one day the water birds returned, settling among the fresh green reeds as they always had in the spring. It was the year Two-Reed, long to be remembered as the year that the Tenocha returned from the dead, and once more took up the mission of their god.

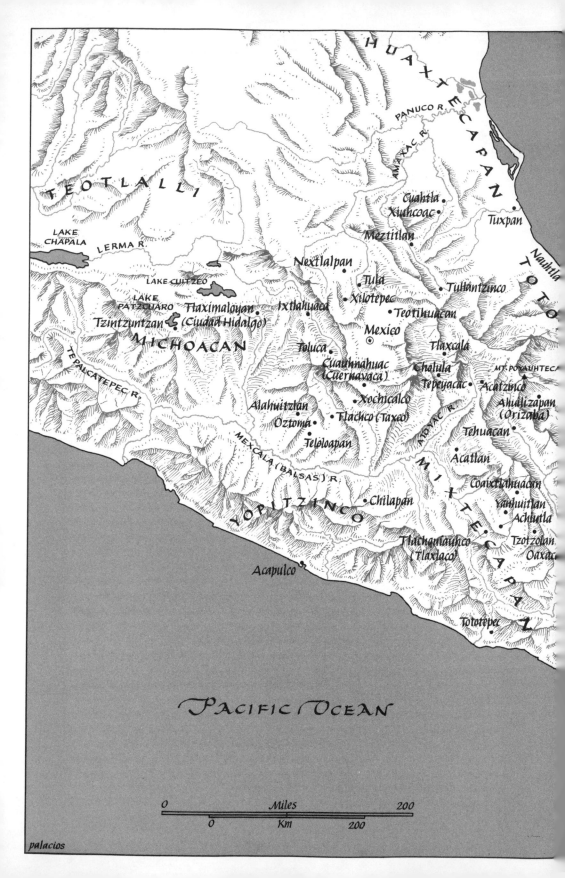

HUAXTECAPAN

PANUCO R.

AMAXAC R.

Cuahtla

Xiuhcoac

Tuxpan

TEOTLALLI

Meztitlan

TOTO

Nauhtla

LAKE
CHAPALA

LERMA R.

Nextlalpan

Tula

Tullantzinco

LAKE CUITZEO

Ixtlahuaca

Xilotepec

Tlaximaloyan
(Ciudad Hidalgo)

LAKE
PATZCUARO

Teotihuacan

Tzintzuntzan

Mexico

MICHOACAN

Toluca

Tlaxcala

Cuauhnahuac
(Cuernavaca)

Chalula

MT. POYAUHTECA

Tepeyacac

Acatzinco

TEPALCATEPEC R.

Xochicalco

Ahuilizapan
(Orizaba)

Alahuitzlan

Tlachco (Taxco)

ATOYAC R.

Oztoma

Tehuacan

MEXCALA (BALSAS) R.

Teloloapan

Acatlan

YOPITZINCO

M I X T E C A

Coaixtlahuacan

Chilapan

Yanhuitlan

Achiutla

Tzotzolan

Tlachquiauhco
(Tlaxiaco)

Oaxaca

Acapulco

P A L

Tototepec

PACIFIC OCEAN

0   Miles   200
0   Km   200

palacios

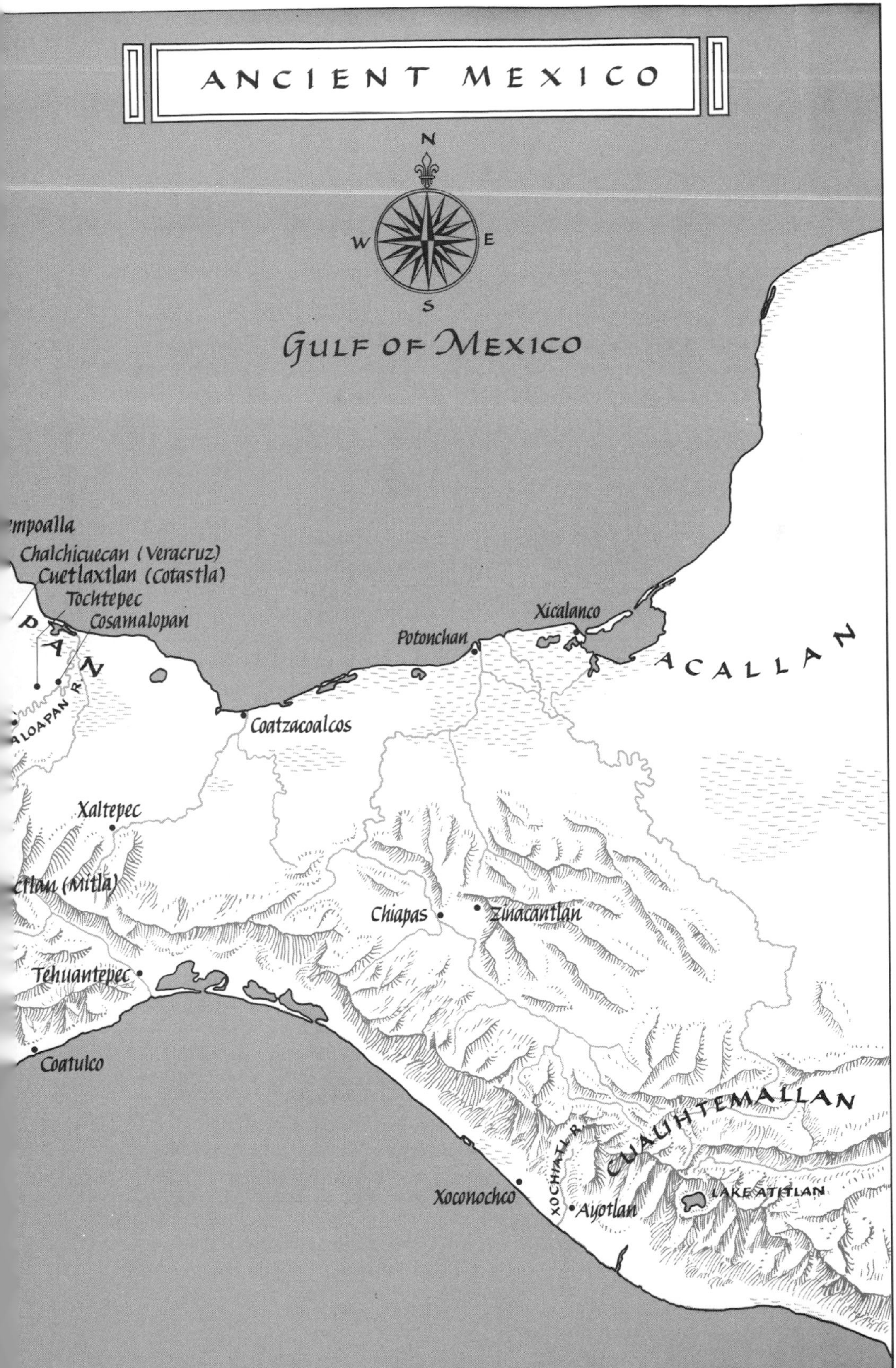

ANCIENT MEXICO

N
W E
S

GULF OF MEXICO

mpoalla
Chalchicuecan (Veracruz)
Cuetlaxtlan (Cotastla)
Tochtepec
Cosamalopan
PAN
Xicalanco
Potonchan
ACALLAN
LOAPAN R.
Coatzacoalcos

Xaltepec

tlan (Mitla)
Chiapas   •Zinacantlan

Tehuantepec •

Coatulco
CUAUHTEMALLAN

XOCHIZTLA
Xoconochco   •Ayotlan   LAKE ATITLAN

III

HUEMAC

1456–1463

1

WITH the famine behind them, the people of Tenochtitlan once more drew sustenance from their Mother, the Earth, nourishing their bodies and reviving the trade in their marketplaces. Work was resumed on the great temple of Huitzilopochtli, and the Mexicans from Tlatelulco joined with the Tenocha in the construction of a new, two-channeled, stone aqueduct to Chapultepec, to assure a steady flow of fresh water to their cities. Once again, the artisans labored patiently in their shops, the women planted flowers in the rooftop gardens, and the fishermen and fowlers silently poled their canoes among the reeds in the Lake.

Yet in the palace of Moteczuma, all the talk was of war. The vision of Tlacaelel shone in the eyes of the warchiefs, and the new decrees concerning the status of warriors had produced an unrelenting state of eagerness and tension among the young men of the city. The sons of lords and the sons of slaves were joined by their equal lack of visible rank, and all furiously sought the chance to establish their worth in battle. The hallways and waiting rooms of the palace were crowded with both the proven and the unproven, all hoping to catch the attention of the Speaker or one of his advisers.

Threading his way between the knots of men, Acolmiztli moved down the main hallway toward his appointment with his father, keeping his eyes level and trying not to be affected by what passed before him. The magnificence of the carved wooden beams high overhead and the painted murals on the walls no longer awed him, for Quinatzin had brought him here many times as a child. But the proud figures of the Eagle and Jaguar Warriors, with their golden lip-plugs and feathered headdresses, excited his respect and envy, and made him keenly aware of his own lack of insignia and rank. He dared not meet their eyes as he went by, lest they should see the naked longing in his own.

Acolmiztli was sixteen years of age, slender yet wiry, and very erect in his bearing. He had completed his studies in the calmecac nine months earlier, and had since taken up residence in the telpochcalli, the Young Men's House, where he was training to be a warrior. Already, he had distinguished himself as a bowman, and as a runner of great speed and stamina, and he hoped that these qualities might earn him the right to accompany the warriors as a shield-carrier on the campaign that was being organized against the Mixteca. There were many others who also wished for this privilege, though, and it was well known that few apprentice warriors were being taken, due to the length of the journey and the relative scarcity of rations. Acolmiztli had appealed to his father for help, and he had come here today in answer to a summons that he hoped would soothe the desperate yearning in his heart.

When he at last arrived at the chamber he sought, he found the door guarded by an enormous warrior whose warclub looked like a child's toy in his huge fist. His head was completely shorn, indicating that he was quachichtin, one of those whose bravery maddened him in battle. But Acolmiztli could tell that simply by looking at the man's face, which was crude and fierce, and utterly lacking in humility. It took the young man a moment to gain the courage to address this forbidding sentry, but when he did, his voice was steady, and he did not flinch in the face of the warrior's sneering gaze.

"Well? Who is it you want to see?" the guard demanded rudely.

"My father," Acolmiztli began, but the warrior cut him off impatiently.

"And who is your father? Does he have a title?"

"He is Quinatzin," Acolmiztli said simply, for his father had no official title, and, as Acolmiztli knew from experience, needed none. He saw this reconfirmed in the way the guard immediately lowered his tone and tried to put some respect into his voice.

"Ah, the Hand of the Demon Heart," he mused, looking the boy over appraisingly. "You may enter. He is there, to the right as you go in."

Acolmiztli entered the chamber, which was one of several anterooms connected to the Hall of the Speaker. Here he could feel the power of the assembled lords as a pressure on his skin, and the splendor of their garments and jewelry dazzled his eyes, so that it took him several moments to locate his father. Quinatzin was standing only a few paces away, locked in conversation with a pair of warchiefs who, from their dress, appeared to be Tepanecs. He leaned upon his staff with one hand, gesturing gracefully with the other as he spoke, so that the attention of his listeners would not wander.

Acolmiztli's admiration for his father was wholehearted, but always, when he saw him under these circumstances, he felt a twinge of embarrassment at the plain figure Quinatzin chose to present in public. He wore no jewelry or insignia of rank, and his long, graying hair flowed onto his shoulders, in the manner of the tlamatinime, the wise men who had become his closest friends in the court. He has proven himself as a warrior, Acolmiztli reminded himself, and there is no one who would question his rank and authority. Still, the young man thought, self-consciously fingering the long hank of hair that hung at the back of his neck, still, once I am allowed to cut this in the manner of a warrior, I will never again wear it long, until I am a white-haired old man without the strength for war. My father could not help his injury, but it has made him appear old before his time . . .

QUINATZIN was aware of his son's presence, and he finished his business with the warchiefs as quickly as he could. He knew the pleasure his news would give Acolmiztli, and he looked forward to presenting him with it, despite his own misgivings about the haste with which this campaign against the Mixteca was being organized. It seemed too soon after the famine to be venturing so far from the city, and the highland cities of the Cloud People were said to be well defended. But the merchants that Moteczuma had sent out to spy for him had been murdered on the trail leading out of the Mixtec capital of Coaixtlahuacan, and not even a lack of preparedness could keep the Tenocha from responding immediately to this blatant provocation.

So Quinatzin had done as his son had requested, understanding the young man's eagerness for recognition, and hoping that the gods would not steal back his life. He had acted as the son of a Tenocha would expect his father to act, and, as he greeted Acolmiztli, he put a properly somber expression upon his face.

"It has been arranged. You are attached to the Jaguar Warriors, and you will report to their house at dusk today. You should know that I could not have gotten you this place, despite my influence in the court, if you had not shown yourself to be capable of filling it. Do not allow yourself to become arrogant, though, for you must work to prove that I and your instructors at the telpochcalli were not wrong."

"Surely, I am unworthy of this honor," Acolmiztli said humbly, though with joy in his eyes. "I will exhaust myself to justify your trust, and sooner would I die than bring disgrace to you and to my city."

"May the gods give you strength," Quinatzin said proudly, looking at his son with unconcealed affection. "Now we must go, so that you can make your farewells to your mother and sister. I am done here, unless . . ."

Quinatzin glanced around the room, nagged by the sense that there was someone else he had meant to speak to today. But he could not think of who it was, and he felt his son's impatience, as well as the pull of his own desire to make the most of whatever time they had left together. Shrugging finally, he looked into Acolmiztli's shining, eager eyes and nodded contentedly.

"Let us go, my son. The rest can wait until after I have eaten a meal with you, and given you my blessing . . ."

WHEN Quinatzin and Acolmiztli entered the courtyard, they found Cocatli sitting on the ground not far from the entrance, arranging stones in patterns in the dust. Her concentration was so total that she did not look up until their shadows fell over her and Acolmiztli laughed, amused as always by the seriousness with which his sister played. Cocatli ran to her father and clung to his waist, and Quinatzin cupped her head with his free hand, fondly ruffling her black hair. The dark-skinned little five-year-old, who had her mother's eyes and features, was his favorite among all of his children, and he always responded to her with an extra measure of protectiveness. She was tiny, even for her age, and though she bruised easily, she never cried out or complained. Quinatzin had already reconciled himself to the fact that she would never achieve her full growth, because of how she had been starved as an infant.

"Your brother has come to say goodbye to you, my flower," Quinatzin said coaxingly. "He is leaving us now to go with the warriors, to fight for our city."

Cocatli peered shyly around her father's leg before running to Acolmiztli, who lifted her high over his head before settling her against his hip.

"Gently," Quinatzin cautioned, and Acolmiztli laughed, proud of his own strength.

"When we have laid waste the city of Coaixtlahuacan," he promised his sister exuberantly, "I will bring you back the jewels of a Mixtec princess to play with."

Ome Xochitl had her loom set up under the huehuetl tree, and she was talking to Chopilotl, Quinatzin and Teuxoch's youngest daughter, as she worked. Chopilotl's first-born child, a girl, lay bundled in a cradle at her mother's feet. She was the fourth grandchild that his daughters had given to Quinatzin, and he knelt to look at her more closely after he had greeted his wife and accepted his daughter's embraces.

"Our son leaves tonight to go with the Jaguar Warriors," he announced to Ome Xochitl as he straightened up. "He is to accompany them to the land of the Mixtecs."

"I am proud, my son," Ome Xochitl said gravely, rising to embrace her son. "I will pray for you, and rise in the night to make offerings for your return."

Acolmiztli thanked his mother in a joyful voice that made his humble words sound oddly boastful. Quinatzin laughed and smiled proudly at his wife, remembering all the hardships they had lived through so that they might enjoy moments like this. But then he saw Teuxoch coming across the courtyard with Huemac in her arms, and his joy vanished in a wave of guilt, as he suddenly remembered who it was he had meant to see that day. Huemac had not yet been pledged to a calmecac, as Teuxoch often reminded her husband, and Quinatzin had been intending for some time to speak to the old men who taught in the calmecac attached to the Tlacatecco, the temple of Huitzilopochtli.

But he had forgotten again today, and worse, he remembered with a pang of remorse, he had forgotten that Acolmiztli also had a brother to bid farewell. Though Huemac was now over a year old, Quinatzin had yet to develop any strong feelings for this strange, homely child. Despite these attacks of guilt, his second son remained unreal to him, a presence the gods would likely remove at any time.

"He is clean now," Teuxoch said in a satisfied voice as she brought the baby in under the tree. "But I think he is hungry."

"He must bear his hunger like a warrior," Acolmiztli said nonchalantly, lifting the child from Teuxoch's arms. "I have come to say goodbye to him before I leave for the battlefield. I am going tonight to serve the Jaguars."

"That is good," Teuxoch said approvingly, watching without concern as Acolmiztli tossed the baby into the air and caught him lightly, reveling in the strength of his arms and the sureness of his hands. But then Huemac began to cry, and Ome Xochitl came to take him from her son.

"I will feed him," she said, "and I will see that the servants begin preparing the meal."

When Ome Xochitl had gone, Quinatzin turned to find Teuxoch waiting at his elbow, obviously desiring to speak to him. He nodded courteously and drew her aside, out of hearing of the others.

"I know that you are very *busy,* my husband," she said pointedly, "but is it not past the time when your younger son should have been promised to one of the calmecacs?"

"Many children are not pledged until their second year," Quinatzin countered, knowing that he concealed none of his negligence from Teuxoch's sharp eyes. "I have not yet decided which would be the best for him."

"Indeed," Teuxoch said sarcastically. "Then it is not too late for me to offer my advice in the matter? Not that it would seem to be a difficult decision. It is only natural that those who serve the Cihuacoatl would want to send their sons to the Tlillan calmecac."

Quinatzin returned her gaze coolly, showing no sign of the aversion he felt at even the mention of the House of Darkness. Though all the calmecacs were under the patronage of Quetzalcoatl, they were run by the priests of the temple to which the particular school was attached. And none of the calmecacs felt the influence of Tlacaelel quite so directly as the Tlillan, which was attached to the temple of the Snake Woman. It was the first place Tlacaelel turned whenever he pondered the education of the Tenocha youth, and how it might be made to better serve the aims of the city and its god. Quinatzin had hoped to spare Huemac the full impact of that influence, as he had his elder son.

"I had also thought of the school run by the priests of the Tlacatecco," he said blandly, attempting an attitude of open-mindedness. "It is where Acolmiztli distinguished himself, after all. And it is the largest of the calmecacs."

"And therefore inferior," Teuxoch snapped impatiently. "I had no hand in the choice of your other son, and the Tlillan was then still under construction. But now it is the place where all the great lords send their sons. Is not Huemac a child of the nobility, is he not *pilli*?"

"Yes, but all of his signs are unpromising," Quinatzin argued lamely. "Perhaps they will not take him."

"Do not insult us both with such quibbling. Are you not the right hand of the Cihuacoatl? Am I not his daughter? They will accept him; you have only to ask."

Quinatzin stood stubbornly silent, unwilling to concede, though he had no good arguments to offer. He was debating the cost of ignoring Teuxoch to her face when she began speaking in a new tone.

"Forgive me, my husband," she said with feigned humility. "Perhaps I have misunderstood the cause of your concern. Perhaps you have already made overtures to the priests at the Tlacatecco, and do not wish to go back on your word . . ."

"No, I have done nothing," Quinatzin admitted wearily. "I will speak to the priests of the Tlillan tomorrow."

"I am pleased that you find my advice worthy," Teuxoch said humbly, and bowed to her husband. "May I speak to you of another thing, then? It also concerns your son."

"What is it?" Quinatzin demanded, allowing his impatience to show.

"It is the way the young wife stares at the child. She loses herself in his eyes, and the child in hers. It is not seemly for a person to go about staring into the faces of others. It is impolite, and if he stares this way at women when he is a man, their husbands will think him an adulterer. The young wife knows this, yet she persists in encouraging his bad habits."

"Can one so young truly possess habits of his own?" Quinatzin inquired ironically, raising his eyebrows.

"He has stared since the day of his naming," Teuxoch insisted stubbornly. "She must provide a better example for him, or he will turn out bug-eyed and rude."

As if it could harm his looks, Quinatzin thought, goaded to cruelty by his sense of guilt and self-disgust. Oh, Huemac, he groaned inwardly, already I am playing my part in your bad fortune.

"I will speak to her about this later," he said to Teuxoch in a chilly tone, and indicated that he wished to return to the feast being set out for Acolmiztli. Teuxoch bowed compliantly, and went ahead to lay a place for him.

LATER THAT night, when the feasting was over and Acolmiztli had departed, Quinatzin remained restless, staying out in the courtyard long after the rest of his family had retired. Though he knew that he did not have to fear Ome Xochitl's scorn, he had not told her of his conversation with Teuxoch, or of the choice he had made concerning Huemac's education. I can face her with the shame of my forgetfulness, he told himself, but how can I reveal to her that I have no feeling for this child of ours? She will think badly of me not just as a father, but as a man. She will judge that my heart is deficient, and I will have no defense. Then, perhaps, I will feel her scorn for the first time.

The middle of the night passed, yet Quinatzin found no solutions for the worries that plagued him. When he heard the baby cry out to be fed, and saw a light kindled within Ome Xochitl's rooms, he decided that it was time to face both his shame and his deficiency, and went in to speak to his wife.

Ome Xochitl had rekindled the fire in the hearth to warm herself, and she was nursing Huemac in the flickering light. And indeed, as Teuxoch had complained, she was staring raptly into the child's eyes as he grasped at her breast. Quinatzin seated himself next to the fire and waited patiently for the feeding to be done, noticing that Ome Xochitl was not in the least self-conscious about her staring, which she immediately resumed after nodding briefly in greeting.

"I must look at my son," Quinatzin said in a tight, determined voice, once the child was through burping and seemed to be asleep. Apparently finding nothing odd in this request, Ome Xochitl laid Huemac out on a blanket close to the fire, well within the circle of light.

Wiping all expression from his face, Quinatzin bent over the sleeping child, finding some unexpected satisfaction in the firmness of his flesh and the straightness of his limbs. His growth, apparently, would not be diminished by the hunger his mother had suffered during her pregnancy. Huemac's face had also grown more distinct, though certainly no more attractive. Quinatzin noted this with a sinking heart. Except for the deep-set eyes, the child's features were flat and undistinguished under the prominent forehead, and folds of loose flesh hung permanently beneath his jaw, like the wattles of a turkey. His skin was the ruddy color of well-dried chili, and his thick, black hair stood up in tufts on the sides of his head, making his ears appear even more outsized and ridiculous.

Quinatzin glanced at Ome Xochitl but did not meet her eyes, and it was several moments before he could bring himself to break the silence.

"Teuxoch has complained to me of this habit you have of staring into the child's face. She thinks this is bad for him."

"I am aware of her opinion in this matter," Ome Xochitl said mildly. "But it is only because she finds it unsettling to look into his eyes herself. Do you also find it so?"

Quinatzin shifted uneasily on his mat. "I cannot say, though I doubt that a child's gaze could truly be unsettling."

"Look for yourself, then," she suggested.

"But he is asleep."

"He is not asleep. Look closely, and you will see that he is watching you."

Quinatzin looked down in surprise, but it seemed to him that Huemac's eyelids, with their many folds and creases, were shut tight. Bending still closer, though, he was able to perceive a sliver of brown and gold peeping out from beneath the hooded eyelids, and he felt his own eyes widen in astonishment.

"Can you really be so devious?" he exclaimed without thinking, and saw Huemac's eyes open fully. They were even larger than Quinatzin remembered, round and dark brown, the pupils surrounded by their inner rings of golden light. He felt himself being drawn down long tunnels and pulled back instinctively, then leaned closer again. When he finally looked up at Ome Xochitl, his vision blurred momentarily, and he realized that he had been holding his breath for the whole time.

"Such power," he gasped in amazement. "His ugliness vanishes."

"They are his gift," Ome Xochitl explained solemnly. "They are his weapon in the battle he will wage with his fate. I am teaching him how to use them."

"But is this deviousness to be encouraged?"

"I did not teach him that. It is his way of escaping Teuxoch when her attentions tire him. Have you never wondered about this calming effect she claims to have upon him?"

Quinatzin laughed, remembering how Teuxoch had boasted to him of this very thing. But then he also remembered his earlier conversation with his first wife, and the thought of the House of Darkness made him frown.

"She spoke to me tonight about pledging him to a calmecac," he confessed in a low voice. "And because I had neglected my duties, I was forced to say that I would promise him to the Tlillan."

Ome Xochitl said nothing, and when he finally brought himself to look at her, expecting disappointment, he was surprised to see an ironic smile on her face.

"This does not distress you?" he asked. "I had hoped to spare him from the influence of Tlacaelel, at least until he was grown."

"We can spare him nothing, my husband. And you should not accuse yourself harshly, for the Tlillan is as fine a calmecac as there is in Tenochtitlan."

"But with his *luck* . . . "

Ome Xochitl shook her head firmly. "You seek to protect him, as if he were the child you were yourself. But he is different, he is not like the children we were. He is like only one person I know: my father. He, too, was an ugly child, and devious at an early age. Or so my grandmother has told me."

"So . . ." Quinatzin concluded, but could go no further. He felt a great sense of relief, both that his negligence had not been harmful and that his repugnance for the child had been alleviated. But he also felt helpless, and confused about how he should confront his duties in the future.

"What must we do for him, then?" he asked finally.

"We must not deny his talents, but encourage them, and see that they are not used for evil purposes. We must love him as we do our other children, but without ever forgetting that he is different. Above all, my husband, we must never allow him to deceive *us*. It will not be easy."

"I will begin tonight," Quinatzin vowed, and reached out a hand to the child on the blanket. Staring at him with his mouth wide open, Huemac grasped one of his father's fingers with his tiny hand and tugged mightily. Quinatzin smiled and tugged back, but gently, so that his son would not lose his grip.

2

I T was over a year later that Acolmiztli finally returned to his father's house, and he was carried in on a litter, with an arrow wound in his leg. The shield-carrier had indeed become a warrior, and had performed well, taking his place among the Jaguar Warriors who had protected the rear of the retreating Mexicans. For the Mixtecs had completely overwhelmed the ill-prepared and underequipped army from the north, ambushing them in the misty highland passes and outnumbering them when the armies met on the plains outside of the city of Coaixtlahuacan. Many of the best of Moteczuma's warriors had fallen before Acolmiztli and the other untested apprentice warriors had been pressed into the ranks out of necessity.

His wound was in the fleshy part of his thigh and was not crippling, but it had festered during the long journey home, and there was danger that the infection might spread. Acolmiztli was at first reluctant to surrender himself to the confinement and inactivity prescribed by the physicians, but then he was visited by a captain of the Jaguars, who praised him and promised that a place would be kept for him in the ranks of warriors. He was told to rest himself thoroughly, for the next campaign against the Mixteca would not be hurried, and would not end in retreat.

Then the captain cut Acolmiztli's hairlock at the nape of his neck and braided it with red cotton tassels, in the manner of the warriors. He also presented the youth with a shield covered with eagle feathers and a pair of crystal earplugs, and left with the further promise that Acolmiztli would be admitted to the order of the Jaguars as soon as he had had the opportunity to take the required three captives. The captain was followed by a steady stream of visitors, as Acolmiztli's relatives, instructors, and friends from the telpochcalli came to congratulate him and listen to his tales of the war against the Cloud People. Even Quinatzin found time to sit with his son and ease the loneliness and boredom of his confinement.

But then the visitors ceased and it was quiet in the room where Acolmiztli lay healing, listening to the familiar sounds that came to him from the courtyard and dreaming of the day he would return to the battlefield. He was passing his time in this fashion one day when he suddenly realized, in the process of moving his mats more directly into the light from the doorway, that someone, or something, was sitting in the far, dark corner of the room. Acolmiztli saw that it was his brother, Huemac, and called to him, and the child came out of the shadows and squatted next to the mats where Acolmiztli lay. Huemac was now almost three years old, and his plump little belly hung in rolls around his middle as he rocked back and forth on his heels with his knees up around his chin, his ears jutting out from the sides of his head like tiny wings. He stared seriously at Acolmiztli's bandaged leg, rocking forward to give it a tentative poke with his finger.

"Ah!" Acolmiztli exclaimed involuntarily, and Huemac quickly hid his finger behind his back. Acolmiztli smiled to hide his pain.

"It is a small wound, my brother," he said to calm the child. "It was given to me by a Mixtec arrow."

"Miss-tuck," Huemac repeated solemnly, his big, bright eyes on Acolmiztli's face.

"Mish-teck," Acolmiztli corrected gently, noticing the way his brother's eyes seemed to follow his lips as he spoke.

"Mish-teck!" Huemac blurted impulsively, and giggled triumphantly when Acolmiztli laughed.

"You learn quickly, little brother. What other words do you know?"

"Nahualli?" Huemac suggested experimentally, tilting his head sideways as if expecting to see a change in his brother's face.

"Nahualli! Do you think me a sorcerer?"

"Sorcerer," Huemac repeated, nodding eagerly and gesturing at Acolmiztli's face with his hand. "Nahualli, nahualli . . ."

"Who teaches you these things, little one? Who has told you that I am a shape-shifter?"

Huemac stared back at him quizzically, beginning to show signs of restlessness and disappointment. So Acolmiztli, remembering a trick of his father's, turned sideways into the light from the doorway and began to make shadow-animals on the wall with his hands. The first image he cast was of a duck, which brought such a loud and accurate quack from Huemac that Acolmiztli started and stared around him stupidly, unable to believe that there was not a duck in the room with them. But then Huemac repeated the sound impatiently, and just as accurately, gesturing at Acolmiztli's hands.

Still stunned, Acolmiztli stretched out his fingers to form a long, thin bill, and Huemac responded with the croak of a heron that was every bit as true-to-life as his duck call. Acolmiztli was too amazed to remember any of the other shapes his father had cast, but he found that all he had to do was to alter the position of his fingers slightly and Huemac would supply an appropriate sound, everything from water birds to night hawks. His imitation of a wolf was so truly frightening that Acolmiztli was compelled to call for his mother for an explanation. Watching his brother's lips, Huemac perfectly echoed his call a moment later.

Ome Xochitl came in carrying her medicine pouch and a drinking bowl filled with milky liquid, which she handed to Acolmiztli, instructing him to drink. Then she put her medicine pouch beside him on the mats and squatted next to Huemac, who put his head under her arm and pressed against her affectionately.

"The octli will give you strength," she said casually, seeing that Acolmiztli continued to stare at her over the rim of the bowl without drinking. "I will put a fresh poultice on your wound. Have you been conversing with your brother?"

"Conversing!" Acolmiztli sputtered. "Is it truly he who makes these uncanny sounds? Where can he have even heard such things?"

"Your father likes to take him to the lake shore; that is where he hears the water birds. And there was a captive wolf caged in the marketplace one day when he was there with the first wife, and he has never forgotten how it growled at him."

Huemac began to growl, deep in his throat, but he ceased immediately when Ome Xochitl tilted her chin in his direction. Acolmiztli watched them both with wary eyes as his mother crushed herbs with a grinding stone and began to mix them with pine resin and powdered charcoal.

"What else has he shown you?" she asked to distract him, as she gingerly pried the old poultice off his wound. Acolmiztli grimaced briefly and spoke in a tight voice, gritting his teeth against the pain.

"He showed an uncommon stealth in entering the room without my seeing him. And who has told him these things about nahuallis?"

"Nahualli," Huemac mimicked, glancing from one to the other. Ome Xochitl smiled and patted the poultice into place.

"The pain will be gone soon, and then the healing will go rapidly," she said in a satisfied voice, before taking up his question. "Teuxoch tells him stories about shape-shifters and enchanters, and the casters of evil spells. She means to frighten him, but she has only aroused his curiosity."

"I am a warrior, but even I am frightened of such things," Acolmiztli confessed reluctantly, with a suspicious glance at his brother. "This cannot be healthy in a child, my mother; it is the result of his evil luck."

"Luck?" Huemac echoed quizzically, and Ome Xochitl's face took on a stern expression.

"He will soon enough learn about his luck, my son, and he will have to live with it for the rest of his days. Should we discourage his curiosity, then, and make him timid? Or should we respect his fearlessness of the things that frighten even warriors?"

Acolmiztli folded his arms across his chest and remained petulantly silent. Huemac also crossed his arms, and stretched his face into a caricature of his brother's expression of stubborn displeasure. He had moved a little apart from his mother. Acolmiztli glanced at him and wanted to laugh, but his pride prevented it, and he turned back to his mother with his head elevated at a haughty angle. Ome Xochitl stared at him with perfect composure, and briefly inclined her head toward the child next to her.

"You see that you are an example to him," she said in an even voice. "If you would treat your mother with arrogance and disrespect, so must he."

Acolmiztli appeared flustered, and dropped his arms to his sides. Mirroring his brother's obvious confusion, Huemac did likewise, and ducked his head between his knees, as if afraid to look at either of them.

"Forgive me, my mother," Acolmiztli began, but Ome Xochitl stayed him with a hand.

"You are a man now, my son. You must not apologize to women. Nor will I ever again presume to correct you. After this, you must be guided by your own heart, in the true manner of a warrior."

Gathering the bowl and her pouch, Ome Xochitl quietly left the room, and both of her sons stared after her for several moments before looking at one another. Acolmiztli, who had been greatly disturbed himself by his mother's display of anger, saw that Huemac was close to tears, and was gradually edging toward the door. Acolmiztli frowned and beckoned him to remain.

"Stay, then, little brother," he said gruffly, "until I have told you *my* stories."

Huemac cast a hasty glance at the door, then looked timidly back at his brother.

"I will tell you about the Cloud People," Acolmiztli coaxed in a softer tone, and Huemac cocked his head inquiringly. Acolmiztli beckoned to him again.

"Sit here with me, little brother, and I will sing you the war songs of the Jaguars . . ."

"Jaguars," Huemac repeated with relish, and crept closer.

3

A FULL year passed before the armies of the Alliance again marched south, passing through the conquered lands of the Tlalhuicans before converging upon the city of Coaixtlahuacan. This time, they came in full force, accompanied by many bearers and apprentices carrying provisions and extra weapons. They met the warriors of the Mixtec chieftain Atonal on the Plain of Serpents, and for days the men fought and died under the blistering southern sun. Finally, the Mixtecs were pushed back behind their defenses, and then into the streets of Coaixtlahuacan, where they surrendered to the Mexicans and their allies to save their temple from burning.

Word of the victory, and the tribute that had been negotiated, came back to Tenochtitlan, where the people rejoiced in the streets. Invigorated by their success, the warriors of the Alliance continued south to conquer the cities of Yanhuitlan and Achiutla, and then marched east along the Papaloapan River, capturing the rich trading center of Tochtepec without a battle. With the fall of the city of Cosamaloapan, the conquest of the Mixtecs was complete, and the Mexicans stood poised on the southern frontier of the Totonac lands, which extended northward along the shore of the Divine Waters.

In the year Seven Flint-Knife, the victorious army of the Tenocha marched homeward, loaded with the tribute they had received in advance, and preceded by long columns of captive warriors yoked together at the neck. The priests and lords of the city came out to greet them, swinging smoking braziers of incense and showering the warriors with flowers. It was the twentieth year of the reign of Moteczuma Ilhuicamina, and the new Sun Stone that had been carved in his honor was dedicated with the blood of many Mixtec captives.

After completing his offerings to the gods and partaking of the feast in the House of Jaguars, Acolmiztli returned to the house of his father, followed by a young apprentice warrior with his arms filled with gifts. Acolmiztli now wore the spotted jaguar-skin headdress of his order, and attached to his shoulders was a shield of white egret plumes. His face had been darkened by exposure to the southern sun, and the golden Mixtec serpent fixed into his upper lip added to the resolute fierceness of his countenance. His parents greeted him with the restraint and respect appropriate to his new status, and the young warrior returned their greetings with a practiced humility that in no way detracted from his dignified bearing.

"I have brought gifts for my family," Acolmiztli announced proudly, once the formalities had been observed. He gestured to the apprentice, who came forward and carefully deposited the cloth-wrapped bundles in a pile at Acolmiztli's feet.

"These are the riches we found in the storehouses of Coaixtlahuacan," Acolmiztli said, unwrapping the bundles one by one and passing them out with great ceremony. For Teuxoch, he had brought a sheaf of fragrant yetl leaves, a bag of cochineal dye, and several skeins of colored thread that had been made from rabbit fur. Cocatli received a bag of seashells mixed with carved pieces of amber, tortoise shell, and mother-of-pearl, and for Ome Xochitl and Quinatzin there was a large bag of cocoa beans and two richly embroidered Totonac mantles fringed with the rare and precious feathers of the red troupial. The last bundle was for Huemac, but as Acolmiztli began to unwrap it, he realized that his brother was not present.

"Where is my younger brother?" he asked Ome Xochitl in surprise, certain that he had seen the child when he entered the courtyard.

"He is there," Ome Xochitl said, gesturing over her son's shoulder, "in Cocatli's garden."

Acolmiztli turned and saw Huemac standing in the middle of the small patch of vegetation that filled the far corner of the courtyard. Cocatli had begun her garden by accident in the first year after the famine, when she had buried some maize and beans as a safeguard against future hunger and then had forgotten them. By the time these sprouted, Cocatli had been weaned from her compulsion to hoard, but her mother had encouraged her to cultivate the garden, anyway, and had helped her plant some maguey and nopal cactus alongside the seasonal crops. Cocatli was now standing next to Huemac and seemed to be offering him her bag of shells, though he would not look at her or take the bag.

"Why does he spurn my gifts?" Acolmiztli demanded, looking back at his mother. "I have brought him a Mixtec shield and a ball of pure rubber, a ball for tlachtli."

"It is not you he spurns, my son," Ome Xochitl said gently. "He is sulking, because he has just learned that Cocatli will soon go to be educated by the priestesses of Quetzalcoatl. She is his only playmate."

"Why does he not play with the other little boys?"

"They spurn him. They say he is ugly, and their parents tell them that he is unlucky. He frightens them with his voices, and his stealth, which they call trickery."

"He must . . ." Acolmiztli began angrily, then remembered himself and fell silent. He looked at Quinatzin, whose impassive face confirmed what Ome Xochitl had said.

"I will bring him to you," Teuxoch said impatiently, but Acolmiztli shook his head vehemently.

"No! No, I will take them to him myself. He must *see* how a warrior shows his generosity."

Taking the shield and the ball, Acolmiztli walked slowly across the court-yard toward the garden. Huemac and Cocatli were standing with their backs to him, and he could see that, in size at least, they were indeed a matched pair. He had to think a moment to recall that Huemac was now five years old and Cocatli almost ten, and the gap in their ages suddenly made their closeness that much more remarkable. Remarkable because Acolmiztli could remember, from the time of his convalescence, how Cocatli would allow Huemac to follow her around, and would explain things to him, and would never complain when he played tricks on her with his voices, which he did whenever she became too absorbed in her solitary games to pay attention to him. Yes, my brother, he thought compassionately, it is indeed painful to lose a companion as devoted as our sister has been to you.

Both children turned to stare at him as he stepped over the neat border of painted stones that surrounded the garden, but Huemac turned his back again as Acolmiztli squatted a few feet away and put the shield and ball down before him. He could see that Cocatli was still a little afraid of him in his warrior's dress, so he smiled and held out his hand to her, and brought her close enough so that he could caress the side of her face.

"You have grown prettier since last I saw you, my sister," he said, and Cocatli lowered her eyes demurely, clutching the bag of shells to her chest. "The heart of the Lord, Quetzalcoatl, will be gladdened by your presence in his temple."

Cocatli smiled shyly and reached out to touch the plumes attached to Acolmiztli's shoulders. He caressed her again and signaled that she should leave him alone with Huemac, and, with a last, concerned glance at Huemac's back, she took her bag of shells and left the garden.

"So, my brother," Acolmiztli began in a hearty tone. "It has been two years since I have seen you. Will you not greet me and accept my gifts?"

Huemac hunched his shoulders slightly but did not turn around, and Acolmiztli had to restrain himself from grabbing his brother and scolding him for his rudeness, as he would have with any other child.

"I have brought you a Mixtec warshield and a ball of pure rubber. Must I leave them here in the dirt, and never know if they have brought you joy?"

Still, Huemac did not turn, and Acolmiztli felt his compassion turning into annoyance.

"Perhaps you wish to be alone, and share your joy with no one. Perhaps it is your luck to be this way . . ."

Huemac whirled suddenly, his face contorted with such pain and rage that Acolmiztli instinctively put up his hands. He was not ready for Huemac's wild attack, though, and went over backward into the dirt when the child threw himself upon him, growling in his throat and beating at his brother with his tiny fists. He landed on Acolmiztli's chest, knocking the headdress from his head, but the young warrior just laughed and did nothing to restrain the child's flailings.

"Yes, my brother," he cried loudly, "such anger is good only for fighting, is it not? Fight me, Huemac, show me the strength of your anger!"

Huemac beat upon his brother's chest until his arms were exhausted and his breath came in sobs, and then Acolmiztli wrapped his arms around him and rolled in the dirt, pretending to be wrestling. Finally he stopped, and Huemac crawled off his body and lay next to him on the ground, gasping for breath. Slowly, Acolmiztli raised himself into a sitting position and gingerly removed a cactus spine from the back of his arm. Huemac lay with his eyes closed, his chest rising and falling rapidly.

"It is a good thing you were not armed, little warrior," Acolmiztli said to him. "I think that you meant to kill me if you could."

Huemac opened his eyes, showing by the deep seriousness of his gaze that his intentions had, indeed, been deadly. Acolmiztli smiled broadly and dusted off his headdress before replacing it upon his head.

"It is not wise to go about attacking Jaguars, though," he said mildly. "Even when armed."

"Jaguar," Huemac repeated, narrowing his eyes thoughtfully as he sat up. Acolmiztli casually lifted the spoked wooden shield from the dirt and twirled it in his hands, causing the light to glint off the green and blue feathers that had been woven into the reed cover.

"The Mixtec who carried this also attacked me, but since he was not my brother, I struck him down. Now he is my captive, and calls me 'father.' "

Huemac's round eyes moved back and forth between the shield and his brother's face, as if putting something together in his mind.

"Was he also unlucky?" he asked finally, and Acolmiztli understood his meaning.

"I do not speak his language, but he fought me with great valor, and from his dress, he must have been a warrior of high renown. And now, when he dies upon the stone, he will go up to the home of the Sun. It is the best of all deaths. It is what I wish for myself, if I cannot die upon the field of battle."

Huemac put out a hand and stopped the spinning shield, so that he could look at the design, which was of green lightning bolts flashing out from a blue center. Gently easing it into his brother's hands, Acolmiztli let him admire it in silence. Then he reached for the round, black ball.

"I have also brought you a ball for tlachtli, the game of the lords. It is a game used to test the course of the future, as well as the skill of the players."

Huemac set the shield down and took the ball from his brother without hesitation, cupping it reverently in his little hands.

"I will show you how to strike it," Acolmiztli offered. "If you have had enough of fighting . . . ?"

The eagerness momentarily disappeared from Huemac's eyes, and he glanced wistfully across the courtyard in the direction Cocatli had gone. Acolmiztli waited until he again had his attention.

"A warrior accepts his luck, my brother," he said. "Cocatli has been promised to the priestesses, and soon you, too, will go to the calmecac. Then our mother will be left alone here. She will be sad, but do you think she will weep and carry on as you have?"

Huemac made no answer, then suddenly seemed to grow tired of his brother's questions and jumped to his feet.

"Tlachtli," he demanded, holding the ball out to his brother with both hands. His lips were clamped shut in a determined expression, and Acolmiztli could tell that he hadn't entirely gotten over his anger and grief. But he will, Acolmiztli thought as he took the ball from Huemac and struck it expertly with his hip, sending it flying against the courtyard wall.

"Be brave, my brother," he said to himself, as Huemac chased after the ball. "There are many others who will leave you before your fate is complete . . . "

4

ON the night before Cocatli was to enter the temple of Quetzalcoatl, her parents took her and her brother to see their grandfather. Nezahual- coyotl had come to Tenochtitlan to help inaugurate the resumption of the war with the Chalcans, which had been postponed during the years of the famine and the Mixtec campaigns. But though the Texcocan Speaker had presided over the ceremonies of war with his usual correctness, it was well known in the Valley that his mind was occupied with other matters. Now nearing sixty years of age, he had recently designated one of his younger sons, Nezahualpilli, as his heir, and he was personally training the boy to succeed him when he died. His court had thus become, more than ever, a center of learning as well as the place of ruling, and the time not spent with his son was shared out among Nezahualcoyotl's other passions: the study of the stars and the painted books, the composition of flower songs, and his conversations with the tlamatinime and the holy men who constantly surrounded him.

He had also created a great controversy with the temple he was constructing in Texcoco. It was to have nine levels, one for each of the heavens, and the shrine at the very top, representing the dwelling place of the God, was to contain no image. This was the temple of Ometeotl, the Lord of the Duality, the god who was both male and female, who created and sustained the world. He was also called Tloque Nahuaque, the Lord of the Near and the Far, and Yohualli Ehecatl, the Night and the Wind, the one who was everywhere, and invisible. Though all prayed to this god, he remained intangible and unseen, and no one had ever built a temple in his honor before this.

Nezahualcoyotl had stirred up even greater emotion by announcing that there would be no blood sacrifices to this god, and that only birds, serpents, and butterflies would be offered in his temple. To explain this, and calm the tempers of the priests, he had called a convocation in his quarters in Motec-zuma's palace, and had sent out invitations to all the important priests and wise men in Tenochtitlan, Tlatelulco, and the neighboring cities. Tlacaelel had sneered at the notion of an "empty temple," and had denounced the lack of blood sacrifice as "effeminate." His scornful decision not to attend had per-suaded many others to also stay away, but still, the hearing chamber had been filled with priests and white-haired old men when the convocation had begun shortly after dawn.

When Quinatzin and Ome Xochitl and their children arrived that same night, at the hour appointed for their interview, they learned that the discus-sion still had not been concluded.

"They have not even stopped to eat," the Texcocan guard confided to Quinatzin. "And such shouting! I did not think that the old ones had such strength left in their lungs!"

"How many remain?" Quinatzin asked.

"Only a few, now. The high priests of the Tlacatecco departed rudely, before noon, and most of the other Tenocha priests left with them. The Tlatelulcans and Tepanecs left in the afternoon, and many more were forced by their duties to depart at sunset."

Quinatzin thanked the guard and returned to his wife and children, who had dressed themselves in their finest garments for the occasion.

"I will go in and listen," he said to Ome Xochitl. "If it threatens to go on for much longer, I will return and find a more comfortable place for the children to wait."

The guard swung the door open and Quinatzin disappeared inside. Ome Xochitl bent to remove a fleck of dirt from Cocatli's spotless white mantle, and, as the little girl held still for her mother's ministrations, she glanced around her and her eyes widened.

"Mother," she said urgently, "Huemac is not here!"

"I know," Ome Xochitl said calmly. "He went inside with his father."

"Will he be punished?" Cocatli asked in a concerned tone.

"That will be up to his father," Ome Xochitl replied, "and his grandfather." She glanced briefly at the door. "I did not feel it was my place to stop him, this time."

HUEMAC TIMED his move perfectly, slipping through the door in such close conjunction with his father that the edge of Quinatzin's mantle brushed against his face as he separated himself from his father and slid into the deep shadows next to the wall. Quinatzin continued on without looking back, crossing the darkened portion of the chamber to join the small group of men who were seated in a circle in the center of the room. The only light came from torches that had been placed in standards set at intervals around the outside of the circle.

Huemac stayed where he was, expecting the door to open at any moment and his mother to come in and get him. He had never been able to fool her before this, and truly, he had expected *someone* to catch him. He had been jealous of all the attention being lavished upon his sister, and had merely been trying to capture some of it for himself. Now that he had succeeded in getting in, he did not know why he wanted to be here. He was sure, though, that he was in trouble, whatever he did. "It is my luck," he told himself ruefully, as he always did whenever his instinct for mischief had landed him in a situation beyond his control.

But the door remained closed and no one came to rescue him, and gradually, his curiosity reasserted itself and drew him toward the lighted circle. Sliding himself noiselessly along the polished stone floor, he crept closer to the seated men, though at an angle that put distance between himself and the place where his father was seated. When he had come within a few feet of the lighted area, he stopped and listened, crouching in the darkness.

He knew that his grandfather, the Fasting Coyote, was in this room, but since he had never seen Nezahualcoyotl before, he did not know which of the dozen or so men he was. He had been told that his grandfather was a king, and a wise man, and a sorcerer. But none of the men wore jewels or a crown, and they were all old and white-haired (except Quinatzin, who was gray), as the tlamatinime were supposed to be. Many, it seemed to Huemac as he scanned their faces, had the luminous, unblinking gaze that Teuxoch had told him was the mark of the sorcerer.

Huemac began to move again but then froze, struck by the sudden sensation that he had been noticed. Instinctively, he flattened himself against the floor and hooded his eyes from the glint of the light. But the voice of the man who was speaking continued in its same calm tone, and Huemac could see no heads turning, or eyes trained in his direction. Yet the feeling persisted, and seemed to grow stronger when Huemac again tried to move. Who knows I am here? he wondered. It did not feel like his father's awareness, and a quick check of the darkness behind him assured him that his mother still had not come after him. Yet *someone* knew he was here.

Frightened by the feeling, Huemac began to back away from the circle, one small movement at a time, expecting someone to cry out and expose him at any moment. But then he drew even with the head of the circle, and saw the man with the long face. He was sitting cross-legged on a mat, his head erect, facing toward the speaker at the other end of the circle. His hair was white and his brow deeply furrowed, and shadows gathered in the hollows of his cheeks and the creases beside his powerful nose. Huemac crawled closer and stared, feeling the power the man radiated in his stillness.

"Nahualli," he whispered to himself, and suddenly the man's features began to blur before his eyes. His nose and chin seemed to melt together into a muzzle, and a brief flash of sharp white teeth appeared out of the blur. Then the torchlight flickered, and the man's face was normal again. Huemac blinked in astonishment, his body frozen into a crouch. He was sure now that the man knew he was there, but he did not care anymore about being caught. He let himself relax, as if he already *had* been caught, and listened attentively as the man began to speak.

"Lords, my friends, it is late now and my mind and tongue have grown weary. I am grateful that you have spoken so frankly of what is in your hearts, and I shall not forget or treat lightly what you have said to me today. I know that even among you, who have stayed this long and have questioned me so closely, there are those who are not persuaded of the wisdom and correctness of what I do. This is as it should be, for no one should convince you of a truth that is not apparent to your own heart. If you had no doubts, you would not be human, and I would not value your opinion as highly as I do."

Huemac understood little of what the man was saying, but he was entranced by the sound of his voice, which came to his ears like a caress. It reminded him of his mother's singing, only it was deeper in tone, and filled with beautiful words he had never heard before.

"It is right and necessary that we should make offerings and do penance before the gods that are close to us, who have been known to the people since the time of the Toltecs. But though they are the lords of our fate, are they not the children of a still greater one, the one called Moyocoyani, He Who Creates Himself? Did he not give life to his son, Quetzalcoatl, who then gave life to us? Is it not this one we address when we pray to Ipalnemohuani, the Giver of Life?"

Moyo-coyani, Huemac thought languidly, listening to the melodious sound the word made in his mind. Ipal-nemo-whanni. The sounds of this man were very pleasing.

"Can we give this one a color, when he is all the colors? Can we seek to give him a form, to dress an image in his likeness, when he is the form of everything, and its foundation? Is he not there, already, in the images we have made of his children? Blind as I am, and poor in my knowledge, I seek only to honor him purely. If I have committed a disgraceful act, I have no excuse beyond this. I ask for your indulgence, and your blessings as you return to your homes."

There was a sudden silence, and the seated men began to gather their belongings and wrap their mantles around them in preparation for departure. But then someone Huemac couldn't see raised a voice and addressed Nezahualcoyotl:

"There is one who has listened in the darkness without speaking. Should we not have his blessing, too, before we leave?"

There was loud laughter around the circle, and all those with their backs to Huemac turned and looked at the spot where he was hiding. Nezahualcoyotl whinnied in his throat and beckoned to the boy.

"Come, Huemac," he said, smiling into the darkness. "You have been invited to join our council."

Huemac felt the eyes upon him, and saw the stern face of his father from where he had risen at the other end of the circle. Slowly, he got up and stepped cautiously into the light, his head hunched between his shoulders as if expecting a blow. Several of the men laughed again, disconcerting him, so that he jerked around when his grandfather laid a cool hand upon his shoulder. But

Nezahualcoyotl's eyes were kind and amused, and Huemac let himself be drawn to his side and turned to face the group.

"You must forgive my grandson," Nezahualcoyotl explained, "for he had not seen his grandfather's face before today, and we know the impatience of the young. His father was also very curious as a young man."

Those who knew Quinatzin or had guessed the relationship laughed and turned in his direction, and Huemac saw a grudging smile creep onto his father's face.

"Tell us, then, little wise one," one of the old men suggested facetiously, "what did you learn there, hiding in the darkness?"

"Moyo-coyani," Huemac said obediently, and grinned when they laughed and applauded him. "Ipalnemohuani," he added, and would have gone on had Nezahualcoyotl not touched him lightly on the shoulder and gestured for him to sit down.

"I thank you again, my friends," Nezahualcoyotl called, as the old men began to file out of the room, carrying their reed mats folded under their arms. Huemac saw his father follow after them and immediately turned toward his grandfather, knowing that he still had some time with this man before he would have to face his parents.

"So, Huemac," Nezahualcoyotl said reprovingly, "you have disobeyed your parents to come in here. Were you so eager to see me that you could not wait with your sister?"

"Yes," Huemac said automatically, believing it to be true. He stared into his grandfather's gentle eyes with utter abandon, not bothering to temper the force of his gaze, as his mother had taught him to do with other people. He knew that his staring could not disturb this man.

"And my nahualli? Did you see that, too?"

"Yes," Huemac breathed reverently, and Nezahualcoyotl smiled at his enthusiasm.

"Your mother was correct in what she has told me about you. Not all children would have seen what I showed to you. Do you know this?"

"Yes," Huemac said simply. "It is because I am unlucky."

A trace of sadness showed in Nezahualcoyotl's eyes as he contemplated the child next to him, and he thoughtfully stroked the few, white hairs that grew from his chin.

"Luck is a very complicated thing, my young one, whether it is good *or* bad. The more of your life you offer to it, the more it will take from you. But there are those who have changed their luck. Your father is such a one, and it was because of this that he was alive to create you."

"How? How changed?" Huemac demanded, his face taking on an intensely hopeful expression.

"It was when he was injured and weak, and the shape of his future appeared fearful to him. Yet he was brave, and did not flee from his fate, though he wanted to. Someday, perhaps, the shape of *your* fate will become clear to you, and perhaps you will want to run from it, or allow it to kill you quickly. That is when you must be most brave, my grandson, that is when you must resolve to change your luck before it can destroy you."

Huemac nodded uncertainly, and Nezahualcoyotl reached out and fingered the amulet, the jade rabbit, that hung on a thong around Huemac's neck.

"Yes, you are the Rabbit child," he said softly. "You must keep this stone with you always, Huemac. It will protect you and give you strength in times of danger."

"Yes, Grandfather," Huemac promised gravely, then jumped to his feet when he saw his parents and sister approaching. He stepped forward to his father's side and bowed with them to Nezahualcoyotl, but after they were all seated, he kept his eyes hooded and did not look at either of his parents.

"Greetings, Quinatzin, my friend," Nezahualcoyotl said graciously. "And you, my daughter; the sight of you and your children gladdens my heart. Come closer, then, Cocatli, my granddaughter, so that I may savor the freshness of your presence. Soon, my precious one, you will go to join the sisters of our Lord, the respected ones, the virgins who serve in the temple . . ."

Huemac watched as his grandfather spoke to Cocatli, petting her affectionately as he warned her of all that would be expected of her in the calmecac, and urged her to conduct herself with diligence and humility. Huemac suddenly found that he no longer felt any jealousy toward his sister, but only a great sadness at her leaving. Tears began to stream down his face and he felt his father look at him, but he could not stop the aching in his heart, or the water that it brought to his eyes.

"You must be prudent, little sister," Nezahualcoyotl was saying, "and turn your eyes from the things of the world. Your heart must become as the precious green stone, the precious turquoise. Take heed, Cocatli, and do not go crooked before the Lord; do not falter in his presence."

Nezahualcoyotl then presented her with a sleeping mat and a new white mantle, along with quantities of copal incense and sheets of fine paper as offerings to the temple. Cocatli thanked him and accepted his blessing, but as she turned to take her seat, she saw Huemac crying and stared at him in surprise.

"Your brother grieves at your departure," Nezahualcoyotl said to her. "He blesses you with his tears."

Ome Xochitl gestured with her eyes, and Cocatli went and sat next to Huemac, who tried to smile at her through his tears. Cocatli patted his knee consolingly, her eyes very serious.

"Let us go to my quarters," Nezahualcoyotl suggested, "where food has been prepared for us. There is much I would discuss with you both."

"First, Lord," Quinatzin interrupted, "I wish to apologize for my negligence; I should not have allowed the boy to escape my notice."

"I have spoken to him about this," Nezahualcoyotl said, forcing Huemac to meet his eyes, "and I do not think he will disobey you so readily the next time. Is that not so, Huemac? You must see that you do not test your parents' forgiveness a second time."

"Yes, Grandfather," Huemac promised, sheepishly glancing sideways at his father and mother. Quinatzin nodded sternly, and then they all rose to leave the room together, with Huemac staying very close to his sister's side.

5

IT was a hot, breathless afternoon in the late summer of the year Nine-Rabbit. The air hung motionless over the courtyard of Quinatzin's house in the Royal Compound, and the locusts buzzed in the branches overhead as Ome Xochitl sat in the shade grinding maize. Occasionally, she paused over her metate and glanced out into the bright sunlight, to the corner of the courtyard near Cocatli's garden, where Huemac was playing with his ball. She listened to the steady thud of rubber against plastered stone, and watched as her son hurled himself into the path of the bounding black ball, struck it forcefully with his hip, then whirled quickly to meet the rebound off the wall. Huemac was only seven years old and not especially quick afoot, but his stocky, wide-hipped build was perfect for the game, and he played it with ferocious energy. The walls where he played were covered solidly with round, black marks, and his ability to keep the ball in continuous motion for minutes at a time was a source of amazement and pride to both of his parents.

But while Ome Xochitl was pleased that he had developed this skill on his own, she was wary of his obsessive attachment to the game. There were tlachtli courts in both Huexotzinco and Texcoco, and as a young girl, she had heard stories of the men whose addiction to the game, and to the betting that always accompanied it, had driven them to ruin. There were men who had gambled away all of their possessions, who then sold themselves into slavery in order to keep playing. And it was a dangerous game for the players, who were often injured by falls on the rough surface of the stone court, and sometimes killed outright by a blow from the hard rubber ball. There were also tales of the games arranged by the rulers to settle disputes between their soothsayers over the course of the future, after which the losing players were made to feel the displeasure of their patron.

As she watched Huemac throw himself headlong into the dust after the ball, Ome Xochitl knew that her son might easily become one of these addicted men, since it was his nature to be both stubborn and imprudent where his passions were concerned. Yet, for all her misgivings, she was reluctant to deny him this pleasure, which kept him out of mischief, and which required the participation of no one else. For Huemac was still a friendless child, though as much because of his age as his personality. Few children had been born in Tenochtitlan during the hard years immediately preceding his birth, and those several years older had already entered the calmecac. And Huemac himself had reached the age when he would not play with children he considered too young for him, which ruled out the large group of infants who had been fathered during the period of recovery after the famine.

The Royal Compound, in fact, on a day less hot, resounded with the noise of babies and small children. The Tenocha warrior lords, the Tecuhtli, had responded to their recent military success by taking on as many wives and other women as they could afford, as a sign of their status. Ome Xochitl knew that Teuxoch had urged Quinatzin to do the same, but she had also known that her husband was satisfied with the children and grandchildren he already possessed, and that he had no desire to display his status in this manner. The Tecuhtli were also beginning to send their sons and daughters to the calmecac at an earlier age, but Ome Xochitl and Quinatzin had agreed that this would not be wise for Huemac, who had yet to develop the patience and discipline for the kinds of tasks the priests would set for him. He would surely be restless and unhappy, and probably disobedient, considering the nature of his powers. It was better for him to be lonely, they thought, than to allow him to blacken his future by failing at the calmecac.

When Ome Xochitl saw Teuxoch leave her rooms and stride angrily toward Huemac's corner of the courtyard, she knew what would follow, and she was reconciled to the fact that the older woman was right: The boy had been playing out in the sun too long, and had probably done more damage to his body. But she also knew that Teuxoch was still angry over the powdered chili Huemac had slipped into her yetl pouch, and so she was prepared to forgive her son even as she readied herself to join in his scolding. It was only when he was bored and unoccupied, after all, that he turned his energies to these annoying tricks.

Huemac was limping slightly as Teuxoch marched him back under the shade of the tree, and his skin and hair were covered with a fine coat of dust. As he came closer, Ome Xochitl could see that his knuckles were bleeding and one knee was badly bruised, and there were fresh scrapes on his chest and the sides of his arms and legs.

"I do not know how you can sit there and watch this happen," Teuxoch said angrily. "Look at what he has done to himself!"

"We have told you that you must wait and not play so hard," Ome Xochitl reminded her son sternly. "Your brother has not yet returned from the land of the Totonacs with the leather protectors he has promised you."

"The game makes me forget," Huemac said, unable to make a real show of repentance. "The ball moves too fast to play lightly."

"That is no excuse," Teuxoch said, and turned him sideways. "Show your mother what you have done to your buttocks."

Huemac reluctantly lifted the side of his dirty maxlatl, revealing the dark purple bruises that covered his hip and the side of his buttock. The skin appeared taut and ready to burst from the liquid trapped underneath, and Huemac squirmed with pain when Teuxoch poked him there.

"The pain should remind you, if nothing else," she said scornfully, as Huemac blinked back his tears.

"Go and wash yourself thoroughly," Ome Xochitl commanded, "and then bring me my medicine pouch. I will have to lance those bruises and clean out the blackened blood. Give me your ball; you will not be able to play again until you have healed."

Huemac clutched the ball tightly against his chest, but then gave it up when he saw the determined look in his mother's eyes. Ome Xochitl briefly softened her expression as she took the ball, letting him know that she sympathized with his reluctance, and that she would repay him for his obedience. Still limping, but bearing his injuries stoically, Huemac went off to cleanse himself.

"You do not scold him enough, or tell him how to behave," Teuxoch said bitterly, the muscles in her jaw forming a hard, oval lump around the yetl in her mouth. "You think it is better to let his wounds discipline him. But he *listens* when I speak sharply to him, and he changes his ways."

It is only that he will not let you catch him twice, Ome Xochitl thought, but she had no desire to argue with Teuxoch. She knew that it vexed the older woman that she, the younger wife, could make Huemac obey her without scolding, without even speaking at all. But Ome Xochitl was not about to reveal her method, for she was training Huemac as her father had trained her: making him read her wishes and feelings in her eyes, face and gestures, developing his sensitivity to hidden meanings by gradually reducing the emotion she displayed to him openly. She had taken care to leave no doubt of her affection, but she had also seen that her displeasure lost none of its force in the translation from a raised voice to a lifted eyebrow. When Huemac finally had to leave her side, he would be able to see much more in people than what they chose to reveal in words.

"He should have been sent to the calmecac already," Teuxoch concluded, seeing that she was not going to get an argument. "They would not spoil him *there.*"

"Perhaps you should speak to our husband," Ome Xochitl suggested innocently. "Perhaps he does not know you feel this way."

Teuxoch spat into the dust and rubbed at the spot with her sandaled foot.

"He knows," she said, turning to go back to her rooms, "but I will remind him nonetheless."

Perhaps I do spoil him, Ome Xochitl thought as she watched Teuxoch walk away. But no more than you, Second Mother, and for the same reason —you love him, and you know that the world is going to treat him roughly. You scold to prepare him; I forbear to make him learn. But we are both his mother, and like all mothers, we will live to see our child suffer.

AT MIDNIGHT, as the priests throughout the city blew their conch trumpets, Ome Xochitl rose quietly from her mat and went out into the courtyard to pray for her son. Acolmiztli was fighting with the armies in the lands of the Totonacs, and she had made a vow that she would rise at this hour every night and make offerings to insure his success and safe return home. Facing north, she pricked her earlobes with a piece of obsidian and smeared her blood on strips of paper, which would later be taken to the temple of Tezcatlipoca to be burned. With these offerings in her hands, she raised her face to the black night sky, crying out in sorrow to Tezcatlipoca, the Lord of the Smoking Mirror, asking that he forbear from stealing back the life of her son. She called upon him by the names Yaotl, the Enemy, and Moquequeloa, the Mocker, for he was known to be both fierce and capricious, the Dark One who played with the fates of men. Ome Xochitl humbled herself before him, praying that her son's heart might not falter, and that if his life must be taken, that he might die a warrior's death.

She sat silently for several moments after she had finished praying, but as she was about to rise, she heard her husband leave Teuxoch's rooms and come across the courtyard toward her, tapping ahead of himself with his staff. He was over fifty now, and was often up in the night, since he longer slept as well or as much as he had as a young man. Ome Xochitl waited patiently while he squatted next to her and bowed to the north, adding his prayers to her own.

"You are faithful to our son, little mother," he said to her affectionately, when he had finished and seated himself across from her.

"Is there any news of him?"

"He has been made a captain of the Jaguars, and a leader of the first scouts. They say that there is no ambush he cannot outrun, and that with his bow he kills silently, from afar."

"This is news for a father," Ome Xochitl chided him mildly. "A mother wishes to know that he is well and will be returning home shortly."

Quinatzin smiled. "He is well. Every day, the army draws closer to the city of Cuetlaxtlan, where the trail leads down from the mountains. But they say that the city is well defended, and that the Tlaxcalans have joined the Totonacs as allies. So it could be many months yet. When he returns this time, we must find him a wife, so that there will be someone else to pray for him."

"Will this warfare never cease?" Ome Xochitl said wearily, then held up a hand before Quinatzin could speak. "I know: Our son is Tenocha, and so are we."

"Yes," Quinatzin said succinctly. "I have been thinking of our other son, as well."

"Has Teuxoch spoken to you again of the calmecac?"

"Of course, but she does not convince me. He is still too impetuous for such confinement."

"He will *always* be too impetuous," Ome Xochitl pointed out. "But he will be better able to endure the chastisement when he is ten."

"So I explained to her. But I could not deny that I am with him too little, and that he needs the company of men. I had thought of trying to keep him with me, but the presence of a child would be too often inappropriate in the palace, and I do not have your sensitivity to his whereabouts. I would be forced to punish him for his curiosity."

Ome Xochitl listened silently, impressed and gratified by his concern for Huemac's welfare, and pleased that he still agreed with her about the calmecac. Yet it was clear that he had reached some decision regarding their son, and that it involved taking him away from her, a possibility that brought a sudden chill to her heart. Quinatzin waited a moment for her reply, then went on:

"While I was thinking of this, however, I had the good fortune to pay a visit to an old friend, and it was in his house that I discovered the solution to our problem. Surely you remember my old friend Tezcatl, the Tlatelulcan I met before the Tepanec War? As his name might suggest, he is now a seller of mirror-stone, and a fine craftsman in the art of cutting and gluing them into mosaic mirrors and jewelry. He is also a gatherer of information for me, because he is friendly and honest to a fault, and people naturally tell him things."

"Does he have no children of his own?" Ome Xochitl asked in a low voice, thinking, despite herself, that Teuxoch would also oppose the notion of leaving Huemac with some childless Tlatelulcan stonecutter. She wondered how her husband could even have conceived of such a thing.

"Ah!" Quinatzin exclaimed triumphantly. "That is what makes it so suitable. He has *two* children: a boy, Nopaltzin, who is a year younger than Huemac, and a girl called Taypachtli, who is younger still. Their mother died two years ago, and they are alone with Tezcatl, who feeds them and keeps them by his side."

"And what is it that makes you believe that these children, who have never seen Huemac, will be willing to have him as their playmate?" Ome Xochitl asked sharply, and Quinatzin paused and considered her silently for several moments.

"It is not like you, my wife, to judge things so quickly," he said quietly. "You have not heard all I have to say. Tezcatl's daughter, Taypachtli, was born without sight. When the mother died, the girl's brother became her caretaker. Nopaltzin is a fine young boy, honest like his father, and always attentive to the needs of his blind sister. But he, too, is lonely, and misses the company of other boys. Perhaps he and Huemac would not like one another, but I had thought to bring them together."

Ome Xochitl sighed, and hung her head briefly.

"Forgive me, my husband," she said. "He is the last of my children, and I cannot help but want to keep him by my side. But you are right: He needs a playmate, and perhaps this child will not mistrust him as the others do. I was wrong to question your judgment."

"It will have to be tested, anyway. And he is not going there to stay, little mother, it is not like the calmecac. He will still be here for you and Teuxoch."

"When will you take him?"

"Two days from now. I have spoken privately to Tezcatl, and he, too, likes the idea. But we have arranged nothing, and we have agreed not to tell the boys in advance. It will be their choice, if they decide to become friends."

"Let us hope they will," Ome Xochitl said in a fervent voice, and was glad of the darkness, which kept her husband from seeing the foolish tears in her eyes.

AS THEY left the plaza and entered the broad street that led to the bridge to Tlatelulco, Quinatzin allowed himself the luxury of concentrating all his attention on his son. Time together like this, in the middle of the day, was a difficult thing to arrange, and Huemac had shown that he was aware of this. He had not even asked where his father was taking him, but he had been waiting in the courtyard since early morning, according to Ome Xochitl, doing nothing in order not to get himself dirty. Quinatzin had seen him swell up with pride and importance at his father's entrance, and he had held his head high, looking neither to the right nor the left, when they had walked together through the narrow streets of the compound.

For his part, Quinatzin found himself pleased by the sight of the stocky child at his elbow. Huemac had washed and dressed himself carefully, wearing a clean maxlatl and a net mantle of maguey fiber, and the jade rabbit around his neck. He had tied his long black hair back with a thong, so that it almost covered his ears, and while his face was not pretty, it was composed and properly somber. Patiently matching his father's halting stride, he strode calmly through the crowded street, appearing indifferent to the many people they passed. Even when a little girl pointed to the poultices on his buttocks and loudly asked her mother what they were, Huemac did not turn his head or otherwise show that he had heard.

Ah, but he probably misses nothing, Quinatzin thought; Ome Xochitl has only taught him to do his staring covertly. To test him, Quinatzin glanced casually over his shoulder, and referred to a man who had passed them several moments before.

"Did you see? Was that an ibis that fisherman was carrying on his pole?"

"It was a heron," Huemac said, without looking. "It would be bad luck to kill an ibis."

"So you remember what you learned from our visits to the fowlers so long ago," Quinatzin said happily, and stopped on the bridge to look at his son. "That gladdens my heart, Huemac, for we have had too little time together, and there is much you have had to learn from others."

Huemac blinked several times, appearing pleased but also slightly embarrassed. Quinatzin stared thoughtfully at the canoes passing beneath them.

"Today I am going to take you to the house of another one of my friends. He is a Tlatelulcan. What have you been told about the Tlatelulcans?"

"They are Mexicans like the Tenocha," Huemac said hesitantly, obviously uncertain of how honest he should be. "But the Second Mother says they are more like Tepanecs. She says they are cowards who have become rich by trading rather than warfare."

"Trading is an honorable profession, my son," Quinatzin said. "And the Tlatelulcans are not cowards. My friend Tezcatl fought with our people against the Tepanecs, and he would probably still be a warrior, even at his age, if he had not fallen from a rooftop in Coyoacan and hurt his back. Now he is a craftsman, and makes the fine mirrors that are used in the houses of the lords."

"I do not like mirrors," Huemac said rudely. "Except the black ones, that make all faces look like my own."

"Self-pity does not become a man," Quinatzin said sternly, and Huemac stiffened penitently. "And you will be careful not to insult my friend with such rudeness."

"I am sorry, Father," Huemac said abjectly, and Quinatzin, remembering his youth, reached out a hand and lifted the boy's chin.

"Be cheerful, Huemac, I am not angry with you. And I do not think you will insult this man, once you have met him. He is that rare thing: a man whom one trusts on sight."

"How did he get this way?" Huemac asked earnestly, once they had resumed walking. Quinatzin shrugged.

"I do not know, and I do not think he could tell you if you asked. You must watch him, and then perhaps you will be able to tell me."

Huemac frowned slightly, as if he could not believe such a disclaimer coming from his father. But he asked no more questions, and they walked the rest of the way in silence.

THE HOUSE of Tezcatl the mirror-stone seller was one of a long row of identical houses that faced outward onto a canal, its only distinguishing mark a large oval piece of shiny black stone embedded in the wall over the open doorway. It was much smaller than any of the houses in the Royal Compound, and its walls were built of whitewashed adobe brick rather than stone and plaster. There were two rooms along the eastern side of the courtyard, a garden against the back wall, and a long, open work-space along the western wall. Exposed beams supported a sloping, thatched roof, under which Tezcatl kept his benches, tools, and piles of materials.

Even before Tezcatl rose to greet them, Huemac recognized him among the small group of men sitting together under the thatched roof. There were several things that made him stand out from the other men: his great size, the loudness of his voice, the wide expanse of white teeth he displayed when he smiled. And he was the only man wearing a leather apron. But what struck Huemac most vividly was the fact that his head was completely bald, and it reflected the light in glimmering plates, nearly as brightly as did the polished pieces of stone he had laid out on a mat before him.

Clapping his hands with pleasure at the sight of Quinatzin, he came out from under the roof, ducking his head with a practiced motion. He was easily half a head taller than Quinatzin, with a massive chest and broad shoulders, and muscles that looked like rocks. He projected an air of such great vigor and physical strength that Huemac felt dwarfed and insignificant, and could only stare upward at him with wide eyes.

"Lord, my friend, Quinatzin," he boomed, gripping Quinatzin's arm so that his whole body shook. "Welcome to my house, poor as it is."

"So, Tezcatl," Quinatzin said wryly, eying the seated men. "As usual, the pleasure of your company adds to the idleness of your city."

Tezcatl laughed loudly, showing more teeth than Huemac had ever seen in one mouth.

"No, my friend, this is business. But we are all honorable tradesmen, and it is not fit to appear too industrious when one is cheating one's colleagues."

The other men laughed, and a couple of them gathered their bundles and began to depart, waving their farewells to their host. Tezcatl returned their salutations, then bent his head to Huemac.

"Greetings also to you, Huemac. Your father honors me by bringing his son to my house."

Huemac knew he should say something, but he was blinded by the broad band of white teeth and the glistening dome of bare skin.

"Quachichtin?" he asked numbly, and Tezcatl threw back his head and laughed.

"No, little one, I am not one of the Shorn Ones. I am angry in battle, but not mad. Still, I have borne my baldness with great courage. Do you not think so, Quinatzin?"

"Especially in the winter," Quinatzin concurred with a straight face, and Tezcatl and the other men exploded into laughter. Huemac joined in happily, staring in amazement at all the smiling faces and laughing mouths. He had never seen his father in such company, and he was immensely proud of the amusement Quinatzin had caused with his joke. It made him feel that this thing called trust was indeed a rare and precious quality.

The men seated themselves under the roof and resumed their conversation, gesturing at the goods laid out before them and calling on Quinatzin to take their sides in the bargaining. Listening eagerly and laughing whenever the men laughed, Huemac wandered around the outside of their circle, examining the knives and chisels on the benches and poking his fingers into the open piles of sand, emery, and charcoal. He avoided looking directly at the finished pieces of silver and black stone, except those whose polished surfaces had been carved into designs or the faces of animals. He was squatting beside a pile of stone shavings, turning the slivers with his hand to make them catch the light, when he saw the other boy watching him from a few feet away.

Immediately, Huemac hooded his eyes and assumed a defensive stance, with his feet wide apart. The other boy was larger than Huemac, and his arms were looped over the wooden yoke balanced on his shoulders, which had a pottery jug attached to each end. He stared back at Huemac openly, making no effort to hide his curiosity.

"Huemac, this is *my* son, Nopaltzin," Tezcatl boomed from the other side of the room. "Where is your sister, Nopalli? You must introduce Huemac to Taypachtli."

"I was going to fetch water," Nopaltzin said, seeming reluctant to put down the yoke.

"Well, do that first," Tezcatl allowed, "but then you must attend to our guest."

"I will help," Huemac suggested impulsively, and Nopaltzin eyed him uncertainly, as if gauging his strength. But finally, he put down the yoke and handed one of the jugs to Huemac.

"It is very heavy when it is full," he warned, seeing how carelessly Huemac handled the empty jug. "And it is a long walk back from the fountain."

"I am strong," Huemac said with a frown, and Nopaltzin just shrugged.

"Let us go, then," he said, and led the way to the door.

ALTHOUGH HE left a trail of spilled water in the dust behind him, Huemac managed to return to Tezcatl's house without dropping the jug. It *was* extraordinarily heavy, and slippery where he had to hold it around the middle, since his arms were not long enough to permit him to hold it by the handle at the top and rest it against his hip, as Nopaltzin did. And Huemac had insisted on filling it to the rim, despite Nopaltzin's efforts to persuade him not to. The last half of the journey back had been a nerve-racking experience for both of them, with Huemac straining every muscle to maintain his precarious grip on the jug, and Nopaltzin anxiously contemplating the punishment he would receive from his father if it were broken.

"Here," Nopaltzin said with relief, when they finally reached the garden and could set the jugs down in the soft dirt. Huemac knelt with his arms still around the jug, unable to control the trembling of his limbs or his tortured breathing. He felt ashamed in front of the other boy and wanted to run away, but he was too exhausted to move.

"So," Nopaltzin said suddenly, attempting to imitate his father's booming voice. "Now that we have done the light chores, we can get down to the *real* work!"

Huemac stared at him in bewilderment, then saw him break into a smile, showing strong, white teeth like his father's, and they both began to laugh. They laughed until they fell down into the dirt holding their sides, subsiding only gradually into spasms of giggles.

"That is what my father always says," Nopaltzin said, when they were able to sit up and look at one another, "whenever he has worn himself out and still has more to do."

"Your father is a man to be trusted," Huemac said respectfully. "That is what my father says." Then he grinned at Nopaltzin. "But he is also very *funny!*"

They laughed some more and then fell silent, glancing shyly at each other as they busied themselves dusting off the dirt from the garden. Finally, Nopaltzin could no longer restrain his curiosity and asked Huemac about the poultices on his buttocks.

"It is from playing tlachtli," Huemac said, finding that it did not embarrass him to explain. "My brother, Acolmiztli, brought me a ball of rubber from the land of the Mixtecs. He is a Jaguar Warrior, and a great fighter."

"I have no brothers," Nopaltzin said wistfully, but then his face brightened. "But come, you must meet my sister. She is only four, but she is very nice. Already, she knows many songs by heart, and perhaps she will sing for us."

Huemac eagerly followed Nopaltzin to one of the rooms across the courtyard, blinking rapidly as they came out of the bright sunlight into the dimness of the room. A servant girl was grinding maize in the corner near the hearth, and sitting on a mat not far away was a moon-faced little girl who appeared to Huemac to be asleep. Yet her head turned toward them as they approached, and Huemac realized with a start that she was blind. She smiled when Nopaltzin squatted in front of her and spoke her name.

"Taypachtli, I have brought you a guest. His name is Huemac, and he is the son of the great lord Quinatzin, the wise man who walks with the staff."

"Has he come to play with us?" the little girl asked in a soft, clear voice. "Or is he an older son?"

"He is a child like us," Nopaltzin explained, glancing at Huemac with sudden reticence. "But I do not know if he has come to play with us. His father is a great lord of the Tenocha."

Huemac did not understand at first, because the children he had met before this had all been the offspring of great lords, and most of them had not wanted to play with *him*. It was a new thing for the choice to be his, and it made him feel a great surge of loyalty toward Nopaltzin.

"I will play if my father will let me," he offered magnanimously. "And if you must carry water, so will I."

The two boys giggled, and grinned at each other.

"Are you close, Huemac?" Taypachtli asked, putting her hands out in front of her. "Come closer . . ."

Encouraged by a nudge from Nopaltzin, Huemac shuffled forward on his heels, touching one of her hands with his own to show her where he was. But when she raised her hands up to his face, he pulled back abruptly.

"What is it?" Taypachtli cried in alarm, and Huemac looked anxiously at Nopaltzin, who urged him on with a nod of his head.

"Do not be afraid. It is her way of seeing you. Close your eyes so that she will not hurt you by accident."

Shrinking inside, Huemac leaned closer and shut his eyes. Now even *she* will know I am ugly, he thought miserably, flinching slightly as her hands found the sides of his face. But her fingers had a light, feathery touch, and they did not linger over the loose, fleshy places under his jaw, about which he was most self-conscious. Quickly, she traced the powerful curve of his forehead and the flat contours of his cheeks and nose, and only when she found his eyes did her tiny fingers hesitate with interest, exploring the depth of his eye sockets and brushing lightly over the creases in his eyelids. Huemac was able to stay still and not resist her examination, but the joy of these new-found friends went out of him as he thought of what she must be discovering about him.

"Your eyes are very large," Taypachtli said finally. "Can you see far away with them?"

"Yes," Huemac said, opening his eyes warily as she removed her fingers from his face. But there was no repugnance on her pretty, moon-shaped face; only what seemed to be curiosity.

"Can you see in the dark?"

"Yes," Huemac admitted, and Nopaltzin snickered, then fell silent when he saw that Huemac was serious.

"That is the only way *I* can see," Taypachtli explained simply, without sadness. "How did you learn?"

"I do not know; I just always could. It is because I am unlucky."

"But how can that be?" Nopaltzin asked. "I would consider myself lucky if I could see in the dark. Then I would never be afraid at night."

Huemac cocked his head at the two of them, wondering if they could really be so different from the other children, who had despised him for his willingness to enter the dark places that frightened them. He had never thought of it as an advantage, because he had never known their fear, and they had always treated him with contempt afterward.

"I can also speak with other people's voices," he admitted timidly, testing their tolerance, "and with the voices of animals."

"What animals?" Taypachtli asked, her face suddenly animated.

"Let us hear you," Nopaltzin pleaded.

"You will not be frightened of me?" Huemac asked incredulously.

"I like the sounds of animals," Taypachtli said. "I will sing for you if you make them for me."

The servant girl jumped when Huemac quacked, but Taypachtli clapped her hands with glee, and Nopaltzin grinned and urged him to do more. *Trust,* Huemac thought happily, and complied with his friends' wishes.

"WHAT WAS that?" Tezcatl demanded. He and Quinatzin were sitting alone under the thatched roof, where the sound of a howling coyote had come to them clearly from across the empty courtyard. Quinatzin laughed at the expression on his friend's face.

"That is Huemac. I have told you of his skill with voices, have I not?"

"Perhaps I did not take you seriously enough," Tezcatl said, his eyes fixed on the room across the way. "But the children have not come running to me, so they must not have found it too frightening."

"He does not mean to be frightening, except when the other children spurn him because of his appearance, and his luck."

"My children would never do such a thing," Tezcatl said confidently. "I have taught them to value what is in the heart, as well as the face." He glanced again at the room. "I think they have taken to Huemac, as we had hoped. It would be good if they could become friends, as our two cities have again become friends."

Quinatzin looked at him skeptically, deciding it was time they talked frankly. Tezcatl was a man of such good heart that it always required some prompting to get him to use the shrewdness he possessed. He heard everything with the same, accepting grace, and he was slow to judge his information or come to conclusions that other people might find displeasing. But he did not forget the unpleasant details, or try to hide them, and Quinatzin valued his information for the very neutrality with which it was held.

"I have meant to speak to you about the relations between our cities," Quinatzin began slowly. "It was your Speaker, Cuauhtlatoa, who won the friendship of Moteczuma and Tlacaelel, but the Talking Eagle has grown old, and some say he will not live for many more years. Have you heard talk of whom the lords of your city favor as his successor?"

"Two of his sons sit in the Council of Lords, and naturally, much of the talk centers around them. But those who speculate also recognize the power Moteczuma will exercise over any choice, and they do not know his preference."

"And of the warchief, Moquiuix? What do they say of him?"

"Ah, Moquiuix"—Tezcatl smiled, his eyes sparkling with pride—"that is another thing! He is young, but what a warrior! His courage has inspired great pride in the young men of my city, and in the old ones, too. Even I want to fight again, when I hear of the things he has said and done."

"Would he inspire the same confidence as your Speaker?"

Tezcatl frowned and sat thinking for several moments.

"Surely, one so brave is bound to rise to a position of leadership," he said finally. "But he is still so young, and he does not come from the families of the rulers. And it is well known that he is hotheaded and impetuous, which are good qualities in a warrior, but defects in a ruler." He looked at Quinatzin and shrugged apologetically. "Frankly, my friend, there are many in Tlatelulco who resent the influence of Tenochtitlan in our affairs, and these same ones look to Moquiuix as their spokesman. I am afraid there would be no peace between our cities if he were made our Tlatoani."

"I understand the resentment of your people," Quinatzin said sympathetically, "and I would hope to see the cause of it abolished. But you must know that Moteczuma looks upon Moquiuix with great favor, and does not see his rashness as a defect. Nor does his brother, but for other reasons."

"What reasons can Tlacaelel have for such a judgment?" Tezcatl demanded incredulously.

"You must understand, my friend," Quinatzin said gently. "Tlacaelel has never desired peace between the Mexicans. He has always been jealous of the wealth of your merchants, the pochteca, and he would like to have it to distribute to the warriors who trade in his marketplace of death."

"Why are there such men?" Tezcatl cried in frustration, clenching his huge fists. "Even now, our warriors fight with the Tenocha against the Totonacs. Are we to turn against one another when that is done?"

"Let us pray that it does not happen. There is still a possibility of a marriage between Moteczuma's granddaughter and one of the sons of Cuauhtlatoa, which could alter the course of this thing. Otherwise, we must hope that the rashness of Moquiuix will leave him lying in the fields of the Totonacs, for if he returns from this campaign a success, I fear that he will be given the girl, and the title."

The two men stared silently at each other for several moments, then turned their heads simultaneously at a sound from the other side of the courtyard. The children were coming toward them in a group, talking and joking among themselves. Huemac and Nopaltzin stood on either side of Taypachtli, each guiding her by a hand. Tezcatl ran a hand over his smooth skull and sighed heavily.

"We are not so young anymore, Quinatzin," he said sadly. "Hope evades our capture far more easily than when we were fresh and innocent. Perhaps there is a way to save these little ones from suffering that we cannot see. We must not allow our lack of hope to blind us to the example of their friendship. Surely, it is not only children who can reach such a simple understanding?"

"Not if there are other men with hearts as good as yours, my friend," Quinatzin said with a weary smile. He glanced at the children and was pleased that they had been brought together, and that they had chosen to be friends. But the sight of their young faces also made him feel, even more keenly, the weight of his age and experience. And unlike his good-hearted friend, he could not believe in his own heart that the friendship of children could prevent a war.

ꗇꗇ 6 ꗇꗇ

IN the year Ten-Reed, the armies of the Alliance began their final drive against the Totonacs. The forces of Nezahualcoyotl came down from the north, through the lands of the already conquered Huaxtecs, and the Mexican garrison in the Mixtec city of Cosamaloapan moved up the coast from the south. A third force came through the mountains from the west, skirting the great mountain Poyauhtecatl to the south and taking control of the pass that led down to the heavily fortified Totonac city of Ahuilizapan. Beyond was the Totonac capital of Cuetlaxtlan, Leather Land, lying open and vulnerable in the hot coastal lowlands that rose from the shores of the Divine Waters.

This third force was composed of the Tenocha under the command of Moteczuma's grandsons—Axayacatl, Tizoc, and Ahuitzotl—as well as contingents from Culhuacan and Tenayuca, and a sizable contingent of Tlatelulcans under their fiery warchief, Moquiuix. As they waited in the pass for expected reinforcements from Texcoco, word of treachery came by runner from Tenochtitlan: the Tlaxcalans, the enemies within the house, had allied themselves with the Totonacs and joined the defenders of Ahuilizapan, while the warriors of Huexotzinco and Cholula were moving in from the rear to seal the ambush. It was Moteczuma's judgment that the forces of the Alliance were outnumbered and should retreat from the trap being prepared for them.

The warchiefs assembled in the pass, and though they were now stronger with the addition of Nezahualcoyotl's son, Acapipioltzin, and his Texcocans, it was generally agreed that retreat was called for. But then Moquiuix leapt to his feet and addressed the chiefs with impassioned words, saying that he was a Mexican and had come to fight, and that even if the others chose to return home, he and his warriors would stay and fight on without them. Without waiting for a reply, he prepared his men for battle, and when he led them screaming down the pass toward Ahuilizapan, the other chiefs, shamed and inspired by his bold words, brought their warriors in behind the Tlatelulcans.

Faced with almost certain death, Moquiuix and his warriors stormed the Totonac defenses with a fury and abandon never seen in that land of slow, green rivers. When Axayacatl and his brothers arrived with their men, the Tlatelulcans had already fought their way into the city, and the Totonacs and their allies were in disarray. All that remained was the taking of captives and the burning of the temple, and though the Tenocha vied with their brother Mexicans for these honors, the day clearly belonged to Moquiuix.

The rich city of Cuetlaxtlan fell shortly thereafter, and when the terms of the Totonac tribute had been negotiated, the armies of the Alliance marched home in triumph. In Tenochtitlan, there was a celebration that went on for five days, surpassing in size and opulence anything previously witnessed by the inhabitants of the city. The warriors were publicly rewarded by Moteczuma with shares in the rich plunder of the campaign, and they danced in lines in the plaza, led by Axayacatl and Moquiuix, who even in this competed like rivals. Songs were composed commemorating the victory, and the lords and their families feasted on spiced cocoa and the almost-unknown delicacies of shrimp, crab, turtles, and sea snails that had come from Ahuilizapan, the city by the Waters of Delight. Thousands of captive Totonacs and Tlaxcalans went to feed the gods, some having their hearts ripped out upon the techcatl, and others dying in ritual combat upon the temalacatl, the gladiatorial stone in the House of Eagles. Many times during the festivities, Moteczuma expressed his deep satisfaction with Moquiuix's bold deeds, and before the celebration was over, he announced to the assembled lords that he had given his granddaughter, Chalchiuhnenetl, to Moquiuix as a wife.

After the public ceremonies had been concluded, the family of Quinatzin gathered in their father's house for a feast honoring the return of his eldest son. Acolmiztli, now a battle-scarred veteran of twenty-three, sat in the place of honor next to his father, once again partaking in the familiar foods of his city.

"So, my son," Quinatzin said fondly, when the feasting was over and they were relaxing with the other men, smoking long reed tubes filled with yetl. "You are now one of the great ones, a Jaguar and a member of the Tecuhtli. It is truly rare for one so young to have risen this high, and my heart is filled with pride for you."

Acolmiztli was silent out of modesty, drawing deeply on the painted tube while the other men murmured their agreement and respect. Quinatzin watched him carefully, wondering if he and Ome Xochitl were correct in thinking that they had detected a new maturity in their son. He seemed more thoughtful now, and less impressed with the trappings of his rank, as witnessed by the small amount of jewelry he was wearing this evening, and the absence of his Jaguar headdress.

"I thank you, my father," Acolmiztli said finally. "It is the hope of all young men to bring pride to the hearts of their parents. I can ask for no greater reward for my labors."

The other men smiled with pleasure at this show of respect, but Quinatzin's smile took on a wry twist.

"None? Have your years in the field so impoverished your imagination? Has the thought of a wife never crossed your mind?"

"Many times," Acolmiztli confessed. "Often, when I was lying on the hard ground, shivering with the cold of the mountains, I thought of this to warm myself."

"It is good that you did not think of it in battle, too," Tezcatl joked, from his place on the other side of Quinatzin. "It is very distracting to carry a spear you cannot throw."

Quinatzin waited for the laughter to die down, seeing that Acolmiztli, despite his own good-natured smile, had given the matter some serious consideration.

"I have made some inquiries," Quinatzin said to him when it was quiet, "and I will arrange for the proper introductions to be made, if it is what you wish. Do your vows as a Jaguar permit such a thing at this time?"

Acolmiztli momentarily furrowed his brow, and Quinatzin understood that it was this consideration, and not a lack of imagination, that made him hesitant. Yes, my son, he thought compassionately, it is decisions such as these that age one, even as they lay the foundation for wisdom.

"There are those in my company," Acolmiztli said slowly, "who are returning immediately to the field, to fight against the Chalcans. It is a time of great opportunity for those who are ambitious, who would bring honor to themselves and sustenance to the Sun. Our vow binds us to this mission, and it is not easy to forsake such an opportunity, whatever one's personal ambitions."

Acolmiztli paused and stared seriously at his father's face, as if looking for a solution there. Finally, he drew a deep breath and went on:

"But I have won many honors already, and while I do not scorn these, you have shown me by your example, my father, that there are other things a man may value. Someday, I would also like to sit beside my son and speak to him as you have spoken to me tonight. It is time that I attended to the lands and tribute that have been given to me by the Speaker, and time I began making a home for myself."

"And some children," Tezcatl boomed exuberantly. "I do not think you should allow Moteczuma to give you *those.*"

"This Tlatelulcan gives me no peace," Acolmiztli complained facetiously, smiling at his father's friend. "But I can forgive you anything, Tezcatl. I was there when Moquiuix spoke to the warchiefs, and never have I heard a bolder man. I would be proud to have such a man as the Speaker of my city."

"And so he will be," Tezcatl said softly, with a glance at Quinatzin. "There can be no question of it now."

"You do not sound pleased," Acolmiztli said, showing his surprise. Tezcatl again glanced at Quinatzin, then inclined his great bald head toward the young warrior.

"Your father and I have seen many bold men during the course of our lives, but very few who were fit to carry the heavy burdens of the Tlatoani. Boldness can be a very dangerous thing in a ruler, if it is not tempered with wisdom and humility."

Acolmiztli frowned and looked questioningly at his father. Quinatzin nodded, but spoke in a conciliatory tone, to relieve the tension he could feel building in his son.

"It is good that the ruling houses of our cities have been joined by a marriage. The Mexica should speak with one voice, like the brothers they are. But you yourself saw the way Axayacatl and Moquiuix danced together in the plaza: They were like fighting cocks. Is this the kind of friendship we should seek for our people? Or," Quinatzin added dramatically, gesturing at the two boys who were playing ball in the corner of the courtyard, "are not these little ones a better example of the trust and cooperation we truly desire?"

As the men turned to watch, Huemac curled one leg behind him, holding the ball in his hand while checking to see that Nopaltzin was ready. Then he swiveled on his planted foot and brought his other leg through forcefully, dropping the ball in front of his body and hitting it a solid blow with his thigh. As the ball sailed toward the wall, he urgently motioned Nopaltzin into position for the rebound, moving in behind him in case he should miss. Each boy was wearing one half of the leather tlachtli outfit—kneepads, gloves, hip and thigh protectors—that Acolmiztli had brought back from Cuetlaxtlan, and since these were man-sized garments, the protectors flapped and gathered on the boys' small bodies, and the kneepads kept slipping down around their ankles.

But despite their ludicrous appearance, they managed to keep the ball in play for several moments before it bounced past them. Nopaltzin, though larger, was clearly the less skillful player, and he listened earnestly to Huemac's advice.

"You must pretend that you are playing on the great court in the plaza, and that all the great lords are watching," Huemac instructed him solemnly, unaware that the men were listening. "The future of your city is at stake, and if the ball gets past you, you will die for it!"

The men laughed, but neither boy noticed, because the ball was moving again, and the fate of the city was on the line.

"He is a fierce one, my brother," Acolmiztli said with a satisfied smile. "It is good that he has found a companion to share his pretending." He glanced shrewdly at Quinatzin and Tezcatl. "Did the two of you arrange this alliance?"

"We encouraged it, certainly," Quinatzin acknowledged, and Acolmiztli looked back at the boys.

"He seems to have lost the anger that once possessed him," he mused aloud, then nodded abruptly to the two men. "Perhaps you are right. Perhaps there are enemies enough to be found elsewhere."

"Perhaps," Quinatzin allowed with a small smile. Relieved that the tension had been dissipated, Tezcatl beamed broadly.

"Ah, that brother of yours makes *friends* for me. He goes with us to the marketplace, and he speaks for me to the foreigners who come to examine my wares. He learns the names of their numbers quickly and can repeat them back during the course of the bartering. I do not think they always understand him, but it makes them feel better just to hear their own tongue."

"And so they buy more," Quinatzin threw in, and Tezcatl laughed loudly along with the others.

"His skill with voices is truly uncanny," he said, shaking his head in admiration. "He has fooled me many times. The only one he cannot fool is my daughter Taypachtli, and that is because she is sightless. She recognizes his presence no matter who he pretends to be."

"So does his mother," Quinatzin said, then turned to Acolmiztli. "*Your* mother, my son. She has composed a flower song in your honor, and I think it is time she sang it for us. Go to her and ask, while I fetch Teuxoch and my daughters."

Acolmiztli went eagerly to the rooms of his mother, but stopped just inside the door to greet his sister, who rose from her mat next to the little blind girl and smiled at him. Cocatli was thirteen, and though still tiny, and thin from the fasting at the calmecac, the signs of her approaching womanhood were clearly apparent. She was wearing a white mantle without design or embroidery, and her black hair was finally growing back from the cropping it had received upon her entrance into the temple.

"Soon, I am told," Acolmiztli said to her, "your vow to the temple will be completed. What will you do then, my sister?"

"The sisters of the god have encouraged me to join their order and become one of them. They especially prize the ornaments and decorations I make for the temple. But our parents speak to me of marriage."

"And do you hear them?" Acolmiztli asked with a grin that made Cocatli lower her eyes in embarrassment.

"I am not permitted to even think of such things," she said modestly, and Acolmiztli laughed.

"Of course not! Forgive me, my sister, I am a warrior, and naturally crude. But I know that you will want to obey our parents' wishes," he added pointedly, "and that pleases me greatly."

"And you, my brother?" Cocatli asked, her dark, oval eyes sparkling with pleasure. "Do not our parents speak of marriage to you, as well?"

"Yes, and I have finally heard them. We must arrange the day so that you will be allowed to attend the wedding."

"I am pleased," Cocatli said, and led him by the hand over to Taypachtli, motioning him to squat close to her.

"Taypachtli, little seashell," she said fondly, "this is Huemac's and my brother, Acolmiztli."

"Closer," Taypachtli said, and Acolmiztli submitted his face to her searching hands. He felt her fingers flit over his features, lingering briefly on the battle scar above his left eyebrow and the large perforation in his upper lip.

"You are a strong man," she said, "but not so old."

"You see well with your hands," Acolmiztli congratulated her, reaching out to gently stroke the roundness of her cheek. Then he touched the pendant in her lap. "But what is this, little one?"

"It is the spindle whorl of our Lord, Quetzalcoatl," Cocatli explained. "It is a gift to my temple from her father, the man who smiles. Taypachtli was showing me how she polishes the small places with a tiny piece of cane. It is her special skill, and the way she helps her father in his work."

"It is fine work," Acolmiztli said sincerely, examining the pattern of descending circles that seemed to disappear into one another, like a whirlpool. "Are you also Huemac's friend, little Taypachtli?"

The little girl's face brightened happily.

"I sing to Huemac, and he speaks to me with the voices of animals. Though sometimes, when he is being bad, he pretends to be Nopaltzin or my father."

"Yes, our Huemac is a *great* pretender," Acolmiztli agreed, glancing up as Ome Xochitl entered the room. She squatted next to them, and Taypachtli immediately turned her head in that direction.

"Huemac's mother," she said, and Ome Xochitl reached out and took the little girl's hand. She looked at her son questioningly.

"I have come to tell you, my mother, that I have decided to remain in Tenochtitlan and to take a wife."

"That is good," Ome Xochitl said, "but forgive me if I am not surprised. I felt, when I saw you again, that you had come to know the needs of your heart."

Acolmiztli gazed at his mother affectionately, forgetting completely that he was a great, stern warrior.

"My father says that you have composed a flower song for this occasion."

"It is a poor one, I am afraid, for I have not had the time for such things for many years. Let us go to the courtyard, and I will recite it for you and the others."

Quinatzin had assembled his family and guests under the huehuetl tree, with Teuxoch and his daughters and their families to his left, and Huemac, Nopaltzin and Tezcatl, and the other guests to his right. Ome Xochitl led Taypachtli to her father, and Cocatli and Acolmiztli took seats beside their father. Swaddled in the leather tlachtli outfit, Huemac grinned up at his brother, who smiled back and motioned for him to face forward and listen to their mother. Standing calmly before the group, Ome Xochitl began to recite:

> "Behold, O Lord, the brave Tenocha warrior.
> He is the Stalwart Lion;
> He is the Jaguar who springs;
> He has sung his war song
> On the fields of blood and burning.
>
> Truly, did he come here a small one,
> A precious herb-green stone,
> A beautiful quetzal feather,
> A gift from the Giver of Life?
>
> Is it he whom the warriors praise
> In the House of Eagles,
> In the land of the Cloud People,
> By the shores of the Great Waters?
> Can a small one have grown so great?
>
> Behold, O Lord, the brave Tenocha warrior.
> Let him prosper, O Giver of Life,
> Reward him with your gifts
>
> Of precious stones, of precious feathers.
> Give him many sons, O Lord,
> Sons to sing as their father did
> On the fields of blood and burning."

"Again!" Tezcatl shouted over and over amid the applause that followed the conclusion of Ome Xochitl's recitation, and the others picked up his request and repeated it until they had persuaded her to give them a second reading. Acolmiztli sat through both performances as if mesmerized, his cheeks warmed by the praise and obvious love in his mother's words. Yet what struck him most powerfully was the sense of wonder she had captured, the same wonder he felt whenever he thought of all he had accomplished in his young life. His deeds had often seemed to him to belong to another person, to some charmed creature whom he watched from the outside, marveling at the man's resourcefulness, and the narrowness of his escapes from death. Now he understood the meaning of that wonder, and experienced a moment of profound humility. It is not I who possess courage, he thought reverently, but courage that possesses me.

The response to the second recitation was more subdued, but only because others had been touched as Acolmiztli had and wished to show their respect in a manner appropriate to the depth of their feelings. It had also grown quite late, and some of the smaller children had fallen asleep in their parents' arms. One by one, the guests brought their families over to praise Ome Xochitl and bid their host good night. Carrying Taypachtli in his arms, Tezcatl was the last to leave, with Huemac escorting him and Nopaltzin all the way to the door.

Then Quinatzin was alone with his wives and his youngest children, and he gathered them around him under the tree in the courtyard. Sitting in the flickering torchlight, he looked at them each in turn, lingering longest on the faces of Teuxoch and Ome Xochitl. At last, he began to speak:

"It has been thirty-five years since I first came to this island," he said quietly, and even Huemac stopped fidgeting to listen. "I did not expect to find my home here, though I had been driven from the home of my birth as a child. I came here as an ally of the Tenocha, who were then a poor people, so poor that they did not even own the land on which they lived. Who would have thought that they were destined to be the rulers of the whole Valley, and of lands far beyond? It is something to be wondered at, even by those who have seen it happen, as I have, and you, my wives."

The children looked at their mother and Teuxoch, then back at their father, who spoke to them directly:

"It was fate that brought me to Tenochtitlan, and kept me here, though my heart yearned for the home I had lost. But you, my children, are Tenocha by birth, and you will never know that yearning. Whatever your fates may be, you will know that this city is your home, and the foundation of all that you are. May that knowledge always be a comfort to you in times of hardship and misfortune. There is great suffering on this earth, my children, and you will not escape it. But remember your home, and your people, and let them give you the courage to bear your fate."

No one stirred when Quinatzin had finished. The torchlight flickered in the darkness, throwing shadows across the faces of the seated figures. The people of Tenochtitlan were at rest, and it was quiet in their city.

IV

THE HOUSE OF DARKNESS

1465–1469

BEFORE Huemac entered the calmecac at the age of ten, his father told him what he should expect there. He was warned that he was going to a house of fasting and penance, where his whole life would be subject to the harsh discipline of the priests, and where he would endure abuse, humiliation, and physical hardship. He would be made to gather firewood and sweep the temple floors, and to work hard in the fields and chinampa plots that belonged to the calmecac. He would be awakened at midnight and forced to bathe in icy waters, and then he would be sent out alone into the darkness to pray and perform acts of penance. Obedience would be expected of him at all times, and any sign of laziness or indifference would be punished severely.

Though he knew these things, Huemac listened with the proper respect, resolving within himself that he would not allow his luck to cause him to fail and bring disappointment to his father. It was not until later, when he was alone with her, that his mother spoke to him. Training her dark eyes upon him, she spoke forcefully, using more words than he had ever heard from her at one time:

"Now you must leave me, my son, and go into the world on your own. You have been warned of the hardships that await you, and in this, your father has not exaggerated. But you will also find that you are more powerful than most of the boys in the calmecac, as well as some of the priests. I tell you this not so that you will become arrogant, but so that you will not be surprised by it and act carelessly. I have trained you to be this way, and you have powers that are yours alone. Some you know, and others you will learn quickly, for you will have need of them. I will not delude you, my son: There will be those in the calmecac who will hate you and treat you scornfully. Some because of your appearance and luck, others because the blood of Texcoco is in your veins, and still others because they will sense that you understand them too well. You are Tenocha, Huemac, you can withstand their hatred and abuse. You must not use it as an excuse to abuse your powers in acts of revenge. There are ways to defend yourself and correct your enemies without causing them harm, and you are clever enough to find them. You must promise me, now, that you will never turn your powers against another unless your life itself is in danger."

Huemac solemnly promised that he would not, and then, unable to hold his tears, he fell weeping into his mother's arms. Ome Xochitl embraced him, and gave him her blessing, and took into her keeping the jade amulet he had worn since childhood. Then, weeping herself, she turned away from him, so that he could leave her, and the house of his parents, with dignity.

THE TLILLAN calmecac was a low, rectangular enclosure attached to the rear of the Temple of the Snake Woman. Its rooms and chambers were joined by colonnaded walkways that opened onto four interconnected courtyards, each containing a deep, round pool. In the main hall stood the image of Quetzalcoatl, patron of the calmecac, dressed in the beaked mask and feather mantle of Ehecatl, the God of Wind. A string of wooden beads had been left at the foot of this image when Huemac had been pledged to the Tlillan as an infant, and these were given to him to wear when he entered the calmecac for the first time. They were a reminder of the vows of obedience, chastity, and humility that had been made on his behalf, vows that Huemac repeated aloud before his head was shaved and he was given the black loincloth and net mantle of the novitiate. Then he and the other boys in his class, fifteen in all, were placed in the charge of the priest who was to oversee their education and the fulfillment of their vows.

The regimen of the calmecac was indeed as harsh and unrelenting as had been promised, and the first months were a terrifying ordeal for all the boys, until their bodies had adjusted to the freezing baths and the constant hunger, and their minds had assimilated the shock of being awakened nightly and made to face the darkness. Since the darkness provided no obstacle for him, Huemac had an easier adjustment to make than the others, a fact that some of the more perceptive of them recognized, despite his efforts to conceal it. Their suspicions did him little harm, though, since the boys were kept too busy during the day to even talk to one another, and their loneliness was enforced at night by being made to sleep alone on the polished floor, with only their thin mantles for covering. Added to the fact that he was the oldest boy in his group, this aura of suspected power, though it won him no friends, made even the sons of the most powerful Tenocha lords hesitate in displaying scorn for him.

Along with their chores and acts of penance, the boys were taught the legends, hymns, and rites of the gods, and they were instructed in the movements of the stars and the complicated workings of the tonalpohualli, the sacred calendar of day signs. They learned how to use the red and black paints, and how to interpret the figures and symbols in the sacred books: the Temicamatl, the Book of Dreams, the Tonalamatl, the Book of Day Signs, and the

Xiuhamatl, the Book of Years, which contained the history of the tribe and its city.

Huemac found all these things fascinating, and with his keen ear was able to recite what he had heard even before he had come to fully understand it. For the better part of his first two years in the calmecac, he encountered no unusual difficulties with the demands made upon him by the priests, and was not punished more frequently than any of the other boys. He had not even had the occasion to remember his vow to his mother until the priest in charge of his class left to fulfill a vow of his own, and Coatleztli came into his life.

Coatleztli, Snake Blood, was a priest known throughout the Tlillan for his strictness, and for the cruelty he displayed toward the boys in his care. He was a thin man, as all the priests were, but his body was hard and vigorous, for he was also Tlamacaztequiuaque, a priest who had fought alongside the warriors and had taken captives in battle. His diamond-shaped face was pitted from a childhood disease, and his long black hair was matted with dried blood, for he was in training to become a sacrificing priest in the temple of the Snake Woman. The first time Huemac laid eyes on him, he sensed that Coatleztli was a harsh and dangerous man, and that he wanted everyone to know it.

Upon taking charge of Huemac's group, Coatleztli called each of the boys to him privately, leaving Huemac for the last. From the instant he entered the room, Huemac felt the hostility emanating from the priest, and he accordingly adopted a humble stance, hooding his eyes as his mother had taught him. Coatleztli stared at him silently for a long time, but Huemac felt only the boldness and hostility, and none of the penetrating sensitivity of his mother. He is vain, Huemac thought; I can hide from him if I have to.

"You are the son of Quinatzin, the Texcocan who serves our Lord, Tlacaelel?" Coatleztli asked without prelude, and without the slightest sign of respect in his voice.

"Yes."

"His wife is Teuxoch, the daughter of the Cihuacoatl?"

"Yes."

"But your mother is his second wife, the daughter of Nezahualcoyotl of Texcoco?"

"Yes."

The priest grunted rudely. "You were born during the nemontemi, in One-Rabbit. How is it that you were not given one of the names appropriate to such a luckless birth?"

"My name was given to me by my second mother—by Teuxoch, the daughter of Tlacaelel. It came to her in a dream sent by the Snake Woman."

Coatleztli made a sound of disgust. "We do not have enough priests and soothsayers for such tasks, I suppose. And Texcocans cannot be expected to honor Tenocha customs. Why were you not sent to one of the calmecacs in Texcoco?"

"I am Tenocha!" Huemac blurted, with more force than he intended, for he felt Coatleztli sneering at his family, and no one had ever done that in his presence.

"So . . . you are impertinent, too," the priest said in an icy voice, his eyes narrowed. "You have not yet proven that you deserve to be here, Impertinent

One, and it is *I* whom you must convince. Be mindful of all that you do here, Huemac, for you have no second mother in this house. I will be watching you always, waiting for your luck to betray you . . .''

HUEMAC TURNED twelve in the year One-Reed. This was the beginning of a new cycle, during which the sign One Reed, the sign of the East, would carry the burden of the years until thirteen more had passed. It was also the sign under which the return of Quetzalcoatl was prophesied, and the possible appearance of the god was awaited with trepidation throughout the Valley. This was especially true in Tenochtitlan, since the Tenocha considered themselves to be the heirs of the Toltecs of Tula, and it was *their* kingdom that Quetzalcoatl had promised to reclaim. The shrines and calmecacs dedicated to the Plumed Serpent were cleaned and furnished with new, more splendid images, and his priests and novices began a long, penitential fast as the feast of Quetzalcoatl's birthday, the day Seven Reed, approached. The skies and winds were studied with great anticipation, and efforts were made by the high priests in all the cities to investigate omens and prevent the rise of false prophets.

In the calmecac, there was an intensive concentration on the legends of Quetzalcoatl, and Huemac applied himself to this study with a fervor born of desperation, for the torments of Coatleztli grew harder to bear with each day. The priest had begun by subjecting him to a constant stream of criticism and verbal abuse, trying to rattle Huemac and force him to slip up. When that did not provide him with sufficient excuses for punishment, he began to create them himself. He would mutter orders to Huemac under his breath, and then punish him for hearing incorrectly, or for asking to be told a second time. He would find dirt on the floor where it could not have escaped Huemac's broom, and he detected errors in recitations that would have satisfied any other priest in the calmecac. Huemac's calves and upper arms were a mass of sores from the maguey spine Coatleztli used for punishment, and since no effort of his own seemed to bring relief, he began to pray to the god for deliverance.

Along with the other boys, he studied Quetzalcoatl in all his various guises: as Ce Acatl, the Morning Star, warrior god of the ancient city of Teotihuacan; as Ehecatl, the God of the Wind; as the Plumed Serpent, son of Ometecuhtli and Omecihuatl, the god who had brought back the bones of man from the Land of the Dead, and who had found maize for the new people to eat, and had taught them craftsmanship and the counting of the days and years. But it was as Quetzalcoatl-Topiltzin, the god-king of the Toltecs, that Huemac related to him most deeply. The sad story of Quetzalcoatl-Topiltzin's corruption and his departure from Tula had been one of Huemac's favorites as a child, and in this aspect, the god was always painted in the sacred books as an old, bearded man with a long nose, bearing an uncanny resemblance to Huemac's grandfather.

It was in this aspect, as well, that the god had promised to return in the year One-Reed, so Huemac began to devote his prayers exclusively to this earthly incarnation of the Plumed Serpent. He had to hide his enthusiasm for Quetzalcoatl-Topiltzin from Coatleztli, of course, because the reason the god-king had been driven from Tula was his refusal to sacrifice men, and as a devotee of the sacrificial cult, Coatleztli felt the threat of his return most directly. In his class, the priest spent as little time as possible on the legends of Quetzalcoatl-Topiltzin, preferring to dwell on the fierce exploits of Ce Acatl instead. When he discovered, shortly before the feast of Seven Reed, that Huemac had gone on his own to one of the wise men attached to the calmecac and had asked questions about the god-king, he punished him with a severity usually reserved for major infractions, tying Huemac's hands and feet and rolling him down the stone steps in front of the Tlillan.

Huemac injured a rib in this fall and could not fully straighten up for several days. But he bore his pain, as he had all of Coatleztli's torments, in silence, like a Tenocha. He knew that the other boys were watching him, and though none would dare to take his side, he could feel that their sympathies were with him in this struggle. Coatleztli felt it, too, and grew even more openly hostile, making disparaging remarks about Nezahualcoyotl's piety and Quinatzin's loyalty in the hope of goading Huemac into an outright act of defiance. Now, the vow he had made to his mother came to Huemac's mind every day, and he performed his penance and fasting with a devastating rigor, praying to Quetzalcoatl to return and deliver him from his tormentor. According to the reckoning he had learned from the priests, there would not be another year One-Reed for fifty-two years, and Huemac did not expect, with his luck, to be alive to see it.

When the day Seven Reed dawned, though, the sky was empty of omens, and the message was brought rapidly to Tenochtitlan by runners from the eastern shores of the Divine Waters: There had been no appearance; Quetzalcoatl had not returned. A wave of relief swept through the assembled Tenocha lords and priests, and the fast many of them had undergone was broken with a massive celebration in the plaza before the Temple of Quetzalcoatl. Huemac swallowed his disappointment along with the food he had denied himself for so long, feeling the gloating eyes of Coatleztli fixed upon him. He did not know what to do now that the god had failed him; the calmecac had indeed become the House of Darkness, offering him not the slightest glimmer of hope in his misery.

It was in such a frame of mind that he went out with his group several days later, to work on the chinampas that belonged to the Tlillan. As the boys waded into the muddy water of the Lake to tend and repair the floating garden plots, Coatleztli squatted on the bank above them, giving instructions. Then he stopped and suddenly began reciting the legend of the temptation of Quetzalcoatl-Topiltzin. Despite his depression, Huemac forced himself to listen carefully, because the tension between himself and the priest had not lessened in any way, and he knew that this particular story had to be aimed at him.

Coatleztli spoke first of the great abundance of all the good things that had existed in the city of Tula when Quetzalcoatl-Topiltzin ruled there: the maize and cotton of many colors, the finely feathered birds, the cocoa trees, the gold and precious stones that lay everywhere. He described the splendid houses of the god-king, and told how, as the priest of Tloque Nahuaque, Quetzalcoatl-Topiltzin guarded his people, the Toltecs, with his purity and his prayers, going out to bathe in the icy waters at midnight and shedding his own blood upon the summit of the mountain. When he reached the part of the story where the three sorcerers, led by Tezcatlipoca, came to corrupt Quetzalcoatl-Topiltzin in his House of Feathers, Coatleztli began to question the boys and call on them to recite.

"And why did the sorcerers decide to drive the priest from the city of Tula?" he demanded of one of the smaller boys, who made no attempt to hide his fear at being called on. "Why did they give him the octli and make him drunk?"

"Because he would not sacrifice men to the gods," the boy said in a choked voice. "But only birds, butterflies, and serpents."

"Only birds, butterflies, and serpents!" Coatleztli repeated scornfully. "Is it any wonder, then, that the sorcerers came against him, and that he fell before their trickery? Could he have been so easily tempted, if he had not offended the gods? Should we mourn his fall, then, and wish for his return? Or should we not instead celebrate the triumph of Tezcatlipoca?"

The boys applied themselves to their work, avoiding the eyes of their teacher, for they had no answers to such questions. They had never heard the god-king described in such scornful terms, and it disturbed them, and made them worry about what was coming next. But Coatleztli did not seem to want an answer; he seemed merely angry, and not to be crossed. Huemac, especially, felt this, and he gathered his wits for the turn that would surely come to him.

The telling of the legend went on, with different boys describing how Quetzalcoatl-Topiltzin had been corrupted with drink and made to lie down with his own sister, and how the disgraced priest had then buried all his treasures and departed from Tula, sending away all the beautiful birds and leaving the land devastated behind him. Coatleztli had grown increasingly impatient as the story progressed, and finally he pointed at Huemac, who stood knee-deep in the muddy water.

"*You,*" he said rudely, avoiding the use of Huemac's name as he always did. "You recite the rest."

Blinking up at the man on the bank, Huemac sent a swift, silent prayer to the Plumed Serpent, begging him to guide his tongue and not let him falter in his recitation. Then he reminded himself that he knew this story as well as any other, and put assurance into his voice as he spoke:

"And when Quetzalcoatl-Topiltzin had reached the mountain of the White Woman, Iztaccihuatl, he stopped and looked back upon Tula for the last time, and he began to weep. The tears sprang from his eyes; they streamed down his face, wetting his beard; they dripped onto the ground, piercing the rocks on which he stood.

"When he finally reached the shores of the Divine and Unlimited Waters, he stopped and wept again. Then he turned to take leave of those who were with him, saying to them:

" 'I must leave you here, my people. I journey now to the east, to Tlillan Tlappan, the Land of the Black and the Red. It is there that I go.'

"Then he spread his great feather mantle upon the waters, and it turned into a raft of serpents, and he placed his jewels and precious feathers upon the raft. And once more he turned to the people and spoke:

" 'I go now, but one day I will return. In the year One-Reed, the year that is mine, I or those who are my sons will come back to this place, and reclaim the kingdom I have lost!'

"Then Quetzalcoatl-Topiltzin stepped upon the raft of serpents, and was gone. Some say that his body was consumed by a great fire, and that his heart rose out of the flames and mounted to the sky, where it became the Morning Star. Others say that he sailed away on the raft, toward the east, toward the Land of Tlillan Tlappan . . ."

Huemac finished and adopted a humble stance toward his teacher, though he was sure in his own heart that he had recited the story perfectly. He gave silent thanks to Quetzalcoatl for having inspired him. Then Coatleztli spoke:

"That was incorrect," he said bluntly. "You will come to me later for punishment."

Huemac's head came up, and he could not help himself.

"How was it incorrect?" he demanded impulsively, forgetting himself completely. Coatleztli came down the bank in one stride, scattering the other boys before him.

"Do you dare to argue with me?" he cried angrily.

"I merely . . ." Huemac began, but the priest slapped him across the face with all his strength, and Huemac went over backward into the water. He had barely come to the surface when he was pushed back down and kicked in the stomach. And then kicked again, and held under so that he could not get his breath and began to swallow water. He choked and struggled to turn himself upright, but then he lost all sense of which way was up and began to drift into unconsciousness, no longer feeling the kicks and blows, no longer able to fight against drowning. A pleasant sense of release came over him and he accepted his end, and let himself go to the embracing waters . . .

Then he was jerked upright by the hair and thrown bodily onto the bank, where he lay coughing and gagging, unable to see and shocked that he was not dead. Things were said to him but he could not hear or understand, and he only knew, after a time, that they had gone and left him. His injured rib was a sharp, searing pain across his left side, and his stomach and throat convulsed periodically, dredging up bile and dirty water. He shivered continuously, digging his body deeper into the mud for warmth. You are Tenocha, he told himself deliriously, you must not die. You must live to revenge yourself upon this man.

And as the shivering began to subside and he could once again feel the warmth of the sun, Huemac suddenly remembered the words his grandfather had said to him so many years before:

"Someday, the shape of your fate will be clear to you, and perhaps you will want to run from it, or allow it to kill you quickly. That is when you must be most brave, that is when you must change your luck before it can destroy you."

Instinctively, Huemac reached for the amulet around his neck, but it wasn't there. Instead, he found the string of wooden beads, and he ran his fingers along it until he located the bead that belonged to Ome Xochitl. It was the roundest, most perfect bead on the string, and as he rolled it gently between his thumb and forefinger, he could feel his mother's dark eyes upon him. You must release me from my vow, Mother, he prayed desperately; you must free me so that I can defend myself.

Next to his mother's bead was the pointed one that belonged to Nezahualcoyotl, and beside that was the dark, pitted bead of Coatleztli. It is not revenge, Huemac told himself; this man is unholy, and he has tried to kill me. Struggling to free himself from the mud, Huemac brought himself by stages to his feet, and stood swaying on legs that shook and buckled beneath him. I will live, he vowed, and began to drag himself back to the calmecac, driven by the conviction that the time had come to change his luck.

2

A s Quinatzin approached the Temple of the Snake Woman and saw the long, low buildings of the calmecac lying beyond, he thought, as he always did now, of Huemac, and of his younger son's proximity to Tlacaelel. Quinatzin had no informants in the Tlillan, and thus had to rely on whatever information he could pick up secondhand, or whatever Tlacaelel chose to reveal to him. He had expected to be reminded constantly of his son's nearness, if for no other reason than that Tlacaelel seldom passed up an opportunity to make him nervous. And he had also thought that Huemac would surely have called attention to himself by now. Yet he had heard nothing, and on the few occasions when he had been allowed to see his son, he had found Huemac thin but otherwise well adapted to the rigors of the priest's school.

Tlacaelel's silence on this subject did not surprise Quinatzin as much as it once might have, though, for his relationship with the Cihuacoatl had been greatly affected by the enormous expansion of the power and influence of their city. The edginess of their early days had been blunted by the sheer volume of matters that required their attention. Treaties had to be signed and taxes collected, honors had to be conferred and accepted, and the vast amounts of tribute pouring into the city had to be counted, catalogued, and distributed to the proper recipients. The schedule of ceremonies and feasts to be arranged and attended was unrelenting, and in itself required the supervision of a staff numbering well over a thousand persons.

Tlacaelel relied absolutely on Quinatzin's loyal cooperation in these matters, out of necessity, and though he still had his subordinate spied upon, he was no longer so inclined to set traps for Quinatzin or those who served him. It was also true, as Quinatzin constantly reminded himself, that Tlacaelel had little need for such precautions anymore. Nezahualcoyotl had maintained his prestige within the Alliance, but he no longer had either the desire or the power to oppose the wishes of the Demon Heart. The other tribes in the Valley were so frightened of the Tenocha that conspirators could find no easy allies, and those who tried were most often betrayed by those they approached. If Tlacaelel had grown lax in his old age, it was because he knew that he had nothing to fear.

The Cihuacoatl was alone in his chambers beneath the temple, seated in front of a black curtain embroidered with silver serpents. Before him on a low serving table were bowls of food and gourds of water and cocoa. Quinatzin seated himself on the other side of the table, with his bad leg stretched out sideways and his staff on the floor beside him. Though he had been too busy to eat since the early morning, he refused Tlacaelel's offer of food and drink, knowing that some of the dishes would certainly be drugged. Expertly, of course, so that the unwary eater might never suspect what had loosened his tongue or brought the sudden fear to his heart during the conversation that followed. Quinatzin had seen many men undone by their inability to live with their hunger.

Now, he and Tlacaelel faced each other with the false frankness of old and tested adversaries. The Cihuacoatl was fast approaching seventy years of age, and his long hair, except where the ends had been dipped in sacrificial blood, was completely white. He had also become somewhat near-sighted, which dimmed the old hunger in his eyes and made him peer owlishly from behind his fierce beak of a nose. Quinatzin found his expressions increasingly hard to read because of this, as well as because, with age, Tlacaelel's moods had become more unpredictable than ever.

Trying to gauge the present mood of his superior, Quinatzin began his report on the preparations being made for the installation of the warchief Moquiuix as the new Speaker of Tlatelulco. This was the culmination of the lobbying Tlacaelel had begun long ago, but he did not seem as pleased by the success of his machinations as Quinatzin would have expected. He seemed, in fact, to be annoyed at something.

"And what do your spies in Tlatelulco tell you?" he demanded impatiently when Quinatzin had finished. "Are the Tlatelulcans impressed by their new importance?"

"I have no spies, Lord," Quinatzin said mildly. "Only friends."

"Your 'friends,' then," Tlacaelel snapped. "Has Moquiuix infected his people with his own arrogance?"

"They are proud that Moteczuma honors their warchief as they themselves do," Quinatzin said carefully. "They feel protected by the respect that exists between our leaders and our cities."

"Respect! Is this why the temple they are building to Huitzilopochtli is larger than our own?"

Tlacaelel glared at him angrily, and Quinatzin was silent, knowing that it was useless to try to reason with him when he was in this state. These fits of righteous indignation came to Tlacaelel frequently, one of the long-term effects of his exertions during the famine, from which he had never fully recovered. He seemed as vigorous as ever, and he was still possessed by those moments of demonic lucidity that placed him in complete command of everything and everyone around him. But there were also moments when he lost his sense of continuity and reacted to events with outraged innocence, seemingly unaware that he had set them in motion himself. Today, Quinatzin thought wearily, he resents the pride of the Tlatelulca; tomorrow, he will remember that their boldness suits his plans, and he will encourage it.

"And what do your friends say about a successor to my brother?" Tlacaelel asked, changing the subject so abruptly that Quinatzin could not at first see the connection. He tried not to show his surprise, though this was Tlacaelel's first recognition, before him, of the widely held belief that Moteczuma's health was failing.

"If such a time should come," Quinatzin said, "it is assumed that *you,* Lord, will succeed Moteczuma."

"What need have I of the title?" Tlacaelel asked, dismissing the possibility with a grand gesture. "Have I not always shared its powers? Have I not worn the turquoise crown, and occupied a seat equal to the ruler's? Besides, I am now too old to lead the warriors in conquest. Who is spoken of among the younger lords?"

"Iquehuac, Moteczuma's only legitimate son, is mentioned with great respect," Quinatzin said in a neutral voice. "As is your own son, Tlilpotonqui."

"And Axayacatl?" Tlacaelel demanded suddenly, and Quinatzin blinked in surprise. Then he understood the connection, and saw where Tlacaelel's righteous anger had been leading. The arrogant ascendancy of Moquiuix in Tlatelulco, which Tlacaelel had helped to engineer, was now to be used as the reason for raising Axayacatl, his arch rival, to the reed seat in Tenochtitlan. The Demon Heart has intended this all along, Quinatzin decided bitterly, yet it is his forgetfulness that allows him to be angry, and provides him with the proper excuse.

"Axayacatl is the youngest of the three grandsons of Moteczuma," Quinatzin said, knowing the uselessness of such an objection even as he raised it. "According to custom, Tizoc, the eldest, should be chosen first."

"Itzcoatl was the son of a slave woman," Tlacaelel reminded him bluntly. "Had we bowed to custom, we would not have had the man we needed to lead us against the Tepanecs."

"Axayacatl is also younger than Moquiuix, and a rival."

"The Speaker of the Tenocha has no rival," Tlacaelel sniffed haughtily, "and certainly none among the Tlatelulca. Even a Texcocan should know this. I do not know why you raise such an objection, Quinatzin. Perhaps you have spent too much time listening to your 'friends' in that city of quackers . . ."

Tlacaelel was smiling, taunting him, and Quinatzin lowered his eyes, afraid that his true feelings were showing in his face. The possibility of a war between the Mexicans distressed him enormously, and Tlacaelel's attempts to stir one up—attempts that seemed so haphazard and willful—aroused a wild, uncontrollable anger in him. He has no vision to guide him, Quinatzin thought; he does this to amuse himself.

"The Fasting Coyote will have to be consulted, of course," Tlacaelel continued blithely, indicating, to Quinatzin's relief, that the interview had reached its end. "And Chimalpopoca of Tlacopan. This is an important decision for all our peoples, and we will need their wisdom. Yes, we must be sure, in this case, to consult with *all* of our 'friends' . . ."

AT MIDNIGHT, the boys in the Tlillan calmecac were awakened by the bellowing of the conch trumpets blown by the priests who kept watch over the hours. Rubbing the sleep from their eyes, the boys rose from the floor of their chamber and went naked into the courtyard, where they stood shivering before the black waters of the sacred pool. Coatleztli came out wearing a long black robe and carrying a hand censer of smoking copal incense, and as he took his place at the edge of the pool, the boys began to chant the hymn of purification in preparation for their ritual bath. One by one, they came before Coatleztli, who waved the censer over them and spoke the words consecrating the penance they were about to perform in the name of Quetzalcoatl, who, as Ehecatl, had dominion over this day, Nine Wind. Then each boy lowered himself into the icy waters of the pool and swam to the other side, without splashing or putting his face into the water.

When Huemac's turn came, he stepped forward with his head bowed before the priest. It had been many days since the drowning incident, but this was only the fourth time he had been allowed to bathe by the healers, who were still amazed that he had survived his illness. They had given him herbal remedies and special foods, including eggs and fish, and they had made him rest and had forbidden him from bathing or drawing blood. But children born during the nemontemi were not thought to have the power to withstand an illness or injury, so even as they had seen him recover his strength, they had expected him to fail. So, too, had the boys in his class, the first time he had come to the pool after the healers had judged him fit. Huemac had felt them watching and had forced himself to go into the water like a Tenocha, even though the fear had nearly made him sick to his stomach, and he had needed to be helped from the pool on the other side.

Tonight, he felt no fear as he stepped to the edge of the pool and Coatleztli passed the censer over him. It was rumored that Coatleztli had been reprimanded by the Tepanteohuatzin, the head priest of the calmecac, for endangering the health of one of his charges, and though he had left Huemac alone since his return, they both knew that nothing was settled between them. Until tonight, Huemac thought darkly, as the priest murmured the prayer of consecration over him. But when Coatleztli was about to utter the name of Quetzalcoatl, Huemac turned his eyes upon the man and stopped his thoughts. It was a dangerous act, for Huemac had not fully perfected his use of this power, but he wanted to put Quetzalcoatl into Coatleztli's mind this night, and in a way that would make him doubt himself.

"Of . . . of . . . of Quetzalcoatl," the priest finally got out, and Huemac hastily lowered his eyes, satisfied with what he had achieved, and fairly certain that Coatleztli had not seen him staring. Then, following the rhythm of the ceremony, he stepped past the priest and let himself down into the pool. The coldness of the water pierced his skin and made him shrink into himself, but he plunged ahead without hesitation, buoyed by his triumph over the priest. He sprang from the pool at the other side and rubbed himself briskly with a towel of maguey fiber, his skin tingling from the shock of the water. He felt light-headed, and there was a slight trembling in his limbs, the result of his having fasted for the last four days. The healers would have punished him had they known he was not eating the foods they had prescribed, but he was about to risk his life in a far more important way tonight, and he had purified himself accordingly. He would have to eat something soon, but he had always been more rigorous in his fasting than was required, so he knew that he could withstand this. He was Tenocha, no matter what Coatleztli tried to make him feel, no matter what was said about his parents and his unlucky birth. Snake Blood would soon be made to know what that meant, and to regret that he had not finished the drowning he had begun.

Dressing himself in a clean maxlatl and a thin mantle of coarse maguey fiber, Huemac gathered his ritual paraphernalia and followed the other boys toward the entrance. But then he slipped down a side passageway and ducked into a little-used storage room. When he emerged, he was carrying a bundle held close against his chest, and he left the calmecac by a side entrance, using all his powers of stealth to avoid being seen.

Soon he was hurrying along the causeway, heading north in the darkness. The fast pace and the excitement in his chest made him feel dizzy and weak, and his injured rib ached painfully, but he did not slow up or stop for breath. He had a long way to go, and there was much to be done before Coatleztli arrived at his place of penance. He also did not want to risk being accosted and questioned, and made to reveal the contents of his bundle. Inside the thin piece of cloth were a ball of maguey twine, a small bundle of quetzal feathers, and a gourd similar to the empty one he wore tied to his waist. This gourd, though, was filled with octli, and like the feathers and twine, he had stolen it from the calmecac. It was sacramental octli, and if he were found with it in his possession, he would be instantly expelled from the calmecac and permanently disgraced, perhaps even killed. Huemac did not wish to change his luck in that direction, so he hurried, and kept to the shadows at the edge of the road.

As he left the causeway and entered the forest at the foot of Mount Tepeyac, he could feel the blood racing in his veins and the air erupting raggedly from his lungs, pulling on the sore muscles in his side. Blue spots appeared before his eyes and silver shadows flashed in the darkness, but he was used to these hallucinations, and did not let them distract him. Weaving his way between the tall firs, he found the path that led steeply upward, winding treacherously past deep, rocky ravines filled with fallen trees. Coatleztli was proud of his courage, and he had a reputation among the other priests as one who went far into the forest, holding his nightly vigils in the most dangerous, lonely places. But Huemac, with his ability to see in the dark, had found the place easily, and he had learned that Coatleztli returned to it every night, without deviation. It was a clearing in the trees, not far from a cliff that fell off sheerly to the rocks far below, and Huemac skirted the cleared space carefully, wanting to leave no warning signs of his presence.

Quickly, he stowed his bundle and the empty gourd beside a tree and began to gather firewood, which he was required to bring back to the calmecac for the temple fires. When he had collected a large enough pile of wood, he took the empty gourd and went hunting scorpions. These, along with spiders and other poisonous insects, were used to make the sacred paint worn by the priests in their ceremonies, and collecting them in the dark was one of the most onerous—and dangerous—duties of the boys from the calmecac. Huemac, though, had always excelled at this task, since he could see what he was doing and thus had no fear of being bitten. He had decided to hunt only scorpions tonight because he was in a hurry, and because they did not have to be brought back alive, since they commonly stung themselves to death in the gourd.

Squatting beside a broken sandstone ledge where the insects made their homes, Huemac tapped lightly on the ground and made a dry, rustling sound in his throat, calling them out of their holes. It was the sound he had heard them make themselves, a sound of threat and warning, and he had learned to imitate it perfectly during the many nights he had spent engaged in this task. When the first scorpion appeared, its forked tail lifted menacingly, he killed it swiftly with a stick. Then he repeated the tapping and the sound, summoning another from its abode. He soon had enough to fill his gourd, and retired to his place by the tree.

When he had rested from his exertions, he made a clearing between the trees, sweeping the ground clean of leaves and twigs with a fir branch. Then he squatted in the center of the clearing and faced the east. Taking a sharp piece of bone from the pouch at his side, he drew blood from his earlobes and forearms and flicked it with his fingers in the direction he was facing. But he did not pray to Quetzalcoatl on this night. Instead, as he had for the past four nights, he prayed to Xolotl, the dark twin of the Plumed Serpent, the god whose name meant both "Monster" and "Double." He was identified in some of the legends as the nahualli of Quetzalcoatl, and he was always painted in the sacred books as a horrifyingly ugly creature with enormous claws and teeth. It was said that he had accompanied Quetzalcoatl on his trip to the underworld to bring back the bones of man, and that he had nourished the first people on the milk of the maguey plant until Quetzalcoatl had found maize for them to eat. He was, besides, one of the patron gods of the tlachtli game, and Huemac had prayed to him before on this account.

But tonight he called upon Xolotl as a god of the underworld, as one familiar with the dark ways of deception and death. Send me the wind that comes from heaven, O Lord, Huemac prayed fervently, give me a vision to guide my actions and make them successful. Above all, Huemac wished to know if he should kill Coatleztli, or simply try to frighten him off, as the sorcerers had done to Quetzalcoatl-Topiltzin. "He must leave this city so that *we* can live here," Tezcatlipoca had said of the god-king of Tula, and Huemac was willing to settle for as much.

In his heart, though, he wanted to kill Coatleztli, and he only awaited the proper sign. The cliff lay somewhere just ahead of him in the darkness. If his plan worked, it would not be hard to coax Coatleztli in that direction. But the forest around him was silent, and no shapes materialized out of the ghostly, glowing lights that swam before his eyes. I am alone in this, Huemac thought, as I am in all things. It is my luck to be alone. He was keenly disappointed that his fasting and prayers had not brought him the guidance he had sought, but he was still determined to go ahead with his plan. Because he had been given no sign, though, and because he did not trust his luck, he decided that he would not try to kill Coatleztli. He would station himself here, between the clearing and the cliff, and he would drive the man in the other direction.

There was still time before the priest would arrive, and as Huemac crouched in the darkness, he pressed the pitted wooden bead between his fingers, wondering, for the last time, why the priest had chosen to make him his enemy. Coatleztli had hated him before he had even seen him, because of his blood, his birth, and his name. But he had also made clear that he hated Huemac's father and grandfather, and considered them his enemies, as well. He had hinted on several occasions that Quinatzin was a spy for Nezahualcoyotl, and was not trusted by the man he served, the Cihuacoatl. This had particularly outraged Huemac, for he was sure of his father's loyalty, and he had been told many times by Teuxoch that his father was considered invaluable by Tlacaelel, and was honored by him. Still, the fact that the priest would even dare to suggest such things had shaken Huemac's confidence, for Coatleztli was an ambitious man, and would not have risked such disrespect if he had thought it could harm him. Huemac could no longer believe, as he had when he had entered the Tlillan, that his father's and his second mother's relationship to Tlacaelel would protect him there.

But you would approve of what I do, Second Mother, Huemac thought fondly, finding Teuxoch's bead, oblong and lumpy like a jaw filled with yetl. You would approve of my vengeance, you who have taught me what it means to be Tenocha. Then he found the perfect bead that belonged to Ome Xochitl. I am sorry that I must break my vow, Mother, he thought, but this man has left me with no choice. He must leave this city so that *I* can live here.

Then Huemac bowed to the east, touched dirt to his tongue, and rose to his feet. Taking the feathers, twine, and the gourd of octli from the bundle beneath the tree, he turned toward the clearing and set to work.

QUINATZIN SAT alone beside the embers of the hearth fire, smoking yetl rolled into a long reed tube. Ome Xochitl lay on the mats on the other side of the room, asleep after their lovemaking. He had also slept, satiated and satisfied that the vigor still remained in his body after fifty-seven years. But then he had awakened from his sleep, and the anger and uneasiness had reasserted itself in his mind. A message had come back from Nezahualcoyotl that afternoon, a response to the news that Tlacaelel was promoting Axayacatl as the next Speaker of the Tenocha. The message had been unusually short and blunt:

"The conflict between the Mexica is unavoidable, no matter who is elected. This only the gods can change. I will place my son safely upon the icpalli before I die."

He has abandoned me in this, Quinatzin thought bitterly, and warns me to look after my own. Yet these Mexica, about whom he cares so little, are the people I call my own, and I have no other kingdom but theirs to leave to my sons. Soon I will be serving only one master, and that one Tlacaelel. Is that a position I would choose to leave to my son? And if we are at war with our brothers, the Tlatelulca? Is that what my fate has brought me, is that the inheritance I must leave to my children?

Quinatzin had already decided that he was going to oppose Tlacaelel in this, but he did not question Nezahualcoyotl's ability to read the future, and he could not easily disregard his warning. Nor could he fully believe that Tlacaelel *could* be thwarted, since such a thing had never happened, though many had tried. Opposing his will seemed as hopeless as opposing fate itself. But still, I must try, Quinatzin thought. I have been his captive for thirty-five years; he must kill me some time. That, too, is unavoidable, and I have always known it. Tezcatlipoca may steal back my life whenever he chooses, but I cannot be a party to this war, I cannot serve the Demon Heart against those I have learned to call my brothers . . .

"The wind!"

Quinatzin started and looked over at his wife, who was sitting up with her eyes wide open.

"The wind!" she repeated in a desperate voice, and Quinatzin crawled across the room to her, dragging his bad leg behind him. When he touched her hand and she turned to look at him, he could see that she had not been awake until that moment.

"You said 'the wind.' 'The wind,'" he repeated gently, as Ome Xochitl continued to stare at him dazedly. "Were you dreaming of this?"

"It is Huemac," she announced abruptly. "He is in danger. There were serpents, and a great wind . . ."

"It is all this talk of Quetzalcoatl," Quinatzin said to calm her. "Was not Huemac full of this the last time he was allowed to visit you?"

Ome Xochitl shook her head impatiently, rejecting his attempt at reasonableness. She sat with her upper body bent forward and her head cocked to one side, as if listening, or trying to remember.

"It is too late," she said at last. "It cannot be prevented."

"What?" Quinatzin demanded, finding such a statement thoroughly alarming in his present state of mind.

"I am not sure. Whatever it is that threatens him."

"Shall I go to the calmecac and inquire?"

"No," Ome Xochitl said decisively. "We will know soon enough if he has come to harm. But we must pray for him," she added, and began to dress herself. Quinatzin thought a moment and found the idea agreeable.

"To whom shall we pray?" he asked over his shoulder, as he preceded her into the courtyard.

"To Quetzalcoatl," Ome Xochitl said. "To Ehecatl, the God of the Wind . . ."

THE GOURD of octli lay on a bed of fir branches in the center of the clearing; tied around its neck were the quetzal feathers that Huemac had stolen from the feather workers who made vestments in the calmecac. Huemac himself crouched behind a low thicket at the edge of the clearing, between it and the cliff to the east. From the tree next to his right hand, a series of taut lines ran off into the foliage in several directions, tripwires that he planned to cut with his flint knife when the time came. He licked his lips anxiously, feeling the tight dryness in his throat and wishing he had thought to bring some water with him. So much depended on the success of his voices, and he did not know how long he could make the call of the rattlesnake before faltering. It became hard to throw his voice, as well, when his throat was too dry, and it was essential that Coatleztli not be able to determine where the voices were coming from.

Huemac had not allowed himself to question his plan before this. It had come to him gradually over the course of the last three nights, as he had hidden here in the darkness, spying on the priest at his prayers. He had seen how sensitive Coatleztli was to sounds and movements in the dark, and he had heard the priest weeping and crying aloud to the gods, as if they had spoken to him directly. Huemac had known then that his voices would work, and Coatleztli had himself provided the final inspiration by revealing the superstitious fear that snakes aroused in him. He had disturbed a rattlesnake on the trail the night before and had immediately fallen to his knees, calling out Quetzalcoatl's name in terror. Had the snake chosen to strike rather than to slither off into the undergrowth, Coatleztli would not have tried to avoid its bite.

But will he drink the octli? Huemac wondered now, as the time approached and his nervousness grew. To a priest such as Coatleztli, the breaking of a vow would have to be more terrifying than the bite of the deadliest serpent. Huemac would have to convince him that it was the voice of the god commanding him, and he was beginning to question the arrogance that had allowed him to assume he possessed such power. But then he heard the first sound, which came to his ears like an explosion, sending shock waves through his body. He stopped breathing, then forced his lungs to work, measuring the distance in his mind as the footsteps came closer. It is in the hands of the gods now, he thought; I cannot turn back.

After what seemed an interminable time, he saw the priest coming through the trees, and just as Coatleztli stepped into the clearing, Huemac slashed through the lowest line with his knife, and the foliage next to the priest seemed to leap upward and out at him. Coatleztli jumped sideways in fright, only to jump forward again when Huemac filled the air behind him with the loud, paralyzing buzz of the rattlesnake. Huemac swept the sound completely around the circle, increasing the volume as he went and making the branches overhead leap and bounce with the swing of his knife. Coatleztli stood frozen in one spot, not daring to move. Huemac ceased rattling and sent a hissing sound coiling across the clearing, forming the undulations with his tongue. Then he spoke, in a voice as large as Tezcatl's and as rock-hard as his mother's when she was angry:

"DRINK FROM THE GOURD!"

Coatleztli stared around him and finally spied the gourd on its bed of branches. He lifted it gingerly and removed the reed stopper, but did not drink. Huemac cut his second-to-last line and swept the rattle halfway around the clearing, feeling the strain on his throat. He could not do much more of this. The priest put the gourd to his lips, then lowered it again.

"It is octli!" he cried fearfully. "I am forbidden!"

Huemac cut the last line and hissed loudly as the branches swished overhead. Then he put everything he had into his voice, because he knew that he could not afford to argue:

"IT IS SACRED OCTLI! YOU MUST DRINK!!"

Huemac's throat and palate felt raw, and he did not think he had the strength left to rattle. Coatleztli again raised the gourd to his lips, but then fell to his knees and began sobbing.

"Can it be you, O Lord?" he cried. "Do you command it?"

"DRINK!" Huemac croaked, but there was no echo in his voice, and Coatleztli looked up uncertainly, staring in the direction where Huemac lay hiding. I am finished, Huemac thought despairingly; my luck has finished me.

But suddenly there was a great rushing sound, and Huemac felt a strange tingling in his midsection as a powerful gust of wind blew over him, flattening the trees and scattering leaves across the clearing. In his first fright, Huemac could think of nothing, and stared about in bewilderment. When his eyes fell upon the priest, he did not recognize him immediately. Coatleztli was kneeling with one arm across his eyes, his long hair tossing around his face, the gourd clutched in his free hand. Huemac felt the tingling in his stomach grow stronger.

"DRINK!" he bellowed with renewed strength, though his command was almost lost in the howling of the wind, which had torn the quetzal feathers from the gourd and sent the fir branches hurtling across the clearing. Raising the gourd over his head in supplication, Coatleztli tipped it to his lips and drank. When he had finished, he attempted to rise but stumbled sideways, and fell upon one knee. The gourd dropped from his hand and blew away in the wind.

"NOW YOU MUST GO!" Huemac shouted over the wind, no longer feeling the pain in his throat. Dust blew into Coatleztli's eyes and he groped drunkenly at his face, calling out to Quetzalcoatl to forgive him.

"Take my life!" he offered piteously. "Tear the heart from my body!"

"GO TO THE EAST!" Huemac commanded. "GO TO THE SHORES OF THE DIVINE WATERS, AND WAIT FOR ME THERE!"

The priest lurched to his feet and looked around dizzily, as the trees tossed wildly and pelted him with twigs and pine needles. There seemed to be a smile on his face as he leaned into the wind, facing the place where Huemac hid.

"GO TO THE DIVINE WATERS!" Huemac shouted, but his voice broke, and the wind tore the words from his mouth and blew them away unheard.

"I am coming!" Coatleztli cried deliriously, throwing his arms over his head, as if to embrace the wind. Then he began to run toward Huemac, who barely had time to dive out of the way before the priest came crashing through the thicket, screaming Quetzalcoatl's name as he ran blindly toward the cliff. Huemac rolled and came up into a crouch, slitting his eyes against the force of the wind. He saw Coatleztli carom off a tree and run into space, still screaming, though the wind swallowed all sounds as the priest plunged to his death.

Then Huemac was alone with the raging wind, which seemed to pull at him, urging him toward the cliff. In a panic, he turned and ran, out across the clearing and into the forest on the other side, oblivious to the branches that slapped at his face and clawed at his legs. Then he tripped over a root and fell heavily to the ground, and lost consciousness.

WHEN HE awoke, later, he remembered instantly all that had happened. I have killed him, he thought, I and the wind. Yet he felt no dread at the thought, even though he knew that he would be suspected and probably questioned. He sat up and again felt the tingling in his stomach, which made him realize that he was hungry, ravenously hungry. Reaching into the pouch at his side, he found the maize cakes he had saved during his fast. They were stale and crumbled in his fingers, but they were the most delicious food he had ever eaten, and he finished them to the last crumb, feeling strength flowing back into his body. Somehow, his throat was neither dry nor sore, and when he stood up, he discovered that his rib no longer caused him pain or hampered his movements.

The night air was very still when he once again ventured out into the clearing, searching its perimeter until he found all the quetzal feathers and then the empty octli gourd, which was wedged tightly against the roots of a large fir. Then he removed the strings he had tied around the tree trunk and gathered the pieces of twine that hung from the branches overhead, and buried them along with the feathers beneath a bush. He did this coldly and methodically, with a self-possession that amazed him, since in his mind he knew that he should get away from this place as soon as possible. But the fears in his mind did not affect him as powerfully as the tingling in his midsection, which made him feel that he was floating, and that all his actions occurred in slow motion.

When he had tucked his flint knife back into his pouch and secured the gourd of scorpions to his waist, he took the octli gourd and walked to the cliff's edge. Far below, he could see a dark figure draped limply over the rocks, but though the drop was sheer, he experienced no vertigo.

"I did not intend to kill you, Snake Blood," Huemac said aloud, in a voice so cold it did not seem to be his own. "But in my heart, I desired your death. It is my luck, and yours, that the gods have ignored my intentions and heeded my desires."

Then he threw the empty gourd down after the body, shouldered his load of firewood, and started back to the calmecac.

3

I N the year Two Flint-Knife, Moteczuma Ilhuicamina, the Angry Lord Who Shoots at the Skies, died in the twenty-eighth year of his reign. Though his death was not sudden or unexpected, it had a profound effect on the people of Tenochtitlan, who had relied on this stern one to carry the burdens of the Speaker for so many years. The ceremonies of mourning went on for eighty days and involved all the inhabitants of the city, so that none should forget the fierce warrior who had led the Tenocha to greatness. Tlacaelel presided over many of the eulogies and dedications himself, delivering long speeches in praise of the deceased Speaker and often weeping openly. At the end of the eighty-day period, the ashes of Moteczuma and those of the retainers who had accompanied him to the underworld, along with the treasures and regalia of the ruler, were buried with great pomp in the courtyard of Moteczuma's palace.

The extent of Tlacaelel's grief over the death of his half brother was the source of much amazement to those who served him, for they had never before seen their master incapacitated by his emotions. Tlacaelel retired to his chambers beneath the Tlillan and brooded openly over the fact that, save for Nezahualcoyotl, he was now the only one left of those who had led the Mexica against the Tepanecs. And he had become strangely indifferent to the subject of a successor to Moteczuma, doing nothing to combat the rumors circulating in the city or the factions forming in the ranks of the lords. He left the task of arranging for the electoral council solely to Quinatzin, giving him no specific instructions concerning seating or protocol, as if he were content with what custom would provide.

When the lords of the Alliance and their subjects had assembled in the council chamber, Tlacaelel welcomed them with a speech that ignored the business at hand and dwelt at length upon the virtues and successes of the past Speaker, a rhapsodic account of the conquests of the Alliance and the security of their power. Quizzical glances were exchanged in the room as Tlacaelel droned on with no apparent aim, speaking only of Moteczuma and things of the past. The Cihuacoatl ended by declining the title before it could even be offered, saying that his true place was, as always, beside the reed seat of the ruler and not upon it. Then he sat down abruptly, seeming to indicate, by his lack of a candidate, that he would be willing to accept the choice of the group.

There was a moment of stunned silence at this apparent abdication of power on Tlacaelel's part, and then all the eyes in the room turned toward Nezahualcoyotl. But the Fasting Coyote, appearing bemused, turned his honorary right to speak over to Chimalpopoca of Tlacopan, and Quinatzin could feel a wave of excitement travel through the assembled lords as the Tepanec Speaker rose to his feet. They sense their freedom, Quinatzin thought; they know who Chimalpopoca will propose, and they are thinking beyond him to their own candidates.

Expressing his deep disappointment at Tlacaelel's refusal of the title, Chimalpopoca bowed to the logic of inheritance by nominating the two who were closest to Moteczuma in both blood and age: his only son, Iquehuac, and his nephew, Tlilpotonqui, who was the eldest son of Tlacaelel. Other lords then rose to speak on behalf of one or the other, though with little conviction, because it was well known that Moteczuma himself had not endorsed Iquehuac, thinking him deficient in judgment, and that Tlacaelel had already chosen Tlilpotonqui to succeed him as the Cihuacoatl.

The floor was thus left open to the most vociferous faction in the room, those who were descended from the line of the former Speaker, Itzcoatl, and who had long resented the transfer of the title to the family of Moteczuma. These strongly put forth the names of the three young warchiefs—Tizoc, Ahuitzotl, and Axayacatl—who were the grandsons of both Moteczuma and Itzcoatl. They were also the brothers of Chalchiuhnenetl, the wife of Moquiuix, which won them the support of the small delegation of Tlatelulca in the room.

Though it was generally acknowledged that Axayacatl was the most brilliant warrior of the three, he was only nineteen years of age, and many of the white heads present were more inclined toward his eldest brother, Tizoc. Despite his tepid war record and sour disposition, Tizoc had rallied support for himself on the grounds of his greater age and administrative experience, and those who spoke for him stressed the traditional reasons for respecting the order of birth and guarding against the jealousy that could arise between brothers. They reminded the assembly of what had befallen the Tepanecs of Azcapotzalco when Tezozomoc had passed over Maxtla and appointed a younger son who could not hold his father's kingdom together.

It was a powerful argument, with all the weight of custom on its side, and the supporters of Tizoc, sensing victory, began to move the meeting toward a decision. But then Tlacaelel suddenly roused himself and rose to deliver a stirring speech on behalf of Axayacatl, claiming that it was crucial at this time to elect a bold warrior to lead the Tenocha, since the loss of Moteczuma might tempt some of their enemies and subjects to test the power of the Alliance. He cited rumors of unrest among the newly conquered Chalcans and reported, without evidence, that the Tlaxcalans were again inciting the Totonacs to revolt, painting a picture of massive incipient rebellion that was in complete contradiction to the successes he had claimed for Moteczuma earlier. The lords who had participated in the savage subjugation of the Chalca looked at one another in disbelief, knowing that none fit to rebel had been left alive in Chalco.

The loud murmurings of dissent that greeted the conclusion of Tlacaelel's speech told Quinatzin that it had not worked. A tight, queasy knot of anticipation grew in his stomach as the murmurings blossomed into open cries of disagreement, prompting angry, incoherent replies from Tlacaelel, who seemed unable to believe that he was being seriously opposed. It was the first time that Quinatzin had ever seen him lose control of an important situation, and it filled him with a wild, dreadful kind of exhilaration, something he had felt only one other time in his life, the day that he had helped to burn the temple in Azcapotzalco. Could it be that the Demon Heart had finally beaten himself? It seemed too impossible to believe, too wonderful to be trusted.

But then the chamber fell silent, for Nezahualcoyotl had risen to speak. Bowing to the lords who had spoken, he affirmed his respect for their opinions and for the frankness with which they had been offered. Yet despite his own regard for tradition, he said, he had to side with the Cihuacoatl in this instance. The work of the Alliance was not finished, Nezahualcoyotl suggested with calm authority. Let Tizoc be raised to the Council of Lords so that he might advise his brother and take his place if the time came, he counseled, but let us now elect a warrior to carry on in the tradition of Moteczuma. The silence continued unbroken after Nezahualcoyotl had seated himself, and no one rose to contradict his advice.

Axayacatl was elected in due course, and many long speeches were made recognizing his worthiness. Tizoc was made Defender of the Temple by acclamation, and Iquehuac was mollified by being named Regent of Tenochtitlan during the time that Axayacatl would be away, gathering captives for his coronation. But Quinatzin heard nothing, and could not bring himself to pay attention to the details of his defeat. His exhilaration was gone, banished by the crushing realization that the inevitable was forever beyond the grasp of his imagination, which always contrived to find hope where none existed.

When the assembly had concluded, Quinatzin waited in the hallway outside until Nezahualcoyotl left his retinue and came over to greet him. Though he bowed courteously to the king, Quinatzin made no effort to conceal the depth of his bitterness and disappointment.

"Do not judge me too hastily, Quinatzin," the Fasting Coyote said calmly. "I have reasons for what I did. I know these brothers, and Axayacatl is the best of them, and the one most open to reason."

"He is also the most impetuous," Quinatzin pointed out. "And you know of his rivalry with Moquiuix."

"Do you think that Tizoc, with his vanity and his pettiness, could abide the arrogance of the Tlatelulcan any better? I have told you, Quinatzin: The conflict between your cities is unavoidable. I prefer Axayacatl because I have influence with him, and because he is the friend of my older son Acapipioltzin, who will be the guardian of Nezahualpilli until he is old enough to rule by himself. It is essential to my people, and advantageous to yours, that there be good relations between Texcoco and Tenochtitlan until that time has come."

"And what of the relations between Tenochtitlan and Tlatelulco?" Quinatzin demanded. "I do not want to live to see war between the tribes of the Mexica."

"Then you will die trying to prevent it," Nezahualcoyotl said savagely, but Quinatzin did not flinch in the face of the king's certainty.

"I know this," he said quietly, and Nezahualcoyotl stared at him in surprise and disbelief.

"Has age taught you nothing, my friend? Do you run after your fate even now?"

"Perhaps I have pursued it long enough," Quinatzin said cryptically. "Perhaps now I can seize it in a way that matters."

"You delude yourself. Tlacaelel will never permit you such an opportunity."

"You saw him falter today. As he grows older, it may happen more frequently."

"He will never falter in striking down those who betray him."

"Then I will die bravely, as a captive should. But I must try. I cannot leave this to fate, or to other men."

Nezahualcoyotl's long face wore the anguished expression of one who saw the future too clearly, but he did not attempt to argue further.

"You have chosen," he said in a resigned voice, stroking his long chin whiskers thoughtfully. Then he looked sharply at Quinatzin. "Tell me, then: When does my grandson finish at the calmecac?"

Quinatzin stared back curiously. "Less than a year from now, in the month of the Great Feast of the Lords."

"You must send him to me in Texcoco when he is finished here."

It was stated as an order, and Quinatzin bowed automatically before the message penetrated.

"But why, Lord? He is Tenocha, he should go to the telpochcalli here."

"Here, where he is suspected of killing a priest?" Nezahualcoyotl demanded harshly. "Yes, Quinatzin, I have other messengers than yourself. Did you think that because nothing was proven, you did not need to tell me?"

"Had they found him guilty"—Quinatzin shrugged—"no one could have saved him. But they had no evidence, Lord. They suspected Huemac only because the priest had mistreated him, and because they know he is different from the other boys. Besides, the priest was a warrior; he was not a man that a twelve-year-old boy could kill."

"Are you certain that *Huemac* could not?"

Quinatzin hesitated for a long moment, and then did not reply at all.

"You have not asked him yourself?" Nezahualcoyotl asked incredulously.

"I was there when he was questioned by the Tepanteohuatzin and the other priests. They accepted his denials, and the affair was ended." Quinatzin looked up at the older man, appealing for understanding with his eyes. "I do not possess his powers, Lord, and I do not understand them. I am his father, I must believe in his innocence."

"That is why you must send him to me," Nezahualcoyotl said flatly. "I am not required to hold such illusions."

"But Lord," Quinatzin argued desperately, "he will soon be a man, and he will leave my house forever. Do not take him from me now, before I have come to know him. I have given him into the keeping of others before this; he will feel that I am sending him away because I do not care for him."

"You will have to convince him yourself that that is not so," Nezahualcoyotl said unsparingly. "But it is dangerous for him here. That priest was one of Tlacaelel's favorites, and I know, though you have not told me, that the Cihuacoatl still wishes to interrogate Huemac personally. Even an *innocent* twelve-year-old boy could not withstand that."

"Tlacaelel uses this threat only to punish me, and he has not acted on it in all this time. Nor has he spoken of it since the death of Moteczuma."

"The Demon Heart forgets nothing, and one day he will remember Huemac. If you will not protect yourself, Quinatzin, how can you protect *him*?"

Quinatzin pursed his lips and did not speak for several moments. Then he shook his head sadly.

"Perhaps it is best that you take him, after all. I have never been able to protect him."

"You will not change your mind, then, about protecting yourself?"

"I could not expect my son to respect me if I did not oppose this evil that threatens our people," Quinatzin said resolutely, and Nezahualcoyotl sighed.

"Very well, then. Do what you must, and I and my sons will aid you in whatever way we can. But use all the cleverness you have learned in serving Tlacaelel to oppose him; do not throw your life away carelessly. In the meantime, I will see that Huemac is prepared for the meeting he must one day have with this man."

"I am grateful, Lord," Quinatzin murmured, obviously anguished by the choice he had been forced to make. Nezahualcoyotl smiled sadly, and the lines deepened in his craggy face, making him suddenly appear much older.

"There is not much time left to me, Quinatzin, and I have given up trying to change the world I will leave behind. Perhaps all that we can truly change are those who will inherit that world. Send Huemac to me, and I will do my duty toward him, as a grandfather should. I will make a warrior of him, and when he asks me, I will explain to him that his father was a man whose bravery maddened him at the end, so that he dared to do battle with fate itself . . . "

FROM WHERE he lay, flattened against the top of the back wall, Huemac had a clear view of the entire courtyard. He could see Tezcatl beneath the thatched ramada, talking to a customer while he mixed glue for the mosaic mirrors and jewelry he made. A serving girl ground maize with a metate in front of the rooms on the other side of the courtyard, and Huemac had just seen a second girl leave the compound with a shopping basket over her arm. Directly below him was the garden with its avocado trees, maguey plants, and beds of flowers and vegetables, all of which were in full bloom, for the time of harvest was very near.

In the center of the garden was a shaded alcove created by trellises arched against the back wall, and through the rich green foliage of climbing roses and morning-glory vines, Huemac could make out a figure moving back and forth. He scanned the courtyard again, the sweet fragrances of the flowers mingling in his nostrils with the smell of lime paint from the wall upon which his chin was resting. He was hoping that the person beneath the trellises was Taypach-tli, but he could afford to take no chances. He had come to Tlatelulco on business for the calmecac, and just because he had concluded that business did not mean that he was permitted pleasure visits, especially not to a female who was not his mother or sister.

When he was sure he could not be observed, he lowered himself over the side of the wall and dropped silently to the ground, landing in a crouch behind a tall row of maize plants. Then he crept forward until he could see into the alcove, being careful to make no sounds. When he saw that the person there was Taypachtli, he relaxed, and felt such a surge of happiness that he did not move, but merely squatted where he was and watched.

His friend had grown much taller since he had last seen her, showing already, at the age of ten, that she would be as large and sturdy a woman as her father was a man. She was pacing back and forth in the alcove with a woven basket balanced on her head, and she was making faces as she paced. No, she is *practicing* faces, Huemac realized, as he saw her expressions go from sad to questioning to surprised in successive circuits. He could not figure out why she was doing this, but he admired the intensity of her concentration, and just looking upon her gentle, moon-shaped face again made him feel light and joyful, as if the dark loneliness that had settled into his bones was beginning to lift. Forgetting about the rules he was breaking, he rose and slowly went forward to the edge of the alcove.

Taypachtli turned at the other side of the shaded space and came halfway back toward him, then stopped abruptly, jolting the basket from her head.

"Huemac!" she breathed, smiling as she put her hands out to him. Then a worried expression passed over her face and she quickly pulled her hands back.

"But there is no festival today, you should not be here. You will be punished if we are seen alone together!"

"No one has seen me," Huemac assured her. "And you would not say that you had, would you?"

Taypachtli hesitated, then laughed softly and held out her hands again.

"You must not stay long, but I am glad that you have come to see me. It is very lonely here, with Nopalli in the calmecac."

"It is very lonely in the calmecac, too," Huemac said, and raised her hands to his face. As her fingers flickered lightly over his features, he wondered if she would feel the changes in him, the dark secrets that stirred coldly in his heart. But his skin warmed to her touch, and when she allowed her hands to linger caressingly upon his neck and shoulders, a delicious shiver passed through his body, and he had to open his eyes to stop the sudden spinning in his head. At that moment, he could not feel the darkness himself.

"You are taller and older, of course," Taypachtli said, as she dropped her hands. "And your face has gotten thinner, and harder. But you are still Huemac."

Still Huemac! He shivered again, grateful that she could not see his face, for he was not sure whether he was going to laugh or break out in tears. Still Huemac, still her friend, still someone she could trust. *No one* trusted him in the calmecac, and there were many times, when the tingling sensation came to him powerfully, that he did not trust himself. The feeling always seemed to be particularly strong when he was dreaming of doing violent things to his enemies, or when his dreams had aroused him sexually, making him think of Taypachtli and other women in a manner that was strictly forbidden by his vows. He had feared that these evil thoughts would overwhelm him when he saw Taypachtli again, and he was grateful now, and relieved, to find that his heart was clean. Though he searched himself thoroughly, he could find no trace of those deep stirrings he had come to think of as the Winds of Xolotl, the unearthly presence that had been with him since the night on Mount Tepeyac.

"Let us sit in the back, where we cannot be seen," he suggested, and led her by the hand to the rear of the alcove, where the densest vegetation surrounded a small earthenware image of Xochiquetzal, the Goddess of Flowers and of Craftsmen. Huemac was struck by the erectness of Taypachtli's posture as she seated herself on the soft bed of sawdust surrounding the image, and by the way she self-consciously lifted her chin after she had located where he was sitting.

"What was it you were doing when I came upon you?" he asked curiously.

"I am learning faces," Taypachtli said shyly. "I have often heard my father say that the face is the mirror of the heart, and though I cannot see the faces of others, still, I must show them what is in *my* heart. It is your mother who has been teaching me this."

Huemac started. *"My* mother?"

"She has come here several times with your sister, Cocatli, who barters with my father for stones and jewelry. You have seen the fine things Cocatli makes, have you not? And now she has a daughter of her own! They said that you have not yet seen your niece, Huemac, and that you have not visited your mother for a very long time. You should not treat your mother so badly . . ."

"I know," Huemac said guiltily, "but I am kept very busy in the calmecac. Once I have graduated, though, and have enrolled in the telpochcalli, then I will be able to visit them often. And you, too, Taypachtli. I will come and tell you everything I have learned, so that you will be as wise as your brother, and will not be forced to put up with his bragging."

"Will you, Huemac?" Taypachtli said excitedly. "I would like that very much. But you must go now, before my father finds you here. He would be angry that you have disobeyed the rules, and that I have not sent you away as I should."

"I will come again, if you will let me. I am often sent to Tlatelulco on errands, because of the good will there is for my father here, and because . . ."

"Because what?" Taypachtli asked, and Huemac hung his head, wishing he had watched his tongue more closely.

"Because I can use my eyes and voices on anyone who tries to abuse me," he confessed, and Taypachtli inhaled sharply.

"That is wrong, Huemac! And it is wrong to break the rules by coming here."

"I know it is wrong, yet . . . I was punished before when I had done no wrong, and the rules meant nothing then. As long as I am not caught, why should I worry about them now?"

"Huemac!" Taypachtli exclaimed, her face expressing the appropriate measures of shock and dismay that such a statement would naturally elicit from a well-bred person.

"Perhaps it is my luck that makes me this way," Huemac said, shamed by her reaction. "But I could not help myself. Surely, it cannot be so wrong to want to see my friend?"

"I will still be your friend when you have graduated from the calmecac, and are no longer bound by these rules. I will be your friend forever, Huemac . . ."

"Forever?" Huemac echoed foolishly, feeling the tears rise suddenly to his eyes. He reached out and touched her affectionately on the cheek, and her face broke into a broad, unrehearsed smile.

"And you will be mine, Taypachtli," he said solemnly, in a voice that wavered and stuck in his throat. "I am glad that I have seen you, but I will not come to you like this again. You will see: I will obey the rules, so that you will be able to think well of me the next time we meet."

"I will practice my faces for that day," Taypachtli promised. "You will *see* that I think well of you."

"Goodbye, my friend," Huemac whispered, touching her hand briefly as he rose and left the alcove. Then he scaled the wall and, with a last glance at the garden, dropped to the ground on the other side, and headed back toward the House of Darkness.

QUINATZIN was examining tribute lists in his chamber in the Tecpan when the guard informed him that his first wife was outside, requesting to see him. After seeing that the scribes who were assisting him knew their duties, he dismissed them and asked that Teuxoch be admitted. Quinatzin had expected that she would come to him soon, since he knew that she had been to see her father the day before, and that she had failed, again, in her attempt to present Huemac to Tlacaelel. He also knew that she had asked Tlacaelel to keep her visit a secret, fully believing that it was a secret her father could keep. Crafty as she was in her own ways, it would never have occurred to her that her husband and her father spied upon one another. She would not have understood why either had a need, since they had worked together in apparent harmony for over thirty-five years.

Nor had she ever been able to understand why Tlacaelel had consistently refused her requests to bring her adopted son before him. Quinatzin had never been grateful for Teuxoch's efforts in the past, but he had lately come to realize that her wholehearted advocacy of Huemac was one of the things that prevented Tlacaelel from summoning him himself. Throughout the period of scandal in the calmecac, her belief in Huemac's innocence had never wavered, and she had expressed her outrage to her father when Quinatzin's efforts had not been enough to have the investigation dropped immediately. Tlacaelel would not want her there, promoting the virtues of her adopted son, when his intention was to wring a confession from the boy. Nor could he risk an interrogation that might harm Huemac without incriminating him, for the cruelty of such a failed attempt would be impossible to explain to his daughter, who knew as little of her father's real nature as she did of Huemac's.

Teuxoch was now fifty-three years old, five years younger than Quinatzin, though her hair was nearly as white. Age had pared the flesh from her body and face, making her appear small and sparrowlike, and exaggerating the bright, prying inquisitiveness of her eyes. Quinatzin noticed that she had forsaken her yetl and whitened her teeth for this visit, and that she was wearing an embroidered Totonac skirt that Acolmiztli had given her.

"Greetings, my wife," Quinatzin said graciously. "I am pleased that you have honored me with this visit."

"I am grateful that you have received me, my Lord," Teuxoch replied, lowering her eyes modestly. "But I do not come on my own account, but on behalf of your younger son."

"What is it you wish for Huemac?" Quinatzin asked, letting her know by the studied innocence of his tone that he did not wish to hear anything he had heard before. She had spoken so vociferously against Huemac's being sent to Texcoco that he had been forced to command her silence on the subject, something he had done so seldom during their years of marriage that the shock still lingered for both of them. Teuxoch seemed to recognize this by speaking in her most humble tone, as if she had reached no conclusions, but merely wished to express her concerns.

"When he was under suspicion, I prayed that he would be found innocent, and so the priests have found him. Yet there is a cloud that lingers over his name in this city, and I fear that it will not be dispelled, but will only grow, if he leaves so suddenly after his graduation. I do not say that it is true, but there are many in Tenochtitlan who believe that Nezahualcoyotl is a sorcerer and a shape-shifter, and these same people might think that Huemac goes to Texcoco to acquire his grandfather's dark skills."

"I cannot be concerned with what some people believe," Quinatzin said succinctly. "There are many more who know him as a priest and a great ruler, and revere his holiness and wisdom. Huemac's reputation cannot suffer from such an association."

"But what of the damage that has already been done? Can it be left to mend itself in his absence, or will it not greet him upon his return?"

"These things happened to a boy," Quinatzin pointed out, indulging her argument in order to see where it was leading. "When Huemac returns, he will be a man, and he will have to prove himself as a warrior, like all the other young men. His past will not matter then; only the strength in his arm and the courage in his heart."

Teuxoch's jaw worked restlessly, but she did not reply. Quinatzin knew that Tlacaelel was one of those who believed that Nezahualcoyotl was a sorcerer, and he deduced from what Teuxoch had said that she had told her father where Huemac was going. She had probably even used Nezahualcoyotl's name to shame Tlacaelel into making his own request for Huemac, not realizing that the Cihuacoatl could not afford to antagonize the Fasting Coyote at this time, since he would need the loyalty and support of Texcoco in any clash with the Tlatelulca. Yes, she does my work for me, Quinatzin thought, as he waited for her next maneuver.

"And what was Huemac's response to this news?" Teuxoch asked finally, adopting a more personal tone as she shifted the ground of the conversation.

"I did not have much time with him," Quinatzin said in a neutral voice, recognizing that he was about to be held accountable for his lack of fatherly feelings. "He spoke the proper words of gratitude, and he asked no questions after I had assured him that he would receive his warrior's training in Texcoco, and that he would be placed with a company of warriors when he returns to Tenochtitlan. If he was disappointed, he concealed it well."

"But of course he would conceal it," Teuxoch said with a mother's certainty. "He honors your wishes too highly to do otherwise. Nor would he ever be so impudent as to remind you of your own words, the words you spoke one night in the courtyard, when you told your family that Tenochtitlan would always be their home. I mean no disrespect in reminding you myself, my husband; I think only of what might be in your son's mind."

"And what do you imagine that to be, my wife?" Quinatzin asked sternly, feeling guilty in spite of himself. Teuxoch gave a small, unassuming shrug.

"I would think that he is proud of his father's importance in this city, and yearns to follow your example. He must wonder if you know this, since you can send him away so easily. He must wonder why you do not wish to keep him by your side, as my own father has done with his sons. As Nezahualcoyotl does with *his* many children."

"Huemac will know my feelings toward him before he leaves for Texcoco," Quinatzin said brusquely, as much to himself as to his wife. "The Tecpan is no place for a young man who wishes to be a warrior. And Huemac knows that *he* could not refuse the request of his grandfather, even if I were rude and selfish enough to suggest such a thing."

"No, my Lord, *you* could not," Teuxoch assured him hurriedly, sensing that his patience was departing. "But there might be another who could be interested in taking Huemac's part, someone who could explain to Nezahualcoyotl that his grandson is needed here, and should thus be trained here."

"There is no such a one," Quinatzin said flatly, then seemed to have a second thought. "Unless . . . but no, that is impossible."

"What is it you are thinking?"

"Only your father could make such a request, but it would not be proper for me to approach him after Nezahualcoyotl had spoken to me. And I could not ask you . . . no, I could not ask you to do such a thing," Quinatzin decided severely. "A man should not send his wife to beg favors for him, even to her own father. Forgive me, Teuxoch: I was swayed by the feelings you have aroused in me with your concern, and I spoke without thinking. I will be grateful if you will forget that such an idea ever entered my mind . . . "

Quinatzin lowered his eyes, as if ashamed of his rashness. When Teuxoch did not reply, he knew that he had beaten her, which filled him with a different kind of shame. He had trapped her in her own secret, and had made her suffer the disappointment of her father's refusal for a second time, while pretending himself to be trying to please her. And of us all, he thought ruefully, it is she whose concern for Huemac is most genuine and selfless.

"I have heard nothing that dishonors you," Teuxoch said at last. "I am sorry for the time I have taken. I will leave you now to your duties."

Holding tightly to her dignity, she bowed to him stiffly and left the chamber with small, quick steps. Nezahualcoyotl is right, Quinatzin thought as he watched her go. There is no protection in innocence, however well-intentioned its source may be. And Teuxoch's innocent regard for her father, which Quinatzin had helped to maintain, had been passed down to Huemac. He must indeed wonder about my feelings toward him, Quinatzin reflected gravely, but he will wonder more when I tell him the truth about this man I have served for so long, this man who is the face and heart of the Tenocha. Perhaps I have spared my son the truth for too long, perhaps he will not be able to believe me now. Perhaps he will think me a traitor to his city and its people, and will never respect me again. But there is no escaping it: He *must* be told.

Quinatzin sighed, and made no move to call in his scribes. He sat with his head bowed, thinking hard on the words he would say to Huemac, wishing that fate had not forced him to disillusion his son at so early an age.

⊟∥ 4 ∥⊟

As the graduates filed out of the Tlillan calmecac, the boys who were remaining behind lined the steps on both sides, chanting a hymn in praise of those who had completed their vows. Huemac blinked as he emerged into the sunlight, but he kept his head high as he passed between the ranks of the singing boys and went down the steps. He was proud of all that he had learned here, and prouder still that he was alive to see this day. It did not matter now what the priests and the other boys thought of him, or what would be whispered about him after he was gone. The fact would remain, recorded forever in the folded books, that he had graduated honorably with the rest.

Led by Axolohua, the priest who had replaced Coatleztli, the line of boys proceeded toward the Temple of Quetzalcoatl, skirting the edges of the great crowds that filled the open plaza area in front of the Tlacatecco, the Temple of Huitzilopochtli and Tlaloc. It was the eighth month, the Great Feast of the Lords, and in this year Three-House, the annual festivities of Xilonen, the Goddess of the Young Maize, were being combined with celebrations in honor of Axayacatl, who had been installed two days earlier as the Speaker of Tenochtitlan. Dressed in their finest feathers and jewels, the warriors of the city danced in long lines beside the young, unmarried women, who carried ears of the new maize in their hands and wore their hair loosened to symbolize the silk of the ripening plant. Groups of singers and drummers maintained a constant rhythm for the dancers, who were surrounded six-deep by onlookers wearing garlands of flowers over their brilliantly colored mantles.

But Huemac could pay little heed to all this activity, for the Winds of Xolotl stirred strongly within him, reminding him that there was one final ceremony to be completed before he would be freed from his pledge to the calmecac. As he climbed the steep steps of Quetzalcoatl's temple, he felt the tingling spread from his stomach into his limbs, so that his muscles flexed involuntarily. Have you allowed me to come this far, O Lord, Huemac wondered desperately, only to loose these powers in me, and bring about my ruin? He felt helpless before the feelings that floated inside him, deep and restless, warning constantly of the great and unpredictable powers that could erupt at any moment.

Following the boy ahead of him, Huemac passed through the opening in the center of the serpent's mouth and entered the shrine itself, which was lit only by torches and seemed very dark after the sunlight in the plaza. Incense burned in ornate copper braziers set at intervals around the circular room, and clouds of rich gray smoke ascended slowly toward the smoke hole in the center of the conical roof. At the far end of the hall, the image of Quetzalcoatl, wearing the beaked mask and feather mantle of Ehecatl, the Wind God, stood upon a gilded altar studded with precious stones. A group of black-robed priests next to the altar began to chant as the boys lined up single file before the image of the god.

Standing beside the image and presiding over the ceremony was the High Priest of Quetzalcoatl, who was also wearing the mask and regalia of the god. After Axolohua waved a hand censer of smoking copal over them, the boys went forward in turn and knelt before the image, touching dirt to their tongues while the priest blessed them and released them from their vows, speaking in the sacred language understood only by the highest of priests. Then the string of wooden beads that each boy had worn since the day of his entrance into the calmecac was removed by the priest and deposited in the deep brazier that stood before the altar, and the boy was free to go.

Huemac stood motionless as Axolohua passed the censer over him, but he could feel, as he had for the past two years, the nervousness he aroused in the priest. Axolohua had never been able to conceal the fact that he was afraid of Huemac, and after what he had risked to change his luck, Huemac had not hesitated to use the man's fear to his own advantage. He had played on his teacher's nerves to just the right extent, so that all of his questions had been promptly answered, and he had never again been punished unjustly. He knew that Axolohua, like many others in the calmecac, would be glad to see him leave.

The image upon the altar had the body of a man and the head of a bird, with a yellow tongue and a row of sharp white teeth protruding from the pointed red beak. On its head was a conical hat painted with stripes of black, white, and yellow, and in its hands were a curved knife and a shield covered with heron and cormorant feathers. As Huemac knelt before the image, he saw the golden wind jewel hanging around its neck, and the Winds of Xolotl roared in his ears, deafening him to the words of the priest. He humbled himself and touched dirt from the floor to his tongue, praying that he might someday learn to understand the powers he felt inside of him, and come to master them before they could bring about his destruction.

When the High Priest ceased murmuring his incantations, Huemac rose and ducked his head so that the string of beads could be taken from around his neck. A surge of emotion went through him when the priest touched him, and the flesh around his neck felt suddenly cool as the beads were removed. Huemac cast a surreptitious glance at the priest and saw him hesitate, his eyes hidden behind the mask of the god. He has been touched by the powers, Huemac felt suddenly, and he senses the same in me. There had been others, though only a few, who had given him this feeling, and he waited in dread for the one who would finally confront him and demand an explanation.

But then the priest began to mutter in a different, higher voice, waving his hand several times over Huemac's beads before turning to cast them into the fire. There was a sharp, sizzling sound as the beads burst into flame, and Huemac knew, as he bowed before the priest, that it was the pitted bead of Coatleztli that had made the sound. He could feel the attention of the High Priest still upon him as he rose and turned to go, but he did not allow himself to hesitate or look back. Nor did the priest try to stop him. He thinks that I am too young, Huemac reasoned, or perhaps he respects the danger I represent too greatly to risk an open confrontation. At this point, Huemac did not care what the reason was. As he stepped out onto the platform, into the sunlight, he was only grateful that he had survived; that he had escaped at last from the House of Darkness.

THE SHORT walk to Axayacatl's palace, where Huemac was to meet his father, quickly drove all thoughts of the past from his mind. The future seemed to beckon to him from all sides: The warriors in their finery, the beautifully plumed and painted women, the flowers, the feasting, the admiring crowds— all these things spoke to him of the promise of manhood, urging him to hurry and prepare himself, for these were the rewards of the brave Tenocha warrior. Huemac's eyes took everything in eagerly, despite the pain it caused him. Even if I must leave for a while, he thought enviously, I will return to claim my share of this; I will not allow anyone to keep me away forever.

Axayacatl's palace lay outside the western wall of the temple precinct, and as he headed toward the colonnaded opening in the Serpent Wall, Huemac passed the Tlachco, the Ball Court of the Lords. A game was obviously in progress, for the long side walls of the sunken court were lined with spectators, and the sounds of their cheering and wagering carried clearly to Huemac's ears. *I* will play there, too, one day, he vowed, as he left the temple precinct and turned left toward the palace. Once past the guards and into the palace courtyard, he paused at a fountain and washed his face and neck, tying back his long black hair with a leather thong, so that it covered his ears.

The palace had been built during the year that Axayacatl had been away gathering captives for his coronation, and despite the flowers that decorated its corridors, the odors of fresh paint, wood shavings, and lime mortar still hung in the air. The main hallway, where Huemac had been told to await his father, was deserted except for an occasional guard, since the Speaker and his court were all at the Tlachco. While he waited, Huemac studied the wall paintings, executed in vivid shades of red, orange, and black, which commemorated the conquests of past Tenocha Speakers.

In successive panels, the same familiar figure was repeated: a crowned man, wrapped in a mantle, seated upon a reed seat, with the curved volutes of speech issuing from his mouth. Above each figure was the glyph indicating the Speaker's name and the symbols of his date of coronation, and listed beside him were the cities he had conquered, each delineated by the picture of a temple with flames rising from its broken roof, accompanied by the glyph that belonged to the city. The conquests of Moteczuma Ilhuicamina, whose glyph was an arrow piercing a temple, covered one entire wall.

The panel belonging to Axayacatl, Water Face, listed as his only conquest the city of Tehuantepec, which he had captured in a daring raid that had taken him all the way to the western shore of the Divine Waters, making him the first Mexican ruler to stand with his army on that coast. It was the act that had solidified Axayacatl's right to the crown and had silenced those who had persisted in questioning his age and experience. It was also an act that had inflamed the ambitions of every young man in Tenochtitlan, and Huemac was no exception. He was now fourteen years of age, and he would soon have to wear his hair in the long, single lock of the unproven, a mark of youth and inexperience that only success in battle could remove. He could not forget that his Speaker was only six years older than himself, with many campaigns ahead of him, and the same youthful urge to prove himself that Huemac felt so deeply.

Why has my father brought me here? Huemac wondered with a sudden surge of resentment. He had reconciled himself to the fact that he was going to Texcoco, had welcomed it, even, in the belief that his grandfather was the one person who could help him deal with the powers inside him. Yet he could not look forward to being a foreigner in an unknown city, and the opportunities he was forsaking by leaving Tenochtitlan at this time filled him with an aching sense of loss. His father had not explained his grandfather's request, and Huemac had not thought it proper to ask for the reason himself. But he wished now, as he stared at Axayacatl's nearly blank panel, that his father had not been so careless in arranging this meeting place, which only served to aggravate the feeling of loss.

"Greetings, my son," Quinatzin said from behind him, and Huemac turned to find his father leaning upon his staff, smiling at him.

"Greetings, my father," Huemac replied hastily, hoping that his father had not seen the displeasure he had been feeling.

"You have been admiring the conquests of our city?" Quinatzin asked, and Huemac nodded, and turned back to Axayacatl's panel.

"What city is to be next, Father?"

"Tlatlauhquitepec," Quinatzin said in a casual voice. "Or possibly Tlatelulco."

Huemac stared at his father in bewilderment, to see if he had heard correctly. Quinatzin stared back at him evenly.

"You have been sequestered in the calmecac, my son," he explained, "so you probably have not heard of the discord that has grown between our cities. No doubt you are unaware of the latest scandal, of the disparaging remarks made by Moquiuix concerning the manliness of Axayacatl?"

Huemac stiffened in surprise and anger, hardly able to believe his own ears.

"No, I have not heard of this," he said in a low voice, wondering how his father could report such an incredible insult with such perfect calm.

"It is true," Quinatzin continued. "I was there when he said these things, at the banquet celebrating the coronation. He spoke very loudly, for he was very drunk. Tlacaelel had seen to that."

"The Cihuacoatl?" Huemac whispered foolishly, totally confused by what he was hearing. Quinatzin nodded sternly.

"Yes, he is the priest of the Snake Woman. But in this, he serves the one called Necoc Yaotl. You have learned of this god?"

"He is the Enemy of Both Sides," Huemac answered obediently. "He is Tezcatlipoca, the Sower of Discord."

"Then you will understand why Tlacaelel saw that Moquiuix was given the strongest octli at the banquet, and why, in his drunkenness, the Tlatelulcan offered this unforgivable insult to our Speaker. There are many now, in both of our cities, who are the victim of Necoc Yaotl, and who serve him unknowingly. This, also, is Tlacaelel's doing."

"But do *you* not serve the Cihuacoatl, Father?" Huemac asked timidly.

"Not in this!" Quinatzin said fiercely, rapping his staff on the polished floor for emphasis. Then he saw Huemac's wide-eyed expression and forced himself to be calm. "As you know, my son, it was fate that brought me to this city and made me the servant of the Demon Heart. Had I chosen to do otherwise, I have been told, it would have cost me my life. Fate has been kind in sparing me this long, so that I might see my children grow and prosper. But if it is my fate now to help bring death and destruction to our brothers in Tlatelulco, I would rather die first."

Huemac stared speechlessly, seeing the deeply lined features and whitened hair of the old man who was his father, yet hearing the angry, resolute voice of a young warrior. The stringy muscles in Quinatzin's bare arms bulged from the force of his grip on his staff, and his eyes had not left Huemac's face. They were the eyes of a stranger, of a man who had revealed himself for the first time, and was not sure he would be understood.

"Is there war between our cities, then?" Huemac asked, still not certain why he was being told these things. Quinatzin relaxed his grip on the staff and adopted an explanatory tone, seeming again like the father Huemac knew, except for the frankness of his words.

"Not yet. Axayacatl would not allow a drunken remark to spoil his coronation, and neither he nor Moquiuix is secure enough in his rule to test the strength of the other. But Nezahualcoyotl has assured me that such a test is inevitable."

"Is that why he has sent for me?"

"No," Quinatzin said, and glanced briefly at the floor, as if ashamed. "No. He has sent for you because I can no longer protect you here."

"But from whom, Father?" Huemac asked in a bewildered voice. "I do not understand. If it is not the Tlatelulca . . . "

"Perhaps you will understand when I tell you that the priest who died, your teacher, was a great favorite of the Cihuacoatl." Quinatzin paused to let his words sink in, then went on: "And that Tlacaelel has shown a great interest in you ever since your name was linked to the death of the priest."

Huemac's limbs went cold and the tingling sensation sharpened to a painful edge in his stomach. Some of the priests in the calmecac, when they could not make him confess, had threatened that Tlacaelel surely could, and would. But when it had not happened, Huemac had forgotten the threat, and had assumed that he was safe. Now he saw that he had never been safe.

"I have told you these things about the Demon Heart," his father continued, "so that you would know what kind of man he is, and why his interest is dangerous to you. If you were to repeat what I have said to anyone, even Teuxoch, it would mean my life."

"I will tell no one," Huemac promised fervently, and Quinatzin smiled.

"I trust you with my life, Huemac," he said softly. "But I cannot trust myself with yours. It grieves me to have to say such a thing to my son, but I have served Tlacaelel for over thirty-five years, and I know that I am no match for him. And whatever your powers, Huemac, neither are you. Perhaps when your grandfather is finished with you, you will be. Perhaps."

Huemac bowed his head briefly, then looked up at Quinatzin with sad eyes.

"Will I see you again, Father?"

"There is no saying how long the inevitable may take before it occurs," Quinatzin said wryly. "I am an old man, but still, I do not *wish* to die tomorrow. There may be many years left to me; it will be as the gods determine. But come, you have heard all that I have to say. We are expected at the house of Acolmiztli."

Huemac nodded politely, and fell into step with his father as they moved down the long, deserted hallway, past the banquet halls and council chambers. They walked with deliberate slowness, in silence, prolonging the little time they had together.

OME XOCHITL sat alone on the edge of one of the reflecting pools in Acolmiztli's courtyard, watching her grandchildren playing a short distance away. There were seven now: six by Acolmiztli's three wives, and Cocatli's first born. None was above the age of four, but all were either crawling or toddling, confined within a loose protective circle of parents and servants, who tried to keep the children away from the cactus and out of the pools. Acolmiztli's second and third wives were seated on the other side of Ome Xochitl's pool, and across from them were Cocatli and her husband Tlacateotzin, who were standing guard in front of a thorny bed of maguey and yucca. The voices of Teuxoch and Atototl, Acolmiztli's first wife, could be heard from the back of the courtyard, where they were directing the servants who were setting out the feast.

Quinatzin and Huemac were late, and the other guests would be arriving soon. Ome Xochitl had hoped, specifically for Huemac's sake, that the family would have some time alone together. Yet she also knew how important this conversation with his father was, to both of them. She had advised Quinatzin to tell their son everything behind Nezahualcoyotl's offer, even to the extent of making Huemac fear for his life in Tenochtitlan. She did not think that less would work, since she had never doubted that Huemac had had a hand in his teacher's death, and since he had avoided being alone with her from that time forward. If he were left to draw his own conclusions, Ome Xochitl had told Quinatzin, he would take the blame upon himself, and assume that they were sending him away because they were ashamed of him.

"So, Mother," Acolmiztli said as he came up to stand next to her. "Where is this brother of mine, and his father?"

Ome Xochitl smiled at her elder son, pleased by the gentleness of his tone. Though still under thirty years of age, Acolmiztli was a wealthy and powerful man—a commander of the Jaguars and the lord of this splendid house, as well as the husband of a daughter of the ruling house of Ixtapalapa. Yet his importance had not made him arrogant or demanding, and he did not display his wealth on his person as did so many of the warrior lords. Except for a pair of golden armbands and the commander's pendent—a shield and four arrows woven in blue feathers—around his neck, he was dressed as modestly as his father usually was, in a blue cotton mantle and a pair of soft leather sandals.

"It was necessary that they talk, my son," Ome Xochitl explained, "before Huemac leaves for Texcoco."

"Yes, he is young to be leaving his family," Acolmiztli agreed. "But our grandfather will look after him, and his comrades will be his family, once he has begun his training as a warrior."

"It is not his homesickness that concerns us," Ome Xochitl said. "It is more important that he understand the reasons for his going."

"His grandfather has requested him," Acolmiztli pointed out. "What other reason need there be?"

"None, of course," Ome Xochitl conceded, and sighed. "You forget that we are talking about Huemac, though. Nothing that happens to him is simple, or easily explained."

Acolmiztli looked away, then back at his mother.

"I always forget this," he confessed. "I always wish, for my brother's sake, that he could be like the other Tenocha boys."

"He can never be that," Ome Xochitl said flatly. "And you should not wish it. For *his* sake, you should not wish it."

"But has he not survived his unlucky birth? And has he not graduated from the calmecac like the other boys? He was not an ordinary child, but must that prevent him from succeeding as the others do? I think sometimes, my mother, that you persist in seeing him as different because it pleases you to do so."

Ome Xochitl stared at him silently. "It does not matter what pleases me," she said coldly. "And I do not have to *see* him to know that he is different. He is here now."

"Where?" Acolmiztli demanded, glancing swiftly at the entrance to the courtyard to assure himself that no one had entered without his notice. Then, just as he was turning back to Ome Xochitl, he caught a movement out of the corner of his eye and stopped to see Huemac and Quinatzin enter the courtyard. Acolmiztli turned slowly to face his mother, who had risen and was staring intently at the pair coming toward them. Finally, she nodded and again looked at Acolmiztli.

"It has gone well," she said, revealing her relief. "I am sorry if I spoke sharply to you, my son."

"I should not have doubted you," Acolmiztli said apologetically. "I will not forget again."

Quinatzin and Huemac had by this time reached the group of parents and children on the other side of the pool. Acolmiztli and Ome Xochitl delayed their approach until after Cocatli and Acolmiztli's wives had finished showing off their children to Huemac, and had ceased scolding him for not having come to see them sooner. Huemac took his scolding manfully, apologizing to each of the mothers in turn and praising their children so profusely that the women were soon laughing at the extravagance of his language.

"They are like the herb-green jade, they are like the smoky blue turquoise," Huemac rhapsodized, parodying the complimentary forms he had learned in the calmecac, using a high, funny voice that made all the children laugh. When he saw his mother and brother join the group, though, he stopped clowning abruptly and went forward to bow before them.

"Greetings, my brother," Acolmiztli said. "I salute you upon your graduation from the calmecac, and I welcome you to my house."

"I am grateful," Huemac said with the proper humility. "And I congratulate you upon your success against the Zapotecs."

"They are good fighters, the people of Tehuantepec," Acolmiztli allowed modestly. "We must eat together, Huemac, and I will tell you about it."

Smiling with pleasure, Huemac bowed again. His face had sobered, though, when he looked up at his mother. He was now taller than she was, so that he could see the streaks of gray in her black hair, but the stance he assumed toward her was even more humble than that which he had assumed toward Acolmiztli.

"My daughters have already scolded you sufficiently for your negligence," Ome Xochitl said mildly, "so I will not add my voice to theirs. I am glad that you could come to us today, so that we might celebrate the completion of your vows. I return this to you as a token of your release . . . "

Ome Xochitl reached forward and Huemac stooped so that she could place the jade amulet around his neck. He looked down at the rabbit against his chest, then back at his mother. She could see the gratitude and relief in his eyes, and she knew then that he had indeed been involved in the killing of the priest, and that he had avoided her out of a feeling of guilt. But she could also tell, from his relief, that he had not acted willfully, and that his success had not hardened him against his guilt.

"This is a joyful day for me," Huemac said at last, unable to express more of his feelings before the others. Ome Xochitl nodded in a way that only he would understand and appreciate, then embraced him briefly, smiling as she let him go. Quinatzin came up and also embraced his wife, laughing when one of his grandsons twined himself around his staff and tugged. Acolmiztli detached the boy and lifted him to his shoulder.

"Now that we are all together," he announced, "let us begin the feasting. My brother must learn again what it is to eat . . . "

IT WAS dark and the torches had been lit in the courtyard before Huemac was able to steal away to a corner to be alone. His father and brother had treated him as the guest of honor, taking turns introducing him to the lords and warriors who now filled the courtyard, and Teuxoch and Atototl had stuffed his fast-shrunken stomach with every delicacy to be had in Tenochtitlan. Huemac had been enormously flattered by all the attention being lavished on him, and had listened eagerly to Acolmiztli's and the other warriors' stories of the campaign against Tehuantepec, thrilled by the details of his brother's courage and daring. But at a certain point, it had all become too much for him, accustomed as he was to silence and solitude, and he had been forced to slip off on his own.

He was glad now that he had come, though there was a while, after his conversation with his father, when he had wished that he could depart unnoticed from the city. He had felt that he now carried his father's secrets in addition to his own, and he had feared that he would be awkward and tongue-tied in the company of his brother's important and successful friends, who he imagined had no secrets like his own. He had also dreaded the meeting with his mother, fearing that she would not have forgiven him for breaking the vow he had made to her.

It was she more than the others that I feared, Huemac reflected, leaning against the palm tree that sheltered this corner of the courtyard. Acolmiztli's house and friends are impressive, and his first wife is an intimidating woman who does not approve of me, but had my mother looked at me with accusing eyes, I could not have stayed to face anyone else. He fingered the amulet around his neck, certain now that Texcoco did not mean permanent exile, and that his family here would not forget him while he was gone. Tlacateotzin, Cocatli's husband, had even encouraged him to apply, upon his return, to Tlacateotzin's company in the ward of Moyotlan, which was renowned for the quality of its tlachtli players.

Rested now, Huemac began to wander back the way he had come, studying the paintings on the columns that lined the interior walkway surrounding the courtyard. Acolmiztli had been made the Tecuhtli, the lord, of this house by Moteczuma, at the time that Acolmiztli had been made a commander of the Jaguars. It was one of the grandest in the ward of Teopan, with two stories of rooms and the enormous, flagstoned courtyard with its pools, fountains, and formal gardens. Huemac was wondering enviously if he would ever achieve such wealth and importance himself when he saw a familiar figure standing in the light of a torch fixed to the wall ahead.

Huemac had not seen Nopaltzin in almost two years, and he saw now that his friend had grown tall and handsome, his strong legs and arms already corded with veins and well-defined muscles. He has not fasted as I have, Huemac thought, to compensate for his sudden feeling of ugliness. He also noticed that his friend bore fewer scars of penance, and that his face seemed fresh and untroubled. He could tell with absolute certainty that Nopaltzin had had no experiences like his own in the calmecac.

As he came closer, Huemac perceived the man who was the object of Nopaltzin's undivided attention. He was a wiry young man wearing the jaguar-skin headdress of Acolmiztli's order, one of many such warriors in the courtyard, but the only one squatting next to the large polished bowl that sat alone upon a specially embroidered reed mat. That bowl, Huemac knew, contained the flesh of the captives Acolmiztli had taken in Tehuantepec and brought back to Tenochtitlan to be sacrificed to Huitzilopochtli. After their hearts had been ripped out and offered to the god, and their bodies tumbled down the side of the temple, the priests had cut off the arms and legs and had given them to Acolmiztli's servants, who had cooked the flesh in a stew with tomatoes, chilies, and squash blossoms. Only full-fledged warriors, the tequihua, could eat from this bowl.

Huemac felt a jolt in his stomach, and the tingling sensation became very strong as he stopped beside Nopaltzin and watched the warrior eating with his fingers from the polished bowl. Before he and his friend could acknowledge each other, though, the warrior whirled on them and rose to his feet, showing his displeasure at being observed.

"Who are you?" he demanded roughly, glaring at them from a few feet away. Despite himself, Huemac stared at the fierce jaguar's head, with its gleaming teeth and obsidian eyes, which surrounded the warrior's angry face.

"I am Huemac, the brother of Acolmiztli."

"I am Nopaltzin, the son of Tezcatl, of the ward of Atezcapan, in Tlatelulco."

"Tlatelulco!" the warrior spat, giving off a strong odor of octli. "I do not eat with quackers! Who has invited you here, boy?"

"It is *I* who was invited," a voice boomed from behind the boys, and Tezcatl suddenly appeared at his son's side. "Do you have something to say to me, my young friend?"

The warrior stared up at Tezcatl, who had straightened his aging body to its full height, his hands hanging huge and ready at his sides.

"I do not eat with those who have insulted my Speaker and my city," the warrior said defiantly, not backing off.

"Then you must be sure to avoid Moquiuix if he is here," Tezcatl replied. "*I* have not insulted Axayacatl, and I have done nothing that deserves the insult you give to me and my son."

"Do you disown your Speaker, then?" the warrior demanded rudely, and Tezcatl began to move toward him. But then Acolmiztli was between them, holding Tezcatl back with an arm as he turned to face the warrior.

"This man is my guest, Colotl," Acolmiztli said in a voice that concealed none of his fury. "You will apologize to him at once, and then you will leave my house!"

Colotl complied immediately, though his apology, uttered in a choked voice, was barely audible. As he turned to stalk off through the crowd that had gathered around him, a sudden gust of wind made the torches flicker, and Huemac hastily lowered his eyes, aware for the first time of the emotions raging inside him, and of the fact that he had trained his eyes upon the warrior. He only half-heard the apologetic words of Acolmiztli as he struggled to calm the violence in his heart, and when he was finally able to pay attention to those around him, he discovered that Nopaltzin was no longer at his side. Tezcatl was conferring privately with Quinatzin in a low voice, but his son was nowhere to be seen.

"Greetings, Huemac," Tezcatl said, looking up from his conversation. Quinatzin beckoned to his son to join them.

"Greetings, Tezcatl," Huemac said courteously, then could not restrain himself. "Where has Nopalli gone?"

"I do not know," Tezcatl confessed. "But it is probably best that he be left alone right now. As I was explaining to your father, the young men of my city are proud of their Speaker, and do not deplore his rashness as their fathers and grandfathers do. Nopalli was no doubt disappointed by my disavowal of Moquiuix."

"Your words did you honor, my friend," Quinatzin said sincerely, then smiled. "Though you have *always* had a talent for correcting the manners of the Tenocha."

Tezcatl laughed and ran one hand over the shiny dome of his head, gesturing affectionately at Quinatzin with the other.

"Did you know, Huemac, that the first time your father met me, he insulted me outrageously?"

"No!" Huemac exclaimed in disbelief, and the men laughed, looking at one another and shaking their heads at the memory.

"It is true," Tezcatl affirmed. "I was so angry that I was close to attacking him with my bare hands. Almost as close as I was to attacking that young man . . . " Tezcatl trailed off, glancing down at his hands, then over at Quinatzin, who nodded solemnly. Then he reached out suddenly and clapped Huemac on the shoulder. "But you do not want to waste your time listening to the reminiscences of old men. You have not paid your respects to my daughter."

"Taypachtli is here? Where?"

"You cannot hear her? Listen . . ."

Faintly, the sound of a chorus of women's voices came to Huemac's ears. Then the chorus finished and a lone voice took up the refrain, a high clear soprano that could not be mistaken. Huemac bowed to his father and Tezcatl.

"With your permission, I will go to her . . . "

"Go, my son, and say your farewells. A messenger has come from your grandfather. He has been in the city for the coronation, but he leaves tomorrow, and he desires that you accompany him to Texcoco."

"I will be ready," Huemac said, then looked up at Tezcatl. "Farewell, Tezcatl. May the gods watch over you and your family until I return."

"I will await that day, Huemac," Tezcatl assured him, his smile gleaming in the torchlight. "Go to Taypachtli," he said, and sent Huemac off, in the direction of the singing.

THE FLOOR of the long room was covered with sleeping children, some bundled in blankets and attended by their mothers, and others snuggled together with their brothers and sisters. The only light in the room came from wicks burning in small bowls of chia oil, but Huemac had no trouble making out Taypachtli among the other women who were sitting against the wall nearest to the doorway. The women were singing a song about Tlalocan, the green paradise far to the south where those who had died in water were taken by Tlaloc, to live forever in warmth and happiness. Taypachtli's voice became softer and softer as she sang the words of the last verse, and as the women began the final chorus, they rose silently from their places by the wall and started filing out of the room, letting their voices trail off into whispers, for all but a few of the children were asleep. Huemac stepped back out of the doorway and allowed the women to pass, noticing how the ones his own age averted their eyes shyly, and how their mothers smiled at one another when they saw him waiting. The last to leave the room were Taypachtli and Cocatli, and when they had stopped before him, Taypachtli turned her face away exactly as the other girls had done, though she did not conceal her smile.

"I will be your chaperon, my brother," Cocatli said, and Huemac laughed fondly, for his sister, though a mother herself, was no taller than Taypachtli, and certainly not as large.

"I am grateful," he said. "I would not want to meet with my friend under circumstances that were improper."

Taypachtli raised her face to him then, and held out her hands, which he clasped briefly. He thought he could detect, even in the dim light, that she was blushing, but the smile she gave him was warm and unembarrassed.

"Congratulations, Huemac," she said. "You have graduated."

"Yes, but now I am afraid I must leave Tenochtitlan. I will not be able to visit you as I had planned."

"Your mother has told me that you are going to Texcoco to be with your grandfather the king. That is a great honor. I will miss you, but I know that I will see you again."

"You must look after Nopalli while I am gone," Huemac said, "and remind him that I am also *his* friend."

"He will not forget," Taypachtli said with conviction, and Huemac smiled sadly, envying his friend her innocence.

"Taypachtli and I have made something for you," Cocatli interrupted gently. "It is from many of us, actually. Tezcatl gave us the stones and glue, and Acolmiztli contributed the leather band. It was I who made the mosaic, and Taypachtli who has given it such a perfect polish."

Cocatli held out a narrow band of dark leather, in the center of which was a round, mirror-stone mosaic of a seashell. The even, scalloped lines glittered brilliantly as Huemac turned the band over in his hands. Then he removed the thong around his forehead and tied the leather band on in its place. Taypachtli lifted her hands and he brought them to his face, closing his eyes as she examined her gift, allowing her fingers to linger over his features, taking her last look.

"Farewell, Taypachtli," he said finally, in a voice filled with emotion. "I will treasure your gift as I treasure your friendship. As I treasure yours, my sister."

Cocatli smiled and embraced him, the top of her head coming just to his chin.

"We will *all* expect to see you upon your return," she said, staring fondly into his eyes, which were wet. He bowed to both of them, and Taypachtli bowed back when Cocatli signaled her by lightly touching the back of her hand.

"Farewell, Huemac," Taypachtli said, weeping openly. "May the gods be with you in Texcoco."

"And with you, here," Huemac said, unable to look directly at either of them. Then, with a courteous nod to his sister, he turned abruptly and headed back toward the courtyard, where his mother and father were preparing to leave.

V

THE CITY
AND THE HILLS

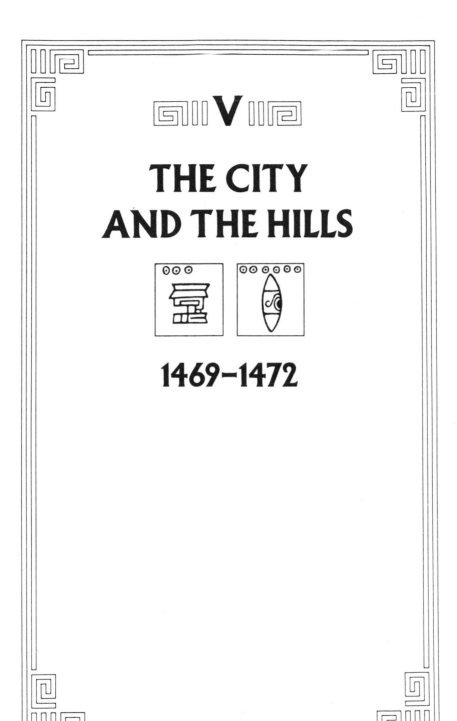

1469–1472

1

I T was not until midnight of his first day in Texcoco that Huemac was finally
summoned to a private audience with his grandfather. He was already
thoroughly exhausted from the excitement of this long day, which had
begun at dawn, when he had boarded a canoe for the trip across the Lake. He
had then spent the rest of the daylight hours on his feet, following in the retinue
of the king and waiting in the hot sun while Nezahualcoyotl paid a visit to each
of the major temples. He had been given a meal at nightfall and was then led
to his quarters in the telpochcalli, where he was introduced to the Master of
Arms, Tlaltecatzin, who would be his instructor. After inquiring in a friendly
manner about Acolmiztli, with whom he had fought in the Totonac wars,
Tlaltecatzin had explained the rules and requirements of the house, a process
that had drained the last of Huemac's energy, since the Master was a methodical man who made sure at every step that he was being understood correctly.

Despite his fatigue, though, a great restlessness came over his body as soon
as he entered the king's chamber. All his muscles seemed to be straining
against themselves, as if he had not moved them in days, and the tingling
sensation pressed upward on his lungs, causing his breath to come erratically.
Trying to ignore his discomfort, Huemac bowed low before Nezahualcoyotl,
who was seated on a reed seat covered with jaguar skin, which stood in front
of a circular screen of brilliant blue and green feathers. Yet when Huemac had
seated himself at his grandfather's command, he could not keep his body still.
His muscles flexed and cramped involuntarily, making him shift and squirm
in ways that Nezahualcoyotl could not fail to notice. Huemac was so chagrined

by this sudden loss of control that he could not bring himself to look up.

"Be still, Huemac," Nezahualcoyotl said in a voice that had a peculiar ring to it, and Huemac felt a sudden pressure upon the top of his head. Then it was as if a hand had pushed down through his skull to the very pit of his stomach, compressing all his thoughts and sensations into a point of blackness that swallowed him up. When he returned to full consciousness, there were golden spots before his eyes, and he felt light and empty, and slightly sick to his stomach. Then that, too, passed, and he felt relaxed and lucid, no longer fatigued.

Nezahualcoyotl was staring at him intently, his long, bony hands folded in his lap. When he was finally satisfied with his study, he relaxed his gaze and spoke softly:

"What do you wish to learn here?"

Huemac was totally unprepared for such a question from his grandfather, and could not think of anything for several moments. When he did speak, his words sounded childish to his own ears, and his voice seemed too high, the voice of a boy:

"I wish to learn the ways of the warrior. And ever since I was a child, I have wished to become an ollamani, a ball player. And . . . "

"And?" Nezahualcoyotl inquired, when Huemac hesitated.

"And I would like to learn the secrets of the sorcerers."

Nezahualcoyotl grunted, as if amused. "You are ambitious. Now: Tell me what you *need* to learn here."

Huemac thought carefully, understanding the distinction his grandfather was making. He remembered his conversation with his father, and realized that nothing he had learned then could be unknown to the man before him.

"I must learn how to defend myself against Tlacaelel, so that I can aid my father against him."

"Your father must act alone in this," Nezahualcoyotl informed him. "But yes, that is why I sent for you. Is that all? Or is there something more that you need?"

The tingling started up in Huemac's stomach with the suddenness of a wind-blown fire, jerking him upright where he sat. Then it stopped, and Huemac realized that his grandfather had been causing the sensation with his eyes.

"These feelings . . . " he said helplessly, and Nezahualcoyotl nodded, as if they had at last come to the true subject of this discussion.

"Tell me about the priest," he commanded. "Tell me *everything* about the priest . . . "

WHEN HUEMAC had finished telling of his interrogation by the priests of the calmecac, Nezahualcoyotl asked him to again describe the wind that had killed Coatleztli, as well as the winds he felt inside himself. Then the king sat for a long time with his eyes closed, thinking.

"You have changed more than your luck, Huemac," he said at last. "This shows plainly, to those whose eyes can see. What I cannot understand is why you survived. You are right: The wind would have killed you that night. You were only an instrument."

"Then I have committed no crime?"

"I did not say that. You were a *willing* instrument, and a necessary one. You drew this upon yourself. Tlacaelel will not fail to notice this."

"But I had done nothing to earn the priest's hatred," Huemac pointed out timidly. He did not want to appear to be avoiding responsibility for his actions, but he truly did not understand how he had drawn this situation upon himself.

"Are you not a person worth hating?" Nezahualcoyotl said sardonically. "Did you not fight him, and use your powers upon him? And have you not used your powers on other people? A warrior does not wonder why he is attacked; a ball player does not question why the ball bounces his way. They know that their powers will always attract a challenge. You should accept this, Huemac, and not burden yourself with false humility. You were not given these powers in order to remain innocent, and avoid being hated. Nor would you be seeking more power, if you truly desired a blameless life. Look inside yourself, and do not ask me again if you are worthy of being hated."

Huemac was not sure if he was being praised or condemned, but he nonetheless felt the truth of his grandfather's statement. My mother knew this about me, he realized, but she could not bring herself to say it so plainly; she thought that her vow could protect me against myself. He looked up at his grandfather, and saw that he was open to more questions.

"Do the gods also hate me? Did they make me their instrument in order to punish me?"

Nezahualcoyotl shrugged and spread his hands wide. "Perhaps they meant to warn you, which could even be a sign of favor. Or perhaps it was only because you had made yourself available. It is impossible to know these things with any exactness. Finally, we are all in the hands of Tezcatlipoca, the Decider of Fates, and he does as he pleases, he amuses himself with us. I do not think that we are worthy of *his* hatred."

The answer chilled Huemac, but he saw that it had been offered in complete seriousness, so he did not permit himself to be disappointed.

"Was it foolish of me, then," he asked meekly, "to have asked for a vision?"

"No, such requests are entirely proper," Nezahualcoyotl allowed, but then grew stern. "But you were foolish to have called upon a god as dangerous as Xolotl, and your plan itself was very risky, needlessly so. You are not strong enough yet to show compassion for your enemies; you should have aimed directly at disabling or killing him. There was no way that you could both keep your vow and break it, just as there is no difference between corrupting a priest and killing him. You should have resolved these matters for yourself, *before* asking for guidance."

Huemac hung his head briefly, feeling the heat rise to his face. But then his grandfather went on, the scolding tone gone from his voice:

"In any case, the gods have shown themselves to be capricious in regard to the granting of visions, even to those who are devoted to them. There are men who spend their whole lives seeking visions, and are never rewarded. And there are other men who, for a fee, will give you the magic mushrooms and help you find lost objects, or locate someone who is trying to harm you. There are many kinds of visions, Huemac, and there is always the problem of understanding what has been shown to you. Had you been given the vision you sought that night, would you have been capable of interpreting it, and acting upon your interpretation?"

"I had thought that its meaning would be plain," Huemac confessed, and

Nezahualcoyotl made an exasperated noise with his lips. Then he shook his head and smiled indulgently.

"I am forgetting the follies of my own youth. I can see that you are instructed in such matters, if you wish it."

"I would be grateful, Lord," Huemac said humbly.

"I have already chosen a man named Xiuhcozcatl, Turquoise Necklace, to instruct you in the uses of the sacred plants. I will inform him that he is to answer whatever questions you may have and teach you what you need to know. He is a man of great knowledge, and he can help you with these stirrings you feel inside. You have met Tlaltecatzin?"

"He has explained to me the rules of the telpochcalli, and he expressed his admiration for my brother, Acolmiztli."

"So you do not think, then, that you will be tempted to kill him?" Nezahualcoyotl asked with a straight face, then grinned wolfishly at Huemac's stricken expression. "You must forgive my sense of humor. These men will be hard with you, but they will not be cruel or unjust. There is one more, who may or may not be your teacher. His name is Icpitl, Firefly, and he is the Master Trainer of the tlachtli players. I will see that you are given a tryout with him, and if he decides that you have promise, you will train with him, and be released from your work duties at the telpochcalli. If he rejects you, you had best give up your ambitions, for he is never wrong when it comes to judging talent. He is in many other ways a thoroughly dissolute man, but in this, he has my complete trust."

"I will accept his judgment," Huemac promised, feeling a sharp pang of dread at the thought of being rejected, and an equally sharp eagerness at the thought of being trained by such a man.

"You will spend your first six months with Tlaltecatzin, and if you have progressed satisfactorily, you will then be allowed to go to Xiuhcozcatl. All your teachers will report directly to me, and I will call you to me from time to time to see for myself. Do not talk to them about Tlacaelel or the other priest; I will tell them all they need to know." Nezahualcoyotl looked at him sharply. "Do you have any questions?"

Huemac hesitated, then began to shake his head negatively, afraid that the question he wanted to ask would make his grandfather think him obtuse, or lacking in courage. But Nezahualcoyotl perceived his hesitancy and gestured for him to speak.

"Will the gods use me again?"

Nezahualcoyotl raised his eyebrows slightly, but did not seem to find the question a foolish one.

"Much will depend on your willingness to be used, which will be determined by the kind, and amount, of power you seek. But still, you *have* been marked, and there is no telling what that might mean to you in the future. You must prepare yourself for any eventuality."

A look of weary anguish passed over Huemac's face, but he bowed to show his compliance. Nezahualcoyotl nodded for him to rise, the bleak smile on his face softened by the sympathy in his eyes.

"I have given you little comfort, my grandson, but I think it is best that you know the terms of the struggle. It is hard and unrelenting, and you must not allow yourself to relax. But I will see that you are properly armed before I die, I promise you this. Go to your teachers, Huemac, and apply yourself to learning all they can teach you. We will talk again later, when your education is under way, and you can share with me the comfort of your new knowledge . . . "

DURING the first month of their training, the new boys in the telpochcalli handled weapons sparingly, learning how to repair and care for them, and how to carry them while running or climbing. Then they progressed to mastering their use, practicing individually with the sling, the macana, the bow and arrow, and the atl-atl, the board for throwing darts. During this time, their only targets were stone statues, straw dummies, and the padded shield Tlaltecatzin used for demonstration purposes. Some of the boys had already distinguished themselves by their marksmanship, and others by their swiftness afoot, but no one had yet had a chance to prove his ability to fight.

One day when it was cool and overcast, the Master suddenly paired the boys off according to their size and strength, and he issued each of them a padded helmet, a wooden shield, and a three-quarter-size macana, which had edges of soft chalk rather than the deadly obsidian. Sensing the excitement he had stirred up in the group, and seeing the ambitious way they handled the flat wooden warclubs, Tlaltecatzin made them sit and took a long time explaining the purpose of this drill, which was to be primarily defensive in nature. Then he arranged them in a wide circle and had one pair fight at a time, while he shouted instructions and pointed out things to the other boys.

"Stay low! Guard your legs!" he reminded them over and over, letting each pair slash at each other until one had been knocked off his feet or marked with the chalk.

"Huemac! Cayolin!" he called. "Begin—now! Stay low! Guard your legs!"

Huemac rushed his partner impetuously, hoping to bowl him over with sheer momentum, since Cayolin was lighter than he and longer in the legs. But he was also quicker, and sprang nimbly out of Huemac's way, dealing a blow that Huemac blocked with his shield as he went by. Then they circled and traded cautious, thigh-high blows, marking each other's shields as they probed for openings.

"A wide stance, Cayolin!" Tlaltecatzin warned. "Bend your knees! Head up, Huemac!"

Cayolin's macana clashed against Huemac's shield, sending shock waves up his arm. He swung back immediately, nearly slipping under the other boy's guard, since Cayolin had risen slightly from his crouch to deliver his last blow. But Cayolin got his shield back down in time to block Huemac's thrust, though the force of the contact sent him staggering backward. Huemac was upon him immediately, sensing his advantage and forgetting entirely the purpose of the drill.

"Stay low!" Tlaltecatzin called as Cayolin tried to dig in and fend off Huemac's attack. Huemac feinted low and to the right, straightened up as Cayolin missed with his macana, then ducked quickly to the left, stepping behind his opponent. With his shield hand, he reached up and grabbed the long lock of hair on the back of Cayolin's head, jerking him back onto his knees. With one swift motion, Huemac drew his macana across the boy's exposed neck, leaving a long white mark. Then he sprang back triumphantly and bowed to Tlaltecatzin.

"That was very clever, Huemac," the Master said dryly. "But why did you go for his throat when his legs were already exposed to you? Do you have a preference for dead captives?"

As he was saying this, Tlaltecatzin walked over to Cayolin, who was still kneeling, rubbing his neck. The boy looked up curiously when the Master held out his hands to him, then understood and surrendered his shield and warclub. Armed now, Tlaltecatzin turned back to Huemac.

"I *have* no hair to grab," he said, displaying his warrior's topknot as he advanced. "How will your trick work with me?"

There was no anger in the Master's voice, and Huemac knew that he had overstepped the bounds of the drill. But as the man came toward him, Huemac again saw Coatleztli descending the bank, and heard his life being threatened. The tingling filled his stomach and he glared at Tlaltecatzin with blazing eyes, showing no intention of giving ground. He would kill this man, too, before he would allow himself to be abused.

The first blow came whistling in knee-high, and Huemac blocked it easily with his shield. But before he could raise his own macana, Tlaltecatzin had swung again, and Huemac had to jump back to avoid being struck. Then the blows came at him one after another as the Master kept him moving ever backward, maintaining a steady, methodical pressure that had Huemac too busy defending himself to strike a blow of his own. He could tell by the shocks against his shield that the Master was swinging with only half his strength, but the placement of his blows was so relentlessly accurate that Huemac was never able to fully regain his balance. Yet he fought on stubbornly, determined not to let this man humiliate him.

"Guard your legs!" Tlaltecatzin advised calmly, even as he landed a blow that numbed Huemac's shield hand. "They are most vulnerable when you are tired, so guard them!"

Sweat stung Huemac's eyes, and his mouth and nostrils were filled with the dust that surrounded them in a stifling cloud. His back and legs were stiff with the pain of maintaining his crouch, and he was getting his shield down later and later. Finally, he could dodge no more, and with a last, desperate effort, he launched himself straight at his teacher, aiming a reckless blow at his upper body. As his macana glanced harmlessly off Tlaltecatzin's shield, he saw—with a sense of helpless frustration—the older man duck beneath him and rap him sharply on the shin with the flat side of his warclub. Then Huemac was rolling in the dust in pain, clutching his shin with both hands. Cayolin and the other boys began to cheer, but the Master cut them off brusquely.

"Silence!" he roared, and the boys obeyed immediately. "I did not do this to humiliate Huemac, but to teach you all a lesson! The purpose of warfare is to take captives, and to avoid being captured yourself. And those who practice the warrior's art most skillfully know the value of a sound fighting stance, and they rely as much on strategy as on strength and speed. They know that even the strongest warrior grows tired and careless if his opponent allows him no opening, and presses him constantly. They know that the last one standing is always he who has best guarded his legs."

Then he turned to Huemac, who stood with his head bowed, stamping his foot to relieve the pain in his shin.

"You defended yourself well, Huemac," the Master said in a kindly voice. "In that respect, at least, you provided a good example for the others."

Huemac stared at him in total amazement, unable to believe that he was not going to be punished further. *Surely,* the Master had seen the hatred in his eyes!

"Nor do I want you to forsake whatever advantage your cleverness can gain for you," Tlaltecatzin continued in his calm, explanatory way. "But you must be sound, you must know all the tricks the other warriors know before you begin devising tricks of your own."

"Forgive me, Lord," Huemac murmured, overcome with shame at how he had acted toward this man. "I forgot myself."

"Such abandon can be very useful," Tlaltecatzin said mildly, and then smiled knowingly at Huemac. "Provided you do not overmatch yourself, and forget to guard your legs." Then the Master turned back to the group and clapped his hands: "And see that the rest of you do not forget! Next!"

HUEMAC was sweeping the floor in the main hall of the telpochcalli late one afternoon when Tlaltecatzin called him over to deliver a message that had come from the king.

"You are to report at once to the Master Trainer of the tlachtli players. He is waiting for you at the Tlachco."

"The court that lies to the north of the palace?" Huemac asked uncertainly, since his knowledge of the city's geography was still vague.

"No, the great ball court, the Court of the Lords, which lies within the temple precinct. And Huemac," the Master added, staying Huemac's departure with his hand. "I wish you success in this venture, but I must warn you about Icpitl. He was once the most famous ollamani in the Valley, but he has long since squandered his reputation on gambling, women, and the herbs that madden the senses. Respect him as a teacher, as you must, but disregard his example as a man. There is no straightness in his heart or face."

Huemac studied the stern features of the Master and listened with an attentiveness bordering on reverence, for he had come to regard him as the fairest man he had ever met, a man whose honesty and judgment he trusted as completely as he did those of Tezcatl. Tlaltecatzin had entered the Young Men's House at the age of thirteen and lived there still, some thirty years later. He had never married, though his broad face was not unattractive, and it was said that he had acquired great wealth as a warrior. He lived modestly and did not gamble or womanize in public, as if always aware of the example he presented to the boys in his care. The other warriors attached to the telpochcalli considered him something of a prude, but that did not prevent them from placing their own sons with him if they could.

"My grandfather has also warned me about this man," Huemac replied seriously. "I am grateful for your advice, Master, and I will watch myself around him."

Before he left the telpochcalli, Huemac went to the image of Tezcatlipoca that stood in the main hall. The Lord of the Smoking Mirror, in his guises as Yaotl, the Enemy, and Telpochtli, the Young Man, was the patron of all the telpochcallis, both here and in Tenochtitlan. His image was as tall as a man and was made of shining black stone, though his features were painted the color of human skin. Dressed in the regalia of a warrior, he wore gold earplugs and a feathered lip-plug, and in his right hand was a highly polished golden shield rimmed with feathers, symbolizing the mirror in which Tezcatlipoca saw everything that happened upon the earth.

Huemac threw a handful of copal incense into the brazier and prostrated himself before the image. Though he had intended to follow the sober example of Tlaltecatzin and to ask for guidance and protection against the corrupting influence of Icpitl, his prayers quickly took a different turn. Be merciful, O Lord, he prayed, do not crush my ambitions and destroy my hope. Surely, it is my fate to be a ball player; surely, it is you who have raised these hopes in me. Give me success, then, let me be the best there is, before you steal back my life.

As he rose and bowed to the image, Huemac remembered his grandfather's words and realized how freely he had just offered himself for the god's use. Already, I am becoming careless, he reflected ruefully, though neither the realization nor his reflections prompted him to try to address the god in a different manner. This was a power he wanted deeply, and, as he turned away from the image of Tezcatlipoca, Huemac knew that there was no risk he would not take to have it.

THE TLACHCO and the area around it were deserted when Huemac arrived. The last rays of the setting sun bathed the plastered walls of the temple precinct in a rich, amber light, throwing long shadows toward the east. A wind from the mountains, filled with the wild, fresh scent of the forest, blew off the smoke from the temple fires and brought a chill to the air, for it was already the twelfth month, and the frosts would be coming soon.

Pulling his net mantle closer around him, Huemac made an uneasy circuit of the ball court, finding no one waiting for him and hearing no voices to indicate that anyone was around. He began to wonder if this Icpitl could be so unreliable as to have forgotten, or if Tlaltecatzin could possibly have sent him to the wrong place. He felt weak with the excitement and anxiety of being so near the ball court, and he desperately wanted to move his body before it, too, became entranced. His childhood dreams of glory seemed to surround him on all sides, tugging at his attention, pulling him away from the nervous reality of the tryout.

The Tlachco was an I-shaped structure with a long, narrow trunk and shorter open areas at each end. The external walls were brilliantly painted with pictures of the gods playing the game and were surrounded by groves of special trees: spreading palms and a tree that bore clusters of red blossoms in season. The walls were about the height of a man, and the court within was sunken to an equal depth. Huemac entered by means of a short flight of steps at the northern end, and, moving very tentatively, crossed the painted line that separated the short end area from the long confines of the main court.

He was not sure that he should be here unaccompanied, for the Tlachco was a sacred place, and had to be blessed in a special ceremony before the game could be played upon it. And there was still no sign of the Master Trainer. But as long as he was here, Huemac could not resist the temptation to examine the court, upon which he had imagined himself performing so many times. It was perhaps a hundred and fifty feet in length and some thirty feet wide, with low ledges that sloped upward at the base of the walls. The floor was painted in quarters of black, red, white, and blue, and its surface was roughened by the grooves and striations of the reliefs that had been carved underfoot. Images of the patron gods of the game had also been painted on the side walls, their shapes and colors vivid and recognizable even in the failing light: the Black and Red Tezcatlipocas, Quetzalcoatl, Coatlique, Ixtlilton, and the special patrons of the ball players, Xochiquetzal and Xolotl.

Huemac stopped short of the black stripe that divided the court in half. Halfway up each wall, in line with the stripe, was a large stone ring with a hole in its center. The left-hand ring was plain on the side facing Huemac, while the one on the right was carved with the face of a monkey, indicating it as the target for those who played on Huemac's side of the center stripe. Huemac stared at the right-hand ring, dreaming of that rare and wonderful day when he would be the one to put the ball through the ring and win the game outright, along with the mantles of his opponent's supporters. How he yearned for that day, even though it was a feat accomplished perhaps only once in a lifetime, even by the most skillful players.

Then his attention was attracted to the circular stone that was set into the floor at the very center of the court. This was carved with the monstrous, froglike image of Tlaltecuhtli, the Lord of the Earth, whose mouth was a hole that some said led to the center of the earth. His gaping jaws were reddened with the dried blood of those unlucky men who had played and lost in the ceremonial games—when the forces of the Sun were pitted against those of the Underworld—and had been sacrificed afterward. Huemac shivered at the thought of such a fate, and felt the tingling stir, deep inside him. Then he heard a familiar sound, and looked up in time to see a ball go whizzing past him.

"One!" someone cried derisively, in a rough voice that echoed off the polished walls. "Did you come here to dream?"

Halfway down the court on the other side of the stripe, a man emerged from the shadows of the western wall, appearing fat and ungainly in the thick leather padding that was wrapped around his hips and thighs. Huemac saw that he had three more balls cupped against his chest, so he backed up quickly, until they were both the same distance from the center stripe.

"Two!" the man shouted, and sent another ball flying toward Huemac, on an angle between him and the left-hand wall. Huemac reacted instantly, but his yucca-fiber sandals slipped on the smooth floor, and he could not intercept the ball before it hit the side wall. He played it on the rebound, but poorly, misjudging its velocity so that it ricocheted painfully off the point of his hip and bounced away behind him.

"Point!" the man called tauntingly, and laughed. Huemac quickly tore off his sandals and threw them after the ball, then turned to face his opponent. The floor felt rough to his bare feet, and he knew that he would pay for his traction in blood. But he also knew that he did not have many more chances to miss, and when the man called "Three!" he responded with a desperate energy that overrode all concern for his flesh.

The ball was looping straight at him, and he rushed to meet it, splaying out his right leg at the last second and catching the ball with his thigh just as it rose from the floor. His timing was perfect, and the ball sprang off his thigh with a force that sent him backward onto his buttocks. His opponent stood flatfooted as the ball soared over his head and rolled toward the back wall, and Huemac had to restrain himself from calling "Point!" on his own behalf. His thigh was throbbing with the promise of a deep bruise, but all Huemac could feel was the satisfying solidity of the shot, and the even more satisfying sensation of having scored on the Master Trainer.

"Four!" the man cried hoarsely, and sent the last ball bounding over the center line with an easy swivel of his hips. It was not hit especially hard, so Huemac had time to plant himself in its path and return it with a hard knee-shot. The return took him to the other side of the court, but also gave him time for a stationary shot, and Huemac realized that the Master was volleying with him. Having learned his lesson from Tlaltecatzin, Huemac restrained himself from attempting anything spectacular, concentrating instead on returning the ball with a minimum of effort and risk. His body was taking a pounding from the hard rubber ball and his feet were raw from skidding across the abrasive floor, and he wanted to minimize that, as well.

But then his opponent began anticipating his returns and returning the ball more sharply, drawing Huemac to the right, and in toward the center stripe. Soon they were facing one another at a distance of perhaps thirty feet, the ball going back and forth between them so rapidly that they could only block it reflexively, without the time to set up for a proper shot. Guard your legs, Huemac told himself wearily, waiting for the Master to hit one past him. For it was clear to him that the older man could continue this volleying indefinitely, so fine were his reflexes and so effortless his returns. Huemac marveled at the economy of the Master's movements, even as his own responses began to grow increasingly ragged. If I could only get a shot at the ring, he thought wistfully, despairing at ever being able to get the ball past this indomitable man.

But then the Master suddenly turned sideways and let the ball glance off his buttock. It soared in a high, lazy arc, giving Huemac the unexpected opportunity to set up for a good shot. The ball was coming down close to the right-hand wall, opening up a wide range of easy cross-court shots, none of which the other man could have blocked. Yet the positioning was also perfect for a shot at the ring. Why go for his neck when his legs are already exposed to you, Huemac remembered, in the last instant before the ball hit the floor, but he did not remember, later, making his choice. He simply put everything into the shot, aiming upward at the ring and throwing his thigh into the ball.

For an instant, it felt true, and a thrill went through his entire body. Then the ball hit off the top of the ring and bounded over the wall, out of the court. He had lost. And lost when I might have won, he thought bitterly as he sank to the floor, too drained to remain on his feet. When he was able to look up, the Master was standing over him, swaying slightly. He was an ugly man, with thick wet lips and a crooked hump of a nose. But the ugliest things about him were his eyes, which were cold and reptilian, and bloodshot. He is drunk,

Huemac realized, recognizing the sour smell of octli mingling with the powerful odors of sweat and leather.

"Tired, boy?" the man inquired without sympathy. "I was easy on you. I once killed a man who dared to play that close to me. The ball hit him in the throat, and he fell dead without making a sound."

Huemac got slowly to his feet, feeling every bruise. He found that he was nearly the same height as the Master, whose muscles had begun to sag, showing the signs of extreme dissipation. Huemac found him thoroughly repulsive, and answered without his usual respect.

"I am grateful that you spared me, then."

"Ha! They do not let me kill *boys,*" he muttered scornfully, stepping close to Huemac and looking him up and down. The stench of his unwashed body and sour breath nearly made Huemac gag, and he gasped with pain when the man suddenly grabbed his right thigh and squeezed it cruelly. For a moment, Huemac was close to striking out at him, not caring who he was, or what opportunities he had to offer. Then the man released him and stepped back, rubbing a hand across his eyes and staggering slightly.

"You will do," he said blearily. "Report to the Cillan Tlachco tomorrow at the same time. *This* one," he said, looking around him in disgust, "is reserved for the great lords, the fine *men* of our city."

Belching so loudly that Huemac jumped, the man turned on his heel and lurched off, following an uncertain line toward the other end of the court. Huemac watched him go, recalling, despite the man's personal repulsiveness, how beautifully he had played the game. And he was *drunk*. Huemac did not know what to think. He had been accepted, but by whom? And for what? He had had a chance to win easily, yet had gone for the ring, and missed. Did this man admire that kind of rashness, the very kind that Tlaltecatzin had warned him against? Huemac was too weary to make sense of such a thing. He turned and went back to find his sandals, and left it for another day to sort out the teachings of his Masters.

QUINATZIN had, of course, been formally introduced to Axayacatl by Tlacaelel, and he knew that both Nezahualcoyotl and his son Acapipi-oltzin had spoken favorably about him to the young Speaker. But he did not hurry to make his influence felt, preferring to wait until his advice would be welcomed, and not simply lost in the flood. He made himself quietly helpful and watched the young man struggle to accustom himself to the burdens of his office: to the many required fasts and sacrifices, the constant round of ceremonies and festivals, and the grave choices that were offered to him daily, along with a welter of conflicting opinions. Axayacatl was so young and strong, and his demeanor so similar to that of his grandfather Moteczuma, that few people saw how his energies were being drained. But Quinatzin recognized the signs of irritability and fatigue, and he noticed that Axayacatl was becoming increasingly short in his responses to Tlacaelel and to his brother Tizoc, neither of whom was shy about demanding the Speaker's attention. He chose to approach the young ruler in the midst of a noisy banquet, when the attention of the other guests was focused on a troup of Mixtec dancers.

He saw immediately that his patience had been worthwhile, for Axayacatl seemed to have anticipated this meeting, and he did away with the usual amenities and asked Quinatzin to speak to him frankly.

"You must have eyes and ears of your own, my Lord," Quinatzin suggested in a respectful voice. "You should not hear things for the first time from others."

"These others you speak of are the same ones who served my grandfather," Axayacatl pointed out, but there was no reprimand in his voice, and he was clearly interested in what Quinatzin had to say.

"I intend no disrepect toward them, for I am one of them myself," Quinatzin said. "But do you not feel lonely, Lord, surrounded by all these white heads?"

"It had not occurred to me to replace them. They have earned their places of honor."

"Still, others might be given a chance. Surely, you have comrades whose advice and trust you would value as highly here as upon the field of battle?"

"Perhaps," Axayacatl said thoughtfully, stroking his smooth chin and studying Quinatzin's face. "How might room be made for them?"

"Promote them, Lord. You are the Speaker."

"But they will be as ignorant of the workings of the court as I am. How could they help me?"

Despite the seeming innocence of the question, there was a shrewdness in the young man's eyes that pleased Quinatzin greatly. He is learning how to guard his choices and make them his own, he thought, as a ruler should.

"Anyone can learn protocol," Quinatzin explained calmly, certain now that Axayacatl was reading his meaning. "Perhaps I could provide teachers for them, since I am in charge of such matters. But only if you order it, Lord."

"It has just occurred to me to do so," the Speaker decided. "I will send my friends to you, Quinatzin, and you will see that they are properly educated."

"With pleasure, Lord," Quinatzin said, bowing obediently, as if he had been summoned here, and was now being dismissed.

IN THE year Four-Rabbit, the second of Axayacatl's reign, the rift between Tenochtitlan and Tlatelulco began to deepen. There were arguments and incidents in the streets and marketplaces of both cities, and acts of vandalism that each blamed on the other. Rumors of purported insults wafted back and forth between the courts of the rulers, the most harmful concerning Moquiuix's treatment of Chalchiuhnenetl, his wife and Axayacatl's sister. It was said that Moquiuix thought her ugly and mistreated her disgracefully, taking the fine mantles that her brother sent her and giving them to his concubines, leaving his wife in rags. Axayacatl was fiercely protective of his sister, who in truth was not attractive, but was loved and honored by all her brothers. When he heard that his sister was being mistreated, he had to be restrained from going to Tlatelulco himself, and only a personal message of denial from Chalchiuhnenetl (solicited secretly by Quinatzin) had prevented a declaration of war.

Quinatzin had no doubt that this rumor had been planted by Tlacaelel, since it had come to the Speaker's ears directly, by-passing the network of listeners and informants he had helped Axayacatl set up. And a counter-rumor had been started in Tlatelulco, to the effect that Axayacatl and his brothers were laughing at Moquiuix for putting up with their ugly sister at all. Quinatzin had tried to combat this lie by means of his contacts among the members of the Tlatelulcan merchants' guild, but it was reported that Moquiuix was so infuriated by the rumor that he had, indeed, begun to mistreat Chalchiuhnenetl. It seemed that Necoc Yaotl, the Enemy of Both Sides, was being true to his name, for as the rumors grew wilder, the willingness of others to believe them increased proportionately.

But while Quinatzin was still at work combating rumors and pondering how to reveal Tlacaelel's hand in them to Axayacatl, Moquiuix began to move on his own. First he established a series of public contests for the young men of his city, offering prizes to those who showed the greatest prowess with the bow and the atl-atl. And though the targets were only wooden statues and flocks of waterfowl, the true purpose of the contests was not lost on the Tenocha, who reacted with nervous anger to the sight of so many armed men so close to their city's boundaries. Then Moquiuix lost all caution and sent ambassadors to the Chalcans, asking them to side with him against the Tenocha. One of the ambassadors was Iquehuac, the unfortunate son of Moteczuma, who had been offered his father's title in return for his treachery.

Quinatzin was not present when the Chalcans brought the ambassadors to Axayacatl, and repeated the offer that had been made to them. Quinatzin only heard of the Speaker's enormous anger, and when he accompanied Tlacaelel to the council chamber later, he saw immediately that Axayacatl had subsided into a mood of cold, quiet fury. It may be the perfect mood, Quinatzin reflected, glancing hopefully at the Speaker's second brother, Ahuitzotl, who was seated three places from the icpalli. Ahuitzotl had shown none of Tizoc's jealousy toward Axayacatl, and he had recently enhanced his standing with his brother by leading the successful conquest of Tlatlauhquitepec. He was also friendly and open to suggestion, and he had eagerly taken up as his own the bold proposal that Quinatzin had leaked to him by means of the Texcocan ambassador. Only boldness would work, Quinatzin had reckoned, now that Moquiuix had initiated hostilities with such consummate clumsiness.

"What are we to do with these traitors, Uncle?" Axayacatl asked Tlacaelel, when the councillors were all seated.

"Chimalpopoca has agreed to take care of the other one," Tlacaelel said darkly, referring to Iquehuac. Then he looked toward Tizoc, who, as always, was waiting impatiently to speak. "Perhaps the Defender of the Temple has a suggestion as to how we should respond to this provocation . . . ?"

Tizoc glanced at Axayacatl, who nodded wearily. The young Speaker had begun to tolerate his brother's advice with less and less grace, since Tizoc could not make a proposal without also claiming full credit for the idea's originality, and since most of his ideas involved the avoidance of warfare, for which Tizoc had little taste. Tlacaelel always encouraged him to speak first when he could, knowing that his proposals could only make Axayacatl more receptive to fiercer alternatives.

Tizoc was a tall, thin man with a high voice and the unattractive habit of looking at the floor and clasping his hands in front of him when he spoke. But today he was inspired by his idea, and he addressed his brother with unusual boldness.

"Lords," he said urgently, "this is a provocation that we cannot ignore. You have seen how Moquiuix trains his warriors in public, and now he seeks alliances behind our backs. Are these things not proof of his vulnerability? And are not Texcoco and Tlacopan solidly on our side in this affair? I say, let us demand Tlatelulco's surrender, *now,* while it is plain to Moquiuix that he is at a disadvantage. Let us demand that he bow to our Speaker and give us hostages, or we will crush him!"

It was Quinatzin's proposal, right down to the hostages, but Tizoc had presented it in absolutely the wrong way, stressing the Tlatelulca's weakness rather than the Tenocha's strength. Had Ahuitzotl proposed it with a warrior's impetuous assurance, it might have seemed like a brilliantly simple solution, rather than a cunning but empty threat. Quinatzin looked at Axayacatl's stern face and cursed Tizoc silently.

"Are we so lacking in honor that we gloat over our enemy's weakness?" the Speaker demanded scornfully, glaring at his brother. "And where should we lodge these hostages? With the traitors we already hold?" He turned swiftly toward Tlacaelel. "What do you say, Uncle?"

"Have the ambassadors executed publicly, and send their heads to Moquiuix," Tlacaelel advised. Then he, too, glared at Tizoc. "We do not make idle threats," he said fiercely, "nor do we begin wars with our neighbors. Let them strike the first blow, but let us be ready when they do."

Axayacatl nodded with satisfaction and gestured to one of his aides to see to the executions. Tizoc left the chamber in a huff, accompanied by his retinue, and the other lords began to suggest ways that the defenses of the city could be shored up without arousing the suspicions of the Tlatelulca. The trap was being laid, and Quinatzin knew that he would not be able to warn his friends in Tlatelulco without becoming a traitor himself, and his first loyalty was to the Tenocha. He sat silently as the talk went on around him, reminding himself that he had chosen to fight this battle, and that he had known his prospects from the beginning. He fought now against his despair, telling himself that at least the war had not begun today, as had seemed possible. But he knew, in his heart, that he had little hope of preventing the conflict as long as Tizoc and Moquiuix continued to do Tlacaelel's work for him . . .

"AND HOW has my grandson progressed in his training?" Nezahualcoyotl asked the man who stood before him with his head bowed. Icpitl shrugged and shuffled his feet. He was very sober, and very uncomfortable under the disapproving gaze of the king.

"He is the best of the boys from the telpochcalli. He has a good enough build, and the instincts . . . all he needs is experience."

Nezahualcoyotl cocked his head. Icpitl seldom said more of a candidate than that he was acceptable, and it was not his nature to flatter someone for the purpose of gaining favor. Indeed, it was not in his nature to try to gain favor at all. Huemac has made an impression, Nezahualcoyotl thought, though he was uncertain if that fact pleased him.

"Is he a good student? Does he attend to your instructions?"

"He attends to the game," the Trainer said curtly. "That is all I ask."

"And what is his attitude toward *you,* Icpitl?" Nezahualcoyotl said pointedly, and the other man looked up at him for the first time, showing a glimmer of anger in his cold eyes.

"I am his trainer. He listens to what I tell him."

"Have you bragged to him about your exploits, then?" the king said contemptuously, goading him. "Does he know why you were finally barred from the game?"

"He has no doubt heard this from others"—Icpitl bridled—"but it has not caused him to shun me. Huemac and I understand each other, you see. We are both ugly, and passionate."

"There is a difference," Nezahualcoyotl said coldly. "He is not corrupt."

"I am not a priest, or his mother," Icpitl muttered, then looked up at the king with an expression that was both sly and defiant. "Would you *have* me tell him of my crimes, Lord? He may only come to respect me more, since he tells me that he is going to Xiuhcozcatl soon, to learn the plants. Perhaps that old sorcerer will give him a taste for tlapatl, too."

"Do not taunt me, you insolent dog!" Nezahualcoyotl snapped, and Icpitl hastily lowered his eyes. "I spared your life, once. Do not give me reason to reconsider that decision."

"As you wish, Lord," Icpitl said softly, straightening up to show that he was not afraid.

"Remove yourself from my sight," Nezahualcoyotl said abruptly, turning his head away as the Trainer bowed and left the chamber. Then the king gestured to one of his aides.

"Summon Xiuhcozcatl. Then inform Tlaltecatzin that my grandson is to report to Xiuhcozcatl in the morning."

Nezahualcoyotl wondered if he had made a grave error. He had foreseen that Huemac might become fascinated by Icpitl, but it had never occurred to him that the Trainer would reciprocate. That miscreant had never shown a fondness for *anyone* before this, yet he had an "understanding" with Huemac! And worse, he was entirely correct about Huemac's passionate nature. He did not say that simply to taunt me, Nezahualcoyotl thought; there was pride in his voice, and recognition, for no one had ever played the game more passionately than Icpitl. It was to heighten his passion, and not because he needed an extra advantage, that he had begun using the power herbs which had led to his being barred.

Nezahualcoyotl knew this because Icpitl had told him so, many years ago, when he was still a famous ball player and had been caught drinking the herbs before an important match. It was not the first time he had been caught, and since it was a ceremonial game, the priests in charge had asked that the punishment be death. But I pardoned him, Nezahualcoyotl thought now, because I, too, understand the yearnings of a passionate heart. Have I spared him only for this, then? So that Huemac may have a mirror in which to see the effect of a life lived *only* for passion?

Nezahualcoyotl smiled, realizing that the situation was perhaps more favorable than he had thought. Huemac would have to look into that mirror for himself, and decide whether he liked what he saw there. Icpitl could possibly be the most valuable teacher he would have here. Still, it was unquestionably best that he go to Xiuhcozcatl immediately. When Huemac returns from his apprenticeship to that man, Nezahualcoyotl thought confidently, he will at least know that there are forces in the world much larger than those which stir in his heart and loins . . .

HUEMAC REPORTED at dawn to the Petlacalco, the Royal Storehouse that was part of the palace complex. He had been told only that he was to meet Xiuhcozcatl here, and that he would be leaving the city for an indefinite period. He had been given no opportunity to raise objections, though if the choice had been his, he would have much preferred to stay in Texcoco and go to this teacher later. He felt that he had secured a place for himself in the telpochcalli, and that his spare time would be more profitably spent with Icpitl than with some old man, however wise. My grandfather must not know how successful I have been here, Huemac thought; he must think me as naïve and uncertain as when I came to him.

Expecting a white-haired old man, Huemac did not pick Xiuhcozcatl out of the crowd, and was surprised by the man who suddenly appeared before him. He was neither young nor old, perhaps the same age as Tlaltecatzin, since there were only a few streaks of gray in his long black hair. Instead of a mantle, he was wearing an old grayish-brown blanket into which he had cut a hole for his head and neck, and he wore no insignia that might have distinguished him as a warrior, priest, or administrator. Huemac might have taken him for a workman or a plain commoner, had the tingling sensation not suddenly sharpened in his stomach.

"Lord," Huemac said quickly, and made a proper, if belated, bow. When he straightened up, he found Xiuhcozcatl studying him critically.

"Take those off," he commanded, pointing to Huemac's sandals. "And that," he added, indicating the net mantle tied at Huemac's shoulder. Huemac dropped his mantle onto the sandals, aware suddenly of the bruises on his exposed body, marks he had worn with pride on the ball court. Xiuhcozcatl seemed to regard them with distaste. Then he stepped closer, and Huemac stood still while the other man examined his headband, the gift of Taypachtli.

"Good," Xiuhcozcatl murmured, then looked at the jade rabbit without touching it. "Very good. Show me what you have in your pouch."

Obediently, Huemac opened the leather pouch that was tied to his waist. One by one, he removed his firesticks, a small packet of salt, a ball of pine resin wrapped in green leaves, some copal incense, and the sharp piece of jaguar bone he used for the drawing of penitential blood.

"Keep the copal. You do not need the rest. Is there anything else?"

Huemac dropped the other items onto his mantle and removed his flint knife from the bottom of the pouch. Xiuhcozcatl stared at him in a peculiar way as Huemac handed over the knife.

"You trust me more than you know," he said, turning the knife over in his hands until its sharp point was aiming at Huemac's midsection. Suddenly, Xiuhcozcatl opened his eyes very wide, and Huemac doubled over in pain, feeling as if he had been stabbed.

"It is this that creates the stirring inside of you," Xiuhcozcatl said. "It must be returned to the place where it helped to take a life. It must be buried there, along with anything else you still have in your possession."

The pain disappeared, and Huemac straightened up warily. The knife was no longer in sight.

"I will keep it for you until you are strong enough to take responsibility for it," the teacher said. "Bring your things, and come with me."

Xiuhcozcatl spoke rapidly to one of the storehouse attendants, and Huemac soon found himself trading his fine mantle and leather sandals for a new knife and a blanket similar to his teacher's. Having Huemac hold it taut, Xiuhcozcatl cut a hole in the center of the blanket and helped Huemac slip it over his head. There was rabbit-fur thread woven into the cotton, and Huemac admired its warmth while Xiuhcozcatl again spoke to the attendant. Provisions changed hands, and Huemac stood like a bearer while Xiuhcozcatl filled his pouch with dried meat and strung two gourds of water and a fiber bag of toasted maize over his shoulders.

"Let us go," the teacher said, and started out of the building at a fast walk. Huemac hefted his burdens and ran after him.

"Where are we going?" Huemac asked, and Xiuhcozcatl answered without slowing his pace.

"Away from the city."

"Will we be gone a long time?" Huemac wondered aloud, and Xiuhcozcatl looked at him over his shoulder.

"Perhaps forever," he said crisply. "One never knows . . . "

3

THEY went north from Texcoco on a well-traveled path, passing through the cities of Tepechpan and Acolman, where the dog market was. Xiuhcozcatl set a hard pace, stopping only to point out the tracks of animals and find more things for Huemac to carry. He kept Huemac's hands filled with leaves, branches, cactus spines, and whatever else could be found along the path, advising Huemac to handle them gently and to get to know them. He also gave him small stones, which Huemac was to carry in his mouth until he had gotten to know their tastes. After he had carried an object for an unspecified time, Xiuhcozcatl would have him select a place beside the trail and bury the object along with an offering of maize and dried meat. Huemac did not know the purpose of this and Xiuhcozcatl did not volunteer an explanation, so Huemac simply did as he was told, feeling slightly absurd until he discovered that stones did, indeed, have distinct flavors, a fact that surprised him into performing these chores with complete seriousness.

On the third day, they came to the town of Teotihuacan, which lay in the shadow of the great pyramid where the god Nanahuatzin had done his penance in preparation for his sacrifice and reincarnation as the Fifth Sun. Many of the ancient temples surrounding the pyramids, said to have built by the Toltecs, were in ruins, their statuary broken and their muraled walls fading in the sun and the rain. Huemac gazed in awe at the enormous pyramids, nearly twice the size of those in Texcoco and Tenochtitlan, and he could feel the presence of the ancients in the wind that howled down the broad avenue leading away from the Temple of the Moon. He left a generous offering of meat and maize at the temple of Tlaloc, the Rain God, praying, at Xiuhcozcatl's urging, for the rains that would make the sacred mushrooms grow.

Though he and his teacher had eaten very little, Huemac had seen the stores in his pouch and the net bag diminish at an alarming rate, due to all the offerings he had made. When they passed the marketplace on their way out of town and did not stop, he felt concerned enough to ask Xiuhcozcatl if they should not replenish their supplies. His teacher looked at him in surprise.

"Have you brought something with which to trade?" he asked, and Huemac shook his head.

"No, Lord, I gave everything to you at the Petlacalco."

"Would you have me barter my blanket, then?"

"No, Lord. But surely, you are the agent of Nez—"

"Here, I am the agent of no one but myself," Xiuhcozcatl said brusquely. He pointed toward the low, brown hills that lay beyond the town. "The hills will provide for us, as they provided for our ancestors, the Chichimecs."

"Yes, Lord," Huemac said glumly, and Xiuhcozcatl stopped on the trail to face him.

"You are a city boy, Huemac, and you have been spoiled by not being made to hunt for your food. No doubt you have been taught that the hill-people are stupid savages, and that the way to hunt is as the lords of Tenochtitlan do, with a hundred servants to drive the game into shooting range!"

Huemac hung his head sullenly and did not respond.

"Your grandfather has asked me to teach you the plants, so that they cannot be used against you by other men," Xiuhcozcatl continued in the same harsh manner. "But your grandfather is not with us now. You must begin to think about what *your* interest in the plants is."

"Is it not proper to seek the visions they bring?" Huemac asked defensively, and Xiuhcozcatl's eyes lit up with scorn.

"You have spent too much time in the company of priests," he spat. "Visions have nothing to do with propriety. They come, or do not, according to the courage and intention of the seeker. What is your intention, Huemac? How great is your courage? You must know these things before I can allow you to partake of the plants' power."

Then the teacher turned, and with Huemac following closely behind, started walking toward the hills.

AS XIUHCOZCATL led him deeper into the hills, into a rough arid country where there were few clear trails and no signs of other people, Huemac began to lose track of the days. After all the years of regimentation at the hands of the priests, for whom keeping the time was a holy task, it was tremendously disconcerting to awaken each morning with no notion of what would happen that day. For a while, he was able to comfort himself with the assumption that they would soon reach their destination and his instruction in the plants would begin, and he would be able to count the days until his return to Texcoco. But the country only grew wilder and more desolate, and as his sense of being lost increased, the prospect of his return provided less and less solace.

His teacher did nothing to alleviate his anxieties, appearing to have *no* destination. They would sometimes march for long stretches without rest, then camp for two days in the same place while Xiuhcozcatl made him learn the names of all the plants and the habits of all the animals in the area. Twice it rained at night, and both times Huemac was made to leave the caves where they were sheltered and dance in the rain, chanting hymns to Tlaloc and the mushrooms until he was exhausted.

Soon their provisions were gone, and Huemac began to experience the dreadful extent of his dependence on his teacher. He could not have found his way out of these hills on his own, and the secrets of finding food and water in this hard land were unknown to him. He had no weapons other than his flint knife, and what little hunting he had done had been in forests, where his skills as a stalker could be put to full use. Here, the cactus and scrub brush provided him no cover, and the slightest sound traveled through the still desert air to warn his prey. For two days after their food had run out, Xiuhcozcatl left him to his own devices, and Huemac subsisted primarily on cactus fruit and the peeled leaves of the nopal, which loosened his bowels and gave him stomach cramps. On the third day, they marched from dawn until late afternoon, and every time Huemac ducked into the bushes to defecate, Xiuhcozcatl left him behind, so that he was forced to track his teacher in order to find him again. Finally, Huemac could stand it no longer, and he gathered his courage to complain. But Xiuhcozcatl spoke first:

"I am hungry," he announced, as if it had just occurred to him. "Perhaps you would like to get us something to eat."

"Yes, Lord," Huemac confessed weakly. "But I do not know how."

"Have you asked the hills to provide for you?"

Huemac looked around him helplessly. "I do not know the gods of these hills."

"You do not *know* any of the gods," Xiuhcozcatl snorted. "But you can *see* the hills. Make yourself known to them, Huemac; find a way to make them hear your prayers."

Huemac knelt uncertainly in the coarse reddish sand, facing the largest of the surrounding hills, which lay to the north. He looked over the rolling expanse of cactus and mesquite, tinted red by the setting sun, a landscape that mocked the churning emptiness in his stomach and the helplessness in his heart. In his mind, he saw his bones whitening on these slopes, and he began to weep at the stark loneliness of the image. Had he lived this long, and learned all that he had learned, only to die here from hunger and thirst?

Suddenly, he had forgotten his teacher and was crying aloud to the hills, begging them to forgive his ignorance and spare his life. The tears streamed down his face and he gathered them on the ends of his fingers and offered them in supplication to the hills.

"I am alone!" he cried. "I know nothing, and I have nothing! All I can offer is the water from my eyes, the precious water that comes from my heart!"

Then Huemac prostrated himself in the sand and was silent for a long time, the image of the barren hills filling his mind. Gradually, the dark shapes behind his eyes lightened and smoothed out, and he slept. When he awoke, Xiuhcozcatl was squatting across from him, staring at him calmly. It was the first time that Huemac had seen satisfaction on his teacher's face.

"The hills have accepted you," he said softly. "Now you can begin to learn how to live like a Chichimec . . ."

NOW HUEMAC awoke each morning with only one thought: How was he going to feed himself that day? He no longer consulted the sky as a marker of time, but as a bearer of weather and a caster of shadows. Xiuhcozcatl had begun to teach him in earnest, and Huemac could not afford a moment's inattention, for the day's sustenance depended on the success of the lesson. He learned how to dig for roots and gather the edible herbs, and how to build snares and set nets for the birds and animals that could not be stalked. He fashioned slings from the fibers of the yucca plant and taught himself to wait patiently for the single shot most of his prey offered him. Many times, he went hungry, and suffered in addition the scornful silence of his teacher.

Like a Chichimec, Huemac learned to eat whatever he could find, and his vision of what constituted food broadened even as it became sharp and predatory. He killed and ate snakes, rabbits, birds, lizards, skunks, weasels, kangaroo rats, and various kinds of beetles, grasshoppers, and locusts. For everything he ate, he gave thanks to the spirits of the animals and plants who fed him, addressing them as he would the gods. Xiuhcozcatl had taught him this, and soon such gratitude became second nature to him, and he began to regard his prey with a certain reverent expectation, convinced that it would not elude him if he approached it with the proper respect.

As he became more proficient as a hunter, Huemac found that he was able to think about other things as he went about gathering his food, and he began to dwell seriously on the question of his intention toward the sacred plants. In this desert, he could think of them only as something to be hunted, as nourishment. But what kind of nourishment were they? And what hunger drove him to want to know? He had never had a vision, and he knew now that he might not understand it if he did. Yet his hunger to know was undeniable, and it had nothing to do with wanting to protect himself against Tlacaelel. Tenochtitlan seemed very far away to him, yet his present quandary seemed to have been with him for as long as he could remember, as old and familiar as his luck.

Noticing his restlessness, Xiuhcozcatl began to talk to him at night, over the embers of the dying fire. He first had Huemac repeat to him everything he knew about his ancestors, on both his mother's and father's sides. After speaking for some time about what his mother had told him about her mother and Nezahualcoyotl, Huemac realized that he had very little to say about his father's parents, except that they had been killed by the Tepanecs.

"That is all I know," Huemac said sheepishly. "We were raised to think of ourselves as Tenocha."

"I see that. It is one of the things that confuses you. I knew your grandfather; his name was Citlalcoatl, Snake of Stars. I hunted deer with him once in the mountains behind Texcoco."

"*You,* Lord?" Huemac exclaimed in surprise. He stared at the deep lines in his teacher's weather-beaten face, but he could not see him as a man old enough to have known his grandfather.

"I am four years older than the Fasting Coyote," Xiuhcozcatl said casually, as if daring Huemac to disbelieve him.

"But you are not old!"

"Not as Nezahualcoyotl is old, no. But I have not spent my life in cities, being a ruler. There were some of us, after Texcoco had fallen to the Tepanecs, who urged him to stay in the hills and live as our ancestors had, for the hills would always be ours. But he had been shown a vision of his life by the Owl Men when he was still a young child, and he could not leave his people and his kingdom."

"Who are the Owl Men, Lord?" Huemac asked.

"They are sorcerers, very powerful men," Xiuhcozcatl explained, staring at him steadily. "They have not been seen for many years, and it is said that they have gone away because they could not abide the power of the priests. The man we are going to tomorrow, Oztooa, knew some of them, for he was alive in the time of Nezahualcoyotl's great-grandfather, the original Quinatzin."

Huemac's knowledge of his grandfather's genealogy was limited, but he knew that this man would have to be over one hundred years old.

"Is this Oztooa also a sorcerer?"

"Of course," Xiuhcozcatl said with a trace of irritation. "That is enough talk for tonight. You must rest now, and prepare yourself for tomorrow."

Huemac lay down and gathered his blankets around him, even though he did not feel ready to sleep. He still had not resolved the question of his intention, and the things he had just been told seemed only to have made it more difficult. I am Tenocha, he told himself, yet my ancestors were Chichimecs, people who hunted these hills as I have learned to hunt them. For the second time, the possibility of not returning to Texcoco occurred to him, though this time he was thinking of living, not dying. Perhaps these people to whom he went tomorrow were his *real* people. His father had said that it was fate that had brought him to Tenochtitlan, and had not Nezahualcoyotl himself made a choice to go back?

For a moment, as he listened to the cries of a nighthawk echo through the desert air, the choice was real to him. He could forsake his family and friends, his place among the warriors and the ball players, his dreams of being a Tenocha lord. He would be free of the stigma of his blood and birth; there would be no one to remind him of the scandal in the calmecac; he would never have to match wits with the Demon Heart, or serve him. Perhaps even his bad luck would be left behind.

But then the faces of his mother and father, of Taypachtli and Cocatli, and even that of his second mother, flooded into his mind, and the thought of never seeing any of them again brought an aching lump to his throat. How could he *not* go back? They loved him and would miss him, never knowing why he had abandoned them. The pain of it was too much to even imagine, and Huemac jerked his thoughts away before he was overcome.

But as he lay in the darkness, struggling to contain these painful speculations, his intention suddenly became clear to him. If he must make the choice of his grandfather, he must also have a vision to guide him. It was this that he would seek from the plants, and as proof of his sincerity and courage, he pledged himself to follow the path that was shown to him, no matter where it led. If you call to me, O hills, he vowed, I will come to you. But if it is my fate to return to the city of my birth, then show me this also, and I will obey. Huemac rose briefly to his knees and bowed to the hills. Then he lay back down and was soon fast asleep.

THE VILLAGE lay in a canyon at the base of the mountains that rose to the east. Huemac and Xiuhcozcatl had been climbing since noon, coming out of the desert into groves of wind-bent juniper and pine, and finally onto a series of sharp ridges that zigzagged upward past land that was increasingly cultivated. The steep slopes on both sides of the ridge were terraced with ancient stone walls and planted with rows of spiky maguey plants and the remains of last season's maize and beans. About a third of the plots had recently been burned, and Huemac wondered, when he first passed one of these blackened plots, whether this was the result of war.

"The land is burned and left to lie fallow so that it can replenish itself," Xiuhcozcatl explained curtly. "A special offering and ceremony is made to Huehueteotl, the Old One, the ancient God of Fire. But no more questions, and do not stare at those we meet."

Though people stopped their work to watch them from the fields as they passed, no one came out to greet them until they had descended into the canyon and crossed the shallow stream that ran down one side. Then they were met by a delegation of warriors who greeted Xiuhcozcatl respectfully, but in a language that Huemac did not know. Huemac scanned the warriors covertly, awed by their fierce and barbaric appearance. They wore necklaces of claws and talons, mantles made of wild-animal skins, and lip-plugs of obsidian and bone. Some wore feathers tied into their long hair, while others had shaved their foreheads and left large tufts of hair sticking up on the backs of their heads. All of them carried bows and quivers of arrows.

The tufted-heads are Otomi, Huemac remembered, having once been corrected by Tezcatl when he had mistaken some for Tepanecs in the marketplace. He remembered, as well, that Tezcatl had found his mistake amusing for some reason. Now he did not know why he was remembering such things, except that he was nervous and—for the first time since Xiuhcozcatl had taken his knife—he was feeling the tingling in his stomach. Xiuhcozcatl had not told him what awaited him here, beyond the one mention of the old man who had known the Owl Men, Oztooa.

Surrounded by the warriors, they were led through the center of the village, which was a collection of straw huts arranged in a loose semicircle around a large ceremonial hearth. Next to every hut were wooden racks upon which skins were being stretched and dried, and the village smelled heavily of smoked meat and the herbs used in the curing of hides. When they had passed the last of the huts, the large crowd of children that had been following them departed, and they formed into a single file to climb the steep path that led to a cave that gaped blackly, halfway up the canyon's back wall.

Just inside the entrance of the cave, Xiuhcozcatl pulled Huemac aside and allowed the others to pass and disappear before them into the darkness. Then he ordered Huemac to strip down to his maxlatl, taking his headband, amulet, pouch, and water gourd and wrapping them into a neat bundle inside Huemac's blanket.

"Be truthful in your answers to the Old One," he warned, "and make no promise that you do not intend to keep. Now you must close your eyes, for you are not permitted to see what is written on the walls in the darkness. Lower your head and take hold of my blanket, and do not open your eyes until I tell you to."

Stooping beneath the low ceiling, Huemac grasped the edge of Xiuhcozcatl's blanket and trailed after him blindly. The cave had a musty odor and was very cold, seeming to grow colder as they wound their way forward, taking several turns and crouching further beneath the lowering ceiling. Huemac felt the breath catch in his throat as the walls closed in around him, and he almost opened his eyes in fright when he heard something scurry away underfoot.

"Crawl!" Xiuhcozcatl commanded in a hoarse whisper, and Huemac got down on his hands and knees in the soft powdery dust that covered the cave floor. He was now so cold that he could not feel his hands and feet, and the perspiration of his effort felt like ice against his bare skin. Then he sensed the ceiling opening out over his head, and his teacher led him to a spot and told him to sit up and open his eyes.

Huemac found himself sitting alone on one side of a circular chamber whose ceiling was somewhere far above him in the darkness. There was a small fire in the center of the room, its flames casting a dancing light on the wall paintings and the row of faces that stared at Huemac from the other side of the fire. The warriors stood or knelt against the wall, and sitting in a second rank in front of them were several white-haired men and women. There even seemed to be some children in the room, but Huemac had little time to notice, for all of his attention was immediately drawn to the old man sitting directly across from him.

Oztooa, the Gray Fox, he thought, staring up at the tiny man. The Old One was seated upon a low platform covered with coyote skins, his body shrouded in a blanket of rabbit fur. One bony hand protruded from the blanket, holding a circular fan of yellow parrot feathers. His white head was bare, and his dark, narrow face looked like a shriveled chili, wrinkles upon furrows upon crevices, a face embedded with shadows. His large, round eyes were like two glittering pieces of obsidian, and Huemac did not attempt to meet them directly. Though the tingling was very strong in his stomach, his limbs felt paralyzed by the cold, and he had to resist the temptation to move closer to the fire.

Xiuhcozcatl was seated next to the platform, and he spoke to the Old One in his own tongue, gesturing occasionally toward Huemac. Oztooa listened without taking his eyes off Huemac, then spoke rapidly and motioned for Xiuhcozcatl to translate.

"I have told him that you come from Tenochtitlan," the teacher explained to Huemac. "He wishes to know if it is true that the Tenocha are building a house where the wild creatures, the birds and the animals, will be held captive."

Huemac had to think a moment before he understood the reference, because he had never conceived of anything being held captive except humans. When he answered, it was with a sense of shame that was new to him, the result of the many prayers he had offered to the spirits of his prey.

"The Speaker receives many live things as tribute," he said as simply as possible, sensing that his answer would not please the old man. "He is constructing a place where they may be kept."

Oztooa spoke sharply, and Xiuhcozcatl again translated.

"He asks: For sacrifice or for eating?"

"Just to keep," Huemac said awkwardly. "To look at."

A murmur of disapproval swept around the chamber when his reply was translated, and Huemac felt anger being directed toward him, which stirred his shame and made him want to disavow what his people were doing. But he knew that he could not, at least not yet.

"The Old One wishes to know," Xiuhcozcatl said, after the old man had again spoken, "if the feathers of the quetzal and the cotinga are available in Tenochtitlan, and if you will send him some, since you have brought no gift this time."

Xiuhcozcatl's eyes reminded him of the warning he had been given concerning promises, but Huemac found the request a perfect opportunity for making his intention clear to both his teacher and Oztooa.

"Tell him that if I return to Tenochtitlan, I will surely send him the feathers he desires."

Xiuhcozcatl stared at Huemac curiously. "There is a chance that you may *not* return?"

"One never knows, Lord."

Xiuhcozcatl looked at him again, then began to translate, taking a long time, since Oztooa had observed the interchange between them and asked many questions, scowling suspiciously.

"He wishes to know the reason for your uncertainty about returning to Tenochtitlan. Do you not wish to return? Or have you committed some crime there?"

"I very much wish to return, for it is the city of my birth, and my family and friends are there." Huemac paused, and seeing that Xiuhcozcatl was waiting, he decided that he had to answer the second question, too. "And yes, I have committed a crime there, but this would not prevent me from returning."

Xiuhcozcatl translated, and Oztooa turned back to Huemac, gesturing impatiently for him to go on.

"I am confused, Old One," Huemac said humbly. "My face and heart were formed in Tenochtitlan, but my blood comes from Texcoco, and thus, I have learned, from these hills. I wish to know where it is that I truly belong. It is for this that I seek the visions given by the sacred plants."

Xiuhcozcatl narrowed his eyes and raised his eyebrows slightly, as if reassessing his student. When he translated for Oztooa and the others, another murmur swept the chamber, this one filled with surprise and, Huemac thought, approval. His teacher proceeded to go on at some length to Oztooa, though the only words Huemac could understand were the names of Nezahualcoyotl, Quinatzin, and Tlacaelel. He took his eyes off Xiuhcozcatl and the Old One for a moment in an attempt to scan the faces behind them, but a heightening of the tingling sensation in his midsection brought his attention right back. The yellow fan in Oztooa's hand was moving, wavering in an almost imperceptible rhythm. Then it stopped, and the feeling in Huemac's stomach also subsided.

"The Old One finds your intention commendable," Xiuhcozcatl informed him. "And he has offered to help you resolve your confusion. He says that the blood of Nezahualcoyotl is good blood, and he wants to know if you will stay here and take a wife from among his great-granddaughters. He will see that you are adopted into the tribe and given a place of honor among his people. Think carefully before you answer, Huemac," he added in a warning voice.

Huemac again raised his eyes to the people behind Oztooa, and this time the old man did not prevent him from searching their faces. He found their features crude and their expressions indecipherable, yet he sensed a great strength in them, and a quality of quietness and waiting that reminded him of these hills. They are people who burn the land to make it grow, he thought, and who eat whatever they can kill. Doubts that he could ever live as they did began to rise in him, but the memory of his vow, and his determination to keep it, drove them from his mind. He took a deep breath and clasped his icy hands together tightly.

"Tell him that I have done nothing to deserve the honor he extends to me, and that I am very grateful. Assure him that if this is the path that is shown to me, I will follow it."

"Do you realize what you are agreeing to?" Xiuhcozcatl inquired sternly, and Huemac realized for the first time that he was placing his teacher in a position as difficult and risky as his own. To return to Texcoco without his pupil would not endear him to the king.

"I must go where I belong, Lord," he insisted quietly. "It is a choice my grandfather made himself, and my father, as well, before he went to live in Tenochtitlan. They would understand why I must make it, too."

"Your grandfather warned me that you were clever and impulsive, and that it would be difficult to bring you along slowly," Xiuhcozcatl said, and shook his head ruefully. "Even at that, he underestimated you."

Xiuhcozcatl spoke to the old man, who questioned him closely until, at last, he appeared satisfied. He gestured to the old woman sitting beside him, and she handed him a brightly painted gourd bowl. The Old One waved his fan over the bowl and uttered a few words in a singsong voice, then reached into the bowl and put a piece of something in his mouth.

"Teonanacatl, the Flesh of the Gods," Xiuhcozcatl interpreted in a similar voice, as the woman brought the bowl over to Huemac. She gestured for him to keep his hands where they were and to open his mouth, and when he did so, she reached into the bowl and deposited a piece of mushroom on his tongue. It was tough and fibrous and tasted like dirt, though as he chewed it, his mouth filled with a bitter juice that numbed his tongue and palate. The woman continued around the chamber, and though not everyone partook of the mushrooms, all the old people did, and a number of the warriors as well. Huemac had just managed to swallow the first mushroom when she returned and gave him another.

Four times Huemac was fed from the bowl, and four times he chewed and swallowed, though there was no feeling left in his mouth and throat. Already, he was feeling warmer, and his muscles began to relax, shifting and uncoiling beneath his skin as if of their own accord. The old people had begun to sing, and though Huemac could not understand their words, he found the sound of their voices very soothing. The Flesh of the Gods, he thought languorously, letting his eyes drift over the wall paintings, which seemed to have grown more distinct, their colors rich and brilliant.

The singing gradually grew louder, its rhythm more pronounced, and the shapes on the walls seemed to move as if they, too, were singing. Then a single voice was raised, singing in Nahua, Huemac's own language. He listened raptly, feeling the words come into his mind even before they came to his ears:

> "It is my net, this net.
> With it, I capture the running deer.
> With it, I bring down the screaming hawk.
> Nothing eludes this net, my net.
> With it, I capture the spirits
> And hold them fast."

Then Huemac realized that it was *he* who was singing, and that he was lying on his back, staring upward. Stretched above him was a silver net, a web of shining lines that billowed out away from him and then settled back down. There were creatures caught in the net, birds and animals of many colors, and strange, glowing creatures that seemed to be neither animal nor human. Huemac stared at them for a long time, finding that he could indeed hold them fast in his net, which billowed and settled in time with his own breathing.

"Huemac . . . Huemac . . . Huemac . . ."

The name seemed to be coming from a great distance, its echoes causing the net to vibrate and then to disintegrate, releasing its catch. Huemac felt a tugging at his midsection, as if a rope had been tied around his waist, and then he was pulled upright, yanked into a sitting position with such force that everything within his field of vision was set to bouncing wildly for several moments. The fire seemed very bright, though not as bright as the eyes of Oztooa, which shone like two glowing discs.

"Look into his eyes, Huemac," a voice intoned. "Look, and follow the path they light for you . . ."

The discs expanded and turned orange, then yellow, and Huemac felt himself being drawn forward along a path that shone with the colors of the fire. He was very warm, and could feel the sweat running off his body. Then a shape appeared before him, and he saw a fox sitting on the path ahead, its thick plume of a tail curled around its legs. Huemac stopped, and the path seemed to be sucked up into the fox's eyes, which blazed with a golden light before blinking out.

Huemac again found himself on his back, and again the force around his middle jerked him upright.

"Follow the path," the voice commanded, and once more the eyes drew him in. Huemac felt that he had gone farther this time when a coyote suddenly appeared on the path before him. The coyote cocked his head briefly as if to warn Huemac off, then tilted his muzzle and let out a howl that made Huemac jump back. The path disappeared into the coyote's eyes, which hung like burning shields in the darkness before vanishing.

The next time Huemac tried the path, he encountered an owl who hooted at him so fiercely that he immediately turned and ran, and never saw what happened to the path. But he had seen, beyond the owl, a kind of clearing, a place where the light seemed to broaden out in all directions. And he knew, somehow, that this was his destination, and he headed for it resolutely the next time the voice set him along the path. Suddenly, he was in the marketplace in Tlatelulco, running through a great crowd of men who seemed to be fighting with one another in slow motion. A shape reared up in front of him, but he was moving too fast to stop himself and ran right through it, feeling it burst apart and blow away behind him. Then he felt himself rising, and the shapes reared up one after another, bursting apart like puffballs upon contact. Huemac was having difficulty seeing, and when he wiped his eyes, his hand came away covered with a reddish film. He went higher and higher, sensing by the warmth that he was near the top, though he was now so coated with the film that he could hardly see. Two shapes appeared before him, barely recognizable, one large and the other small and misshapen. But they fled before Huemac could reach them, and as they disappeared from his sight, he felt himself being dragged down by the film that covered his body, and he fell into blackness.

When Huemac next came to, an old man was squatting beside him, holding him up in a sitting position with one arm. There was a golden haze hanging over everything, blurring his vision, but when Huemac tried to wipe his eyes, the old man restrained his arm. Then he realized that the old man was Xiuhcozcatl, and wanted to say something about how he had aged, but he could not find the words.

"Where were you, Huemac? Where did the path take you, this last time?"

Xiuhcozcatl had to repeat the questions several times, because his words seemed to be coming to Huemac at different speeds, and it was difficult to catch them in the right order. And he was distracted by the color of the air, and by the way his teacher's face kept changing: first young, then old and gray, then suddenly sharp and predatory, his features tattooed with the head feathers of a hawk. Huemac wanted to comment on all these things at once, as well as answer Xiuhcozcatl's question, but there were too many thoughts crowding into his mind to put any one of them into words.

"Where, Huemac, *where*?" his teacher prompted, and a cool wind blew in Huemac's face, clearing the air before his eyes. He saw that the Old One was waving his fan in his direction.

"Tlatelulco," he managed finally, and Xiuhcozcatl left his side to confer with the old man. Huemac found that he could sit upright quite easily by himself. His body felt strong, in fact, though the commotion in his mind had not ceased. He tried to focus in on his teacher and Oztooa, who seemed to be arguing. Huemac could see the words issuing from their mouths in little puffs of reddish smoke, though the sounds of their speech seemed to come at him from the most surprising places, often from behind or beneath him. Xiuhcozcatl returned to his side, his face old and grave.

"You must go down the path one more time, Huemac," he said, and shook him roughly by the arm. "But do not linger there, do you understand? It is very dangerous. Look once, and then turn your back on what you have seen. *Be brave, little brother,*" he added in a whisper that thrilled Huemac with its sudden note of intimacy and concern. He wanted to smile and reassure his teacher, but a sharp tug at his midsection prevented the effort, and then he saw the yellow eyes of the Old One.

"Follow the path . . ."

This time, Huemac seemed to reach the clearing in one bound. Then he was standing in Tenochtitlan, close to the Eagle Gate that led into the city. Ahead of him, a great crowd of people, mostly old men, were standing on both sides of the gate, obviously waiting for someone to enter. Their hands were filled with garlands of flowers, and they were singing a song of praise to the returning warriors. Huemac heard someone call his name from behind him, but before he could turn to see who it was, an old man standing a short distance away turned to face in his direction.

At first, Huemac was too startled to recognize what he was seeing. The old man looked past him impatiently, then turned back toward the gate, craning his neck expectantly. But Huemac had seen the amulet around his neck, and the face, though greatly aged, was his own. Huemac started toward him eagerly, then again heard his name being called, fainter this time, but with a note of pleading that caught his attention. He stopped, and the old man began to draw away from him, edging forward into the crowd. Huemac did not want to lose him, but the voice behind him had made him feel guilty, as if he had forgotten a promise, and he turned . . .

It was wet and cold, and he was being bounced up and down, over and over again, so that it seemed, when he was finally able to open his eyes, that the world would never be still again. The motion was making him sick to his stomach, and he retched violently, feeling strong hands upon his body. Then he could see, though he was covered with a cold sweat and shivered uncontrollably. Xiuhcozcatl was holding one of his arms and the old woman who had given him the mushrooms was holding the other. A blanket was wrapped around his shoulders, and gradually he could think, and was able to hear his teacher's questions.

"Tenochtitlan," he croaked painfully. There was a murmuring in the room, and the old woman next to him patted Huemac's arm and said something he could not understand. She smiled at him, revealing teeth that had been painted red.

"She says that she believes you," Xiuhcozcatl explained, "but she wishes that your path had brought you here instead. She admires your courage, and the sounds that you made."

There was laughter in the room, but it died abruptly when the Old One spoke. Huemac was given some water, which washed the bitter taste from his mouth and cooled the rawness in his throat. He felt very tired, and had trouble keeping his eyes open to watch the conversation between Oztooa and Xiuhcoz-catl.

"He says that he is satisfied," his teacher explained at last. "But he reminds you that you must send him the feathers you promised."

Huemac nodded weakly, and felt a warm wind wash over him, taking away the last of his strength. The last thing he saw, before sleep took him, was the yellow fan swaying gently, swaying softly, back and forth . . .

THE journey back to Texcoco seemed very short. They had provisioned themselves before leaving Oztooa's village, so they did not spend any time hunting, and reached the outskirts of Teotihuacan after four days of steady traveling. In contrast to his forbidding silence on the trip out, Xiuhcozcatl talked almost constantly on the way back. He made Huemac go over and over the details of his experiences with the mushrooms, discussing every aspect of his visions with him and explaining what he understood them to mean. He told Huemac that the animals he had seen—the fox, coyote, and owl—were Oztooa's nahuallis, his animal doubles, and that the howling and hooting he had heard had been made by Huemac himself. Even the Old One, he revealed, had been amused by the sounds that Huemac had made, and by how greatly he had frightened himself with his own hooting. Some of the old people present had referred to him afterward as Owl Boy, laughing every time they said the name.

Xiuhcozcatl also told him frankly that the vision of Tlatelulco was mysterious, and troubling. Possibly, he would have to kill someone there, and might even be killed himself, despite what the second vision had shown him. A vision so violent and unclear had to be regarded with great wariness, for it offered the possibility of an occurrence so devastating that fate itself, and all previous visions of it, would be irrevocably altered. He warned Huemac to avoid the Tlatelulco marketplace as much as possible, and to never go there carelessly.

As they made their camp for the night outside of Teotihuacan, the teacher informed Huemac that this was the last night that they would talk about these things, and that he should ask whatever questions remained in his mind. Tomorrow, he said, Huemac would have to begin searching for the objects he had buried the first time they had come this way. Those that allowed themselves to be located would be power objects for him, and would thereafter aid him when he came to the desert. Eventually, if he gained a sufficient affinity with them, he could use them as tools and weapons, as Oztooa did with his parrot-feather fan.

"He cast winds at me with it," Huemac remembered, still amazed. "And I could feel its movements in my stomach."

"He hooked you there, in the hole in your spirit. That is how he pulled you up from the floor."

"I have a hole in my spirit?"

"It was apparent to all who took the mushrooms with you. It is because of the knife. You will not be whole until you return it to its resting place."

"Will you keep it for me, Lord?" Huemac requested anxiously.

Xiuhcozcatl raised his eyebrows mockingly. "What, there is a source of danger you do not gladly embrace? You, who would barter your life with a man of Oztooa's powers? I should have thought that you would want it back, so that you could trade with it in the marketplace, or gamble it away with your friend Icpitl."

Huemac endured his teacher's jibes good-naturedly, taking the teasing as a sign of how their relationship had progressed. Nor had he forgotten the solicitude Xiuhcozcatl had shown toward him before he had ventured down the path for the last time.

"What would have happened to me," he asked, "if I had gone after the old man in the vision instead of turning back?"

"If you had caught up with him, you would not be here today. You would be lost to yourself, and to the world."

"Why did the Old One insist on my going, then?"

"He would not accept Tlatelulco as proof that he had lost the bargain, and he was willing to risk your life to be sure. It is not often that a young man of your blood offers himself so freely, and the Old One wanted you very much, much more than the feathers. Now, of course, you may go to him whenever you wish, and there will be a place for you, as long as you do not forget the feathers. But come now, it is late, and you have hard work ahead of you. Do you have any more questions?"

"The old man in the vision," Huemac said without hesitation, returning to the part of his experience that had touched him most deeply. "He had feathers in his hair; he was an Old Eagle, a warrior who had survived with honor. Can it be true that I will live so long?"

"I have warned you of the other vision," Xiuhcozcatl reminded him, "but what reason have you to doubt what was shown to you? Your intention and courage were strong, whatever might be said about your judgment in making such a bargain."

"But my luck is very bad," Huemac objected. "I have told you the circumstances of my birth . . ."

"Luck is an invention of the priests and soothsayers," the teacher said disdainfully. "It allows them to make a living with their books. Besides, there is no reason to assume that a long life is an indication of *good* luck. It is sometimes harder to stay alive, and bear what fate brings you."

Huemac had no more questions. He remained silent, watching the stars rise over the hills. He would return to them, he knew, for Xiuhcozcatl had made it clear that his training with the plants was far from over. He bowed to the hills, promising not to forget what he had learned from them. Then he began to think, for the first time in many days, about the city.

THEN HE was immersed in it once again, rising to the sound of the priests' conch trumpets, eating food other hands had prepared, hastening to fulfill a routine that never varied in its intensity. Huemac had no more than rolled his power objects up in his blanket and put them away when Tlaltecatzin had him out on the target range, practicing with the throwing board. The annual contests for the boys in the telpochcalli were coming up at the end of the month, and to make himself competitive, Huemac not only had to practice for extra hours with the weapons, but he also had to attend sessions with boys younger than himself in order to catch up on what he had missed.

But though he was busier than he had ever been previously, he did not allow himself to feel rushed or harried, and he dealt with his tasks one by one, with an efficiency that impressed the Master of Arms.

"The desert seems to have agreed with you, Huemac," he said one afternoon, several days after Huemac had returned. "You are thinner, but no less strong, I think. And you seem more patient."

"The hills are too old for haste," Huemac said, then felt sheepish about speaking in such a manner before the Master, who had lived all his life in the city. "Everyone here seems possessed by an urgency that consumes them, and shortens their days."

Tlaltecatzin smiled. "I remember one who could not wait to show me all his cleverness. But I am not mocking you, Huemac, and I respect what you have learned from Xiuhcozcatl. Another of your teachers has inquired about you several times, as well, and Icpitl even came here once himself, to see if I was hiding you from him."

Huemac frowned. "How soon does he expect me to resume my lessons with him?"

"He cannot have you until after the contests, by order of your grandfather," the Master said, and smiled at Huemac's obvious relief and pleasure. "There is a possibility that we will soon be at war with the people of Tullantzinco, and the warriors will need shield and weapons carriers. Those who excel in the contests will qualify for this honor."

Huemac bowed. "If you will forgive my urgency, Lord, I would like to return to the practice range."

"Go," Tlaltecatzin said indulgently. "But patiently, Huemac, as patiently as you know how . . ."

WHEN HUEMAC did finally show up at the Tlachco, Icpitl was as hard on him as he had expected, keeping him long after the other boys for individual instruction, and running him until his legs began to knot and cramp from pounding against the unyielding surface of the court. It was dark when they finished, and Huemac could barely drag himself to the training room. Icpitl lit a torch on the wall and ordered him to take off his leathers and his maxlatl and lie face down on a low table covered with reed matting.

First, the Trainer put poultices on Huemac's scrapes and the new bruises on his buttocks. Then he knelt beside the table and rubbed his hands with an aromatic oil, and began to massage the knots out of Huemac's calf muscles, talking as he kneaded deeply with his blunt fingers.

"So," he said irritably, "you have been a good little sorcerer, like your grandfather would want. And now you have been a good little warrior, too."

"I took a first with the sling," Huemac said proudly, unaffected by the Trainer's scorn. "And I was second in the dueling with macanas. Tlaltecatzin has promised me a place with the warriors if they march on Tullantzinco."

"You mean a place *behind* the warriors," Icpitl said with a disdainful snort, working upward to Huemac's back and shoulders. Huemac grunted softly as the rough fingers bore down on tender places, but the overall release of tension felt wonderful.

"Turn over," the Trainer commanded curtly, and Huemac stretched out on his back and closed his eyes, feeling the fingers go to work on the aching muscles beneath his shins. He ignored Icpitl's peevish mutterings and fell into a doze, lulled by the rich aroma of the liniment. Dimly, he felt a pleasurable stirring in his groin and squirmed luxuriously, his mind filling with vague images of naked flesh. Then he was wide awake, and aware of an oiled hand sliding up and down his penis. He tried to sit up, but a strong hand immediately came down on his chest, pinning him to the table. Icpitl's face loomed over him, his thick lips fixed in a cruel leer.

"And what did you learn about *this* in the desert?" he hissed, pressing down on Huemac's chest while his other hand continued to stroke Huemac's erect penis. "Did that old sorcerer show you what the savages do when there are no women about? Or perhaps Tlaltecatzin, that pompous eunuch, told you that you should let it hang uselessly, like the lock on the back of your head. Then, when you become a great warrior, you can have it cut off, like *he* did."

Suddenly, Icpitl removed his hands and stood back. Huemac leaped to his feet, livid with anger and shame, his swollen member bobbing straight out before him. Only his nakedness and the memory of that powerful hand upon his chest prevented him from attacking the Trainer with his bare hands.

"You are suchioa, a pervert!" he spat. "I could have you killed for this!"

"You are no priest," Icpitl sneered. "You lie there squirming, then pretend you did not enjoy it!"

Icpitl's own maxlatl was distended, and with a swift, practiced movement, he reached into the folds of cloth and produced his own member, which was enormously engorged. Despite himself, Huemac stared, for he had never seen another man's erection before this.

"You see, *I* am not ashamed of my manliness," the Trainer boasted. "I know what to do with this, besides squeezing it with my own hands. But perhaps you are just a boy, Huemac, and still frightened of such things."

"I fear nothing," Huemac said tightly, deliberately raising his eyes to Icpitl's face. The older man laughed triumphantly and put his hands on his hips, leaving himself exposed.

"Then go and wash yourself, and use the soap root. Wash *all* of your parts," Icpitl said, and laughed again. "You can always have me killed later, if you still wish it, but first you are going to meet a teacher whose lessons you will not want to forgo . . ."

THE APARTMENT to which Icpitl led Huemac was one of a great number of identical one-room dwellings that were crowded together along the narrow, uneven streets near the canoe docks. This one had a small flowerbox upon the sill of its single window and a border of red flowers painted around the shrouded doorway, which opened directly onto the street. But its truly distinguishing feature was that there were no children around it. This was the poorest calpulli in the city, and most of these apartments were overflowing with the families of immigrants, or the refugees from the most recent wars. Even at this hour, gangs of half-naked children, some very young, roamed through the streets, and Huemac could feel their curious eyes upon him as he waited outside the apartment.

They know what I am here for, he thought, still smoldering from the shameful way Icpitl had tricked him into this. And what kind of woman had he brought him to? Her name itself—Ce Malinalli—was one of the worst of the day signs, and proof of her bad fortune. There were many kinds of auianime, street women, and the most beautiful were kept as concubines by the lords and warriors, and were allowed to dance in certain of the festivals. The others plied their trade among the older boys in the telpochcalli, or else they lived in hovels like this and sold their bodies to anyone, either in the marketplace or on the streets.

She is probably old and greatly used, Huemac thought angrily: a flabby old woman afflicted with the itching buttocks. Yet she will be as lewd and brazen as Icpitl, and will expect me to throw myself upon her like a dog upon food. Huemac hated the idea of lying with a woman who had already given herself to that filthy man, and he had no intention of accepting such a woman as his teacher. I will finish what I have come for quickly, he vowed, and she will see the scorn I have for her.

Icpitl emerged from the room and grinned at him.

"Ce Malinalli asks for her pupil. I will be back for you later."

"I will not be here," Huemac said stonily. "I do not wish to linger where *you* have been."

"Perhaps you had better leave now, then. You might find that your desires are not so easily satisfied."

"I do not have your desires," Huemac snapped, and stepped past him, hearing the sound of the other man's laughter behind him as he pushed through the blanket draped across the door. Most of the tiny room was in darkness, except for the corner farthest from the door, where a ring of oil wicks created a circle of soft yellow light. Standing in the midst of the circle was a young, slender woman only a few years older than Huemac himself. She was wearing a flower-patterned shift and a short skirt that revealed her shapely legs, which were tattooed with intricate designs. Her long black hair hung loose and flowing on one side of her face and was bound back on the other, leaving two twists of hair, like horns, on the very top of her head. She smiled and bowed courteously, and Huemac bowed back automatically, disconcerted by her youth and apparent beauty.

"I am Ce Malinalli, my Lord," she said, in a voice meant to be enticing. "May I offer you a drink of sweet water? Or, if you prefer, I can send for some octli . . . ?"

"I do not drink octli," Huemac said rudely, having advanced to the edge of the lighted area. He could smell the sweet scents of rose water and the poyomatli herb, with which she had anointed her body, and he could see that her cheeks and lips had been artificially reddened. He opened his eyes wide and glared at her, as if seeing through her disguise. "Nor have I come here to drink with you."

To Huemac's surprise, she did not flinch before the force of his eyes, but only gave him a knowing smile and began to untie the knot at the shoulder of her shift.

"I understand your urgency, Lord," she said, slowly baring one breast and then the other. Still smiling at him, she untied her skirt and peeled it off from around her hips, showing him the dark triangle between her legs. Then she knelt on the pile of mats that lay within the circle of light and looked up at him invitingly, spreading the tendrils of her loosened hair across her bare shoulder and over one breast.

"How would you have me lie?" she asked, and Huemac blinked rapidly, feeling the tingling beginning to build inside him. He wondered, now, how he had expected to get this over with quickly, when he did not even know how to begin. He had been told, of course, but the words he remembered did not seem to explain anything about the splendid creature he saw before him, her gleaming body stretched out and waiting for him. Feeling that he was dreaming, he went forward and lowered himself to the mats . . .

Ce Malinalli looked at him expectantly, then seemed to sense his uncertainty and reached out to gently caress his arm.

"I am glad that you have decided not to hurry," she said, and ran her hands up to his shoulder to untie his mantle. Huemac was sitting with his legs stretched out before him, and when she raised up on her knees to dispose of his mantle, her firm round breasts were within inches of his face. Cupping a hand behind his head, she brought his lips to her nipple, which stiffened when he touched it with his tongue. Ce Malinalli took his free hand and guided it to her hip, then slowly turned her body into him, so that his fingers slid across the smooth contours of her buttocks as he buried his face in her breasts.

Ce Malinalli's breath whistled in his ear as they fell to the mats together and pressed their bodies tightly against each other. She murmured languidly and rubbed her breasts against his chest, locking a leg over his hip and thrusting her pelvis against the burgeoning lump in his groin. Then he was rising out of his maxlatl, and when her hands closed upon his member, he moved without thinking or seeing. Ce Malinalli rolled onto her back and maneuvered him between her legs, and suddenly, he was gliding forward into a tunnel of liquid warmth, wrapped in the silky grasp of sensations too delicious to be believed. There was a roaring in Huemac's ears, and he gasped with helpless pleasure when she began to move beneath him. Yellow light splashed against his eyes as he rocked and thrust, feeling the tingling in his stomach build and peak, shaking him with a violence that frightened him even in the midst of his excitement. Then the tingling seemed to swoop suddenly downward, into his loins, where it burst out of him in a great, shuddering flood.

He was still rocking when his senses returned, and for a moment, he was stricken by the awful feeling that he had harmed her with the violence of his consummation. But then he could hear her breathing, and the way she continued to move beneath him revealed no sign of injury. Gradually, certain that she was unharmed, he uncoupled himself and fell panting by her side. Ce Malinalli smiled at him and stroked the side of his face.

"Surely, it was wise to put off your thirst," she suggested softly, and Huemac could only smile at her deliriously. Icpitl did not return as he had promised, after all, and Huemac continued his lessons long into the night, proving his desire to learn again and again. When he finally crept back to the telpochcalli just before dawn, his legs were rubbery and his eyes gritty from lack of sleep, but he could not think of a better way to feel.

EARLY in the fall of the year Five-Reed, the warriors of Texcoco marched on the city of Tullantzinco, which had refused to pay its taxes to Neza-hualcoyotl. After a short siege, the defenders of the city were easily over-come, so easily that many of the apprentice warriors were allowed into the fighting before a truce was called. The company to which Huemac was at-tached, however, was one of the few that encountered stiff opposition, and thus its apprentices were never summoned into action. Though he was a witness to some heavy fighting and helped in the securing of captives, Huemac did not get to fight himself, and had to undertake the long, triumphant march back to Texcoco with his apprentice status unchanged.

When his company had reached Teotihuacan, Huemac was called out by his captain and delivered over to Xiuhcozcatl, who had brought Huemac's blanket, pouch, and power objects from the city. Without giving him time to rest, Xiuhcozcatl led Huemac back into the hills, saying only that they were going to hunt Peyotl, the One Who Glows. Trying to put aside the thoughts of Ce Malinalli's warm body, which had sustained him through the frustration of the campaign, Huemac trudged wearily after his teacher.

From the first, he had trouble readjusting to life in the desert. He slept poorly on the hard ground, tired easily during the long marches, and was slow in regaining his skills as a hunter. Xiuhcozcatl observed his fatigue and clumsi-ness with a silence every bit as punishing as the hunger Huemac brought on himself, since the openness and banter of their last days together were still fresh in Huemac's mind. Then, while climbing over a stone wall near Oztooa's village, Huemac slipped on a loose stone and fell heavily, spraining his ankle. Leaving him lying on the ground in pain, Xiuhcozcatl went ahead to the village and brought back some strong men, who carried Huemac down into the canyon and left him by the side of the stream, so that he could soak his swollen ankle in the icy spring water. When they were finally alone, Xiuhcozcatl spoke to him sternly:

"Now you must tell me what you have done with the jade rabbit."

Grimacing with pain, Huemac was nonetheless relieved by the chance to talk, and began to explain about Ce Malinalli, and how he had lost his amulet to Icpitl.

"He loaned me cloth, and yetl, and octli, and I had nothing with which to repay him. So I gave him my headband and the amulet to hold as my pledge of payment. Now I play for him in the games he arranges, and my winnings are subtracted from my debt. That is how I was able to redeem my headband."

"And if you lose?" Xiuhcozcatl asked skeptically, and Huemac looked down at his ankle.

"Then I owe him more. But my age gives us an advantage in the betting, because the older men tend to underestimate my ability."

"*Us?* You must owe him a great deal, for that amulet is very valuable. I can only assume that you have continued your visits to this woman."

"Yes," Huemac said tonelessly. "I have not been able to stop myself."

"Why have you not gone to your grandfather? *He* would understand about a woman."

"I did not think of it in time," Huemac admitted, "and now it is too late. He gave the amulet as a prize to my mother, who gave it to me. And he warned me, long ago, never to lose it. I could not bring myself to tell him into whose hands it has fallen."

"Keep your foot in the water," Xiuhcozcatl commanded, and then lost himself in thought, glancing occasionally at Huemac and shaking his head.

"This is very serious," he said at last. "But since it seems to be your way to gamble with your life, that is the only way you can rescue yourself. You must tell me truthfully: Can you play against this man, can you beat him?"

Huemac thought for a moment, then shook his head sadly.

"I do not think so. I am faster than he is, and I have more endurance, but he is too clever for me. He tricks me into bad shots before I can wear him down."

"Why is that?" the teacher demanded, and Huemac shrugged helplessly.

"He knows me too well. He knows how to tempt me."

"That can be remedied," Xiuhcozcatl assured him. "There is an old woman in the village who can help you break this spell that Icpitl has cast over you. But you must give up the other woman. She is the source of your debt, and a symbol of your weakness."

Huemac frowned and pursed his lips, feeling suddenly hopeless. He could make such a promise here, but he did not feel at all certain that he could keep it once he returned to Texcoco. And that uncertainty made him feel even less confident that he could ever defeat Icpitl in a one-man game.

"It is no use, Lord," he said despairingly. "My debt is even greater than the value of the rabbit, and even if I were to lower it, he will never let me play for all of it at once. I have nothing to offer him as a stake."

"There is one thing that I am sure he will play for," the teacher said, showing a trace of disgust at Huemac's weakness. "That is tlapatl, the power herb. I will give you all that you will need to tempt him into a game, but you must abstain completely from this woman, and you must not offer him the herbs until you are ready to play him and win. Do not think that you can simply trade with him for the rabbit; that would never free you. And Huemac: If you try to cheat on this bargain, or if you play him too soon and lose, do not come to me for help. Do not ever come back to me at all."

"But Lord," Huemac pleaded, his eyes widening anxiously, "you have told me yourself that I have much left to learn. Who would teach me?"

"I do not care. You will not be good for anything if you cannot free yourself from this debt. You will have become what *he* is. If you try to approach me in that condition, I will kill you with your own knife, for you will deserve to die."

Huemac stared down his leg at the many scrapes and bruises he had accumulated from the ball game, and then at the grotesquely misshapen ankle dangling in the water. Beyond his toes, he could see the reflection of his face, and he felt every bit as ugly and evasive as that distorted, shifting image. He glanced up at his teacher.

"I am very tired, Lord. Why is it that I must always do battle with my teachers?"

Xiuhcozcatl laughed. "That is what a student *ought* to do! What better way is there to prepare you for the enemies you will meet?"

"But must my life always be at stake?" Huemac demanded, failing to see the humor in the situation.

"Do you have anything better to offer?" Xiuhcozcatl asked sharply, and Huemac opened his mouth to reply, then closed it stubbornly.

"Now I will be in debt to you and the old woman," he said finally, in a defeated voice.

"If you win and return the tlapatl to me, you will owe me nothing. The old woman will not demand from you something that you cannot pay."

"You leave me no choice, then."

"You have left yourself none. You have allowed this man to choose for you for too long; now you must take back what is yours. Be brave, little brother," Xiuhcozcatl added, with a note of sarcasm that stung Huemac deeply, despite his fatigue and despair. Tears of anger came to his eyes, and he pulled his foot out of the water abruptly.

"Cut me a staff, Lord," he said hoarsely, "and then take me to this woman . . ."

DURING THE curing ceremony, Huemac was told to imagine himself a hawk circling high over his prey, floating effortlessly on a cushion of air, waiting in silence for the speck far below him to move into the open. There is a man, a man with a net, the curing woman sang, and he waits for you below, in hiding, he waits to trap you with his net. But he cannot touch you while you glide upon the air, she continued, and you have the eyes of a hawk, and the patience of a true hunter. You will circle, and hang in the air, and only when you have perfectly measured the distance, only when you are certain that he cannot reach you with his net, only then will you plummet from the sky, and make your strike . . .

When Huemac returned to Texcoco, his ankle had healed fully and he was walking normally, though with a grim sense of purpose that did not allow him to take any joy in the sight of the now-familiar streets. Slung over his shoulder was a deer-hide bag filled with the roots, leaves, and flowers of the tlapatl plant, the herb of power. After presenting himself to Tlaltecatzin and offering incense to the image of Tezcatlipoca, Huemac rolled the bag up in his blanket and put it away. Then he went to the Tlachco to dress for practice.

Icpitl greeted his appearance with his usual sarcasm, calling him the sorcerer's apprentice and asking him what spells he had learned to cast this time. Huemac stared back at him coolly, as if from a great height, and did not respond. Very deliberately, he untied his mantle and removed it, revealing the tiny rabbitskin pouch that hung on a thong around his neck.

"So, you have been buying jewelry from the savages, eh?" the Trainer suggested derisively, and some of the other boys in the training room laughed, pleased to hear their teacher taking this tone with his favorite pupil. Again, Huemac did not answer. One by one, he took his leather protectors down from their pegs and rubbed them with chia oil, until their suppleness was restored. Then, using a cactus thorn and maguey-fiber thread, he carefully sewed a small bundle of tufted hawk feathers to each piece before putting it on. By this time, all the other boys had left the room, and Huemac was alone with the Trainer.

"What is all this?" Icpitl demanded. "Did you purchase magic charms from the Otomi, too? What do savages know about tlachtli?"

"I am ready to play now," Huemac said calmly, ignoring the questions.

"And what will you do afterward? You must be ready for some relaxation, as well, after all this time in the field. Ce Malinalli has missed you, you know. Perhaps, if I offered to buy them from her, she might even be persuaded to accept these charms of yours as payment . . ."

Huemac picked up a ball and started past him, heading for the steps that led up to the court. Icpitl put a restraining hand on his arm, but dropped it immediately when Huemac's eyes blazed at him.

"You will come to your senses," the Trainer said in a threatening voice. "You will remember soon enough that you are a man, and then all of the Otomi charms in the world will not keep you satisfied. You will come to me again, Huemac, and you had better hope that I will hear you when you do . . ."

You will hear me, Huemac thought, but he said nothing, and continued up the stairs.

NOR DID Huemac again go to Ce Malinalli, though Icpitl flaunted the invitation constantly, and though she sent him messages of her own, filled with distress at his prolonged absence. Now, after practices and games, he went instead to the Young Men's House, where he squatted in the steamy darkness of the sweathouse and flogged his body with maize husks, scouring the temptation from his heart. Never before had self-denial been so difficult for him, and despite his efforts to exhaust himself totally, he spent many nights tossing sleeplessly on his mat, tormented by the memories of Ce Malinalli that lingered in his flesh. Several times during this period, Tlaltecatzin reprimanded him for using excessive force in the drills, and once punished him with extra work duty for initiating a fistfight with another boy.

Then, one night, Huemac fell into a deep sleep and dreamed of the hawk, and when he awoke, he realized that the spell had been broken. The yearning in his loins was gone, and he could begin to think clearly about his mission. Now he was on his own, for although the curing woman had helped to free him from Icpitl's influence, she could not tell him how the Master could be beaten in the game. But after he had completed the curing ceremony, Huemac had gone to hunt Peyotl in the desert, and the One Who Glows had given him a vision that had provided him with a clue as to how he should proceed. In the vision, he had seen himself as an older man, perhaps forty years of age, and he was teaching a group of young men how to play tlachtli. Huemac had not been able to make out what it was that he was saying to them, and the scene soon disintegrated and vanished from his sight. Yet it left him with the intriguing image of himself in the role of teacher, and opened his mind to speculations that had not occurred to him while he was a mere student trying to please his own teacher. For the first time, he began to wonder about *how* he had been taught, and what might have been left out of his education. He became a student not of a man, but of the game itself.

Icpitl, of course, taught his trainees to play the way he himself had played in his prime, when he had set standards still unmatched. He had once gone undefeated for two consecutive years, and it was said that he had volunteered to captain a team in the ceremonial games ten times, and that ten times he had sent the opposing captain to his death upon the itzompan, the sacrificial stone in the center of the court. Huemac had heard all this many times from Icpitl himself, but now he sought out some of the older, retired players and asked for their versions.

Many still shook their heads in amazement as they recalled the utter abandon with which Icpitl had played. Like a whirlwind, they said: always moving, always attacking, always hitting as hard as possible, without regard for his own safety or that of his opponents. Several showed Huemac the injuries they had suffered at Icpitl's hands, and two claimed to have seen him kill a man on the court. There were also complaints and rumors about his use of tlapatl, and unanimous approval of the ban Nezahualcoyotl had enforced against him. But no one denied that he was the most formidable player they had ever seen or played against, and few showed a desire to play against him even now.

Trying not to be daunted by Icpitl's reputation, Huemac gathered as much information as he could, using it as a standard against which to judge the Trainer's present prowess. And he gradually came to realize, as he watched with his new detachment, that Icpitl now employed a style of play that differed fundamentally from the one that had made him famous. He was still capable of awesome bursts of skill, and he always began the game with a flurry of activity designed to intimidate his opponent. But beyond the initial burst, the intensity was not sustained, and his strategy became one of anticipation rather than attack, reflexes rather than running, and plain, simple deception. For Icpitl was a master of the feigned vulnerability, the deliberate stumble, the unearned but all-too-inviting opportunity, and once he had established a reckless tempo, he slacked off and let his opponents make the mistakes. It was, finally, the appearance of abandon disguising a highly calculated attack, a style that goaded the opposition into errors rather than forcing them.

It was also a style, Huemac perceived, that totally wasted many of the natural advantages of youth. Yet he and all his fellow trainees had accepted it unquestioningly, as the only way to play the game. It made for fast, high-scoring games that took place at close quarters, largely within the central third of the court, and that featured frequent and spectacular shots at the rings. The players hit with maximum force and played every ball on the first hop, rather than running for deeper position. Whenever possible, they aimed directly for the opposing player, having learned from Icpitl's bragging recollections that there was no better way to intimidate a man than to try to hurt him.

He has prolonged his competitiveness at our expense, Huemac realized; he has adapted us to a style that favors the limitations of his age and rewards his greater cunning. Resentment blossomed in Huemac's heart, providing him with the courage to break with his teacher and begin to forge a style of his own. Yet even as the outline of a game plan began to take shape in his mind, he continued to play the way he had been taught, working on his own game only when he was alone or Icpitl was not around. He also began to build up his strength and stamina, running long distances along the lake shore and volunteering for the heavy work projects assigned to the young men of the telpochcalli. This alone improved his playing, but the improvement was lost on Icpitl, who had begun to consistently overmatch Huemac in competition, absorbing losses of his own simply to keep Huemac in his debt. It made him suspicious when Huemac did not complain of this, but his suspicions only increased his determination to maintain his hold on the jade rabbit.

"You will *have* to come to me, one day," he would threaten periodically, whenever Huemac's apparent indifference to him began to get on his nerves. But Huemac did not come to him, even after he had begun to feel that he was ready; that he could play the Trainer and beat him. The days passed and the bag of tlapatl remained rolled up in Huemac's blanket in the store room of the telpochcalli, while Huemac equivocated in the face of the final test. Though the thought of never seeing Xiuhcozcatl again brought a chill to his heart, it was not only the fear of losing that made him hesitate. Nor was it really the prospect of falling more deeply under Icpitl's influence. His true obstacle, Huemac realized, was the unshakable regard he had for the man who had taught him virtually everything he knew about the game. Playing across from Icpitl in a practice game, Huemac felt capable of beating him. But alone in the telpochcalli, contemplating the bag of tlapatl and all it represented, his courage failed him, and he could only think that *this* game would be different from any other he had ever played. Icpitl would somehow transform himself into the player he had once been, attacking with his old abandon, and then Huemac would learn that he was not ready to take on his teacher after all, and never would be.

It was his mother who finally made up Huemac's mind for him. A message came down from Nezahualcoyotl that Ome Xochitl was coming to Texcoco for a visit in only a few days, and that Huemac was to be released from his duties at that time so that he could meet with his mother and grandfather. Huemac had already met with Nezahualcoyotl once without the amulet and had not been found out, but he knew that he would never be able to deceive his mother in a similar fashion. She would recognize its absence at once, if she did not know of it beforehand. Convinced, finally, that he could not afford to hesitate any longer, Huemac unwrapped the bag from his blanket roll and went to arrange for the game, feeling a wild rush of excitement in his lungs, like the wind of a hawk coming down for the kill.

ALL THE prayers had been said, all the offerings made to the gods of the game, to the Sun and stars, to the hills, to the hawk whose feathers Huemac wore. With only a short time left until noon, he made his final preparations, tightening the straps on his rubber-soled sandals and smearing pitch on his cheekbones to cut the glare of the sun. Icpitl suddenly strode into the training room, dressed in leathers fluttering with the ribbons and feathers he had won in past games.

"I have come to pay my last respects," he announced arrogantly. "You have brought the tlapatl?"

"Tlaltecatzin holds it for me, in the center box. You have the rabbit?"

"Ce Malinalli holds it for me. The Master of Arms will no doubt find her company pleasing. Certainly more pleasing than you will find mine."

Then he smiled strangely at Huemac, who gradually realized that the proud, possessive smirk on the Trainer's face was his way of showing affection, or what passed for it in Icpitl's heart.

"Still, I admire the rashness of your challenge. You are much like I was as a young man, except for these charms, and this ridiculous abstinence."

"I am *nothing* like you were," Huemac stated flatly, his eyes shining out of blackened sockets. "You will understand this before we are through today. We will play until one of us drops or admits defeat, correct?"

"You will know when you are beaten," Icpitl assured him angrily, and turned on his heel toward the court, with Huemac not far behind.

ICPITL BEGAN the game with his customary ferocity, charging the ball recklessly and hitting low, slashing knee shots that came at Huemac like a humming, black blur. Though he could not match the velocity of the Trainer's shots, Huemac tried not to give ground, grunting audibly as he took the full force of the ball against his pads and sent it flying back. The gasps and cheers of the crowd sitting atop the walls confirmed the fact that Icpitl was playing up to his reputation, and Huemac fought back with wild desperation, telling himself not to be discouraged as one, then a second ball sped past him and rolled all the way to the dead zone at the end of the court. A third went by him, and almost a fourth, which he luckily blocked with a last-moment, instinctive swivel of his hips. But as the ball sailed back toward Icpitl, Huemac saw that he did not charge it, and that his return was deceptively weak. Huemac knew, then, that the time had come to play his own game.

Instead of rushing in to meet the ball, he turned and ran backward, striking it with his thigh as it rebounded off the wall and sending a high, looping shot deep into Icpitl's side of the court. The Trainer had plenty of time to retreat under the ball, and he returned it on a hard line, rushing forward behind his shot in anticipation of an advance on Huemac's part. But Huemac only faked a rush of his own, and again dropped back and hit one over his opponent's head. This time, Icpitl was caught flatfooted, and could only watch as the ball bounded into the dead zone.

"Play like a man!" he hollered scornfully, as another ball was thrown out and they began again. Huemac, though, showed no inclinations toward taking his teacher's advice, and continued to retreat and hit deep, running from one side of the court to the other, and making Icpitl do the same. High like a hawk, he told himself, refusing the opportunities the Trainer gave him to try to hit past him, running in circles at times in order not to be forced into a low shot. The bettors along the wall began to hiss and call out to him to attack, but Huemac paid them no heed, concentrating instead on the effect his tactics were having on Icpitl. A lesser player of his age and conditioning would already have been exhausted, but the Trainer would not be so easily coaxed into wasting his energies, and Huemac knew better than to underestimate his strength.

But he also perceived that Icpitl was concentrating so hard on his returns that he had forgotten about attacking, or about the possibility of being attacked himself. When one of his returns came in low and short, Huemac unexpectedly made a rush for it, and slashed a knee shot that flew past the Trainer at waist height, so fast that he could not move for it.

Now Huemac was only one behind, and the crowd had fallen silent. When a new ball came into play, Huemac rushed it impetuously, and almost put another one past his disconcerted opponent. But though Icpitl's face was grim as he returned to the attack, Huemac knew that he was probably crowing in his heart, thinking that Huemac's success had gone to his head. Huemac continued to press the attack, battling at close quarters until he felt Icpitl begin to hit harder, in preparation for an all-out assault. Just as the Trainer launched himself at the ball, Huemac turned and ran backward as fast as he could, looking back over his shoulder to gauge the angle of the shot. It was hit with devastating force, and most likely would have knocked him down if he had stayed where he was and tried to block it. As it was, Huemac had to make a desperate dash simply to intercept the rebound off the wall, and his return was not as high and deep as he would have liked. But the expression on Icpitl's face as he turned to chase the ball more than made up for the weakness of the shot, for Huemac could almost hear him sigh and curse his aging legs as he forced them into a run.

Huemac's own legs were aching and his breathing was deep and ragged, but he could feel the reserves of strength that his extra training had given him. He stayed deep and continued to run, knowing that every bit of effort took that much more out of the older man. Try though he might to conserve his energy, Icpitl was slower and slower getting under the high, arching shots, until at last he lost one in the sun and the game was tied.

Now he is in the open, Huemac thought fiercely, now I must strike. And he began to alternate his deep shots with sporadic rushes toward the center line, controlling the rhythm of the game and keeping Icpitl permanently off balance. Two more shots went past the Trainer, and a third point went to Huemac when Icpitl shot for the ring and missed, sending the ball out of the court. He stared at the spot where it had disappeared for a long moment, his chest heaving and his eyes glazed, unable to bring his attention back to the court. One of his kneepads was askew, but he made no effort to adjust it. Then he looked over at Huemac and his shoulders seemed to sag, and Huemac knew that it was over, that he had won. The fatigue suddenly lifted from his body, pushed out by a rush of energy that made him feel reckless and buoyant, heady with the knowledge that he could do anything he wanted and Icpitl could not stop him.

The presiding judge hesitated with the next ball, then threw it out with a shrug when Icpitl hollered hoarsely to put it into play. The best the Trainer could manage, though, was a lackluster knee shot, which Huemac immediately pounced on and fired back with such force that Icpitl grimaced and staggered backward as it slammed off his hip pad. Huemac allowed him no chance to recover his strength, charging the center line and hitting hard, low shots that made Icpitl strain simply to thrust his body in the way in time. All he had left were his marvelous reflexes, which Huemac stretched to their limit and beyond, until Icpitl's body jerked helplessly at the sound of the ball striking Huemac's pads.

Having volleyed with him long enough, Huemac put three more balls past him in quick succession, the last ricocheting painfully off Icpitl's side as he lunged and missed, and went sprawling onto the floor. There was movement among the spectators on the wall, and voices began to call out to Icpitl to quit. But the Trainer rose unsteadily to his feet and signaled for another ball. His chest was one massive abrasion, the blood running down to stain his sweat-soaked leathers, which were plastered with the limp remnants of feathers and ribbons. Huemac was close enough to him to see the fluttering muscles in his arms and the agony that clouded his narrow eyes.

"Do not make me kill you!" he called out, and the Trainer's face curled upward into an ugly snarl. Lurching forward, he met the new ball in midhop and butted it clumsily with his knee, sending it back across the line on a leisurely bounce. As Huemac wound himself up for a thigh shot, he saw Icpitl step into the direct line of the shot and drop his hands, offering his chest as a bloody target that Huemac could not possibly miss. But this time Huemac did not forget himself, and at the last moment, he swiveled on his heel and let the ball glance off his buttock, sending it high into the air. Icpitl tilted his head back, trying to follow the path of the ball as it arched over him, then lost his balance, waved his arms once, and fell like a tree to the floor. His legs jerked once and he lay flat, not moving in the sudden silence.

Removing his gloves as he went, Huemac crossed the line and knelt beside his fallen opponent. Blood welled from the lacerations on Icpitl's heaving chest, and his eyes opened and closed spasmodically.

"Sorcery," he mumbled incoherently, fastening on Huemac with one eye. "Someone has been teaching you . . . "

"Many people have been teaching me," Huemac said, still struggling to catch his own breath. "But you showed me your weaknesses yourself; you were my only teacher in that."

Icpitl groaned. "I would have made you famous . . . I did not care about the debt . . . "

"There is no debt now," Huemac reminded him proudly. "Farewell, Icpitl, you have taught me more than you know . . . "

Then Huemac rose slowly to his feet, and went to reclaim the jade rabbit.

NEZAHUALCOYOTL'S famous baths lay a half-day's walk to the east of Texcoco, upon Texcotzinco Hill, one of the red-rocked foothills that reared up in the shadows of the mountains of Tlaloc. A smooth path of fitted stones wound upward and around the western face of the hill, cresting and leveling off at a place two thirds of the way up, where stone statues of Nezahualcoyotl and his father Ixtlilxochitl gazed sternly down from a platform carved out of the red, porous bedrock. A vine-draped arbor covered the path with a lush green shade as it continued around the hill, intersected at points by steep flights of stone steps, some of which led upward to the summer palace on the summit of the hill, and others which descended to the bathing pools situated on the flat ridge below. An intricate network of stone channels and open masonry pipes carried water through the dense, junglelike foliage, creating artificial streams and waterfalls, filling the pools and grottoes used for bathing, and watering the groves of fruit trees and the beds of exotic plants and flowers that had been imported from the Hot Lands.

When Huemac first arrived at Texcotzinco, he was awed by its lushness and beauty, which reminded him of Tlalocan, the legendary paradise of the Rain God. He felt honored to have been summoned here by the king, and he had come proudly, wearing his amulet over his best mantle. At last, it seemed, he would have his chance to share his accomplishments with his grandfather, to show him how he had grown and matured. Even more than the praise he expected, though, Huemac wanted the opportunity to discuss his experiences with Nezahualcoyotl, to hear his interpretation of the visions and his assessment of the victory over Icpitl. His training here would not be complete, Huemac felt, without this final summing up.

Yet one day went by, and then another, and Huemac was not allowed so much as a glimpse of his grandfather. Protocol was very strict, because the king had revealed that he was dying, and the demand for audiences with him was tremendous. One whole set of buildings next to the palace had been reserved for the delegations from foreign cities, and the palace itself was filled to overflowing with Nezahualcoyotl's many relatives, wives, children, and grandchildren. These, especially the women, possessed a keen and abiding awareness of their rank and proximity to the throne, and they were not shy about pushing their claims upon the king's attention. Lodged in their midst, Huemac was quickly made to feel the insignificance of his own relationship to Nezahualcoyotl, and his hopes for a private interview began to fade.

Rapidly, his pride in being here turned to rancor at the way he was treated by these sneering city folk, who condescended to speak to him only long enough to ascertain his genealogy, and thereafter ignored him as they might a servant. They commented openly on his clothing and his Mexican accent, and made him feel that he was no one, not even a Texcocan: just a boy almost seventeen years old who was still an apprentice warrior, still unranked as a tlachtli player, still in the hands of his teachers.

Bored and resentful, Huemac began to regard them with the defensive scorn of the hill people, inwardly despising these imperious women with their long fingernails and dyed hair, and their children, some half his own age, who went about trailed by retinues of their own. They would die in the desert, all of them, he thought disdainfully, watching them feed themselves from the many dishes laid out on long tables in the courtyard where he was quartered. He also had not failed to notice the many birds that were kept in painted wooden cages suspended over the flower beds, and to amuse himself one afternoon, he began to call and whistle to the ones whose songs he knew.

Before long, he had all the birds chattering and flitting about in their cages, filling the courtyard with a musical racket. Children began to gather around him, laughing at the great noise he had created and adding to it with their own, childish bird calls. Huemac conducted them like a chorus for a while, enjoying being the center of attention, then began to demonstrate his other voices, answering their requests with roars and growls that silenced the birds and sent them fluttering frantically against the bars of their cages.

Suddenly, all the children turned their heads and began to move aside, making room for a young boy who strode right up to Huemac, followed closely by an extensive retinue of tutors and attendants. Huemac had only to look upon the narrow intelligent face beneath the stiff blue crown to know that this was Nezahualpilli, his grandfather's son and appointed heir. Speaking in a commanding tone, the Fasting Prince demanded a second performance, offering Huemac fine mantles and quills of gold dust for his trouble, as if he were a paid entertainer. Declining payment, Huemac bowed low to the boy, who was some ten years his junior.

"I could not take payment from my 'uncle,' Lord," Huemac said pointedly, and though some of Nezahualpilli's guardians appeared offended by this veiled reprimand, the prince himself clapped his hands and laughed with pleasure.

"You must allow me to give you a gift, then, 'nephew.' What would please you?"

Huemac was about to make another gracious refusal, but the lingering resentment of these last days made him feel bold and slightly vengeful, and he suddenly perceived a way to express the alienation he had been suffering in the midst of all these great lords and ladies.

"There is *one* thing, Lord," he suggested slowly, and the prince gestured grandly for him to go on. "There are many birds here, imprisoned within cages so that we may enjoy their beautiful songs. But near the observatory, also in cages, are the hunting birds, the hawks and falcons that are made to soar silently through the skies rather than to sing. It would please me greatly to see them returned to the sky."

Nezahualpilli stared back at Huemac intently, ignoring the heated objections of his tutors.

"Why would this please you?" he asked curiously.

"I have spent time among the hill-people," Huemac explained, "and I have come to regard the wild creatures as our ancestors, the Chichimecs, once did. It is wrong to hold them captive without reason."

Several of the prince's guardians were now glaring openly at Huemac, but he paid them no mind, sensing that he had touched something deep within Nezahualpilli. He has heard of the Chichimecs, Huemac thought, but he knows only the memory of their greatness. That should not be enough to satisfy the son of Nezahualcoyotl.

"You must tell me more of this," Nezahualpilli said at last, waving off the querulous complaints of his tutors as if they were not there. Then he smiled and nodded to Huemac. "But first, nephew, let me hear your voices. Then, I promise you, the hawks will go free . . . "

AS HE descended a steep flight of stone steps the next morning, in answer to a sudden summons from the king, Huemac first noticed an unusual quietness. Then he began to see all the empty cages, and he realized that the prince had not confined himself to freeing only the hawks. I have been called to answer for this, he thought, suffering a flash of anxiety that just as quickly turned to anger, and then to laughter. If the only way he could get to see his grandfather was by leading his son into mischief, then he could not be sorry he had done it. Death would steal Nezahualcoyotl forever, soon enough; Huemac was willing to risk some punishment to see him while he still lived.

The summons was to the Bath of the Three Frogs, a large, circular pool sunken into a flat, terraced ridge, providing its bathers with a magnificent view to the west, over the rolling hills striped with rows of green maguey, the groves of willow and cypress along the river, the rich maize lands that surrounded Texcoco itself, gleaming whitely on the shore of the sky-blue Lake. Huemac lost himself in the immense beauty of the scene for a moment, shedding his rancor, thinking: Yes, it was worth it to have come back out of the hills to create this; Nezahualcoyotl has been well rewarded for his choice, and for his dying.

Huemac stopped near the three stone frogs that squatted in front of the pool, and gave his name to the guards who were in charge of the many people waiting to see the king. Among them were a high priest from Cholula, a delegation of Tlaxcalan warriors, and several of the great ladies who had snubbed Huemac previously. Yet he was immediately ushered past them to the front of the line, and then sent forward to the place next to the pool where Nezahualcoyotl was holding court. The king was sitting in the shade of an arched trellis covered with palm fronds and flowering vines, surrounded by a group of people of varying ages, all so splendidly dressed that Huemac could not tell the lords from the attendants. Other guests splashed in the clear waters of the pool, their naked presence ignored by the court out of modesty. Huemac sensed the nearness of his mother, but he could not locate her with the one quick glance he was permitted before he had to bow before the king.

"Greetings, Huemac," Nezahualcoyotl said abruptly. "I suppose you know why I have sent for you?"

An impudent response hovered on Huemac's tongue, waiting to burst forth with all the repressed impatience of these past days of idleness, but the sight of his grandfather's fleshless body and hollowed face shocked him into momentary silence. He had not expected the decline to be so apparent. When he finally answered, his voice was husky with apology.

"If I have caused you to be angry with your son, Lord, I can only offer my deepest regrets, and ask that you punish me, and not the Fasting Prince. The idea was mine."

"Why did you even suggest such a thing to him?" the large, fair-skinned woman next to Nezahualcoyotl demanded, and Huemac guessed that she was the queen, Matlatzihuatzin, the sister of Chimalpopoca of Tlacopan and the mother of Nezahualpilli. It was obviously she who was most angry about this, for Nezahualcoyotl's long face, on second glance, bore an expression of serene detachment, his already gentle eyes softened even further by the knowledge of impending death. Huemac explained his reasons to the queen as he had to her son, but he failed to stir her imagination in a similar fashion.

"And what savage taught you this nonsense?" she inquired contemptuously when he had finished, and Huemac had to glance away briefly to conceal the sudden anger in his eyes.

"His name was Oztooa, my Lady," he said tightly. "And he has lived in this land since the time of Quinatzin, when our people first came out of the hills. I do not believe that he would tell me nonsense."

"Nor *would* he," Nezahualcoyotl interjected, then laid a comforting hand on the queen's arm. "You must forgive me, my wife, but in this case I must side with my grandson. He did not ask to free your beloved songbirds; that was Nezahualpilli's own idea."

"It would never have occurred to him on his own," Matlatzihuatzin insisted angrily, flashing fire at Huemac with her eyes.

"Perhaps it *should* have," Nezahualcoyotl said, so sharply that the queen, though clearly not satisfied, closed her mouth and nodded reluctantly. Then she requested permission to leave, and swept off with her retinue, darting a last, unforgiving glance in Huemac's direction. The king smiled ruefully.

"Is there nowhere you can go, Huemac, without creating an enemy for yourself?" he asked lightly, and Huemac also smiled, hearing the voice of a man he did not have to pity. He allowed himself to ignore the people surrounding the king, sensing that they did not matter to Nezahualcoyotl; that he did not seek privacy because he was already alone.

"It is a talent I was born with, Lord," Huemac said, in a bantering tone he had never used with his grandfather before. "I will be pleased to tell Oztooa, when I see him again, that you defended his wisdom."

Nezahualcoyotl laughed his high, whinnying laugh, curling back his lips to reveal a broad expanse of pink gums.

"Tell him, by all means. And tell him that I am honored that he tried to steal you from me."

"You have spoken to Xiuhcozcatl, then?" Huemac asked.

"I have spoken to *all* your teachers," Nezahualcoyotl assured him, and shook his head in amusement. "You have led an interesting life here, Huemac. Perhaps, at times, even more interesting than you would have desired . . . ?"

"The dangers of my impulsiveness have been brought to my attention, more than once," Huemac admitted, submitting to his grandfather's teasing with pleasure.

"Ah! So you are no longer thinking of it as your bad luck! That *is* a good sign. Come closer, Huemac, and look into my eyes. But do not lose yourself there . . . "

Huemac squatted in front of his grandfather and immediately felt Nezahualcoyotl's gaze lock onto his own, narrowing his focus and diminishing the space between them. Huemac saw the white hair and wasted features, the long, narrow nose, the webbed lines surrounding the utter blackness at the center of his eyes . . . there was an urgent tugging at Huemac's midsection, and he consciously tugged back, widening his eyes little by little, until he had established a comfortable tension. Then he could see the whole of his grandfather's face, and he could make out the images that began to pass across it, welling up and fading out like shimmering, evanescent masks. There was the coyote he had once seen as a child; an eagle with translucent golden eyes; the face of a man with black mirrorlike eyes and sharp reddened teeth; a spotted, snarling jaguar; a narrow, elongated face tattooed with serpents that coiled and uncoiled in time with Huemac's breathing; and, finally, the grim white visage of a naked skull. Then the air before Huemac was empty, without shape or color, a vision of nothingness.

Nezahualcoyotl released him gently, and Huemac rocked backward onto his heels, but kept his balance. His grandfather's face appeared even more drawn and haggard, but satisfaction shone through the weariness in his eyes.

"Now you have seen the faces of my life," he said, "as well as the face of my death. And I have seen yours. Your end will not come to you soon, Huemac; there is much that you will have to live through, and suffer. I cannot offer you any more comfort than when you first came to me, but I do not think that you need comfort—or seek it—any longer."

"Am I prepared, then, to face the Demon Heart?"

"You must go once more to the desert with Xiuhcozcatl, to finish with the plants. But then you will return directly to Tenochtitlan."

Huemac stared at him without speaking, and Nezahualcoyotl read his thoughts from the expression on his face.

"No, you will not see me again. But it is time that you returned to your home, and though I have told my people not to mourn my passing, they will do so anyway, and the ceremonies might delay your departure unnecessarily. When you are finished in the desert, go to the lakeside city of Chiconauhtla. There you can hire a canoe to take you across to Tepeyac, where I understand you have some business to complete."

Huemac nodded mutely, and the king waved a finger at him admonishingly.

"You must not mourn for me, either. It will only distract you from the challenges of your own fate, and make you weak in the face of your enemies. Straighten your heart, my grandson, and be at peace with yourself, for you have brought me great joy in your time on the earth." Then Nezahualcoyotl smiled and adopted a more matter-of-fact tone. "Now: I know that you have rescued yourself from debt, but there must be those whom you would wish to reward for their services and friendship. Tell me what you desire for them, and it will be yours."

Huemac bowed gratefully, and cleared his throat before speaking: "I have promised the Old One a bundle of quetzal and cotinga feathers, and there is a curing woman to whom I owe a bag of coral and turquoise beads. I would also like to give something to Tlaltecatzin and Xiuhcozcatl."

"A fine Huaxtec mantle for the Master of Arms, and some trade goods for the Turquoise Necklace," Nezahualcoyotl said to one of his attendants, before turning back to Huemac. "What else? Come, do not be shy, my time for generosity is limited."

"There is a woman whose name is Ce Malinalli . . . "

"Ah, the one teacher I did not consult," Nezahualcoyotl said with a knowing smile. "She will have mantles and skirts that will cause her to remember you with fondness. But is there not another? What would you have me give Icpitl?"

Huemac frowned and spread his hands indecisively, then had a thought that brought a wicked smile to his face.

"Perhaps a mirror, Lord . . . a fine mosaic of silver mirror-stone, in which he could see himself clearly."

Nezahualcoyotl gave a short, appreciative laugh. "Yes, I think you are ready to leave me; you have learned to show the proper amount of compassion for your adversaries." The king paused, then went on in a gentler voice, signaling the end of the interview: "Your mother awaits you in the plaza beside the great aqueduct. Rise, and let me look upon you once more."

"Farewell, Grandfather," Huemac whispered as he rose to his feet, his eyes glittering with unsuppressed emotion.

"Farewell, Huemac," Nezahualcoyotl said, smiling at his grandson for what both knew would be the last time. "May the gods of the Tenocha, and the gods of your ancestors, watch over you and give you strength. May the Giver of Life be merciful, and let you live for a while upon the earth . . . "

OME XOCHITL crossed the plaza quickly and collapsed, gasping for breath, on a stone bench that lay in the shadow of the high aqueduct wall. She was no longer so slender, at forty-eight, as she had once been, and the air here was much thinner than that of Tenochtitlan. She had rushed over from the Bath of the Three Frogs with intemperate haste, having stayed longer than she had intended, listening to all but the very end of her son's conversation with the king. She needed time, now, to gather her thoughts about what she had heard and, more importantly, *felt* during the interview.

For although she had hidden herself behind the other people and had allowed herself only one short glimpse of her son, she had clearly felt every one of Huemac's emotions: his shock at Nezahualcoyotl's appearance, his outrage at the queen's ignorant snobbery, the secret shame aroused in him by the mention of this man Icpitl. Even when he had been looking into his grandfather's eyes, and she could not know what was being revealed to him, she had nonetheless felt the thrill produced in him by what he was seeing. A thrill very different, in its reverence, from what had passed through him when he spoke the name of the woman . . .

This is not proper, she thought self-consciously; he will be marrying before too long, and only his wife should have this knowledge of his inner feelings. Ome Xochitl had originally decided to come to Texcoco because of a premonition that Huemac's life was in danger, but her anxiety had passed before she had even left Tenochtitlan, and one of the first stories she had heard upon her arrival here was the tale of Huemac's successful duel with Icpitl. It was apparent to her from this, and from the conversation she had just heard, that Huemac no longer needed her protection, and probably would not appreciate her anxieties on his behalf. As a result, she had resolved to conceal the real reason for her visit, and to let him think that she had come here to share her father's last days.

She sensed Huemac's approach long before he came around the bend in the path and started across the plaza toward her. Watching his eyes, she could tell that he had been deeply affected by the audience with his grandfather, but she also could not help noticing the way his gaze swept over her appraisingly before meeting her own. My son has the eyes of a man, she thought ruefully, experiencing a sudden awareness of the wrinkles in her face and the silver in her hair. She rose from the bench and embraced him, feeling the strength and solidity of his body.

"Sit beside me, my son, and let me look upon you," she said, and Huemac dutifully took a seat on the bench, calmly opening himself to her inspection.

"You were there, Mother," he said curiously. "Why did you not join our discussion?"

"Your grandfather had asked me to be present," Ome Xochitl explained, "but I knew that it would be your last conversation with him, and I did not wish to intrude. I will have more time with my father after you have gone to the desert."

"You heard everything, though?" Huemac asked, and she nodded.

"Your grandfather spoke to me beforehand, so I knew of the things to which you referred. This latest mischief of yours did not surprise me, either," she added dryly, and Huemac laughed.

"These people are my kin, yet they treated me with less respect than the savages they scorn so freely. Only the prince treated me with the courtesy for which Texcoco is famous."

Ome Xochitl contemplated him silently, hearing the note of bitterness behind the seemingly casual response.

"Since your pride is still so sensitive," she said, "I must warn you to be careful when you return to Tenochtitlan, especially if you come by way of Tepeyac. There are incidents with the Tlatelulca every day, and young men have died because they were careless enough to display their pride in the wrong place."

Huemac sobered instantly. "And the older men?" he demanded. "What of my father?"

"He fights to preserve his people, as he always has. But even he no longer believes that an open battle can be avoided. He seeks merely to delay the final provocation, and to minimize the amount of blood that must be shed. He has been successful so far, but I do not think he will be able to continue for long after the Fasting Coyote dies. His death is certain to make both Moquiuix *and* Tlacaelel bolder in their provocations."

"Necoc Yaotl," Huemac murmured thoughtfully, then looked up at his mother. "Will there be time for me to return and help him?"

"Possibly," Ome Xochitl said, then spoke without thinking: "But I do not think that he will want you to share his danger."

Huemac heard the possessiveness in his mother's voice and frowned sternly. "You forget, Mother, that I was sent here because I *already* share in that danger. I do not think that Grandfather would send me back to Tenochtitlan if he did not feel that I was capable of defending myself."

"Forgive me, my son," Ome Xochitl said, lowering her eyes apologetically. "I should not have allowed my grief and sorrow to speak for me."

"Grief? For your father?"

Ome Xochitl shook her head wearily. "I have seen much death in my time upon the earth, Huemac. I saw my mother die when I was still a girl, and I buried four of my children during the Rabbit years. Now my father is dying, as he prophesied, and I fear that my husband will soon follow him to the Land of the Fleshless. Can you blame me for wanting to save you?"

Huemac opened and closed his mouth several times, rejecting the first, impulsive words that came into his head. Ome Xochitl saw him gradually master the uneasiness she had created in him, until he could look at her with an expression that showed an appreciation for her pain.

"You must forgive my pride, as well," he said softly. "But Grandfather has asked that we not grieve for him, and you have always known of the dangers that Father has chosen to face. As his son, I cannot be saddened by the bravery of his choice."

"That is as it should be," Ome Xochitl agreed solemnly. "Nor have I ever tried to dissuade him from his choice, for I know that there is no other way for him to live. My grief is for the hope I cannot allow myself to have, and for the cold certainty that fills my heart in its place."

Huemac laid a hand on hers, and they sat in silence for several moments, listening to the muted whisperings of the water flowing above their heads. Ome Xochitl looked eastward along the length of the great stone aqueduct, which topped the next hill and then reappeared at the crest of the one after that, snaking its way toward the springs on the side of Mount Tlaloc. It seemed a colossal feat of craftsmanship, yet she could not help contrasting its apparent permanence with the fleeting lives of the men who had built it.

"I have been given visions of a long life," Huemac said, gently breaking into her thoughts, "and you yourself heard Grandfather confirm this. No doubt you also know that I had a vision of Tlatelulco which threatens the others, and robs them of certainty. I have not forgotten this, my mother; I will not be so careless in Tenochtitlan as I have sometimes been here."

Hearing the utter sincerity of his attempt to comfort her, Ome Xochitl felt tears well up in her eyes. Taking his blunt, callused hand into her own, she tried her best to smile at him.

"That is all that I can ask of you," she said, blinking back her tears. "Hurry back to us, my son, do not delay your return. The time now is very short, and your city will soon need *all* her men . . ."

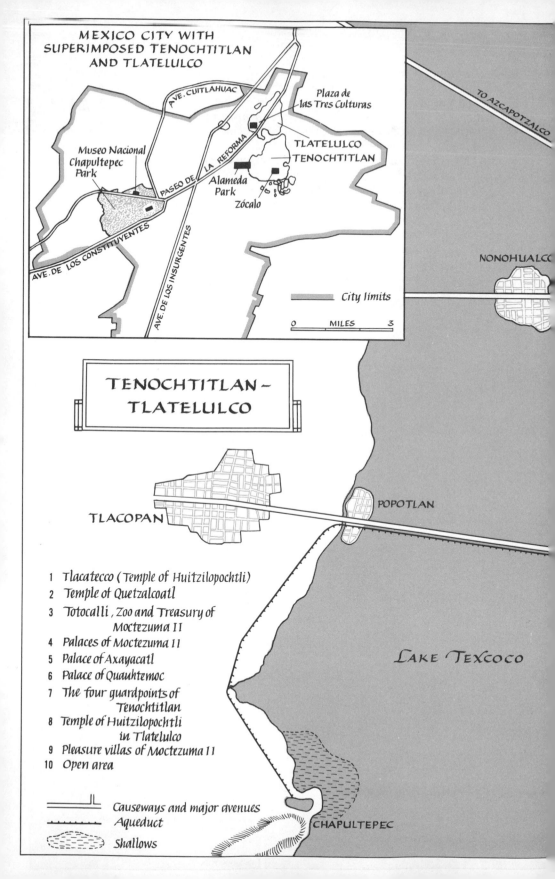

MEXICO CITY WITH SUPERIMPOSED TENOCHTITLAN AND TLATELULCO

AVE. CUITLAHUAC

Plaza de las Tres Culturas

Museo Nacional
Chapultepec
Park

PASEO DE LA REFORMA

TLATELULCO
TENOCHTITLAN

Alameda
Park

Zócalo

AVE. DE LOS CONSTITUYENTES

AVE. DE LOS INSURGENTES

City limits

0   MILES   3

TO AZCAPOTZALCO

NONOHUALCO

TENOCHTITLAN ~ TLATELULCO

TLACOPAN

POPOTLAN

LAKE TEXCOCO

CHAPULTEPEC

1   Tlacatecco (Temple of Huitzilopochtli)
2   Temple of Quetzalcoatl
3   Totocalli , Zoo and Treasury of
     Moctezuma II
4   Palaces of Moctezuma II
5   Palace of Axayacatl
6   Palace of Quauhtemoc
7   The four guardpoints of
     Tenochtitlan
8   Temple of Huitzilopochtli
     in Tlatelulco
9   Pleasure villas of Moctezuma II
10   Open area

Causeways and major avenues
Aqueduct
Shallows

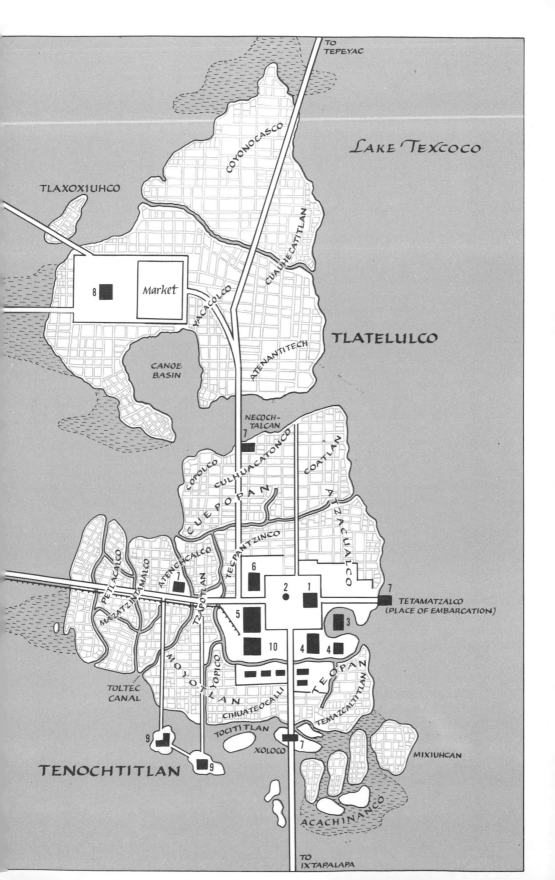

TO
TEPEYAC

Lake Texcoco

COYONOCASCO

TLAXOXIUHCO

CUAUHECATITLAN

8 Market

YACACOLCO

TLATELULCO

ATENANTITECH

CANOE
BASIN

NECOCH-
TALCAN

7

COATLAN

COPOLCO

CULHUACATONCO

C U E P O P A N

TECPANTZINCO

A T Z A C U A L C O

6

PETLACALCO

MAZATZINTAMALCO

ATENCHCALCO

7

TZAPOTLAN

2   1

7 TETAMATZALCO
(PLACE OF EMBARCATION)

5

3

10   4   4

M O Y O T L A N

TOPICO

T E O P A N

TOLTEC
CANAL

CIHUATEOCALLI

TEMAZCALTITLAN

9

TOCITITLAN

9

XOLOCO   7

MIXIUHCAN

TENOCHTITLAN

ACACHINANCO

TO
IXTAPALAPA

VI

TLAZOLYAOYOTL:
The War
of Defilement

1472–1473

1

NEZAHUALCOYOTL, Ruler of Acolhuacan, Lord of the Chichimecs, died in the year Six Flint-Knife, at the age of seventy, and his ashes were buried beside those of his ancestors at the place called Cuauhyacac, the Forest's Edge. Less than a month later, while ceremonies of mourning were still being held in Texcoco, Moquiuix sent envoys to the regent, Acapipioltzin, offering him a calpulli of his own in Tenochtitlan and lands for all his sons, if he would betray the Triple Alliance and join with the Tlatelulca. It was also hinted, with the requisite subtlety, that Moquiuix would be willing to help Acapipioltzin overthrow the prince and claim the icpalli for himself. Acapipioltzin, however, was as much his father's son as Nezahualpilli, and he responded to the offer with an outrage that showed that his loyalty could not be bought. He sent the envoys back to Tlatelulco with harsh words and reported their offer to Axayacatl, reconfirming Texcoco's steadfast support of the Tenocha and the Alliance.

Undaunted, Moquiuix next made overtures to the Tlaxcalans and Huexotzincans, whose lands beyond the eastern mountains had been gradually encircled by the conquests of the Alliance, and who had sharpened their hatred of the Tenocha during the long series of flower wars that had been held on their borders since the time of the famine. Yet Xicotencatl and the other leaders hated *all* of the Mexica, and they could not be persuaded that the Tlatelulcan offer was not a trick designed to lure them to their destruction. Again, Moquiuix's ambassadors were received with suspicion and mistrust, and were sent away without the pact they had hoped to secure.

In Tenochtitlan, the usual protests were issued, but no more decisive action was taken. This was Axayacatl's own doing, for the young Speaker, surrounded now by confederates of his own choosing, had grown more comfortable upon the reed seat, and seemed to have taken a firm grip on Tenocha policy. Kept informed by many of the same people who served Quinatzin, he had succeeded in neutralizing the dissident factions led by Tizoc and the disgruntled relatives of Iquehuac, and when Tlacaelel voluntarily removed himself from the court, claiming ill health, Axayacatl was freed to rule as he saw fit.

Yet despite this apparent freedom, and his reputation for impetuousness, the Speaker reacted to the Tlatelulcan threat with a complacency that struck all but his closest advisers as curious, if not actually dangerous. He appeared content to wait for a provocation that would put justice on his side, no matter how long it might take, and he displayed little concern when it was learned that Moquiuix had secured some potential allies among the Matlatzinca to the west, and was seeking others in the Otomi and Tepanec cities to the north. His brother Ahuitzotl and the leaders of the Eagle and Jaguar Warriors, who had seen no action in months, pressed him repeatedly to launch an immediate attack, but Axayacatl could not be budged. He would say only that his sister and the nephew who had been named for him lived in Tlatelulco, and as long as they were safe and well treated, he would not allow himself to be provoked into an attack on his brother-in-law.

Quinatzin placed as little credence in this explanation as he did in Tlacaelel's claim of illness, for he had himself heard Axayacatl, on more than one occasion, express his yearning for the chance to face Moquiuix man-to-man. And as he listened to the Speaker's statements now, he detected an arrogance in Axayacatl's attitude toward the Tlatelulca that was not warranted by the facts as he knew them, and as he had assumed they were being reported to the ruler. He is *too* comfortable, Quinatzin reflected ominously, and he underestimates the strength and ferocity of his enemy. Obviously, someone had his ear, someone whose information he trusted and prized more highly than that of the sources he shared with Quinatzin.

Quinatzin suspected that it was one of the handful of young warchiefs who were Axayacatl's closest confidants, but *which* one remained a mystery, for Quinatzin's only reliable contact among their ranks had recently been sent to command the garrison at Cuetlaxtlan. This was the fourth informant who had suddenly become unavailable to him, and the final bit of proof that Tlacaelel was not languishing in his illness, if he was indeed ill at all. The removal of the warchief could have been a coincidence, had the loss of the other three not shown all the earmarks of the Demon Heart's vicious handiwork. One had been the maidservant of Chalchiuhnenetl, Moquiuix's queen, and had acted as a valuable intermediary for Quinatzin, before she was charged with adultery and summarily put to death. The other two, both of lower rank, had simply disappeared, and were not heard from again.

As a result of these depredations, Quinatzin was forced to move with extreme caution, and to restrict his visits to his most important sources. He began to feel, as he had during his early years in Tenochtitlan, that he was proceeding in darkness, and being outflanked by his enemies on all sides. Yet he did not cease in his efforts to penetrate the circle around Axayacatl, and, with the fatalism that had gradually become his sustaining force, he began, at night, alone, to devise his final strategy, a plan that would only be put into effect after his own death.

He was sitting beneath the huehuetl tree late one night, thinking of this, when he saw Ome Xochitl leave her rooms and come across the courtyard toward him.

"Huemac is coming," she explained, and Quinatzin retrieved his staff and rose laboriously to his feet, without bothering to question how she knew.

"Good," he said curtly. "I have been thinking of him."

Moments later, Huemac appeared in the courtyard entrance, a bow and quiver of arrows slung over his shoulder and a large bundle tucked under one arm. He was still wearing his desert blanket, and both of his parents glanced down at his bare feet when he stopped to bow before them.

"Greetings, my son," Quinatzin said. "The sight of you brings joy to my heart, and pleasure to these old eyes."

"Always, I have prayed that I might see you again," Huemac replied. "The gods have been merciful, my father."

"Shall I awaken the first wife?" Ome Xochitl inquired of her husband, but Quinatzin shook his head peremptorily.

"No. I have much to say to my son, and he to me. Prepare some food, and we will come inside."

Ome Xochitl took the bundle—which contained Huemac's city clothes, sandals, and tlachtli gear—from under Huemac's arm and left the two of them alone under the tree. Huemac seemed suddenly ill at ease, almost furtive in his father's presence, and Quinatzin, with a rare stroke of insight into his son, realized that something was disturbing him intensely, something that might have just happened to him.

"You are troubled, Huemac. What is it?"

"I have seen Nopaltzin," Huemac said immediately, then closed his mouth and swallowed, as if it hurt him too much to go on.

"Where? In Tlatelulco? You took a chance going there at . . ."

"Not in Tlatelulco," Huemac interrupted. "I saw him on Mount Tepeyac, only a little while ago."

"Did he greet you?" Quinatzin prompted, having been told by Ome Xochitl that Huemac was returning by way of Tepeyac, but not why.

"He did not see me," Huemac said in a flat voice. "I was hiding, watching while my friend took an oath to kill me and all my people. It was a blood oath; they drank a potion made from the itzpacalatl, the water from the washing of the sacrificial knives."

"I am sorry that you had to see this, my son," Quinatzin said quietly, "but I am not surprised. Tell me: How many were there, and who conducted the ceremony?"

"There were perhaps fifty young men, some with their hair still uncut, like mine. There was a warchief, a powerful man with a hooked nose, accompanied by a squad of Otomi Warriors. And there was a priest who wore the mask and carried the Serpent Staff of Huitzilopochtli. It was he who mixed the potion and administered the oath."

"That was the High Priest, Poyahuitl," Quinatzin informed him. "And the man with the hooked nose is Teconal, Moquiuix's brother-in-law. He is the leader of the Tlatelulcan war party, and it is obvious he intends to press every

available man and boy into his service. This information will be very useful
to me, my son. You showed great courage in staying to watch."

"Useful!" Huemac flared angrily, astonished and insulted by his father's
cool assimilation of the news. "I wanted to kill him! I had an arrow in my bow,
aimed at Nopalli's heart. How can this be useful to anyone, except Necoc
Yaotl?"

"Lower your voice," Quinatzin commanded sternly. "And stop being sentimental. There is no time for it. Do you think that you feel worse than Tezcatl,
whose son no longer comes to visit him?"

"So it is too late," Huemac said in a softer voice, though his bitterness was
no less apparent. "I have only returned in order to help kill those who were
my friends."

"You may have to," Quinatzin said unsparingly, "and you must not hesitate
when the time comes. But I am glad that you did not begin tonight. I have
need of you alive."

Huemac's face wore a rueful expression. "I came back to help you, Father.
But is it not plain that nothing more can be done? You cannot hope to forestall
the war any longer . . ."

"I do not wish to," Quinatzin said swiftly. "I have been trying to precipitate
it for over a month now, and I would have it begin tomorrow, if I could. This
surprises you?"

"Very much," Huemac managed weakly, and Quinatzin smiled.

"I have no doubt that you were well taught in Texcoco, my son, but there
is an area of your education that is still incomplete. You know nothing of the
world I have inhabited for the past forty years, the world of the rulers, and
of those who would be rulers. It is not your fault, for I have not had the time
to teach you before this."

"But you will now?" Huemac inquired hopefully.

"As I said, I have need of you, and there is no one who could teach you
more than I. But perhaps you are still filled with despair over your friend, and
would rather surrender yourself to the Enemy of Both Sides . . . ?"

"I do not understand what you hope to accomplish," Huemac said frankly,
"but I will serve you in whatever way I can."

"Let us go inside, then, where we can speak without the risk of arousing
Teuxoch. You will understand soon enough," Quinatzin promised, as they
moved toward the rooms. "As much, at least, as *I* understand . . ."

"YOU MUST understand, first of all," Quinatzin began, after they had shared
food together, "that while both cities consider a conflict to be inevitable,
neither wants to be responsible for starting it. Moquiuix and his people have
long resented the sovereignty exercised over them by Tenochtitlan, but they
know, despite their recent successes, that they are still outnumbered, especially
in terms of experienced warriors. Even the drinking of the itzpacalatl will not
make an apprentice the equal of an Eagle or a Jaguar. So there are great
pressures on Moquiuix to contain the pride of his warchiefs and avoid a battle
until he has secured reliable allies. These pressures come from the artisans and
merchants of his city, who have much to lose but little to gain from a war, and
from his wife, Chalchiuhnenetl, whose presence in Tlatelulco reminds everyone of the strong ties of blood that exist between our peoples.

"Axayacatl, for his part, does not want to dishonor himself by attacking his brothers without sufficient provocation. He feels, perhaps unreasonably, that he is certain of victory, and it is a matter of pride to him that he not be seen to have acted too hastily, out of nervousness and fear. He knows that the Tlatelulca would never have dared to challenge Moteczuma as they have challenged him, so he strives to withhold his wrath as his grandfather would have, and will not permit himself to be goaded into a rash and ill-considered attack. The warrior orders, of course, who have vows to Tonatiuh to fulfill, have put great pressure on him to let them fight, or at least to arrange a flower war with the Tlaxcalans. They are very unhappy in their idleness, but so far Axayacatl has held out firmly, and continues to wait for Moquiuix to bring the battle to him."

"And Tlacaelel?" Huemac asked impetuously, eager to show, despite his earlier bewilderment, that he was not *totally* naïve.

"Ah, Tlacaelel," Quinatzin exclaimed softly. "I can never know all that is in *his* heart. He has retired from the court and allowed it to be known that he is ailing, but I do not believe this for an instant. He knows that his absence encourages Moquiuix and Teconal in their mad daring, and he moves behind the scenes as viciously as ever. He has made it very difficult for me to operate with any safety. I also believe that he has an agent among Axayacatl's advisers, and that this agent is deliberately leading the Speaker to underestimate the strength of the Tlatelulca."

Huemac tried, vainly, to mask his incomprehension behind a thoughtful frown, but he could not make sense of such a thing.

"Why would he want to mislead the Speaker in such a way? It can only lead to a weakening of our defenses."

"Precisely. But the Demon Heart does not recognize weakness, and he has no interest in defending the warriors of our city. Always, my son, his only goal has been to bring glory to Huitzilopochtli, and the more who die fighting in the god's name, the greater the glory. It does not matter to him if those who die are our enemy, or our own people—their blood equally feeds the god."

"Even those who worship other gods share this belief," Huemac pointed out, "but it does not lead them to expose their warriors to unnecessary danger. That is inviting disaster!"

"You are beginning to understand," Quinatzin assured him sardonically. "If Tlacaelel has his way, he will unleash all the hatred and envy that have existed between our cities since the time that the Tenocha first came to this island. He will see that the killing does not stop until the streets are red with blood, and there is no one left to beg for surrender. He knows the Tenocha; he knows the vengeful wrath that wells up in their hearts when they are strongly opposed by an enemy. Especially an enemy whose prowess they have underestimated."

"So *this* is why you have tried to hasten the war," Huemac concluded, impressed but not heartened by his new knowledge. Quinatzin nodded somberly.

"It is only a matter of time before Moquiuix feels bold enough, or desperate enough, to launch a surprise attack. I doubt that the Tenocha will be truly surprised, but they will be unprepared for the ferocity of their enemy, and it will cost them greatly to beat the Tlatelulca off. Then, feeling that he is the aggrieved party, and angered by his unexpected losses, Axayacatl will throw all his warriors into the battle, and Tlatelulco will finally be destroyed."

There was a long silence, and Huemac glanced over at his mother, who was sitting a few paces away with her head bowed over her folded hands. But though he knew she was listening, she did not look up. Quinatzin went on in a voice remarkable for its lack of emotion, the voice of a man who put his faith in nothing, yet rejected no possibilities out-of-hand:

"If, on the other hand, the Tenocha could be made to attack first, then they would be most bound by their sense of honor, and most inclined to mercy. If the temple in Tlatelulco could be taken quickly and put to the torch, perhaps both sides would come to their senses, and a general slaughter could be averted. Some months ago, before Moquiuix began to seek allies, the merchants' guilds of his city and ours secretly proposed to him and Axayacatl that a mock battle be arranged, a flower war in disguise, which would allow both cities to avoid disgrace as well as destruction. The proposal was rejected, of course, but I have not forgotten what I learned during those discussions. I have not forgotten about the temple."

Quinatzin's eyes looked past his son, to the future, perhaps, or to the end of the future. Huemac waited patiently until his father's attention returned to him.

"How could the Tenocha be encouraged to make such an attack?" he asked, and Quinatzin acknowledged the pertinence of the question with a satisfied nod.

"Chalchiuhnenetl is being mistreated by her husband, and I have used this to try to convince her brothers that they should reclaim her from Moquiuix. Perhaps that would be insult enough to stir Axayacatl into action, though I doubt it. I am also trying to discover which of his advisers is giving him false information about the strength of the Tlatelulca, and to make him take their threat seriously. What you have told me tonight will be useful in this regard, for it shows clearly that Moquiuix is not relying solely on whatever allies he can secure, and that his numbers might be much greater than we have suspected. It will also give Teconal pause, to think that we know everything he does. Perhaps, if I use this information cleverly enough, it will even help me to learn which of Axayacatl's young warchiefs is Tlacaelel's agent . . ."

"How can it do that?"

Quinatzin smiled modestly. "I will leak it to the adviser I suspect most highly, in such a way that he will think that he can conceal it if he wishes. Then I will leak it to someone else, and wait to see if Axayacatl has already been told."

Huemac let out an involuntary gasp at the simplicity of the ploy, and its utter deviousness. He smiled at his father, but Quinatzin deflected his admiration with a stern gesture.

"Simply knowing who it is does not mean that I will be able to counteract his influence, or bring on the war any sooner. You must not be so impressed by small successes, or you will grow complacent and careless."

"I understand," Huemac said apologetically. "But you have not told me how I can help you, beyond what I have already done."

Quinatzin glanced at his wife, who still did not raise her head. Then he looked straight at Huemac and took a deep breath, as if mustering all his determination.

"I want you to join Tlacateotzin's company in Moyotlan and continue with your training as a warrior, as any other young man would. Continue playing tlachtli, as well, if you wish. Act as if you have no opinions about this war, other than those shared by your comrades."

"But of what use can I be among our own warriors?" Huemac complained, disappointed by the safety of the assignment, which he suspected was a concession to his mother.

"I have not finished," Quinatzin snapped irritably, with another glance at Ome Xochitl. "You will listen to your comrades, and keep me informed of what they are thinking and feeling. And you will also act as my messenger, though you will have no message to deliver until after I am dead."

Huemac was not certain he had heard correctly, until his mother's stiffly staring face convinced him that he had.

"To whom will I deliver this message?" he asked quietly.

"To Tlacateotzin and Acolmiztli. When you hear that I have been killed, you will know that I have failed, and that the worst is about to occur for our cities. Then you must go to them and show them the way to Tlatelulco, the way I will show to you tomorrow. Once this war begins, the only thing that will stop it is the burning of the temple. The sooner that is accomplished, the fewer the lives that will be lost. If all else fails, my son, you must lead the way to the temple, and conquer anyone who stands in your way."

"I swear that I will do this," Huemac vowed, though there was pain in his eyes. "But what if the war begins, and there is no news that you have been killed?"

"Then you will know that I have succeeded beyond all hope," Quinatzin said, smiling bleakly, "and that I have found a way to make peace with the inevitable." He glanced over at the gray light seeping through the open doorway. "Rest now, for it is almost morning. I will take you to Tlatelulco this afternoon."

Rising from his mat, Quinatzin leaned upon his staff and limped out of the room. Huemac stood and stretched his legs and shoulders, yawning and rubbing his eyes ostentatiously. He had not slept in a day and a half, and his nerves felt raw and exposed from what he had been through in the last hours. He needed time and rest to assimilate what he had seen and heard, and to accustom himself once more to the sounds and smells of a city. But his mother's attention pulled on him powerfully, demandingly, a force that he could not ignore no matter how weary or unwilling he was. Suddenly angry that she could exert such pressure upon him, he whirled and knelt facing her, a few paces away.

"What do you expect from me, my mother?" he demanded, his voice rising beyond his control. "What could I possibly say that would bring you any comfort? My father has chosen, and I must honor his wishes!"

Ome Xochitl measured him impassively, an accusing glint in her dark oval eyes.

"You did not tell him everything that happened to you tonight," she said flatly, and Huemac sat back onto his heels, then rose and walked in a small circle away from her, collecting himself.

"I could not tell him why I was on Tepeyac," he said sullenly, "and he did not ask me. He would not have understood. I do not understand all of it myself."

"What really happened to you tonight, Huemac? It was not only seeing Nopalli, and wanting to kill him."

Huemac pursed his lips and nodded grudgingly, a defeated look in his eyes.

"I went to Tepeyac," he said slowly, "to make myself whole again, to mend the damage I had done to my spirit, long ago. I accomplished this according to Xiuhcozcatl's instructions, and the feeling that has been with me for many years went away, or so it seemed. I did not feel much different, but I had been warned not to expect a sudden change. As I was leaving the mountain, I saw lights in the forest and went to spy upon the ceremony. That is where I saw Nopalli . . . "

"What happened to you then?"

"The feeling . . . the one I had been having . . . came back, into my hands." Huemac flexed his fingers before his body, regarding them warily. "They *shone,* they glowed in the darkness with a reddish light that would have exposed me if I had not hidden them beneath my mantle. I could feel their heat against my skin, and a power so strong that I was sure I could have torn a man to pieces as easily as a child plucks apart a flower."

"And then?" Ome Xochitl prodded, for Huemac's eyes had turned inward at the memory. He blinked and continued:

"When I saw Nopalli drink the potion, willingly, joyfully, pledging himself to destroy every man, woman, and child in Tenochtitlan, when I saw him begin to dance around the fire, smiling a terrible smile . . . I could think only that I had to kill him. And my hands, as if of their own will, lifted my bow and armed it, aiming for his heart. Never have I had the strength to bend a bow so far; I would have put the arrow completely through his body. I know it. My amazement at that saved me, for my hands would not shoot on their own, and I had time to come to my senses. I decided that if I must kill my friend, I will not do it from hiding."

"That was very honorable of you," Ome Xochitl said, with a sarcastic edge to her voice that he had never heard before. "So you did not think that you needed to confide any of this to your father before accepting the task he has bestowed upon you?"

"He does not know all my secrets, as you do," Huemac said in a tight voice. "Yet he trusts me, and I will honor that trust, and the promise I made to him."

"And what of the promise you made to me? Have you forgotten your vision of Tlatelulco? How will you watch yourself, how will you guard your spirit, when you cannot even control your hands?"

"I did not shoot!" Huemac thundered, overwhelmed by his anger. "And I do not need you to guard my spirit for me!"

Aghast at his own outburst, Huemac hung his head and did not look his mother in the face. Ome Xochitl rose and folded her arms across her chest.

"I see," she said stiffly. "You are a man now; you must make your own decisions. Forgive me for questioning your judgment."

"Forgive my rudeness," Huemac said, though there was still anger in his voice. He spread his hands in supplication, then dropped them abruptly, as if the need to apologize only added to his resentment.

"You need not say anything more," his mother told him, and walked past him out of the room. Huemac stood where he was, staring down at this hands.

I am home less than a day, he thought, and already I am at war with my best friend, and my mother. This, too, must be the work of Necoc Yaotl, the Enemy of Both Sides. But he will not have me, Huemac vowed, he will not have me *or* my city. Then Huemac lay down and tried to sleep, in the room where he had been born, where his father had just spoken to him of dying, where he had finally told his mother that he must be free.

2

CROSSING over the bridge into Tlatelulco, Quinatzin led Huemac to Pochtlan, the largest of the seven contiguous calpullis inhabited by the merchants of the city. Here, as required by protocol, they first paid a visit to the house of Popoyotzin, who was one of the top leaders of the pochteca, the Guild of Principal Merchants. Each of the seven calpullis had its own leadership, Quinatzin explained, as well as many clan-based trade associations, but all were under the authority of the guild. Not only did the pochteca regulate the main marketplace and organize the trading journeys to foreign lands, but they also appointed judges and ran their own law courts, independent of the official legal apparatus. Thus, though Popoyotzin had been appointed to his post by Moquiuix himself, his power within the community relied upon no outside source, and no one could hope to conduct business among the merchants without his knowledge and approval.

Since the pochteca were renowned for their wealth, Huemac was momentarily puzzled by the unpretentiousness of their leader's house, which appeared to be crowded in amongst others of an equally modest size. But once inside, he realized that it was all one house, and that the many separate entrances all led—by means of a deliberately complex network of interior passageways and blind courtyards—into a central courtyard every bit as large and spacious as that belonging to Acolmiztli. It seemed even more spacious, in fact, because the house itself was only one story, and none of the trees planted around the perimeter had been allowed to grow higher than the interior walls. Though there were fewer servants in evidence than Huemac would have expected in such a grand house, a long row of beehive-shaped clay ovens against the far wall revealed that, at least on occasion, this courtyard was the scene of large gatherings.

Popoyotzin was a short, rotund man whose large belly was not hidden by the loose folds of his mantle. He wore no jewelry or insignia, and his garments were of drab maguey-fiber cloth, rather than cotton. He greeted Quinatzin with effusive cordiality, appearing greatly flattered by the visit, and by the fact that Quinatzin had brought his son to meet him. He bowed to Huemac and welcomed him to his house, bemoaning its humbleness with a diffidence that echoed insincerely off the walls of the enormous courtyard. After many such courtesies had been exchanged, and a servant had brought them cups of whipped cocoa and maize cakes sweetened with honey, the two men went off to confer privately and left Huemac to wait in the courtyard.

Seated on the edge of a pool filled with white water lilies, Huemac watched the people who came and went around him, aware that he was being watched himself. He was struck by the poverty of their dress, especially after having seen the gaudy finery worn by the warriors of both cities. Even in the three years that he had been gone, the garments and insignia of the warriors seemed to have grown more resplendent, thick with precious stones and the brilliantly colored feathers of birds never before seen in Anahuac. Yet these merchants, who dressed themselves more poorly than the boys from the calmecac, were the very ones who brought the stones and rare feathers, the jaguar skins, from the far-off lands where they could be found: from Xicalanco and Ayotlan, Xoconochco and Zinacantlan, places the armies of the Alliance had never visited. They braved the dangers of the trail, and of hostile tribes, so that those who served the gods on the field of battle could be rewarded with the symbols of their rank and valor.

For this, Huemac thought, their wealth is tolerated and they are allowed to live in our midst like arrogant strangers, providing supplies but no warriors to the warchiefs, ruling over themselves, marrying only their own kind and permitting no one else into the guild. They were even allowed, during certain of the festivals, to sacrifice slaves they had bought rather than captured, a privilege that many of the warriors considered a direct affront to their calling. They are wise not to flaunt their prosperity, Huemac decided; they must know how much they are resented.

As an apprentice warrior, Huemac himself was not immune to this resentment, and he was not certain that the *pretense* of poverty he saw around him was not as offensive as the wealth it was meant to conceal. Popoyotzin's humility had not been convincing, and these other people, despite their coarse clothing, did not carry themselves as if they were poor or humble. And the cocoa he had been given was among the finest he had ever tasted. It was obvious that they only eschewed the *visible* trappings of wealth, a prudence that in no way lessened their essential presumptuousness.

When he saw Popoyotzin and Quinatzin coming across the courtyard toward him, Huemac rose, reminding himself to be courteous, and not to allow his true feelings to show. My father must deal with these people, he told himself, and I have promised to aid and obey him. Perhaps he will even be able to tell me why I should respect them.

But it was difficult for him to listen to Popoyotzin fawn over his father, flattering him shamelessly, extending his compliments to Huemac himself. Huemac heard the pride and shrewdness that lurked behind every seemingly humble word, yet Quinatzin responded as graciously as he always did, refusing the praise with modest words, as if it were genuine though undeserved. When they were at last on the street again, and alone, Huemac could not restrain himself from exhaling loudly in relief.

"Is waiting so hard for you?" Quinatzin inquired mildly. "I thought the cocoa was quite adequate."

"Yes," Huemac agreed curtly, then could not contain himself. "But I do not know who they hope to fool with this, this *illusion* of poverty!"

"It is no illusion. It is the way that they live. Only on the feast days of their gods do they display their wealth, and then they are required to give much of it to the guests they invite on such occasions. These always include the warriors of the city."

"I am sorry," Huemac said immediately. "Perhaps I judged them too quickly. I have heard many bad things about them."

"No doubt," Quinatzin averred. "Teuxoch is like her father in thinking that the pochteca are cowardly and disloyal, a people who value a clever bargain more highly than the taking of a captive. But if you come to understand them, you will see that they are brave and honorable in their own right, and very correct in their attitudes toward the gods."

"I will clear my mind of what I have heard," Huemac promised in a chastened voice. "I will try harder to understand what is before me."

"You must form your own opinion, in any case," Quinatzin said easily, dismissing the need for apology. "I will take you to a man who may be able to help you. His name is Cuetzpaltzin, and he is a member of the oztomeca, the Guild of Vanguard Merchants. They are of course part of the pochteca, but they have rites and duties all their own. Cuetzpaltzin is one of those known as nahualoztomeca, the 'disguised vanguard merchants.' "

"How is he different from the other pochteca?"

"You will see. Now you must begin to pay attention to where things are, for after we visit Cuetzpaltzin, I will show you the path to the temple. Come, and do not be disturbed by those who will observe us. We are safe here."

They were in the southwestern quarter of the city, moving westward, away from the great canoe basin that opened into the channel that separated Tlatelulco from Tenochtitlan. Behind them, just to the north, was the plaza containing the marketplace and the temple of Huitzilopochtli, which was considerably larger than its counterpart in Tenochtitlan and could be seen from anywhere on either island. The calpullis through which they passed were honeycombed with canals and canoe slips, bridged by wooden platforms that also served as docks, and could be moved from place to place. Many of the warehouses were raised on pilings over the water, unreachable from the street once the bridges had been cut. Huemac looked down the dark passageways between buildings: narrow, twisting paths lined with hidden doorways and side alleys that were barred by wooden gates. He could feel eyes watching him from those doorways, waiting in ambush behind the shadowed gates. I would not want to fight in those alleys, Huemac thought; they would have every advantage over a stranger. Can it be through here that Father wishes the attack to come?

But Quinatzin said nothing, leading the way with assurance, oblivious to the armed men who trailed him through the winding streets. Even the children, playing at being merchants with tiny staves and makeshift bundles, stopped to observe their passage in silence, and one of their number slipped away from the group and ran on ahead, in the direction Quinatzin was going. Huemac saw water birds overhead and sensed a stiffening in the breeze, which led him to believe that they were nearing the western shore of the island. But then Quinatzin turned abruptly into one of the side passages, and Huemac saw the child who had preceded them waiting just ahead, at the first bend in the path.

Quinatzin nodded to the boy, and they followed him around the corner, then around another corner, and still another, turning and doubling back on themselves until Huemac could barely retain his sense of the direction from which he had come, much less how to find his way back. Armed men appeared in the side entrances they passed, standing silently in the semidarkness, making no attempt to block the way.

Finally, the boy led them through a gate and directly into a house that was a single room with only the one entrance and no windows. The floor was of wood covered with reed matting, and Huemac could hear the dim murmur of water somewhere below his feet as he quickly scanned the room, taking in the fish nets and spare paddles in one corner; the crossed black staves standing like an altar in another, with an incense burner smoking before them; the exotic masks, shields, and skins that decorated the walls. He wanted to examine the things on the walls more closely, but he had no time as he bowed with his father and seated himself next to Quinatzin, on one side of the square of light provided by an open trap in the ceiling. On the other side were three men, one seated several feet in front of those who flanked him on either side. Huemac noticed that the two behind had macanas balanced across their laps.

"You must forgive the precautions, my friend," the man in front said to Quinatzin, in an accent that Huemac could not quite place. "My people trust no one these days."

"It is understandable," Quinatzin said simply. "This is my younger son, Huemac. He has just returned from Texcoco, where he was under the tutelage of his grandfather, the late king."

"The wisdom of the Fasting Coyote is sorely missed, throughout Anahuac," the man said, nodding with sympathy and respect in Huemac's direction. "I am Cuetzpaltzin, and although this is not my home, I welcome you to my calpulli."

Huemac bowed, tantalized and intrigued by the man's accent, which did not seem Mexican. Nor, though he could see him clearly across the square of light, could Huemac tell more about Cuetzpaltzin than that he was about thirty years of age, rather slight in build, and dark complected. His face evaded easy description, seeming one moment flat and moronic, and the next shrewd and sharply defined. He was wearing a blue-and-green cotton mantle of a foreign weave and design, with long tassels hanging from the border.

"I have heard, my friend," Quinatzin said, "that there is again trouble in the lands of the Zapotecs."

Cuetzpaltzin nodded earnestly. "Some of our men, returning from Xoconochco, were ambushed near the city of Mictlan. There is trouble in many places, because the armies of the Mexica have not been seen in many months, and attacks such as this go unavenged. It is wasteful," the merchant said angrily. "The warriors of our cities sit here idle, waiting to tear at one another, while rich lands lie unconquered, closed even to trade."

"Yet Moquiuix still rejects your peace proposals?"

"He rejects even the entreaties of his queen, who, it is said, has seen portents of disaster in her dreams. He is blinded by the tribute he sees pouring into Tenochtitlan, tribute that might easily be his. He has forgotten that our forefathers were traders as well as warriors, and relied as much upon the strength of their backs as that of their arms."

"It has been reported," Quinatzin said delicately, "that Moquiuix has found allies in the cities of Culhuacan, Huitzilopochco, and Cuitlahuac."

"That is interesting," Cuetzpaltzin said in a neutral voice. "How has Axayacatl responded to this rumor?"

"He finds it unlikely, of course. He has invited the rulers of those cities to Tenochtitlan to celebrate next month's festivities to Ilamatecuhtli, to whom there will be many sacrifices. No doubt he will ask them then."

"No doubt," the merchant repeated absently. "It is a curious rumor."

They sat in silence for a few moments, while a woman brought in three cups of cocoa and tubes of rolled yetl for the two older men. While his father and the merchant went through the ritual of lighting and sharing the yetl, Huemac sipped his cocoa and pondered the significance of the conversation he had just heard. Information was obviously being exchanged, but it was impossible to determine just what each had told the other that had not been known to both of them beforehand. Were the queen's dreams useful to his father? And what was the meaning of the invitations to the rulers? It had seemed to Huemac, when he was listening, that the two men had spoken with unusual frankness, yet he was not sure now that anything had been openly revealed by either of them.

Still, they seemed to have completed their discussion, for when Quinatzin resumed speaking, between puffs on the smoking tube, it was in a more casual tone:

"My son wishes to know how the members of your guild are different from the other pochteca. I thought perhaps you would show him the feathers you brought back from Zinacantlan."

Cuetzpaltzin gestured to one of the men behind him, who rose and went to remove something from the wall. Then he laid a reed mat within the square of light and placed a small bundle of long, green feathers upon it. They were a shimmering, brilliant green, fully three feet long, shading to an iridescent grayish-white toward their delicately fringed tips. Huemac nearly gasped at their beauty.

"They are the tail feathers of the quetzal," Cuetzpaltzin explained. "I bartered for them myself, less than a year ago, in the marketplace of Zinacantlan."

Huemac looked quickly to his father and saw that it was all right to ask questions.

"Forgive my ignorance," he said to the merchant, "but how were you able to trade there? My brother, Acolmiztli, has told me that all the lands south of Tehuantepec are hostile territory, and that the Chiapanecs of the highlands are especially unfriendly."

"You have been correctly informed," Cuetzpaltzin said, with just a trace of a smile. "But they are not unfriendly to those who look and speak as they do." Narrowing his eyes and puffing out his cheeks, the merchant suddenly began to speak in a rapid, high-pitched dialect that was as unlike Nahua as anything Huemac had ever heard, yet seemed, somehow, to fit the face out of which it was issuing. Then Cuetzpaltzin relaxed his features and spoke normally: "You see, we are the merchants of the vanguard, and we often have no protection except that which our cleverness gives us."

"It is a great risk to take," Huemac said, thoroughly impressed by the demonstration.

"We are warriors," the merchant said flatly. "We know that if we die on the trail, our bodies will be painted and burned, and we will ascend to the heavens, to the abode of the Sun."

Huemac started visibly, and he again glanced at his father, who nodded to him to speak his mind.

"Forgive me, I mean no offense," he said carefully, "but I have been taught since I was very young that the honor of escorting the Sun through the sky belonged exclusively to those who died in battle or upon the techcatl."

"Forgive me, also, if I say that the warriors of Tenochtitlan do not do us justice. It is *we* who go in advance of the armies, mapping the trails and penetrating the defenses of the enemy, preparing the way for the warriors of Huitzilopochtli. Who is to say when the battle begins? Is it only when the warriors meet in great numbers, dressed for war? What of the warriors who scout for the army? Are they not accorded the same honors as those who march within its ranks, even if they die far from the battlefield?"

"This is true," Huemac conceded.

"*Our* battlefield is on the trail," Cuetzpaltzin continued in an impassioned voice, "and in the wilderness, and the marketplaces of foreign cities. There we spy for the army, and fight for Huitzilopochtli. Surely, the blood we shed must go to increase his glory."

"I had not thought of it in such a way," Huemac admitted reluctantly, and the merchant gave him a sardonic smile, as if he were familiar with the difficulty Huemac was having in accepting such a view.

"It is good that you had the boldness to ask, then. I know how some of the Tenocha think of us, but I am not affected by their opinion. I know that I walk correctly before the gods, and serve them with all my heart."

This was stated with such utter conviction that Huemac could only nod in agreement. Cuetzpaltzin nodded back.

"Do you have any more questions?"

Huemac thought a moment. "Just one, my Lord. Why, if you are the warriors of Huitzilopochtli, do you not seek to wear the insignia of those who serve him?"

"Our special god is Yacatecuhtli, the Lord of the Vanguard. He teaches us to live humbly, and to be thankful for the poor food and clothing that sustain us on the trail. Amongst ourselves, we know the names of those who are honored. Besides," the merchant added, giving Quinatzin a sly, conspiratorial smile, "at the present time, it would not be granted to us."

The two older men laughed loudly, and after a moment, Huemac grinned weakly, realizing that this sudden departure from seriousness had been intended to teach him a lesson. So *this* is the world of my father, he thought, this place where the demands of the gods can so quickly give way to the opinions of men, so that it is hard to tell one from the other. This place where candor is a kind of code, where men can speak sincerely of their beliefs yet bow in their minds to other realities. Huemac was staggered by the simplicity of the worlds he had known before this, and the overwhelming sense of his own naïveté made him feel suddenly tired.

"I thank you, my friend," Quinatzin was saying. "If you can have us guided to the dike along the western shore, I would like to spend a moment admiring the sunset upon the water before we go on."

"It is very beautiful, at this time of day," Cuetzpaltzin agreed, and gestured to one of the men behind him. "May the gods protect you in your travels, Quinatzin . . ."

WATER BIRDS wheeled through the slanting rays of the falling sun, while fishermen, rocking with the waves, pulled black nets from blood-red water. Huemac breathed deeply of the cold salty air, trying to clear his mind of the fatigue that had descended upon him. He and his father were standing upon a dike of mortared stone, looking westward to the island of Nonohualco, and beyond, to the land that had once belonged to the Tepanecs. Several feet below them was a second landing where canoes were being unloaded, but they were far enough away that they could not be overheard.

"I know that there is much you wish to ask me," Quinatzin said without preliminary, "but right now you must listen, and use your eyes. This is the place to which you must lead Acolmiztli, when the time comes. You see the great huehuetl tree there, on the corner of Nonohualco? That is the landmark that will guide you here; you must not turn the canoes until you are even with it, in order to avoid the shoals that lie close to the shore farther south."

Shading his eyes, Huemac stared at the shaggy black silhouette of the tree, committing its shape to memory.

"This is the one safe place to land," Quinatzin continued, "for it is a bridge that cannot be cut. It will be fiercely defended, but once you have won your way onto it, the oztomeca will retreat to their houses and expect to fight you there. The warriors must not be allowed to pursue them, or you will be trapped and destroyed. Lead them instead to the street that lies ahead to our right; it leads directly from the Nonohualco causeway to the temple plaza. There will be guards behind you on the causeway, but they will most likely be engaged with our allies from Tlacopan."

"Will not the oztomeca attack us from behind when they see where we have gone?" Huemac asked.

"It is not their responsibility. They will hold the canoe basin and defend their calpullis against all invaders, as they have agreed with Moquiuix, but they will not do more than this. You have seen their independent ways yourself."

"Indeed," Huemac said. "The plaza will be heavily defended, will it not?"

"Most of Moquiuix's forces will probably be concentrated in the marketplace, since the main Tenocha attack will come from that direction. You may not be able to take the temple yourselves, but the confusion you create will bring the battle in around it. That, at least, is my hope."

Huemac nodded silently, and spent several more moments memorizing the details of the landscape. When he was finished, he turned to his father and studied him with the same intensity. Quinatzin was sixty-three, but his face had aged well, the skin still taut across his high cheekbones, the forehead virtually unlined beneath the mane of white hair. It was a distinguished face, calm and unblinking, a face that invited trust. As always, Huemac was painfully aware of how little he resembled his father; he imagined that his own face, in contrast, was flat, dark, and devious, his eyes a source of discomfort for other people. Yet he also felt, looking at his father now, that his own face was far less of a mask, his heart far more worthy of the trust Quinatzin inspired so easily.

"Have you seen enough?" Quinatzin inquired gently, and Huemac sheepishly dropped his eyes and shrugged.

"I feel that I am just beginning to see you. From the time that I was a small child, I knew that you did not have my mother's powers, and that I could fool you if I wanted to. Always, I have felt that I was the more crafty one. But now that I have seen your world of secrets, I feel that I am still that small child. Do not misunderstand: I still wish to learn. But I am not certain that I will ever belong in your world."

Quinatzin laughed softly and rolled his eyes skyward.

"Neither did I, once. But your grandfather and your mother taught me to accept what fate had thrust upon me. No doubt you will have to learn the same thing in your own way." Quinatzin reached out and laid a hand on Huemac's shoulder. "There is no need to apologize for your feelings. You know the sort of man I have served. Perhaps if I had had your kind of craftiness, I would never have come under his power. That is what I hope will save you from a similar fate."

"I have been shown a vision of myself as an Old Eagle," Huemac announced impulsively, watching closely for his father's reactions, alert for the slightest sign of disapproval or disbelief. But Quinatzin appeared genuinely pleased.

"That is a fortunate prospect, indeed. Perhaps you have escaped the luck with which you were born."

"Perhaps," Huemac said dubiously. "I should also tell you that I have had a vision of something that would happen to me in this city. It was a strange and violent vision, filled with danger, yet its meaning was unclear."

Quinatzin removed his hand and looked at Huemac with concern.

"Perhaps I have asked too much of you, then."

"I knew this when I accepted your trust. I did not tell you then because I was afraid you would misunderstand and refuse to let me help you. But I could not speak to you about fate and keep these things to myself."

"Will they interfere with the duties I have entrusted to you?" Quinatzin asked, and Huemac straightened his shoulders and put a determined expression upon his face.

"My mother thinks so, but I do not. I will not let them," he added sternly. "I have been trained not to run from the challenge they present to my spirit."

"Then I must trust your judgment," Quinatzin said decisively. Hefting his staff, he took a step backward, off the dike. "But come, the sun has set, and the streets of this city will not be safe for us after dark. When you are settled in Moyotlan, we will return and see our friends Tezcatl and Taypachtli."

"Yes," Huemac agreed wearily. "I have been away for so long that even Tenochtitlan seems foreign to me."

"Let us go home, then," Quinatzin said, and started walking, leading the way back through the calpullis of the pochteca, and out of Tlatelulco.

HUEMAC was welcomed to the company of the ward of Moyotlan by his brother-in-law, Tlacateotzin, who was one of the company commanders. Acolmiztli, whose contingent of Jaguar Warriors was attached to the ward, was also present to greet him, but Huemac saw immediately that this was not the time to be asking about his sister or his nephews and nieces. He bowed formally and listened as they reminded him that the task of warfare was stern and demanding, and warned him that he must apply himself rigorously and not expect any favored treatment from them.

"We know of your victory over Icpitl," Tlacateotzin said, his normally pleasant features frozen into the lines of sober authority, "but you will not be given a tryout with our team until you have been tested as a warrior. You have five days in which to renew your skills with the weapons, and then you will be expected to defend yourself against the other apprentices in the daily drills. It is up to you to prepare yourself."

Huemac looked at both of their faces, seeing in their eyes the belief that he could not have learned anything important in Texcoco, since he still had not proven himself in combat. It was the only test that mattered to them, the only proof that one was a Tenocha. Huemac had believed the same thing for most of his life, yet at that moment, as he stood beneath their stern, admonitory gaze, he could only see it as one of the many tests he had already undergone and had yet to undergo, and not the most crucial of those. He had his visions to face, and the task his father had given him, and the eventual confrontation with Tlacaelel. And had he not already killed a man, and risked his life against the likes of Icpitl and the Old One?

"I will be ready," he said firmly, perhaps too firmly, for both Tlacateotzin and Acolmiztli frowned at his apparent lack of humility.

"This is not the telpochcalli," Acolmiztli said. "There are apprentices here who are older than yourself, and who have never studied anything but the arts of war. They will show no respect for how *you* have spent your time."

"I understand," Huemac said with the same firmness, unwilling to yield to his brother's estimation of how well he had been trained in Texcoco. I have *seen* that I am Tenocha, he thought belligerently, and I will prove it to anyone who cares to come against me. But I will not pretend that such a challenge fills me with awe.

"Go and prepare yourself, then," Acolmiztli said, curt to the point of anger. Tlacateotzin made a gesture of dismissal, and Huemac bowed again and went off, alone, to begin his life as a warrior.

IT TOOK Huemac less than a day among the apprentice warriors to discover how badly the morale of the Tenocha had deteriorated during this long and uneasy period of armistice. Some of the young men had left the calmecac even earlier than Huemac and had come here directly upon graduating from the telpochcalli, lured by the rich opportunity for glory and advancement promised by the reign of Axayacatl. Yet the Speaker had undertaken little action of any magnitude since his initial campaigns, and the armies of the Tenocha had not gone into the field in almost two years. Instead of rising swiftly through the ranks as they had expected, the apprentices found themselves growing older with their status unchanged, still unable to drink octli, smoke yetl, or wear cotton clothing, denied even the privilege of eating in the same room with the proven warriors. Some were fast approaching the age of marriage, yet possessed neither the means nor the rank to ask for a wife.

Meanwhile, they had seen more boys come out of the telpochcalli and crowd into their quarters, competing not only for space but also for what little distinction there was to be won in the daily drills. Huemac quickly perceived that these exercises had long ago lost whatever value they might once have had for the learning of technique. They were run by the older warriors, who were themselves so bored and frustrated by their enforced idleness that they allowed the trainees to attack one another without restraint, sometimes even making bets on the outcome. Serious cuts and broken bones were frequent occurrences, and bad fighting habits were often overlooked and left uncorrected in the general outpouring of energy and emotion. No one, including Tlacateotzin and Acolmiztli, seemed to notice the sloppiness of the fighting, and no one seemed concerned that the apprentices regarded one another as opponents, rather than comrades.

When the sixth day arrived, Huemac took his place on the practice field, aware of the scrutiny of his brother and Tlacateotzin, and of the other apprentices vying for the chance to take advantage of the newcomer. For just a moment, his old rashness came back to him, and he was tempted to attack with the kind of abandon that he knew would impress Acolmiztli, no matter how he might endanger himself. But when he was finally called on to fight, he remembered his responsibility to his father, and his angry rejection of his mother's concern, and he came out warily, concentrating on guarding his legs and avoiding an injury that might incapacitate him.

He heard catcalls as he closed with his first opponent, who showered him with abuse while slashing viciously at his head and shoulders. Let him waste his breath, Huemac thought coolly; let them *all* waste their breath. Fending off his opponent's wild attacks, Huemac hammered away at him with a precision Tlaltecatzin would have admired, wearing him down and making him pay for every mistake. Soon he had the man reeling helplessly and gasping for breath, and when no one moved to stop the contest, Huemac finished him off with a stinging but harmless blow to the knee, similar to a blow he had once received himself.

The catcalls ceased immediately, and as the afternoon wore on, Huemac became increasingly grateful for the soundness and patience that Tlaltecatzin had instilled in him, and for the endurance he had built up in the desert and on the tlachtli court. He fought three more times, each time against an older and larger opponent. His matches took twice as long as any of the others, and though two of them ended in a virtual draw, he knew that no one would be lining up to face him tomorrow.

"Your style is too conservative," Acolmiztli said to him afterward, then admitted grudgingly: "But you have been well trained."

Better than you know, my brother, Huemac thought insolently, though he accepted the compliment with a gracious nod. Acolmiztli gave him a hard stare before turning on his heel and stalking off, obviously disappointed. Huemac felt the pain of that, briefly, then hardened himself against such a sentimental response. Though I do not wish to ever carry my father's message, he thought as he watched his brother depart, you will someday learn that I was not sent here simply to please you . . .

THE TINGLING sensation, which Huemac had not experienced since the night on Mount Tepeyac, returned for the second time during his tryout with the Moyotlan tlachtli team. It began in his right foot and gradually spread upward to his knee, a warm, prickly feeling that made him want to stamp his foot. When he felt the muscles in his calf begin to flex and swell, he cast an anxious glance downward, but the leg *looked* normal.

At the time, he was playing in a six-man game, stationed to the rear of his two teammates. He was relaxed and slightly bored, for he did not see much action back here. The ball players of Moyotlan all played the fast, low-trajectory game pioneered by Icpitl, so that the third man merely served to back up the main action that occurred at midcourt. Huemac had come to the tryout prepared to reveal the secret of how he had defeated Icpitl, thinking that he owed it to them out of loyalty to the team. But none of the other ball players asked him. Instead, they had gone out of their way to show him how unimpressed they were with his victory, since it was supposedly well known that Icpitl had lost his skills with age. Huemac was made to understand that he was in Tenochtitlan now, and he would have to make his reputation *here.*

So Huemac had kept his secrets to himself and played the game as they did, since he could tell even in warm-ups that not one of them played with Icpitl's grace and mastery. He systematically humiliated his first opponent, a young man his own age who had obviously just taken up the game, and who should not have been sent against him. As if admitting their mistake, the team leaders seated atop the wall next sent out a man several years older than Huemac who was wearing the black-and-red colors of a regular team member. Huemac later learned that he was the number three man on the team, but he treated the man no better than he had his first opponent, running him from side to side and tempting him into foolish mistakes. When he felt that he had sufficiently demonstrated his skill, he was able to slacken the tempo and chance a glance at the team box on top of the wall at midcourt. But no one was watching him; they were all too involved in making and settling bets.

Now, as he stood idly in the backcourt, he could see that the activity of the most intense interest was not the action on the court, but the gambling among the spectators. He felt a strong surge of disgust at this, followed by the desire to wake them up. As if in response, the tingling in his leg grew stronger, and moved upward into his thigh. Though the leg looked outwardly the same, Huemac could feel the muscles bulging with an incredible strength.

Dare I use this power? he wondered. Despite his attempt to bury it with the knife, it had followed him off the mountain, and he had to reckon with it. He remembered what his mother had said to him, and he to her; he remembered his grandfather saying that whether or not the gods used him again depended on the kind of power he sought. This was enormous power, deadly power. Can

I guard my spirit against this kind of power? he asked himself sternly; can I use it and not have it destroy me?

Yet as he returned his attention to the game and the raucous crowd that surrounded it, he knew that the real question was whether he had any other choice but to try. He could not ignore the sensation of power in his leg, which seemed to only grow stronger when he tried to neglect its presence. I must learn to control it, he decided suddenly, or it will control *me.*

Huemac gauged the distance to the stone ring fixed into the wall just below the team box. No one ever shot at it from this far; that was always left to the up-men. Huemac bounced slightly on his right leg, lifting himself off the ground without effort. He knew then that he could do it, and he could think of no better way to bring everyone's attention back to the game. When the ball rose over the heads of the men in front of him and came bounding toward him, then, he did not back up for the expected lob, but charged it with all his might. Digging in with his left foot, he threw his right leg into the ball with such force that he did a complete back-flip and came down hard on his buttocks. The ball was a black blur that sailed over the upturned faces of Huemac's teammates and suddenly flattened itself against the stone ring with a loud *thwack,* missing the hole by a hand's-breath.

The rebound came all the way back to where Huemac was sitting, but since he could not hit it again, he simply let it go by. After a moment of complete, astonished silence, the crowd let out a roar, and the game had to be stopped momentarily while attendants collected the flowers and tubes of yetl that were thrown onto the court. When the game began again, Huemac saw that the spectators were watching now, if for no other reason than to see what he would do the next time he got the ball. Though his buttocks were throbbing from the fall, his right leg was flowing with power, literally twitching for another try. When the ball finally came through to him, he slammed it again, and this time it hit the outermost edge of the ring and ricocheted past the opposing team, who were too amazed to try to move for it.

The uproar along the top of the wall was tumultuous, and mantles and lengths of cloth were thrown down onto the court by the excited bettors. The chant of "Again! Again!" was taken up by the crowd, and when Huemac looked up at the team box, he saw that the men sitting there had their heads turned away from the court, and were frantically making bets with one another. So I have only provided them with another reason to wager, Huemac thought bitterly, and decided that it was time to put an end to this game.

There was no pretense of continuing the competition when the ball was next thrown out. After one volley, it came directly to Huemac, who hit it with the same astounding force yet dipped under it slightly to give it a higher trajectory. It rose straight toward the ring, evoking a shout from the crowd, then kept rising, soaring over the ring and right into the team box, where the spectators ducked and scattered in panic, dumping their betting goods off both sides of the wall.

Apparently, no one was hurt, but another ball was not thrown out, and as if by common consent, the spectators rose and began to leave. Huemac turned and walked toward the training room, aware suddenly that the tingling in his leg was gone. So it can be used, he thought, and used *up.* He was met at the end of the court by several attendants with their arms filled with the flowers, yetl, and cloth that had been thrown onto the court. Their leader looked at

Huemac with awe and asked where he would like his gifts taken. It was more wealth than Huemac had ever had, yet he did not hesitate in making his decision.

"Take them to the shrine of Xolotl, our patron," he said. "It is *his* power that has done this, not mine . . ."

AT THE END of his first month with the company, Huemac was finally given a day of leave. He went first to his father's chamber in the Tecpan. After they had eaten together, Quinatzin had his attendants remove the dishes and then sent them out of the room.

"I am told that you have adjusted well to your company," he said to Huemac when they were alone. Huemac shrugged ironically.

"I was well trained in Texcoco."

"Indeed," Quinatzin replied absently, before getting down to serious business. "Let me tell you first what I have learned, since the information you brought to me helped in the discovery. The warchief who has captured Axayacatl's ear is named Ocomatli. He is related to Tlacaelel on his mother's side, though distantly, and I have not been able to confirm a connection between them. The reason that this Ocomatli has gained the Speaker's trust is that he has a highly placed spy in Tlatelulco."

Huemac widened his eyes quizzically, but Quinatzin shook his head.

"No, I do not know who this spy is, but from what I have ascertained, he must be close enough to the Tlatelulcan War Council to know all of Moquiuix's plans. Axayacatl, at least, feels that he knows all of his enemy's intentions. This is the source of his overconfidence, and his patience. He means to lure the Tlatelulca into an ambush."

"Perhaps he has reason to feel confident, then," Huemac suggested. "And perhaps if Moquiuix were to walk into an ambush, his courage would be shattered and he would sue for peace."

Quinatzin smiled tolerantly. "That assumes that the word of this spy is trustworthy, and that all of what he says is communicated to the Speaker. As I said, I do not know that Ocomatli is an agent of Tlacaelel, but I *suspect* it."

"Would Tlacaelel truly allow our own men to fall into a trap?"

"He is capable of such a thing," Quinatzin assured him, "when the mood is upon him. I do not see much of him these days, and when I do, he is playing sick. Sometimes I do not think that he is playing, for the spirit waxes and wanes in him. But you can be sure that he will have his strength when the war comes."

"When do you think it will come?" Huemac asked softly.

"There is another month until the nemontemi. I do not think that anyone will act until they are over, and then the ceremonies of the first month, the Calling for Rain, will have to be held. Soon after that, I expect that Tizoc and Ahuitzotl will bring Chalchiuhnenetl back from Tlatelulco. The war will no doubt begin within days of her return."

"I have your message," Huemac said gravely, "but I continue to pray that I will not be called on to deliver it."

"It will be as the gods will it. Now you must tell me what you have learned among the warriors of our city."

Holding nothing back, Huemac spoke bluntly of what he had seen in Moyotlan: the bad morale of the apprentices, the injuries and sloppiness permitted in the drills, the gambling and womanizing going on among the older warriors, the blindness of the leaders to what was happening beneath their very eyes.

"It is because they, too, are mystified by the reasons for this waiting," Quinatzin said of the leaders, "though I assume that they have been told to blame it on the Tlatelulca."

Huemac nodded disgustedly. "It is what all the men believe. They are being made to forget that the Tlatelulca are people of our own blood. A great number of shields are being made, all bearing the seven eagle feathers of Tenochtitlan, so that we will be able to tell ourselves from the enemy."

"I know this," Quinatzin said, and smiled calmly in the face of his son's obvious disillusionment. "But what you have told me of the morale of the warriors is interesting; it required a fresh eye to see it so clearly. I will see that it is brought to the Speaker's attention, independently of Ocomatli. But now you must go to see Tezcatl and Taypachtli. I cannot accompany you, but I will give you the insignia of a messenger, so that you may travel freely. Make good use of your time, my son, for easy access to our friends may be denied to us very shortly."

"I will go now, if we are finished."

"Go," Quinatzin said with a wave of his hand, "and give my regards to Tezcatl and his daughter. Do not be shocked by how our friend has aged, or by the fact that he never speaks of Nopaltzin. It would probably be best not to mention that you have seen Nopalli. It can only deepen Tezcatl's pain to be reminded."

"And mine, as well," Huemac said sadly, and bowed to his father in leaving.

WHEN HUEMAC stepped through the doorway of Tezcatl's house, he found himself at the starting point of a series of paths that had been laid out in precise lines across the courtyard. The paths were made of dry rushes that crackled slightly underfoot, and they were bordered by small, round stones that had been embedded in the dirt floor. One branch went off to the rooms on the far side of the courtyard, another to the thatched ramada where Tezcatl worked, and still another cut straight across the courtyard between the rooms and the ramada, intersected by two shorter paths that went to the garden in the back. Wind chimes made of various kinds of materials had been hung at strategic points around the courtyard, and their tinkling music provided the only sounds, for there were none of the usual idlers gathered to talk and barter with Tezcatl.

Tezcatl himself was seated at his bench beneath the ramada, his shiny dome of a head bent over his work, accompanied by two young apprentices who looked up at Huemac's approach but made no attempt to alert their master. As Huemac seated himself on the other side of the bench, he saw what his father had warned him about: Tezcatl's once-handsome face had grown gaunt and sorrowful, with deep frowning lines etched into his forehead. He was the same age as Quinatzin, yet looked years older.

"Greetings, Tezcatl," Huemac said politely. "I bring you my father's regards, as well as his apologies for not coming himself."

"Ah, Huemac," Tezcatl murmured softly, looking him up and down with eyes too sad to smile. "You have returned to us at last." He gestured to one of the apprentices: "Have the women prepare food and drink for our guest."

He turned back to Huemac and stared at him in silence for a long time, his hollowed face gradually taking on an expression of helpless, wistful yearning. Huemac remembered what a splendid figure of a man Nopaltzin had seemed on the mountain, every bit as large and powerful as his father, and with the same handsome features. Huemac knew that he himself was no substitute, but only a painful reminder of all that had been lost. He tried to smile in a way that would not be taken for unwanted sympathy.

"So, my friend, how is your business?" he asked, attempting the bluff tones he had often heard his father use. "I must tell you, I saw no mirrors in Texcoco as fine as those you make."

Tezcatl laughed shortly and seemed to recover himself.

"So they have taught you how to flatter in that fine city," he said gruffly, then gestured at the workbenches and mats strewn with mirrors and pieces of jewelry. "My business is fine. I have two clever apprentices and a daughter who orders all of us about, so it does not matter that I have grown slow and forgetful in my old age."

"I cannot believe such a thing," Huemac said graciously. "Is your daughter here?"

"Taypachtli has gone to the marketplace with one of the serving women, to purchase a turkey for the upcoming festivities. She should return at any time. She is no longer a little girl, you know," Tezcatl added, with just enough edge to his voice to make Huemac meet his eyes. "She has the body of a woman, though she is only fifteen."

Huemac felt the heat rise to his cheeks, and he knew that the memory of Ce Malinalli was there in his face for Tezcatl to see.

"Surely, then," he said tentatively, "the young men of your city must come to visit her?"

"There were some, the friends of . . ." Tezcatl trailed off abruptly and frowned. "But they come no more. You are special to her, Huemac; she has waited for you to return. I would not wish to see you take advantage of her youth, and the trust she has in you."

Huemac told himself not to be offended; that Tezcatl would not be speaking this way if he had not already lost a son.

"I would not betray her trust, or yours," he said evenly, opening his face to Tezcatl's inspection. The older man squinted at him skeptically.

"She told me that you visited her once, alone, when you were still in the calmecac."

"I did," Huemac admitted. "But when she convinced me that it was wrong, I left and did not try to come again. I was a young boy and very lonely."

"She told me these things, as well. I did not mean to imply that you could not be trusted, but you know as I do that there is going to be a war. I can still remember, in the times before the Tepanec War, that there were many young men who could not wait for the proper ceremonies to be performed. There were children born to women who could not even call themselves widows."

"I know that you speak to me as a father," Huemac said stiffly, "but I must answer you as a warrior. And I would not go seeking to involve myself in disgrace at a time like this, when I might be called on to go into battle at any moment. Perhaps you also remember that there are young men capable of showing restraint."

Tezcatl sighed heavily, letting his broad shoulders slump. When he looked up at Huemac, there was apology in his eyes.

"Forgive me, Huemac. I had indeed forgotten that restraint existed anywhere anymore. I could see that you had become a man, but my belief that manhood brings maturity has been greatly shaken in recent months, and I did not see *how much* of a man you are. Eat with me now, and tell me of Texcoco. When my daughter returns, I promise that you will be allowed to speak with her privately . . ."

IMMEDIATELY upon entering the courtyard, Taypachtli removed her sandals and handed them to the woman who accompanied her. Whispering in Taypachtli's ear, the woman pointed uselessly toward the ramada, and Taypachtli turned in that direction and lifted her hands to her hair. The woman helped her smooth down the feathery bangs over her forehead and straightened the long braids that hung almost to her waist. Then Taypachtli turned again and began to follow the path that led toward the ramada, moving slowly yet certainly, guiding herself by the rushes beneath her feet and the sounds of the wooden wind chimes that hung from the crossbeam at the end of the ramada.

Huemac stopped talking in midsentence and turned to stare as Taypachtli touched the post that supported the crossbeam and came around the corner of the ramada toward him. Even sitting down, he could see that she was nearly as tall as he was, and the weight of her breasts against the thin cloth of her shift showed that Tezcatl had not exaggerated her womanliness. But it was her face that truly struck Huemac dumb. As if sculpted by some deft hand, the beauty of her features had emerged distinctly from the soft, childish roundness of her face, revealing the firm contours of her cheeks and the ripeness of her lips. Though her eyes were closed, she carried her head high and wore an animated expression that quickly dispelled any notion that she was walking in her sleep.

Smiling fully for the first time, Tezcatl motioned for Huemac to greet her, and Huemac rose without hesitation. Taypachtli stopped a few feet away from him and cocked her head inquisitively, then suddenly broke out into a radiant smile.

"Greetings, Taypachtli," Huemac managed, still disconcerted by her beauty. Taypachtli put out her hands, then drew them back, as if realizing that they were too old for such touching.

"Greetings, Huemac," she said shyly, still smiling. "Your voice has changed greatly, and you are taller."

"And you, my friend, you . . ." Huemac stammered, unable to express how beautiful she seemed to him. "You have also grown up!"

They both laughed at that, as did Tezcatl, who had risen to join them. The old warrior's enormous body had bent and stiffened from the injuries he had incurred long ago, and he seemed to loom over them like a great shadow as he took his daughter's hand and led her and Huemac to some mats at the far end of the ramada.

"Huemac has already told me his tales," he explained to Taypachtli, "and I must get back to my work. But perhaps you can entertain him until it is time for him to return to his company."

Then Tezcatl left them alone, sitting across from one another in an awkward silence that was due less to shyness than to an overabundance of things to say.

"There is so much to tell," Huemac began, and spread his hands helplessly, but Taypachtli broke in eagerly.

"You must tell me everything. Your mother has told me that you lived for a time among the hill-people, and that you went on a campaign with the warriors."

"This is true," Huemac said warily. "Has my mother been here often?"

"Many times, though not so much recently. She helped to lay out my paths for me, and had Cocatli make the wind chimes. Have you not spoken to her?"

"Only once. We had a disagreement. She does not trust my judgment."

Her distress showed plainly on Taypachtli's face, making Huemac reflect, ruefully, on how well his mother had taught her.

"You cannot let this be, Huemac," she said in a concerned voice. "You must explain your reasons to her and try to reach an agreement. Do not hurt your mother as Nopalli has hurt Father."

"My mother knows my reasons, as she knows everything else about me. I have no desire to hurt her, but I must prove to her that I am capable of making my own decisions and carrying them out. Perhaps Nopalli is only doing the same thing . . . ?"

"My brother is lost to us forever," Taypachtli murmured, incredulous yet resigned to the loss. "He was angry because our father had spoken on behalf of one of the peace proposals put forth by the pochteca, and then Father refused to contribute any more prizes for the contests Teconal holds for the warriors. Nopalli denounced him in the presence of others, swearing that he would never return to the house of a traitor."

Tears welled out from under Taypachtli's eyelids and ran slowly down her cheeks. Huemac was tempted to reach out and wipe them from her face, to hold her against him and comfort her, but he restrained himself. Necoc Yaotl causes this sadness, he thought bitterly, feeling the war looming ominously over all their lives.

"There may not be much time left to us," he said suddenly, possessed by an urgency he could no longer repress. "I could speak to you as I have to your father, and tell you of the places I have seen and the things I have done. I could entertain you with these stories and never speak of what is in my heart. But it is the secrets of my heart that I long to show you more than anything else."

Taypachtli inhaled sharply at this proposal, which went beyond friendship to the intimacy usually reserved for marriage. Huemac scanned her face anxiously for signs of disappointment or rejection. He had not known until that moment that he was going to make such an appeal; it had sprung unconsidered from his lips. Now, with each moment that she deliberated, he began to feel more and more ugly and presumptuous. He remembered the "others" that Tezcatl had mentioned, others who were no doubt handsomer than he, and less haunted by their luck.

"I must warn you," he went on before she could respond, "that my secrets are not those of an innocent boy. No doubt they would shock and frighten you, and fill you with disgust. They are the result of this evil luck with which I was born."

"Yet you would tell me everything?" Taypachtli asked, and the innocent wonder in her voice convinced Huemac that he had made an improper request.

"Not if it would cause you to think badly of me. I would rather keep my secrets buried in my heart and remain your friend, than reveal them to you and have you shun me."

"I would never shun you," Taypachtli said gently. "And I have always hoped that one day you would speak to me like this. That has been the secret of *my* heart, for I have always been afraid that you would no longer want to be burdened with a blind girl when you had become a man."

"But you are very beautiful," Huemac protested, "and surely, your fingers have told you that I am uglier than other men."

"I do not know how others may regard you. I know only that it is *your* face, and that it has always looked upon me with kindness. I feel that even now it smiles at me . . ."

"As does my heart," Huemac said hoarsely. "If I return from this war," he added impulsively, "I will ask for you as my wife, if you will accept me."

"I am too young to speak of such things," Taypachtli scolded him, but she made no effort to conceal her pleasure. "But now you must tell me everything, as you promised."

"Yes," Huemac agreed gratefully, and took a breath that filled him with buoyancy. "I must begin in the year One-Reed, when I was still in the calmecac . . ."

4

THE five unlucky days of the nemontemi came and were passed in deliberate and anxious idleness, and the year Seven-House was greeted in Tenochtitlan with the traditional ceremonies to Tlaloc, the Rain God. Huemac entered his eighteenth year in a state of high anticipation, certain now that a confrontation with his fate was as inevitable as the war between the Mexica. The tingling power came to him with greater and greater frequency, flowing into ever larger portions of his body as he struggled to learn how to control and contain it. He knew now that it came to him most easily when he was angry or upset, or when he was anywhere near the marketplace and temple plaza in Tlatelulco. This latter fact had convinced him that the power was tied in with the mysterious vision he had had, as well as with the mission his father had entrusted to him. Suddenly, the tangled strands of his life seemed to be coming together, as if the pattern had been long in the weaving, and only now was the design of his fate becoming clear. It was for this, Huemac felt, that he had been trained and tested; for this, that he had been rescued from Oztooa and Icpitl and allowed to return to Tenochtitlan.

Aware that he had no room for carelessness, and nowhere to turn for help, Huemac forced himself to exercise an almost priestly discipline over the affairs of his daily life. Preoccupied with his own internal stirrings, he went about his duties in silence, seldom socializing with the other apprentices and taking no part in the gambling that went on constantly in their quarters. When he was given leave, he was most often gone, visiting his father or Taypachtli, or praying in the shrine of Xolotl. These were the only places where he felt able to relax, since the tingling never came to him in any of them. After an afternoon of talk with Taypachtli, he could return to his stern, self-imposed regimen with renewed determination, watching everything around him—and inside of him—with wary eyes.

Even as he brought order to his life, though, Huemac saw his reputation among the other members of his company deteriorate. His distracted silence was mistaken for arrogance, and his steady performances in the drills and tlachtli games earned him more suspicion than admiration, for there had been other occasions, since the day of his tryout, when he had not been able to control the awesome power that came to him. On one such occasion, when he had been provoked into losing his temper during the drills, he had totally crushed four straight opponents, injuring two of them.

Appalled at this lapse, and grateful that he had not killed anyone, Huemac had resolved never to let it happen again. But when he reverted to his former methodical fighting style, he was at first thought to be holding back out of laziness or pride, for it was inconceivable that any apprentice would hesitate to show his best for any other reason. He was coaxed, then taunted, but when he failed to repeat his previous performance—and worse, displayed no concern over his failure—rumors began to circulate about him. If these were truly *his* powers, it was wondered, why did he not use them to impress his superiors, as any other apprentice would have done? The scandal in the calmecac was recalled and embellished, and it was rumored that he had learned sorcery in Texcoco and had used it to cast a spell over the warriors he had beaten. Several of the other apprentices went to Tlacateotzin and asked that Huemac be prevented from wearing his headband and amulet in the drills, suspecting that these were evil charms being used against them.

On the last day of the festivities to Tlaloc, Huemac was invited to a feast at the house of his brother, Acolmiztli. As soon as he entered the courtyard and saw Acolmiztli and Tlacateotzin wearing their commander's insignia and a full array of jewelry, with Acolmiztli especially fierce and resplendent in his Jaguar headdress, Huemac knew that an effort was being made to impress him. This was confirmed by the coolness of his brother's greeting, which included a pointed reference to the uncut lock of hair on the back of Huemac's head. Huemac did his best to appear chastened, and began to prepare himself for the reprimand that he knew was coming.

After the ceremonies to the gods had been observed, the feasting began in one of the smaller banquet rooms, since there were only a few guests and the air in the courtyard was chilly. Quinatzin and Ome Xochitl were attending a feast in the palace of Axayacatl, so Teuxoch had been invited in their place, and she did her best to keep Huemac eating from the many dishes that had been placed in front of them. Humoring her attentions, Huemac nonetheless managed to eat sparingly, keeping an expectant eye on his brother's unsmiling face. Several times during the course of the evening, he made himself available for a private conversation, each time sensing how deeply he puzzled Acolmiztli, who did not avail himself of any of these opportunities. Have I misread his intentions, Huemac wondered, or does he seek to punish me with silence?

Finally, the children were put to bed, the other guests departed, and only the immediate family was left sitting around the copper brazier that warmed the banquet room. Huemac sat with Teuxoch on one side of him and Cocatli and Tlacateotzin on the other, facing Acolmiztli and his first wife, Atototl, across the fire. After Teuxoch had repeated the story of how she had rescued Cocatli from the coyote during the famine, a story she always told on such occasions, Acolmiztli drew himself up and looked straight at Huemac.

"I have asked your commander's permission to speak to you, my brother," he began, with a deferential nod in Tlacateotzin's direction, "because I am greatly concerned about the attitude you have displayed toward your calling."

"What attitude is this?" Teuxoch demanded in the silence that followed, glancing back and forth from one brother to the other.

"Please, Mother," Acolmiztli said impatiently, "you must let me speak. Huemac knows of what I speak."

Huemac felt his skin go cold, then hot as the attention of the group focused in on him. The unfairness of being reprimanded in front of his family filled him with a deep, burning anger that threatened to get the better of his self-control, and he had to take several calming breaths before he could bring himself to speak:

"What have I done that displeases you?"

"You show no eagerness for fighting," Acolmiztli burst out in an accusing tone, "you *deliberately* hold yourself back in the drills! You are not yet blooded, yet you seem lazy and unconcerned about proving your worth. It is hard for me to admit that such a person is my brother!"

Anger flared up behind Huemac's eyes, momentarily blinding him, and then he felt the tingling begin at the base of his spine and travel swiftly upward into his neck and head. His jaw locked and his vision blurred, and he had to struggle to remain upright. Then his vision returned, and with it a clarity of mind such as he had never experienced before, even under the influence of the plants. He could *feel* the attitudes of everyone around him: the shock and disbelief of Teuxoch and Cocatli, Tlacateotzin's unease, Acolmiztli's righteous annoyance, the haughty scorn that Atototl displayed toward him more or less consistently. Huemac perceived these things without any emotion of his own, other than the supremely arrogant conviction that he was more powerful than any of them. He looked back at his brother with a detachment so complete that it carried him beyond insolence.

"My record in the drills speaks for itself; I have not been felled by anyone I have faced. And I do not think that it is laziness that causes my matches to last twice as long as the others. As for this eagerness of which you speak, I see little of it among the other apprentices. Frustration and hostility, *yes,* for there are many who should have been given a *real* chance to prove themselves long ago."

"Do not be impertinent, Huemac," Tlacateotzin cautioned, trying to ease the tension in the group, but Acolmiztli waved him off.

"They will have their chance soon enough," he said. "It is still no excuse for you to hold back in the drills. Do you think that it is up to you when you will fight and when you will not? You fight when you are told, and with all your heart!" Acolmiztli's nostrils flared angrily, and the rising and falling of his chest caused the strings of shells around his neck to clink together softly. He glared at Huemac with furious incomprehension. "Many people have told me of the day you felled four warriors in a row, and of how badly you beat them. Yet you have done nothing like it since! Explain this to me."

"One of those warriors now has a broken arm," Huemac pointed out coolly, "and will be of no use to us in the coming war. I have always thought that the purpose of the drills was to prepare us for the enemy, not do his work *for* him."

The audacity of this response drew expressions of disapproval from everyone around him, but Huemac did not back down from his brother's gaze. It was too late to apologize; if he did not stand up to Acolmiztli now, he would never be able to go to him later and make him listen to their father's plan. And he could see, behind the anger in his brother's eyes, a grudging recognition of the truth of Huemac's statements.

"So you disapprove of how the drills are conducted?" Acolmiztli inquired dryly, and Huemac noticed Tlacateotzin lean forward attentively.

"My approval or disapproval does not matter, as you know, and I have never complained to anyone. But every warrior, no matter how humble, is entitled to his own opinion of what he sees, and I have seen many men injured uselessly while their officers stood by making wagers, ignoring the sloppiness of the fighting." Huemac paused and stared straight at his brother, holding back none of the power in his eyes. "Perhaps you can explain the usefulness of this to me."

"Are you saying that our warriors are not prepared?" Tlacateotzin interrupted, and Huemac hooded his eyes slightly before turning in his brother-in-law's direction.

"I am saying, Lord, that they have been prepared for too long. The edge of their readiness has been blunted by all this waiting. Would they not be fasting and abstaining from women if they were about to embark upon a campaign? Yet they do not do so now, even though the war could come to us tomorrow."

Tlacateotzin and Acolmiztli exchanged a glance, and Tlacateotzin nodded for his fellow commander to speak.

"You would know soon enough," Acolmiztli said; "all the warriors are to begin purifying themselves tomorrow. Perhaps that will ease your mind about the competence of our leaders."

"I have never questioned the competence of my leaders, or their wisdom," Huemac said sincerely. "It is an impossible task, to prepare for a war that never comes."

Acolmiztli considered him in silence, his chin resting on his hand, his eyes narrowed in concentration. Huemac felt the power leaving him and blinked rapidly against the darkening of his vision; his mind suddenly felt dull and fatigued, and he could no longer sense the feelings of those around him. He lowered his eyes in confusion, gripped by the memory of his own eloquence yet uncertain of what he had accomplished by it. I have explained nothing, he realized with belated anxiety, except that I owe him no explanations.

"Perhaps I have underestimated you," Acolmiztli said at last, and Huemac jerked his head up in surprise. "Your concerns are not those of a typical apprentice, but then, you have not had the usual training. Accept my apologies, Huemac, if I have doubted you unfairly."

Huemac could only bow with relief and gratitude amid the general release of tension. Teuxoch, though, was not so willing to let the matter drop.

"It is plain that you have doubted your brother unfairly," she scolded Acolmiztli. "Even an old woman like myself can see that. But what he has told you about the warriors is a more serious matter. You must tell this to Axayacatl and convince him to attack at once. If my father were healthy, this would have been done long ago."

"We miss your father's counsel," Acolmiztli said judiciously, receiving a sympathetic glance from Tlacateotzin, "but I do not have his access to the Speaker."

Tired as he was, Huemac did not miss the exchange of glances between the two commanders, and he heard the lack of concern in his brother's response. They know about the ambush, he realized with a last burst of intuition; Axayacatl has confided his plans to them at last. But before this realization could sink in, Teuxoch spoke again:

"Speak to Ocomatli, then," she said with stubborn insistence. "He is close to both the Speaker *and* my father."

"I will do what I can, my mother," Acolmiztli promised politely, and bowed to signal that he had heard enough on this subject. Then he turned his attention to Huemac.

"It is time that you returned to your company, my brother. You have spoken boldly to me tonight, but not without justice. Sometimes it is necessary for brothers to express their differences."

"I am grateful for your concern and understanding," Huemac said respectfully. "And I think that we can have few real differences, since we are both Tenocha, and love our city."

Both Teuxoch and Tlacateotzin nodded in emphatic agreement, and Acolmiztli smiled with renewed fondness. Huemac began to make his farewells to each member of the group, begging their forgiveness for causing them to listen to his justifications. But he was not sorry that he had stood up to his brother, or about what he had learned as a result. His head was beginning to ache and the walk back to his quarters suddenly seemed very long, but even as he wearily found his way out of Acolmiztli's courtyard, he was already thinking about when he could see his father, and what he would tell him when he did.

QUINATZIN was present in the Council Chamber on the day that Chalchiuhnenetl was brought back to Tenochtitlan. Though everyone had known that this would happen, Tenocha pride demanded that surprise and outrage be shown, and the hallways of the palace rang with the warriors' vows of revenge on her behalf. This was the sister of their Speaker, the princess given to Moquiuix by Moteczuma himself, the living bond of blood between the two cities. She had been rejected by Moquiuix, repudiated before the entire Tlatelulcan court, it was said, and when her brothers Tizoc and Ahuitzotl came to reclaim her, Moquiuix allowed her to be taken without interference. Many heads were lowered in shame when Chalchiuhnenetl entered the chamber in the company of her brothers, with her two children beside her.

Yet the woman who came before Axayacatl, though she had clearly suffered much, was not a person in need of pity. Nor did she feed the appetite for vengeance that her return had so easily whetted. She was tall and bony like her brother Tizoc, yet the blood of Moteczuma showed in the strength of her jaw and the power of the appeal she made to her brother. She told him of the respect Moquiuix secretly harbored for him, and of the dreams and portents that had haunted her life in Tlatelulco: the voices that came from her womb, crying disaster in the middle of the night; the dark old men who appeared out of nowhere and the birds that were seen dancing in a pot of boiling water; the mask that spoke to her husband from the wall, warning him of his doom.

"Moquiuix does not want this war, my Lord," she insisted. "He knows that it is unholy, and will go against him. It is Teconal and Poyahuitl who continue to stir the Council to war, but even they would have to recognize an offer of peace, if it came from you personally, my brother. The pochteca are ready to pay you tribute, and flower wars could be arranged between the warriors." She gestured dramatically toward the boy at her side, who bowed to his uncle. "I and my son, who bears your name, will convey this offer ourselves, if you will permit us the honor."

Voices were raised in approbation of Chalchiuhnenetl's courage, and Quinatzin could see that Axayacatl had been powerfully affected by her appeal. He will not be able to refuse her, Quinatzin thought, seeing the open pride in the young Speaker's face. Quinatzin also knew that Axayacatl had nothing to lose by making an offer of peace now. His spy in the Tlatelulcan court was very reliable, and kept him apprised of all of Moquiuix's plans; an ambush had already been prepared, should the Tlatelulca mistake his generosity for weakness and decide to attack. Axayacatl risked nothing with this offer, yet it would assure his innocence in whatever followed. Quinatzin did not think that Moquiuix could accept a peace offer at this point, but he did not find this discouraging, for a Tlatelulcan refusal would force the Tenocha to formally declare war, and it was this kind of war that Quinatzin had sought all along.

"You have moved my heart, my sister," Axayacatl announced grandly, without consulting with his advisers. "I will ask the Tlatelulca to meet with us to discuss the terms of a peace. But I would prefer to keep you and my nephew by my side, for the sight of you pleases me greatly. Our uncle, Cueyatzin, will carry my offer to Moquiuix. He is a man of honor, and his word will be trusted."

A thin, dignified man stepped from the ranks of the white-haired old men and bowed before the Speaker, to the applause of both his peers and the young warchiefs surrounding Axayacatl. Despite his innate pessimism, Quinatzin was moved by the scene, as were those around him. He watched the young ruler bestow the white plumes of ambassadorship upon the venerable Cueyatzin, a man who had served Moteczuma, and he saw tears form in the old man's eyes as he listened to Axayacatl speak with a magnanimity and sureness of power reminiscent of his grandfather. The peace offered to the Tlatelulca was stated in terms so lofty, and yet so final, that no one could ever doubt either his sincerity or his willingness to fight if he were refused. It was a magnificent performance, and Quinatzin felt tears of nostalgia coming to his own eyes. I have accomplished what I was brought here for, he thought; I have given the Tenocha faces to match the greatness of their hearts.

And what of the Demon Heart? he wondered automatically. When will *he* show his face? Quinatzin headed for the door, his eyes already dry. He could not believe that Tlacaelel would allow anything to dull the hatred he had stirred up between the Mexica, but events were moving fast, and perhaps this time they would outrun even Tlacaelel's ability to bend them to his will. But it is not over yet, Quinatzin thought as he hurried out of the chamber, already framing the messages he had to dispatch, and wondering if there would be time for one more meeting with his son.

HUEMAC listened to his father's voice with his eyes closed, visualizing himself saying these same words to Acolmiztli, convincing his brother to allow him to guide the war canoes to Tlatelulco. He now knew the complete details of Axayacatl's planned ambush; more, surely, than the Speaker and his warchiefs had confided to any one of their commanders. Acolmiztli would have to be impressed, and he would have to believe that the information had come from Quinatzin.

"And if the Tenocha attack first, and there is no ambush?" Huemac asked, opening his eyes when his father paused for breath. Quinatzin smiled skeptically.

"Then you will have no message to deliver, and I will reveal the strategy to the warchiefs myself, and help to end the conflict quickly. But we must not hope for so much," he cautioned. "Tlacaelel has not yet shown himself, and it is *his* agent who controls the spy in Moquiuix's court. So much depends on this spy, whose name, as I have told you, is Ehecatzitzimitl, the Wind Demon. The ambush has been laid according to his advice, and if it were to fail, the Tenocha would be vulnerable."

"When will Cueyatzin return with Moquiuix's answer?"

"Soon, if it is a refusal," Quinatzin said with assurance. "I must go now, in order to be there when he returns."

Father and son stared at one another, sharing an excitement that made it difficult for either to stand still. Yet both were reluctant to have this meeting end.

"You have served me well, Huemac," Quinatzin said. "You have made me proud. Whatever fate brings to me, I will be grateful for these last months with my son."

"I will eat with you when this war is over," Huemac promised in a husky voice. "May the gods watch over you, my father."

"And *you,* my son," Quinatzin whispered, and turned abruptly to go.

EVEN BEFORE the appearance of Tlacaelel, Quinatzin had learned of the refusal of the peace offer. He was waiting outside the Council Chamber, hoping for a last message from Tlatelulco, when he saw the Cihuacoatl and his entourage coming down the hallway, dressed for war. Tlacaelel was wearing jade earplugs and a headdress of eagle feathers, and his shrunken body was visibly weighed down with the mass of feathers and jeweled insignia he had won in his days as a warrior. The standard of heron feathers attached to his scrawny shoulders waved ludicrously, far above his head, and the shield and spear he carried were half-sized, of the kind used to train boys. Blind to anything except his own righteous glory, he swept past into the Council Chamber without recognizing Quinatzin.

Tizoc and Ahuitzotl also came by, carrying weapons and accompanied by armed retainers. Quinatzin knew that he could not wait much longer. Just as he was about to give up and enter the chamber, he saw a man coming toward him, wearing the uniform of one of Axayacatl's messengers. Quinatzin was sure that he had seen the messenger before, somewhere, but before he could identify him, the man had stopped before him, and Quinatzin realized that it was his friend Cuetzpaltzin.

"You have taken a great risk, my friend," he said gratefully, and the vanguard merchant shrugged.

"I have taken greater. You know of the refusal of the peace offer?"

Quinatzin nodded.

"Something has happened since then," Cuetzpaltzin said in a flat Tenocha accent. "A spy has been discovered in our midst. He was called the Wind Demon, when he was alive. He had much to say before he died."

"That is unfortunate. No doubt your people now question the sincerity of the peace offer."

"No doubt. Since there will be war, I came myself to secure our agreement in person."

"It is secure," Quinatzin assured him. "The attack from the west will by-pass your calpullis in favor of the temple. I have entrusted this to my sons in the case of my own death."

"I hope that I will not have to kill them," Cuetzpaltzin said without emotion. "Farewell, my friend. May we meet again in Pochtlan."

"May the gods protect you, Cuetzpaltzin," Quinatzin said, and watched the merchant march off with a swagger appropriate to his assumed station. Then he turned and went into the Council Chamber.

The speeches had already begun, but the old man who was holding forth immediately yielded the floor when Tlacaelel indicated his desire to speak. He had removed the standard from his shoulders and surrendered his spear and shield, yet the golden bands on his arms and the precious stones on his chest glittered fiercely when he rose from his reed seat next to Axayacatl.

"Lords!" he exclaimed in his harsh, rasping voice, peering out at the warriors assembled in the room. "We have acted honorably toward these people who call themselves our brothers! We have offered them peace, yet they have spurned us, and called us cowards! We have no choice!" he shouted above the uproar his words had created. "We must declare war upon them! Let the priests be consulted for a propitious day to begin . . ."

The warriors shook their weapons over their heads and shouted the name of Tenochtitlan, and Tlacaelel listened with a satisfied smile on his face before returning to his seat. After he had succeeded in quieting the room, Axayacatl turned again to Tlacaelel.

"And who, Uncle, should have the honor of declaring this war? Who will go to Moquiuix and give him weapons, and paint him with the paint of the dead?"

"Let it be Cueyatzin," Tlacaelel said dramatically, and the warriors again raised their weapons and shouted the name of the ambassador. Quinatzin suddenly understood what Tlacaelel was up to. It was *he* who had betrayed the Wind Demon to his own people, just at this moment. Moquiuix would be infuriated by this proof of Axayacatl's treachery, and he would have no patience with the formalities of war. He would kill Cueyatzin and attack as soon as possible, before Axayacatl could learn of the discovery of his spy. The ambush would fail, and the Tlatelulca would inflict heavy losses on the Tenocha before they could be beaten back. Yet without allies, Moquiuix would not be able to press his advantage on a second day, and when the Tenocha counterattacked, they would not stop killing until the deaths of Cueyatzin and those lost in the ambush had been avenged a thousand times over. It would be a slaughter of the greatest magnitude.

Unless . . . Cueyatzin was still being dressed for his mission, and it would take time for the weapons and paint to be blessed by the priests and brought to the palace. If Axayacatl could be told of the death of the Wind Demon, many lives might be saved, perhaps even that of Cueyatzin. Quinatzin saw Axayacatl rise and lead his entourage through a curtained exit in the rear of the chamber. When Tlacaelel followed the Speaker through the curtain shortly afterward, Quinatzin left his place and began to work his way around the circumference of the chamber, pausing occasionally to greet someone he knew, in order to conceal his real destination from whatever eyes were watching him in the crowd. When he reached the curtain, he nodded perfunctorily to the guards flanking it and pushed his way into the darkness that lay beyond.

Suddenly, rough hands seized both of his arms, and a hand was clamped over his mouth as he was borne forcibly down a passageway that led off to the left. His staff fell to the polished floor with a loud clatter and was kicked away into the darkness.

Then he was taken through another curtain into a lighted room, where his arms were released with a thrust that made him sag upon his bad leg. But he straightened up when he saw Tlacaelel come out of the shadows and stand in front of him, looking him up and down with eyes as hard and hungry as on the night Quinatzin had first met him.

"So . . ." he rasped scornfully. "You betray me at last."

"I would," Quinatzin admitted easily. "But I do not betray my city. You do not serve your people in this, Demon Heart; you have no vision to guide you."

"Silence, traitor! These impudent quackers deserve to be taught a lesson, once and for all!"

"There will be much useless killing, on both sides."

"I would not have anything less," Tlacaelel sneered, then glanced at the guards and made a dismissive gesture. "Go, then, Texcocan, I have pretended to let you fool me for too many years. Make your farewells to my daughter and that whelp of Nezahualcoyotl. You are going to Moquiuix with Cueyatzin. You will anoint him with the paint of the dead and give him weapons with which to fight us."

"And if I refuse?"

"Then you will not be permitted any farewells, and your death will be blamed on Tlatelulcan spies."

Quinatzin stared at the sharp, cruel features of the man he had served and hated for forty years, the man who had always worn the face of his fate. Tlacaelel's eyes burned with their old hunger, but wildly, without the penetrating gleam of divine conviction. Perhaps Huemac has a chance, Quinatzin thought; perhaps his visions will allow him to succeed where I have failed. Thinking of this, Quinatzin let out a long breath and smiled.

"At last, I shall be free of you, Demon Heart," he said. "No more will I be your captive, and witness to your evil. I welcome my death."

Tlacaelel blinked suspiciously and appeared confused for a moment. Then the glare returned to his eyes and he smiled disdainfully.

"You speak like a Tenocha, but I know you for what you are."

"You will *see* what I am," Quinatzin said proudly, and turned to accompany the guards from the room.

HAVING HEARD nothing from his father, Huemac waited in his quarters with the other apprentices, cleaning his weapons and listening absently to the excited voices of those around him. He was ready to fight, but he did not share the common joy at the declaration of war, for he had no taste for glory that would come at the expense of people he loved. On his last visit to Taypachtli, he had tried to persuade her to go and stay with his mother, but she had refused to leave her father. Now when he thought of leading the warriors into the marketplace in Tlatelulco, he had also to think, with dread, of the house of Tezcatl, which lay so near at hand.

Suddenly, the tingling began at the base of his skull and filled his head so quickly that he dropped the macana he was holding and fell over onto his back. The apprentices next to him stopped talking and turned to stare at him curiously, but Huemac was unable to pay them any mind. When his dizziness had passed, he rose from his mat and walked past their curious eyes without a word of explanation. Just outside the doorway, he met Tlacateotzin coming in, and his brother-in-law, after recovering from his surprise, pointed back toward the courtyard.

"Your father," he said bleakly. "Acolmiztli is waiting for you."

Huemac nodded and started past him, but Tlacateotzin stopped him with a hand on his shoulder.

"We will avenge his death, Huemac. We will make them pay in blood."

"Yes," Huemac replied impatiently, and continued on toward the two figures standing beneath the torch attached to the courtyard wall. He bowed to his brother and to Teuxoch, seeing the pain of sudden loss in their eyes, a pain very different from the one that stabbed at his own heart.

"How was he killed?" he asked brusquely, before either of them could speak. Acolmiztli stiffened at Huemac's tone, but he allowed Teuxoch to answer.

"He went with Cueyatzin to Tlatelulco," she said, her voice quivering with outrage. "They were ambassadors! Yet Moquiuix slew them like dogs and threw their bodies away!"

"Who sent him to Tlatelulco?"

"The Cihuacoatl," Acolmiztli said, frowning at Huemac's apparent lack of emotion. Teuxoch opened the long cloth-wrapped bundle she was holding and showed Huemac the warclub inside.

"I have brought you your father's macana," she said. "He would want you to use it against his enemies."

"Yes," Huemac said, lifting the warclub gingerly from its wrappings. It was over forty years old, its flat, wooden surface fissured with age. But it had been kept oiled, and its obsidian edges had lost none of their deadly sharpness. Huemac hefted it experimentally, feeling the tingling power flow from his hand up into his arm.

"Yes," he repeated, "I will use this well."

"He also left you a message," Teuxoch continued. "I still do not understand it, but he said that you would." She screwed up her face in an effort to recall the message exactly. "He said . . . these were his exact words: 'The wind has died. Yours is the only secret.' "

Teuxoch and Acolmiztli both looked at him inquisitively, but Huemac said nothing, his gaze fixed on the macana swinging loosely in his hand.

"Thank you, my mother," he said finally. "This gives me great courage. How is our mother?"

"Cocatli is with her, and weeps more than she. I do not think that she can believe it is true. I do not wish to myself."

Huemac put his free arm around the tiny woman and drew her against his chest, feeling the shudderings of her grief. He stared over her white head at his brother, who was watching him with a wary, expectant expression on his face.

"Come, Mother," Acolmiztli said, gently disengaging Teuxoch from Huemac's embrace and leading her toward the doorway. "I will see that you are safely escorted home."

When Acolmiztli returned, Huemac wasted no time in beginning his explanation.

"Now you must listen to me, my brother," he said commandingly, "and know that what I will tell you comes from our father. He has made me his messenger."

"Why did he not tell me himself?" Acolmiztli demanded, and Huemac glared at him with such force that he recoiled and raised an arm in front of his face.

"That does not matter. Listen! Axayacatl's ambush will fail if the Tlatelulca strike quickly, as I think they will. The forces of Moyotlan, and the other companies in the rear, must be ready for the Tlatelulca when they break through."

"How do you know this? How do you know *any* of this?"

"You heard our father's message: The only secret is *mine,*" Huemac said, holding the macana flat across his chest. "I can lead you safely to the temple in Tlatelulco. I can take you there before Moquiuix knows that you have landed on his island."

Some of the surprise and anger faded from Acolmiztli's features, and he considered Huemac seriously.

"If this is true, I will tell the warchiefs myself."

"No!" Huemac exclaimed, unconsciously raising the macana in front of his body. "I will not let you squander this out of ignorance and trust!"

"Do you threaten me?" Acolmiztli demanded in an icy voice.

"I will kill you before I will let you give our father's secret to the men who sent him to his death," Huemac assured him with equal coldness. "Do not make me do the work of Necoc Yaotl, he who sets brother against brother. It is too late to prevent what will happen tomorrow. Moquiuix will attack first, and the ambush will fail, as I have told you. After you have seen this happen, and the order is given for the Tenocha to attack, you must let me lead the canoes of Moyotlan."

"You? An apprentice?"

"I will not be an apprentice after tomorrow. The Tlatelulca will leave none of us unblooded, I promise you."

Acolmiztli stared at him until Huemac realized that he was still holding out his macana and lowered it to his side. His brother seemed to relax slightly, though his face was stern.

"And if the ambush does not fail?" he asked.

"Then my secret will not be needed, and you may punish me for how I have spoken to you tonight. But only after we have sacked the temple in Tlatelulco."

Acolmiztli smiled. "So be it. I do not share your concern about tomorrow, and I do not think that I could convince any of the warchiefs to believe you, either. We shall let events decide whether you will lead the canoes to Tlatelulco or carry shields in the rear."

"Fate will decide," Huemac said flatly, and turned to go back to his quarters, to prepare himself for war.

THE Tlatelulca attacked at the first light of dawn. A large force of warriors, their shaven heads painted red and their leaders wearing the standards of the Otomi Warriors, smashed through the undermanned barricades on the main bridge and surged recklessly into the streets of Tenochtitlan, blowing on bone war whistles and shouting "Tlatelulco! Tlatelulco!" The Tenocha allowed them to progress part of the way up the broad avenue that led to the temple plaza before springing their trap: A host of men armed with bows, slings, and throwing boards suddenly rose up on the rooftops and sent down a hail of darts, arrows, and stones, while contingents of Eagles and Jaguars poured out of the houses and side streets where they had been concealed, surrounding the Tlatelulca on all sides.

Yet as the men in the street were systematically cut down, the Tenocha saw how young they were beneath their war paint, and realized that they had been tricked. These were not Moquiuix's finest warriors; these were only apprentices dressed to look like veterans! Then the Tenocha heard, from behind them, the horrible war cries of the *real* Otomi Warriors, who had come silently across the water in canoes and were attacking the ambushers from both sides. The apprentices in the street, who had offered themselves for this suicide mission, now turned and fought back with the wild fury of those who expect to die, creating a cross fire in which the Tenocha began to waver and fall in confusion.

The forces of Moyotlan were stationed on the far side of the wide canal that intersected the main avenue at a point some two thirds of the way to the temple precinct. From his vantage point atop a small calpulli temple, Acolmiztli could see the reinforcements massed in the streets several blocks closer to the scene of the fighting, waiting for the order to move in and finish off the survivors of the ambush. Of the fighting itself, all he could see was the dust and smoke rising above the rooftops, though the sounds of drums, whistles, and screaming men carried clearly to his ears.

Suddenly, the reinforcements formed up and began to move out at a trot, and the other commanders standing beside Acolmiztli stirred uneasily and looked at one another with questions in their eyes.

"It is too soon," Tlacateotzin said, voicing what was in all their minds. Acolmiztli instinctively turned to look behind him, seeing the tops of the temples towering above the Serpent Wall, the smoke from the temple fires curling lazily upward in gray spirals. Then he looked down and saw the warriors of Moyotlan waiting in thick groups on the bridges over the canal, prepared to follow the first wave of reinforcements and carry the war to Tlatelulco. If Huemac has been proven correct, Acolmiztli thought, then we must no longer think of ourselves as an attack force, but as the last line of defense before the temple precinct itself.

Even as he had this realization, the first runners began to arrive, gasping and bloody, telling of how the ambush had failed. The Tlatelulca had attacked in unexpected numbers, with such terrible ferocity that the number of Eagles and Jaguars who had fallen before them could not be counted. None of the other commanders were prepared for such a setback, and the suggestions they offered up were half-hearted and uncertain. Some thought that the reinforcements would turn the tide; others disagreed, and suggested sending their own men into the battle, though no order had been given. Meanwhile, they could see the fighting moving toward them inexorably, fast approaching the positions the reinforcements had just abandoned.

"We must withdraw our men to this side of the canal," Acolmiztli announced abruptly, startling the other commanders out of their quibbling. "And we must cut the bridges."

This created another uproar, with the more confident of the commanders insinuating that Acolmiztli was a coward, and even the most prudent among them denying that the Tlatelulca would ever get this far. But Acolmiztli resolutely stood his ground, feeling that his father's wisdom had been confirmed and, thus, had to be heeded.

"This is no time for foolish pride," he snapped. "We may be all that stands between the enemy and the sacred temples. Let us break up the bridges and build barricades along the far bank of the canal, so that we can destroy them if they try to cross. We can easily cross the canal ourselves if we are called on to advance."

Acolmiztli was not the highest-ranking warrior among them, but his decisiveness carried great weight in this unforeseen situation, and even the boldest commanders could not ignore the terrible risk of allowing the Tlatelulca to reach the temple precinct. Feeling keenly the shame of such a thing, and remembering who had advised it, they went down to arrange their men into defensive positions.

LATE THAT night, Huemac stood in the courtyard of his company's quarters while his hair was cut and tied into a knot on the top of his head with red tassels. He had been engaged in the massive battle waged at the canal, taking his place on the ramparts when the veteran warrior ahead of him fell and holding it until the Tlatelulca were finally driven back, late in the afternoon. His arrows had been found in three of the dead left behind on the opposite bank, and he had killed one and captured another of the many who had tried to fight their way through his position. Except for some minor wounds on his arms and legs, and a deep bruise on his ribs from a stone, he had not been injured, and he had saved himself from total exhaustion by not joining in the pursuit of the retreating Tlatelulca. Some of the apprentices had added two or three captives to their credit simply by picking off the wounded stragglers, but Huemac was satisfied with his share of the glory, and he knew that the real test still lay ahead of him.

After the ceremony was completed, he went up to accept the congratulations of Tlacateotzin, who gripped his arm and smiled broadly, pleased as both a commander and a relative.

"So, Huemac," he said proudly, "now you have had a full taste of Teoatl Tlachinolli, the blood and burning of war. Have you visited your captive?"

"He is in the hands of the healers, but he is a brave man, and he will live to die gloriously upon the stone. He called me his father and asked when he would be given to the gods." Huemac cast a glance over the ranks of the leaders and then looked back at Tlacateotzin. "Where is Acolmiztli?"

"He has only just returned from the House of Eagles, where the warchiefs have been planning tomorrow's attack. Your brother is a great hero, you know. It was he who saw the danger and made us build defenses, so that we were not overrun when the Tlatelulca broke through the front lines. He has asked that you come to him in his room."

Huemac had seen his brother frequently during the daylong battle, since Acolmiztli had roamed back and forth behind the lines with a select group of Jaguars, filling in wherever the attack was heaviest. Once, they had found themselves standing side by side with their bows stretched taut, both aiming for the commander of the forces directly across the canal. Huemac had felt the tingling power come into his hands and had bent his Otomi bow an extra inch before freeing his arrow, which sped through the air with terrible force and lodged in the man's chest, completely penetrating his thick cotton armor. Releasing only an instant later, Acolmiztli sent an arrow through the man's throat as he fell. Then, caught up in the delirium of battle, Acolmiztli had thrown back his head and shouted to the sky: "Watch my brother, O Sun! Watch how he kills for you!"

Huemac could see, as he entered his brother's room and bowed to him, that Acolmiztli had not forgotten that moment, either. The wariness and suspicion were gone. Acolmiztli sat with his back against the wall, some bowls and dishes on a low table by his side. There were fresh bandages on both of his legs and on one of his arms, and in his lower lip was a curving lip-plug of blue stone, from which hung a shimmering blue hummingbird feather.

"Be seated, and rest yourself," Acolmiztli said. "Tomorrow you will ride in the lead canoe with me when we take the battle to Tlatelulco."

"I am grateful," Huemac began, but his brother cut him off with a curt shake of his head.

"I have already received too much credit that was not due me. It was only because of you, and our father, that I was able to act as I did." Acolmiztli scowled, and his voice turned bitter. "I was with the army when it last met defeat, at the hands of the Mixtecs. We were beaten as badly, but I did not feel then what I do now; I did not feel that our own leaders had conspired against us."

"Tlacaelel serves the hunger of the gods," Huemac said bluntly. "This was his doing, not Axayacatl's."

"Then it was he who sent our father to his death."

Huemac nodded. "Our father chose to oppose him in this. He hoped to prevent a general slaughter by bringing the war to a rapid conclusion. That is why he showed me the way to the temple."

Acolmiztli frowned and bowed his head, making Huemac wonder how much of his innocence his brother really wished to shed. This was no time for bitterness, and he did not think that Acolmiztli could face the full truth without being borne down by it. He was relieved when his brother sighed and looked up at him with an expression that was weary but resolute.

"We must honor his wishes, then. I have been given full command of the canoes of Moyotlan, and I will take them wherever you say. But you must tell me everything you know."

Huemac told him about the landing place on the dike, and the attitude of the pochteca, and the streets that would lead them to the temple plaza. He warned his brother just as he had been warned himself about the dangers of pursuing the pochteca into their calpullis.

"I will see that everyone follows my standard," Acolmiztli promised. "There will be no more useless deaths." He stared at Huemac with a curiosity that made him hesitate before speaking: "Do you know what will happen tomorrow, as you did today?"

"No. I know only that I will be tested by my fate, and that I must meet the challenge or die."

"Then you must eat with me."

Acolmiztli turned to the table beside him and placed a small, polished bowl in front of Huemac. It was tan in color, decorated with red suns on its sides and red fire serpents around the rim. When Acolmiztli removed the lid, the rich aroma of herbs, meat, and chili peppers wafted to Huemac's nose.

"You have served the gods of war today," Acolmiztli said solemnly. "You have become tequihua, one who has a task. Here is the flesh of a man who was my captive, a man who died beautifully, as a god. Let him give you strength as he has given it to Huitzilopochtli, to the Sun."

Huemac bowed his head over the bowl, thinking of the next day's battle, of his vision, of the gods who fed on the hearts and blood of men. The tingling, which had come to him only intermittently during the day, was like a vibrating energy beneath his skin, pressing against the backs of his eyeballs and the top of his skull. He knew that there would be no turning back once he had eaten; that the power would be with him until he had used it up or been destroyed by it. He thought of his mother's warning, and then of his father's death, and he knew that he could no longer guard his spirit. I have eaten the Flesh of the Gods, and received a vision, he thought; now I must eat the flesh of men and follow my vision to its end.

Huemac reached for the bowl, and ate . . .

THE CANOES glided silently through the mist that hung over the black water, startling a feeding heron, who rose from the reeds with great, heavy beats of his wings and disappeared into the grayness overhead. Huemac crouched near the bow of the lead boat, next to Acolmiztli, who wore the red butterfly device of the fire goddess attached to his back, topped by a high crest of green feathers. Huemac gripped the side of the canoe and felt the power ebbing and flowing inside him, leaving him weak one moment and aching with excess energy the next. He had not eaten or slept since the night before, lying wide awake and helpless on his mat as the winds of Xolotl swept through him, filling his ears with the roaring of his own blood. He felt agitated and slightly dizzy, which made him worry about his balance as he rose up to look for landmarks.

He strained his eyes against the hanging fog, which was harder for him to penetrate than darkness. Already, he could hear drums and shouting off to his right, where the main attacks against the canoe basin and the bridge were just beginning. The air around him turned white, then pink as the sun broke over the mountains far to the east. The shoals and cane thickets marking the edge of the channel were now clearly visible, and soon the great gnarled shape of the huehuetl tree loomed out of the mist to Huemac's left. He signaled to his brother, who raised his macana over his head, and the paddlers behind them dug in and bore for shore.

Arrows and darts began to fall into the water around them before they could even see the dike, but then the fog lifted, and the air was rent by the shrill sounds of bone whistles and conch trumpets, and by the thudding of stones and flint-tipped arrows against wooden shields and armored bodies. Huemac peered at the enemy from beneath his shield, preparing himself for the shock of landing, for he could see the wooden stakes that had been planted in the water at the base of the dike. There was a loud crunch as the bow of the dugout canoe hit the stakes and plowed up over them, smashing into the earthworks that had been erected along the lower landing.

Acolmiztli and the two Jaguars with him leapt from the canoe upon impact, throwing the defenders back with sheer momentum, and Huemac followed into the space they had cleared, slashing out with his macana to the right and left as the Tlatelulca sought to close back in around them. The crush became enormous as more warriors stormed over the earthworks and locked themselves against the enemy, shield-to-shield, pushing and straining for the room to strike a decisive blow. Clouds of arrows from the canoes behind hummed overhead as the Tenocha gradually fought their way to the top of the dike, climbing over the bodies of the dead and wounded to strike at the defenders above.

Huemac followed his brother's crested standard and got to the top just as the defenders began to give ground and fall back to the shelter of their houses. From the plainness of their battle dress, and the animal skins and foreign insignia that some of them wore, Huemac could tell that they were pochteca. He stopped beside Acolmiztli, who was plucking an arrow from the armor girding his hips while he surveyed the situation.

"Perhaps we should burn some of their houses," Acolmiztli suggested, "so that they will not be tempted to attack us from behind."

"No, leave them!" Huemac shouted above the din of the fighting. "*There* is the way to the temple; we must not linger here!"

Nodding his reluctant agreement, Acolmiztli called to his captains and gave orders for the boatmen to take the wounded away in the canoes. He had lost perhaps fifty men out of his original five hundred, which left him with a large enough force to assault the plaza, if he used surprise to his advantage. With his standard waving fiercely over his head, Acolmiztli moved his men out at a run, sending his best scouts ahead and leaving a small rear guard of bowmen to keep the pochteca pinned to their houses.

They met little resistance as they ran silently past the boarded-up houses and barricaded side streets, trading arrows with the bowmen who fired on them sporadically from the rooftops. Huemac felt a wild exhilaration from the churning movements of his legs and the cool misty air rushing past his face. To his left, he could see a battle raging on the island of Nonohualco, where the Tepanecs had come across in force to support the Tenocha. The Tlatelulca troops lining the causeway that led to the island were also under a heavy attack by a fleet of war canoes bearing the standard of Tlacopan. Just before they reached the corner of the broad avenue that led east to the temple plaza, Acolmiztli halted his warriors and consulted with the scouts. The gate to the plaza was still open, they reported, and the guard force was small and unprepared for an immediate attack. Acolmiztli looked back at the fighting on the causeway, deciding whether to help the Tepanecs or forge ahead alone, and hope that the Tepanecs would soon come in support. Then he glanced at Huemac and made up his mind.

"Let us take the war to Moquiuix," he proclaimed loudly, and waved his warclub in the direction of the temple.

The Tlatelulca guards at the gate stood frozen in shock as the screaming crowd of Tenocha warriors swept around the corner and bore down upon them, blowing on whistles and shrieking their war cries. Then the guards sprang into action and rushed to close the gate, leaving some of their number outside to perish in the first onslaught. The Tenocha vanguard attacked the wooden gate with copper-headed axes while their comrades cleared the few defenders from the top of the wall with well-placed arrows. They had broken through the gate and dispatched the last guards just as a running wave of Tlatelulcan reinforcements appeared from behind the great pyramid of Huitzilopochtli, some two hundred yards away, and started across the open plaza area to meet them.

It was immediately clear to Acolmiztli that he was outnumbered, and that he could not survive here in the open until the Tepanecs arrived. Spying a smaller temple directly off to his left, he waved his macana in the air and started toward it.

"To the temple!" he cried, and led the rush for the platform. It was the Temple of the Snake Woman, a long black shrine set atop a steep, two-tiered pyramid, surrounded on both sides by courtyards and outbuildings. The Tenocha quickly overran the priests defending it and took up positions in the courtyards and all up and down the steep sides of the pyramid, from which the bowmen could fire down upon the advancing Tlatelulca.

"We must let Moquiuix know why we have come," Acolmiztli said to his men, when they had reached the top platform and killed the last of the priests. Taking a piece of firewood from a pile next to the smoking brazier, he ignited it on the coals and threw it onto the roof of the shrine. The other men quickly followed his example, and as the wooden structure went up in flames and billowing clouds of black smoke, a great silence fell over the hundreds of Tlatelulcan warriors who had formed a circle around the temple, just out of the range of arrows. Huemac unslung his bow and looked out over the surrounding crowd of warriors, counting at least four times their own number before his eyes reached those massed in ranks around the base of the gigantic temple of Huitzilopochtli. Still more could be seen pouring in through the gate at the eastern end of the plaza, where the marketplace fronted onto the temple.

"Perhaps we have come too soon," Huemac ventured, as the silence below was replaced by a growing roar of anger.

"Then we must defend ourselves until the others arrive," Acolmiztli said calmly, moving away from the shrine as it began to pop and spew cinders into the air. Fitting an arrow into his bow, he braced an elbow against a stone serpent's head and aimed downward at the charging line of Tlatelulcan warriors, letting fly just as the first of them came into range.

THERE WERE only forty men left alive on the Temple of the Snake Woman when the Tepanecs finally arrived and laid siege to the western gate, drawing the Tlatelulca away. Heavy fighting was also occurring around the eastern gate, where Eagles and Jaguars could be seen struggling against the shaven-headed Otomi Warriors. It will not be long now, Huemac thought, as the last of his attackers backed down the temple steps and ran to join the defense of one or the other of the gates. He lowered his macana, then discarded it altogether when he noticed that it was cracked down the middle. His father's warclub had been lost long ago; this was the third he had taken from the bodies of dead warriors. The shield he carried in his other hand was gouged and splintered so that its markings were no longer recognizable, and his torn cotton armor freely spilled its batting onto the blood-soaked platform. The dead lay around him in piles, sprawled and broken over the sharp stone steps. Huemac had an arrow wound in his right foot and gashes everywhere on his body, including a deep, oozing cut over one ear, but he thought that his thirst alone might kill him.

Acolmiztli lay behind him on the ground, breathing raggedly, his knee shattered by a macana blow. Huemac had killed the man before he could finish Acolmiztli off, and had then stood guard over his brother's body, using all the power in his body to keep the attackers off. Now, as the battle retreated from him, he let his arms hang limp and useless by his sides, in too much pain to know if the tingling was still with him. Am I through? he wondered. Was this what my vision foretold? Raising his head with an effort, he gazed across the body-strewn plaza to the great temple. There, at the very top, he could see a tiny figure wearing the turquoise mantle of the Speaker. He was pacing back and forth in front of the black shrine of Tezcatlipoca, trailed by a smaller figure, perhaps a child. Huemac remembered the two figures that had fled from him in his vision, and he knew that he was not finished.

He turned and knelt beside Acolmiztli, whose head was cushioned by his Jaguar headdress and the remnants of his feathered standard, and whose leg Huemac had bandaged with a mantle taken off a corpse. His face was streaked with blood and soot, and when Huemac grasped his hand, it was cold and without strength. Very slowly, Acolmiztli opened his eyes, and Huemac saw, as he had not in many years, how much his brother looked like Ome Xochitl.

"I must leave you, my brother," Huemac said, his voice a mere croak from the dryness in his throat. "For I do not have the strength to carry you down these stairs."

"There are others who will tend to me," Acolmiztli said, his eyes dim and barely able to focus. Huemac took his brother's hand and laid it upon Huemac's Otomi bow and the last of his arrows, which he had placed on the ground beside Acolmiztli.

"I leave you my bow and three arrows, in case the enemy should return."

Acolmiztli closed his eyes and swallowed laboriously, too weak to close his fingers around the bow.

"Go, Huemac," he whispered. "Go and put an end to this filthy war."

Huemac turned and began to descend the steep stairs one at a time, grimacing every time he put pressure on his wounded foot. He was halfway down the steps before he realized that he might not see his brother alive again, and as he picked his way between the corpses piled at the bottom, the reality of death struck his senses like a blow held back while the killing was actually going on. My father is dead, he thought; somewhere, his eyes stare as sightlessly as these, and his spirit wanders in Mictlan, the Region of the Fleshless. Soon, my brother may join him there.

Huemac no longer knew where he was going, or what he hoped to do there. He had no weapon and not even the strength to wield one; he was on the verge of tears, certain that he would collapse completely if he gave way to them. Warriors were running past him, Tepanecs who had broken through the western defenses and were heading for the front of the Temple of Huitzilopochtli, where the Tlatelulca were making their last stand. Huemac followed them blindly, limping and panting from the effort of simply putting one foot ahead of the other. He felt used up and the war seemed very far away, but he could not bring himself to stop.

Then he came upon the body. It was lying directly in Huemac's path, a large man stretched rigid on his side, one leg curled and braced backward beneath the other, his back arched against the arrow that had penetrated his chest and killed him instantly. His lips were curled back from his teeth, his face frozen in a last, shocked grimace. It was Nopaltzin.

Huemac bent over him and with one quick motion snapped the feathered shaft of the arrow and threw it clattering across the flagstones. He did not wish to know if it had been his own. Then the grief broke inside him and flooded his eyes, and he knelt and wept over the body of his friend, tilting his head back and letting the tears stream down his face.

"You have taken my father," he cried to the sky, "and Nopalli, and Acol-miztli! Will you have me, too, O Gods?"

Huemac was shaking, every muscle quivering uncontrollably, and he suddenly realized that the tingling had returned. His body was pulsing with heat, and he could no longer feel his pain or the thirst in his throat. His hands felt swollen with power as he gathered up the macana that lay beside Nopaltzin's body and leapt to his feet.

"Let me finish it, then!" he shouted furiously, brandishing the warclub at the vultures circling lazily overhead. "Use me if you will, but give me the power!"

Strapping his shield to his left arm, he took a two-handed grip on the macana and began to run toward the temple, leaping over the bodies that lay in his way, screaming the names of his father, his brother, and his friend. The Tepanecs stared in amazement and made way for him as he overtook them and charged into the lead, running headlong for the Tlatelulcan troops that stood in a solid mass at the base of the temple steps. Some of the Tlatelulca rushed out to meet the charge, and Huemac ran right over the first man he met, smashing him in the face with his shield and hurling him backward, unconscious. Then he swung his macana to the right and tore the legs from beneath two Tlatelulca with one blow, sending the others retreating back to their ranks in disarray.

"Cuachic! Cuachic!" the Tepanecs shouted in admiration for the madness of Huemac's bravery, and they poured in behind him as he leapt forward to assault the warriors guarding the temple steps. Huemac could see the terror in the eyes of the warriors in the first rank as he threw himself upon them, knocking three of them to the ground before those behind pushed him back. Huemac slashed his way forward again, splintering shields with the force of his blows, but the wall of men was too thick, and he could make no headway against it.

Backing away, he ran behind the front lines to the center of the fighting, where he could see Axayacatl himself, dressed in his turquoise mantle, struggling in the midst of a tangled mass of Eagles, Jaguars, and Otomi Warriors. The Tenocha were on the verge of breaking through, and Huemac could see the Tlatelulca beyond the front line beginning to back away, up the temple steps. Holding his warclub in both hands over his head, Huemac ran toward the tangle of men, planting his foot on the back of a bent-over Eagle Warrior and springing clear over the entire group.

"Tenochtitlan!" he shouted, as he landed on his feet behind the startled Tlatelulca and spun in a circle, clearing the space around him with his macana. The warriors in front of him broke and ran, and as he whirled back toward the entangled Tenocha, the sharp edge of his macana caught an unsuspecting Otomi Warrior on the side of the neck and sent his head flying from his body. With that, the Tlatelulcan line gave way, and Axayacatl and his men surged toward the steps, close on Huemac's heels.

"Moquiuix is mine!" Axayacatl commanded, but Huemac did not hear him, for he was rising now, effortlessly, as he had in his vision, not feeling the power in his legs that propelled him up the steep stone stairs. There was a reddish glow directly in front of his eyes, and he could not see the Tlatelulca priests and warriors scattering out of his way in fright. Stones and arrows whistled past him harmlessly as he gained the third tier and started up the last flight of steps, Axayacatl and the others now far behind.

Then he was to the top, and saw a black-robed priest rushing at him through the red light, swinging a warclub at his head. Ducking instinctively, he stuck his shield in the priest's stomach and lifted him high over his head, before tossing him backward down the steps. As Huemac turned to face the other priests on the platform, an incredible howl burst from his lungs, a shriek composed of all the voices he had ever learned, the deadly buzz of the rattle-snake foremost among them. The priests froze, then bolted and ran for the shrines. Huemac cut down three of them before the rest scurried through the veiled entrances that lay behind the bloody sacrificial stones.

"Die with your gods, then!" Huemac shouted contemptuously, lighting torches from the firewood next to the braziers and throwing them onto the roofs of the shrines and through the doorways. "That is for my father!" he cried deliriously. "And for Acolmiztli! And Nopalli! Burn, you cowards!"

Axayacatl and four of his warriors had now reached the platform, and they saw Moquiuix and his dwarf run out from behind the shrine of Tezcatlipoca at the same time that Huemac did.

"He is mine!" Axayacatl yelled, but Huemac was closer, and he did not heed the Speaker's order as he advanced upon the two figures, his lips fixed into a snarl, his eyes blazing with hatred and anger. Before he could reach them, though, Moquiuix and the dwarf turned and ran for the edge of the platform, and with a final scream threw themselves over the side.

The reddish glow seemed to move away from Huemac, and he followed it with his eyes until it melted into the flames pouring from the shrines, and disappeared into smoke. The tingling diminished until he could feel only a small tremor of it, somewhere below his stomach. Axayacatl and the other warriors were staring at him, horror-struck by Moquiuix's suicide, or perhaps by whatever it was in Huemac's face that had driven him to it. The warriors drew in around Axayacatl protectively as Huemac approached with his war-club still in his hand. The shrines crackled noisily as they burned behind him, lighting the Speaker's young face.

"It is over, my Lord," Huemac said, and bowed before him. The guards relaxed slightly but kept their hands on their weapons, as if not sure what to expect.

"Who are you?" Axayacatl demanded. "And why did you not heed my command?"

"I am Huemac, the son of Quinatzin," Huemac said, and saw his father's name register on the Speaker's face, though he tried not to show it. "I did not hear your command, or I would have obeyed it."

"You were as one maddened," Axayacatl assured him, "and truly terrible to behold! What was it that possessed you, Huemac? Was it vengeance against those who killed your father?"

Emboldened by the awe in Axayacatl's voice, Huemac stared into his eyes, trying to gauge the innocence of the question. Axayacatl was only six years older than himself, but the weight of his authority had aged him, and his apparent guilelessness had an air of calculation about it. *He is offering me a respectable excuse for my madness,* Huemac realized, *and asking in return that I do not question the manner of my father's death. If he suspects Tlacaelel, he does not want to know for sure.*

"No," Huemac said at last, "it was not vengeance. It was grief that he had died so needlessly. May I go now, Lord? I am tired of seeing Mexicans die."

This last was stated bitterly, and the warriors around the Speaker frowned and shifted uneasily. Axayacatl stayed them with his hand, but the stiffness of his features showed that he, too, was displeased.

"Go now, if that is your wish," he said. "I will summon you later to reward you for the courage you have shown today."

Huemac bowed again, aware that he had just refused the favor of the most powerful man in Anahuac. But he wanted no favor that made a lie of his father's death, and helped to conceal the hand of the Demon Heart. *I will not inherit my father's life of deception,* he vowed, *no matter what it may cost me.*

When he reached the stairs, he glanced back over his shoulder and saw Axayacatl and his warriors standing at the edge of the platform, staring down at the place where Moquiuix had fallen.

WITHOUT STOPPING to drink or wash his wounds, Huemac hurried through the crowded streets, heading for the calpulli of Atezcapan. He was limping again and did not know where the strength to even move was coming from, but the desperate fear in his heart drove him onward. Many of the houses he passed were in flames, and the laughter of the looters mingled with the screams of those who ran fleeing along the street, their possessions and children clutched to their breasts. Near one of the bridges, a Tlatelulcan family had been driven into the canal by a group of Tenocha apprentices, who were forcing their victims to quack and splash like ducks in the water. Although the order to stop the killing had been given, bodies lay everywhere.

Tezcatl's body lay sprawled just inside the doorway of his house, surrounded by the benches and timbers he had used to barricade the entrance, and by the five warriors he had killed before he died. Standing in the center of the courtyard were two Jaguar Warriors, one holding a bulging bag of loot, the other engaged in pinioning the arms of Tezcatl's serving woman, who struggled against him. They were both laughing, their attention trained on the scene occurring at the edge of the garden.

Huemac recognized the third warrior instantly: It was Colotl, the Jaguar who had once argued with Tezcatl at Acolmiztli's house. He was dancing in a circle around Taypachtli, taunting her so that she whirled and jabbed wildly with the maguey thorn in her hand. The fresh blood on Colotl's arms showed that she had defended herself well, but exhaustion and despair were making her thrusts more and more futile and pathetic. Rage welled up in Huemac's heart, and he felt his eyes widen and grow bright, radiating the power that he had always kept hidden from other people, as his mother had taught him. He started forward, paying no heed to the fact that he was outnumbered three to one.

"A blind she-cub!" Colotl crowed exultantly, seizing Taypachtli's wrist from behind and forcing her to drop the thorn with one cruel squeeze of his hand. He pulled her in to him and grabbed for her breasts, then noticed Huemac coming toward him.

"Release her," Huemac growled, and Colotl's face darkened with anger. He threw Taypachtli roughly to the ground and whirled quickly to scoop his macana up, turning back with his legs spread in a fighting stance, a malicious smile on his face. Huemac saw, out of the corner of his eye, that the other two Jaguars had also picked up their weapons and were edging toward him.

"Who are *you*, boy, to give me orders?" Colotl demanded, appraising Huemac's torn and bloody figure as he advanced.

"I am Tenocha," Huemac said, "but I am not a coward like you, Colotl."

The name brought the Jaguar's head up, and he looked fully into Huemac's eyes. His sneer vanished instantly, and then he gasped once and fell to the ground, clutching at his chest. Huemac turned hastily to face the other Jaguars, who had recovered from their shock and were moving toward him. But one look at Huemac's eyes made them back off and then run for the doorway, leaving their loot behind.

"Is it you, Huemac?" Taypachtli said, as he turned and came toward her. The serving woman had helped her rise and was brushing the dust from her clothing, casting fearful glances over her shoulder at Huemac. He took Taypachtli's outstretched hands and brought them gently to his face.

"Yes, it is you," she said joyfully, but then cocked her head and frowned to show her bewilderment. "But what has happened to the others? I heard no fighting."

"I stopped his heart with my eyes," Huemac said bluntly. "The others chose not to fight. You are safe now," he added, softening his tone, for he saw that he had frightened her. He glanced over at Colotl, who lay writhing in the dust a few feet away, his face contorted with the pain of trying to recapture his breath. There is another who will fear me and speak ill of my name, Huemac thought. But it did not matter, for he understood his luck now, and never again would he hide his powers for the sake of a reputation he could not have.

"Come, let us go to Tenochtitlan," he said quietly, and discarded his battered shield to let Taypachtli take his arm. She did so without hesitation, though he sensed that she also felt the change in him and was disturbed by it. Leaving Colotl lying among the other bodies in the deserted courtyard, they walked out into the street with the serving woman following a few steps behind, wary of Huemac yet glad to carry the bag of loot he had rescued.

OME XOCHITL was sitting next to the hearth in her rooms, staring into the coals of the fire, as if hoping to find some sign of when her waiting would be over. She could not deny the emptiness that had come suddenly into her heart during the afternoon, an absence of feeling so abrupt and total that it had left her immobilized. Yet she could not accept the fact that Huemac was dead. He is gone, she told herself over and over, persuaded but unbelieving.

Then she heard a noise and looked up to see him standing just inside the doorway, bloody and disheveled, watching her with an expression she could not read.

"I had thought," he said slowly, "that one day I would come to you to hear your apology. But I am grateful simply to see you again, my mother."

"I thought that you had died," she said helplessly, and Huemac smiled at her confusion.

"And I thought the same of Acolmiztli, though Teuxoch has informed me that he is alive, and will recover. If I had died upon the temple today, I would have died a hero. But that is not my luck."

Huemac swayed on his feet, and Ome Xochitl rose and came to his side, realizing that he was hurt. He continued to talk, beginning to ramble from fatigue as she removed the ragged armor from his body.

"No, it is my luck to be feared and misunderstood, and always looked on with suspicion," he said loudly, as she led him to a mat near the fire and made him lie down on his back. "I know that now, and I accept it. Never will I have my father's smooth face and tongue, never will I be trusted as he was. But I have a power that is equally valuable, if not more so: I can make even the Tenocha *fear* me."

Ome Xochitl dabbed at the cut over his ear with a wet cloth, and Huemac winced and closed his eyes, his voice trailing off to an incoherent murmur.

"It is over now," she said soothingly, but Huemac's eyes popped open and he unconsciously put a hand on his stomach, as if to still a movement inside.

"No," he said in a whisper, "I have still to meet with the Demon Heart. You must heal me, Mother, so that I will be ready."

"Yes, my son," Ome Xochitl agreed, watching his face until he again closed his eyes and his breathing deepened. Then, offering a fervent prayer to the gods that had spared her son, she opened her medicine bag and, with tears flowing from her eyes, began to tend to his wounds.

6

DURING the ceremonies in the plaza, Huemac stood beside his brother in the front ranks of the surviving members of the company of Moyotlan. Their daring raid into the temple precinct had been credited with demoralizing the Tlatelulca and so disorganizing Moquiuix's defenses that the Tenocha victory had come much more easily than expected. Acolmiztli had been elevated to the rank of warchief for leading the attack, and all the warriors had been given the insignia of heroes, as well as rich shares in the spoils of the war. Huemac was especially splendid in his new dress, for in addition to the rewards of Axayacatl, the Tepanecs with whom he had fought had presented him with several fine mantles and a pair of golden butterfly earplugs. These dangled near his shoulders, and set into his perforated lower lip was a lip-plug of blood-red stone, placed there by Axayacatl himself. His cotton mantle bore the twisted wind jewel sign in yellow on the front and had long yellow tassels on the bottom, as the mantles of the lords did, and the gold and leather bands that girded his arms and legs bore sprays of precious feathers.

Yet although he was in many ways the most famous warrior in Tenochtitlan, Huemac had not been singled out for particular distinction by the Speaker, and neither of the warrior orders had asked him to join their ranks, despite the strong advocacy of Acolmiztli. Huemac had had to tell his brother that it was no use; that although the Tenocha esteemed madness in battle, whatever its source, they regarded the quachic with great wariness, as if he were an ungovernable weapon. And to this suspicion Huemac had added his notoriety as the man who had scared Moquiuix to his death, and who had dropped a Jaguar in his tracks with one look. Acolmiztli had gradually come to see that such a reputation could not be combated or outlived, and that Huemac's decision to embrace it was the only choice left open to him. Now, when people questioned him about his brother's reputed powers, Acolmiztli would nod mysteriously and advise the questioner to thank the gods that Huemac was a Tenocha, and not their enemy.

After the requisite sacrifices had been made to Huitzilopochtli and the ceremonies had been brought to an end, Huemac was notified that the Cihuacoatl wished to see him in his chambers beneath the Temple of the Snake Woman. Huemac took a deep breath and looked at his brother, who leaned upon a crutch to support his injured leg.

"You must put all thoughts of our father's death out of your mind," Acolmiztli cautioned. "There is no way that you can avenge yourself upon this man."

"I know this," Huemac assured him. "I seek only to prevent him from adding my name to his list of victims. I have been preparing myself for this day for many years."

"May the gods protect you, then," Acolmiztli said. "I will wait to hear from you."

Huemac nodded and strode off across the plaza, his golden earplugs gleaming in the sunlight. After watching him leave, Acolmiztli called two of his highest-ranking captains to him, men who had fought alongside Huemac in Tlatelulco, and told them to wait outside the Temple of the Snake Woman.

"If my brother has not emerged by sundown," he commanded, "inquire of him in my name, and do not let them turn you away without an answer . . ."

AS HUEMAC walked down the dark passageway beneath the temple, he directed all his attention to the tiny tremor of tingling that still remained with him, like a flutter in his stomach. He had forgotten it during the ceremony, and even now, despite his rising excitement, he could not detect any growth in its intensity. I must rely on my own powers, he thought, feeling more relieved than anxious, for he was sure that Tlacaelel would try to anger him and goad him into making a fatal mistake, and his anger was nearly impossible to control when the power was upon him.

Tlacaelel was sitting on a raised dais at the end of the chamber, with torches in holders behind him casting a lurid yellow light on the silver serpents embroidered into the black curtain that shrouded the back wall. He was wearing the long white robe of his priestly office, and his bare arms bore the bloody marks of a recent act of penance. The resemblance to Teuxoch was very apparent to Huemac, until Tlacaelel smiled, a smile that was chilling and utterly heartless, more like the grimace of a wild beast that has sighted its prey.

"So this is the famous Huemac," Tlacaelel rasped, gesturing for him to sit on a mat only a few feet away, though below the level of the dais. "I have heard many things about you, son of Quinatzin. But first you must drink with me, you must share some of the fine octli brewed by our brothers the Tlatelulca."

Huemac took the offered cup and tipped it to his lips as if drinking deeply, though he only allowed a small quantity of the pungent maguey wine into his mouth, swirling it around carefully with his tongue before swallowing. Xiuh-cozcatl had taught him to discern the various tastes of all the drugs, even in the minutest amounts, so that he was sure, when he lowered his cup, that there was nothing in it but octli.

"It is indeed fine octli," he said casually. "I thank you, my Lord."

Tlacaelel laughed mirthlessly and poured more into Huemac's cup, before setting the painted gourd on a low table beside him. Then he squinted knowingly at Huemac and spoke sharply:

"Your father is dead."

"Yes," Huemac said, staring briefly into the prying eyes to gauge their power, which was considerable. Yet no more powerful than my own, Huemac thought, if it comes to that.

"It has been said," Tlacaelel continued, "that you do not blame your father's death on the Tlatelulca. I would know whom you *do* blame."

"I blame no one," Huemac said evenly, hooding his eyes slightly against Tlacaelel's relentless gaze. "It was fate that brought him to this city, and fate that made him an ambassador at such an unfortunate time. When I spoke to Axayacatl upon the temple, it was with the grief of a son who loved his father and hoped to learn from him, one who could not accept his fate as easily as he did himself."

"It is also said," Tlacaelel said harshly, frowning to show his disbelief, "that you were displeased by the number of Mexicans who died gloriously in the battle. That is a coward's attitude!"

"Indeed," Huemac agreed. "And I do not know how it could have been attributed to me, since the number of Tlatelulca I killed myself is well known. But I cannot be responsible for all the lies that are told about me."

Tlacaelel glared at him silently, seeming to grow more angry by the moment, but Huemac merely sipped from his cup and pretended not to notice, feeling the octli spread its warmth into his stomach. He glanced at Tlacaelel from beneath his hooded eyelids, seeing the fury in the old man's eyes and rejoicing in his own calm. He is used to unnerving people with his ruthlessness, Huemac thought disdainfully, but he does not have that advantage over me. He took another swallow of octli and waited for the next accusation, feeling aloof and impenetrable. Tlacaelel grunted softly and blew air out through his nostrils, as if frustrated.

"Your father was valuable to me," he said, "for I could read his heart and make him serve me. He hated me, but he feared me, too, as any wise man would. But you, Huemac, you do not fear me . . . "

"Perhaps I do not have my father's wisdom," Huemac said dryly, risking a trace of sarcasm. "I was raised a Tenocha, by your own daughter, and taught that a Tenocha fears no one. I have always tried to honor her teachings."

"I can see that," Tlacaelel said angrily, spraying tiny drops of saliva into the air. "You have too much courage for a Texcocan. I made your father my captive, but I do not think that I could do the same with you. You are much too dangerous to be trusted!"

"I am dangerous only to the enemies of the Tenocha," Huemac began, but Tlacaelel lost all control and shouted at him:

"You are dangerous to *me*!"

Then Tlacaelel abruptly dropped his eyes and reached for the gourd, as if ashamed of his admission. He poured with shaking hands, splashing octli onto the table, and hastily raised his cup to his lips. Huemac took one, polite drink of the sour liquid and decided that he had had enough, for he was beginning to feel pleasantly dizzy, and he did not want to celebrate his victory too soon.

"I would have you killed, if you were not so famous," Tlacaelel resumed in a low voice. "Instead, I am going to see that you are inducted into the Eagle Warriors, and pledged to fight for the Sun. Soon, we will turn ourselves to the task of punishing those who conspired with Moquiuix against us, and the warriors will again be marching to far-off lands. You will be in the vanguard, Huemac, and I will see that you are kept away from Tenochtitlan for a long time. Perhaps someone will kill you *for* me."

Huemac sneered openly, unmoved by such a cowardly threat. I will outlive your hatred of me, Demon Heart, he thought contemptuously, remembering the vision he had had of himself as an Old Eagle. I will live in this city long after you have died, poisoned by your own evil . . .

Then he found himself in the act of reaching for his cup, and he realized that there was an intolerable sourness in his mouth, and a prickling, burning sensation in the back of his throat. The taste was unmistakable: It was ololiuhqui, the seeds of the green-serpent vine. Tlacaelel must have slipped them into his cup sometime after the first pouring. Huemac's stomach suddenly convulsed and he shuddered violently, seeing colored flashes in front of his eyes. He retched and tried to vomit, but produced only a small amount of milky liquid, for he had fasted for a day prior to the ceremony.

"That is poor gratitude for the offer I have made you," Tlacaelel said unctuously, his voice buzzing in Huemac's ears. "There is no way the Eagles would have you, otherwise. They know, as I do, that you are a spell-caster and a murderer of priests!"

Huemac tried to cover his ears against the awful echoing of Tlacaelel's voice, but the reverberations coursed through his body unimpeded, as if he were hearing with his skin.

"What good is your fearlessness now?" the voice goaded. "Now, I think, you will begin to tell me the *truth.*"

Huemac felt Tlacaelel's words dig into him like tiny claws, and though he knew that he should make no answer, he felt no control over his tongue, and he was hearing sounds that might have been his own. The air in front of him was thick and swimming with darting minnows of light, and behind it—through it—loomed that sharp predatory face, those insatiable eyes. I will be helpless soon, Huemac thought frantically, grasping the jade amulet around his neck and trying to make his mind work, make it remember what he had been taught, remember how to shut out the one who would steal his visions . . .

"Speak, murderer!" the buzzing voice commanded. "Tell me what you did to Coatleztli, tell me how you drove him to his death . . . "

Death! The silver serpents writhed against the blackness of the curtain, and behind them were the shapes of a mountain, and trees that waved and shook, and a knife that glowed with the color of the serpents. Huemac recoiled and tried to cry out, calling to Xolotl to save him. But the other voice was louder and drowned out his prayers, screaming instead of murder and death. *I am lost* flashed through his mind, and he felt his heart sink within him, a dead weight descending into turbulent darkness . . . but there, in the darkness, he suddenly saw—felt—a small glowing ball, and he caught himself upon it desperately, grasping with his whole being, feeling the claws that tried to tear him loose, the blows that buffeted his head. He fell backward, still clutching the tingling ball, and suddenly went rigid . . .

He found himself standing on a high place, something like the cliffs at Chapultepec, except that he was looking straight down over the whole of Tenochtitlan. So stunning was the view of the temples and painted buildings, the intricate network of streets, bridges, and canals, that he did not notice at first that a war was being waged below him. Or perhaps it only began as he watched, for the flames roared up and spread with astonishing quickness, giving off clouds of black smoke that obscured the men fighting in the streets and around the temple plaza. Who is it that attacks us? Huemac wondered, unable to recognize the enemy through the smoke and dust of battle. He heard a great booming sound that was repeated several times, and then a low rumbling vibration started up beneath his feet and grew until the air itself seemed to be quivering. He saw cracks appear in the walls and roofs of the houses, and then the temples began to tremble and break apart, shedding large chunks of painted plaster that exploded on contact, showering a multicolored dust over the broken statuary littering the pyramid steps. My city is being destroyed, he realized; it is dying before my eyes.

Then he was aware of voices, and felt a weight settle upon his right shoulder. He turned his head very slowly, straining against the sudden reluctance of his neck muscles, and saw the hawk perched on the end of his shoulder. He did not know how the hawk had landed without being seen, but he was not frightened by it. The reddish-brown filigree of its sleek feathers trapped light in shimmering patterns, and it stared at him out of one wide, unblinking yellow eye. Reflected in the blackness of its pupil was the deeply lined face of a white-haired old man, the man Huemac had seen once before, the old man who was himself. The face spoke to him in a commanding voice:

"You must stop it."

The words echoed in his ears, and then were taken up and repeated, dimly, by the chorus of voices he had heard earlier. Looking down, he saw, far below, as if he had become a giant, a crowd of tiny people: some dark and misshapen, others shining with light, yet all crying out to him, beseeching him to stop the destruction. Drawing courage from their pleas, he looked back over the burning city and widened his eyes to their furthest extent, exerting all his power to make the destruction cease.

The rumbling vibration began to diminish, then faded out altogether. Gradually, the smoke thinned and the flames shrank away, and he could see the solid outlines of the temples, their painted exteriors restored to their former perfection. Tenochtitlan was whole again, its peaceful streets empty of warriors.

"I have done it!" Huemac cried exultantly, and began to laugh, intoxicated by his own power. I have saved my city, he told himself triumphantly, sending his laughter echoing off the blue vault of the sky.

But then the earth shivered, and suddenly the rumbling began with even greater force, sending shock waves through the air. Huemac gaped in horror as the city erupted into flames and once more began to fall into ruin. He stared desperately and held out his hands in supplication, but this time he was powerless to stop the devastation, and he saw the red shrine of Huitzilopochtli burst into splinters as the image of the god was thrown from its altar and went crashing down the temple steps, leaving a trail of fire behind it. Screams of pain filled Huemac's ears, and then the ground beneath his feet gave way and he plummeted downward, surrounded by flames and falling pieces of shattered stone, seeing the hawk spiraling upward in flight, its red tail feathers flashing once before disappearing into the smoke . . .

FOR A LONG time after the vision had passed, Huemac lay flat on his back, eyes staring upward sightlessly, unable to bring himself out of his trance. He remembered clearly what had happened: the drug's taking effect, Tlacaelel's questions, his desperate focusing upon the tingling ball in his stomach. Yet none of it seemed to matter in itself, being merely the occasion for this vision, this final glimpse of what fate held for him. So I am to see the end of Tenochtitlan, he thought sorrowfully, and to fail in my attempt to prevent its downfall. That is my luck, the way the gods have chosen to use me. He felt no desire to leave his trance and reenter the world where such a fate awaited him.

But feeling was slowly coming back into his body, and he was aware of faces above him, and the angry mutterings of a voice he recognized as Tlacaelel's. Then water was poured over him and he was slapped sharply across the face; unseen hands lifted him into a sitting position and held him there forcibly. Huemac felt full awareness returning and fought against it angrily, hating these people for bringing him back. Then his vision cleared and he saw the hand poised near his face, and he struck out at it ferociously, feeling the sting in his own hand as he knocked it away. His arms were immediately pinned behind him, and the hand struck him twice across the face, jarring blows that sobered him instantly. He saw that the hand belonged to Tlacaelel, and that he was being held on both sides by strong guards.

"Why do you only beat me?" he demanded, finding that his voice had returned. "Why do you not kill me while I am helpless?"

Tlacaelel signaled to the guards to loosen their grip on Huemac's arms, though not to let him go entirely. Huemac saw the anger in the old man's face transform itself into a satisfied smirk.

"After what you have told me," he said insinuatingly, "I do not wonder that you beg to be killed."

"I told you nothing," Huemac said scornfully. "I *laughed* at you!"

Huemac had spoken impulsively, in anger at being soaked and slapped, but he saw Tlacaelel's face darken and knew that he had guessed at the truth: that he had indeed laughed aloud during his vision. He knew then that he had escaped into the vision, and had confessed to nothing.

"You were laughing over the death of Coatleztli," Tlacaelel said harshly. "You said: 'I have done it!' "

"I spoke in a vision; I did not speak to *you.*"

"You confessed to me!" Tlacaelel insisted imperiously, "and to all the others who are here."

"Their testimony means nothing, for *I* was not here. I was seeing things shown to me by the goddess of the green-serpent plant; I was seeing my future."

"You have no future, murderer!" Tlacaelel thundered.

"Kill me, then," Huemac said recklessly. "Prove to me that you are stronger than fate. I have had my vision, and I am tired of your threats."

The guards stiffened in shock and retightened their grip on his arms, and Huemac prepared himself to be slapped again. But he had no fear of anything that Tlacaelel could do to him, and he could see the old man hesitate as the knowledge of this penetrated. Then Tlacaelel lowered his hand and turned impatiently to the black-robed priest who had been kneeling beside him for some time, obviously waiting to deliver a message. The priest whispered urgently in his ear, flinching at the anger that appeared on Tlacaelel's face.

"Send them away!" Tlacaelel snapped, and the priest cast an anxious glance in Huemac's direction before continuing in an agitated voice.

"They refuse to leave, my Lord. They are captains . . . and they speak in the name of the warchief Acolmiztli."

Tlacaelel slapped the man across the mouth, and the priest immediately prostrated himself before his master, ready to absorb more blows. But Tlacaelel simply made a disgusted sound and turned back to Huemac, who straightened up expectantly in his captors' arms.

"You will report tomorrow to the House of Eagles," Tlacaelel said through his teeth. "May your fate claim you before you again come into my presence, Huemac."

Then he waved his arm toward the door and shouted at the guards, who rose hurriedly and bore Huemac away, out of the chamber of the Cihuacoatl.

OME XOCHITL knelt at the end of the line of mourners, which included herself, Cocatli, Teuxoch, and two of Teuxoch's daughters. Before them on a bed of fresh pine branches was a small stone image of Mictlancihuatl, the Goddess of the Dead, who had eyes of black mirror-stone and gaping jaws at the joints of her twisted limbs. Teuxoch, her hair loosened and her face smeared with pitch, used a long-handled incense ladle to add more copal to the smoldering coals in the brazier next to the image. Swaying from side to side, she began to sing in a high keening voice, with the other women chanting in low tones behind her. She sang of Mictlan, the Place of Our Common Sleep, where the spirit of Quinatzin was destined to wander for four years, undergoing many trials before he was allowed to rest.

When Ome Xochitl saw Huemac enter the courtyard and head toward the room he had taken as his own—the room where Acolmiztli had once convalesced as a young man—she rose quietly from her place and went to meet him. He was wearing the jade rabbit over a plain mantle and carried a wet bundle under one arm; there were fresh bruises on his cheeks and forehead, and his eyes were glassy with fatigue.

"It is over," he said to her. "I have met Tlacaelel, and he has made me an Eagle in order to banish me from the city."

"You are free, then!"

"Free? Of him, yes," Huemac growled, casting a baleful glance at the mourners. "See that Teuxoch is kept away from me until I am rested."

"Yes, my son," Ome Xochitl said compliantly, seeing the unreasoning anger in his eyes. "But she is very excited that you have been made the master of this house, and have been given such rich rewards. She will be very anxious to hear of your interview with her father."

"I could not look upon her with kindness now—I would only see him! Tell her that I will eat with her tomorrow before I go to the House of Eagles, but keep her away from me tonight, or I will say unforgivable things!"

Exhausted by his anger, Huemac turned on his heel and went into his room, dropping his bundle by the door and throwing himself onto the sleeping mats, sleeping almost at once. Ome Xochitl covered him with a blanket and lifted the wet bundle from the floor, discovering that it was his mantle with all his jewelry and insignia rolled up inside. She stared sadly at the golden butterflies, the finely worked armbands with their sprays of red and yellow parrot feathers, the strings of coral and turquoise beads. To possess the symbols of such high honor, she thought, yet never to be able to claim them in innocence, proudly, as one's own. It was a hard fate to visit on one so young.

She took the mantle to her own room and hung it up near the fire, laying the jewelry and feathers out on a mat to dry. The smell of copal and burning rubber came from the next room, where Taypachtli was conducting her own ceremony of mourning for her father and brother, alone, as she had requested. Taypachtli had become silent and withdrawn during the course of the last several days, ever since she had overheard Teuxoch discussing possible marriage matches for Huemac, which Teuxoch spoke of solely in terms of the eligible young women in her father's family and that of Moteczuma. Ome Xochitl knew that there was nothing she could say to comfort Taypachtli; that only Huemac could reassure her, and he had been too preoccupied with other things lately to pay any attention to her.

And now Tlacaelel had made him an Eagle Warrior, pledging him to a life of fighting, and to the expectation of an early death. She wondered if Huemac would tell her about the interview, or if he would keep it inside himself, as he had with whatever had happened to him in Tlatelulco. She had heard the stories of his wild bravery from others, but he had not spoken of it himself, except for his delirious gloating over the fear he had inspired. He has freed himself from everyone, she thought ruefully; even I can no longer read his heart, if he does not choose to open it to me.

Ome Xochitl returned to her place in the ceremony, and when it was over, she told the others of Huemac's interview with Tlacaelel and of his imminent induction into the order of Eagles. Teuxoch, her eyes glistening with pride and happiness, wanted to awaken him immediately, but Ome Xochitl persuaded her to let him rest, pointing out that he was still recovering from his wounds, and repeating his promise to eat with his second mother in the morning. Teuxoch finally went off to her own rooms, already making plans for the feast that she was sure Huemac would want to hold to celebrate his success.

When everyone had gone, Ome Xochitl washed her face and seated herself on the mats beneath the huehuetl tree, wrapping a blanket around herself to ward off the chill of the air. A bright half-moon rose as she waited, and the hard-packed floor of the courtyard gleamed like burnished silver. Sometime after midnight, Huemac came out of his room with a blanket draped over his shoulders, and she called to him softly. The swollen bruise on his cheek showed plainly in the moonlight as he seated himself across from her, but the tension and anger had left him.

"I needed very much to rest," he apologized. "I am grateful that you waited for me."

"I hoped that you would wish to speak to me," she admitted frankly. "I know that you no longer need to."

Huemac looked at her sadly, but did not deny her statement.

"The power that was within me is gone," he said quietly. "It came to me today for the last time, in the form of a vision. It was a vision that made the threat of banishment seem trivial, that made even Tlacaelel himself impotent to affect my fate. It was a vision of the end of Tenochtitlan."

"You had this vision in the presence of Tlacaelel?" Ome Xochitl asked, and Huemac nodded.

"It saved me from him. I am to live a long life, so that I may be a witness to the destruction of my people."

"You must . . ." Ome Xochitl began impulsively, then caught herself. "Do you wish my advice in this matter?"

Huemac smiled at his mother's deference, then winced at the pain the smile caused in his bruised cheek.

"Even when I was angry with you," he said, "I did not cease to honor your wisdom. You have always been the mirror that showed me to myself most clearly."

"Speak, then, my son," Ome Xochitl said in a gratified voice. "Tell me all that you wish me to know."

"I must begin with the priest," Huemac said, turning his eyes inward. "And the powers I called upon to kill him."

BY THE TIME Huemac finished his recitation, the moon had dipped low in the west, casting its ghostly light over only the topmost branches of the tree. The priests throughout the city blew their conch trumpets, signaling the third division of the night.

"I did not wish to return to this world," Huemac concluded wearily. "And when Tlacaelel brought me back, I dared him to kill me. I could not see how I could bear to carry this terrible knowledge with me through the rest of my life."

"Do you now?" Ome Xochitl asked suggestively, and Huemac shrugged in resignation.

"I have been taught to accept my fate, and the challenge of my visions. I will do what I must to bear this. Yet I cannot help but think of the man for whom I was named, the Huemac who ruled over the Toltecs in the time of the fall of Tula."

Hearing no self-pity in his voice, Ome Xochitl allowed him a few moments to reflect on the enormity of his fate. She knew that she would have to lead him gently, and not appear to be pushing.

"Once, in your vision, you were able to stop the destruction," she said when he was looking at her again. "And once you could not. Can you assume from this that you are doomed to failure?"

Huemac cocked his head and considered her in silence, then smiled grudgingly at her shrewdness.

"You are right," he admitted finally. "I have taken only the meaning that was most plain to me. But it will be a long time before I am able to return to Texcoco, and my teachers in the hills."

"You *have* time," Ome Xochitl reminded him, "and someday you must go to those who can help you interpret this vision correctly and show you how to live it out, or perhaps even change it. But should you wait until you are free to wander? *This* is where your fate awaits you; you must find allies here, as your father did. Do not forget the tiny people in your vision."

Huemac lowered his eyes and rubbed a weary hand across his chin.

"My father tried to teach me this before he died. But I do not have his face, or his reputation for trust. I cannot win allies among those who fear me."

"You made an ally of your brother," Ome Xochitl pointed out. "And is there not another who trusts you?"

Huemac glanced toward the rooms where Taypachtli slept, then back into his mother's dark eyes.

"She fears me, as well," he said ruefully.

"She fears only that you do not care for her. How else can she feel when you tell her nothing of what is in your heart?"

"I intend to make her my wife," Huemac said defensively. "But I could not bring myself to tell her about Nopaltzin, and how I wished for his death."

"She will not hate you when you tell her how you grieved for his death," Ome Xochitl assured him. "Do not hide your heart from her, my son. Do not let the greatness of your vision blind you to the strength she can give you. You will never have the power you need if you lose your heart in the search."

"I will speak to her," Huemac decided abruptly. "Perhaps I can make her trust me again."

Ome Xochitl nodded her approval, then reached out to touch the jade rabbit on his chest.

"I will compose a flower song for your wedding," she promised, and Huemac smiled gratefully. Then he bowed his head while she passed a hand over him in blessing.

"You have been promised a long life," she said solemnly. "Perhaps the greatness of misfortune will overtake you in the end, but you will have time to prepare yourself, and you must use it. In all things, my son, from now until the end, you must go gathering power . . ."

VII

CAPTIVES

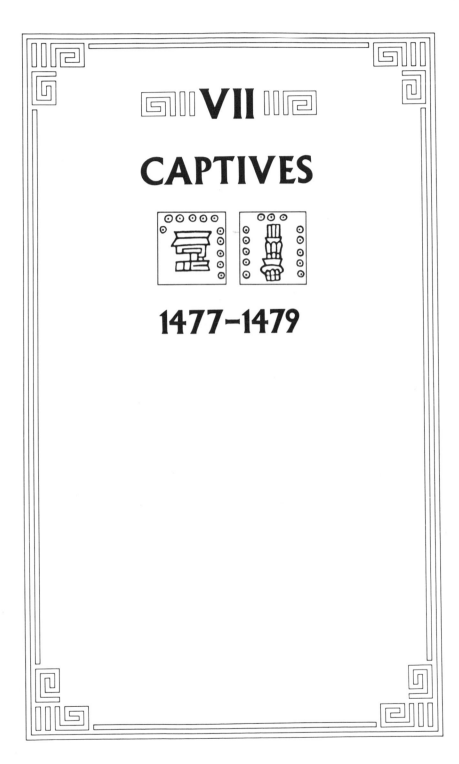

1477–1479

1

As the victorious army of the Mexica came across the western causeway toward Tenochtitlan, the people of the city came out to greet them, streaming through the Eagle Gate to the blowing of conch trumpets and the beating of drums. The army was preceded by a long line of captives: Matlatzinca, Mazahua, and Ocuilteca who had been taken in the campaign against the tribes of the Toluca Valley. The number of captives was unusually large, for this was the second time in three years that the Tenocha had crossed the western mountains to conquer them, and there was never any mercy shown to subjects who had the audacity to rebel. The people on the causeway raised their voices approvingly as the length of the line became apparent, for there were a new gladitorial stone and a new Eagle Vessel to be dedicated, as well as the traditionally large number of sacrifices to be made during this, the Month of the Flaying of Men, the second month of the year Eleven-House.

At the head of the line, dressed in the finest jewels and feathers and carried on litters, were the two captives that belonged to Axayacatl. These men were the objects of much admiration and reverence, and their praises were sung by a chorus of priests, since they would go to sustain the Sun in the name of the Great Speaker himself. After they had been incensed by the priests and presented with garlands of flowers and tubes of yetl, an honor guard of white-haired Old Eagles escorted them through the gate and into the city, moving at a slow, stately pace, so that the crowds could see and admire them fully.

Behind the litters came the captives of the high warchiefs and those of the members of the warrior orders, ranked according to the status of their captors and the degree of valor they had displayed before being captured. Some wept and sang their death songs; others kept their heads raised proudly as they slowly shuffled forward with their hands tied in front of them, guarded by their captors' apprentices. The Old Eagles acted as criers, questioning the apprentices and then relaying the information to the eager throngs lining the street, proclaiming the name and rank of the captive and describing how he had fought before being subdued. Jostling one another for a better view, the people in the crowd cheered each announcement and showered the captives with flowers, repeating their names aloud.

In the midst of the first group of captives was a tall, hard-faced Matlatzincan who wore a white bandage wrapped around his forehead beneath his tufted, Otomi-style haircut. His haughty face was impassive, and he did not respond to the shouts of the crowd when it was announced that he had slain two Eagles and a Puma Warrior before being taken. He was guarded by an exuberant, fifteen-year-old apprentice named Michpilli, who wore a standard of black turkey feathers surmounted by a crest made from the feathers of the red-tailed hawk, the personal standard of the Eagle Warrior, Huemac.

Though he tried to emulate the composure of his captive, Michpilli's youthful face broke continuously into a broad excited smile, accentuating the prettiness of his features, which were almost girlish, especially the long silken lashes surrounding his brown eyes and the sensuous bow of his lips. He was good-sized for his age and had proven his fighting ability in the telpochcalli, but the delicacy of his appearance had caused every other warrior in the House of Eagles to scorn him as an apprentice. Only Huemac had given him a fair chance to prove himself, and Michpilli repaid his master's trust with a devotion so fierce and uncompromising that the other apprentices had long ago learned not to gossip about Huemac when he was present.

"There is the family of your captor," he said to the Matlatzincan, when they had come abreast of Teuxoch, Ome Xochitl, and Taypachtli, who shared a place in the first rank of the crowd with the wives and children of Acolmiztli and Tlacateotzin.

"Which are wives?" the prisoner asked in crude Nahua, scanning the line of women with seeming indifference.

"My master has no wife," Michpilli explained, struck by the oddity of this fact for the first time. "But the beautiful round-faced woman, the one who has no sight, she is to be his asked-for woman."

Frowning at the effort of comprehension, the Matlatzincan looked again, then nodded that he understood.

"Tell that I bow to her," he said to Michpilli, and waited until an Old Eagle could relay the message before inclining his tufted head in Taypachtli's direction. Blushing at the honor being accorded to her, Taypachtli respectfully returned the bow, while the women around her beamed with pride. Michpilli felt like shouting with joy, and only restrained himself with difficulty. His own mother was a Tlatelulcan, a relative of Moquiuix, and he had always believed that Huemac's regard for Taypachtli had been extended to her people, and thus had had a great deal to do with his own acceptability as an apprentice. He hoped that Huemac would marry her, and he wondered again, as the procession moved on, why his master had not done so before this.

After the last of the captives had passed through the Eagle Gate, the ornate litters carrying Axayacatl and Chimalpopoca of Tlacopan came into view, and the crowd let out an enormous, adoring cheer. Now in the eighth year of his reign, the young Speaker had spent most of the four years since the civil war in the field, extending the dominance of the Tenocha to the north and west and covering himself with glory. His features properly stern, Axayacatl sat cross-legged beneath a woven canopy of green feathers, wearing the turquoise diadem of the ruler. His litter was flanked by the brilliantly costumed figures of his warchiefs, among them his brothers Tizoc and Ahuitzotl, Ocomatli and Acolmiztli, Eztetl, the supreme commander of the Eagles, and Colotl, who was now the supreme commander of the Jaguars.

Immediately behind the warchiefs came the select group of Eagles known as the Cuachic, their heads shaven except for the stiff ridge of hair that denoted their extraordinary courage, which they had demonstrated by accomplishing at least twenty exceptional deeds of valor. They were followed by the Eagles and Jaguars, marching in mixed pairs, and then by the Puma Warriors—those who had distinguished themselves in battle, yet whose common blood prevented their admission to the major orders. Taking up the rear, before the mass of regular warriors, was a small contingent of Tlatelulcan Otomi Warriors, who had only recently been allowed to march beside the Tenocha.

Because of the illustrious captive he had taken, Huemac occupied a place of honor directly behind the captains of his order. He was wearing cotton armor painted to look like feathers, and his face was half hidden by the golden visors of his headdress, which resembled the gaping beak of a screaming eagle. His shield and standard were attached to his back, and in his hands he carried the weapons of the man he had captured.

As was proper, he displayed no sign of recognition as he marched past the proud faces of his family. He had yet to make his penance and the offerings that would complete his vows to Tonatiuh and Huitzilopochtli, and contact with women was not permitted until that had been done. Even then, Huemac doubted that he would be given an expedient release, for his contingent of Eagles was under the command of the warchief Ocomatli, who was in turn the willing agent of Tlacaelel. Huemac had been allowed back to Tenochtitlan only twice in the last four years, and each time for a matter of days. He had spoken to Taypachtli on exactly four occasions since the day he entered the House of Eagles.

Huemac had borne his banishment in silence, but not idly, and now he felt that his luck was about to change, if it had not in fact changed already. The Matlatzincan was a great prize, and even before his capture, Huemac had begun to win the favor of the Superior Eagle, Eztetl, providing him with useful information from the sources that Huemac tried to cultivate wherever he went. Even Ocomatli could not harass him if Eztetl took his side, and the commander of the Eagles seemed to be leaning in that direction, despite—or perhaps because of—the continued vicious slanders of Colotl.

More than this, though, Huemac felt a growing power that had its source in the vows he had taken, and the strictness with which he had kept them. Tlacaelel had sent him to the Eagles as a punishment, and he had not been welcomed into their ranks with rejoicing, or even respect. He might easily have taken his vows indifferently, even cynically, knowing that his vision of a long life would protect him. Yet if he had learned one thing from all that had happened to him, it was the power of correctness, and when the time had come to pledge himself to Tonatiuh, the Sun, he had done so without reservation. Perhaps his life was not his own to give, but he would act as if it were, and thus make his offer an honest one.

It was because of this, and not the desire to win favor, that he had thrown himself against the Matlatzincan, a man who was ten years his senior in fighting experience and who had already done terrible damage to the best of the Tenocha. And it was also because of this, Huemac felt, that he had been able to strike the blow that had saved his own life and made the man his captive. It was correctness, not courage, that had kept him fighting past the point when all seemed lost, that had let him think only of fighting, and not of dying.

Now, as he followed the men ahead of him into the temple precinct, Huemac remembered his first conversation with the vanguard merchant, Cuetzpaltzin, a man who also walked correctly before his god, yet who was not oblivious to the power wielded by men. Huemac had spoken to him several times since that day, and he had learned from him that all favor was not tainted, and that it was as incorrect to flee from it as it was to seek it too avidly. I have fulfilled my pledge to you, O Lord, Huemac thought, glancing up at the sun, and I ask only that you accept this man in my name. He is very brave, and his courage will gladden your heart and give you strength. And if other rewards should come to me because of him, Lord, do not be angry; let us both have that which sustains us.

Lowering his eyes, Huemac let his mind go quiet for a few moments. Then he began to think ahead to seeing his captive, and what he would say to him, and beyond that to the possibility, the glimmering hope, that this man would be the means to his freedom . . .

AFTER SECURING his prisoner in one of the barred enclosures behind the Hall of Eagles, Michpilli hurried to fetch food and water and sleeping mats for him, mindful of Huemac's strict instructions that the Matlatzincan be made as comfortable as possible. He had only just returned with the supplies when Huemac himself arrived, carrying two cups and a gourd of octli. He had removed his uniform and wore his hair loose, still damp from the washing he had given it. Michpilli jumped to open the latticed gate for his master and lay a mat for him to sit on, then ducked respectfully out of the way while Huemac greeted his captive, first in Nahua, then in the language of the Matlatzinca.

"Greetings, my son," he said to the older man, who smiled sardonically before he bowed back.

"Greetings, my father."

"You may leave us," Huemac said to Michpilli, after the apprentice had placed the food and drink on a mat between the two men. Michpilli swung the gate to but did not tie it, noticing that both of the guards nearby, as well as the prisoners in the adjacent enclosures, were watching this interview curiously. None of the other warriors had come to visit their captives so quickly, and none, certainly, had concerned themselves with providing food and drink. They would in time, of course, but most likely not until after tonight's feast.

Michpilli did not understand the reason for his master's excessive display of courtesy. Without question, the Matlatzincan was a great warrior, but had not Huemac proven himself to be greater? And why go to the trouble of learning the man's barbarous language, when he would surely die soon, and when he already knew enough Nahua to converse adequately?

But then, there were many things that Michpilli did not understand about the ways his master chose to spend his time: conversing with the pochteca he met on the trail rather than gambling with the other warriors around the campfire; visiting the white-haired old men rather than the women of the streets in the cities where he was stationed; allowing some of the Puma Warriors to address him as an equal and share food with him. Michpilli was still too afraid of Huemac, and too grateful to him, to question his master's actions. But that did not prevent him from wondering, and from thinking occasionally, despite himself, that perhaps the other apprentices were not wrong when they referred to Huemac as nahualli, sorcerer . . .

Huemac poured octli for himself and the Matlatzincan, whose name in Nahua was Huactli, the Night Heron. Huemac always thought of him by this name, since the man's name in his own tongue had two of the *r* sounds that Huemac, despite his ability with voices, still found difficult to pronounce. Otherwise, the language was quite similar to Otomi, which he had begun to learn during his visits to the hill-people.

"You are to die, day after tomorrow," Huemac said, signing *two* to make his meaning clearer. "In ceremonies to Xipe Totec, and to Tonatiuh."

"They are ancient gods, venerable gods," Huactli allowed, suitably impressed. "How do I die?"

Huemac had learned, on the first campaign to Toluca, that the Matlatzinca used only one form of sacrifice, crushing their victims to death in strong rope nets. And though he knew that Huactli was acquainted with some of the ways that the Mexica sacrificed, he felt that it was important that his captive be fully aware of what was to happen to him. For the sake of correctness, Huemac told himself, though he was not averse to the prospect of *his* captive dying in a noteworthy fashion.

"You die upon the temalacatl, the spindle-whorl stone," he explained, making a circular motion with his hands. "You fight with Eagles and Jaguars."

"I will be given weapons?" Huactli asked incredulously.

"Your weapons are . . . " Huemac sought the proper word in vain, and had to lapse momentarily into Nahua: *"Ceremonial.* Not true weapons: clubs of wood; a macana armed with feathers, not obsidian. Eagles and Jaguars have *true* weapons."

The Matlatzincan squinted at him suspiciously.

"How many do I fight?"

"Four—two Eagles, two Jaguars. But you fight one at a time. Until you fall."

"And if I choose not to fight?" Huactli asked, and Huemac curled his hand and made a ripping motion at his chest.

"Then heart torn out on stone. Die fast. And quiet."

Huactli's black eyes glittered brightly as he examined Huemac's face over the rim of his cup. Then he set down his cup and smiled disdainfully.

"The weapons do not matter. I will kill them anyway."

Huemac nodded gravely, not allowing himself to smile, even though the answer pleased him greatly. He did not wish to appear *too* eager on his captive's behalf, since the man was a foreigner and an enemy, and might choose to withhold his cooperation as an act of spite. For, despite all their conversations and Huactli's acceptance of the ritual form of address, Huemac was still not certain how much the older man respected him. He had been on the verge of dealing Huemac his deathblow when Huemac, with a last desperate effort, had thrown his macana and struck him in the head. It had been a lucky escape, and an even luckier capture. The Matlatzincan was a proud, scornful man, and perhaps to him, his fate seemed undeserved, and no reason to honor his captor's wishes.

Taking a sip of octli, Huemac reminded himself to ask Michpilli later how the man had acted during their entrance into the city. Then, putting a great strain on his Matlatzincan vocabulary, Huemac attempted to explain the meaning of the various stages of the sacrificial ceremony: how he would be the representative of all the Warriors of the Sun when he mounted to the temalacatl, and how his struggle on the stone symbolized their task on the earth. And how, after he had fallen, he would be carried to the top of the Temple of the Sun and sacrificed on the Eagle Vessel, where his heart and blood would be offered as sustenance to Tonatiuh. Finally, Huemac explained how the skin would later be flayed from his body and given to an apprentice priest to wear, symbolizing the way that Xipe Totec, the God of Seedtime and Planting, brought a new skin to the earth each spring.

Huactli listened silently, his expressionless face unchanging, even when Huemac told him that he was to be one of the first to honor the new stones with his death, and that all the great lords of Tenochtitlan, as well as those from other cities, would be in attendance. Uncertain of the impression he was making, Huemac decided that he had said enough. He had an enormous desire to tell him that the first man he would face—the Elder Jaguar—was a man who feared and hated Huemac greatly. But such a revelation might make the Matlatzincan suspicious of his motives, and it seemed, in itself, somehow incorrect. Better to let him meet Colotl on his own, and let the gods decide.

"Rest now, my son," Huemac said formally, and made a motion to rise. But Huactli gestured for him to stay and spoke to him in Matlatzinca:

"I have heard the others of your tribe, the young ones, say that you are a sorcerer. Was this how you captured me?"

Huemac's eyes widened angrily, but he succeeded in restraining the power of his gaze. He drew himself up with dignity.

"You left time for sorcery?" he demanded, annoyed by his awkwardness in the man's language. "I am almost killed by you, I am lucky to live. Where is sorcery?"

Huactli pursed his lips and considered Huemac through narrowed eyes. Then he shrugged and nodded in agreement, and Huemac suddenly understood that the man had only been testing him; that he accepted his capture as valid. Giving him a sly look, Huactli spoke in Nahua:

"Why, Father, you have no wife?"

Huemac stared at him in astonishment, and saw the man grin with delight at his own joke.

"I have been away," Huemac said gruffly, frowning with mock annoyance. "There has been too much trouble in Toluca!"

"Ah, *much* trouble!" Huactli repeated, then looked at Huemac and roared with laughter. Knowing that they understood one another at last, Huemac smiled broadly and rose to his feet. He bowed to his captive, who was still laughing, then closed the gate behind him and tied it fast, aware of the incredulous stares of the guards. Have you never heard a man laugh at death? he wanted to say, but he resisted such a boastful urge. Better to let them wonder, and whisper, and add to the anticipation.

"Farewell, my son," he said to Huactli. "I will come for you, when it is time."

THE CEREMONY began shortly before noon in the courtyard of the walled enclosure known as the House of Eagles. Axayacatl, Tlacaelel, and the other lords of Tenochtitlan had taken their places in the royal box above the eastern entrance, and beside them were the leaders of their allies and subjects. In specially constructed booths at one end of the royal box, screened off from public view by flower-covered nets, were the warrior lords from the enemy cities of Tlaxcala, Huexotzinco, and Cempoalla. The courtyard below was jammed with warriors and guests, and other spectators sat atop the freshly whitewashed walls, which gleamed brilliantly under the midday sun.

In the center of the courtyard was a square platform with a short flight of steps at each of the four directions, and upon this platform was the temalacatl —a flat circular stone two feet thick and ten feet in diameter. Its hard gray surface was carved with scenes of warfare and conquest, and a short length of rope was coiled around the hole in its center. The area around the platform had been carefully swept clean of debris, and a cordon of uniformed Eagles and Jaguars kept the crowd from encroaching too closely on the ceremonial area.

At the western end of the enclosure was the pyramid of the Temple of the Sun, which rose in two steep tiers to the shrine of Tonatiuh, painted a flaming red. Descending the temple steps were the first members of a long procession, led by nine priests who wore the skins of captives who had been sacrificed to Xipe Totec earlier that day. Over the bloody skins, each priest wore the mask and regalia of the god to whom the captive had been offered, the first wearing the red headdress and carrying the rattle-staff of Xipe Totec. Next came Tonatiuh, Huitzilopochtli, Quetzalcoatl, and the five lesser gods celebrated on this occasion.

After the priests came the singers and those who played the drums and sacred instruments, all wearing tall white plumes and woven replicas of the temalacatl on their backs. Following them down the temple stairs were four armed members of the warrior orders, two Eagles and two Jaguars, specially chosen for their rank and honor. The priests seated themselves in a circle around the platform, and the singers and musicians formed another circle around them and began a loud, rhythmic hymn to Tonatiuh. The four warriors climbed to the platform and began to dance around the temalacatl in time with the beating of the drums, shaking their feathered shields and feinting with their obsidian-edged warclubs. The voices of the singers grew stronger, echoing off the gleaming walls and rising heavenward, preparing the way for those about to die.

An opening was made in the ranked circles of men, and through it came a double line of captors and captives, tied together at the knee, so tht they had to go supporting one another. All were naked except for paper maxlatls, and their bodies had been painted with the thick white paint of the dead, to which balls of white goose down had been pasted. They wore turkey feathers stuck into their hair, and their faces had been smeared with pitch in broad streaks.

Huemac and Huactli were the second in the line, and after the pair ahead of them had ascended to the platform, they were met by a priest who incensed them with a hand censer of smoking copal. Huemac was in a high state of excitement, feeling light-headed from the past day of fasting and rigorous penance, and shivering slightly with anticipation. He glanced once at Huactli as the priest untied their legs and saw that the Matlatzincan's eyes were closed in prayer. Then they blinked open and Huactli stamped his foot, flexing the leg that had just been unbound. He looked back at Huemac, his lips curling upward into his customary disdainful expression, making cracks in the thick coat of paint around his mouth.

The first captive fell quickly, appearing overwhelmed by the singing and the noise of the crowd, and confused as to what was expected of him. He was not even certain what direction to face, and when Colotl, the Elder Jaguar, leapt on him from the east, he tripped over the rope that tied him to the stone and lost his shield parrying the first blow. Colotl slashed the legs out from under him with two vicious strokes of his macana, then danced victoriously around the stone as the priests called the Four Dawns lifted the captive to their shoulders and carried him up the temple steps to be sacrificed.

Accompanied by two black-robed priests, Huemac and Huactli climbed the steps to the platform, where they were met by a third priest. Standing above them on the stone, the priest addressed the captive:

> "Brave Matlatzincan,
> Warrior from the rugged land of Toluca,
> You have not come here
> Because of weakness,
> But because of your manliness.
> You will die here,
> But your fame will last forever."

Then he gave Huactli a bowl of teooctli, the sacred wine of the priests, and the Matlatzincan, as Huemac had instructed, offered the bowl to the four directions before drinking from it through a hollow piece of cane. A second priest tore the head off a quail and sprinkled the bird's blood over a feathered shield, raising it high in offering to the Sun. Then he gave the shield to Huactli, and the other priests helped him to stand upon the temalacatl, where he turned to look down upon Huemac.

"I am ready to die, Mexican," he said fiercely. "Let them come to kill me!"

"Farewell, brave friend," Huemac answered in Matlatzinca. "You bring me great honor!"

Huemac stepped back and descended from the platform, taking his shield and warclub from Michpilli, who awaited him, wide-eyed, at the foot of the stairs. Huemac knew that his own eyes were glowing brightly, and he opened them wider when he saw Colotl facing him from the platform above, dancing and shaking his weapon menacingly. Huemac added his voice to those of the singers and began to dance in opposition to Colotl, fighting a symbolic battle that carried all the hatred of the real thing. Their macanas hummed as they cut the air between them, avoiding contact by only inches.

A priest wearing the skin of a mountain lion mounted to the stone and tied the free end of the rope around Huactli's waist, jerking on it to make sure that the other end was still secured to the temalacatl. As the singing increased in volume, the priest presented Huactli with a warclub edged with beautiful feathers, and left four pine clubs on the stone, one at each of the four directions. Carefully coiling the excess rope away from his legs, the Matlatzincan raised his shield and macana in front of him and began to sing his death song as the priests left the platform and came to stand behind Huemac, who continued his dancing, mimicking the motions of the man on the stone.

The sounds of bone war whistles rose above the singing as Colotl attacked from the east, swinging his warclub at the legs of the captive, who parried the blow expertly and struck back with the feathered macana, driving Colotl back off the stone. Pieces of wood flew from their shields as they hacked at each other, Huactli maintaining his advantage upon the stone by the sheer fury of his blows. Soon the feathered warclub was cracked and splintered and Huactli was bleeding in several places, but he still refused to give ground. Enraged, Colotl hammered away at him ferociously, and finally succeeded in mounting to the stone. But Huactli rushed him immediately, banging him backward with his shield, and before Colotl could recover his balance, the Matlatzincan spun sideways and hurled his warclub at close range, knocking Colotl's headdress free and sending him sprawling off the edge of the stone, unconscious.

The noise of the whistles and the singing was deafening, and Huemac danced furiously at the foot of the platform, exulting in the victory of his captive, as if it had been his own. Sweat glistened on Huactli's body, running down his legs in a white stream and joining with the blood that dripped onto the temalacatl. With a fierce cry, the Matlatzincan scooped up one of the pine clubs and whirled to meet the Elder Eagle, who charged onto the stone from the west and tore the battered shield from Huactli's hand with one slashing blow of his macana. Huactli dodged sideways, and Huemac, on the ground, did likewise, imagining the restraining pull of the rope and swinging his warclub in imitation of the blow that Huactli delivered to the shield of the Eagle Warrior. The man backed off and then closed for the kill, raising his shield in front of his face to deflect the club Huactli threw at him. It seemed to Huemac that the end was at hand, but Huactli ducked under the swinging warclub of his attacker and ran past him, gathering the rope into a taut line that cut the legs out from under the lurching Eagle. Huactli turned swiftly and kicked the man in the head as he fell, then shoved him off the stone.

The air was now filled with the sounds of rejoicing and praise for the captive, and the Younger Jaguar from the south waited, out of respect, for the exhausted Matlatzincan to gather his breath and pick up another club with which to defend himself. Huemac turned and danced before the crowd, shaking his weapon with proud gestures as the Sun shone upon his head and the sweat stung his eyes. He was completely beside himself with joy, shouting his captive's name into the din.

On the stone, Huactli fought on with his club, but wearily, spilling more and more of his own blood. Finally, with the last club lost from his grasp, he threw himself upon the Jaguar with his bare hands as his only weapons, but the warrior dodged easily to the side, slashing deeply across the back of the Matlatzincan's legs with the edge of his macana, severing the tendons and causing the bright blood to spurt skyward. Huactli was vanquished.

Immediately, the Four Dawns rushed to the platform and lifted the dying warrior onto their strong shoulders. The crowd was in a pandemonium, and parted reluctantly to let the priests through, closing in again to touch the trailing hands of the captive, or the shields of Huemac and the Younger Jaguar, who followed closely behind. Huemac felt the hands touching his body, yet the faces attached to them seemed far away, and their ecstatic cries melted into the great ringing noise in his head. We are rising to meet you, O Tonatiuh, he prayed, tilting his head back as he began to climb the steep temple stairs behind the priests, his eyes slit against the fierce yellow light that filled the sky. The priests ahead of him moved in unison, never faltering, leaving bloody footprints for him to follow as they mounted to the place of the god.

Then Huemac reached the top platform and saw the image of the Sun hanging in the open shrine: It was reddish gold and seemed both a butterfly and an eagle, yet faceless, a winged creature trapped within a golden ball that spread its rays in radiant lines. Huemac bowed deeply before the tapestry and touched dirt to his tongue, humbling himself.

Above the image of the Sun was the glyph for its name, Four Movement, the name of the Fifth Sun, the Sun born at Teotihuacan by the sacrifice of the gods. Standing before the tapestry was the quauhxicalli, the Eagle Vessel, a round stone similar to the temalacatl yet slightly smaller. Carved on its outer edges were the twenty day signs, and on its flat surface was the face of Tonatiuh, his mouth a shallow depression still filled with the blood of the previous captive.

The Four Dawns threw Huactli onto this stone on his back, with his head hanging over the edge and each of his limbs pinned by one of the priests. Dressed as an Eagle, the high priest of Tonatiuh stepped forward, holding a heavy obsidian blade aloft in invocation:

> "Here is our offering, O Tonatiuh,
> You Who Go Forth Shining,
> Warrior of the Skies.
> Here is his heart, his courage;
> Here is his blood to sustain you.
> Rise, Great Eagle,
> Bless us with your warmth,
> Bless us with your holy fire."

Then, at an order from the high priest, the Younger Jaguar severed Huactli's head from his body with one stroke of his macana, and the captive's blood flowed over the edge of the stone. The high priest moved quickly, opening the Matlatzincan's chest with one swift rip of the knife and reaching in to tear out his heart. This, still pulsing with life, he offered to the Sun, calling it "eagle-cactus fruit" and begging Tonatiuh to accept it in the name of his people.

Huemac danced wildly around the stone, beating on his shield with his war-club, his head and limbs jerking up and down to the demanding rhythm of the emotions that surged through him. The sky wheeled overhead, filled with a presence that pulled at him and made his head swim. He danced until he was exhausted and collapsed on the platform, feeling that it was he who had died.

WHEN MICHPILLI found him later, Huemac had cleansed his face and body of paint and was dressed in all his feathers and jewels. He noticed the way the boy looked at him, at first fearfully, then with obvious relief.

"Was I so frightening to behold?" he asked gently, and Michpilli started, as if his thoughts had been read. He nodded weakly.

"You looked like a demon of the night, and I feared that you were going to attack Colotl yourself. I would not have wanted to be him."

"Nor must he, at this moment, with the pain he must have in his head." Huemac shook his head in awe. "You saw how Huactli threw his warclub? It *was* I who attacked Colotl."

"There has been none other like him," Michpilli said proudly.

"It still goes on?"

"The Cihuacoatl has ordered many killed today, to dedicate the stones. But the temalacatl is slippery with blood, and many of the captives have lost their courage from watching their comrades die." Michpilli frowned unconsciously. "The fighting is not good."

Huemac stared at him silently, and the apprentice hastily tried to make up for the looseness of his tongue.

"Forgive my presumption, Lord . . . "

"It is no presumption to speak the truth," Huemac said brusquely. "The Speaker has called for me. You may accompany me to his chamber."

"I do not merit such an honor," Michpilli said quickly, lowering his eyes.

"You have been correct in your duties. I honor that as I do the truth. Come, let us go to Axayacatl . . ."

"WHAT IS IT you wish, Huemac?" the Speaker said grandly, his natural generosity swollen by the success of the ceremony, and by the speeches of praise that had been made to Huemac upon his entrance. "I am doubling your share of the tribute from Toluca, but that is not enough. Speak, my son, tell me how I can repay you for the glory you have brought to our city."

Huemac appeared to smile modestly, while his eyes scoured the faces in the chamber. He had noticed immediately that Tlacaelel and Ocomatli were not present, though Tlacaelel's son, Tlilpotonqui, was. His brother Acolmiztli was standing behind the Speaker, next to Ahuitzotl and Eztetl, whom Huemac had seen nodding approvingly during the speeches. The two young boys sitting at the foot of Axayacatl's reed seat had to be his eldest sons, Tlacahuepan and Moteczuma the Younger, which perhaps accounted for the Speaker's fatherly tone. Huemac knew that his credit with the ruler would never be higher, and he could sense that Axayacatl was ready to forgive him fully for his actions in Tlatelulco, provided he was given some sign of repentance.

There was only one thing that Huemac sought, but he had considered two different ways of asking for it. One was to simply request permission to marry, and hope that Ocomatli would allow him the time. The other was to ask to be placed under the command of Acolmiztli or Ahuitzotl, either of whom would no doubt give him the permission and the necessary time. He would also be freed from Tlacaelel's direct control, and the prospect of thwarting the Demon Heart was very tempting.

Huemac looked up at Axayacatl, knowing that the meaning of the second request would not be lost on him. Ocomatli had ceased being his close confidant after the civil war, but Axayacatl had never openly acknowledged the reasons for the failure of the ambush. A request for a transfer would be a clear message that Huemac had not forgotten and did not wish to. Thinking of his father, Huemac pondered the value of such a message for a few moments before he spoke:

"I am grateful for your favor, my Lord, but there is little that I require. I ask only that you grant me permission to marry."

"Granted," Axayacatl said expansively. "There is nothing else? Perhaps there is a match I can help arrange . . . ?"

"I know the woman I will ask for," Huemac replied, seeing a smile come onto Acolmiztli's face. "There is no one who could please me as much."

"Take her with my blessing, then. I will send food from my own kitchens for your wedding feast."

Huemac bowed, feeling that his decision had been the correct one, one his father would have approved. His presence was no doubt a sufficient reminder of the past, and it was foolish to attempt to use Axayacatl against Tlacaelel. Huemac readied himself to go, but Axayacatl gestured for him to remain.

"My son witnessed the ceremony today, and has a question for you. Speak, Moteczuma."

The boy who bore the name of his famous great-grandfather was the younger of the two sons, perhaps nine or ten years of age. He was also smaller than his brother and his face was narrower, bearing more of a resemblance to Tizoc and Chalchiuhnenetl than his father or Ahuitzotl. His eyes, though, were bright and intelligent, and the courtliness of his speech indicated that he was already being educated.

"I am honored to be in your presence, brave Eagle," he said in a high-pitched voice, blushing at the attention he had drawn to himself. "It is said that before your captive fought, you spoke to him in his own tongue. What was it you said?"

Huemac saw knowing looks being exchanged between the men surrounding the Speaker, and he realized that, even today, he had managed to add to his questionable reputation. He smiled at the boy, though without any of the irony he was feeling.

"He told me that he was ready to die, and I saluted his bravery."

"But how did you come to learn the language of the enemy?" Moteczuma pressed him shyly, glancing over his shoulder at his father, who encouraged him with a nod.

"My captive taught me," Huemac said simply, and saw amazement register on other faces besides the boy's. Now I have done it, he thought ruefully; now they will find excuses for Colotl.

"You came to know your captive?" Axayacatl inquired incredulously.

"As much as one might come to know a foreigner, Lord, in a short time. I called him my son, so I felt that he should know the meaning of our ceremonies and the manner of his death, so that he might act correctly."

"I have never heard of such a thing," Axayacatl confessed, turning to the men behind him, who also shrugged and shook their heads. "You are a most baffling man, Huemac."

"Yes, most baffling," Moteczuma agreed in an awed voice, unaware that he had spoken aloud until his father laughed. Then his brother and the other men in the room joined in, and Moteczuma ducked his head and shrank with embarrassment. So curious yet so timid, Huemac thought: strange qualities for the son of such a bold ruler. It will not be easy for him to live with his name. He gave the boy a sympathetic glance, but Moteczuma would not raise his head.

"You may go," Axayacatl said, and Huemac bowed and backed out of the Speaker's presence, feeling the eyes upon him and knowing that he had made his usual mystifying impression. So be it, he thought, then put the matter out of his mind and went to find Taypachtli.

2

HUEMAC and Taypachtli were married in the late spring of the year Eleven-House. They tied the ends of their mantles together before the hearth in the house that now belonged to Huemac, with Cocatli and Tlacateotzin taking the role of Taypachtli's parents, and Acolmiztli standing in as the father of the groom. The feasting began on the fifth day after the ceremony, when the wedding couple emerged from their seclusion and blushingly revealed the reddened mat upon which they had consummated their marriage.

Teuxoch, of course, was in charge of the feast, and though the old woman was hampered by the painful stiffness that age had put into her joints, she had taken command of the servants like a warchief on his first campaign. Every corner of the courtyard had been swept, the walls freshly whitewashed, and the huehuetl tree hung with streamers of bright flowers. Displayed on mats and tables beneath the tree was the wonderful array of delicacies sent by Axayacatl, as he had promised. There were roast turkeys and fat little dogs cooked in mole sauce; duck, pheasant, and venison stewed with onions, tomatoes, and chilis; maize cakes stuffed with fish, frogs, and axolotls (newts); shrimp and oysters brought fresh by runners from the lands of the Totonacs; and fine rich cocoa that had been whipped and sweetened with honey and vanilla. There were also baskets of fruit and bags of maize, beans, and chia seeds, as well as quantities of cooking oil and octli.

"I should only have friends enough to eat all this," Huemac said to Taypach-tli, as they readied themselves to meet their guests.

"You shall, my husband," she assured him. "This will be a house to which people will always want to return."

Huemac smiled at her confidence. Though the courtyard had been laid out with paths and markers long ago, and though Taypachtli had gained increasing poise under his mother's tutelage, he had not expected her to be ready so soon to assume the position of mistress of the house. Not with a personality as strong as Teuxoch's to contend with. Yet she had not only done so, she had even enlisted Teuxoch's aid in an ambitious project to make their household a special place, one whose graciousness would offset Huemac's dubious reputation. In addition to her ferocious memory for details, Huemac had discovered that his wife possessed a quality he lacked so totally that he had not even known it existed: the ability to make people *want* to help her. Though she had no choice but to trust others, Taypachtli somehow made her dependency seem like a gift, an opportunity rather than an obligation. There was no greater proof of this than the fact that Teuxoch, who had never approved of their marriage, was arranging this feast as much to please Taypachtli as to glorify her adopted son.

"Tell me who is here," Taypachtli requested, stopping him just outside the doorway to their rooms.

"Acolmiztli and Tlacateotzin are here with their families," Huemac said, scanning the small crowd in the courtyard. "And so are the daughters of Teuxoch. My apprentice, Michpilli, has brought his mother and sister. His mother's family, I believe, were friends of your father's."

"Yes, I remember them," Taypachtli said softly, repressing her sadness at the memory of those who had died in the civil war. "Are there any other of my people here?"

"My friend Cuetzpaltzin, the man of many faces of whom I have told you, has brought his family. And there are others of my friends among the pochteca, most of whom you have not met."

"They do not get invited to Tenochtitlan very often anymore," Taypachtli said of the merchants. "We must help them to mingle with the other guests. Which of the warriors have come?"

Still considering her shrewd assessment concerning the merchants of Tlatelulco, Huemac studied the group of men who had stationed themselves at a deliberate distance from the pochteca.

"There are some of my former comrades from Moyotlan, and two members of the Texcocan embassy, old friends of my mother's. Ah, and my commander, Eztetl, has chosen to honor us with his presence. He has brought some warriors with him, two from the order of Eagles, and two Pumas. One of the Pumas is my friend: His name is Opochtli, and he is also a ball player. He fought beside me in Toluca."

"And the other warriors?" Taypachtli asked pointedly. "Are they not also your friends?"

"No, I could not truly call them that. They have honored my invitation out of respect. Though one of them is a great eater," Huemac added sardonically, "and may only have come for the food."

"I will put him in Teuxoch's hands, and he will be your friend before the night is through," Taypachtli promised. "But take me first to Acolmiztli. There is something I must discuss with him."

"With my brother?" Huemac asked curiously, surprised by the purposefulness of her tone. "What is it?"

"It is a secret, part of the surprise your mother and I have been preparing for you. Though your mother knows nothing of this."

"Is it the flower song?" Huemac guessed, though he could not imagine what Acolmiztli could have to do with the recitation his mother had promised him. Or Taypachtli, either.

"You will see in time," Taypachtli said archly, pulling him into motion along the pathway that led from the door. "You do not *always* have to know the future . . . "

"SOON YOU will have more grandchildren," Cocatli said to her mother, watching from a distance as Huemac and Taypachtli began to greet their guests. Ome Xochitl heard the wistful note in her daughter's voice and looked at her with sympathy, seeing the lines of strain that Cocatli's last pregnancy had etched into her face. She had lost the child, the second such occurrence after three difficult but successful pregnancies, and Ome Xochitl knew—for she had spoken to the midwives herself—that it was doubtful that Cocatli would be able to bear any more children.

"You have two fine sons and a daughter," Ome Xochitl said gently, reaching out to smooth her daughter's dark, serious features. "You have no reason to be envious of Taypachtli."

Cocatli rested her cheek against her mother's hand and sighed.

"Perhaps now Tlacateotzin will take a second wife," she suggested listlessly, and Ome Xochitl cupped her chin and looked into her eyes.

"He can afford to," she said matter-of-factly. "But you will always be the first wife; in every way, I think."

"Yes, I think so, too," Cocatli admitted, freeing her chin from her mother's grasp by turning to take another look at Taypachtli. A distracted expression passed across her face. "I do not know what it is that truly bothers me. I have felt sad lately, and filled with fear about the future."

"Is it this campaign that the men are planning?" Ome Xochitl asked with open concern, and Cocatli shrugged helplessly.

"Perhaps, though I usually do not worry about Tlacateotzin until he has actually gone into the field. I am sorry, my mother," she said plaintively, "I do not wish to wear a sad face to my brother's wedding feast."

"He knows the joy you feel for him," Ome Xochitl said, glancing over at her son and daughter-in-law, "and so does Taypachtli. It is Teuxoch who would never forgive you."

Cocatli grimaced wryly and followed her mother's eyes.

"She has Tezcatl's wonderful smile," she observed of Taypachtli, "but none of his loudness. Do you know that she reminds me in many ways of you, my mother?"

"Of me?" Ome Xochitl scoffed. "You are only seeing the mannerisms I have taught her. She has a natural graciousness that is hers alone."

"I agree, but I have also noticed that she hears everything, and forgets none of it." Cocatli raised an eyebrow at her mother. "When Huemac and I were children, we listened to Teuxoch's scoldings, but we never doubted who truly ruled the household. I have the same feeling around my brother's wife."

"Perhaps then Huemac's future, at least, is secure," Ome Xochitl suggested mildly. "And if we can say that of him, can the future truly be so fearful for the rest of us?"

Cocatli had no answer, and could only shake her head and smile at the persuasiveness of her mother's logic.

"I never thought that Huemac's luck would be a source of comfort to me," she confessed, and Ome Xochitl patted her hand encouragingly.

"Let it be a cause for celebration. Share in his joy until your own returns to you, as it will."

"I will try," Cocatli promised wearily, "I will try . . ."

"I MUST greet the pochteca," Huemac said reluctantly, glancing uncertainly from his wife to his brother. "Come to me when you are finished, my wife. I will be near the first garden path."

"I will bring her to you myself," Acolmiztli promised in a hearty voice, enjoying Huemac's discomfiture immensely. He took Taypachtli's hand and bowed to Huemac, who gave him another puzzled look before slowly walking away. Acolmiztli gave the hand a conspiratorial squeeze and leaned closer to speak:

"You do not know, Sister-in-Law, how long I have waited to see such a look on my brother's face! He truly knows nothing of our plan?"

"He has guessed that it has to do with his mother's flower song," Taypachtli said, "but that, too, will be a surprise for him." She hesitated for a polite moment, then could not contain her eagerness to know: "Were you able to speak to Ahuitzotl?"

"There was a meeting of the warchiefs yesterday," Acolmiztli said in a satisfied voice, "and I spoke to him afterward. Since I had already bragged to him about Huemac's skill at tlachtli, he was receptive to hearing more. He loves feasts, and you should have seen him smile when I told him there would be singing! He has a passion for singing that is nearly equal to his love for the ball game."

"Did he accept the invitation, then?"

"He has another feast to attend tonight, but he promised to come here later. If he likes what he sees and hears, I do not doubt that he will ask to have Huemac attached to his command."

"We will make him welcome," Taypachtli said. "I do not know how to thank you for what you have done, my brother-in-law."

"I owe my brother a great deal," Acolmiztli told her. "I would have asked for him myself, if Ocomatli were not my superior. But Ahuitzotl will treat Huemac as fairly as I would myself, perhaps even better, once he sees what a ball player he is. It is not right that Huemac should be kept away from you, or from the children you will soon have."

Taypachtli ducked her head shyly, though her pleasure at the prospect of motherhood was apparent. Acolmiztli gazed at her with admiration. We may yet rescue my brother from his luck, he thought, *despite* the things he says and does.

"Shall I take you to Huemac now?" he asked, laying her hand on the crook of his arm.

"I can easily find my own way," Taypachtli assured him with a gracious smile. "But I would be most honored if you would accompany me, and allow me to introduce you to the merchants of my city."

Acolmiztli pursed his lips and glanced over at the group of pochteca—dressed modestly even on this occasion—who were sitting with his brother. So that is how Huemac knows so much, he mused, viewing the merchants with the deep-rooted distaste of the warrior class. The pochteca of Tlatelulco had been subjected to a heavy tax after the war, their leaders barred from the Council and the court, and their right to sacrifice slaves rescinded by Tlacaelel. Acolmiztli had agreed fully with these measures, and he turned back to Taypachtli with a stern expression on his face, knowing that she must have been aware of the diminishment of the merchants' status before she had asked him to meet them.

"Why do you ask me such a thing?" he demanded. "You are the wife of a Tenocha, you must know how the warriors feel about the pochteca."

Taypachtli stiffened slightly and carefully removed her hand from Acolmiztli's arm.

"Forgive me if I have been presumptuous, my Lord. But as you must know, my husband does not share your scorn for the merchants. They are his friends, and he barters with them for information."

"And what does he offer in trade?"

"His respect," Taypachtli said evenly. "It is from your father and the man named Cuetzpaltzin, he says, that he learned that respect is a commodity precious to all men."

"Yes," Acolmiztli agreed automatically, "as mine is to me. Why would you have me offer it to these merchants?"

"Your acquaintance would be a gift to them," Taypachtli explained, "and thus, to Huemac."

Acolmiztli considered her innocent features in silence, his annoyance beginning to fade. He remembered that this was her wedding feast, a day she might easily have spent rejoicing, rather than negotiating favors for her husband.

"You are very ambitious on my brother's behalf," he said suggestively, and Taypachtli made no effort to deny it.

"He has said the same thing of you, my Lord," she murmured. "That is why he would not take you to the merchants himself, and risk your disapproval."

Acolmiztli looked over at his brother and knew that she was telling him the truth; that Huemac spared him the confidences he knew might be disturbing. He had said nothing about communicating with his captive, for instance, until young Moteczuma had drawn it out of him. Had I known, Acolmiztli thought, I might have warned him not to speak of it so casually; it does not help for him to keep things from me.

"Come," he said abruptly, "you may introduce me to the pochteca. But I have one condition: You must say that I *asked* to be introduced. I want my brother to know that he is not the only one who is unpredictable."

Taypachtli smiled and held out her hand.

"He will be very surprised. You do me a great honor, my Lord."

"You have bartered well for the privilege, Taypachtli," he said gruffly. "Come, my sister-in-law, let us make this a *day* of surprises for him . . ."

WHEN HUEMAC noticed the merchants sitting across from him suddenly come to attention, he looked instinctively over his shoulder, and saw Taypachtli and Acolmiztli approaching along the path of hard-packed crushed stone. Expecting them to stop a short distance away, he rose to his feet, and remained standing awkwardly when they walked right up to the group. Then Taypachtli explained, to his utter astonishment, that Acolmiztli had asked to be introduced to his friends, and she proceeded to call out the names of those pochteca she knew to be present. The men responded to her greeting and bowed to Acolmiztli, who bowed back with complete courtesy. Huemac recovered from his initial surprise in time to finish the introductions, presenting first his brother and then his wife, to those she did not know.

"I will join the other wives," Taypachtli said to Huemac when he was through, "and leave you to converse with the men."

"Yes, my wife," Huemac said dazedly, unable to take his eyes off Acolmiztli, who had seated himself between two pochteca and was offering them octli from one of the gourds laid out on mats in the center of the circle. With difficulty, Huemac returned his attention to Taypachtli, and saw that she was smiling at him.

"So this was your surprise!" he whispered as he led her back to the path. Taypachtli shook her head.

"No," she said simply. "This is your brother's surprise." She cocked her head sharply. "The women are near the entrance to our rooms?"

"Yes," Huemac replied, and before he could say more, she had slipped free of the arm he had around her waist and walked away, one hand held out in front of her, listening intently for the sounds of anything that might be in her path. Huemac turned back to the group, noticing the wonder and approval on their faces as they watched Taypachtli depart unassisted. You do not know how *truly* astonishing she is, he thought, blessing the luck that had brought him such a wife.

"I did not mean to interrupt your conversation," Acolmiztli said politely. "Please go on."

Cuetzpaltzin and the other merchants looked to Huemac, as did Michpilli and the Puma Warrior Opochtli, who was the only other warrior Huemac had been able to lure into the group. They had been discussing the campaign being planned against the Tarascans of Michoacan, the land beyond the great mountains to the northwest of Toluca. Huemac knew that this was a sensitive subject for Acolmiztli, who was still coming to grips with the fact that his injured knee would prevent his participation in this particular campaign. He had proven himself capable of long marches, but hard climbing caused him agonizing pain, and the mountain passes to Michoacan were steep and treacherous. Acolmiztli would have to stay behind to guard the women and children of Tenochtitlan, a duty that naturally rankled a warchief of his young age. He had been moody and difficult lately, which only made his sudden willingness to be introduced to the pochteca that much more puzzling to Huemac. But he had no choice but to try to capitalize on his good fortune, and hope he would not antagonize his brother in the process.

"I was explaining to my friends," he said, gesturing to include the whole circle, "that there are many reasons for the campaign we will undertake next year. I have told them that some of the rebel Matlatzinca have found safety in Michoacan, and that Tlacaelel has requested captives for the dedication of the great Sun Stone that is being carved."

"It is also fifty years since our victory over the Tepanecs, and the founding of the Three-City Alliance," Acolmiztli added, his eyes settling on Cuetzpalt-zin as the most important among the merchants. "Young Nezahualpilli and Chimalpopoca of Tlacopan have expressed their eagerness to join us in this venture. They, too, have heard of the great wealth of the Tarascans."

"This is true," Cuetzpaltzin agreed. "They are rich in cotton, and are very skilled with metals and precious stones. But it is wise that you are going in force, for there are very many of them."

"I know little of them, myself," Acolmiztli said casually. "It is said that they are descendants of the Chichimecs, and that Aztlan, the home of the first Mexica, lies somewhere in the northern reaches of their territory. We will know better after we have conquered them."

As if to underscore his indifference, Acolmiztli reached out to pour more octli for himself, forgetting to offer any to the men around him, or to the man to whom he had just spoken. Cuetzpaltzin's elastic features turned to stone, but he waited patiently, and pretended not to notice Acolmiztli's rudeness. Huemac knew the merchant well enough by now to know that he was probably more offended by Acolmiztli's willful ignorance than by his lack of manners.

"I have heard this," Cuetzpaltzin said finally, "but I do not know if it is true. I have been to Michoacan only once, and then only as far as the city of Tlaximaloyan."

Huemac leaned forward to look at his brother, hoping that he would have the courtesy to put down his cup and respond. If not, Huemac would have to change the subject, for he could not ask Cuetzpaltzin to reveal his knowledge to someone who did not care. Huemac noticed that Michpilli was also leaning forward expectantly, obviously baffled by Acolmiztli's lack of curiosity, since he himself had been fascinated by the things the merchants had to say. If nothing else, this will be an education for him, Huemac thought; he will learn the costs of snobbery.

Acolmiztli finally saw Huemac glaring at him and seemed to remember that he had asked to join this conversation. He set his cup down abruptly and asked the first question that came into his head:

"And how far is it to this place, Tlaximaloyan?"

"It is perhaps a day's march from the city of Ixtlahuaca to the mountains," Cuetzpaltzin reckoned, "then two or three days more to Tlaximaloyan, depending on the weather and the state of the passes. The land is very rugged and is like a desert in some places, though there are many lakes further in, where the cities are. That is why they are called Michoaque—Those Who Have Fish."

"Are they not also called Tarascans?" Acolmiztli inquired with too much cleverness, as if he were a teacher testing the limits of his student's knowledge.

"Their god, in our language, is called Mixcoatl, the Cloud Serpent, the ancient hunting god of the Chichimecs. But in their own language, he is called Taras, and so they call themselves Tarascans."

"You know a great deal for only one visit," Acolmiztli remarked, becoming

more animated in the face of Cuetzpaltzin's calm explanatory manner. Huemac let himself relax, confident that his brother could not provoke Cuetzpaltzin into anything that might be interpreted as insolence, since that was a luxury
in which the pochteca never trafficked.

"What manner of people are they?" Acolmiztli prompted, when Cuetzpaltzin took his statement as a compliment and chose not to respond. "How do
they sacrifice to their god, for instance?"

"They have great ceremonial hunts, as we do in the month of Quecholli. But
they sacrifice only snakes, birds, and rabbits—they do not sacrifice men. Those
they capture in war, they make into their slaves."

"They do not give their captives an honorable death? That is barbarous!"
Acolmiztli burst out, and Cuetzpaltzin nodded solemnly in agreement, allowing none of Acolmiztli's anger to settle on him.

"I am told that they are fierce fighters," he said quietly, "and that they do
not spare many on the battlefield when they are victorious."

Acolmiztli was now considering him with genuine seriousness, and Huemac
noticed that Tlacateotzin, Eztetl, and one of the Eagles—no doubt drawn by
Acolmiztli's presence—had come up and were squatting just outside the circle,
listening intently to the conversation. Acolmiztli noticed them, as well, and
seemed to think more carefully before asking his next question:

"What sort of weapons do they use?"

"They are very good with the bow and the sling, like the hunters that they
are," Cuetzpaltzin explained. "I do not think they use the throwing board, but
they have macanas and spears like ours, and axes made of a metal that is like
copper only much harder. I am told that they use these axes in battle, to break
the shields of their enemy."

Acolmiztli looked over his shoulder to exchange a glance with Eztetl, who
frowned with concern and indicated his desire to ask a question. This required
that he be introduced, and Huemac gladly did the honors, introducing Tlacateotzin and the Eagle as well. The merchants bowed low each time, their faces
fixed in a curiously impassive expression that Huemac had only recently come
to recognize as pride.

"How many warriors can they muster?" Eztetl asked, once room had been
made for him and the others to join the group.

"The lord of Tlaximaloyan is called Chichicha. He is a powerful man, and
alone can probably raise an army of several thousand warriors. The overlord
of all the Tarascans resides in the city of Tzintzuntzan, which is further west,
on the shore of the lake called Patzcuaro. Few foreigners are ever allowed to
enter his city, but it is said that his warriors number in the tens of thousands."

There was a deep, common silence among the warriors when Cuetzpaltzin
had finished, and Huemac realized that if there was going to be an argument,
it would begin now. It was dangerous to reveal unpleasant truths to the
Tenocha once they were committed to a course of action; since they did not
feel that they could fail, they did not appreciate having their judgment questioned. Huemac saw a scowl appear first on the face of Tlacateotzin, who was
to command Acolmiztli's company in his place.

"You would advise that these fish eaters be approached with caution, then?"
he inquired in a challenging tone, using "fish eaters" in the same way that
"quackers" was scornfully applied to the Tlatelulca. Cuetzpaltzin stared at
him for a long moment.

"Even if I dared to offer advice to the Tenocha," he said humbly, "I would never recommend caution. Your courage does not allow for it. I would say only: Go in sufficient numbers, and carry a supply of extra shields."

Huemac felt the tension dissipate as quickly as it had arisen, and he smiled when he was certain that Cuetzpaltzin's diplomatic answer had satisfied all the warriors. Now they could act on this information and communicate it to the other warchiefs, without feeling that it reflected on their bravery.

"Let us eat together, my friends," Huemac suggested, reassuming his role as host. "Let us drink to the strength of our shields . . ."

AFTER THE younger children had been put to bed, the guests gathered under the tree in the torch-lit courtyard and waited for the singing to begin. Huemac was seated in the place of honor, with Teuxoch by his side and the other guests ranged around him in a loose crescent. In the center of the courtyard, Taypachtli tested her voice while Ome Xochitl positioned the chorus of women and the three professional musicians around her. Glowing with the octli inside him, Huemac heaped praise on his second mother for her part in making this feast a success.

"You have brought me great prestige, and great happiness, my mother," he said, holding her tiny, gnarled hands between his own to warm the stiffened joints. He could tell that she was very tired, and aching from the effort of sitting up.

"I did little," she scoffed. "It was your prestige that brought us this wonderful food, and your wife who has arranged the entertainment. She listens, that one, as you certainly never did. She seeks my advice before I can even offer it."

"Then you think she is an acceptable wife?" Huemac inquired innocently, and smiled when Teuxoch avoided his eyes.

"I cannot complain of her presence; she is less trouble than I had supposed. But she has no lineage. She would have been grateful to be the second wife, had you not been so foolish as to reject Axayacatl's offer."

"I know, my mother," Huemac said patiently. "It is my luck to be foolish concerning those I care about. I think it is because I was spoiled as a child."

"You were indeed," Teuxoch agreed fiercely, "but not by me!"

"No, never by you." Huemac laughed, looking at her with unconcealed fondness. Her resemblance to Tlacaelel had long ago ceased to disturb him, and the way she had aged in just the last few years had made him realize how much he would miss her scolding and solicitude when she was gone.

The singers began with a song of the Eagle Warriors, accompanied by the musicians on flute, drum, and gourd rattles. Huemac listened without joining in, mesmerized by the clarity and perfection of Taypachtli's voice, which she had begun to train in his absence. He watched her through a film of tears, feeling that he could never be happier than he was at this moment.

Then there was a sudden commotion at the entrance to the courtyard, and he looked up to see two torchbearers come in, followed immediately by the commanding figure of Ahuitzotl, who wore a cape of yellow feathers over his broad shoulders. His retinue of warriors and women poured in noisily behind him, but hushed instantly when Ahuitzotl heard the singing and gestured to them for silence. Unable to see the cause of the disturbance, Taypachtli kept on singing, carrying the other singers with her when they began to falter. Then Ahuitzotl gestured strenuously for them to continue, and they picked up the chorus so enthusiastically that they almost startled Taypachtli into faltering herself. But she took command of the last verse and brought the song to a rousing conclusion, to the loud applause of the guests.

Huemac rose and helped Teuxoch to her feet, then led her forward to the place where Acolmiztli was already introducing Ahuitzotl to Taypachtli and Ome Xochitl. The brother of Axayacatl was of medium height though built like a stone column, with broad heavy features and close-set black eyes that lit up like a child's when something pleased him. Those same eyes were said to be truly terrifying when he was angry, but Huemac could tell at first glance that such would not be the case tonight.

"Greetings, Ahuitzotl," Huemac said. "My house is honored by your presence. May I present Teuxoch, the first wife of my father . . . ?"

"I am acquainted with the daughter of our esteemed uncle, Tlacaelel," Ahuitzotl replied, bowing to Teuxoch with a smile. "But please, do not let me interrupt the singing. It was to hear this little songbird," he added, indicating Taypachtli, "that I came, at the invitation of your brother. Let her continue."

Huemac offered his seat of honor to the warchief, but Ahuitzotl refused the courtesy and took a seat to Huemac's left; Teuxoch and Acolmiztli were to his right. The members of Ahuitzotl's retinue blended easily into the crowd, and servants—who appeared to be quite prepared for this eventuality—brought them cups of octli and freshly whipped cocoa, and rolled tubes of yetl. The excitement had made the throats of the singers dry, so there was a pause while water was brought to them. Huemac lit a tube of yetl in the bowl of glowing coals held by a servant and passed it to Ahuitzotl ceremoniously, after drawing the pungent smoke deeply into his lungs. He knew now what this surprise was all about, though he could not begin to express his admiration for the resourcefulness of his brother and his wife. It seemed another example of the power of correctness: That which he had refrained from seeking himself was being brought to him by other hands.

"Is it true that you are a ball player?" Ahuitzotl asked as he passed back the smoking tube, and Huemac resisted an urge to look in Acolmiztli's direction. But he sensed his brother's hand in this, and he decided that he should not waste this opportunity by seeming shy or indifferent.

"I trained in Texcoco with the Master Trainer, Icpitl, and was the third-ranked player on the Moyotlan team before I became an Eagle. I have not had the opportunity to play since."

"I have heard of the game you played against Icpitl," Ahuitzotl said gruffly, as if the statement itself were sufficient praise. "Have you seen my brother's team perform?"

"Only once. They overpowered the team from Culhuacan."

"Could you raise a team to beat them?"

Huemac paused deliberately, so as not to seem merely rash and boastful.

"If I were allowed to choose my teammates and given the time to train them . . . yes, I have no doubt it could be done."

Ahuitzotl's eyes glittered brightly beneath his heavy brow, and a slow smile crept onto his face. But then the musicians began to play, and he abruptly turned his eyes away.

"We will speak more of this later."

Their voices refreshed, the singers joined together in several of the traditional Tenocha feast songs, including a long, inspiring rendition of the journey of the Mexica from their homeland in Aztlan. Then, after she and Ome Xochitl had sung a two-voice song about the ball game, Taypachtli led them all in a marching song of the pochteca, which Ahuitzotl, for one, had never heard before and applauded vigorously, to the delight of the merchants present.

After twice repeating the last chorus at the insistence of Ahuitzotl, the other women filed off and Taypachtli, Ome Xochitl, and the musicians moved in closer to the tree, with the guests forming a complete circle around them. Ome Xochitl stepped forward and bowed before she spoke:

"I have composed a flower song in honor of your wedding, my son. Taypachtli has found music to carry the words and will sing them with me."

A murmur swept the courtyard, and then the crowd fell silent. The drum boomed once and then the flute began to play, with the rattles buzzing low in the background. Taypachtli sang the short verses herself, and was joined by Ome Xochitl on the long:

> "Rabbit Child, Rabbit Child,
> Born in the days of hunger
> Born in the years of dying.
>
> Who are the people
> Who live in your blood?
> Who are your fathers
> Of old?
> The Toltecs, the Chichimecs,
> The warriors of Aztlan.
>
> Rabbit Child, Tenocha Boy,
> Reared in the City of Eagles
> Taught in the House of Tears.
>
> Who are the gods
> That guard your people?
> Who are the gods
> That give them life?
> The God of Wind, the God of Rain,
> The Hummingbird from the Left.
>
> Rabbit Child, Apprentice Youth,
> Student of the warriors
> Listener to the wise.
>
> Who were the Masters
> Who trained you?
> Who were the mirrors
> Of your heart?
> The able men, the learned ones,
> The Lord of Acolhuacan.

Rabbit Child, Eagle Man,
Servant of the War Gods
Captor in their name.

Who are the ones
Who pray for you?
Who are those
You sustain?
The blind ones, the aged ones,
Your people in Tenochtitlan.
The widows and the fatherless,
Your people in Tenochtitlan."

Amid the shouting and applause, Huemac found that Ahuitzotl was gripping his arm—had been gripping it for some time, in fact. Tears were streaming unabashedly down the warchief's face, and his voice was fervent as he pulled Huemac closer to speak:

"The gods have given her a great gift in return for her sight. You were wise to accept no other prize from my brother."

Huemac nodded through his own tears, too moved to speak. Ahuitzotl released his arm and they both rose, and with Teuxoch and Acolmiztli beside them began to make their way through the crowd surrounding Taypachtli and Ome Xochitl. Ahuitzotl made a long speech of praise, punctuated by shouts of agreement from the other guests, then removed his cape of yellow feathers and draped it around Taypachtli's shoulders. To Ome Xochitl, he gave the necklace of golden flowers set with pieces of amber stone that had hung around his neck, and he had members of his retinue reward the musicians and the other singers with items of jewelry from their own persons.

"This evening has gladdened my heart," he said to Huemac as he prepared to depart. "I will send for you after I have spoken to Eztetl and Ocomatli."

After the warchief and his retinue had left, Huemac stood with his arm around Taypachtli's feather-covered shoulders and made his farewells to the other guests, who carried off great quantities of the excess food as gifts. Cuetzpaltzin and the other pochteca called Taypachtli "Daughter" and "Sister" and promised to bring her spices and cocoa from Ayotlan; they needed to make no promises to Huemac, who knew that he would be amply rewarded for the prestige they had gained this evening. Then the warriors paid their respects one by one, bowing awkwardly to Taypachtli and repeating the flowery phrases they had learned in the calmecac so long ago. Finally, Michpilli and his family filed past, glowing with gratitude, and then Acolmiztli and Tlacateotzin and their wives came up, their arms filled with sleepy children.

"It has been a feast like no other, my brother," Acolmiztli said. "May the gods bless your house with many children."

"Ahuitzotl is going to ask for me," Huemac told him, "as you no doubt planned. I am deeply grateful, my brother, even though you fooled me so thoroughly."

"Ah!" Acolmiztli laughed. "It was not so hard, was it, Taypachtli?"

"Indeed," Taypachtli agreed, smiling in Acolmiztli's direction. "The only fool is he who thinks he cannot be surprised."

Then Huemac was alone under the tree with Taypachtli and Ome Xochitl, while the servants moved around them, clearing away the debris of the feast. Huemac embraced his wife and his mother in turn, reiterating the inadequacy of any thanks he might give them.

"But where is the second mother?" Taypachtli asked.

"I saw her go to her rooms," Ome Xochitl said. "Perhaps she was overtaken by fatigue."

But then they saw Teuxoch emerge from her rooms and come across the courtyard toward them, taking small, deliberate steps. In her hands was the necklace of turquoise flowers that Ome Xochitl had given her so many years before, on the day that Huemac was bathed and given his name. She stopped a few feet away from them, her eyes bright in her narrow face, her chin held high with self-conscious dignity. She gestured solemnly toward the huehuetl tree.

"Once, my son, the vultures sat in this tree, waiting for us to die. Acolmiztli shot them with your father's bow, and we ate their foul flesh to keep ourselves alive. Now the warchiefs of our city sit beneath its sheltering branches and converse with you as a friend. I can have no greater satisfaction; I will be honored to die in this house."

"You have honored it with your living, my mother," Huemac said with emotion, and embraced her warmly while she held the necklace tight against her chest. When he released her, she stepped up to Taypachtli and tied the necklace around her neck.

"My son has taken you for his wife," she said simply. "I commend him to your care, my daughter."

Tears welled out from under Taypachtli's eyes as she ran her fingers over the flowers, and she could not bring herself to speak. Huemac embraced her jubilantly, then embraced each of his mothers again.

"Thank you, O Gods, for this day," he cried to the sky. "Thank you for these good women, who give me everything, and make my life upon this earth a thing of joy . . . "

MICHPILLI awoke to the sound of rain falling on the rocks outside the cave in which he was lying. He had only a dim recollection of coming here in the darkness, dragging one of the wounded in after him before collapsing on the stone floor. He was lying on his side facing the entrance, a circle of gray light made dimmer by a drumming sheet of rain. He looked at the cascading water yearningly, running a dry tongue over lips that were cracked and blistered with thirst. He hurt everywhere, especially in his head, and his muscles protested every attempt to move. Gradually, he raised his hand to the worst of his wounds, a deep slash that ran from his left temple to his jaw, narrowly missing his eye. The edges of the wound were puckered and caked with blood and pieces of dirt and sand, and the whole left side of his face began to throb with pain at his touch, causing him to jerk his fingers away.

Little by little, he raised his head and then his upper body, so that he could see the other inhabitants of the cave. Just behind him, Huemac lay motionless on his back, with one heavily bandaged hand clamped tightly against his chest. My master lives, Michpilli thought with relief, seeing Huemac's chest fall and rise again. On the other side of the cave, Opochtli the Puma Warrior sat with his back against the wall, his eyes open but glazed with pain and fatigue. He gestured limply toward the two bodies that lay beside him and shook his head negatively.

We must have water, Michpilli thought, or we, too, will die. He raised himself to his knees and began to crawl toward the entrance, causing the blood to pound in his head with the same force and loudness as the rain hitting the rocks outside. He felt sick and broke out in a cold sweat, but he continued to drag himself forward, until with a last lunge, he managed to thrust his head and arms out under the downpour. The wound on his face stung furiously and he coughed and sputtered as the water splashed up his nose and into his mouth. Cupping a hand over the wound, he rolled over onto his back and opened his mouth, letting the precious liquid batter against his teeth and flow down his parched throat.

Then Opochtli was lying beside him, and the two of them let the rain beat against their skin until they had replenished their moisture-starved bodies. Opochtli sat back first, and helped Michpilli to sit up next to him.

"My master," Michpilli croaked, indicating that they must bring him water. Opochtli nodded and reached to untie the bundle attached to Michpilli's back. It contained the mantle and insignia of Huemac's brother-in-law, Tlacateotzin, who had fallen in the first day of fighting with the Tarascans. Michpilli had forgotten that it was there, but he nodded in eager agreement when Opochtli removed the cloth-lined wooden helmet from the bundle and held it out upside-down to catch the rain. When it was full, they crawled back to Huemac, who groaned and struggled feebly against them when they lifted him into a sitting position. His eyes fluttered open when Michpilli patted water onto his cheeks with his fingers, then closed with relief and pleasure when the helmet was tipped to his lips so that he could drink.

"Ah . . . that is good," Huemac said, when he had revived sufficiently to sit up by himself. He shot a glance at the motionless bodies on the other side of the cave. "Colotl is dead?"

"Both he and the other Eagle are dead," Opochtli informed him, and Huemac took the news without blinking, in silence. He had carried Colotl most of the way here himself, after finding him lying wounded on the trail. It had been a futile gesture from the beginning, but no one had been able to persuade Huemac to leave his enemy to die, least of all Colotl himself, who had cursed Huemac and tried to fight him off while he was still conscious.

"I apologize for risking your lives to try to save his," Huemac said quietly, looking at each of them in turn. Both shook their heads in denial.

"Only you could have led us here in the darkness," Opochtli said, glancing out at the slackening rain. "But we must not stay here much longer."

"No," Huemac agreed wearily. "I have medicines in my pouch, and yetl to numb our pain. Can both of you walk?"

They nodded in unison, and looked questioningly at Huemac's bandaged hand.

"It is only broken," he explained. "The bleeding was not much. Get me more water for the medicines," he said to Opochtli, then pointed Michpilli toward the bodies. "Remove their insignia and bundle it. We leave here as soon as the rain stops."

THREE DAYS before, Axayacatl and his allies had crossed the mountains into Michoacan with an army of twenty-four thousand men. They had known, before they marched onto the plain outside of Tlaximaloyan, that the Tarascans facing them numbered some forty thousand, including large contingents of their own Eagles and Jaguars. But there had been no one in the Tenocha camp who wished to return to Tlacaelel without at least having tested the strength of the enemy, and there were many who had seen greater odds overcome in the past. Despite a last warning from the Tarascan chief to depart in peace, Axayacatl had sent his men into battle with an admonition to show these savages the courage that had conquered Anahuac.

Eight thousand of his men fell in the first hours of fighting, the ranks of the Eagles and Jaguars were decimated, and those of the Cuachic—who could not retreat—nearly wiped out. Before the day was over, the Mexica and their allies were in open retreat, leaving the plain littered with their dead. Nightfall found them at the place called Zamacoyahuac, Big Mouth, where the warchiefs again had to make a decision, since the terrain prevented an orderly retreat. Again it was decided to fight rather than flee, and large quantities of a maize-and-water mixture called yolatl, the "broth of the brave," were distributed to the warriors, who vowed to vindicate themselves the next day.

The Tarascans swept down on them at the first light of day, their battle-axes shining in the sun and their war cries filling the air. Axayacatl fed rank after rank of his warriors into the battle, committing all the reserve troops from Chalco, Xochimilco, and the Tlahuica cities. Even the apprentices, who had long since run out of shields to carry, were sent into the fray, though few lived long enough to savor the opportunity. When a cousin of Axayacatl's, a member of the Council of Lords, was killed, the spirit of the army was broken, and those that remained fled for their lives with the Tarascans in hot pursuit.

As he limped along the trail behind Opochtli, who carried the dead Eagle's insignia upon his back, Michpilli could take no satisfaction in the memory of how well he had defended himself. He remembered only the pain and exhaustion and thirst, and the terror of being constantly surrounded and under attack by a mass of warriors so thick that their number never seemed to diminish, no matter how many were killed. He had stayed as close as possible to Huemac, one of a small knot of men who had banded together out of desperation and had guarded one another's backs during the retreat. Huemac had kept them going, declaring over and over again, with wild-eyed conviction, that he was not destined to die here. Michpilli believed him now, though there had been many times when he had lost all hope himself, and had hated his master for forcing him to fight on.

When they had found another cave to shelter them for the night, Huemac built a small fire and began to prepare fresh poultices for their wounds. Hoping to take advantage of the last hours of light, Opochtli took his sling and went hunting. Michpilli sat as still as possible while Huemac dabbed at his wound with a piece of cotton torn from his armor and moistened with healing herbs.

"You are no longer so pretty, my friend," Huemac said with grim amusement, making no effort to disguise the shaking that weakness and hunger had put into his hands. "But at least no one will ever wonder if you have been to war."

"I do not hope to ever go to war like this again," Michpilli blurted, surprising himself with his own frankness. Huemac merely nodded and continued his ministrations.

"Perhaps Axayacatl will have learned a lesson, if not Tlacaelel."

Huemac chose not to elaborate on what that lesson was, but Michpilli had not forgotten the conversation between Acolmiztli and the merchants. The night of the feast, and its joy, seemed far in the past, though less than a year had gone by.

"I am sorry that your sister's husband was killed, Master," Michpilli said respectfully, when the press of Huemac's other hand made him aware of the bundle on his back. Huemac sat back on his haunches and looked at the boy, who had turned sixteen shortly before leaving on this campaign.

"Thank you, Michpilli. I would like you to be with me when I deliver his insignia to Cocatli. No, do not bow, you will only start yourself bleeding again. And you must now address me as an equal, for we have fought together. There will be many places to fill within the ranks of the Eagles; I will recommend to Eztetl that you be given one."

"I am grateful, Ma . . . Huemac," Michpilli said awkwardly, his smile lopsided and wincing. "I would like to serve with you if it is possible."

"Of course," Huemac said, then smiled wickedly. "You are no longer afraid of my sorcery, then?"

"I feel that I am alive because of it," Michpilli said truthfully. "You are the only one of us who did not lose his hope. But I still do not understand why you tried to save Colotl. He would not have done the same for you, certainly."

"He was my enemy," Huemac said with a shrug, "but I did not fear him. Perhaps I hoped to kill him myself someday. Perhaps he served me, by reminding me that I am worthy of being hated."

Michpilli squinted at him dubiously, and Huemac smiled.

"I doubt very much, Michpilli, that you will ever have my talent for making enemies. But I will tell you as my grandfather told me: Do not ever be surprised by the men who will come against you without cause. Just see that you respond to their unwanted attentions as the Tarascans responded to ours."

They sat silently, watching the twilight deepen and the mists roll into the canyon below. Then Opochtli appeared suddenly between the trees, carrying a rabbit in his hand, and all thoughts of fighting and dying fled from their minds, and they prepared themselves to eat.

HUEMAC and his companions joined up with the remainder of Axayacatl's army in the Matlatzincan city of Ecatepec. Only four thousand of their original number had survived the flight over the mountains, many dying from thirst and exhaustion in the passes. It was far worse than Huemac had imagined in his most pessimistic moments, a lesson too costly to be easily contemplated.

Ahuitzotl and Eztetl expressed their gratitude that Huemac was still alive, but their voices and eyes, like those of the other warchiefs, were hollowed by the shock of defeat. Axayacatl was said to be beside himself with grief, tortured by the feeling that he had somehow failed in his duties as a leader and a priest. The warriors said little to one another as they sat around their campfires, tending their wounds and gathering strength for the march home. The reality of the defeat they had suffered hung over them like a heavy cloud, invisible yet oppressive, a presence with which few of them had ever had to live.

The city had been informed of the sad news, and an honor guard of Old Eagles met the returning troops at Chapultepec and escorted them across the causeway to the mournful lowing of conch trumpets and the measured beating of a drum. The crowds lining both sides of the Eagle Gate were silent, anxiously scanning the faces of the warriors to determine if their husbands, brothers, and fathers were among the living. As the warriors displayed the bundles they carried and the Old Eagles relayed the names of those known to be dead, women in the crowd began to shriek and tear at themselves, flailing about in grief. The sounds of the grieving soon rose to a tumult, and many in the crowd were overcome and had to be carried off by their relatives and friends.

After the warriors had done their penance and completed their vows, Tlacaelel himself addressed them from the steps of the Tlacatecco. Though he wore the war garb of Huitzilopochtli, the old man could not keep his voice from quavering as he surveyed the sad remnants of the once-proud Tenocha:

"Take heart, my sons, and do not be dismayed. Remember that your comrades did not die on their sleeping mats, or sitting at home with the women. They died fighting, like the warriors they were! Their hearts and blood have gone to sustain Tonatiuh and Huitzilopochtli, and to Our Mother the Snake Woman, and to Yaotl, the Enemy. I am proud that I have lived this long, to see such honor paid to the gods! I wish only that I had died with them!"

Tlacaelel threw back his head and began to weep, and many of the men assembled below him did likewise. Michpilli felt little urge to weep, himself, and he noticed that Huemac was staring at the Cihuacoatl with hard, unforgiving eyes. He is right, Michpilli thought; the lesson *has* been wasted, except on those of us who had to live through it. He exchanged a knowing glance with his former master as they walked slowly from the plaza after being dismissed.

"Remember this day," Huemac said gravely. "In all the glory that may come to you, remember the feelings you had today, and let them humble you and make you wise. Come, let us go to see my sister."

MICHPILLI bowed once more to Cocatli, then rose and bowed to Huemac and Acolmiztli before leaving the room. Cocatli stared absently at her brothers, then looked down at the jewels and insignia spread out on the torn and bloody mantle in front of her. Surrounded by her loosened hair, her dark face seemed pinched and tiny, the face of a child grown prematurely old. She wore a black band of mourning around her forehead.

"I had premonitions of this," she said in a dim voice. "I said nothing to

Tlacateotzin, for I knew he could not allow himself to pay heed to my fears."

Acolmiztli glanced uneasily at Huemac. Throughout the city, people were reexamining the doubts they had had about this campaign, and some—though strictly in private—were even questioning the mission of conquest that had guided the Tenocha in their rise to glory. And it was not only the widows who were expressing such doubts. The entire male line of some families had been wiped out, leaving cousins and in-laws with the responsibility for more mouths than they could feed, and many of the farmers and fishermen who provided food for the marketplaces had been taken from their tasks out of the necessity of posting a heavy guard during this time of weakness. The normal processes of the city were in disarray, and the only things being produced in abundance were rumors and the sightings of omens and apparitions. Huemac looked back at his brother impassively, as if to say that the burden of denial was not his, and he would not argue with Cocatli's feelings. Acolmiztli sighed, seeing that he, as the elder, would have to be the voice of cold practicality in the midst of their sorrow.

"He is gone, my sister," he said gently. "You cannot blame yourself for the workings of the gods. But since your husband's only surviving brother has not claimed you, you must now decide where it is that you wish to live. Both of our houses are open to you."

Cocatli glanced from one to the other politely, appearing to weigh her decision, though both of the brothers were fairly certain of how she would choose.

"I am grateful to you, Acolmiztli," she said after a considered pause, "but I would prefer to reside with Huemac and our mothers, in the house where we were born."

"I understand," Acolmiztli said easily. He turned to Huemac: "I entrust our sister and her children to you, my brother, though you may always count on my assistance in matters of their welfare."

"Your children will be as my own, Cocatli," Huemac promised. "And you will have whatever you need."

Cocatli thanked them both profusely, though her mind did not truly seem to be on the subject at hand. When the demands of politeness had at last been met, she drew a long breath and looked directly at Huemac.

"After my husband had left me," she said portentously, "I had a very vivid dream. I was lost and troubled in this dream, and then Quetzalcoatl came to me, in the shape of a man. He was very old and looked much like our grandfather, though his beard was long and white. His skin was also very pale, and he spoke in a tongue I could not understand. He took me into his arms and comforted me, singing to me as our mother sang to us when we were children."

A tremor passed through Huemac at the mention of the Plumed Serpent, the god who had watched over his punishment and revenge in the calmecac, the twin of Xolotl. But he told himself that it was a mere coincidence; that Cocatli had, after all, received her education at the temple of Quetzalcoatl. He considered his sister silently, aware that Acolmiztli was also waiting for his assessment of this dream.

"Was there anyone else in the dream?" he asked carefully.

"There was only one: a beautiful woman who had glowing eyes . . . eyes very much like your own, my brother. She stood behind the god and looked at me as if she knew me."

"But you did not know her?"

"No, though I felt her friendliness."

Huemac frowned, unwilling to contemplate the meaning of the woman's eyes. Instead, he spoke authoritatively about that which was clear to him, concealing the unruly speculations that were running through his mind.

"It is rare for a god—any god—to appear in such a kindly fashion, without threat. It is clearly a summons to his service."

"That was also the opinion of our mother," Cocatli said. "I have already gone to the temple, and offered my services to the women there."

"But you have a family!" Acolmiztli protested. "It would not be right to abandon your children for the priesthood."

"I do not intend to do so," Cocatli explained calmly. "I will serve only in the time that is free to me. Then, when my children are grown and settled, I will ask to join the ranks of the priestesses, if the god will have me."

Acolmiztli fell silent, appealing to his brother with his eyes. Huemac knew how he felt, for he also did not relish the thought of his sister dedicating herself to the hard, lonely life of the women of the temple; it made his heart ache to think of the beauty and gentleness that would be lost from the world he inhabited. But he also saw Cocatli's determination, and knew that she would not be dissuaded. He nodded unconsciously, comforting himself with the memory of a statement his father had once made, to the effect that there was no way to know how long the inevitable might take to occur.

"There is correctness in your decision," he admitted at last. "But we must first make men of your sons, and see that Illancueitl is properly wed."

"Of course," Cocatli agreed. "That is my duty, and my joy. I thank you for your advice, my brothers. I would like to be alone now, if I may."

Huemac and Acolmiztli bowed to her and walked out of the room she had once shared with her husband. Acolmiztli hastily consulted the sky, as if remembering all the matters that needed his attention. He glanced at Huemac's splinted hand, which he carried in a sling in front of him.

"How long before your hand will be healed?"

"The healers say several months, and then I will have to work to regain its strength. How soon is the next campaign?"

Acolmiztli looked at him sharply. "How do you know of this?"

"I know Tlacaelel. The Tenocha have lost an enormous amount of prestige; he will want to recapture it before he dies."

Acolmiztli glanced away, as he always did when the name of the Demon Heart came up between them. He had shown his willingness to aid and protect Huemac in whatever way he could, but he had also let it be known that he considered Huemac's struggle with Tlacaelel to be a personal matter, and one he could not allow to interfere with his judgments as a warchief of the Tenocha.

"Do you disapprove of our recapturing our prestige?"

"Of course not," Huemac said scornfully. "If we wait too long to demonstrate our strength, we will have to fight *everyone*. I only hope it will not be attempted in undue haste."

"The leaders know they have failed," Acolmiztli said bluntly, "and they do not wish to repeat their mistake. We cannot move before next year, in any case. I tell you this because you are being promoted to the rank of Captain of the Eagles, and I have suggested to Eztetl that you be placed in charge of training the new recruits to your order."

"I am honored," Huemac said, and smiled insinuatingly at his brother. "You do not fear that my teaching methods will be too conservative?"

"We cannot afford to lose more men," Acolmiztli said curtly, ignoring his brother's teasing, "and your ability to stay alive is unquestioned. Teach them as you wish, but help us to keep our prestige alive!"

Seeing his brother's emotion, and the obvious strain he was under, Huemac simply bowed in compliance. He knew that Acolmiztli was acting correctly, though with the guilty urgency of the unwilling survivor; he would never forgive himself for being spared the terrors of Michoacan.

"I will do my best," Huemac promised, and Acolmiztli nodded sternly.

"So will the leaders," he said in a resolute voice, and hurried off to the tasks that awaited him. Huemac watched him with compassion, thinking: He has no vision, no dream, to guide him—only the words of other men, and the demands of his honor. He had always envied his brother the simplicity of his life, but he understood now that those with simple lives, and simple loyalties, were least equipped to deal with disaster. It is *theirs,* he thought, whether they have helped to bring it about or not.

Adjusting the sling around his neck, he thought briefly of the disaster he had been shown in his vision, and of the woman in Cocatli's dream, and of the prophecy of Quetzalcoatl. Then he shrugged and smiled, and went to see his niece and nephews.

HUEMAC LAY on his back in the flickering light of the fire, his injured hand resting beside him and Taypachtli clasped tightly against his chest. It was the first time that they had been alone since his return, and he whispered of how often she had been in his thoughts while he was away, and of how her image had sustained him during the arduous journey home. The night was warm, and he wore only a maxlatl and she only a skirt.

"And have you returned with all of your parts, my husband?" Taypachtli asked softly, sitting up next to him on the mats.

"Perhaps you should check," Huemac suggested, feeling himself rise even as she began to loosen the folds of his maxlatl. Her marvelously sensitive fingers slid over the ridge of his pelvis and across his abdomen, closing unerringly around his stiffening member.

"Oh!" she exclaimed suddenly, feigning fright. "They have left an arrow in you!"

Huemac laughed with delight and reached up to cup one of her breasts, which filled his palm completely. Feeling for his legs, Taypachtli hiked up her skirt and threw one leg over him, so that she sat straddling his thighs. Bunching her skirt up around her waist, she curled her fingers around his penis and gently pulled upward, drawing an involuntary moan from Huemac's lips.

"It pains you greatly, I see," Taypachtli remarked, lifting her eyebrows. "Perhaps I should pull it out before you bleed to death."

"Oh no," Huemac protested languidly. "A warm poultice would surely be sufficient."

Taypachtli laughed and took her hands away. Huemac reached for her skirt, but she caught his hand and held it against her thigh. Her face grew suddenly serious.

"It is not kind of me to keep the news to myself," she announced, "even if you have not had the intelligence to ask me. My bleeding did not come last month."

"What? You are . . . ?"

"The midwife says that she will know for certain by next month. But *I* know."

"Taypachtli," he murmured affectionately, tugging gently on her hand until she brought her face close and found his lips with her own. Then she sat back up and removed the skirt from around her hips, and once again took hold of him.

"Your mother has told me how it must be done when one is with child," she said, rising up on her knees. "Besides, you are injured, and must not strain yourself."

"Then you must tend to me, my wife," Huemac said gratefully, and cried out with pleasure when she sank slowly downward, impaling herself upon him, joining their bodies together while the shadows danced around them, unseen.

STAY low!" Huemac shouted hoarsely. "Guard your legs!"

The two young recruits battered at one another from a near-crouch, feinting with their macanas and scuttling from side to side like crabs, marking each other's shields with chalk but leaving no openings for deadlier blows. When they had fought long enough without either gaining a decisive advantage, Huemac grunted with satisfaction and commanded them to stop. He looked at their youthful faces as he commented on their performances, wondering if he would ever be able to trust that they were ready. Most had not seen combat before Michoacan, and then only as apprentices in the back lines, and these last months of working with them had made Huemac feel like an Old Eagle, at the age of twenty-four. It was the year Thirteen-Reed, and the campaign against the Mazahua of Xiquipilco was less than a month off. He would soon see if his charges were as good as he hoped.

"That is enough!" he announced to the group. "You almost looked like Eagles today," he said sardonically. "I would say that I am pleased, but that would only make you arrogant and lazy. Instead, as your reward, you have only to run to the Tlatelulco bridge and back. Double shields and spears, and no stopping for rest!"

The young warriors greeted their reward with loud jeers, but they obeyed the command without complaint, for they were used to being driven by Huemac, and they were proud that they were finally beginning to measure up to his demanding standards. It had been days since he had turned his eyes on them in anger, and that in itself was a reward that far outweighed any words of praise. Picking up their extra weapons from the rack against the wall, they formed themselves into ranks and began to jog out of the courtyard.

Huemac debated whether to join them as he sometimes did, then noticed Michpilli beckoning to him from the colonnaded walkway that led to the Hall of Eagles. His young assistant was standing as he always did now, with his face turned slightly to the left, which, because of the long red scar and drooping eyelid on that side of his face, gave him the appearance of looking disdainfully down his nose. But Huemac could tell from his gestures that he was excited about something, and when he saw Cocatli's oldest son, Omeocelotl, standing behind him, he hurried over immediately.

"What is it?" he demanded, and saw his nephew jump at the loudness of his voice.

"Your wife's time has come," Michpilli explained in an urgent tone. "The midwives have taken her into the sweathouse."

"You are in command here until I return," Huemac said to Michpilli, then turned and knelt beside Omeocelotl. His nephew was eight years old, the middle child, and the one most deeply affected by his father's death. He had become restless and easily discouraged, and though he idolized his uncle, Huemac was always careful not to intimidate him with sudden challenges.

"Thank you for bringing this message so promptly, Little Jaguar," he said to the boy, smiling and putting a hand on his shoulder to calm him. "We must return quickly. Will you run with me, and show me the swiftness of your feet?"

Omeocelotl nodded eagerly and dashed off ahead of his uncle, throwing up the pale bottoms of his bare feet. Huemac turned once more to Michpilli:

"Do you know the sign of this day?"

Michpilli frowned but could only shrug helplessly, so Huemac left him and took off after his nephew, who was already out of the compound and heading for the gate in the Serpent Wall. Huemac overtook him just outside the gate and curbed his own stride to match the boy's as they turned up the street that led to the Royal Compound. Soon they had drawn even with the double line of jogging recruits, who stared and grinned when they saw their captain racing past them with a child at his side.

"He even runs the young ones!" one of them called in mock amazement.

"Is this *your* reward, Little Eaglet?"

Inspired by their attention, Omeocelotl ran even faster, and Huemac cursed the warriors good-naturedly before chasing off after the boy. They were both gasping for breath by the time they got to the entrance to the compound, where Huemac slowed them to a walk.

"Those legs will carry you far, my nephew," Huemac praised him. "Perhaps even to Tehuantepec."

Tlacateotzin had gone to Tehuantepec with Axayacatl's army, and his return from that far-off land remained one of the most powerful memories of

Omeocelotl's young life. It had given the boy a consuming interest in foreign lands, which had grown recently into an obsessive desire to travel.

"I want to go even farther," the boy proclaimed, still catching his breath. "I want to go to Xoconochco, and Ayotlan."

"Ayotlan!" Huemac laughed. "That is indeed far."

"That is where I want to go," Omeocelotl insisted. "Do you know anyone who has gone that far, Uncle?"

"Do I?" Huemac said distractedly, as they came within view of his house. He forced himself to attend to his nephew's question. "Indeed, I know a man who has not only been to Ayotlan, but also to Zinacantlan, the Place of Bats. Perhaps he will tell you about it, if you ask him with the proper respect."

"Zinacantlan," the boy murmured experimentally. "When can I meet this man, Uncle?"

"Soon," Huemac promised absently, as they turned into the courtyard of his house. Teuxoch was sitting under the huehuetl tree with the other two children, Illancueitl and Azcatzin, who were ten and five years of age, respectively. Huemac stopped before them, jerking his head toward his rooms when he heard Taypachtli cry out in pain.

"They have bathed her and given her the ciuapatli root," Teuxoch explained calmly, as if she had not heard the cry. "But it is a large child and its movements are slow."

"Can I go to her?" Huemac asked, and Teuxoch snorted and spat yetl juice into the dust.

"Your sister and the second wife are with her, as well as the midwives. They do not need a *man* getting in their way. Watch over the children. I am tired now, and must rest."

Huemac helped her to her feet and escorted her to her rooms, reminding himself, in his distraction, not to hurry the old woman, whose slow, hobbled movements still left her short of breath. He also had to look out for little Azcatzin, who had hold of the back of Huemac's mantle and kept threatening to get between his legs. When a serving woman came to help her, Teuxoch paused another moment with her hand on Huemac's arm.

"Do not worry, my son," she said, looking into his eyes. "She is young and healthy, and I have prayed to the Snake Woman for her. She will bring forth her captive unharmed."

"Thank you, my mother," Huemac said gratefully. "Do you happen to know the sign that rules over this day?"

Teuxoch worked her jaw wearily, counting in her head.

"It has been ten days or more since the dances of One Flower . . . it must be close to the end of the thirteen. I am afraid I have lost count."

"Rest now," Huemac advised, trying to count backward himself. "I will alert you as soon as the child has arrived."

"Ah! To be weary at such a time," Teuxoch grumbled fitfully, as the serving woman led her to her sleeping mats. Huemac had already lost sight of her as he calculated rapidly in his mind: Eleven Dog, Twelve Monkey, Thirteen Grass. There were twenty signs in the Tonalamatl, the Book of Day Signs, and they were assigned in a fixed order to a rotating series of thirteen days each, with each series ruled by the sign that fell on the number one. One Flower was considered a generally favorable sign, and though Eleven Dog and Twelve

Monkey were preferable to Thirteen Grass, all the numbers after ten were thought to be fortunate. If it *was* Thirteen Grass, though, that meant that the new series would begin tomorrow under the rule of the sign One Reed . . . the sign that belonged to Quetzalcoatl.

Huemac felt a tugging at his mantle and looked down out of his thoughts to find his youngest nephew holding something out to him. It was the small rubber ball that Huemac had been using to exercise his injured hand. Huemac stooped and lifted the boy into his arms, balancing him on his hip, with the ball still in his tiny hands.

"So Little Ant, you have brought me my ball," Huemac said, but Azcatzin only stared at him without speaking, glancing past him once at the entrance to Teuxoch's rooms. He was feather-light in Huemac's arms, a skinny child with a head too large for his body and eyes too large for his head. He had always been Huemac's favorite, for in him Huemac saw Cocatli as he first remembered her: grave, dark, and pensive—a rabbit child.

"You are not frightened by the sounds, are you?" Huemac coaxed gently, when the boy still did not speak. "You know that your aunt Taypachtli is fighting like a warrior, in order to bring a child into the world . . . ?"

"I am not frightened," Azcatzin said, his eyes wide but unafraid. "But the Old Grandmother said I must be still."

"Well . . . you know that you must always respect your grandmother's wishes."

"Yes," the boy agreed automatically. "But she is gone now. Must I still be still?"

Huemac laughed and set him down on the ground.

"No, you may play if you wish. Only you must not disturb the women or your grandmother."

Azcatzin ran ahead with the ball still in his possession, and Huemac followed him slowly, his nervousness returning as he again came within hearing range of his wife's cries. He decided to try to concentrate on the children instead. Omeocelotl was talking to Illancueitl under the tree, telling his sister about outrunning the warriors, and about the man who had been to Zinacantlan. He would make a fine vanguard merchant, Huemac thought idly, if the pochteca ever took in outsiders. It would be interesting to see what his nephew made of Cuetzpaltzin.

"Can I bring you food and drink, my uncle?" Illancueitl asked when he took a seat beside her, and Huemac graciously indicated that he wanted nothing, smiling at the dark-eyed girl. He had decided long ago that she was every bit the Splendid Feather of her name, as tolerant of her brothers as Cocatli had been of him, but much more outgoing and attentive, with none of her mother's intense self-absorption. Huemac knew that he would miss her quiet, easeful presence when she left in a few months to be educated at the temple.

"Do you remember the birth of your brother, Illancueitl?" Huemac asked, watching Azcatzin, who was kicking the ball, chasing it, and then kicking it back, intent upon the trails he was making in the dust of the courtyard.

"I remember only that it took a long time," the girl recalled, "and that my father was very nervous. I was as young as Azcatzin is now."

Taypachtli cried out from her room and Huemac jumped reflexively, then grimaced sheepishly at the children.

"Yes, and I am as nervous as your father," he confessed, and Omeocelotl stared at him with his mouth open.

"But you are a great warrior, Uncle," he blurted. "You have been to Michoacan! There can be nothing that frightens you."

Huemac smiled patiently, aware that Omeocelotl's devotion had its source in the death of his father, and that it should not be casually rebuffed.

"Every warrior is nervous until he has been tested," he said to the boy. "And this is Taypachtli's first test. I am nervous on her account."

"But she is not alone, my uncle," Illancueitl pointed out, looking at Huemac with such concern that he hurriedly patted her hand. He did not wish to make *them* nervous.

"You are right, my niece; she is surrounded by worthy and experienced comrades. It is *I* who am alone, in my waiting."

"But *I* am here," Omeocelotl said staunchly.

"And I, my uncle," Illancueitl added shyly, and Huemac smiled gratefully at both of them, remembering the time he had spent comforting them when they had first come into his house. He had not expected to be repaid for his kindness so soon.

"Then I will not be nervous," he lied, "and we will wait together, my children . . ."

LATE THAT night, Huemac sat alone under the tree, still waiting to be released from his anxiety. Sleep had taken the children long ago, despite their loyal efforts to stay awake and keep him company. His mother and sister had each come to sit with him briefly, and once he had helped carry Taypachtli to the sweathouse in the corner of the courtyard, where the midwives had massaged her for the second time. Everyone had assured him that there was nothing wrong, that it was simply a long labor, but he had felt that his heart was being squeezed and twisted when he had looked upon Taypachtli's weary, pain-contorted face. He had seen that same expression on the faces of warriors, late in a battle, when they only wanted the struggle to be over.

Huemac was sure that Cocatli would know what the day sign was, especially if One Reed was close, but he had found himself unable to ask her when she had visited with him, and she had not volunteered the information. She had also given no indication that she had made the connection between her dream and his child, so he had thought it best to simply not bring the matter up. Perhaps it was not One Reed, after all, or perhaps the child would be a boy. And he had no real reason to suppose the dream pertained to him, except for Cocatli's mention of the woman's eyes and his own abiding sense of the influence of Quetzalcoatl upon his life. He had had no further experiences of the tingling power since the last vision. Surely, he had paid his debt to the gods? Surely, they did not use him still, through his sister and his child?

The air was suddenly filled with the sound of the priests' conch trumpets, signaling the middle of the night, and Huemac shook himself and drew his blanket closer around his shoulders. Now it is another day, he thought, and a different sign for my child. And what if it is One Reed? he wondered boldly. And what if it is a girl child, and has my eyes? If the gods were plotting the destruction of Tenochtitlan, as his vision indicated, there was no one whose fate would be exempt. He could do nothing to alter that for anyone's children, if the gods willed it.

Momentarily reconciled, he listened for sounds from his rooms, but heard only low voices and an occasional moan. It was foolish of him to worry over things beyond his control, he decided. He should be grateful, with his luck, to have a child under any circumstances, and he should only pray that it would not be a gift given only to be snatched away too soon. Inheriting the responsibility for Cocatli's children had gotten him used to the idea of having children of his own, but he knew that this was a blessing not guaranteed even to normal men. His recent run of good fortune had not deluded him into believing that he had escaped his luck, or that the gods would not inflict further punishment upon him before he faced his final test. Like everything else, the matter of his child's fate had to be addressed with correctness.

While this decision calmed him somewhat, it brought him right back to the problem of his child's sign. One Reed, he knew from his studies of the Tonalamatl, was an unfavorable sign, with a strongly negative effect on the days that followed immediately in the series. Acolmiztli had given him the name of a well-known soothsayer, a man who could no doubt use his skill with the painted charts to modify and diminish the influence of the birth sign, if it were indeed unfavorable. But Huemac had a strong antipathy toward the tonalpouhque, the soothsayers, which was why he had not contacted the man before this.

This feeling was based on several things. One was his own knowledge of how little actual power the soothsayer had to counteract a bad sign, since the book could not be made to lie. Another was his teacher Xiuhcozcatl's statement that luck was a mere invention of the priests and tonalpouhque, so that they could make a living from their books. Finally, there was the fact that the soothsayers had played no role in his own life, and would certainly have given him no chance if they had. He could not imagine how he might have fared had the tyranny of his luck been impressed upon him more firmly as a young child, and made official for all those around him. He had suffered enough without them.

But while he believed that any luck could be changed, he was equally certain that it could not be avoided, and he knew, when the time came, that he would consult the tonalpouhque for his child's sake, Xiuhcozcatl and his other objections notwithstanding. If the sign was good, the bathing and naming of the child should be done as soon as possible; if not, a better day would have to be found for the bathing, to offset the power of the birth sign. Huemac could not deny the importance of these rituals, which were all governed by the Tonalamatl. And whether he approved of soothsayers or not, he would have to know his child's fortune, so that he could be vigilant against its bad possibilities. He would have to see that the reading was done correctly, and that a suitable name was chosen, one strong enough to bear whatever fate was attached to it.

The third division of the night passed and Huemac's stomach began to growl, making him wish that he had eaten something when it had been offered. But then there was a sudden commotion among the women in his rooms, and shortly afterward the stillness of the night air was shattered by loud, piercing shouts—the war cries of the midwives—which brought him instantly to his feet. Then he heard the shuddering wails of an infant, and one of the midwives appeared in the doorway to call to him:

"She has taken her captive! She has brought you a small shield, a precious girl child!"

"My daughter," Huemac whispered, and fell to his knees, giving thanks to the Snake Woman, to Yoalticitl, the Goddess of Childbirth. He prostrated himself and touched dirt to his tongue in humility, asking to be forgiven for his worries and his doubting.

Cocatli was the first to come out to him, and he leapt to his feet to embrace her.

"Taypachtli asks for you," she said, smiling calmly at his enthusiasm. "She and your daughter are both well. It is a beautiful child."

"She does not look like me, then?"

"She looks like her mother, and perhaps also a little like *our* mother."

"And her eyes?" Huemac inquired anxiously. "Does she see?"

"No one has seen her eyes yet," Cocatli said, searching his face in the darkness. "But I would not be surprised if she has your eyes, my brother. You know that it is the day One Reed, the day of our Lord, Quetzalcoatl?"

"Yes," Huemac said automatically, as if he had known it all along. He realized that there was no hurry for a soothsayer. "Will you pray for her, Cocatli? Despite the beauty of your dream, it is a very unfavorable sign for a child."

"She belongs to the god," Cocatli said serenely. "He will watch over her fate. Go to your wife, Huemac. Look upon her, and upon your daughter, and show them the love you hold in your heart. I will fetch the second mother."

Huemac leaned forward to embrace her again, feeling the tears come to his eyes as the fact of his daughter's birth finally penetrated and relief washed over him in waves.

"Bring the children, too, if you think it is wise," he suggested giddily. "They were my comrades in waiting."

"I will see if I can rouse them. Go now, do not stand there smiling, as if you were drunk . . ."

The atmosphere of the dimly lit room was warm and steamy, smelling of pine smoke and herbs. The two younger midwives squatted beneath the one remaining torch, digging a hole in the hard-packed floor next to the hearth. The eldest midwife stood behind them out of the light, murmuring prayers over the cloth-wrapped child Ome Xochitl held in her arms. Huemac saw that he had come in during a pause in the ceremony and immediately he knelt beside Taypachtli, who lay half propped up on a pile of mats against the wall, her legs covered with a blanket. Her face had been washed and her hair pulled back, and her fingers were cold against his skin when Huemac lifted her hand to his face.

"Huemac," she whispered in a hoarse voice. "We have a daughter."

Huemac squeezed her hand and brushed her cheek with his lips.

"It was a long battle, my wife. I worried for you."

Taypachtli smiled wearily. "Am I not the wife of a great warrior? But hush now, let us listen to the words of the midwife . . ."

Huemac sat back against the wall, turning his head as Teuxoch entered the room, followed by Cocatli and the two oldest children. Huemac held out his arm and Illancueitl guided her sleepy brother over to his side; Huemac put his arm around Omeocelotl and shook him gently to help him awaken. Cocatli continued across the room and took her place beside the other women.

The younger midwives had now finished their digging, and the eldest midwife held out a bundle wrapped in many layers of cloth, and spoke to the child in Ome Xochitl's arms:

"Here is the cord I have taken from your side, your middle, my precious feather. It is your gift to him who sent you here, to Tloque Nahuaque, the Lord of the Far and the Near. And here is where I shall bury it, here by the hearth fire. Just so does our Lord, the Giver of Life, place you here upon the earth, Little Woman, thus does he plant you here. This is where you will dwell, this is where you will be the heart of the home, the banked fire, the hearth stones. In this house you will stay, and never wander. Your duties will always be those of the home, the spinning and weaving, the grinding of maize and the cooking of food. You will suffer fatigue here; you will sweat beside these ashes and grow weary. Such is your fate, such is the place given to you."

Lulled by the warmth of the room and the soothing rhythms of the ritual, Huemac watched contentedly as the bundle was placed into the ground and covered over. His earlier worries suddenly seemed distant, and abstract. It occurred to him that these same words had been spoken over Cocatli in this very same room, and here she was today, still beside the hearth. Perhaps the god would be content to watch over his daughter in the same manner, and not take her away from him. His hopes for her no longer seemed so vain, surrounded as she was by the wisdom and correctness of these women.

The women now seated themselves in a line facing Taypachtli, and the baby was given to Teuxoch, who spoke to her solemnly, warning her of the hardships she would suffer in this life, and of the tasks that would be hers. Then Teuxoch exhorted the new mother to be humble and grateful for the gift the gods had given her, and to guard this precious necklace and keep it from harm. The baby had begun to cry during this recitation, and she continued crying as she was passed to Ome Xochitl, who rocked her gently while addressing similar words to her and her mother. Still, the child did not cease her wailing, and Huemac felt Taypachtli grow tense beside him, and Omeocelotl shift uncomfortably on his other side. Ome Xochitl's last words were nearly drowned out by her granddaughter's crying, but she merely smiled tolerantly, murmured a blessing over the child, and passed her to Cocatli.

The child ceased crying so abruptly that everyone in the room suddenly sat up straight, as if they had been leaning backward, away from the force of the sound. Cocatli glanced once at Huemac, then looked down at the child in her arms, holding the bundle away from her body, so that the women around her could also see the child's face. Ome Xochitl looked up at Huemac and nodded gravely.

"I have told you all of my dream," Cocatli said slowly. "And now this child has arrived on the day of the god, the day that is sacred to Quetzalcoatl. I offer you the final proof, my brother."

Helped by the midwife, Cocatli rose and carried the child over to her parents. She knelt before them, turning sideways so that her shadow would not block the light. Huemac saw the puckered little face, the tiny, copper-colored fist clenched next to the cheek, the wet mouth moving aimlessly. And then he saw his daughter's eyes: They were round and dark brown, smaller than his own and lacking his thick eyelids, but with the same golden rings around the pupils. Eyes he had seen only in mirrors before this.

"She sees, Taypachtli," Huemac said softly. "And she has eyes like my own."

"She is a dream child," Cocatli murmured fondly. "A precious stone in the crown of our Lord, Quetzalcoatl-Topiltzin. I will pray for her at the temple, and make offerings in her name."

Cocatli carefully placed the bundle into Taypachtli's outstretched arms, and the baby curled deeper into the blankets and closed her eyes in sleep. The other women had also risen and come in around the parents, and Taypachtli raised her face to address them:

"I am grateful to all of you," she said, her voice still hoarse and whispery. "Never did I feel that I was alone in my struggle. I will honor you always for helping to deliver this gift to me."

"Come, we must let them rest now," the elder midwife said, rising along with her assistants. "We will be in the next room if we are needed."

Since she had to go to the temple in only a few hours to help prepare for the ceremonies of One Reed, Cocatli also left, taking the children with her after they had paid their respects to Taypachtli and their new cousin. Huemac was glad that his mothers stayed behind, and that they so clearly expected to be consulted further.

"I had much time to think, while I waited," he said, "and I considered many things concerning my child's luck. I worried over how I might protect her and change her fortune. But now that I have seen her, I know that I am not capable, alone, of acting correctly on her behalf. I ask your advice, my mothers, and yours, my wife."

The two older women exchanged a knowing smile, as if sharing a common memory. Ome Xochitl deferred to Teuxoch with a gracious nod.

"She is clearly no ordinary child," Teuxoch said flatly. "You have not contacted the soothsayers yet?"

"There is no hurry," Huemac assured her. "The most fortunate day for the bathing is Seven Rain, six days off."

"Then there is time to consider a name," Ome Xochitl said boldly, and turned to Teuxoch. "Once, when you were called on, my mother, you proved quite skillful at choosing a suitable name."

"But that was under extraordinary circumstances," Teuxoch protested. "And there were no soothsayers to be consulted."

"Leave the tonalpouhque to me," Huemac suggested dryly, and the reluctance vanished from Teuxoch's face.

"I will try, if you both wish me to," she said, and they all looked at Taypachtli.

"After all you have given me, my mother," she said, "I could not ask you for more. But I would be honored to accept the name you suggest."

"As would I," Huemac added quickly, and Teuxoch nodded and struggled to her feet.

"I must go now," she said succinctly. "I will pray to the Snake Woman and then I will sleep, and I will dream for this child."

TWO DAYS after the birth, the soothsayer came to Huemac's house. Though he was aware of the reputation of the man to whose house he had been invited, he did not enter the courtyard with any greater humility than he usually assumed toward his clients. He was a man of wealth himself, after all, the soothsayer to the lords, and he was used to having his authority respected by powerful people. He felt this most keenly at this particular time, since his skills were in high demand among the warriors going to Xiquipilco. He wore a fine mantle and walked with his head high and his hands free, accompanied by two assistants, one to carry his writing materials and the other to bear the Tonalamatl, the Book of Day Signs.

As the servant led him and his assistants along a neatly marked path of crushed stone, the soothsayer paused to bow to two older women who were tending some children at the edge of the garden. He also catalogued at a glance the goods that had been laid out beneath the tree as his payment: several large stacks of cloth, each stack a different color, and at least ten turkeys in wicker cages. A most generous offering, the soothsayer thought, though it only confirmed what he already knew about his client: that he was young, and wealthy, and that this was his first-born child. Therefore, he would naturally be willing to pay a great deal for a favorable reading, especially since he was educated and would know the bad fortune attached to One Reed. He would no doubt be grateful for whatever effort the soothsayer could make to improve his child's luck, and he might even be inspired to add to the goods already on display.

The soothsayer's confidence grew further when he entered the room, which was well lit with torches, and saw the young couple sitting beside the hearth. The woman holding the child, he quickly discerned, was blind, and her husband appeared half-asleep, his heavily hooded eyes barely open. He was a remarkably ugly man, the soothsayer thought, though the wife was quite presentable, despite her blindness. No doubt they were well acquainted with bad luck, from the looks of them; the soothsayer made an instinctive judgment to be unsparing at the outset, so that they would be that much more grateful for the comfort he would give them later.

"Greetings, Tonalpouhqui," Huemac said respectfully. "Please, refresh yourself with food and drink before you begin."

The soothsayer bowed politely and permitted himself a few bites of food and a taste of cocoa while his assistants laid the painted charts out on a mat before him. Then he inquired as to the exact time of the child's birth, and began to go down the long columns of numbers—each with one of the twenty day signs attached—using a painted piece of reed as a pointer. He already knew what he would say, but he did not hurry to break the suspense.

"Your daughter's tonalli, her day sign," he said at last, "is the sign One Reed. It is the sign that belongs to our Lord, Quetzalcoatl, the God of Wind, and as worthless as is the wind, so will be her life. All that she might possess, everything that she is, will be swept away by the wind. It is a most unfavorable sign, as are those that immediately follow."

The baby suddenly began to cry, and the soothsayer frowned at the noise, then modestly glanced away when he saw the mother begin to loosen her shift in preparation for feeding. He was about to go on with his recitation when he noticed—*felt,* actually—that the man's eyes were wide open and staring right at him. The soothsayer swallowed slowly, his mouth suddenly dry.

"We know the nature of our daughter's sign," Huemac said. "What can be done to improve her fortune?"

The soothsayer wanted to explain the difficulties involved, the intricacies of modifying one sign with another, but he realized—*felt,* again—that he dared not waste words with this man; that his help was *expected* rather than sought. The child had continued to cry, despite her mother's ministrations, and the soothsayer was relieved when the man turned his glowing eyes away to attend to his daughter.

"I will take her, Taypachtli," he said in a soft voice, and lifted the bundled child against his own chest, where it quieted instantly. In the sudden silence, the soothsayer decided that everything he had heard about this man was true, and that he must do what he could to befriend him and make him happy.

"The fourth day from this one, Lord," he said ingratiatingly, "falls under the sign Seven Rain, a very propitious day. I would recommend that the child be bathed on this day, so that good fortune may rain down upon her, and wash away the stain of her birthright."

Huemac looked up from the child at his chest and nodded in agreement, giving the soothsayer the unsettling feeling that it was not only *he* who was being consulted.

"An offering might also be made to the priests of Quetzalcoatl," the soothsayer suggested, "so that they may remember the child in their prayers."

"This has already been seen to," Huemac said curtly, as if such advice were superfluous. The soothsayer cast about for something more to say, but it was almost impossible to think with those eyes on him. He glanced down at his charts but could make no sense of them, and decided to proceed directly to the naming. "May I suggest, then, that the child take the name of this propitious day: Chicome Quiahuitl?"

"That is not suitable," Huemac replied. "I would not have her birth sign overlooked entirely."

The soothsayer blinked rapidly, baffled by such an attitude. Did he want to improve his daughter's fortune or not? Beginning to sweat slightly, the soothsayer again consulted his painted books, wondering what would satisfy this strange and terrifying man.

"Perhaps, then, you would wish to call her Quetzal Acatl: Precious Reed?" he suggested tentatively, but this time it was the wife who shook her head in denial.

"A reed is too easily scattered by the wind," she said firmly. "Her grandmother has recommended that she be given the name Quetzal Papalotl, Precious Butterfly, so that she may dance before the wind, and spread her shining wings in the light of the Sun, to whom her father is pledged."

The soothsayer licked his lips, but he could not bring himself to protest. He swore, though, that he would never return to this house, no matter how much payment was offered.

"It is somewhat irregular," he said tightly. "But let it be as you wish. I will have this painted for you in a folded book, and I will send it to you on the day of the bathing."

336

"We are grateful to you," Huemac said in a satisfied voice. "Your payment awaits you in the courtyard; my servants will help you convey it to your house."

The soothsayer bowed to both of them, then rose and waited while his assistants gathered up his books and materials. He bowed again and backed out of the room, trying not to show how anxious he was to get away. As he turned to go through the door, he thought he heard the child sigh loudly, as if expressing a relief equal to his own.

"SHE IS indeed a special child, our Little Butterfly," Huemac said when the soothsayer was gone, marveling at how she had grown quiet in his arms. He did not recall what had possessed him to ask for her, since he had never had such an effect upon any other child, and since he was still wary of dropping her.

"I did not think that she was hungry," Taypachtli said with a shrug. "She must have known that you were speaking for her."

"She is waking," Huemac reported. "Sing to her, Taypachtli," he suggested impulsively. "Let her *hear* the beauty that dwells within her mother."

Taypachtli began a soft, rhythmic chant, and the baby wriggled luxuriously in Huemac's arms before lapsing back into sleep. Rest now, my little Papalotl, he thought contentedly, rest and dream of the life that awaits you, and of the loved ones who will guard you, here in the home of your birth, here in the city of Tenochtitlan . . .

VIII

THE GAME OF AUGURY

1481–1484

1

AXAYACATL, the sixth Speaker of the Tenocha, died in the year Two-House, at the age of thirty-three. There had been earthquakes and an eclipse of the sun in the months prior to his death, omens that seemed to reflect as much upon the young ruler's past as upon the future that was so soon to be cut short. For Axayacatl would always be remembered as the ruler who had presided over the war between the Mexica, and had led the Tenocha to the most terrible defeat in their history in Michoacan. He had added the names of many cities to the conquest lists and had displayed great personal bravery, but he had not truly extended the boundaries of the power he had inherited from Moteczuma Ilhuicamina, and he died before recapturing all the prestige that had been lost at Michoacan.

His last campaign had been the successful sacking of the Mazahua city of Xiquipilco, two years earlier, and it was there that he had received the wounds that led to his death. Victory alone had not been enough to satisfy his need for vindication, and he had thrown himself into the thick of the fighting with utter abandon, as if the spirits of those who had died in Michoacan stood behind him, goading him on. After taking two captives single-handedly and helping to put the Mazahua to flight, he had dashed off alone in pursuit of the Mazahua ruler, ignoring the calls of his comrades and disappearing from their sight into a field of man-sized maguey plants. When they found him again, Axayacatl had been cut down in an ambush and was being borne off as a captive by the Mazahua, and though he was rescued and rushed into the hands of the healers, he never recovered from his wounds, and finally succumbed in the twelfth year of his reign.

With the reed seat of the ruler empty, Tlacaelel once more emerged from his chamber in the House of Darkness to take charge of the fate of his people. The Demon Heart was now over eighty, his eyes half-blind and his limbs so withered by age that he had to be carried everywhere on a litter, yet he took command of the city with a vigor and decisiveness that belied his apparent infirmity. He ordered that Axayacatl's likeness be carved into the cliffs at Chapultepec, next to those of Itzcoatl and Moteczuma Ilhuicamina, and that all the official eulogies should laud Axayacatl for having died a hero's death. Security was tightened around Tenochtitlan and within the subject cities, and Tlacaelel's agents moved with their customary ruthlessness to suppress rumor and dissent. A date was set for the election of a new Speaker, and invitations were sent out to the lords of the Three-City Alliance. The people of Tenochtitlan waited patiently, confident that Tlacaelel would guide the choice of their ruler as wisely as he had in the past.

HUEMAC DID not feel the impact of Tlacaelel's ascendancy immediately. He was twenty-six years old in the year of Axayacatl's death, and he enjoyed the favor of both his commander, Ahuitzotl, and the Supreme Eagle, Eztetl, because the young Eagles he had trained had performed well at Xiquipilco. It seemed a certainty that he would be promoted to the rank of sub-commander, though this, as with most military matters, had been put off during the period of Axayacatl's decline. Satisfied with his duties as a captain and trainer, Huemac was content to wait and spend his free time with his family, for his daughter Papalotl was now two, and Taypachtli was in the last months of her second pregnancy.

But then, as the day of the election approached, things began to happen that he could not ignore. His promotion was again brought up for consideration, and was denied. Eztetl, who brought him the news, could not meet his eyes as he explained, lamely, that the lords had decided that Huemac was too young for the rank. Then some of Huemac's best trainees, all with family connections to Tlacaelel, transferred to other squads, giving equally lame excuses for their defections. Invitations to feasts did not come as expected, and men who had known him for years now avoided his company.

Huemac had already begun to reconsider his future when he received the summons to his brother's house. After greeting Acolmiztli's wives and children, and sharing the obligatory meal, he followed his brother to a private room. Acolmiztli was almost forty, his hair graying where it was pulled back from his forehead, and new lines around his eyes and mouth adding gravity to his features. Over his mantle he wore the striped stole of a judge of the Teccalco, the court where complaints were heard and judgments rendered for both commoners and noblemen. He came to the point immediately upon seating himself across from Huemac:

"Were you told why your promotion was denied?"

"It was decided that I am too young," Huemac said sardonically. "Or so I was told."

"But you know the real reason," Acolmiztli prompted.

"I assume that the Demon Heart has remembered that I am alive."

"I was there when your name came up for consideration," Acolmiztli said tightly, his face darkening at the memory. "Eztetl and Ahuitzotl were both prepared to speak on your behalf, but Tlacaelel never gave them a chance. He had said nothing up to that point in the meeting, but then he burst out with such anger and hatred that everyone was too stunned to respond. He called you a sorcerer and a traitorous coward, and an evil influence upon the young men of our city."

Acolmiztli ended his recitation abruptly, breathing hard through his nose.

"He did this in front of you, my brother?" Huemac asked quietly, and Acolmiztli nodded stiffly, shaking with the indignity of the affront.

"He did it in front of everyone. I do not know how much he sees, anymore, but he did not care who heard him."

"What did Ahuitzotl do?"

"I do not know, because I left the chamber in protest. Several of the lords who were present expressed their sympathy to me, later," Acolmiztli added bitterly, "but none of them joined me in leaving."

"That was to be expected," Huemac said calmly, looking at his brother with sympathy of his own. "I am sorry that you had to suffer this insult on my behalf, my brother. But that was also to be expected. It was foolish to ever think that I could live in this city and avoid him forever, no matter whose favor I had won."

The resignation in Huemac's voice brought Acolmiztli's head up and made him forget his anger.

"Have you had a vision of this?" he demanded, but Huemac slowly shook his head.

"I have not. But I knew the risk when I chose to escape from my banishment and return here to begin a family. I knew that I would not be safe as long as breath remained in his body."

"What will you do, then? If Ahuitzotl did not know that he was your protector before this, he knows now. He is a ruthless man, Huemac. He will not hesitate to use you to further his own ambitions."

"I am told that his current ambition is to replace his brother Axayacatl upon the reed seat," Huemac said, hooding his eyes suggestively. Acolmiztli spoke sharply:

"Ahuitzotl is rash as well as ruthless. Tlacaelel promised the crown to Tizoc long ago, and he will see that Tizoc has it. Ahuitzotl has only angered him by putting forth his own candidacy. There is no one who will support him, and when the time comes to win back Tlacaelel's favor, he will do whatever he has to. He will give you to Tlacaelel as a gift."

"Why do you suppose he has not done so already?" Huemac inquired, widening his eyes in mock innocence, and Acolmiztli's face grew stern.

"I do not like what you are thinking," he said in a disapproving voice. "There is nothing, short of treason, that you or anyone else can do to prevent Tizoc's election. To ally yourself with Ahuitzotl's ambitions would be suicide."

"Should I accept my banishment, then?" Huemac demanded harshly, the playfulness gone from his face. "Should I leave my family and go wherever Tlacaelel decides to send me?"

"I will look after your family," Acolmiztli assured him. "Tlacaelel cannot live forever. You will still be young when he has gone to the Land of the Dead."

Huemac lowered his eyes and toyed with the edge of the reed mat on which he was seated. When he looked up again, there was a dangerous glint in his eye that made Acolmiztli shudder involuntarily. He had not seen his brother this way since the civil war, and he had hoped to never see that look of deadly decision again.

"And if he lives another ten years?" Huemac asked softly. "My children will have grown up without knowing me. No, my brother. I am grateful for your offer, and I will accept it if I am given no other choice. But if there *is* a way to stay here, I will take it, no matter what the risk. This is my city, and I will not allow the Demon Heart to drive me out of it again."

"You were saved by a vision the last time you confronted him," Acolmiztli reminded him sharply. "But you have no vision to guide you now; you have said so yourself. It is your pride that makes you want to tempt your fate so rashly."

"It is not pride," Huemac said curtly. "How many insults and injuries must I suffer at his hands? How many did our father suffer, before Tlacaelel sent him to his death? Do you not remember how he spoke to us once, under the huehuetl tree? He gave us this city as our home. It is our rightful inheritance, earned with his blood."

"An inheritance may be claimed at any time," Acolmiztli pointed out judiciously, openly alarmed by Huemac's tone. "Why must you confront him now? You have a family to protect, and there is no one who can stand in Tlacaelel's way anymore. His power is greater than ever, and his use of it unrestrained. If not of yourself, think of the risk to those you love, should anything happen to you."

"I *have* thought of this, my brother," Huemac replied. "And I have decided that those I love are as much a part of my fate as anything shown to me in a vision. They, too, are the gifts of the gods, and I cannot abandon my responsibilities to them. I do not have a vision to guide me in this, or a father to give me advice. I must use my own judgment, and it tells me that I cannot avoid the Demon Heart any longer. I have chosen to involve others in my fate, and for their sake as well as my own, I must settle my place in this city once and for all."

Acolmiztli sighed and fell silent, examining his brother's implacable features.

"You will tell me," he inquired finally, "when you have spoken with Ahuitzotl?"

"If you wish. If it is safe for you to know."

"Will it never end for you, my brother?" Acolmiztli wondered sadly. "Will you never be free to live your life as other men do?"

Huemac smiled ruefully and rose to leave.

"You have helped to give me several years of such freedom," he said, "and I am grateful to you, Acolmiztli. But I am not like other men, and now I must act on my own behalf, as I have been trained to do. It is not *I* who tempt fate, but my fate that tempts *me.*"

BACKED BY the full weight of Tlacaelel's prestige, Tizoc, the Pierced One, the eldest grandson of Moteczuma Ilhuicamina, was elected by the assembled lords to wear the turquoise crown and carry the burdens of the Speaker.

Ahuitzotl was the only one to oppose his brother's candidacy, and what little support he had gathered melted away beneath Tlacaclel's unforgiving gaze. In recognition of his prowess as a warchief, Ahuitzotl was raised to the Council of Four Lords that would advise the Speaker, which also put him in line to succeed should anything happen to Tizoc. But Tlacaelel pointedly refused to promise him the succession, in order to punish him for his opposition.

The Huaxtec city of Metztitlan had recently mistreated some Tenocha merchants, and so it was chosen as the place where the Speaker-elect would go to obtain the necessary captives for his coronation. In an act of spite against Ahuitzotl, whom he hated and envied, Tizoc appointed his brother to the post of Regent, to guard the city in his absence. Because Huemac served under Ahuitzotl's command, he was also left behind when the army marched eastward, much to the dismay of the ambitious young Eagles under him. Several more of his best recruits arranged transfers in order to join in the campaign, but Huemac could not be concerned with these petty blows to his prestige. Ahuitzotl had not yet spoken to him, but neither had he been given orders to leave. He spent his time thinking and scheming, gathering information, and consulting with his mother and Taypachtli. And he began to visit the ball court more frequently, holding tryouts for the third member of the team he was forming with his friend Opochtli.

As he left the practice court one day, he was intercepted by a messenger from Ahuitzotl, who told him that the Regent wished to meet with him immediately, in secret. Expressing no surprise, Huemac let the man lead him away, following a circuitous route through the streets that brought them finally to a back entrance of the palace. Here Huemac was placed in the care of a second guard, who led him down a series of empty interior passageways, all of which had the air of being deliberately deserted. They came at last to a large wooden door, which swung open at a coded knock from the guard, who stepped aside and left Huemac to the guards inside. As he brushed through the gauze curtain covering the doorway, Huemac's ears were assaulted by a great chattering noise, and his nostrils were filled with a hothouse stench composed of the mingled odors of fish, damp vegetation, and caged animals. He stopped short and stared, realizing that he was in the Totocalli, the Royal House of Birds.

Before him, disguising what had once been a courtyard, was a lush green jungle of ferns, fruit trees, and flowering shrubs from the Hot Lands, with vine-draped palms rising from their midst to almost touch the billowing cotton net that formed a tented roof overhead. Gravel paths wound their way between the banks of greenery and the many shallow pools, and the birds were everywhere: Herons, egrets, and red spoonbills waded delicately among the ducks and swans in the pools, and the warm, heavy air resounded with the hoarse shrieks of parrots and the cacophonous din produced by the hundreds of smaller birds that flitted about in the foliage. Against the near wall, away from the pools, were the shrouded wooden cages that housed the hawks, eagles, and other birds of prey.

Huemac shuddered, struck by memories and associations so vivid they seemed like premonitions. The Old One asking him disgustedly if it was true that the Tenocha held the wild creatures captive in their city. The hawk feathers he had worn to give him power in his duel with Icpitl. Nezahualpilli setting free the birds at Texcotzinco. The hawk who had perched upon his shoulder in his final vision, the creature who might one day be his nahualli.

The guards were looking at him curiously, but Huemac ignored their stares. Ahuitzotl could have had no notion of the irony of inviting him to this place, but Huemac suddenly saw it as an omen, a sign of the correctness of his decision. He had not escaped from the grasp of the Old One, and of Icpitl, merely to be caged here like one of these unfortunate creatures. He glanced scornfully at the clipped wings of the wading birds, and at the flimsy net stretched overhead. I have the means to free myself, he thought, if I am given the opportunity. I need only the courage to seize it, and once again risk the nets of those who would trap me.

With a last look at the birds of prey, Huemac nodded to the guards and followed them into the maze of greenery, stopping abruptly, once, when a covey of tawny-crested quail dashed across the path in front of him. The unnatural abundance of game had aroused his hunting instincts, and he sought to focus them upon the coming conversation, for everything now told him that this was to be no ordinary meeting. The benches where the royal goldsmiths and lapidaries usually worked were empty, and the long-handled rakes used to comb feathers from the water had been abandoned by their attendants at the side of the path. The only people present were members of Ahuitzotl's personal guard, and even those who knew Huemac looked away, as if they had not seen him pass.

Ahuitzotl was sitting cross-legged on a low stone bench sheltered by a high thicket of bright-green cane, and he sent the guards away and motioned silently for Huemac to sit beside him. He was dressed without any of his usual magnificence, and his thick features seemed puffy and strained, already show-ing the ill effects of the enforced idleness to which his brother had consigned him. The black eyes that flickered briefly across Huemac's face were brutally cold, hardly the eyes that had once run with tears at the sound of Taypachtli's singing. Huemac sensed that they were truly alone; that there was no one listening behind the cane.

"I was not aware, when I asked for you," Ahuitzotl began, in a tone meant to sound both aggrieved and disappointed, "that you had made a personal enemy of the Cihuacoatl. I would not have thought that the son of Quinatzin could have aroused the sort of feeling that Tlacaelel has lately displayed toward you."

Huemac stared straight ahead and did not answer, watching a stately white swan glide past in the pool, furrowing the water noiselessly. The elegant, fixed curve of its neck reminded him of some of Taypachtli's poses, and made him more anxious than ever to reach an arrangement with Ahuitzotl. But it would be a sign of weakness to seem too accommodating, too fast.

"If I have become a liability to you, my Lord," Huemac replied, putting a chilly trace of Texcocan disdain into his voice, "by all means, send me back to my former company."

Ahuitzotl's face darkened at the ingratitude of the reply, but Huemac sat stolidly, letting him know that he intended to offer no explanations, and would not be led.

"That is not where Tlacaelel would have you sent!" Ahuitzotl snapped. "He wishes to send you on a special mission to the city of Teloloapan, which has recently begun to resist our rule. It seemed possible to me—no, *likely*—that you would be mistaken for a common spy and would be killed. That is why I decided that you could not be spared from your duties as an instructor of the younger warriors."

"I am humbled by your concern for my safety," Huemac said, without any pretense of humility whatsoever. "It could not have been easy for you to risk Tlacaelel's displeasure again, so soon after the election."

"You are in my debt," Ahuitzotl threatened crudely. "And it continues to cost me the Cihuacoatl's favor to protect you."

"So you have called me here, in secret, in order to collect?" Huemac suggested, not hiding his disbelief. "What can I possibly offer you, Lord, since the one thing you covet has already been given to your brother?"

"Do not mock me," Ahuitzotl growled, genuinely angry, and Huemac grew serious and put more respect into his voice:

"I do not mock you, Lord. I simply wish to make the terms of our bargaining plain. You must feel that I can be of great use to you, or you would have given me to Tlacaelel long ago. What is it that you think I can do?"

Ahuitzotl looked away, as if suddenly embarrassed to say aloud what was in his mind.

"You have powers," he muttered. "It is said that you once stopped a man's heart with your eyes."

Huemac stared at him, then laughed rudely.

"So, you offer me a chance to be an assassin, rather than a spy! That is no bargain, my Lord; that is treason."

"Go then, and good luck in Teloloapan!" Ahuitzotl burst out angrily, and turned to wave his arms at the swan, which had lumbered up to him to be fed. The big bird spread its wings and hissed viciously, standing its ground. Huemac silently took a handful of cracked maize from the basket beside the bench and threw it into the water. The swan dropped its wings and went after it.

"You are going about this in the wrong way, my Lord," Huemac said calmly, "though your impatience is justified. We need a warrior to lead us now, a man with the courage and strength to recapture our prestige and strike fear into the hearts of our enemies. I know that you are such a man, and that Tizoc never will be."

The flattery worked even better than Huemac had intended; he now had Ahuitzotl's full attention. He paused a moment longer, listening to the buzz of a hummingbird in the undergrowth behind him, then met Ahuitzotl's expectant gaze.

"Your brother is a young man, but he is weak, and the burdens on the Speaker are very heavy. They have crushed many a stronger man. You must see that Tizoc's strength is fully tested; you must see that he is not allowed to shirk his responsibilities."

"Go on," Ahuitzotl prompted, his eyes narrowed with interest.

"You spoke a moment ago about the unrest in Teloloapan," Huemac reminded him. "There is now unrest in a great many places, yet it is not spoken of aloud, even in the palace. Tlacaelel himself keeps such information from the ears of the people. Someone must make the lords and the warriors aware of the threats to our prestige and the provocations of our enemies. Someone must remind Tizoc, over and over, that it is his duty to lead the troops in war."

"It is, indeed," Ahuitzotl agreed fiercely. "But how would that someone get *his* information?"

"The pochteca see and hear many things, but they are not often summoned to the palace anymore, now that Tlacaelel rules. I have no doubt that they would be greatly honored if the Regent of our city invited them into his presence, and entrusted them with his goods to trade. Words might also be traded at the same time, provided that the confidentiality of the bargain were assured."

"You can arrange such a meeting?" Ahuitzotl inquired bluntly, and Huemac nodded in confirmation. The warchief lowered his head and rubbed his chin thoughtfully.

"My ambition is well known, though," he said ruefully. "I will be accused of trying to drive my brother to his death."

"If your stated concern, always, is for the prestige of the Tenocha," Huemac explained hastily, "it need not be seen as ambition. Offer to lead the troops yourself, and say nothing against your brother. It was others who placed Tizoc upon the reed seat; let it be *their* duty to see that he fulfills his obligations. Be especially attentive to Tlacaelel. Apologize to him for opposing his will. Show him the respect you have for the greatness he has brought us in the past, and express your concern that death may overtake him before the Tenocha have been restored to their full glory. Do not let him forget that his time upon the earth is short, and the situation grave. You have no need to contest your brother openly, my Lord; you have only to force Tlacaelel and the other lords to take responsibility for what *they* have wrought."

Huemac finished breathlessly. Ahuitzotl clasped his hands in front of him and frowned deeply, so that Huemac could not tell if he was debating the merits of the scheme or questioning his own ability to carry it out. Ahuitzotl had all the courage that Huemac had claimed for him, but he was not a subtle man. Huemac was wondering if he would be forced to present his last bargaining item when Ahuitzotl spoke:

"You are crafty, Huemac," he said abruptly. "But what you are advising is that I wait and let others do my work for me. That is not my nature. I will grow impatient, and Tizoc will goad me, and I will not be able to keep myself from contesting him. Then my ambition will be perceived for what it is, and your plan will be useless. But meanwhile, *you* will have been protected, at *my* cost."

Huemac could barely conceal his disgust. *This* was the man he would help to become Speaker, a man who could not even be counted on to control his temper! But then he reminded himself of what was at stake, and spoke boldly:

"Then I will contest Tizoc *for* you, my Lord. On the Ball Court of the Lords."

Ahuitzotl's eyebrows shot up, and the suspicion dropped away from his face.

"*Yes,*" he whispered appreciatively. "It could be a game of augury, his fortune against my own." He looked sharply at Huemac. "But you must not lose."

"I will not lose, if you will give me the time to prepare, and the men I need."

"They are yours," Ahuitzotl said grandly, clapping Huemac on the shoulder in his enthusiasm. Then he seemed to remember himself, and how this agreement had been reached, and he sobered and took his eyes from Huemac's expressionless face.

"I am satisfied," he said gruffly. "Tlacaelel will have to understand that the captain of my team cannot be sent on special missions. Make the arrangements with the pochteca; tell them that I have a surplus of blankets and golden jewelry. Go now, and take my regards to your wife . . ."

Huemac rose and bowed stiffly. He looked around him carefully as he retraced his steps along the path, fixing this place in his mind, and resolving never to return.

TAYPACHTLI lay in darkness, her fingers tracing the familiar jagged shape of the scar on the back of Huemac's left hand, where he had been wounded at Michoacan. She could tell by the tinkling sounds of the bells tied around Papalotl's ankles that the child was climbing all over her father, and Huemac's nervous twitchings showed that he was having trouble keeping a grip on her with only one hand. He has spoken to Ahuitzotl, Taypachtli thought, feeling the tension he had brought into the room with him, a tension that was now being focused upon her condition.

"Perhaps another midwife should be consulted," Huemac suggested in a low voice, so that the midwives on the other side of the room would not overhear him and be offended. "Or one of the healers from the palace."

"They could do nothing that your mother and the other women have not done already," Taypachtli said firmly. "It is only an injury to the muscles that support the weight of the child. It will heal if I do not try to walk or move around."

"Then you must not try," Huemac said, removing his hand from her grasp as the tinkling increased and Papalotl began to giggle. The child inside of Taypachtli kicked violently, and she gasped at the impact, feeling a dull burning pain low in her abdomen, beneath the great, swelling weight that filled her middle.

"Quiet, Papalotl," Huemac said sharply, and Taypachtli felt him lean closer. "The pain is bad?"

"It is wearisome," Taypachtli said tightly, unable to conceal her discomfort. "He is so large and heavy, and he kicks as if he wished to injure me."

"Rest, then," Huemac said anxiously. "I will take the children with me to Tlatelulco. They can play with Cuetzpaltzin's children while we talk. Do you remember the boy you played with, Papalotl, the quiet boy?" Huemac asked their daughter, speaking very slowly and clearly. "His name was Pinotl. Would you like to go and see him again?"

"Pee-notl," Papalotl repeated happily, announcing her assent with a flurry of eager tinkling sounds. Taypachtli reached out for the hand of her nephew Azcatzin, who crouched vigilantly on her other side. The little seven-year-old had been her guide and support during these last difficult weeks, seeing that she did not stumble or fall from the weight of her child.

"Go with your uncle, my faithful one," she said warmly. "I will not need you to guide me for a while."

"I am grateful to you, Azcatzin," Huemac said. "You may have the honor of informing Omeocelotl that he may accompany us to Tlatelulco, as long as he has stacked enough wood for the sweathouse. Take Papalotl with you, while I speak to my wife."

The tinkling sounds receded, and Taypachtli felt her husband lie down on the mats beside her. Her hand was taken in his, and she turned her face toward the sound of his breathing.

"You have spoken to Ahuitzotl?" she asked in a whisper.

Huemac hesitated, and she sensed his reluctance to burden her with his own troubles. She squeezed his hand encouragingly.

"I must know the state of the world into which I will bring our child," she reminded him, and he sighed softly.

"I spoke to him. As I thought, Tlacaelel has been pressuring him to have me sent away again. But he has agreed to protect me and keep me here. He sent his regards to you," Huemac added sardonically, "after we had arrived at an adequate form of compensation for his protection."

"What has his favor cost you?"

"Little so far, though perhaps a great deal later on. I have involved myself in his ambitions, and they are very dangerous. I had almost forgotten how it feels to put myself into the power of another."

"So had I," Taypachtli said wearily, wincing as the child kicked again. "This one is so large that I no longer know who is the captive, and who the captor. But I will bring him forth unharmed," she added bravely.

"You are certain it is not a girl child?" Huemac asked, lightly resting a hand on the enormous mound between her spraddled legs.

"No woman would kick so rudely," she scoffed, and was pleased to hear him laugh. He pressed his lips against her cheek and they lay silently for a few moments, their faces very close.

"The children are waiting," she reminded him finally, with great reluctance. He stroked her face and swallowed thickly.

"I did not ever want to involve myself in my father's world," he confessed. "It is a world of false smiles and hollow words, where men betray one another for power. But I would enter it gladly, again and again, rather than leave you now."

"You are not alone, my husband," Taypachtli murmured. "We will not desert you, and you will always know that our smiles are real. But go now. We will talk more, later . . ."

"Yes, my wife," Huemac whispered gratefully, and then was gone, leaving her alone in the darkness, alone with the creature that stirred and jostled inside of her, waiting to be freed.

YOU will now have sole charge of the afternoon drills," Huemac said to Michpilli, when they met the next day. "Speak to the captain of the Puma Warriors, and see that Opochtli and Chiquatli are also released from their duties at that time. Say that it is by the order of Ahuitzotl."

"Chiquatli?" Michpilli asked with a grimace, looking at Huemac curiously. "Why that one?"

"You have become lofty in your judgments of men, Michpilli," Huemac said dryly, and his assistant's face flushed darkly, illuminating the livid furrow across his left cheek. "You do not agree that he has a great potential as a ball player?"

"Yes, of course," Michpilli said. "But he has no discipline, and will not take orders. Surely, Ahuitzotl would allow you to hire someone who would be less trouble?"

"I need a man of unusual capabilities, and Chiquatli is the only one in the city who might have them. He can be taught to take orders."

"I wish you luck." Michpilli shrugged. "No one has been able to teach him yet."

"Perhaps no one has *needed* to teach him as I do," Huemac said cryptically. "Find out to whom he owes things, and see that his debts are paid."

Michpilli nodded obediently, though he was puzzled by the intensity, and the suddenness, of Huemac's renewed interest in the ball game. With his name being slandered and his best recruits leaving his command, it seemed a frivolous distraction, though Michpilli could not truly believe that his master did anything frivolously.

"Were there any messages for me?" Huemac asked, and Michpilli briefly consulted his memory.

"Two. The first was from Ahuitzotl: He said that the merchants you had recommended were satisfactory. The other was from your sister, the widow of Tlacateotzin: She said to remind you that your nephew Omeocelotl enters the calmecac tomorrow, and that you have promised to attend the ceremony."

"Lords and little people," Huemac murmured, smiling to himself at the incongruity. He looked up at Michpilli. "Has there been any word from the army?"

Michpilli frowned. "The Huaxtecs continue to hold their defenses, yet Tizoc refuses to replace Ocomatli as the commander-in-chief. It does not seem likely that they will be home by the feast of Four Movement."

"That is unfortunate," Huemac said absently, showing little remorse at the news. "We have been blessed with great leaders in the past; it will not be easy to tolerate Tizoc's ineptitude."

Michpilli drew a sharp breath, shocked by how casually Huemac had offered the opinion, which was extreme even for him. None of the warriors in the city respected Tizoc, but it was considered disloyal to criticize the Speaker openly, especially when Tlacaelel was acting as his adviser.

"Perhaps he will learn from the Cihuacoatl's guidance," Michpilli offered, and saw Huemac's face harden.

"Yes, perhaps the Demon Heart can find a Michoacan for *him,* too," he suggested darkly, looking steadily into Michpilli's eyes. Michpilli remembered the day they had stood together on the plaza, listening to Tlacaelel weep for the men he had so carelessly sent to their deaths, and he looked back at Huemac with sudden comprehension. He did not know what Huemac hoped to accomplish with his ball team, but he no longer doubted the seriousness of the stakes, if Tlacaelel was somehow involved.

"I am at your service, my Lord," he said loyally. "In any way . . ."

"Thank you, my friend," Huemac said warmly, resting a hand on his shoulder. "I would be grateful if you would look after the needs of the troops, for I may not be able to pay them my full attention in the days ahead."

"I will be honored. Is there anything else?"

"Just one," Huemac said, looking past him with determined eyes. "Tell Opochtli and Chiquatli that we begin training this afternoon."

A LIGHT RAIN began to fall as Azcatzin trotted out of the courtyard and turned in the direction that his mother had told him to go. He already knew the way to the palace ball court well enough, having been past it many times on exploring trips around the city with Omeocelotl, but it had not occurred to him to tell his mother that as she had detailed the exact way that he must go. She had spoken loudly, over the screams coming from his aunt's room and the terrified crying of Papalotl, who was clinging to his mother's legs. He had concentrated on her words, feeling very proud that this task was being entrusted to him, and taking pleasure for the first time in the fact that Omeocelotl was in the calmecac, and was no longer available for missions like this. It was a relief, too, to get away from the noise of his aunt's struggle and the incessant wailing of little Papalotl, who was too young to understand about how women took captives.

Jumping over a puddle that had collected before the white west portal of the ball court, Azcatzin entered a stone-floored vestibule that was littered with dried flowers and the crushed remains of yetl tubes. Finding no one around, he went up the flight of steps directly in front of him and came out into the open in the midst of the boxes that sat atop the wall at midcourt. Here he found his uncle's helper, Michpilli, the man with the cut on his face. He was standing with a cloak held over his head to ward off the rain, but he turned and bent low when Azcatzin pulled gently on the edge of his cloak.

"Azcatzin! What are you doing here, boy? Is it Taypachtli?"

"I must see my uncle Huemac," Azcatzin said solemnly, staring wide-eyed at the cut on the man's face. "The baby has come."

"Ah . . ." Michpilli murmured, straightening up to take a step over to the front of the box, where he could look down into the court. Azcatzin followed him obediently, and Michpilli drew him in under the cloak before the box's retaining wall, which came up to Azcatzin's stomach.

At first, the boy was simply dazzled by the brilliant colors of the court floor, and by the fierce, godlike figures painted on the surrounding walls, which gleamed wetly in the muted light. It looked like a temple to him, but there were no steps or shrines, and the walls had been laid flat and open to the sky, making him wonder where the priests said their prayers. Then he saw the two men in rain-darkened leathers, one on either side of the black dividing line, hitting a ball back and forth between them.

"It had to happen sooner or later," a deep voice said from above and behind him, and Azcatzin looked up at a tall, long-legged man who, like the men on the court, was wearing thick leather pads around his hips and knees, scuffed leather gloves on his hands, and a shiny, close-fitting helmet on his head. He smiled down at Azcatzin, seeming vaguely familiar to the boy.

"Can we interrupt him, Opochtli?" Michpilli asked. "His wife is delivering."

"We cannot stop it now," the tall man said. "Chiquatli has been spoiling for this duel ever since Huemac took him on. He must learn, the hard way, who is the captain of the team."

Seeing that they were paying no attention to him, Azcatzin turned back to the court, wiping moisture from his face. The two men below him had drawn closer to the dividing line, and he could now tell that the one on the left—the smaller one—was his uncle. The ball flew between them at incredible speed, hitting off their pads with a *swack!* that could be heard clearly above the steady splattering of the rain. Azcatzin could feel each blow in the pit of his stomach, and he arched his body against the wall, filled with a sudden restless excitement.

"They could both be injured, playing so close," Michpilli's disapproving voice said above him. "Chiquatli hits harder than anyone I have ever seen, and Huemac could slip in this rain."

"I see only Chiquatli slipping," the tall man said calmly. "And he is lucky to be hitting the ball at all. Huemac is baiting him. Here, boy," he said, leaning over to thrust a hard black ball into Azcatzin's hands. "Help your uncle to finish this quickly. Stand back, Michpilli, so that Huemac will see him; he will understand why he is here. Go on, boy, throw it . . . "

Cupping his hand around the big ball with some difficulty, Azcatzin reared back from the wall and threw it as far as he could, seeing his uncle shade his eyes against the rain and look up at him as the ball sailed down. Then Huemac's body jerked in recognition, and he instantly sprang for the ball, striking it with his knee and advancing toward the line behind his shot.

Though he had played ball with his uncle, Azcatzin had never seen him run, much less *really* play ball, and he was amazed to see a grown person leaping and throwing himself about with such wild abandon. Having understood little of what the men behind him had said—except for the name *Chiquatli,* Screech Owl—he recognized only that his uncle was the smaller of the two men, which gave him an extra thrill when it became clear that Huemac was winning. He wiggled his hips in imitation, marveling at the way his uncle could thrust part of his body in front of the ball at the last moment, hitting it with a solid *swack!* every time, and then not fall down from the impact, as the other man had just done for the second time. Azcatzin suddenly decided that he was going to be a ball player when he was old enough. His brother Omeocelotl had confided to him, just before entering the calmecac, that his secret desire was to become a vanguard merchant when he graduated, and Azcatzin had been worrying ever since about what *he* would be. But now he knew, and would not have to worry about it again.

The tall man allowed him to throw out three more balls, one right after another, it seemed. The men were directly below him now, so close that he could hear the squeak of their rubber sandals on the wet stone floor and see the expressions on their streaming faces. But the man opposite his uncle was hardly moving anymore, except to brace himself and bare his teeth every time the ball came flying back at him.

"He is dead on his feet," the tall man said. "Now it is Huemac who must be careful not to cause an injury."

Swack! The ball slammed off the other man's pads and came back to Huemac on one easy bounce. Azcatzin saw the other man cringe and raise his hands defensively as his uncle, poised on one leg, brought his other leg whipping through for the shot. But he hit down on the ball, so that it landed a few feet in front of the other man and bounded straight up at his chin. White showed around the man's eyes as he threw himself backward, landing heavily on his back as the ball flew past where his head had been.

Azcatzin turned to get another ball, but the tall man was no longer there. Somehow, he had gotten down onto the court, and when Azcatzin looked again, he was standing over the fallen man, who was still lying on his back in the rain. Huemac was halfway down the court, walking rapidly toward the open end.

"Come," Michpilli said in a kindly voice, "let us go deliver your message."

HUEMAC'S SON was born on the day Two-Eagle, the second day in the series ruled by the sign One-Jaguar, the sign of wild beasts and dangerous places. Both were signs belonging to the warriors, but in this case, the soothsayer Huemac consulted could only confirm what was already obvious to the eye: This was a child destined to spend his days upon the field of battle. He was prodigiously large, the largest baby the head midwife had ever delivered, and he had come into the world fighting, injuring his mother with the violence of his struggles and greeting his captors with a bellow of protest. Pledging him to the service of the Sun, the midwife cut his birthcord and presented it to Huemac, who would bury it upon the battlefield when he next went to war.

The bathing of the child took place two days later, at dawn on the day Four Movement. The warriors who attended were all dressed in full battle regalia, for this was a holy day in Tenochtitlan, a day especially sacred to the warrior orders, whose patron, the Sun, had been born under the sign Four Movement. All the people of the city, even to the smallest children, fasted and shed their blood in penance on this day, in commemoration of the sacrifice the gods had made to bring the Sun into being. The period of fasting was scheduled to end at noon, when special captives would be slain in a public ceremony at the Temple of the Sun.

Conducted under such circumstances, the bathing was an unusually grave and portentous affair, though some of the warriors present could not contain their shouts of approval when the enormous infant struggled with the midwife, and caused her to call for assistance. When the child had finally been cleansed, he was presented with a tiny shield and four tiny arrows, and he was given the name Xolotlpilli, Monster Prince. This name was again the inspiration of Teuxoch, who had exclaimed, upon seeing the baby for the first time, that he was a monster, a true prodigy.

Taypachtli had suffered some additional bleeding after the delivery, and then had begun to feel feverish, causing concern among the midwives, who packed her womb with herbal dressings and fed her a medicinal broth to combat the fever. Though the danger was not thought to be great, she was not allowed to attend the ceremonies at the Temple of the Sun, and she did not join Huemac in welcoming the guests who afterward came to the feast celebrating their son's birth. Among the first to come to Taypachtli's room to pay his respects was Cuetzpaltzin, the head of the vanguard merchants. He greeted the new mother fondly and made a great fuss over the baby, who lay bundled in his cradle beside Taypachtli.

"Already, he fills his cradle!" Cuetzpaltzin exclaimed. "Huemac will have to discipline him early, before he becomes too large to handle."

"He is a good-tempered baby," Taypachtli assured him. "He simply has a restlessness to match his size."

Xolotlpilli waved his hands up at Cuetzpaltzin's face, and his tiny foot thudded against the end of the cradle. But there was a smile on his face, and his big brown eyes stared upward placidly, a peaceful contrast to the wild shock of black hair on his head.

"He has Huemac's nose and forehead," Cuetzpaltzin said, "but his cheeks are round like yours, and his jaw is strong and clean." The vanguard merchant paused respectfully. "Like your father's, actually."

"Very much like my father's," Taypachtli agreed softly, resting a hand on the edge of the cradle. She was sitting with her back against the wall, and there were dark red spots, high up on her cheeks.

"I do not wish to tire you, my daughter," Cuetzpaltzin said apologetically, "and you must forgive me for asking at a time like this. But there is something I do not understand about your husband."

"Can there be a secret the two of you have not traded?" Taypachtli asked lightly, and smiled. "But speak, my friend. We are both Tlatelulca."

"I am glad that you have not chosen to forget. So, you must explain to me Huemac's attraction to the ball game. He does not usually share the passions of the other Tenocha, and I have never known him to be interested in gambling. Many of the men who spend their time around the Tlachco are among the worst to be found."

"But tlachtli is also the sport of the lords," Taypachtli pointed out, "especially of those lords who might otherwise contend with one another in more harmful ways. Huemac is forming a team at the request of Ahuitzotl."

"Ah," Cuetzpaltzin exclaimed softly. "Then his passion for the game is feigned?"

"No, it is genuine. He has been playing since he was a young boy, and he was trained by the Master Trainer of Texcoco. He has told me of his matches, and made me feel the excitement of it."

"There is not enough excitement in a man's life?" the merchant asked incredulously. "Especially for a man like Huemac! I am grateful for your explanation, but I am afraid I still do not understand such a passion. I will know better than to say so to Huemac, but it seems a passion more natural to a child than to a man."

Taypachtli started to laugh, then grimaced at the pain it caused her. Cuetzpaltzin reached across the cradle and rested his hand upon hers.

"I can assure you," she said with a weak attempt at a smile, "that his passions are those of a man."

"I cannot doubt the proof," the merchant agreed. "My blessings upon you, Taypachtli, and upon you, Xolotlpilli, Monster Prince. Let us hope, little warrior," he whispered, bending low over the cradle, "that you will soon provide all the excitement that your father will need."

AS SHE stepped from the noise of the courtyard into the quiet of Teuxoch's rooms, Ome Xochitl heard the faint tinkling of bells somewhere ahead of her in the darkness. The only light came from the fire smoldering in the hearth, but she knew that that would not impede her granddaughter, who saw in the dark nearly as well as Huemac himself.

"Papalotl!" she called softly, feeling her way forward while her eyes adjusted to the darkness. She found the little girl crouched next to Teuxoch's blanket-wrapped body, and she quickly knelt beside her to prevent her from awakening the old woman. But Teuxoch was already awake, and seemed to be smiling at Papalotl.

"*You* did not forget your old grandmother, did you?" she said hoarsely, wheezing slightly as she struggled to free herself from her blankets.

"Grandma come brother's feast," Papalotl said exuberantly, and Teuxoch chuckled and coughed.

"Help me dress, Ome Xochitl," she said. "I will join my family for a while."

Ome Xochitl put an arm under her back and helped her to sit up. Teuxoch was sixty-six now and seemed to weigh nothing, certainly not as much as Xolotlpilli. She had been bedridden for most of the last year, and Ome Xochitl worried about the effect the excitement of the feast might have on her. But there was no point in trying to dissuade her, now that she was awake, so Ome Xochitl rose and lit a torch and began to gather Teuxoch's clothes.

"You are a good child, Quetzal Papalotl," Teuxoch was saying when Ome Xochitl returned. "At your age, your father was already playing tricks on his old mother."

"Tricks?" Papalotl echoed dubiously.

"Do not put ideas into her head," Ome Xochitl warned, though she was not really concerned about Papalotl's impressionability. She had watched her granddaughter carefully throughout these first two years, and beyond her extraordinary eyesight, the child had shown no unusual powers, and certainly none of the deviousness that had come to Huemac so early. Her golden eyes were open and trusting, and she was in every other way a normal child, a pretty child, with her mother's round face and just the slightest resemblance to Nezahualcoyotl in the fineness of her nose and chin. If the god had indeed put his mark upon her, it had not yet begun to show.

"Did you fast today, my child?" Teuxoch asked. "Did you do penance for the Sun?"

"Tonatiuh," Papalotl repeated without enthusiasm, rubbing the place on her forearm where her father had gently pricked her with the thorn of penance. Even Cocatli had not been able to quiet her then, Ome Xochitl thought wryly, remembering her granddaughter's unholy screams of pain and surprise.

After she had helped Teuxoch to wash herself and redden her lips and cheeks, Ome Xochitl wrapped the tiny withered body in a warm, colorfully embroidered shift and combed the tangles out of Teuxoch's silvery hair.

"Come feast, come feast," Papalotl said happily, swinging her arms and prancing in a jingling circle as Ome Xochitl helped Teuxoch to her feet.

"Such energy," Teuxoch sighed. "These little ones make me feel the weight of my years."

"Without them, though, we might come to feel nothing," Ome Xochitl murmured, and followed Papalotl out into the light, leading Teuxoch by the arm.

AZCATZIN had seen the set of leather pads and the helmet when they were brought out with the other gifts, late in the afternoon, and they had not been out of his mind for a moment since. Again and again, he had drifted over near the mats that had been laid out near the courtyard entrance, making sure that the neat, buff-colored bundle and the shiny wicker headpiece had not moved from their place between the pile of red blankets and the basket of chia seeds. There were many other children here, including two of Acolmiztli's sons, and Azcatzin had not yet found the courage to tell his uncle about his own desire to be a ball player. He *had* told his mother, though, which gave him reason enough to hope, and to keep a sharp lookout over what was being dispensed.

The torches atop the high poles surrounding the gifts had been lit shortly after the singing and dancing had ended, and as the guests began to make their farewells, Huemac would accompany them to the door and fill their arms with gifts. Azcatzin trailed him at a distance as he led a large group of Puma Warriors, all in their fur headdresses and vests, over to the mats, joking with them about the poor quality of the gifts he had to offer. Azcatzin relaxed when he saw his uncle walk past the leathers and begin distributing mantles from one of the piles, and he let his attention wander to the Puma Warrior who stood alone at the edge of the group. He was half-turned away from the others, gazing about aimlessly, as if he did not expect to be given any gifts.

He was one of the most muscular men that Azcatzin had ever seen, and he held himself arrogantly, conscious of his power even in repose. He was light-skinned and quite handsome, with broad, even features and thick black eyebrows. But what drew Azcatzin's interest was the tattoo on the outside of the man's thigh: a large, swooping bird of some kind. Then the man noticed him staring and grinned, showing sharp white teeth. He came up close to the boy and flexed his thigh in the light, and Azcatzin saw that the bird was an owl, its sharp ears flaring away from deep-set eyes and a cruelly hooked beak, its wings spread in descent and its talons outstretched.

"*Tecul,* owl," Azcatzin said numbly, trying to tear his eyes away from the ominous bird.

"It is *chiquatli,* the screech owl," the man said, still grinning. "It is the evil bird that cried out in warning on the day that I was born. The day that my mother died."

Azcatzin stared at him in surprise, a connection forming in his mind.

"You played tlachtli against my uncle," he blurted. "In the rain."

"Your uncle? Oh . . . so you are the nephew of my brave captain. Has he made *you* his apprentice yet?"

"I have not asked him," Azcatzin said stiffly, sensing that he was being mocked. "I am only seven."

"That is just the right age! You will not mind being ordered about, and sent out to run in the rain."

"Leave him alone, Chiquatli," Huemac said in a cold voice, deliberately stepping in front of his nephew. Chiquatli looked at him disdainfully, then gave a short laugh and backed off a few feet. Huemac turned and knelt before Azcatzin, whose face lit up when he saw the pads and helmet in his uncle's hands.

"I wanted to reward you, Azcatzin, for how well you have served your aunt, and your mother suggested to me that you had formed an interest in the ball game. Besides, you are alone here now, without a playmate your own age, as I was when _I_ learned." Huemac smiled at him and held out the pads. "Come, let us see what my friends the leather workers have done for you . . ."

Huemac showed him how to strap the pads around his narrow hips, and he carefully tightened the laces on the kneepads so that they would not bind or slip. Azcatzin's black eyes sparkled beneath the shiny rim of the helmet, which teetered slightly above his ears, leaving room for growth.

"Go and show your mother," Huemac said. "We will begin your lessons tomorrow."

With a last wary look at the man with the tattoo, Azcatzin dashed off, and Huemac stood up and walked over to Chiquatli, who grinned at him sarcastically. Then he noticed the small, cloth-wrapped bundle in Huemac's hands.

"I have brought you a gift, as well. I sent to Texcoco for these."

Standing with his back to the men waiting by the door, Huemac carefully unfolded the cloth, revealing a sheaf of finely textured, reddish-gray feathers, and a pair of gnarled yellow talons tufted with gray down. Chiquatli's handsome face went pale, and he tucked his hands behind him in refusal.

"I will have nothing to do with your sorcery," he hissed, and Huemac suddenly reached out and jabbed him in the thigh.

"What is _this_, then? You wear _this_ owl out of bravado, yet you do not have the courage to even touch these feathers. There is power in these objects, Chiquatli, if you are man enough to try to claim it."

Chiquatli rubbed his thigh sullenly, unable to meet Huemac's eyes, and aware of the men watching them from the doorway, his captain among them. They were not close enough to hear, but they could not fail to see it if he threw the first blow.

"Must we speak of this here?" he asked helplessly.

"We _must_," Huemac insisted, his eyes unrelenting. "I have indulged your stupidity long enough. Now you must choose: Either apprentice yourself to me, fully and completely, or go back to the life I took you from. You would soon enough gamble your way into slavery."

"That is my luck," Chiquatli muttered. "I did not ask you to save me from it."

"Your _luck_," Huemac said with disgust. "In your whole life, you have never truly looked at your luck. You have been a slave to the fears you were taught as a child; you have thrown away your luck because you do not have the courage to face it. I am offering you a chance to reclaim it."

"Why should you . . ."

"Choose! And do not think that you can betray your promise later. If I am forced to duel with you again, I will not hesitate to kill you."

Chiquatli looked down at the feathers in Huemac's hand, then up at his face.

"I will obey you," he said finally, in a low, choked voice. "But I do not think that even you can change my luck."

"It will be *your* doing, if it is done," Huemac said, and folded the cloth back over the feathers. "I will keep these for you until you have proven yourself worthy of their possession. Go now; we begin to practice seriously tomorrow."

Chiquatli turned and walked toward the entrance, not looking at the men who parted to let him pass. The men exchanged curious glances among themselves, then stared back at Huemac. But Huemac merely bowed and waved a final farewell, as if nothing unusual had occurred. He had planned to speak to Chiquatli tonight, and Azcatzin had provided him with the perfect opportunity, before the proper audience. Tomorrow the whole city would know that he and Chiquatli could not get along, and had argued openly at his feast. Let them think the worst, Huemac thought, as he turned away. Let them think it for as long as possible . . .

LATE THAT night, after the last guests had departed, Huemac had an urge to gather his family together and speak to them under the tree, as his own father had done. But he learned from the servants that Teuxoch, Cocatli, and the children were already asleep, and he found his mother sitting in the darkness beside Taypachtli, who was sleeping peacefully. Raising a finger to her lips, Ome Xochitl checked on Xolotlpilli in his cradle, then led Huemac back out into the courtyard. The night air was cool and damp, smelling of the Lake, and the stars glittered coldly in the blackness overhead.

"Her fever flared up during the evening," Ome Xochitl said of Taypachtli. "But then it broke, and began to subside. She can rest now, and she will be much better in the morning."

"The gods have been kind to me," Huemac said quietly, gazing around the deserted courtyard with a kind of wonder. "I have done nothing to deserve the people I have been given."

"You have acted with correctness," his mother said firmly. "Both as a warrior and as a man. But I saw something tonight that disturbed me greatly."

"Chiquatli?" Huemac suggested knowingly, and Ome Xochitl nodded.

"There were many standing around me who were certain that there would be a fight. They could not comprehend why you would want a man like that for your apprentice."

Huemac laughed shortly, a barking sound that echoed off the courtyard walls.

"They have forgotten the man to whom *I* was apprenticed," he said dryly. "Chiquatli will do what is required of him, when the time comes."

"How do you know this?"

Surprised by his mother's skepticism, Huemac almost spoke sharply to her. But then he realized that although he had told her what he had promised Ahuitzotl, he had not revealed any of his plans for his team. He had not yet told anyone, in fact, except for his teammate Opochtli.

"Forgive me if this sounds arrogant, my mother," he said. "But I have decided that I am going to change the way that the ball game is played in this city. That has been my intention ever since I returned from Texcoco nine years ago. Chiquatli does not yet know how well my plans will suit him, but he will learn."

"It does indeed sound arrogant," Ome Xochitl said sternly, "though not because of your ambitions toward the game. I do not doubt your skill as both a player and a strategist, and certainly you have proven yourself as a teacher. I question only your intentions toward this young man. His fear and hatred were plain to see."

Seeking to explain himself, Huemac told her of his offer of power, and how he had used it to bend Chiquatli to his will. He described, further, the combination of intimidation, surprise, and reward he planned to use to keep his apprentice in line. Before he was even finished, Ome Xochitl began shaking her head in disapproval.

"You will never win his trust that way," she stated flatly. "He will always feel that you are using him."

"What if I am?" Huemac demanded irritably. "I will give him discipline, and probably make him wealthy. Most men should be so well used."

Ome Xochitl stared at him silently, until the sound of his own ruthlessness began to echo in his ears. He dropped his eyes and shifted his feet uneasily.

"Is this the attitude with which you would enter a ceremonial game, a test of fates?" she asked. "As the captain of the team, your life would be forfeit if you lost. Can you be sure that your visions of a long life will protect you if you offend the gods in your search for power?"

"I have named my first son after Xolotl, the patron of the ball game," Huemac said defensively, and his mother's eyes flashed her dissatisfaction.

"Do you think that is enough? In Texcoco, you had to rely only upon yourself. But now you have a *team*. I am disturbed, Huemac, because I see you forgetting what you have learned in the years since the civil war. Once, you may remember, you thought that your only power lay in the fear you could inspire in others. Yet you have made friends for yourself in this city, men like Michpilli and Opochtli, and Cuetzpaltzin. And surely, the women and children in your care do not fear you. Why do you forsake trust now, when it has served you so well?"

"I do not know," Huemac admitted sullenly. "Perhaps because I did not think that it would work with Chiquatli. Or because there is so little trust in the world I have entered."

"That only makes it more precious," Ome Xochitl countered. "But I will not press you further, my son. You must converse with your own heart concerning the correctness of your intentions, and how they might best be carried out. You must do this especially in regard to Chiquatli."

Huemac looked at her for a long moment, then lowered his head and bowed deeply.

"It has been a long time since you last scolded me, my mother," he said in a chastened voice. "But I have heard you."

"I trust that you will understand my concern, and forgive my boldness. It was *I* who urged you to gather power, though I know the difficulties of its use. Will you have to contest Tizoc's team soon?"

"I have just begun; it could be years before such a match would be meaningful. Tizoc must be allowed to fail on his own for a while."

"Use your time, then," Ome Xochitl said, and looked at him with unconcealed pride. "Make yourself as correct in the eyes of the gods as you are in mine, and those of your family. I will pray for you, my son. I will pray that *this* time you will find your freedom, and it will be yours forever . . ."

LATE in the year Two-House, Tizoc returned from Metztitlan, ahead of the army, and went directly to his private place of prayer, making no pronouncements concerning the success or failure of the campaign against the Huaxtecs. The troops marched into Tenochtitlan a half-day later, unheralded by the usual fanfare of drums and criers, and the expressions on the warriors' sunburned faces silenced the crowds who turned out to greet them. They had taken only forty Huaxtec captives, and had lost three hundred of their own men. Tizoc had not even visited the front lines during the fighting, and the attack had been so poorly organized that apprentices had been forced into the battle while veterans stood idle at other places on the field. Some of the apprentices, most notably Tlacahuepan, the eldest son of Axayacatl, had performed well, but that was small consolation for the disgrace the army had suffered.

Tizoc was nonetheless crowned as the seventh Speaker of the Tenocha, and at Tlacaelel's order, a great display of power and unity was put on for the guests who attended the coronation. Nezahualpilli of Texcoco, now sixteen years old, placed the turquoise diadem upon Tizoc's head, and both he and Chimalpopoca of Tlacopan reaffirmed their loyalty to the Three-City Alliance. Similar declarations were made by the representatives of the allied and subject cities, and a vast array of gifts were exchanged during the four days of feasting that followed the coronation.

Unlike previous years, however, the traditional enemies of the Tenocha, such as the Tlaxcalans and Huexotzincans, did not even bother to respond to their invitations, and they sent no one to honor the new ruler. Other cities, especially those outside of the Valley, sent delegations that did not include their ruler or top leaders, offering pledges of loyalty in tones that reflected indifference, if not outright insolence. Though no official notice was taken of these breaches of courtesy, they did not escape the attention of Ahuitzotl, who was developing a long memory for the insults that would one day have to be avenged.

Yet a full year passed, and still Tizoc did not stir from the palace. At the insistence of the warchiefs and the heads of the warrior orders, a series of flower wars had been arranged with the warriors of Tlaxcala and Huexotzinco, but no formal campaigns were announced, despite an abundance of provocations. Tlacaelel was again said to be ill, and Tizoc used his time to further ingratiate himself with the priesthood, who had become his major source of political support. Statuary was commissioned, and the festivals of the ritual calendar were observed with great rigor and expense, though fewer and fewer captives were available for sacrifice.

Then, in the year Four-Reed, Tlacaelel called for a convocation of the leaders of all the cities under the command of the Alliance. The purpose of the convocation was to announce a major enlargement of the great Temple of Huitzilopochtli, and to enlist the aid of all those invited in the completion of this sacred task. It was a diversion worthy of Tlacaelel's manipulative genius, and it succeeded in silencing those who had begun to grow openly restless with Tizoc's lack of military initiative. Unable to question or deny the worthiness of the project, the warriors laid down their arms and helped with the hauling of timber and building stone, which had to be brought from great distances on log rollers.

Ahuitzotl was beside himself with frustration, and as a gesture of his displeasure, he allowed Huemac to be sent to Cholula as part of a delegation bearing Tlacaelel's invitation to the convocation. This was a dangerous mission, for Cholula lay close to the territory of the Tlaxcalans, whose raiding parties operated with impunity on the mountain trails leading to the holy city. Huemac's party was ambushed both going in and coming out of Cholula, but they managed to fight their way clear each time, losing only two men in the process. There were others in the group, besides Huemac, who suspected that their plans had been betrayed to the Tlaxcalans in advance, but unlike him, they blamed the treachery on the Cholulans.

After he had made his report at the palace, Huemac was summoned to the temple plaza by Ahuitzotl. The warchief stood alone on a high wooden scaffold, overseeing the men who were piling up logs and blocks of stone around the base of the great pyramid. Ahuitzotl glanced once at the fresh bandage on Huemac's arm, but no sympathy dimmed the anger in his eyes.

"I could not stand the thought of you playing on the ball court while I was here, doing *this,*" he said bitterly, as his only explanation for his sudden withdrawal of protection. He glared at Huemac as if he wished to hurl him from the scaffold onto the stones below. "What good is your cleverness now? You see how my brother taunts me! Yet you continue to waste your time in matches with the ward teams, and secret practices that require a guard around the Tlachco. You mock my trust, Huemac!"

"You promised me time to prepare," Huemac reminded him coldly. "And Tizoc has only just begun to form the team that will represent him. There is no point in contesting them now; neither team has the stature to give the game the importance it deserves."

"How long must I wait for that?" Ahuitzotl demanded impatiently, and Huemac stared at him for a moment before answering in a flat, challenging tone:

"As long as it takes."

Ahuitzotl seemed about to lose control completely, but Huemac locked eyes with him and put enough force into his gaze to make him keep his distance. He knew, too well, how vicious Ahuitzotl could be when he had been crossed, but the trip to Cholula had destroyed whatever patience he had formerly had for tolerating these fits of temper. They had become more frequent, the longer that Ahuitzotl was made to wait.

"I have made a bargain with you," Huemac said finally, hooding his eyes to break the tension between them, "and I will keep my promise. But I cannot make time move to suit you, and I *cannot* prepare my team when I am in Cholula. When the time has come to test your fortune against that of your brother, you will know it, for the whole city will be betting on the outcome."

Ahuitzotl appraised him narrowly.

"You have become bold in your predictions, and even bolder in the way you speak to me," he said in a warning tone.

"When you are the Speaker," Huemac said evenly, "I will bow before you, and touch dirt to my tongue. But do not ask me to be meek about what I have undertaken on your behalf. You would not ask a warrior to bow to you upon the battlefield."

Ahuitzotl gave him a hard look, then relaxed his face and laughed loudly.

"You are incorrigible, Huemac. No doubt you will still speak to me this way, even when I *am* the Speaker. But at least you do not try to please me with lies and flattery, like those who surround my brother. He hears nothing that would move *him* to the battlefield."

Huemac looked out over the piles of stone and the laboring groups of men, understanding from Ahuitzotl's tone that he had shed his anger and was now open to advice. The suddenness of these shifts disturbed Huemac nearly as much as the anger itself, and always made him wonder how much influence he cared to have with this tempestuous man. It seemed more and more likely that he could make himself more necessary to Ahuitzotl than his father had ever been to Tlacaelel, and thus even more thoroughly trapped. But now was not the time to be thinking of limiting his influence.

"With all these workers available," he suggested, gesturing at the busy scene below them, "would this not be a good time to suggest to Tlacaelel that he have his own face carved next to those on the cliffs at Chapultepec?"

"It would, given his age and the recent state of his health," Ahuitzotl said with a shrewd smile, and nodded for Huemac to go on.

"Your nephew, Tlacahuepan, became a warrior at Metztitlan, and he has been invited to participate in the next flower war. You should make him your favorite, so that Tizoc will not be able to use him to enhance his own prestige. Also, as your protégé, he would be less likely to challenge you at the next election."

Ahuitzotl bridled at the suggestion that *anyone* would dare to contest his right to the reed seat, but his anger passed quickly, and he accepted the advice with a curt nod.

"Yes, it is no doubt wise to guard against the future." He looked at Huemac searchingly, and saw that he had nothing more to offer. "So. When are you going to abandon this new style of yours and begin to play seriously?"

"We have not lost yet—is that not serious?" Huemac demanded, with some irritation of his own. "This is the style that will win for us, no matter whom Tizoc fields. When the time comes, it will be seen clearly that you represent the new and original, and your brother the old and discredited. It will distinguish you even further."

"You are satisfied with Chiquatli?"

"He is learning."

"But why bother with someone who needs teaching?" Ahuitzotl suggested expansively. "The Texcocan champion is available; I will hire him for you."

"I have the man I want," Huemac insisted calmly. "Your wealth would be better employed, Lord, if you were to offer bonuses for our victories. We are already becoming favorites in the betting, and I do not doubt that Chiquatli will be approached with bribes."

"I will come to your next game and award the prizes myself. That will help to identify me with the team, and it will take my mind off these *chores*. Is there anything else that you need?"

"Just time," Huemac said succinctly, looking up at the shrines atop the great pyramid. "And the favor of the gods."

WHILE THE convocation was being held in the palace in Tenochtitlan, Huemac practiced with his team on a rented court in Tlatelulco. There was a guard posted at each entrance to keep out the curious, and the only people allowed onto the court with the team were the five trusted apprentices whom Huemac had recruited as a practice team. All the other teams in the city were by now familiar with the style of play that Huemac had introduced, and many had already begun to devise strategies against it, or were altering their own styles in emulation of the team's success. But Huemac had not stopped refining his method, and there were some secrets that he did not wish to give away until the time was right.

The style had touched off a great controversy when he had first exposed it to public view, for he had done away entirely with the conventional alignment of two players close to the center line and one deep. Instead, he was alone in the front line, with the long-legged Opochtli (who, as his name suggested, was left-handed) several steps behind him and to the left, and Chiquatli, with his young powerful legs, stationed in the deep position behind them both. Their style depended on their ability to change the flow of the game at will, which they did by means of a complex series of shifts and passed shots, cued by voice and hand signals known only to themselves.

At his choice, Huemac could leave anything hit to his left to Opochtli, who could in turn pass the shot to Chiquatli, who might either volley deep or pass a soft shot forward to his teammates. At selected times, Huemac and Opochtli passed everything to Chiquatli and let him run his deep opponent ragged with volley after volley, until one of the front-line players would have to drop back to help. Then Opochtli would charge up to the front line to join Huemac in a sudden, concerted attack that usually caught the opposition off-balance.

New variations on these basic shifts were being worked out every day, especially now that Chiquatli knew that he could call for his own shot whenever he wanted it, and that his teammates would trust his judgment if he spotted an opportunity they had not perceived. Knowing that he was more than a mere backup, Chiquatli had come to take great pride in his own steadiness and stamina, a pride he reinforced every time he was able to wear out his opposite number on the other team. Already, some teams had begun moving their strongest hitter to the back line, weakening their attack in an attempt to defend against Chiquatli's booming shots. So far, none had succeeded, and Chiquatli, along with his teammates, was rapidly becoming a wealthy man, due to Ahuitzotl's generosity and the continued bad judgment of rival bettors.

Huemac ended the practice with a half-hour scrimmage against all five apprentices at once, to exaggerate the pressure of a real game, then concluded as he always did by setting up first Opochtli, then Chiquatli, then himself for a shot at the stone ring fixed high on the midcourt wall. Calling to Chiquatli to stay behind, he sent everyone else in to wash and dress, and waited for his apprentice at the center line.

Chiquatli had learned to relax in Huemac's presence, and though there was still no affection between them, Huemac had not had to speak harshly to him since the night of the feast. He has profited handsomely from his discipline, Huemac thought; but soon, perhaps, that will not be enough. He bounced the ball he was holding, watching Chiquatli approach with his customary swagger. He waited an extra moment before speaking.

"Come, now just the two of us will play," he said nonchalantly, and felt Chiquatli freeze where he stood.

"I have not disobeyed you," the young man protested weakly, and Huemac looked at him closely before smiling.

"I know that. This is your reward: I am going to teach you how to play the front line."

Chiquatli stared at him in bewilderment, knitting his brow.

"But that is not my position," he said foolishly.

"Not yet, it is not. But perhaps, late in some game, I might decide to call you up to the front line. The force with which you hit would be very distressing to a tired opponent, especially once I have taught you how to control your power."

Chiquatli regarded him suspiciously, even though he was clearly tempted by the offer. Huemac thought again, as he had many times, of what his mother had said, and he wished that he could tell Chiquatli the truth: that, at twenty-eight, he was not as young as he once was, and that his body was absorbing a tremendous beating, due to his playing alone in the front line. The cleverer teams were already hitting at him on purpose, which made the option of Chiquatli's relieving him a possible matter of survival. But Huemac was afraid that such an admission of weakness would undermine his authority, and give Chiquatli ideas about replacing him, so he let his offer stand, and did not elaborate upon his reasons.

"Perhaps you only want to prove your power over me," Chiquatli said warily. "I do not want to be humiliated again."

"I am going to *give* you power," Huemac said with annoyance. "I have already told you that. You must learn to be more accepting."

"I do not want your feathers and charms," Chiquatli blurted, with a nervous jerk of his head and shoulders. Huemac smiled at him with a conviction he did not truly feel.

"You will, when you are ready," he said, and turned to cross over the center line, wondering why that time seemed ever farther off, the harder he tried to bring it about.

WORK ON the Temple of Huitzilopochtli went forward, and several more months passed, with only a single flower war to exercise the warriors. Interest in the ball game increased as a direct result of this idleness, and the stands were filled for every game, with the betting reaching ferocious heights. Huemac's team was still undefeated, as was Tizoc's, and the time when the two teams would have to face one another was fast approaching. Ahuitzotl, at Huemac's instigation, had already begun talking up the importance of the game, describing it as a contest between the "new" and the "old," and leaving no question that the terms also applied to himself and his brother. The betting was beginning to follow political lines, giving rise to speculation about the possibility of a ceremonial game, a game of augury.

Despite the success of the team, and the constant improvement of Chiquatli, Huemac could not feel the confidence he wanted. He had scouted Tizoc's team and had seen that it was the equal of his own in talent, with perhaps a slight edge in experience and physical size. Tizoc had himself hired the Texcocan champion, so that he now had men of Chiquatli's size and strength at every position, veterans who would not be easily fooled by crossing patterns and tricky shifts. Huemac gave his own team an edge in terms of strategy and teamwork, but that only evened the odds, and left the outcome in the hands of the gods.

Realizing that he had come to the end of his cleverness, Huemac had begun visiting the shrine of Xolotl after every game, praying to his patron for guidance and making generous contributions to the maintenance of the priests out of his winnings. He sat in darkness before the image of the god, trying to shut off the scheming of his mind so that his heart would be open to inspiration. He had controlled Chiquatli through intimidation and enticement, and Ahuitzotl had helped to keep the young man free from the temptation of bribery. But Huemac had still not persuaded him to take the owl feathers and commit himself totally, and he could sense that Chiquatli was becoming increasingly distracted by his wealth, and thus even harder to reach. His mother's prediction was proving to be all too accurate, and Huemac felt trapped by his own tactics, unable to change his attitude toward Chiquatli without making him even more suspicious.

As he left the training room after his latest victory, his arms filled with the blankets and jewelry he had won, he found Azcatzin outside, waiting to walk with him to the temple, as he always did on those occasions when Huemac brought him to the game. Azcatzin was now nine years old, a year away from the calmecac, and although he was wiry and well proportioned, he was still small for his age, and probably always would be. He congratulated Huemac on his victory, and they discussed how the game had been played as they left the Tlachco and walked toward the Temple of Xolotl.

"May I go in with you, Uncle?" the boy asked unexpectedly, when they had come to the base of the stepped platform upon which the shrine stood. Huemac shifted the bundle of goods in his arms and considered his nephew seriously.

"But you have not yet been trained in the rites of penance."

"I will watch you," Azcatzin pleaded. "I will be correct in every way, I promise."

Huemac examined him for a long moment, wondering what it was he wished to pray for. Size? Strength? Or simply the chance to play on the Court of the Lords someday? He doubted that it was anything more than that, for he had tried to nurture in Azcatzin the same pure love of the game that he himself had had as a boy, before his life had become complicated by the likes of Icpitl. Still, perhaps such simple wishes were more worthy than his own. Smiling suddenly, Huemac held out the bundle in his arms.

"Take these as your offering, then," he said. "And let us go to meet the patron of our game . . ."

THE SHRINE of Xolotl was dark except for the coals that smoldered in the brazier before the altar, giving off the resinous aroma of copal and casting a reddish glow over the grimly bestial countenance of the image of the god. Clamping his jaw muscles tightly against the pain, Huemac pricked his ear-lobes with a piece of sharpened bone and flicked blood in the direction of the altar with his fingers. Then he blotted at his ears and fingers with strips of white paper, and reached forward to deposit the papers in the brazier.

Out of the corner of his eye, he saw Azcatzin go through the same ritual, handling the piece of bone with awkward determination and blinking back the tears that rose to his eyes at the sharp, stinging pain. Huemac nodded encouragingly as the boy dropped his bloodied papers into the brazier, where they flared up and vanished almost immediately into a puff of white smoke. A priest touched a gong lightly—twice—and the novitiates with him chanted in a low rhythm as they withdrew from the chamber and left the devotees to their prayers.

Huemac sat cross-legged, his arms on his thighs, his head bowed on his chest. Azcatzin, he saw, imitated him perfectly, lapsing into his own prayerful state without a second sidelong glance. Huemac allowed himself a moment of pride on his nephew's behalf, then sought to silence his own thoughts, immersing himself in the sensations of his body: the thirst in his throat, the tight, aching muscles beneath his knees and shins, the searing pain in the fleshy part of his buttocks, which were a mass of scar tissue from the daily pounding they absorbed. These, too, were his marks of penance, his offerings to the god of the game. He was taking an inordinate beating in his attempt to implement a new style, but if he was successful, *all* the teams would change, and the game would ultimately be safer and less punishing to its participants. It would also enhance the beauty of the game, favoring skill over brute strength, and Huemac hoped that this was pleasing to the god; the fact that he had so far managed to avoid serious injury seemed an indication that this hope was not misplaced.

Still, Huemac approached Xolotl with great wariness. He was no longer certain about which of the gods had helped him kill the priest and had then visited the tingling power upon him, but he had not forgotten that the Dark Twin of Quetzalcoatl was the one he had asked. Huemac did not wish to be used in that manner ever again, so he addressed the god with humility and restraint, seeking only guidance, rather than the god's active intervention. He felt that he already possessed the power to defeat Tizoc's team, but he had to be sure that he was using it correctly, in conformance with the divine will.

This restraint had placed a severe limitation on what he could offer the god in return for his guidance, and the need for a suitably serious offering had been nagging at him for months. In recalling his preparations for the game with Icpitl, he had been unable to deny the crucial importance of his struggle to relinquish his desire for Ce Malinalli. A comparable sacrifice seemed essential, since this, too, would be a game for his life. But Huemac's desires were now met within the boundaries of his marriage vows, and he had never had a taste for the vices of other men. What was there to offer, since he could not give up the people he loved, and dared not offer himself for the god's use?

Huemac's eyes blinked open in frustration, and he glanced sideways at Azcatzin, whose posture was unchanged. The boy's straight, slender body reminded him, again, of the vision he had been given by Peyotl, the One Who Glows, the vision of himself as a teacher of the game. Since the vision had also contributed to his ability to beat Icpitl, he had examined his memory of it many times, searching for hidden meanings. Always, though, he had regarded the teaching itself as a distant eventuality, an occupation to be pursued only after the completion of his competitive career. And that was at least five years off, barring injury.

But now, with the boy beside him as a living reminder, Huemac suddenly understood that the vision represented a commitment that could be made at any time, freely, as an offering. And he realized at the same time that his love for the game was a passion as great—greater, in the end—than his hunger for Ce Malinalli. He had not thought beyond the game against Tizoc's team, but the possibility of quitting would not have occurred to him in any event. He still loved the competition, and once he had established his style as the only way to play the game, he would be the undisputed master of the sport. He would be famous, and would have the power to raise the game to a new level of skill and beauty. He would finally reap the full benefits of the years of pain and dedication he had put in.

The thought of giving all this up filled him with such pain that his body shook, and he raised his face beseechingly to the image of the god. But Xolotl's jeweled eyes glittered redly in the darkness, showing no pity for Huemac's loss. It is the proper offering, Huemac thought sadly, realizing, despite his regrets, what it was that he had to do. He had to purify himself of ulterior motives and devote himself solely to the game, recapturing the single-minded dedication he had possessed as a boy. He would play each game to the utmost of his ability, as if he were an apprentice who had not yet proven himself. As a guarantee of his sincerity, he would pledge that the game against Tizoc's team would be his last. If he won, he would retire from competition and become the teacher in his vision, training generations of apprentices like Azcatzin, who would play the game with both correctness and zeal, and who would have Xolotl as their only patron.

The solution to his problem with Chiquatli seemed equally simple. He must force nothing on his apprentice, influencing him, if at all, by example alone. If that meant surrendering his authority and exposing himself to unwanted challenges, so be it. He would suffer the consequences of his former arrogance willingly, in order to further humble himself in the eyes of his god.

Huemac suddenly felt lighter, the aches and pains in his body forgotten. He did indeed have a vision to guide him, though he had been blind to it until now. A fluttering sensation started up in his stomach, giving him a moment's panic, before he recognized the feeling and assured himself that the tingling power of his youth had not returned. It was only the nervous stirring of anticipation, the anxiety of the novice before his first match. Huemac had not experienced such nervousness in years, at least since he had begun playing professionally, but it felt good to have the feeling back. It seemed a sign that the god had heard his vow, and approved of it.

Prostrating himself before the image, Huemac touched dirt to his tongue in obeisance. Azcatzin had felt his movements and had done the same, straightening up only a few moments after Huemac did. Huemac looked at his nephew with a gratitude that he could not express, and that Azcatzin would not have understood had Huemac tried. Here is the power of which my mother spoke, Huemac thought: the power that those we love and trust have to inspire us. He nodded to the boy to show that they were finished, and together they backed out of the presence of the god.

"WAR! WAR!" little Xolotlpilli cried happily as he ran across the courtyard toward his father, the copper bells around his ankles jingling wildly. Huemac saw that Papalotl had been dressing her brother up again, for Xolotlpilli's round face was painted with streaks of soot, and there was a crown of paper feathers tied around his forehead. Laughing, he caught the boy up and gave him a hug, feeling Xolotlpilli's strong little arms go around his neck to return the embrace. Despite the signs surrounding his birth, the two-year-old had always been an extraordinarily affectionate child, loving to be held and fondled. At this moment, with his senses enlivened by his recent revelation, Huemac felt that the body pressed against his own was the most precious thing on the earth, and his heart swelled with love and pride.

"What war, my son?" he asked jovially, smiling sideways at Azcatzin as he shifted the child's considerable weight in his arms. But Xolotlpilli mistook the question for agreement, and only bobbed his head more enthusiastically.

"War!" he crowed loudly, hugging his father again. Huemac now saw the group gathered under the tree, and he scanned their familiar faces affectionately: Michpilli, Ome Xochitl and Taypachtli, Cocatli and Papalotl, and his niece, Illancueitl, who had recently finished her studies at the temple. He noticed that Michpilli was standing as close to Illancueitl as was respectable, and that he stole an admiring glance at the girl even as Huemac approached. She is as beautiful as Cocatli, and my assistant is of marrying age, Huemac reflected musingly, then promptly turned his attention to what Michpilli was saying:

"The Matlatzinca have revolted again. They have killed our ambassadors and blocked the roads to Toluca. Tizoc has decided to march against them."

Nodding absently, Huemac put Xolotlpilli down and held his arms out to Papalotl, who left Cocatli's side and came toward him slowly, displaying the reserve she had developed in response to her brother's overflowing affections.

"Come, my little butterfly," Huemac coaxed. "I will be leaving you soon, and I wish to take your memory with me wherever I go."

Papalotl came to him quickly at that, burying her face in the hollow of his neck. Huemac stroked her shiny black hair and rocked her gently, aware that Michpilli was regarding him uncertainly, disconcerted by this display of fatherly emotion at such an urgent time.

"Ahuitzotl and Eztetl have given me permission to command the squadron," Michpilli said hesitantly, "if you wish to remain here with your team."

"You may have the command," Huemac said, smiling at Michpilli's reluctance to presume on their relationship. "But I will be going with you. I wish to serve Tonatiuh one last time, before I ask the Sun Priests to release me from my vows. When I return from the field, I will have to pledge myself to Xolotl."

"Show-lotl," Xolotlpilli repeated proudly, in the sudden silence that greeted his father's statement. Sensing the change in mood, Papalotl raised her face from Huemac's neck and looked around curiously. It was Ome Xochitl who spoke first:

"You are certain that this is the correct path, my son?"

"There can be no other," Huemac replied calmly. "Tizoc is himself the living image of Huitzilopochtli, whom we revere as the warrior aspect of the Sun. Therefore, his team will naturally represent the Sun in any ceremonial game, and his opponents the forces of the underworld. I can rejoin the Eagles later, but I cannot serve two masters on the ball court."

Michpilli was staring at him with open perplexity, and the faces of the others reflected various degrees of puzzlement. Only Ome Xochitl nodded with understanding and acceptance. Huemac smiled at each of them in turn, bestowing special fondness upon Azcatzin and Illancueitl and his own children.

"Do not be alarmed, my people," he said gently. "It is *you* who have given me the conviction of my actions, and the inspiration to carry them out. Perhaps someday I will be able to explain this to you so that you will understand. But you have my gratitude, and the love that fills my heart at the sight of you."

Only Taypachtli had ever heard him speak of his feelings so unabashedly, and her eyes were wet, too, as she felt her way to his side. The other members of his family crowded in around him, touching, weeping, and murmuring words of affection and loyalty. Michpilli stood by awkwardly, just outside the group, until Huemac freed an arm to reach over the heads around him and grasp his assistant's hand.

"It is for this that we live and struggle, my friend," Huemac said, as the tears streamed down his face. "It is for this that we give our hearts and lives to the gods."

⌐║|| 4 ||╒⌐

THE campaign against the Matlatzinca was organized rapidly, and the army marched out of Tenochtitlan late in the twelfth month of Four Reed, after the harvest and the feast celebrating the return of the gods had been completed. Though hampered by heavy rains and plagued by the same problems of leadership that had made the Huaxtec campaign a failure, the warriors nonetheless managed to cross over the mountains, crushing the Matlatzincan resistance easily and putting the torch to the temple in the center of the capital city of Toluca. Tizoc then arrived and took up residence in the palace of the Matlatzincan chieftain, sending his warriors out to scour the hills for those who had fled the attack. This brought him a significant number of additional captives, though it also served to encourage acts of looting and helped to lay waste to the countryside. Eventually, even the apprentice warriors balked at hunting down helpless farmers, and Tizoc was persuaded to settle the terms of peace and return to Tenochtitlan in triumph.

Huemac had taken two captives in the fighting, and he gave these to the Sun Priests as a gift, in return for his release from his vows to Tonatiuh. He surrendered his Eagle's insignia without misgivings, for he knew in his heart that he had served the god well. Nor could he believe that a defeat of Tizoc would be a defeat for the Sun, since Tizoc had served the gods of war so poorly. The rounding up of defenseless captives in Toluca had disgusted many of the veteran warriors, and immediately on his return, Tizoc had commissioned the carving of a new Eagle Vessel, ordering that his own name be inscribed above scenes depicting conquests that actually belonged to Axayacatl. Huemac no longer doubted that he served the right man, and that the fate of the Tenocha would be better off in the hands of Ahuitzotl, unstable as he was.

Tizoc was now eager to test his luck, and shortly after the year Five Flint-Knife had been ushered in, he urged that a ceremonial game be arranged immediately. But the priests attached to the Tlachco would not be pressured, and they set the match for one month hence, on the propitious day One Dog, traditionally a day on which new rulers were elected. The spoils of war, so recently the property of the Matlatzinca, were transformed overnight into the betting goods of the Tenocha lords, who wagered massively on the outcome of this fateful match.

Huemac scheduled three games for his team in the time that remained, still hoping to somehow win Chiquatli's trust. It seemed an impossible task, for the young Puma Warrior had run down several easy captives in Toluca, and then had spent the rest of his time in looting and eating. He had gotten himself visibly out of shape, but Huemac had not reprimanded him, and he had not insisted that Chiquatli accompany him during the extra running he was doing himself. This was in accordance with his vows to Xolotl, which Huemac had made official after his release by the Sun Priests.

On the morning of the first of these matches, Huemac rose and went to the shrine of Xolotl to pray. Then he returned to his house and went to the wicker chest in his room, sending Taypachtli and the children and the servants out into the courtyard. Digging down past his accumulated awards and insignia, he found the blanket Xiuhcozcatl had given him to wear in the hills. Wrapped up in it were the deer-hide pouch containing his power objects, his flint knife and sling, some net carrying bags, and the leathers he had worn against Icpitl.

Taking out the leathers, he replaced the other items, holding the medicine bag for a few moments before carefully wrapping it back up in the blanket. Then he rubbed the leathers with chia oil until their flexibility was restored and their scuffed surfaces shone, and he straightened and smoothed the tufts of hawk feathers sewn into the seams. After assuring himself that they were still serviceable, he tucked them into a neat bundle under his arm. Then he walked back out into the light of the sun, feeling the first flutter of anticipation in his stomach . . .

FROM THE very start, the match went badly for Huemac's team, even though they were heavily favored over their opponents, the ward team from Coatlan. Opochtli was still slightly hampered by an injury incurred at Toluca, and he was slow in warming up to his full potential; the first point went past him when he tried for a running shot off the side wall and missed. But the team's real weakness was Chiquatli, who had arrived for the game looking as if he had not slept the night before. The Coatlan team spotted his sluggish responses immediately and began to hit everything deep, running Chiquatli from side to side until he missed. Huemac got to touch the ball exactly twice as his team lost the first game by a score of five to one.

Either team had only to win two out of three games to win the match, and when Chiquatli's continued ineptitude put the Coatlan team up two to nothing in the second game, they relaxed and began to take frequent shots at the stone ring. This allowed Huemac back into the action, and he tied the game at two apiece with a hard thigh shot, after a Coatlan attempt at the ring had gone into the stands. In response, his opponents quickly reverted to their former strategy, sending volley after volley over Huemac's head.

Chiquatli was now playing his position with angry desperation, his face contorted in a scowl of shame. He was running and hitting better, but his timing was still poor, and his impatience made him want to accomplish too much too soon. Going for the big play, he called Opochtli off a shot at the last moment, intending to hit the ball on the run and send it over everyone's head. But he misjudged the bounce and caught the ball too low, spraying an errant line drive that hit the ducking Opochtli squarely in the back, felling him instantly.

The game was stopped while Chiquatli and Huemac knelt beside their fallen teammate, who thrashed about in agony for several moments before his breathing returned. Water was brought out to him, and while Opochtli recovered his senses, Huemac stood and looked up at the stands, which were in a tumult. Across the court, in the western boxes, he could see Ahuitzotl sitting with his nephew Tlacahuepan and several other warchiefs, including Huemac's brother, Acolmiztli. Ahuitzotl was gesticulating angrily, but the others sat looking straight ahead, ignoring the bettors who were clamoring for their attention on all sides.

They do not give us much chance, Huemac thought, turning to look up at the royal box behind him. Tizoc was seated in the midst of his retinue, which included Axayacatl's other son, Moteczuma the Younger, as well as the members of Tizoc's team. This group was laughing and exchanging further wagers, and several of their number had thrown flowers to Chiquatli as a sarcastic gesture of respect for his aim. A loss now would not hurt us greatly, Huemac thought shrewdly; their overconfidence would work to our advantage later.

But then he felt the eyes of Moteczuma upon him and stared back at the young prince, remembering the first time they had met, and the impression he had made on the boy. Suddenly his own shrewdness disgusted him, and aroused all the determination that had gone into his vows to Xolotl. Turning back to his teammates, he found Opochtli resting on one knee and Chiquatli standing with his head bowed, unable to face either of them. Huemac spoke with deliberate softness, though loudly enough to be heard over the crowd:

"So, my friends. We are losing three to two, and we are down one game. Are you ready to learn how it feels to lose?"

"No," Opochtli croaked stubbornly, looking up at Huemac with pain in his eyes.

"Chiquatli?"

The young man's face twisted miserably, and he jerked a thumb at his own chest, his voice shaking with emotion.

"It is *my* . . ." he began, but could not finish.

"I did not ask for an apology," Huemac said evenly. "I asked only if you were ready to lose. Have you wagered heavily on this match?"

Chiquatli nodded speechlessly.

"Then double your bets," Huemac told him, "and pledge all your winnings to the temple of Xolotl. He is going to help us win."

Opochtli nodded and rose to his feet, beckoning to one of the court attendants to act as their messenger. Chiquatli could only stare at Huemac, his eyes straying involuntarily to the hawk feathers fluttering on his leathers. Huemac spoke to him with exaggerated simplicity, as he might have spoken to a child:

"You must allow me to rescue us from this game. Play defensively. Pass everything forward to me, and watch what I do with it. We are going to attack, Opochtli," he said to the tall man, "and we are not going to give them an opportunity to hit over us."

Huemac paused, then again addressed Chiquatli.

"If we are successful, they will begin hitting to you again in the next game, and we will not be able to prevent them. When you hear me give the cry of the hawk, you and I are going to exchange places."

"You cannot replace me everywhere," Chiquatli said dully, and was startled when Huemac smiled and placed a hand on his shoulder.

"That is what *they* will think, too," Huemac said. "But I am not replacing you, my friend; I am giving you a chance to redeem yourself. They do not know how well you can play the front line, but *I* do. They will be very surprised at how difficult it is to take advantage of you at close range. And you do not need to fear for your mistakes, for I will be behind you."

The attendant had arrived and was awaiting their instructions, and Chiquatli saw that his teammates were looking to him to give the order. Just then, another wreath of flowers came sailing down, followed by a shouted demand to resume play. Chiquatli's eyes flashed angrily and he turned to the attendant.

"Double my stakes," he barked. "With everyone."

An enormous roar went up as the news spread through the crowd, and the noise did not abate as a ball was tossed out and the game recommenced. Opochtli rushed up to join Huemac in the front line, and the two of them launched a blistering attack that would have done credit to Icpitl himself. The Coatlan team was caught completely off-guard and swiftly lost their lead, then fell behind by a point as Huemac hit shot after shot at the man opposite him, until the man was forced to hit the ball into the stands to avoid being injured. Huemac threw himself into every shot as if it were his last, and though his opponents tried to hit over him, Chiquatli consistently passed the ball back to his captain, who renewed the assault with a ferocity that stunned the spectators nearly as much as it did the other team. When Huemac sent a low shot along the side wall and into the scoring zone, winning the game, the crowd erupted and the attendants had to be called out to sweep up the flowers that were showered onto the court.

Huemac was wringing with sweat and was close to exhaustion, but he had done what he had promised, and one look at Chiquatli's eyes as they prepared to resume play convinced him that this game would be an anticlimax. After Opochtli had scored the first point on a fine pass from Chiquatli, Huemac screamed like a hunting hawk and retreated to the back line, grinning fiercely at his apprentice as they passed one another on the run. As Huemac had expected, the Coatlan team chose to concentrate on Chiquatli rather than running Huemac deep, and they found themselves down three to nothing before they realized their error. Chiquatli played grimly, not letting up on himself even when his opponents, their defenses in total disarray, began to dodge out of the way of his shots. When the final ball bounced past the last defender, ending the match, he still remained crouched, ready for the return, until the flowers showering down upon him broke his concentration and told him that he had won.

Pushing his way through the cheering crowds that poured onto the court, Chiquatli found Huemac waiting for him at the entrance to the training room.

"I must speak with you," Chiquatli said, shouting in Huemac's ear to be heard above the noise of the crowd.

"There will be time, later," Huemac shouted back. "Let us first go to the temple, and thank the god for the luck that was granted to us."

"Yes," the young man agreed emphatically, and followed his captain down the stone stairs, into the depths of the Tlachco.

IT WAS after dark before Huemac was able to return to his house, and he forced his tired legs into a rapid walk, anxious to tell Taypachtli about his miraculous victory. But as he turned onto his street, he saw the warriors standing outside his doorway, dressed in the uniform of the Cihuacoatl's personal guard, and he slowed his pace. So . . . the Demon Heart has finally come to see his daughter before she dies, he thought, drawing himself up with dignity as he approached the guards.

"What is your business here?" one of them demanded, blocking the entrance, and Huemac glared at him silently until he saw recognition dawn in the man's eyes.

"This is my house," he said then, and the man bowed and moved aside to let him enter. Huemac heard the names of Tizoc and Ahuitzotl whispered behind him as he walked into the courtyard, turning without hesitation in the direction of the covered litter that was standing outside of Teuxoch's rooms. There were other warriors stationed at various points around the courtyard, and Huemac's family was gathered in a tight group under the tree, looking like prisoners in their own home. Huemac raised a hand to them in greeting, then walked past the cluster of litter bearers and boldly entered Teuxoch's rooms, parting the guards at the entrance with a single look.

Tlacaelel was sitting with his back against the wall, a few feet away from the bundled form of his daughter. His angular face in the flickering torchlight seemed shrunken and pared of all living flesh, an eagle mask carved from some ancient, fissured stone. His eyes fluttered open, then closed, then opened again as Huemac stepped past him to bend over Teuxoch.

"She is sleeping," Tlacaelel rasped irritably, waving him away. When Huemac instead seated himself across from him, the old man leaned forward to peer into his face.

"So. It is you."

"Welcome to my house," Huemac said in a measured tone, "to the house of Quinatzin. Would you care for something to drink, my Lord?"

Tlacaelel laughed hoarsely, then tilted his head back against the wall, as if the effort had exhausted him. Huemac watched him warily, distrusting any show of weakness. His eyes had been dim and watery, but he had recognized Huemac quickly enough.

"You have your father's manners, Huemac," Tlacaelel said lazily, "if not his wisdom. *He* did not throw his life away in a game."

"There are many who think that I will keep my life," Huemac said in the same even voice. "I am certain that you can find someone who will take your wager."

Tlacaelel laughed again and coughed into his hand.

"Do you really think that you can defeat me so easily?" he asked, when his throat had cleared. "Ahuitzotl will do my bidding as well as Tizoc. Perhaps even better."

"Is it by your bidding," Huemac asked insolently, "that Tizoc allows our prestige to erode, and brings disgrace upon us?"

Tlacaelel considered him silently, not rising to the provocation, which had been deliberate. Huemac had no real interest in angering the old man, but he did not fear it, and he had begun to find Tlacaelel's bantering tone offensive. He did not wish to be a source of amusement to his enemy, not in his own house.

"I could have you killed for such a remark," Tlacaelel said finally. "But I prefer that you meet your death publicly, upon the stone in the Tlachco. That way, the whole city will see what happens to those who conspire against me."

"And if it is Tizoc's captain who dies?" Huemac suggested, letting the question hang in the air between them for a few moments before concluding: "I would think that Huitzilopochtli's disappointment with his representative would be indisputable."

"Do not speak to *me* of the god," Tlacaelel snapped angrily, then narrowed his eyes and smiled mirthlessly. "You obviously have not heard that the

Texcocan champion, Cacalotl, has volunteered to captain Tizoc's team. He is a man you know, of course."

Concealing his surprise, Huemac shrugged ostentatiously.

"I know him only slightly. He was among the youngest of Icpitl's apprentices when I was there."

"They say that he became Icpitl's favorite after you left," Tlacaelel continued goadingly. "Until he put out one of Icpitl's eyes and ended his career as a trainer. They say that he wishes to do the same to you, because of the way that you are ruining the game."

Huemac widened his eyes, but not out of the fear that Tlacaelel was trying to inspire in him. He remembered Cacalotl as one of those who had most envied and disliked him for being Icpitl's favorite, and who had hated him even more for turning on their teacher later. The fact that *he* would be the opposing captain only confirmed Huemac's belief that this game was the result, and the culmination, of something begun long ago in Texcoco, something vitally concerned with Huemac's personal fate, whatever its repercussions for the fate of the Tenocha. Without knowing it, Tlacaelel had demonstrated, again, his lack of influence over Huemac's fate. A surge of confidence went through Huemac, and he smiled at the old man.

"Cacalotl will have his chance to test me. Just as you had yours, my Lord."

"So you think that you are through with me?" Tlacaelel inquired sarcastically, and Huemac looked at him and nodded.

"Whatever the outcome of this match," he said with conviction, "it will not be *you* who decides my fate. A win would make me untouchable, by you or anyone else. A loss would also put me beyond your grasp, once and for all. Know that, old man: If the gods claim my life, it will be *my* doing, not yours."

"No one is untouchable in my city!" Tlacaelel exclaimed violently, then leaned back against the wall, clapping a hand to his chest to calm his emotions. Huemac stared at him impassively.

"Remember that, Lord, when it is time to deal with Tizoc."

Tlacaelel's head came up, but he was breathing too hard to speak. He looked past Huemac at Teuxoch, then clapped his hands sharply, and a half-dozen attendants entered the room. Tlacaelel stayed them with a hand and turned back to Huemac.

"We have spoken for the last time, son of Quinatzin. But I will live long enough to see you suffer the wrath of Huitzilopochtli."

"Farewell, Lord Cihuacoatl," Huemac said, as the attendants lifted the old man into their arms and prepared to carry him from the room. "May you have your reward for the things that you have done upon this earth . . ."

Then Huemac was alone with his second mother, and he moved closer to her, to watch for signs of wakefulness. The presence of her father lingered in the room, cold and oppressive, and Huemac could feel the tense wariness that remained in his muscles. He had visited Teuxoch daily since she had begun to fail, and every day she had asked him why her father had not responded to any of Huemac's repeated summonings. If only she could have heard us, he thought wearily, his lips puckering at the cruel irony of his relationship to the woman in front of him.

Finally, Teuxoch stirred in her blankets, and a dim light shone in the hollows of her eyes when he bent over her face.

"Greetings, my mother," he said softly.

"My father was here," Teuxoch said in an uncertain voice, as if unable to trust her own recollection.

"I spoke with him," Huemac assured her. "We watched over you together."

Teuxoch smiled and let her eyes close, sinking back into the blankets. Then she shuddered and came to again, pain showing in the crabbed lines of her face. Huemac moved his mouth helplessly and put a comforting hand on top of the blankets.

"It will not be long, my son," she said. "Ghosts walk with me in my dreams, and the wind that blows around them is very cold."

"We are all praying for you. Even the little ones."

"The little ones," Teuxoch repeated aimlessly, her eyes blinking up at him. Then her gaze steadied, and she spoke with an urgency that seemed impossible in one so frail: "Make them Tenocha, Huemac. As I made you."

"Yes, my mother," Huemac promised, watching her slip back into unconsciousness. Tears came into his eyes, and he let them slide down his cheeks unashamedly. Ah, my mother, he thought sadly, you who wanted so much for me, and never knew who it was that stood in my way. You who raised me to be a man whom your father would admire, and only succeeded in making me a more worthy enemy for him. It has been your fate to love us both, father and son, enemies until we die . . .

Huemac shook himself and rose to put more wood onto the fire. As the flames flared up and heated the air around him, he felt the tension begin to go out of his muscles. Tlacaelel was gone, and would come no more into his life. The test that remains is with my fate, and my fate alone, Huemac thought fiercely, and drove the image of the Demon Heart from his mind. Warming his limbs next to the fire, he began to prepare himself for the man who had taken his place in Texcoco, the man who would have to die so that Huemac would one day be able to return there himself . . .

5

TEUXOCH died in her sleep five days before Huemac's final game. She was sixty-nine-years old. On the night after her funeral, Huemac had a dream. He dreamed that he was in the desert with his teacher Xiuhcozcatl, sitting beside a sweet-smelling fire of juniper sticks. They were speaking in Otomi, discussing the hunting of birds, when Teuxoch suddenly came out of the darkness and stood on the other side of the fire. Giving Xiuhcozcatl a contemptuous look, she shook a finger at Huemac and scolded him:

"What do savages know about tlachtli?"

Embarrassed by his mother's rudeness, Huemac did not want to meet Xiuhcozcatl's eyes, but he finally had to. His teacher answered the question in Otomi, without hesitation, as if they had been discussing this very thing all along.

"We know how to endure," he said gravely. "We know how to wait with our pain."

Pleased that his teacher had not been offended, Huemac turned back to Teuxoch to translate, but she was no longer there, and neither was the fire. Huemac was so startled that he jumped to his feet, and woke up.

Taypachtli was beside him, breathing deeply and regularly, and a quick sideways glance assured him that the children were also safe and asleep. But the dream lingered uneasily in his mind, Xiuhcozcatl's words seeming, upon reflection, to be a warning of possible injury. What is it that *I* will have to endure? he wondered, running his fingertips lightly over his cheeks to his eyes. The mere thought of losing his sight filled him with an overwhelming dread, and he had to struggle to hold on to his courage. Perhaps the god had planned to end his career all along; perhaps his offering had not been made in time; perhaps . . .

But Huemac had made his vows, fully knowing the risks involved. The consequences would have to be endured, the pain borne with patience. There was no other choice, except death. Closing his eyes tightly, he offered a brief prayer to both Xolotl and the gods of the hills. Then he rolled onto his side and tried to find his way back into sleep.

ON THE night before the ceremonial game, the teams and their sponsors assembled around the itzompan, the round stone at the very center of the ball court. The high priest of the Tlachco presided over the ceremony, flanked on his left by a priest wearing the blue hummingbird regalia of Huitzilopochtli, and on his right by a priest wearing the striped dog-mask and conical cap of Xolotl. Tizoc's team would represent the ball, the Sun, and Ahuitzotl's team would represent the court, the dark Underworld through which the Sun had to pass after completing its daily journey across the sky. The game would thus be a reenactment of the nocturnal struggle of the Sun to free itself from the powers of the night and rise again over the earth.

A low, three-legged brazier stood over the hole in the middle of the itzompan, and one by one the priests and players each threw a handful of incense onto the coals and drew their own blood in penance. Then, with Tizoc and Ahuitzotl kneeling with their teams on opposite sides of the freshly painted center line, the priest of the Tlachco presented each of the imitators of the gods with a ball and commanded that they be thrown toward the southern end of the court. This procedure was repeated for each of the other three directions, and once the balls had been retrieved by the priest's attendants, they were distributed evenly among the players and sponsors. The players wore only loincloths, for their leathers and sandals had been left at the temples of the gods, along with offerings of food and octli that the players themselves would eat before tomorrow's game.

"And what is it that you wish the gods to decide, Lord Tizoc?" the priest asked solemnly, when the ritual of purification had been completed.

"I ask that they confirm my right to the reed seat of the Speaker," Tizoc said in a high, nervous voice. "And that they command my brother's submission to my authority."

"And you, Lord Ahuitzotl?"

"I ask the gods to judge my brother's fitness to rule," Ahuitzotl growled in a low voice, trying to disguise his own nervousness. "And to match it against my own."

Huemac's head was bowed in an attitude of reverent attention, but he was not truly listening to the vows being taken by the two brothers. From beneath his hooded eyelids, he was watching Cacalotl, who was kneeling directly across from him. The young man had black eyes and aggressive features, and he was as large and powerfully built as Chiquatli. His head was unbowed and he was staring at Huemac with open disrespect, his lips curled in a sneer of disdain. The arrogance of his bearing, in the presence of the priests, made clear that his motives for being here were purely personal, and required no higher justification.

Despite the differences in their ages and physical appearance, though, Huemac could not help but see himself in Cacalotl. Here is the man *I* would have been, he thought with a kind of awe, had I been unable to free myself from Icpitl's influence—had I lost my jade rabbit and never returned to Xiuhcozcatl, or to the place on Tepeyac where I buried the knife. Icpitl would have made *me* the Texcocan champion, and I would have tried to drown my remorse with octli, women, and the herbs of power. In time, I, too, would have come to scorn the gods as Cacalotl does, valuing my pride above all other things, even life itself. I would be as reckless with my spirit as he is, and just as dangerous in my hatred.

"Huemac . . . Cacalotl . . ." the priest intoned. "Rise and face one another, across the stone where one of you will find his end."

Staring at his opponent with rapt recognition, as if into a mirror, Huemac fended off the hatred emanating from Cacalotl's eyes without putting any undue force into his own. He could feel, like a memory in his own nerves, the completeness of Cacalotl's belief in his own power. He has the confidence of youth, Huemac thought, and a pride that permits him no awareness of his own limitations. He cannot imagine being beaten, so he will not recognize it, and adjust, when it begins to happen to him. Believing himself to be indomitable, he will fight to the end, and be surprised when it is over. Huemac bowed deeply.

"Play well, my brother," he said. "Let us honor the gods with our performance."

"We will honor them with your death," Cacalotl said crudely, drawing frowns from the priests and a reproving glance from Tizoc. Huemac repressed a smile, glad that the young man had shattered the mirror with his foolish threat, breaking the identification between them. Now he was just another opponent, and there would be no remorse in vanquishing him. He is a person within myself who died long ago, Huemac thought, and bowed again.

"In the name of Xolotl," he said, softly but clearly, "I welcome your challenge with all my heart."

THE NOISE of the crowd above came through the walls of the training room as a low, distant rumble, a muted foretaste of the pandemonium that was to come. Chiquatli tightened the last knot on his hip protector, letting his eyes wander over the tufted owl feathers that hung from his side, to the image of the bird itself tattooed on his thigh. He had been drunk on octli when he had had the tattoo put on, as a sign of his contempt for the world into which he had been born. Now, it fused with the image Huemac had put into his mind, not a wild, terrifying creature, but a patient, sharp-eyed hunter, who swooped unerringly out of the silence to seize his prey. It was a curing ceremony that Huemac had taken him through, ridding him of the disrespect that had clouded his vision for so long, so that he might discover the powers that lay hidden within himself.

Chiquatli stood up and stretched, and the image vanished from his mind, along with the momentary solace it had provided. Despite his having rested and eaten in the usual way, his legs seemed unusually weak, and his insides felt as damp and icy as his sweating palms. *All* our lives should be at stake, he thought irritably, flexing against the weakness in his limbs. It did not seem fair to him that the cost of defeat would not be shared as equally as the rewards of victory. Huemac had taught him how to change his luck, but what if it were *his* mistakes that sent his benefactor to his death? What would his luck be worth then? It would be better to die with him than to have to live on with the guilt, Chiquatli decided, feeling his misgivings settle like knots in his muscles.

"Be brave, little brother," a voice whispered suddenly in his ear, and Chiquatli jumped in surprise, nearly striking his head on the low ceiling. He looked at Huemac sheepishly, his cheeks warming with embarrassment.

"Your reflexes, at least, are excellent," Huemac said dryly, smiling compassionately at his apprentice's nervousness. "You were thinking about your luck, were you not? You were thinking that you have asked too much of it; that, no matter how much you may have changed, you have no business in a game of such importance."

Chiquatli nodded and swallowed with difficulty.

"Yes, all that. And much more."

"You are gaining wisdom, my friend," Huemac said approvingly. "You would be a fool *not* to ask yourself these questions."

"Even if it makes me weak?"

"It makes you *ready*," Huemac corrected, his eyes bright with recognition. "Is it not better to face your doubts here, rather than on the court? If you respect them and give them a place in your heart, you will see, once we begin to play, that you have the means to resolve them."

Opochtli came up to join them, and they stood silently for a few moments, looking at one another, before Huemac spoke:

"I must tell you now, my friends, that this will be my last game. After we win today, I will not compete again as a player."

Opochtli's eyes widened, but he said nothing. Chiquatli's disappointment, though, was too keen for him to remain silent.

"But the *team*," he said in disbelief. "The work we have done together . . ."

"I will train another to take my place," Huemac assured him. "And it is precisely our work as a *team* that will win for us today. But I must act in accordance with my fate, and I have made a vow to the god that I will quit after this match. I will become a teacher of the game, and I will send my students to watch the two of you in your prime."

Chiquatli looked to Opochtli for support, but the tall man merely shrugged acceptingly before turning back to Huemac.

"You have brought us to the brink of great wealth and fame, yet you offer it all to the god," Opochtli said, with both wonder and admiration in his voice. "It is a worthy offering, Huemac, and I will be proud to serve you this last time."

"As will I," Chiquatli added quickly, wiping the disappointment from his face. Huemac smiled gratefully at both of them, then nodded once and grew serious.

"Listen, then, to my strategy," he said commandingly, sweeping them with a determined gaze. "They are an experienced team, and they have scouted us carefully; they will not be surprised by any of our shifts. But Cacalotl has decided that this is a contest just between the two of us, and he will try to attack me at every opportunity. When the time is right, I will allow him to engage me man-to-man, and that is when the two of you must do your hardest work. You must back me up, but more importantly, you must concentrate on keeping yourselves ready. I will duel with him for as long as it is necessary, but meanwhile, you must do whatever you must to stay warm and alert."

"But that is playing into his hands," Chiquatli protested. "He is not the kind of man who can be easily worn down."

"Neither am I," Huemac reminded him sharply. "And it is not *him* that I will be trying to wear down, but his teammates. Cacalotl will forget them in his eagerness to get at me, and they will forget themselves if they are kept idle long enough. They will become selfish and overeager, and forget that they must play together. But *you* must not forget."

Huemac paused to stress this last point, then addressed Chiquatli:

"When I raise my hand and give the cry of the hawk, you will exchange places with me. But as soon as you have done so, we will resume our regular style of play. Even if I have tired Cacalotl, you *must* not duel with him, do you understand? The temptation will be great, but I am placing all my trust that you will be able to resist it. Hit the first ball back with all your force, to mislead them, but then pass the second to Opochtli or me. You will be rewarded for your discipline, Chiquatli, I promise you. The ring will be open to you at the end, if you are patient."

In the silence that followed, Chiquatli raised his eyes to meet Huemac's and saw that there was no demand, and no pleading, in his captain's gaze; just the steady encouragement of his trust.

"I will wait for my moment," he promised, and was filled with pride when neither of his teammates appeared relieved, or gave any other sign that they had doubted him. The fear of failing Huemac left him abruptly, replaced by a deep, heartening sense of their mutual reliance. In whatever was to come, he would not be alone; they would decide their fates together.

"Let us go, then," Huemac said, motioning toward the stairs that led up to the court. "The gods, and the people of our city, await our appearance . . ."

CRUSHED together with her family in the box next to Ahuitzotl's, Taypachtli held tight to the jade rabbit around her neck, trying not to let the roars of the crowd bewilder her. Huemac had given her the amulet to hold for him, for luck, but Taypachtli was grateful simply to have something solid to anchor her in this din, which seemed at times to be lifting her right out of her seat.

"What is happening, Azcatzin?" she asked her nephew, who, along with his brother, had been released from the calmecac to attend the match. He was acting as her eyes, since Michpilli, on her other side, was busy explaining things to Cocatli and Illancueitl.

"Tizoc's team has just scored," Azcatzin informed her, when a pause in the game brought a momentary lull to the crowd. "They are leading three to one in the second game."

Huemac's team had won the opening game, the first of five games, or of however many it took until one team had won three games.

"Cacalotl caught Uncle out of position, and hit it past him," Azcatzin continued. "He is anticipating the shifts very well."

Taypachtli made an anxious sound that was lost in the renewed cheering of the crowd. Ome Xochitl would not have stayed home with the children and sent *me* here, she reasoned to reassure herself, if she thought that Huemac might fail. Huemac himself had confided everything to her—his vision and the vow to Xolotl, Chiquatli's conversion, his assessment of Cacalotl's personality —and he had convinced her completely of the correctness of his actions. Yet Taypachtli had felt some lingering reservation in him, some uncertainty so large and vague that he could not express it, even to himself. It was as if, now that his freedom was so close at hand, he could not recognize how it would come to him, or how he would know that it had. Always, she thought, there has been someone controlling his life, someone standing between him and his fate. To be free would be like reaching for a familiar doorway and finding that you had already passed through, into a room where there were no boundaries, and no guideposts.

"What is happening now?" she asked anxiously, as the people around her surged forward in their seats.

"Chiquatli hit an excellent shot, but it was returned," Azcatzin said in his clinical way, then seemed to realize her nervousness and took her hand comfortingly. "Do not worry, my aunt. His team will win."

"You are certain?" Taypachtli asked in a lighter voice, both chastened and encouraged by the boy's unquestioning confidence in his uncle's ability.

"I prayed for him," Azcatzin said gravely, in his deepest voice. "I prayed that he would live to teach me everything he knows. It was done correctly, at the temple of Xolotl himself."

The noise engulfed them again, but this time Taypachtli's heart was buoyed up by the voices she heard shouting her husband's name. She smiled in Azcatzin's direction and squeezed his hand gratefully.

"He will win, then," she said succinctly. "There can be no question of that now."

THE THIRD game was tied at two points apiece when Huemac decided that it was time to challenge Cacalotl. Each team had won one game, using up most of their stock of shifts and trick plays in the process, and Huemac knew that his opponents' greater size and strength would soon begin to tell if he did not change the flow of play. Cacalotl had been taunting him since the beginning of the match, jeering every time that Huemac dodged one of his hard, slashing shots. But the Texcocan had himself played with unusual restraint, passing shots and varying his timing to test Huemac and Opochtli's reactions, and generally using his teammates well. Only twice had he deliberately aimed for Huemac, and both times, Huemac had ducked out of the way at the last instant and let Chiquatli hit what proved to be winning shots. Huemac had no doubt that Cacalotl would be ready to take up the challenge.

Indeed, a grin of genuine delight appeared on the younger man's face when he saw Huemac move up toward the dividing line and hit the ball directly at him. Motioning for his teammate to leave him alone in the front line, Cacalotl sent a low, singing thigh shot back at Huemac, and the duel was joined.

Standing face-to-face in the center of the court, the two men began trading shots, scorning, by unspoken yet mutual consent, all opportunities to hit past one another. If points were going to be scored, it would be off the body of the other, or on missed shots that went into the stands. *Now* the gods will see something, Huemac thought exultantly, striking each shot with maximum force, and not backing off a step from Cacalotl's returns. The Texcocan had obviously not expected such power from Huemac, and the grin disappeared from his face as he dug in his heels and worked for an advantage.

Those who witnessed it would say later that it was the longest point they had ever seen played, and that never had two players been more evenly matched. Shot after shot flew between them, the ball a black blur that would suddenly coalesce against a deftly turned pad, flying back before the opponent could possibly ready himself. Yet miraculously, he always was. Huemac lunged and whirled, moving by instinct alone, the brightly figured floor vibrating with color beneath his eyes, which stung from the sweat pouring off his body. The range of his vision had narrowed to the tunnel of space between himself and Cacalotl, and he did not hear the screaming of the crowd. There was just the ball, the black line, and the helmeted target across from him.

Gradually, though, Huemac noticed that his opponent's shots were rising, coming in hard and high as Cacalotl dipped low to get his full strength behind the ball. Backing off slightly, Huemac was still forced to jump to get his hip in the way of the ball, and he knew that the return would come in chest-high if he tried to hold his ground. Instead, he suddenly charged the line and caught Cacalotl's return with his thigh just as the ball began to rise from the floor, driving it on a line back at his opponent's feet. Cacalotl's upper body jerked helplessly, and he grimaced with pain as the ball ricocheted off his shin and spun crazily away. Point to Huemac's team.

Golden spots swam in front of Huemac's eyes as he stood gasping, half bent over to accommodate the heaving of his chest, sweat dripping off his face onto the stone floor. The spectators were on their feet, and the other players were holding up their arms to dissuade the crowd from throwing more flowers onto the court. As an attendant brought him a towel and then began to mop up the sweat around his feet, Huemac turned to look at his teammates, who rewarded his efforts with enthusiastic gestures of support. Chiquatli even jogged in place, widening his eyes in a pantomime of alertness.

When Huemac turned back, Cacalotl was scowling at him from the other side of the line, standing impatiently while his team's healer massaged his leg. Then he pushed the man away from him and hobbled in a circle until he had restored the bounce to his movements. He, too, can bear his pain, Huemac thought admiringly, though he knew that Cacalotl would now be more intent on injuring him than ever. He also knew that he had only to hold the Texcocan off for a while longer to disrupt the rest of his team, but despite the cautionary memory of his dream, Huemac could not allow himself to think of merely playing out his advantage or protecting himself. This was a game for the gods, and it had to be played with abandon, as he had promised.

A new ball was thrown out, and Cacalotl closed with him again, concentrating now on keeping the ball low, to avoid another rush by Huemac. So Huemac began to hit high, backing his opponent up and keeping him off-balance for several moments, until Cacalotl retaliated by hitting down on the ball and sending it back on the bounce. Though the rebounds off the grooved floor were tricky to handle, they arrived with less force, and Huemac was grateful for the respite, for his knees, hips, and buttocks were beginning to throb from the pounding they had already absorbed. He is feeling it, too, Huemac told himself, shutting his mind against the pain.

Cacalotl was too strong, though, to be kept at bay forever, and soon he had closed the gap between them and was again coming through the ball with all his power. He began to raise the trajectory of his shots little by little, rocking Huemac backward, and daring him to make another charge. But Huemac held his ground, taking blow after blow, until finally the ball came in too high to handle, and he was forced to duck out of the way and let Chiquatli make the deep return.

As the ball was chased down and passed forward to Cacalotl, Huemac could hear the sudden amplification in the noise of the crowd, and he knew that Cacalotl would be sensing the kill. Patience, he told himself, gathering his courage for the coming onslaught. Cacalotl attacked him mercilessly, as expected, and Huemac fought him off as best he could, making no effort to disguise his desperation. The Texcocan's teeth were bared, as if he could taste victory, and when Huemac saw him coil his legs under him, he knew that it was now or never. Throwing up his arms to distract Cacalotl's attention, he made an exaggerated lunge forward, faking a rush to the line, then pulled himself back abruptly, almost losing his balance in the effort. Perceiving only the first movement, Cacalotl changed his shot at the last instant, sending back a low liner designed to catch Huemac in the midst of his charge. Then he charged forward himself, only to find Huemac where he was, and the ball coming back at him waist-high. Unable to check his own momentum, he threw himself to the side, and the ball caromed off his hip protector and went into the stands.

Four to two, Huemac, with only one point needed to seal the victory. Again, the attendants had to come out to clear the court and bring towels to the players. Opochtli came up to Huemac, who was swaying on his feet. He inclined his head toward the opposing team, who were arguing among themselves, the other two players obviously trying to convince Cacalotl to allow one of them to return to the front line.

"We have won," Opochtli said. "Let us return to our regular style of play. It is for *you* that I ask this."

"Not yet," Huemac said, dazed but determined. "If Cacalotl has his way,

I must accommodate him. He is almost convinced that it is only *me* he must beat. Be ready to back me up, and tell Chiquatli to prepare himself."

Opochtli did not argue, and Huemac let him take the first shot when the new ball came in. Cacalotl had won *his* argument, and he stood alone in the front line, a vengeful expression on his face as he waited to resume the attack. One of his teammates stood behind him with his hands on his hips, and Huemac took heart from the man's obvious disgruntlement, telling himself that all he had to do was wait, and endure.

Cacalotl engaged him warily, mixing up his shots to avoid falling into a recognizable pattern, and watching Huemac's reactions carefully. Seeing a way to turn this hesitancy to his own advantage, Huemac began to use every form of deception he had ever learned from Icpitl, feinting to mask his true intentions, and making his shots as unpredictable as possible. He was able to rest himself in this way, but as the pain in his body diminished and strength began to flow back into his legs, shame overtook him. This was the old style of play, the style he had vowed to supplant; he could not return to it now and hope to keep the gods' favor. He had been lucky so far, but only, he felt, because he had not backed off from punishment.

Even as he thought this, he sprang back to the attack, nearly overpowering Cacalotl with the suddenness of his reversal. Again the ball began to fly between them, as both players pushed themselves past their limits to maintain the intensity of the exchange. There was a roaring in Huemac's ears that was not coming from the crowd, but he disregarded it as he disregarded his pain, losing himself in the game, feeling nothing but the sudden, shocking impact of the ball against his pads. I am going to *win,* he thought wildly, unleashing a shot that made Cacalotl wince and recoil as it slammed off his pads. Huemac hit the return with a slashing motion of his knee and advanced toward the line behind it, certain that he had his opponent on the defensive.

Unable to retreat in time, Cacalotl threw himself desperately at the ball, flipping himself onto his back as he miraculously connected with his thigh. The ball came flying up at Huemac's stomach with incredible force, and as he brought himself to a skidding halt, his sandals slipped on a wet spot on the floor—dampened by his own sweat—and he fell backward, throwing up his hands to protect himself. The ball struck him as he fell, smashing his left hand back into his chest with a force that hurled him to the ground.

When Huemac's head cleared, he was lying on his back, and there was an enormous, crushing pain in his hand. Opochtli and Chiquatli helped him to sit up, holding him upright when a sudden dizziness made him retch and vomit onto the floor beside him. Water was lifted to his lips, and after he had cleansed his mouth and drunk a little, he felt well enough to allow the healer to tend to his broken hand. Gritting his teeth against the pain, he commanded that it be bound tightly, and then had his teammates lift him to his feet and walk him around until the heat returned to his body. With an arm looped over each of their shoulders, he made a slow circuit of the midcourt area, followed by the eyes of the now-silent crowd.

"Forgive me, my friends," he said hoarsely. "I forgot that it is *we* who must win this game. Now we must return to our game."

"Are you strong enough to play the deep position?" Opochtli asked, reluctantly releasing Huemac's arm so that he could stand on his own. Huemac tested the bounce in his legs, holding his bandaged hand close to his chest.

"I still have my legs," he averred, seeing the concern in their eyes. "Whatever I cannot hit back, I will pass forward to the two of you. We are a *team*, are we not? I will give the signal to you, Chiquatli, as soon as the ball is put into play."

"I am ready," the young man said fervently. "And I have not forgotten our plan."

"It will bring you glory," Huemac promised him, and smiled through his pain. "Let us go and claim it . . ."

The crowd broke out in amazed shouts when Huemac again took up his place in the front line, opposite Cacalotl, whose eagerness to take up the attack was all too apparent. But when the new ball was thrown in, Huemac raised his good hand over his head and screamed like a hawk, and Chiquatli came up to take his place. Shouting contemptuously, Cacalotl tested his new opponent immediately, giving Huemac time to run back to his position. Chiquatli returned the shot easily, and then the second one as well, shouting back at Cacalotl as if he intended to take up the duel on Huemac's behalf. But with a hand held behind his back, he was already signaling Opochtli, and when the ball came back, the two of them ran a crossing pattern, with Chiquatli screening for the running shot that Opochtli slammed off the side wall to Cacalotl's right. The ball ricocheted off the wall and bounded between the two startled deep men before they could move for it, rolling all the way into the scoring zone at the far end of the court. Five to three, game to Huemac's team.

The crowd surrounding the royal box had grown very quiet, and one of Cacalotl's teammates had joined him in the front line and was refusing to move, turning his back on his captain's arguments. Huemac saw it all from his place in the backcourt and raised his eyes to the sky, thanking the gods for the favor they had shown to his team. He held his throbbing hand over his heart, letting the joy in one assuage the pain in the other, knowing that there was no pain great enough to defeat him now.

His opponents began the fourth game with a half-hearted attempt to force Huemac into a deep volleying game, but he stubbornly ran everything down and passed it forward, wobbling like a wounded hawk yet letting nothing by. Chiquatli and Opochtli kept shifting constantly, calling and signaling to each other with an assurance that impressed even Huemac. Cacalotl continued playing with astounding energy, but he had only moving targets to shoot at, and his teammates, in their frustration, stopped passing to him when they had shots of their own. As their attack lost all coordination and they fell behind in the score, they began to shoot for the stone ring, hoping for the once-in-a-lifetime shot that would win everything. But Huemac's team kept the ball in the center of the court, and very quickly they were leading four to nothing, as Cacalotl and then one of his teammates hit the ball into the stands in vain attempts at the ring.

From his deep position, Huemac had seen Chiquatli pass up three good shots at the ring himself, each time playing it back so that his opponents would have no shot of their own. The crowd had fallen completely silent, drawing in a collective breath every time a shot went up at the ring. Deciding that it was time his apprentice was freed to take his own chance, Huemac tightened his throat and let out a high, descending wail that echoed off the stone walls and caused the spectators to recoil in their seats.

"The ring, Chiquatli!" Huemac called. "It is yours!"

Chiquatli glanced back over his shoulder at the signal, then took a few steps backward and to his right, giving himself a better angle at the ring. When the next shot came deep to Huemac, he looped it forward to Chiquatli, who timed the ball's bounce and ran beside it for a few steps before slashing upward with the side of his knee. The crowd gasped as the ball slammed off the side of the ring and fell back into Chiquatli's court, and then they broke their silence with applause for the near miss, cheering even though the try had cost Huemac's team a point.

"Again!" Huemac shouted encouragingly, and Chiquatli tried once more off the toss-in, this time putting the ball clear over the stands. He played more conservatively after that, leaving the ring's temptation to his opponents, who seemed certain to put one of their own into the stands to end the match. But Cacalotl's next shot hit the wall below his ring and came all the way back to Huemac, who again screeched like Chiquatli's namesake as he passed the ball forward. The angle was perfect, and Chiquatli's swooping thigh shot was a masterpiece of timing and execution. As the ball arched toward the ring, Huemac thought that he was finally going to see one go through, and he held his breath along with everyone else.

Then—almost too fast to see—the ball passed *over* the ring, causing the line of craning faces along the top of the wall to fall backward in a wave. But even as the judge was gesturing to indicate that there had been no score, the ball curved in its flight and fell back into the court, missing the top of the side wall by less than the width of a finger. Cacalotl's team had all been staring upward, too, and they jerked in unison as the ball landed and took a gigantic bounce toward the end zone, sailing over the head of the last man who could possibly reach it, who nonetheless flattened himself against the wall in his attempt. The match was over; the gods had made their choice.

THE TRAINING room used by Huemac's team was a scene of loud celebration afterward, except for a small screened-off area in the rear, where Huemac lay on a table with his eyes closed, breathing deeply while the healers labored over the task of splinting his broken hand. It was the same hand he had injured in Michoacan, but this time it was much worse; he could tell that by the pain alone, even without listening to the daunted tone of the healers' consultations. I am through as a warrior as well as a ball player, he thought; I will never have the strength to hold a bow or a shield. Xolotl has freed me more completely than I ever dared to hope.

The tightening of a bandage filled his head with a red burst of pain, obscuring his thoughts, and he began to drift, the noise of the celebrants outside blending into a single sound, a humming pressure against his ears. Images from the match's concluding ceremony rose to the surface of his mind in vivid fragments: The heavy obsidian blade glittering in the sunlight . . . Tizoc frozen in the background, his stricken face the color of ashes . . . Ahuitzotl standing beside Huemac, giving off a heat equal to his own . . . the wide brown eyes of young Moteczuma as he unconsciously shrank away from his uncle's side.

And then the blue-feathered priest of Huitzilopochtli raising the knife to the Sun, the swift, shining arc of its descent, the bright vermilion blood splashing over the edges of the itzompan as the wildly staring head of Cacalotl rolled from his body . . .

Huemac felt the healers finish their ministrations and leave him, and he opened his eyes to see Ahuitzotl standing over him. The warchief stared at him blankly for several moments, as if he did not recognize him, or was not sure that he was human.

"You have paid dearly for our victory, my friend," he said at last. "Now it is *I* who am in your debt."

"Yes," Huemac said, softly but emphatically, and Ahuitzotl laughed.

"I am glad that we are agreed," he said jovially, and helped Huemac to sit up on the edge of the table, steadying him with a hand before stepping back to examine his face.

"Opochtli has told me that you will not play again. Is this true?"

"I made a vow to the god. From now on, I will only *teach* the game."

"And?" Ahuitzotl inquired with unusual tact, nodding slightly toward Huemac's bandaged hand.

"I will not fight again, either," Huemac said bluntly, without self-pity. "I will ask to be readmitted to the Eagles, so that I may train others, but I have no illusions about joining them on the battlefield."

Ahuitzotl crossed his arms on his chest and cupped his chin with a hand.

"You are not yet thirty; that will not be enough for a man of your talents," he said thoughtfully. "You know that I will soon be the Speaker, and you know my desire to restore our city to its full power. I will need good men to help me manage the affairs of our people."

"There is only one favor that I would ask of you, Lord," Huemac said decisively, "and I would like to ask for it now, since it would be impossible later to deny the request of the Speaker."

"Speak, and it is yours."

Huemac stared at him for a long moment, as if to give him a chance to reconsider his promise. Then he nodded and spoke in a flat voice:

"Do not ever ask me to serve you in the palace. In any other way, I am yours, but I do not wish to inhabit the world of my father."

Ahuitzotl's disappointment was apparent in his face, and for a brief instant, anger came into his eyes. But then he sighed and let his shoulders drop in a shrug of resignation.

"You do not trust me," he said ruefully, "because of the way I forced you into my service."

"It was my fate to serve you," Huemac said simply. "But now there are other things I must pursue. I am like the caged birds in the Totocalli: My powers are wasted in confinement."

"I understand your feelings," Ahuitzotl admitted reluctantly, "for it is the way I have felt for all these years, while the reed seat was being denied to me. I know that when it is mine, I will regret having granted you this favor, but you have it with my gratitude. Do whatever it is that you must, Huemac, but do not hesitate to approach me again if you change your mind."

Holding his hand carefully out of the way, Huemac bowed to show his own gratitude.

"Thank you, my Lord. May the gods grant you the glory you wish to bring to our city."

"They will," Ahuitzotl vowed fiercely. "They will be pleased to see that the Tenocha have not forgotten their mission, and their destiny!"

"Yes," Huemac murmured absently, thinking of his own vision of that destiny, and of the fact that he was now free to pursue its meaning. Then he roused himself and held out his good hand so that Ahuitzotl could help him to his feet.

"Let us join my teammates and drink to our victory," he suggested. "And to the future we have won."

IX

LESSONS

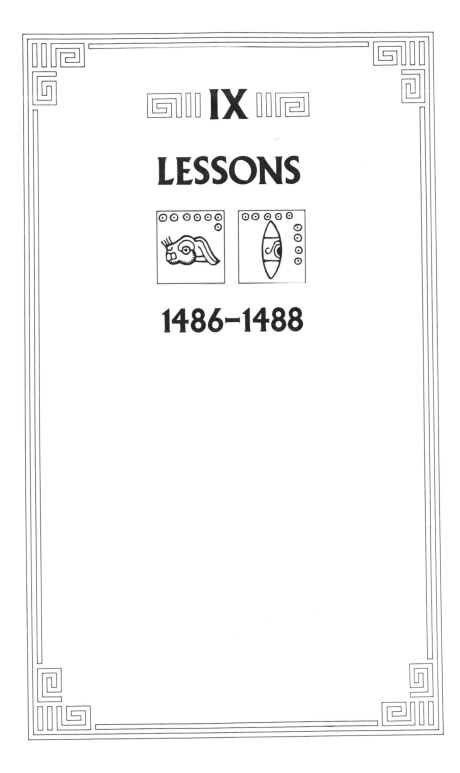

1486–1488

1

A COOL breeze blew from the north, riffling the waters of the Lake and sending wispy white clouds scudding by overhead. The heavy dugout canoes bore steadily eastward, propelled through the choppy water by the strong, rhythmic strokes of their paddlers. Huemac sat in the lead canoe with the other senior members of his delegation, watching as the city of Texcoco loomed ever larger ahead. It was the year Seven-Rabbit, fourteen years since he had left Texcoco, at the age of seventeen. Now he returned wearing the white plumes of an ambassador, bearing the greetings and the invitation of the Speaker-elect of the Tenocha, Ahuitzotl, to the ruler of the Acolhua, Nezahualpilli.

Shifting to his knees, Huemac raised his face into the fine cool spray coming over the bow, feeling the residual fatigue in his body. Only two days earlier, he had returned from Ahuitzotl's coronation campaign, an extended foray against the Mazahua cities of Xiquipilco, Chiapan, and Xilotepec. Huemac had served as a rear-guard commander, arranging the reserves and committing them to battle at the proper time, but taking no part in the fighting himself. Still, Ahuitzotl had driven the troops harder than they had been driven in years, and his constant presence had placed a heavy demand upon his commanders to drive themselves even harder. The field had not been abandoned until all three cities had fallen, and over a thousand captives had been obtained for the coronation ceremonies.

But Huemac had not been able to plead fatigue when Ahuitzotl had appointed him to carry his invitation to Nezahualpilli, and neither had he brought up the fact that he lacked the proper rank to head such a delegation. This was Ahuitzotl's way of showing his continued favor, and after having specifically rejected any role as an adviser, Huemac had not considered it prudent to correct the ruler on matters of protocol. Besides, Ahuitzotl had already shown that he intended to rule according to his own inclinations, moving his friends and favorites into positions of power without much regard for their previous status or training.

The canoes were met at the docks by a procession of high-ranking Texcocan officials, who led the delegation through the crowded streets to the Cillan, the Royal Palace. There, in the Council Chamber, Nezahualpilli sat in state upon a raised seat covered with jaguar skins, surrounded by his lords and advisers. He bore a striking resemblance to his father, and even at a distance, Huemac could feel his power and intelligence, and his sensitivity to everyone around him.

After the requisite greetings had been exchanged, and long speeches had been made inviting Nezahualpilli's participation in the coronation ceremonies, Huemac came forward alone and touched dirt to his tongue before the young king. Nezahualpilli had just turned twenty-one, and though he had been the titular ruler for almost fourteen years, he had only recently been able to claim the full regalia and titles of his father. He was tall and slender, as Nezahual-coyotl had been, though on closer inspection, Huemac found him more handsome than his father, the length of his features being less pronounced.

"Greetings, nephew," he said lightly, the memory of their first meeting alive in his eyes. Huemac smiled, feeling the probing force of those eyes and matching it easily with his own.

"Greetings, my uncle," he replied with equal irony. "You must excuse my lack of rank in heading this delegation. My Lord, Ahuitzotl, honors me beyond my deserts."

"I am always pleased to receive a kinsman," Nezahualpilli said smoothly. "And I am doubly honored to greet the man who vanquished our champion. There is no need for apology, Huemac, for you are a most famous man."

Huemac accepted the flattery with a gracious bow, impressed, despite himself, by the ease and elegance of Nezahualpilli's manner. He had not been made to feel his own crudeness so keenly in years.

"And how is Ome Xochitl, your mother?" Nezahualpilli asked.

"She is over sixty years of age, my Lord, but she is well, and she asks to be remembered to you and those of your family."

"And your wives?"

"I have but one wife, Lord . . . "

"Only *one*?" Nezahualpilli interrupted incredulously, having already taken several wives of his own, including a niece of Tizoc's and one of Axayacatl's daughters. Huemac continued smiling, but he put a stern edge of warning into his eyes, to remind the young man that he was still his senior, at least in terms of age and experience.

"It is my choice, Lord," he said evenly. "There is no other who could possibly compete for the favor of my heart."

"That is most unusual, but praiseworthy," Nezahualpilli decided, seeing from Huemac's eyes that the offer he had been about to make would not be appreciated. He rose abruptly from his seat and gestured to include the entire delegation.

"Come, my friends, you must share food with me, and see the gardens I am building . . ."

Throughout the elaborate meal that followed, Nezahualpilli praised Ahuitzotl and the renewed boldness he had brought to the Tenocha, and he repeatedly expressed his enthusiasm for the campaign against the Huaxtecs that Ahuitzotl had proposed as the next undertaking of the Alliance. Huemac listened politely, aware, as was everyone present, that it had taken the young king until the age of nineteen to prove himself as a warrior, and that there were many, even among his own people, who still questioned Nezahualpilli's appetite for warfare. Huemac did not share this skepticism, but he had to wonder if this urbane young man, so at home with the niceties of protocol and politeness, was really prepared to meet the expectations of a man like Ahuitzotl.

As to Nezahualpilli's skill as an architect, there could be no question as he led them through the palace gardens, which he had enlarged and made superior to anything constructed by his father, with secret grottoes hidden by waterfalls and arbored bridges arching gracefully over pools filled with water lilies and exotic fish. Leaving the others to admire the flowers, he asked Huemac to accompany him, and the two of them ascended to the top of the viewing tower that Nezahualpilli had built for himself in the corner of the courtyard. The platform at the top was barely large enough for two men, and it was here that the young king came alone, at night, to perform his penances and observe the stars.

From this height, the whole city was spread out beneath them, the many temples thrusting their brilliantly painted shrines up out of the maze of gleaming walls and rooftop gardens, the orderly rows of maize and maguey marching into the shadows of the distant hills. Huemac could feel the pride in the young man standing so closely beside him: a calm, unassailable pride unlike anything known to the Tenocha, based as it was on an inheritance carefully preserved for many generations, rather than upon a legacy still in the making. Again, Huemac admired the wisdom and courage, and the vision, that had brought Nezahualcoyotl back out of the hills to reclaim the city of his fathers. Then he turned to meet the eyes of his grandfather's heir, who was examining him curiously, without any pretense of kingly distance.

"You must speak frankly with me, Huemac," he said, "as your father did with mine. You must tell me of the man who sent you here; I do not know him as well as I would like."

Huemac nodded agreeably, pleased that it had been stated as a request rather than a demand, and secure in the knowledge that his refusal to serve in the court protected him from ever having to perform the function his father had for Nezahualcoyotl.

"Ahuitzotl is a wild beast who has been caged for too long," he said with deliberate bluntness. "Yet he is also a man, with a man's need for respect, and an equal capacity for revenge. He is not the kind of man who will tolerate equivocation on the part of those he calls his friends."

"I will remember that," Nezahualpilli said judiciously, then hesitated for several moments before asking his next question: "And what is your opinion of how Tizoc died?"

"You have no doubt heard the same rumors as I, my Lord," Huemac said easily. "Does it truly matter if it was the work of sorcerers, or of a subtle poison? The gods had deserted him, and so, obviously, had all those who might have protected him."

"Including Tlacaelel?"

"In *my* city," Huemac said pointedly, "even the Cihuacoatl must bow to the wishes of the war gods. We are the chosen people of Huitzilopochtli, and we serve him above all others."

Nezahualpilli nodded and turned his eyes back over the city, seeming to focus on the nine-storied temple that his father had dedicated to Ometeotl, the God of the Duality, so long ago. Huemac stared at the black shrine covered with silver stars, the shrine that contained no image, and he was struck again by the vast difference in the traditions that he and his companion had separately inherited.

"Moyocoyani," he murmured softly, recalling that it was in defense of this temple that his grandfather had come to Tenochtitlan at the time of their first meeting. He turned back to find Nezahualpilli regarding him with fresh appreciation, the curiosity tinged with empathy.

"You were also trained here, Huemac," he said suggestively. "Have you gained all the knowledge you wish to possess?"

"No, my Lord," Huemac admitted without hesitation. "I had thought that perhaps I might see my teacher while I am here. His name is Xiuhcozcatl, the Turquoise Necklace."

Nezahualpilli raised his eyebrows and seemed to stiffen slightly.

"He has not been seen since my father died. It is said that he lives in the hills, among the Otomi and the Chichimecs."

"I will have to come back and find him, then," Huemac said resolutely, politely ignoring the faint tone of disapproval, or disappointment, in Nezahualpilli's voice. "Perhaps, Lord, sometime after the Temple of Huitzilopochtli has been dedicated, you could ask that I be sent to you. I could repay your kindness by sharing my knowledge of tlachtli with the ball players of your city."

"I will be pleased to do so," Nezahualpilli replied, almost too quickly. "You could even return with me after the coronation, if you so desire."

"I am grateful, Lord, but I must see to the marriage of my niece, and one of my nephews is about to be inducted into the pochteca. Besides," he added, holding up his crippled hand, "the armies will be marching soon after the coronation, and though I can no longer fight, my leadership will be needed."

"Yes, and mine, as well," the king agreed. "But I will not forget your request. I would like to be your friend, Huemac, and speak with you on matters other than the relations between our cities. I can tell that you, too, have been touched by the winds from heaven."

Nezahualpilli's eyes were glowing, and Huemac felt himself being drawn in against his will. Yet he was also tantalized, and he knew that he was not resisting the pull with his whole heart. It had been a long time since he had met anyone who understood these things. Too long, he thought with a flash of fear, which broke the spell. Huemac drew back respectfully, making a short bow in the space permitted to him.

"Forgive me, my Lord," he said humbly, "but you overestimate my powers, which I have not used in years. I am honored by your offer of friendship, and I accept it gratefully. But my training was very limited, and I must prepare myself to be able to converse with you adequately."

Nezahualpilli seemed slightly surprised, but not disappointed by the answer.

"I respect your prudence," he said simply. "And I have seen enough to know that we *will* talk, and be friends. Let us return to the others now, and go with them to the Temple of Huitzilopochtli, to make an offering to your god. We must prepare ourselves for the wars that Ahuitzotl is making for us."

"That is more than prudent, my Lord," Huemac agreed, and followed the king down the steep observatory steps, descending in stages to the earth below.

THE MARRIAGE of Michpilli and Illancueitl took place shortly after the coronation of the new Speaker, in the house that Michpilli had been given by Ahuitzotl himself, as a reward for the exceptional valor that Michpilli had displayed in the recent campaign against the Mazahua. At the age of twenty-four, Huemac's former apprentice was now a member of the Tecuhtli, the warrior lords, as well as a full captain in the Eagles.

On the fifth day after the ceremony, Huemac and his family prepared themselves to return to Michpilli's house for the wedding feast. Leaving Taypachtli to her dressing, Huemac went out into the courtyard to find his children, conscious of how little time he had had with them lately, and of how much less he might have in the future. Papalotl was already seven and Xolotlpilli five, and after the effort that Huemac had expended to free himself, he was determined to share in their growth as much as he could.

His daughter was standing under the huehuetl tree with her friend Pinotl, the son of the vanguard merchant Cuetzpaltzin, and Huemac stopped for a moment to admire her, amazed as always that he had fathered such a beauty. He did not think that it was solely a father's pride that made the combination of her round cheeks and golden eyes seem so irresistible, and he had seen the way that other adults took special notice of her.

The dark-skinned little boy standing next to her made an odd partner, for Pinotl was every bit as homely as she was striking. He had the hooked nose, receding chin, and high sloping forehead of his Huaxtec mother, and his sleepy, hooded eyes and slow speech made him appear stupid. His name, the Stranger, seemed to suit him well, though Huemac had come to realize long ago that he was just as quick of mind as Papalotl, and probably more observant.

The two older children were talking to Xolotlpilli when Huemac came up, and it was obvious from the tone of the conversation that Papalotl was displeased with something that her little brother had done.

"He has given away his armbands, Father," she complained to Huemac. "The ones Aunt Cocatli made for him."

"I did not give away!" Xolotlpilli protested vigorously. "I traded!"

"For what did you trade, my son?" Huemac asked gently, squatting beside the sturdy little boy, who was already nearly as tall as his sister. Xolotlpilli's wide brown eyes blinked rapidly, showing his dread at the possibility that his sister—as usual—was right.

"For this," he said defensively, holding out the painted wooden flute that he had been hiding behind his back. "It is the flute of Tezcatlipoca himself!"

"It is not," Papalotl said, with the cold certainty of her superior age and wisdom. "You have been cheated again."

"The boys who did this were older than he is," Pinotl broke in unexpectedly, in his flat, uninflected voice. "They all pretended to want the flute very much, but then they let Xolotlpilli win the bidding."

"Why did you not stop them?" Papalotl demanded, turning her righteous indignation upon Pinotl, who veiled his eyes and seemed to become somehow indistinct in the face of her accusatory glare.

"They were Tenocha"—he shrugged—"and I had not been invited to participate in the bartering."

Tears suddenly appeared in Xolotlpilli's eyes, and he threw down the flute and balled up his meaty little fists, his lips curling back in a truly threatening snarl.

"I will get them back," he vowed, and would have gone off immediately to seek his revenge had Huemac not restrained him. Huemac chose his words carefully, for this was not the first time that something like this had happened, and he knew how much it hurt his son to be thought stupid.

"No, my son, you must not go back on your bargain once it is made. Is that not correct, Pinotl?"

The older boy nodded emphatically, still avoiding Papalotl's eyes. Huemac picked up the flute and turned it over in his hands, speaking to all of them:

"Once, I knew a man in Texcoco, and I gave him my finest mantle, my good leather sandals, and all the contents of my pouch. And do you know what he gave me in return? An old blanket with a hole in it for my head, some gourds of water, and a sack of toasted maize!"

Even Xolotlpilli understood the foolishness of this trade, and all three children looked at Huemac with varying degrees of astonishment and disbelief on their faces.

"But you see," Huemac continued calmly, "that man was my teacher, and the blanket kept me very warm when he took me with him into the desert, and the maize and water soothed my hunger and thirst as nothing in my pouch could have. I learned many things from that man, and I never regretted the bargain I made with him."

Huemac could see that Xolotlpilli was still slightly baffled, but the tone of the story had calmed his anger and made him forget that he wanted to cry.

"Now, my son," Huemac said patiently, "you must learn from these boys, as I did from my teacher. You must come to know the value of things, and you must not be so eager to possess the things that are prized by others. From now on, you should ask your mother or sister, or Pinotl, before you barter away the things that are yours."

"Yes, Father," Xolotlpilli promised, with such aching sincerity that Huemac felt a pang of remorse, and wanted to embrace his son and tell him not to worry about anything. Xolotlpilli was such a kind and generous child that it did not seem right to teach him calculation and distrust. Yet Huemac also knew that the boy had to learn these things or he would *always* be left with no recourse but revenge. Given his size, it would not be long before he hurt one of the other boys, and made himself a pariah.

"This is a nice flute, nonetheless," he said, handing it back to the boy. "Your mother or grandmother could no doubt teach you how to play it, if you asked them. And perhaps, if you played a tune for her, your Aunt Cocatli would forgive you for trading away her gift."

Xolotlpilli put the painted tube to his lips and blew a single, quavering note that made them all laugh.

"That is enough for now," Huemac said lightly, seeing, out of the corner of his eye, Taypachtli emerge from her rooms. "Here is your mother. Let us forget these things and be joyful, so that we may properly celebrate your cousin's marriage."

"YOU MUST be more patient with your brother," Ome Xochitl said later, after Papalotl had finished telling her and Cocatli about the bartered armbands. The three of them were sitting in a circle beside the hearth in Michpilli's house, filling thinly rolled maize cakes with ground meat for the feast that was going on outside in the courtyard.

"He is younger than you are," Ome Xochitl continued, "and he does not learn as quickly. You must be kind to him, as Cocatli was to your father when *they* were children."

Papalotl gave her aunt a puzzled look, as if trying to imagine her as a child, and Cocatli smiled and shook her head with mock exasperation at the memory.

"Your father looked up to me as Xolotlpilli does to you, but he also used to play tricks on me with his voices, and jump out at me from dark places. You should be grateful that *your* brother is not so mischievous."

"I will try to be better," Papalotl promised, more to Ome Xochitl than her aunt. Her attachment to Cocatli was deep and abiding, but so was her curiosity, and she had recently discovered that her grandmother knew things beyond the range of what her aunt was interested in teaching her, which had mostly to do with the rituals of the priests and priestesses. Papalotl took a certain illicit pleasure in plumbing this new source of information, a feeling that was heightened by Cocatli's presence, and which made her hesitate. But then the question overwhelmed her loyalty, and she put it directly to Ome Xochitl:

"What did Father do in the desert? He told us today that he learned many things there."

"His grandfather, Nezahualcoyotl the king," Ome Xochitl explained easily, "sent him there to learn the secrets of the plants and wild creatures. He lived for a while among the hill-people, and learned the ways of our ancestors, the Chichimecs."

"Chichimecs?" Papalotl repeated doubtfully. "But the Toltecs are our ancestors, are they not? That is what they teach at the temple."

"They are *both* our ancestors," Ome Xochitl said. "That is another thing your father learned in the desert."

"Will he take *me* there?"

The two women exchanged a silent glance, and Ome Xochitl nodded to her daughter to speak first.

"You are too young for such a thing now," Cocatli said, "and you have been promised to the priestesses when you reach the age of ten. That is only a few years off; I doubt that you will be given the opportunity to travel."

"But *after* I leave the temple?" Papalotl insisted hopefully. "Perhaps he will take me there before I am married."

"Your father has been speaking to you of marriage?" Ome Xochitl asked in a neutral tone, feeling Cocatli's palpable disapproval of the notion.

"I *told* him that I was promised to the temple," Papalotl said, with an anxious glance at her aunt. "But he said that there are many ways to serve the god. He said that *you* had married, my aunt."

"It will be up to the god to decide," Cocatli conceded grudgingly, and reached over to fill the maize cakes that her niece had been ignoring. Ome Xochitl gave her daughter a long look, then gestured at the completed tray.

"Take these to the ovens, my daughter," she said to Papalotl. "We will join you in a moment."

The little girl looked from one to the other, sensing the disagreement she had stirred up between them, and obviously wishing that she could stay to hear its resolution. But then she took the tray and did as she was told, glancing back over her shoulder once.

"Huemac is right, of course," Ome Xochitl said when the child had left the room. "She has shown no evidence that she is meant for the priesthood."

"Are the signs of her birth insufficient?" Cocatli demanded with unusual sharpness. "Her behavior at the temple is always perfect, and most pleasing to the priests and priestesses."

"That is because she is with you," Ome Xochitl pointed out, "and would not do anything to displease you. It is *you* that she worships, my daughter. Need I remind you of how good Huemac has been to *your* children? Why do you not trust him with his own?"

"Because I suspect that he does not trust my god," Cocatli said bluntly. "And that he does not wish to surrender his daughter into Quetzalcoatl's keeping, no matter what the signs indicate."

"Perhaps he has reason not to trust the god as you do," Ome Xochitl replied with equal frankness. "Your brother has been exposed to great powers, both here and in Texcoco."

"But must he pass such knowledge along to his daughter? When she has been so clearly marked for the god's service?"

"Can he leave it to his son?" Ome Xochitl said harshly, then softened her tone. "I love Xolotlpilli as you do, but his limitations are apparent to all of us. And it has been five years since his birth; Huemac may have no others."

Cocatli lowered her eyes and did not respond, and they were silent for several moments, listening to the sounds from the courtyard.

"Besides," Ome Xochitl resumed quietly, "there is someone you are forgetting. Have you asked Taypachtli what *she* wishes for her daughter?"

Cocatli looked up with a troubled expression on her face.

"She does not object to my taking Papalotl to the temple with me. I asked her permission."

"That is because she wants her daughter to see all the things she has never seen, and cannot show her herself. She respects the specialness of your attachment to Papalotl, but I do not think that she would object if Huemac chose to take the child into the hills with him."

"And you, my mother?" Cocatli inquired knowingly. "I do not think that you would object, either."

"It is not I who will decide," Ome Xochitl said curtly. "But neither will I pretend to be ashamed of my Chichimec heritage, or discourage the child from knowing about it. It is hers, as well."

They stared at each other without speaking, then rose from their mats and began to walk toward the door.

"I wish to do what is right," Cocatli said apologetically. "I do not wish to contend with my brother for the heart of his child."

"I know this," Ome Xochitl said gently, placing an arm around her daughter's shoulders. "Let us *all* be patient, then, and trust that the god will make his wishes clear to us. As he will, when it is time for us to know."

LATE THAT same night, while the feasting continued in Michpilli's courtyard, Huemac and Cocatli made their farewells to the wedding couple and hurried through the deserted streets toward Tlatelulco. At midnight, the day One-Serpent would begin, a day most propitious to the traveling merchants, who called it the Straight Way. An expedition under the command of Cuetzpaltzin would be leaving as this day commenced, headed for the trade center of Xicalanco, which lay many hundreds of miles away, close to the lands of the Maya. With them would go Cocatli's elder son, Omeocelotl, whom the vanguard merchant had taken on as an apprentice.

It had not been easy for Huemac to persuade the pochteca to allow an outsider into their ranks. Cuetzpaltzin, who appreciated the sincerity of Omeocelotl's desire, had been willing from the outset, but the decision had not been his alone. Huemac had made an appearance before the council of principal merchants, reminding them of his father's friendship, and of his own part in winning them the favor they currently enjoyed with Ahuitzotl. He proposed to them that their respectability could only be increased by the presence of the son of a Tenocha commander in their midst, and that one day soon, when the civil war had been forgotten, the two tribes of the Mexica would again have to learn how to treat one another as brothers. It was in the belief that from such small beginnings great changes grew, he told them, that he entrusted his nephew into their care.

As they crossed the bridge and turned into the dark, crooked streets of the calpulli of Pochtlan, Huemac came out of his reverie and realized that he and his sister had hardly spoken, and that Cocatli seemed to be avoiding his presence, even while she stayed by his side.

"You are not having second thoughts, my sister?" he asked cautiously, taking her arm as they crossed a narrow, swaying bridge.

"Not about my son," Cocatli blurted, startled out of her own deliberations. "This is the life he has chosen for himself, and as you know, the god of the merchants, Yacatecuhtli, the Lord Who Guides, is one of the aspects of my Lord, Quetzalcoatl. He summons my son to his service, just as he summoned me. As he will one day summon your daughter."

"One day?" Huemac repeated in surprise. "You do not think that he has already called her?"

"I *do,*" Cocatli said firmly. "But I suspect, my brother, that you do not."

Huemac stopped in the street to examine his sister's face, which had been sharpened and clarified by the fasting she had undertaken, and seemed not to have aged. He had never spoken to her of his ambivalence toward Quetzalcoatl, feeling that her unquestioning piety would not permit him to express himself honestly. But he saw now that it had been even more dishonest to remain silent.

"Forgive me, Cocatli, for not being open with you," he said with genuine regret. Then he drew a deep breath. "I was once touched by the god. I felt his terrible power flowing through my body, possessing my heart and my will. I cannot wish this on my daughter. You do not know the pain that the gods can bring to those who approach them too closely."

"I know only the pain of my distance," Cocatli murmured sadly. She looked up at him with a rueful smile on her face. "But I can no longer reproach you for your feelings, my brother, as I have been doing in my heart. I had assumed that your experiences had caused you to scorn the priesthood."

"Perhaps I question the completeness of their knowledge," Huemac said frankly, "but I do not despise their calling. If it is what Papalotl is drawn to, I will not stand in her way. But I will also give her every opportunity to change her fate, if she so chooses. It is the same choice that our father and grandfather gave to me."

"Perhaps it is *I* who have not had enough trust in the god," Cocatli admitted thoughtfully. "For surely, he will guide such a choice." She reached out suddenly and put her hand on Huemac's arm, looking deep into his eyes. "I am glad that we have finally spoken of this, my brother."

Huemac covered her hand with his own and nodded in agreement.

"Come, then," Cocatli urged, "let us hurry. I have already given away a daughter today. I would see my son again before he, too, leaves me."

FINALLY, the last prayers had been spoken, the ashes of the burnt offerings buried, the concluding exhortations of the white-haired old men and women delivered and acknowledged. As the priests' conch trumpets sounded the middle of the night, the members of the expedition rose from their places and attended to their goods, arranging the loads upon their carrying frames and binding them tightly with strips of rawhide. Then the leaders distributed the loads amongst themselves and their followers, giving the heaviest to the hired bearers and the lightest to the young apprentice boys, overburdening no one. This was done with strict adherence to order, in silence, and then the pochteca, the principal merchants, and the oztomeca, the vanguard merchants, formed themselves into two separate lines, with their respective leaders at the head of each line and the apprentices in the rear.

Cocatli watched her son take his place toward the end of Cuetzpaltzin's line, though not too close to the end, for Omeocelotl was almost fifteen, and was as tall as his uncle. He was easily the oldest of the untried apprentices, because his Uncle Acolmiztli had insisted that he complete one year of military training after his graduation from the calmecac, in the vain hope that this would convince his nephew to change his mind and become a warrior. Instead, Omeocelotl had spent his free time in the telpochcalli learning languages from the warriors who had traveled to foreign lands, in eager anticipation of his own travels.

A great bonfire had been lit close to where the guests were seated, near the courtyard entrance. Two by two, the merchants came forward, each taking a handful of fine white copal from the green gourd vessel and casting it into the fire. Then they proceeded through the open doorway to the canoes waiting in the darkness, saying nothing, and above all not looking back. All but the bearers and the youngest apprentices carried weapons, and Omeocelotl wore the Otomi bow that Huemac had given him stretched over the pack upon his back. His head had been washed and his hair cut short according to custom, which demanded that he not wash or cut it again, all the time that he was on the trail.

How young he is, and how much he has come to resemble his father, Cocatli thought, as the men paraded past the fire and Omeocelotl edged forward in the line, so that she could see his face. Tears came to her eyes, but she did not try to hide them, knowing that her son could not look back at her, or any other woman, now that he was purified. Then he was directly before the fire, stooping for a handful of incense, a stern young man with no thought for anything but the journey ahead. Return him to me, O Lord, Cocatli prayed; see that he does not perish from thirst on the trail, or fall before the arrows of his enemies.

Then, looking straight ahead, he disappeared through the doorway and was gone. The last boys followed him into the darkness, leaving the fire crackling in the silence behind them. No one moved in the courtyard for a long time, until the head merchant finally gave the signal and the guests rose and began to depart. Huemac helped Cocatli to her feet and stood beside her, the flames casting dancing lights across their faces.

"He will come back to you a man, my sister," he said soothingly. "With stories to tell the grandchildren he will want to give you."

"Yes," Cocatli agreed numbly. "Yes, I must look forward to that, and learn not to miss him."

"I will take you to the temple," Huemac said, leading her toward the doorway, "and we will pray for him together."

2

THE work on the Temple of Huitzilopochtli was scheduled to be finished near the end of the year Eight-Reed, and it was for the purpose of obtaining captives for its dedication that Ahuitzotl had proposed the Huaxtec campaign to Nezahualpilli. But there was another matter to be attended to first, a matter of pride and prestige, subjects to which Ahuitzotl was particularly sensitive. The province of Teloloapan, conquered long ago by the first Motecuma, had chosen the occasion of Ahuitzotl's coronation to rebel openly, sending no one to honor the new Speaker and then closing their roads to the Mexican merchants. They were not alone in refusing Ahuitzotl's invitation, since the enemy tribes had displayed the same scornful indifference they had shown toward Tizoc's coronation, but their defection gave Ahuitzotl a focus for all the wrath that had been building in him for years.

Accompanied by his allies from Tlacopan and the other lakeside cities, Ahuitzotl crossed over the mountains south of Cuauhnahuac and descended in force on the cities of Teloloapan, Alahuiztlan, and Oztoma. One by one, the cities were sacked and burned, and the leaders who came to Ahuitzotl begging for peace were summarily killed, as were all the men and women not considered suitable as captives. The orphaned children, some forty thousand in number, were divided between the allies and carried off as slaves. The Tenocha marched home victorious, leaving behind a smoking ruin devoid of all life, except for the vultures circling greedily overhead.

While the shock of the devastation inflicted upon Teloloapan was still being absorbed by the inhabitants of the Valley, Ahuitzotl replenished his supplies and marched his army eastward, joining forces with the troops of Nezahualpilli at the northern frontier of Texcocan territory. Together they launched a massive attack on the still-unconquered Huaxtecs, who had congregated their forces around the city of Xiuhcoac. After days of fierce fighting, the defenses were stormed and the city taken, and the Huaxtecs laid down their arms and sued for peace. A heavy tribute was imposed upon them, to be paid in eighty days, and then Ahuitzotl began the journey back to Tenochtitlan, taking three thousand Huaxtec captives with him, binding them together by means of a thin line passed through the perforations in their noses.

On the night before they were to arrive home, Huemac received a summons to the tent of the Speaker, where he found Ahuitzotl lounging on a low cot, accompanied only by his two nephews, Tlacahuepan and Moteczuma Xocoyotzin. Both of the young men had distinguished themselves in the fighting— Moteczuma for the first time—and like their uncle, they were wearing fine Huaxtec mantles and standards of red parrot feathers as marks of their bravery. Huemac bowed low and touched dirt to his tongue, aware that his presence here was a matter of some indifference to Tlacahuepan, but that Moteczuma was watching him closely. He noticed, as he rose, that there was a new confidence in the prince's narrow face, and that he was measuring Huemac with his eyes.

"Greetings, my friend," Ahuitzotl said casually, only reluctantly raising himself to a sitting position. "I have asked you to join our deliberations because you know, better than anyone, my desire to restore the prestige of our city. We have made a good beginning, have we not?"

"Very good, my Lord," Huemac agreed, showing none of the revulsion he still felt for the slaughter that had occurred in Teloloapan. Ahuitzotl smiled with unconcealed pride.

"But it is *only* the beginning," he assured Huemac grandly. "The next step is the dedication of Huitzilopochtli's temple. I want it to be an occasion that will live forever in the hearts and minds of everyone, especially those of our enemies. I want to be sure this time that my invitations are received with the respect they deserve, even in Tlaxcala and Michoacan!"

The indignities of the past welled up in Ahuitzotl's eyes, and Huemac waited patiently for the Speaker's anger to pass before he spoke himself:

"Then you must send ambassadors who will impress them with your seriousness. The lords here, for instance," Huemac said, gesturing toward the young men standing behind Ahuitzotl, "and others from among the ranks of our most illustrious warriors. Make them aware that they are dealing with those closest to the ruler, those who will carry out your revenge should they dare to refuse your hospitality."

Ahuitzotl appeared startled by the suggestion, and Huemac saw Moteczuma's eyes narrow suspiciously.

"But what if they were to be taken captive?" Ahuitzotl demanded with
uncharacteristic cautiousness. "We would be risking our most important leaders."

"Those who have mistreated our ambassadors have always suffered for it in
the past," Huemac said pointedly. "Moteczuma Ilhuicamina himself was once
held captive by the Chalca, but he escaped, and he returned later to lay waste
to their cities."

"Perhaps, then," young Moteczuma interjected, eying Huemac deviously,
"your brother, the warchief Acolmiztli, would also make a fit ambassador . . . ?"

Huemac was surprised and offended by the crude implications of the question, but he saw that Ahuitzotl did not seem to find it discourteous, and was
waiting for his answer.

"Most fit, my Lord Moteczuma," Huemac replied coldly, biting off his
words. "I did not mention my brother out of modesty, but surely, he would
not forgive me for implying that he wished to be spared such duty. He was
alive in the time of your great-grandfather, when it was the tradition to send
our finest men to represent the Speaker."

Moteczuma flushed deeply at the rebuke, but he clamped his thin lips
together and did not respond. Ahuitzotl laughed loudly.

"You should know by now, my nephew, not to trade words with Huemac.
He does not wield them lightly."

"If that is all, my Lord . . . ?" Huemac inquired politely, though he was still
angry about the exchange. Ahuitzotl nodded, smiling wryly, as if in recognition of Huemac's feelings.

"I am grateful for your candor, as usual. You may return to your company."

Huemac bowed and backed out of the tent, not straightening up until he had
pushed through the flap and was standing among the guards outside. He
breathed deeply as he walked away, calming himself, realizing that he was as
shaken by the suspicions of self-interest and the ignorance of tradition as he
was by the insult he had been offered. The largeness of spirit that his father
had labored so hard to instill in the Tenocha seemed sadly diminished, de-
graded by an unthinking reliance upon brute force.

The Demon Heart was right, Huemac thought bitterly: Ahuitzotl will continue to do his bidding even after he is gone, for it is the only example he
knows. Head down, Huemac headed for his brother's company to warn him,
and to tell him of what he had heard. For once, he knew, Acolmiztli would
understand his feelings perfectly.

"EVEN NOW, after twelve months, I feel that I have had too little of you,"
Illancueitl murmured, lightly tracing the smooth ridges of muscle across her
husband's naked chest. It was shortly after Michpilli's return from Xiuhcoac,
and they were lying together in the warm yellow light of the hearth fire.

"And I of you," Michpilli replied in a muted voice, running the flat of his
hand across her nipple and down over her ribs. Illancueitl arched her body

against him sensually, no longer demure in her hunger for him. Boldly, she reached down between his legs . . .

But he was limp; completely limp. Feeling the cold heat of panic and shame rise to her face, Illancueitl cautiously took her hand away. When Michpilli did not seem to notice, her panic began to mount. The old women had told her that such things happened to men, but to happen so soon! Had he tired of her already? She tried to remember some of the special caresses the old women had described to her, but she had not really listened, so certain had she been that *her* man would never need such prompting. He has not needed it since his return, she told herself; quite the contrary.

Filled with dread, she raised her eyes to Michpilli's face, and saw immediately that his mind was elsewhere, and his expression deeply troubled. It cannot be me, she thought with relief. Forgetting about caresses, she brought her hand slowly up to the left side of his face, to the scar that split his cheek. Michpilli blinked and widened his eyes, but he kept himself from flinching as she laid her fingers upon him.

"Do you remember, my husband," she asked softly, "what we discovered on our second day of seclusion?"

"Yes," Michpilli said, leaning his cheek against her cupped hand. "That was the day I told you that Huemac had advised me to reveal everything to you, and you told me that your mother had advised *you* to seek just such a revelation. It was the day that I first told you of Michoacan, and let you touch me like this."

"You must tell me, then, what it is that troubles you so greatly. Can it possibly be worse than what you told me that day?"

Michpilli shook his head and put her hand to his lips, remaining silent for a long time, his brow furrowed in thought. When he finally began to speak, Illancueitl did not try to interrupt him, even in the long silences that ensued while he struggled for words, or perhaps against having to say them aloud:

"There was a valley, on the way to the city of Alahuitztlan. We came over a hill and saw it suddenly, and everyone, even the Cuachic, fell silent and stared. It was as beautiful a place as I have ever seen. There were groves of cocoa trees, and trees heavy with many kinds of fruit, and fields of cotton and maguey, and the plants from which rubber is taken. It was watered by canals and ditches lined with stone and equipped with wooden gates, and everything was the bright, shiny green of parrot feathers, so green that it made you blink in wonder."

Michpilli paused and swallowed arduously.

"We destroyed everything. We cut down the trees and threw dirt into the ditches, and we set fire to the cotton, which smoked horribly. We left the farmers fixed upon the stakes that had supported their grape vines. It was all by the order of Ahuitzotl. It was a *lesson* . . .

"Then today, I went to visit my captives. There are five of them, two of whom are Mazahua, captured almost a year ago. They wanted to know when they would be allowed to die; they asked me if they were animals, to be caged and fattened for the dedication ceremonies. I could not meet their eyes. The crowding is terrible, for there are *thousands.* Ahuitzotl is hoarding them for another lesson.

"I am sickened by it!" Michpilli burst out suddenly. "It is not right to keep men like this, like dogs for the market. They will die badly, and bring no honor to the gods."

He broke off abruptly, panting, his eyes inflamed with emotion. Illancueitl lowered her eyes respectfully, recognizing that what her husband had just said came very close to treason, and that he had spoken from the heart.

"Perhaps we should go elsewhere, then," she said quietly, when it was clear that he had nothing to add. Michpilli stared at her in disbelief.

"Leave Tenochtitlan? But this is our *home.*"

"We should not live in a place that makes you so unhappy; it would be unhealthy for our children. Ahuitzotl does not rule in Texcoco, and my uncle has many friends there."

"But I cannot, I do not think . . . " Michpilli stammered helplessly. "Huemac would never do such a thing!"

"Yet it was he, was it not, who taught you the lesson of Michoacan? Is this any different?"

Michpilli examined her with sad eyes.

"No, it is not," he said finally. "I must think about this more thoroughly, and then I will speak to him. I am grate—" he began to add, but Illancueitl hastily covered his mouth with her hand.

"Do not speak," she whispered, pressing herself against him, her breath quickening as his arms came around her tightly.

"You do not think me . . . unmanly, then?" Michpilli asked plaintively, turning his mouth away from her hand. Illancueitl put the hand back and pulled him over on top of her, feeling a growing tautness against her thigh.

"No, my husband," she assured him joyfully. "I could never think such a thing. Not now, not ever . . ."

ON THE DAY of the dedication, the temple precinct was a solid mass of people, all dressed in their finest clothing, jostling and competing with one another for a clear view of Huitzilopochtli's new temple. The entire population of the city —men, women, and children—had been ordered to attend the ceremony on the penalty of death, and to their number were added the thousands of invited nobility from the allied and subject cities. These occupied places of honor close to the temple, beside the screened-off enclosures containing the delegations sent by the enemies of the Tenocha: the Tlaxcalans and Huexotzincans, the Yopi, and the Tarascans of Michoacan. The other temples within the precinct were crowded with priests and visiting dignitaries, as were the tops of the walls of the compound itself, and every high place as far away as Tlatelulco held its share of spectators. The murmur of voices and shuffling of feet produced a constant, low racket behind the solemn beating of drums.

The face of the great pyramid lay in deep shadow as the orange glare of the rising sun broke over the topmost platform, revealing the four sacrificial stones that had been erected in front of the shrines of Huitzilopochtli and Tlaloc. The people in the crowd became still and craned their necks to see as Tlacaelel was carried up the temple steps, accompanied by the stately figures of Ahuitzotl, Nezahualpilli, and Chimalpopoca of Tlacopan. Rays of sunlight flashed off their crowns and golden jewelry as they reached the top platform and took their places beside the stones.

Their bodies coated with the white paint of the dead, the captives entered the compound from all four directions at once, closely guarded on both sides by armed Eagle and Jaguar Warriors, who cleared a way for them through the crowd. Standing atop the front wall of the House of Eagles, in the southwestern corner of the temple precinct, Huemac could see the southern line of captives stretching out through the gate and down the street, all the way to the beginning of thc causcway to Ixtapalapa. Thousands, he thought grimly; a feast beyond all reckoning, except that of the gods.

Michpilli stood beside him, with the members of their families arranged along the edge of the wall in front of them, the two children safely secured between the women. Both men had had the right to a more prestigious station, closer to the temple, but they had chosen by mutual consent to maintain their distance, and patrol the precinct of Tonatiuh instead. Having positioned their men carefully, they had no choice now but to stand and watch, since it was clearly impossible to patrol with the crowd packed around them so densely.

Four white figures began to climb the shadowed temple steps, four suns rising between the painted serpents' heads and the ranks of black-robed priests stationed up and down the face of the pyramid. The drums thudded hollowly, and the spectators sucked in their breath with a vast, excited hiss. When the captives finally reached the top platform, they were seized by priests and thrown onto their backs upon the stones, and the four rulers stepped forward, their obsidian knives held skyward. A single voice sang out, echoing over the multitudes below. Swiftly, the knives were plunged into the chests of the victims, and their hearts were torn out and raised high in offering to Huitzilopochtli. Then the bodies were toppled over the side of the pyramid, and the crowd exhaled loudly and broke out in loud, sustained cheers of approval. The rulers moved aside, and teams of priests took their places as the captives began to move up the temple steps four at a time, in steady, synchronized waves . . .

BY MIDAFTERNOON, the sun was high and hot, and the smell of the blood streaming down the face of the temple hung over the entire precinct like a clinging, sickly-sweet cloud. Children began to cry and gag, and both men and women fainted away and fell against their neighbors. Loosened by these disturbances, the crowd began to shift and move, with some people gradually detaching themselves and edging toward the precinct entrance, passing those who pushed in to take their places. The blood on the temple stairs was now so thick that the captives were slipping and being forced to crawl on their hands and knees up the steep steps.

"I have seen enough," Ome Xochitl finally announced, after her granddaughter had become violently ill and had vomited onto the heads of the people below. Huemac and Michpilli helped the women safely to their feet and cleared the way down the stairs to the courtyard. Ome Xochitl put each of the children between two adults, and then made sure that everyone was holding hands. Huemac hugged his son and daughter and stood close to Taypachtli for a moment.

"Take them home, and do not come back," he commanded hoarsely, his throat closing at the dense, mingled odors of sweat, vomit, and blood. "No one will be missed after today."

Taypachtli nodded and shuddered in the warm sunlight, perspiration standing out on her forehead.

"For the first time," she said in a choked voice, "I am grateful that I cannot see." She removed the wreath of flowers from around her neck and held it out until Huemac could duck his head through the circle of fragrant blossoms. "Attend to your duties, my husband, and come to me when you can."

Huemac plucked a flower from the wreath and handed it to Michpilli as they watched their loved ones, chained together, snake their way through the crowd. Michpilli lifted the flower to his nose and looked at Huemac with hollow eyes.

"Now we must stay to see the end of this," he said tonelessly, and Huemac rested a hand on his shoulder.

"Let us bear it with the bravery for which the Tenocha were once known," he said in a hard voice. "Before we became butchers . . . "

THE KILLING went on continuously for four days, from sunrise to sunset. The horrible stench of the clotting blood was inescapable after the second day, and the sky was darkened by the clouds of carrion birds who had come to feast upon the bodies that were being dumped into the Lake. Huemac and Michpilli were summoned from their posts to help control the lines of captives, who had become progressively more terror-stricken and unruly. The prisoners wept and bumped against one another in confusion, their eyes wild from the drugs in the octli they had been given. Fewer and fewer were able to make their way up the steep stairs without slipping on the blood, and it had become impossible to distinguish those who fell to their deaths from those who jumped. The reddish-black pool at the base of the temple was ankle-deep, and a constant procession of harried priests came to fill gourd bowls with the divine liquid, which they carried off to paint the faces of the images in the various temples throughout the city. The crowd that remained, their weariness and discomfort apparent, made only a low moaning sound in recognition of each new death.

The guests departed gratefully at the end of the fourth day, bearing the terrible tale of what they had seen along with the sumptuous gifts they had been given by Ahuitzotl. Over ten thousand captives had died, but many of those who had witnessed the slaughter went away convinced that the number was many times that. The city of Tenochtitlan had been bathed in blood, its reputation enlarged and irrevocably stained by the magnitude of its holy ambition.

"I, too, have seen enough," Michpilli said to Huemac, as they walked slowly away from the temple precinct, where a new skull rack was already being constructed to accommodate the heads of the most recent victims. Neither man had eaten in two days, but more than food, they craved the dark solitude of the sweathouse, and the chance to cleanse the smell of death from their skin.

"You are leaving, then," Huemac said in a dull voice, showing no desire to dissuade his friend. "Where will you go?"

"It is said that we will soon be sending people to resettle Teloloapan, to keep it from the Yopi. I will go there, if the opportunity is presented to me."

"I will miss you, and my niece," Huemac said sadly. "But you know my feelings, and I have already given you my blessing."

"You will not consider coming with us, then?" Michpilli asked, without much hope. Huemac looked at his friend's face beneath the Eagle headdress, seeing again the timid, too-pretty boy who had come to him so long ago, so desperate for an apprenticeship that he would accept even a reputed sorcerer for his master. Then Huemac blinked and saw his comrade of many campaigns, the man who had walked beside him out of Michoacan. He felt suddenly old, wearied by the swift passage of the years.

"No, my fate lies here," he said slowly. "Now more than ever. I helped to raise Ahuitzotl to the reed seat; I must stay and bear my responsibility for what he has done."

"May the gods give you strength," Michpilli prayed, his eyes wet. They clasped hands and stood for a moment, gripping one another tightly.

"Farewell, Michpilli, my friend," Huemac said finally. "May the gods look with favor upon your new home, and take from you the memories of the one you left behind. Go now, and begin the life that awaits you, far from this city of blood . . ."

THE leaders of the Three-City Alliance stayed behind in Tenochtitlan after the dedication of the temple, in order to negotiate the terms under which the province of Teloloapan would be resettled. After much debate, it was decided that each of the three cities would send two hundred families, and that their allies and subjects would be invited to send up to twenty families apiece. Nezahualpilli urged, for the sake of future harmony, that these all be volunteers, and that the rulers themselves should provide them with all they would need in the way of seed, tools, and temporary provisions. This was agreed to, and a propitious day was selected for the departure. Acolmiztli, who had previously served as Ahuitzotl's ambassador to Huexotzinco, was named as one of the commissioners who would lead the settlers to their new homes and see to the distribution of land, and to the eventual election of their own leaders.

Despite all his duties, Nezahualpilli had not forgotten his promise to Huemac, and before he left Tenochtitlan, he secured Ahuitzotl's permission to invite Huemac to Texcoco. At the king's suggestion—aided by some prompting by Ome Xochitl and Taypachtli—Huemac decided to take his whole family with him. The spring rains had not yet come to wash the city clean, and the lingering odor of blood had robbed all but the indefatigably hardy Xolotlpilli of their appetites. Papalotl had been irritable and lethargic ever since the day of the dedication, complaining frequently of headaches and nausea, and becoming a trial to her mother.

Cocatli chose this time to enter the temple and begin her training as a priestess of Quetzalcoatl. Her daughter had left with Michpilli for Teloloapan, her elder son had gone off with the pochteca, and Azcatzin had recently taken up quarters in the Young Men's House, to learn the ways of the warriors. As she had explained to Huemac and her mother, now was the proper time for her to begin serving her novitiate, the first two years of which would be spent in virtual seclusion. By the time that Omeocelotl and Azcatzin reached the age of marriage, she would have finalized her vows and attained a rank that would allow her to attend her sons' weddings. Cocatli was thirty-seven years old and would be sequestered with girls still in their teens, but this in no way diminished the enthusiasm with which she approached the taking of her vows.

Except for her niece, the members of Cocatli's family accepted her decision with equanimity. Papalotl treated it as a personal abandonment, and became even more moody and difficult as the preparations to leave for Texcoco went on around her. Cocatli tried to reason with her, and Huemac scolded her sharply several times, but Papalotl clung to her disgruntlement with the same insistent righteousness that characterized all her other attachments.

Finally, the day of leaving dawned, and the family proceeded to the canoe dock on the eastern shore of the island, accompanied by Cocatli, Azcatzin, and a small band of servants carrying the family's possessions. As Huemac arranged his wife and son in the bow of the first canoe, Cocatli squatted beside Papalotl for one last attempt at reconciliation.

"There are many sad partings in this life, my child," she said earnestly, "but this need not be one of them. In two years' time, you will enter the temple yourself, and then we will be together again."

Papalotl coughed into her hand and twisted sullenly, refusing to meet her aunt's eyes.

"Will you leave me without a proper farewell, then?" Cocatli asked. "Have I injured you so greatly that you must punish me in return, and leave me with a heavy heart?"

Papalotl looked at her then, her lips and chin puckered stubbornly.

"Who will take me to the temple when you are gone?"

"Our Lord has a temple in Texcoco, too," Cocatli informed her gently. "Perhaps your grandmother would take you, or your mother; you are old enough to guide her now."

"Perhaps you will forget me," Papalotl suggested in a trembling voice.

"Never," Cocatli said forcefully. "You are the dream child sent to me by the god; you are as precious to me as any of my own children. I could never forget you, Papalotl, never."

Then the child was sobbing in her arms, begging her aunt's forgiveness, and Cocatli held her to her breast, letting her own tears come.

"Farewell, my precious butterfly," she murmured in Papalotl's ear, stroking her hair until she stopped shaking. Over her niece's shoulder, she saw Huemac waiting, but he held up a hand to indicate that he would not rush them. Gradually, she released herself from Papalotl's embrace and dried the girl's eyes with the edge of her shift. Papalotl stared at her searchingly, her golden eyes wide with pain and remorse.

"Go with your father," Cocatli said. "I will await you in the temple."

Unable to speak, Papalotl jerked her chin up and down twice, then turned and ran to Huemac, who lowered her into the canoe beside Ome Xochitl. Then he, too, came to embrace Cocatli.

"Farewell, my sister. I have told Azcatzin that he may go to Opochtli or Chiquatli if there is anything he needs. May the god hear your vows, and receive you into his order."

"I will pray for you, as well," Cocatli promised as she escorted him back to the canoes. Huemac lowered himself in behind Taypachtli and reached up to grasp Azcatzin's hand for one last time. Then the oarsmen pushed off from the dock, and the heavy canoes sloughed sideways for a moment, before straightening and heading out onto the Lake. Soon they were visible only as narrow black gashes across the sun's brilliant reflection, and Cocatli and Azcatzin turned away, and went back to the city.

HEADING NORTH from Texcoco several days later, Huemac passed through the towns of Tepechpan and Acolman, marveling at how they had grown and spread in the fifteen years since he had last come this way. Much more land was under cultivation, and the traffic on the road was far heavier than he remembered, especially in terms of the numbers of warriors traveling under the royal standard of Texcoco. There was a garrison stationed at Teotihuacan, and the warriors gave Huemac a suspicious once-over in the marketplace, obviously unable to reconcile the Mexican warrior's lock on the top of his head with the fact that he was weaponless, and wore only a plain blanket for a mantle. Huemac slept outside of town that night, returning only briefly, before dawn, to make an offering at the ancient temple of Tlaloc, where he prayed to the Rain God to withhold the storms that would impede his travels.

It was another two days before he had left the last settlements behind, along with the logging camps and stone quarries around which they had grown. These enterprises now reached far back into the hills, and the trail that Huemac followed was well worn, compensating for the fact that many of the landmarks he remembered had been obliterated. On the third day, he came down out of the forested hills into the desert, and the trail became increasingly indistinct, finally vanishing altogether in the coarse red sand that lay underfoot. Now Huemac would have to guide himself by the sun and the rounded peaks of the distant mountains, and by whatever other landmarks he could remember.

But first it was necessary to deal with the person who had been following him ever since he had left Teotihuacan. Huemac had heard his sounds in the night, and had several times seen dust hanging in the air, far behind him. Though he knew that it would not be difficult to lose such a clumsy pursuer, he was sufficiently angered by his own suspicions to want to know for sure who it was that wanted him followed. He made his net out of yucca-fiber rope and weighted the ends with stones, then lay in wait behind a rock ledge that jutted out beside the path he had been taking.

He had chosen the path because of its steepness, and he heard the man puffing with exertion before he came into view: a fully armed Texcocan warrior, macana in hand, his head and back bent under a heavy load of food bags and water gourds. He never saw the net until it settled over his head and bore him to the ground, and he did not see Huemac until the knife was already at his throat.

"Do not move or you are dead," Huemac warned, kicking the macana aside and reaching through the folds of the net to remove the man's flint knife from his waist. Then he dug his knee into the man's side and tilted his chin back with a touch of the cold blade against his throat.

"Now speak: Who sent you to follow me?"

"I came only to hunt," the man began, but stopped immediately when Huemac flicked his wrist and opened a cut on the man's chin.

"You hunt with a macana?" Huemac demanded savagely. "One more lie and . . ."

"The king!" the man blurted frantically. "My Lord Nezahualpilli . . ."

Huemac lifted himself slowly off the man's body, commanding him to lie on his stomach and put his face into the dirt. Then he removed the net and used his knife to sever the string on the man's bow and the straps on his bags, gourds, and quiver of arrows. Depositing these items behind him, he told the man to rise to his knees and face him. The man did so sullenly, his face and mantle smeared with blood and dirt.

"Tell your king that I am disappointed in him. Tell him that I shall want to know the explanation for this when I return."

"It would be better if you killed me now," the man muttered.

"Perhaps, but you will deliver my message, anyhow, *if* you make it back alive," Huemac said ominously. "Take your life and go. These things you have brought will be offered to the gods of the hills."

"But without water . . ."

"Go! Your thirst does not interest me."

With a last, longing stare at the gourds behind Huemac, the man rose to his feet and backed down the path, finally turning and breaking into a jog. Huemac watched him until he was out of sight, then turned back to the pile of provisions on the ground, laughing to himself at the size of the load. Gathering everything up in his net, he proceeded up the path to where he had sequestered his own goods.

Beside the pile in the net, the few bags and gourds he had brought seemed insignificant, yet the sight of them suddenly struck him as a reproachful reminder of how little Xiuhcozcatl had ever permitted him to carry. I, too, have shown little faith in my skill as a hunter, he thought ruefully, and even less in these hills, which provided so well for me in the past. He had been intent upon reaching Oztooa's village as quickly as possible, because he had promised Taypachtli that he would be back in three months' time, in order to help celebrate Xolotlpilli's sixth birthday. It had seemed more practical, in Texcoco, to find his teacher first and begin discussions with him, before spending the time to relearn the ways of the hill-people.

Now such a plan seemed utterly foolish. He would need all his former skills, plus some luck, simply to find his way to his destination. And to appear before Xiuhcozcatl or the Old One as a man of the city would be to invite their contempt, for he no longer had youth or inexperience to excuse him. They certainly would not share their knowledge with him, and they might even refuse to speak to him at all. No, even though he could never truly be one of them, he had to approach them on their own terms; he had to make himself a Chichimec again.

First, he removed the colored threads that held his topknot in place and shook his hair out over the back of his neck. Then he took out his knife and began digging in the loose sand, and when the hole was large enough, he filled it with the weapons and food he had captured, along with the rest of his own provisions, except for a small sack of toasted maize. Covering everything with dirt, he proceeded to pour the contents of the water gourds over the mound, one gourd at a time, praying to the hills to sustain him. He saved the last gourd, and slung it over his shoulder with his net and the sack of maize as he rose to his feet. At his waist were his knife and sling, the leather pouch containing his power objects, and a second pouch filled with the feathers and precious stones he had brought as gifts.

Tying the headband that Taypachtli had given him so long ago around his forehead, Huemac stood for a moment on a promontory, gazing out over the desert, feeling its emptiness and its power. He realized, with a sudden pang of guilt, that his promise to Taypachtli had been rash, the product of desire rather than true confidence. Out here, one never knew if he would be allowed to return, or when.

Still, when he remembered at the last moment to remove his leather sandals, he chose not to discard them. Instead, he bound them together and tied them to his water gourd, as a reminder of the promise he had made to his wife and family. Even in this land, he told himself as he walked down into the desert, promises must be kept. Then he corrected himself: *Especially* in this land, promises must be kept. Then he went on, sharpening his senses to the sights and sounds that would have eluded the attention of a man from the city.

"DO YOU know this man whom Huemac has gone to find?" Nezahualpilli asked, when Taypachtli had been led to the bench across from his own and the necessary greetings had been exchanged. Taypachtli cocked her head quizzically.

"No, my Lord. Do you disapprove of him for some reason?"

Nezahualpilli sat up a little straighter, beginning to understand the high regard in which Huemac held this woman. Few people, including most of his wives, could have sensed the feeling that lay behind his question.

"You hear me perhaps better than I would wish," he admitted wryly. "Yes, there has been trouble between Xiuhcozcatl's people and my own. I said nothing of this to Huemac, however, because I respect the esteem in which he holds his teacher."

Taypachtli did not respond, and it took Nezahualpilli a moment to realize that her silence was a reproach.

"Most likely, he sensed my feelings himself," he added hastily. "I have instructed some of my men to see that he is not endangered by the conflict, in any case. Perhaps I have acted wrongly," he suggested, when she still did not respond.

"I cannot speak for my husband, my Lord," Taypachtli said modestly. "But I have heard him say, many times, that ignorance is always the greatest danger."

Nezahualpilli flushed with shame, and he was grateful that she could not see the effect her words had had upon him. He decided to change the subject.

"I am told that you have a wonderful voice, my Lady. Perhaps some time you will be kind enough to sing for me."

"I would be honored," Taypachtli agreed without hesitation. "You and your people have shown great kindness to me and my children, for which I am grateful."

"Yes," Nezahualpilli said belatedly, realizing that it was not enough to merely nod. He examined her round, impassive face for clues to the frustration he was feeling, but he could see nothing that hinted at secretiveness or a desire to thwart his curiosity. He had not thought that it would be this difficult to steer the conversation toward the things he wished to know, but he saw now that he might be forced to hurt her feelings to do so.

"Are you aware, my Lady," he said slowly, "that on your husband's last visit to Texcoco, I was prepared to offer him one of my cousins as a wife? And that he discouraged me from even making the offer? Please, I tell you this to flatter you," he added when Taypachtli hung her head. "He told me that there was no other who could ever compete for the favor of his heart."

"I had a fever, after the birth of my son," Taypachtli said in a low voice. "It is this that the midwives think has made me barren, though I have not had the courage to tell Huemac. I have been selfish in not encouraging him to take another wife myself."

"You must not reproach yourself," Nezahualpilli said guiltily. "It is *his* choice, and an honorable one. But I must confess, I am puzzled by his lack of concern for the future. After all, it is only natural for a man to want many children to comfort him in his old age, and to speak well of his name after he is gone. Does Huemac not share this desire?"

"I do not know, my Lord."

"Perhaps it is something else, then?" Nezahualpilli prodded. "Some vision of what the future holds for him?"

"Perhaps," Taypachtli conceded reluctantly. "You must ask him these things yourself, my Lord. It is not my place to speak of his visions."

"Of course; forgive my curiosity. There is much about your husband that interests me, and I have had too little time with him," Nezahualpilli explained apologetically, gesturing brusquely for the attendant who had brought Taypachtli to him. "I will let you go now, my Lady. But soon, I hope, you will favor me with your singing."

"Whenever you wish, my Lord," Taypachtli promised, and bowed to him before she was led away. Nezahualpilli narrowed his eyes and scanned her figure as she left the garden, letting his vision blur and then expand as he had been taught, until he could see only the colors surrounding her body. As a technique for reading the future, it was not as accurate as what he could see in a person's eyes, but it was accurate enough. She will die within five years, perhaps ten, he thought sadly, unable to interpret the thin band of black around her body in any other way.

He realized, as he let his eyes go back to normal, that Huemac had spoken truthfully about the extent of his powers. He could not know this about his wife, or he would not face the long years ahead of him with such confidence; he probably would not even have left her to go into the desert. Nezahualpilli's eyes filled with tears of remorse at the thought of the cruel way he had tried to use her. And all because I cannot see my own future, he grieved, and would help myself to whatever knowledge Huemac possesses. I have wronged them both, and I have done so in the guise of friendship.

Waving his attendants away with a frown, the young king submerged himself in thought, and began to consider the ways in which he might make amends.

WHEN THE path finally wound its way out of the scrub oak and juniper covering the foothills and began to climb a steep barren ridge at the base of the mountains, Huemac knew that he had found his way back. He was thirsty and very hungry, but he moved at a deliberate pace, taking careful note of everything around him. The walled-in plots sloping away from the sides of the path had been recently burned, but not selectively, and there were sandaled footprints trampled into the cinders. Huemac had previously seen signs of the movements of groups of men, and he had suffered unduly from the scarcity of game and the depletion of the water holes. But this was the final proof that war had come into the hills.

He was not surprised, then, on reaching the canyon, to find that the village had been destroyed and abandoned. Even the willows along the stream had been burned, and their blackened leaves rustled bleakly as Huemac bent beneath them to drink from the icy water. He was aware that he was being watched, but he could not determine from where, or by whom. A lone woodpecker tapped in the stillness as Huemac walked through the charred ruins of the village, stooping once to examine the shaft of an arrow left sticking in a lodgepole. The markings were Texcocan.

Thinking to draw whoever was watching him out of hiding, Huemac began to climb toward the cave where he had first taken the mushrooms, high up in the canyon wall. As he drew near to the cave, though, he felt the hair rise on the back of his neck, and he suddenly knew that his observer was ahead of him, in the cave. He paused momentarily, trying to locate the cause of his certainty, but he could not account for it by means of his ordinary senses. Leaving his hands open at his sides, he climbed the last few feet to the flat stone ledge at the mouth of the cave and stood looking in at the darkness. It was not easy even for him to penetrate the darkness from outside in the light, but he was *sure* that someone was there, and he did not understand why he could not at least make out his shape. But the blackness was solid.

"Come out," he said in Otomi. "I am a friend."

Suddenly two tiny half-moons of light appeared in the darkness, and then a slender figure emerged, bow in hand, with an arrow aimed directly at Huemac's heart. It was a woman.

"Who are you?" she demanded, not loosening the tension on her bowstring. She was dark and wiry, and the muscles in her bare arms stood out like rawhide cords. Her face was partially obscured by the bow, but Huemac guessed that she was around twenty. She was wearing a tunic made of some kind of black fur and leggings of dark leather, which only partially explained her previous invisibility.

"My name is Huemac," he answered, standing very still. "I am looking for a man named Xiuhcozcatl."

"What do you want with him?"

"He was my teacher, many years ago. I hope to learn more from him."

"You are old to have a teacher," she said suspiciously, "and you do not speak our language well. Where do you come from?"

"Tenochtitlan."

The flint tip of the arrow wavered, and then the young woman slackened the string and lowered her bow, allowing Huemac a good look at her face. It seemed at first glance a typically fierce, expressionless Chichimec face: high cheekbones, narrow eyes, few lines to betray age or temperament. But her nose was small and pointed, like a fox's, and her lips were nearly as full as his own. Most striking were her eyes, which shone with unusual brightness from beneath a fringe of thick lashes, reminding him of the lights he had seen in the cave only moments before.

"You are the Owl Boy," she said suddenly, and Huemac started at the sound of the title he had earned so long ago, in this very place.

"How do you know that?"

"I was in the cave that day, although I was very young. I am Chimalman, Shield Hand, the great-great-granddaughter of Oztooa."

Now Huemac understood why he had felt her presence, and why she had been able to avoid his detection. He stared at the necklace of teeth and claws around her neck, and then at the dimly spotted fur of her tunic, realizing that it had been made from the skin of a black jaguar.

"Will you take me to the Old One?" he asked.

"He is gone."

"Dead?" Huemac queried, and she frowned darkly.

"Gone," she repeated, then gestured with her bow. "Come, I will take you to Xiuhcozcatl . . ."

Setting a hard pace, Chimalman led him up into the mountains along a path that twisted upward between sharp rock ledges and leaning stands of pine, often skirting close to the edge of precipitous drops. Ignoring his hunger, Huemac followed the long black braid, wrapped with feathers and colored threads, that bounced against her slender buttocks as she climbed ahead of him. The sun began to sink behind them and the air grew chilly, even though they were still in the light. Sentries appeared from behind rocks as they passed, tufted-headed warriors in feathers and furs who nodded to Chimalman and examined Huemac with hard, suspicious eyes.

The smell of wood smoke and cooking meat came to them before the village was in sight, and Huemac's mouth began to water in anticipation. But first they had to pass an ancient stone sweathouse, which stood beside a deep pool fed by one of the mountain streams, and Huemac announced that he wished to cleanse himself before meeting Xiuhcozcatl. Chimalman shrugged compliantly and set to work building a fire against the one blackened wall of the sweathouse, ignoring Huemac's offer to do it himself.

When the fire was blazing against the outer wall, Chimalman stood up and pulled her necklace and tunic off over her head, and dropped her leggings to the ground. Huemac froze where he stood, transfixed by the image of her naked body even after she had turned away from him and ducked through the low, round entrance. This had not been his intention—he had hoped for some time alone to collect himself. He supposed, though, that he should have expected it, since it was the custom in Tenochtitlan, as well, for men and women to bathe together. But this woman was not his wife, or even a relative.

Nagged by the sight of the sandals tied to his water gourd, Huemac dropped his blanket and maxlatl over them and crouched to enter the sweathouse. It was already hot and steamy inside, and the thin wall of porous rock glowed red in the darkness. Huemac dipped his hands into the bowl of water near the entrance and threw some against the wall, which hissed and sizzled. He was squatting beside Chimalman in the cramped space, so close that their knees were touching. Despite himself, Huemac could not keep his eyes from wandering, sidelong, over the sleek contours of her body. The sight of her small, upturned breasts and the smooth curves of her belly and thighs reminded him of how long he had been alone in the desert, and he felt a heaviness begin to grow in his loins. Then he noticed the glittering light beneath her thick eyelashes, and realized that she was looking back.

"You also see," he said in a mortified voice.

"Of course," she said, with what sounded like amusement. "Do you like what *you* see?"

"Ah, you . . . you are very different from my wife," Huemac mumbled, crossing his arms over his thighs in confusion. Then he took a handful of green cedar fronds from the pile beside him and began to switch himself vigorously across the back.

"I did not ask you about your wife," Chimalman hissed scornfully, and suddenly put a hand on his thigh, digging her nails into his skin. To his shock, Huemac felt his penis stiffen further, twitching upward so that it grazed her knuckles. Chimalman gave an abrupt laugh and took her hand away.

"That is what I thought," she said. "At least *part* of you tells the truth."

Then she squeezed by behind him, rubbing her slick body against his back, and left the sweathouse. Stewing in a heat of his own making, Huemac switched at himself violently, trying to flog her vision from his mind. When he could stand it no longer, he ran from the sweathouse and plunged directly into the pool, hearing her laugh again just before his head hit the water . . .

THE COUNCIL lodge in which Xiuhcozcatl received Huemac was not as large or finely made as the one in Oztooa's village, and its roof beams had yet to be carved or painted. Seated on the fur-covered dais of the chief, Xiuhcozcatl treated Huemac coldly at first, asking him in Otomi if he had come bearing the regards of the king.

"He pretended to know little of you," Huemac explained, straining his vocabulary to make himself understood to the men and women who surrounded him in a tight circle, filling every corner of the room. "He sent a man to follow me. I sent him back without his weapons."

Several of the warriors standing behind Xiuhcozcatl grunted in approval, but the chief himself spoke angrily, in Nahua:

"He has demanded that we send warriors to fight in his wars, and his people come into the hills to steal our timber and stone, even our water. For this, he offers us a place in his Council, and the promise of his *protection.*"

Huemac nodded glumly, feeling a dim urge to come to his kinsman's defense, but knowing that this was not the proper time or place. Xiuhcozcatl had good reason for his anger, and he seemed, in his role as chief, even more intimidating than Huemac remembered. His hair was now mostly gray, but his gaze had lost none of its penetrating power, and every word, every gesture, carried the weight of unquestioned authority. He wore a piece of shiny black obsidian through his upper lip, and his arms and shoulders had been tattooed with what looked like feathers and serpents' eyes. In his hand was a short carved stick that had the sharp curving talons of a hawk tied to its end.

"Why do you no longer carry your bow?" he inquired abruptly, reverting back to Otomi. Huemac took a moment to compose himself, then displayed the crooked fingers of his left hand, keenly aware of Chimalman watching him from her place to Xiuhcozcatl's left.

"I cannot hold it properly," he confessed. "I injured my hand in the ball game. In a game of augury."

Xiuhcozcatl shook his head and smiled for the first time.

"You have not changed, then; you still love to gamble with your life. Perhaps that is why you have come back to me . . . ?"

"No, my Lord," Huemac said firmly, resisting the insinuation concerning his first visit to the hills. "I gambled only to free myself, so that I might pursue the meaning of my visions. It is for *this* that I have come to you."

"What have you brought me as a gift, then?" Xiuhcozcatl demanded harshly, in response to Huemac's suddenly businesslike tone. Huemac calmly removed his second pouch and laid the stones and feathers out on the hard-packed ground in front of him.

"I have brought you these . . . and my friendship."

The chief's lips curled back and he snorted disdainfully, as if he had heard these words before.

"Of what use is your friendship to me?" he demanded rudely. "Can you return the game to these hills, and drive off the foreigners who prey on us? Are you so important to the king that he will listen to you, and change his ways?"

"He is the son of Nezahualcoyotl," Huemac snapped, lapsing into Nahua in his anger. "He will have to answer to his father's memory. I intend to remind him upon my return."

A wave of puzzlement swept through the room, and Xiuhcozcatl gestured to Chimalman to translate. So she, too, knows my tongue, Huemac thought, though he was too offended by Xiuhcozcatl's response to dwell on his discovery. Even here, it seemed, tradition was overlooked and friendship poorly rewarded. Huemac felt a kind of despair that drove all caution from his mind, and made him forget the powers of the man with whom he was dealing. When Chimalman had finished speaking, and the room was again quiet, Huemac looked up at his teacher with unforgiving eyes.

"Since you scorn my friendship," he said, still in Nahua, "I will not burden you with it any longer. Please accept these poor gifts, though, as a token of my respect for our past acquaintance."

The people around him murmured uneasily, having understood his tone if little else, and Huemac saw the hands of the warriors tighten on their weapons. Chimalman looked questioningly at Xiuhcozcatl, but he was staring hard at Huemac, and made no sign for her to interpret for the others. Huemac felt the force of his teacher's eyes pressing down on him, and he widened his own to their fullest extent, fighting back with all the strength of his anger and pride. Kill me, then, he thought wildly; let yours be the final injustice . . .

Then the stick in Xiuhcozcatl's hand moved slightly, and silver streaks danced in the air between them. The streaks became claws, silver talons that rushed toward him, lashing out at his face and eyes. Huemac blinked rapidly but refused to flinch, and he felt the talons rake harmlessly over his face, with a sting like wind-blown sand. Then the air was still, and dizziness descended upon him, making him throw out his hands for balance.

"Octli," Xiuhcozcatl commanded, and a gourd bowl of the pungent liquid was lifted to Huemac's lips. He felt utterly weak, and his face burned hotly as the octli slid down his throat. His eyes were gritty, and it was several moments before he was again able to focus on Xiuhcozcatl.

"Forgive me for doubting you, Huemac," the chief said in Otomi, bowing deeply for emphasis. "I had to test the strength of your intentions, after all these years. You must allow me the chance to win back your friendship."

"Yes," Huemac agreed dazedly, and Xiuhcozcatl clapped his hands sharply.

"Let us share food together, and renew our acquaintanceship," he said. "Tomorrow, we can begin to talk about your reasons for coming here."

THE NEXT morning, after Huemac had eaten, Chimalman led him up the mountainside to meet with the chief. She had avoided Huemac during last night's feasting, and she said little now, though her manner was highly respectful. Huemac wondered if she had been insulted by his confusion in the sweathouse, and he longed to speak with her in his own tongue, and know that his apology was understood. But her silence was forbidding, and he decided to leave such matters for later.

They found Xiuhcozcatl sitting beneath a gnarled pine, on a promontory that overlooked a deep, stream-filled gorge. In the distance, the hills were surrendering their shadows to the new light.

"You will not mind if my daughter-in-law," Xiuhcozcatl said, indicating Chimalman, "listens to our conversation? She is a woman of great powers."

Huemac looked from one to the other in surprise.

"Chimalman was the wife of my eldest son," Xiuhcozcatl explained. "He was killed by the Texcocans while out hunting alone."

"I am sorry," Huemac said solemnly, understanding a little better why he had been treated with such distrust. He turned to the young woman. "I would be honored to have you sit with us, my Lady."

Chimalman frowned uncomfortably, and Xiuhcozcatl laughed.

"Those are the manners of the city, my daughter," he chided, motioning for both of them to sit across from him.

"Now, my friend," he said to Huemac, settling his arms across his lap. "Begin with your knife . . ."

Pausing frequently to drink from the bowl of water beside him, Huemac talked steadily until the sun was high overhead. He described the power that had come to him on Mount Tepeyac, and how he had wrestled with it, and how it had finally taken total possession of him during the war with Tlatelulco. He told of frightening Moquiuix to his death, and of stopping Colotl's heart, glancing once at Chimalman as he described the rescue of Taypachtli. He concluded with the story of his interview with Tlacaelel, reciting the details of his vision as precisely as possible.

Feeling that he had reached a crucial juncture, Huemac thought to stop at this point for his teacher's comments, but Xiuhcozcatl urged him to go on, claiming that he had to know everything. And indeed, though he listened carefully to the details of Huemac's relations with Axayacatl, Ahuitzotl, and Tlacaelel, and of his experiences as an Eagle Warrior and a ball player, he seemed equally concerned with Huemac's performance as a teacher and an uncle, and he asked a great many questions about Michpilli, Illancueitl, and Huemac's nephews. Chiquatli's transformation also aroused his curiosity, though he told Huemac flatly that the owl feathers had been a ludicrous invention. The ceremonial game and its outcome held only minimal interest for him, once he had heard about Huemac's dream, and about the connection between his Peyotl vision and his vow to Xolotl.

The last part of the conversation, concerning Huemac's family and the birth of his children, seemed to take longer than all the rest. And although he was hoarse and weary, Huemac found himself stating his conclusions emphatically, with a frankness and detachment he had never before assumed toward this subject. Perhaps it was the influence of his surroundings—the thin, clear mountain air, the sunlight filtering through the pine needles, the deep quiet and attention of his listeners—that made him discard the pretenses of sentimentality. Or perhaps he had simply kept the truth to himself for too long. But as he heard himself speaking of losing Papalotl to the priesthood, of Xolotlpilli's limited mental capacities, and of the likelihood that Taypachtli would bear him no more children, he was struck by how thoroughly he had come to accept these things as facts—the natural result of his luck. He realized, with a kind of shock, that his vision of the end had bred a great resignation in him, and that he had forsworn the prospect of more children out of a guilty foreboding that he would have nothing to leave them as an inheritance.

Xiuhcozcatl finally held up his taloned stick to indicate that he had heard enough, and Huemac ended his recitation with a grateful sigh. The sun was nearly down in the west, and the distant hills shone a burnished red. From somewhere above where they sat, the querulous squawk of a mountain jay rang out in the stillness.

"Your experiences have aged you, Huemac," Xiuhcozcatl said softly. "In many ways, you are already the Old Eagle in your visions. But the same experiences might easily have corrupted you, or crushed your spirit. It is to your credit that you continue to confront your fate with such bravery."

Huemac nodded modestly, though the praise warmed him.

"As to your vision," the chief continued, "I do not know that I can help you, for I fear that your instincts are correct. I know of no one living today who has the power—in himself—to avert the disaster you have described. Even were I to teach you everything I know, I could not give you such power."

"Perhaps, though, with the aid of the others, the little people . . . ?" Huemac suggested hopefully, though he did not really feel much hope. It seemed that he had known this all along, in his heart, yet the pain of his disappointment was too real and immediate to allow him to fully accept it.

"Perhaps," Xiuhcozcatl said with undiminished skepticism. "That is something you will have to explore for yourself. This is not the first I have heard of this, you know; others have reported similar premonitions. Before he left us, the Old One advised me not to waste my men in resisting the city people. 'Their time is limited,' he told me, 'but these hills will be ours forever.' "

"But what could bring such a thing about?" Huemac cried hoarsely, giving way to his despair.

"The accounts I have heard have all mentioned invaders," Xiuhcozcatl said gravely. "Foreigners with powers unknown to us."

"Can it be Quetzalcoatl, as the Toltecs prophesied?"

"I cannot judge the wisdom of the Toltecs." Xiuhcozcatl shrugged. "It did not save them from their own demise. But if these invaders are indeed gods, then you must ask yourself if your city deserves to be spared from their judgment."

Huemac was silent, having judged his people harshly only the night before, in describing the dedication ceremony and its attendant slaughter. He thought briefly of the man for whom he had been named, the last ruler of Tula. Then he shook himself roughly and looked up at the chief.

"And if they are men?" he asked in a determined voice, and Xiuhcozcatl laughed.

"Then you must fight them!" he said heartily, appearing quite pleased with the question. "For that, I will be glad to help you prepare yourself. I only wished to empty you of illusions beforehand, so that they would not interfere with your learning."

Huemac looked at him sharply, but saw that his despair was being acknowledged, not mocked. He nodded wearily.

"You have not allotted much time for this visit," Xiuhcozcatl resumed after a respectful pause, "but I understand your sense of obligation to the members of your family. They are important to your fate, and you must nurture them. This means, of course, that much will have to wait until you can stay with me for a longer period. It could take years to locate your nahualli, and tame him. But I can give you the power to deal with Nezahualpilli before you leave this time."

"I would be grateful," Huemac replied. "He must be made to see the error of his ways."

Xiuhcozcatl nodded agreeably, though his eyes remained skeptical. He glanced at the fading colors of the sky, then at Chimalman.

"I will leave the two of you now, so that you may speak in private."

Huemac hastened to struggle to his feet, one of which had grown numb from inactivity. He bowed awkwardly, then hobbled in a circle, stamping his foot against the knife-pricks of returning sensation. But finally he was forced to face Chimalman, who stood with her back against the tree, examining him silently. When he stared back at her, she raised her hand—self-consciously, he thought —to the necklace around her neck, revealing a fishhook-shaped scar on the back of her hand. To his relief, she chose to speak to him in Nahua, which seemed to soften her voice.

"It was the chief," she explained, "who sent me to the old village yesterday. I was to make sure that the cave had not been defiled."

"But you found me instead."

"I had foreseen that someone would come to me; I assumed that you were the one. Perhaps you know that our women are not allowed to marry twice within the tribe."

"Yes," Huemac admitted. "Then you are no longer sure that I am the one foretold to you?"

"Your shyness did not dissuade me," she said frankly. "It was at my request that the chief tested your intentions last night, to see if you could not be made to stay. I did not need to hear again today of your devotion to your wife, to know that you would be returning to her."

"I am sorry . . ." Huemac began, but stopped immediately when Chimalman's black eyes flashed with anger.

"I, too, can live without illusions," she snapped, raising her chin proudly. "And I still wish to know if you are the one."

Huemac stared at her with a mixture of admiration and anxiety, unable to deny his excitement at the prospect, yet uncertain of where it might lead. It might be years before he was able to return, and the possibility of taking her back to the city with him was out of the question. It might only hurt her to know. And himself, as well. But then he saw the determination in her eyes and knew that it was equal to his own, and that he could not refuse her the chance to know her fate.

"I will not thwart you, then," he said decisively. "How can we settle this matter?"

"Meet me tonight by the sweathouse, when the moon is high. We will have our proof then."

"I will be there," Huemac promised, and bowed courteously as she left him.

A THICK mass of clouds had rolled in over the mountains after nightfall, and the air was damp and chilly when Huemac left his hut and walked toward the sweathouse. The hidden moon lit the clouds from behind, illuminating their swift passage across the night sky. Though he had no weapons and was known to everyone in the camp, Huemac moved down the center of the path with deliberate openness, taking it as a sign of Chimalman's rank within the tribe that he was not accosted by any of the sentries.

The surface of the pool reflected the gray roilings of the clouds overhead, and Huemac saw that a fire had already been lit beside the sweathouse. So, she will test me that way again, he thought, and wondered what more she could hope to learn. He himself had stopped resisting his desire for her, now that he knew that his return to Taypachtli was certain. It would be no betrayal of her to lie with another woman, and he wanted to feel Chimalman's hands upon him, and her lithe young body pressed against his own. If fate offered her to him again, he would be more than willing to obey its command.

Though no clothing had been left outside the sweathouse, Huemac stripped off everything except the jade rabbit and entered the building without further hesitation, aroused despite the chill in the air. But the sweathouse was empty. Settling himself impatiently, he threw water against the glowing wall and waited, becoming enormously erect as the heated odors in the room brought back the image of Chimalman's nakedness and he indulged himself in fantasies of love-making. But as time passed and the heat began to sap his strength, his penis drooped and he wondered if he had miscalculated her intentions. Still, *someone* had lit the fire outside. He decided to see and crawled back out through the low entrance, feeling the air hit his streaming body with an invigorating slap.

There was no one to be seen, but his clothes had been moved some distance away, to the edge of the pool. Huemac started toward them but stopped halfway when he saw that they had been torn and shredded beyond any further use. Then he heard the cough behind him, deep and dry, like the rattling of pebbles in a gourd. It was definitely not the kind of cough made by humans.

Huemac turned slowly, and at first he saw only the eyes, gleaming at him like two pieces of polished mirror-stone. The breath caught in his throat as the jaguar suddenly raised its blunt head and crouched lower, black spots rippling down its sinewy golden back. Momentarily oblivious to his danger, Huemac stared at the animal in rapt fascination, never having seen a live jaguar before. Its long tawny tail twitched once in the air behind it, but otherwise, the cat was absolutely motionless, a frozen image of beauty and menace.

Then Huemac's fear overtook him, and he thought immediately of the water. He did not know if jaguars could swim, but he doubted that any animal could both swim *and* attack. He took a slow, deliberate step sideways and stopped. Only the eyes followed him. He began to slide his foot sideways again, but this time the jaguar bared its teeth and moved with him, gliding forward at an angle that prevented any possibility of a mad dash for the pool.

The fire, Huemac thought next, trying to calm the wild pounding of his heart. But he had only begun to edge back toward the sweathouse when the cat snarled and slid back to cut him off. The sweat had completely dried on Huemac's body, and he felt himself begin to shiver with the utter coldness of his fear. In his hopelessness, he stared straight into the eyes of the beast confronting him. He opened his mouth to scream but no sound came out, and suddenly he was being drawn forward by the eerie light emanating from the jaguar's eyes . . . pulled inexorably until he was no longer standing but running, with the jaguar running ahead of him, its long tail and spotted hindquarters just barely visible. Pine needles crunched softly underfoot, and he seemed to be going at incredible speed, somehow missing the rocks that jutted up in his path and the swinging boughs that danced at the edges of his vision.

He burst into a clearing in the trees and slid to a stop, the air erupting from his lungs in explosive gasps. The jaguar was no longer in sight, but Huemac did not know whether to feel relieved or disappointed. He was in the grips of some kind of delirium, the thoughts spinning through his head too quickly to be captured. Then a powerfully sour aroma enveloped him where he stood, and suddenly the jaguar appeared at his side, rubbing its smooth, warm flank against his calf. Huemac froze in wonder as the animal stretched out its front paws and arched its back from head to haunches—briefly unsheathing its long, deadly claws—and then brushed against the front of his knees, emitting a low rumbling sound from deep within its body. It circled Huemac closely, twisting sinuously between his legs and spraying him with its odor. *Her* odor, Huemac thought suddenly, and before he understood how he knew this, he looked down and saw the lighter marking on the black fur of the right front paw, the distinctive barbed curve of a fishhook . . .

"Chimalman!" he whispered in an awed voice, and the rhythmic rumbling sound increased in volume. No longer afraid, Huemac closed his eyes and gave himself to the delicious friction of fur against skin, to the hot, rough tongue that licked at his loins, raising the temperature of his blood. Breathing heavily, he reached down for the cat, but before he could touch her, she sprang away from him with a bound that took her halfway across the clearing, where she seemed to disappear into the air. Then Huemac saw the hut in among the trees and went toward it, the jaguar smell thick in his nostrils, his stiff member cutting a hard arc through the air before him.

Chimalman was kneeling on a bed of gray fur, her black hair spread loosely over her back, her luminous eyes gleaming brightly as she stared back at him over her shoulder. Her dark slender body was lathered with sweat, and as Huemac knelt behind her, she pushed back against him with her buttocks, demanding to be mounted. Huemac put his hands upon her instead, caressing the supple flesh of her belly and thighs, probing the wetness between her legs. Chimalman made a moaning, growling sound and let her head loll between her arms, swaying from side to side as Huemac positioned himself behind her. His erection seemed so immense, and she so small, that he entered her with as much care as his passion would permit, gripping her narrow hips to restrain himself and feeling the soft folds of flesh catch and give at his penetration.

Then he was fully sheathed, his abdomen taut against her buttocks, his penis caught tight in a luscious grip that took his breath away. Chimalman tossed her head and wriggled under him, her thin arms outstretched for balance, her fingers clawing at the gray fur. Murmuring her name, Huemac ran his hands over the undulations of her ribs and grasped her small, pointed breasts, feeling her nipples harden against his palms. They began to move in unison, sliding apart only to plunge back together, rocking back and forth with greater and greater abandon. Bucking wildly, Chimalman yowled and buried her face in the fur, the muscles in her back and shoulders jumping spasmodically as successive shudders passed through her body. Blind with pleasure, Huemac wrapped his arms around her middle and thrust as deeply as possible, shouting incoherently as his passion built to a peak and spilled out of him in a flood . . .

Long moments later, he returned to awareness to find Chimalman curled up beside him, her black hair spread out around her head. Propping himself on an elbow, he ran a hand admiringly over her body, gently stroking her shoulder and neck, touching his fingers to the flat planes of her cheeks and the soft, swollen bow of her lips. Her eyes were open, contemplating his face, their brightness shadowed by the black, luxuriant lashes.

"You are very beautiful," he whispered, and she smiled languorously, her teeth a thin white band against the darkness of her skin.

"You are very skillful, and very passionate for a city man."

Huemac laughed quietly, then examined her face for a moment before speaking:

"It was your nahualli that brought me here," he said tentatively, and Chimalman nodded once in acknowledgment.

"When you did not run, but followed," she explained, "she chose you for her mate. She will die when I die, but her spirit will belong to our child when I am gone."

Huemac cocked his head and looked at her sharply.

"You know this? And it is what you want?"

"The choice was not mine," Chimalman said simply, without regret. "But I am certain now that you will return to me, someday. Part of your fate will always lie here, in the land of your ancestors. The last of your line will not perish with the city."

Tears of gratitude rose to Huemac's eyes, and he gazed at her longingly, already feeling the pain his departure would cause him.

"You offer me more than I can ever repay," he said humbly, and she raised a hand to his face, astonished and then moved by his tears.

"That is *my* fate," she reminded him gently. "And after tonight, I cannot be sorry that it brought you to me. I will have our child to comfort me, until my mate returns . . ."

Touching her wet fingertips to his lips, she pressed herself against him, and did not let him think again about leaving.

𝄢‖ **4** ‖𝄢

COME out, my children," the voice said. "You have nothing to fear from me."

Concealed behind a bank of feathery green ferns, Papalotl glared accusingly at Xolotlpilli, certain that it was her brother's anxious stirrings that had given them away. He looked back at her with terrified eyes, ready to run if she gave the word. Papalotl sniffed disdainfully, even though she had put this fear into him herself by exaggerating the possible consequences of discovery, in order to give their secret exploring an added aura of danger. Now she simply stepped out into the open, deciding that Xolotlpilli could be dealt with later.

The woman who had spoken was sitting on a bench at the edge of the garden path, surrounded by her attendants. She smiled brightly as the children approached her tentatively, Xolotlpilli lagging back a little, as if to hide himself behind his sister's slender figure. Papalotl gazed admiringly at the woman's sky-blue mantle, and at the turquoise jewelry around her neck and the golden rosette at her forehead. Her skin was pale and flawless, and her face and eyes projected a lightness and good humor that Papalotl had never experienced in such abundance in one person.

"How lovely!" she exclaimed softly, in a silky voice that disarmed the girl completely. "What is your name, my child?"

"Quetzal Papalotl, my Lady. This is my brother, Xolotlpilli."

"What unusual names," the woman murmured, seeming to take pleasure in the fact. She motioned them closer. "And whose children are you?"

"My father is Huemac," Papalotl explained. "We are Tenocha."

"Yes, I have heard of him, and of your mother, as well. It is said that she has a beautiful voice, and that she is a composer of flower songs."

"She is *my* mother, too!" Xolotlpilli threw in proudly, and grinned when the attendants all laughed. The woman in the blue mantle smiled at him patiently.

"I am called the Lady of Tula," she said. "I am the third wife of Nezahualpilli, the king."

"The queen," Papalotl breathed, and bowed hastily, nudging her brother to do likewise.

"I am also a composer of flower songs," the woman continued when they had straightened up. "Would you like to hear the song I was composing when you came into my garden?"

The children nodded eagerly, and the Lady of Tula folded her hands in her lap and began to recite from memory, her eyes fastened warmly on Papalotl's face:

> "Like the shy cotinga,
> I sing from the shade,
> From the hidden places.
> I dwell in the cloud forest,
> In the tops of high trees.
> My songs fall lightly to the ground,
> Like precious blue feathers,
> Like the petals of rare flowers,
> Like the shadows of the gods."

Papalotl stood mesmerized, totally captivated by the woman's melodious voice and queenly bearing.

"What is a cotinga?" Xolotlpilli suddenly whispered in her ear, and Papalotl jerked away from him violently. Then she saw the Lady of Tula frowning at her in mild reproof, and she turned to put an arm around her brother's broad shoulders.

"It is a bird, Xolotlpilli," she explained apologetically.

"A beautiful *blue* bird," the woman added, and held out her arms to both of them. "Come, my children, and sit with me for a while. Your company pleases me . . ."

Papalotl was supposed to go to the temple with her grandmother that afternoon, but Xolotlpilli was not aware of this, and probably would not have thought to remind her even if he had known. As it was, the memory of her appointment did not so much as enter Papalotl's mind as she stepped forward eagerly, and took a seat by the side of the Lady of Tula.

NEZAHUALPILLI stood alone in the narrow covered gallery that ran the length of the western end of the palace, opening onto a broad view of the Lake. Dark storm clouds hung low over the water, dropping rain in ragged sheets onto the dimpled surface of the Lake and hiding the distant islands of Tenochtitlan and Tlatelulco from the king's eyes. Nezahualpilli wiped moisture from his face and straightened the golden crown upon his head, so that the inset circle of black mirror-stone was centered directly above and between his eyes. When he sensed Huemac's approach, he turned away from the Lake and faced the entrance through which his visitor would come.

The guards who brought Huemac in hesitated about leaving him alone with the king, for Huemac had come directly from the desert, and he both looked and acted like a wild Chichimec tribesman. His feet were bare and his hair was loose under a leather headband, and he was wearing a dirty blanket as a mantle. A fiber sack and a water gourd were slung over his shoulder, and there was a spotted band of jaguar fur around his left wrist. Even his sun-darkened face seemed to have become harsher and less expressive. He made a crude, perfunctory bow and did not bother to touch dirt to his tongue, drawing a warning growl from the guards. Nezahualpilli ignored the slight and commanded the guards to withdraw, which they did only reluctantly.

Huemac was regarding him silently, his hooded impenetrable eyes moving from the king's face to his crown to the rain falling behind him, as if all were a matter of equal indifference to him. His right hand rested lightly on the flint knife sheathed at his waist, a violation of the royal presence that Nezahualpilli knew had to be deliberate.

"You have not been to see your family," the king said tentatively, uncertain of how to begin.

"I wanted to know first if we would be leaving Texcoco," Huemac told him bluntly. "I trust that you received my message?"

"Yes, though the messenger was half-dead from thirst."

"Perhaps, then, you can also explain *this,*" Huemac replied, and removed the broken shaft of an arrow from the bag over his shoulder. "I found it in the ruins of Xiuhcozcatl's former village," he added as he handed the arrow to the king. "It seems a fit symbol of the protection you provide to your people."

Nezahualpilli examined the markings on the arrow with a rueful expression on his face, turning it slowly in his hands as the rain drummed rhythmically on the roof overhead. Then he looked up and met Huemac's eyes, clenching the arrow tightly in one hand.

"I cannot justify what I have done, Huemac. Nor, as the king, do I need to. But I have studied this matter carefully, and I would like you to listen to my explanation."

"Speak, then," Huemac said curtly. "I am anxious to hear your reasoning."

Nezahualpilli nodded and took a moment to compose himself, unconsciously tapping the jagged end of the arrow against his open palm. His eyes were large and dark when he began to speak:

"As you know, my father died when I was very young, too young to have learned all he needed to teach me. The time after his death was a period of great uncertainty and readjustment—even I felt this—and there was competition among the lords and priests to preserve their position and power. It was during this time that many of the men like Xiuhcozcatl left the city and did not return. As a result, the prospect of going into the desert was never presented to me by my guardians, and I received all my training here. What I know of the Chichimecs I learned from the lips of the old wise men and the pages of the painted books."

"Certainly," Huemac interjected knowingly, *"they* did not cause you to scorn your ancestors."

"No, it was the Mexica, and my own insecurity, that caused me to do that," Nezahualpilli said with bitter self-reproach. "The encroachment of your people upon our lands and prerogatives has been constant since the time of my father, but Ahuitzotl has done more than perpetuate the tendency; he has made it an active policy. I thought that to combat him, and protect what was mine, I would have to exercise a control over my people that was every bit as ruthless and absolute as his own. You warned me of his ambition, Huemac, but you did not tell me how his demands could be met without hardship to my people. It was to meet Ahuitzotl's request for stone and timber for the Temple of Huitzilopochtli that I sent my men into the hills, and it was because of *his* wars that I asked the Chichimecs for fighting men. I did not think that I should accept their refusal any more easily than he would accept mine."

"And now, my Lord?" Huemac asked guardedly. "Has your thinking been changed?"

"It has been corrected," Nezahualpilli admitted, looking at Huemac steadily. "Tlacaelel died while you were away, and I went to Tenochtitlan for the funeral ceremonies. It was there that I learned the uselessness of trying to respond to Ahuitzotl in kind. He has initiated two new campaigns, which he plans to lead himself, and to insure the allegiance of his allies while he is away, he has begun to install his own relatives as rulers in the cities around the Lake. He has already put his nephew Cuitlahuac in Ixtapalapa, and others from among his friends and family now rule in Tula, Azcapotzalco, Culhuacan, and Xochimilco. The members of the Alliance were not consulted about this, or about the similar changes he is planning for Coyoacan and Chalco."

Huemac grunted appreciatively, no longer concealing the sympathy and concern in his eyes. The sound of thunder rolled in off the Lake, and Nezahualpilli waited for it to pass before going on.

"I understood then that even if I were to turn my people into a nation of warriors, I would not be able to make my kingdom safe. Our participation in Ahuitzotl's wars is scorned at the same time that it is expected, for the Mexica will never believe that they require assistance in the matter of war. Considering the size of the army that Ahuitzotl is raising in your city, our numbers will soon be as superfluous as our consent.

"Yet," Nezahualpilli said after a pause, holding up the arrow with an air of discovery, "in matters of ritual and custom, their deference to me is complete. Ahuitzotl has no respect for the traditions of others, but in his own city he is anxious that things be done correctly. It is there, in the court, that I truly have power, for he needs the reassurance of my prestige. *That* is my only weapon, and I must wield it *for* my people, rather than warring upon them out of my own fear. Ahuitzotl will have the benefit of my knowledge and prestige as often as he likes, and I will shower him with such respect and attention that he will never think to count the numbers of warriors I send to him.

"That is why," he continued hastily, holding up the arrow to keep Huemac from interrupting, "I have given orders that the hill-people—all of them—are not to be disturbed within the boundaries of their ancestral territory, and that they are to be compensated for the injuries they have suffered at my hands. I do this because I have wronged them, and I wish to regain their respect. But I also know now that they are *my* protection as much as I am theirs. With a man like Ahuitzotl in power, I can no longer be certain that I will not be dispossessed of my city, and have to flee to the mountains as my father did."

Nezahualpilli lowered the arrow self-consciously. He had delivered his speech with his typical assurance, yet as he looked to Huemac for a reaction, his long face wore the shy, stricken expression of a man who needed approval, and was not accustomed to asking for it. Huemac seemed entranced, and could only stare at the king's face, the golden rings around his pupils expanding and contracting with his breathing. Then, very deliberately, he squatted before Nezahualpilli and touched dirt to his tongue.

"Then you will accept my apologies for what I have done to you?" the king asked softly, his relief and gratitude unconcealed.

"Apologies are wasted between friends, my Lord," Huemac said, and grimaced wryly. "I came here to accuse you of your crimes and shame you with the memory of your father. I was fully prepared to incur your wrath and be banished forever from your city. You would not have been the first ruler I had seen who had been corrupted by his own power. Nor would you have been the first to send me away in anger."

Huemac paused, his eyes glowing with the force of his feelings.

"Instead, you have shown me that it is possible for wisdom and humility to live within the shadow of power, and to grow in the heart of the one who possesses it. I heard the sound of the Fasting Coyote in your voice, and I recognized his wisdom, his correctness, in the decisions you have reached. I am satisfied that you will do what you must to redeem yourself in the eyes of your people. You have already done so in mine."

Nezahualpilli smiled gratefully and rested a hand lightly on Huemac's shoulder.

"Go to your family, my friend. We will talk more when you have rested and visited with them."

"I will tell them that we are staying in Texcoco," Huemac said, and bowed deeply before leaving the king's presence. Nezahualpilli watched him go, then turned back to the rain-darkened scene behind him. The smooth shaft of the arrow fit neatly into the crease of his palm, and he closed his long fingers around it thoughtfully, staring at the sharply chipped edges of the flint tip. Then he looked west, toward Tenochtitlan, and decided that he would keep the arrow, as a reminder of the kind of protection that *he* would provide for his people . . .

🔲ǁ 5 ǁ🔲

EARLY in the year Nine Flint-Knife, on the day belonging to his birth sign, Nezahualpilli celebrated his twenty-third birthday with a gigantic feast in the banquet hall of the Cillan. Wearing one of the fine mantles that the king had given her, Ome Xochitl accompanied her family to the feast, which spread out of the great hall and into the surrounding gardens and courtyards. Palm fronds and fresh boughs of cedar and pine decorated the walls and rafters, and streamers of fragrant flowers hung just above the heads of the guests. Groups of professional singers and dancers performed in the court-yards, largely ignored by the milling guests, who entertained themselves with the artful conversation for which Texcoco was famous. The array of foods set out against the walls was staggering: stews of turkey, venison, and dog; spit-roasted ducks, rabbits, and quail; fish, crabs, and shrimp cooked with tomatoes and chilies; baked maize cakes filled with fish eggs and the ground meat of newts and frogs. There were also bowls of plums and sapotas of many colors, avocados and tuna cactus fruit, and more kinds of greens than anyone could have named. Servants moved through the crowd with bowls of octli and gourds of freshly whipped cocoa sweetened with honey and vanilla.

After she had eaten, Ome Xochitl remained seated on her mat while the other members of her family mingled with the celebrants. She felt subdued by her nostalgia, for she had spent many days in this hall as a young girl, and she would be leaving it—and Texcoco—in just a few days' time. Huemac had been summoned back to his duties in the House of Eagles, and they had all agreed that Papalotl would need some time to readjust to her own city before she entered the temple. Tenochtitlan will be a shock to all of us, Ome Xochitl thought ruefully; we have flourished here.

She glanced over at her son, who was engaged in an animated conversation with a white-haired old man who carried a beaded yetl pouch over his shoulder. With a kind of wonder that made her feel her own age, she noticed the strands of gray in Huemac's hair, and the lines that creased his broad cheeks. His time in the desert had wrought a profound and subtle change in him, as if the natural fatalism of that hard land had finally conquered the restlessness with which he had contemplated his fate. Ome Xochitl had seen him turn to the task of acquiring knowledge and power with a new maturity and patience, spending long hours conversing with the king and his wise men, and applying himself to the study of Texcoco's extensive library of painted books. She knew that he did this in the face of a catastrophe he now considered inevitable, and she admired his calm, and the attention he was still able to give to his family, and to the young ball players he had trained here.

Her thoughts were interrupted by Papalotl, who had come for her grand-mother's inspection, the third time she had done so since they had arrived a short time ago. Ome Xochitl smiled tolerantly and plucked a piece of thread from the back of Papalotl's embroidered shift, which was a gift from the Lady of Tula. The girl had become completely enamored with the life of the court, and she was relentless in her curiosity concerning the niceties of Texcocan speech and manners, and the fine distinctions of rank that were revealed in the way the lords and ladies dressed. She had not asked Huemac a single question about the desert, and had in fact been speechless with horror when he had appeared before her in his Chichimec clothing.

"Have you been introduced to the other wives of the king, my child?" Ome Xochitl asked, after indicating to Papalotl that her appearance was perfect in every detail.

"Oh, yes. The first wife is the niece of Tizoc," Papalotl explained earnestly, as if this vital piece of information were equally new and fascinating to her grandmother. "She is very tall and thin, and very aloof."

Ome Xochitl raised her eyebrows slightly at the diplomacy of the term, since she knew the woman in question to be basically cold and arrogant, and not fond of children. Papalotl went on in the same serious tone:

"The second wife is the daughter of Axayacatl and bears the name of her aunt, Chalchiuhnenetl. She is the sister of Tlacahuepan and Moteczuma. She has long hair and bright black eyes and is one of the most beautiful women in Texcoco," Papalotl added breathlessly, pronouncing the word "Tet-su-ko-ko," as the members of the Texcocan court did. Ome Xochitl had heard rumors that this queen had eyes for men other than the king, but she did not wish to begin disillusioning her granddaughter so soon. The niceties of court gossip could wait until she was older.

"The Lady of Tula is beckoning to you," Ome Xochitl said instead. "She is with your mother."

Despite her obvious eagerness, Papalotl bowed formally to her grandmother and walked carefully through the crowd, her chin held at the proper level and her pace restrained. Cocatli will not recognize her, Ome Xochitl thought wryly. But she understood the attraction that the elegance of the court held for her granddaughter, and she did not wonder at the attachment that Papalotl had formed for the Lady of Tula. There were few with the queen's graciousness and love of beauty in Tenochtitlan, and fewer still who would bestow them so easily upon a child.

Ome Xochitl was pleased, as well, that the Lady of Tula had extended her friendship to include Papalotl's mother, and that she had done so even before Taypachtli had begun to earn a reputation for her singing. The two women were partially obscured from Ome Xochitl's view by the shifting crowd, but even so, the pleasure they took in each other's company was easily apparent. And this despite the fact that they were the main competitors for the prizes Nezahualpilli had offered to the composers of flower songs, who would deliver their compositions later. Like her father, Taypachtli enjoyed good company, and Ome Xochitl knew that she was not taken with the elegance of the Texcocans so much as with their gentleness and humor. "There is more laughter here, but it is not as loud and boisterous," Taypachtli had said after attending her first gathering in Texcoco. "And they do not talk so much of war and dying."

Then her view of Taypachtli was blocked completely, and Ome Xochitl began to search the crowd for her grandson. The blossoming of Xolotlpilli was perhaps the most startling development of their entire stay, since the boy might easily have felt diminished by all the attention being lavished on his sister by the Lady of Tula. Instead, he had managed, on his own, to make friends with just about every young child in the palace, as well as most of the guards, cooks, and serving women. Nearly as broad as he was tall, Xolotlpilli struck most people as a comical figure, with his big ingenuous eyes and the slender bone flute clutched in one meaty hand. But once he began to play the painted flute, which his father had brought back for him from the hills, he commanded everyone's respectful attention, and the incongruity between his great size and his skill with the delicate instrument gave him an undeniable charm. Ome Xochitl was still astonished at how adept he already was at the age of six, and she gave all the credit to Taypachtli, since she could not account for such a talent from her side of the family.

Xolotlpilli, however, was nowhere to be seen, and Ome Xochitl guessed that he had found himself some new friend or friends to entertain. She glanced up and smiled as Huemac lowered himself to the mat beside her. He examined her face questioningly, as if looking for signs of ill health. But then he nodded in recognition and smiled at her knowingly.

"Memories, my mother?"

"My wedding feast was celebrated in this hall, almost fifty years ago," she said wistfully, mildly incredulous. She reached out to touch the jade rabbit around his neck. "Then, this was only a trinket in my father's chest, a prize offered casually for his own pleasure."

" 'We dream here, thinking we are free,' " Huemac quoted with quiet pride. "Do you think that Taypachtli will take the prize tonight?"

Ome Xochitl shrugged and spread her hands.

"It is her own composition, and she has not recited it to me. I only know that it is very different from anything that she has done before. The Lady of Tula is also a fine composer," she added. "It will not be an easy decision for the king."

"He is growing used to that," Huemac said wryly. "Would you like to walk with me," he asked, "and meet the man to whom I was speaking? He was a friend of your father's."

"Give him my regards," Ome Xochitl demurred. "I am happy here, with my memories, and my family to watch. I will join you later, my son, when it is time for the contest."

SEATED IN the center of the dais, Nezahualpilli was flanked on both sides by his wives and relatives. A small circle of space had been cleared directly in front of him, with the seated guests spreading out around it like a multicolored fan, their heads bobbing gently to the rhythms of the flower songs. Torches burned in holders high up on the walls, casting a thick golden light over the proceedings.

There were eight different composers, both men and women, who were offering their songs to the king, and Nezahualpilli listened to each with an attitude of complete concentration. But in his heart, he was looking forward to the last two recitations, which he had reserved for the Lady of Tula and Taypachtli. He was immensely proud of his clever wife, whose charm and wit never failed to please him, and who was second in his affections only to Chalchiuhnenetl. He thought so highly of her flower songs that he had wanted to give her the last position, out of fairness to Taypachtli, who was not so well known to the audience, and might not be able to recapture their attention after the Lady of Tula had played upon their senses. But his wife had insisted that her friend should have the place of honor, and Nezahualpilli had indulged her wishes, as he always did.

Taypachtli herself remained an enigma to him, despite all he had come to know about her husband. He had not spoken to her privately since the day he had seen her death, and in public she seemed shy in his presence, smiling her beautiful smile but saying little. He had been astonished, after Huemac had told him how deeply he confided in her, to learn that she was the daughter of a Tlatelulcan artisan, and that she had had no formal education. Nezahualpilli did not confide in *anyone* to such an extent, even those who were his equals in knowledge, and he could not imagine what a woman who had been blind from birth—who had never been off the islands of Mexico before this—could possibly make of the things Huemac must have described to her. And how could she hope to compete as a composer with someone like the Lady of Tula? He knew that she had not collaborated with her mother-in-law, and he hoped that she would at least use her lovely voice to good advantage, so that her performance would not be completely eclipsed by the one that had gone before.

But then it was the Lady of Tula's turn, and Nezahualpilli abandoned his speculations as his wife left her place on the dais and bowed before him. Her long skirt swirled around her legs as she turned to bow to the audience, which greeted her appearance with an expectant round of applause. Then, pausing briefly to hold her listeners, she recited her song of the shy cotinga, starting high in the back of her throat and then letting her smooth, liquid voice drift down at the end of the last lines, the individual sounds falling lightly upon the ears of her audience, like the petals of rare flowers, like the shadows of the gods . . .

It was by far the shortest of the flower songs that had been offered, and the first to draw applause so prolonged that a second recitation was required to quiet the guests. As the Lady of Tula repeated her performance for the enthusiastic crowd, Nezahualpilli noticed the identical, glowing eyes of Huemac and his daughter staring up at her from their places at the edge of the circle. He hoped that they would not be disappointed by what was to follow, and that he would not be forced to regret his indulgence.

When the applause had died down for the second time, Taypachtli rose from her place beside her husband and stepped tentatively into the circle, feeling her way forward to the whispered instructions of Ome Xochitl. She was wearing a yellow mantle and a magnificent cape of yellow feathers, and there was a necklace of blue turquoise flowers around her neck.

"The name of my flower song is 'Texcoco,' " she announced in a clear voice, and Nezahualpilli sensed a sharpening of attention in the crowd, which shifted and murmured inarticulately. It was a bold subject for a foreigner to choose, especially a Mexican, and Nezahualpilli wondered what she would dare to tell them about themselves. He could tell nothing from her face, but then, as the guests fell silent, she began to speak:

"I feel Texcoco
In my dreams;

I know her touch
Upon my skin.
It is the fresh pine breeze
Of the mountains;
The constant whisper
Of the Lake;
The watchful silence
Of wise men, thinking.

Is it true that we have knowledge?
Is it true that we learn?
The movements of the gods
Pass before us unseen;
Their ways become a memory.
The red ink fades;
The black ink peels from the page;
The words of understanding
Go dry on our tongues.

Perhaps here, in Texcoco,
City of forest winds,
City of sighing water:
Here where the books are stored
And copied;
Here where the stars are watched
At night;
Here where the words and pictures
Are captured by heart.
Perhaps here, in Texcoco,
Amid the songs and laughter,
There is still remembering."

The crowd hesitated only an instant—to be sure there was no more—before bursting into wild applause. Several guests leapt spontaneously to their feet to place wreaths of flowers around Taypachtli's neck and shoulders, shouting their praises in her ear. Taypachtli appeared bewildered, and Nezahualpilli realized that she did not understand how she had flattered them. But *he* knew the vanity of his people, and he knew that it had caused them to miss the somber note of nostalgia in the second set of verses, and to ignore entirely the "perhaps" in the last. There was a hidden charge behind the surface admiration, a warning of the fragility of all that was truly precious.

The king saw this begin to dawn on his people during Taypachtli's second recitation, and he felt its final realization in the deep, absorbed silence with which they received her performance for a third time. Nezahualpilli suddenly remembered what Huemac had once said to him: "She sees in me the person who, in my heart, I would most like to be." At the time, Nezahualpilli had dismissed the possibility of such insight, thinking that it would have to be naïve and idealistic, if not actually delusionary. But now he saw the power it had to inspire others, when its essential generosity was combined with a fine sense of discrimination and a genuine wariness of the future. These should also be the qualities of a good ruler, he thought fiercely, deriving his own personal meaning from Taypachtli's song.

The silence continued for a moment after Taypachtli had finished her third recitation, and then the audience rose as one and began to clap their hands in unison, at first with respectful moderation, but then harder and harder, until the sound of their clapping boomed off the walls of the long hall. Nezahualpilli had risen with them, and he could tell from the faces around him on the dais that his choice of the winner would not be disputed. It has taken a Mexican to show us the kind of people we should be, he thought wonderingly, with a sense of gratitude too deep to allow any resentment.

Raising his hand for quiet, the king summoned the other composers before him and rewarded them one by one, with such generosity that no one could have thought him- or herself the loser. To the Lady of Tula, as runner-up, he presented a vest woven from the bronze and golden feathers of the pheasant and a pair of earrings carved from the finest amber. Then he stood before Taypachtli and placed upon her head a golden crown which had a cluster of five golden flowers, inlaid with mother-of-pearl, at the brow: the symbol of Macuilxochitl, Five Flower, the God of Flower and Song.

"You have reached into our hearts, Taypachtli, and you have inspired us," he said, smiling down on her and the members of her family. "I would also like you to have this necklace of turquoise and coral, as a reminder of the joy you have brought to our city."

Taypachtli unexpectedly held out her hands for the gift, and after a moment's hesitation, the king gently draped the necklace—a thick string of tiny red-and-blue birds—over her outstretched fingers. Taypachtli delicately pressed the birds between her thumbs and fingertips, smiling as she recognized their shape. She cocked her chin in Nezahualpilli's direction.

"I would like to remember the one who taught me the art of composition, my Lord. She is a woman of your own blood."

"Ome Xochitl," the king said without hesitation. "Come forward, my sister."

Ome Xochitl accepted an excited hug from Papalotl, glancing once at Huemac as she released herself and went to Taypachtli's side.

"You bring me great joy, my daughter," she said quietly, her eyes shimmering with tears. Taypachtli smiled again and held the necklace open until Ome Xochitl could duck her white head through it. Then the two women embraced one another fondly, and the king led the applause for both of them.

The contest marked the end of the feast, and the crowd began to break up as the king's servants came out with their arms filled with the gifts to be distributed to the departing guests. Accepting congratulations from those who remained behind, Taypachtli removed some of the wreaths from around her shoulders and gave them to Papalotl, Xolotlpilli, and the Lady of Tula.

"You must promise me, Taypachtli," Nezahualpilli said, "that you will not hide yourself from us in Tenochtitlan. When I next call a convocation of composers in my city, you must honor us with your presence."

"It is *I* who will be honored, my Lord," Taypachtli assured him modestly, the crown on her head gleaming brilliantly as she bowed before him. Nezahualpilli contemplated her thoughtfully, almost sadly, it seemed, then turned to

Huemac, who stood smiling proudly, his hands on the shoulders of his bleary-eyed son.

"And you, Huemac? When will you return to us?"

"I do not know, my Lord," Huemac said frankly, then glanced sideways at Papalotl, who was staring at him with an expression of anguished longing on her face. Meeting her eyes, he held out his hand to her, and she came eagerly to his side.

"Perhaps in a few years, when my children have grown," he said to the king, "we will all come back to visit you. I do not doubt that I will see you often in Tenochtitlan."

Nezahualpilli smiled wryly at the reference to their conversation of so many months ago, the first occasion on which he had allowed the Mexicans to counsel him. He passed a hand over Huemac and his family in blessing.

"I have profited from your stay here. I will not forget your friendship."

Everyone bowed as the king and his retinue left the dais and proceeded toward the royal chambers. Glowing with pride, Huemac embraced his wife, then gave way so that his children could show their love for their mother. Finally, as the torches were beginning to be extinguished, he gathered them all around him and led them slowly from the hall, exchanging farewells with the many friends they had made in Texcoco.

X

AHUITZOTL:
The Water Monster

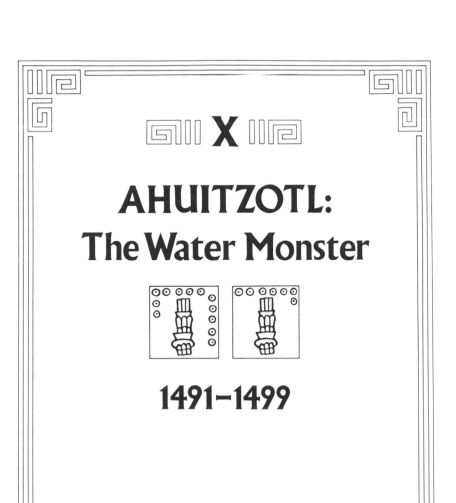

1491–1499

1

A s he followed the slender figure of Pinotl through the narrow streets of Pochtlan, Azcatzin reflected on the fact that it had been almost ten years since he had been in Tlatelulco for any other reason than to trade in the marketplace. The last occasion had been the time that Huemac had taken him and his brother Omeocelotl to visit the house of Cuetzpaltzin, the vanguard merchant whose tales of far-off places had so excited Omeocelotl. Now Omeocelotl was a vanguard merchant himself, a man of some standing among the pochteca, according to Huemac, with a house of his own here in Pochtlan. This was the first opportunity that Azcatzin had had to visit him in the last four years, for Omeocelotl had been away for most of that time on trading expeditions, and Azcatzin himself had recently participated in two long campaigns with the army.

It was the year Twelve-Reed, and Azcatzin was seventeen; his brother, twenty. Azcatzin was still short and slight of build, but his wiry body was hard and compact, and he carried himself with the coiled dignity of a man who does not easily give way in the face of a threat. The lock on the back of his head had been cut and wrapped into a topknot with red and green threads, in recognition of the three captures in which he had jointly participated, and he was wearing the fine mantle and obsidian lip-plug that Ahuitzotl had given him as a reward for his bravery in the last campaign. This had been a thrust over the mountains to the south and west of the resettled province of Teloloapan, into the hot coastal lowlands that stretched south for many miles to the northern frontier of the Yopi territory. The Tenocha and their allies had conquered the cities of Zacatula and Acapulco, as well as many smaller towns, and Azcatzin and the other young warriors had bathed for the first time in the salty surf of the Divine Waters.

That will not impress Omeocelotl very much, Azcatzin thought, as Pinotl led him down a dark alleyway between the houses, skirting along a canal barely wide enough to accommodate one canoe at a time. His brother had already been to both coasts, to Xicalanco in the east and Tehuantepec in the west, traversing distances that seemed unimaginable to Azcatzin. He wondered, with a trace of anxiety, what his brother would be like, and whether they would still be able to converse with each other.

Pinotl suddenly turned right, and Azcatzin came behind him into a courtyard so tiny that the clay ovens in one corner and the sweathouse in another made it seem crowded. The house itself was so low that its rooftop garden could clearly be seen from the ground directly in front of it, and the ceiling inside made Azcatzin feel tall until his brother rose to greet him, and had to duck his head to avoid the roof beams that were still a hand's-breadth above Azcatzin's topknot. Omeocelotl was as large a man as their father had been, and he looked like him, as well, though his broad face was darkened from exposure to the sun and his eyes were narrowed in a perpetual squint. He was wearing a plain brown mantle, and his hair hung to his shoulders, bound back from his face by a strip of black cloth around his forehead. He gripped Azcatzin's hand strongly, breaking into a smile so effusive that Azcatzin could not help but smile back.

"Welcome to my house, my brother!" he said happily, clapping Azcatzin on the shoulder while he looked him up and down. "That is a splendid mantle; no doubt the gift of the Speaker. I was told that you had ended your apprenticeship in glory, and here is the proof!"

Azcatzin beamed foolishly at his brother's praise, uncertain of just how to return the compliment. This was such a tiny house, and its one room, except for a jaguar skin and some feathered devices on the far wall, was as barren of adornment as Omeocelotl himself.

"And I am told," Azcatzin ventured, imitating his brother's hearty manner, "that you are a vanguard merchant of great repute. You must possess many goods."

"Oh, no," Omeocelotl disagreed, shaking his head in self-deprecation as he led Azcatzin to a seat. "I possess very little, very little, indeed. The things I trade all belong to my uncles, the principal merchants. Rest, my brother, and tell me about your journey to Acapulco. I have never been there."

Omeocelotl sat down across from him, lit from behind by the shaft of light that came through the open trap in the ceiling overhead. He put his elbows on his knees and leaned forward with such overt curiosity that Azcatzin felt compelled to talk about himself, which he did with a certain relief, since he did not know how to proceed in the face of his brother's professions of poverty.

"First, I must bring you the greetings of our sister and her husband," Azcatzin said, and described how the troops had been quartered in Teloloapan before pushing over the mountains, and how he had gone with Huemac, Opochtli, and Chiquatli to visit the new home of Michpilli and Illancueitl.

"Our nephew already walks and speaks," he said of Illancueitl's first-born, "and our niece is dark and beautiful like her mother, a veritable precious feather. Michpilli is an important man in his city, and he took us to the valley where the cotton fields and orchards are being replanted. He made farmers of us with his enthusiasm, and we spent half of our leave up to our knees in mud, helping to dig irrigation ditches!"

Omeocelotl laughed appreciatively, nodding to a serving woman, who placed gourds of cocoa and empty cups before each of them and withdrew without a sound. Azcatzin sipped the cool frothy liquid, identifying honey, vanilla, and cinnamon among the many flavors mingling with the rich chocolate taste of the drink. Cocoa was still a new experience to Azcatzin, who had only recently earned the right to drink it, and he savored it slowly, allowing his brother to deal with a series of visitors who came to him one at a time and conferred in low voices. Azcatzin noted the respect with which they approached Omeocelotl, and the curt, decisive way he replied to their requests, wasting no words. Like a captain, Azcatzin thought; he had already ascertained that the feathered devices on the wall behind his brother were warrior's standards, though from none of the tribes he knew.

"Forgive these interruptions," Omeocelotl apologized, when the last of the visitors had gone. "You must go on with your story."

"First you must tell me about the standards on the wall," Azcatzin countered. "Where are they from?"

"Two are from the Chontal of Acallan, the swampy land to the west of Xicalanco. The third belonged to a member of a Zoque raiding party that attacked us outside the city of Cimatan."

Azcatzin waited for his brother to elaborate on their capture, but Omeocelotl had lowered his eyes and was toying silently with the stirring stick in his cocoa.

"Did you capture their owners?" Azcatzin asked, and his brother gave him a guarded look, as if it breached his sense of modesty to speak of such things.

"I killed them," he said simply.

"Then you must be a great warrior!" Azcatzin exclaimed, but again Omeocelotl resolutely shook his head in denial.

"I am but a poor merchant, my brother, I fight only to protect the goods entrusted to me. But let us speak no more of this. Tell me, how are our uncles?"

Azcatzin frowned openly, frustrated and baffled by his brother's unwillingness to talk about himself. What has happened to his pride? he wondered, remembering how Omeocelotl used to boast to him of his exploits when they were children. But courtesy demanded that he reply to the question of his host, so Azcatzin could not probe further.

"I did not see much of Huemac on this campaign, for he was serving as a rear-guard commander. He is even busier now that we have returned to Tenochtitlan, for he is one of those in charge of building Ahuitzotl's army. He is a hard taskmaster, and it is said that all the young apprentices are afraid of him."

"Is he still teaching you to be a ball player?" Omeocelotl inquired, and Azcatzin brightened despite himself.

"When there is time. He is preparing me for a tryout with Chiquatli's team. You must come to see me play some time."

"That would be a pleasure," Omeocelotl said, then paused before going on: "And how is our Uncle Acolmiztli?"

442

Azcatzin examined his brother curiously.

"You have not seen him? He has been in Tenochtitlan all along, you know. He no longer goes into the field with the warriors, because of his bad leg."

"I know this," Omeocelotl said in a neutral tone. "He is well respected for his work as a judge in the Teccalco, and for the services he has performed as an ambassador and counselor to Ahuitzotl. But I know that my presence no longer pleases him; he is disappointed that I did not choose to join the ranks of the warriors."

"Then you must go to him," Azcatzin urged, "and tell him of the men you have conquered. He will be proud of you when he learns that you are a warrior in your own right."

Omeocelotl let out a long breath and did not speak for several moments. Then he looked into Azcatzin's eyes.

"It is not your fault that you do not understand the ways of the pochteca, my brother, and it will take more than one visit for me to instruct you properly. So I will speak to you in a way that you will understand, as one Tenocha to another. But you must promise me that you will not take offense until you have heard *all* that I have to say. And you must also promise that you will not repeat my words to *anyone*: not to your own people, and not to anyone to whom I might introduce you in the future."

Azcatzin spent a moment considering the implications of his brother's *choosing* to speak to him as a Tenocha, as if the same blood did not run in their veins. Then, since he *did* wish to understand, he nodded solemnly in agreement.

"You have my promise."

"Good. Then tell me: You have already participated in two campaigns, and you have demonstrated your valor in battle. How have you been rewarded for this?"

"I have been allowed to cut my hair in the manner of the warriors," Azcatzin said, trusting that his brother had a reason for asking him to explain what both of them already knew. "And I can now sit with the seasoned warriors, and partake with them of yetl and cocoa and octli. And I am allowed to wear this lip-plug and the cotton garments given me by the Speaker."

Omeocelotl paused respectfully, as if to soften the impact of his next questions:

"Yet it is true, is it not, that you still sleep in the Young Men's House? And that until you have taken four captives, you will have no house of your own, and no share in the tribute from the lands you have helped to conquer?"

"That is true," Azcatzin admitted grudgingly, beginning to see where this line of inquiry was leading and not liking it.

"Is it not also true that until you have taken your fourth captive, you will be rewarded solely with the feathers and jewels that signify your rank?"

"I do not fight for 'things,' my brother," Azcatzin replied testily, "any more than our father did. I fight for the glory of the gods and our city."

"I do not question the worthiness of your motives," Omeocelotl said, holding up a hand to remind his brother to hold his temper as he had promised. "I am speaking only of the manner in which you are repaid for your efforts. Every time that Ahuitzotl summons the fighting men to war, he gives them insignia to wear into battle. And when they have returned successful, he gives them more insignia in recognition of their courage. That is as it should be. But have you never wondered where the Speaker finds such great quantities of feathers and precious stones?"

Azcatzin shrugged involuntarily, showing that he had not.

"They are the spoils of war," he supposed, "and part of the tribute sent by our subjects."

"Partly, that is true," Omeocelotl allowed. "But consider the present size of the army, and how active it has been. We *have* no subjects in the lands where the precious birds are found in abundance, and where the emerald-green jade and the yellow amber are dug from the ground. Without the merchants to obtain these things for him, the Speaker would be forced to reward the warriors with bags of maize and lengths of cloth."

"No one denies the usefulness of the pochteca," Azcatzin said impatiently. "But we are still speaking of 'things.' "

"We are speaking of the *value* of things," Omeocelotl corrected. "Let me tell you a story: In the swamps of Acallan, the land of the Chontals, we came upon a forester who lived alone, in a hut raised on poles over the water. He wore a yellow nose-bead and cut his hair like an Otomi, and he did not smile once. But he also did not flee from us, and so we talked with him, sometimes in his language, sometimes in ours. He was a man who trapped birds for his living, and when he learned that we were traders, he brought out bundles of precious feathers: those of the quetzal and the blue cotinga, the red troupial and the black guan, and parrot feathers of many colors . . ."

Omeocelotl gestured with his chin toward Azcatzin's chest.

"I had twenty mantles with me, very much like the one that you are wearing, but I did not even bother to show them to this man. He wanted flint and obsidian, copper ax heads and cochineal dye, and a mirror in which to see himself. In return for these things—perhaps half the value of your mantle— we received enough feathers to make insignia for an entire regiment. Our canoe was so crowded with the bundles that we had to kneel on them to paddle."

Azcatzin made an unpleasant face, blinking at the effort of imagining such wealth. But he did not try to interrupt as his brother went on:

"I do not tell you this to impress you with our cleverness, or to imply that this man was stupid. He got as much as he would have from the feather merchants in Xicalanco, and he did not have to pay the marketplace tax. And the true cost to us was much greater than it appeared, for we had traveled for many months just to reach that land, and we had lost several of our number along the way. We would lose even more on the journey back to Tenochtitlan. But still, my brother," Omeocelotl added in a humble tone, "we would be the first to admit that our sacrifice was very small compared to the blood that the warriors will shed to obtain those feathers the second time."

"Are you saying," Azcatzin demanded quizzically, "that the warriors have made a poor bargain for themselves?"

"I am saying that *they* are the ones who put the final value on these things," Omeocelotl explained patiently. "Their pact is with the gods of war, and they have no choice but to barter with their lives. We honor them for this, for the warrior's calling has been sacred since the beginning of time. And *that* is why we make no claims to being warriors ourselves, even though we fight and die as you do. Nor do we ever boast of our possessions, since these are the very things for which you shed your blood so freely. We know that the warriors regard us with suspicion and disdain, because we do not seek glory for ourselves. But were we to live less humbly, we would be sure to excite their hatred and envy, and cause them to come against us."

Now Azcatzin understood the source of his brother's reticence, and he saw that it was rooted in a pride in his calling that was as deep-seated as Azcatzin's own. Yet a pride that hid itself so resolutely from view was contrary to everything that he and Omeocelotl had been taught as boys, and though he knew the reasons for it now, he still did not comprehend how his brother had come to accept such an attitude as his own.

"Speaking as one Tenocha to another," he said carefully, "I have to wonder, my brother, if you do not sometimes wish to claim the honor that is rightfully yours."

Omeocelotl smiled slowly, without denial.

"Because of my upbringing, I feel this more than the other pochteca," he admitted. "But no one in Tlatelulco is contented with the fact that our temple to Huitzilopochtli has lain in ruins since the civil war, and that our city is ruled by an Eagle Speaker appointed in Tenochtitlan. Perhaps, though, that will change soon, when it is again seen that we serve Huitzilopochtli in our own way, in advance of the warriors."

"How will this be seen?" Azcatzin asked quickly, catching a momentary glimpse of ambition in his brother's eyes. Omeocelotl gave him a shrewd look and smiled again.

"Much has changed in the Valley since the time of our suppression. The lands close at hand, save for those of the Tarascans and the Tlaxcalans, have all been conquered, many so long ago that their tribute has since been forgiven. Ahuitzotl is forced to go farther and farther afield in search of new conquests, and thus, the service we perform as his eyes and ears has increased in importance. A great expedition is being planned at this very moment, to depart in the coming year. There will be more than a thousand of us, and we will be bearing Ahuitzotl's goods as well as our own. One half of the group will go to the east, to Xicalanco and beyond, testing the strength of the Chontals. The other half will go west and south, to Xoconochco and Ayotlan, in the land called Cuauhtemallan. We will be going in force, without disguise, in order to scout for the army that will soon follow after us."

Azcatzin raised his eyebrows, imagining the hostility that such a group would draw upon itself, since the spying activities of the pochteca were well known everywhere.

"That will be very dangerous," he ventured.

"We do not fear danger," Omeocelotl assured him. "Like you, we fear only the humiliation of failing in our appointed task."

The statement had a familiar ring—an echo of their mutual past—and Azcatzin smiled suddenly, reconciled completely to his brother's position.

"I wish you success," he said sincerely. "You used to speak often of Xoconochco and Ayotlan. Are you going there?"

"Yes," Omeocelotl said with unmistakable satisfaction. "Perhaps you will go there yourself, before too long."

"You must be sure to mark the trail, then."

Omeocelotl nodded agreeably and glanced behind him at the fading light coming through the overhead trap.

"Will you stay and share food with me? You still have not told me of your captures."

"I will trade with you for the story of yours," Azcatzin proposed slyly. "You need not fear: I will not forget that you are but a *poor* merchant."

"In that case, I accept," Omeocelotl said easily, and reached out to grasp his brother's hand, sealing the bargain.

XOLOTLPILLI awoke with a start, surrounded by darkness. He was sprawled face down on the bed of fir branches he had been using as an altar, and the rest of his body was very cold, for he was wearing only a thin maxlatl and a net mantle. Jumping guiltily to his feet, he looked up at the stars to see how long he had slept, shaking his legs and flapping his arms to restore circulation.

Ce Acatl, the morning star of Quetzalcoatl, was already high in the east, and the sky had turned somewhat lighter. Xolotlpilli would be expected back at the calmecac soon, and he had yet to gather any firewood or collect his quota of the poisonous insects the priests used in their paint. A familiar anxiety began to churn in his empty stomach, awakening the gnawing sense of misery that had been his constant—and only—companion since the day he entered the priests' school. He had been warned of the hardships he would have to endure, of course, but he had not expected them to prove so unyielding to his strength and courage. Sleep was an enemy he could not fight, since it always took him by surprise. He knew that it was hunger that made him so sleepy, but the priests refused to give him any more to eat than the other boys received, even though he was as large as any two of them together. His skin hung in loose folds over his bones, which stood out like the rack upon which meat had been dried. Many times he had been tempted to eat the things he found in the forest, but he had always managed to restrain himself. So far. If only I could have my flute, he thought hopelessly; *that* would keep my mind off my stomach. I could play for the gods, and they would know the prayers that are in my heart.

Again he roused himself, and began to look for the gourd he had brought with him. Wishing did him no good, he knew, though it was a lesson that came hard to him, and had to be relearned time and again. Despite all his suffering, he still had not forgotten how happy he had once been, in the days before he had become a student. He had had many friends then, boys who liked him and who vied with one another to have him on their side in the mock battles they fought. And he had been able to sleep the whole night through, and eat his fill, and he could listen to the stories of his mother and grandmother without being made to repeat them back . . .

No more, he warned himself, feeling his misery sharpen. Picking up the stoppered gourd, he took one of the fir branches in his other hand and groped his way to the rock pile that lay at the edge of the clearing. Turning over a rock with his foot, he grimaced with disgust at the long many-legged centipedes that scurried briefly back and forth before coiling themselves into protective circles. Unable to restrain the force of his arm, Xolotlpilli brought the fir branch down with a crashing blow, flattening all those underneath. About half of them were crushed beyond recognition, but the rest wriggled feebly, curling back upon themselves, and he scooped these into his gourd, using twigs as tongs. The priests sometimes objected to the mangled state of his offerings, but Xolotlpilli had been bitten too many times to risk a more subtle form of capture. He loathed hunting these creatures in the dark nearly as much as he loathed the darkness itself, and he always felt that he used up vast amounts of courage simply to make himself stay here. But he feared the priests, and their disciplinary thorns, more than anything, so he continued turning over rocks until his gourd was filled with hairy, twisting bodies.

He had just finished when he heard, distantly, the sound of the priests' conch trumpets, confirming the fact that he was already late. Xolotlpilli felt a sob catch in his throat, and he wondered desperately why he had been born to suffer like this, and still to fail. You are worthless, *worthless,* he reproached himself, anticipating the reprimands of the priests, as well as the punishments they would inflict upon him. He wished that he could run away, and live in these woods by himself, and never have to go back to the calmecac. But it was impossible for him to contemplate the disgrace he would bring on his parents —*they* were not the cause of his stupidity.

Tears welled up in his eyes, and with them came a wild unreasoning rage. He jumped up and ran to the edge of the clearing, staring blindly at the trees. He had no time to search the underbrush for dry sticks; he barely had time to get back before daybreak. But he would not return without wood. He would give them so much wood that they would not know what to do with it. Selecting a sturdy long-needle pine about his own height, he seized its rough-barked trunk in both hands and began to jerk it back and forth, grunting with effort. The tree cracked near the base with a loud rending sound, and Xolotl-pilli tugged and twisted until the trunk tore free, sending him backward to the ground. He was up in an instant, growling ferociously as he ripped the limbs loose and stripped them of their needles, his hands sticky with pine resin and his own blood. When the trunk was completely bare, he planted its narrow end in the earth and bent it back upon itself, straining mightily until he had broken it into two pieces.

Then he stood panting over the pile of jagged, broken limbs, his anger turning to regret at the sight of the tree's gleaming white flesh. He would have to propitiate the forest for what he had done to the tree and the spirit that dwelled within it, but there was no time for that now. Bundling the entire pile together with maguey twine, he heaved it to his shoulder and started back to the calmecac. Behind him, forgotten, was his gourd, left lying on the bed of pine needles surrounding the splintered stump, as if in recompense for the damage he had done.

WHEN THEY had arrived at the entrance to the women's quarters, Taypachtli thanked the servant who had brought her to the temple and asked her to return when the great Wind Drum was sounded at sunset. Cocatli was waiting just inside the entrance, and she formally welcomed her sister-in-law to the precinct of Quetzalcoatl, taking Taypachtli's hand in lieu of an embrace. Then she led her guest to a bench in a quiet corner of the interior courtyard, and the two women sat down together to talk.

"I am pleased that you have come to see me," Cocatli said. "Though I hope that you are not concerned about Papalotl. She has emerged from her seclusion and is doing quite well."

"I am glad to hear that," Taypachtli admitted, "though it was more to see you that I came. The house can be very lonely sometimes, with all the children gone, and Huemac away so much tending to his duties. I miss your company, my sister."

Touched by the plaintive note in Taypachtli's voice, Cocatli covered her hand with one of her own.

"I think of you often, as well, though I do not lack for company here. I have spoken to Papalotl twice recently, and the last time, she recited your flower song for me. I do not wonder that you won the first prize."

"Does my daughter still yearn for Texcoco, and the life of royalty?"

"I am sure that she has saved her memories," Cocatli said wryly. "But there have been no more complaints of her daydreaming, and she has lost her Texcocan accent. Her memory is excellent, and she is quick to grasp the many meanings of the songs and legends. The priestesses are most pleased with her."

"Has she grown?"

"Oh, yes," Cocatli said emphatically. "Our Butterfly is becoming a woman, my sister, a most *beautiful* woman. Even the priests have noticed this, though Papalotl herself is given no opportunity to dwell on such earthly matters."

Taypachtli frowned slightly and lapsed into a thoughtful silence, as if afraid of offending Cocatli with her response.

"She appears to be contented with her studies and her service," Cocatli said, guessing at her companion's thoughts. "But I do not think that she means to make the priesthood her vocation. Not yet, anyway."

"She is only twelve," Taypachtli offered consolingly, though her own relief was plain. Cocatli smiled and patted her hand again.

"I do not blame you for wanting to see her married, and a mother," she said tolerantly. "I have made my peace with Huemac on this subject, and I would say the same thing to you: Let us both be patient, and trust in the decision of the god."

Taypachtli nodded gratefully, and they were silent for a few moments, listening to the dim echoes of a recitation being conducted somewhere within the nearby rooms.

"It seems odd, and propitious, that you should have come to visit me today," Cocatli mused aloud. "For I have been asked about Huemac on two different occasions recently. How is it that my brother knows Patecatl, the High Priest of my order?"

"I do not know," Taypachtli confessed. "I have never heard this man's name."

"He is a very holy man, and kind to those beneath him," Cocatli said reverently. "He told me to encourage Huemac to come to see him. He said only that it concerned certain rumors that Huemac is said to have been investigating in Texcoco. Perhaps Nezahualpilli sent word to him."

"Perhaps," Taypachtli allowed thoughtfully. "I will give Huemac the message. To whom else have you spoken?"

"The young lord, Moteczuma. He is often at the temple, for he, like Papalotl, was dedicated to the Plumed Serpent at birth. He was born in the year One-Reed, the year of my Lord."

"Huemac knows him," Taypachtli said, with a curtness that surprised Cocatli. "What did he ask you?"

Cocatli stared at her briefly, impressed by the intensity of her involvement in her husband's affairs. My brother is lucky, she thought, to have one with whom he can share so much.

"Once he had approached me," she explained, "he became very shy, and it was not easy to ascertain what it was he wanted. He seemed curious about what Huemac had done in Texcoco, and what his relationship to Nezahualpilli was. Perhaps he had also heard of these rumors the High Priest mentioned . . . ?"

A gong sounded suddenly from the pyramid that rose up behind the courtyard, and Cocatli put a cautionary hand on Taypachtli's arm.

"The Wind Drum of our Lord is about to be sounded," she warned. "Do not be startled."

Taypachtli nodded and sat calmly as the great thunder of the drum rose into the air above them, booming out over the entire city. It was a signal given twice each day—at sunrise and sunset—the sound to which the Tenocha both began and ended their work day.

"I must go now," Taypachtli said, when the last, rumbling echo had died away. "Tell our daughter that we look forward to the feast of Seven-Reed, when we may see her again. Oh yes, and give her the regards of her friend Pinotl, Cuetzpaltzin's son. He will be leaving soon for Cuauhtemallan with Omeocelotl, to whom he has apprenticed himself."

"I will tell her," Cocatli promised, squinting curiously at Taypachtli. "I do not wish you to violate your husband's confidence, my sister," she said hesitantly, "but you must tell me one thing before you go. Do these rumors have to do with Quetzalcoatl?"

"Possibly," Taypachtli admitted reluctantly, after a long pause. "Forgive me, my sister. I do not know how frank he would wish me to be with you on this subject."

"He has told me that he was once visited by the god, and that it was a very frightening experience. But you do not have to tell me more. Only tell *him* that Patecatl is a man to be trusted."

"He will be grateful," Taypachtli assured her. "As I am grateful for your understanding."

"I have always honored my brother's need for secrecy," Cocatli said simply. "Give my regards to my mother and brothers," she added, "and come to see me again. My vows should not separate us more than is necessary."

"I will return soon, then," Taypachtli said, as she rose from the bench. "Though I fear that I bring too much of the world into this holy place."

"We *all* live upon the earth," Cocatli demurred, taking Taypachtli's hand and glancing up at the round, painted shrine atop the temple pyramid. "However much we may wish to inhabit some better place . . ."

THE wind came up suddenly in the night, rattling the windchimes in the courtyard and making the huehuetl tree creak and shudder in protest. Waking instinctively, Huemac identified the sounds as harmless and began to lapse back into sleep. But then he sensed that Taypachtli was also awake, and he rolled over to find her sitting with her back against the wall, a blanket pulled up to her chin.

"Did the wind also awaken you, my wife?" he asked softly, trying not to startle her. Her head turned slowly in his direction, and her voice seemed curiously flat, almost dreamy, when she finally responded.

"I was awake when it rose, though I do not know what woke me. Perhaps I had a dream, though I do not remember dreaming. I could not go back to sleep."

Huemac sat up beside her and found her hand under the blanket. He recalled the discussion they had had before going to sleep, wondering if he had not soothed her anxieties as well as he had thought.

"Were you worrying about Xolotlpilli again?"

"I was thinking about him," Taypachtli allowed, in the same musing tone. "But I was thinking of many other things, as well. I was thinking of my father, and Nopalli. And of the child in the hills who grows without a father. I could not seem to control the things that came into my mind."

"These are somber thoughts," Huemac offered sympathetically, rubbing her hand between his own.

"They did not *seem* somber," Taypachtli replied mildly, without real disagreement. "Some were in fact quite pleasant. I was also thinking of Michpilli in his valley, and of the Lady of Tula's promise to find a match for Papalotl."

Huemac could see no connection between any of these thoughts, and he began to wonder if his wife were truly awake, even though she was answering him quite coherently. Could she be speaking out of a dream?

"Perhaps I am getting old and foolish," Taypachtli suggested when he did not respond, "like the white-haired old women who have only their memories left."

"You are only thirty-three years of age, my wife," Huemac reminded her sternly. "And you have me, and our children, and the grandchildren who will one day fill this house with their noise. I know that you are lonely now, and I am sorry that my duties take me away from you so much. These young men today are fools for glory, even worse than I was at their age. I cannot allow them to go into the field undisciplined."

"I was not complaining, my husband," Taypachtli assured him, squeezing his hand under the blanket. "You came back to me from the desert. That is a thought that warms me always, despite my compassion for the woman and the child in the hills."

Huemac moved closer, slipping an arm under her back.

"It is our fate, and our blessing, to stay together like this," Huemac whispered, his lips close to her ear. Taypachtli smiled and turned her body into his, and they gradually lowered themselves to their mats. But before they could begin their love-making, they heard a small, timid voice crying out from the doorway, asking for the parents of Quetzal Papalotl.

"What is it?" Huemac demanded, bolting upright beside his wife. Taypachtli put a restraining hand on his arm, to keep him from frightening the speaker away.

"Come in, whoever it is," she said in a welcoming tone. "We are the parents of Quetzal Papalotl."

"I am from the temple," the voice said. "You must come quickly. Your daughter has had an accident."

Taypachtli rose and dressed hurriedly while Huemac went to rouse Ome Xochitl, who promised to follow after them. The young girl from the temple, though flustered by the powerful wind and Huemac's insistent questions, nevertheless managed to convey what little information she knew as they hurried through the deserted streets toward the temple precinct. Papalotl had collapsed in the midst of a ceremony marking the end of a long fast to Ehecatl, the God of Wind; she did not appear to have injured herself in her fall, but she had lain unconscious for some time, beyond the reach of the priestesses' efforts to awaken her, weeping loudly and calling out her mother's name. The Priestess Cocatli had sent the girl for them as soon as Papalotl had been returned to consciousness.

Huemac propelled Taypachtli over the smooth flagstones of the plaza, following the girl around to the side of the Temple of Quetzalcoatl. Cocatli met them at the entrance to the women's quarters, and she immediately took Taypachtli's hands and spoke comfortingly:

"She is not injured, my sister. She has had an attack of some kind, perhaps brought on by a weakness in the blood. She had fasted with the rest of us, and only two days ago, she began to bleed like a woman for the first time. I will take you to her. You can go no further, my brother," she said to Huemac, "but the High Priest awaits you in his chamber. The girl will take you there."

Huemac nodded helplessly, watching as the two women disappeared into the interior of the building. Then he stepped back into the wind and let the girl lead him to another entrance, and down a long, dimly lit corridor to the chamber of the High Priest. Huemac paused before entering, remembering the message Cocatli had delivered for this man, an invitation to which Huemac had never responded. He did not think that he knew anyone called Patecatl, and once he had entered and had seen the old man seated beneath the chamber's single torch, he was certain that he did not know him. Patecatl was a vigorous man of perhaps sixty years, with snow-white hair and a deeply lined face. He was wearing a golden wind jewel over his long white robe, and his waist-length hair had been braided with strips of white cloth. His black eyes were bright yet very gentle, reminding Huemac of his grandfather.

"I am Patecatl, the High Priest of our order," he said in a friendly tone, beckoning to Huemac to sit across from him. "I have been waiting to speak with you, and now your daughter has provided me with the occasion."

"What has happened to her?" Huemac asked abruptly, forgetting his manners in his concern for Papalotl. He had not believed for an instant that anything that happened to his daughter in the Temple of Quetzalcoatl could be an "accident."

"When the wind rose outside the temple," Patecatl explained, overlooking the breach of politeness, "your daughter cried out and fell to the floor, unconscious. Then she had a dream, or perhaps a vision." The priest paused to examine Huemac's face. "She dreamed that she heard a loud sound, like many drums beating, and then the earth and the sky began to shake, as if about to fall into pieces. She found herself in the water with her mother, and they were sinking, and then she could not find her mother, and she was certain that she had drowned. She called her mother's name many times while she was seeing this."

Huemac swallowed with difficulty and lowered his eyes from Patecatl's face, feeling a chill spread through his body. So . . . the god had finally reached out for his daughter. Or perhaps for his wife.

"It could mean nothing," the priest continued in a practical voice. "Many of the girls have visions when they are fasting, though few are so totally overcome by them. And the signs surrounding your daughter's birth are very powerful. She will not be permitted to fast for a while, and I will see that she is watched during the times of her bleeding. When she has recovered from her fright, I will talk to her myself, and see what more I can learn."

"I am grateful, Your Holiness," Huemac managed, still preoccupied with the unsettling details of Papalotl's vision. The loud sound and the shaking bore a striking similarity to certain details of his own vision of the end, so much so that he was certain that it had been no mere dream. Then he realized that the priest had not spoken, but was watching him with a smile on his wrinkled face.

"You do not remember me, then," the old man said, seeming only mildly surprised. "I suppose that is understandable, since you never saw my face. Perhaps, though, you still remember the ceremony that was held in this temple on the day that you graduated from the calmecac. It was *I* who wore the mask of the god on that day, *I* who took your beads from you and released you into the world."

Huemac stiffened, remembering the power that had tingled within him that day, and the eerie way that his beads had sizzled when the priest had thrown them into the brazier. *This* priest, he thought warily, recalling how certain he had been that the man in the beaked mask had sensed his power, and had been touched by it himself.

"That was a long time ago," he said carefully. "Forgive me for not recognizing your name, Your Holiness."

"I have followed your career closely since that day," Patecatl told him frankly, brushing aside his apology. "I have examined the public record of your exploits, and I have listened to all the rumors. You have a most extraordinary reputation, my son, both here and in Texcoco."

"You have friends in Texcoco?" Huemac asked suspiciously, feeling very uncomfortable with the fact that this man, about whom he knew so little, seemed to know a great deal about him. He did not like being at such a disadvantage, especially with a priest.

"None in the hills," Patecatl said modestly, "but enough in the city to know the kinds of questions you were asking there. We both know how dangerous such speculations could be to you in this city, so I do not wonder that you do not trust me. But I want you to believe that I am not one of those whom you need to fear, and that you are not alone in your seeking for answers."

Hearing the invitation in the old man's words, Huemac stared deeply into his gentle black eyes, assessing his truthfulness by the straightness of his gaze, a technique that Nezahualpilli had taught him. He saw, in addition to Patecatl's essential honesty, that the priest had no nahuallis and no coercive powers. All his forces were directed inward, and upward. There was indeed nothing to fear from him. Huemac withdrew his gaze and bowed respectfully.

"I believe you, my father, and I would be honored to share with you what I know."

"That is good," Patecatl said gruffly. "As you know, a great test is being prepared for our people. The signs are undeniable. Those with the courage to face this must band together, and not allow themselves to be suppressed."

"Are there others in this city, besides ourselves?" Huemac asked hopefully. "What of young Moteczuma?"

Patecatl hesitated, squinting at him guardedly, then broke into a rueful smile.

"Already, you put my frankness to a test. I had heard that you are like that." Then the priest shook his head and grew serious. "Moteczuma has enormous curiosity concerning the ways of the gods, and he is very learned for his age. But he is also very close to the reed seat, and I know that in his heart he regards the prophecy of Quetzalcoatl's return as a threat to his inheritance. He wishes to propitiate the god, not welcome him into his city."

"And you, my Lord?" Huemac inquired with equal seriousness. "Would you welcome the god even if it meant our destruction?"

"Without question," Patecatl said emphatically. "But the Plumed Serpent is not a god of destruction and killing. Indeed, it was his unwillingness to spill the blood of his people that caused him to be driven out of Tula. But we are getting ahead of the things that we must discuss. Go to your wife, my son; she will need your comfort on this night."

Huemac nodded gratefully and bowed to the priest before rising.

"I will come back to speak to you soon, my Lord," he promised.

"Surely. Though there is still time for us to prepare," Patecatl added, giving Huemac a knowing glance in parting. "As you know . . ."

CUAUHTEMALLAN, Omeocelotl repeated silently as he followed the men ahead along the trail, brushing back the grasping vegetation and keeping an eye to the ground for snakes. It was a land as strange and awesome as he had imagined, fiercely hot yet always wet, with jungles like this, where the flowering plants grew to the size of trees and seemed to drip their brilliant colors onto the spongy earth underfoot. Where monkeys and parrots screamed in the branches overhead and enormous spiders spun webs large enough to capture birds; where the sudden, deep night was filled with the sustained screech of thousands of insects, punctuated occasionally by the chilling cough of a jaguar prowling close by, felt but never seen.

Yet then the trail would rise out of the cloud forest into a land of swift rivers and misty valleys, the views of the distant mountains broken only by stands of pine and oak and shelves of jagged black rock. The ground underfoot crunched like cinders and could be felt to vibrate whenever the trail passed within sight of one of the smoking mountains, which growled ominously and spat ashes into the air. This, too, was Cuauhtemallan, home of the Maya, a land unknown until now by the pochteca of Mexico.

Omeocelotl saw a bright light ahead, indicating a clearing in the jungle, and he reflexively checked his weapons. According to what they had been told in Xoconochco, they should soon be reaching the river called Xochiatl, the last major barrier between them and their goal: the city of Ayotlan. This would be as far as the merchants would penetrate on this journey, for they had been on the trail for almost two years, and most of their goods had already been traded for the cocoa, jade, and precious feathers that were found here in such abundance. There was also a growing sense that the opposition to their presence was building, and that they would not be allowed to return, with their accumulation of wealth and their carefully drawn maps, as easily as they had come.

In recognition of the danger, Cuetzpaltzin had chosen to personally lead the party to Ayotlan, and he had hand-picked those who would accompany him, leaving the rest behind to guard the encampment outside of Xoconochco. Omeocelotl knew that he and his fellows, largely from the Guild of Vanguard Merchants, had been chosen because of their steadiness and restraint. A provocation could not be risked, and many of the young men, traveling openly under the banner of Ahuitzotl, had become more and more Mexican in their attitudes the farther they got from home, and sometimes their impatience to communicate was interpreted as aggression. Cuetzpaltzin was taking no chances this late in the journey, this far from any hope of rescue should trouble arise.

Cuetzpaltzin reassembled his men at the edge of the jungle, and all stood reverently while prayers were offered to Huitzilopochtli and Yacatecuhtli, the Lord Who Guides. Then the fighting men like Omeocelotl gave their black walking staves to their apprentices and formed a protective wedge behind Cuetzpaltzin and the other leaders, their shields and warclubs at the ready. The archers fitted arrows into their bows and took up places inside the wedge, surrounding the porters and the loosely yoked line of slaves at the center. Proceeding at a stately pace, Cuetzpaltzin led the group in a mass across the grassy plain that led down to the river.

A large fleet of high-bowed war canoes was drawn up on the bank, and in front of them, seven or eight deep, were the ranks of warriors who had come across to meet the merchants. They were fierce-looking men, resplendent in feathers and face paint, their golden jewelry gleaming in the sun. The leader who came forward to greet Cuetzpaltzin wore a headdress of parrot feathers over his tufted topknot, and his earlobes hung almost to his shoulders from the weight of the golden plugs inserted through them. He wore a vest of blue cotinga feathers over his cotton armor and carried a throwing board and a shield of turquoise mosaic with a circle of gold in the center. Pieces of jade and mirror-stone had been fitted between his teeth, which sparkled with green and silver light when the man opened his mouth to speak. Using a dialect similar to the language of the Zoques, he gestured to himself and his warriors, proudly naming them as the Quiche, the lords of Ayotlan.

Standing in the front of the wedge, Omeocelotl saw the man's eyes roam appraisingly over the merchants as Cuetzpaltzin sought to reply to him in a tongue he would understand. He sees our smaller numbers, and our lack of battle insignia, Omeocelotl thought, and he wonders why he should not simply kill us and take our goods. Omeocelotl tightened his grip on his macana, remembering the conversation he had had with Azcatzin. We *should* be allowed the markings of our bravery, he thought with sudden anger, so that foreigners like these would not be tempted to take us lightly, and mistreat us at their will. We will make them sorry if they try, he vowed fiercely, scanning the ranks of warriors for signs of restlessness.

Yet no one stirred among the Quiche, and Omeocelotl saw that Cuetzpaltzin was gradually winning over their leader. Gesturing frequently and speaking always in a calm, humble tone, Cuetzpaltzin had succeeded in drawing all the man's attention to himself, and soon he was plying the man with gifts in a manner designed to win his favor without arousing his greed. Omeocelotl found himself being won over, and his anger of the moment before faded into shame at his own impulsiveness. *That* is the true courage of the pochteca, he thought ruefully: to meet all threats with a calm face and cunning words, defying the enemy by passing safely through his midst. And to never raise your arm precipitously, out of fear or the suggestion of disrespect.

I am still too much a Tenocha, Omeocelotl told himself, as one of the slave traders from Azcapotzalco brought forward a young Huaxtec girl who had been captured in Ahuitzotl's campaign against Cuauhtla. Because her Huaxtec features were so similar to those considered beautiful by the broad-headed, hook-nosed Maya, the girl had been heavily bid upon in Xoconochco. But now Omeocelotl could see, in the delighted smile on the Quiche leader's face, the reason for Cuetzpaltzin's refusal to allow her to be sold before this. She was the final, winning gift.

Then the Quiche leader was embracing Cuetzpaltzin and signaling to his men to make room for the merchants in their canoes, and the party began to make its way down to the river. Omeocelotl gave silent thanks to the gods for the wisdom and patience of his leader, and for the lesson he had learned this day. Never again would he forget the kind of courage he must have: the courage that had guided him, at last, to the land of his dreams, to the city of Ayotlan.

ABOVE THE shouts of the men and the clash of warclubs against wooden shields, Chiquatli heard, faintly, the high hollow sound of someone playing the flute. Even without being able to see the player, he knew from the mournfulness of the tune that it had to be Xolotlpilli. The boy had been moping around the House of Eagles for almost ten days, having been placed in his father's care after he had punched another boy senseless in the Young Men's House. It had been Xolotlpilli's first day in the telpochcalli, and the other boy had been stupid enough to smirk and point to him as the boy who had just been sent away from the calmecac. He had even been foolish enough to call Xolotlpilli "stupid" to his face.

Chiquatli did not really understand why all this had upset Huemac so greatly. Many boys were not fit for the calmecac, whether the sons of lords or not, and Xolotlpilli was not the first boy to ever be temporarily banished from the telpochcalli for fighting. It had happened many times to Chiquatli as a boy, and he had never had as good a reason for *his* fights. What amazed him even more, though, was the way that Huemac indulged his son's hurt feelings and permitted him to sulk. Huemac was very busy, of course, and distracted by the problems his daughter was having in the temple, but Chiquatli had never seen him have even a moment's patience with self-pity on the part of his apprentices and trainees. Certainly, he never showed any to *me,* Chiquatli thought sardonically, and grinned to himself. He had come to take a perverse pride in the incorrigibility of his youth, now that he had grown into a man of responsibility: captain of the Puma Warriors, captain of the royal ball team, and one of Huemac's head trainers. He had even married recently, and he hoped, soon, to be a father himself.

Still, he remembered what it was like to be a bad boy, and he suddenly decided that he might be just the one to snap Xolotlpilli out of his trance. Huemac seemed unable, or unwilling, to make his son own up to his shame, but then, Chiquatli suspected that Huemac had had little experience with shame himself. Surely, he was not the expert Chiquatli was. Choosing two more men to skirmish with the chalk-edged warclubs, Chiquatli instructed his assistant to take over the drill for him. Away from the noise of the fighting, he followed the sound of the flute easily, and found Xolotlpilli sitting in the shade of the warriors' gallery, his back against one of the painted columns. He stopped playing when the warrior's huge shadow blocked out the sun, but it was several moments before he brought himself to look up at the man.

Despite the stern intentions with which he had come, Chiquatli felt himself soften at the sight of Xolotlpilli's utterly abject expression. His broad features seemed puffy with despair, his big brown eyes clouded by the memory of the friends he had left behind in the calmecac, along with most of what he had thought of as his honor. Chiquatli thought he knew something about friendlessness and lost honor, and compassion made him try a gentle approach first.

"Why do you not come over and watch us?" he suggested in a kindly voice. "There are ways to fight that do not get you into trouble, you know."

Xolotlpilli winced slightly at the mention of fighting and did not respond to the offer. Chiquatli had an impulse to invite him to participate, but he realized quickly that that would be overstepping his authority, and possibly dangerous, besides. Xolotlpilli was extraordinarily large for his twelve years, but he was too young to be matched with any of the trainees, all of whom were over sixteen and already trained in the telpochcalli. Some had even served in battle as apprentices. Chiquatli decided to try another tack, and assumed a knowing tone:

"I was often in trouble when I was a boy," he confessed. "But your father showed me how to face my past and put it behind me. You can do this, too."

Far from being cheered by this information, the boy gave him a baleful glance, as if the comparison insulted him. Chiquatli began to realize that he did not know the slightest thing about how to talk to children, but he felt that he had come too far to stop trying now.

"Why sulk about it?" he prodded, making a gesture of casual dismissal with his hand. "You had good reason to strike that boy. I would have done the same, and I never got to go to the calmecac at all."

"That is because you are macehuale—a commoner," Xolotlpilli muttered rudely, and Chiquatli's head jerked back as if he had been slapped. Baring his teeth, he reached down and gathered a handful of mantle and yanked the boy to his feet.

"*Stand* when you speak to a warrior!" he barked, pulling the boy away from the painted column and pointing to it with his other hand. "You do not deserve to cool your insolent self in this shade, which is the shadow of brave men. Come with me!"

He strode off without looking back, too angry to even contemplate what he might do if the boy refused to follow. But Xolotlpilli was right behind him when he walked into the middle of the drill and stopped it with a single furious gesture. The circle of young men fell silent and backed away slightly, bewildered by the wrath this overgrown child had inspired in their trainer. Chiquatli pointed at two men who stood on opposite sides of the circle, one the largest and the other the smallest of the trainees.

"You two will fight," he rasped harshly, then took a shield and macana from his assistant and dropped them at Xolotlpilli's feet.

"Your stupidity has been indulged long enough," he announced. "Your father loves you too much to let you suffer like a man, but I do not have his sympathy. Take those weapons and be of some use! I leave it to you to decide whom you should help . . ."

Chiquatli clapped his hands to begin the drill, and the smaller man gamely circled his massive opponent, staying low as he had been taught. Xolotlpilli stood as if paralyzed, his eyes fixed upon the weapons at his feet, not responding to the urgings of the men nearest to where he stood. The big man closed in on his opponent and landed a crunching blow upon his upraised shield, sending him staggering backward. Xolotlpilli looked up at the sound and jerked around foolishly when one of the men behind him poked him in the back, adding some scorn to his encouragement.

"It is your choice!" Chiquatli called. "Help him or watch him fall!"

Under desperate attack, the small man did a somersault in the dust and slashed out at the bigger man's legs with his macana, momentarily clearing some space for himself. But then the big man was upon him again, battering away at his shield in an almost leisurely manner, letting the weight of his blows take their toll. Glancing over at Xolotlpilli, he called out in a contemptuous tone:

"Would you like to finish him for me?"

The circle of men let out a collective growl of displeasure at the arrogance of this suggestion, which so angered the small man that he forgot himself and made a wild leap at his opponent. But the big man's nonchalance had been a ruse, and he calmly ducked the swinging warclub and struck the smaller man across the ribs with the flat of his macana, sending him reeling to the ground. The big man laughed, and Chiquatli spat into the dust, disgusted with himself for having created this situation. He had allowed one of his men to be openly humiliated, and for nothing. He was reaching for a weapon of his own, to teach the big man a lesson in humility, when out of the corner of his eye, he saw Xolotlpilli move across the circle.

His jaw clenched tightly and his eyes red with anger and shame, the boy stood in front of the fallen trainee and glared up at the big man, who was a full head taller.

"You will not touch him," Xolotlpilli said in a thick voice, making it a vow as well as a warning. With the shield and warclub raised in front of him, he no longer seemed so young, and the big man paused to reassess him before breaking into a grin.

"Just try to stop me, little man," he sneered, and started forward confidently. But before he could take a second step, Xolotlpilli let out a bloodthirsty scream and sprang at his opponent, slashing first right, then left with his macana, jarring the shield that the big man just managed to get into the way in time. It was the classic opening attack, executed so skillfully that the circle of men gasped in admiration before breaking into amazed cheers. Now where did he learn *that*? Chiquatli wondered, knowing that it was not the kind of move the boys picked up in their street games.

Recovering from his surprise, the big man glowered menacingly at Xolotlpilli and advanced again, no longer playing. Feinting with his shield, he dipped low and swung at the boy's legs, but Xolotlpilli jumped back nimbly and deflected the blow with his shield, turning the big man into the path of his own swing. The man jumped back himself, but not before the edge of Xolotlpilli's warclub left a streak of white across his shoulder. The men cheered again, but Xolotlpilli did not pause to celebrate his touch, moving in on his opponent behind a flurry of well-aimed blows. Chiquatli was now certain that he was witnessing something marvelous, the emergence of a true prodigy, a natural warrior. At the same time, though, he began to worry about how to stop this. Xolotlpilli had no helmet or armor, and it was plain to see that the big man would not hesitate to hurt him to save himself further embarrassment. Already, he was aiming disabling blows at the boy, who gave ground with a dangerous reluctance.

"Next touch wins!" Chiquatli shouted, waving his arms to quiet the cheering and restore the normal ambience of the drill, in the hope that this would remind the combatants that they were not fighting for real. The men fell silent, but Xolotlpilli and his opponent did not seem to notice, and continued hacking away at each other as forcefully as ever. Both were clearly exhausted, the maddened expressions on their streaming faces showing the emotion that sustained them. Chiquatli nudged his assistant and moved up to the edge of the circle, ready to intervene if necessary.

The two opponents crashed against each other, shields first, then bounced off and swung from the hip, each for the other's midsection, each aiming to kill. Chiquatli jerked forward involuntarily, then caught his breath as the warclubs met in midair, colliding with such force that they shattered and flew from their owners' hands in pieces, sailing over the heads of the ducking observers. Xolotlpilli and the big man could only stare at each other, stunned, and Chiquatli was between them in an instant.

"That is enough. Well fought, both of you," he added, nodding to the big man to show that he meant it. "I apologize for not warning you of Xolotlpilli's prowess."

"He is indeed a monster," the big man agreed with grudging admiration. Xolotlpilli seemed embarrassed by their attention, now that his anger had left him, and he ducked his head shyly and went over to the man he had defended, who remained seated on the ground, holding his side.

"I . . . I am ashamed that I did not help you sooner," Xolotlpilli stammered apologetically. "Perhaps you would like to strike me as you were struck."

458

The man stared at him incredulously, then laughed and held out his hand for Xolotlpilli to help him up.

"It was you who needed no help," he said admiringly, and clapped the boy on the shoulder as a gesture of forgiveness. Xolotlpilli beamed with gratitude, and the childlike innocence of his smile made the men around him laugh and give him another cheer, shouting his name three times.

"Continue with the drill," Chiquatli said curtly when they were through, and led Xolotlpilli back to the quiet shade of the warriors' gallery. Without speaking, the older man picked up the flute the boy had dropped beside the column and handed it back to him. Xolotlpilli looked at it for a long time before he raised his eyes to Chiquatli's face.

"I am sorry for what I said to you, my Lord," he said in a low voice, and Chiquatli laughed softly.

"If you had not made me angry, we might not have learned of the brave warrior hiding behind your sad face. Go back to the Young Men's House, Xolotlpilli," he said seriously. "I do not think that they will be able to keep you for long, and then you can come back here and train with the men. With your father."

"I would like to train with *you*," Xolotlpilli replied, a note of pleading in his voice. "My father *is* too kind to me."

Chiquatli frowned uncomfortably.

"I spoke in anger, and did not think first," he said weakly. "I am no one to be criticizing your father's wisdom."

"But you were right," the boy insisted. "He will *always* be too kind to me. You said yourself, I must be allowed to suffer like a man."

"Do not keep reminding me of my words," Chiquatli said gruffly, embarrassed by the devotion shining from the boy's eyes. "I will speak to your father when he returns tonight, and I will abide by his wishes. But I will tell him how much I would like to have you," he added in a softer tone, not wanting to dim that shine completely.

"You will not tell him what I said to you?" Xolotlpilli asked anxiously, and Chiquatli looked at him for a moment before answering.

"Only if you wish me to," he said pointedly, and Xolotlpilli blinked several times as the older man's meaning sank in. Then he drew himself up with dignity.

"I do," he said in a resolute voice. "I want him to know *all* the shame that I bear."

"Good," Chiquatli agreed. "Then he will understand, fully, how you earned my forgiveness. Go now, boy, and visit with your mother before you return to the telpochcalli. I will see you again, I know, when you come back to join the ranks of the men."

3

ACOLMIZTLI stood in the midst of the cheering crowd at the Eagle Gate, flanked by his mother, sister-in-law, and niece, watching the army march into the city. It was a familiar circumstance to him by now, since, in recent years, he more often greeted the warriors than accompanied them. Yet today was different, decidedly different, and everything seemed slightly strange to him, the sounds off-key and the images a bit too vivid. This was the year Three-Reed, Acolmiztli's fifty-fourth year upon the earth, and while he had celebrated many triumphs in that time, he had never expected to see the day when the warriors would form an honor guard for the merchants, leading the pochteca into Tenochtitlan as conquering heroes.

Only the year before, word had reached the city that the expedition bearing Ahuitzotl's goods had been attacked while returning from Ayotlan, and that the merchants had gone to ground at a place called Quauhtenanco, somewhere south of Tehuantepec. Ahuitzotl had immediately raised an army and sent it off under the command of his nephew Moteczuma, who had recently been promoted to the rank of warchief. None of Acolmiztli's sons had gone along, three of them being previously pledged to a flower war in Atlixco, and a fourth lying injured from his last campaign. But Huemac, Azcatzin, and Xolotlpilli had all volunteered, and they had joined the other warriors in their vow to either rescue the merchants or die trying.

But the army had barely reached the boundary of the Tlalhuican territory when they had met the merchants coming the other way, returning home under their own power. And the story that had been sent ahead to Tenochtitlan by runner was even more incredible: The expedition had been besieged at Quauhtenanco for nearly two years, surrounded by a coalition of warriors from the many tribes that lived between Tehuantepec and Ayotlan. Though outnumbered and desperately short of food and water, the merchants had held their defenses against attack after attack, until finally they had beaten back their attackers and routed them in the open field. It was said that they were returning to Tenochtitlan loaded down with the shields and standards they had taken from the warriors they had slain in making their escape.

Still pondering the import of this astonishing victory, Acolmiztli bent an ear away from the crowd to listen to the voice of his niece, who was standing beside him, describing the scene to Taypachtli.

"Here are the Eagles and Jaguars, Mother," Papalotl was saying. "But they are not as grave as they usually are; they are smiling with pride, in honor of the pochteca! And there is Father, wearing his Eagle headdress!"

Acolmiztli looked over the crowd at Huemac, then back at his niece. So beautiful, he thought; even a man of my years chooses to stand beside her when he can. He glanced down at Papalotl's right arm, which was splinted and held immobile in a cloth sling tied around her graceful neck. It was such a pity, he thought, that she was plagued by those dreams and fits, which caused her to injure herself, and which had put the look of fear into her golden eyes. He was wondering if she would *ever* be able to marry, when Papalotl suddenly looked up and caught him staring at her. Acolmiztli jerked his eyes away abruptly, but not before he had seen the apprehension in her gaze and the worried crease that was forming between her eyes. Only sixteen, he thought sadly, and already haunted by her fate . . .

"Here are Opochtli and the other Puma Warriors," Papalotl continued to her mother, though with a self-conscious tremor in her voice. "And here is Chiquatli—I can even see the tattoo on his leg! Oh, Mother, Xolotlpilli is even bigger than when he went away! He looks very brave, my brother . . ."

Xolotlpilli was indeed so large that Acolmiztli had to remind himself that the boy was only fourteen. He was only a few fingers shorter than Chiquatli and was already heavier than his master, whose owl-feather standard he carried. Acolmiztli had not approved of his nephew apprenticing himself to a Puma, a commoner, but Huemac, as usual, had allowed the boy to have his own way. It did not seem to have harmed him, though, Acolmiztli admitted grudgingly, noting the pride and confidence with which Xolotlpilli carried his weapons. He remembered how crushed the boy had been after being sent away from the calmecac, and how utterly his own attempts to rouse him had failed. Now, if what all the warriors were saying was true, the son of Huemac was destined for great things, and it was not expected that he would wear his apprentice's lock for long.

Acolmiztli again felt the sense of unreality descend upon him. Prodigies and merchant warriors: Had the inexplicable become commonplace in the city of his birth? Did nothing hold with the traditions he had always followed? Staring about helplessly, Acolmiztli spied his nephew Azcatzin coming through the gate, and immediately, some of his calm returned. Azcatzin marched only a few steps behind the seasoned warriors, since he needed but one captive to join their ranks. Papalotl told her mother that her cousin also looked very brave, and Acolmiztli could only concur, admiring the young man all the more because he was so small. Azcatzin was his favorite nephew, his attachment to the ball game easily forgiven in the light of the tenacity with which he pursued the warrior's task. He reminded Acolmiztli of himself: someone who had never wanted to be a sorcerer or a vanguard merchant, someone who had always had to work at the warrior's craft, like a normal man.

But then the noise of the crowd rose to a deafening roar, for the triumphant merchants had come into view. Acolmiztli experienced a queasy, shifting sensation in his stomach, and for several moments, he could not bring himself to look. Yet he knew that he had to, as surely as he had to take his next breath. He inhaled, braced himself, and looked.

The merchants wore their usual plain garb, but their long, unwashed hair hung in tangles, far down their backs, and many leaned on their black staves as they walked, due to the injuries they had incurred. The principal merchants and the vanguard merchants came two-by-two, and at their sides were their apprentices, their arms filled with the insignia their masters had captured. Acolmiztli located Omeocelotl several paces behind Cuetzpaltzin, though his face was so darkened by the sun as to be hardly recognizable. He was wearing an amber lip-plug, and he carried one bandaged arm in a sling, his weapons strapped to his back.

Next to him was his apprentice, the dark son of Cuetzpaltzin whose name

Acolmiztli could never remember. In contrast to his master, the boy was a blaze of brilliant color, with a beautifully inlaid shield hanging from each of his shoulders and his arms filled with feather crests and jeweled devices that glittered with gold and turquoise and mother-of-pearl. Acolmiztli counted at least ten separate standards in the boy's arms before he could bring himself to count no more. He listened to his niece's excited description as if from a great distance.

"Pinotl is limping, but he seems to have grown larger and more manly. He must wish that Omeocelotl were not such a great warrior, for he is terribly loaded down with all the insignia he carries! Oh, and the feathers, my mother! There are shimmering blue ones, and some red as flames, and long, exquisite, emerald-green ones such as I have never seen before."

"Those are the tail feathers of the quetzal," Acolmiztli supplied curtly, drawing a surprised glance from Papalotl, who had not known he was listening. His eyes were still fixed upon the parade of merchants, and when he spoke again, it was in a slow, musing tone, almost as if he thought himself alone in this crowd: "My nephew, the vanguard merchant, is also a great warrior."

Papalotl looked past her mother to Ome Xochitl, showing her puzzlement in her eyes. Had she not just said the same thing herself?

"That should not surprise you so, my brother-in-law," Taypachtli reminded him in a mild tone. "The merchants of my city have always been brave fighters. And he is *your* nephew."

Acolmiztli heard the intended flattery in her words, but he could not take them into his heart. On the one hand, he felt a great relief, as if a burden had been lifted from his shoulders, and he no longer had to strain against its weight. Yet he also felt a sense of loss, an emptiness where something solid and binding had once stood. He realized that his mother had moved in closer, and that she and his niece and sister-in-law were all waiting for his response.

"The meaning of what it is to be a warrior has changed forever today," he said, and sighed heavily. "Or perhaps I simply have not seen it until now. My father and Huemac saw it years ago. They knew that we would someday have to call the pochteca our equals."

"And do *you* accept it, my son?" Ome Xochitl asked, raising her voice to be heard above the crowd, which was loudly admiring the goods being carried past by the porters.

Acolmiztli stared at his mother, remembering the war he had fought against the Tlatelulca, and the scorn he and the other warriors had always felt for those who spent their lives seeking wealth rather than glory. What would it mean, now that the two were no longer separate and distinct? What would happen to the sacred nature of the warrior's calling? He did not know; only that it had already been done.

"I have no choice now," he said in a resigned voice, and bowed to his mother. "Forgive me, but I must leave you now. I want to be in attendance when these merchants are greeted by Ahuitzotl. I want my nephew to see that I pay him all the honor and respect that he deserves."

Bowing again to his niece, Acolmiztli slowly made his way to the front of the crowd. Then, drawing his graying head up with dignity, he joined those who were following the last of the porters toward the Palace of the Speaker.

AS WAS his nature, Ahuitzotl reacted immediately to the provocation that had been offered him. He asked that war be declared upon the people of Tehuantepec and all the tribes to the south, and he sent messengers to his allies and subjects requesting troops. Opening the royal storehouses to them, he ordered his own commanders to muster an army of twice the normal size, for they would be fighting over six hundred miles from home, and they would need to take their own reinforcements with them. Due to the great distances, it was decided beforehand that no captives would be taken, though the warriors would be given credit for their kills.

With all the training schedules accelerated, and regiments to be organized, Huemac found himself swamped with work, and he decided that he dared not put off the conversation with his daughter any longer, since the press of his duties might soon absorb him completely. He went alone, after sunset, to the rooms formerly occupied by Teuxoch, which Papalotl had requested for herself on being sent home from the temple. Patecatl and Taypachtli had made this decision in Huemac's absence, since this last fit had been more violent than the others and had resulted in actual physical injury. It was the ninth such attack since the night of the first, some four years earlier, and though Papalotl no longer remembered what she saw while unconscious, the sense that her mother was threatened had only grown stronger and more agonizing. Her formal training at the temple had been completed a year ago, but she had refused to leave her cloistered life, hoping that her prayers and purity might somehow dispel that threat.

As he accepted the food and drink that she had prepared for him, Huemac could feel his daughter's nervousness. He knew that she wanted to return to the temple as soon as her arm was healed, and that she was afraid that he had other ideas concerning her future. After discussing the matter thoroughly with Taypachtli, Patecatl, and his mother, he most definitely did, but he also had no desire to rush this conversation. With so little time and so much at stake, he did not want his daughter leaping to false conclusions.

So he had her put more wood on the hearth fire and asked her to sit across from him, encouraging her to eat from his bowls, since her priestly thinness appalled him. He spoke in a calming voice, chatting easily about the honors that had been conferred upon the merchants, the Tlatelulcan woman that Omeocelotl had chosen for his wife, the unrepressed excitement that Xolotlpilli was displaying at the prospect of his first campaign. Soon her eyes had ceased their nervous straying from his own, and he paused for a few moments to indicate that he had something serious to say.

"I know that you think that you are responsible for your mother's safety," he began slowly. "It is a notion with which your mother disagrees, and so do I. So does Patecatl. Each of us has a fate that is ours alone, my daughter, given to us by the gods. And while our thoughts and actions may affect the fate of another, even change it, it is not within our power to decide the final outcome."

"Is it not true, though," Papalotl asked, "that the evil of our desires can do great harm, and even kill?"

The image of a priest disappearing over a cliff flashed briefly through Huemac's mind, but he recovered himself quickly, and saw that his daughter had asked the question innocently, and was referring to herself.

"What evil desires do *you* have, my daughter?" he scoffed. "There is nothing evil about wishing to be a lady of the court rather than a priestess. Or wishing to know the man who would be your husband. Even Cocatli would tell you this."

Papalotl stared at him silently, her golden eyes shadowed by the dark circles of sleeplessness. Then she lowered her eyes and spoke in a voice made husky by guilt:

"There was a time, in Texcoco, when I wished that I had no mother, so that the Lady of Tula might adopt me."

Huemac examined her abject features with sympathy, seeing how fearful she had become of herself. Taypachtli was right—she could not be allowed to go on this way, blaming herself for things beyond all human control.

"That was a child's wish, and you are no longer a child," he said, with a sternness that brought her eyes up. "I do not wish to be harsh with you, Papalotl, for I know what you are suffering. I know the fear that the touch of the gods can inspire; I have felt it myself. Perhaps that is why you are also being touched. Perhaps *I* am the cause of this vision of doom. But I cannot know for sure, and so I must grant you the dignity of possessing a fate that is yours alone. Just as you must grant the same to your mother."

"What does she wish me to do?" Papalotl asked in a helpless voice, lacking the curiosity to even question her father's experience, which he had never revealed to her before this. There will be a time of great explaining, one day, Huemac thought ruefully. But then he looked at his daughter and assumed a tone of decision.

"Nezahualpilli has called a convocation of flower-song composers in his city for the year Four Flint-Knife, only five months hence. He has invited your mother to attend, and she wishes to go. She would like to take you with her, and see if a marriage match can be made for you."

Papalotl cringed visibly, her eyes widening in distress.

"But we would have to cross the waters of the Lake! Father, you cannot permit her to take such a risk!"

"She knows the risk," Huemac said calmly, keeping a tight check on his own anxieties, "and she will not allow me to dissuade her. She feels that there is a greater risk to *you,* if you continue in the temple. The healers have tried all their cures, and even Patecatl can find no solution in his prayers. Your mother convinced him, and me, that you should be allowed to seek a remedy, and a life, in the world of men and women, outside of the sacred confines of the god."

"I could not live with the guilt, if something happened to her," Papalotl murmured, tears streaming down her face.

"Do you think that it would be easier for *me*?" Huemac demanded with sudden impatience. "I have not agreed to this lightly, Papalotl, and I intend to take every precaution I can. The priests of the wind and water gods will be consulted, and offerings will be made, and I will not let your mother go near the water if there is anything threatening in the sky above it."

"Will you go with us?" Papalotl asked meekly, sorry that she had angered her father by doubting his own concern. Huemac shook his head slowly, taking deep breaths to recover his composure.

"My duties will not permit me to leave the city for some time. But I will hire the best boatmen, and I have asked Pinotl to accompany you in the canoe, both when you go and when you return. He has consented to do me this favor. He is a fine swimmer, and good with a canoe."

"But is he strong enough?"

"Do not underestimate your friend: He killed three men at Quauhtenanco. Besides," Huemac added briskly, "he will have only one person to save, should there be an accident."

Papalotl stared at him blankly, certain that her mother could swim no better than she could herself.

"When your arm has healed," Huemac continued, "you will go to the house of Cuetzpaltzin and meet his daughters. They are the ones who taught Pinotl to swim when he was small, and they know of a secluded pool in Tlatelulco where you can learn in privacy. Their company will be good for you, as well. But you must be diligent, my daughter. You must be ready and able to save yourself when the time comes."

Papalotl could only nod in compliance, knowing from the tone of her father's voice that he would not be swayed. She brushed the tears from her cheeks with the back of her hand and sighed with such enormous weariness that Huemac reached out and took her other hand into his own. Papalotl looked up in surprise at this violation of the rules of intimacy, and she was stirred by the emotion she saw in her father's eyes.

"There is a saying among the Otomi, my daughter. 'If you go through this life weeping, it will be over in an instant.' You must welcome the time that is given to you, even though it be filled with hardship and suffering. You will be given no more upon this earth."

Papalotl lowered her eyes modestly, but she was glad that he did not release her hand, and grateful that he waited patiently while she struggled to blink back the new tears that had risen to her eyes. Finally, she was sufficiently composed to meet his gaze, and he smiled as he let go of her hand.

"I will weep no more," she promised in a resolute voice. "I will be strong and brave, like my mother. *Whatever* our fates may provide for us . . ."

ONLY DAYS after Ahuitzotl had departed with his army for Tehuantepec, the sun over Tenochtitlan turned red in the middle of the day, and seemed to falter in the sky. Blackness crept across its face, devouring its brightness and casting the earth into sudden night. Papalotl was standing waist-deep in the water when the sky above her darkened, and two of Pinotl's sisters, though terrified themselves, jumped into the pool to help her. But Papalotl felt no dizziness, no rushing of wind in her head. It was a powerful omen, but it did not affect her. Pushing the other women away, she swam out of their reach, as if tempting the gods to strike her. Despite the pleas of her companions, she refused to come out of the water until the sun had regained its full shape and the sky was once more bright. Then, as the other women watched her with stunned eyes, she began to speak to them, for the first time, of going to Texcoco with her mother.

When the day chosen for their departure finally arrived, the sky was calm and clear, without a cloud to obscure the distant peaks of the mountains of

Tlaloc. Pinotl met them at the canoe dock, accompanied by the two Tlatelul-can boatmen whom his father had personally selected for this voyage. Ome Xochitl and Cocatli had also come to see the women off, and they took Papalotl off to one side so that Huemac and Taypachtli could speak privately.

Huemac lifted his wife's hands to his face and let her fingers linger there, tracing the deep creases in his cheeks and the warrior's perforation in his upper lip. Her smooth, round face seemed very beautiful to him, and he put his arms around her waist, swallowing the lump that had risen in his throat before speaking.

"That is so you will not forget me," he said with forced lightness, moving his lips against her fingers, "in the midst of all the praise and attention you will be receiving."

"I will wish every moment that you were with me," Taypachtli said softly, and Huemac again had to struggle against his emotions.

"Someone must guard the city while the warriors are gone," he said without conviction. "You must send me any news, and I will do the same when I have word of Xolotlpilli. I will be here to greet you when you return."

"Do not worry for me, my husband," she replied with sudden seriousness, letting him know that he had hidden none of his anxiety from her. "Only pray that our daughter may find a way to be at peace with herself, as I have always been with you."

Unable to speak, Huemac pulled her against him and held her tightly, blinking back his tears. Then, because the others were waiting, he reluctantly released her from his embrace and led her over to the canoe. Pinotl helped him lower her to a seat behind the bow paddler, then jumped into the canoe himself, placing himself between mother and daughter. Cocatli stepped forward, and all bowed their heads in silence as she blessed the boat and said a prayer for a safe journey.

"Farewell, my wife," Huemac said in a thick voice. "Farewell, my daughter. Remember me to our friends in Texcoco."

Then Taypachtli waved and the canoe pushed off, and Huemac had a last glimpse of his daughter's face as she looked back over her shoulder. Her eyes, he noted with some satisfaction, were bright and dry.

"I hope that I have done the right thing in allowing this," he said to his mother and sister, staring out after the canoe. Ome Xochitl brushed a strand of white hair back from her face and laid a comforting hand on his arm.

"It is what she wished, my son," she said. "Let us pray that the gods will answer her with kindness."

"I will go now to begin my vigil for their safety," Cocatli said resolutely, and led them back along the dock, in the direction of the Temple of Quetzal-coatl.

NEZAHUALPILLI did not find the time to speak privately to Taypachtli until the convocation was nearly over. Even then, he sounded distracted to her sensitive ears, though it might only have been the distance that a heightened sense of authority had put into his voice since she had spoken with him last. She knew that he was thirty-one years old, seven years younger than herself, but there were times when he sounded as old as the aged ones who were his advisers. He has grown in wisdom, Taypachtli thought, though she wondered, with a vague anxiety, why her presence had inspired this distance in him.

"My healers have told me that they can find no flaw in your daughter," Nezahualpilli said, after the formal greetings had been exchanged. "And I trust that she has had no more of these attacks while under my roof?"

"None, my Lord," Taypachtli replied with undisguised satisfaction, "even on days when there were great winds. She has been able to rest here, and regain her strength."

"Ah, but she has put great *unrest* into the hearts of my young men," the king said wryly, sounding very much like a man of thirty-one. "They vie with one another in singing her praises to my wife. When do you wish a match to be made?"

"She must go back to Tenochtitlan first to be examined by her father and the High Priest of her order. If they are agreeable, she could then return here to make her choice of a husband."

"My city will be blessed by her beauty," Nezahualpilli said graciously. "I am honored that Huemac would permit his daughter to come live among us. And now, of course, we shall see more of you, as well."

Taypachtli caught her breath and cocked her head sharply, hearing a false note in this last statement. It had sounded very similar to the tone that Huemac had used with her on the dock, but while her husband's attempted heartiness had been rife with concern, Nezahualpilli's echoed a certainty that could not be denied. He, too, knows the details of Papalotl's vision, she thought, and it is said that he sees the future in visions of his own. He had lied to her, and in lying, he had told her that she was indeed going to die. Taypachtli's hands turned cold, and she gripped the edges of her skirt, feeling more alone in her darkness than ever before.

"Your song about Texcoco," Nezahualpilli said, breaking in on her thoughts with self-conscious abruptness, "has been among those most often requested during the convocation. Your name is being mentioned in the same breath with those of the most famous composers, men like Tecayehautzin and Prince Ayocan."

"I am not worthy of such mention, my Lord," Taypachtli murmured, in a hollow voice that did not seem like her own.

"I doubt that the judges will agree. They are waiting eagerly, as I am waiting, to hear your new song."

"Perhaps they will be disappointed. Perhaps they will find my subject trivial and my meaning mysterious."

"Knowing your talent as I do," the king assured her admiringly, "I cannot envision such a response."

"I am grateful for your encouragement, my Lord," Taypachtli replied politely. Then she could not help herself and went on in a tone that quavered on the edge of accusation: "I cannot imagine that *anything* escapes the range of your vision."

Nezahualpilli remained silent for several moments, evidence that he had understood her meaning. When he finally spoke, his voice was again that of an old man, wearied by the world but not immune to the sufferings of those who dwelled in it.

"No, my daughter," he said sympathetically, in agreement. "Often, I must see that which grieves me deeply, but of which there is no point in speaking. Is there some favor that I might grant you, before you leave my city?"

Taypachtli bowed with genuine gratitude, then sat for a long moment, her brow furrowed in thought.

"Only that you invite me back, and that you do this in front of my daughter," she said quietly, and Nezahualpilli gave a small grunt of surprise before nodding shrewdly in agreement.

"I will give her no reason to doubt my sincerity," he promised. "And someday, I will tell her of your caring, and your courage."

Taypachtli bowed again, but said nothing.

"Go to her, then," Nezahualpilli advised in a gentle voice, "and share in the joy that beauty brings to a young heart. I will save my farewells, until the time of our true parting . . ."

"THIS IS most ominous news," Patecatl said gravely, when Huemac had finished his recitation. Word had just come from the ceremonial battlefield in Atlixco: Tlacahuepan, the eldest son of Axayacatl, member of the Council of Four Lords and the most likely successor to Ahuitzotl, had been slain in a flower war with the Huexotzinca. The great warrior had strewn the ground around him with the bodies of the dead before his strength had failed him, and then he had demanded to be sacrificed on the field where he had distinguished himself. Praises for his bravery were being sung in cities throughout Anahuac, but in Tenochtitlan, the songs also mourned the leader who had been lost.

"Our success ruins us," Huemac said, in a voice that was almost a snarl. "We shed our blood in lands too distant to permit the taking of captives, so our warriors must also gamble their lives in the wars of flowers. We spread ourselves too thin, and thus we suffer from many wounds."

"The lords will now look to Moteczuma as the next Speaker," Patecatl said suggestively, diverting Huemac from his anger. "He would be the ninth to rule our city, if such a thing comes to pass. You are aware of his affinity for the Toltecs; both his mother and one of his wives come from Tula. He has mentioned to me many times that it was the ninth in the line of Tula who oversaw the collapse of the Toltec kingdom."

"The 'Huemac' for whom I am named," Huemac said sourly. "His interest in me has always been unhealthy."

"You must be very careful around him," Patecatl warned. "He is given to sudden fears and impulses, and he often looks to find the cause outside of himself."

Huemac looked up at the older man and smiled sardonically; the priest had been very cautious and discreet in the discussions they had had concerning Moteczuma in the past.

"Frankness grows on you, my friend," he said teasingly, though with a challenging edge to his voice. "Perhaps dangerously so. You must be careful of voicing such criticisms aloud, even to me. Moteczuma is also a devious man, and no doubt he has large ears for the things that are said against him."

"I speak only the truth," the priest insisted sternly. "Remember my warning, Huemac."

Huemac sobered instantly and nodded to show his earnestness.

"I will not be careless. I must go now, my Lord, if I am to be there when my wife and daughter arrive from Texcoco."

Patecatl walked with him into the courtyard beyond the priest's chamber, and then out onto the plaza itself. They watched the processions of priests and pilgrims moving between the brightly painted temples, carrying ladles of smoking incense, and they discussed the reported improvement of Papalotl's health, and the possibility that she was well enough to marry. They had just agreed on the time of their next meeting when they felt the ground begin to tremble beneath their feet. They looked at each other in bewilderment, and then a great jolt shook them where they stood, and the walls of the temples began to dance before their eyes.

"No!" Huemac shouted, and turned as if to run. He had taken only one stride before another jolt bounced him into the air, where he seemed to hang for an interminable instant, his ears filled with the crashing of falling walls. Then he came down hard on the buckling flagstones, and the breath was driven from his body, and he descended into darkness . . .

"PERHAPS, my Lady," Pinotl had suggested to Taypachtli before they set out, "it would be wise to remove your beautiful crown. Were it to slip from your forehead, it might be lost forever."

"Then it would be my offering to Tlaloc," Taypachtli had replied in an oddly casual tone, and she had taken her place in the canoe with the golden circlet of five flowers still on her head. Since the Lake, on this day chosen by the Wind and Water priests, was as smooth and flat as a piece of polished mirror-stone, and since there were so many important-looking people standing on the dock listening, Pinotl had quickly decided that it was not his place to argue. It offended his sense of values, though, to see such an exquisite piece of jewelry handled with such carelessness.

Due to all the people who had come to pay Taypachtli and Papalotl their farewells, it was a long time before they were able to push off from the dock. Pinotl learned many things about his friend while he waited, and most of them brought little pleasure to his heart. He had perceived the improvement in Papalotl's health, of course, but that was the only thing that brought him any cheer. It was more than obvious that she had won a circle of admirers for herself among the young lords of Texcoco, and that she would be coming back soon to choose one for her husband. In Tenochtitlan, he would at least have been able to see her occasionally, but in this city, among such people, she would be forever closed off to him. Even if she and her husband were willing to overlook his lowly status, his lack of education and manners would be an embarrassment to everyone, himself most of all.

Pinotl was glad, then, when they had finally pushed off, that he was able to sit with his back to Papalotl. Not that he would ever tire of gazing upon her beautiful face. But he knew well enough how he must look to her, and he was too old now, and too much a man, to enjoy the sisterly affection with which she had always regarded him. It only made him feel darker and uglier, so that he yearned to be done with this task and back on the trail. Among the Maya, he had been considered quite handsome; perhaps he would have to go there to find himself a wife when he was older.

Still, he did not close his ears when Papalotl began to speak to him, telling him about the flower-song convocation and the success that her mother had enjoyed. She referred to her mother constantly, with a regard that astonished Pinotl, so closely did it border on reverence. He could still remember the way she had been when she had returned from Texcoco six years ago, her head filled with the names of lords and ladies and her eyes seeing only reflections of herself. Then she had not been able to say enough about the Lady of Tula and the other queens, and her mother had impressed her only because she had won *their* approval with her flower songs.

Taypachtli had again won the prize—several, in fact—but this time Papalotl seemed to share in the glory directly, on her mother's behalf. Stretching her hand along the side of the canoe next to Pinotl, she showed him the ring that her mother had given her. Mixtec, Pinotl decided immediately, recognizing the delicate workmanship with which the gold had been cast and polished. The ring was in the shape of a butterfly, inlaid with black and silver mirror-stone that glittered more powerfully than the water lapping around the canoe.

"That is excellent craftsmanship," Pinotl murmured in praise, wishing that he had the courage to take her hand and examine the ring more closely. Instead, he lifted his paddle and dug into the water on the other side of the canoe, so vigorously that the bow paddler glared at him over his shoulder for steering them off course. But at least the hand was gone when he brought his paddle back into the canoe.

"It was the king's personal gift to my mother," Papalotl said proudly. "But she gave it to me, as a memento of our visit."

Pinotl nodded to show that he had heard, but then a sudden wave splashed over the bow, and he quickly slid his paddle into the water to steady the rocking boat. The bow man called out a warning just before a second wave sprayed over them, and suddenly they were fighting against a steady chop, the water all around them breaking into whitecaps that lashed against the canoe from several directions at once.

"What is it?" Taypachtli cried anxiously, holding one hand to her crown as she turned back toward Pinotl. But he could not tell her, for there was still no wind, and they were not close to any of the known whirlpools in the Lake. Then they heard a deep rumbling sound, followed by a vast, sucking hiss that seemed to be rushing at them out of the west. Looking sideways past Taypachtli's bobbing figure, Pinotl's eyes widened in terror as he saw the enormous, foaming wave that was bearing down on them. He immediately discarded his paddle and reached out for Taypachtli's shoulders.

"Take hold of my daughter!" she shouted fiercely, twisting loose from his grasp and throwing him backward onto Papalotl. She, too, struggled against him, but there was no time to argue, so he ducked under her arms and locked his hands around her back, stiffening himself against the shock he knew was coming.

"Mother!" Papalotl screamed in his ear, and then the canoe was lifted out of the water and thrown backward, and Pinotl clutched Papalotl to him as they plunged into the water, thinking only that he must not let her be lost . . .

IN the dream, Huemac was sitting on the top of a hill, watching the warriors who were fighting below. He was wearing the plumes of a messenger, and he knew that he had come to tell Ahuitzotl about the earthquake. But then he saw Xolotlpilli, who was still just a boy, struggling up the hill toward him, carrying a feathered shield that was almost as large as he was. Huemac started to call out to his son, to encourage him, but then he remembered that he had not yet told the boy that his mother was dead. The words "your mother is dead" sprang from his lips as he thought them, and with a horrified gesture, he tried to summon them back. Slowly, they began to return, then faster, blurring until he saw them as silver claws, claws that stabbed into his eyes and made him weep . . .

He woke suddenly, and knew that he had been dreaming. Yet his eyes were indeed wet. Even in my dreams, I weep, he thought, with a weary kind of self-disgust. He was lying on his side, facing the wall, and because he felt no desire to move, he let his eyes linger over the deep crack that zigzagged through the plastered surface of the wall, running from floor to ceiling. Gradually, he became aware of the sounds of pounding and chipping coming from somewhere behind him, perhaps from his own courtyard, and these sounds finally proved annoying enough to make him throw off his blanket and roll over to investigate.

He found his mother sitting a few paces away, next to the hearth fire, tending to a pot of soup. She glanced over at him wordlessly, and did not cease her stirring.

"What is that noise?" he demanded irritably.

"I sent for the workmen," Ome Xochitl said curtly. "It is time that this house was repaired."

Huemac heard the scornful tone in her voice, the deliberate use of "this" rather than "your." So she, too, has lost her sympathy for me, he thought, and would shame me back to life. As if my heart could still feel a pain so petty . . .

"Send them away," he said listlessly. "They will disturb Papalotl's rest."

"Papalotl is not here. She has gone to the temple to consult with Cocatli and Patecatl. She built a fire next to the sweathouse before she left; it should be ready now. Go and use it, my son. Your body smells of neglect."

Huemac forced himself into a kneeling position, becoming angry despite himself. But his mother did not give him a chance to speak.

"Go," she commanded. "I have something to say to you, but you will not be able to hear it with misery clinging to your skin. Cleanse yourself thoroughly; use the soap root."

Huemac glared at her angrily, but she merely turned back to her soup and refused to pay any more attention to him. He saw that she had laid out clean garments next to his sleeping mat, and he snatched these up in one hand, intending to say something disrespectful. But his anger failed him before he could speak, so he clamped his lips shut and went to do as his mother had ordered.

Though he did not want to admit it, he felt much better upon his return, and he even had some appetite for the turkey broth and maize cakes that his mother set in front of him. He allowed himself some curiosity as he ate, wondering what it was that she had to say to him. But Ome Xochitl's aged face surrendered no clues. She was now over seventy, her hair completely white, her features grown spare and tight, trapping lines in dense webs around her mouth and eyes. Her nose and chin showed more plainly than ever that she was the daughter of Nezahualcoyotl.

"What is it that you have to tell me, my mother?" Huemac said at last, when she showed no inclination to open the conversation. Ome Xochitl looked at him then, her dark eyes examining his face for several moments before she spoke:

"I think that it is time that you heard Taypachtli's last flower song."

Huemac felt his scalp prickle and grow damp, and a wave of weakness swept over him. In his grief, he had given no thought to anything that had happened *before* the earthquake, and no one had forced such information upon him, not even Papalotl. He was not sure, even now, if he was ready to hear it.

"She recited it for me before she left for Texcoco," Ome Xochitl went on, calm but relentless. "I did not understand it then, and neither, truly, did Papalotl when she heard it at the convocation. But your daughter had a dream last night, and when she awoke this morning, she began to remember her mother's words, and she came to discuss them with me. Now you must hear them, too."

"What sort of dream?" Huemac demanded, but Ome Xochitl simply shook her head, and would not let him interrupt.

"It is called 'The Spindle-Whorl Shell,' " she said in a formal voice, then straightened her back and began:

> "The spindle-whorl shells,
> Empty now,
> Hollowed of life,
> Wash up on the shores
> Of the Divine Waters.
>
> They are gathered by the shell merchants
> And traded in the marketplace
> Of Ahuilizapan;
> They come to Anahuac
> As tribute,
> As gifts,
> As objects of barter.
>
> The spindle-whorl shell,
> Empty now,
> Hollowed of life.
> Yet a trumpet in the hands of priests,
> Dividing the night;

A mold for the goldsmiths,
Casting wind jewels;
A pattern for the weavers,
Spinning mantles;
A toy for a grandfather,
Making strange sounds
To please a laughing child.

This spindle-whorl shell,
So filled now,
So noisy with life.
Let us hear the lessons
That spill from emptiness."

Huemac felt the hard knot of his grief begin to unravel inside him, and he bowed his head and let the hot tears stream down his face, wetting the front of his mantle. Taypachtli, his precious shell . . . hollowed now of life, yet speaking to him still, touching him with the lesson of her courage . . .

Silently, Ome Xochitl passed him a bowl of warm water and a towel, and waited while he washed and dried his face. The sounds of the workmen outside again came to his ears, but he was no longer annoyed by their noise.

"I am grateful, my mother," he said. "And I am ready to hear you now."

Ome Xochitl searched his reddened eyes, then nodded briefly.

"I also think it is time that you went back to the hills. The Regent," she said, referring to Tlacaelel's son, Tlilpotonqui, "loves you no more than his father did. He should be glad to grant you your release in Ahuitzotl's absence."

Huemac's eyebrows lifted slightly, and a glimmer of enthusiasm crept into his eyes. He had not thought of Chimalman, either, since Taypachtli's death. Or of the child he may have fathered. He rubbed his chin thoughtfully, remembering his other children, and the dream he had had.

"But who will tell Xolotlpilli about his mother, when he returns from Tehuantepec? And who will preside at Papalotl's marriage?"

"Acolmiztli and I can tell Xolotlpilli," Ome Xochitl assured him. "Papalotl wishes to accompany you to the hills. That is why she went to consult with the priest and Cocatli."

Huemac opened his mouth in protest, then paused in recollection.

"Did she dream this?" he asked, and Ome Xochitl nodded.

"She described the hills to me in much the same way that you once did, though without knowing the names of things. She said that she saw a Chichimec village, and a man with a claw instead of a hand. She believes that this man can help her understand her fate, and the reason for her attacks."

"Do you agree with this?" Huemac inquired dubiously. "It would be a hard journey for a girl who has never left the city."

"Did she not survive the earthquake?" Ome Xochitl retorted. "Pinotl is not merely being modest when he says that they saved each other; she made him stay and look for her mother until they were both exhausted. Why do you question her fortitude? Or do you fear the explanations you will have to make?"

Huemac lowered his eyes, showing that she had hit on the true source of his hesitation.

"I will have to tell her everything," he said in a low voice. "I will have to tell her about the priest I killed, and my vision of the end . . . "

"And of Chimalman, as well," Ome Xochitl finished for him. "She is your daughter. Do you doubt your ability to make her understand?"

Huemac sighed and shook his head wearily.

"I had hoped to never involve my children in the trials of my fate," he said, and Ome Xochitl looked at him with sympathy.

"So did *your* father," she reminded him softly. "Papalotl will not let herself be excluded, any more than you would. Now you must learn, as I learned, the cost of your child's trust."

Huemac was silent for a few moments, then shook himself vigorously, as if to awaken his muscles. He bowed to his mother, seeming both resigned and grateful.

"I will speak to Patecatl," he said. "And then I will go to arrange for my release."

AS THE sun rose higher in the sky and her father still did not return from his hunt, Papalotl crawled farther under the clump of mesquite where he had left her to wait. She spent a moment listening for sounds and trying to identify their sources, as Huemac was constantly urging her to do, but nothing seemed to stir in the breathless heat surrounding her meager shelter. She ran a finger through the fine coat of dust that covered the skin of her arm, remembering how the utter dryness of this land had made her weak and dizzy until her body had adjusted. She had made many adjustments during these long days on the trail, most without complaint, and she was proud of the way that she had impressed her father with her hardiness, even though it was the memory of her mother's courage that had given her the strength.

Again hearing no sounds, she allowed herself to dwell upon the equally long evenings of conversation she had had with her father as they rested beside the glowing embers of the campfire. She now knew his complete history, from the signs surrounding his birth to his battles with Tlacaelel, even to his most recent discussions with Patecatl. It had not been easy for either of them, and there were times when she had felt herself in the presence of a murderous stranger, whose hard words made her shudder at the coldness and cruelty that could live in the hearts of men. Gradually, though, as the implacable logic that had ruled his actions became clear to her, she had begun to see him anew: not merely as the father who had smiled upon her from birth, but as a powerful man who carried the experiences of his forty-one years with thoughtfulness and honor, displaying the marks of his successes and failures in his lined face, his graying hair, and his scarred body. She could not look upon him now without seeing everything that he had been and done, and feeling herself forever incapable of judgment.

Swatting at the insects that had found her in her hiding place, Papalotl began to wonder when her father would appear. He had gone off to hunt for gift meat, he had said, because they were now very close to the Chichimec village, and he did not want to arrive empty-handed. Only the night before, with some uneasiness, he had finally told her of his last visit to the hills, and of his mating with the woman called Shield Hand. And somehow, though her images of

Nezahualcoyotl and even the Old One were extraordinarily vivid, Papalotl still could not conjure a face for this sorceress, this Jaguar Woman. Her father had left it to her to decide how to conduct herself when they met, but her mind remained a blank, resisting the thought of anyone's taking her mother's place, and intimidated in advance by the fact that she utterly lacked the kinds of powers that this woman supposedly possessed.

Then she heard the sound, and froze where she lay. When it was not repeated, she knew that she had heard correctly: Someone was near. She waited for a long time, scarcely breathing, but when her father did not show himself, she began to wonder if he was testing her again. He had crept up on her many times before this, in order to sharpen her sensitivity to the approach of man. This time, she thought suddenly, she would surprise *him;* she would catch him from behind when he jumped out to startle her. Moving slowly and silently, she began to crawl out from under the sheltering mesquite, but she had barely risen to a crouch when she was surrounded.

Her heart seemed to stop for an instant, even as she saw that the arrows pointing at her were held by three boys no more than nine or ten years of age, and that their bows were only half-size. Trying to calm the renewed beating of her heart, she rose slowly and held up her open palm in the gesture of friendship her father had taught her. The boys, their heads tufted with high, stiff clumps of hair, shouted at her threateningly in a language she did not understand, but they nonetheless backed away from her slightly. Attempting a smile, Papalotl spoke to them in Nahua:

"I am Quetzal Papalotl. Who are you?"

Two of the boys looked questioningly to the third, who was the smallest of the three but apparently their leader. He regarded Papalotl from beneath hooded eyes, an exaggerated scowl upon his young face.

"You are our captive," he said suddenly in Nahua, shaking his bow at her in a menacing gesture.

"You know my language," Papalotl said in surprise, but then did not go on, for she had seen the child's eyes at the same moment that he had seen hers.

Suddenly something crashed in the underbrush behind her, and the boys instantly went into a crouch, pulling their bowstrings taut. Papalotl had also turned toward the sound, and the next thing she knew, the boys were sent sprawling to the ground and Huemac was standing beside her with his knife in his hand. He knelt quickly next to the boy who had spoken and lifted his head by means of his hair tuft, holding the knife under his throat and spitting out a command in a foreign tongue. Though unhurt and poised to flee, the other boys stayed where they were, as did Papalotl, frozen in shock by the icy brutality of her father's voice. Finally, Huemac spoke again, and the boys rose to their feet and stood silently in front of him, as if awaiting their punishment.

"Father," Papalotl said urgently, recovering her wits, "this one speaks Nahua, and his . . . "

But then she saw that her father was already staring intently at the youth, who was in turn staring at the band of jaguar skin around Huemac's left wrist.

"What is your name, my son?" Huemac asked gently; and the boy looked up at him wide-eyed, showing the golden rings that surrounded his brilliant black eyes.

"Tepeyollotl," he said in Nahua, "Heart of the Mountains."

"The Jaguar God," Papalotl whispered breathlessly. "This is my brother . . . "

The boy shot her a quick glance, his eyes wild and unsettled, and Huemac rested a hand lightly upon his shoulder to calm him.

"Slowly, my daughter," he said to Papalotl, then again addressed the boy: "Where is your mother, Tepeyollotl?"

"At the village."

Huemac replaced his knife in his sheath and gestured to all three of them.

"Pick up your bows, then, and take us to her. No doubt, she is expecting our arrival."

NEZAHUALPILLI has kept his word, Huemac noted with satisfaction, as he and Papalotl followed the boys along the ridge that led up to the original site of the Chichimec village. The stone walls and sloping plots of maize and maguey at the sides of the trail had been restored, and the occasional burned-out plot was clearly the work of the farmers, not the warriors. Huemac also realized that his own reputation had been greatly enhanced by the king's actions, as even the sentries stepped from their hiding places to salute him, and the men and women working in the fields shouldered their tools and came to pay him their respects. Their show of deference was elaborate and sustained, almost as if it were *he* who had brought peace to their land.

Even before the formal greetings were concluded, though, he felt the weight of their attention begin to shift toward Papalotl. He could not wonder at this, for in this crowd his daughter stood out like a jewel among stones. She was taller than the other women and her hands and body showed none of the effects of work and childbearing; her skin was smooth and unmarked by any of the scars and tattoos with which the Chichimec women decorated themselves, and her teeth were neither filed nor stained with color. But beyond these obvious differences, there was the ineffable effect of the very way in which she carried her beauty, which was of a kind never before seen in this land. In the court of Texcoco, she excited admiration; here, she inspired awe.

With Huemac's encouragement, young Tepeyollotl assumed the role of crier, and it was to him that the people began addressing their questions once the welcoming had been completed. Huemac felt a strange thrill go through him when he heard the dark little boy describe him as "my father from Mexico," and, hearing the approving murmurs of the crowd, he was glad for the prestige that Nezahualpilli had conferred upon him. He could never make up for his years of absence, but perhaps his appearance could give the boy cause for pride.

Another, louder murmur rose when Tepeyollotl informed the people that the woman beside Huemac was his daughter, and the next question came quickly, from several sources. Tepeyollotl glanced shyly at Papalotl, then chose to repeat the question to Huemac in Otomi:

"They wish to know—where is her husband?"

Huemac smiled slowly and moved a little closer to Papalotl, who kept her eyes lowered self-consciously, clearly feeling the attention being paid to her.

"She has no husband, nor is she pledged," Huemac answered in Nahua, for his daughter's benefit. "She has been a woman of the temple, and now she comes to Xiuhcozcatl for his help in determining her future."

This caused an even greater reaction in the onlookers, once Tepeyollotl had translated, but it also persuaded them to clear the way so that the boys could lead the visitors to the chief. As they began to move again, Huemac leaned close to Papalotl and spoke into her ear:

"I will warn you, my daughter, as I was once warned: Speak only the truth here, and make no promises you do not intend to keep."

Papalotl gave him a sideways glance, confusion and anxiety in her eyes.

"Do they hate me, Father?" she whispered plaintively. "The women stare at me so fiercely!"

"That is envy, not hatred," Huemac explained. "Remember what I have said, and do not be quick to judge them, or yourself."

"It is so *strange,*" Papalotl admitted helplessly, and Huemac gave her a knowing smile.

"Be brave, my daughter," he whispered reassuringly, then turned his eyes straight ahead, to the village now coming into view.

CHIMALMAN was not among the notables who joined Xiuhcozcatl in welcoming Huemac back. She wished to see Huemac's daughter alone in her hut, the chief said, and Papalotl bowed to him numbly, unable to gauge the significance of this request, unable even to feel the anxiety it should have awakened in her. The stench of the bodies crowded into the lodge had nearly made her gag, and then to stand at the center of all those fierce, inscrutable faces, feeling the pressure of their curiosity, and their judgment. She felt assaulted, close to tears in her bewilderment, and the sight of the tattooed man with the talon-stick— much more forbidding than he had seemed in her dream—did nothing to soothe her jangled nerves. Nor did her father seem familiar to her any longer, dressed in his Chichimec clothing and speaking their tongue, paying great deference to the man with the stick.

Without looking back at her father or the chief, Papalotl followed Tepeyollotl out of the lodge, her eyes downcast before the curious stares that pursued her. She did not really notice where the boy—her half-brother, she had to remind herself—took her, or if he said anything. She had not had an attack since leaving the temple, but never had she felt more vulnerable than she did at this moment. Even her grief at her mother's death had not left her so completely unbalanced, and so close to the edge of collapse.

But then she was inside the darkened hut and saw the woman sitting next to the fire. A small woman, Papalotl realized with some surprise, feeling herself being drawn across the room by the glowing light in the woman's eyes. The fire crackled briefly, giving off a white smoke that filled the hut with the sweet aroma of desert grass.

"Welcome, Quetzal Papalotl," the woman said in a flat, unaccented Nahua. "You will sit with me? I am Chimalman."

Papalotl bowed formally and seated herself on a bed of soft rabbit fur across from the woman. Until she sat down, she had not realized how weak and tired she was, and she struggled against an overwhelming desire to close her eyes and sleep.

"Drink this," Chimalman said abruptly, holding out a painted gourd cup that gave off wisps of steam in the firelight. "It will ease your fatigue and clear your mind."

Obediently, Papalotl took the cup and raised it to her lips, tasting the sourness of the octli even as its pungent aroma filled her head. A swift fire spread through her body, and she felt her strength returning almost immediately. When she looked up from the cup, though, the woman's shining eyes bored into her own, and she was seized by a sudden dizziness that made her throw out a hand for balance. Chimalman instantly dimmed her eyes and took the cup from Papalotl before she could spill it.

"Forgive me," she said hastily. "When I saw your eyes, I assumed that you possessed the same powers as your father. I sought to lend you my support."

"I have no powers," Papalotl confessed, blinking with mild surprise at the sound of her own voice. But the dizziness had passed, and she found that she felt quite a bit better, less anxious as well as clearer-headed. As if to give her time to recover fully, Chimalman turned aside to put another stick and more sweet grass on the fire, and Papalotl examined her swiftly, noting the wiry hardness of her body, the fur vest and claw necklace, the absence of markings on her dark, narrow face. Papalotl did not find her attractive in any conventional sense, but there was something distinctly compelling about her presence, something that set her apart from the other Chichimec women Papalotl had seen. She resolved, for her father's sake, to do her best to make friends with this woman, who had yet to smile at her.

Chimalman had been studying her in return, but she gave no sign whether she was pleased by what she saw.

"Who told you that you have no powers?" she asked suddenly, throwing Papalotl off-balance, since she had been expecting a question about her father. She was about to say "everyone" when she hesitated, realizing that no one had ever told her such a thing outright; it was an assumption she had never felt qualified to challenge. She looked up at Chimalman, remembering her father's warning to speak only the truth.

"I have simply never demonstrated any," she said diffidently. "I have had dreams, and once a vision, but I did not seek them, and I could not control how they came to me. I was finally forced to leave the temple because of them."

"That is why you have come here, then?" Chimalman inquired, and Papalotl nodded tentatively, unable to read the woman's face or voice, and thus to determine the nature of her interest. It was disconcerting to be interrogated so closely by someone she had just met, someone who gave away so little of herself. Was all the truth-telling to be on her part? Papalotl wondered, but decided nevertheless to be as frank as possible.

"I wish to know if I should return to the temple," she explained. "Or if I am free to marry and raise a family."

"The priests could not tell you this?" Chimalman asked incredulously. "Or your father?"

Papalotl shook her head in denial, realizing again that no one had actually tried to reach such a determination. She had been examined and questioned, but all her questioners had assumed that the answer would have to show itself in some other way.

"I was born under the sign of Quetzalcoatl," Papalotl said, reaching for what had always seemed the most basic assumption governing her life. "My aunt, who is a priestess of the god, had a dream that foretold my coming. We have always waited for the god to make his will known to us."

Chimalman grunted forcefully, with a scorn that even Papalotl could not mistake. She stared at the woman blankly, shocked by the irreverence of her reply.

"Your father was not so lazy about pursuing his own fate," Chimalman observed dryly. "How old are you?"

"Seventeen," Papalotl replied automatically, though she was stunned to hear her father criticized so openly.

"And you have never known a man?"

"Of course not!" Papalotl blurted, flushing at the rudeness of the suggestion. She suddenly did not care if this woman became her friend; she wanted this interview to end. Chimalman, though, seemed unaffected by her outburst, as if unaware that she had given any cause for offense.

"There is a way, then," she mused thoughtfully. "There is the Ceremony of Dreaming. But it could be very dangerous to you," she added. "Powers could be unleashed that would possess your spirit forever if you did not have the strength to master them."

"Perhaps we should consult with my father, and the chief," Papalotl said in a stiff voice, feeling in no mood to take advice from this woman. Chimalman cocked her head quizzically.

"It is not their choice to make," she said flatly. Then she lowered her voice, as if to soften it: "I do not know how I may have offended you, Quetzal Papalotl. I am not familiar with how women converse with one another in the city. But you have told me that you do not know what powers you own, and that you have been at the mercy of dreams that no one has explained to you. You are no longer a child: If you have truly come here to discover your fate, why do you try to avoid the choices that are yours to make?"

Papalotl opened and closed her mouth helplessly, at a loss for how to respond. She felt no sympathy from this woman, yet she was the first to have offered her a way to cope with her dreams. And she was right: No one *had* assessed her powers or forced her to confront the meaning of her dreams. But could she be believed?

"There is one other thing that you should know before you choose," Chimalman said, as if in recognition of Papalotl's uncertainty. "You must have someone to guide you through this ceremony, a knowledgeable woman. I am the only one among those in the village who speaks your language."

Papalotl sighed heavily, feeling trapped. Why had she told this woman so much? Yet she had told as much to many people, and none of them had ever challenged her so seriously. Why *did* she shy away from the first hope she had been offered? Why did she not seize it gratefully, eagerly? As she thought this, Papalotl felt something snap within her, and she experienced a moment of sudden lightness, as if she had torn free from some invisible bonds. She looked up into Chimalman's steady gaze, seeing a patience that was as far beyond sympathy as these hills.

"Will you be my guide, Chimalman?" she asked softly, and was rewarded by a sudden brightening of the older woman's eyes.

"It would bring great gladness to my heart, Quetzal Papalotl," she said with undeniable sincerity. "I would regard my responsibility to you most solemnly."

"That is my choice, then," Papalotl said firmly, and Chimalman nodded with what seemed like satisfaction.

"We must call one another 'sister,' then, from this time onward. That way, you will always remember that I serve you as guide and support, but not as guardian. I can open you to the powers that lie within you, and I can prepare you to meet them, but I cannot protect you from yourself."

"I have been sheltered long enough," Papalotl decided thoughtfully. "Perhaps too long. I will attend carefully to your teachings, my sister."

Chimalman nodded again, lowering her eyes at the loyalty in Papalotl's voice. Then she raised her head and smiled awkwardly, seeming almost embarrassed by her next question:

"Perhaps now, my sister," she said shyly, "you will tell me about your father . . ."

LEANING against an empty meat rack, Huemac stood at the side of Chimalman's hut, watching Tepeyollotl distributing his gifts among his cousins, the children of his uncles. Since he had not known the sex of his child, Huemac had brought two sets of gifts: necklaces and colored thread and a bone-handled mirror for a girl; tasseled loincloths, a tlachtli ball, and a flint knife with a tortoise-shell handle for a boy. He had given everything to his son, making him fabulously wealthy by Chichimec standards, if only for a short while. Tepeyollotl had paused over his gifts just long enough to assure Huemac that he appreciated their value, and then he had proceeded to give everything away, except for the knife.

Watching this happen, Huemac marveled at the boy's generosity, knowing that it far exceeded what was required by custom. Perhaps he compensates for being an only child, and fatherless, Huemac thought, though what he had seen of his son so far had convinced him that the boy suffered no insecurity about his place in the tribe. Xiuhcozcatl and Tepeyollotl's uncles had seen to that, along with Chimalman herself. But no one, in Huemac's hearing, had claimed credit for the boy's extraordinary poise and self-possession, though all had remarked upon it. He was perhaps the least-reprimanded child in the village, yet not from a lack of high spirits; his good behavior seemed to grow out of some kind of personal decision, rather than a desire to please or an avoidance of punishment.

Because Chimalman and Papalotl had sequestered themselves in a hut at the edge of the village, off-limits to all men, Huemac had been forced to spend a great deal of time alone with his son. And his problem remained the same one that he had voiced to Xiuhcozcatl soon after his arrival: How could he be of use to the boy, how could he win his respect and friendship, when all of his knowledge applied to a world that Tepeyollotl would probably never see? The Chichimecs did not live in cities and wage campaigns of conquest, and their version of tlachtli was played on dirt courts in the middle of the open plain, with a ball made of tightly wrapped skins. And surely, Tepeyollotl could learn nothing from Huemac about the desert, or sorcery, since he had already begun his instruction in the magic plants with Xiuhcozcatl himself.

But the chief had merely laughed and told Huemac that he, as the father, would have to find the entrance to his son's heart for himself. Huemac had tried many different things these last nights, but although Tepeyollotl had listened attentively to the stories of wars, ball games, and far-off places, Huemac could tell that he had not really reached the boy.

When he had finished accepting the gratitude of his cousins, Tepeyollotl came over and respectfully presented himself to his father.

"I am most impressed by your generosity, my son," Huemac said admiringly. "Is it the custom in your mother's family to give away all that is given to you?"

Tepeyollotl appeared disconcerted by the question, and he lowered his eyes with a shyness Huemac had not seen before. Feeling that he had touched upon something important, Huemac proceeded gently, putting encouragement into his voice:

"Perhaps it is your own custom," he suggested, and the boy looked up at him intently and shook his tufted head.

"It is the custom of those who would be chief," he said softly, watching Huemac for signs of disapproval or disbelief. Huemac merely raised his eyebrows, controlling his surprise.

"Is it your intention to be chief one day?" he asked.

"Yes. It is a dream I had long ago."

"And what sort of ruler do you plan to be?"

"A just and kind ruler, one who is loved by his people," the boy replied without hesitation, giving Huemac a glimpse of the depth of both his innocence and his self-esteem.

"I have known many rulers," Huemac said, "and few of them have lived up to such a lofty ideal. The power that surrounds the man who rules is a great burden, and an even larger temptation. All his acts have great consequences, yet like any normal man, he is subject to mistakes in judgment. It becomes very difficult to acknowledge your errors when there are few who would dare to remind you, and many more who would see such acknowledgment as a sign of weakness."

Huemac stopped abruptly, realizing that he had launched into a speech, inspired by the rapt fascination in Tepeyollotl's eyes. So *this* is what inflames my son's heart, he thought wonderingly, amazed by the irony of the situation. That he, who had spent so much of his life avoiding the world of the powerful, should now give instructions to one who avidly sought entrance to that world, and at the tender age of nine . . .

"I did not mean to make a speech," he apologized, and Tepeyollotl came out of his trance, shaking his head in an involuntary gesture of denial. "There are also rulers of the kind you mentioned, like your great-grandfather, Nezahualcoyotl. Perhaps you would be interested in hearing how *he* conducted himself as ruler . . . "

"Yes, yes," Tepeyollotl repeated, unable to find more words to express his eagerness. Huemac smiled and put a hand on his shoulder.

"Come, then. Let us find a suitable place, where we can sit and discuss the nature of a fit ruler . . . "

THE HUT where Chimalman and Papalotl had gone to live was at the back of the canyon, on the other side of the stream from the village. Food was brought out to them every fourth day, but Papalotl seldom saw anyone, even at a distance. The people of the village seemed to know the places where Chimalman was likely to take her, and they avoided the possibility of accidental contact, especially the men. Yet this was in no sense a confinement, for they were away from their hut for a large part of every day, and Chimalman had insisted from the outset that Papalotl be the one to decide their daily routine. She offered the younger woman a number of options every morning, teaching her to consider each one with equal care, to feel the kind and amount of energy that each inspired in her.

"The energy can either be fearful or desirous," she explained. "Either one indicates an activity that is necessary to you. Those are the only kinds of activities that you should ever pursue. If the energy is not present, it is better to simply sit or sleep."

They began each day by climbing the steep trail behind their hut to plunge themselves into the icy waters of a mountain pool. This was part of the regimen that Chimalman had established, with Papalotl's consent, to build up the younger woman's endurance. They also climbed rocks and trees, ran long distances through the hills, and hunted for their own meat. Papalotl learned how to take the lives of her prey in the proper manner, and she took her part in the gutting and skinning that had always been left to the servants in her father's household. Even the making of fire, so difficult at first without the proper board and firesticks, soon became instinctual and effortless.

Woven in around these chores would be Papalotl's chosen subject of study, usually a single aspect of the world around them, which they would pursue until both were satisfied that it had been exhausted. Whole days would be spent in the examination of stones, trees, or a single animal, and at night, they might lie under the stars, listening to the song of a rushing stream, or tracking the moon's journey across the sky. Chimalman urged Papalotl to experience these things with fresh senses, discarding her knowledge of the uses to which they could be put as well as the ritual connotations she had been taught to associate with them. She was encouraged instead to study their shapes and the shadows they cast, the sounds they made at different times of the day and night, and the colors and odors that gave them their beauty and power.

When it rained or when Papalotl was tired, they would sit beside the fire in their hut, talking about their experiences and the people they had known. They spoke with absolute frankness, for Chimalman put no limits on the kinds of questions she would ask and answer, and she encouraged Papalotl to free her curiosity from the restrictions of "forbidden" or "offensive" subjects. They spoke so often of sexual matters, and so openly, that Papalotl soon lost the habit of blushing, even on those occasions when Chimalman chose to use Huemac as her example. Chimalman told her about her first husband and her great-great-grandfather Oztooa, and they laughed together, like sisters, at the story of Huemac the Owl Boy, bartering for his life with the Old One.

In return, Papalotl told her about her family and the people she had known in the temple and the Texcocan court, spending the largest amount of time on her mother, Cocatli, and the Lady of Tula. And because the world of her past seemed so far away, so divorced from her present reality, Papalotl found herself able to judge it dispassionately for the first time. She listened to Chimalman's insights, knowing that her companion knew nothing of city life, yet recognizing the essential accuracy of the motives she ascribed to those who had influenced Papalotl's life. She began to understand how she had been shaped, and why, and at what point the influences on her had come into contradiction. Gradually, she even learned to criticize those she loved and trusted, feeling not disloyal, but simply separate, the owner and sole guardian of her own fate.

At frequent intervals throughout their time together, Chimalman would remind her to pay particular attention to her dreams, and to the sensations that came to her during her time of bleeding, persisting in her urgings even though Papalotl consistently reported nothing unusual. The purpose of this did not become apparent to Papalotl until she had spent two full days acquainting herself with the wind, the subject Chimalman had left for last. She had seen the way it bent trees and scattered their seeds, heard it sigh over the grasslands and howl in lonely canyons, watched it create invisible demons that whipped sand in brown funnels across the face of the desert. Then, one warm, overcast afternoon, with an east wind blowing down off the mountains, Chimalman made her sit on an exposed hillside and coaxed her to give herself to the wind.

Almost immediately, the rushing sensation filled her head, and she fell into a dream. She saw the city of Texcoco cloaked in gloom, the people moving through the streets with their eyes downcast, murmuring vaguely of scandal and death. Then she saw the Lady of Tula, her face hollowed with grief, and beside her the king, his eyes reflecting the mingled pain of anger and regret. In his hands, Nezahualpilli held a coiled rope such as the executioners used. Someone behind him spoke, saying: "The Mexicans will be angry."

But just as the dreadful nature of these images began to make her afraid, Papalotl saw them recede and Chimalman appear in their place. She was kneeling in front of Papalotl, blowing in her face and rubbing one of Papalotl's palms over the butterfly ring she wore on her other hand. Whatever Chimalman had been chewing had given her breath a powerfully obnoxious odor, which made Papalotl choke and cough until her eyes watered and her nose ran. But she had come through the dream sitting up, and with only a little prompting, she was able to remember clearly everything she had seen.

"It is as I thought, my sister," Chimalman said solemnly, once Papalotl had recovered fully. "You are possessed of a great power, the power to dream the future."

Papalotl considered this quietly, showing both the awe and the anxiety that it inspired in her.

"Where does such a power come from?" she asked finally.

"Often it is inherited," Chimalman explained. "Other times it is the gift of the gods, or their punishment. The source is not as important as the use you make of it, though. When it came to you for the first time, you did not recognize it, and so it fastened on the conflict that existed in your heart. You wanted very much to return to Texcoco, yet you also wanted to please your aunt and be faithful to your vows. You were divided in your yearnings, and thus vulnerable."

"But why, then, did I dream of my mother's death?"

"The dream did not truly concern your mother," Chimalman said, nodding forcefully to make Papalotl listen before interrupting. "It was a dream of your own conflict: of being torn between your yearning for Texcoco and your commitment to Tenochtitlan. It was a warning that *you* were in danger, but you chose only to see the danger to your mother. You might very well have been killed yourself, drowned in your own indecision."

Papalotl lowered her eyes as the truth of this sank in, and she no longer felt so eager to disagree. Chimalman helped her to her feet and made her loosen her limbs before leading her down the hill.

"Can I learn to master this power?" Papalotl asked at last, as they found the trail that led back to their hut.

"Perhaps," Chimalman said in a neutral voice. "You must learn to observe your dreams without fear, and to bring yourself back without injury. Your ring will be a touchstone for you, an anchor in this world. The same is true of the herb I blew in your face. But come," she added briskly, urging Papalotl into a trot, "we must not get ahead of ourselves. The *serious* part of our work has just begun."

FOR AN entire day before the ceremony, Papalotl was not allowed to either sleep or dream. Chimalman brought her small quantities of water and dried meat while she sat quietly in their hut, contemplating, for the last time, all that she had learned. In the past weeks, Papalotl had dreamed of virtually every person who was important to her, of places both familiar and utterly foreign, of events that brought her joy and distress in equal measure. She had learned how to trigger the dreams and how to pull herself out of them at will; she had even begun to differentiate, on the basis of the clarity of detail, their relative distances in time. The only thing she had yet to dream of was herself.

"You must save yourself totally for the ceremony," Chimalman had insisted, and Papalotl had complied by immediately pulling back from any dream in which she saw her own image.

Early on, she had experienced an enormous exhilaration at her new-found power, reveling in her ability to visit the members of her family without moving from these hills. She saw her grandmother buying a turkey in the marketplace in Tlatelulco, Cocatli praying in the temple, her father teaching tlachtli to a group of young men. One of her most vivid dreams concerned her brother Xolotlpilli, who appeared to her with his head completely shaved and his face painted black and yellow, carrying a shield and macana that looked like toys in his huge hands. He was extremely angry about something, but the men at whom he was shouting all wore the insignia of the Tenocha, and they answered him by name. They, too, were very angry, but they backed away from Xolotlpilli's threatening gestures, muttering into their hands.

As she had with several others, Chimalman had advised Papalotl to consult her father later about this dream, since neither woman possessed sufficient knowledge of the ways of the warriors to interpret its significance. Papalotl had looked forward to this confirmation, and to the wonder she would inspire in her brother when she told him what she knew. But then, soon after this dream, she had had another, equally vivid, in which she had seen the city of Tenochtitlan flooded and falling into the Lake, the people streaming out along the causeways with their goods upon their backs. This dream had ended with a vision of her Uncle Acolmiztli upon his deathbed, and had left her shaken for days afterward.

"Now you know the burden of this power and the knowledge it brings," Chimalman had told her. "You will have to decide the consequences of revealing what you know, or of keeping it to yourself. You will also have to be responsible for correctly interpreting what you see, though you are as apt to be mistrusted for an accurate prediction as for one that fails. Many people will appeal to you to read their fates, but few of these will have the courage to desire the whole truth."

Papalotl considered all these things as she prepared for the ceremony, remembering that her father had once gambled *his* life for the knowledge of where he belonged. Chimalman had warned her that her own risk was much greater, since she traded not with a man, but with the spirit powers themselves. She was reaching for a power far beyond any possessed by her father, who had received his knowledge of the future involuntarily and had never sought more. Sitting in the cool darkness of the hut, moving as little as possible, Papalotl nonetheless began to sweat in anticipation.

At dusk, she and Chimalman went out to the circle they had cleared and marked with stones in the desert. At the center of the circle was the open-sided shelter that Papalotl had built with her own hands: a small circular hut made of arched cedar branches joined at the peak with maguey twine, with a wide opening at each of the four directions. Papalotl stripped off her clothing outside the circle and let Chimalman paint her naked body with alternating horizontal stripes of white and red.

After Chimalman had painted her own face in a similar fashion and had disposed of the paints and clothing, the two women took freshly cut fir branches and carefully swept the circle from the outside in, effacing their own footprints and the many tracks left by animals and birds.

"This way, we will know who comes to visit you while you are dreaming," Chimalman explained. "Perhaps we will even find the footprints of a man, if there is one nearby who is right for you. Likewise, the tracks of any other creature will provide us with clues to the identity of your proper mate, if such a one exists. But you must not concern yourself with watching, or hoping."

Chimalman next instructed her to sit on the blanket in the center of the hut and face the west, where the sky still glowed orange from the light of the dying sun. She removed the butterfly ring from Papalotl's finger and spoke to her softly:

"You must abandon all control now; you must allow the wind to bring the dreams to you. Open yourself, my sister, do not resist what is shown to you, do not turn your eyes away in fear. I will not lose you if you are strong. Call out to the wind, Quetzal Papalotl, tell him of your name and your intention, the knowledge that you seek. Open yourself to his guidance, my sister . . ."

Night fell around them silently, without a whisper of a breeze to stir the darkness. Papalotl sang her wind song over and over, facing each of the directions at intervals determined by Chimalman, who sat behind her at all times. There were occasional rustlings in the underbrush outside the circle, and once heavy wings beat by close overhead, startling Papalotl out of her concentration. Chimalman quietly coaxed her back into the properly receptive state, reminding her to be open and unresisting.

She was facing the south when the wind finally rose. In her excitement, Papalotl began to sweat, and the hot, dry wind immediately covered her painted body with a fine coat of dust. Sand blew into her eyes, but Chimalman spoke even before Papalotl could raise her hands, warning her not to rub them against her eyes. Heeding the admonition with difficulty, Papalotl blinked rapidly against the painful particles, and suddenly went into a dream:

She saw herself from above, a slender figure in a white robe with a ring sparkling on one hand. She walked across a courtyard she recognized as part of Nezahualpilli's palace, and ahead, she saw the Lady of Tula waiting for her. The older woman's face was at first sorrowful and apologetic, and her gestures were consoling. But then her expression changed to one of bafflement, and finally to a disappointment she could not conceal.

She cannot comprehend my lack of grief, Papalotl thought, and was briefly saddened for her friend, before the scene disappeared in a sudden haze of whiteness . . .

She was floating over Tenochtitlan, rain falling all around her. The streets below were awash in a flood that reached to the tops of the doors of some of the poorer houses, and people were being rescued from their rooftops by men in canoes. Then she was on the ground, splashing through ankle-deep water in the midst of a great crowd that was heading out of the city along the southern causeway. Looking back, she saw her Uncle Acolmiztli standing atop the Xoloco rampart, gray-haired and long-faced, watching the crowd leave.

Farewell, my uncle, she cried voicelessly, knowing with absolute certainty that she would not see him alive again. Again, the whiteness descended around her like a pall, and Tenochtitlan was gone . . .

She was walking down a broad avenue in a strange city, surrounded by a crowd composed solely of girls and young women, all dressed in white robes like the one she wore herself. They were talking gaily among themselves, as if on their way to a feast, but though Nahua was predominant among the many languages being spoken, Papalotl found all their words incomprehensible. Those ahead began to turn to the left, disappearing around the corner of a building, but a sudden wind came up around Papalotl, pushing her straight ahead with such force that she had soon left the crowd far behind, without ever being able to turn her head to see where they were going.

Then she saw the temple pyramid ahead and was stunned by its enormity, and by the fact that she had not seen it until this moment. It was perhaps twice as large as the Temple of Huitzilopochtli in Tenochtitlan, and its terraced steps seemed to rise by stages into the heavens, the top lost in whiteness, as if the blue dome of the sky had been pierced. The wind pushed her across the broad flagstoned plaza in front of the pyramid, past scores of people who seemed frozen in place, their heads bowed in attitudes of reverence and humility. All around her were representations of the Plumed Serpent, carved into balustrades and standing pieces of stone, and painted onto long wall murals in lurid shades of orange, ochre, and blue.

She found Pinotl standing at the base of the temple steps, his head bowed over the black staff in his hands. Papalotl held back against the insistent pressure of the wind and looked into her friend's dark, Huaxtec face. Pinotl opened his hooded eyes and stared back at her longingly, showing the depth of the love and devotion he held for her. He pointed silently at the temple.

Tlachiualtepetl, Papalotl heard, or thought, as the wind pushed her up the steps and Pinotl was left behind. She knew then that she was in Cholula, the holy city of Quetzalcoatl, and that this was his temple, the greatest in all of Anahuac, the one called Man-Made Mountain. The wind swirling around her became stronger and colder as she climbed, and she realized that her robe was gone, and she was again naked.

On a platform halfway up, she came upon Cocatli, who was braced against a stone serpent's head, barely able to withstand the force of the wind. With her hair tossing around her face, Cocatli tried to look back at Papalotl, but her attempt at a smile failed and she had to turn her face away.

Her awe blinds her to me, Papalotl thought, and then was swept upward again, past white-robed forms that huddled by the sides of the stairs, cowering before the wind. She was now so cold that she could not feel her limbs, but she felt no fear at the wind, which propelled her upward, step by step.

At the last platform before the top, she met Patecatl, his hands clasping the golden wind jewel around his neck, his white hair streaming straight out from the sides of his head. He bowed to her formally, but then ran his eyes down her body and frowned deeply before turning away, as if unable to look upon her any longer.

He disapproves of my nakedness, she thought, and went on, filled with a vague disappointment. But the feeling vanished instantly when she saw her father waiting for her at the top of the last flight of steps, his eyes glowing brightly, his hands outstretched to help her. He was wearing his jade rabbit and his jaguar-skin wristband, and his face was set in the proud, wistful lines of a father who had completed his duty to his child.

Now you are here, his eyes said to her, *now I must leave you . . .*

Papalotl felt his calloused hand in hers for only an instant, for just as she set her foot upon the platform, he was transformed into a brilliant, golden-eyed hawk and vanished from her sight in a blaze of reddish-brown feathers. Looking around for him, she saw only the great mountains that surrounded the city on all sides, the snow-capped peak of Popocatepetl, the Mountain That Smokes, rising directly ahead of her, behind the circular shrine at the far end of the platform. Bending her head into the wind, Papalotl started toward the shrine, toward the red serpent's mouth that surrounded its entrance. There was no one else on the platform with her, and the shrine, too, proved to be empty. Completely empty. Papalotl stopped abruptly, stricken by a sudden, intense fear at the sight of the empty altar where the image of the god should have stood. The air seemed filled with shifting, barely perceptible shapes, and she jerked in fright when something dry and smooth rubbed against her leg, and invisible feathers brushed the back of her neck. She felt a terrible grittiness in her eyes and wanted to turn them away from the altar, but then she heard, or remembered, Chimalman's encouraging voice:

Be steadfast, my sister, do not look away . . .

The wind howled in circles around the shrine, and the room seemed filled with a low, moaning respiration. The shapes were all around her, brushing her legs and breasts with a feathery touch that made her skin crawl and her nipples harden. Trembling with fear, she walked blindly toward the altar, trying not to see the shapes materializing in the air around her, the billowing plumage and shimmering blue-green scales . . .

Falling to her knees before the altar, Papalotl raised up her hands and placed them flat upon the polished stone surface, feeling a great warmth rise up through her palms. She cried out in gratitude and began to weep, pouring out the coldness of her fear in tears that splashed onto the stone floor and spread in puddles of iridescent green feathers. The shapes pressed in around her, close to her skin, but the fear left her as the warmth traveled down her arms and into her body, and a greenish glow appeared before her tear-washed eyes. Then she felt herself falling, drifting gently downward, swaying lightly from side to side, caressed by the air in which she moved. There was a great wetness between her legs, a circle of liquid sensation that suddenly expanded and sent waves of pleasure pulsating through her body, a delicious tingling that seemed to fill every part of her, bathing her with pleasure. Yet her heart beat calmly, possessed by a sense of peace and well-being such as she had never known, a joy too deep to be felt as excitement. She breathed deeply, and let herself fall . . .

Quetzal Papalotl. A voice. *Quetzal Papalotl.* A hard shape against her palm, familiar. *Come back, my sister.* The shape again, harder now. *Come back.* Then a terrible odor, also familiar . . .

Then she was awake, struggling in Chimalman's arms, her head jerking away from the breath being blown in her face. She could not control the resistance of her body, and fought against the protective embrace until exhaustion overtook her and she went limp. Chimalman spoke to her softly, soothingly, bringing her back to coherence. When Papalotl was able to look at her with recognition, Chimalman pointed to the reddish stain on the blanket where Papalotl was sitting.

"You broke the shield of your womanhood, my sister. Who was it that came to you in your dream?"

Papalotl stared down at the stain, then sighed languidly and allowed Chimalman to lower her onto her back. Her eyes glowed with happiness as she looked up at the older woman, who covered her naked body with another blanket.

"The god," Papalotl murmured, and tilted her head back, her eyes closed and a smile on her face. "It was the god . . ."

AFTER delaying for many months, Huemac and Papalotl finally set their departure for early in the year Six-Rabbit, before the spring rains could impede their traveling. Many of the village women came out to bid them farewell, bringing their children to be blessed by the "holy woman," as they had come to regard Papalotl, the woman who had dreamed on clear ground. They brought her a bow and a quiver of arrows, and presented her with a rabbit-fur blanket to which each had contributed a special skin. Papalotl's eyes glistened as she accepted their gifts, but in the manner of the hill-people, she would not shed tears at a parting. Standing tall in their midst, she spoke to the women in their own tongue:

"I will never forget you, my people," she promised. "I will come to your village in my dreams, and I will guard your children with my prayers."

Only Chimalman and Tepeyollotl accompanied them past the boundaries of the village, stopping when they reached the head of the trail leading down into the desert. Huemac placed his hands on Tepeyollotl's shoulders and addressed him with the proper paternal gravity, telling him to think about the things they had discussed and to test the conclusions they had reached, so that they would have a basis for further conversations when he returned.

"I will look for hawks, my father," the boy offered eagerly. "Perhaps I can be of help when you go to hunt for your nahualli."

"I will count on your aid," Huemac said, his eyes glowing with satisfaction. He held his son's shoulders for a moment longer, then released him with a nod that spoke only of the promise of their future together.

Then he was staring into Chimalman's sparkling black eyes, feeling the strength that flowed into him at her regard. He remembered, as if from a bad dream, the pain and loss he had carried in his heart when he had come here, the emptiness that this woman and her son had filled with their caring.

"I leave my heart in your keeping, Chimalman," he said softly. "You are the one who has healed it, and given me life."

Chimalman lowered her eyes at this display of emotion, then raised them again just as quickly. A trace of a smile played around her lips, showing that she had lost her embarrassment at such compliments, and had come to like their sound. She let him embrace her briefly, then stepped back for a last look.

"Return to us when your affairs in the city are settled," she said with her usual directness. "Your son and I will be waiting, holding your heart until you come to reclaim it."

HUEMAC and Papalotl marched south toward Texcoco, noticing immediately that the lack of rain of which the hill-people had complained was much worse in the lowlands, and that it had severely affected the supply of game. They were forced to go into the towns for their food much sooner than they had planned, and here they found the bartering unusually contentious, the patience of the traders foreshortened by a sense of desperation that was still being denied, and thus had no other outlet. The small stone shrines that stood beside even the humblest fields shone with new paint and fluttered with the blue ribbons that had been left as offerings to the water gods, and many eyes were fixed hopefully upon the sky.

"I do not foresee a flood from these conditions," Huemac grumbled one afternoon, as they followed a dry stream bed away from the trail in search of water. Papalotl smiled tolerantly, well acquainted with her father's skepticism by now and aware that he would not fully share her belief in her dreams until they had been tested.

"Was it not *your* father," she inquired lightly, "who said that there is no way of telling how long the inevitable may take to occur?"

Huemac gave a short laugh and looked at her with the wistful expression he had worn in her dream, the look that told her that he had reconciled himself to her fate, however much he might still wish for proof. Papalotl gazed back at him fondly, savoring the closeness that had developed between them, knowing that they would be separated from each other all too soon.

Texcoco provided the first positive proof of Papalotl's dreaming power, though it was not a confirmation in which either of them could take much joy. They found the usually lively city shrouded in gloom, its people in a state of stunned depression, exactly as Papalotl had foreseen. Those who knew them at the palace seemed ashamed to meet their eyes, and they were told, without explanation, that the king was in seclusion and was receiving no visitors. After a long wait, they were finally granted an interview with the Lady of Tula, who told them in grief-stricken tones what had happened:

Chalchiuhnenetl, the king's Mexican wife, had finally committed a fatal indiscretion, giving a piece of jewelry—a gift from Nezahualpilli himself—to one of her lovers. Having heard and ignored the rumors of his wife's waywardness for years, the king nevertheless could not shut his eyes to the evidence when it appeared before him so brazenly, worn on the person of a man in his own court. So he had made an unexpected late-night visit to his wife's quarters, and there he had found her naked, reveling shamelessly in the company of not one, but four, young men.

The king had requested of Ahuitzotl that he be the one to pronounce judgment upon his niece, but the Tenocha Speaker had refused to involve himself in the matter. So Nezahualpilli's own judges had conducted the trial, hearing all sides before finding Chalchiuhnenetl and the four men guilty of adultery and condemning them to death. In a ceremony witnessed by the entire city, the queen and her companions had been strangled by the executioner's ropes, along with all the retainers who had cooperated in deceiving the king.

"The lords of *your* city, of course, were greatly angered that the execution took place in public," the Lady of Tula explained, her eyes downcast in apology. "I am afraid, my child, that a match for you in this city, at this time, is impossible."

Huemac and Papalotl exchanged a brief glance, and then Papalotl spoke to her friend and sponsor in a comforting tone:

"It does not matter, my Lady. I am going back to the temple, where I belong. But I will always be grateful for your kindness, and for the interest you have shown in me."

The Lady of Tula looked from daughter to father in distress, shaking her head in unconscious denial. But then, gradually, she saw that they were of one mind on this matter, and her eyes darkened with disappointment.

"I have been claimed by Quetzalcoatl, my Lady," Papalotl told her gently as they parted. "There is no other to whom I may belong, now."

THE EFFECT of the drought on Tenochtitlan was apparent to Huemac even before his canoe had docked. He saw how drastically the level of the Lake had receded around the island, exposing patches of lake bottom to the baking sun and leaving the chinampa beds to rot, high up on the dry shores. There cannot be much fresh produce in the city anymore, he thought, seeing only half the usual number of fishermen poling through the shallow water, which gave off a powerful stagnant odor. Acolmiztli and Ome Xochitl had come to greet them on their return, and though they did not seem thin or underfed, Huemac saw the memory of the Rabbit Years, the years of starving, in the lines of both their faces.

"Greetings, my brother," Acolmiztli said as Huemac stepped from the canoe, his desert garments bundled under one arm. They gripped each other's arms, Acolmiztli glancing with surprise at the amount of gray in Huemac's hair.

"I must tell you, my brother," he said apologetically, "that Ahuitzotl has told me to bring you to him as soon as possible."

"Tell us first of Xolotlpilli," Huemac requested, after embracing his mother and allowing Acolmiztli to bow to his niece. Acolmiztli drew himself up proudly and put a hand on Huemac's shoulder.

"He is here, Huemac; you will see him. But do not be surprised if your ears are filled with tales of your son's glory even before you lay eyes on him. He distinguished himself beyond all others at Tehuantepec; he was inducted into the ranks of the Cuachic upon the field of battle, the youngest ever to join their order. They are calling him Xolotl Mexicatl, the Monster of Mexico."

Huemac had glanced in Papalotl's direction at the mention of the Cuachic, wondering if she would recognize the reference to these "shaved heads," and understand how it fit with her dream of Xolotlpilli. But his daughter did not catch his look; she was staring at Acolmiztli pensively, struggling against an emotion that moistened her golden eyes. She has not told me of all her dreams, Huemac realized, putting a proud smile onto his face for Acolmiztli's benefit. He gently placed his bundle into his mother's keeping.

"I will go with you to Ahuitzotl, then," he decided, and spoke to Papalotl in a crisp voice, bringing her instantly out of her trancelike state: "Go with your grandmother, my daughter; tell her of your decision. I will go with you to Patecatl, later."

Papalotl bowed hastily, showing the Chichimec bow and quiver stretched across her back. Acolmiztli raised his eyebrows at Huemac.

"Have you become a hunter, my niece?" he inquired in a bluff voice, and Papalotl looked up at him evenly, her control once more complete.

"A hunter of dreams, my uncle," she said softly, and bowed again, remaining bent over the rabbit-fur blanket in her arms until Huemac had led Acolmiztli away.

STANDING with his brother in the back of Ahuitzotl's audience chamber, Huemac surveyed the crowd with whom he waited, amazed at the diversity of those who were the guests of the court. Warriors, priests, and lords stood shoulder-to-shoulder with ball players, entertainers, merchants, and women of the street, commoners and noblemen mingling with only a minimal regard for the distinctions of rank. The calpixque, those functionaries who served as tax collectors and the stewards of the royal stores, were also much in evidence, their tribute rolls held across their chests like weapons.

Huemac was also impressed by the general gaudiness of dress and make-up, staring like a Chichimec at the yellowed cheeks and bluish hair of the women and the profusion of rare feathers and jewels that decorated the insignia of the warriors. He began to wonder if he should not have taken some time to reaccustom himself to the city before coming here. The noisy murmur of many voices seemed to invade his awareness against his will, and he was constantly being distracted by the commotions created by Ahuitzotl's dwarves and clowns, misshapen men with painted faces and tunics feathered with mock insignia.

"What would our father have thought of this?" he wondered aloud, and Acolmiztli shook his head slowly, a rueful expression on his face.

"The old conventions are gone," he said solemnly. "They began to die when our father did. But then, you have never been a respecter of convention yourself, my brother."

"No," Huemac admitted, unconsciously fingering his hair, which he had neglected to tie up in the proper fashion. "Tell me about Tehuantepec," he asked. "Why was Ahuitzotl forced to return so soon? Surely, he could not have lacked for warriors?"

"The Tehuantepeca fought fiercely, and the heat of that land took its toll on our men. And there was the water shortage to be dealt with here."

"And?" Huemac inquired, seeing his brother hesitate and glance about to see who might be listening. Apparently satisfied that they were not being overheard, Acolmiztli continued in a low voice:

"And there were some troops who had to be taken out of the field for a while. Even after Tehuantepec surrendered, and the order to cease fighting had gone out, the looting of the city continued for several days. Many of the commanders could control their men only by means of threats, and sometimes not even then. Ahuitzotl was forced to promise them gifts from his own stores in order to halt the looting, and he found it prudent to provide for this before proceeding on to Xoconochco."

Huemac rubbed his chin thoughtfully, remembering Papalotl's dream.

"Was my son involved in this?"

"He was one of those who helped to restore order," Acolmiztli assured him. "Chiquatli was another. Your former apprentice is now a commander of the Pumas, and he has been invited into the circle that advises the Speaker."

"And you, my brother?" Huemac asked shrewdly. "Is your voice respected in the Council?"

Acolmiztli examined him silently, as if to assure himself that he was not being taunted.

"When an appeal is made to tradition," he said evenly, "I am often called on to speak. Otherwise, I accept all that passes before me, just as I accepted the merchants being honored as warriors. I do whatever I can on behalf of our people, especially those who do not have a share in the spoils of war."

Huemac nodded respectfully and was about to commend his brother for his tolerance when he heard his own name being announced above the murmuring of the crowd. Acolmiztli walked forward with him, then separated himself and went to join those on the dais with Ahuitzotl. The Speaker was seated on a seat covered with mountain-lion skin, wearing a scarlet mantle with an eagle's face pattern and a border of serpent's eyes. Attached to his broad shoulders were the long, jade-green tail feathers of the quetzal, the crest that he had adopted as his own after the conquest of Tehuantepec. Crouched at his feet was a dwarf with a blackened face and a bonnet of red feathers on his head.

Huemac bowed low and touched dirt to his tongue, hesitating when he heard a ripple of laughter pass through the people standing behind him. When he straightened up, he saw that the dwarf had been parodying his actions, and was licking his thick lips as if he had just enjoyed a tasty meal. Anger rose up in Huemac, and he immediately turned his eyes on the tiny man, pinning him where he sat and making him so uncomfortable that he finally had to cover his face with his hands. The room had grown very quiet while this was happening, but then Ahuitzotl laughed abruptly, and many of those around him quickly joined in, shedding the tense expressions they had assumed upon seeing Huemac glare so threateningly at the Speaker's favorite dwarf.

"So, Huemac," Ahuitzotl said heartily. "I can see that you have lost none of your self-esteem while you were away. I should be angry with you for the way that you took advantage of Tlilpotonqui in my absence, but my regard for your son makes me willing to overlook your dereliction. I was sorry to hear about your wife, as well."

Huemac nodded silently, making no attempt to express a gratitude he did not feel. The quiet in the room deepened, but Ahuitzotl only smiled sardonically, as if he had not expected to be treated any differently. Huemac scanned the faces behind him, seeing his brother and Chiquatli and Tlilpotonqui among the many lords he recognized, but seeing no sign of Moteczuma.

"I have need of you now, though," Ahuitzotl went on, "and I expect that you will return to your duties immediately. I need more warriors, Huemac. Xoconochco awaits me, and the Tlaxcalans will need to be taught a lesson soon. I will need an ambassador to represent me in Texcoco, as well. There are not many here," he added pointedly, glancing around at the men on the dais, "whom I could trust to be courteous in that city."

"The Mexicans will be angry," Huemac thought, remembering Papalotl's dream. He wondered briefly if it was mourning for his sister that had caused Moteczuma's absence.

"What would be the purpose of my mission?" he asked, readdressing himself to the Speaker's proposition. Ahuitzotl answered him in a voice obviously intended to be heard by everyone in the room:

"Our city has grown, as you have no doubt seen. Even before this drought, we needed more fresh water. I have decided to build another aqueduct to bring it here from Coyoacan. There are five springs there that would more than fulfill our needs." The Speaker suddenly narrowed his eyes and lowered his voice slightly: "What do you know of the ruler of Coyoacan, the man called Tzotzoma?"

Huemac had heard this name from some of the wise men in Texcoco, always with admiration, but he was careful in his response, sensing the nearness of Ahuitzotl's anger.

"He is from the ruling house of Azcapotzalco, and he is said to be very learned in the ways of the ancestors, and the gods."

"He is a fool!" Ahuitzotl bellowed, his anger fully upon him. "He hesitates with me; he tells me these waters are too unruly to be harnessed. He dares to ask me to think again!"

The men behind the Speaker had all come stiffly to attention, and Huemac saw the dwarf creep quietly out of the range of his master's feet. Huemac thought of his conversations with Tepeyollotl, and of the fact that he had helped to place this man upon the seat of the ruler. He found himself hating the frightened silence he felt all around him, and looked up into Ahuitzotl's infuriated eyes.

"Perhaps he tells you the truth, my Lord," he suggested calmly, and saw Ahuitzotl hesitate for just an instant—his eyes startled into self-reflection— before he burst out with renewed force:

"He should better concern himself with his safety! I will have his water, and his life, as well, if he puts me off again! *No one* refuses the Tenocha what they desire . . ."

Ahuitzotl trailed off venomously, his chest heaving, his heavy face contorted with spite. The people in the chamber were deathly still, hardly daring to move even their eyes. Tzotzoma is a dead man, Huemac thought; neither tradition nor truth have any hold on *this* ruler. From beneath his hooded eyelids, he again scanned the faces behind Ahuitzotl, seeing that only Acolmiztli gazed back at him. Even Chiquatli had turned his eyes away.

"What would you have me do in Texcoco, my Lord?" Huemac asked again, when it seemed that Ahuitzotl had regained control of his temper. The Speaker cleared his throat noisily and again spoke in a public voice:

"I will need stone and timber, and workmen, and men who know about building. Since our esteemed ally, the Fasting Prince, has seen fit to absent himself from this last campaign, he will no doubt have a great deal of time and energy to devote to this task. I will leave it to you to convince him of the wisdom of his cooperation."

Huemac bowed compliantly.

"When do you wish me to leave?"

"I will tell you," Ahuitzotl muttered in a surly tone. "Go back to your warriors for now. And Huemac . . ."

"Yes, my Lord?" Huemac said attentively, but Ahuitzotl merely stared at him for a long moment, letting him know how close he had come to drawing the Speaker's anger upon himself. I have used up the last of his gratitude, Huemac thought; he will not accept boldness, or the truth, from me again.

"You may go," Ahuitzotl said at last. "But do not forget that past favor might easily be lost, by *anyone* . . ."

"I shall remember, my Lord," Huemac said politely, and backed out of the ruler's presence, taking his only pleasure in having brought silence to this chamber.

THE ROOM in which Xolotlpilli sat was crammed with the goods and honors he had won: sacks of maize and beans pushed in between the stacks of mantles and loincloths, shields and standards leaning against the walls, his jewelry and feathered insignia laid out on mats around his own. He glanced up irritably when Papalotl came into the room and seated herself across from him, her arms filled with a furry gray bundle.

"I asked not to be disturbed, my sister," he said sternly, in a voice as deep as his father's. Even seated, he seemed immense, his muscles bulging beneath the golden armbands around his biceps. His head had been completely shaved except for a stiff, narrow ridge of hair above his left ear, and a claw-shaped piece of shiny black obsidian protruded from his upper lip. Papalotl, however, appeared to find nothing unusual, or even particularly imposing, about his appearance.

"There are many people waiting to see you," she said simply. "They drink up all of our grandmother's octli."

"I will buy her more," Xolotlpilli muttered, and Papalotl cast a meaningful glance around the room.

"Yes, you are a very wealthy man, my brother. Why is it that you seem so unhappy?"

"Where is it ever taught that wealth brings happiness?" Xolotlpilli snapped. "It brings envy and disagreement and ugliness between men. It is nothing worth killing for."

"Do you not fight for the gods, my brother?" Papalotl asked innocently. "And for the glory of our city?"

"Each man fights for his own glory, it seems, and for the things that glory will bring him," Xolotlpilli said bitterly. "The honor of our name means nothing anymore; the warriors must be bribed in order to fight."

"Why is that?" Papalotl prompted, and though Xolotlpilli grimaced, he did not seem unwilling to explain.

"We fight far from home, and we are gone for many months. Many of those who must go with us are not warriors by trade, and they worry over the idleness of their fields and shops while they are away. They complain that the largest share of the spoils always goes to the ruler and the warrior orders, and that they have no share in the tribute at all. Many of the apprentices and warriors without rank feel the same way."

"Are their complaints just?" Papalotl asked gently, and Xolotlpilli shrugged his huge shoulders uncomfortably.

"Yes," he admitted reluctantly. "But that is no justification for looting the homes of defenseless people. I was forced to raise my arm against my fellow warriors, to make them stop."

Now Papalotl understood the significance of her dream, and she gazed sympathetically into her brother's plaintive eyes.

"Why is there not a more equitable distribution of the spoils?" she asked, and saw Xolotlpilli's bitterness return, hardening his face.

"I proposed this to Chiquatli and the other commanders," he said in a soft voice, obviously pained by the memory. "They laughed and reminded me of my age. They told me to wait until I had wives and children, and to *then* see if I desired such a change."

"Perhaps you should give away what you own, then," Papalotl suggested boldly, "and be an example to them. They might be tempted to laugh at you some more, but there would be no question as to what *you* fight for."

Xolotlpilli cocked his gleaming head and examined her thoughtfully while turning the idea over in his mind.

"It would be a controversial gesture," he noted aloud. "It might be said that I was trying to shame them."

"They would only shame themselves with such an accusation," Papalotl said flatly. "Your instincts are sound, my brother; you *know* what is right. You should hope never to gain the sort of wisdom they recommend."

"I will do it, then," Xolotlpilli decided impulsively, nodding to himself with satisfaction. Then he looked back at Papalotl and smiled for the first time. "I am grateful for your advice, my sister, and for the confidence you have shown in my judgment. Perhaps, while it is still here, you would like to choose something for yourself, as my gift," he added, gesturing expansively to include the contents of the room. But Papalotl only shook her head.

"I am returning to the temple, Xolotlpilli," she told him solemnly. "I will have need of nothing there. But I have brought *you* a gift, my brother."

She laid the bundled blanket before him and watched as he rubbed a massive hand over the soft fur, feeling its warmth. His large brown eyes grew gentle, making his face seem as young as his seventeen years.

"There is something else inside," Papalotl added, and smiled at the expression that appeared on Xolotlpilli's face as he opened the bundle and lifted up the painted bone flute.

"My last one was lost months ago, in the mountains beyond Oaxaca," he murmured thickly, blinking against the tears that rose to his eyes. "Your kindness overwhelms me, Papalotl."

"Are you not the very model of Telpochtli, the Young Warrior?" Papalotl asked rhetorically. "Should you not also have a flute?"

Xolotlpilli nodded and smiled weakly, too touched to speak. Papalotl gave him a moment to recover himself before adopting a more serious tone:

"Our time together is very short, my brother, so you must forgive me if I speak boldly to you. I learned many things in the hills, but my purpose in going there was to understand my fate, and to discover the powers I had been given to cope with it. Clearly, you were meant to discover these same things upon the fields of blood and burning; the very fame that troubles you so attests to that. Therefore, you must not allow yourself to be confused by the names and titles that are given to you, or by the way that others regard you. You must learn to converse with your own heart, so that you will always remember who you are. That is why I have brought you these things: the Chichimec blanket, to remind you that the blood of Nezahualcoyotl flows in your veins, blood as old and wise as the hills; and the flute, to remind you of the boy whose heart was generous and kind. *Both* are to remind you that you are my brother."

"They will be my dearest possessions," Xolotlpilli promised, clearly impressed by her speech. "You have gained great wisdom in the hills, my sister. I am grateful that you have chosen to share it with me."

"I have very little wisdom," Papalotl said ruefully. "But I know that a heart in conflict with itself is a very dangerous thing; I know that it makes you vulnerable to the worst that is in your fate. I learned this at great risk, and there is already enough risk in the life that fate has given you. You were meant to be an extraordinary warrior, Xolotlpilli, all the signs say so. But you must be truthful with yourself, and use your powers in concert with the best that is in your heart. Then you will be as extraordinary a man as you are a fighter."

His eyes glowing, Xolotlpilli briefly bowed his head, as if to give thanks. Then he looked up at Papalotl.

"I will miss you when you have gone into the temple," he said quietly. "But I will make a donation there, in your name, before I return to the battlefield."

"You must come to see me when you return. And you must bring your children to visit me in Cholula, when I go there."

Xolotlpilli raised his eyebrows slightly at this revelation, but he merely nodded in agreement. Papalotl smiled and inclined her head toward the painted flute, which was all but lost in his huge hands.

"Perhaps you will play me a tune now, as you used to in Texcoco," she suggested. "Perhaps we can be as children again, before we are separated, and go off in pursuit of the tasks our fates have given to us."

⌐⌐| 6 ||⌐

T HE messenger from Patecatl arrived just as Huemac was leaving the House of Eagles, so he turned left instead of right and followed the shaven-headed novice toward the Temple of Quetzalcoatl. To his right, climbing the steps of the great pyramid, was a long procession of black-robed priests; heading, Huemac knew, not for the shrine of Huitzilopochtli, but for the blue-and-white shrine beside it, the home of Tlaloc, God of Rain. There had been a little rain during the previous season, but not enough to break the drought. The year Seven-Reed had begun without any alteration in the pattern of clear skies and dry weather, and the city of Tenochtitlan lay parched beneath the sun, suffocating under a layer of dust and the stench of its own wastes.

When he arrived before the priest, Huemac explained that he was expected at the construction site just outside the precinct gates, and he asked to be allowed to return later for their talk. But Patecatl seemed to feel strongly that what he had to say could not be put off, so he offered instead to accompany Huemac to the place where the aqueduct was being built.

"The walk will be good for these old legs," the priest said gruffly, as they walked across the plaza together, heading south. "What is your part in building this water-carrier, my son?"

"I am the liaison between the Regent, Tlilpotonqui, and Nezahualpilli, who is in charge of the actual construction," Huemac said without enthusiasm. "It is a waste of words designed to show Ahuitzotl's displeasure over the execution of his niece. It is also his way of punishing both Nezahualpilli and myself for defending Tzotzoma."

Patecatl shook his head sadly but said nothing, the common response to the mention of the unfortunate ruler of Coyoacan. Even now, with the aqueduct nearing completion, the memory of Tzotzoma's murder hung over the project like an ominous cloud. His last words, before the rope had tightened around his neck, had prophesied that Tenochtitlan would be destroyed by the waters that Ahuitzotl had stolen. Perhaps because of this, the elaborate ceremonies of dedication, which would not take place until Ahuitzotl returned from Xoconochco, were already in preparation, as if to ward off danger in advance.

"I must speak to you about your daughter," Patecatl said abruptly, when the subject of Tzotzoma had been allowed to settle. "I must tell you of the strictures under which I have placed her."

"What has she done?" Huemac asked in surprise. "She has not spoken to anyone of her dreams, has she?"

"No, she has abided by that agreement," the priest acknowledged. "But she has not stopped her practice of dreaming."

"She did not promise to forsake her powers, my father," Huemac reminded him respectfully. "Only to keep her knowledge to herself. Has she created some disturbance?"

"Quite the contrary; she has only become more covert. She has learned to do without the foul-smelling herbs she used to burn, and she no longer shows any inattention afterward. I know that she continues only because I thought to ask her, and she confessed to me freely."

"Do you punish her for her honesty, then?" Huemac inquired, with an edge to his voice that brought the old man's head up.

"That has nothing to do with it. She dreams when she should be sleeping, or praying. And she continues to harbor this absurd notion of serving in Cholula. Why, in this city alone, there are at least twenty priestesses more deserving of such an honor! And where is there any sign of this flood she has predicted?"

They had come out through the south gate of the temple precinct, and just ahead, they could see the scaffolds and platforms of the men working on the aqueduct. Supported by earthworks that were buttressed by thick logs and lined with mortared stone, the open, double-channeled conduit snaked off into the distance, following the line of the causeway that went south toward Coyoacan. Huemac gave the priest a hard look and gestured at the massive wall of earth and stone.

"Perhaps it is being brought to us," he suggested darkly, and Patecatl's normally gentle eyes flashed a stern warning.

"You forget yourself, Huemac. Such a suggestion is neither amusing nor proper. I agreed to allow Papalotl to go into the desert to be healed, and I did not complain of the unorthodox fashion in which this was accomplished. Nor did I show any disapproval toward the things she claimed to have seen and experienced. But I cannot allow one of our priestesses to practice sorcery in our midst. Therefore, I have forbidden any further dreaming, even in private."

"You would force her to choose between the gift of the god and her obedience to you?" Huemac demanded incredulously. "That is a serious mistake, my father. You *do* disapprove of her nakedness, even if it is only of the heart."

"I disapprove of anything that diminishes the purity of our order," Patecatl snapped. "Papalotl is looked up to by many of the younger girls, because of her beauty and her kindness. I cannot allow her to have such an influence while she is still practicing barbarian rites in secret; it cannot be wholesome."

"Our ancestors, the Chichimecs, are not barbarians, and we owe as much to their wisdom as to that of the Toltecs," Huemac said stiffly. "Do you never wonder that they continue to flourish in the hills, while the Toltecs are gone? Perhaps this is where our ways must part, my father, for I could not disagree with your thinking more completely."

"Do not be so proud, Huemac," the priest scolded him sharply, "and so quick to place yourself in opposition. You have few enough friends among the powerful in this city. I released you from an obligation once, but I will not do so now. We have shared too much for you to turn on me in disrespect."

Huemac stared at him silently, breathing deeply through his nose. Then he exhaled loudly and let his shoulders relax.

"Forgive my impetuousness, Father," he apologized. "Papalotl will obey your wishes, as she should. But we must reach a new agreement. She must be allowed some chance to win her release; you must name what it is that will convince you of the holiness of her powers."

Patecatl hesitated stubbornly, then allowed a grudging smile to appear on his aged face.

"Always, you seek to bargain with fate, Huemac. Let it be, then. When I see that Tenochtitlan has more water than its needs require, I will send your daughter to Cholula with a personal request that she be interviewed. But until such a time, she must put aside her dreaming."

"Tell her that I have agreed to this," Huemac said. Then, before taking his leave, he gave the priest an inquisitive glance: "I notice that you have not chosen to share the contents of my daughter's dreaming with me. Did you not ask her?"

"I did," Patecatl admitted reluctantly. He looked up into Huemac's expectant eyes and sighed. "She said that she had seen the temple of our god being rebuilt, by the command of Moteczuma, who wore the turquoise diadem of the Speaker. Then she saw this same temple in flames, burning against the night sky. Perhaps now you see why I do not wish her to continue this practice."

"I see," Huemac said in a neutral voice, without agreement. He bowed to the priest in parting. "Farewell, my father. Be vigilant in your duties. As to our judgments, the future will test them, soon enough."

EVER SINCE Papalotl's return from the desert, Cocatli had been waiting to learn what had happened to her there. She had been told only that her niece had undergone some kind of curing ceremony, during which the young woman had discovered, at last, that her true place was in the temple. But this much was obvious to anyone with eyes, and even more obvious to those who had come into contact with Papalotl, and had experienced the serenity that seemed to flow from her every word and gesture. Cocatli had felt this herself, and she had seen the calming effect that Papalotl had upon the younger women, especially those who had just come into the temple. They seemed to sense immediately that she was at home here, comfortable with the harsh living conditions and the even more perplexing demands of devotional duty.

Cocatli had wanted to embrace her many times, and share her joy and wonder at this change. And she had sensed—at their first, brief meeting—that Papalotl had wanted to give her the opportunity. But by the time an occasion for personal conversation had presented itself to them, Papalotl had no longer seemed anxious to confide in her, and had conducted herself in a subdued manner. She had consistently led the conversation away from the subject of her sojourn in the desert, and she had withdrawn completely the only time that Cocatli had brought it up herself.

Though hurt by this secrecy, Cocatli had nonetheless accepted her niece's right to remain silent, and she had not pressed the matter during all the months since. But then, very recently, she had heard rumors that the High Priest was somehow displeased with Papalotl, a possibility that puzzled even those priestesses envious enough to have tried to find fault with her. Nor were the rumors ever confirmed by any action on Patecatl's part. Yet Cocatli had noticed a perceptible dimming of Papalotl's enthusiasm, as if she *were* being punished. This had gone on for almost a month, and seemed to be growing worse when Cocatli finally decided to confront her niece directly.

She went to Papalotl's sleeping chamber early one morning, before the rest of the women had risen, using as her excuse the news that had only reached the city late the night before, while Papalotl had been sleeping. She found her niece alone in the tiny, barren cubicle, sitting cross-legged on a reed mat, her face still lined and puffy with sleep. Yet Papalotl noticed her presence immediately and beckoned for her to come into the room.

"Xoconochco has fallen," Cocatli announced in a soft voice. "Xolotlpilli and the other warriors will be returning home soon."

Papalotl stared back at her without surprise, seeming so unaffected by the news that Cocatli wondered if she were truly awake and had heard her. Then the younger woman spoke, in a crisp voice that left no question as to her alertness:

"Yes," she agreed succinctly. "And the rains will be returning with them."

"Did you dream this, my sister?" Cocatli asked, struck by the conviction with which the statement had been offered. Papalotl smiled very deliberately, more a rueful grimace than an expression of amusement.

"I am not allowed to dream," she said. "And I did not seek that which was shown to me. Soon, though, I shall not be so constrained. Soon, I shall be free again."

"Free?" Cocatli echoed helplessly, feeling a chill spread through her body. She remembered Papalotl's first attack, and the dream of Taypachtli's drowning. I am losing her, she thought suddenly, just as I lost her mother. She knelt before her niece, clasping her hands in front of her imploringly.

"Remember your vow, Papalotl," she pleaded. "You must not entertain these thoughts of freedom any longer. You have pledged yourself, and you have been accepted. You cannot choose again."

"You misunderstand, my aunt," Papalotl said sympathetically, reaching out to wrap Cocatli's hands with her own. "And you have no need to fear: My dedication to the god is not in question. Be patient, my sister. One day, I will be able to explain everything to you."

"When?" Cocatli demanded plaintively, her distress and confusion only partially alleviated.

"When Patecatl has satisfied his doubts," Papalotl replied, then held up a hand to indicate that she did not wish to discuss the matter further. "I can tell you no more, my sister. Only that it will not be long . . ."

AS AHUITZOTL and his army marched back into Tenochtitlan, the clouds that had been hanging over the city for several days released their water in a sudden, brief downpour, soaking both the warriors and the crowd that had come out to greet them. It was the first such rain in over two years, and the people received it joyously, taking it as an omen as powerful as that of the victory itself. The aqueduct from Coyoacan had been completed only a few days earlier, and, regarding this shower as a propitious sign, the Water Priests quickly set the date for its dedication. After rewarding his warriors for their success in Xoconochco, Ahuitzotl put aside his armor and donned the ceremonial robes of his office, and summoned the requisite dignitaries from Tlatelulco, Tlacopan, and the surrounding towns and cities.

At dawn on the chosen day, the order was given, and the main lock at the reservoir in Coyoacan was opened for the first time. Only moments later, it seemed, the water flowed into Tenochtitlan, where it was greeted by a full complement of priests and nobles, led by a priest wearing the blue mantle and heron-feather headdress of Acuecueyotl, the Goddess of Waves. Quail were beheaded and their blood was poured upon the rushing water, along with offerings of blue maize flour, incense, paper, and liquid rubber. The priest dipped handfuls of the sacred water and threw it out over the assembled crowd, who danced to the music of flutes and conch trumpets and sang songs of praise to Tlaloc and his consort, Chalchihuitlicue, She of the Jade Skirt. White-haired old men brought forth containers of live fish, frogs, and newts, and these were blessed before being emptied into the pipe, which would carry them to the Lake to reproduce.

In a last solemn ceremony, four young children were led forward, dressed in the blue raiment of the Water Goddess. One by one, they were stretched out over the foaming culvert, and the priest opened their chests and tore out their hearts, adding their precious lifeblood to the flowing waters. Ahuitzotl gave a long speech welcoming the waters to his city, and then he threw golden jewels in the shape of fishes and frogs into the pools near his palace. As the joyous crowd began to disperse, the Speaker ordered his stewards to distribute seed from his own stores, so that his people might revive their chinampa plots and rooftop gardens, and once more feed their families.

The Tenocha planted under clear skies, wetting their fields by hand as prayers were again offered up to the Rain God. Shortly after the festival of Toxcatl, Tlaloc answered with a thunderstorm that provided more noise than actual moisture, startling those who had grown unaccustomed to the booming voice of the god. Then dark clouds piled up over the mountains to the east, and the rains began in earnest. Day after day, the water poured down from an unrelenting sky, as if to make up for the scarcity of years in a single season. The mood of the Tenocha turned from joy to trepidation, and the dying words of Tzotzoma were recalled and repeated in nervous whispers.

The Lake quickly rose to its original level, and then, as the ruler of Coyoacan had warned, the pools and holding tanks within the city began to overflow from the combination of the heavy rains and the abundant waters that poured through the aqueduct with undiminished force. Ahuitzotl commanded that the spillways south of the city be opened, diverting the water into the salty part of the Lake, beyond the protective dike that had been erected in the time of the first Moteczuma. And when the rains continued, and the dike began to erode and show signs of giving way, he hastily sent out crews to repair and enlarge it. But even the lash of his anger could not enable them to work fast enough. Soon the canals of the city were overflowing their banks and the recently restored chinampas were being washed out into the Lake, and the people began to fear for their own safety.

The huts of the commoners who lived along the shore were the first to fall, collapsed by the unceasing pressure of the tides against the pilings upon which they rested. Rescuing what possessions they could, the beleaguered people fled to the mainland in their canoes, touching off a panic in those who remained behind and saw the water rising to the tops of the causeways. With a final roar that could be heard all the way to Tenochtitlan, the rain-swollen waters collected at Coyoacan burst through the dam meant to hold them back, and the flood spread into all parts of the city. Powerless to do anything more, Ahuitzotl reluctantly gave the order, and the evacuation of Tenochtitlan began.

THE NOVITIATES and students attached to the Temple of Quetzalcoatl were sent home to their parents as soon as the danger to the city became apparent. Then, having determined the few old ones who would stay on with him, Patecatl began to dispatch the younger priests and priestesses in groups of two or three, responding to the offers of shelter that came to him from their relatives, and from the temples in other cities. The first offer concerning Cocatli and Papalotl came from the lord Acolmiztli: He was sending his wives and younger children to Ixtapalapa, the home of his first wife; the ruler of that city would also be pleased to provide shelter for Acolmiztli's sister and niece, should the High Priest choose to send them there. The second offer came from the Jaguar Warrior Azcatzin, who had been granted his release and was taking his wife and his aging grandmother, Ome Xochitl, to Texcoco. He, too, welcomed the presence of his mother and his cousin in his canoes.

Patecatl politely refused both offers, and then he sent a message of his own to Huemac, who had taken up quarters in his son's house, on the high ground near the Speaker's palace. The priest watched his messenger depart, wading laboriously through the knee-high water that covered the plaza, then turned and went back to his chamber, calling to his attendants for a roll of treated leather and bowls of red and black ink. He had only just finished his work when Pinotl arrived with Huemac's reply, and he received the vanguard merchant along with the two women, who came bearing the things he had told them to gather.

Pinotl planted his black staff before the priest and bowed behind it, touching dirt to his tongue. He had a full complement of weapons strapped across his back, beneath a thick maguey-fiber cloak, and he began by apologizing for wearing them into the temple.

"I am ready to leave immediately for Cholula, my father," he explained. "The lord Huemac has entrusted me with taking these two women there safely."

Cocatli started slightly, glancing sidelong at her niece, who sat motionless, her eyes fastened expectantly on the priest.

"Did Huemac have any other message for me?" Patecatl asked, his hands curled around the roll of leather in his lap.

"He sends his respect for your wisdom and judgment, my father," Pinotl reported, "and he remembers his obligation to you as a friend. I am also to tell his daughter that he and his son will be staying behind to guard the city, but that they will come to visit her in Cholula soon."

"Thank you, my son," the priest commended him, then turned to the two women. "The priests in Cholula have agreed to accept you into their midst as a pilgrim, Cocatli, for the duration of the trouble here. Arrangements will be made for your return when such a thing becomes feasible.

"As for you, my daughter," he said to Papalotl, who drew herself up with dignity, not quite concealing the excitement in her eyes. "I have drawn a record of your life, indicating the signs surrounding your birth, the quality of your service in the temple, and the nature of the dreams you have described to me. You must supply the High Priest with the details that are missing, and you must be prepared to defend yourself against his skepticism. You are free to do this in any way that you believe wise; you no longer have to prove your holiness to me."

Papalotl bowed gratefully.

"The god will prepare me, my father," she said in a soft voice, "as he does in all things. I would request your permission, though, to also tell these things to my aunt, and to my friend," she added, indicating Pinotl.

"Tell whomever you wish, as you see fit," Patecatl instructed. "You have powers beyond my reckoning, Quetzal Papalotl. I can only ask that you use them with honesty and compassion, and strive always to increase the glory of the one we serve. Go now with the blessing of our Lord, Quetzalcoatl," he said, raising a hand over them and lightly touching Pinotl's staff. "And of Yacate-cuhtli, the Lord Who Guides, god of the vanguard merchants."

All three bowed again before rising and leaving the priest's chamber, Papa-lotl bearing the roll of leather he had given to her. Pinotl showed the women how to bundle their sandals and ritual implements in the midst of their extra clothing, then had them pull their cloaks up over their heads before leading them out onto the rain-swept platform in front of the shrine. Papalotl paused at the top of the steps and had them wait while she gazed out over the deserted plaza and the great Temple of Huitzilopochtli that rose out of its waters.

"Farewell, my city," she murmured, her tears mingling with the raindrops on her cheeks. "May the gods of our ancestors watch over you, and bring your people home once again. I leave you now."

Then, placing herself between Pinotl and her aunt, she nodded that she was ready and started down the temple stairs.

THOUGH HE had remained in the city, inhabiting the one wing of his palace that stood above water, Ahuitzotl was so demoralized that for two months he was able to do little more than listen glumly to the daily round of messages, requests for aid, and reports of further emergencies that were brought to him by canoe. And while the rains had stopped, the city was still flooded, and would remain so as long as the waters from Coyoacan continued to flow into the Lake. Yet Ahuitzotl could not bring himself to face the total destruction of the project begun in his own name, and so he temporized pointlessly, insulating himself from advice he did not want to hear.

Finally, though, at the coaxing of Acolmiztli and others, the Speaker sent an appeal to Nezahualpilli, who came across the Lake without hesitation. He strode into Ahuitzotl's audience chamber wearing a dark blue mantle deco-rated with silver stars, the smoking mirror of Tezcatlipoca set in a golden crown around his elegant head. He surveyed the gloomy faces of the Mexicans, noting the absence of clowns and entertainers in their midst, and the silence that hung over the crowded, unswept room. His own abundant vitality shone in his face, but he waited calmly for the dejected Ahuitzotl to remember his manners and address him.

"Greetings, my Lord," Ahuitzotl said at last, his eyes dulled with misery. "You see the terrible state we are in. I appeal to you: What is to be done?"

Nezahualpilli nodded, but without sympathy, and when he spoke, his voice was as hard and polished as the floor on which he stood:

"Now, when it is too late, you ask what is to be done. But who could convince you to consider beforehand the consequences of your actions? Would you listen to Tzotzoma when he gave you good advice, warning you of danger as a loyal subject should? Would you listen to his uncle, the ruler of Tlacopan, when he vouched for his nephew's intentions and pleaded for Tzotzoma's life? No, you chose instead to slay him and steal his waters, disregarding all the warnings that were given to you!"

Slapped by the king's words, Ahuitzotl had straightened up on his seat, but Nezahualpilli continued in the same unrelenting manner, speaking with a voice that seemed not his alone, but that of many:

"And how had Tzotzoma sinned against you? Did he steal from your possessions or conspire against your rule? Had he disregarded his obligations to you, or shown you disrespect? Can you say with the assurance of the just that he *deserved* to die? You have offended, Ahuitzotl, you have angered the gods. And so, you and your people have been visited with an enemy against which you are helpless. Even the strong arms of your warriors are no proof against the swelling waters, the punishment of the gods."

Nezahualpilli paused and swept the room with a stern gaze that invited no interruption, then went on:

"It is my opinion that the dam you built must be completely destroyed and the waters returned to their original course. You must also make solemn offerings to Chalchihuitlicue, she who rules over all waters that are confined. You must give her jewels and precious feathers and all the things that are known to be pleasing to her, including the blood of young children. Perhaps these things will placate her, and cause her to withhold the wrath she has lately rained down upon you. I would also recommend that restitution be made to the heirs of Tzotzoma and the people of Coyoacan for the grief you have brought to their city."

Nezahualpilli bowed when he was finished, then stood waiting before Ahuitzotl, who seemed to be having trouble swallowing. The men standing behind him appeared braced for an outburst, but when Ahuitzotl finally spoke, it was with the voice of one who had met defeat, a voice that no one had heard from him in all his years upon the reed seat:

"I will do as you advise," he promised, and then could say no more, gesturing to Nezahualpilli in a half-hearted attempt to convey gratitude. The king bowed to him again and left as he had come, his head held high, in the manner of the righteous.

Acolmiztli had listened to Nezahualpilli's speech from the side of the chamber, having arrived too late to take his customary place on the dais. He had at first been incredulous that *anyone* would dare to scold Ahuitzotl in such a forthright manner, but as he heard the Fasting Prince speak the thoughts that were in the minds of everyone in Anahuac—thoughts that had hung dangerously on his own tongue for months—he swelled with pride for the courage of his kinsman, and blessed the wisdom that Nezahualcoyotl had invested in his son. Only with great difficulty could he conceal his immense satisfaction with how Ahuitzotl had capitulated in the face of his chastisement.

A low murmuring swept the room after the Speaker rose from his seat, his shoulders slumping, and left the room in the company of his advisers and the slender retinue that remained with him. Then Acolmiztli felt a hand on his elbow, and turned to find Huemac standing beside him.

"This will not be a friendly place for you tonight, my brother," Huemac said matter-of-factly. "I bring you an invitation to visit with those of us who have taken up residence at the house of Xolotlpilli. Will you come?"

"I would be honored," Acolmiztli said gratefully. "I will know, at least, that one person shares my feelings on this night."

"Indeed," Huemac agreed knowingly. "Come, I have a canoe. My son and his friends await us."

AS A REWARD for his deeds of valor, Xolotlpilli had been given a house within walking distance of the Speaker's palace, an enormous edifice with two separate courtyards and two full stories of rooms. It had formerly belonged to an illustrious warrior who had died in Xoconochco, leaving no sons of sufficient rank to inherit. Since he had not yet taken a wife, Xolotlpilli had promptly invited a number of young warriors to leave the telpochcalli and lodge with him, thus enlarging his already sizable reputation for generosity at the same time that he provided himself with company. These friends were the core of the group of perhaps twenty young men who were now living in the dry second-floor rooms with Huemac and his son. By day, they patrolled the flooded city in their canoes, discouraging looters and bringing food and firewood to the priests and priestesses stranded in their island temples. At night, they gathered together in one of the gardens on the roof to cook their simple meals and talk among themselves.

Huemac explained this to Acolmiztli as they walked through a long room crowded with sleeping mats and climbed the ladder to the roof, emerging into the rich golden light of the setting sun. There were three fires burning around the perimeter of a broad circle that had been cleared in the dirt, and the men —all between the ages of sixteen and twenty—were standing or squatting near the flames, tending to food, talking quietly, or simply gazing out at the brilliant colors in the sky to the west. Except for the presence of the surrounding buildings and the steady lapping of water in the street below, this might well have been a campsite somewhere on the trail, an illusion that aroused nostalgic longings in Acolmiztli as Huemac began to introduce him to the men.

From their speech, Acolmiztli could tell that some had been educated in the calmecac and others had not, and that at least three came from other cities. But all wore the same plain clothing, without insignia, and no mention was made of rank or family as they were introduced. Nor did there seem to be any unspoken hierarchy among them; even Xolotlpilli, the owner of this house, was taking his turn at the cooking, exercising none of the prerogatives of the host. They seemed to relate to one another as comrades and equals, paying deference only to him and Huemac, who wore the distinguishing marks of their age.

Accepting a bowl of bean stew and a cup of water, Acolmiztli seated himself between his brother and his nephew, noticing that all sat facing inward, sharing in the general conversation as they ate. They seemed extraordinarily relaxed and good-natured for a group of warriors who had been deprived of their chosen task, trapped here in this deserted city, without ball games, dances, or other amusements to keep their minds off their inactivity. What can they have done with their ambition, Acolmiztli wondered, struck by the absence of boasting and the kind of competitive edginess he remembered so well from his own days as an aspiring warrior.

As Huemac began to recite the details of Nezahualpilli's speech, Acolmiztli scanned the circle of young faces, waiting to see how they would react to the news of Ahuitzotl's shaming. But though their faces were properly grave, not one of them frowned or made any other sign of disagreement. They seemed, in fact, to be as satisfied with the outcome as he had been himself.

"It is a good thing," one of them offered when Huemac had finished, "that our allies have the courage to say those things that are too harsh for our own tongues."

"Yes," another agreed. "It is better that they risk injuring our pride, rather than remaining silent and allowing it to diminish further in the eyes of the gods."

"It is time that positive actions were taken," a third speaker said, then added, somewhat sadly: "Soon, our work here will be over."

The others around the circle nodded silently, wearing expressions of similar regret. Acolmiztli glanced swiftly at his brother for an explanation of this sadness, but Huemac merely smiled and indicated that he should ask for himself.

"Forgive me, my young friends," Acolmiztli said, breaking the silence, "but I do not understand what saddens you. Surely, guarding a flooded city cannot be such a satisfying duty. Surely, you must yearn for more important work than this?"

"We consider our work very important, my uncle," Xolotlpilli said, glancing around the group before assuming the right to answer for them. "And we do not merely guard. We have become the stewards of our city."

Acolmiztli wrinkled his brow and gestured for him to go on.

"In our patrols, we often find things that will be spoiled by the water if they are not put to immediate use. So we take them to those who need them the most. Likewise, we sometimes find that the storerooms of one house are crowded with goods, while those of another are empty. So we move a few things from the first place to the second. There have also been occasions when we have borrowed some things that would not be missed by their owners and traded them for food and wood on the mainland."

"How does this differ from looting?" Acolmiztli demanded sternly, aghast at what his nephew had just described. A young man on the other side of the circle broke in in Xolotlpilli's defense, though there was nothing defensive about his explanation:

"We keep nothing for ourselves," he said simply. "Everything goes to those in need. Why should we trouble the Speaker with requests for stores, when they are so readily provided by the lords of our city?"

"Provided without their knowledge," Acolmiztli pointed out harshly. He turned to Huemac. "And you, my brother. As their commander, you are responsible for this."

"As responsible as any other," Huemac admitted with a slight shrug. "But I do not command here. We are all here voluntarily, because we enjoy the company and the work. We decide everything together."

"The idea came to us of itself," Xolotlpilli added. "We had asked my cousin Omeocelotl and the other merchants still in Tlatelulco for supplies, and they gave them to us freely. We did not think that the lords of Tenochtitlan would wish to be thought any less generous, even in their absence. What Tenocha would refuse to give aid to his brothers in their need?"

Acolmiztli shook his head but had no reply, and he listened numbly as still another young man sought to convince him:

"That is why we think of ourselves as stewards, rather than thieves. We merely redistribute the spoils that were won in the name of our god and *all* our people. We are all the wealthier for it."

There was a long silence while Acolmiztli pondered their explanations, finding that no eyes avoided his own or showed any resentment at the way he had challenged their honesty. It was their utter frankness that finally persuaded him; that, and the fact that they possessed an energy and sense of mission that was lacking everywhere else in the city, particularly in the palace.

"Do not ask me to approve," he said at last. "But every army must provision itself, and clearly, we are engaged in a war for our survival. Everyone must give what he can spare."

"Whether he knows it or not!" Huemac concluded emphatically, and the group roared with laughter, releasing all the tension within the circle. Several of the men got up to relieve themselves off the side of the building, and new conversations were started as the others stretched their legs and formed smaller, more intimate groupings.

Acolmiztli soon found himself at the center of one such group, being pressed for stories of the campaigns in which he had fought and of the warchiefs he had served. Even as he responded to their interest—so different from that of the ambitious young warriors in the court—he wondered if Huemac had asked them to flatter him in this way. But then he saw that his brother was being questioned in a similar manner, and the persistence of his own companions quickly convinced him that their interest was personal, and quite genuine.

When the stars had risen over the city and the fires had burnt down to ash, the young men began to retire to the floor below, finally leaving the two brothers alone on the roof. They stood together without speaking, listening to the haunting strains of Xolotlpilli's flute, which drifted upward through the open trap. He played the simple melodies that all had learned as children, bending and lengthening the notes to reveal their full poignance, soothing his fellow warriors to sleep.

"They are fine young men," Acolmiztli said softly. "I have not enjoyed myself so thoroughly in months. I am grateful that you brought me here, my brother."

"The credit belongs entirely to Xolotlpilli," Huemac demurred. "He is unerring in his choice of friends, when he might easily have surrounded himself with sycophants. I did not teach him this, and I do not know who might have."

"He reminds me more and more of Tezcatl, though he seems to have his mother's reserve. I watched him carefully tonight. He carries his prestige lightly, as if he has discerned the difference between mere power and the greatness that can be built upon it. That is a rare perception for a Tenocha of his generation. You have reason to be proud, my brother."

Huemac nodded in acknowledgment, cocking his head as he realized that the music from below had stopped, fading without a trace into the watery sounds of the night.

"Will you come to us again?" he asked, examining his brother's face in the darkness. "I know that the others would benefit from your company, but I also ask for myself. We are not so young anymore, and I would like to share this time before our duties are once more upon us."

"I will come gladly," Acolmiztli said quickly, touched by the obvious sincerity of the request. "You are still my little brother, even if your hair is as gray as my own."

"Let us sleep, then," Huemac suggested with a smile. "It has been a long and eventful day."

"Go to your rest, my brother," Acolmiztli replied, turning to gaze out over the shadowed rooftops. "I wish to be alone for a while with my city. I wish to enjoy the feeling that tonight there is justice in Tenochtitlan, and hope for the future of her people."

WEARING ONLY a maxlatl over his loins and a sweat rag around his forehead, Huemac stood with his hands on his hips, resting with the other members of his crew. They were working in the ruined hall that had once been the Mixcoacalli, the House of Cloud Serpents, where Ahuitzotl used to listen to his favorite singers and composers. The air in the hall was very humid and smelled of mildew, and sounds echoed in a distorted fashion due to the water that still covered most of the floor. The painted cloud serpents were peeling off the walls in great scabrous chunks, reminding Huemac that the enormous task in which he was engaged, simply to make the city habitable, was only the prelude to the even larger effort of again making Tenochtitlan a place of beauty.

Huemac took a deep breath, hardening himself against the multitude of aches in his forty-four-year-old body. He was getting too old for this kind of labor, especially with one nearly useless hand. Then he looked down at the dais on which he stood, feeling a different kind of ache as he remembered the times that Taypachtli had stood upon this very spot, sending her clear, sweet voice to the ears of an adoring crowd. I have not left *all* my heart in the hills, he thought ruefully; there is still enough to feel the pain of those I have lost.

Then he heard his name being called, and as he turned and saw the pained expression on the face of the messenger hastening toward him, he knew suddenly why he had been having these melancholy thoughts.

"My brother," he said abruptly, and the man blinked at him once in surprise before blurting out his message:

"He has been injured. So has the Speaker. They were inspecting one of the storehouses when the roof caved in upon their heads. I am afraid that their injuries are grave . . ."

Huemac dispatched the man to find Xolotlpilli, then wound his way through the slippery, rubble-strewn hallways to the rooms where the injured had been taken. A wall of armed guards stood before the hushed chamber where the healers were tending to Ahuitzotl, and one of them pointed Huemac toward the next room down the corridor. He entered just as the healer rose from beside Acolmiztli's body and spread his hands in a mute gesture of futility.

Two of Acolmiztli's sons had preceded Huemac into the room, and they quickly knelt on either side of their father and took his hands into their own, speaking in whispers. Acolmiztli was resting on one shoulder, his opposite hip twisted beneath him at a grotesque angle. His head had been wrapped with a loose bandage, and blood was soaking through the side of his mantle.

Though he had seen the knowledge of this in Papalotl's eyes, Huemac had never asked for confirmation, and he was as unprepared for his pain as if he had never suspected that the end might be near. Tears flooded his eyes as he remembered the time that he had stood in the plaza in Tlatelulco, screaming his grief to the gods, thinking that he had left his brother behind to die on the temple. Now there was nothing that could bring him back, as nothing had brought back their father, and Tezcatl, and Nopalli. The old way dies with you, my brother, he thought sadly; the old way that brought us so much glory, and so much death.

Huemac raised his head to see one of his nephews beckoning to him from where he knelt beside Acolmiztli.

"He asks for you, my uncle."

Huemac squatted beside his brother and leaned his face over Acolmiztli's, which was very pale. The eyes opened briefly in the contorted face, flashing recognition before they closed again, and Acolmiztli began to speak, groaning out his words:

"You are the oldest now, Huemac. Guard our people . . . our city. Our inheritance, bought with our father's blood. Fight for it, my brother. Save it . . ."

A shudder went through his body, twisting his features, and then he was still. Reaching forward with a trembling hand, Huemac wiped one of his own tears from Acolmiztli's face, as if to smooth away the pain of his death.

"Farewell, my brother," he said softly, then rose and left the dead man to his sons. Xolotlpilli was standing just inside the doorway, and he briefly rested a hand on his father's shoulder before letting him pass. Huemac wandered aimlessly along the corridor the way he had come, stepping back as the guards outside Ahuitzotl's chamber parted to allow someone to leave. It was Moteczuma. He started at seeing Huemac, then glanced past him down the hallway, his narrow features softening with sympathy.

"Is he gone?" he inquired gently, and Huemac nodded.

"And your uncle?"

"His head," Moteczuma began, then seemed to remember the guards behind him. "It is serious, but he will recover."

"We are fortunate," Huemac said, with an equal lack of conviction. He could see, from the distracted dartings of the prince's dark eyes, that Moteczuma was already thinking about the future: about his own likely ascension to the reed seat. Then his eyes focused in on Huemac, taking on a troubled light.

"I have been aware of you since I was a child," he said slowly. "I saw you defeat Cacalotl on the ball court, and I know of the other services that you have performed for my uncle. Yet I am still uncertain as to what sort of man you truly are."

"I am Tenocha, my Lord," Huemac said evenly. "Like yourself."

"Yet you attached yourself to the Texcocan court, after refusing to serve my uncle here."

"The Fasting Prince is my kinsman. I was his guest, not his servant."

"Clearly, though, you preferred his court to our own," Moteczuma said accusingly. "Perhaps you found the Tenocha lacking in manners. Or perhaps you do not see a long future for yourself here?"

Huemac stared back at him stolidly, refusing to respond to his insinuations. He remembered Patecatl's warning about this man, a warning he had not really needed.

"Perhaps I am simply not suited to the life of the court," he said finally. "Perhaps *that* is the sort of man I am."

Moteczuma frowned in disbelief, obviously finding this answer to be an evasion. Huemac was surprised to see disappointment appear on the younger man's face, and he wondered suddenly if these accusations had been intended as an invitation to take the prince into his confidence. He remembered that Moteczuma himself had been an infrequent visitor to Ahuitzotl's court, allegedly because he had disapproved of its lack of decorum. But if he had, indeed, been making an overture of friendship, the opportunity for seizing it had clearly passed.

"No one will force you into such a position, then," Moteczuma told him angrily. "It is doubtful, anyway, that good luck could ever follow anyone bearing your name."

Turning on his heel, Moteczuma strode off down the hall, followed closely by several of the guards. There is the new way, Huemac thought wearily, the way that will guide our future. He could not help but think of his vision; of Tenochtitlan falling into ruins.

Xolotlpilli had been standing out of earshot, and now he came up to join his father, glancing curiously in the direction of the retreating prince.

"He seemed angry with you, my father," Xolotlpilli said, and Huemac shrugged.

"It is a talent I have," he said lightly. Then he looked up into his son's face, admiring the strength and openness he saw there. This, too, is the new way, he thought suddenly, and felt some of his weariness leave him.

"Come, my son," he said warmly. "Let us consume our grief in work, as Acolmiztli would have wanted. We have a city to rebuild."

XI

THE SHAPES
OF MEN

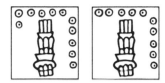

1503–1515

1

THE vanguard merchant Pinotl came to Cholula from the great Mixtec trading center of Tochtepec, far to the south, where he had been overseeing the construction of a new warehouse for his guild. It was late in the year Eleven-Reed, and he shivered as he came down onto the plateau where the city lay, finding the air only a little warmer than it had been in the mountains. But then, he had never truly felt comfortable in the holy city, despite the strength of its merchants' guilds and the predominance of the cult of Quetzalcoatl, patron of the merchants in his guise as Yacatecuhtli, the Lord Who Guides. The territory of the Tlaxcalans lay too close at hand, and the landscape itself was overpowering, the great mountains that surrounded the city on all sides seeming to press in upon the space in which he breathed. The crowds of pilgrims in their white robes also unsettled him with their habit of begging and their public outbursts of religious fervor. He, who had mingled unnoticed with the people of Xoconochco and Ayotlan, had little tolerance for those who called attention to themselves so extravagantly, and even less sympathy for anyone who begged instead of bartering.

Yet he considered the time he was able to spend with Papalotl as precious, and he looked forward to these visits with an eagerness that more than made up for his discomfort. He had long ago stopped thinking of himself as merely a messenger between father and daughter, though he performed this function willingly, bringing Papalotl news of her relatives and friends in Tenochtitlan and relaying her messages to Huemac. Still, he always knew that he would learn more from her insights and speculations than she from his recitation of plain fact, and he was able now to admire her beauty with safety, his emotions protected by her priestly status. It gave him great pleasure simply to sit in her presence, calmed by the sense of well-being that surrounded her, and stimulated by the astonishing range of her knowledge.

As always, she greeted him in the small temple courtyard that was her favorite, since it was decorated with murals depicting the life of Quetzalcoatl-Topiltzin, the god-king of Tula. She sat waiting on a low bench, wearing a blue-green stole over her white robe, the butterfly ring on her finger glowing softly in the late-afternoon sunlight. Pinotl bowed deeply to her and would have touched dirt to his tongue had she not prevented him, smiling and denying that she was worthy of such obeisance, especially from her old friend.

Since his last visit had occurred just prior to the coronation of Moteczuma Xocoyotzin as the ninth Speaker of the Tenocha, their conversation naturally turned to the state of his rule, once the news from her family had been discussed. Pinotl suspected that much of what he would say was already known to her, but he proceeded as if no such suspicion existed in his mind, reporting the facts as he might have to the council of merchants. Better to let her select what was important, what trivial; it was always interesting to know what did *not* surprise her.

"Moteczuma is a most exacting ruler," he began. "Nothing that pertains to his city and his people, however small, escapes his attention. He has already replaced many of the people who served Ahuitzotl, including the entire palace staff. He has removed all those not of noble blood, saying that the Speaker did not stand out sufficiently when surrounded by commoners."

"Who serves him now?" Papalotl asked.

"Only the sons of lords and those of his subject rulers. They have been taken from the calmecacs and specially trained to wait upon his needs. Perfection is expected of them in all things, and they are punished with death if they fumble in their serving or their speech while in his presence."

"That is rigorous duty," Papalotl observed mildly. "The lords cannot be happy to see their sons so severely used."

"Whatever their feelings," Pinotl said with a shrug, "they dare not express them improperly, lest they be humbled completely. As it is, they can only approach the Speaker with their feet bare and their bodies clothed in coarse garments, and they are not allowed to raise their eyes to Moteczuma's face unless they are bidden to do so. It is death for a commoner to *ever* look upon his divine person."

"He has always been inordinately proud of his Toltec lineage," Papalotl mused aloud, glancing at the murals that surrounded her. "No wonder my father suffers under his rule. How have the merchants of Tlatelulco fared at his hand?"

Pinotl looked at her sharply, knowing that he had given no hint of Huemac's difficulties in what he had said earlier.

"We have been forced to surrender many of our goods on behalf of our city," he said to answer her question. "Moteczuma has demanded that we once again pay the full tribute levied after the civil war, even though most of this had been forgiven us by Ahuitzotl. My father and your cousin Omeocelotl were among those who counseled our people to pay rather than fight, and we have given him even more than he asked, in order to reassure him of our loyalty and respect."

"That is wise," Papalotl told him. "He is not a man who trusts easily; he must test even his friends and allies. No doubt, he has many spies in his employ."

Despite himself, Pinotl glanced uneasily around the deserted courtyard.

"It is said that he even disguises himself, in order to see if his orders have been carried out in every detail. Even the Cihuacoatl, Tlilpotonqui, is subject to such scrutiny."

Papalotl nodded absently, as if she knew this, as well, or simply found it logical. Pinotl marveled at how easily she seemed to comprehend Moteczuma's character, when even the Speaker's closest relatives had been surprised by the sudden loftiness of his ways. In Tenochtitlan, none could know him now except as he wished to be known: as the most powerful ruler in Anahuac, a man above all other men, answerable only to the gods.

"I have dreamed only sparingly of late," Papalotl said, breaking into his thoughts. "It is as if the power were conserving itself for the future. Nonetheless, there are three messages I would ask you to repeat to my father."

Pinotl inclined his head attentively, clearing his mind to receive her words.

"The first concerns my cousin Azcatzin," she said in a measured tone. "I have seen him on the Ball Court of the Lords, being carried on the shoulders of a cheering crowd of men. Many of the men were bare-chested. I do not know what any of this means, but it will happen very soon, if it has not happened by the time you return.

"Second, I have seen the New Fire kindled once more upon the Hill of the Stars. And I have seen my grandmother comforting a small boy as he does his penance for the renewal of the years. I assume that this child is my brother's son, Cuauhcoatl."

Pinotl blinked once at the awesomeness of this revelation: to know of the success of the New Fire Ceremony, four years in advance! Papalotl, though, seemed to find her grandmother's participation in this vision to be equally important, repeating the message a second time to be sure he had heard all of it. Then she went on in the same earnest tone:

"Lastly, I have seen my father in the hills. I have seen him undergoing a painful ordeal. It is important during this struggle that he remember himself as a man. He must arm himself with the joys and sorrows of his life, the memories that make him feel. These will be his weapons in the struggle."

Pinotl closed his eyes and repeated the words silently to himself until he was sure he would not forget. When he looked back up at Papalotl, she was smiling at him, her golden eyes sparkling with affection.

"There is one other message," she said, then paused, as if to savor this last piece of news. "You must tell Eptli, your wife, that I have seen her taking on the shape of motherhood. I have seen this happening in the time of planting."

Starting with his hooded eyes, Pinotl's veiled countenance seemed to open like a flower, one of his rare smiles breaking across the sharp vertical plane of his face. Then the smile was gone and he was bowing deeply, repeating the gesture several times in his happiness.

"I am grateful, my Lady," he said in a husky voice. "We have both been hoping for such a gift from the gods."

"I will pray for Eptli's well-being during her time of waiting," Papalotl promised. "Perhaps, when next you come to me, your ears will be ringing with the crying of an infant, and your heart will be swelled with the pride of a father . . ."

AFTER SENDING the servants searching throughout Xolotlpilli's house, Ome Xochitl finally found her son in the nursery. Huemac was seated beside the blanket-wrapped form of his grandson, softly singing a song that Ome Xochitl recognized as one of Taypachtli's favorites. And even though his voice was rough and untrained, it was having the desired effect upon little Cuauhcoatl, who snuggled deeper into his blankets and stuck a thumb into his mouth, his eyes closed contentedly.

Ome Xochitl waited in the doorway, watching with contentment of her own as Huemac ended his song and briefly held his hand over the two-year-old's head in blessing. Then he rose quietly and came over to her, showing that he had been aware of her presence.

"Your visitors have all arrived," she said in a low voice, so as not to awaken the child. "They have been sent to await you in your room, as you instructed. I assume that you have called them together to say that you are leaving."

Huemac looked at her fondly, impressed but not surprised by her prescience. Ome Xochitl was now almost eighty, her body bent and brittle, her hair completely white. Yet her dark oval eyes shone with their usual alertness, the same eyes that had seen his every move when he had been as young as Cuauhcoatl.

"I assume, then, that I do not need to tell you my reasons," he said rhetorically. "You have seen what my life here has become. It is time that I went to claim my full powers."

"I am only surprised that you have waited so long," Ome Xochitl told him. "I have suspected that it is my age that made you hesitate."

"You know me too well, my mother," Huemac said ruefully, shaking his head. "Papalotl, though, has just assured me that you will be alive to witness the next kindling of the New Fire. Therefore, I can leave with an easy heart, knowing that you will be here when I return."

Ome Xochitl sighed and bared her teeth in a thin smile.

"I have had years enough already," she said quietly. "But I will be grateful for all that the gods will give me, so that I may see my grandchildren and great-grandchildren grow. And I will look forward to your return, so that I may see *your* growth, as well. But come, my son—go to your friends. They are most uncomfortable with one another."

"That is how I wish them to be," Huemac informed her, smiling wickedly. Then he glanced over at the sleeping boy and his face sobered. "He will not remember me when I return, but perhaps that is just as well. *His* life, at least, will not be tainted by my reputation."

"He will recognize you, one day," Ome Xochitl assured him, and went to sit beside the boy as Huemac left to meet with his friends.

AFTER RELINQUISHING his house for redistribution by the Speaker, Huemac had accepted a second-floor room in the western wing of Xolotlpilli's house, which had been restored to its former elegance after the flood. He could feel the tension as soon as he entered the low-ceilinged room, which took its light from the open trap overhead. Yet he did not hurry to break the uneasy silence once he had seated himself on his customary mat. Instead, he let his eyes wander around the room in a leisurely fashion, considering each of the five men in turn. To his right sat Chiquatli, now thirty-nine years of age yet again practicing the sullen ways of his youth, his downcast eyes refusing to meet those of the others in the room. Beside him, distinguished by their plain clothing and long hair, were Omeocelotl and Pinotl, thirty-two and twenty-four years of age, respectively. Both sat motionless, trying to appear as unobtrusive as possible in the company of the warriors in the room. Wearing a fine mantle and an amber lip-plug, the twenty-nine-year-old Azcatzin, a captain of the Jaguar Warriors, sat to Huemac's left, as far away from Chiquatli as space and politeness permitted. Finally, appearing the most uneasy of all, there was Xolotlpilli, now twenty-two and the most famous warrior in Tenochtitlan, next to Moteczuma himself. He stood leaning against the wall beside the doorway, his shaven head almost reaching to the raftered ceiling.

When he had allowed them to suffer the silence long enough, Huemac began to speak, gesturing to include them all:

"First, my friends, I would ask you to look around at the faces in this room. Do you see anyone here who is not bound to you by blood or obligation? Do you perhaps see someone who might be a spy for Moteczuma? Then why is there this silence, this tension, among you? Can one man have made it impossible for even friends and relatives to speak their feelings to one another, and thus renew their trust? Or perhaps, with your silence, do you not do the work of his spies *for* him?"

Huemac paused. There had been no scorn in his voice, yet he could see shame appear in their faces as they gradually took their eyes off him and glanced at one another.

"I know each of your hearts, my friends," Huemac continued, "and so I am distressed by the distance that has grown up between you. So it is that I am going to tell you what each of you knows but cannot say to your friends. I will speak the truths of our lives, so that we may know one another again."

Huemac turned first to his former apprentice, whose handsome face was set in combative lines, his jaw clenched tightly.

"You, Chiquatli, are a man betrayed by the powers you trusted and served. You have been rudely reminded of your common blood and thrust from the palace. The captaincy of the royal ball team has been taken from you. You see Xolotlpilli, who once scorned your advice, now enjoying the favor you lost through no fault of your own; you see Azcatzin, whom you helped to train, being considered for your captain's post. And so you envy and despise them, and blame them for taking the things that are rightfully yours."

"Yes," Chiquatli hissed angrily, raising his head to glare at the other two men. Huemac nodded once in recognition before looking past Chiquatli to Omeocelotl.

"And you, my nephew," he said calmly. "You are resentful at the tribute that has been reimposed on you by the people of your own blood, to whom you should have nothing more to prove. You are too wise to show it, but it is not easy for you to share a room with your Tenocha brothers anymore. One part of you wishes to don the jewels and insignia that Ahuitzotl awarded you after Quauhtenanco, and to challenge those who would demean your honor."

Omeocelotl stared back at his uncle without speaking, his face empty of all expression, not agreeing, not denying. Huemac smiled as if his point had been proven, then raised his chin to the dark-skinned youth next to Omeocelotl.

"Pinotl, my friend," he said gently. "You are the youngest here except for Xolotlpilli, and you do not have his rank. So you would be silent out of modesty, though your eyes and ears have no doubt already told you all that I am saying. Perhaps you disguise yourself too well, my friend; perhaps you hide that part of yourself that others need most."

Knowing that he was causing Pinotl pain by this exposure, Huemac turned quickly to his left, to Azcatzin.

"My nephew, you who have worked so hard to prove yourself in this city, despite your lack of size. You know that you are at your peak as a ball player, a match for any man. You know that you are deserving of the captaincy of the royal team, though you would have been willing to wait until Chiquatli relinquished the post voluntarily. Since it is open, however, you wish to claim it, and this makes you feel disloyal, and uncomfortable in Chiquatli's presence. Perhaps you are also aware that the reason Moteczuma has not offered it to you already is because of your connection with me, and so you have similar feelings toward me."

Azcatzin cocked his head, as if to shake it in denial, but then stopped himself. He looked from his uncle to Chiquatli, then lowered his eyes and sighed wearily, his shoulders slumping. Huemac looked up at his son.

"Xolotlpilli," he said softly, musingly. "Who does not know of your fame, my son? Certainly, Moteczuma does, for he lets you sit beside him and calls you his strong arm, the shelter of the people. And you have reason to admire him in return, for he has rewarded you fairly, and he has fought bravely beside you upon the ramparts of Icpatepec. Yours is the hardest task of all, for you must bear the burden of the Speaker's favor in this room of men who have been wronged by him. You are above his harassments, and so you feel guilty that you have done nothing to defend Chiquatli or myself, or your friends in Tlatelulco. You wish that you could be innocent and unaware of these things, but your heart is too large not to be troubled."

Nodding intently, Xolotlpilli spread his huge hands and glanced around the room, his eyes filled with apology. Huemac waited until the attention of the men had again returned to him.

"Lastly, you see me, whose deeds and reputation you know. Perhaps you have also seen how my duties as a commander and a trainer of young men were reduced until they became meaningless, so that I was driven to join the ranks of the Old Eagles, though my hair is not yet white. And perhaps you know that Moteczuma has spoken disparagingly of me as both a man and a ball player, so that only the boys who can find no other teacher come to me now. I am forty-eight years old, still strong and competent, yet I have no place in my own city."

Huemac paused and scanned their attentive faces, showing no sign that he either recognized or needed the sympathy he saw in their eyes. He was interested only in the fact that the truth seemed to have worked; that they had forgotten their differences along with their uneasiness.

"I have told you these things because I must leave you for a while," he continued, "and because I wish you to join together as allies. The years ahead are going to be a time of great testing for our leaders and our people. Honesty and courage will become more rare and precious than ever before, and the traditional loyalties that have bound us together will be strained and broken. You have already begun to see this happen among yourselves, though you are brothers, and cousins, and comrades in arms.

"Your situations will no doubt be improved by my absence," Huemac added with a rueful grimace, "since I remind Moteczuma of too many things he would rather forget. But I have not forgotten my duty to you. I have arranged certain things, and you must forgive me for speaking of your private affairs in front of the group. It is essential that you share the truth equally, even at the expense of your privacy."

Taking a deep breath, Huemac turned to Chiquatli, who met his eyes without any of his previous sullenness. Yet his expression was guarded, as if he knew that his own situation was perhaps the least susceptible to amelioration.

"Your ambitions are ill-served here, my friend," Huemac said bluntly. "Here, where lineage has been raised above merit. Nezahualpilli, though, is in need of a Master Trainer for his team, and he has asked me if you would be willing to accept this post in his city. There is a place for you among the commanders, as well, if you wish it. I can assure you that you will be treated with the respect you deserve in Texcoco. Consider."

Seeing Chiquatli's features soften, Huemac quickly turned back toward Azcatzin, linking the two men with a sweeping gesture of his hand, and waiting until they acknowledged each other.

"Whatever Chiquatli's decision," he said to his nephew, "the captain's place here is still open, and you are the logical choice to fill it. Moteczuma vacillates only because he remembers the defeat of his uncle Tizoc, and my hand in it. He cannot determine if that makes you lucky or unlucky to him. But I have reason to believe that this will be resolved very shortly, and in your favor. So you must concentrate totally upon playing your best, and not involve yourself in any connivance. Disregard the rumors you will hear, for I have started many of these myself."

Azcatzin's mouth dropped open momentarily, but then he looked at Chiquatli and the two of them began to laugh, and were quickly joined by the other men in the room. Smiling at his own slyness, Huemac next gestured toward Omeocelotl and Pinotl.

"My friends, the merchants. Moteczuma wars no less than his predecessors, and he has just as many warriors to satisfy and just as many mouths to feed. He will remember your importance to him soon enough, and you will again be welcomed into our midst as brothers. In the meantime, you must remember your kinship to the men in this room, as I hope they will remember theirs to you. I hope that you will come to them as equals, and share what is in your hearts and minds."

Omeocelotl glanced warily at the other men, receiving a firm nod of agreement from each of them. Finally, he looked to Pinotl, who also nodded without hesitation.

"We will come gladly," Omeocelotl said in a dignified tone. "And our houses in Tlatelulco will always be open to our fellow Mexicans."

"As mine will be in Texcoco," Chiquatli added, his smile showing that he had already reached his decision. Huemac waited patiently, allowing them to share this moment of camaraderie, which he had planned for so diligently. Then he raised his eyes to the expectant face of his son.

"I spoke to you a moment ago, Xolotlpilli, about the difficulty of your position. I would now ask you to assume an even harder task. You must first be the protector of this group. Perhaps, one day, you will be called on to intercede for us, but for now, your friendship is quite enough. Only in the shade of a reputation such as yours will the truth be able to flourish in safety.

"But there is no safety in innocence," Huemac added, adopting a cautionary tone, "and that is what will make your role so difficult. For you must allow these men to help you shed your innocence concerning Moteczuma, but you must not be tempted by your new knowledge into defying him rashly, and thus losing his favor. You must change and learn, but outwardly you must go on as before, so that your house will always be a place where we may gather to speak our minds without fear of intimidation. It will not be easy, my son."

Xolotlpilli drew himself up against the wall, the outward thrust of his jaw showing the firmness of his resolve.

"Let us meet often, my friends," he urged, appealing to the others with his eyes and hands. "Let this very room be a place empty of envy and suspicion, a place where only the truth is spoken."

The others immediately voiced their assent, each according to his own sense of propriety, though even the merchants were affected by Xolotlpilli's enthusiasm. Seeing that he had accomplished his goal, Huemac rose from his mat, and the others also got to their feet and came in around him in a tight circle, acknowledging their closeness with smiles and small gestures.

"I will return in time for the New Fire Ceremony," Huemac told them, then spent a moment gazing at their faces. "Farewell, my friends; be vigilant in your duties. I leave you with an easy heart, knowing that our people are in safe hands."

<h1 style="text-align:center">◨◫ 2 ◫◧</h1>

FOR almost half a day, Huemac followed the signs that told him of Chimalman's presence: the few golden hairs caught upon a cactus thorn; faint pug marks left in the coarse red sand; the lingering odor of cat. He saw that she was leading him away from the main trail, on a path that led more directly to the mountains, and he followed willingly, enjoying this teasing, this testing of his tracking skills. Several times he thought that he caught sight of her, but only, he knew, because she wanted him to.

Finally, Chimalman appeared from behind a bush ahead of him, an arrow pulled taut in her bow, aimed at his heart. Huemac smiled at the fierce image she presented, remembering that this was how he had first seen her, emerging from the cave above the village. He came up until the flint tip of her arrow was almost touching his chest, gazing with pleasure upon her sharp unlined face and her glossy black hair, the thick-lashed eyes glittering at him from behind the bow. She did not look like a woman old enough to have a fifteen-year-old son, a fact that made Huemac feel his own age most keenly.

"You are my captive," Chimalman informed him in a peremptory tone. "You must come with me."

"Where will you take me?" Huemac asked lightly.

"I know a place, in the mountains, where a captive might be bathed and kept safely. He might even be permitted certain freedoms."

"Perhaps I also know this place," Huemac suggested. "Perhaps I would even go there willingly. But should I not be taken before the chief first, and allowed to state my business?"

"The chief will be away from the village for several more days. And he already knows your business. So do I," she added, and slackened her bow. "That is why I would have you to myself for a while. There is no telling how long your business will take you. You could be a white-haired old man by the time you return."

"Sometimes," Huemac confessed, "I feel that I am an old man already. The ground seems harder to my bones, the hills steeper to my legs."

"I am not interested in those parts of you," Chimalman said scornfully, and Huemac straightened up, an expression of mock outrage on his face.

"You would take liberties with your captive?"

"I would make him serve me with all his strength," she assured him bluntly. "I would have no respect for his age."

"Perhaps you would kill him."

"It would be a worthy sacrifice. It would be his punishment for staying away from me for so long."

Repressing a joyful laugh, Huemac bowed in surrender.

"Take me, then, my captor," he said without regret. "I have not the will to resist you . . ."

XIUHCOZCATL still had not returned to the village when Huemac and Chimalman finally came down from their sojourn in the mountains, so Huemac seized this time to renew his acquaintanceship with his son. Tepeyollotl had grown considerably, the top of his tufted head now coming up to Huemac's chin. And though he resembled his mother in the slenderness of his body, he also had her wiry strength and force of presence, which he had exerted to make himself the leader of one of the young warriors' lodges. He wore a single eagle feather tied into his hair, evidence that he had ventured out successfully on the path of war.

Together, they went out into the hills to study the hawks that Tepeyollotl had located for him. From blinds of their own construction, they watched the birds hunting and making kills, and they helped each other climb the high rock ledges to examine the nests that had been built there. Other times, they simply lay on their backs in the tall grass, watching the broad-winged predators riding the air currents high overhead, concentrating on those with whitish breasts and bright reddish-brown tail feathers. Huemac used these quiet times to listen to the tales of his son's exploits, and to tell Tepeyollotl about the disasters of Ahuitzotl's last years, and about the harsh beginning of the reign of Motec- zuma Xocoyotzin. Never had the perversity and arrogance of Moteczuma's ways seemed more apparent, Huemac thought, than when mirrored in the earnest, disbelieving eyes of his son.

They returned late one afternoon to learn that Xiuhcozcatl had returned, and that he was awaiting them both in the cave behind the village. After purifying themselves in the sweathouse, they climbed the steep path and groped their way down the dark tunnel with their eyes closed, so that they would not see the sacred markings on the cave walls. Only when they had crawled into the final chamber and could see the yellow light of the fire through their eyelids did they allow themselves to look. Xiuhcozcatl was sitting on a bed of skins, his hunched back shrouded in a blanket of thick brown fur; Chimalman was seated beside him, wrapped in a cloak of the same material.

The chief signaled brusquely with his talon-stick, indicating that they should sit across from him, on the other side of the fire. Huemac stared at his former teacher, struck by how suddenly age had overtaken Xiuhcozcatl, and by how much he had come to resemble the Old One. His weathered face was a maze of deeply chiseled lines, and his brilliant eyes glowed from sockets that seemed to recede far into his head. His hair was completely white, coiling onto his fur-covered shoulders like ropes of snow. Huemac felt the probing force of those eyes, and he allowed himself to be examined without resistance or loss of self-control. Xiuhcozcatl subjected Tepeyollotl to a similar scrutiny, and, from the tension in his son's body, Huemac could tell that he, too, could feel the pressure of the old man's power.

"I assume that you have come to find your nahualli," Xiuhcozcatl said to Huemac without prelude. "I have summoned you to this place to remind you of the impulsive youth who came here once, seeking the power of a vision. He earned the name of Owl Boy, and is remembered in this village for the rashness of his courage. I wish to remind you that you are not so young anymore, Huemac. Perhaps you are not as willing as you think to put your whole being to risk."

Huemac had considered this many times, both before leaving Tenochtitlan and on his journey to the hills. He had even tested himself after seeing Chimal- man again, but the answer had still been the same. He offered it plainly:

"There was a time in my life when this was true; when my concern for my family and my duties made me wary to risk my spirit. But even then, my fate forced me to gamble with my life, and I found the courage to act. I feel now that the time of my final vision approaches rapidly. I have seen to the welfare of my people, the 'little people' who might aid me. I have developed sources who reveal to me the signs and rumors that are in the land. But I am disliked by the new ruler, who is a vicious and unpredictable man. I must have the power to resist whatever attempts he might make to ruin me."

Xiuhcozcatl leaned forward slightly, resting his chin on the smooth curve of his talon-headed stick.

"And you think that your nahualli can give you this power?" he asked.

"I have discussed this with Nezahualpilli," Huemac revealed, "and he has assured me that Moteczuma is capable of *feeling* such a presence, if not of comprehending its source. And he is a man who fears that which he cannot understand. But since it is unlikely that he would confront me directly, I think of the ability to change my shape as a protection against assassins or the threat of imprisonment. Those are the usual ways he moves against his enemies."

"You do not want the killing power, then?" Xiuhcozcatl demanded. "You sought this once, I know. A nahualli who is used for the purpose of killing can never be freed, and must die with its master."

"I have killed enough in my lifetime," Huemac assured him. "I would not waste my powers on murder."

"I see that this is true," the chief said, after examining him so closely that Huemac's head began to ache from the pressure against his eyes. "I must warn you, then," Xiuhcozcatl went on, "that what you are about to attempt is more dangerous than anything you have ever done; save, perhaps, for the time that you summoned the killing power to yourself as a boy. If you lose your courage and try to pull back once the process has begun, you could be irreparably damaged, and left with the mental powers of a child, or a beast. I saw a man once who had been conquered by the animal he sought to tame; he howled and snapped at people in a most pathetic manner. The members of his family were finally forced to kill him, out of compassion."

"Should I similarly fail," Huemac replied firmly, "I hope that you will treat me with the same kindness."

Xiuhcozcatl studied him for a moment, then sat back, as if satisfied with the answer. He relaxed the shape into which his features had been set, forcing Huemac to see that the resemblance to the Old One had been intentional, not natural. Xiuhcozcatl was a larger man, and he still carried part of his strength in his flesh. Oztooa's had all been in his eyes. The chief gestured to Chimalman with his stick, and she leaned forward to put some sweet grass onto the fire, reviving the musty air in the chamber.

"A man, or a woman," Xiuhcozcatl explained, with a nod to Chimalman, "may have various kinds of relationships with his or her animal double. A nahualli may be held entirely within the person who owns it, as a manifestation of the owner's spirit. Or it may be allowed to roam freely until called on, a magical yet independent creature. Some sorcerers do both. Chimalman, for instance, has chosen to allow her nahualli its independence, even though she has tamed it fully. She feels that this makes both of them stronger, and younger. No doubt this is true. I have always held mine within myself, and you see how I have aged."

The chief permitted himself a sly smile as the humor of his statement penetrated and the others widened their eyes in surprise. He was, after all, some years over one hundred. Huemac's heart swelled with encouragement at this uncharacteristic jest, which he took as a sign of his teacher's approval and confidence.

"Clearly," Xiuhcozcatl continued seriously, "*you* must possess your nahualli completely, for there would be no fit habitat for a hawk near a city. Thus, you must take its independence along with its shape. You have a great affinity for this animal, Huemac. It has shown itself to you in the visions of both yourself and your daughter; its spirit was visible to some of us as long ago as the day on which you ate the flesh of the gods in this very room. Do you have any memory of the song you sang on that day?"

Huemac shook his head and shrugged helplessly.

"I do not even remember making the sounds that earned me the name of Owl Boy," he confessed, and Xiuhcozcatl smiled again.

"I did not call it to your attention at the time," he said, "because I could not be sure that you would persist in your search for power. Perhaps, my daughter, you would like to remind him now."

"It is what I remember best from that day," Chimalman recalled in an odd, musing tone, looking at Huemac with what seemed like fondness. "The children of the village used to sing it in Otomi, but for some reason, I had to know the real words, the ones I had heard. That is how I began to learn Nahua."

"We are not discussing your fate, my daughter," the chief reminded her gruffly, breaking into her reverie. "Sing."

Chimalman bowed apologetically, then straightened her back and sang the Owl Boy's song, her eyes focused somewhere above Huemac's head:

> "It is my net, this net.
> With it, I capture the running deer.
> With it, I bring down the screaming hawk.
> Nothing eludes this net, my net.
> With it, I capture the spirits
> And hold them fast."

Huemac glanced upward involuntarily, remembering lying on his back on this floor, staring up at the net suspended magically over his head, filled with equally magical creatures. He had sung it to *them,* his nahualli no doubt in their midst, though he had no way of knowing it then.

"Yes, I remember," he said simply, nodding gratefully to Chimalman.

"That is the song you will sing when you are ready to summon your nahualli to you," Xiuhcozcatl told him. "Do not sing it aloud, even to yourself, until that day has come. You have long months of preparation and purification ahead of you. Do you have any questions before you begin your task?"

Huemac glanced sideways at the young man sitting next to him.

"Will I be able to leave my nahualli to my son?"

"If you free it in time. Its departure will leave you very vulnerable, so be sure that you reckon the moment correctly."

"I shall not mistake it," Huemac said gravely, and bowed to the chief. "Let us begin, then . . ."

AS THEY came out of the scrub oak and topped the rise, Tepeyollotl stopped beside a patch of nopal cactus and pointed upward at the sky. Raising a hand to shield his eyes against the harsh glare of the sun, Huemac gazed upward at the circling bird.

"Tzopilotl, a black vulture," he decided, noting the short tail and bare, grayish head. "Let us leave something for him, as a sign of our good will."

"Fresh meat, for the eater of filth?" Tepeyollotl murmured dubiously, even as he offered up the string of skinned carcasses they had captured earlier in the day. Huemac ignored the query as he picked through their kills, finally settling on a small rabbit. He laid this conspicuously upon a flat rock at the side of the path, knowing that the sharp eyes of the carrion bird would not miss it. Then he turned back to his son and gestured that they should continue walking.

"You have been very patient, my son," he said to the youth. "I know that I lack your deftness as a hunter, especially with my net. And I, too, have noticed the scarcity of game since the rains failed to come. But that is all the more reason to be generous in our offerings. There was a time, before I knew how to hunt at all, when Xiuhcozcatl made me give away every bit of food I carried. It was a wonderful surprise, and a gift, to learn that the hills would provide for my survival.

"Besides," he went on, waving off Tepeyollotl's apology, "I feel that my nahualli is now very close. I have been awakened in the night by its screamings, which you have not heard."

"I will be even more patient, my father," Tepeyollotl promised, though he could not conceal the look of relief that passed across his face. They had been away from the village for over a year, having walked as far north as the frontier of Texcocan territory before circling back to the west and south. Huemac no longer knew what month it was, only that the season was spring, and the rains had not yet arrived. He was as tired as his son of the diet on which they had been subsisting, a diet composed almost solely of those animals that were his nahualli's natural prey: rabbits, mice, gophers, the long-legged desert rats, and an occasional lizard. He was tired, as well, of sleeping on the hard ground and seeing no other people, though he knew that this isolation hurt him less than it did his ambitious sixteen-year-old son.

"Perhaps we will be able to return for the summer hunt," Huemac suggested casually, knowing that Tepeyollotl would never bring up the subject himself, however much it might be on his mind. With his customary correctness, he had placed his obligation to his father above all the others he had taken on, and he would not look ahead until this task was completed.

"Perhaps," he agreed in a neutral tone, then fell silent, obviously pondering something Huemac had said earlier.

"You have a question?" Huemac prompted gently, and Tepeyollotl nodded, showing the concern in his eyes.

"I do not wish you to misunderstand or think me ungrateful, my father," he said carefully. "But I have sensed that you feel some need to reward me, as if it were not my privilege to serve you in this way. This causes me to wonder why you wish to leave your nahualli to me, rather than to one of your other children."

Huemac stopped and stared into his son's golden-ringed eyes, impressed by his sensitivity.

"You are correct in what you sense," he said, "for I know your ambitions, and I know what your prolonged absence from your lodge might cost you. But I never considered leaving my nahualli to anyone else. Both of my other children have powers more suitable to the lives they lead, and if my vision is correct, it is likely that you will be the only one of my blood to survive me."

"But I will inherit my mother's nahualli," Tepeyollotl pointed out, "and probably one of those belonging to the Old One."

Huemac blinked in surprise, until he remembered that the younger Chichimecs—those who had never known Oztooa—referred to Xiuhcozcatl by this title.

"You will need all the power you can own," Huemac told him. "The disaster may strike the cities first, but the hills will not be spared forever. But come, let us put these thoughts out of our minds. There will be time later, when the present task has been concluded, to discuss the future. But not now, my son, not yet."

"*YOUR NAHUALLI will only show itself to you once,*" Xiuhcozcatl had said. "And there is no way to foresee how it will come to you. It might be waiting for you on a limb beside the path, or it might attack you from above. It might even come to you unseen, though such a thing is highly unusual. However it comes, you will either lose it then or make it your own. But you will not look upon it again, from the outside, until the time that you set it free."

The chief's words flashed into Huemac's mind only an instant after the excitement took him over, making his heart race and his hands sweat. The maguey-fiber net slipped out of his grasp and dropped to the ground, startling the quail he had been stalking into flight. His lips felt rubbery and his eyes hot and swollen, reminding him of the onset of some of the magic plants. Trying to gather his wits, he strove to remember the other things that Xiuhcozcatl had told him:

"Despite the affinity that exists between you," the old man had warned, "it will fight you for your freedom. First it will try to take you over, and then it will try to escape. The time when you are still between your man-shape and the shape of your nahualli is the most dangerous. Tepeyollotl must see that no one comes upon you unaware, for you will be both vulnerable and dangerous to anyone who approaches you. But he will not be able to help you if you injure yourself or lose your senses. He *must not* help you, even if you scream in agony at the pains being inflicted upon you, even if you seem to be dying. You are strong enough to withstand the pain, Huemac, but you must not allow yourself to grow fearful or weary. It is a truly bewildering experience, enough to try the strongest spirit."

It comes, Huemac thought, though the sky above him was empty and nothing stirred in the brush. He stripped off his clothes and piled them neatly on top of the net, so that Tepeyollotl would understand when he came to find him, and would take up his vigil. Then Huemac drank the last of the water in his gourd, knowing that he ran the risk of dying of thirst if his struggle with the nahualli went on too long. The excitement was building in him, making his body tremble, but he did not want to sing his song until he had prepared himself, and could predict where the nahualli might appear.

He peered around him at the brush and cacti, wiping sweat from his eyes as he tried to determine where a hawk would be drawn to settle. Then, just when he thought that he could wait no longer, his eyes fell upon the large, spreading cactus that rose out of the midst of a clump of mesquite. It was the hard, thorny, prickly pear cactus, the tenochtli for which his city had been named, on which the great eagle had shown himself to the first of the Tenocha. *That* is where he will show himself, Huemac thought with sudden certainty, and lifted his voice in song:

> "It is my net, this net.
> With it, I capture the running deer.
> With it, I bring down the screaming hawk . . ."

The hawk descended with a rush of feathers that went through Huemac from his head to his feet, making him curl his toes into the sand to keep his balance. There, perched on the cactus, was his nahualli, wings tucked neatly behind, his sleek, copper-colored head swiveling warily from side to side. There was a thick band of brownish feathers across his white breast, and the eyes that finally fastened on Huemac, bulging prominently on either side of the sharply curved beak, were a deep yellow, almost orange in color.

Huemac stared at the hawk until it became agitated, spreading its broad, powerful wings and screeching at him in short, hoarse bursts. *Remember yourself as a man,* Huemac told himself, then raised his arms over his head and flicked his hands at the bird, as if casting a net. The hawk flapped once and rose off the cactus, floating toward him with its wings fully spread and its talons outstretched, aimed at Huemac's heart . . .

Huemac forced himself to keep his eyes open, yet he could not see for several moments, as wave after wave of images—of feathers, talons, red meat, and blue sky—passed through his mind in quick succession, too rapidly to be comprehended. The sensation of merger was unlike anything he had ever experienced: like being the body of water into which an object had been plunged, yet being that object himself, and sharing in its feeling of immersion. Then his mind was clear, and he could see again.

For one long moment, he felt completely normal, lacking even the excitement that had come to him earlier. Stretching his limbs experimentally, he held his arms out in front of him and looked down. They seemed to be his arms, yet gradually the dark reddish color of his skin grayed and faded, and the contours of his veins and muscles stood out with greater and greater distinction, until the fine, sparse hairs on his forearms looked like black thorns, and his pores like deep holes. Huemac blinked, dizzied by the sensation that his arms had risen to meet his eyes. Then he looked out over the desert and saw how the whole world had changed. Colors were muted and shadows accentuated, and every object had an extraordinary definition that did not diminish quickly with distance. He could count each individual thorn on the cactus, along with the ants and cochineal bugs that crawled over the flat, dull-green leaves. Far off, something moved in the underbrush, and Huemac's eyes flashed to it instantly, perceiving the twitching nose and dark liquid eyes even before he knew that he was looking at a rabbit.

Even as he marveled at the power of his vision, Huemac began to perceive the other changes that were occurring in his body. His tongue felt narrow and pointed, probing a dry, bony mouth devoid of taste; his breathing was rapid, streaming through the thin slits of his nostrils with a sound like a bone whistle. His limbs felt hollow and buoyant, and when he looked again at his arms, he saw a pattern of feathers spreading across his skin, his fingers becoming stiff and bushy.

"I am a man!" he shouted, but the only sound that came to his ears was a hoarse, high-pitched scream. He felt himself being lifted off the ground, and he struggled against the sudden feeling of weightlessness, exerting all his force to keep himself from rising off the earth. But his muscles responded sluggishly, and he succeeded only in throwing himself face-first into the sand. His hand came in contact with a rock, and he gripped it instinctively, his other arm flapping uncontrollably, his legs digging furiously beneath him like claws seeking a purchase in the loose sand. Focusing all his awareness upon the hand that gripped the rock, Huemac hung on stubbornly, ignoring the frantic spasms that racked his body.

Then he was still, and gradually the feeling that had all been in his hand crept up his arm and into his shoulders and neck, so that he was able to raise his head. His body was his own again, but now he was aware of the adversary inside of him, aware that it was waiting, gathering strength.

"I am a *man,*" he announced fiercely, placing his other hand on the rock and pulling himself to his knees. A warning flutter came from within his chest, and he immediately ducked his head between his arms, which bowed and wobbled and were nearly pulled loose from the rock by the force that tried to jerk him upward. Huemac panted for breath after the seizure had passed, noticing that he had dislodged the rock from its hole in the ground. I need a firmer handhold, he thought, and felt—as surely as if he had seen it—the hawk within him cock its head, as if listening.

"No thoughts!" Huemac shouted to confuse his adversary, and then made an impulsive break for the mesquite, hands outstretched to grasp the first strong limb. But his vision changed in midcourse and the underbrush seemed to rush up at him, so that he faltered and grabbed too soon, throwing himself off-balance. Then he was rising, his arms becoming wings that would take him over the mesquite. He let out a scream and flailed out with his legs, which seemed to be shrinking beneath him. Just as he felt the air catch beneath his wings, his trailing foot struck the topmost limb of the cactus, and the pain of the thorns piercing his flesh immediately brought him crashing down in the mesquite.

Though stunned by the impact, Huemac felt his own powers returning more quickly than those of his nahualli. We men know better how to fall, he thought, as he checked himself and found nothing broken. He lowered himself gingerly to the ground, wincing as he inadvertently drove one of the barbed thorns deeper into his foot. He sat down and slid backward on his buttocks until his back was resting against the gnarled trunk of the tree upon which he had landed. Pulling his foot into his lap, he worked the stinging thorns out of his flesh one by one, the familiar throbbing pain awakening memories of the calmecac and Coatleztli, who had wielded the disciplinary thorn so freely.

Now the rest of Papalotl's message came back to him, and he understood why Xiuhcozcatl had urged him so strongly to heed her advice. He must arm himself with the "memories that make him feel"; he must hold onto himself, rather than any *thing.* Feeling a watchful stirring within, he nonetheless abandoned his seat under the tree and limped out into the open, deliberately bearing down on his wounded foot to keep the pain alive.

"I am a man who has suffered," he said aloud, and was gratified when the creature within seemed quizzical, and hesitant. He took his left hand and banged himself on the chest until the pain in his crooked fingers brought tears to his eyes.

"*This,* I broke in Michoacan, and again on the Ball Court of the Lords," he said proudly, holding the hand in front of his face to see if his vision was changing. It was not. Excited by his discovery, Huemac concentrated all his attention on the details of how he had injured the hand, remembering the Tarascan warrior who had shattered his shield with a copper-headed ax, and Cacalotl smashing the black rubber ball back at him. As long as he kept the images of past pain firmly in his mind, his vision remained the same. But once his concentration lapsed and the memories began to fade, the hawklike clarity would begin to reassert itself, and he could feel the spirit within grow bolder.

Stamping his bleeding foot, he again recalled the calmecac, running through all the punishments that Coatleztli had ever inflicted upon him, including the near-drowning. This last memory awakened real fear in Huemac, and he indulged it freely when he felt the nahualli shrink and hide itself, as if participating in the emotion. When he had exhausted his memories of the calmecac, Huemac began to search his body for scars, identifying each aloud and calling up every memory he could associate with it. He dug his fingers into the scarred flesh of his buttocks, remembering the punishing practices to which he had subjected himself as a boy, before he had pads to protect himself. And he recalled his mother's lancing the blistered skin, freeing the blackened blood to the sharp sting of the air. For the first time in his life, he was truly grateful for all the suffering he had undergone.

He kept this up without pause until nightfall, when he felt the creature within him grow completely quiescent. It is a good thing that you are not a night hunter as well, Huemac thought wearily, as he dragged himself in under the mesquite tree to rest. His mind was nearly as exhausted as his body, and though he knew that he had won the first part of the struggle, it had cost him dearly. He could only hope that the cost to his nahualli had been just as great. In his exhaustion, Huemac let his chin sink to his chest, and as his eyes closed, he fell immediately into a dream. He was soaring effortlessly over the desert, held aloft by the cushion of warm air trapped beneath his outspread wings, his sharp eyes alert to the slightest movement below. He saw the legs of a man protruding from beneath a tree, saw especially the man's bloody foot, then felt himself being pulled into an updraft, spiraling higher and higher, leaving the earth behind . . .

Fear at the great height brought Huemac back to consciousness, though for a long time he seemed to be swimming up from a suffocating depth. Then the air burst from his lungs and he could see the shapes in the darkness around him and feel the coarse sand under his legs and hands. I must not sleep, he told himself harshly, and I must not let *him* rest. Again, he remembered his daughter's message, as Pinotl had related it to him: "You must arm yourself with the joys and sorrows of your life, the memories that make you feel. *These* will be your weapons in the struggle."

"I am a man who has loved," Huemac said loudly, and felt a startled, querulous movement inside. Certain, then, that the nahualli had no choice but to listen and participate in his remembering, Huemac began to call up the images of all the people who had shared their hearts with him. Imagining their faces staring at him out of the darkness, he spoke to them lovingly, reminding himself of what they had meant to him. He recalled the moments of understanding that he had shared with his mother and father, and with Teuxoch, his second mother, and with Acolmiztli, Cocatli, and his own children. Many times, he wept, sensing, somehow, that this was particularly puzzling and annoying to his nahualli, who rustled uncomfortably within him.

To keep his memories from turning into dreams, Huemac talked loudly to himself and got up to limp in circles, slapping his naked body against the chill of the night air. Once, when fatigue seemed to be overtaking him, he picked several fat leaves from the cactus and scraped them on a rock, sucking the juice from the fibrous pulp to alleviate his thirst and revive himself. As he swallowed the tart cactus water, he could feel the hawk shiver and try to turn away, producing a strange twisting sensation in Huemac's midsection.

He saved his memories of Taypachtli until the sky had turned from black to gray and the air around him had begun to lighten. He was half delirious from the effort of remembering, but he immediately noticed a change in his nahualli when he brought up the image of the little blind girl who had befriended him so long ago. Ah, so you understand the feeling of having a mate, Huemac thought, and suddenly lost his desire to annoy the creature inside him. Instead, he spoke in a gentle tone, caressing both of them with the memories of tenderness that clung to his image of Taypachtli. He recalled the details of their courtship and marriage, feeling a responsive quiver to his imaginings of love-making, and he recited Taypachtli's flower songs aloud, enjoying the remarkable sensation of the bird preening himself languidly as the rhythms washed over him. Yes, my friend, Huemac thought fondly, there are *pleasures* we can share, as well . . .

He did not remember falling asleep, but he awoke in pain, his arms and legs racked with muscle spasms and his stomach cramping against the sharp, rending pain in his middle. Gasping in agony, he doubled over and rolled forward in the sand, clutching helplessly at his stomach, which felt as if it were being torn apart from the inside. Blackness hovered at the edge of his vision, offering release, but he fought it off, unable to think what was causing this. Then he felt a blinding pain between his eyes and a wild battering in his chest, and he knew that his nahualli was trying to escape.

"Never!" he shouted, and felt the creature's struggles grow wilder, hacking at his head and stomach with its beak and claws and buffeting his heart and lungs with its wings. Huemac rolled over and over and came to his knees screaming, his body a pain-ridden cage for the frantic creature within. A sudden surge sent him sprawling forward, toward the deadly, hooked barbs of a barrel cactus. *He is trying to kill me,* Huemac thought, and threw himself to one side, rolling his body out of danger. The pain, however, did not cease, and it took all his strength simply to remain conscious. The nahualli surged again and again with undiminished force, propelling Huemac across the ground and through the underbrush, where he was clawed by the cactus and bruised by the rocks. He managed to grab the scaly limb of a tree and clung to it briefly, until the branch broke and tore free as he was pulled away.

Huemac did not know how long this went on, or at what point he could feel the nahualli beginning to tire. But suddenly the pain was gone and he was on his feet, staggering like a drunken man as the surges continued to pass through him. He careened from tree to tree, grasping just long enough to direct himself away from the nearest cactus, then lurching on, wondering when this was going to end. Blundering his way across a bed of loose shale, he lost his footing and fell hard on his buttocks. Then he heard a sound that froze his blood and made the nahualli go rigid inside of him.

The rattlesnake lay only a few feet away, coiled and ready to strike, its golden tail buzzing a steady warning. Huemac stared at the gaping mouth and gleaming fangs, hardly daring to breathe. But then he felt the nahualli gather itself inside of him, and he knew that in a last, suicidal gesture, it was going to attack the snake and kill them both. A feeling of helplessness swept over him, for he knew that he was too weak to hold back against another surge. In his desperation, he cast about with his eyes for a weapon, his head ringing with the angry rattling of the serpent. What memory will protect me now? He thought despairingly, and in his despair, the image of a priest upon a mountain came back to him.

My voice! he thought, and before the nahualli could launch itself, Huemac let out with a rattle of his own, casting the sound at the snake with all the force he could muster. The rattlesnake reared back, its head swaying from side to side, then quickly uncoiled itself and slithered off into the underbrush, its pebbled body glimmering in the sunlight.

The nahualli was now completely still, and Huemac sat where he was until the heat of the sun made him heave his aching body to his feet and seek the shade of a stunted tree. It was over, he was certain of that; he could feel surrender in the creature's quietness.

"Now we are one, my friend," he said softly, weary but triumphant. "Now you can teach me what it means *not* to be a man . . ."

TEPEYOLLOTL had heard no sound from his father in almost three days, and he had not seen the hawk for a day and a half. His task had become that of simply waiting, once the screaming and crashing in the underbrush had ceased, and he had seen the hawk begin its clumsy maneuvers over the desert, flying low and staying aloft only for short periods, like an immature bird. Nor was there any longer any point in patrolling the area or trying to conceal his own presence, not after the sharp-eyed hunter had deliberately circled over Tepeyollotl's hiding place on two separate occasions, screeching audibly, as if in recognition.

The young man was burying the remains of his meal beneath a tree when he heard the whoosh of wings behind him. Controlling his impulses, he turned slowly, and saw his father standing a few feet away. Huemac's naked body was scratched and bruised in many places, and one of his eyebrows was badly swollen, but there was a smile on his face.

"Greetings, my son," he said heartily. "I have come to take you home."

"I congratulate you upon your success," Tepeyollotl said as he came closer, examining his father's face with sudden curiosity. The golden rings around his pupils seemed larger and darker, and his broad features seemed somehow sharper and more mobile. But most striking was the streak of white that now ran through the center of his gray hair.

"I know," Huemac said patiently. "The effects are still visible. Your mother told me that last night. She also told me that your lodge is awaiting your return, so that you can lead them in the summer hunt."

Tepeyollotl brightened, then paused to consider fully what he had just been told.

"You have visited the village?" he asked incredulously, and Huemac smiled again.

"It is not so far as it once was. But come, we must travel as fast as our legs will carry us if we are to return in time for the hunt."

While Huemac dressed, Tepeyollotl hastily gathered their water gourds and carrying nets, and strung his bow and quiver over his back. He handed his father the maguey-fiber net he had left behind with his clothes, and Huemac gazed at it briefly before slinging it over his shoulder. Then they set off through the desert at a fast walk.

"Would that we both had wings," Tepeyollotl said impatiently, staring ahead at the distant hills. Huemac laid a comforting hand on his arm but did not slacken his pace.

"In time, my son," he promised. "In time, you will know this wonderful power. And you will own it."

3

THE terror that came to Xolotlpilli in his sleep was blind and unreckoning, the fear of total extinction, and it jarred him rudely awake, into the very blackness of which he had dreamed. He blinked helplessly, his fingers clawing the mat beneath him in panic. Then he could make out shapes in the darkness, and heard Chalchiuhtona's steady breathing beside him, and he knew that he was in his own room, and that the world had not ended. He lay rigid for a few moments, smelling his own sweat, then quietly rolled away from his wife and slipped out of the room, snatching up his loincloth and a blanket as he left.

The corridor was cold, for the side that faced inward onto the courtyard below was open to the night air, and this was the last month of the year, a time of dampness and chill winds. Xolotlpilli stopped to tie on the loincloth and wrap the blanket around his broad shoulders, then proceeded down the hall, his way illuminated by the bright silver moon that hung low in the west. The path to his father's room was familiar to him, even in darkness, for he had gone there frequently, of late, to play his flute and calm the trembling of his heart.

Though the room was empty, he stood in the doorway for a moment, as if to fill it with his hoping. Then he stepped into the darkness with his arms raised over his head, groping for the trap door in the center of the ceiling. Thrusting upward, he threw the door open, letting in a blinding shaft of moonlight. When his eyes had adjusted, he made a slow circuit of the room, touching the things that he and his friends had hung from pegs on the walls. He ran his fingers over the cracked leather of Chiquatli's old tlachtli pads, flicking lightly at the fringe of limp owl feathers that hung from the seams. Each of the men had contributed an item of personal importance to the room's decoration, leaving a memory of himself for those times when he could not actually be present. There were the still-shiny pads that Azcatzin had worn on the day that he had put the ball through the ring, the jaguar skin that Omeocelotl had brought back from his second trip to Xoconochco, and the black mask of the Bat God that Pinotl had obtained in Zinacantlan, when he had gone there in disguise to scout for the Speaker.

Xolotlpilli himself had donated the weapons and eagle-feather standard of the captive he had taken in the last attack upon Tlaxcala, some two years earlier. These were pegged in a neat bundle against the south wall, and resting atop of the bundle was the painted bone flute that Papalotl had given him, a symbol of his character that was every bit as important as the weapons. Xolotlpilli took down the flute and seated himself on the reed mat that was his by custom, facing the empty mat where his father had sat four years earlier. He began a tune that had no recognizable melody, letting his lips and fingers play out the emotions that alternated in his heart, hope rising out of the somber depths of despair, then falling again in quavering protest.

Alone in the silvery light, he played out the mood of his city and its people, giving voice to the anxiety that had settled over all of Anahuac as the year approached its end. For this was the year One-Rabbit, the last in the count begun fifty-two years earlier, the year that would complete the sacred bundle and bring to a close the circle of years in which the people had lived. Soon, the New Fire Ceremony would be performed upon the Hill of Stars, and the moment of decision would arrive: Either the fire would be kindled and time would begin anew, or else the forces of Night would prevail over the earth, extinguishing the Fifth Sun and bringing all life to an end. It was a time of hope held in balance by fear, a time to review the sins of the past and pray for the forgiveness of a future.

Uneducated as he was, Xolotlpilli had no knowledge with which to resolve this tension, and even his great courage, proven time and again upon the battlefield, seemed of little consequence in the face of a threat so enormous and otherworldly. He could only wait and suffer, and hope that the time of testing of which his father had spoken was not to come to an end so soon. For surely, the Tenocha *had* been tested in the four years that Huemac had been gone: tested by the failure of their attacks on the Tlaxcalans, by the revolt of their subjects among the Mixtecs and Zapotecs, and by the drought that was now in its second year. None of *these* matters had been resolved, either, despite the efforts of Moteczuma and his warriors, and the prospect of real famine cast a dark shadow over all hopes of renewal.

Most ominous, though, at least to Xolotlpilli, was the fact that his father had not returned as he had promised. The New Fire Ceremony was only ten days off, yet no message had been received, and Huemac had not been seen in either Texcoco or Cholula, the two places where Xolotlpilli had thought to inquire. It was inconceivable to him that his father would break his word, but then, this was a time when all people contemplated the inconceivable, opening their hearts to doubt. Xolotlpilli was no different, especially since he had only the vaguest of notions concerning where his father had gone or what he hoped to do there.

Letting the last note trail off plaintively, Xolotlpilli withdrew the flute from his lips and put his hands in his lap, listening attentively in the sudden silence. He thought that he had heard a sound above him, on the roof, though it might merely have been an echo, or the product of his imagination. Just when he had decided that it was nothing, he heard a soft, rustling sound, and the ceiling above him creaked audibly. Rising by degrees, Xolotlpilli silently went to the wall and took down the warclub, leaving the flute in its place. He crouched in the darkness near the wall, watching as the shadow of a man broke the shaft of moonlight and dimmed the room. The shadow hesitated over the opening for a long time, and then a familiar voice spoke, so startling Xolotlpilli that he jumped backward and banged his elbow against the wall.

"The ladder," the voice commanded. "I am no thief, whoever you are. But I am too old for jumping through trap doors."

Still holding the warclub, Xolotlpilli lifted the ladder from the floor with his other hand and leaned it carefully against the edge of the opening. Then he stood back and watched the man climb down, unable to believe what he was seeing. Truly, those were his father's eyes, his father's face, but such a thing was not possible!

"No, you are not dreaming, my son," Huemac said gently, and held out his hand so that Xolotlpilli could touch him, and assure himself that he was real. Realizing that the macana was still in his hand, Xolotlpilli dropped it with a clatter that made him wince in surprise. Then he gripped his father's wrist, and was gripped in return with reassuring firmness. Tears sprang to his eyes, and he wrapped his father in an impulsive embrace, half lifting him off the floor. Huemac grunted and laughed, pounding his son lightly on the back to make him remember his own strength.

"Surely, this is magic," Xolotlpilli murmured as he released his father, continuing to stare at him in amazement.

"Did you not call me with your flute?" Huemac asked in an amused tone. "I thought that it was you, but the tune you played seemed troubled and uncertain, and then you hid yourself from me. It did not seem like you to wait in ambush for a thief."

"These are uncertain times," Xolotlpilli said apologetically. "I have not been myself lately. I had even begun to doubt that you would return as you had promised."

Huemac considered him seriously for a moment, then gestured that they should sit. Xolotlpilli watched as his father removed the pouches and knife from his waist, noticing the white streak in his hair for the first time.

"I see that I have not been fair with you," Huemac said abruptly. "I left you with a stern warning concerning the future, but I did not reassure you as I should have. Would it help you to know that the New Fire will be kindled, and our lives will go on?"

Xolotlpilli straightened in surprise, his sense of relief turning quickly into one of betrayal, and anger.

"You knew this before you left?" he demanded incredulously. "And you did not tell me?"

"I did not wish to complicate your task," Huemac said. "I did not think that it would help you to have knowledge you could not explain, even to yourself. But the things in this room," he added ruefully, "tell me that you have performed your task admirably. You must forgive me for underestimating you, and allow me to make up for my unfairness."

Xolotlpilli stared at him dubiously.

"Perhaps, then, you will now tell me how you know this about the New Fire?" he asked, and Huemac nodded agreeably.

"Your sister has the power to see the future," he said with deliberate bluntness. "Your grandmother knows this, as do Cocatli and Pinotl. We kept it from you as much for Papalotl's protection as your own, since augury can be a dangerous gift. I have just been to see her, and she told me that you have a new daughter. She wonders how long it will take you to notify her."

"I sent the message yesterday," Xolotlpilli said defensively, then stopped as he realized the implications of his own admission. He finished weakly: "We have given her the name Xiuhcue, Turquoise Skirt, in honor of Xiuhtecuhtli, Lord of the Year."

"I am pleased," Huemac said with a proud smile. "And how is your wife, and my grandson?"

"Chalchiuhtona is well, and Cuauhcoatl grows with each new day. Grandmother is also well, though the dampness stiffens her limbs and makes her bones ache. They will be as surprised as I by your return. How would you have me explain it?"

"It will be enough to say that I came by night and did not wish to disturb the household. Only you must know the truth. That is," Huemac added, with a significant pause, "if you wish to know."

"You offer me a choice?"

"I have chosen for you for too long, perhaps unfairly. But there is unfairness, too, in forcing you to know things that may trouble your heart. I *wish* to tell you, do not doubt that. I only want you to know beforehand that the truth —and certain kinds of knowledge—do not always make life simpler, or the future easier to face."

"I have learned this in your absence," Xolotlpilli said, proud yet rueful. "I have learned it in this room, and in the presence of Moteczuma. I can no longer choose *not* to know."

Huemac examined him for a moment, then nodded approvingly.

"I will keep my secrets from you no longer, then," he promised. "There can be no hiding, for I have come back to claim my place in this city, and I will need you by my side."

"I am here," Xolotlpilli said staunchly, "as I have always been."

"Then you must listen carefully, and question anything that escapes your understanding. You know, of course, that I was born in the last year One-Rabbit, fifty-two years ago, in the time of starving?"

"During the nemontemi, the unlucky days," Xolotlpilli supplied obediently, his eyes large and expectant. Huemac nodded slowly and drew a deep breath.

"Let me tell you of the luck that was mine, then, and how I set about to change it . . ."

ON THE second day after his return, Huemac left his son's house and went, alone, to the temple precinct. He intended to pay his respects to his friend Patecatl, but he also intended for himself to be seen. This proved as easy as he had suspected, for Moteczuma had his eyes and ears everywhere in the city, and Huemac was sure that he had been recognized at least twice before he had even reached the precinct gate. He walked slowly, with his head bent and his eyes hooded, further exaggerating the appearance of age that his lined face and white-streaked hair had given to him prematurely.

The Temple of Quetzalcoatl stood in its same place at the center of the plaza, though it rested now upon a greatly enlarged platform, and its shrine was surrounded by scaffolding and shrouded with protective coverings. As Papalotl had predicted, the temple had been rebuilt by Moteczuma in the year after his coronation, and then, a little more than a year later, the thatched roof of the circular shrine had mysteriously caught fire in the night. According to what Huemac had learned in Cholula, only the precautions that Patecatl had taken against such an emergency and the frantic efforts of the priests and novices had saved the shrine from being totally destroyed. He could see, as he approached, that the roof was still in ruins, and that there was no one working upon the scaffolds. Obviously, this was another project that would not be undertaken until a fresh bundle of years had been assured.

The High Priest himself stood on the top platform before the shrine, giving his blessing to a group of barefoot, shaven-headed students from the calmecac. These filed past Huemac as he climbed the steep steps, their eyes downcast and their young bodies marked by the thorn of penance. Patecatl was waiting for him at the top of the stairs, and Huemac knelt before him and touched dirt to his tongue, receiving the priest's blessing before any greetings were exchanged.

"Welcome home, my son," Patecatl said, as the two men examined each other, each noticing how the other had aged. The priest seemed visibly less robust, his shoulders shrunken within the folds of his white robe, his lips and hands seized occasionally by involuntary quivers. His face and eyes seemed even more gentle than Huemac remembered, as if time, or perhaps resignation, had further softened the heart within.

"Let us retire to my chambers," the priest suggested, but Huemac restrained him with a glance.

"Perhaps we should talk here, while there is time. Unless I have overestimated Moteczuma, his men will be here for me soon."

"There is no overestimating his caution," Patecatl assured him. "Were you anyone else, I would wonder how you had gotten this far into the city without his knowledge. You intend to face him directly, then?"

"I am told that he allows few people *that* privilege," Huemac said dryly. "But I am ready now to claim the other privileges that rightfully belong to me. He must be made to learn that I will not avoid him any longer."

Patecatl raised an eyebrow skeptically, then glanced to his right, squinting down across the plaza.

"I think I see the men of whom you speak," he said, and adopted a more urgent tone. "I should tell you, then, that Moteczuma has heard of Papalotl's powers. The priests in Cholula could not keep quiet after the temple here burned; they place great faith in her predictions, now."

"I have just seen her," Huemac said with a nod. "She is still careful in what she chooses to reveal."

"So must you be," Patecatl warned in a low voice, raising his eyes to include the men who had come up behind Huemac. There were four of them, two polite young men from the palace staff and two large warriors who wore the fringed mantle of the Speaker's personal guard. The latter two took up positions on either side of Huemac, ostentatiously displaying the weapons they carried. In contrast, the two courtiers bowed deeply to both Patecatl and Huemac, stating the Speaker's desire in terms that were almost apologetic.

"I will be glad to accompany you," Huemac said obediently. "Farewell, my father. It has been my pleasure to see you again."

"We will continue our conversation at another time," the priest said in a casual tone, ignoring the ominous presence of the warriors. But he blessed Huemac for a second time in parting, and he stood watching until his friend, surrounded by the four men, had passed through the south gate of the precinct and disappeared from sight.

THE PALACE of Moteczuma lay to the southeast of the temple precinct and occupied an area perhaps two thirds as large, with two floors of rooms surrounding a maze of interior courtyards. It was much larger than the old palaces of Axayacatl and Ahuitzotl, and close enough to the eastern shore of the island that visitors could come directly into the palace by canoe. Xolotlpilli had tried to describe the magnificence of its halls and gardens to Huemac, finding the palace in Texcoco a poor comparison, at least in size. Each of Moteczuma's five principal wives had her own quarters and staff, and the Speaker's collection of animals and birds was housed in a wing of its own, with wading ponds of both fresh and salty water, and hundreds of caretakers to look after the health of the animals. The entire palace staff—all sons of noble blood —was said to number over two thousand.

In a small room next to the gate, Huemac was ordered to shed his sandals and cotton mantle and don the coarse maguey-fiber mantle that was provided for him. He did this with the same apparently decrepit lack of haste that had characterized their walk to the palace, a pace that had had the warriors stepping on their own feet, wondering why a guard was necessary for a doddering old man. After being instructed by the courtiers not to speak or raise his eyes until he was commanded to do so, Huemac was led up a flight of stairs and down a long corridor, past the entrances to at least a dozen large banquet halls and audience chambers.

Out of the corners of his eyes, Huemac noted the windows and porches that gave onto the open air, cataloguing the exits that appeared wide enough to accommodate the spread wings of a hawk. He hoped to use his powers only as a last resort, but there was no telling, with Moteczuma, how quickly that moment might arrive. Nezahualpilli had advised him to act the part of an Old Eagle, a man protected by his years and past honors. He had told him that Moteczuma was sometimes affected by appeals to tradition, and that it might be useful to remind him of his predecessors, the father and uncles that Huemac himself had served. But Nezahualpilli had been granted as little private access to Moteczuma as he allowed to his own lords, and his last words to Huemac had been to be ready for anything, especially a treacherous attack.

The courtiers left Huemac alone with the two warriors in a small, high-ceilinged anteroom, and Huemac wondered if the attack was going to come this soon. But the indifferent stances of the warriors showed that they had no such orders, and that they had, in addition, accepted his feebleness at face value. Grateful that they were too young to know of his reputation, Huemac relaxed and tried to prepare himself for his interview. Though she had tried on several occasions, Papalotl had had no dreams that might aid him, and Xolotlpilli's experiences were of limited value, since they were those of a favorite. Xolotlpilli had told him, though, that he would most likely find Moteczuma alone, except for the ubiquitous young men who waited on him, and the dwarves and hunchbacks who entertained him and who were, in fact, his closest personal companions. The lords, Xolotlpilli had said, were seldom allowed to attend him in a group, except for council meetings and on ceremonial occasions, when their access to him was limited by protocol. Moteczuma maintained himself in splendid isolation, where *his* was the only voice to be heard, the only will to be heeded.

Perhaps this will work to my advantage, Huemac thought, as the courtiers returned for him, warning him again to keep his eyes on the ground from this point forward. He nodded absently, feeling his nahualli come to full alertness in response to the sudden tension that flowed into Huemac's body as he was led into the Speaker's chamber. From beneath his hooded eyelids, Huemac saw immediately that Xolotlpilli had underestimated the respect that Moteczuma had for him: In addition to the two serving men who flanked the reed seat, and the dwarf crouched at the foot of the dais, there were at least a half-dozen armed guards stationed at intervals around the platform upon which Moteczuma sat.

Allowing himself to be guided as if he were indeed sightless, Huemac squatted on command and touched dirt to his tongue in humility. When the order to rise did not come immediately, he knew that he was to be humiliated further, and he prepared himself for a long wait. The only person within his limited view was the dwarf, obviously a young boy, despite his prematurely wizened features. Huemac saw intelligence in the boy's eyes, and sensed something like compassion in the quiet way he observed Huemac's abasement. It cannot be any easier to be Moteczuma's favorite than to be his enemy, Huemac thought, to take his mind off the mounting pain in his hunched back and straining legs. He did not conceal the effort that the awkward position was costing him, though, and he even allowed his legs to buckle slightly, to enhance the pathetic image he knew he was presenting.

"Rise," a cold, scornful voice said at last, and Huemac straightened up slowly, as if every joint were protesting the ascent. He kept his head bowed and his eyes hooded, but now he could see Moteczuma plainly. He was sitting upon a seat covered with jaguar skin, wearing a blue mantle, golden armbands, and earplugs of clear, shimmering crystal. The turquoise crown on his head stood out brilliantly against the rich green fan of quetzal feathers attached to the backrest of his seat. Moteczuma was now close to forty, yet he appeared several years younger, his body still slender and his face unlined. His dark eyes were filled with a disdain that made Huemac suspect that he had not been taken in by the pretense of old age.

"So, you have returned, Huemac," he said in a voice that matched his eyes. "What made you think that your presence here would be tolerated any better than before? Did you think that something had changed? You know that I do not trust you."

Huemac stood silently, head down, his humble posture offering no argument in his own defense.

"Did you truly believe that this appearance of age would make me think you harmless?" Moteczuma went on, openly scoffing. "Or perhaps you felt that the favor I have shown toward Xolotlpilli and Azcatzin would now be extended to you. They have served me well, but I do not see what *you* can offer me. Speak, then: Tell me why I should consider allowing you to stay here."

"My fate lies in this city, my Lord," Huemac said, quietly but clearly, as if it were a fact beyond dispute. "I have known this since the time of the civil war, when your father was the Speaker. I can avoid my fate no more than he could."

A look of uneasiness passed briefly across Moteczuma's face at the mention of his father, and Huemac knew that he had called up the appropriate ghosts, making him reach for the hazy memories of childhood.

"Your fate, and that of all the Tenocha, is in *my* hands," Moteczuma reminded him sharply, then faltered slightly and went on in an agitated tone: "And in the hands of the gods. Perhaps you have chosen to come at this time," he added suspiciously, "because you know that there is little time left to any of us. Speak, I command you! Do you expect the end to come shortly?"

"No, my Lord," Huemac assured him. "I expect that the New Fire will be kindled, and time will go on. I expect to grow old in this city."

"You have *seen* this?" Moteczuma demanded urgently, leaning forward in his seat. Huemac was aware of the wide eyes of the dwarf at his feet, and he knew that Moteczuma shared the boy's obvious need for reassurance, despite his hatred of the source.

"Yes, my Lord," Huemac said firmly, and Moteczuma sat back and was silent for several moments, considering. Then a shrewdly nasty expression crept onto the Speaker's narrow face, and Huemac knew, as well, that there would be no gratitude for having answered the man's need.

"So . . . *this* accounts for the boldness you have shown all these years, to my father, my uncle, and myself. Do you think, even now, that your future is safe?"

Even before the dwarf's head turned, Huemac saw Moteczuma's hand signal to the warrior standing at the right corner of the dais. Huemac let the man take one step toward him, his macana rising in his hand. Then, so swiftly that no one saw him raise his eyes, Huemac threw the shape of his nahualli at the warrior, a brief, taloned shadow that struck at the man's unprotected face and sent him reeling backward in panic. The other guards immediately leapt onto the dais to surround the Speaker, but no one else made a move toward Huemac. The warrior lay where he had fallen, stunned but unhurt, and too frightened to rise.

"You dare to threaten me?" Moteczuma shrieked, standing now, but behind his guards. Huemac heard other men come into the room behind him, and he tensed himself internally, quelling the anxious stirrings of his nahualli.

"I bear you no threat, my Lord," he said calmly. "But it is every man's duty to protect himself against an unwarranted attack. I have told you that I intend to grow old here."

"You are a sorcerer!"

"I am an Old Eagle," Huemac replied. "I did not beg for the honors that were granted to me by Axayacatl, and Tizoc, and Ahuitzotl. Must I beg you, Lord, for my very safety?"

"Yes!" Moteczuma shouted, so beside himself with anger that he struck out at the guards in front of him with his hands. Spreading his arms wide in appeal, Huemac suddenly dropped to one knee, and spoke in a voice that carried to every ear in the room:

"Then I beg you humbly to spare my life, and allow me to live here . . ."

Gambling that his unexpected action had dumfounded everyone in the room, Huemac assumed the full penitent's position and again touched dirt to his tongue. The utter silence in the chamber told him that he had judged correctly, but he kept his eyes on the frightened face of the dwarf, knowing that he would see the attack coming in the boy's eyes, if his other senses failed to warn him. The silence continued, uninterrupted by even the slightest movement. Finally, Moteczuma spoke, in a voice that struggled to make resignation sound like decisiveness.

"Nahui Olin," he said, and the dwarf stirred and looked back over his shoulder. "Go to him, and raise him up."

Bouncing obediently to his feet, the dwarf hesitated, then slowly walked to where Huemac squatted on the floor. Reaching down, he placed a tiny, dimpled hand onto Huemac's arm and tugged gently. Keeping his head bowed, Huemac rose to his feet, letting his hooded gaze fall upon the boy in front of him. For a brief moment, their eyes met, and Huemac bathed the boy with a glow of encouragement and respect, sharing an instant of secret triumph.

"Raise your face, Huemac, and look upon me," Moteczuma commanded, and Huemac saw that he had resumed his seat, and sent the guards back to their places. He also saw no trust on the Speaker's face, merely the grudging acceptance of a man who did not wish to fail twice in his attacks on an unarmed man.

"Perhaps you have spoken truly concerning the power of your fate," Moteczuma continued, with a slight shrug. "But it was your humility that softened my heart today. I trust that you will remember that in the future. Go now, and let me hear no evil of you. Let me hear *nothing* of you, if you wish to remain here . . ."

Huemac bowed deeply and backed slowly out of the Speaker's presence, without again raising his eyes. The last thing he saw, before turning to leave the chamber, was the dwarf looking after him, his old man's face wearing an expression of boyish wonder, his black eyes deep with fascination.

"YOU MUST stay awake," Ome Xochitl murmured to Cuauhcoatl, shifting his considerable weight in her blanket-covered lap. "We must all be awake to welcome the New Fire."

She and her great-grandson were sitting on the rooftop, at one end of a line that had Xolotlpilli and Huemac in the middle and Chalchiuhtona at the other end, holding her daughter in her arms. Several of the young warriors who boarded with Xolotlpilli sat behind him and Huemac, and all were facing south, toward Ixtapalapa and the Hill of Stars. The rooftops all around were similarly crowded with people, as were most of the high places in the silent, darkened city.

Cuauhcoatl squirmed uncomfortably and rubbed at his gritty eyes, wishing that he could bury himself in the Old Grandmother's blankets and sleep forever. The tension and activity of the last several days had completely worn him out, by keeping him in a state of perpetual excitement. It had all been so unusual: seeing his father and grandfather sweeping and cleaning with the women, using their brooms like weapons on an enemy. And then joining in the procession to the shore of the Lake, where the stone images of the household gods had been cast into the water, along with the soot-blackened stones from the cooking fires, and all the old dishes and grinding stones. Cuauhcoatl had bravely discarded his toy weapons, encouraged by a hint from his mother that he would be given new ones later.

Even eating cold, uncooked food and having no light at night had been stimulating, giving rise to fantasies of camping with the army in hostile territory, where no fires were permitted. But now, this long after his bedtime, even the novelty of being up on the roof with the adults could not sustain him any longer. He heard his baby sister begin to cry at the other end of the line, and he wished that he could cry, too, and be cuddled in his mother's soft arms. But he was six years old now, no longer a baby, and he knew that his father would not tolerate tears and whining from him on this occasion, when all were suffering the same wait.

"The stars have reached the center of the sky," Huemac announced solemnly, and Ome Xochitl took this as a cue to gently dislodge Cuauhcoatl from her lap.

"You are too heavy for these old bones, my son," she told him. "It will not be long now, though."

As he reluctantly resettled himself next to his great-grandmother, Cuauhcoatl's eyes fell upon the bone implements laid out on a mat in front of his father. It was a sight he had been trying to avoid all evening, and a shudder passed through him at the thought of those sharp points piercing his own flesh. He had bravely accepted the idea when it had been explained to him, but he had not been so tired then. Now he was sure that he would cry out and shed tears at the pain, a prospect that frightened him nearly as much as the pain itself. He was considering the possibility of pretending to be asleep, when suddenly the men beside him let out a great shout, which found its echo in all parts of the city, and soon became a sustained cheering.

"Look," the Old Grandmother said, pointing to the south. There, upon a distant hilltop, a great bonfire blazed brightly, a lone beacon against the night sky.

"The New Fire!" Cuauhcoatl exclaimed exuberantly, forgetting his fatigue in the sudden excitement, and touching off a wave of approving laughter in the men behind him. Rising from his place of honor, Xolotlpilli distributed the sharp pieces of bone to those around him, and was himself the first to pierce his earlobes and forearms, flicking blood in the direction of the fire. Cuauhcoatl watched wide-eyed as the other adults followed his father's example, but he jerked away involuntarily when Ome Xochitl placed her hand on his arm.

Then his sister let out a wail of pain and he jerked again, staring wildly around him.

"Yes, even little Xiuhcue must do penance for the time in which we live," Ome Xochitl told him softly. "Be brave, my son. Remember yourself as the warrior you are."

Cuauhcoatl clenched his teeth, trembling uncontrollably as his great-grandmother pinched his left earlobe between her fingers and rubbed it briskly, stretching and numbing the skin. Then her other hand flashed swiftly out of the corner of his eye, and a bright flame of pain blossomed in his head. But he caught the sob before it could burst from his throat, and that unexpected success gave him the courage to turn his head, so that she could pierce his other earlobe. So intense was the pain in his ears, and so determined was he to hold back his tears, that he did not feel the bone as it scratched his forearms.

"Now offer your blood, my son," his father said in a proud voice, and Cuauhcoatl gingerly raised his fingers to his ears, barely feeling the wetness that covered his wounds. Glancing once at his father, who nodded encouragingly, he awkwardly flicked blood in the direction of the distant hill, feeling the stinging heat of the fire touching his torn flesh.

"Recognize this boy's courage, O Gods!" his father cried out to the sky, and Cuauhcoatl's heart swelled with pride as he accepted Ome Xochitl's comforting embrace, covertly drying his eyes on the blankets wrapped around her frail body.

The rest of the night went by in a blur, half dream and half noisy reality. He must have slept for part of the time, for the sky was already lightening with dawn when he found himself being borne through the streets on his father's shoulders, perched high over a streaming crowd of joyous people. Then they were in the courtyard of the old palace of Axayacatl, where a great bonfire had been lit by the fire bearers from Ixtapalapa. Young warriors danced around the blaze, dashing in close to light torches, as if daring the flames to singe their bodies. Cuauhcoatl was given to another warrior, and he watched as his father joined the dance, towering over the other warriors and drawing cheers of recognition from the crowd.

Then he was lowered to his feet and could not see through the crowd, and fatigue again overtook him as he clung desperately to the edge of his mother's skirt to keep from being separated. He did not remember much after that, and he awoke to the sensation of movement, and something hard pressing against his chest. He realized that he was being carried, but it was several moments before he had the strength to raise his head and look at the face of the man upon whose shoulder he had been resting.

"Grandfather," he said sleepily, and Huemac slowed to a halt, rearranging his arms so that the boy could look at him directly. Cuauhcoatl yawned and grimaced, reaching down to find the jade rabbit that had been trapped between their bodies. He fingered the stone absently, becoming self-conscious in the warm glow emanating from his grandfather's eyes.

"That was given to me by my mother, the woman you call the Old Grandmother," Huemac explained. "She gave it to me on the day of my birth, in the time of the last New Fire Ceremony."

"I want to get down," Cuauhcoatl said uneasily, and Huemac lowered him to his feet, holding him upright by the shoulders. When Cuauhcoatl continued to avoid his eyes, he knelt before him and tipped the boy's chin up to his own.

"We do not know each other well, Cuauhcoatl," he said gently. "You must forgive me for being gone while you were growing up. But I am here for you now, my grandson."

Cuauhcoatl stared back at him timidly, unsettled by the glowing eyes and the uncanny streak of white in his long gray hair. Although he knew that he should not think such a thing, he thought that his grandfather was ugly, his face flat and deeply lined, his jaw sagging with extra folds of flesh. He did not smile often, as Cuauhcoatl's father did, and many of the family's servants were afraid to even go near him. Though he would not have admitted it, Cuauhcoatl was deeply disappointed that the grandfather he had been told about for so long had turned out to be such a strange and disturbing man.

"No, I am not pleasant to look at," Huemac said ruefully, reading the boy's thoughts in his eyes. "But look into my eyes, Cuauhcoatl, and you will know that I hold you in my heart, and care for your well-being."

Blinking hesitantly, Cuauhcoatl forced himself to look, and then gave himself up to the steady golden glow that seemed to blot out the rest of his grandfather's features. He felt a gradual warmth spread throughout his body, and then saw the image of his own face, smiling at him as if from a mirror. The image faded slowly, melting away until it merged with the smile that his grandfather now wore. Cuauhcoatl blinked again as the transition became complete, and he was aware of himself standing in the street, with people passing by on both sides. His grandfather rose and reached down for his hand.

"Come, my grandson. The years have begun anew; let us share the time that the gods have given us."

"Yes, Grandfather," Cuauhcoatl said in an awed whisper, and took the hand, willing to be led.

⌐╖║ **4** ║╓¬

THE rains returned to the Valley of Anahuac in the spring of Two-Reed, the first year of the new bundle. With the drought broken and a good crop assured, the Tenocha were again able to turn their energies toward the fulfillment of their vision of greatness. Moteczuma assembled a great army under the command of his brother, Cuitlahuac, and sent his warriors south to deal once and for all with the rebellious Mixtecs and Zapotecs. To insure the continued favor of the gods, he ordered that many of the temples be repainted and given new images, and he presided over the dedication of a gigantic statue of Coatlique, the Earth Goddess who was the mother of Huitzilopochtli. Construction again went forward on the Temple of Quetzalcoatl, which was finally completed in the year Three Flint-Knife.

News of this last event reached Papalotl in the fall of Three Flint-Knife, in a message from her Aunt Cocatli, who had been present at the dedication. That same night, Papalotl attempted to go to her aunt in a dream. But, as had been happening with increasing frequency, her power failed her and she fell instead into a deep, dreamless sleep that left her feeling restless and irritable when she awoke. Papalotl had so far resisted the possibility that she might be losing her powers with age, but now she began to consider it seriously, to the extent of discussing the matter with the High Priest. He, too, was disappointed, for her auguries had brought added prestige to his temple. But it was the way of the gods, he told her sadly, to sometimes take back the gifts they had granted to men and women.

As fall turned to winter, and the year Four-House approached, Papalotl's ability to dream disappeared entirely. When she closed her eyes to sleep, she descended into an uneasy blackness, from which she would bolt awake, trembling, several times during the course of the night. Four-House would be her thirtieth year on the earth, her tenth since coming to Cholula. She had risen high within her order, and was also well liked by her sister priestesses. But now they began to watch her with apprehension, seeing the strain in her face and the dark circles that appeared beneath her beautiful golden eyes, and suffering the effects of an irascibility she had never shown before.

In the second month of Four-House, her bleeding came to her with painful force, accompanied by aches in all her joints and agonizing cramps that incapacitated her totally. By order of the High Priest, she was not taken to the usual place of bleeding, but was sequestered separately, under the care of three older women. She lay in pain for five days, until the bleeding ceased and the torment she had been under passed from her body like a fever. Then she fell into a sleep that lasted from one night to the next, so worrying the women with its depth that they summoned a healer to examine her for signs of life. The healer listened to her heart and breathing and assured the women that she would recover, though she would no doubt be weak for a long time.

Papalotl awoke some time after the healer's departure and found that all three women had dozed off, even the one who was sitting up beside her. A strange whistling sound came to her from the hallway outside, and it was several moments before she could identify it. The wind, she thought, remembering the way it sometimes swirled around the great temple, penetrating even into these subterranean rooms. She listened to the wind's muffled suspirations, which came and went with a soothing regularity, like a whispered song. Then she closed her eyes and went into a dream.

The first images came to her in quick succession. A hawk circling high over a city, looking down on a boy crouching on a rooftop below. Her father and Nezahualpilli sitting together in the stands of the Tlachco, watching a ball game. Her brother being carried wounded from the battlefield, then recovering in his house. Cocatli weeping beside the body of her mother, who wore the white paint of the dead.

There were other familiar faces on the edges of these scenes, but they went by too fast to permit reflection. Papalotl had the overwhelming sense that these revelations were unimportant, that she was simply using them up in order to empty herself, and open her spirit to an even greater power. The last of the images—of herself standing in the courtyard of Quetzalcoatl-Topiltzin—faded into a vast whiteness, like the inside of a cloud, and the only sound she could hear was the steady howling of the wind.

Then she was staring at the night sky, the dark, familiar shapes of the mountains in the foreground telling her that she was looking to the east. A star plummeted from its place in the blackness, leaving behind a silver streak in the center of the sky, a hovering apparition that caught and held Papalotl's eye. As she watched, the streak solidified and transformed itself into a single green reed. *Ce Acatl, One-Reed,* Papalotl thought, and saw the reed begin to vibrate, then to spin, its bottom end whirling in a wider circle than its tip, describing the shape of a great spindle-stone in the sky. The spindle shape spun faster and faster around its upper end, becoming solid and turning from green to orange, and then to a deep, burning red. It grew until it filled the center of the sky, a great shimmering pillar of fire that obscured the stars all around it.

Gazing upon it, Papalotl felt the same all-encompassing sense of well-being that she had experienced in her dream of the god's visitation, and she knew that the Lord was near. She smiled and raised her arms to the omen in the sky, feeling strength flow down from her fingertips into her body, filling her like a warm liquid. She cried out in joy and gratitude, and as she heard her own voice calling the god's name, her eyes suddenly blinked open. Then she could feel the cold wind against her cheeks, and she was aware that she had been dreaming. Yet the pillar of fire was still there, exactly as she had seen it, lighting the entire eastern sky with a lurid red glow. She continued to stare at it in amazement, until she heard a voice at her elbow:

"Can you hear me, my daughter?" the High Priest asked softly, and Papalotl turned to look around her for the first time. The High Priest threw an arm up in front of his face as her eyes fell upon him, and the crowd of white-robed women behind him ducked their heads in unison, their long hair tossing in the wind. Papalotl hastily hooded her eyes, but not before she had seen the mural on the wall beyond the bowed heads of the women, telling her that she had somehow come to the courtyard of Quetzalcoatl-Topiltzin.

"I hear you, my father," she said, and the priest lowered his arm to look at her. Papalotl glanced back at the awesome light in the sky, expecting him to turn with her. But he merely regarded her curiously, as if he saw nothing to distract him. Nor were any of the women looking at the sky.

"Do you not see it?" she asked incredulously. "There, in the east?"

"I see nothing but the sky and stars," he said, gazing at her steadily. "What do *you* see, my daughter?"

Papalotl caught her breath, for the pillar of fire was unchanged, and cast a reddish light over all their faces. She described it in great detail to the priest, who listened intently but showed no signs of recognition. The women murmured and stared at her in awe, and several fell to their knees and bowed their heads.

"How do you feel, my daughter?" the High Priest asked when she had concluded her description, and Papalotl had to think for a moment and flex her limbs before she could answer.

"I feel well, and strong," she decided, recalling, for the first time, the pain and weakness she had recently suffered. "How did I come to be here?"

"The women say that you sat up and called out in your sleep, crying 'One-Reed,' the year of our Lord. Then, though your eyes were still closed, you rose under your own power and walked straight to this place. The women followed you, but you did not need their aid. You walked with the certainty of one who sees."

Papalotl bowed her head and shrugged helplessly, having no memory of her journey. Then she looked again at the omen in the sky.

"It is still there, my father," she said, and the High Priest gently took her arm and encouraged her to sit with him on the mats that had been brought for him.

"Keep your eyes upon it, then, while you tell me what else you dreamed," he suggested, then corrected himself: "While you tell me what else you *saw . . .*"

THE QUARTERS of the royal jesters were in the south wing of the palace, on the second floor. The floor below contained the cages and jars that housed the Speaker's collection of serpents and wild animals, and the deep growls of bears and mountain lions reverberated through the floor above, penetrating the rooms where Moteczuma's dwarves, hunchbacks, and albinos lived. Alone in his cubicle, the ten-year-old Nahui Olin lay trembling on his sleeping mat, the victim of a nightmare in which he had been pursued by wild beasts. Familiar as they were, the sounds from below did not make him want to close his eyes again, and be alone in the darkness from which he had just escaped.

He started to cry, then stopped himself, knowing that no one would come to comfort him. Instead, he rose and dressed himself, and went out into the hallway, which was dimly lit by a torch set in the wall at the far end, near the stairs to the roof. Nahui Olin wandered naturally toward the light, waddling slightly from the permanent bow in his thick stubby legs. He glanced into each of the rooms he passed, looking for companionship, but no one else was awake. Nahui Olin told himself that it did not matter, that they would not have sat with him, anyway. No one was a friend to the "favorite."

Feeling the ache of his loneliness, he stood aimlessly in the circle of light beneath the torch, as if visibility might cause him to be found. Then he grew restless and went up the stairs to the viewing deck on the roof above. The vast blackness of the sky made him hesitant to leave the light on the stairs, but he finally summoned the courage to run across the platform and crouch at the base of the stone railing that surrounded the deck. Grasping one of the pillars that supported the railing, he peered out over the sleeping city, seeing figures moving around a fire atop one of the calpulli temples. In the far distance was the dark hulk of the Xoloco, the fortress-like gate that led to the causeway to Ixtapalapa.

More aware than ever of being alone, Nahui Olin very quickly began to wonder why he had come here. But just as he was gathering the courage to dash back to the stairs, he heard the sound of rushing wings above him and instinctively ducked his head. When he could finally bring himself to look, the first thing he saw were two golden eyes staring at him out of the darkness, and he cried out in fright and tried to squeeze himself between the pillars of the railing. But a kindly voice called him back.

"Do not be afraid, Nahui Olin. I am a friend. Do you not remember me?"

Huddled against the pillars, the boy forced himself to look again, and this time made out the face and figure of the man squatting a few feet away from him.

"You are the man called Huemac," he said in a trembling voice. "Have you come to kill me?"

Huemac laughed softly, and Nahui Olin uncoiled slightly at the reassuringly human sound.

"No, my friend. I have come because I, too, am a man with a difficult task. And I also have few friends with whom I can share my troubles."

"How do you know this about me?" the boy asked suspiciously, though he had let go of the pillar, and was no longer poised for flight.

"I know the master you serve," Huemac said simply. "And I know what it is to be thought strange, and ugly. How old are you, my son?"

"I am ten. I was born in the year Seven-Reed."

"And you were born under the sign Four Movement, the birth sign of our Sun?"

Nahui Olin nodded and grimaced bitterly, making slits of his eyes; his mouth puckered like an infant's deprived of suck.

"I was destined to be a great warrior, an Eagle or a Jaguar," he said thickly. "Then, when I was three, we knew . . ."

Nahui Olin trailed off, his voice failing him completely. Tears trickled from the corners of his eyes, rolling down over the fat rolls of his cheeks. Huemac could easily imagine the disappointment of the parents upon learning that their son would grow but a little, always to be stunted and misshapen, a parody of a man. But he could *feel* the devastating pain that their disappointment and rejection had inflicted upon the boy before him.

"So you were sent here," Huemac supplied in a soft voice, "where you are thought to be a little man, without the natural feelings of a child. I myself was blessed with parents who understood my uniqueness and cherished it. I would offer the same understanding to you, Nahui Olin, if you would be my friend."

Instead of being touched by the offer, the boy squinted at Huemac with renewed suspicion, his lips curling into a sneer of practiced disdain.

"*No one* is a friend of the favorite," he muttered cynically. "I am not such a child. You only want to use me for your own purposes."

"Perhaps," Huemac allowed, "but not as others would use you. Not as Moteczuma uses you. You will not have to roll on the floor and make comical faces to win my regard; you will not have to pretend to be happy. You will only have to be the brave warrior that you were fated to be, and face up to the task that is yours."

Nahui Olin glanced down at his feet, then back at Huemac.

"I do not know what task you mean."

"I told the Speaker that my fate lies in this city," Huemac said, "but I did not tell him all that I have foreseen. I have had a vision of the destruction of Tenochtitlan. Soon there will be omens to corroborate this. But there is a chance that we might be saved; that I, and those who aid me, might still avert this disaster. That is why I risked my life to stay here, and why I have come to you tonight. You are one of a very few who might have influence with Moteczuma."

"*Me?*" Nahui Olin exclaimed incredulously. "I am nothing, merely a servant. I did not choose to become his favorite."

"Have you never wondered what he sees in you? Have you never thought that he bears a name as powerful as your own, and that perhaps it reminds him of the weight of his own destiny, and of his inadequacy in the face of it? He can pity you, and laugh at the cruel trick fate has played upon you, but he can never allow himself to be pitied or laughed at.

"Also, like you," Huemac went on pointedly, "he feels himself to be an orphan, abandoned to the stern expectations of his fate. His father died when he was not much older than you are now, and the uncle who took him under his protection was later murdered by his own lords. Nor can he ever forget that his brother, Tlacahuepan, should have ruled before him. You are the child locked away within his heart, the little man who craves protection and comfort, but can find none."

"I do not understand all this," Nahui Olin protested, shaking his large, round head. "And *you* could not protect me; he hates you too much."

"He will no doubt try to kill me again," Huemac agreed calmly. "The only protection I can offer you is the knowledge of your true task. For, if you go on trying to please him out of ignorance, you will surely make a mistake someday, and then he will cast you out or have you killed. That is why you must *choose* to be his favorite. You must learn to gauge his moods and respond to them correctly; you must be his counterpart in all things, demeaning everything he dislikes, glorifying that which he honors. He must come to think of you as a representation of himself, so that he could not conceive of harming you. Later, perhaps, when the danger to our people is clear, you will know how to use your influence."

"You ask too much of me," the boy said plaintively, sinking his chin into his hands.

"It is not I who gave you your name, and your fate. There are many kinds of warriors, my son, of all ages and shapes. Our city will need all of them when the time of decision comes. I ask you to dedicate yourself now, before it is too late. You will see the omens for yourself, soon enough."

"But what if I forget what you have told me?" Nahui Olin asked in a wheedling tone. "Perhaps you will not come to me again."

"I do not desert those I call friend," Huemac assured him. "Unless I am out of the city, I will come to this place every tenth night. I offer you my hand as a token of this promise."

Nahui Olin stared at the hand indecisively, then looked around him, seeing only darkness. With a noise that was half desperation and half relief, he pushed himself away from the pillar and crawled forward to take Huemac's hand. Huemac went to his knees and spread his other arm wide, gently drawing the boy into his embrace. Nahui Olin's arms went around him tightly, and he began to weep against Huemac's chest.

"Yes, my little warrior," Huemac murmured soothingly. "It is a hard fate that you have been given. But you will not have to bear it alone any longer, I promise you that."

NEZAHUALPILLI, now forty-four years old, had not been a frequent guest in Tenochtitlan since the time of the flood, some ten years earlier. The harsh words he had spoken to Ahuitzotl on that occasion, and the shame they had caused, had not been forgotten by the Tenocha, or forgiven by Ahuitzotl's successor. Nor would Moteczuma ever forgive Nezahualpilli for the public execution of his sister, Chalchiuhnenetl, or for the effrontery of having a reputation greater than his own. The Fasting Prince was still sent for when ceremony demanded his presence, but Moteczuma had been heard to proclaim, on more than one occasion, that he was the *sole* ruler of Anahuac, and that he had little respect for the other members of the Three-City Alliance.

None of these things touched Nezahualpilli any longer, and he did not feel any satisfaction when the fiery pillar appeared in the sky over Tenochtitlan, even though he knew that this omen would provide him with one last triumph over his rival. He had foreseen the omen's coming several months ago, and it had, in fact, been visible to him for many days before it was first sighted in Tenochtitlan. Knowing that he would be consulted eventually, he listened calmly to the reports of Moteczuma's panicked reaction, which had led to the untimely deaths of all the soothsayers and diviners who had failed to warn him. Undiminished in power and brightness, the omen continued to appear night after night, fading only with the rising of the Sun.

After ten days of indecision and dread—a true measure, Nezahualpilli thought, of the envy and hatred Moteczuma felt toward him—the Tenocha Speaker finally sent a messenger to Texcoco, requesting aid. With deliberate formality, Nezahualpilli gathered his retinue and came across the Lake, grave with the knowledge he had waited months to deliver. After his stormy interview with Moteczuma had been concluded, he went unannounced to the house of Xolotlpilli, paying no heed to the suspicious eyes that followed him through the streets.

Huemac was sitting with his mother and grandson when the king and his retainers descended upon him, filling the courtyard with their numbers. Nezahualpilli greeted his "nephew" and half-sister fondly, seeing by the startled look of recognition in their eyes that they, too, noticed his growing resemblance to his father. He stared quietly at young Cuauhcoatl for a moment, making the boy nervous, then looked at Huemac with equal sadness.

"You know why I have come here, my friend," he said bluntly. "So I will tell you as I told Moteczuma: This omen is only the first that will warn us of our coming doom. In not too many years—perhaps five, perhaps ten—death will walk this land, and our cities will be destroyed, our people ruined. Nothing will be spared. You have inquired of this very thing in the past, Huemac. I can tell you now that it is a certainty, though I myself will not be alive to see it."

Huemac bowed his head respectfully, aware of the terror on Cuauhcoatl's face as he glanced from the king to his grandfather, hoping to hear a denial.

"I do not suppose," Huemac said finally, "that Moteczuma wished to believe what you told him. When will the ball game be played?"

Nezahualpilli cocked his head and squinted down his long nose at Huemac.

"I forget that you are in communication with your daughter," he said with a thin smile. "I also told Moteczuma that as a further sign of what is to come, he will never again be successful in battle against his enemies, the Tlaxcalans and Huexotzincans. This, he will no doubt wish to test for himself. In the meantime, he has challenged me to a game of augury, wagering his kingdom against three turkey cocks. This will take place in three days' time. I have already sent for Chiquatli and my team."

"His men and Azcatzin's have each defeated the other once," Huemac recalled, "and both play the game I taught them. This will be a real test of the fates, my Lord."

"The gods have already spoken," Nezahualpilli said, with a certainty that was almost casual. "Do you wish to accompany me to the match?"

"I would be honored," Huemac said wryly. "I do not expect that Moteczuma will invite me."

"I will send a man for you, then. Be well, my sister," Nezahualpilli said, bowing graciously to Ome Xochitl. "And you, my son," he added, nodding to Cuauhcoatl before turning to leave, taking his retinue with him. Huemac exchanged a long, knowing glance with his mother, then jumped when his grandson's nails dug into his arm. Cuauhcoatl's eyes were brimming with tears, and his voice quavered desperately.

"He is wrong! He *must* be wrong! Tell me it is not true, Grandfather!"

Huemac stared at the boy with sympathy, feeling a familiar ache at the resemblance he bore to Taypachtli, his smooth round cheeks aflame with emotion.

"He is a wiser man than I, my son," Huemac said quietly. "I cannot deny the truth of what he tells me. I can only hope . . ."

But Cuauhcoatl would not stay to hear more. Shaking his head so vehemently that his tears flew through the air, he thrust Huemac's arm away from him and ran from the courtyard crying.

"I will bring him back," Ome Xochitl said firmly. "He is too old to be permitted such rudeness."

"Let him go, my mother," Huemac advised. "Let him find whatever consolation he can. This is not a truth that any of us wish to face, myself included. He will come back to me when he cannot avoid it any longer. Let him be a child until then, let him retain the innocence of his hopes."

THE LIGHT-WOOD trees that surrounded the Ball Court of the Lords were in full bloom, dropping their blood-red blossoms onto the heads and shoulders of the crowd that had been unable to find seats inside. These people turned and parted silently as Nezahualpilli's guards cleared a way to the entrance, with the king and his retinue close behind, staying together in a tight group. Walking beside the king, Huemac noticed the hostile faces in the crowd, though many more seemed simply anxious and fearful. He was also aware of the murmurs of recognition that greeted his own appearance, for he was well known here, his defeat of Cacalotl still a favorite story among fanciers of the game. The fact that he now chose to walk with the Texcocans was not lost on those old enough to remember the game of augury that had helped to bring Ahuitzotl to the reed seat.

Huemac had not been certain of his own motives when he had made the choice; he had accepted Nezahualpilli's offer on the basis of Papalotl's dream alone. But further reflection had convinced him that it was the correct one, however dangerous it might prove later. If there was to be any hope of defending the city, Moteczuma had to be shocked out of his arrogance, and made to realize the necessity of cooperation. Huemac could not foresee what he might gain from being associated with the events that might bring this about, but he knew, given his present status, that he had little to lose in the eyes of the Speaker.

The stands on both sides of the brightly painted court were filled to capacity, and more people lined the walls at the far ends. Yet the crowd was subdued and undemonstrative, and if wagers had been laid on this match, they were not being negotiated publicly. A canopied seat had been erected for Nezahualpilli next to the royal box, separated from Moteczuma's own seat only by a narrow, stepped aisle. After Nezahualpilli had greeted the Speaker and taken his seat, Huemac stepped forward to bow before Moteczuma, who pretended not to see him. Nahui Olin, though, who wore a bonnet of yellow parrot feathers and an orange mantle bearing the emblem of his namesake, raised his head haughtily and deliberately turned his back on Huemac.

"There are *some* men upon whom the Sun never shines," the dwarf explained scornfully, his pudgy hands wedged against his hips, his face wrinkled with exaggerated disdain. Permitting himself one of his rare smiles, Moteczuma dismissed Huemac with a curt wave of his hand. Huemac faltered as he bowed a second time, as if flustered by the dwarf's insult. In his heart, though, he applauded Nahui Olin's performance, and was pleased to have been the object of it.

Seating himself in the place that had been left vacant beside Nezahualpilli, Huemac scanned the crowd for familiar faces, again struck by the ominous silence that hung over the stands. Directly across from where he sat, he could see Chiquatli and Azcatzin in the team boxes, surrounded by their assistants and substitutes. Both had invited him to visit their teams in the training room, but Huemac had stayed away out of fairness, knowing that he could not encourage both teams with the same sincerity. He was grateful, though, that Chiquatli had retired from active play long ago, and that an ankle injury had forced Azcatzin to the sidelines the year before. At least neither of them would suffer the fate of the losing captain, though Huemac had already begun to worry about his nephew's future in this city, should the match turn out as Nezahualpilli expected.

A low murmur of anticipation swept through the spectators as the teams came out onto the court to warm up. Moteczuma's team, representing the Sun, was playing under the patronage of Huitzilopochtli, and wore blue helmets and loincloths. Nezahualpilli's team was dressed in black, in honor of their patron Tezcatlipoca, Lord of the Night Sky. The symbolism of the match was thus abundantly clear to everyone, yet Huemac could feel the presence of a third powerful god hovering over the court. He could not help but see this match —between two of his own apprentices—as the end result of the vow he had made to Xolotl so long ago. And would not the Dark Twin of Quetzalcoatl naturally work to confirm the prophecy of his master and double?

"And where are *your* hopes, my friend?" Nezahualpilli asked suddenly, breaking into Huemac's thoughts. "Does your knowledge nonetheless allow you to wish?"

Huemac heard a wistful note in the king's voice, contrasting sharply with the implacable certainty in Nezahualpilli's deep, gentle eyes.

"I do not wish against the inevitable," Huemac said flatly. "But the sooner it is recognized, the sooner we can prepare ourselves to combat its evil effects."

Nezahualpilli grunted softly and hooded his eyes, stroking his narrow chin thoughtfully.

"You honor your father's memory," he said admiringly, "as well as the responsibility created by your vision. Perhaps those are more useful motivations than hope, if no less futile. That is my only sorrow in knowing my own end: I will not witness the courage with which our people will resist their destruction."

Then both men turned their attention to the court, for the teams were ready, and the judge was crying his last instructions before throwing out the first ball. As the opening game began, Huemac put aside his thoughts concerning the outcome and tried, despite himself, to simply enjoy the spectacle of two such fine teams in action. Both played the game he had created, passing unselfishly and shifting alignments with frequency and ease, constantly altering the flow of the game as they vied for an advantage. They played beautifully, with both grace and power, exactly as Huemac had always dreamed the game could be played. Tears came to his eyes as he watched the blue and black patterns unfold on the court below, the black blur of the ball always providing the final connection. Try as he might, the irony of what he had wrought continued to overwhelm him, reminding him that this awesome display of skill could not alter the fate that had been so recently written in the night sky. There would be no winners today.

The first game was long and hotly contested, but the Tenocha team took an early advantage and then matched scores to win, five to four. When they again jumped out ahead of the Texcocans in the second game, the crowd came suddenly to life, and their wild cheering carried the Tenocha to an easy five-to-two victory. Flowers were showered down onto the blue team, and play had to be stopped while the attendants came out to clear the court, although this in no way quieted the crowd. The members of the black team were standing in a group beneath their team's box, trying to hear the instructions that Chiquatli was shouting down to them. Huemac exchanged an inquiring glance with Nezahualpilli, who appeared unperturbed by the din.

"Your *people* have not forsaken their hopes," he said dryly, looking over at Moteczuma, who sat rigid on his seat, as if afraid that any movement might break the spell. The Tenocha now needed only one game out of the remaining three to win the match, and the spectators screamed wildly as the next ball was thrown out, hoping to add to their opponents' confusion.

The Texcocans showed their courage and determination in the third game, attacking relentlessly and forcing the Tenocha into a series of careless mistakes that finally cost them the game. But the score was close, and the Tenocha seemed to have lost none of their confidence, or the backing of the crowd, as the fourth game began. They scored the first point, then lost one on an unnecessary attempt at the ring, then went out ahead again. The score was tied at two when things started to go wrong for the Tenocha.

Huemac had seen bad luck overtake good teams before, but never with such stunning completeness. Traction seemed to disappear from beneath the players' feet, and the ball suddenly became erratic and unpredictable in its bounces once it had crossed into the blue court. Trying to compensate, the Tenocha players became hesitant and overcautious, making poor use of the few opportunities they were able to set up for themselves. The encouragement of the crowd became ragged, then querulous. Sensing their sudden advantage, the Texcocans attacked with greater and greater boldness, mixing power with deception to keep their hapless opponents off balance. The game ended in total silence, with the black team ahead, five to one.

The only voice raised during the final game belonged to Azcatzin, who kept up a steady stream of encouragement and instruction to his men. But it was to no avail. Desperation had begun to work against the blue team, each man trying to perform the feat that would turn the game around, but only succeeding in placing himself or his teammates out of position. One man knocked himself unconscious against the wall and had to be replaced; another shed his rubber sandals for better traction and then slipped on his own bloody footprints. The Texcocans showed them no mercy, ignoring the ring even when they were far ahead. The Tenocha took the last shot, an errant try for the ring that flew over the place where Moteczuma sat and landed outside the court. The final score was Texcocans five, Tenocha nothing.

The stands emptied with astonishing quickness, led by an ashen-faced Moteczuma, who did not even pause to bid his guests farewell. Soon only the presiding priests and the Texcocans were left, along with the men who gathered solemnly around the bloody stone circle in the center of the court.

"I must see to the concluding ceremonies," Nezahualpilli said in a toneless voice, rising wearily from his seat. Huemac could see how little he had enjoyed his triumph.

"I will leave you, then," Huemac said. "I must go to the shrine of Xolotl, and pray for the courage to bear what we have been shown today."

"Watch behind you, as well," the king cautioned. "Moteczuma will take what revenge he can."

"I will not make it easy for him," Huemac promised. "Farewell, my Lord. May the gods protect you while you remain among us."

Nezahualpilli smiled bleakly and raised a hand over Huemac in blessing.

"I will see you before I go, my friend. If there is any luck left to us, Huemac, may it belong to you, and to all those who likewise struggle to save our people."

5

THE pillar of fire appeared over Tenochtitlan every night for a full year, then vanished as abruptly as it had come. The armies of the Tenocha and their allies had remained idle during the whole time that the omen was visible, and with its disappearance, the warchiefs began to clamor for action for their men, and the priests of the war gods called the Speaker's attention to the lack of captives for their ceremonies. So Moteczuma arranged a flower war with the Tlaxcalans and Huexotzincans, who responded eagerly to his challenge, promising to have the agreed-upon number of warriors waiting at the ceremonial field outside of Atlixco. They, too, had heard of Nezahualpilli's prophecy, and of the game of augury that had already tested it once.

Moteczuma had left Huemac alone, as well, during the time of the omen, but he came after him as soon as Xolotlpilli had marched out of the city with the warriors. It happened as Huemac was returning from Tlatelulco, where he had been visiting his old friend Cuetzpaltzin, who was bedridden with a fever contracted in the Hot Lands. Behind him, at the usual safe distance, was the man that Huemac had come to think of as his "Shadow": several different men, actually, who took turns in following him whenever he went out into the city on foot. Huemac knew them all, by feel as much as by sight, and he had made a point of losing each individual Shadow at least once, usually the first time the man was assigned to follow him. He wanted them to be aware that they existed on his sufferance, and that he could embarrass them at any time, thus exposing them to the deadly anger of Moteczuma.

This night, though, as he turned onto a dark, narrow street not far from his son's house, he sensed that there were men waiting ahead of him, too. He stopped abruptly in the middle of the street, scanning the shadows next to the houses with his night vision. One man, knife in hand, was clearly visible to him, for the man had foolishly assumed that darkness alone would conceal his presence. The foot of another man could also be seen, sticking out from behind a wall. Combining his night vision with the sharp focus of his nahualli, Huemac was also able to see the end of the assassin's rope held by the second, concealed man. He waited until he was certain that there were only these two, and that the one behind had come no closer, before he decided to call the murderers out of hiding. He could simply have changed his shape and disappeared into the air, but he preferred to leave Moteczuma a message in parting.

"Come out, my friends," he called in a loud voice. "Surely, you do not need to ambush an unarmed old man."

There was a long silence, and then the man with the knife stepped out into the open, his teeth bared in a menacing grin. His companion with the rope stayed close to the houses, but he, too, began to edge toward the place where Huemac stood. Huemac allowed the man with the knife to come almost within striking range, then gestured swiftly with his hand, attracting the man's gaze to his own and fixing him with his eyes. He had not used his full powers on a man since the day he had stopped Colotl's heart, so long ago, but he held nothing back in the face of this assassin. The knife dropped out of the man's hand before he could begin to raise it; he screamed once and fell to the ground, clawing at the sides of his head and spitting blood onto the paving stones.

The man with the rope immediately turned and ran off into the darkness, and Huemac whirled and took several quick steps toward the hiding place of the man behind him.

"Show yourself," he cried fiercely, "or I will kill you where you stand!"

Huemac had no powers to back up his threat, but the bluff brought the man out into the open, where he stood trembling, his eyes averted in terror.

"Tell Moteczuma that his assassins share his luck," Huemac snarled. "Tell him that I am beyond his reach, and that I will remain so until he comes to his senses, and remembers that I am Tenocha, too. Go now, and tell him what I have said!"

The man ran off without looking back, and Huemac went over to examine the man on the ground. He was dead. Huemac knew that he had to leave the city, and soon, before his presence brought danger to his friends, or forced him to kill again. But he had to see his mother first, and Nahui Olin would be expecting him at midnight. There was no time to travel at the pace of a man, with a man's vulnerability. His vision suddenly sharpened, and the contorted features of the corpse leaped up at him, greatly magnified, looking like a landscape of porous gray rock. Huemac smiled at his nahualli's eagerness to be freed, and he allowed the creature to expand within himself, feeling a familiar shrinking sensation begin in his muscles and bones. With the last of his human awareness, he stepped carefully away from the corpse and raised what had been his arms over his head, exploding into the air in a burst of flashing feathers . . .

SHORTLY AFTER Xolotlpilli had left for the flower war, Ome Xochitl had sat down with Chalchiuhtona and told her about Papalotl's dream, in order to prepare the young woman for the shock of seeing her husband injured. Not that Xolotlpilli had not come home bloodied many times in the past, but he had always returned on his own feet. This, from what Huemac had communicated before he also left the city, was likely to be much more serious, perhaps even crippling. Ome Xochitl could still remember the day that Acolmiztli had been brought to her on a stretcher, so she did her best to at least spare Chalchiuhtona the pain of surprise. She encouraged the younger woman to store extra water and wood, and to begin preparing bandages and medicines, knowing that being able to *do* something was the surest way to hold off hysteria.

Word was not long in coming back from Atlixco, and it was even worse than expected: The flower war had been a complete disaster for the Tenocha and their allies. The Tlaxcalans and Huexotzincans had taken command of the field from the outset, killing or capturing ten men for every loss of their own. The ranks of the warrior orders had been decimated, and one of the members of the Council of Four Lords had been killed. Moteczuma had ordered the city into mourning, and had himself gone into seclusion in the House of Darkness.

When the sound of muffled drums signaled the warriors' return, Ome Xochitl rose from her warm blankets beside the fire, ignoring the pains in her chest. Taking charge of the household, she sent Cuauhcoatl for the healers and had the servants build fires to boil water; she spoke calmingly to Chalchiuhtona, reminding her that she would have to be her husband's strength in this time of crisis.

The women were composed and waiting in the courtyard when Xolotlpilli was carried in, his enormous body hanging off the sides of the stretcher, bloody bandages covering his left hip and side. But they had barely choked back their grief at seeing him in this state when they received an additional shock: Azcatzin had also been wounded, and even more grievously than his cousin. As if he had saved the last of his strength for just this purpose, Xolotlpilli forced open his pain-reddened eyes and spoke to his grandmother in a fierce whisper:

"Azcatzin must stay here with me," he insisted with a wild and flickering determination. "Moteczuma must not be allowed another chance at him."

Ome Xochitl obeyed him without question, instructing the servants to make room for another man and sending one of them for Azcatzin's wife. But though she did not fully understand the meaning of Xolotlpilli's words, she had only to see the full extent of Azcatzin's wounds to know that neither Moteczuma nor anyone else would need another chance at him. In that instant, she herself began to die, giving in to the pain and weariness that had been with her for so long, even as she continued to struggle to save the lives of her grandsons. She had known from Huemac's overly elaborate farewell that her end was near, but now, as she surveyed the torn flesh of the men she had helped to raise, she began to welcome the blackness that would finally swallow up her grief.

When Cuauhcoatl returned with the healers, she sent him off again to summon Cocatli and Omeocelotl. Under the skilled hands of the healers, Xolotlpilli quickly regained consciousness, and though Ome Xochitl pleaded with him to conserve his strength, he insisted on telling his story, as if the memory itself was a wound that required immediate cleansing.

Huemac had warned him, he said hoarsely, that Azcatzin's life was in jeopardy because of the ball game. So he had attached himself to his cousin's company and had stayed as close to Azcatzin as possible. But he and the other Cuachic had been called into battle first, so he had not truly seen which of the commanders had betrayed Azcatzin. He only knew that when he was finally able to clear some space for himself, in order to look, he saw that Azcatzin was surrounded by Huexotzincans, and that no one was being sent to support him. He had fought his way to his cousin's side just as Azcatzin was cut down, and he had stood over his fallen friend, single-handedly holding off the Huexotzincans until his fellow Cuachic had come to his aid. He had stayed by Azcatzin's side all the way back to Tenochtitlan, allowing only those he trusted to tend to him.

When Xolotlpilli had finished his recitation, Ome Xochitl persuaded him to sleep, and she did not tell him that his heroism had been in vain. Then she went to join the circle of mourners around Azcatzin, sitting by her grandson's side for a day and a night while he slowly died. He was thirty-six years old, born in her fiftieth year, little more than a year after the death of her husband, who had been betrayed by the man *he* served. Ome Xochitl marveled at how sharp the bite of grief remained after all this time, and all the deaths she had witnessed. She had made this city her home, and become a Tenocha in her heart, but she could bear no more of the bitterness and pain that her chosen people brought on themselves.

Cuauhcoatl was the only one in the courtyard when she hobbled out of the darkened inner rooms, blinking at the harsh glare of the sun. The entire left side of her body had gone numb from sitting, and there was a painful burning beneath her ribs, which she attributed to not having eaten in almost two days. Yet her mind seemed very clear and lucid, as if in compensation, and she recognized immediately that Cuauhcoatl was suffering troubles of his own. He had been shaken by the sight of his father's wounds, but he had seemed to recover quickly enough when both she and Chalchiuhtona had assured him that Xolotlpilli would survive. What he was feeling now, she knew, was abandonment, for he had just turned ten and would enter the calmecac in two days' time. With Huemac gone and his father off fighting, there had been no one to counsel him and deliver the traditional words of admonition and encouragement concerning the ordeal he was about to undergo.

Short of breath and dizzied by the sunlight, Ome Xochitl seated herself in the shade of the palms that lined one of the reflecting pools and called her great-grandson to her. Cuauhcoatl came willingly, obviously desirous of company, but before she could begin to speak, a squadron of armed men came through the entrance and began to deploy themselves around the courtyard. They all wore the black fringed mantle of the Arrow Warriors, the warrior order that Moteczuma had recently created for the members of his personal guard. Their leader strode up to Ome Xochitl and Cuauhcoatl and explained his mission without bothering to bow:

"I have come for Huemac, with orders to arrest him. Where is he hiding?"

Reaching out a hand so that Cuauhcoatl could help her, Ome Xochitl rose laboriously to her feet. But when she looked at the guard, her dark eyes burned like coals in the deeply hollowed sockets of her withered face.

"There has been a death in this house," she said coldly, "and one of our city's greatest warriors lies wounded. Remember some respect."

Flustered by her eyes, the man bowed hastily.

"Forgive me, my Lady. But I must have Huemac; it is by the Speaker's orders."

"My son left the city several days ago," Ome Xochitl informed him in the same tone. "Moteczuma knows this, and why. You will not find him here."

"He was seen in Tlatelulco this morning," the guard said abruptly, as if to shock her into compliance. "We will have to search the house."

He gestured to his men and made a move to step past her, but Ome Xochitl blocked his path with a nimbleness that surprised both the guard and Cuauhcoatl, who quickly drew himself up next to her.

"I say that you will not disturb the mourning of this household," Ome Xochitl said harshly, steadfast in her anger. "I have been alive since the time of the first Moteczuma, and never in my memory have warriors been known to violate the sanctity of their own fallen comrades. Would *you* be the first? Kill me, then, for I shall not move."

The guard hesitated, shamefaced, as he glanced around at his men, some of whom had hung their heads at her words. Then he bowed again, and began to back out of Ome Xochitl's presence.

"Obviously, Huemac is not here," he said, his voice loud and false. "I ask you to pardon our intrusion, my Lady . . ."

Cuauhcoatl watched the guards withdraw, then turned to glance admiringly at his great-grandmother, his eyes widening with sudden concern at the gray pallor that had swept over her features. Gasping for breath, Ome Xochitl clutched his shoulder and let him guide her to the bench before she collapsed. She clung tightly to his arm, though, and kept herself upright, refusing to lay down upon the bench as he wanted.

"No," she wheezed, feeling that the air was being crushed from her body. "There is no time. My son . . . your grandfather . . . was coming back to see you . . ."

"Do not talk, Grandmother," Cuauhcoatl pleaded, but he did not let her go. Her eyes swimming with pain, Ome Xochitl struggled to look into his face, seeing the faces that were in his blood: Tezcatl, Taypachtli, Xolotlpilli, even a trace of Quinatzin.

"He wanted to bless you . . . and tell you," she managed feebly. "Prepare yourself. Be a great warrior . . . and help our people. Help *him*, Cuauhcoatl . . . trust him when he calls to you."

"I will, Grandmother," the boy promised, his lashes thick with gathering tears. "I will always remember!"

"He was coming for you," Ome Xochitl repeated, her voice sinking to a whisper as she allowed herself to be lowered onto her back. "Go now . . . bring the others . . ."

Cuauhcoatl disappeared and the pain closed in around her like a clenched fist, blackening her vision. She knew, as the life seeped out of her, that she had lied with her last breath; that Huemac had been coming to see *her*. But Cuauhcoatl would not be harmed by the deception, and perhaps he would help Huemac, and be one of the little people in his vision. It was little enough that she could do for her son, this unlucky child that she had brought into the world, that she had loved and worried over for so long. Now there was nothing more that she could do for him, nothing more upon this earth, where he would struggle on alone, until his own end came . . .

THE OLD woman came to the temple in the late afternoon, a basket of flowers in her arms, her head shrouded in a dark shawl that completed the picture of humility she presented. She was obviously a commoner, and she kept her face shyly averted as she spoke to the young woman at the entrance to the priestesses' quarters, requesting an audience with the Priestess Cocatli. She identified herself only as the wife of Tezcatl, the mirror-stone seller.

The young woman received her courteously, guiding her to a bench in the inner courtyard and encouraging her to wait. She returned a short time later with Cocatli, who shook her head quizzically, without recognition, when the old woman was pointed out to her. Cocatli was herself almost sixty, her hands gnarled and spotted with age, her face hollowed and drawn in around largely toothless gums, showing, finally, the full effects of having been born in a time of famine. But her dark oval eyes had lost none of their vitality, and she carried herself with the calm certitude of one who had found her true task. She approached the old woman on the bench respectfully, displaying a deference that paid no heed to the obvious differences in their dress and status.

The old woman rose and bowed with awkward effusiveness, seeming large and curiously graceless, as if Cocatli's stately presence had robbed her of all coordination. Cocatli helped her retrieve the flowers that had spilled from her basket, then made her sit beside her on the bench, smiling with tolerant sympathy when the woman turned her face toward the wall, hiding in her cowl.

"You wished to see me, my sister?" Cocatli inquired gently. "I once knew a man with your husband's name, but he has been dead for many years. I do not suppose that you come from Tlatelulco?"

"There, and elsewhere," the woman said in a surprisingly deep voice, and slowly turned her head away from the wall, raising her face to Cocatli's view.

"Huemac!" Cocatli breathed, and glanced quickly around the courtyard before reaching forward to grasp the blunt, calloused hands that her brother held open in his lap. His golden-brown eyes looked into hers, and, softly, they both began to weep, finally sharing their grief at the deaths of their mother and Azcatzin, grief that only the other could fully comprehend. Tears ran freely down their faces, and they clung to each other's hands tightly, unable to speak for several moments.

"Now we are the only ones left, my sister," Huemac said at last. "Forgive me for coming to you here, but I had to see you again. My son's house is closely watched, as were the funeral ceremonies."

"Did you know?" Cocatli asked tearfully. "Did you know, beforehand, that they were both to go?"

"Our mother, yes," Huemac allowed, "and even of my son's injury. But Papalotl had seen nothing concerning Azcatzin. Perhaps it was not in his fate to die, until Moteczuma intervened. I am sorry, my sister; it was *I* who taught him to be a ball player."

"You did so out of kindness, and it brought great joy into his life," Cocatli said staunchly, and paused to dry her eyes on the edge of her sleeve. "But what are *you* going to do, Huemac? It saddens me to see you like this, a fugitive in your own city."

Huemac sighed heavily, a flash of stubborn anger briefly lighting the resignation in his eyes.

"I thought that the time had come to return and reestablish myself here, and help prepare for what is coming," he said bitterly. "But Moteczuma learns slowly, and I remain a danger to those who shelter me and provide me with disguises. I do not wish to see your other son or Pinotl marked for death on my account."

"Omeocelotl is clever, and he can defend himself," Cocatli said bravely. "You have earned your place in this city."

"Still, I can do no good here now. I have decided to return to the hills for a while, and give Moteczuma time to dwell upon the omens, and exhaust his viciousness upon others. I had hoped to see Patecatl, as well, before I left."

"He is very ill," Cocatli informed him in a low voice. "I do not think that there is much time left to him."

Huemac sighed again and let his shoulders slump. He plucked idly at the flowers in the basket beside him and did not speak for a long time.

"My friends leave me too soon," he said tonelessly. "Cuetzpaltzin is also failing, and Nezahualpilli waits calmly for the end he has already seen. Perhaps, though, they are the lucky ones."

Cocatli frowned instinctively and took his hand to make him look at her.

"Surely, my brother," she insisted, "you do not share Moteczuma's dread at the sight of these omens? They signal the return of our Lord, Quetzalcoatl, just as he prophesied so long ago. Surely you trust the interpretation that has been placed on Papalotl's experiences?"

"My daughter's dreams have grown in significance," Huemac admitted, "but she has only just begun to perceive the larger fate of our people. I have told you before that I have had experiences of my own, and that they do not lead me to trust your god as you do. And Nezahualpilli, for one, does not share

Papalotl's certainty concerning the source of these omens. His choice of a patron for his ball team reminded me that it was Tezcatlipoca who drove the Plumed Serpent from this land. Perhaps the Lord of the Smoking Mirror plays tricks with us, and mocks our hopes."

"Nezahualpilli is a man of great wisdom," Cocatli said respectfully. "But Papalotl saw the pillar of fire long before it was visible to anyone else, including the king. She is revered in the Holy City, and people come from great distances to consult with her, and bask in her presence. I cannot question the holiness of what she is shown."

"I will not argue with you, my sister," Huemac said quietly. "I would prefer to believe as you do, but there is too much that prevents me. Perhaps things will be clearer, by the time I return."

"When will that be?"

"When I can be of some real use. I will come when the signs are right, whether it is safe or not. Until then, my sister, I commend my family to your care."

"I will watch over them in my prayers," Cocatli assured him. "Come back to us soon, my brother."

Huemac nodded and squeezed her hand in farewell. Then he gestured to the basket of flowers on the bench beside them.

"Perhaps you will take these to the shrine for me, as my offering to Quetzalcoatl. I must live with my doubts, but they have not robbed me of respect."

"I will be honored," Cocatli said, and picked up the basket as she rose to her feet. Arranging the shawl around his face, Huemac also rose and accompanied her to the entrance, his back again bent and his footsteps slow and hobbled. Cocatli blessed him solemnly in parting.

"Farewell, wife of Tezcatl," she said, for the benefit of the young woman minding the gate. "May the gods show you their favor, and resolve your doubts. May the wisdom of Quetzalcoatl guide you always."

THE BROAD, marshy lagoon of Xicalanco lay soaking in the orange glare of the setting sun, its many islands and sand-spits casting long shadows toward the east. A slight breeze blew from that direction, bringing no coolness, but bearing the salty smell and the low tidal rumble of the Divine Waters, which beat against the reef at the eastern mouth of the lagoon. Omeocelotl sat alone in one of the waterfront houses owned by the vanguard merchants, sweating in the oppressive afternoon heat, which had brought canoe traffic to a standstill and had silenced the birds and monkeys in the nearby trees. No one moved along the docks, where a lone pelican sat atop a piling, its long-billed head tucked wearily beneath its wing.

The house where Omeocelotl sat was a raised platform covered by a thatched roof, its sides open except for gauzy curtains of insect netting. It belonged to him by virtue of his rank, which was now that of Pochteca Tlatoque, Merchant Chief. The other members of the expedition he had brought to Xicalanco lay sleeping in their hammocks in the men's quarters, waiting for the end of the day, and for their leader to give the order to depart for home. The goods they had collected were all packed and tied to their carrying frames, and they had already said their farewells to their friends and relatives in Xicalanco, expecting the order to be given before this. Omeocelotl understood their restlessness, for their business here had been completed several days ago, and they had been away from Tlatelulco for over two years. But he was also determined, despite the entreaties of his lieutenants, that he would not leave for home without Pinotl.

He had last seen his friend in the mountain city of Zinacantlan, the Place of Bats, where the two of them had gone to reconnoiter for Moteczuma, disguised as Chontal traders. After scouting the defenses of the city, Omeocelotl had led the rest of the party back to Xicalanco, drawing careful maps of the route that the army should take through the lands of the Chontals and the Zoques. Pinotl had gone on, alone, to explore the trade routes to the south and west of Zinacantlan, promising to return in eight months' time. Certainly, of all the vanguard merchants, Pinotl was the only one capable of going so far —and staying so long among the suspicious Zinacantecos—without being detected. But he was already almost ten days overdue, and no messages had been sent ahead.

The sun sank lower in the sky, and the moist tropical air lay like a fever upon Omeocelotl's skin. He knew that he would have more than just the delay, and his men's impatience, to answer for, if Pinotl did not return. The Council of Principal Merchants had authorized the exploration to Zinacantlan only to humor Moteczuma, for they saw no wisdom in venturing into unconquered territory when Mexico's control was slipping in so many other areas. They would have preferred that Moteczuma concentrate his energies on subduing the rebellions that had broken out as a result of the omens and prophecies of doom, rebellions that had effectively closed the western trade corridor from Tehuantepec to Xoconochco. Thus, they would take even less pleasure in an effort to penetrate *beyond* Zinacantlan, and they would hold Omeocelotl responsible if a man as valuable as Pinotl were lost in the course of an unauthorized and highly risky venture. They might even interpret the ambitiousness of Omeocelotl's scheme as a reassertion of his Tenocha blood, and refuse to trust him in the future.

Omeocelotl was certain in his own heart that he served the interests of his guild, but he could not deny that his motive for exceeding his authority was personal, and that his knowledge of the Tenocha mentality had led him to devise a particularly audacious plan. The instinct of the merchants, in times of danger and unrest, was to withdraw and regroup, and then proceed cautiously. They did not understand why Moteczuma, plagued by rebellion and disarray within the lands he already controlled, would wish to undertake a new conquest so far from the center of his power. But Omeocelotl understood only too well; he knew that Moteczuma, in true Tenocha fashion, would rather have a noteworthy triumph to celebrate than a thousand treaties insuring safe travel and peaceful relations. The prophecies of doom, the rebellions in the west, even the continued defiance of the Tlaxcalans: all would be made easier to bear, and to disguise, by a new addition to the list of conquests, with all its attendant fanfare and self-congratulation. The appearance of success, Omeocelotl knew, was in itself a powerful means of control and persuasion.

But then a moving shape out on the lagoon caught Omeocelotl's attention, and brought his ruminations to an abrupt end. He rose hopefully to his feet and pushed the mesh curtain aside, shading his eyes against the harsh glare reflecting off the water. The shape disappeared momentarily behind a low hummock of mangrove and cane, then reappeared into the light, clearly distinguishable as a canoe with only a single passenger. Omeocelotl squinted, straining to make out the markings on the high bow of the canoe. It was Pinotl. At last.

Omeocelotl met him at the dock, kneeling to hold the canoe fast against the pilings. Pinotl sat with his paddle across his lap, rocking gently in the water, too exhausted to move. His hair was tied up in the tasseled, forward-curving knot favored by the Mayans, and the end of his long, hooked nose was blistered and peeling from exposure to the sun. Sweat had drawn broad streaks through the noxious black ointment that coated his wiry body, revealing the many tiny wounds inflicted upon him by insects and jungle thorns. Omeocelotl stared at him with open relief, only now feeling the full force of the anxiety he had suffered on his friend's behalf. He realized, for the first time since Azcatzin's death, how much he had come to look upon Pinotl as a younger brother.

"I am glad to see you, my friend," he said, trying to restrain the effusiveness of his emotions. "How far beyond Zinacantlan were you able to go?"

"All the way to Xoconochco," Pinotl croaked, his lips and throat parched with thirst. He gestured wearily toward the copper ax heads and cheap shells piled into the bottom of the canoe with his weapons and staff. "That is my payment. I was a bearer for a Zoque merchant trading out of Zinacantlan."

"We will receive better payment from Moteczuma," Omeocelotl assured him, and extended a hand. "Come, let me help you to the guild house . . ."

While Pinotl was bathing and eating, Omeocelotl went to tell the rest of his men that they would be leaving in the morning. Then he sent for cocoa and yetl and arranged his paints, brushes, and sheets of treated leather, giving orders that he and Pinotl were not to be disturbed. Once his friend had refreshed himself, they sat down together beneath a smoking torch, and Omeocelotl began to draw maps of the trade route from Zinacantlan to Xoconochco, which Pinotl had committed to memory. They worked steadily, without extraneous comment, though both were aware of the enormous value of Pinotl's accomplishment. Now they could prove to Moteczuma that in addition to seizing the riches of Zinacantlan, he would also be opening a route by which the tribute owed to the Tenocha could again flow from Xoconochco.

Formerly, the tribute deriving from the last of Ahuitzotl's conquests had gone north along the coast to Tehuantepec, and then north and east to Oaxaca and Tochtepec. But the arrival of the omens, and the subsequent rebellion of the Tehuantepeca, had closed this route to Moteczuma's tribute gatherers. The path that Pinotl had charted was separated from this hostile territory by a range of high mountains, and it was entirely controlled by the Zinacantecos, or by whoever might come to conquer the Zinacantecos.

"Moteczuma will be more than grateful," Omeocelotl said when they had finished, and the maps were lying flat before them, sprinkled with mirror-stone dust to help the paint harden. "He is too distracted to muster a campaign to Tehuantepec, but he has long been interested in opening a way to Zinacantlan. We can offer him the means to solve two of his problems at once. You have performed a great feat, my friend, perhaps the greatest of any vanguard merchant."

Pinotl nodded sanguinely, his eyes hooded against the glow of Omeocelotl's praise.

"We of the vanguard are not interested in greatness," he said in his flat nasal voice, still sounding slightly like a Zoque. "Can we trade this information for Huemac's pardon?"

"We will have to offer it freely to the Speaker, as the merchants always do," Omeocelotl said. "But I have sufficient rank now to make sure that proper credit will accrue to the two of us. With Xolotlpilli lending his prestige to our cause, Moteczuma will have to listen. His need for a success must outweigh his hatred for Huemac by now."

"What about the Council, and the head of our own guild? They will see how we have put ourselves forward."

"Let them blame it on my Tenocha blood, then," Omeocelotl decided. "Huemac is *my* uncle, and you have only to say that you were following my orders, if you are criticized. But I would like you to have the credit you deserve, if you will take it."

Pinotl took a sip of cocoa and looked out into the night, which vibrated with the sounds of thousands of restless insects. Omeocelotl could see his friend's natural modesty fighting against the spirit of boldness that had impelled Pinotl to lend himself to this scheme so readily, and which had no doubt sustained him throughout his explorations. It was a spirit that had only a little to do with Huemac, though both men had agreed at the outset that the time of testing was clearly at hand, and that Huemac should not be kept away from Tenochtitlan any longer. But Pinotl did not carry the debt of past favors that Omeocelotl felt he owed to his uncle; Pinotl had, in fact, done many favors *for* Huemac. His enthusiasm for this venture came from a different source.

Omeocelotl remembered the courtyard beside the great temple in Cholula, where Quetzal Papalotl had received them two years earlier, when they were on their way to Xicalanco. The courtyard had been crowded with priests, and pilgrims, and foreign lords who had brought their families to be blessed by the priestess. Yet Papalotl had singled them out in the crowd, and had left the lords and priests waiting while she took them to an inner chamber for a private interview. That is when he had first seen the spirit arise in Pinotl, though not as boldness. He was as respectful toward Papalotl as any pilgrim, yet he sat straighter than usual, and did not hood his eyes or speak in his customary shy murmur. It was a subtle change, but enormous in its implications for someone who knew Pinotl as well as Omeocelotl thought he did. Never before had he seen Pinotl display his sense of self-worth as clearly as he had that day in Papalotl's presence.

"I will take my share of both credit *and* blame," Pinotl said at last, his expression still reluctant. "It was Huemac who suggested that I sometimes disguise myself too well. If we are criticized by the Council members, it is *I* who should remind them of the things that Huemac has done for all of us in the past."

Omeocelotl nodded, eying his friend with new respect. Unobtrusiveness was a definite advantage to a vanguard merchant, but he had always felt that Pinotl's diffidence ran so deep that it handicapped him as a man. To see him show this spirit made Omeocelotl feel that perhaps they *both* shared some of the conquering impulse of the Tenocha, and made him even prouder to claim Pinotl as a brother.

As if aware of his friend's admiration, Pinotl took a last hasty sip of cocoa and rose from his mat.

"We must go far tomorrow. I will sleep now," he said simply, and went toward the back of the room, where a hammock had been strung for him. Omeocelotl stayed behind, carefully rolling up the maps one by one, wondering what it was like to love someone so much, someone who was untouchable in her holiness, who could be served but never loved in the way that was natural to men and women. Still, Pinotl was too much a merchant to strike a bargain that brought him no return, and it was obvious that Papalotl's friendship gave him a confidence and sense of self-esteem that no one else, not even his wife, could provide. Certainly that was a gift worth the pain of physical distance.

Gathering the maps together in his lap, Omeocelotl bound them with a piece of twine and rose to his feet. He mused briefly on the possibility that it had been Quetzalcoatl himself, acting through his priestess, who was responsible for the success of this enterprise. It was more than just skill that had guided Pinotl safely to Xoconochco and back. But whoever was to be thanked, the rest of the plan was now in Omeocelotl's hands. As he extinguished the torch and walked toward his hammock in the darkness, he began to rehearse the words he would say to the Council, and to Moteczuma, when he finally returned to the islands of Mexico.

<h1 style="text-align:center">᠍᠍ 6 </h1>

AWAKENING in the night, Huemac left Chimalman's side and went out to relieve himself in the high grass behind the circled huts of the village. The air was clear and crisp, and he stood for a long time in the quiet darkness, staring upward at the stars. They seemed familiar and reassuring, untroubled in their movements. Looking at them, it was almost impossible to imagine the sky as it had been, transfigured by omens never before seen in Anahuac. Two years after the pillar of fire had appeared, a great comet had swept across the heavens while it was still daytime, showering the earth with fiery sparks before breaking into three parts and falling beyond the eastern horizon. Some among the Chichimecs—reasonably, to Huemac's mind—had expected to see the stars jarred into new positions afterward, and even though the sky looked the same, they did not trust it as they used to.

It was the year Ten-Reed, Huemac's sixtieth upon the earth, and except for periodic visits to Texcoco and Cholula, he had spent the last four years in the hills. In recent months, he had even stopped going to Texcoco, for the news of Tenochtitlan had taken on a depressing familiarity. There had been a series of other omens: mysterious, unextinguishable fires in the shrines of Huitzilopochtli and Xiuhtecuhtli, a boiling upheaval in the Lake on a windless day, reports of cowled women who roamed the streets of Tenochtitlan at night, crying that the end was coming. All these had been predicted in advance, by

Papalotl among others, but Moteczuma continued to equivocate, vacillating between terror-stricken passivity and ruthless acts of assertion. He had his agents scour the countryside for those who had had visions or witnessed omens, only to then deny the validity of the stories he was told, and to kill those who had had the bad judgment to tell him the truth. Others besides Huemac had gone into hiding, among them many of the most capable and trustworthy of the soothsayers and wise men. Moteczuma had surrounded himself with those who were left, allowing himself to be deceived by their lies and self-serving assurances, while doing nothing to prepare his people for the trials ahead.

Huemac had not expected to remain in the hills this long, but there was a part of him that did not wish to go back to the city at all. He missed his family and friends, those who were still alive, but Chimalman had not lost her ability to soothe that particular ache, and he had had the chance to watch his son Tepeyollotl rise to a place of prominence beside the chief. Instead of creeping about in disguise and fending off assassins, he had spent fruitful days with Xiuhcozcatl and the other sorcerers in the village, refining his powers and developing his relationship with his nahualli. He had adapted his nerves and muscles to the timeless rhythms of this land, and he was as contented here as the knowledge of his real fate would allow.

The time of reckoning was approaching, though, and he did not know how much longer he could wait for a summons or a sign. The year prophesied for Quetzalcoatl's return—One-Reed—was only four years off, and Papalotl, for one, was certain that those who were coming would arrive in that year. Soon, perhaps, Huemac thought, it would be too late to try to influence Moteczuma, if such a thing were indeed possible at *any* time. My friends will have disappeared or forgotten me, he thought wearily, and I will have only my own powers to put in the way of fate.

Shaking his head, he started back toward Chimalman's hut, but he stopped abruptly when he felt his nahualli break into a sustained fluttering inside him. He recognized the signal instantly, and knew that another nahualli was near. But he could tell, by his own nahualli's alertness, that this was not a familiar spirit-animal, not one of the nahuallis that belonged to the other sorcerers in the village. But how had it gotten so close to the huts without alerting the others? Unless, of course, it was *allowed* to come to him . . .

There was a rustling in the grass, and then a coyote stepped onto the path and sat down on its haunches, not more than ten feet from where Huemac stood. Its mottled fur had a silvery tinge, and its yellow eyes glowed balefully from behind the pointed muzzle. Yet Huemac felt no menace emanating from its presence, and he noticed that his own nahualli had subsided into a watchful calm. Huemac stared back at the animal, nagged by a familiarity that eluded him, until the coyote turned its elongated head sideways, its teeth glinting eerily in what almost seemed to be a smile. Then Huemac remembered the meeting room in Tenochtitlan, where his grandfather had spied him out in the darkness as he crept around the circle of old men. That was the first time that this nahualli had been shown to him. The second had come during his last visit with Nezahualcoyotl, when the dying king had revealed to him the shapes of his life and death.

It is Nezahualpilli who calls to me, Huemac realized, and saw the coyote's pointed ears twitch, as if the thought had been spoken aloud. The animal stared for a moment longer, then turned and trotted down the path, leaving a trail of silver paw-prints that evaporated in its wake. Huemac followed at a distance, seeing the coyote turn again, down the trail that led off into the desert to the south and west, toward Texcoco. It paused once, looking back at him over its shoulder, then broke into a loping run and disappeared into the night.

Huemac knew that he had been given his sign. Did he dare to hope that it meant the end of his exile? Did he truly wish for such a thing, since it would mean that his final struggle had begun? But he had learned, in his sixty years, the uselessness of hopes and wishes; he did not need them to know when to follow the signs of his fate. Shrugging obediently, he started back toward the hut, to tell Chimalman that he would be leaving in the morning for Texcoco . . .

NEZAHUALPILLI had left orders in Texcoco that Huemac should be brought to him at the royal gardens at Texcotzinco, where Nezahualcoyotl had gone to die. The king was seated, half reclining on a fur-covered bench, in the arbored plaza at the very top of the hill. He was attended only by the Lady of Tula, who greeted Huemac fondly and brought him forward to sit on a bench opposite the king's. Nezahualpilli was only fifty years old, but his hair had gone completely white, and the skin on his long, narrow face seemed cracked and fragile, like old bark paper. He rested his bright, gentle eyes on Huemac for a long moment, a dreamy, nostalgic smile playing around his lips.

"So, my friend," he said in a musing voice. "It does not seem so long ago that I found you in the courtyard below, entertaining the children with your voices."

"This life passes quickly," Huemac agreed, his eyes on Nezahualpilli's face. "More quickly for some than for others. I am glad that you summoned me, my Lord."

"I wished to see you for one last time. Your friendship has meant a great deal to me in my time on this earth. Is there anything more that you wish to know about what is to come? I have *seen* the invaders . . ."

Huemac looked at him sharply, his interest in such things still a reflex, despite all his time in the hills. Nezahualpilli's eyes were hooded, seemingly amused, though the offer had been serious. It cannot be *good* news he has to tell me, Huemac decided, and smiled ruefully at the blind courage of his own desire to know.

"Will they be gods or men?" he asked, and Nezahualpilli nodded with satisfaction, as if pleased by Huemac's predictability.

"They will be men," he said succinctly. "But they will prove as irresistible as the gods. How many times have the years been bound since the fall of Tula? Yet the prophecy of Quetzalcoatl-Topiltzin has not been forgotten; we remain here not as his heirs, but as invaders ourselves, usurpers of his kingdom. He once offered us deliverance from the cult of sacrifice, and we scorned him for his kindness. Yet the people yearn for his return, even now."

"Perhaps, though," Huemac suggested, "they will not accept the men who come in his place. Perhaps they will fight instead."

"Perhaps," the king allowed easily. "I know, at least, that *you* will. I would not count on many others."

"Including your sons? I know that you have named no heir. I could not help but hear this, for it is being discussed everywhere in the city."

Nezahualpilli gave him a knowing smile.

"Your first influence on me, Huemac, was to persuade me to set free my father's birds. Do you wonder, now, that I would free my people to choose their own ruler?"

"Yes," Huemac said flatly. "Because you know as well as I that Moteczuma will be the one to choose, if you do not."

"He will, in any case. Do you remember when you described Ahuitzotl to me as a caged beast? Now it is Moteczuma who is trapped, and I would not have all my people perish with him. If we are united under one ruler, we will fall with him, or cause him to come against us. I have three sons who are in line to rule. Let Moteczuma choose his favorite; the other two will know their peril, and they will keep their independence, as my father did. They will remember, as you once made me remember, that our safety lies in the hills and mountains."

Nezahualpilli reached into the folds of the furs beneath him and produced the broken shaft of an arrow, which he handed ceremoniously to Huemac.

"I will not need this symbol of error any longer," he said. "I have used it many times, to remind myself of the true duty of a just ruler. Perhaps you will find someone to whom it would be useful, someone who can still accept the task of protecting the people."

"I know the very person," Huemac said gratefully, handling the arrow with care, like a talisman. The king raised a thin, bony hand over him in blessing.

"Farewell, then, Huemac. I can do no more for you. Your son awaits you below. Go to him; the future is now yours."

Huemac bowed and touched dirt to his tongue. Then he stood staring at the king, his eyes glittering with emotion, reluctant to leave this man, who was one of the last links to so much of his past. Finally, he bowed again, dropping tears onto the arrow in his hands.

"Farewell, Lord Nezahualpilli. May your name always be honored in this land, where you ruled so wisely."

Then Huemac bowed to the Lady of Tula and backed out of the king's presence, and went down to meet his future.

XOLOTLPILLI was not hard to find in the crowded courtyard below. His shaven head stood out over the heads of those around him like a glistening red beacon, and though other people were standing shoulder-to-shoulder, a respectful space had been left vacant around the giant warrior, the Monster of Mexico. Xolotlpilli was thirty-four years old, a truly venerable age for a Cuachic, though he had only a slight limp to show for his years of battle. His powerful jaw had hardened and his cheeks had lost some of their roundness, making him look, except for his flattened nose, like the very image of Tezcatl. He greeted Huemac enthusiastically, smiling with such joyful abandon that he drew disapproving glances from the crowd, many of whom had already begun their mourning for the king. Huemac discreetly led him away, down the paved path that led around the hill to the aqueduct.

"There is more white in your hair, my father," Xolotlpilli said lightly. "But otherwise, you seem no older."

"I am older," Huemac assured him gruffly, flexing the arm that Xolotlpilli had squeezed. "And you are still strong. What has brought you to Texcoco, my son?"

"I am on my way to Huexotzinco. They have broken with the Tlaxcalans and placed themselves under our protection." Xolotlpilli paused and shrugged, showing his father that he regarded the situation with some skepticism. Then he widened his big brown eyes and smiled the brilliant, heart-winning smile he had inherited from his mother and Tezcatl. "I have also come to tell you that you may return to Tenochtitlan."

They had come to the plaza beside the great wall of the aqueduct, which snaked off into the distance over the dun-colored hills, its precious burden of water a silver streak along its back. Huemac put his hands on his hips and exhaled forcefully.

"Moteczuma has decided this?"

"He was persuaded," Xolotlpilli said, with a relish that came close to boastfulness. Seeing his father's raised eyebrows, he quickly went on in a more humble tone: "Though mostly by Omeocelotl and Pinotl. It was they who scouted the way to Zinacantlan and showed Moteczuma its value. I only helped to conquer it. We made our appeal to Moteczuma together, and he has granted you a full pardon for the crimes he felt you had committed."

"That is very generous of him," Huemac said dryly. "But I am grateful to you, my son, and to my nephew and Pinotl. You have done an old man a great favor."

"We feel that we serve our people in bringing you back," Xolotlpilli said, gazing at his father proudly. "The breakdown of loyalty and trust of which you warned us is happening everywhere, though especially in Tenochtitlan. The burden of maintaining the truth has become very heavy, and we did not wish to conduct our meetings without you any longer."

"You have made me very proud," Huemac murmured, returning his son's gaze with such affectionate force that Xolotlpilli smiled bashfully and lowered his eyes. "Have you admitted any others to the group?"

"A few of my friends sit with us occasionally, as well as Chiquatli when he is in the city with his team. But we still have not filled Azcatzin's place."

"What about your son?" Huemac asked. "He must have graduated from the calmecac by now."

Xolotlpilli hesitated, looking out over the hills for a moment before meeting Huemac's eyes.

"Cuauhcoatl is in the Young Men's House. He is only fourteen, but he is large for his age, and he has already been named a Leader of Youths. He has apprenticed himself to a member of the Eagles, and will probably be coming to Huexotzinco soon himself."

"You have not answered my question," Huemac pointed out shrewdly. "Perhaps you are no better at telling your secrets to your son than I was."

Xolotlpilli shrugged ruefully, spreading his huge hands in appeal.

"He entered the priests' school while I was still injured, and he did very well there. His mind is quick and he is popular with the other young men; already, he carries himself like a lord. His future seems bright to him, despite the omens, and I could not bring myself to darken his attitude with the truth. I know that I am wrong to spare him, but . . ."

Huemac laid an understanding hand on his son's shoulder.

"There is still time for him to enjoy his innocence and youth," he said softly. "We will all know when that time is past. Tell me, has there been any change in Moteczuma's court?"

"It is very different," Xolotlpilli said emphatically. "He keeps some of the lords around him at all times, as witnesses. People have come before him and told him, or shown him, truly remarkable things. But often they have vanished before a second interrogation was possible, even though they were imprisoned and kept under guard. It is not as open as the court of Ahuitzotl, but it is somewhat better than it was."

"And the Speaker's dwarf? The one who fancies himself the Sun?"

"He is still the favorite, I am afraid," Xolotlpilli said with distaste, "and more adept than ever at humiliating visitors. He is Moteczuma's pride in all its worst aspects."

Huemac nodded thoughtfully, but made no comment. He gestured that they should go back the way they had come.

"Come, let us go find Chiquatli, and make him feed us. Then my business in this city will be completed."

"I have told my wife to prepare your room for you," Xolotlpilli said, as they followed the path back around the hill. "And I have notified my aunt, the Priestess Cocatli, of your return."

"I am grateful," Huemac said, and held up the broken arrow that he had carried all this time without explanation. Nor did he attempt to explain it now, contemplating the arrow with an intentness that avoided Xolotlpilli's questioning gaze.

"You must send them a message," he said absently, his attention still fixed on the arrow. "You must tell them that I will be delayed for a few days. I must take this to its rightful owner, and say farewell to another piece of my past . . ."

HUEMAC HAD already been overtaken by nostalgia before he reached the village, thinking of the desert and the hills through which he passed as his second home, and the land of his ancestors. He anticipated solemn speeches and a last, fond sharing of memories with the friends he had made here, once he had revealed to them that he was leaving them forever. In an uncharacteristic gesture, he saluted the sentries he passed as he climbed the trail to the canyon, receiving only curious stares and curt nods of recognition in reply, as if they found nothing particularly special about his coming back to them, as he had done so many times before.

The village, though, was in a state of intense activity, the people bustling about in a celebratory mood, making preparations for a feast. Huemac wandered through their midst with a puzzled smile on his face, not wishing to admit his ignorance of the occasion for this celebration, since he had thought that his knowledge of tribal custom was complete by now. But he could tell nothing from the kinds of foods and decorations being prepared, and the snatches of conversation he overheard seemed vague and empty of ceremonial references. When he finally brought himself to ask a group of women, they simply laughed and chattered to one another in Otomi, too rapidly for him to understand.

Huemac wondered if something had happened in the short time he was away, or if this was one of those feasts that was only celebrated at great intervals, so that he had missed it in the past. His ignorance made him suddenly feel like an outsider, a sensation he found painful to endure in his present state of mind. He did not think he deserved to feel like a stranger just as he was leaving.

He found Tepeyollotl with some of his lodge brothers, cutting up the carcass of a deer outside their meeting house. They looked up at Huemac with blank expressions on their faces, doing nothing to ease the embarrassment that came over him as he asked his son the reason for this feast. Tepeyollotl hesitated for a long moment, as if sharing his father's shame, and his friends politely averted their eyes in the silence.

"You truly do not know?" Tepeyollotl asked reluctantly, as if to give Huemac one last chance to redeem himself.

"I would not ask you if I knew," Huemac snapped, and Tepeyollotl raised his palms in apology. Then, glancing around at his friends, he leaned forward and spoke in a significant whisper:

"The Owl Boy is leaving us."

Huemac blinked uncomprehendingly, and saw a smile creep onto his son's face, and onto the faces around him, as well. Then they all burst into laughter and slapped one another on the shoulder as the joke penetrated and Huemac understood that they had been teasing him. This feast was for *him,* in honor of his leaving.

"Your mother knew?" he managed weakly, as the young men crowded around him and Tepeyollotl, eager to show the good feelings behind their jest.

"And the Old One," Tepeyollotl confirmed. "They sent us out for meat as soon as you left for Texcoco. But we have always known that you would leave us for good, one day."

"Of course," Huemac murmured dazedly, overwhelmed by the joy in the faces around him, and by the utter lack of regret in his son's voice. There would be no solemn speeches, he realized, no sadness at his parting, which had been determined long ago, when Oztooa bore the title of the Old One. "If you go through this life grieving," Huemac recalled, "it will be over in an instant."

"Let the feast begin, then," he said, with a heartiness that brought cries of approval from the crowd that had gathered around him. "I have not left you yet!"

THE SINGING and dancing went on long into the night, and great quantities of venison and octli were consumed by the revelers. Huemac sat between Chimalman and Xiuhcozcatl, shouting his compliments to the dancers and greeting the many people who came to say a personal farewell and give him gifts, which would all be left with Tepeyollotl to distribute to the needy of the village. A white-haired old man with whom Huemac had exchanged confidences brought three of his grandsons up with him.

"He is a man who came here to find his fate," the old man explained to the boys, who examined Huemac with timid respect. "Now he is going back to his city to die."

The boys all bowed deeply, and Huemac accepted their deference, and their grandfather's blunt statement, with gratitude and pride, understanding that he was being complimented.

"My people admire constancy above all else," Xiuhcozcatl had told him earlier, smiling at Huemac's bemused response to this celebration. "You were not the first student I brought here. One even married one of our women and took her away with him. But you are the only one who chose to mingle his fate with ours, and who let us see the further stages of your growth. You have gone away from us many times, to places and tasks that most of my people cannot even imagine. Yet you have always returned, seeking another piece of the knowledge you need to confront your fate. In our eyes, you have never moved off the path that first brought you here, and that now takes you to your end. You have shown us the shape of your life, and it is solid and whole, a source of satisfaction, not sorrow."

Tepeyollotl came up and squatted before his father, his face flushed and sweating from the dancing. He indicated the brightly painted people moving around the fire behind him.

"They ask that you and my mother join them," he explained breathlessly. "It is a couples' dance."

Huemac turned to Chimalman, who nodded agreeably, puckering her lips in wry anticipation, since she had always found Huemac's dancing eccentric and amusing.

"We will do so gladly," Huemac said. "But first, there is something I must give you."

He unrolled the broken arrow from the bundle beside him and passed it over to Tepeyollotl, who squinted at it closely, examining its markings in the flickering light from the fire. Huemac was aware of the sudden attentiveness of both Chimalman and the chief, but he spoke only to his son:

"Before you were even born, I took that arrow to Nezahualpilli, to shame him for attacks he had made on your people. He has kept it all this time, as a reminder of the temptations of power, and of the obligations of a just ruler. Nor has he come against the hill-people while it has been in his possession. I pass it on to you with a single request: that you look with kindness on those who will come to you for protection in the years ahead. They will be at your mercy, but you must show them the greatness of your heart. You must forget your past differences, and join together to fight against the invaders."

Tepeyollotl seemed frozen in place, his head bent over the arrow in his hands. Huemac slowly turned his head to face Xiuhcozcatl, feeling his nahualli stir uneasily within him as the chief tapped his talon-stick against his palm. Xiuhcozcatl's deep-set eyes glittered sardonically as he studied Huemac's face.

"Even in leaving," he said with mock exasperation, "you must do something to surprise and goad me. Is it the octli, or just your incorrigible impulsiveness that makes you think you have the right to select your son as my successor?"

"The tribe will select him, when the time comes," Huemac said calmly. "They have seen the way he has prepared himself for the task. I only give him the arrow in recognition of what is apparent to everyone."

Xiuhcozcatl grunted scornfully and looked at Tepeyollotl, who was regarding him with guarded optimism.

"Your father is ambitious for you, my son; he speaks for your candidacy before the position is even available. It is a good thing for you that you have not inherited his rashness. It is the only thing that might have disqualified you. As it is, my choice will not be a difficult one." Xiuhcozcatl gestured toward the arrow with his talon-stick. "That is a fit symbol of what is to come, and of the choices that will be presented to you. Invest it with your own power, and wield it carefully."

Tepeyollotl bowed with an earnestness that approached reverence. Then he pressed the arrow against his chest and looked at Huemac with glowing eyes.

"Thank you, my father. I promise . . ."

"No more speeches," Xiuhcozcatl broke in gruffly, and waved his stick at Huemac and Chimalman. "Dance now, you two, and let us all remember the joyousness of this occasion."

WHEN THE feasting was over, and all the farewells had been said, Huemac and Chimalman went up into the mountains to be alone. They had not discussed the date of his departure with any exactness, but both felt that they would know when it was time. They hunted together and climbed to the highest lookouts, gazing out over the expanse of pine forest to the hills and desert beyond, able, from this height, to imagine themselves the only people upon the earth. They bathed in the icy pool beside the sweathouse at sunset, and they woke at first light and lay together in silence, listening to the songs of the birds outside their hut. Only the urgency of their love-making reflected their awareness that days, and not years, were all that was left to them.

Finally, one afternoon, they found themselves on the promontory where they had once sat with Xiuhcozcatl, shortly after Huemac had come back to the hills for the first time. Huemac knew that she had not brought him here by accident, so he settled himself with his back against the rough bark of the twisted pine tree and waited for her to speak. Chimalman stood staring down into the gorge below for a long time, then came over and squatted purposefully before him.

"I have always known that you would leave me," she said bluntly, her eyes narrowed against any display of emotion. "I have accepted that from the beginning. But twice more, since I have known you, I have had the dream of a man coming to me out of the desert. Even though it was a younger man, I thought that he was you, for he wore the jade rabbit around his neck. But then, when I heard you speak to Tepeyollotl at the feast, I began to question these dreams more closely."

"What did I say to cause this reconsideration?" Huemac asked curiously, and Chimalman leaned forward slightly, betraying an eagerness that did not show in her face.

"You spoke of those who would come here for protection in the years ahead. You seemed to be speaking only of the Texcocans, as if you did not have people of your own. As if you had not considered the members of your own family."

"*My* family!" Huemac exclaimed, and opened his mouth to frame a protest. Then he stopped himself. "What did the young man in your dream look like?"

"I did not clearly see his face," Chimalman admitted, "but he was larger than you, and dressed in city clothes. In one of the dreams, he was accompanied by a young girl, whom I took to be Papalotl. Now I have begun to think that she was his sister."

"Xiuhcue, my granddaughter," Huemac responded automatically, then frowned and shook his head doubtfully. "If it is indeed my grandson of whom you dreamed, I doubt that he would be one to flee his city in a time of trouble. He is training to be a warrior, and his vows would not permit him to desert."

"Who can say what will happen when the invaders come?" Chimalman demanded sharply. "Such a thing could call all your vows into question. But you are resisting me, Huemac. Where has it been shown to you that all the 'little people' of your vision will perish with you?"

Huemac stared at her thoughtfully, unable to argue on his own behalf. He remembered Cuauhcoatl's furious denial of Nezahualpilli's prophecy, a denial that apparently still governed the boy's life, from what Xolotlpilli had said. Perhaps he knows his own fate better than I, Huemac thought; perhaps the innocence of his hopes is justified.

"It might not be easy to win his confidence, and persuade him to leave in time," he said at last. "But I will consider how it might be done."

Chimalman crossed her arms on her thighs and shook the black braid off her shoulder with an impatient toss of her head, showing that she was not satisfied with his response.

"You once told me, with tears in your eyes, that you could not repay me for all I had given you," she reminded him aggressively. "And it is true: You have given me only one son, and your daughter left me as you are about to. You must send me these two who appeared in my dream."

"So, you would barter with me?" Huemac suggested lightly, smiling at her insistence. "The future for my past?"

"Is it not a fair trade?" Chimalman demanded archly, her black eyes alive with the memory of their love-making. Huemac laughed and reached out for her hands, gazing for a moment at the familiar fishhook-shaped scar. Then he rose to his feet, bringing her up with him. They walked to the edge of the cliff and looked out over the spreading landscape, watching an eagle circling over a distant hill.

"I will send them to you, Chimalman," he said softly, rubbing the scarred hand between his own. "They will be my last offering to these hills, which have provided me with so much. Which brought me to you, and the joy you have given me."

They watched in silence until the eagle had descended, and the sky was once again empty, except for the wind. Then Chimalman turned and started down the path between the rocks, her black braid bouncing against the back of her fur vest. Huemac took a last look at the land below: the hard, unyielding land that had taught him so much; the land of his ancestors, the Chichimecs. Then he started after Chimalman, his heart as empty as the sky, knowing that the time had come to leave . . .

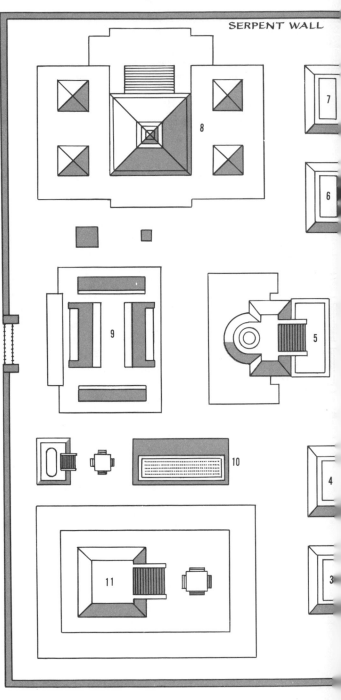

STREET

SERPENT WALL

STREET

N
W E
S

AVENUE
← TO TLACOPAN

Palace of
Axayacatl

7

6

8

9

5

10

4

11

3

STREET

AVENU
TO
IXTAPA

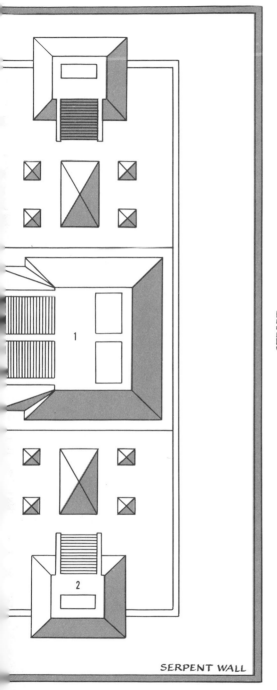

TEMPLE PRECINCT OF TENOCHTITLAN

ACCORDING TO IGNACIO MARQUINA

KEY
TO TEMPLE PRECINCT

1 Tlacatecco, Temple of
    Huitzilopochtli and Tlaloc
2 Temple of Tezcatlipoca
3 Temple of Chicomecoatl,
    Goddess of Maize
4 Temple of Xochipilli
5 Temple of Quetzalcoatl
6 Temple of Cihuacoatl
    (House of Darkness)
7 Coacalca,
    Temple of Captive Gods
8 Calmecac
9 Tlachco, Ball Court of the Lords
10 Tzompantli Skull Rack
11 House of Eagles, Temples of
    Tonatiuh and Xipe Totec

STREET

SERPENT WALL

Palace of Moctezuma II

XII

ONE-REED

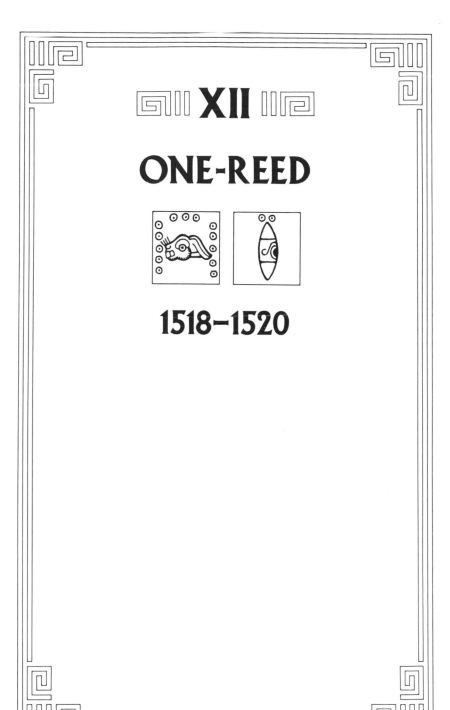

1518–1520

XOLOTLPILLI came to Cholula late in the year Thirteen-Rabbit, making the journey in two days from his camp in Huexotzinco. A cold, stinging rain had accompanied him most of the way, and gusts of the freezing droplets spun through the streets of the Holy City, lashing at the unprotected heads of the pilgrims crowded into the temple plazas. The population of the city seemed to have doubled again since Xolotlpilli's last visit, and he did not doubt that it would continue to grow as the year One-Reed approached. Cholula had become the site of an ongoing religious festival, with the public acts of penance and displays of hysteria becoming increasingly extreme, and all manner of prophecy being proclaimed and debated, sometimes violently. Xolotlpilli shouldered his way through the aimlessly wandering throngs of pilgrims, ignoring the solicitations of soothsayers and charm sellers, stepping carefully around a blood-streaked man who stood naked in the rain, weeping convulsively. The priests had clearly lost their control of events, and Xolotlpilli could not imagine what this city would be like when One-Reed actually arrived, and the foreign gods returned.

They had already been sighted twice within the past two years, first among the Mayans far to the south and east of Xicalanco; and then again, just this past spring, when they had come as close as Coatzacoalcos, and had met with the stewards who served as Moteczuma's tax collectors among the subject Totonacs. They had come from the east, traveling over the Divine Waters in floating temples that looked like small hills upon the water. They were said to be pale-faced beings, some with yellow hair and some with black, and all with long beards the same color as their hair. They kept their bodies completely covered except for their faces, and some wore battle helmets and armor made of a metal that shone like silver. After consulting all the oracles and deliberating for a long time, the council called by Moteczuma in Tenochtitlan had decided that these beings were indeed gods, the descendants of Quetzalcoatl-Topiltzin.

Now, with the advent of One-Reed only thirty days off, all of Anahuac looked anxiously toward the east, where watchers had been posted along the coast. Those who could not abide the wait for such confirmation had come to Cholula to consult with the oracles, among whom Quetzal Papalotl was prominent. The number of people desiring an audience with her was so great that they filled two courtyards and spilled over into the streets, forcing Xolotlpilli to stand in the rain for half a day before he was able to present his credentials to the priests guarding the entrance to the inner rooms. After a further delay, during which they made Xolotlpilli divest himself of his weapons, the priests ushered him in to Papalotl's private chamber, apologizing to the long line of supplicants who were already waiting.

Papalotl was seated on a wicker seat with a backrest draped with white cloth, lit from behind by torches attached to the wall. Xolotlpilli stared at the severe lines of her face for a moment before remembering to bow, an act that Papalotl cut short with a weary wave of her hand, gesturing him closer to the glowing copper brazier beside her seat.

"Warm yourself, my brother," she said in a hoarse voice, the butterfly ring gleaming on her finger as she resettled her hands in her lap. Xolotlpilli shook the moisture from his cloak and held his huge hands over the fire, trying to conceal his shock at her appearance. Her beautiful face seemed shrunken back to the bone, almost angular in the shifting light, and there were dark circles under her golden eyes. Two years older than himself, Papalotl was only thirty-nine, yet there were deep lines around her mouth and wisps of gray among the black hair pulled back from her temples. She has aged five years since I saw her last, Xolotlpilli thought sadly, avoiding her eyes until he had composed himself and taken a seat in front of her.

"Forgive the urgency of my summons," she said. "I hope I did not take you away from an important battle. Not that the fighting can go on much longer," she added, cocking her head knowingly. Xolotlpilli nodded in weary agreement.

"It has gone on too long already. We have never had a sufficient force to overcome the Tlaxcalans, especially when our top warchiefs are constantly being called back to Tenochtitlan to sit in council. And now the Huexotzincans, whose lands we have supposedly been protecting, have bolted from our custody and gone over to the Tlaxcalans. Moteczuma has given the order for one last battle, and then we are to withdraw and return to Tenochtitlan."

"You have been away from your family for a long time," Papalotl observed with sympathy. "Is your son still with you?"

"He is back in the camp, preparing for the battle," Xolotlpilli acknowledged. "He needs but one captive to become a seasoned warrior, so he is still eager for the fight. His ambitions blind him to the pointlessness of what we do."

"You have lost your own eagerness for battle?" Papalotl inquired shrewdly, and though Xolotlpilli lowered his eyes, he made no denial.

"These last years have aged me," he said bluntly, raising his eyes to show that he felt no self-pity. "Knowing the things that Father told me, seeing the signs and omens everywhere . . . and then to participate in a campaign that accomplishes nothing! We squander our energies and blood to no purpose, when we should be preparing ourselves for the invaders. I have been fighting since I was thirteen, Papalotl, often against people we had already conquered once. But never has the goal of conquest seemed more futile than it does to me now."

"Soon, these will be things of the past," Papalotl told him brusquely. "Those who are coming to our land will be here within six months' time. These *invaders,* as you call them," she added dryly. "Has our father won you over to his point of view?"

"Not completely," Xolotlpilli replied in a careful tone, meeting his sister's insistent gaze. "I have great respect for your powers, my sister, but I cannot abandon the responsibility for forming my own judgments. And those who came to our coast last spring are said to resemble men, despite their terrible powers. They inflicted a great slaughter upon the Chontal when they came ashore there, at Champoton. Whether they be gods or men, surely we cannot allow ourselves to be slaughtered?"

"There is no choice but to welcome them," Papalotl said forcefully, dismissing his concerns with a toss of her head. "They have weapons more powerful than any we have seen, and great beasts that serve them in battle. I have *seen* this, my brother, and much, much more. Enough to know that we must not resist them."

Xolotlpilli was silent for a moment, staring at her haggard face, which had once been so peaceful and radiant.

"Do you know, then, that they will approach us with kindness?" he asked gently. "Have you *seen* this?"

"No, I have not," Papalotl admitted. "Many things come to me now, but so rapidly that I have to strain to grasp their meaning. There is not time, anymore, to dwell upon the images that I choose, or to recapture those that escape me. My dreams rush upon me and are gone like the wind in the canyons, and I can only struggle to retain the sensation of their passing. Most concern the arrival of the gods, but I recently dreamed of your son, Cuauhcoatl. That is why I summoned you here."

Papalotl's voice had picked up speed, losing its huskiness, and she went on before Xolotlpilli could respond, her eyes turned inward:

"He was larger than when you last brought him to see me, and his face was fierce and frightening. There was fighting . . . and bloodshed . . . and then I had the sensation of falling and could see no more. Yet I am certain that something extraordinary is about to happen to him."

"Will he be killed?" Xolotlpilli asked, when she was again looking at him, and Papalotl spread her hands helplessly.

"I do not know," she confessed, her voice suddenly heavy with fatigue. "But you must go to him, Xolotlpilli, and watch over him in the days ahead."

"I will leave immediately," Xolotlpilli said, placing a hand flat on the floor, as if to rise. But then he stopped himself and gave his sister a long, significant look, allowing his concern for her to show in his face. Papalotl seemed startled by the intimacy of his gaze, as if no one had dared such a thing with her in a very long time.

"Or is there something more that we must say, my sister?" he suggested quietly. "Neither of us is so young anymore, and I have seen the hunger of the people outside, whose numbers increase constantly. They will drain you of your strength, Papalotl, before One-Reed even arrives. They will devour you alive, if you let them."

"There can be no rest for any of us," Papalotl recited in a weary monotone, "until our Lord has shown himself, and has been accepted by his people."

"Surely, your god would not use you as cruelly as you are using yourself," Xolotlpilli said sharply. "You must forgive my intrusion into your affairs, but it is my duty as a brother to remind you of your health. I do not wish to lose you before your time."

Papalotl had seemed almost angry for a moment, but her face slowly relaxed into a smile, and she held out her hands to him in apology.

"I see that you have lost none of your generosity with age, my brother. And I will heed the advice you have given me. But my faith in the kindness of the Plumed Serpent has not diminished, Xolotlpilli; I will not believe that this is our final farewell."

Xolotlpilli squeezed her hands warmly, and then rose by stages to his full height. His shaven skull shone in the torchlight as he inclined his head to receive her blessing.

"Till we meet again, then," he said in a satisfied voice as he retrieved his cloak from beside the brazier. Then he shot her a sudden, bold glance. "Are you fasting now, my sister?"

"No," Papalotl replied in a mystified voice, cocking her head at the curiousness of the question. Xolotlpilli smiled broadly, a hint of mischief widening his big brown eyes, making him look like the brother of her childhood.

"I will tell the women outside that you are hungry, then," he offered in a gruff, off-handed way, raising an eyebrow challengingly, as if daring her to resist his solicitude. Then he turned quickly and left the chamber, so that the last thing that he heard, as he stepped out into the tense, crowded corridor, was the sound of his sister's laughter.

CUAUHCOATL was standing in the center of his tent, holding one arm carefully crooked against his hip, so that his apprentice could finish sewing the spray of blue hummingbird feathers onto the sleeve of his white cotton armor. An enormous painted head thrust itself through the open tent-flap, and then his father was standing before him, stooping beneath the tent's ridgepole but still blocking out all the light.

"That is good enough," Cuauhcoatl said to the apprentice, who collected his thread and bone awl from the floor and left the tent. Xolotlpilli turned sideways, allowing some light to enter, and Cuauhcoatl saw that he was holding the black battle helmet that he had been given for his part in the capture of Zinacantlan. The helmet's wooden surface had been polished to a deep, glossy shine, and the raised ridge that ran from forehead to neckpiece glittered with an inlay of black mirror-stone. Long black guan feathers flared away behind the ear holes, like trailing wings.

"I have had this altered to fit your head," Xolotlpilli explained as he placed the helmet into his son's hands. "I have a feeling that great deeds await you this day, my son, and I would like to be sure of locating you easily on the field."

Cuauhcoatl accepted the helmet gratefully, but his eyes were uneasy as he looked up into his father's face, searching for signs that this might be his last battle.

"You have been told this in Cholula?" he asked hesitantly, and Xolotlpilli nodded in agreement.

"Your aunt, the priestess, has seen that something extraordinary will happen to you on the battlefield. She has not seen your death, however. I give you the helmet only to remind you to keep your head," he added in a lighter tone. "I have little doubt that you will return from this battle as tequihua, a man who has a task."

"I will wear it with honor," Cuauhcoatl promised, flattening his topknot with one hand before placing the helmet on his head. Beneath the beaked visor, his painted face looked older than his seventeen years, and Xolotlpilli could not restrain a smile of pride.

"Have you decided yet which order you will join," he asked, "once you have taken your final captive?"

Cuauhcoatl averted his eyes and toyed with the helmet's chin strap. Then he drew himself up to his full height, as if determined not to be overpowered by his father's prodigious size.

"I know the Eagles and Jaguars have spoken to you, my father, and I do not wish to disappoint your hopes. But like many of my friends, I am drawn to the order of Arrow Warriors."

Xolotlpilli had suspected this for some time, so he was able to keep most of his disappointment to himself. But he knew that his son had seen how he felt.

"You would make your vows to the Speaker, instead of to the Sun?" he inquired with deliberate mildness. "You prefer to serve in the court rather than in the field?"

"There is no future in the field," Cuauhcoatl explained, adopting the same tone, since neither wanted to argue on the eve of a battle. "There is little glory to be won chasing Texcocan rebels through the hills, or fighting set battles with the Tlaxcalans. And now we are being recalled to the city, anyway."

"No future," Xolotlpilli echoed, shaking his head ruefully. "No doubt you are correct in your assessment, my son. But I will ask you to think again, later, about joining Moteczuma's guard. If your answer is the same, I will not stand in your way."

"I am grateful for your understanding," Cuauhcoatl said politely, though the stiffness of his bow showed that he did not have much intention of changing his mind. Xolotlpilli sighed inaudibly, vexed by the knowledge of how little *real* understanding existed between himself and his son.

"Let us go, then," he said, with forced heartiness. "The enemy awaits our arrival . . ."

A THIN VEIL of mist rose off the well-trampled field as the two armies marched out to meet one another, waving their feathered standards and blowing on bone war whistles. After almost two years of inconclusive struggle, their meetings had taken on the ritualized aspect of a flower war, a trading of captives that threatened neither side with annihilation. The Tlaxcalans knew that the Mexicans and their allies did not have the numbers to breach the defenses that protected the Tlaxcalan cities; they likewise knew that they could never completely vanquish the Mexicans without paying a great cost in blood. So they were content with the face-off, willing to commit a force equal to whatever the Mexicans sent out, yet able to withdraw to safety if the day appeared to be going badly.

In recent months, though, it had been the Mexicans who had most often called the first retreat, reflecting the indecisive mood emanating from Tenochtitlan as One-Reed approached. For this last battle, Moteczuma had sent out his half-brother Cuitlahuac as the commanding warchief, with orders to make a strong showing before leaving the field. A large force of three hundred and fifty warriors had been mustered for this purpose, including a large contingent of apprentices being given a last opportunity to cut their hair-lock. The Tlaxcalans had accepted the challenge willingly, having bolstered their ranks with the rebel Huexotzincans, who were eager to avenge themselves upon their former protectors.

Standing on a barren knoll overlooking the battlefield, Xolotlpilli saw the two armies converge, the warriors holding their painted shields over their heads in a last salute to the Sun. He was standing among the group of advisers surrounding Cuitlahuac, but all his attention was focused upon the glittering black helmet of his son, which could be seen among the white plumes of those in the first ranks of the Tenocha. Spare his life, O Lord, and give him glory, Xolotlpilli prayed to his patron, Tonatiuh, who shone dimly through a cover of high clouds.

Cuauhcoatl charged forward impetuously, slashing out with his macana as the two sides met with an audible crunch in the center of the field. Then all was a confusion of hurtling bodies and swinging weapons, with many men going down in the crush of warriors. This was the most dangerous moment of the fighting, and Xolotlpilli watched the black helmet appear and disappear, as Cuauhcoatl fought furiously to keep his feet and fend off those who were being thrown against him.

Then the fighting spread out over the field, and there were spaces between the rival squadrons of warriors, who came at each other one-for-one, keeping comrades at their backs so that they could not be surrounded. The young apprentices stood in pairs at the rear of their assigned squadrons, ready to tie up and carry off those who fell captive to their masters. Cuauhcoatl found work for his apprentices immediately, cutting the legs out from under a Tlaxcalan in his very first encounter. Xolotlpilli let out a cheer that drew puzzled glances from his colleagues on the knoll, but Cuauhcoatl paused over his captive only long enough to allow his white-plumed comrades to surge in around him, then again sprang to the attack. Another man fell beneath his arm but was dragged away by his comrades before he could be secured, though not before Cuauhcoatl had stripped the man of his insignia and thrown it back to his own apprentices.

Xolotlpilli soon perceived that his son's squadron was pushing out ahead of the other Mexican units, and he was the first to spy the squadron of Huexotzincans who were coming to the Tlaxcalans' aid. On his own initiative, he ordered a reserve squadron forward in support and had the trumpeter sound a warning signal, alerting the white-plumed warriors to their danger. The Huexotzincans attacked before the Tenocha reinforcements could get to the scene of the battle, showering down a hail of darts, stones, and arrows. Most of the whites began to pull back, protecting their flanks, but the black-helmeted Cuauhcoatl stubbornly stood his ground, refusing to yield the captive he had just taken.

"Leave him," Xolotlpilli muttered under his breath, as he saw his son becoming increasingly isolated in the midst of the attacking Huexotzincans. Suddenly, the black helmet was sent flying through the air and Cuauhcoatl dropped from sight, obscured by the enemy warriors milling around the place where he had stood.

Seizing a shield and warclub from the hands of a startled apprentice, Xolotlpilli raced down the hill, bellowing to the Cuachic he passed to join him. But there were many men between himself and his son, so he saw nothing of what occurred during the time it took him to reach Cuauhcoatl. It was those among Cuauhcoatl's comrades still present at the scene who later told the story:

When they saw Cuauhcoatl fall, they rushed forward to his defense, making a loud cry. But the Huexotzincans were there before them, and in larger numbers, and they pushed the rescuers back. Their apprentices darted in behind them and knelt beside Cuauhcoatl's body, their ropes in hand. It was then, the warriors reported, that Cuauhcoatl awoke from the dead and threw his captors off. Springing to his feet, he whirled upon the surprised Huexotzincans, slashing out at them with the warclub that had apparently never left his hand. He killed two outright, and wounded several others before they could get out of his way, swinging his macana with a wild abandon that soon cleared a large space around him.

Then the Tenocha reinforcements poured in behind him, followed closely by Xolotlpilli and his cohorts, and the Huexotzincans panicked and ran, leaving the field to this warrior who refused to die. Suddenly alone, Cuauhcoatl fell blindly upon one of the corpses at his feet and hacked at it in a frenzy, covering himself with blood. When his father finally reached his side, he was insensible, beating his splintered warclub against the earth and commanding it to awaken.

Like those around him, Xolotlpilli stood back in awe, until his son's fury had exhausted itself and Cuauhcoatl again fell unconscious. Then he knelt and gingerly pried the weapon from his son's hand, standing aside as four of his fellow Cuachic lifted Cuauhcoatl to their shoulders. The Tlaxcalans and Huexotzincans were now in full flight, trying to protect their rear from the eager Mexican apprentices who pursued them. Those of the Tenocha who had not gone off after an easy captive fell in behind Xolotlpilli, who carried the shattered black helmet under his arm. Following the limp form swaying on the shoulders of the Cuachic, they began to sing Cuauhcoatl's praises as he was carried from the field.

FOR THE first time since he had become an Old Eagle, Huemac put on the golden mantle he had been given upon his retirement, and tied eagle feathers into his whitening hair. Then he went out to join the crowd forming at the Eagle Gate, waiting to greet the warriors returning from Huexotzinco. His rank allowed him a place at the front, among the criers, but he did not push forward to claim his privilege. It was better that he not be identified with Cuauhcoatl on his grandson's day of glory, and he was still puzzling over the stories that had come back to Tenochtitlan. Had Cuauhcoatl truly been maddened by the fighting, like one of the Cuachic? Or had he been possessed by some other force?

The spectators began to cheer and throw flowers as the captives were led through the gate, and despite his reluctance to be seen, Huemac took a few steps forward into the crowd, craning his neck to see. Then he thought he heard his name being called from behind him, and he turned and impatiently scanned the people to his rear. But he saw no familiar faces, and no one seemed to be trying to capture his attention. Only after he had turned back to view the procession did the memory strike him, making him stiffen where he stood. He remembered the vision that had come to him in the cave in the hills, and he realized that this was how he had first seen himself—as an old man with eagle feathers in his hair, standing in the midst of a crowd at the Eagle Gate.

So it has finally come to pass, he thought, and it is my own grandson who has provided the occasion. He began to edge forward in the crowd, suddenly curious for a better look at the young man whom fate had brought him here to see . . .

CUAUHCOATL finally saw his chance and slipped away from the feast during the dancing. Many people tried to accost him on his way to the stairs, offering congratulations, invitations to other feasts, and introductions to their daughters, but they all backed off respectfully when he gestured toward his bandaged head, as if it had begun to hurt him again. Actually, it was a far different kind of pain from which he was suffering, feeling besieged by all the admiration, which only made him feel like an impostor. No one would accept modesty from him after the way he had been praised by Moteczuma and the other leaders, yet he dared not tell any of them the truth about what he had experienced on the battlefield. There was only one man he felt he could trust with that, but his grandfather had not reappeared since they had briefly exchanged greetings earlier in the afternoon.

As he turned down the corridor toward Huemac's room, Cuauhcoatl reflected on the formality of that meeting, their first in almost seven years. His grandfather had been wearing the garb of an Old Eagle, and they had spoken as one warrior to another, using the standard phrases of praise and respect. Nothing unusual, or even very personal, had passed between them, at least not in the form of words. Yet Cuauhcoatl had been left with the undeniable sense that his grandfather understood what had happened to him. It was a feeling that he could not account for, which made him wonder if he had not merely imagined it, since he wanted so much for it to be true. But then he was at the entrance to the room, and saw his grandfather sitting in the light of a single torch on the wall, facing the door expectantly.

Cuauhcoatl bowed deeply in his relief, and would have begun speaking immediately had Huemac not held up a hand, motioning him to a place at his left.

"This will be your place from this time onward," he said as the young man seated himself. "It once belonged to the Jaguar Warrior Azcatzin, your father's cousin."

Cuauhcoatl bowed again, understanding that an honor was being extended to him, even though he was ignorant of its nature. He noticed the masks, banners, and tlachtli pads on the walls, wondering what sort of business had been conducted here in the past, and what would be expected of him in the future. Then his grandfather spoke, putting an end to one kind of wondering.

"You have had a vision, Cuauhcoatl," he said softly, his eyes glowing visibly in the dim yellow light. "Do you wish to tell me about it?"

"A vision," Cuauhcoatl repeated breathlessly, as if testing the word against what he had experienced. He shook his head helplessly. "It was like nothing else I have ever known, or hope to know again."

"Tell me, then," Huemac prompted. "This is a place of truth; your trust will not be betrayed here."

Cuauhcoatl glanced briefly around the room, as if to reassure himself. But he did not truly need any further urging, and he took a deep, determined breath, furrowing his bandaged brow in recollection.

"I saw the Huexotzincans coming," he began, "and I knew that I should leave my captive and withdraw. I even remembered my father's warning to keep my head. But something held me there, and gave me the notion that I could hold them off until help arrived. I never saw what struck me. Everything suddenly went red with pain, and then I was falling into blackness, as if from a great height. I fell like this for a long time . . ."

Cuauhcoatl had been staring intently at a spot in the air before him, as if mesmerized by the sound of his own voice. Then he blinked, saw Huemac watching him attentively, and continued:

"Then I was standing, and at my feet was a man tied with ropes, asleep. And I saw that the man was Moteczuma, the Speaker. He lay bound and helpless, his eyes shut tight against the light. I called to him to awaken, but he continued to sleep. Only after I had untied him and placed my hand upon his head did he rouse himself, and then he was as one gone mad. He seized a weapon and threw himself upon me, and I had to fight to save myself. Three times, I struck him down, and each time he rose to come at me again, so that I was afraid I would be forced to kill him. I called to him not to fight with me, but he would not hear me, he would not listen . . ."

Obviously shaken by the memory, Cuauhcoatl paused to lick his dry lips and compose himself. Then he went on in a calmer voice:

"It had grown dark as we fought, and then I could no longer see him or feel his blows. I reached out to find him and stumbled over his body lying on the ground, again bound and sleeping, although he might even have been dead. All was darkness, so that I could only feel him, and though I laid my hands upon him and shook his body over and over, he would not awaken. That is all I remember until I awoke in the camp, and was told the things I had done."

The young man sighed with audible relief and let his shoulders slump. His grandfather's eyes were hooded thoughtfully, shutting off the glow that had grown in brightness during the retelling.

"Until today, Cuauhcoatl," he said at last, "I was not fully aware of how closely your fate is tied to my own. But I, too, was given a vision, when I was not much older than you are now, and had performed deeds as inexplicable as your own. I saw Tenochtitlan being destroyed before my eyes, and although I was able to stop it once, I could not prevent the final destruction from occurring. Nezahualpilli knew this when he spoke to me of doom, on that day you spurned me. But he also knew—and you should know it now—that I intend to fight for my city and my people to the last of my strength."

Cuauhcoatl's features brightened at the boldness of his grandfather's declaration, but then he frowned as the overall bleakness of what he had been told penetrated.

"But if these are gods who come to us," he asked warily, "what hope do we have of fighting them?"

"I do not trade in hope," Huemac said flatly. "I have only the responsibility of my vision to guide and sustain me. As you now have yours. Moteczuma has asked you to come to him tomorrow?"

Cuauhcoatl started at the question, and his eyes widened as he saw the connection his grandfather was making.

"Yes, but I . . ."

"You must go to him. But first you must make known your desire to join the Arrow Warriors, and pledge yourself to his protection. Was this not your original intention?"

"Yes, of course, but . . ." Cuauhcoatl sputtered in protest. "But I could not even bring myself to look at him today, though he commanded me to do so. I looked, but I did not let myself see him."

"That was probably just as well," Huemac allowed easily. "But you cannot avoid your fate forever, my son. *You* must not be the one who sleeps. Remember the boldness you showed in your vision: You placed your hands upon him, and tried to shake him into wakefulness. Can you doubt that your place is at his side?"

"But he *attacked* me!" Cuauhcoatl blurted desperately, and his grandfather gave him a dry, sardonic smile.

"You are not the first. Though, like me, you are one of the few who have survived to tell about it. He will no doubt test you again; he will threaten and humiliate you, to be sure that you are not *actually* like me. You must go to him humbly, in innocence and good faith, as if you were the same man who wished to join the Arrows solely for the sake of your own advancement."

"But I am not that man anymore," Cuauhcoatl said stubbornly. "And I still do not understand the 'responsibility' of my vision, as you call it."

"Your responsibility is that of wakefulness," Huemac told him. "You must perform the duties required by the vow you will take to Moteczuma, and you must do so without reservation. But you must also keep yourself alert to the true meaning of all that goes on around you, especially of the dangers that others do not see. You must be ready to act when the sleep of helplessness descends upon the ruler."

Cuauhcoatl sighed in resignation, still uncertain of his role but unable to deny the logic of his grandfather's interpretation. He remembered what the Old Grandmother had said to him before she died, and he knew that this was the time of which she had spoken, the time when he should trust his grandfather and heed his request for aid.

"How will this help you in your fight?" he asked quietly, and Huemac returned his gaze with unconcealed pride.

"There is much that still requires explanation," he admitted, "but I promise you that I will not disappear from your life, as I did in the past. We will speak whenever you come to this house, but never outside this room. You will understand soon enough about the kind of knowledge that is useful to us. I will tell you no more now, so that you may approach Moteczuma with an uncluttered heart. Prepare yourself only for that."

"I will do as you say," Cuauhcoatl promised. "May I speak to my father, though, so that he will not think that I am spurning his wishes for me?"

"He is one of us," Huemac said. "But I will tell him. You should also know that we have a friend in the court, though he is one who may show his friendship in strange ways. It is better that you should discover his identity for yourself, so that you will not appear to be looking for him."

Cuauhcoatl cocked his head curiously at this piece of information, but he soon saw that his grandfather was not going to tell him more.

"I feel that I am walking into darkness," he said, as he prepared himself to leave. Huemac looked at him sharply, then smiled when he saw that it was not a complaint.

"Grow used to the feeling, my son," he advised. "Make yourself a friend to the darkness, and walk lightly."

AT THE appointed hour, Cuauhcoatl appeared outside the audience chamber to which he had been summoned by Moteczuma. He had been stopped and questioned four separate times since entering the palace, and he felt that his progress had been observed the whole way. So he saw no point in identifying himself to the men in black-fringed mantles who stood in a group before the heavy wooden door of the chamber. He simply presented himself for their appraisal, as any candidate to their order might, knowing that his record had already been examined. The silent scrutiny went on for several moments, and then the Arrow Warriors all seemed to relax at once, breaking into smiles and approving nods. A slender young man with a long, elegant face came forward and bowed from the waist, stiffly, in the palace manner.

"Allow me to greet you, Cuauhcoatzin," he said graciously, using the honorific form of Cuauhcoatl's name. "I am Ehecatzin, the Wind Prince, and it is my duty to prepare you for your interview."

Placing a hand lightly beneath Cuauhcoatl's elbow, he steered him away from the others, speaking in a more confidential tone:

"Of course we are all pleased, and honored, that you have applied to join our order, Cuauhcoatl. It is often said that we do not accept warriors of stature into our midst, unless they are related to one of the royal families. But this simply is not true; we are always ready to recognize a man of quality, whatever his blood. We are all your admirers, Cuauhcoatl. Your performance in Huexotzinco has made life here easier for all of us, if you understand my meaning."

Cuauhcoatl nodded sagely, although he had no idea of what the man meant. The words seemed to pour into his ears like warm oil, filled with assumptions and insinuations that were disconcerting as well as flattering, since they hinted at a knowledge he did not yet share. He felt much the same way he had when his grandfather had assigned him a place in his room, and it occurred to him that Ehecatzin might be the friend Huemac had mentioned. But then he pushed the thought roughly from his mind, reminding himself that he came here in innocence. He gave his attention to Ehecatzin, who was going on with his instructions:

"I know that I do not need to remind you to leave your sandals out here, and to keep your eyes lowered until the Speaker invites you to look upon him. I mention this only out of duty. As a friend and admirer, though, let me warn you to beware of Nahui Olin, the Speaker's dwarf. He has been a terror today; he has been calling people Huaxtec and Otomi and insulting them outrageously. It would be disgraceful of him to do this to a warrior of your stature," Ehecatzin added, his eyes flaring briefly with sympathetic outrage, "but there is nothing the Speaker will not permit him. Therefore, you must not try to ignore his questions or be rude to him in any way. Men have died for less."

Cuauhcoatl looked at him sharply, and Ehecatzin nodded solemnly to show that he was serious.

"I will find you later, in the House of Arrows," he promised, "and tell you more of the things you should know."

"I am grateful for your kindness," Cuauhcoatl said, and allowed the man to grip his arm in the manner of a comrade, though they had never fought together.

"You are called, my friend," Ehecatzin told him, as the great door swung open silently and the other Arrows beckoned him forward. Once across the threshold—his sandals left behind—he was surrounded on all sides by armed guards, two of whom took his arms to guide him forward. With his eyes lowered, Cuauhcoatl could see only the polished stone floor, though he sensed the presence of many people beyond those who surrounded him. A voice was speaking ahead of him, but it ceased as he approached, and then the guards stopped him, and Cuauhcoatl squatted immediately and bowed low, touching dirt to his tongue. He felt the guards depart but did not move, awaiting the word of the Speaker.

Suddenly, two small bare feet, the feet of a child, appeared on the floor before him, just within the sight of his lowered eyes. Then the voice of a man boomed out above him:

"How well he bows, my Lord! Not at all like a filthy Huaxtec! And someone has taught the savage to hide his parts with a maxlatl. That is *most* impressive," the voice boomed in mockery, and laughter echoed from many parts of the room. Then the voice took on a note of exaggerated anxiety. "But Lord, what if he has reddened his teeth with dye? O, my Lord, it is too horrible to contemplate—the bloody smile of a Huaxtec!"

Now the laughter was enormous, and Cuauhcoatl felt the heat of embarrassment course through his prostrate body. He was grateful that he had been warned to expect humiliation, for he was not sure that he could have withheld his anger had he been subjected to this in *complete* innocence.

"Still, I must be brave," the voice continued above him. "I must force myself to see. Look at me, Huaxtec!"

Cuauhcoatl sat back on his heels, and looked up into the eyes of Moteczuma's dwarf. He was no taller than a normal man's waist, his head round like a pumpkin upon his slightly crooked shoulders. On his head was a headpiece of rabbit fur, made to look like the face of a monster, with yellow stones for eyes and a ring of serpent's teeth for a mouth. The dwarf's eyes blazed from slits in a face that was round and swollen with rolls of flesh, like that of an infant.

"Ah, this is no Huaxtec!" the dwarf cried, feigning great relief. Then he looked directly at Cuauhcoatl and spoke in a normal tone. "No, this one is Tenocha, a warrior of the Sun. Know then, Young Warrior, that I am called Nahui Olin, he who is the Sun of our era upon the earth. Bend your back, Young Warrior, so that Nahui Olin may mount to the heavens upon your strong shoulders, and shine down upon the Tenocha, the People of the Sun."

Tensing his muscles, Cuauhcoatl obediently knelt on the polished floor and allowed the dwarf to scramble up his back and stand upon his shoulders. Then, at Nahui Olin's command, he rose slowly to his feet, holding onto the dwarf's ankles while keeping his own eyes on the floor.

"Turn, Young Warrior," the dwarf commanded. "To the west," he added arrogantly, bearing down slightly with his right foot, so that Cuauhcoatl turned naturally in that direction, before he even realized that he was being guided. Voices were raised in approval amid the general laughter, which grew as Cuauhcoatl turned slowly in a circle with the dwarf upon his shoulders. He could feel the movements of the little man's body above his head, but he dared not raise his eyes to see what was causing all the laughter. Then he felt the dwarf's buttocks briefly touch the top of his head, and Nahui Olin shouted gleefully:

"*There* is gold for you, Young Warrior! Be glad, for the Sun has soiled you with his wealth!"

Cuauhcoatl stopped, facing in his original direction, and the dwarf freed himself from the hands on his ankles and jumped from Cuauhcoatl's shoulders, turning a flip in the air and landing on his feet. Again there was approving laughter, and then another voice was raised—the dark, solemn voice of Motec-zuma:

"That is enough, Nahui Olin. Raise your face to me, Cuauhcoatl, so that I may look upon you again."

Cuauhcoatl did so cautiously, allowing no boldness to show in his gaze as he looked at the Speaker. Moteczuma was seated upon a throne of gold, surrounded by a fan-shaped screen of blue and gold feathers. He was a slender man, perhaps fifty years of age, with a stern, narrow face that did not seem capable of amusement. But his dark eyes, Cuauhcoatl noted with relief, were bright and inquisitive, so that he hardly seemed like the man in Cuauhcoatl's vision. He was surrounded on the dais by a large group of men, priests and lords mixed in with the ubiquitous Arrow Warriors, but the only one whom Cuauhcoatl recognized was the Speaker's brother, the warchief Cuitlahuac.

"You are tolerant as well as brave, Cuauhcoatl," Moteczuma said. "You have shown great humility, and provided me with much amusement. You will be rewarded for this."

"Your pleasure is my reward, my Lord," Cuauhcoatl replied when given the signal to speak, trying to keep his eyes steadily upon the Speaker while Nahui Olin did two rolling somersaults and came to rest sitting up at the feet of Moteczuma. The Speaker looked down at the dwarf and laughed, a hoarse, coughing sound that he seemed to summon from his throat by tugging on the long, thin strands of hair on the end of his chin. Then he stopped laughing abruptly and turned back to Cuauhcoatl.

"You have asked to serve me, here in the palace," he demanded harshly. "Why have you made this request?"

Cuauhcoatl hesitated, quite genuinely dumfounded that the Speaker would ask such a question.

"It is where all the young warriors wish to serve, my Lord. Close to the face and heart of our people."

"Both the Eagles and the Jaguars have asked for you," Moteczuma continued in a suspicious tone. "Your grandfather was an Eagle, was he not?"

"Yes, my Lord," Cuauhcoatl admitted. "I consulted him, but my decision was not altered by his advice."

Moteczuma grunted softly and was silent, as were all the others in the chamber. Cuitlahuac stepped forward and whispered something in his brother's ear, and Moteczuma nodded curtly, his hand on his chin. Nahui Olin lolled back on one elbow like a courtesan, crossing one stubby leg over the upraised knee of the other. The headpiece had fallen forward to cover his face, making him look so ridiculous that Cuauhcoatl had to jerk his eyes away to keep from laughing. Moteczuma finally spoke, his eyes and voice hard, as if he were passing sentence:

"Tomorrow you will come here to serve me, Cuauhcoatl. You will join the Order of the Arrows, and perhaps, in time, you will be allowed to carry weapons in my presence. But if you fail me in anything, you will die for it instantly, for in this house live the descendants of the Toltecs, those who were perfect in everything they performed. You will fast and do penance until the morning, when you will take your vows and be given new insignia. Go now, for I have spoken."

Cuauhcoatl bowed again and backed away from the dais with his eyes lowered, not daring to turn until he was almost to the door and the guards had intercepted him. These men he looked in the eyes, seeing there the recognition of his new status. But behind him, as the great door swung open, came the loud, insulting voice of Nahui Olin:

"Farewell, Huaxtec! Farewell, Gold Head!"

The laughter disappeared as the door closed on his back, and Cuauhcoatl experienced an enormous release of tension, so powerful that it made him feel light-headed. Everything seemed far away to his eyes, and his hands were clumsy as he tied his sandals back on. He had sometimes felt like this after a battle, but only long afterward, when the nearness of death came to him in his dreams. Though he could not quite believe it, even now, he realized that he had deliberately lied to the Speaker in pretending to have rejected his grandfather's advice. He had done so on an impulse, without reckoning what he would say if Moteczuma had asked him what that advice had been. He had assumed, somehow, that Moteczuma would make his own assumption, as he indeed had. But how could I have known that? he wondered, marveling at the boldness of his own intuition.

Ehecatzin was waiting for him when he was ready to leave, and they walked down the main hall together. The slender young man spoke sympathetically to Cuauhcoatl, repeating what the guards had told him: that Nahui Olin had been unmerciful in his insults, pretending to be the Sun defecating on Cuauhcoatl's head.

"Surely, this despicable little man is permitted too much," Ehecatzin said sternly, then smiled at his companion. "But you were too wise for him, Cuauhcoatl; he could not trick you with his commands. They say that even the Speaker himself applauded when you turned unerringly toward the west."

The memory of the pressure of the dwarf's foot upon his shoulder suddenly came back to Cuauhcoatl, along with Huemac's warning that his "friend" might choose to show his friendship in strange ways. He realized, belatedly, the favor that Nahui Olin had done him, softening his master with laughter. How much more suspicious might Moteczuma have been, had he not been given the chance to assure himself of Cuauhcoatl's humility? Cuauhcoatl glanced at the man beside him, his own suspicions rising at how familiar Ehecatzin already seemed.

"It is not ours to question what the Speaker permits, my friend," he said gently, chiding Ehecatzin, whose smile stiffened before he nodded enthusiastically.

"You are correct, Cuauhcoatzin, please forgive the looseness of my tongue. It is only my warrior's anger at the indignities done to you."

"You honor me too greatly. I must go to begin my fast now, but I will see you again, Ehecatzin."

Then, not knowing quite why he did so, he impulsively gripped Ehecatzin's arm, stealing the man's own gesture with such suddenness that Ehecatzin was caught off-guard, and his response lacked its earlier assurance. Cuauhcoatl turned and continued down the hall alone, taking a perverse kind of pleasure in the confusion he had created in Ehecatzin, who was so polished, and so knowing in his manner. It was a pleasure new to him, and one that seemed somehow dishonorable. Surely, he thought with amazement and pride, surely I am not so innocent as my grandfather thinks . . .

2

THE House of Animals was a long, dark hallway lined on both sides with wooden cages and large pottery urns, which held the beasts and serpents that belonged to the Speaker. Their growling and hissing reverberated endlessly throughout the high-ceilinged room, and the air was rank with the odors of fur and feces, overlaid with the rich smell of blood, for the meat eaters were fed with the trunks and entrails of sacrificial victims. Cuauhcoatl felt his spirit shrink back in dismay as he entered the gloomy hall, but like the warrior he was, he kept his shoulders straight and his head erect as he proceeded toward the place where Nahui Olin stood waiting.

The attendants at the door had greeted Cuauhcoatl with sympathy, for it was common knowledge in the palace that the young Arrow Warrior was the favorite whipping boy of Moteczuma's dwarf, and they did not doubt that Nahui Olin had summoned him here to inflict further torments upon him. Given the circumstances, Cuauhcoatl had found no difficulty in playing to their expectations, wearing a glum face that clearly bemoaned his fate at being the chosen victim of the dwarf's malicious sense of humor. Yet there was a well-hidden tremor of excitement in his heart, for this was the first time, in the five months that Cuauhcoatl had been serving in the palace, that Nahui Olin had summoned him for a face-to-face meeting.

The dwarf was standing in front of a large cage that was shrouded in black cloth, and with an imperious gesture, he ordered Cuauhcoatl to squat beside him. Then he stretched his rubbery face into a gleeful, taunting expression and laughed loudly, sending the raucous sound echoing down the hallway to the attendants watching from the door.

"That is right," he said to Cuauhcoatl in a low voice, as if commending him, "look as uncomfortable as possible; let them see how I torment you."

Cuauhcoatl shifted his weight on his haunches and glanced around him uneasily, as if looking for a way to escape. What he noticed, though, was that Nahui Olin had chosen a perfect place for them to speak without the danger of being overheard.

"So we meet at last," he said to the dwarf, "without tricks or jokes to perform."

"Yes," Nahui Olin said curtly. "One of my purposes in sending for you this afternoon was to see that you were shifted to the night watch. Has this been done?"

Cuauhcoatl nodded, frowning slightly at the realization that he had been manipulated without his knowledge.

"I could have arranged that myself, if I had only been told."

"There was no time," Nahui Olin said with a dismissive gesture. "Your grandfather says to prepare yourself. The messengers that Moteczuma sent to contact the foreign gods have done their duty, and are hastening toward Tenochtitlan. They will arrive soon, perhaps this very night. That is why you had to be switched to night duty, for I am not with the Speaker when he sleeps."

"I will be alert," Cuauhcoatl assured him. "Did my grandfather call them 'gods'?"

"No, he called them 'invaders,' as he always does. But in this palace, as you know, they are *gods.*"

"I will not forget myself," Cuauhcoatl replied stiffly, resenting the superior tone that this little man was taking with him. "How did my grandfather get a message to *you*?"

Nahui Olin's thick lips tightened into a chilly smile.

"He came to see me, as he always does."

"*Here?* In the palace?" Cuauhcoatl demanded incredulously, and Nahui Olin made an impatient noise.

"You sound as much offended as surprised, Cuauhcoatl. Did you expect to learn all his secrets in such a short time? I have been his friend for ten years, and I have learned that it is best to be satisfied with what he wishes you to know. Let us not waste our time being envious of each other."

Cuauhcoatl realized abruptly that it was, indeed, jealousy that he had been feeling. His time in the palace had convinced him of the importance of his grandfather's scheming, and the time that he had spent in Huemac's room, listening to his father and the other men, had deepened his loyalty to the point where he resented even the suggestion that his grandfather trusted someone else more than himself. But he saw now how foolish and immature this was, and, still squatting, he bowed apologetically to the dwarf.

"Forgive me, Nahui Olin," he said sincerely. "I would like to be your friend, as well, even though we may never be able to show it publicly."

"Yes, we *should* be friends," Nahui Olin said quietly, looking into Cuauhcoatl's eyes. "And you must forgive me, for I have long envied you for the way your grandfather cares for you. It is not the same, being a 'friend.' Perhaps I have even enjoyed tormenting you more than I know."

"It renders me harmless in Moteczuma's eyes," Cuauhcoatl pointed out. "I know that at the beginning he thought of me as a hostage against my grandfather."

"That is why you must stay close to him now. As he feels his end approaching, he will think of Huemac, the ninth and last ruler of Tula. He may reach out to your grandfather through you. But be careful, Cuauhcoatl," the dwarf warned. "He might also see you as a symbol of what threatens him, and try to destroy you."

"I know the danger," Cuauhcoatl agreed. "But I am grateful for your advice, and your friendship."

They stared at one another silently, sharing a moment of comradeship. Then Nahui Olin remembered himself and cackled maniacally, for the benefit of those watching.

"Let me show you something," he said to Cuauhcoatl, gesturing him closer to the shrouded cage. Then he lifted the edge of the cloth and peeled the covering back, warning Cuauhcoatl not to get too close to the wooden bars.

The dim light of the hallway penetrated only a short way into the cage, and at first Cuauhcoatl could only see a black mass lying against the black wall. But then two large yellow eyes appeared in the darkness, glowing menacingly, and Cuauhcoatl caught his breath as he made out the whole shape of the jaguar in the cage.

"Do his eyes not remind you of someone else?" Nahui Olin asked suggestively. "Now watch . . ."

Taking the edge of the shroud, Nahui Olin gave it a slight flick with his fingers as he let it drop, and before the cloth could even hit the cage, a paw shot through the bars and snagged the fabric on its sharp claws. There was a ripping sound, and then a low coughing snarl, all in such fast succession that Cuauhcoatl felt them as one blow, and went over backward onto his buttocks. The fear hit him an instant later, making his heart race so furiously that he held a hand to his chest.

Nahui Olin's laughter boomed out over the room, and though he extended a hand to Cuauhcoatl and seemed to be trying to apologize for the fright he had given him, he could not restrain the mirth that shook his stubby body from head to toe.

"I am sorry, Cuauhcoatl," he managed finally, his eyes tearing with laughter. "But that is how *we* must be: watchful in the darkness, and ready to strike in an instant."

"There is no chance of my sleeping now," Cuauhcoatl said with a rueful grimace. "You have made my wakefulness complete, Nahui Olin," he added sardonically. "In your usual friendly manner . . ."

THAT NIGHT, Cuauhcoatl was one of a dozen Arrow Warriors stationed in the hallway outside Moteczuma's sleeping chamber. And although he was probably the youngest of the twelve, he was easily the largest, and their captain had placed him in command of the detail. This had been happening to Cuauhcoatl almost from the moment he entered the order, when he had quickly discovered that he was one of only a few truly seasoned warriors in their ranks. Many, like Ehecatzin, had taken only the one captive required to cut their hair-locks before joining the order, relying upon their family connections for admittance. The best of Cuauhcoatl's warrior friends had all been rejected for palace service, a disappointment he had learned to accept as being ultimately for the best, since it had increased his own stature and had given him access to positions of authority.

But while the Arrows' fighting ability might have been suspect, Cuauhcoatl felt no shame in wearing the fringed mantle, for he had no doubts concerning their discipline and readiness. No one entered or left the palace unobserved, and every visitor's business was known and his movements monitored accordingly. In addition, every Arrow had memorized an elaborate set of emergency procedures and had familiarized himself with all the various hidden passages and escape routes within the palace. They were subjected to constant drills, often unannounced, and those who made mistakes were gone the next day. There was no possibility that Moteczuma would ever be taken by surprise, and he could be smuggled out of the palace on a moment's notice, before his attackers could even find his chambers.

As he surveyed the men ranged before the door, Cuauhcoatl wondered if any of them had ever paused to consider the purpose of their training. Who, for instance, was *likely* to attack Moteczuma in his own palace, when there were no enemies even remotely within striking distance of Tenochtitlan, and an army of sentries was stationed around and outside the city? And under what possible circumstances would the Speaker need to escape with such well-practiced haste? But Cuauhcoatl knew that no one but himself asked such questions, and he only in the sanctity of his grandfather's room. The rest slept the sleep of obedience, alert only to the requirements of their duties, and blind to the reasons for what they did.

We all stand facing outward, Cuauhcoatl thought ruefully, yet the real enemy is already behind us, in the heart of Moteczuma. He respected Nahui Olin's warning to beware of the Speaker's misplaced anger, but from what he had seen of Moteczuma recently, he frankly doubted that the ruler any longer had the capacity for viciousness. He had been downcast ever since the foreign gods had first been sighted a month ago, exclaiming aloud about his bad luck and eating and sleeping poorly. From certain conversations that had taken place within Cuauhcoatl's hearing, it seemed that only the priests of the war gods, and a coalition of warchiefs led by Cuitlahuac, acting in concert, had prevented Moteczuma from journeying to the coast himself in order to surrender his kingdom to the gods.

But then a runner came racing down the corridor, and Cuauhcoatl immediately dropped his speculations and stepped forward to meet him, the other

Arrows coming to attention behind him. The runner's face, despite his exertions, seemed pale and bloodless.

"The messengers have come from the coast," the man blurted breathlessly. "They have seen the gods, and met with them. They request that the Speaker be roused to hear them."

"He gave this instruction himself," Cuauhcoatl agreed, and turned to order one of his men into the Speaker's chamber. But they were all avoiding his eyes, and he knew that none of them wanted to be the one to rouse Moteczuma and tell him of this long-dreaded news. Tightening his lips disdainfully, Cuauhcoatl handed his shield and warclub to the nearest man and gestured for the door to be opened, and went into the chamber himself.

A single wick was burning in a bowl of oil beside the cushioned platform on which Moteczuma slept.

"My Lord," Cuauhcoatl called softly, but the figure on the platform did not stir. Knowing, somehow, that his calls would be in vain, he still announced his presence several more times before climbing onto the platform and kneeling beside the blanket-wrapped form, which was curled into a protective ball, like a child.

"My Lord," Cuauhcoatl said once more, before placing a hand lightly on the man's shoulder. Instantly, Moteczuma jerked awake, throwing out an arm that knocked Cuauhcoatl backward off the platform. Feeling that he was reliving a dream, the young man rolled to his knees and started speaking rapidly, for Moteczuma's eyes were wild and there was a knife in his hand. Attracted by the commotion, other guards had appeared from previously concealed exits in the chamber, but they stayed where they were, listening to Cuauhcoatl explain himself:

"I am Cuauhcoatl, my Lord, a member of your guard. You asked to be awakened if a message came from the coast. It has come."

"When?" Moteczuma demanded incoherently. "Now? Have they seen the gods?"

"So they say, my Lord. Where shall we bring them?"

"Not here," Moteczuma said immediately. "Take them to the Coacalli, the Serpent House, and have the priests prepare two captives." Then he seemed to recognize Cuauhcoatl for the first time. "And you—why are *you* guarding my chamber tonight?"

"Your jester, my Lord, Nahui Olin, had use for me this afternoon."

"Of course," Moteczuma said absently, his mind having already strayed from the question. He dropped his knife onto the blankets and rose. "Go see to what I have ordered. Lead the messengers to the Coacalli yourself, and see that they do not speak to anyone else. I will be right behind you."

THEIR BODIES painted with chalk, the captives were sacrificed in front of Moteczuma, and their blood was sprinkled over the messengers, who had looked into the faces of the gods, and had even spoken to them. The head of the delegation was a tall man much trusted by Moteczuma, and he bore the title Tlillancalqui, the Keeper of the House of Ink. It was he who told Moteczuma how the gods had met him and his companions on the beach and had rowed them out to the gods' floating temple, where a ladder had been lowered to allow them to climb up.

"And were they the same as those who came before?" Moteczuma demanded. "Were their faces pale and bearded, and their hair sometimes yellow, sometimes black?"

"The very same, my Lord, except for a few, whose faces were dirty and black," the Tlillancalqui replied, and Moteczuma gestured silently for him to go on.

"The gods also have a woman of our own kind with them, a woman from Teticpac named Malintzin, the Grass Princess. She showed us the one who is the head god, and he allowed us to adorn him with the raiment of Quetzalcoatl: the turquoise mask with the quetzal feather head-fan, the sleeveless jacket and back mirror, and the shield of banded gold and mother-of-pearl. Truly, the god wore these things with ease, as if they belonged to him."

Moteczuma sighed loudly through his nose, and the messenger was silent while his master pondered this weighty fact. Moteczuma finally made a limp gesture for him to continue.

"We had also brought food to them, my Lord, as you commanded," the man said. "And after making us taste of it ourselves, they ate the maize cakes and fruit with great relish. They especially enjoyed the cocoa we had brought. In return, they gave us some of what they eat, and it is like fasting food—very large and white, and somewhat sweet to the taste. We have brought back what they gave to us."

The Tlillancalqui opened a cloth bundle and carefully laid it on a mat before the Speaker, who made no attempt to touch the white chunks, but simply stared at them with downcast eyes. It was a long time before he asked to hear more, listening now without moving his eyes or interrupting.

The messenger went on to describe the metal weapons and metal armor worn by the gods, and the terrible weapon they possessed, a long, black tube that thundered and spat a stone into the air, making a noise that stole one's senses and emitting an odor that was foul and overpowering, like rotten mud. And if the stone struck a tree, the tree was instantly broken into splinters, as if it had exploded from the inside. The gods also had, as servant-beasts, great hornless deer that were as tall as a housetop, and other beasts that looked like lions or jaguars, except that they had hanging jowls and flat, folded ears, and were very gaunt in the body. They growled ferociously and went everywhere panting, their teeth showing and their tongues hanging out.

"The gods wanted to fight with us the next day, to test our strength," the Tlillancalqui said in conclusion. "But we left for Tenochtitlan as soon as we were put ashore, so that we might not be drawn into an unholy act."

"You have done well," Moteczuma said in a dull voice. "Rest now, for you are fatigued . . ."

The messengers were led out, and Moteczuma sat without moving, his chin on his hand. Everyone in the chamber—priests, stewards, and guards—waited with him, their anxiety mirrored in their faces. Cuauhcoatl observed them coolly, the only one unaffected by the revelations, since he had heard them all before this. Quetzal Papalotl had been correct in every detail, including the fact that the gods would have a woman with them, which she had communicated to Huemac a month ago. But Cuauhcoatl did not allow himself to dwell upon his aunt's awesome power, cause for wonder in itself. He could feel the paralysis setting in among those around him—the sleep of awe.

"Stewards!" Moteczuma cried suddenly, and all the men in the chamber jumped at once, the stewards immediately presenting themselves for instruction. In a commanding voice, Moteczuma began issuing orders in a rapid stream. The priests were sent off to carry the holy food to the Temple of Huitzilopochtli. A list was made of those who would go to the gods as ambassadors and what they would carry: gold and jewels as gifts; provisions for both the gods and their beasts, including captives, in case they drank blood; ink and paper to draw the gods' likenesses. Sorcerers and spell-casters were also to accompany the ambassadors, to test the extent of the gods' magical powers. The lords, warchiefs, and priests of the major orders were to be summoned for a meeting the next day at noon.

Cuauhcoatl was at first surprised, then impressed by the way that Moteczuma had recovered from his shock and had taken command of the situation, although it was unclear what he hoped to accomplish with all this activity. The stewards scurried out one by one, accompanied by guards when necessary. All appeared greatly relieved to have something to do, the sleep of obedience being preferable to that of fear. Soon only Cuauhcoatl and a half-dozen other Arrows were left in the chamber, and Moteczuma again fell into one of his long silences. Then his head jerked up and he lurched to his feet, his face working furiously, as if he were grappling with some momentous realization.

"They are coming for me," he said in a strangled voice. "I must leave here immediately."

Cuauhcoatl responded as automatically as the rest, dropping his shield to snatch a torch from the wall, then falling into step with the Speaker as he headed for the door hidden behind the dais. One of the Arrows stayed behind as a rear guard and two others ran on ahead, giving out a low, keening whistle that was met by an answering signal from far down the dark passageway. Cuauhcoatl and the other three Arrows moved in unison, two on either side of the Speaker, who had broken into a fast run.

At the turnoff to the first escape exit, Moteczuma slowed for a moment but then continued straight ahead, losing the two men who had gone ahead to the exit. It occurred to Cuauhcoatl briefly that this was another drill; that Moteczuma wanted to see if all his alternative escape routes were operable and properly manned. But the Speaker was not running at the pace suitable for a fifty-year-old man, especially one who had eaten and slept poorly for months. Cuauhcoatl found his own young lungs and legs being stretched to their limits, and he knew that only a powerful emotion could be sustaining the man beside him. Daring a glance in that direction, he saw, without question, that Moteczuma was truly trying to escape.

Then, just as all the Arrows were beginning to falter, their lungs bursting and their arms aching from the weight of the weapons they carried, Moteczuma chose his exit, and they burst out of the enclosed passageway and into the night air. The torches were hastily extinguished, but not before Cuauhcoatl had caught sight of the men waiting by the canoes ahead. The night went black and the guards drew close around Moteczuma, panting for breath while their eyes adjusted to the lack of light. They could smell the water and hear it lapping against the shore, but they could not see where the Lake began.

"What do I face?" Moteczuma demanded suddenly. "What lies ahead of me?"

"East, my Lord," Cuauhcoatl gasped. "Texcoco is directly across the Lake."

When Moteczuma did not respond, but seemed only to slump where he stood, Cuauhcoatl realized that his master had been speaking in a larger sense, about his own future. He has run to the end of his fear, the young man thought, and there is nowhere for him to go.

"Perhaps you will end this drill now, my Lord," Cuauhcoatl suggested diplomatically. "You have tested us to our limits."

"Yes," Moteczuma agreed, looking around him dazedly, as if he had forgotten what had brought him here. He stared directly at Cuauhcoatl but seemed not to see him. "You have all performed splendidly. But it is over now. There is no use in going on . . ."

"Let me send for a litter, my Lord."

"Yes, a litter," Moteczuma repeated in a murmur, suddenly as pliant as a child. "It is over," he said, as the guards shifted uneasily around him. "Now it is all over . . ."

THE SKY turned red, then violet as the sun slowly sank behind Popocatepetl, and the great smoking mountain spread its shadow over the city of Cholula. As the murals surrounding her began to lose their colors to the gathering dusk, Papalotl roused herself from her lethargy and again took up her broom. Though she could hear the sounds of the celebrants in the streets outside, she was utterly alone in the courtyard, which showed the effects of its recent use, and of the neglect that had followed upon that. As she swept the refuse into small piles, she gazed down at the dried, crushed flowers, the spilled incense mingling with the dust, the glimmering bits of feathers that had broken off garments or ritual implements. She felt that she could remember the face that had belonged to each tiny piece of trash, faces that had seemed unending until, abruptly, they had ceased coming to her altogether. Now, the cleaning of this courtyard was her act of penance for the trust those faces had placed in her, a trust that would be held falsely, or would simply be forfeit in her absence.

As the great Wind Drum on the temple above began to boom out the end of the day, she leaned upon her broom and bowed her head reverently, so that she neither saw nor heard the hawk that plummeted to a landing behind her. It was the sound of heavy breathing, once the thunder of the drum had died away, that made her start in fright and turn to see who was there.

"Father," she whispered, glancing anxiously toward the inner door of the courtyard as she went to his side. His chest rising and falling from his exertions, Huemac also glanced at the door, but scornfully, as if to mock her fear of discovery. Only with reluctance did he allow her to lead him to a bench in the shadows away from the door, acting like a young warrior spoiling for a fight.

"So, my daughter," he said when they were seated. "You are not ill at all, as they tried to make me believe. You are a prisoner here."

"The High Priest has ordered my confinement," Papalotl explained in a low voice. "I could not disobey him, even to tell you that I had agreed to this."

"Tell me now, then," Huemac demanded, making no effort to lower his own tone. "What has happened to make you agree to such a thing?"

"You are very aggressive, my father," Papalotl observed quietly. "Do you wish us to be discovered here?"

"Can a daughter be denied to her father?" Huemac inquired roughly. "I have spent three days in this city, trying by every means to get to see you. I have been lied to and rebuffed, and I have come very close to using my powers on a priest. My patience is at an end, Papalotl. The invaders have already begun to march inland, toward the lands of the Tlaxcalans. Why are you being silenced at this time?"

"I have dreamed for the last time, my father," she told him gravely. "And the people cannot be told what I saw. It is too late now to admit that I was wrong."

The harshness faded from Huemac's lined features, and he stared at her sympathetically.

"I am not one of the madmen in the streets, my daughter," he said softly. "Tell me what you have seen."

"I went to the shrine above," Papalotl explained, indicating the great pyramid that towered over them. "I was permitted to go there alone, at night. I sat with my back to the image of the god, facing east, and I gave myself to the Wind. The Lord came to me as a warm breeze, smelling of hot sand and salty water, and I was filled with the joyous, restful peace of his presence . . .

"If only he had taken me then," she continued after a pause, her voice losing its lightness. "For I next found myself in a strange town, in a land where the rivers were slow and green, and great palm trees grew along their banks. The people spoke a foreign tongue and were in a state of great excitement, for the foreign gods, the invaders, had come to live among them."

"It was Cempoalla," Huemac supplied for her, "in the land of the Totonacs."

"It was night and there were many fires lit," Papalotl went on, oblivious to the interruption, "but I passed by everyone unseen. The gods were eating, and polishing their weapons, and feeding grass to their deer. They seemed no different from our own warriors, except for their pale skins and loud voices. I thought: If they are gods, why do they not see me, or feel my presence?

"But none did, though I stood beside them and stared into their faces. Then I came to the shrine that had belonged to the people of the town. And beside it, on the ground, were the sacrificial stone and the image of Huitzilopochtli, broken into pieces. The shrine had been painted white and all its hangings and statues had been removed. The gods had erected their own image inside, an image that had no head or body, and no garments or jewelry of any kind. It seemed to be no more than two crossed sticks, and the only offerings they had left before it were small white torches that gave off a strong odor as they burned.

"I went into the shrine," Papalotl said, her voice echoing the hesitation she had felt. "But nothing happened to me, and I felt no different than I do now. Nowhere did I sense the presence of my Lord, or of any other god familiar to me."

"And then?" Huemac prompted, when she suddenly seemed unwilling to go on. Papalotl stared at him for a moment, frowning unconsciously, as if struggling with her sense of modesty.

"Then I was drawn to the largest house in the town, the house of the chief," she said. "It had a greenish glow around it, emanating from an inner room. That is where I found the regalia of the god, his mask and shield, and the crooked staff of the Wind God." Papalotl's face tightened as she looked up at her father. "They were piled into a wooden chest, one atop of the other. And the one who possessed these things was lying naked on mats on the floor. His skin was pale and hairy, and with him was one of our women, lying with him like a wife."

Papalotl spoke these last words with a bitterness that seemed to exhaust her of emotion, so that she went on in a toneless voice:

"I fled from that room without wishing to see more, and then I found myself walking in sand, with a great expanse of water stretching out before me. There, at the shore, was the raft of serpents, the raft spoken of in the legends of Quetzalcoatl-Topiltzin. It swayed upon the water as the serpents coiled and uncoiled, plumed with feathers that glowed a bluish-green in the darkness. And then I saw the Lord, wearing a long robe that was as white as his hair and beard, and holding his staff aloft, as if passing judgment. He spoke to me in a flower song:

> "Long did I journey to come here;
> Many days from the Land of Tlillan Tlappan,
> The Land of the Black and the Red,
> The land of wisdom.
>
> Were there no omens?
> Were there no signs of my coming?
> Yet here the stones are reddened
> With blood;
> Here the fields are blackened
> With the ashes of the dead;
> Here there is cruelty and killing,
> But no wisdom.
>
> My heart is heavy;
> I can find no comfort.
> Tezcatlipoca,
> Lord of the Smoking Mirror,
> Laughs at my grief,
> And mocks my childlessness.
> He will protect no one
> When I am gone . . ."

Papalotl fell silent, staring off into the deepening shadows, as if still seeing the raft.

"Did you go to him, my child?" Huemac prompted gently, and she nodded sadly, without looking up at him.

"I ran to him, crying to be taken, and I saw that my aunt was already with him. But then he raised his staff and stopped my approach, and commanded that I look behind me. And I saw the city of Cholula, as if it were just over the next hill. And the whole city was in flames; even the great temple was burning. In the distance, but still within my sight, was the Lake, with its two island cities, side by side. These also burst into flames as I watched, lighting up the whole sky . . .

"When I turned back," Papalotl concluded quietly, "the raft was far out on the water, so that I could barely make out the form of the Lord, with the golden wind jewel shining upon his chest. A voice called to me, saying only: 'The faithful will not be forgotten.' I fell to my knees in the sand, and then I awoke, and was again in the shrine."

Seeing the tears in her eyes, Huemac waited respectfully for her to compose herself. But then a priestess in a white robe stepped through the inner door and saw the two of them sitting together. Making a small, startled noise, the woman disappeared as quickly as she had come.

"We have been seen," Huemac said brusquely. "You must decide quickly, my daughter. I can take you out of here myself, or I can have Moteczuma demand your release. They cannot silence you if you wish the truth to be known."

Papalotl put a hand on his arm and looked at him gratefully, showing that she appreciated his concern for her. But then she shook her head slowly, and spoke in a firm voice:

"It is too late. There are too many, now, who could not bring themselves to believe it, and who would only turn in scorn upon my order. And the faithful would only be confused by knowing this, and might succumb to their doubts. I have no right to deprive them of the redemption the god has promised. No, my father," she added apologetically. "You are free to do whatever you wish with this knowledge, but I cannot violate my vows of obedience. I must wait here, in silence and humility, and hope that the god will return for me."

Voices could be heard coming toward the courtyard, and Huemac rose instinctively from the bench. Then he collected himself and gazed longingly at his daughter's beautiful face, at the golden eyes that mirrored his own.

"It is my luck that he should have you," he said softly. "Just as it has always been your fate to go to him. He will return for you, Papalotl, for there is wisdom here, where you are. I leave you with pride, for you have brought great gladness to my heart, and honor to everything you have touched. Farewell, my daughter," he whispered, shrinking back into the shadows as the voices drew nearer. "Now I must leave you . . . "

The golden eyes vanished, then reappeared briefly, wild and predatory amid the flashing coppery feathers, as the hawk burst into flight and disappeared upward into the night. A great cry was raised from the doorway behind her, but Papalotl did not turn, continuing to stare at the place where her father had last stood.

"Farewell, my father," she murmured under her breath, and bowed her head, letting her tears fall freely onto the dusty courtyard floor.

3

THOUGH he was one of the last to enter the Council Chamber, Xolotlpilli did not rush to assume his customary place in the circle of seated men. He stopped just inside the door and surveyed the assembly of familiar faces, all in their usual places, grouped according to the factions of opinion that had developed around the issue of how to respond to the foreigners. Moteczuma's reed seat was at the head of the circle, and to his left were those who favored a policy of accommodation with the "gods"; to his right was the coalition of priests and warriors who believed that the advance of the "invaders" should be resisted with firmness. The moderates—those still willing to weigh the arguments of both sides—occupied the places between, facing Moteczuma across the center of the circle.

These groups had gone through many changes during the seven months since the arrival of the foreigners, remaining roughly equal in number even as their respective positions hardened and became increasingly predictable. Xolotlpilli had been associated with the moderates from the very beginning, and he had maintained his neutrality throughout the summer, listening carefully to the reports of the foreigners' progress as they marched inland from their base among the Totonacs. He had never doubted, since hearing of Papalotl's vision, that he would one day join the opposition. But there had seemed no point in making his commitment known while Moteczuma continued to lean so strongly toward the party of accommodation; it was better to save his prestige for a time when his choice might make a greater impression.

Now, however, that time had come, hastened by necessity, and Xolotlpilli had decided to make his defection from the ranks of the neutral as noticeable as possible. He was aware that he was attracting nervous glances from the Arrow Warriors guarding the door, but he delayed a moment longer, until all the men in front of him had taken their seats. Then he walked forward, toward the place that had been left vacant for him next to Itzquauhtzin, the Eagle Speaker of Tlatelulco. Some of the seated men turned at his approach and opened a path for him into their midst, a courtesy that Xolotlpilli acknowledged with a slight bow. But then he turned away from them and continued around the outside of the circle, his great, gleaming head held erect with deliberate dignity. A murmuring began around the circle, and he could see heads turning in his direction as he approached to within a few places of Moteczuma's right hand and took a seat beside the warchief Cuitlahuac, the leader of those opposed to the foreigners. Putting their heads together, the two men exchanged a few words in private, then straightened up at the sound of the gong announcing Moteczuma's entrance.

All the men around the circle bowed low and touched dirt to their tongues, remaining bowed as the High Priest of Huitzilopochtli said the prayers of consecration over this gathering. When the gong sounded again and Xolotlpilli was able to look up, he saw the Speaker staring at him, his narrow features frozen into an expression of weary disappointment. Xolotlpilli politely lowered his own eyes, but his posture, while not defiant, clearly showed the stubbornness of the conviction that had caused him to change places. Then Moteczuma called on the Cihuacoatl to give the latest reports concerning the "gods," making the term sound like a warning.

Though Xolotlpilli had already heard these reports—had, indeed, based his actions directly upon them—he could not repress the hot flash of anxiety that went through him at the first mention of Cholula. Only days earlier, the foreigners, guided by their Totonac allies, had advanced into Tlaxcalan territory, and had inflicted terrible defeats upon both the Tlaxcalans and their subjects, the Otomi of Tecoac. The Tlaxcalans had surrendered and had welcomed the foreigners into their cities as conquering gods, giving them their women and pledging themselves as allies. The Huexotzincans had come over soon after, and now it was said that these two deadly enemies of the Mexicans were urging the foreigners to go south, toward the Holy City.

The report of the Cihuacoatl confirmed this, though he, being a member of the party of accommodation, did not elaborate on the reason for the Tlaxcalans' urgings. But everyone in the room knew of the bad feelings that existed between the Tlaxcalans and the Choluteca, and few could doubt that the Tlaxcalans hoped to bring war on Cholula with the aid of the foreigners. Xolotlpilli, for one, had no doubts whatsoever, and it was this that had made him join the party of resistance. Perhaps his father and sister could resign themselves to the inevitability of something terrible happening in Cholula, but it was his own nature, and his fate, to fight on like a warrior, no matter what the odds. He knew only one way to respond to the danger advancing upon his sister, and that was to join those who would oppose it. It was doubtful that Moteczuma would be any more open to persuasion today than he had been in the past, but Xolotlpilli had come prepared to try.

As usual, though, Moteczuma chose to hear first from those who favored accommodation, a group that included the Cihuacoatl, the Tlillancalqui who had first met with the foreigners, and the ruler of Texcoco, Cacama. It was this young man, the twenty-five-year-old son of Nezahualpilli, the nephew whom Moteczuma had installed in Texcoco by force, who rose to speak.

"Surely, my lords," Cacama began, in his smooth, polished Texcocan manner, "surely, we can have nothing to fear from allowing the gods to proceed to the Holy City. Have we not judged them to be the sons of Quetzalcoatl-Topiltzin, who is worshiped in that city? Will they not be welcome in their home? Indeed, perhaps they will be content to stay in Cholula, and inhabit the shrines that have already been built for them, and advance no farther. And while it is impossible to say what is in their minds, have their words to us not been friendly, and respectful of our rule?"

Cacama paused briefly, inclining his head toward the group of warriors and priests around Cuitlahuac.

"And yes," he went on in an agreeable tone, "I know that there are those who will say that the Tlaxcalans will lie to them, and mislead them into attacking the Choluteca. But will the gods allow their ears to be soiled by the lies of these treacherous men? And are the priests of Cholula without their own protection? It has been said many times in the past that the great temple, the Man-Made Mountain, is sacrosanct, and that its very stones will pour forth a flood of fire and water upon anyone who dares to violate its sanctity. Can we so lightly abandon our trust, my lords, in these things that our fathers have believed to be true? Rather, I say, let us hold fast to our traditions, and do nothing that will undermine our dignity."

Cacama's words received the usual murmurs of approbation from his co-horts, and Moteczuma nodded to show that he, too, was not displeased by the young man's oratory. With some reluctance, the Speaker turned back to recognize the group to his right, gesturing for his brother Cuitlahuac to raise the expected objections. But the warchief gave the floor to Xolotlpilli, who rose to his full height and stared around the circle for a moment, flexing his huge hands unconsciously, as if yearning for a weapon.

"My lords," he said in a blunt voice, eschewing any pretense of courtliness. "I have said little in our meetings so far, yet you all know me, and know that I am a man of actions, not words. Our esteemed ally from Texcoco has spoken with his usual eloquence, and his opinion is to be respected. He has told us that it is impossible to know what is in the minds of these foreign gods, and with this, I can only agree. They accept our gifts and send messages of friend-ship, even while they are inciting our subjects among the Totonacs to rebel against our rule. They speak in tones of respect to our ambassadors, yet they desecrate the temples of our god and cause our tax collectors to be abused. It is indeed impossible to conceive the meaning that friendship and respect have in their minds.

"And who are those they have chosen to befriend thus far?" Xolotlpilli demanded, sweeping the men around Cacama with a stern gaze. "The rebel Totonacs count for little, but is the strength of the Tlaxcalans and Huexotzin-cans so easily dismissed? And we have also heard that the leader of the renegade Texcocans, your brother, my Lord," he said pointedly, staring straight at Cacama, "has asked to join this unholy alliance. Can anything *but* treacherous advice be expected from rebels and enemies?"

Cacama's face had darkened at the mention of his brother, and there were loud murmurs of both agreement and disapproval in many parts of the room, for Cacama's dependence on Tenocha power was a sensitive and much-avoided issue. Xolotlpilli waited for quiet, pretending not to notice the frown on Moteczuma's face.

"Perhaps the foreign gods are indeed as invincible as they showed against the Tlaxcalans," he suggested in a rueful tone. "Perhaps we cannot resist them with the weapons at our disposal. But their numbers are small, some four hundred, as you know. Is there any wisdom, then, in allowing them to amass an army of allies as they advance toward Tenochtitlan? Would it not be better to meet them in the passes leading to Cholula, where their deer could not trample on us as easily as they did against the Otomi? If their intentions are truly peaceful, they will place themselves in our protection, instead of that of our enemies. But if they insist on a battle, let it be *us* who choose the ground."

Xolotlpilli sat down abruptly, appearing oblivious to the controversy he had touched off. He had not suggested anything that Cuitlahuac and the others had not been saying for months, but he had spoken with a fresh voice, as one who had weighed things carefully before rendering his opinion. And though he had argued calmly and logically, his personal sense of the urgency of the situation had not been lost on his listeners. The very *nearness* of the foreigners could no longer be denied, whatever their intentions.

Further arguments were raised on both sides, with Itzquauhtzin and the other moderates interjecting themselves to keep the debate from becoming acrimonious. Xolotlpilli had tried, before the meeting, to persuade the ruler of Tlatelulco to defect with him, calling on Omeocelotl and the pochteca for support, since the merchants had suffered greatly from the disorder and rebellion caused by the foreigners. But Itzquauhtzin had been appointed to his post by Moteczuma, and he was as yet unwilling to risk a loss of the Speaker's favor, though he had listened to Xolotlpilli with sympathy.

It soon became apparent, despite a strong speech by Cuitlahuac, that more than sympathy would be required to force Moteczuma to act. While admitting that the influence of the Tlaxcalans was a reason for concern, he claimed, with a senseless kind of arrogance, that an "ambush in the mountains" did not comport with the greatness of his rule. He would send another message to the gods, warning them not to listen to the Tlaxcalans, and asking them again to come no further toward Tenochtitlan. And he agreed to alert the Cholulans to their danger, and to order the Mexican garrisons at Itzucan and Acatzinco —near Cholula—to be ready in case of trouble. But he would not block the way to the Holy City, preferring to rely on the protections that Cacama had mentioned. Above all men, he said in closing, the Speaker had the obligation to uphold the traditions of the past.

Xolotlpilli bowed with the rest as Moteczuma went out, then rose and stood with Cuitlahuac, seeing the same look of frustration and defeat in the war-chief's eyes that he felt in his own heart. It is his *brother* who does this to us, Xolotlpilli reminded himself, but that only made him think of Papalotl, and his bitterness spilled out on its own.

"Is it no longer the tradition to defend our allies, and ourselves?" he asked with a scowl, and Cuitlahuac put a hand on his shoulder to calm him.

"Perhaps not today," he allowed in a low voice, then squeezed Xolotlpilli's shoulder encouragingly. "But there is always tomorrow, my friend. You know how quickly his mind can change. We must keep trying."

"Of course," Xolotlpilli agreed absently, as they walked out of the chamber together. But he could not help but feel that they were running out of tomorrows, and that no amount of effort would bring back the opportunities that were being squandered now. Already, it was too late for his sister. Holding his head erect, Xolotlpilli walked slowly out of the palace, his warrior's heart heavy with the knowledge that he would never see Papalotl again.

DISGUISED as an aged Mayan pilgrim, his long hair dyed gray and his walk a practiced hobble, Pinotl shuffled through the crowds in the streets of Cholula without attracting attention. Few of the guards stationed around the temples and courtyards even bothered to question him, and those who did were quickly disarmed by his apparent harmlessness, and then exhausted by being chattered at in Mayan. But the tension in the city was palpable, and the warriors were everywhere, breaking up gatherings and keeping the curious crowds away from the quarters of the foreigners, who had arrived in Cholula two days earlier. It was not an easy task, nor a duty that made the warriors themselves comfortable, since the foreigners were accompanied by Tlaxcalan porters, and had left a thousand Tlaxcalan warriors camped outside the city. This did not inspire trust in the Choluteca, and the leader of the foreigners—speaking through the woman, Malintzin—had made matters worse by proposing, in his very first speech to the heads of the city, that the people should abandon their old gods and adopt the god they had brought from afar.

The priests of the city were now having trouble within their own ranks, and Pinotl had heard a rumor that a secret sacrifice—expressly forbidden by the foreigners—had been made to the war gods, and that both Huitzilopochtli and Tezcatlipoca had commanded their priests to bring war upon the arrogant visitors. Pinotl did not know how much such rumors had to do with the presence of Moteczuma's agents, who were also everywhere in the city, but the mood in the streets was growing increasingly ugly. The foreigners had announced their intention of leaving the next day for Tenochtitlan, but it seemed less and less likely that their departure would be accomplished without bloodshed. Already, Pinotl had seen small groups of women and children, with bundles on their backs, heading for the roads that led out of the city.

When night fell, he again journeyed to the courtyard beside the great temple, using his black staff for balance as the crowds jostled him in passing. Several of the streets he had intended to use had been closed by the warriors, so that he was forced to make a wide detour before circling back to his goal. As had been the case earlier, there was an armed guard standing in front of the barred gate, and he eyed Pinotl suspiciously as he hobbled past, muttering to himself in Mayan. There was no choice but to wait, and hope that the guard would fall asleep or leave. So Pinotl found an alleyway between two nearby buildings and slumped down in the shadows, pretending to be asleep himself.

Dawn was just breaking over the city when two other warriors came down the street and began to talk to the man at the gate in excited voices, pointing back toward the temple plaza and obviously encouraging the man to leave. *Go,* Pinotl urged silently, certain now that something was going to happen soon. He felt for the flint knife hidden under his dirty gray robe, resolving to make his move whether the man left or not. But then the warrior acceded to the urgings of his companions, and went down the street with them, leaving the gate unattended.

Lurching to his feet, Pinotl staggered aimlessly out into the street, his movements bringing him to the gate seemingly by accident. He leaned against it as if to rest, testing its strength with his shoulder. It would not give, but there was room enough between it and the wall above to permit a man of his size to wriggle through. Glancing swiftly up and down the deserted street, he tossed his staff over the top and scaled the gate behind it, dropping to his feet in the courtyard below.

Even in the gray light of dawn, the extreme cleanliness of the courtyard impressed itself upon him forcibly, its flagstones freshly scrubbed and the wall murals touched up and polished to a new brightness. Papalotl was seated on a bench in the center of the enclosure, facing the place where his staff had come clattering down. There was a smile on her face, and as he came closer, and could feel the quiet weight of her presence, he knew that he would not be able to take her away from here. She seemed as rooted and immovable as the great temple pyramid behind her, and the mountains beyond that.

"You have come, my friend," she said, in a voice that seemed to float to his ears, like a voice out of a dream. Her golden eyes glowed deeply, their light turned inward.

"I wanted to see you," Pinotl said simply. "Your father said that you would not leave here, but I did not want to believe him."

"The Lord is very close, Pinotl. Can you not feel his presence?"

Pinotl could feel only *her* presence, so powerfully that his heart swelled inside of him and tears rose to his eyes.

"There is great peace here," he said. "Unlike the rest of the city."

"Yes," Papalotl said musingly. "I do not have to dream to know this. You must leave, my friend, before it is too late. *You* were not meant to die here."

Pinotl swallowed so loudly that he was too embarrassed to speak for several moments. Then he made a last desperate attempt to persuade her.

"Your brother, Xolotlpilli, sends me to remind you that he has not been allowed to make his final farewell, and that he cannot come to you here."

Papalotl smiled fondly, but as if at a memory, not an obligation. She put one hand into the other and gently twisted her fingers.

"You must take my last greetings to him, Pinotl," she said, and held out her hand, revealing the golden ring in her open palm. "And you must give this to my niece, to Xiuhcue. You must tell her that a sister awaits her in the hills."

Pinotl clasped his fingers around the ring, feeling the warmth of the precious metal against his skin. A trumpet sounded from the temple plaza, and he was suddenly aware of the noises coming from that direction, the sounds of a large gathering. Laying his staff at the foot of Papalotl's bench, he looked up at her beseechingly, unable to find words for all he wished to say.

"I know what is in your heart, Pinotl," she said for him. "I know how you have loved me, and served me all these years. You are another of the blessings given to me by the god, and I am glad that it is your face I shall remember until the end. Farewell, my friend; may the gods be kind to you and your people."

Pinotl bowed low over the clean flagstones, then picked up his staff and retreated slowly from her presence, walking backward so that he could look at her. He stood for a long time before the gate, until she raised a hand in blessing and called to him to go. Lifting his staff in a brief salute, he turned quickly and climbed back over the gate, landing once more amid the noise and dirt of the street, which echoed with the sounds of contentious men.

PAPALOTL HEARD only the first explosion, like a small burst of thunder from the temple plaza. But the screams and sounds of fighting that followed came only briefly to her ears, and were then swallowed up by the wind that had risen around her, taking away her senses. Her last thought was one of joy that the Lord had come for her, and then she was enveloped by his warmth and his caring, and filled with the utter contentment that attended those he loved. She opened her eyes to a feathery greenish mist, and then an old man appeared before her, the old man in the murals, with his long white beard and conical cap of jaguar skin, the golden wind jewel of Quetzalcoatl-Topiltzin around his neck. Curled in his arms, like a child, was her aunt Cocatli. The god was singing to her, his eyes glittering gently out of the mist:

"Come to me, my daughter.
Come to the rest that awaits you;
Come to the home that is yours . . . "

Then Papalotl was carried forward by the wind and heard no more, and did not see the metal-shirted warriors who burst into the courtyard behind her, and did not feel the shining warclubs that fell upon her already lifeless body . . .

FOR THE second time in four days, Cuauhcoatl was called away from his duties by a summons from his father's house. The first had been due to the death of his great-aunt Cocatli, who had gone swiftly and silently during her morning prayers, the victim of a heart attack. That same night, word had come to Tenochtitlan of the fighting that had broken out in Cholula, and Cuauhcoatl had been waiting ever since for the summons concerning his aunt, the Priestess Quetzal Papalotl. Now it had come, a late addition to the sad and horrifying news that had been pouring out of the Holy City for the last two days.

It was no longer only Cuauhcoatl's family who were in mourning; the whole city was in a state of desolation, the streets silent and empty of their usual commerce. Moteczuma had gone into seclusion in the House of Darkness, and all the temples were filled with people doing penance, while their priests appealed to the gods for an understanding of what had occurred in Cholula. For Quetzalcoatl had protected none of his people, and he had allowed his shrine to be burned and his image cast down. The foreigners had asked for two thousand men to accompany them as porters, and when these were assembled in the plaza before the great temple, they had sealed off the exits and had fallen upon the Choluteca without mercy, firing their flaming tubes into the midst of the crowd and trampling them with their deer. It had been an enormous massacre, even before the Tlaxcalans outside the city had come pouring in to finish off the survivors and loot the homes of their enemies. Hundreds had been slaughtered, and neither the god nor the Mexican garrisons at Itzucan and Acatzinco had gone to their rescue.

And now they will be coming *here,* Cuauhcoatl thought dejectedly, feeling grief spreading all around him, from his family outward. He found his mother in the courtyard, part of a line of mourning women, and he waited respectfully until she could come to him. Her hair was loosened and her eyes seemed wild in her pitch-smeared face, which quivered with barely checked emotions. Through clenched teeth, she told him that the vanguard merchant Pinotl had brought the news of Papalotl's death, having waited outside Cholula for two days until peace had been restored, and he could confirm it for himself.

"He and the other men await you in your grandfather's room," she concluded in a harsh whisper. "Your sister is with them, as well."

"Xiuhcue!" Cuauhcoatl exclaimed softly. "She has been sent home from the temple?"

"Your father and grandfather sent for her. She arrived before you."

Abruptly, Chalchiuhtona turned back to her duties among the mourners, leaving her son to discover the meaning of this for himself. Cuauhcoatl walked slowly from the courtyard, as was proper, but his pace quickened once he was out of sight of the mourners, and he took the steps to the second floor two at a time. But then he stopped, unsettled by his mother's strange manner, and feeling light-headed from all the speculations spinning through his mind.

He barely knew his sister, who was little more than a girl, not yet thirteen. She had been a small child when he had left this house to enter the calmecac, and he had seen her only infrequently since, due to his duties as a warrior and a member of the Arrows. Why had *she* been invited into the room of truth? Surely, she was too young to have had a vision like his own, or to be useful in their grandfather's schemes. The situation could not be *that* desperate, that Xiuhcue's life had to be put to risk.

Cuauhcoatl found himself growing vaguely angry as he again moved down the corridor, wondering if grief had unsettled everyone's thinking. What more could his grandfather feel was needed? He and Nahui Olin were close to the Speaker, his father had begun to speak out in council, and the merchants were slowly bringing their guild around to the position of resistance. Surely, after Cholula, their message would not be so hard to put across; even Moteczuma would have to recognize the danger now. Soon everyone would know that the foreigners were *men,* and then we could finally join together to destroy them.

His grandfather's room was as crowded as Cuauhcoatl had ever seen it. His father was seated in his usual place beside the door, and Pinotl and Omeocelotl were against the wall where Cuauhcoatl's shattered black helmet had been mounted. His sister was sitting on a mat that had been placed between his and that of his grandfather. She glanced up at him timidly as he took his seat beside her, and he noticed how much she had grown since he had last seen her, her face having taken on the definition and her body the shape of early woman-hood. But he also noticed the golden ring on her finger, and Cholula was still too much on his mind for him not to recognize where it had come from. He looked inquisitively at his grandfather, whose aged face showed none of the expected signs of bereavement. He seemed, in fact, quite satisfied with himself, as if he had found the solution to some nagging problem.

"I have already spoken to your sister, my son," Huemac said. "But her presence here concerns you, as well. I have asked you here to give you back your hope, and your future."

Cuauhcoatl stared at him speechlessly, as if he had been told a cruel joke. He glanced sideways at Xiuhcue, who ducked her head shyly. But her eyes did not seem to share his shock, and he realized again how little he knew of her, of her hopes and ambitions. But his grandfather was waiting for him to respond.

"Forgive me," he said in confusion. "But I do not understand your meaning, Grandfather."

"Do you not, truly?" Huemac asked knowingly. "Do you not remember the boy who scorned me once, and insisted that Nezahualpilli could not be correct concerning our fate? It did not occur to me, then, that you might know your own fate better than I, and that there might be another place for you. But you —and your sister—have been *seen,* and asked for, by a woman in the hills. I intend for you to go to her when you have completed your responsibilities here."

"Escape?" Cuauhcoatl blurted indignantly. "Flee from my duties? It was you, Grandfather, who advised me to join the Arrows. Would you now have me break the vows I have taken?"

"Of course not," Huemac said sharply. "But your vow is to Moteczuma himself; you are pledged to defend his person for as long as he is Speaker, and wears the mask and garments of Huitzilopochtli. Should be abandon his obligations—or die—you would be freed from yours, would you not?"

"But then I must stay and fight," Cuauhcoatl insisted, appealing to Xolotlpilli for support. "Father . . . "

"I understand your feelings, my son," Xolotlpilli said evenly. "You were born under the sign Ten Eagle, and you are destined to be a great warrior. But there are warriors everywhere, and there is one in the hills who is the chief, and is of your own blood. My sister, before she died, sent her ring to Xiuhcue, and commended her to the woman in the hills. You must protect *your* sister, Cuauhcoatl, as I could not protect my own."

Cuauhcoatl saw grief in his father's eyes and lowered his own out of respect. But he could not collect his thoughts to make a response; this had all come to him too quickly.

"Omeocelotl has prepared a map, according to my instructions," Huemac told him. "I will tell you everything you need to know before the time comes. It will not be an easy journey for either of you, nor an easy adjustment to the ways of the Chichimecs. But you must think of the boy who cried for his future, Cuauhcoatl, and of the youth who rose from the dead to fight again. Accept the life that fate has offered you, my son."

"But how could I leave you, and my family and city, in a time of danger?"

"You will face your share of danger before you go," Huemac assured him. "But you must trust us to carry on the fight without you. Perhaps there is yet a chance that we will succeed, and I will come to find you in the hills. If not," he added somberly, "I will die knowing that you will live on, and keep alive the memory of our people."

Cuauhcoatl glanced around at the other men for support, but found no allies in his father or the stone-faced merchants. Finally, he looked at Xiuhcue.

"And you, my sister?" he asked in a tone of resignation. "Are you prepared to undertake this journey?"

"Everyone is so frightened here," Xiuhcue said meekly. "Even the priests do not hide their hopelessness. I do not wish to leave our parents, either, but Father has said to go. We must respect his judgment, my brother, for he cares for us."

Xolotlpilli hastily bowed his head, making a barely audible sound. This can be no easier for them, Cuauhcoatl thought, forcing himself to remember, as he looked upon Huemac's composed features, that his grandfather had lost both a sister and a daughter within the last four days.

"I will do as you say," Cuauhcoatl promised. "But not until I have seen, for myself, that Moteczuma cannot be awakened."

Huemac nodded and smiled bleakly.

"We will need your courage," he said to Cuauhcoatl, and allowed his gaze to travel around the room, "for our task is only just beginning. Be watchful, my friends. I do not have to tell you how soon the invaders will be in our very midst . . . "

4

THE foreigners came to Mexico in the thirteenth month of One-Reed, the month called Quecholli, the Red Spoonbill. Moteczuma had tried three more times to convince them to turn back, sending rich gifts of the gold the foreigners loved, and using both Cuitlahuac and Cacama as his ambassadors. But the strangers would not be deterred, and they were well received in the cities of Chalco and Mizquic and Ixtapalapa, where many of Moteczuma's former subjects and allies joined those who supported the foreigners' advance. On the day Eight Wind, the white men, accompanied by their servant beasts and several thousand Tlaxcalan warriors, marched onto the southern causeway toward Tenochtitlan, escorted out of Ixtapalapa by Cuitlahuac and a crowd of dignitaries.

From his grandson, Huemac had learned that Moteczuma intended to meet the foreigners just outside the Xoloco, the great rampart that guarded the southern entrance to the city. Already, a space was being swept by priests, and gourds of flowers were being laid out on a ground cover of fine cotton cloth. The guards around this area were particularly rough, pushing all the spectators of insufficient rank farther down the causeway, and preventing any more from spilling out of the city. Huemac had dressed himself in all his finest jewels and insignia, and he positioned himself at the forward edge of the cleared space, staring down any guard who tried to make him move. The causeway was lined on both sides with curious people, and thousands more floated alongside in canoes, or stood watching from the walls and temples of the city. There was no one in the entire city who did not wish to witness this momentous meeting.

Huemac, however, had come out of more than mere curiosity, and he began to gather his powers as he saw the great crowd advancing toward him, making an enormous din and raising a large cloud of dust. First came the dignitaries who had preceded the foreigners up the causeway, led by Cuitlahuac and Cacama and many of the other high lords of the Alliance. These took their places around the cleared area, some changing into fresher and even more splendid garments, over which they placed garlands of cocoa and popcorn flowers. Huemac was obliged to move farther down the causeway, but he stubbornly maintained his place in the front rank, his glowing eyes enough to keep those who pressed him too closely at a distance.

A sound like a volley of heavy stones hitting the ground came to his ears, and he felt his nahualli become momentarily frantic as four of the foreigners' deer came into view, each bearing a metal-shirted warrior on its back. The sound was made by the feet of the deer striking the ground, for they were as tall as a housetop and lifted their legs high as they came along, their dark coats shiny and flecked with foaming sweat. The warriors upon their backs stopped them before they came to the cleared space, turning them in circles and pulling on the leather thongs attached to the mouths of the deer.

Beyond the deer, Huemac could see other warriors dressed in the shining metal armor, and then the hornless heads of more deer rising above the crowd. The rest of the column, and its true length, could not be made out, though the metal tips of the foreigners' lances flashed in the sunlight like a cloud of stars. In the distance, dimly, could be heard the whooping and singing of the Tlaxcalans, who were no doubt making a great display of defiance at coming into Tenochtitlan so boldly.

Then the conch trumpet announcing the Speaker's approach was sounded, and Huemac bowed his head with those around him, gazing up from under his hooded eyelids. He saw Moteczuma carried in on a litter studded with gold and precious stones, borne by four of his sons and nephews, all beautifully dressed but with their feet bare. Moteczuma stepped from the litter, wearing the full regalia of his office and sandals with soles of beaten gold, and at his side were Cacama, Cuitlahuac, Itzquauhtzin, and the members of the Council of Lords. These kept their eyes downcast in the Speaker's presence, raising them only when the leader of the foreigners stepped forward from between the four deer, accompanied by several of his captains and the woman, Malintzin, who spoke for him.

He was not a large man, this warchief, perhaps the same size as Moteczuma, though he walked with a slight stoop to his shoulders. He had a pale face and a thick black beard beneath his gleaming metal helmet, and he wore a shirt of the same metal and cloth leggings that puffed out at his knees; his ankles were wrapped tightly with white cloth, and his feet were hidden in leather sandals that covered them completely. Removing his helmet to show his head of black hair, he addressed Moteczuma in his barbarous tongue, and his woman translated for him:

"Is it not you? Are you not the one called Moteczuma?"

"I am he," Moteczuma replied in Nahua, and came forward to place a garland of sweet flowers around the warchief's neck. Then he also placed the golden wind jewel of Quetzalcoatl around the man's neck, and stepped back to address him in greeting:

"O my Lord, you have suffered hardship, you have wearied yourself in coming here. Now you have arrived in your city of Mexico, you have come to occupy the reed seat that I have held for you, that I have guarded in my short time as ruler. For your other rulers have departed: the Speakers Itzcoatl, Moteczuma the Elder, Axayacatl, Tizoc, and Ahuitzotl, who was the last to rule before me. Do they perhaps watch us still? O, that one of them might see what is before me, what marvel occurs in their absence!

"I know that I am not sleeping," Moteczuma continued in an awed voice, "I know that I do not dream the face that looks into mine. For a long time, I have been afflicted with uncertainty, I have suffered from not knowing. I have stared into the region of mystery, the place of clouds and mist, seeking the knowledge of your coming. And so it is: The old rulers departed saying that you would come one day to visit your city, that you would return to claim your reed seat. And now it has been fulfilled, now you have arrived. Rest now, my lords, for you are fatigued. Rest now, and be at home in your city."

Huemac turned his head away in disgust, no longer interested in hearing how the foreigner would respond, once his woman had interpreted Moteczuma's words for him. He resolved now not merely to investigate the foreigners' powers, as he had originally intended, but to use his eyes on them, and create an incident if he could. He trained his attention upon the metal-shirted warrior who stood only a short distance away, holding a battle standard made of black, red, and gold cloth. This man had been turning periodically to survey the crowd behind him, though whether he was nervous or simply curious was impossible for Huemac to tell.

He has no nahualli, Huemac ascertained quickly, by feel alone, since the man offered only brief glimpses of his black eyes as he swept them over the crowd. *Look at me,* Huemac commanded silently, concentrating all his power in his eyes, which made the people around and behind him stir uneasily in their places, disturbed by the unknown force emanating from their midst. But the foreigner kept his back turned, listening to what his leader was saying to Moteczuma. *Look at me,* Huemac repeated, unable to believe that the man did not feel his presence.

Then the foreigner turned once more to gaze over the crowd, and his eyes paused on Huemac. Pouring his full force upon the man, Huemac threw the shape of his nahualli at him, quickly and powerfully, so that no one else would see what had felled the man. But the foreigner did not fall. He did not even blink. His eyes remained blank and impenetrable, and soon he had turned away again, seeming completely unaffected by what he had seen.

Huemac stood stunned, exhausted by the force of his effort, and crushed by his failure. He noticed, dimly, that Moteczuma had departed in his litter, and that the column of foreigners was beginning to move off after him. The man with the standard had soon disappeared, followed in rapid order by more metal-shirted men, more men on deer, and warriors who carried strange metal bows and the shining tubes that were said to spit fire. But Huemac could not bring himself to look, and allowed the column to pass by him unseen. Only when the first of the Tlaxcalan porters appeared did he allow the crowd to bear him along, back toward the city.

They are impervious to our sorcery, he thought, feeling a great emptiness descend on him as he passed under the Xoloco rampart. Truly, he told himself wearily; truly, we will have to fight them like *men* . . .

NAHUI OLIN squatted quietly to one side of Moteczuma's low seat, between it and the finely worked wooden screen that sheltered the Speaker from the eyes of his cooks and servants, who labored noiselessly on the other side. There were perhaps two dozen dishes laid out on the cloth-covered table before him, and Moteczuma picked and tasted from these while he talked to the four old men who attended him as advisers. It was his habit, when he was in a good mood, to share his favorite dishes with his guests, and since he was in a particularly good mood today, he kept the mouths of the old men filled while he spoke to them about the manners and religion of the foreigners.

"Is not their god, the One Who Is Three," he suggested, "is he not very similar to our own Ometeotl, the Lord of the Duality? He is the Creator God and the Mother Goddess in one, as well as the son who offers himself in sacrifice, as Nanahuatzin did on our behalf."

The old men nodded politely, their eyes downcast, their jaws working carefully around the tidbits they had been offered. Nahui Olin could understand the confusion they must be suffering, their astonishment that Moteczuma could discuss these things with so much ease, as if considering some esoteric piece of wisdom, some old legend that had never been fully interpreted. Nahui Olin was astounded himself, for this was the first time his master had sent for him since the foreigners arrived five days earlier, and he had expected to find the ruler in dire need of amusement. Instead, he had to cast back to the days before the omens, some ten years earlier, to remember when he had last seen Moteczuma in better spirits. Given the things the foreigners had done, and the mood of the city, it was more than astonishing; it was quite simply beyond belief.

"You must discuss these matters with Lord Malintzin himself," Moteczuma continued expansively. "He is a fine man, and as learned as any priest. No doubt the opportunity will present itself shortly, and I will have you summoned. You may leave me now."

Nahui Olin gave his head a quick shake as the old men left, trying to get the echo of that word, "man," out of his ears. Almost immediately after welcoming the foreigners into the city as the heirs of Quetzalcoatl, Moteczuma had ceased referring to them as "gods," going so far as to tell Lord Malintzin in public that he saw him as a man of flesh and blood like himself. This had caused great consternation among the lords who had heard Moteczuma's speech of greeting, and who now felt justified in wondering why their city should have been turned over without a fight.

Nahui Olin wondered along with the rest, but he knew better than to allow such concerns to distract him from the performance of his duties. Rolling forward in a series of somersaults, he came to his knees before the Speaker and began to mimic the actions of the foreigners' servant lions, growling and panting with his tongue hanging out, and pretending to lift his leg against an imaginary wall. Moteczuma laughed hoarsely, stroking his long chin whiskers, but then gestured for Nahui Olin to stop and sit before him.

"Now you will smoke with me, Nahui Olin," he said in a commanding tone, and a serving woman immediately appeared from behind the screen, carrying a small brazier of lit coals and a tray of painted yetl tubes. Moteczuma performed the ceremony of lighting the tubes, and gave one to Nahui Olin with his own hand, an honor he seldom extended to even his most favored guests.

"So what do *you* think of our visitors?" he asked casually, settling back in his seat and blowing rings of smoke into the air above his head. "Have our people grown accustomed to their presence? Have they lost their fear of the servant beasts, and the tubes that thunder and spit fire? Look upon me, my son, and speak."

Nahui Olin did so warily, for he had never been asked to express his opinion before this. Always, *he* had been the one to guess what was in the other's mind, and act it out. And surely Moteczuma had better sources of information. He saw a devious glint in his master's eyes, and understood that his own opinion was not really important; that Moteczuma merely wished to use him as a mirror for his own thoughts.

"Here in the palace, my Lord," he said carefully, "they have become very familiar. They look into everything, and ask a great many questions. They laugh a great deal, and do not seem to know they are being rude."

"Yes, even Lord Malintzin sometimes forgets his manners," Moteczuma agreed, with a slight expression of disgust. "He embarrassed me at the temple in Tlatelulco yesterday, when he asked to plant the image of his god there. That was very rude, indeed."

An edge of anger had crept into the Speaker's tone as he spoke of the incident, and Nahui Olin watched the man's features harden as he puffed silently on his smoking tube. The insulting behavior of the foreigners had been widely reported throughout the city, due to the extremity of the anger of the priests who had been present, and had heard the scornful way that Lord Malintzin had spoken of their gods. It was rumored that Moteczuma had had to perform special penances of his own in order to placate them, and Nahui Olin guessed, from the look on the Speaker's face, that this was true. But then Moteczuma's expression softened, and he went on in a wistful tone:

"But I forgive him for this. There are ways in which he reminds me of my own father, so rash, and heedless of his own danger. My father was always one who plunged into the midst of the enemy without looking around for his comrades." Moteczuma paused and pulled on his beard, eying Nahui Olin with some of his earlier deviousness. "Did you know, my son, that before he left the coast, Lord Malintzin destroyed the floating temples that had brought him here?"

"No, my Lord," Nahui Olin replied honestly, as Moteczuma's gaze went over his head, into the distance. The Speaker waved his smoking tube languidly, as if casting a net.

"Yes, and he left only a small number behind to guard the camp he built at Chalchicuecan. Suppose these were to be attacked and taken captive," he suggested lazily. "Might not that curb the impetuousness of the one who had surged ahead?"

"It might indeed, my Lord," Nahui Olin agreed politely, wondering why he had heard nothing of this in the reports he received on the workings of the Council. Unless, of course, the Speaker had ordered this on his own, or had yet to suggest it to his lords. No, he has ordered it done, Nahui Olin decided, seeing the obvious satisfaction on Moteczuma's face. He intends to temper his friendliness toward the foreigners with a reminder of his power, the dwarf thought, and to win back the trust of his own lords in the process.

Moteczuma suddenly turned his eyes back on Nahui Olin, and smiled when he saw that he had made the impression he desired.

"Yes, my son, I know how to deal with men such as these," he said smugly. "They are brave and fierce fighters, but they are *our* guests now. They must learn to have more respect for their hosts; they must learn that there are limits to their rashness."

Nahui Olin sat silently, forgetting the smoking tube in his hands. He now understood his master's high spirits, but there was something about this plot that did not inspire a similar confidence in his own heart. What if the foreigners turned angry rather than respectful? It seemed rash not to have notified the Council of his plans, and put the warriors on alert. And why had he compared Lord Malintzin to his father? That puzzled Nahui Olin more than anything else, since he did not think that a good son would so lightly risk his father's anger.

"I see that I have wearied you with things beyond your simple understanding," Moteczuma said in a condescending tone. "You may go now, but speak of this to no one. Let it be *our* secret, my son."

Nahui Olin bowed low and touched dirt to his tongue, then somersaulted backward and came to his feet, bowing again to the sound of Moteczuma's laughter. Then he headed back toward his quarters, wondering if there was time—and a way—to notify Huemac of what was about to occur, before the foreigners heard of it themselves.

THE MESSENGER from the foreigners, who were quartered in the Palace of Axayacatl, said only that Lord Malintzin wished to come to the palace to meet with the Speaker on matters of mutual interest. That was all he had been authorized to say, and though he would have been willing to tell Cuauhcoatl more concerning the mood of the foreigners, he could only shrug and apologize, explaining that he still could not read their faces. Cuauhcoatl thanked him and led him to a nearby waiting room, before returning to the other Arrows in front of the chamber door.

Their faces he could read only too well, for he had heard the same report that they had, earlier in the day. Cuauhpopoca, ruler of the Totonac city of Nauhtla and a loyal subject of Moteczuma, had led an attack on the foreigners' camp at Chalchicuecan, employing both Mexican and Totonac troops. One foreigner had been killed and several others wounded, and one of the deer had also been killed. But the foreigners had succeeded in driving off their attackers, and then their Totonac allies had come to their assistance. The whole coast was now in a state of war, but it could not be said that Moteczuma had gained any definite advantage from the attempt.

Ehecatzin, as always the willing spokesman, addressed Cuauhcoatl in urgent tones:

"You must make the request for us, Cuauhcoatl. The foreigners cannot be allowed to come into his presence armed. We have no way to defend him!"

"Especially not today," another of the Arrows put in. "Suppose they have heard of the attack on their people?"

"He favors you, Cuauhcoatl," Ehecatzin added, "and he does not question your courage. He will not punish you for expressing our concern."

Cuauhcoatl eyed them coldly, knowing that not one of them would be willing to take a similar risk, even the ones who were related to Moteczuma by blood.

"Our captains have made this request from the beginning," he reminded them, "and the Speaker has always refused them. Is my favor a greater protection than their rank?"

Ehecatzin did not answer, and he and the others moved out of the way as Cuauhcoatl pushed past them and entered the chamber. He had already decided, on his own, to make the request, but it angered him that no one had offered to accompany him, and to share the possible consequences. It made him as nervous as anyone that the foreigners were allowed to go everywhere armed, creating a situation for which the Arrows had no contingency plans, since their whole training had been designed to prevent such a thing from happening in the first place. But he did not go about frantically seeking someone else to shoulder the responsibility and to decide how to act. That was the sleep of anxiety, and Cuauhcoatl had no desire to soothe their nerves as they wished.

Moteczuma was conferring with Cacama, Cuitlahuac, and Itzquauhtzin when Cuauhcoatl approached, and the young man stopped a short distance away and waited to be recognized, his eyes fixed firmly on the ground. He heard the name of Cuauhpopoca being mentioned, sounding different on each tongue, since Moteczuma seemed very calm, constraining his lords to express their concern in indirect ways. Cuauhcoatl remembered the night that news of the foreigners' arrival had first come to Tenochtitlan, and he realized that his fate, his vision, was again at work, having put him in position to deliver this message, as well.

"What is it?" Moteczuma demanded at last. "Speak, Cuauhcoatl."

"The Lord Malintzin, my Lord, wishes to come here to see you. On matters of mutual interest, my Lord."

The silence that followed his words was so deep that Cuauhcoatl was sure that he could hear the beating of his own heart. But Moteczuma did not hesitate long in answering, and his voice was as assured as it had been previously:

"Tell him that he may come whenever he wishes. I will await him here."

"Forgive me, my brother," Cuitlahuac interrupted hastily. "But you must not do this! We have killed one of their people, perhaps more. *Now* is the time to change the terms of our friendship, and make them leave. Say that you will speak with them another time, but do not allow them to come here and accuse you in your own palace."

"But *I* have done nothing of which they can accuse me, my brother," Moteczuma said in a mild tone. "I will explain, if they have indeed been informed of this, that Cuauhpopoca acted on his own. I will apologize to Malintzin and order Cuauhpopoca's arrest, though perhaps he will somehow escape. Malintzin will be angry, but he will have to accept my explanation, and he will begin to see how much he depends on me for protection, and how he has endangered himself by undermining my authority among my subjects. He is an impetuous man, Cuitlahuac, he must be made to learn slowly."

"There is no telling what the man might dare!" Cuitlahuac protested, then fell abruptly silent, obviously at a gesture from his brother.

"Take my message, Cuauhcoatl," Moteczuma said pointedly, and the young man bowed in compliance. But he did not immediately back out of the Speaker's presence.

"There is something else?" Moteczuma demanded. "Speak!"

"My Lord," Cuauhcoatl said humbly. "Forgive my impertinence, but the men of the guard ask if the foreigners cannot be made to leave their weapons outside the palace. We are concerned about our ability to protect you if they are allowed so close."

"That is not only impertinent, it is stupid!" Moteczuma thundered angrily. "It would only demonstrate that I have some reason to fear their anger. I have already made my wishes in this matter known to your captains. Have they not informed you?"

"They have, my Lord . . ."

"Yet you still dare to raise it with me? Go to your quarters, you insolent fool! No," he added immediately, a note of malice creeping into his voice. "Better still, take your sorry self to Nahui Olin and tell him that I have sent you to him to keep as a slave. Go now, leave my sight!"

Cuauhcoatl bowed again and backed out of the chamber, hearing Cuitlahuac come to his defense as the door swung shut behind him. The other Arrows could not meet his eyes, and their faces clearly showed their chagrin.

"The answer is 'no,'" Cuauhcoatl said to Ehecatzin. "You are now in charge. Show some courage of your own, my friend; be prepared to fight as I would have been, had I not been banished to the keeping of the Speaker's dwarf."

Cuauhcoatl picked up his shield and warclub and walked away from them, knowing that his words would have far less effect upon them than the fact of his punishment. He was now certain that something important was about to happen, and that he would not be present to lend his wakefulness to the situation. But he could not feel any guilt. He had done what he thought was best; he had lived up to his responsibility, and it had only caused the Speaker to attack him. That is the second time, he thought as he headed toward the House of Animals; once more, and I am free to pursue my fate elsewhere. For the first time since Huemac had proposed leaving to him, Cuauhcoatl began to find the prospect acceptable, even appealing. The task of trying to rouse the Speaker had grown tiresome, and he knew that soon—if something did not change—he would himself begin to lapse, and fall into the sleep of bitterness.

THE NEWS came to him later, while he sat with Nahui Olin in the jesters' quarters above the House of Animals. Lord Malintzin had come to the palace at noon, accompanied by his woman and thirty of his warriors, all armed. They had been allowed into the Speaker's chamber, where the foreign leader had indeed accused Moteczuma of organizing the attack on Chalchicuecan. Moteczuma had protested his innocence just as he had described earlier, calling on his lords for corroboration and making a great display of his anger toward Cuauhpopoca. But the foreigners had not been deceived, and they had suddenly closed in around the Speaker, demanding that he return with them to their quarters. They did not hesitate in telling him that they would kill him immediately if he refused or called out to his guards.

A long argument had ensued, during which the chamber had filled with Arrow Warriors, and it had seemed that the killing would start at any moment. It was said that Cuitlahuac had urged his brother to die now, like a warrior, and free his people to take their revenge. But Moteczuma had merely sighed, as if disappointed in everything he had heard, and then he had sent his guards away, claiming that he had chosen to accompany the foreigners voluntarily, out of respect for signs that the gods had given him the night before. No one had believed him, but they could not attack without putting his life in danger, so they had allowed him to be taken out of the palace on a litter surrounded by the foreign warriors. Cacama, Cuitlahuac, and Itzquauhtzin had also been taken to the Palace of Axayacatl, each with a separate guard of his own.

"So now he is *truly* a prisoner in his own city," Cuauhcoatl said to Nahui Olin, after the messenger had left. The dwarf was sitting across from him on a pile of mats, surrounded by his fellow jesters. They were boys, mostly, dwarves and midgets and hunchbacks, and one shy boy who had pink eyes and white hair, and skin paler than that of the foreigners. They were obviously devoted to Nahui Olin, who treated them with fatherly fondness, letting the youngest ones lean against him and play around his legs. Their deformities still shocked Cuauhcoatl's eyes, but they had accepted his presence with unexpected warmth and familiarity, making it instantly plain that he would not have to play his usual humiliating role with Nahui Olin. That was enough in itself to make him feel grateful, but he had been additionally touched by the fact that not one of them had yet referred to him as Gold Head, though all apparently knew the nickname.

"He thinks of Lord Malintzin as his father," Nahui Olin explained, shifting a tiny boy with big, bulging eyes off his lap. "When he could not lie his way out of trouble, he accepted his punishment, as any son must."

"Will we be made to go to him, Nahui Olin?" one of the other dwarves asked tremulously. "I am frightened of the foreigners and their beasts. Their lions are big enough to eat me!"

"Apparently, he is being given his own rooms," Nahui Olin said in a calming tone. "But if any one of us is summoned, it will be me." He looked up at Cuauhcoatl and grinned. "And I will be sure to take my slave with me, for protection. But now you must all sleep, and not think of this anymore. We are safe here, and we have lions of our own below. Excuse me, Cuauhcoatl, while I see to the little ones . . ."

Nahui Olin returned a few moments later and beckoned for Cuauhcoatl to join him in the corridor. Checking his stride with difficulty, Cuauhcoatl accompanied the little man as he led the way to the stairs at the end of the hall.

"You have made a family for yourself, my friend," Cuauhcoatl said admiringly, as they climbed the stairs to the roof.

"I remember my own loneliness too well," Nahui Olin said with gruff modesty. "And your grandfather made me aware that the prerogatives of the Speaker's favorite could be put to some *good* uses."

Then they stepped out into the darkness, and paused to allow their eyes to adjust. Cuauhcoatl leaned his head back to gaze at the stars overhead, lapsing into a musing tone at the sight of the beauty above him.

"Were you able to tell my grandfather about your conversation with the Speaker?" he asked lazily, shedding some of his tension in the quiet coolness of the night air.

"No," Nahui Olin replied in a dry, almost sarcastic voice. "But I plan to tell him now."

Cuauhcoatl jerked his head down in surprise, then followed the line of Nahui Olin's extended arm, just making out the dark shape leaning against the far railing. Numbly, he walked behind Nahui Olin across the roof, until he could see the golden rings of his grandfather's eyes, and then his face.

"You are early, my friend," Nahui Olin said in a voice that revealed his pleasure. "Look whom I have brought with me. Moteczuma made him a gift to me today, for being so foolish as to mistrust the foreigners' good intentions."

"That was indeed rash," Huemac said with a slight smile. "But it seems that Moteczuma has done us both a favor before surrendering himself. Greetings, my son," he said to Cuauhcoatl. "You must tell me everything that Moteczuma said to you."

Shaking off his bewilderment, Cuauhcoatl quickly described what he had overheard in the court, his memory prodded by Huemac's questions concerning the tone of the Speaker's voice, as well as his words themselves. Then Nahui Olin told of his conversation with Moteczuma, including his thoughts concerning the ruler's attitude toward Lord Malintzin.

"Your insights are very keen," Huemac commended him. "I think that you will find that his high spirits will return, once he has grown accustomed to his father's keeping. It seems unlikely that an attempt will be made to rescue him. Xolotlpilli has just returned to the Council meeting, and he says that they are deadlocked, and will be unable to act as long as both Moteczuma and Cuitlahuac are held captive. I believe at this point that the greater concern is for Cuitlahuac."

"Has Cuauhpopoca been sent for?" Cuauhcoatl asked.

"He will be found," Huemac said bluntly. "There are some who still hope that his presence will persuade Moteczuma to act with courage. Others hope that it will cause Malintzin to kill him."

"What must *we* do?" Nahui Olin asked, and Huemac included both of them in his gaze.

"I have told you both, separately, that there is no magic we can work upon them. So we must learn as much about their habits and their weapons as we can, so we can decide how they may best be fought. You must both study these things if you are allowed into their midst, especially you, Cuauhcoatl. Learn how *you* would fight them. Moteczuma must also be encouraged to request the release of Cuitlahuac and the other lords. Perhaps you would be in a position to accomplish this, Nahui Olin."

Both young men nodded earnestly, and Huemac smiled at them with open pride.

"You must also learn the times and places when Moteczuma will be alone," he went on, "and all the entrances to his chambers, especially the courtyards and high windows. I may have to visit him myself before long."

He looked from one to the other encouragingly, to see if they had any questions, then embraced them each in turn, kneeling to hold Nahui Olin against his chest. The dwarf clung to him unabashedly, making Cuauhcoatl ashamed of the awkwardness he had felt in his grandfather's arms.

"I am proud of you both," Huemac said, looking up at Cuauhcoatl from his crouch, "and pleased that you can be together as comrades and friends. Go to your rest now, my sons; I will see you again when there is more for us to share."

Nahui Olin bowed and started back across the roof without another word, but Cuauhcoatl hung back, looking at the ground and the railing behind his grandfather for signs of a rope or a ladder. Knowing the vigilance of the guards, Cuauhcoatl could not conceive of how his grandfather had climbed up here without being seen.

"How . . . ?" he began, but Huemac stopped him with a curt gesture of his hand.

"You will understand these things later, my son," he said gently. "And in a setting where they will make more sense to you. Go after your friend, and save your questions for the proper time."

Cuauhcoatl bowed compliantly and did as he had been told. But he could not resist a backward glance when he had reached the top of the stairs, and he saw immediately that Huemac was already gone. He tantalizes me, Cuauhcoatl thought, to make me yearn for the future he has offered. And he realized, as he went back down the stairs into the palace, that it was beginning to work . . .

5

AFTER Moteczuma had gone to lodge in Axayacatl's palace, he sent for the Council of Lords to meet with him there, giving Lord Malintzin's assurances that none of them would be detained. But only those of his own family, and the old men who were his personal advisers, came to visit him. Servants were sent to attend him, and all the food, firewood, and other materials that he and the foreigners had requested were supplied. But the lords themselves refused to meet with him while he was in captivity, and many returned his invitations with scornful messages of their own.

Nahui Olin was thus summoned to his master sooner than he had expected, and he found Moteczuma alone in his audience chamber, except for Cacama, Itzquauhtzin, and some relatives of unimportant rank; Cuitlahuac was apparently being held elsewhere. The Speaker had been given a series of connected rooms well within the interior of the palace, a collection that included chambers for eating, sleeping, and holding audiences; a deep pool for bathing; and his own courtyard and garden. The trappings of his life did not lack in splendor even here, although the entrances to his rooms were kept under constant guard by the foreigners, and all his visitors were searched for weapons and were carefully questioned by Lord Malintzin's steward, who had learned some Nahua.

As Huemac had predicted, Moteczuma seemed not to be suffering from his confinement, showing an unfeigned enthusiasm for the frequent visits paid to him by the leader of the foreigners and his captains, and remarking often on the courtesy and deference shown to him by his guards. Nahui Olin did not waste any time in catering to this enthusiasm, playing to the foreign guards as much as to Moteczuma himself, so that his master could explain his jokes to the foreigners and win the favor of their amusement. He had brought Cuauhcoatl along as his personal servant, and he treated the seemingly abject young man with outrageous condescension, calling him Gold Head and finding fault with everything he did. Moteczuma enjoyed this immensely, laughing at the mere sight of the muscular young warrior trailing after the crooked little man like a disobedient child. He seemed to have entirely forgotten how Cuauhcoatl's enslavement had come about, or his own hand in it.

The foreigners' passion for gold was well known, and it was not long before some of the guards began asking about Cuauhcoatl's nickname. One day, they even brought in one of their captains, the one whom the Mexicans called Tonatiuh, because his eyes were the blue of the sky and his hair was the flaming gold of the Sun itself. The captain removed his metal helmet and bowed to Moteczuma, which brought a tolerant smile to the Speaker's face. Using Malintzin's steward as an interpreter, he asked very seriously to know the meaning of Cuauhcoatl's name, as if he did not understand that it was a joke. He seemed slightly disappointed when Moteczuma explained that the Nahua word for gold, teocuitlatl, meant "the excrement of the god," and that Nahui Olin, whose name was that of the Sun, had once pretended to deposit this on Cuauhcoatl's head. But he, and the other foreign guards, was quite amused when Nahui Olin obligingly repeated his trick, waggling his buttocks obscenely over Cuauhcoatl's defenseless head.

After word of this got around, the dwarf and his hulking companion were welcomed into all the various squadrons that comprised the foreign army, performing their act many times before crowds of laughing warriors. Except for Lord Malintzin, who was often in consultation with the foreigners' priest, their access to the quarters of the foreigners was virtually unlimited. Even Cuauhcoatl's size aroused no suspicion, since he played the role of servant beast to dumb perfection.

In this way, he and Nahui Olin were able to scout the defenses the foreigners had set up around and within the palace, and they saw firsthand how the warriors cared for their weapons and their servant beasts. Once they had come to better understand the moods and expressions of the foreigners, and the differences in their ranks, they also began to see how nervous many of the common warriors were, and how weary they were becoming from their constant round of guard duty. They clearly expected to be attacked at any time, and from those remarks that the steward would translate, they did not feel that the person of Moteczuma was much protection against the thousands of warriors surrounding them in the city. The mention of gold often brought forth a show of real rancor, apparently directed at Lord Malintzin himself, but the steward would not translate these grumblings at all.

Early in the month of Atemoztli, the month dedicated to the rain gods, Cuauhpopoca was finally brought to Tenochtitlan to account for his attack on the foreigners. The Totonac ruler was first given to Lord Malintzin, who in turn delivered him to Moteczuma, accompanied only by the steward who spoke Nahua. Nahui Olin and Cuauhcoatl were in the Speaker's chamber when the man was brought in, but only Nahui Olin was in a position to see how Moteczuma's face paled at the sight of his subject. He was unable to speak for the longest time, until Cacama leaned forward to whisper in his ear, and bring him out of his trance.

"Why did you do this, Cuauhpopoca?" Moteczuma demanded in a high voice, glancing nervously at the foreign steward. "Why did you attack the servants of our friend, Lord Malintzin?"

Forgetting that he had not been commanded to raise his eyes, Cuauhpopoca stared back at his master in blank incomprehension.

"Have you forgotten, my Lord?" he asked in a stunned voice. "It was you who ordered me to do this."

"That is a lie!" Moteczuma burst out, his voice rising still higher. "I never ordered such a thing! Would you betray me, you treasonous dog? I will hear no more from you!"

Clamping his lips tightly, Moteczuma turned his face away from the man in front of him, who had fallen to his knees in supplication. When the steward understood that nothing more was to be said, he gestured to the guards to remove Cuauhpopoca, and followed after them with a parting bow to Moteczuma. Cacama waited only until they were gone before speaking out on Cuauhpopoca's behalf:

"You cannot do this, my uncle! You must speak for his innocence, and accept the blame that is yours! You will lose all respect if you allow him to be punished in your place."

"Silence, Cacama," Moteczuma hissed. "You forget yourself."

Cacama glanced over at Itzquauhtzin, who returned his gaze impassively, then turned on his heel and walked away from the reed seat where Moteczuma sat. Nahui Olin and Cuauhcoatl sat very still, controlling their own disgust at what they had just witnessed. The silence in the chamber remained unbroken for a long time, until the door was suddenly thrust open and Lord Malintzin came in with his woman and his captains. The foreign leader's pale face was darkened by anger, and he did not even bother to speak himself, gesturing to his woman to relay his message.

Cuauhpopoca had been questioned, she told Moteczuma, and he had confessed that it was Moteczuma who had given him the order to attack. Lord Malintzin believed this confession, and therefore judged Moteczuma guilty of murder, for which he should rightfully die under the laws of the foreigners' king and god. But since he loved Moteczuma like a son and could not bring himself to see him harmed, the Lord had decided to spare him. But Cuauhpopoca would have to die for his crimes, and Moteczuma was to be put in chains and made to watch as punishment for his complicity.

Unable to believe his ears, Moteczuma angrily protested this affront to his dignity, appealing to Lord Malintzin to have more trust in his honesty. But the foreign leader refused to hear him, and ordered two of his captains to attach the metal bonds to Moteczuma's wrists and ankles. A litter was brought to carry him, and everyone in the chamber was commanded to join the procession that walked slowly to the balcony overlooking the palace's main courtyard.

There below, Cuauhpopoca and several of his captains were tied to large posts that had been thrust into the ground between the flagstones. Cuauhpopoca hung unconscious in his bonds, his flesh torn and bleeding in many places, as if he had been in a battle. Dried grass had been piled up around his feet and those of his captains, and as those on the balcony watched, several of the foreign warriors came out into the courtyard, their arms filled with the warclubs, arrows, and throwing boards they had looted from the palace arsenal. They added these to the piles around the captives' feet and stood back, awaiting a signal from their leader.

Lord Malintzin raised his hand, and two of his men below went forward with torches in their hands and began to set fire to the grass and wood stacked around the unfortunate Totonacs. The Mexicans in the box reacted with cries of horror, and then turned their eyes away, weeping, as the burning men began to scream. It was an unholy death, a senseless way for a warrior to die, unblessed by the rituals that accompanied sacrifice and cremation.

When it was finally over, Lord Malintzin escorted Moteczuma back to his chamber and removed the chains with his own hands. He spoke soothingly to the dejected ruler, telling him again that he loved him like a son and wished to see no harm come to him. He even claimed, through Malintzin, that he trusted Moteczuma so much that he would be willing to set him free. Moteczuma, who had been rubbing his wrists and weeping like a hurt child, became suddenly alert and interested; the transformation was instantaneous, and quite startling to behold. Nahui Olin would say later, in describing it to Cuauhcoatl, that it was as if the man had suddenly emerged from behind the child who had been hiding him.

But then the woman added—on her own, it seemed—that she doubted very much that the Lord's captains would permit him to do such a thing. Moteczuma glanced at the captains, who appeared to glower at him from behind their leader, Tonatiuh with his red hair prominent among them. Then he looked at Lord Malintzin himself, and his face took on a shrewd kind of sympathy, as if he well understood the problem of unruly followers. He replied to the woman that he was grateful for the Lord's generosity, but that for the time being it was better that he remained in their custody, since if he were freed, his own lords would force him to bring war upon his friends and guests. He asked if he might have the steward who spoke Nahua to attend him, so that he might learn more about the ways of the foreigners, and Lord Malintzin granted this request with a further show of magnanimity.

Nahui Olin and Cuauhcoatl sat on together after Moteczuma had retired and the chamber had been emptied of all but themselves. Neither could speak of what they had seen and heard; the screams of the dying rang in their ears, and the smell of burning flesh closed their throats.

"We must go," Nahui Olin said at last. "Perhaps the sweathouse will wash the stain of this day from our bodies and hearts."

"I do not think so," Cuauhcoatl said thickly. "I do not know that I can ever return to this place."

"You will find the courage," Nahui Olin told him. "Our work here is not finished."

"I would finish it with my own hands, if I could," Cuauhcoatl declared, rising unsteadily to his feet to follow his friend from the room. "I would break my vows in an instant, without second thoughts, as *he* has broken his . . ."

SHORTLY BEFORE the end of the year One-Reed, Cacama made his escape from the palace. After bribing a servant to change clothes with him, the young lord simply walked out in the midst of a crowd of porters, unnoticed by the foreign guards. He fled immediately to Texcoco and sent out a call to war, ignoring Moteczuma's angry demands for his return. In Tenochtitlan, security was tightened around Axayacatl's palace, and the foreign warriors made more frequent forays into the city, galloping up and down the streets on their deer and firing their thundering tubes to frighten the people.

At Huemac's request, Cuauhcoatl brought Nahui Olin to his father's house one afternoon, after they had been released from their duties by Moteczuma. Though it was only a short distance from the palace to Xolotlpilli's house, the winter wind was cold and raw, and the young men were grateful for the glowing copper brazier that warmed Huemac's room. All the other men were there, and after introductions had been made, Nahui Olin was ceremonially given a place to sit between Cuauhcoatl and his father.

"I have brought us together, my friends," Huemac explained, "because it seems that war could be very near. I think it is best that we should *all* possess the information these young men have been gathering for me, for we can never tell, in the days ahead, who might be in the best position to use it."

"Has Cacama been successful, then," Cuauhcoatl asked, "in raising an army against Moteczuma and the foreigners?"

The older men exchanged skeptical glances, and Huemac gestured toward the vanguard merchants to his right.

"Pinotl can tell you best. He recently went to Texcoco and spoke to our friend Chiquatli, who has been up in the hills, fighting with the rebels."

Nodding deferentially, Pinotl toyed with the black staff on the floor before him for a few moments, then looked across at Cuauhcoatl and spoke in his flat, unidentifiable voice:

"When Cacama was taken prisoner, his brother, Coanacoch, the ruler of Huexotla, came to Texcoco to rule in his place. He also invited his other brother, Ixtlilxochitl, to bring his rebels out of the hills and join him there. Both have little love for Cacama, whom they regard as the tool of Moteczuma. Chiquatli does not think that they will join with him, and he says that his own camp is divided over whether to send him back to Moteczuma as he deserves. Only Ixtlilxochitl's hatred for the Speaker has prevented this from happening so far."

"Cacama is also too young and inexperienced to command respect elsewhere," Xolotlpilli interjected. "And there are many who still fear the reach of Moteczuma's power. Yes, my son," he assured Cuauhcoatl. "Incredible as it may seem, there are still those who will do his bidding for him, and not only those he has bribed, or who are related to him by blood. He still wears the mask and garb of Huitzilopochtli, and he has continued to defy Lord Malintzin by making sacrifices on those occasions when he is allowed to go to the temple. His claim that the god supports his captivity is accepted by many who should know better."

"So our people are still too divided to act," Cuauhcoatl concluded bitterly. "Who is it, then, who will bring this war?"

"The foreigners may well provoke it themselves," Huemac said patiently, ignoring his grandson's disgust. "Or Cuitlahuac, if we can win his release. Have you had any luck with this, Nahui Olin?"

"Every time Moteczuma has need of a high-ranking ambassador," the dwarf replied, "I recommend his brother. But Cuitlahuac is kept in a separate place, and he refuses to meet or even speak with Moteczuma."

Xolotlpilli grunted with obvious approval, and Omeocelotl leaned forward in his place to address Nahui Olin:

"And Itzquauhtzin? The people of Tlatelulco wish to know how their ruler comports himself, since they have not been allowed to see him since Cacama's escape."

"He is the same as Cuitlahuac," Nahui Olin assured him. "He carries himself with great dignity, and will not make friends with his captors as Moteczuma does."

Omeocelotl nodded with satisfaction and sat back in his place, looking toward Huemac, who was waiting to bring the discussion back to its original subject.

"Tell us, then, my son," he said to Cuauhcoatl. "What are your suggestions as to how these men might be fought?"

Cuauhcoatl had considered this matter carefully during his nights alone with Nahui Olin, and he proceeded to lay his thoughts out in an orderly fashion. He told them first how the foreign warriors went everywhere in tight groups, and were severely punished by their captains if they broke ranks or went off on their own. He recommended that they be attacked in the same way, by masses of men who would not themselves break ranks to take captives or claim insignia. The foreigners' armor and metal weapons were superior in individual encounters, he said, so that it was necessary to overwhelm them by sheer force of numbers.

As to the deer, Cuauhcoatl went on, he himself had observed how tender their feet and legs were, and how often the foreigners had to bind and dress them for injuries incurred simply in traveling through the city streets. He suggested that the ground be torn up in front of them, and that oil should be spread to make them slip, and trip lines strung to make them fall. Always their legs, and not their bodies, he contended, should be the target.

Finally, he spoke of the metal tubes, both large and small, which the foreigners made to spit fire and thunder. He had seen, he said, the piles of round stones and the chests of gray, foul-smelling dust that the foreigners pushed into their tubes with long sticks. It was his opinion, from the care the foreigners took in handling these materials, that they were dangerous in themselves, and that their power might be released accidentally. Never were they allowed near fire or water, as if these elements were harmful to them. Perhaps, he concluded, a rain of flaming darts and arrows could be directed at the tubes and those who operated them.

"Thank you, my son," Huemac said. "And you, Nahui Olin? What are your thoughts on this matter?"

"I am not a warrior," the dwarf said tentatively, glancing at the huge form of Xolotlpilli beside him. "So I cannot speak of how to meet these men in battle. But if it were left to me, I would kill them as they killed Cuauhpopoca: without honor or ceremony. I would put a slow-actng poison into their food, or into the pipe that brings water into the palace. I would watch them die in silence, without pity. I would even drink the water myself, to convince them that it was safe."

The utter savagery of the little man's words left a shocked silence in the room, and even Cuauhcoatl looked upon his friend with new eyes. Huemac smiled grimly, showing that he, for one, did not find the suggestion shocking.

"I am grateful for your opinion, as well," he said to Nahui Olin, then glanced in his son's direction. "Though I doubt that the warriors of our city will wish to surrender their chance for glory and revenge to the deadly herbs."

"They are men like us," Xolotlpilli blurted in protest. "We would dishonor our gods, and ourselves, if we did not meet them in battle, and try to make them our captives."

"Yes," Huemac said dryly, with a sardonic finality that silenced his son. "It is time that we ate together, and spoke of more pleasing matters. But I must first remind you that what was spoken here today is the possession of us all, and if it is possible, we should all decide when and with whom it should be shared. I do not think that leader is yet among us, and we would squander our knowledge by giving it to the wrong man. Let us all endeavor to notify the others, should the time to act come upon us suddenly."

The men rose and started out of the room, but Huemac motioned for Cuauhcoatl and Nahui Olin to remain behind. He looked at each of them in turn, impressing them with his seriousness.

"You have shown great courage, my sons," he told them finally. "Especially in mastering your disgust for the man you serve. But you must not be too courageous. You must recognize when it is time to remove yourselves from the palace for good."

The young men glanced at one another briefly, then nodded in unison.

"Good," Huemac said emphatically. "Come, then, Nahui Olin, let us share the meal we have postponed for so long. It will give me great pleasure to sit with my grandsons on either side of me."

Nahui Olin's eyes became large and moist, but then he looked quickly at Cuauhcoatl, to see if his friend resented Huemac's gesture. But Cuauhcoatl only smiled and laid a hand on the smaller man's shoulder.

"And I, too, will be pleased," he said, feeling a warmth that did not come from the brazier, "to sit with my brother."

THEN THE empty days of the nemontemi came, and the year One-Reed was put behind, and Two Flint-Knife welcomed in. The people of Tenochtitlan suddenly seemed to awaken from their shock, and to realize fully what had happened to them. They began to avoid the foreigners whenever they came out into the city, leaving the streets deserted and their goods unattended in the marketplace rather than meet with them. The foreigners' Tlaxcalan allies were unable to leave the palace compound without creating an incident, and stones were thrown over the walls at night, accompanied by shouted threats and blood-curdling screams intended to keep the guards in a state of nervousness and constant unrest.

Insulated from these disturbances by the thickness of the palace walls, Moteczuma managed to remain oblivious to the situation outside longer than anyone else. He had learned the names of all his guards, and he spent many hours conversing with them through the steward, their friendship and attention assured by frequent gifts of gold and precious stones. When he did go out into the city to perform his duties at the temples, he was closely guarded by a contingent of foreign warriors who never left his side, and who kept others away. Bad news simply did not reach his ears, for the steward was his constant companion, and everyone knew that their words would be immediately reported to Lord Malintzin.

But the artificial tranquillity of his life was abruptly shattered, one day near the end of the first month of Two Flint-Knife, when a delegation of priests representing the rain gods came to visit him. Paying no heed to the presence of the steward, they made their concerns known to Moteczuma in blunt language. There had been no rain since the time of Cuauhpopoca's burning, and now it was again a month that belonged to Tlaloc. There would surely be a prolonged drought, the priests warned, if the necessary sacrifices of children were not made, and they feared that the foreigners might try to interfere, and only increase the god's wrath. As it was, they complained, the white cross that the foreigners had erected atop the pyramid of Huitzilopochtli hung over the temple precinct like a bad omen, confusing and obscuring the messages received from the other gods.

Moteczuma was so disturbed by this warning that he went into seclusion for two days, and then sent a formal request to Lord Malintzin, begging him to leave the city before the gods and the people rose in revolt. The foreign leader refused politely, claiming that the boats—the floating temples—in which he and his men had come had been destroyed, and that they would need time to build new ones. Moteczuma sent orders to his remaining subjects on the coast to provide the foreigners there with wood and workmen, but the promised delay did nothing to relieve his depression. Priests from the other orders began to come regularly to complain, and the Speaker had no choice but to listen, and to feel the foundation of his power crumbling away beneath him. Men, even rulers, could be ignored or replaced, but the gods were beyond such intimidation.

Though they saw Moteczuma's anxiety as a positive sign, Nahui Olin and Cuauhcoatl were hard-pressed during this time to keep him amused, and they learned when it was best to simply withdraw and leave him to his unhappy speculations. When it was reported one afternoon that Cacama had been brought back to Tenochtitlan, they both braced themselves for the worst, expecting that Moteczuma, too, would remember the awful lesson of Cuauhpopoca.

But the Speaker asked only to know who had accomplished this capture, and when he was told that the captors were his own agents, he smiled for the first time in many days, and immediately went off to dress himself for the occasion. He returned wearing the full insignia of his office and carrying the painted reed stick that he wielded when passing judgment in the court. In a voice resonant with new-found authority, he commanded the steward to have the guards bring Cacama in.

The young Texcocan ruler appeared before him with his head unbowed, his face drawn with fatigue and fixed in an attitude of resignation. His own features enlivened with vindication, Moteczuma gestured at him contemptuously with his stick.

"*So,* traitor," he drawled with obvious relish, "you who thought you could betray my trust, and still avoid my wrath. You see now who is the more powerful; you see that you are nothing but what I have made you."

Cacama stared back at him silently, showing no signs of regret or the desire for forgiveness.

"Did you think that I would allow you to defy me forever?" Moteczuma demanded disdainfully. "Did you think that I could not have you whenever I wished? Speak, traitor!"

"You have me only because my brothers chose to give me up," Cacama snarled suddenly, his eyes bright with defiance. "And I came knowing that my death will be the end of you. Now the people will know that there is no one you will not betray, Moteczuma."

"I have not granted you the privilege of using my name," Moteczuma cried angrily. "You will die for your disrespect!"

"Your name is worth nothing," Cacama snapped. "And I do not fear your threats. Have your 'friends' kill me, if they will do that much for you . . ."

"Let him die!" Moteczuma shouted at the steward, waving his stick at the foreign guards who stood behind Cacama. "Now!"

Appearing deeply flustered, the steward replied in broken Nahua that only Lord Malintzin could order such a thing, and that there would have to be a trial and a confession first. He simply shook his head sadly at Moteczuma's offer of payment in gold.

"I will confess to anything!" Cacama proposed boldly, offering his chest to the guards behind him, who merely looked at one another in bewilderment and backed away from him. Moteczuma rose from his seat and whirled to glare at those around him on the dais, seeing only white heads and lowered eyes. Then his gaze fell upon the form of Cuauhcoatl, huddled at the corner of the dais beside Nahui Olin.

"You! Cuauhcoatl!" he said in a loud voice, his eyes wild with anger. "Come before me!"

Giving Nahui Olin a sidelong glance, Cuauhcoatl rose slowly from his crouch and went to stand before the Speaker, his head bowed upon his chest.

"You are pledged to obey me to the death," Moteczuma reminded him. "I command you to kill this man who defies me! I have no weapon to offer you, but surely, your hands are strong enough to break the neck of a traitor!"

Cuauhcoatl's whole body began to tremble, and the muscles in his neck stood out like cords as he struggled to keep himself still. But he did not respond, and he made no move toward Cacama.

"Do as I say!" Moteczuma screamed, and lashed Cuauhcoatl across the side of his face with the painted stick. Cuauhcoatl rose up slightly on his toes, his hands clenching and unclenching at his sides. But he did not move, even when Moteczuma whipped him about the head and shoulders twice more, sending shards of colored reed flying through the air.

"He is but a slave, my Lord," Nahui Olin interjected carefully, when Moteczuma had lowered his arm and stood panting for breath. "Killing is beyond his lowly powers. I will sell him in the marketplace tomorrow and get one who is more useful."

The splintered stick dropped from Moteczuma's hand as he looked down at the dwarf, and then his eyes glazed over and he turned away, weaving so unsteadily that two of his advisers rushed to support him by the elbows. The steward stood briefly in his way, asking what should be done with Cacama.

"Sell him," Moteczuma murmured incoherently. "Give him to Malintzin . . ."

Cuauhcoatl felt the restraining hand on his wrist before he even realized that he had begun to move forward, and it was his confusion as much as Nahui Olin's weight that stopped him from going after Moteczuma. His chest began to heave violently as the fullness of his hatred washed over him, and Nahui Olin held on to him tightly with both hands, long after the Speaker had departed and Cacama had been taken away. Finally, Cuauhcoatl's trembling ceased and his breathing returned to normal, and he was able to look down at his friend without a film of anger over his eyes. Nahui Olin released his wrist warily, patting him several times on the hip and thigh, as if to remind him of himself. There was a long red welt across the side of Cuauhcoatl's face.

"That was too much courage, my brother," the dwarf said hoarsely. "Our work here is finished; we must not come back."

"Yes," Cuauhcoatl murmured, raising his fingers to his burning cheek. "Yes, he has attacked me for the last time. I am through with him now." Then he blinked and truly focused in on Nahui Olin. "But what if he sends for *you*?"

"He will not find me," Nahui Olin said flatly. "It is as Cacama said—there is no one who will help him now. Besides," he added confidently, "I know that *my* brother will not give me up."

"Never," Cuauhcoatl agreed, and the two of them walked out together, side by side, passing through the halls of the Palace of Axayacatl for the last time.

HUEMAC found his son alone in his room, tying on a net mantle and a headdress of forked heron feathers. Xolotlpilli's face and head had been painted with diagonal stripes of blue and black, and there were tufts of feathers attached to his elbows and knees; a flower-covered shield was on the floor beside him. He glanced up once to acknowledge his father's presence, but he did not stop what he was doing until his costume was complete.

"I must ask you again, my son," Huemac said patiently, "not to participate in this dance. I beg you to remember what the foreigners did in the temple plaza of Cholula."

"But Lord Malintzin is not with them now," Xolotlpilli argued. "And perhaps he will have the luck not to return from the coast. In any case, we are soon going to destroy those who are still here, and we must celebrate the feast of the war gods to insure their support."

Huemac pursed his lips, exasperated by the simplicity and wishfulness of his son's thinking. How easily hope had returned to his warrior's heart!

"Do not underestimate Lord Malintzin, or the ones he has left behind," Huemac warned him. "The Tlatelulcans, as you know, have decided not to attend our festivities."

"And I have decided that *I* must," Xolotlpilli replied stubbornly, and Huemac gave in with a sigh.

"Then you must take this with you," he said, and held out a long flat knife sheathed in leather. "You can strap it to the inside of your shield, where the presiding priests will not see it."

"But it is unlawful to carry a weapon into the dance," Xolotlpilli protested, keeping his hands at his sides. Huemac's face and voice hardened perceptibly.

"You heard Papalotl's vision: Tezcatlipoca will protect no one. And the Feast of Toxcatl belonged to the Dark One before we even brought Huitzilopochtli into this land. You are a man, Xolotlpilli. But as your father, I insist that you take this."

Surprised by his father's vehemence, Xolotlpilli took the knife with a chastened nod and fixed it into the wicker frame of his shield, beneath the leather arm-strap. Huemac examined it himself, to be sure that it would not shake free, and then stood back with a satisfied nod.

"Dance well, my son," he said in farewell. "And return to us quickly when it is over . . ."

AS HE walked back toward his own room, Huemac struggled to come to grips with the sense of foreboding that this dance had awakened in him. It was true that permission had been sought and been granted by Lord Malintzin before he went away, so that the foreigners should have no reason for alarm at the assembly of warriors. And it was also true that the foreigners appeared to be in greater disarray than at any time since their arrival. Another fleet of the great boats used by the foreigners had recently appeared on the coast, and the leader of this group—much larger than Malintzin's—had sent messengers to Tenochtitlan, stating that he was Lord Malintzin's superior and had come to arrest him. This had caused Lord Malintzin to set out immediately for the coast, taking half of his men and most of his deer with him, and leaving his captain, Tonatiuh, in charge of the rest.

But Huemac could not share in the hope that this news had aroused in so many Tenocha hearts. He knew the way that Lord Malintzin had dealt with Moteczuma, giving with one hand while taking away with the other, and he suspected that this apparent disagreement between the groups of foreigners was simply another trick. And there was the lesson of Cholula to be considered, no matter who was in command of the foreigners; treachery seemed to come naturally to them.

He had little more to sustain his suspicions, though, now that Cuauhcoatl and Nahui Olin were no longer inside the palace to gather information for him. He had gone several times to the shrine of Xolotl, praying for the guidance of a dream or a vision, but nothing had come to fill the emptiness left by his daughter's death. He felt that he was walking in darkness toward an end that he had already seen, but which might still come upon him unexpectedly. I am as blind as the others, he thought bitterly, yet I am not permitted their saving capacity for hope.

He had decided, then, that it was time to go to Moteczuma; perhaps even past the time, since the Speaker no longer had the power to command the respect of even his most lowly subjects. After allowing Cacama to be thrown into chains with Itzquauhtzin and Cuitlahuac, Moteczuma had bowed to Lord Malintzin's demand that he formally surrender his kingdom, and he had turned over both his own treasure and that of his father as tribute. The people had watched in horror and disgust as the foreigners had stripped the gold and jewels from the headdresses, shields, and royal vestments, and had then burned the precious feathers, the shadows of the gods, in a big pile in the palace courtyard. The last vestiges of belief in the foreigners' godliness had gone up with those flames, leaving Moteczuma's reputation in ashes and smoke.

Still, Huemac reasoned, he might yet find a way to win Cuitlahuac's release, if someone were to drive him to it. Huemac was not certain how this could be done, but he intended to try, and it did not seem wise to wait any longer to make his attempt. Tonatiuh, the foreign captain, had made known his desire to observe the dancing, which would leave fewer people in the palace to witness or possibly obstruct Huemac's entry. There might not be a better time than now.

Cuauhcoatl and his sister Xiuhcue were sitting together in Huemac's room, with the map of their proposed journey spread out on the floor in front of them. They were practicing their Otomi when Huemac came in, Cuauhcoatl laboriously repeating the words and phrases that Huemac had taught Xiuhcue in the last months. They both looked up at him as he took the ladder from against the wall and propped it against the edge of the open trap door.

"I must leave you for a while," he said. "Do not come up after me. Arm yourself, Cuauhcoatl, and bar the gate if you hear any unusual sounds coming from the temple precinct."

"Our father has gone, then?" Cuauhcoatl asked, and Huemac nodded ruefully.

"I could not prevent him. But he will be able to defend himself if there is trouble. See that you do so, as well."

Without another word, Huemac turned and began to ascend the ladder to the roof, feeling his nahualli stir within him as he came out into the open air.

THE LONG line of dancers entered the temple precinct by the south gate and snaked their way through the crowd of spectators, finally breaking out into the open area in front of the great pyramid. They swayed and stamped rhythmically to the beating of the hollow wooden drums and the singing of a thousand voices, their path strewn with flower petals and the air they breathed rich with the odor of copal incense. Xolotlpilli danced near the head of the line, and was one of the first to pass the place where the image of Huitzilopochtli stood at the foot of the temple steps, surrounded by the black robes of the presiding priests. These gaunt men had fasted for a year in preparation for the Feast of Toxcatl, and they held pine staves in their hands and kept a sharp eye out for anyone improperly attired or unworthy of a place in the Winding Dance. Xolotlpilli experienced a pang of guilt as he hefted his shield and felt the extra weight of the knife beneath his forearm, but the priests did not waste their attention on the great ones at the head of the line, except to bow to them with admiration and respect.

The line turned at the far edge of the dancing area and began to wind back the way it had come. Through an opening in the crowd, Xolotlpilli caught a bobbing glimpse of the gleaming metal shirts of the foreigners who stood watching in a group near the north gate. Since they had obviously chosen not to mingle with the crowd, the people had left a way clear for them to see, because they wanted the foreigners to see the magnificence of the Tenocha's best warriors, and the stately devotion they paid to their war god. Let them see our greatness before they die, Xolotlpilli thought; let them know that we have not forgotten the traditions that made us the conquerors of this land.

The singing suddenly grew louder, and Xolotlpilli raised his shield over his head and plunged it down, turning his back on the foreigners as he followed the dancing men in front of him. Cooling sweat broke out on his body, and his heart lifted exultantly as the singing washed over him in resounding waves. Legs pumping to the beating of the drums, he forgot about the foreigners, and about his father and the knife, and lost himself in the dancing. The air around him was filled with dazzling colors and seemed to vibrate with the glorious energy of the god. A sensation of great strength and vitality pulsed through his veins and muscles, and at that moment, Xolotlpilli felt that he possessed the full power of the Tenocha, the Warriors of the Sun, and that there was no one he could not conquer . . .

"WHOM WOULD you call, Moteczuma?" Huemac asked in a dry voice, and the Speaker froze where he stood, his body twisted around in surprise, his mouth open to cry out.

"The Tlaxcalans are all on the other side of the roof, watching the dancing," Huemac went on calmly. "I doubt that they could hear you over the drums, or that they would want to rescue you if they did." He inclined his head toward the door that led from the courtyard into the rooms beyond. "Or perhaps you would like to summon one of your foreign friends, and offer him gold to protect you?"

"You have come to kill me," Moteczuma said weakly, glancing over his shoulder at the door, as if gauging the chances of a sudden dash for safety. Huemac abruptly sat down on a bench across from the one Moteczuma had been occupying.

"I would not deprive Lord Malintzin of the pleasure," he scoffed. "I have come to give you my advice, since you never saw fit to ask for it yourself."

"I do not require your advice," Moteczuma retorted with more boldness, though he remained standing.

"You do, though," Huemac assured him. "I am perhaps the only man in Tenochtitlan whose bad luck approaches your own. Surely, you have not forgotten the man for whom I am named? I was born to face this disaster, just as you were. Sit, Moteczuma. Can you possibly pretend that you are needed elsewhere?"

"My people, my city, need me," Moteczuma muttered sullenly, but he nonetheless seated himself on the edge of the bench. The booming of the drums and the keening of celebratory voices came clearly to their ears as they faced one another in silence. Moteczuma's dark eyes shifted nervously from side to side, refusing to meet Huemac's steady gaze.

"Your people prepare for war without you," Huemac said, gesturing in the direction of the dance. "They know that you do not have the heart for it any longer. When did you lose your heart, Moteczuma? Did you still have it when your uncle died, and you became the ninth to rule, as Huemac was the ninth? Or had you lost it before then, when your father and brother died, and your other uncle was poisoned by his own lords?"

"These are impertinent questions," Moteczuma said stiffly. "I do not have to listen to your insults."

"Go, then. Fill your ears with the flattering lies of the foreigners who hold you captive. See if they will give you back the heart you have lost."

"*You* would give me this?" Moteczuma sneered. "You, who have always belittled and defied me? I would sooner ask the Tlaxcalans."

"Perhaps you should," Huemac replied easily. "Perhaps their taunts would remind you of the courage that once lived within you. A brave man needs his enemies, and respects them for what they are. You knew this once, yet you forgot it, and tried to make friends with those who had come to enslave you. Rouse yourself, Moteczuma!" he said harshly, raising his voice abruptly. "Recognize your enemies, and let them remind you of your courage. Your power and your reputation are gone, lost forever. You have nothing left to lose except your life."

Moteczuma had straightened up angrily at Huemac's shout, but now he let his shoulders slump, and gazed down at his hands.

"I do not want even that, any longer," he said softly. "I pray every night for an end to my misery."

Though filled with disgust at the self-pity in the man's voice, Huemac restrained the sarcastic response that sprang to his lips, and forced himself to adopt a gentle tone:

"Your fate is a hard one, my Lord. I do not envy you your burdens. But you must not put them down just yet. First you must heal the division your capture has created among your people. You must do what you can to gain your brother's release. Let the reed seat pass to one of your own blood before it is too late for all of us."

Moteczuma looked up at him with sad, languid eyes, basking in Huemac's apparent sympathy. Spreading his hands wide, he shook his head slowly and began to explain all that he had learned about the foreigners: their great numbers and wondrous war machines, and the power of their Triple God, who had commanded that all other gods be subjugated to him. But then the drumming in the distance suddenly stopped, so abruptly that both men instinctively cocked their heads at its disappearance. The steady, unified voice of the singers faltered, then broke off raggedly, torn by the piercing screams of people in pain.

"What is happening?" Moteczuma blurted helplessly, and Huemac trained his eyes upon the man, seizing his attention before he could look away.

"The war has begun," Huemac snapped, enveloping Moteczuma with his power, pulling him into his eyes. "Remember your blood. Remember Cuitlahuac!" he commanded. "Do not fail your people, and yourself, this last time!"

Then he released him, and Moteczuma fell backward onto his elbows, his head lolling dizzily on his neck. Huemac rose from the bench and spread his arms, raising them high over his head.

"*Remember,* Moteczuma!" he roared with his last breath, before the transformation overtook him and he burst into flight, spiraling upward out of the courtyard and over the roof of the palace, over the city now at war . . .

XOLOTLPILLI was in the center of the dancing when the foreigners suddenly attacked without warning. He looked up to see a metal-shirted warrior swing his shining warclub at an unsuspecting drummer, sending the man's head flying from his body. Then the foreigners were wading into the crowd from all sides, slashing and stabbing at the defenseless people, who screamed and ran in all directions, slipping on the blood of their fellows and trampling one another in panic. In an instant, the dead and wounded were lying everywhere.

Caught in the midst of the pandemonium, Xolotlpilli began to run himself, until he remembered his courage, and the knife attached to his shield. A number of the dancers had not moved from their places, frozen in shocked disbelief, and he went from one to the other in a rapid circuit, grabbing them roughly by the shoulders and rousing them to action.

"Warriors!" he shouted, brandishing his knife before their dazed faces. "Let us fight our way free!"

Herding them with his shield, Xolotlpilli mustered a group of about ten men around him and plunged into the milling crowd, heading instinctively for the place where the ranks of the surrounding foreigners seemed thinnest. The movement cleared his head completely, and he shut out the noise and confusion around him, focusing all his attention upon the enemy ahead. Their tight ranks reminded him of what Cuauhcoatl had said about attacking in a mass, and he made sure he did not outdistance his companions, gathering more in around him with his shield as he pushed ahead.

Then he could see the faces of the foreigners over the heads of the people struggling against them, fighting metal blades with their bare hands. Stepping over a corpse, Xolotlpilli plowed into the back of the crowd without slowing, heaving those ahead of him forward with his shield, so that they fell bodily upon the foreign warriors. Surging into the middle of the tangled mass, he cut the throats of two of the foreigners before they could free their arms, and fended off another with a jolt from his shield. Sharp blades whistled as they cut the air around him and tore at his flesh, but he stayed in constant motion, whirling and thrusting and knocking bodies about with abandon.

"Tenochtitlan!" he screamed, and leapt at the last man standing between him and freedom. The foreigner crouched and raised his metal-studded shield in front of his body, his thin, deadly warclub extended at his side. But just as the man swung his blade, Xolotlpilli threw his battered shield and hit him in the face. The swinging warclub missed Xolotlpilli's shoulder by a handbreadth as he closed with the man, placing a great hand flat against the man's shield and sending him sprawling to the flagstones.

Several of his former companions had also broken through, and they raced ahead of Xolotlpilli, toward the Serpent Wall that surrounded the precinct. As the first of these reached the wall and leaped for the top, a single foreigner detached himself from those guarding the gate and came toward them, unleashing one of the great spotted lions. Motioning to the others to climb, Xolotlpilli turned and placed himself in the path of the beast, the bloody knife held out before his body. He could hear the creature's maddened growling as it bounded toward him; he could see the sharp gleam of its fangs and the stiff hairs along its back.

Then something swooped out of the air and impaled itself upon the lion's shoulders, flattening the beast with the force of its impact. The lion and its attacker rolled in a wild tumble of fur and feathers, until the furiously beating wings of the hawk lifted it free, leaving the lion writhing on the ground, biting at its own shoulders. The foreigner stopped where he was, gazing up at the fluttering bird, which squawked hoarsely and made another dive at the lion, which leapt for it and missed, landing heavily on its back.

"Jump!" the men on top of the wall called to Xolotlpilli, and he dropped his knife and sprang upward, pulled to the top by the other men as soon as his hands had grasped the edge. The hawk had disappeared into the air overhead, but there was no time to watch after it as Xolotlpilli and his companions dropped to the street below and ran toward their homes, shouting at all they passed to arm themselves, and come forth to bring war upon the foreigners.

"I HAVE never fought in a war from which I could return to my home each night," Cuauhcoatl said aloud, addressing his words to the whole family, who were gathered around him in the courtyard. It was an attempt at lightness, for they all seemed glum and anxious to him; still shaken, he thought, by his close brush with death that afternoon. A stone from the foreigners' exploding tube had passed so closely over his head that he had felt its wind, and then it had smashed into the wall behind him, showering him with shattered brick. But he had escaped with only minor cuts, which Xiuhcue was bandaging for him while he sat with his back against the edge of a reflecting pool.

"I fought such a war, once," Huemac said darkly, standing over him to examine Xiuhcue's handiwork. "It was the war against the Tlatelulca, the War of Defilement."

Cuauhcoatl flinched at the comparison, which seemed unduly morbid. His grandfather turned away restlessly and walked the few feet to where Xolotlpilli and Chalchiuhtona were sitting, fingering the jade rabbit around his neck. Cuauhcoatl noticed that he was no longer carrying his bad left hand in a sling, as he had been since the day of the massacre in the plaza. Just how he had hurt himself had never been explained to Cuauhcoatl, though it had had something to do with his father's escape from the temple precinct.

"And now it is the Tlatelulca we must rely on for leadership," Xolotlpilli said ruefully, lifting his huge head to the sounds that broke the stillness of the night: the shouts and war cries of those harassing the besieged foreigners, and —closer—the muted wails of mourning women. Over six hundred of the Tenocha's highest-ranking warriors had been killed in the massacre, bringing grief into nearly every one of the surrounding houses.

Cuauhcoatl stared curiously at his father, unable to understand the undercurrent of despair, or sadness, he heard in his voice. Only hours before, they had been fighting together on the ramparts that had been erected around the Palace of Axayacatl, showering down a hail of stones, darts, and flaming arrows on those inside, and making periodic attacks on the foreigners and Tlaxcalans defending the walls. Twice they had pushed through to the inner courtyard before being driven back, killing as many as they lost to the foreigners' crossbows and exploding tubes. And it had been seven days since any food or fresh water had gone into the palace; thirst and starvation were certain to become the Mexicans' allies soon, and then they would move in to finish off the foreigners who were left.

But as he opened his mouth to remind his father of these things, Cuauhcoatl realized the hopes that he was indulging, hopes that his father had shown no sign of sharing, however hard he continued to fight. It was anger that brought his father to the ramparts every day; his hopes for a glorious victory had died with the other dancers in the plaza.

Cuauhcoatl glanced down at the capable hands of his sister, wrapping a bandage around a cut on his arm. He pulled away from her slightly, forcing her to look up into his eyes. Xiuhcue did so with her usual reserve, offering him only a glimpse of her handsome brown eyes before returning her attention to his arm. But Cuauhcoatl knew her well enough by now to recognize her tension and excitement, and to know that some decision had been reached.

"There is something I do not know," he said in a flat voice, glancing over at his parents and grandfather. Huemac nodded solemnly and came back a few steps toward him.

"Word has come from the coast. Lord Malintzin has met with the other foreigners and has won them over to his side. He is returning with a much larger force of men, including several thousand Tlaxcalans and Totonacs. They are expected to reach Tepeyacac by tomorrow, and to be here within five days' time. I have decided, my son, that it is time for you and your sister to leave."

"The Arrow Warriors have been disbanded," Xolotlpilli put in, before his son could object, "and we have not yet absorbed your numbers into the other orders. Soon, though, if Cuitlahuac is not released, we will have to reorganize ourselves under the Tlatelulca. Then you will be asked to take new vows, and it would be desertion for you to leave."

"Your task here is finished, my son," Huemac added gently. "I tried, one last time, to rouse Moteczuma, and get him to release Cuitlahuac. But he has not done so, or has not been able to do so. We have only the strength of our arms to rely on now. You must use your wakefulness to see that you and your sister reach the hills in safety."

Cuauhcoatl took a moment to consider their arguments, even though he knew that protest was useless. He had made his agreement, accepted his fate. Yet it was this same fate that had given him the capacity for hope, which now made it so painful for him to leave. He sighed once and spoke in a low voice:

"When are we to leave?"

"Tomorrow morning," Huemac said. "I have arranged with Pinotl to have you taken to Chiconauhtla by canoe. You are going along to help guard his goods, should anyone ask. After that, you have your map, and you know what to do."

"Yes," Cuauhcoatl replied automatically, though his eyes were on the shaking form of his mother, who was weeping in Xolotlpilli's arms.

"Is there not another to whom you should bid farewell?" Huemac asked his grandson. "One who has been like a brother to you?"

"I did not think to tell him of this," Cuauhcoatl admitted, once he had understood his grandfather's meaning. "Even while I was preparing myself, I had hoped that it would not come to pass."

"He knows," Huemac assured him. "But he will wish to hear it from your own lips. Go to him now; I have told him to expect you. The rest of your family will be here when you return."

AS SOON as Cuauhcoatl arrived, Nahui Olin left his charges and took him up onto the roof of Moteczuma's palace. A bright sliver of moon hung in the sky, and there was a warm spring breeze blowing off the Lake, driving away the smoke from the fires still burning in the besieged palace to the west. The noise of the fighting was less noticeable here, obscured by distance and the occasional roars of the caged beasts below. The two men sat together on the far railing, Nahui Olin crossing his pudgy legs under him atop the broad, flat surface while Cuauhcoatl remained perched uneasily on the railing's inward edge.

"Still, I am sorry that I did not tell you myself," Cuauhcoatl apologized resolutely, refusing to accept his friend's easy forgiveness. "We shared too much for me to have kept such a secret from you."

"Perhaps you feared arousing my envy," Nahui Olin suggested soothingly. "It does not matter now, my friend. We have shared our time as comrades, and it has been good. But it is as our grandfather says: Our task is completed."

Cuauhcoatl shook his head stubbornly, pushing himself off the railing and onto his feet. He turned back to Nahui Olin wearing a shrewd, determined expression.

"I have not asked Grandfather," he said, "but why do you not come with us to the hills?"

Nahui Olin laughed softly, putting a tiny hand on Cuauhcoatl's arm to assure him that he was not being ridiculed.

"He told me that you would suggest this," the dwarf said in a kindly voice. "He said that you would try to share your hope with me. He even gave me permission to accept your offer if I wished, even though the woman in the hills has seen no one like *me.*"

"You will come, then?" Cuauhcoatl asked eagerly, covering the little man's hand with his own. But Nahui Olin simply smiled and shook his head.

"I cannot leave the little ones. There is no one who would look after them, and calm their fears. You have seen how they look to me for strength, my brother. Could *you* leave them if you were in my place?"

"No," Cuauhcoatl admitted, after a long pause. "No, you are precious to them. I should never have thought to tempt you with such a thing."

"I am grateful that you did," Nahui Olin said, with a sincerity that made both of them fall silent. They stared at one another with tears in their eyes, sharing the memory of the dangers, and the pleasures, of their unlikely friendship. Then Nahui Olin stood up on the railing and held out his arms to Cuauhcoatl.

"I will miss you, Gold Head," he said hoarsely, wrapping his arms around Cuauhcoatl's back as the young man lifted him off the railing and pressed him against his broad chest. They embraced for a long moment, weeping upon one another's shoulders, and then Cuauhcoatl set him gently upon his feet.

"I will carry you in my heart, my brother, wherever I go," Cuauhcoatl promised, drying his eyes with his bandaged arm. When they had both composed themselves, Nahui Olin started them moving back across the roof.

"Let us go down to the others," he said. "They, too, will wish to say farewell to their friend, before he leaves us forever . . ."

A THIN shaft of dawn light split the crowded buildings of the ward of Pochtlan, casting a murky gray pallor over those who moved silently on the dock beside the canal. The rich scent of the spices being loaded aboard the canoes mingled incongruously with the stagnant, salty smell of the water lapping gently against the pilings. Kneeling on the oily boards of the dock beside his son, Huemac removed the jade rabbit from around his neck and leaned forward to loop it over the bowed head of Cuauhcoatl, who sat with his sister in the canoe below.

"You must wear this always," Huemac said. "It came from the hand of Nezahualcoyotl himself, and it will bring you good luck in the years ahead."

Cuauhcoatl ran his fingers lightly over the amulet against his chest, then looked up at his grandfather.

"Is there any message you would like me to convey to the woman in the hills?"

"Your arrival will say everything," Huemac assured him. "Farewell, my children. May you prosper in your new lives, and bring honor to the memory of your parents."

Huemac rose and stepped away, leaving Xolotlpilli alone beside the canoe, which he held in place with one great hand. The warrior gazed down at the faces of his son and daughter, knowing that there was nothing more to be said. He had given them his advice and praise, and had embraced each of them for the last time. They knew what he felt at their leaving.

"I am sending your mother to her parents in Tlacopan," he began, and quickly stopped himself. "But you know this. I have nothing more to say . . . except that you are more precious to me than life itself. Go now, my children," he said in a choked voice, "I must leave you now . . ."

Xolotlpilli broke off abruptly and rose to his feet, signaling to Pinotl and his sons, who stood ready to cast off. The merchants nimbly lowered themselves into the sterns of the canoes and pushed off from the dock with their paddles. Huemac and Xolotlpilli walked alongside as the canoes slowly gathered momentum and began to move forward out of the canal.

"Farewell, my father," Cuauhcoatl called softly, as the canoe in which he and his sister were riding passed the end of the dock. Xiuhcue looked back over her shoulder with wet eyes and raised her hand in a last wave, and then the canoes turned into the main channel and were lost from sight behind the intervening buildings.

The two men stood for a long time without speaking, watching the air grow brighter around them and listening to the calls of the water birds as they wheeled high overhead. Huemac unconsciously raised a hand to his chest, then let it fall to his side.

"I am ready to die now," Xolotlpilli announced to no one, his words echoing hollowly in the narrow space before being swallowed up by the lapping wake left by the canoes.

"Let us go to find our enemy," Huemac replied, and stepped up on the well-beaten pathway that would lead them back to Tenochtitlan.

7

LATE in the sixth month of Two Flint-Knife, Lord Malintzin again led his troops up the southern causeway toward Tenochtitlan. But this time there were no dignitaries to guide him, and no curious crowds to greet his approach. The causeway was deserted, and the Lake completely empty of canoes; only the rising smoke from the temple fires gave evidence of life in the city ahead. The deep, eerie silence affected even the Tlaxcalans and Totonacs at the rear, who stopped their singing and glanced nervously at the rooftops and side alleys as they passed under the Xoloco and followed the foreigners into the streets. They could feel the eyes watching them from the houses along the way, but no one answered their bold taunts to come out and be seen.

The Palace of Axayacatl lay surrounded by the abandoned earthworks of its attackers, its plastered walls broken in many places and blackened by fire. The gate was opened by those inside, and the foreigners and their allies streamed into the main courtyard unhindered. Once inside, the foreigners shot off their exploding tubes in a thunderous barrage, as if to awaken the city to their return.

Before the echoes of the tubes had even died away, they were met by an answering volley of war cries, and a thick cloud of stones, darts, and arrows descended on the palace grounds. Painted Mexican warriors appeared on all the surrounding rooftops, and thousands more rushed out of the streets to man the earthworks, heaving flint-tipped lances and flaming torches over the court-yard walls. A straggling contingent of Totonacs were caught in front of the gate and cut to pieces as they tried to reach safety, and the gate itself was nearly breached before the foreigners fired their great tubes into the attacking mass and drove the Mexicans back.

The fighting went on all afternoon without pause, until the dead lay heaped around the palace walls and the smoke of the fires burning within darkened the sky. The foreigners took a great toll with their exploding tubes and the hissing metal darts shot by their crossbowmen, but there were always more warriors to challenge them, screaming threats and filling the air with arrows and stones. Even with the coming of night, there was no slackening in the ferocity of the attack; the battle to the death had begun.

THE DAY outside was hot and humid, and as Huemac entered the stifling atmosphere of the Council Chamber, he was nearly overcome by a sudden dizziness that made him sway upon his feet. He followed Xolotlpilli blindly, wondering if he were actually going to faint here, and disgrace himself before the assembled lords. He did not know what was causing this, but he had not felt right since the day he had given his jade rabbit to his grandson. Surely, he was old—at sixty-four—to be taking his place upon the ramparts with the young men. But he had fought mostly with his sling—stones being more effective than arrows against the foreigners' armor—and he did not think that he had exerted himself unduly. This mysterious weakness did not seem ac-countable to mere fatigue, reminding him instead of what he had sometimes suffered after using the magic plants.

He was grateful when Xolotlpilli finally chose a place to sit, and he lowered himself heavily to the mat beside his son, feeling a cold sweat break out on his forehead. Xolotlpilli looked at him with concern.

"You are ill, my father," the big man said solicitously, but Huemac shook his head in denial, causing the blood to pound in his temples.

"It is only the heat," he said gruffly, turning away from his son to examine the men around the circle, pretending that their images did not waver and jump before his eyes. It was several moments, though, before his vision had steadied sufficiently for him to make sense of the situation in the room.

Occupying the side of the circle directly across from him was a strong contingent of warchiefs and high-tufted Otomi Warriors from Tlatelulco, led by Cuauhtemoc, the son of Ahuitzotl who had been elected Eagle Speaker by the Tlatelulca themselves, following the imprisonment of Itzquauhtzin. They left no doubt, by the belligerence of their bearing, that they did not intend to assume their usual secondary position to the Tenocha. Several high-ranking members of the pochteca were seated with them, included in this council because of the large number of canoes they could offer to the war effort. Huemac located Omeocelotl in their ranks and nodded to his nephew, who had apparently been waiting to be recognized for some time.

What he saw on his own side of the circle did nothing to relieve the ache in Huemac's head, for the divisions between the Tenocha seemed as clearly drawn as ever. A small coterie of priests and merchants attached to the Cihuacoatl were clustered near the dais, their backs turned to the group around Xolotlpilli, who were the remnants of Cuitlahuac's opposition party. Diverse elements from among the decimated ranks of the Eagles, Jaguars, and Pumas completed the group, but even these had left spaces between their respective cliques, indicating that there was competition for supremacy both between and within the individual orders.

As the second-in-command to the captive Speaker, the Cihuacoatl convened the meeting, but the discussion had barely begun before the lords were embroiled in a quarrel concerning who should have the honor of presiding over the assembly. Pointing to the superiority of their forces, the comrades of Cuauhtemoc put forward a demand that their leader should share the rule equally with the Cihuacoatl, and that two ranking Tlatelulca should be elected to the new Council of Four Lords. The Tenocha lords rose immediately to denounce this proposal as arrogant and presumptuous, and all the resentment that still lingered from the days of the civil war began to boil to the surface.

"Is *this* where we are to find our enemies?" Huemac murmured disgustedly to Xolotlpilli, who grunted angrily and shifted on his haunches, wiping sweat from his glistening head.

Suddenly, with a total disregard for the protocol of the occasion, a messenger rushed into the chamber and sprang to the center of the circle, shocking the arguing lords into silence.

"Cuitlahuac has been released!" he announced exuberantly. "He is coming here now!"

The men around the circle were on their feet in an instant, all talking at once, waving their arms and embracing one another. Huemac had risen with the rest, and he looked up to find Xolotlpilli regarding him with proud and admiring eyes.

"This is *your* doing, my father," he said, stooping to be heard over the din. "It must be."

"Perhaps," Huemac said with a doubtful shrug, confused as much by what he felt within himself as by the mood of mounting exhilaration in the room. For the dizziness and aching in his head were gone, and he felt stronger than he had in days, strong enough to want to march out of here and lead the attack on the foreigners himself. The oppressive heat of the closely packed bodies in the room suddenly seemed to flow into his aging muscles, making them feel supple and alive.

It seemed only moments later that the warchief himself strode into the chamber, and the lords greeted him with one thunderous voice, shouting his name with a common sense of joy and relief. Cuauhtemoc went immediately to bow before his cousin and, with the Cihuacoatl on the other side, to lead him to the empty reed seat at the head of the circle.

Then Cuitlahuac stood before them, alone on the dais as the other men settled themselves to listen. The warchief appeared thin and weary, his movements betraying the listlessness of long captivity. But the fierce gleam in his eyes left no doubt as to the spirit that remained within him.

"My Lords," he said in a resonant voice. "You have offered me the reed seat of the Speaker, and I humbly accept this honor, and the burdens you have placed upon my unworthy shoulders. But the gods will forgive me, I am sure, if I do not perform the usual rites of fasting and meditation before taking up my task. There is only one rite that can be of importance to us now, and that is the rite of war!"

The lords again leapt to their feet in acclamation, and it was several moments before the cheering died down and quiet could be restored.

"I have seen the hunger that already exists within the ranks of the enemy," Cuitlahuac went on. "And now they have many more mouths to feed. This, in fact, was the reason for my release," he added with a sardonic smile. "Moteczuma has sent me, at the request of Lord Malintzin, to ask you to reopen the marketplace."

This revelation was greeted by a chorus of derisive laughter, followed by rude suggestions as to the kind of bartering that ought to be done with the white men. Huemac again felt Xolotlpilli looking at him, but he was too lost in his own speculations to do more than nod in acceptance of his son's tribute. For he had suddenly understood that his vision was beginning to unfold before him. He had used his eyes, in the vision, to stop the destruction of the city. Just as he had used them, in reality, to impress Cuitlahuac's release upon Moteczuma. And the exultation he felt in the lords around him was the same as that he had felt himself at the moment when he had fended off the disaster in his vision. Perhaps Cuitlahuac's release would, in fact, have the same effect. Bowing his head in the midst of the jeering crowd, Huemac gave silent thanks to those who had taught him to use his powers, and he paid a solitary homage to Moteczuma, who had remembered something of himself, after all.

When he looked up again, the room had once more fallen silent, and Cuitlahuac was holding his wrists out for all to see, displaying the marks left by his metal bonds.

"We owe these murderers too much to let even one of them live," the warchief proclaimed in a seething voice. "We must feed the gods with their hearts and blood, and erase the stain they have spread over our reputation for manliness! There is much glory to be won, my friends," he said in a lower tone, sweeping his eyes around the circle. "And we will all share in it equally. The foreigners have looted the treasures of both my father and brother, treasures that are mine by right. But I will not seek to reclaim any of this when they have all been killed. Let each warrior claim whatever he can win with the strength of his arm; let it be his own. But let us put an end to these invaders once and for all!"

Exhausted by his speech, Cuitlahuac collapsed upon the reed seat, gasping for breath while the cheers of the assembled lords resounded around him. Overflowing with emotion, Xolotlpilli wrapped an arm around his father and shook him up and down, and Huemac could only smile indulgently, feeling the power of the enthusiasm in the room.

"Now there is nothing to stop us from destroying them," Xolotlpilli said forcefully, coiling a great fist in front of his face.

"May it last . . . may it only last," Huemac murmured fervently, and went up to join those who were crowding close to Cuitlahuac, paying homage to the new hope of Mexico.

SUBORDINATED to the need to maintain the siege, the reorganization of the army proceeded slowly, and it was several days before Huemac was summoned for an interview with Cuitlahuac. This took place on a rooftop overlooking the palace grounds, for the foreigners had already made a number of attempts to venture out into the city, and Cuitlahuac wanted to be able to respond instantly to any move his enemy made.

The new Speaker was sitting with his back against the second of two earthen walls that had been erected as defenses against the foreigners' thundering tubes. He smiled easily at Huemac's bow and gestured for him to sit.

"Greetings, my father," he said respectfully. "I am grateful for the leadership you have offered us. I have fought in the past with the men you trained so well for my uncle, Ahuitzotl." Cuitlahuac paused, forcing his face into a sterner mold after the requisite flattery had been dispensed. "But I must tell you that I am not pleased that you and Xolotlpilli allowed Cuauhcoatl to leave the city at this time."

"It was not the choice of Cuauhcoatl, or his father," Huemac replied firmly. "*I* insisted that he go. It was his fate to leave at this time, just as it is mine, and yours, to be here until the end of this. Even the foreigners, my Lord, have not caused me to abandon my respect for fate."

Cuitlahuac frowned uncomfortably, a warchief confronted with the logic of a priest, or a wise man. Huemac put a trace of force into his gleaming eyes, knowing that Cuitlahuac was now remembering the other things he had heard about the old man in front of him, the rumors that had nothing to do with Huemac's war record. Huemac was willing to gamble that he would back off rather than enter this realm of discussion, and indeed, Cuitlahuac finally nodded and indicated that he did not wish to pursue the subject any further.

"Where, then, do you think you might best serve us?" he asked instead, cocking his head to listen to the sounds of fighting behind them. Huemac waited patiently until he had the Speaker's full attention before replying:

"I have studied our defenses, my Lord," he said with deliberate modesty, "which have so far kept the foreigners caged within the palace. But soon, if we do not break in upon them, they will be forced by hunger to try to escape."

"I do not intend to give them that chance," Cuitlahuac said flatly. "But go on . . . "

"It is difficult to predict Lord Malintzin's actions," Huemac confessed, "but in his place, I would take the shortest route out of the city. I would flee to the west, across the causeway to the mainland. As you know—and no doubt Lord Malintzin knows, as well—the people of Tlacopan have not shown a great willingness to support us, due to the way your brother scorned their importance to the Alliance."

"We will settle with them later," Cuitlahuac vowed. "But you are right; we will have to defend the causeway ourselves."

"Then we must do more than has been done so far," Huemac told him. "There are five canals that intersect the road leading to the causeway, and only at the first of these—the one nearest the palace—has the bridge been cut and the canal widened, and barricades put up on the far bank. I would recommend that the same be done at the other four locations, and that they each be garrisoned by troops drawn from the calpullis in which they lie. I would offer myself to organize this work, and to command one of the garrisons, if this idea meets with your approval."

"You believe that the foreigners could get so far as the fifth canal?" Cuitlahuac queried. "Or even the third?"

"They have not yet ventured out in full force," Huemac pointed out. "And they will be desperate. They must all be destroyed *this time,* my Lord," he added emphatically. "None of them must be allowed to escape."

"I have told you that I share this view," Cuitlahuac said with a trace of impatience. "Why do you doubt our ability to prevent their escape?"

"I do not doubt our ability," Huemac said, and took a deep breath before going on: "My only fear is that the men will be distracted by the taking of captives or the gathering of loot, and will let some of them slip through. Many more foreigners will come to our land, my Lord, and we will not be safe as long as Lord Malintzin is alive to lead them against us."

"Lord Malintzin will die with the rest," Cuitlahuac said with a dismissive gesture, his eyes hard upon Huemac's face. "But you are questioning the rewards I promised to the men in the Council Chamber, and to the gods, as well. We have always fought for captives, and for the fine things that are the proof of our courage. How can you say that these things are distractions, you who have spoken to me of what is fated? Surely, you would not have us change the way we conduct ourselves as warriors?"

"These foreigners have shown themselves to be murderers, men without honor," Huemac said stubbornly. "It matters only *that* they be killed, not how or why."

Cuitlahuac's nostrils flared, and his eyes widened with reproach.

"But *we* must fight and die like *warriors,*" he reminded Huemac sharply, "in a way that is pleasing to the gods. Frankly, my father, I am surprised that you hold such an irreverent attitude."

Seeing that he was being regarded with actual suspicion, Huemac simply bowed his head in acquiescence, knowing that he had done as much as he could. Now the matter was truly in the hands of fate.

"However," the Speaker went on in a thoughtful tone, "there is some merit in what you said earlier. I cannot spare many men from the siege, but I will give you enough to begin the erection of defenses on the second and third canals. I will also give you the authority to recruit men from those calpullis. But I warn you: You will not be able to convince the best warriors to stay so far from the scene of battle."

"I will gather those I can," Huemac promised, bowing to show his gratitude. Cuitlahuac summoned one of his aides and explained the powers that Huemac was to be given, and the men to be released to his use. He had only just finished giving these orders when all three men noticed—simultaneously—that the sounds of the fighting had stopped. Cuitlahuac jumped to his feet and vaulted over the barricade, shouting for an explanation.

"They are waving the white plumes of truce," Huemac heard someone say as he followed the Speaker to the forward barricade. "They have brought someone out to speak to us."

Huemac found a space for himself between the men pressed against the earthworks and craned forward to see. Across the street littered with bodies, on the roof of one of the palace buildings just within the courtyard wall, stood a small knot of metal-armored warriors, their shields raised in front of them and the white banner of truce floating over their helmeted heads. The Mexicans along the rooftops and ramparts had fallen silent, but a deep, sustained murmuring swept through their ranks when the foreign warriors parted to reveal the figures of Moteczuma and Itzquauhtzin, their faces unmistakable even at a distance. The wrists and ankles of both men were loosely bound with braids of shining metal, and Itzquauhtzin made a clanking sound as he shuffled forward to speak.

"Hear me, Mexicans, men of Tenochtitlan and Tlatelulco!" he shouted to the watching warriors. "Your ruler, the Great Speaker Moteczuma, implores you to listen, and heed his words. He says to lower your weapons and abandon this battle, for we are not the equals of the foreigners! He begs you to think of the women and children, the old ones, the ones unable to protect themselves. They will suffer great misery, they will be left unfortunate, if you do not cease your attacks. For this reason does he tell you: 'We are not their equals.' See how they have placed him in bondage!"

Moteczuma was pushed forward by his captors until he stood next to Itzquauhtzin, but he did not speak himself, and he held his slender body erect as the jeers of his people washed over him.

"Moteczuma and his words mean nothing to us!" one of the men on the roof beside Huemac shouted back. "We have our own Speaker, and we no longer pay heed to cowards!"

The threats and insults increased in both volume and violence, and it was Cuitlahuac himself who cast the first stone, bouncing it sharply off his brother's shins. Then the stones and arrows came pelting down like hail, and the foreign warriors hastened to draw their prisoners back into their midst and retreat from the roof, holding their shields over their heads for protection. The taunts of the Mexicans continued long after Moteczuma had disappeared, and the fighting around the walls had resumed with all its former ferocity.

But Huemac had seen, with the vision of his nahualli, the smile that had been on Moteczuma's lips when the stones had begun to fall around him, and he knew then that he had not been wrong about the reason for Cuitlahuac's release, and his own hand in it. This is our one chance, he thought as he left the roof with Cuitlahuac's aide: We must stop it *now*.

THE MESSAGE came to Omeocelotl while he was supervising the loading and unloading of the canoes outside his guild's warehouse. Unlike the other messages he had been receiving all morning, this was not an urgent communication; simply a request from Xolotlpilli that he and Pinotl come to the warrior's house for the evening meal, if possible. Surrounded by all the furious activity on the dock, the warrior who had acted as Xolotlpilli's messenger showed his embarrassment at delivering such an apparently trivial message, explaining that he had run across Xolotlpilli in the temple plaza and had been unable to refuse the favor the great warrior asked, since he was coming to Tlatelulco on other business, anyway. He apologized to Omeocelotl for not being able to return with his reply, and the merchant thanked him and sent him off to deal with the business that had brought him here.

Since Pinotl was supposed to return from Chalco this evening with a load of much-needed supplies—which would have to be dispatched immediately to the warriors standing siege around the palace—Omeocelotl knew that he would have no time to spare for a meal with his friends, and he put Xolotlpilli's message out of his mind without further consideration. It was not until well past the middle of the day, when he found himself in the vicinity of the temple precinct in Tenochtitlan, that he thought of it again. Deciding that it would be kinder to give his regrets in person, if he could indeed find his cousin without too much lost time, he left his lieutenants in charge at the dock and went to inquire among the guards at the precinct gate.

Though he was wearing cotton armor and had a shield and warclub strapped across his back, Omeocelotl's long gray hair was loose beneath a plain wooden helmet, and he wore or carried no insignia except for the black staff of his trade. The Tenocha guards greeted him with suspicion at first, but their attitude changed immediately when he explained that he was looking for his cousin, the Cuachic Xolotlpilli. Speaking with new respect, they pointed to the ring of warriors stationed around the base of the Temple of Huitzilopochtli, explaining that Xolotlpilli was a part of the honor guard of high-ranking warriors that had been assigned to protect the temple after the Toxcatl massacre. They sent Omeocelotl to find him without further questioning, and did not bother to provide him with the usual escort accorded to visitors without credentials.

Exposed to the full force of the sunlight bathing the plaza, Omeocelotl hooded his eyes against the glare reflecting from the well-swept flagstones. He noticed, though, that neither the sparse spring rains nor the brooms of the apprentice priests had been able to totally efface the memory of the awful slaughter that had occurred here. The flagstones still bore a faint, pinkish tinge around their edges, and the narrow cracks between them were filled with a caked red powder. No wonder they have left some of their best warriors here, Omeocelotl thought grimly, even though they were a good distance from the besieged palace and were unlikely to be in the path of any escape attempt on the part of the foreigners.

In accordance with his rank, Xolotlpilli was stationed at the foot of the steep stairs that went up the face of the great pyramid. He was standing beside a painted stone serpent's head and was dressed in his full battle gear, with brilliantly feathered devices attached to his back and shoulders and a plumed helmet on his head. He was gazing out over the deserted plaza toward the west, where the fighting was going on just beyond the precinct walls. Omeocelotl noticed that he was carrying the turquoise-mosaic shield that he had captured in the conquest of Zinacantlan, some five years earlier.

It seemed to take him a moment to recognize Omeocelotl, as if his thoughts were lost somewhere in the distance, but then he smiled quietly and raised his painted warclub in salute.

"Greetings, my cousin. You are the first to respond to my summons. Has Pinotl also been told?"

"He is bringing arrows from Chalco, and will not be back to the city until later tonight," Omeocelotl explained. "And I am afraid that I, too, will be unable to dine with you, my friend. Was there something you wished to say to us?"

"No," Xolotlpilli admitted, drawing the word out slowly. "I only hoped that we might be together again for a short time. No doubt it was a foolish wish. My father works day and night, dredging the canals and trying to make warriors out of old men and boys; and it is not really safe for Nahui Olin to go about alone, since the servants of Moteczuma are the targets of such hatred. Yes, it was quite foolish . . . "

Xolotlpilli trailed off in a subdued tone, again staring into the distance, past the round shrine of Quetzalcoatl, which hid the Palace of Axayacatl from their view. Omeocelotl glanced briefly in that direction, seeing nothing unusual except for the black smoke rising from the scene of the battle.

"I am sorry, my cousin," he ventured, unable to determine the source of Xolotlpilli's distraction. "Perhaps when we have brought in all the supplies we need . . . "

"Yes," Xolotlpilli agreed absently. Then he looked directly at the merchant and studied him for a few moments, as if memorizing his features. "But stay a while, Omeocelotl," he suggested in a soft voice. "I would like your company for a few moments longer."

"What is it, Xolotlpilli?" Omeocelotl asked with concern. "You seem saddened. Have you lost a close comrade today?"

Xolotlpilli slowly shook his head, making his dangling golden earplugs dance over his shoulders. His brown eyes were large and solemn, unblinking in the fierce glare of the sun.

"Have you never heard the warriors speak of feeling the nearness of their own death?" he asked in a musing tone. "They say that it is a presence that hovers over you like a shadow, just above the surface of your skin. They say that it makes you feel the life that is within you, as if it were a precious liquid that might be spilled with ease. So they say . . . "

Omeocelotl was silent, hearing the confirming note in Xolotlpilli's voice and understanding that the great warrior was speaking about himself.

"I am old for a Cuachic," Xolotlpilli continued presently. "The gods have given me great glory in my lifetime. They have allowed me to see Xoconochco and Zinacantlan, following in the wake of the brave vanguard merchants."

"Our way was made easier," Omeocelotl said, returning the compliment, "by the reputation of the warriors who would come after us. Especially by that of the man called Xolotl Mexicatl, the Monster of Mexico."

"May our fame never be forgotten," Xolotlpilli concluded quietly, and the two men bowed to each other, acknowledging the past they had shared. One of the foreigners' thundering tubes boomed in the distance, echoing across the empty plaza to where they stood. Then there was another explosion, and another and another, following so closely upon one another that their sound broke over the temple precinct like a great thunderclap. A cloud of gray smoke billowed up against the western sky, and the shouts of fighting men could be heard above the concerted crackling of the foreigners' smaller tubes. Word was quickly passed down the line from those warriors in a position to see the western gate of the compound: The foreigners had broken into the precinct, and were coming this way.

"Go to your duties, my friend," Xolotlpilli said hastily. "It is not your place to be here, defending our temple."

Omeocelotl hesitated for only a moment, then leaned his staff against the stone serpent's head and began to remove the weapons from his back.

"You forget the blood we share," he said curtly. "Am I not the brother of Azcatzin? Is my place not at the side of our comrade?"

Xolotlpilli stared at his cousin's adamant features, then bared his teeth in a fierce smile of gratitude and affection. He raised his glittering shield over his head and shook it joyfully at the sun.

"It is a good day to die, my friend!" he shouted over the noise of the approaching enemy, and turned to climb the steps to the platform above, keeping Omeocelotl close beside him.

HUEMAC was standing waist-deep in the dirty water of the canal when the tubes sounded and a great commotion arose from the direction of the palace, some two blocks away. But he did not leap for his weapons as the young men working with him did; he waited instead for a message to be sent down from the nearby calpulli temple, where the priests kept a sharp lookout over the entire scene of the battle. A young apprentice priest appeared shortly, on the run, and breathlessly reported that the foreigners had launched an attack on the temple precinct, and had already broken through the guards at the west gate.

As he climbed to the bank and took a towel from the pile beside his weapons, Huemac could feel the eyes of his eager young recruits on him. He knew that they would be of little use in this fight, and would probably not even be allowed near it by the higher commanders. But he could not deny the spirit that made them want to try, or the fact that they had worked hard for the chance. Drying his hair with the towel, he ordered them first into their four-man fighting groups, and then into their full ranks, making them wait until everyone had his whole complement of weapons. Placing his chief lieutenant—an old warrior like himself—in charge, he sent them off at a measured trot, with orders to advance to the first canal and place themselves at the disposal of the commander there.

Wrapping the towel around his shoulders, Huemac took his shield and warclub and walked quickly toward the calpulli temple, which was dedicated to Tezcatlipoca. It was a pyramid perhaps only four stories in height, but it rose high enough over the intervening buildings to provide a clear view of Axayacatl's palace and the temple precinct beyond. Huemac felt his breath grow short as he climbed the steep steps, and he realized that a tight knot of anxiety had formed in his stomach, a nameless dread that seemed a spiteful counterpoint to the coolness of his mind. What comes to me now? he wondered, panting helplessly as he reached the summit of the temple and bowed to the image set back within the wooden shrine.

Despite his disreputable appearance, he was totally ignored by the cluster of excited priests, who were squinting furiously in an effort to make out the course of the distant battle. Dripping water from the ends of his loincloth, he walked to one side of the platform and carefully laid his weapons down, feeling the anxiety in his midsection harden like a rock as he bent over. He glanced once more at the black shrine of Tezcatlipoca, then turned very slowly to look toward the east.

A cloud of dust and smoke hung over the temple precinct, which appeared, at first glance, to be a whitewashed box aswarm with men the size of ants. Then Huemac summoned the vision of his nahualli, and saw the colors fade from the warriors' costumes as their figures—and then their faces—came into focus. The compact group of foreigners in their midst stood out brilliantly, their metal shirts and helmets shining like polished silver in the bright sunlight. The foreigners were marching very quickly, the men with the shooting sticks and crossbows in the vanguard, taking methodical turns at loading and firing, so that some of them were shooting at all times. The men on the deer charged out into the open spaces, spearing Mexicans with their lances and retreating back to the main group whenever the opposition became too thick for them to maneuver. Though the group was vastly outnumbered by the crowd of warriors surrounding them, the superior strength of their weapons and their discipline propelled them inexorably forward, toward the great temple.

"They will be stopped," one of the priests declared with forced conviction. "Huitzilopochtli will not allow his image to be defiled a second time."

Huemac's eyes bulged painfully against the sides of their sockets as he strained to see the men on the temple itself, which was beyond the range of even his nahualli's vision. But then a sharp, sudden pain knifed through his midsection, and the knot of anxiety shattered and vanished, washed away by a tingling rush of power that went straight to his head. Suddenly he could see everything, as clearly as he had in his last vision, almost fifty years earlier.

I have failed, Huemac thought as he gazed down at the battle; *it has begun again, and this time it will not be stopped.* The thunder of the explosions seemed to fill his ears and make the platform vibrate beneath his feet as he scanned the ranks of warriors positioned up and down the face of the pyramid. The foreigners had fought their way to the base of the steps, and now they trained their great, rolling tubes on the defenders above, setting off blast after blast that threw men into the air and tore huge chunks of plastered stone out of the face of the temple. The Mexicans retreated to the higher platforms, showering stones and arrows down upon the foreign warriors who had begun to climb the steps, slashing and stabbing with their metal warclubs.

Gripped by the power that was upon him, Huemac could only watch as the foreigners advanced upward, throwing down all those who opposed them. Then a great log came bouncing down the steps, knocking two of the metal-shirted warriors to their deaths, and Huemac's eyes jerked upward, instantly locating the huge man who had heaved the log from the top platform. *My son,* he thought helplessly, seeing Xolotlpilli grimace with effort as he lifted a large stone over his head and tossed it over the side. Beside him on the platform was another familiar figure, a long-haired man in blood-streaked armor who put his shield and body in front of Xolotlpilli while the great warrior stooped for another stone. And you, Omeocelotl, Huemac cried in his heart: Must I watch you die, as well?

But he could not turn his eyes away, even as the foreigners forged their way to the top and began to grapple with the last line of the Mexican defense. Men from both sides were pushed screaming over the edge, tumbling with sickening speed down the side of the pyramid, breaking their bodies on the sharp ledges and stone outcroppings. Huemac saw Omeocelotl's black staff flailing above the heads of the combatants, and then the merchant went down, and Xolotl-pilli was alone in the midst of a crowd of enemies. The great warrior struggled valiantly, fighting with his bare hands long after his shield and warclub had been stripped away. But then he, too, went down, and the platform belonged to the foreigners.

Moments later, flames began to lick around the roofs of the shrines of Tlaloc and Huitzilopochtli, and then the foreigners and their Tlaxcalan allies rushed forward, dragging the image of Huitzilopochtli behind them. Setting its vestments afire with a torch, they pushed the stone figure over the edge and sent it crashing down the face of the pyramid to shatter on the plaza below.

This, too, I have seen, Huemac thought, and as the tears rose to his eyes, the power suddenly left him, and his vision snapped back to normal, making him lurch forward onto his knees. In the distance, the shrines atop the great temple were obscured by a billowing cloud of black smoke and orange flame, and the dead were dark bruises on the face of the pyramid. The priests on the platform with Huemac had also fallen to their knees, weeping loudly and calling to the gods for forgiveness. Some had even taken out their thorns and were pricking their legs and forearms in penance. Huemac turned to pick up his shield and macana, grunting at their heaviness, then pushed himself to his feet and began to walk toward the stairs.

The priests were blocking his way, and they all turned to look at him as he approached, his warclub trailing along the platform in the looseness of his grip. They were facing the shrine of their god, and outrage came into their faces when they saw that Huemac intended to walk past them without turning to bow to Tezcatlipoca.

"Have you forgotten yourself, Warrior?" the eldest priest demanded, rising quickly to stand in Huemac's path. "Dare you show disrespect at such a time, when we need the protection of the gods more than ever?"

"Get out of my way, Priest," Huemac said coldly. "It is *we* who have been forgotten."

Incoherent with anger, the priest sputtered threateningly and thrust out his arms to prevent Huemac's passage. But then he felt the eyes boring into his own and pulled his arms back, covering his face with his hands.

"The Dark One mocks us," Huemac spat. "He protects no one. It is over, Priest. Now let me go to collect the body of my son."

The priests shrank away from him in terror, and Huemac walked through their midst and began to descend the steps, never once turning back to acknowledge the glowering image of Tezcatlipoca, the Decider of Fates.

8

O N the last night of the seventh month, a fine misty rain began to fall, and a gusty east wind came up off the Lake to blow the rain through the dark streets of Tenochtitlan. Halfway down the wide avenue that led to the western causeway, behind the earthworks at the third canal, Huemac huddled beneath a makeshift shelter of sticks and cloth, listening to the distorted echoes of far-off sounds, borne to him by the wind. He was alone on the ramparts, the rest of his squadron having been permitted by their commander to find shelter for themselves in the nearby houses. Huemac was here by his own choice, preferring the dampness of solitude to the company of the boys and old men left to guard this canal, most of whom avoided his presence, as if in fear of contamination.

Huemac smiled to himself in the darkness, tasting the irony of his latest— and last—demotion at the hands of a Tenocha ruler. Even now, at the end, he thought, I have not lost my talent for offending my own leaders. It had taken the priest of Tezcatlipoca two days to gain an audience with Cuitlahuac, but the Speaker, despite all his other worries, had not lost any time in depriving Huemac of his command and returning him to the ranks of the ordinary warriors. The first act of the new commander had been to break up the four-man groups that Huemac had organized to give his raw recruits a fighting chance against the foreigners. His second had been to send Huemac back to the third canal and to forbid him to go near any of the calpulli temples.

Now we will be safe from the wrath of the gods, Huemac thought sardonically, if not from that of our enemy. He raised his head above the barricade, wiping uselessly at the moisture that immediately coated his face, blurring his vision of the defenses farther down the street. There were a few men ranged along the earthworks at the second canal, and many more at the first. But still, there were far too few, by Huemac's reckoning, to fend off the foreigners if they came in force. The unbroken silence around the palace did not deceive him, for he knew that the stomachs of the foreigners and their allies had to be shouting with hunger by now. And although they had retreated back into the palace after sacking the Temple of Huitzilopochtli, they had to be aware of the damage they had done to the spirit of the Mexicans. Only two days ago, as if to emphasize their disdain for the fury of their adversaries, they had thrown out the dead bodies of Cacama, Itzquauhtzin, and Moteczuma. Cacama had been strangled, and the other two men stabbed in many places.

It cannot be long now, Huemac thought, as he settled himself back under his shelter. But then he heard something bump against the side of the canal behind him, and he was up in an instant, his shield and warclub in hand. Raising himself silently above the bulwark, he looked down to see Pinotl sitting in a canoe below.

"Greetings, my friend," Huemac said softly. "You are foolish to be out in this weather, but I am grateful that you have come."

Pinotl tied his canoe to a piling and climbed to the bank, glancing curiously down the length of the deserted barricade. He had brought a dry cloak for Huemac and a gourd of octli for the two of them to share.

"*You* are out in this weather," he observed mildly, removing the reed stopper and handing the gourd to Huemac. "Perhaps you should come to Tlatelulco with me and warm yourself. You will not be missed here."

"This is warming enough," Huemac replied, taking a second sip before returning the gourd. "Have you been able to visit Nahui Olin?"

Pinotl lowered the gourd from his lips and nodded.

"I took more supplies to him and his friends, along with some tools he had asked for. They have begun to farm one of the palace gardens. Nahui Olin said that he had spoken to you."

"Yes, we have made our farewells," Huemac averred. "And now the two of us must do the same. I have already seen my city die, Pinotl. Do not stay to see the end of yours. Take your family and go while there is time."

"Where is there to go?" Pinotl asked quietly.

"Go to your wife's parents in Xicalanco," Huemac suggested. "Or to Michpilli in Teloloapan, or to Texcoco. Chiquatli's men have made a pact with the foreigners; they will give you protection in their midst."

"Have you not heard? There is a great sickness sweeping through the cities on the coast. It is believed that the foreigners brought it with them. And the other trails are not safe for us any longer. There is no escape for any of us, my father; you are not the only one who has come to accept this."

"Of course," Huemac agreed with a sigh. "Go to your family, then, my son. Share with them whatever time is left."

Pinotl replaced the stopper and presented the gourd to Huemac with a slight bow.

"We have shared many memories," he said in an awkwardly formal tone. "It has been my honor to serve you as a friend."

"And mine, to be so well served," Huemac replied gently, seeing the emotion with which his friend was struggling. "Farewell, Pinotl. May your way be the Straight One . . ."

His long, homely face clenched against the feelings that had robbed him of the power to respond, Pinotl nodded stiffly and reached out to briefly touch Huemac on the shoulder. Then he ducked out of the shelter and disappeared over the barricade. Huemac heard a paddle thud against the side of the canal, and then he was alone with the rain and wind.

Now there were no more who would come to him; no more to touch his heart for a last time and remind him of the life he had lived. Yet there *was* one more to be released, and as he contemplated the barren street around him, he decided that the time to free his nahualli had come at last. He had no further use for its powers, and he wished to see it once more before he died, and admire its strength and beauty.

Casting off his cloak and helmet, he rose from his shelter and stood in the middle of the street, allowing the rain to blow over him in wet gusts. When he was certain that no one was watching him, he raised his arms over his head and began to chant in a low voice:

"This net, my net;
With it, I have captured your spirit;

With it, I have held you fast.
But now its coils are loosened,
Now it rises from around you,
Now it casts you free . . ."

With a sudden wrench that made Huemac's eyes roll back in his head, the nahualli erupted within him and burst out through his skin, raking all his nerves with a hot pain and making him stagger in circles to keep his balance. Then the hawk hung in the air before him, its copper wings beating furiously, its sharp beak gaping between the deep yellow eyes.

"Go to Tepeyollotl, my friend," Huemac called softly. "Go to the hills, where my son awaits you . . ."

The hawk screeched hoarsely, then flew in a small circle over Huemac's head before opening its wings fully and disappearing upward, offering him a last glimpse of its reddish tail feathers before it was lost in the darkness above.

Huemac barely made it back to his shelter before he collapsed to the ground, shivering from the sudden cold that surrounded his body. He felt bruised all over and too fatigued to lift his head from the mud beneath him. But he managed to cover himself with his cloak, and he gulped down the last of Pinotl's octli before the gourd dropped from his numbed hands. He had felt no urge to sleep since the day of Xolotlpilli's death, but now his eyes closed of their own accord, and the memories that he had used to capture his nahualli began to flood through his mind. He saw his mother and father again, and Nezahualcoyotl, and Taypachtli and Chimalman, and his children and nephews and all the others who had played a role in his fate. He saw a young man and a girl journeying together through the desert, and the image soothed his ragged nerves and stopped the shaking of his body. As he fell into a deep sleep, he saw, like a shadow hovering over him, the shape of his life, and he perceived that it was solid, and whole . . .

THE FOREIGNERS made their escape at midnight, as the priests were blowing their conch trumpets over the rain-drenched city. Moving silently through the darkness, the advance party of Tlaxcalans made it most of the way to the first canal before they were detected, and the shouts of the sentries broke the peace. The Mexican guards poured out of the surrounding houses and manned the barricades, cutting down the Tlaxcalans who had tried to swim across the canal. Then the main body of the foreigners charged up, bearing a large wooden platform in their midst. Using their thundering tubes to clear away the Mexican defenders, they lowered the platform over the canal and surged across to the opposite bank.

Huemac awoke at the first shout, reaching for his weapons before he had fully regained consciousness. Rising up behind the earthworks, he put his bone whistle to his lips and blew furiously, hearing answering shrieks from all over the city. The foreigners were now engaged in heavy fighting at the second canal, where the Mexican reinforcements were arriving at an amazing rate by means of the side streets. As his own squadron rushed out to join him on the ramparts, Huemac climbed up to look down the canal, and saw canoes filled with warriors coming from both directions. We will make them pay for their departure, at least, he thought fiercely, letting out a war cry as the rain whipped against his face.

The street ahead of him was solid with warriors by the time the foreigners had fought their way across the second canal, and more poured down stones and arrows from the surrounding rooftops. The foreigners' great deer reared up on their hind legs and plunged recklessly into the crowd of warriors, who covered the beasts like insects and pulled them and their riders down by the sheer weight of numbers. The close quarters soon rendered the foreigners' crossbows and shooting sticks useless, and the fighting became hand-to-hand, flint and obsidian against metal.

Gradually, the foreigners pushed their way up to the third canal, throwing the last defenders into the water ahead of them. Then their tubes began to boom again, and flaming stones burst against the earthworks and tore through the bodies of the warriors who failed to duck. The canal became a roiling pit of men, deer, and overturned canoes, with the foreigners behind crossing over upon a bridge composed of dead bodies. Standing atop the ramparts, Huemac and his comrades repulsed the first of these, hacking them to pieces as they struggled for a purchase on the slippery bank. But then a volley of hissing metal darts from the crossbowmen cut through the defenders like a wind made of knives, killing so many of them that the rest, Huemac among them, were forced to fall back and allow the foreign warriors to climb over the barricade.

Step by step, the escaping enemy pushed the Mexicans back down the street, with hundreds dying on both sides. Huemac fought with the calculation of his age, staying just out of the reach of the foreigners' blades until he saw a crack in their ranks, or had the chance to team up with one of his comrades against a single foreigner. Then he attacked without consideration of the risk, going in low and swinging for his enemy's legs. He was bleeding in a dozen places and felt numbed with fatigue, but still he fought on, seizing one of the foreigners' metal warclubs from the hands of a corpse after his own macana had been shattered and lost.

The fourth canal was forded in the same manner as the third, and those defending it quickly retreated to the banks of the fifth, the Tolteca canal, where they massed themselves in a last effort to keep the enemy from the causeway. Too exhausted to swing his borrowed warclub any longer, Huemac crossed the canal over the tops of the war canoes that filled it, and then positioned himself well back of the warriors on the banks, so that he could sling stones over their heads at the approaching enemy.

The fighting at the Tolteca canal went on for hours, until the sky began to grow light, revealing the full extent of the terrible slaughter. A large crowd of Mexican reinforcements had come up behind the foreigners and had succeeded in cutting off and surrounding a group of about a hundred men who had lagged too far behind the main group. These soon lost all hope of going forward and retreated down a side street, harassed and pursued by the screaming band of reinforcements. But this diversion allowed the rest of the foreigners to push across the canal, driving the defenders before them with renewed vigor now that the causeway was within sight.

Backing away in the face of the foreigners' fierce assault, Huemac suddenly saw the opposition to them begin to melt away. Warriors broke off from the group in twos and threes, drifting away into the side streets until the foreigners had passed, and then heading back in the direction of the Tolteca canal. Exhausted and bloodied, they were content to fall upon the wounded stragglers, taking easy captives and robbing the dead of their armor and weapons, and of whatever gold they might have been carrying. No reinforcements came to take their places, having themselves stopped at the canal to gather loot.

Huemac stayed among those who resisted the foreigners' advance all the way to the causeway, but the numbers around him continued to shrink, and there were no troops coming across from Tlacopan in support. Then the metal-shirted warriors were very close, and he could see their warchief, Lord Malintzin, in their midst, along with his woman and the red-haired captain known as Tonatiuh. Now it is truly over, Huemac thought wearily; now my luck is at an end. Feeling no fear, and no regret, he raised the metal warclub in both hands and rushed at his enemy.

"Tenochtitlan!" he screamed with his last breath, throwing himself upon the shining blades that were thrust out to meet his attack. He felt the searing pain that pierced his heart, and then he felt no more, as the life left him and his body fell limply to the blood-stained earth . . .

Epilogue: The Men

THOUGH pursued by the Mexicans and their allies all the way into Acolhua territory, the foreigners finally reached the safety of the Tlaxcalan
frontier, after fighting a last, decisive battle outside of Teotihuacan, the
Place of the Gods. Lord Malintzin had lost almost three quarters of his men
in the escape, but more foreign ships soon arrived on the coast, bringing new
supplies of weapons and fresh men. And the foreigners had left an even
deadlier ally behind in Tenochtitlan: huey zahual, the disease that covered
men's bodies with pustules and robbed them of all strength, so that they simply
lay down to die. This sickness came upon the Mexicans in the thirteenth month
of Two Flint-Knife and lasted for sixty days, killing thousands, including the
Speaker of the Tenocha, Cuitlahuac.

Cuauhtemoc, the son of Ahuitzotl, was in turn elected to the reed seat, and
it was he who organized the defenses of the two cities and prepared his people
to meet the foreigners for the second time. Lord Malintzin returned early in
the year Three-House, leading a force of some eight hundred foreign warriors,
eighty-five deer, and over twenty thousand Tlaxcalan and Huexotzincan allies.
Basing himself across the Lake in Texcoco, he methodically set about winning
over the former allies and subjects of the Mexicans, bringing war upon those
who resisted his offer of an alliance. Chalco fell, and then Xochimilco and
Mizquic and Coyoacan, until all the cities around the southern part of the Lake
belonged to the foreigners. While this was being accomplished, Lord Malintzin's boat builders completed their work on the twelve fighting ships he had
ordered, each equipped with the white banners that made them fly across the
water and the thundering tubes that destroyed any canoe that came within
range. With these, the foreigners took control of the Lake itself.

In the month of Toxcatl, the foreigners and their thousands of allies came
up from the south and laid waste to the mainland city of Tlacopan. Seizing
control of all three causeways, they began their siege, breaking the aqueduct
from Chapultepec and cutting off the Mexicans' supply of fresh water. But
Cuauhtemoc and his warriors refused to surrender, and they came out every
day to fight with their enemy, yielding no part of their defenses without a great
cost in blood. Tenochtitlan fell first, and then the war was carried into Tlatelulco, street by street.

The siege lasted over eighty days, with large parts of both cities being
destroyed in the fierce fighting. With thousands already killed and more dying
daily of hunger and thirst, Cuauhtemoc could hold out no longer, and tried
to flee the city by canoe. But he was intercepted by one of the foreign warships
and gave himself up without a fight, asking to be taken to Lord Malintzin to
surrender. Thus did the era of Mexican power come to an end, with the capture
of Cuauhtemoc, the Descending Eagle. This occurred on the day One Serpent,
in the month Xocotlhuetzi, in the year Three-House. It was, by the count of
the conquerors, August 13, in the Year of Our Lord, 1521.